RAYMOND CARVER

Raymond Carver

Collected Stories

Edited by
William L. Stull
Maureen P. Carroll

THE LIBRARY OF AMERICA

───

Raymond Carver: Collected Stories
is published with support from

THE GLADYS KRIEBLE DELMAS FOUNDATION

Contents

WILL YOU PLEASE
BE QUIET, PLEASE?

This book is for Maryann

Fat

I AM sitting over coffee and cigarets at my friend Rita's and I am telling her about it.

Here is what I tell her.

It is late of a slow Wednesday when Herb seats the fat man at my station.

This fat man is the fattest person I have ever seen, though he is neat-appearing and well dressed enough. Everything about him is big. But it is the fingers I remember best. When I stop at the table near his to see to the old couple, I first notice the fingers. They look three times the size of a normal person's fingers—long, thick, creamy fingers.

I see to my other tables, a party of four businessmen, very demanding, another party of four, three men and a woman, and this old couple. Leander has poured the fat man's water, and I give the fat man plenty of time to make up his mind before going over.

Good evening, I say. May I serve you? I say.

Rita, he was big, I mean big.

Good evening, he says. Hello. Yes, he says. I think we're ready to order now, he says.

He has this way of speaking—strange, don't you know. And he makes a little puffing sound every so often.

I think we will begin with a Caesar salad, he says. And then a bowl of soup with some extra bread and butter, if you please. The lamb chops, I believe, he says. And baked potato with sour cream. We'll see about dessert later. Thank you very much, he says, and hands me the menu.

God, Rita, but those were fingers.

I hurry away to the kitchen and turn in the order to Rudy, who takes it with a face. You know Rudy. Rudy is that way when he works.

As I come out of the kitchen, Margo—I've told you about Margo? The one who chases Rudy? Margo says to me, Who's your fat friend? He's really a fatty.

—

3

Now that's part of it. I think that is really part of it.

I make the Caesar salad there at his table, him watching my every move, meanwhile buttering pieces of bread and laying them off to one side, all the time making this puffing noise. Anyway, I am so keyed up or something, I knock over his glass of water.

I'm so sorry, I say. It always happens when you get into a hurry. I'm very sorry, I say. Are you all right? I say. I'll get the boy to clean up right away, I say.

It's nothing, he says. It's all right, he says, and he puffs. Don't worry about it, we don't mind, he says. He smiles and waves as I go off to get Leander, and when I come back to serve the salad, I see the fat man has eaten all his bread and butter.

A little later, when I bring him more bread, he has finished his salad. You know the size of those Caesar salads?

You're very kind, he says. This bread is marvelous, he says.

Thank you, I say.

Well, it is very good, he says, and we mean that. We don't often enjoy bread like this, he says.

Where are you from? I ask him. I don't believe I've seen you before, I say.

He's not the kind of person you'd forget, Rita puts in with a snicker.

Denver, he says.

I don't say anything more on the subject, though I am curious.

Your soup will be along in a few minutes, sir, I say, and I go off to put the finishing touches to my party of four business-men, very demanding.

When I serve his soup, I see the bread has disappeared again. He is just putting the last piece of bread into his mouth.

Believe me, he says, we don't eat like this all the time, he says. And puffs. You'll have to excuse us, he says.

Don't think a thing about it, please, I say. I like to see a man eat and enjoy himself, I say.

I don't know, he says. I guess that's what you'd call it. And puffs. He arranges the napkin. Then he picks up his spoon.

God, he's fat! says Leander.

He can't help it, I say, so shut up.

I put down another basket of bread and more butter. How was the soup? I say.

Thank you. Good, he says. Very good, he says. He wipes his lips and dabs his chin. Do you think it's warm in here, or is it just me? he says.

No, it is warm in here, I say.

Maybe we'll take off our coat, he says.

Go right ahead, I say. A person has to be comfortable, I say.

That's true, he says, that is very, very true, he says.

But I see a little later that he is still wearing his coat.

My large parties are gone now and also the old couple. The place is emptying out. By the time I serve the fat man his chops and baked potato, along with more bread and butter, he is the only one left.

I drop lots of sour cream onto his potato. I sprinkle bacon and chives over his sour cream. I bring him more bread and butter.

Is everything all right? I say.

Fine, he says, and he puffs. Excellent, thank you, he says, and puffs again.

Enjoy your dinner, I say. I raise the lid of his sugar bowl and look in. He nods and keeps looking at me until I move away.

I know now I was after something. But I don't know what.

How is old tub-of-guts doing? He's going to run your legs off, says Harriet. You know Harriet.

For dessert, I say to the fat man, there is the Green Lantern Special, which is a pudding cake with sauce, or there is cheese-cake or vanilla ice cream or pineapple sherbet.

We're not making you late, are we? he says, puffing and looking concerned.

Not at all, I say. Of course not, I say. Take your time, I say. I'll bring you more coffee while you make up your mind.

We'll be honest with you, he says. And he moves in the seat. We would like the Special, but we may have a dish of vanilla ice cream as well. With just a drop of chocolate syrup, if you please. We told you we were hungry, he says.

I go off to the kitchen to see after his dessert myself, and Rudy says, Harriet says you got a fat man from the circus out there. That true?

Rudy has his apron and hat off now, if you see what I mean.

Rudy, he is fat, I say, but that is not the whole story.

Rudy just laughs.

Sounds to me like she's sweet on fat-stuff, he says.

Better watch out, Rudy, says Joanne, who just that minute comes into the kitchen.

I'm getting jealous, Rudy says to Joanne.

I put the Special in front of the fat man and a big bowl of vanilla ice cream with chocolate syrup to the side.

Thank you, he says.

You are very welcome, I say—and a feeling comes over me.

Believe it or not, he says, we have not always eaten like this.

Me, I eat and I eat and I can't gain, I say. I'd like to gain, I say.

No, he says. If we had our choice, no. But there is no choice.

Then he picks up his spoon and eats.

What else? Rita says, lighting one of my cigarets and pulling her chair closer to the table. This story's getting interesting now, Rita says.

That's it. Nothing else. He eats his desserts, and then he leaves and then we go home, Rudy and me.

Some fatty, Rudy says, stretching like he does when he's tired. Then he just laughs and goes back to watching the TV.

I put the water on to boil for tea and take a shower. I put my hand on my middle and wonder what would happen if I had children and one of them turned out to look like that, so fat.

I pour the water in the pot, arrange the cups, the sugar bowl, carton of half and half, and take the tray in to Rudy. As if he's been thinking about it, Rudy says, I knew a fat guy once, a couple of fat guys, really fat guys, when I was a kid. They were tubbies, my God. I don't remember their names. Fat, that's the only name this one kid had. We called him Fat, the kid who lived next door to me. He was a neighbor. The other kid came along later. His name was Wobbly. Everybody called him Wobbly except the teachers. Wobbly and Fat. Wish I had their pictures, Rudy says.

I can't think of anything to say, so we drink our tea and pretty soon I get up to go to bed. Rudy gets up too, turns off the TV, locks the front door, and begins his unbuttoning.

I get into bed and move clear over to the edge and lie there on my stomach. But right away, as soon as he turns off the light and gets into bed, Rudy begins. I turn on my back and relax some, though it is against my will. But here is the thing. When he gets on me, I suddenly feel I am fat. I feel I am terrifically fat, so fat that Rudy is a tiny thing and hardly there at all.

That's a funny story, Rita says, but I can see she doesn't know what to make of it.

I feel depressed. But I won't go into it with her. I've already told her too much.

She sits there waiting, her dainty fingers poking her hair.

Waiting for what? I'd like to know.

It is August.

My life is going to change. I feel it.

Neighbors

Bill and Arlene Miller were a happy couple. But now and then they felt they alone among their circle had been passed by somehow, leaving Bill to attend to his bookkeeping duties and Arlene occupied with secretarial chores. They talked about it sometimes, mostly in comparison with the lives of their neighbors, Harriet and Jim Stone. It seemed to the Millers that the Stones lived a fuller and brighter life. The Stones were always going out for dinner, or entertaining at home, or traveling about the country somewhere in connection with Jim's work.

The Stones lived across the hall from the Millers. Jim was a salesman for a machine-parts firm and often managed to combine business with pleasure trips, and on this occasion the Stones would be away for ten days, first to Cheyenne, then on to St. Louis to visit relatives. In their absence, the Millers would look after the Stones' apartment, feed Kitty, and water the plants.

Bill and Jim shook hands beside the car. Harriet and Arlene held each other by the elbows and kissed lightly on the lips.

"Have fun," Bill said to Harriet.

"We will," said Harriet. "You kids have fun too."

Arlene nodded.

Jim winked at her. "Bye, Arlene. Take good care of the old man."

"I will," Arlene said.

"Have fun," Bill said.

"You bet," Jim said, clipping Bill lightly on the arm. "And thanks again, you guys."

The Stones waved as they drove away, and the Millers waved too.

"Well, I wish it was us," Bill said.

"God knows, we could use a vacation," Arlene said. She took his arm and put it around her waist as they climbed the stairs to their apartment.

After dinner Arlene said, "Don't forget. Kitty gets liver flavor the first night." She stood in the kitchen doorway folding the handmade tablecloth that Harriet had bought for her last year in Santa Fe.

Bill took a deep breath as he entered the Stones' apartment. The air was already heavy and it was vaguely sweet. The sunburst clock over the television said half past eight. He remembered when Harriet had come home with the clock, how she had crossed the hall to show it to Arlene, cradling the brass case in her arms and talking to it through the tissue paper as if it were an infant.

Kitty rubbed her face against his slippers and then turned onto her side, but jumped up quickly as Bill moved to the kitchen and selected one of the stacked cans from the gleaming drainboard. Leaving the cat to pick at her food, he headed for the bathroom. He looked at himself in the mirror and then closed his eyes and then looked again. He opened the medicine chest. He found a container of pills and read the label— *Harriet Stone. One each day as directed*—and slipped it into his pocket. He went back to the kitchen, drew a pitcher of water, and returned to the living room. He finished watering, set the pitcher on the rug, and opened the liquor cabinet. He reached in back for the bottle of Chivas Regal. He took two drinks from the bottle, wiped his lips on his sleeve, and replaced the bottle in the cabinet.

Kitty was on the couch sleeping. He switched off the lights, slowly closing and checking the door. He had the feeling he had left something.

"What kept you?" Arlene said. She sat with her legs turned under her, watching television.

"Nothing. Playing with Kitty," he said, and went over to her and touched her breasts.

"Let's go to bed, honey," he said.

The next day Bill took only ten minutes of the twenty-minute break allotted for the afternoon and left at fifteen minutes before five. He parked the car in the lot just as Arlene hopped down from the bus. He waited until she entered the building, then ran up the stairs to catch her as she stepped out of the elevator.

"Bill! God, you scared me. You're early," she said.

He shrugged. "Nothing to do at work," he said.

She let him use her key to open the door. He looked at the door across the hall before following her inside.

"Let's go to bed," he said.

"Now?" She laughed. "What's gotten into you?"

"Nothing. Take your dress off." He grabbed for her awkwardly, and she said, "Good God, Bill."

He unfastened his belt.

Later they sent out for Chinese food, and when it arrived they ate hungrily, without speaking, and listened to records.

"Let's not forget to feed Kitty," she said.

"I was just thinking about that," he said. "I'll go right over."

He selected a can of fish flavor for the cat, then filled the pitcher and went to water. When he returned to the kitchen, the cat was scratching in her box. She looked at him steadily before she turned back to the litter. He opened all the cupboards and examined the canned goods, the cereals, the packaged foods, the cocktail and wine glasses, the china, the pots and pans. He opened the refrigerator. He sniffed some celery, took two bites of cheddar cheese, and chewed on an apple as he walked into the bedroom. The bed seemed enormous, with a fluffy white bedspread draped to the floor. He pulled out a nightstand drawer, found a half-empty package of cigarets and stuffed them into his pocket. Then he stepped to the closet and was opening it when the knock sounded at the front door.

He stopped by the bathroom and flushed the toilet on his way.

"What's been keeping you?" Arlene said. "You've been over here more than an hour."

"Have I really?" he said.

"Yes, you have," she said.

"I had to go to the toilet," he said.

"You have your own toilet," she said.

"I couldn't wait," he said.

That night they made love again.

In the morning he had Arlene call in for him. He showered, dressed, and made a light breakfast. He tried to start a book.

He went out for a walk and felt better. But after a while, hands still in his pockets, he returned to the apartment. He stopped at the Stones' door on the chance he might hear the cat moving about. Then he let himself in at his own door and went to the kitchen for the key.

Inside it seemed cooler than his apartment, and darker too. He wondered if the plants had something to do with the temperature of the air. He looked out the window, and then he moved slowly through each room considering everything that fell under his gaze, carefully, one object at a time. He saw ashtrays, items of furniture, kitchen utensils, the clock. He saw everything. At last he entered the bedroom, and the cat appeared at his feet. He stroked her once, carried her into the bathroom, and shut the door.

He lay down on the bed and stared at the ceiling. He lay for a while with his eyes closed, and then he moved his hand under his belt. He tried to recall what day it was. He tried to remember when the Stones were due back, and then he wondered if they would ever return. He could not remember their faces or the way they talked and dressed. He sighed and with effort rolled off the bed to lean over the dresser and look at himself in the mirror.

He opened the closet and selected a Hawaiian shirt. He looked until he found Bermudas, neatly pressed and hanging over a pair of brown twill slacks. He shed his own clothes and slipped into the shorts and the shirt. He looked in the mirror again. He went to the living room and poured himself a drink and sipped it on his way back to the bedroom. He put on a blue shirt, a dark suit, a blue and white tie, black wing-tip shoes. The glass was empty and he went for another drink.

In the bedroom again, he sat on a chair, crossed his legs, and smiled, observing himself in the mirror. The telephone rang twice and fell silent. He finished the drink and took off the suit. He rummaged through the top drawers until he found a pair of panties and a brassiere. He stepped into the panties and fastened the brassiere, then looked through the closet for an outfit. He put on a black and white checkered skirt and tried to zip it up. He put on a burgundy blouse that buttoned up the front. He considered her shoes, but understood they would not fit. For a long time he looked out the living-room window from behind the curtain. Then he returned to the bedroom and put everything away.

He was not hungry. She did not eat much, either. They looked at each other shyly and smiled. She got up from the table and checked that the key was on the shelf and then she quickly cleared the dishes.

He stood in the kitchen doorway and smoked a cigaret and watched her pick up the key.

"Make yourself comfortable while I go across the hall," she said. "Read the paper or something." She closed her fingers over the key. He was, she said, looking tired.

He tried to concentrate on the news. He read the paper and turned on the television. Finally he went across the hall. The door was locked.

"It's me. Are you still there, honey?" he called.

After a time the lock released and Arlene stepped outside and shut the door. "Was I gone so long?" she said.

"Well, you were," he said.

"Was I?" she said. "I guess I must have been playing with Kitty."

He studied her, and she looked away, her hand still resting on the doorknob.

"It's funny," she said. "You know—to go in someone's place like that."

He nodded, took her hand from the knob, and guided her toward their own door. He let them into their apartment.

"It *is* funny," he said.

He noticed white lint clinging to the back of her sweater, and the color was high in her cheeks. He began kissing her on the neck and hair and she turned and kissed him back.

"Oh, damn," she said. "Damn, damn," she sang, girlishly clapping her hands. "I just remembered. I really and truly forgot to do what I went over there to do. I didn't feed Kitty or do any watering." She looked at him. "Isn't that stupid?"

"I don't think so," he said. "Just a minute. I'll get my cigarets and go back with you."

She waited until he had closed and locked their door, and then she took his arm at the muscle and said, "I guess I should tell you. I found some pictures."

He stopped in the middle of the hall. "What kind of pictures?"

"You can see for yourself," she said, and she watched him.

"No kidding." He grinned. "Where?"

"In a drawer," she said.

"No kidding," he said.

And then she said, "Maybe they won't come back," and was at once astonished at her words.

"It could happen," he said. "Anything could happen."

"Or maybe they'll come back and . . ." but she did not finish.

They held hands for the short walk across the hall, and when he spoke she could barely hear his voice.

"The key," he said. "Give it to me."

"What?" she said. She gazed at the door.

"The key," he said. "You have the key."

"My God," she said, "I left the key inside."

He tried the knob. It was locked. Then she tried the knob. It would not turn. Her lips were parted, and her breathing was hard, expectant. He opened his arms and she moved into them.

"Don't worry," he said into her ear. "For God's sake, don't worry."

They stayed there. They held each other. They leaned into the door as if against a wind, and braced themselves.

The Idea

W E'D finished supper and I'd been at the kitchen table with the light out for the last hour, watching. If he was going to do it tonight, it was time, past time. I hadn't seen him in three nights. But tonight the bedroom shade was up over there and the light burning.

I had a feeling tonight.

Then I saw him. He opened the screen and walked out onto his back porch wearing a T-shirt and something like Bermuda shorts or a swimsuit. He looked around once and hopped off the porch into the shadows and began to move along the side of the house. He was fast. If I hadn't been watching, I wouldn't have seen him. He stopped in front of the lighted window and looked in.

"Vern," I called. "Vern, hurry up! He's out there. You'd better hurry!"

Vern was in the living room reading his paper with the TV going. I heard him throw down the paper.

"Don't let him see you!" Vern said. "Don't get up too close to the window!"

Vern always says that: Don't get up too close. Vern's a little embarrassed about watching, I think. But I know he enjoys it. He's said so.

"He can't see us with the light out." It's what I always say. This has been going on for three months. Since September 3, to be exact. Anyway, that's the first night I saw him over there. I don't know how long it was going on before that.

I almost got on the phone to the sheriff that night, until I recognized who it was out there. It took Vern to explain it to me. Even then it took a while for it to penetrate. But since that night I've watched, and I can tell you he averages one out of every two or three nights, sometimes more. I've seen him out there when it's been raining too. In fact, if it *is* raining, you can bet on seeing him. But tonight it was clear and windy. There was a moon.

We got down on our knees behind the window and Vern cleared his throat.

"Look at him," Vern said. Vern was smoking, knocking the ash into his hand when he needed. He held the cigaret away from the window when he puffed. Vern smokes all the time; there's no stopping him. He even sleeps with an ashtray three inches from his head. At night I'm awake and he wakes up and smokes.

"By God," Vern said.

"What does she have that other women don't have?" I said to Vern after a minute. We were hunkered on the floor with just our heads showing over the windowsill and were looking at a man who was standing and looking into his own bedroom window.

"That's just it," Vern said. He cleared his throat right next to my ear.

We kept watching.

I could make out someone behind the curtain now. It must have been her undressing. But I couldn't see any detail. I strained my eyes. Vern was wearing his reading glasses, so he could see everything better than I could. Suddenly the curtain was drawn aside and the woman turned her back to the window.

"What's she doing now?" I said, knowing full well.

"By God," Vern said.

"What's she doing, Vern?" I said.

"She's taking off her clothes," Vern said. "What do you think she's doing?"

Then the bedroom light went out and the man started back along the side of his house. He opened the screen door and slipped inside, and a little later the rest of the lights went out.

Vern coughed, coughed again, and shook his head. I turned on the light. Vern just sat there on his knees. Then he got to his feet and lighted a cigaret.

"Someday I'm going to tell that trash what I think of her," I said and looked at Vern.

Vern laughed sort of.

"I mean it," I said. "I'll see her in the market someday and I'll tell her to her face."

"I wouldn't do that. What the hell would you do that for?" Vern said.

But I could tell he didn't think I was serious. He frowned and looked at his nails. He rolled his tongue in his mouth and narrowed his eyes like he does when he's concentrating. Then his expression changed and he scratched his chin. "You wouldn't do anything like that," he said.

"You'll see," I said.

"Shit," Vern said.

I followed him into the living room. We were jumpy. It gets us like that.

"You wait," I said.

Vern ground his cigaret out in the big ashtray. He stood beside his leather chair and looked at the TV a minute.

"There's never anything on," he said. Then he said something else. He said, "Maybe he *has* something there." Vern lighted another cigaret. "You don't know."

"Anybody comes looking in my window," I said, "they'll have the cops on them. Except maybe Cary Grant," I said.

Vern shrugged. "You don't know," he said.

I had an appetite. I went to the kitchen cupboard and looked, and then I opened the fridge.

"Vern, you want something to eat?" I called.

He didn't answer. I could hear water running in the bathroom. But I thought he might want something. We get hungry this time of night. I put bread and lunchmeat on the table and I opened a can of soup. I got out crackers and peanut butter, cold meat loaf, pickles, olives, potato chips. I put everything on the table. Then I thought of the apple pie.

Vern came out in his robe and flannel pajamas. His hair was wet and slicked down over the back of his head, and he smelled of toilet water. He looked at the things on the table. He said, "What about a bowl of corn flakes with brown sugar?" Then he sat down and spread his paper out to the side of his plate.

We ate our snack. The ashtray filled up with olive pits and his butts.

When he'd finished, Vern grinned and said, "What's that good smell?"

I went to the oven and took out the two pieces of apple pie topped with melted cheese.

"That looks fine," Vern said.

In a little while, he said, "I can't eat any more. I'm going to bed."

"I'm coming too," I said. "I'll clear this table."

I was scraping plates into the garbage can when I saw the ants. I looked closer. They came from somewhere beneath the pipes under the sink, a steady stream of them, up one side of the can and down the other, coming and going. I found the spray in one of the drawers and sprayed the outside and the inside of the garbage can, and I sprayed as far back under the sink as I could reach. Then I washed my hands and took a last look around the kitchen.

Vern was asleep. He was snoring. He'd wake up in a few hours, go to the bathroom, and smoke. The little TV at the foot of the bed was on, but the picture was rolling.

I'd wanted to tell Vern about the ants.

I took my own time getting ready for bed, fixed the picture, and crawled in. Vern made the noises he does in his sleep.

I watched for a while, but it was a talk show and I don't like talk shows. I started thinking about the ants again.

Pretty soon I imagined them all over the house. I wondered if I should wake Vern and tell him I was having a bad dream. Instead, I got up and went for the can of spray. I looked under the sink again. But there was no ants left. I turned on every light in the house until I had the house blazing.

I kept spraying.

Finally I raised the shade in the kitchen and looked out. It was late. The wind blew and I heard branches snap.

"That trash," I said. "The idea!"

I used even worse language, things I can't repeat.

They're Not Your Husband

EARL OBER was between jobs as a salesman. But Doreen, his wife, had gone to work nights as a waitress at a twenty-four-hour coffee shop at the edge of town. One night, when he was drinking, Earl decided to stop by the coffee shop and have something to eat. He wanted to see where Doreen worked, and he wanted to see if he could order something on the house.

He sat at the counter and studied the menu.

"What are you doing here?" Doreen said when she saw him sitting there.

She handed over an order to the cook. "What are you going to order, Earl?" she said. "The kids okay?"

"They're fine," Earl said. "I'll have coffee and one of those Number Two sandwiches."

Doreen wrote it down.

"Any chance of, you know?" he said to her and winked.

"No," she said. "Don't talk to me now. I'm busy."

Earl drank his coffee and waited for the sandwich. Two men in business suits, their ties undone, their collars open, sat down next to him and asked for coffee. As Doreen walked away with the coffeepot, one of the men said to the other, "Look at the ass on that. I don't believe it."

The other man laughed. "I've seen better," he said.

"That's what I mean," the first man said. "But some jokers like their quim fat."

"Not me," the other man said.

"Not me, neither," the first man said. "That's what I was saying."

Doreen put the sandwich in front of Earl. Around the sandwich there were French fries, coleslaw, dill pickle.

"Anything else?" she said. "A glass of milk?"

He didn't say anything. He shook his head when she kept standing there.

"I'll get you more coffee," she said.

She came back with the pot and poured coffee for him and for the two men. Then she picked up a dish and turned to get some ice cream. She reached down into the container and with

18

the dipper began to scoop up the ice cream. The white skirt yanked against her hips and crawled up her legs. What showed was girdle, and it was pink, thighs that were rumpled and gray and a little hairy, and veins that spread in a berserk display.

The two men sitting beside Earl exchanged looks. One of them raised his eyebrows. The other man grinned and kept looking at Doreen over his cup as she spooned chocolate syrup over the ice cream. When she began shaking the can of whipped cream, Earl got up, leaving his food, and headed for the door. He heard her call his name, but he kept going.

He checked on the children and then went to the other bedroom and took off his clothes. He pulled the covers up, closed his eyes, and allowed himself to think. The feeling started in his face and worked down into his stomach and legs. He opened his eyes and rolled his head back and forth on the pillow. Then he turned on his side and fell asleep.

In the morning, after she had sent the children off to school, Doreen came into the bedroom and raised the shade. Earl was already awake.

"Look at yourself in the mirror," he said.

"What?" she said. "What are you talking about?"

"Just look at yourself in the mirror," he said.

"What am I supposed to see?" she said. But she looked in the mirror over the dresser and pushed the hair away from her shoulders.

"Well?" he said.

"Well, what?" she said.

"I hate to say anything," Earl said, "but I think you better give a diet some thought. I mean it. I'm serious. I think you could lose a few pounds. Don't get mad."

"What are you saying?" she said.

"Just what I said. I think you could lose a few pounds. A few pounds, anyway," he said.

"You never said anything before," she said. She raised her nightgown over her hips and turned to look at her stomach in the mirror.

"I never felt it was a problem before," he said. He tried to pick his words.

The nightgown still gathered around her waist, Doreen

turned her back to the mirror and looked over her shoulder. She raised one buttock in her hand and let it drop.

Earl closed his eyes. "Maybe I'm all wet," he said.

"I guess I could afford to lose. But it'd be hard," she said.

"You're right, it won't be easy," he said. "But I'll help."

"Maybe you're right," she said. She dropped her nightgown and looked at him and then she took her nightgown off.

They talked about diets. They talked about the protein diets, the vegetable-only diets, the grapefruit-juice diets. But they decided they didn't have the money to buy the steaks the protein diet called for. And Doreen said she didn't care for all that many vegetables. And since she didn't like grapefruit juice that much, she didn't see how she could do that one, either.

"Okay, forget it," he said.

"No, you're right," she said. "I'll do something."

"What about exercises?" he said.

"I'm getting all the exercise I need down there," she said.

"Just quit eating," Earl said. "For a few days, anyway."

"All right," she said. "I'll try. For a few days I'll give it a try. You've convinced me."

"I'm a closer," Earl said.

He figured up the balance in their checking account, then drove to the discount store and bought a bathroom scale. He looked the clerk over as she rang up the sale.

At home he had Doreen take off all her clothes and get on the scale. He frowned when he saw the veins. He ran his finger the length of one that sprouted up her thigh.

"What are you doing?" she asked.

"Nothing," he said.

He looked at the scale and wrote the figure down on a piece of paper.

"All right," Earl said. "All right."

The next day he was gone for most of the afternoon on an interview. The employer, a heavyset man who limped as he showed Earl around the plumbing fixtures in the warehouse, asked if Earl were free to travel.

"You bet I'm free," Earl said.

The man nodded.

Earl smiled.

—

He could hear the television before he opened the door to the house. The children did not look up as he walked through the living room. In the kitchen, Doreen, dressed for work, was eating scrambled eggs and bacon.

"What are you doing?" Earl said.

She continued to chew the food, cheeks puffed. But then she spit everything into a napkin.

"I couldn't help myself," she said.

"Slob," Earl said. "*Go ahead, eat! Go on!*" He went to the bedroom, closed the door, and lay on the covers. He could still hear the television. He put his hands behind his head and stared at the ceiling.

She opened the door.

"I'm going to try again," Doreen said.

"Okay," he said.

Two mornings later she called him into the bathroom. "Look," she said.

He read the scale. He opened a drawer and took out the paper and read the scale again while she grinned.

"Three-quarters of a pound," she said.

"It's something," he said and patted her hip.

He read the classifieds. He went to the state employment office. Every three or four days he drove someplace for an interview, and at night he counted her tips. He smoothed out the dollar bills on the table and stacked the nickels, dimes, and quarters in piles of one dollar. Each morning he put her on the scale.

In two weeks she had lost three and a half pounds.

"I pick," she said. "I starve myself all day, and then I pick at work. It adds up."

But a week later she had lost five pounds. The week after that, nine and a half pounds. Her clothes were loose on her. She had to cut into the rent money to buy a new uniform.

"People are saying things at work," she said.

"What kind of things?" Earl said.

"That I'm too pale, for one thing," she said. "That I don't look like myself. They're afraid I'm losing too much weight."

"What is wrong with losing?" he said. "Don't you pay any

attention to them. Tell them to mind their own business. They're not your husband. You don't have to live with them."

"I have to work with them," Doreen said.

"That's right," Earl said. "But they're not your husband."

Each morning he followed her into the bathroom and waited while she stepped onto the scale. He got down on his knees with a pencil and the piece of paper. The paper was covered with dates, days of the week, numbers. He read the number on the scale, consulted the paper, and either nodded his head or pursed his lips.

Doreen spent more time in bed now. She went back to bed after the children had left for school, and she napped in the afternoons before going to work. Earl helped around the house, watched television, and let her sleep. He did all the shopping, and once in a while he went on an interview.

One night he put the children to bed, turned off the television, and decided to go for a few drinks. When the bar closed, he drove to the coffee shop.

He sat at the counter and waited. When she saw him, she said, "Kids okay?"

Earl nodded.

He took his time ordering. He kept looking at her as she moved up and down behind the counter. He finally ordered a cheeseburger. She gave the order to the cook and went to wait on someone else.

Another waitress came by with a coffeepot and filled Earl's cup.

"Who's your friend?" he said and nodded at his wife.

"Her name's Doreen," the waitress said.

"She looks a lot different than the last time I was in here," he said.

"I wouldn't know," the waitress said.

He ate the cheeseburger and drank the coffee. People kept sitting down and getting up at the counter. Doreen waited on most of the people at the counter, though now and then the other waitress came along to take an order. Earl watched his wife and listened carefully. Twice he had to leave his place to go to the bathroom. Each time he wondered if he might have missed hearing something. When he came back the second time, he found his cup gone and someone in his place. He took a stool at the end of the counter next to an older man in a striped shirt.

"What do you want?" Doreen said to Earl when she saw him again. "Shouldn't you be home?"

"Give me some coffee," he said.

The man next to Earl was reading a newspaper. He looked up and watched Doreen pour Earl a cup of coffee. He glanced at Doreen as she walked away. Then he went back to his newspaper.

Earl sipped his coffee and waited for the man to say something. He watched the man out of the corner of his eye. The man had finished eating and his plate was pushed to the side. The man lit a cigaret, folded the newspaper in front of him, and continued to read.

Doreen came by and removed the dirty plate and poured the man more coffee.

"What do you think of that?" Earl said to the man, nodding at Doreen as she moved down the counter. "Don't you think that's something special?"

The man looked up. He looked at Doreen and then at Earl, and then went back to his newspaper.

"Well, what do you think?" Earl said. "I'm asking. Does it look good or not? Tell me."

The man rattled the newspaper.

When Doreen started down the counter again, Earl nudged the man's shoulder and said, "I'm telling you something. Listen. Look at the ass on her. Now you watch this now. Could I have a chocolate sundae?" Earl called to Doreen.

She stopped in front of him and let out her breath. Then she turned and picked up a dish and the ice-cream dipper. She leaned over the freezer, reached down, and began to press the dipper into the ice cream. Earl looked at the man and winked as Doreen's skirt traveled up her thighs. But the man's eyes caught the eyes of the other waitress. And then the man put the newspaper under his arm and reached into his pocket.

The other waitress came straight to Doreen. "Who is this character?" she said.

"Who?" Doreen said and looked around with the ice-cream dish in her hand.

"Him," the other waitress said and nodded at Earl. "Who is this joker, anyway?"

Earl put on his best smile. He held it. He held it until he felt his face pulling out of shape.

But the other waitress just studied him, and Doreen began to shake her head slowly. The man had put some change beside his cup and stood up, but he too waited to hear the answer. They all stared at Earl.

"He's a salesman. He's my husband," Doreen said at last, shrugging. Then she put the unfinished chocolate sundae in front of him and went to total up his check.

Are You a Doctor?

IN slippers, pajamas, and robe, he hurried out of the study when the telephone began to ring. Since it was past ten, the call would be his wife. She phoned—late like this, after a few drinks—each night when she was out of town. She was a buyer, and all this week she had been away on business.

"Hello, dear," he said. "Hello," he said again.

"Who is this?" a woman asked.

"Well, who is *this*?" he said. "What number do you want?"

"Just a minute," the woman said. "It's 273-8063."

"That's my number," he said. "How did you get it?"

"I don't know. It was written down on a piece of paper when I got in from work," the woman said.

"Who wrote it down?"

"I don't know," the woman said. "The sitter, I guess. It must be her."

"Well, I don't know how she got it," he said, "but it's my telephone number, and it's unlisted. I'd appreciate it if you'd just toss it away. Hello? Did you hear me?"

"Yes, I heard," the woman said.

"Is there anything else?" he said. "It's late and I'm busy." He hadn't meant to be curt, but one couldn't take chances. He sat down on the chair by the telephone and said, "I hadn't meant to be curt. I only meant that it's late, and I'm concerned how you happen to have my number." He pulled off his slipper and began massaging his foot, waiting.

"I don't know either," she said. "I told you I just found the number written down, no note or anything. I'll ask Annette—that's the sitter—when I see her tomorrow. I didn't mean to disturb you. I only just now found the note. I've been in the kitchen ever since I came in from work."

"It's all right," he said. "Forget it. Just throw it away or something and forget it. There's no problem, so don't worry." He moved the receiver from one ear to the other.

"You sound like a nice man," the woman said.

"Do I? Well, that's nice of you to say." He knew he should

25

hang up now, but it was good to hear a voice, even his own, in the quiet room.

"Oh, yes," she said. "I can tell."

He let go his foot.

"What's your name, if you don't mind my asking?" she said.

"My name is Arnold," he said.

"And what's your first name?" she said.

"Arnold is my first name," he said.

"Oh, forgive me," she said. "Arnold is your *first* name. And your second name, Arnold? What's your second name?"

"I really must hang up," he said.

"Arnold, for goodness sake, I'm Clara Holt. Now *your* name is Mr. Arnold what?"

"Arnold Breit," he said and then quickly added, "Clara Holt. That's nice. But I really think I should hang up now, Miss Holt. I'm expecting a call."

"I'm sorry, Arnold. I didn't mean to take up your time," she said.

"That's all right," he said. "It's been nice talking with you."

"You're kind to say that, Arnold."

"Will you hold the phone a minute?" he said. "I have to check on something." He went into the study for a cigar, took a minute lighting it up with the desk lighter, then removed his glasses and looked at himself in the mirror over the fireplace. When he returned to the telephone, he was half afraid she might be off the line.

"Hello?"

"Hello, Arnold," she said.

"I thought you might have hung up."

"Oh no," she said.

"About your having my number," he said. "Nothing to worry about, I don't suppose. Just throw it away, I suppose."

"I will, Arnold," she said.

"Well, I must say goodbye, then."

"Yes, of course," she said. "I'll say good night now."

He heard her draw a breath.

"I know I'm imposing, Arnold, but do you think we could meet somewhere we could talk? Just for a few minutes?"

"I'm afraid that's impossible," he said.

"Just for a minute, Arnold. My finding your number and everything. I feel strongly about this, Arnold."

"I'm an old man," he said.

"Oh, you're not," she said.

"Really, I'm old," he said.

"Could we meet somewhere, Arnold? You see, I haven't told you everything. There's something else," the woman said.

"What do you mean?" he said. "What is this exactly? Hello?"

She had hung up.

When he was preparing for bed, his wife called, somewhat intoxicated, he could tell, and they chatted for a while, but he said nothing about the other call. Later, as he was turning the covers down, the telephone rang again.

He picked up the receiver. "Hello. Arnold Breit speaking."

"Arnold, I'm sorry we got cut off. As I was saying, I think it's important we meet."

The next afternoon as he put the key into the lock, he could hear the telephone ringing. He dropped his briefcase and, still in hat, coat, and gloves, hurried over to the table and picked up the receiver.

"Arnold, I'm sorry to bother you again," the woman said. "But you must come to my house tonight around nine or nine-thirty. Can you do that for me, Arnold?"

His heart moved when he heard her use his name. "I couldn't do that," he said.

"Please, Arnold," she said. "It's important or I wouldn't be asking. I can't leave the house tonight because Cheryl is sick with a cold and now I'm afraid for the boy."

"And your husband?" He waited.

"I'm not married," she said. "You will come, won't you?"

"I can't promise," he said.

"I implore you to come," she said and then quickly gave him the address and hung up.

"*I implore you to come*," he repeated, still holding the receiver. He slowly took off his gloves and then his coat. He felt he had to be careful. He went to wash up. When he looked in the bathroom mirror, he discovered the hat. It was then that he made the decision to see her, and he took off his hat and glasses and soaped his face. He checked his nails.

"You're sure this is the right street?" he asked the driver.

"This is the street and there's the building," the driver said.

"Keep going," he said. "Let me out at the end of the block."

He paid the driver. Lights from the upper windows illuminated the balconies. He could see planters on the balustrades and here and there a piece of lawn furniture. At one balcony a large man in a sweatshirt leaned over the railing and watched him walk toward the door.

He pushed the button under C. HOLT. The buzzer sounded, and he stepped back to the door and entered. He climbed the stairs slowly, stopping to rest briefly at each landing. He remembered the hotel in Luxembourg, the five flights he and his wife had climbed so many years ago. He felt a sudden pain in his side, imagined his heart, imagined his legs folding under him, imagined a loud fall to the bottom of the stairs. He took out his handkerchief and wiped his forehead. Then he removed his glasses and wiped the lenses, waiting for his heart to quiet.

He looked down the hall. The apartment house was very quiet. He stopped at her door, removed his hat, and knocked lightly. The door opened a crack to reveal a plump little girl in pajamas.

"Are you Arnold Breit?" she said.

"Yes, I am," he said. "Is your mother home?"

"She said for you to come in. She said to tell you she went to the drugstore for some cough syrup and aspirin."

He shut the door behind him. "What is your name? Your mother told me, but I forgot."

When the girl said nothing, he tried again.

"What is your name? Isn't your name Shirley?"

"Cheryl," she said. "C-h-e-r-y-l."

"Yes, now I remember. Well, I was close, you must admit."

She sat on a hassock across the room and looked at him.

"So you're sick, are you?" he said.

She shook her head.

"Not sick?"

"No," she said.

He looked around. The room was lighted by a gold floor lamp that had a large ashtray and a magazine rack affixed to the pole. A television set stood against the far wall, the picture on, the volume low. A narrow hallway led to the back of the apartment. The furnace was turned up, the air close with a medicinal smell. Hairpins and rollers lay on the coffee table, a pink bathrobe lay on the couch.

He looked at the child again, then raised his eyes toward the kitchen and the glass doors that gave off the kitchen onto the balcony. The doors stood slightly ajar, and a little chill went through him as he recalled the large man in the sweatshirt.

"Mama went out for a minute," the child said, as if suddenly waking up.

He leaned forward on his toes, hat in hand, and stared at her. "I think I'd better go," he said.

A key turned in the lock, the door swung open, and a small, pale, freckled woman entered carrying a paper sack.

"Arnold! I'm glad to see you!" She glanced at him quickly, uneasily, and shook her head strangely from side to side as she walked to the kitchen with the sack. He heard a cupboard door shut. The child sat on the hassock and watched him. He leaned his weight first on one leg and then the other, then placed the hat on his head and removed it in the same motion as the woman reappeared.

"Are you a doctor?" she asked.

"No," he said, startled. "No, I am not."

"Cheryl is sick, you see. I've been out buying things. Why didn't you take the man's coat?" she said, turning to the child. "Please forgive her. We're not used to company."

"I can't stay," he said. "I really shouldn't have come."

"Please sit down," she said. "We can't talk like this. Let me give her some medicine first. Then we can talk."

"I really must go," he said. "From the tone of your voice, I thought there something urgent. But I really must go." He looked down at his hands and was aware he had been gesturing feebly.

"I'll put on tea water," he heard her say, as if she hadn't been listening. "Then I'll give Cheryl her medicine, and then we can talk."

She took the child by the shoulders and steered her into the kitchen. He saw the woman pick up a spoon, open a bottle of something after scanning the label, and pour out two doses.

"Now, you say good night to Mr. Breit, sweetness, and go to your room."

He nodded to the child and then followed the woman to the kitchen. He did not take the chair she indicated, but instead one that let him face the balcony, the hallway, and the small living room. "Do you mind if I smoke a cigar?" he asked.

"I don't mind," she said. "I don't think it will bother me, Arnold. Please do."

He decided against it. He put his hands on his knees and gave his face a serious expression.

"This is still very much of a mystery to me," he said. "It's quite out of the ordinary, I assure you."

"I understand, Arnold," she said. "You'd probably like to hear the story of how I got your number?"

"I would indeed," he said.

They sat across from each other waiting for the water to boil. He could hear the television. He looked around the kitchen and then out toward the balcony again. The water began to bubble.

"You were going to tell me about the number," he said.

"What, Arnold? I'm sorry," she said.

He cleared his throat. "Tell me how you acquired my number," he said.

"I checked with Annette. The sitter—but of course you know that. Anyway, she told me the phone rang while she was here and it was somebody wanting me. They left a number to call, and it was your number she took down. That's all I know." She moved a cup around in front of her. "I'm sorry I can't tell you any more."

"Your water is boiling," he said.

She put out spoons, milk, sugar and poured the steaming water over the tea bags.

He added sugar and stirred his tea. "You said it was urgent that I come."

"Oh, *that*, Arnold," she said, turning away. "I don't know what made me say that. I can't imagine what I was thinking."

"Then there's nothing?" he said.

"No. I mean *yes*." She shook her head. "What you said, I mean. Nothing."

"I see," he said. He went on stirring his tea. "It's unusual," he said after a time, almost to himself. "Quite unusual." He smiled weakly, then moved the cup to one side and touched his lips with the napkin.

"You aren't leaving?" she said.

"I must," he said. "I'm expecting a call at home."

"Not yet, Arnold."

She scraped her chair back and stood up. Her eyes were a pale green, set deep in her pale face and surrounded by what he had at first thought was dark makeup. Appalled at himself, knowing he would despise himself for it, he stood and put his arms clumsily around her waist. She let herself be kissed, fluttering and closing her eyelids briefly.

"It's late," he said, letting go, turning away unsteadily. "You've been very gracious. But I must be leaving, Mrs. Holt. Thank you for the tea."

"You will come again, won't you, Arnold?" she said.

He shook his head.

She followed him to the door, where he held out his hand. He could hear the television. He was sure the volume had been turned up. He remembered the other child then—the *boy*. Where was he?

She took his hand, raised it quickly to her lips.

"You mustn't forget me, Arnold."

"I won't," he said. "Clara. Clara Holt," he said.

"We had a good talk," she said. She picked at something, a hair, a thread, on his suit collar. "I'm very glad you came, and I feel certain you'll come again." He looked at her carefully, but she was staring past him now as if she were trying to remember something. "Now—good night, Arnold," she said, and with that she shut the door, almost catching his overcoat.

"Strange," he said as he started down the stairs. He took a long breath when he reached the sidewalk and paused a moment to look back at the building. But he was unable to determine which balcony was hers. The large man in the sweatshirt moved slightly against the railing and continued looking down at him.

He began walking, hands deep in his coat pockets. When he reached home, the telephone was ringing. He stood very quietly in the middle of the room, holding the key between his fingers until the ringing stopped. Then, tenderly, he put a hand against his chest and felt, through the layers of clothes, his beating heart. After a time he made his way into the bedroom.

Almost immediately the telephone came alive again, and this time he answered it. "Arnold. Arnold Breit speaking," he said.

"Arnold? My, aren't we formal tonight!" his wife said, her voice strong, teasing. "I've been calling since nine. Out living it up, Arnold?"

He remained silent and considered her voice.

"Are you there, Arnold?" she said. "You don't sound like yourself."

The Father

THE baby lay in a basket beside the bed, dressed in a white bonnet and sleeper. The basket had been newly painted and tied with ice blue ribbons and padded with blue quilts. The three little sisters and the mother, who had just gotten out of bed and was still not herself, and the grandmother all stood around the baby, watching it stare and sometimes raise its fist to its mouth. He did not smile or laugh, but now and then he blinked his eyes and flicked his tongue back and forth through his lips when one of the girls rubbed his chin.

The father was in the kitchen and could hear them playing with the baby.

"Who do you love, baby?" Phyllis said and tickled his chin.

"He loves us all," Phyllis said, "but he really loves Daddy because Daddy's a boy too!"

The grandmother sat down on the edge of the bed and said, "Look at its little arm! So fat. And those little fingers! Just like its mother."

"Isn't he sweet?" the mother said. "So healthy, my little baby." And bending over, she kissed the baby on its forehead and touched the cover over its arm. "We love him too."

"But who does he look like, who does he look like?" Alice cried, and they all moved up closer around the basket to see who the baby looked like.

"He has pretty eyes," Carol said.

"*All* babies have pretty eyes," Phyllis said.

"He has his grandfather's lips," the grandmother said. "Look at those lips."

"I don't know . . ." the mother said. "I wouldn't say."

"The nose! The nose!" Alice cried.

"What about his nose?" the mother asked.

"It looks like somebody's nose," the girl answered.

"No, I don't know," the mother said. "I don't think so."

"Those lips . . ." the grandmother murmured. "Those little fingers . . ." she said, uncovering the baby's hand and spreading out its fingers.

"Who does the baby look like?"

"He doesn't look like anybody," Phyllis said. And they moved even closer.

"*I* know! *I* know!" Carol said. "He looks like *Daddy!*" Then they looked closer at the baby.

"But who does Daddy *look* like?" Phyllis asked.

"Who does Daddy *look* like?" Alice repeated, and they all at once looked through to the kitchen where the father was sitting at the table with his back to them.

"Why, nobody!" Phyllis said and began to cry a little.

"Hush," the grandmother said and looked away and then back at the baby.

"Daddy doesn't look like *anybody!*" Alice said.

"But he has to look like *somebody,*" Phyllis said, wiping her eyes with one of the ribbons. And all of them except the grandmother looked at the father, sitting at the table.

He had turned around in his chair and his face was white and without expression.

Nobody Said Anything

I COULD hear them out in the kitchen. I couldn't hear what they were saying, but they were arguing. Then it got quiet and she started to cry. I elbowed George. I thought he would wake up and say something to them so they would feel guilty and stop. But George is such an asshole. He started kicking and hollering.

"Stop gouging me, you bastard," he said. "I'm going to tell!"

"You dumb chickenshit," I said. "Can't you wise up for once? They're fighting and Mom's crying. Listen."

He listened with his head off the pillow. "I don't care," he said and turned over toward the wall and went back to sleep. George is a royal asshole.

Later I heard Dad leave to catch his bus. He slammed the front door. She had told me before he wanted to tear up the family. I didn't want to listen.

After a while she came to call us for school. Her voice sounded funny—I don't know. I said I felt sick at my stomach. It was the first week in October and I hadn't missed any school yet, so what could she say? She looked at me, but it was like she was thinking of something else. George was awake and listening. I could tell he was awake by the way he moved in the bed. He was waiting to see how it turned out so he could make his move.

"All right." She shook her head. "I just don't know. Stay home, then. But no TV, remember that."

George reared up. "I'm sick too," he said to her. "I have a headache. He gouged me and kicked me all night. I didn't get to sleep at all."

"That's enough!" she said. "You are going to school, George! You're not going to stay here and fight with your brother all day. Now get up and get dressed. I mean it. I don't feel like another battle this morning."

George waited until she left the room. Then he climbed out over the foot of the bed. "You bastard," he said and yanked all the covers off me. He dodged into the bathroom.

35

"I'll kill you," I said but not so loud that she could hear.

I stayed in bed until George left for school. When she started to get ready for work, I asked if she would make a bed for me on the couch. I said I wanted to study. On the coffee table I had the Edgar Rice Burroughs books I had gotten for my birthday and my Social Studies book. But I didn't feel like reading. I wanted her to leave so I could watch TV.

She flushed the toilet.

I couldn't wait any longer. I turned the picture on without the volume. I went out to the kitchen where she had left her pack of weeds and shook out three. I put them in the cupboard and went back to the couch and started reading *The Princess of Mars*. She came out and glanced at the TV but didn't say anything. I had the book open. She poked at her hair in front of the mirror and then went into the kitchen. I looked back at the book when she came out.

"I'm late. Goodbye, sweetheart." She wasn't going to bring up the TV. Last night she'd said she wouldn't know what it meant any more to go to work without being "stirred up."

"Don't cook anything. You don't need to turn the burners on for a thing. There's tuna fish in the icebox if you feel hungry." She looked at me. "But if your stomach is sick, I don't think you should put anything on it. Anyway, you don't need to turn the burners on. Do you hear? You take that medicine, sweetheart, and I hope your stomach feels better by tonight. Maybe we'll all feel better by tonight."

She stood in the doorway and turned the knob. She looked as if she wanted to say something else. She wore the white blouse, the wide black belt, and the black skirt. Sometimes she called it her outfit, sometimes her uniform. For as long as I could remember, it was always hanging in the closet or hanging on the clothesline or getting washed out by hand at night or being ironed in the kitchen.

She worked Wednesdays through Sundays.

"Bye, Mom."

I waited until she had started the car and had it warm. I listened as she pulled away from the curb. Then I got up and turned the sound on loud and went for the weeds. I smoked one and beat off while I watched a show about doctors and nurses.

Then I turned to the other channel. Then I turned off the TV.
I didn't feel like watching.

I finished the chapter where Tars Tarkas falls for a green
woman, only to see her get her head chopped off the next
morning by this jealous brother-in-law. It was about the fifth
time I had read it. Then I went to their bedroom and looked
around. I wasn't after anything in particular unless it was rub-
bers again and though I had looked all over I had never found
any. Once I found a jar of Vaseline at the back of a drawer. I
knew it must have something to do with it, but I didn't know
what. I studied the label and hoped it would reveal something,
a description of what people did, or else about how you applied
the Vaseline, that sort of thing. But it didn't. *Pure Petroleum
Jelly*, that was all it said on the front label. But just reading that
was enough to give you a boner. *An Excellent Aid in the Nursery*,
it said on the back. I tried to make the connection between
Nursery—the swings and slides, the sandboxes, monkeybars—
and what went on in bed between them. I had opened the jar
lots of times and smelled inside and looked to see how much
had been used since last time. This time I passed up the *Pure
Petroleum Jelly*. I mean, all I did was look to see the jar was still
there. I went through a few drawers, not really expecting to
find anything. I looked under the bed. Nothing anywhere. I
looked in the jar in the closet where they kept the grocery
money. There was no change, only a five and a one. They
would miss that. Then I thought I would get dressed and walk
to Birch Creek. Trout season was open for another week or so,
but almost everybody had quit fishing. Everybody was just sitting around now waiting for deer and pheasant to open.

I got out my old clothes. I put wool socks over my regular
socks and took my time lacing up the boots. I made a couple
of tuna sandwiches and some double-decker peanut-butter
crackers. I filled my canteen and attached the hunting knife
and the canteen to my belt. As I was going out the door, I decided to leave a note. So I wrote: "Feeling better and going to
Birch Creek. Back soon. R. 3:15." That was about four hours
from now. And about fifteen minutes before George would
come in from school. Before I left, I ate one of the sandwiches
and had a glass of milk with it.

—

It was nice out. It was fall. But it wasn't cold yet except at night. At night they would light the smudgepots in the orchards and you would wake up in the morning with a black ring of stuff in your nose. But nobody said anything. They said the smudging kept the young pears from freezing, so it was all right.

To get to Birch Creek, you go to the end of our street where you hit Sixteenth Avenue. You turn left on Sixteenth and go up the hill past the cemetery and down to Lennox, where there is a Chinese restaurant. From the crossroads there, you can see the airport, and Birch Creek is below the airport. Sixteenth changes to View Road at the crossroads. You follow View for a little way until you come to the bridge. There are orchards on both sides of the road. Sometimes when you go by the orchards you see pheasants running down the rows, but you can't hunt there because you might get shot by a Greek named Matsos. I guess it is about a forty-minute walk all in all.

I was halfway down Sixteenth when a woman in a red car pulled onto the shoulder ahead of me. She rolled down the window on the passenger's side and asked if I wanted a lift. She was thin and had little pimples around her mouth. Her hair was up in curlers. But she was sharp enough. She had a brown sweater with nice boobs inside.

"Playing hooky?"

"Guess so."

"Want a ride?"

I nodded.

"Get in. I'm kind of in a hurry."

I put the fly rod and the creel on the back seat. There were a lot of grocery sacks from Mel's on the floorboards and back seat. I tried to think of something to say.

"I'm going fishing," I said. I took off my cap, hitched the canteen around so I could sit, and parked myself next to the window.

"Well, I never would have guessed." She laughed. She pulled back onto the road. "Where are you going? Birch Creek?"

I nodded again. I looked at my cap. My uncle had bought it for me in Seattle when he had gone to watch a hockey game. I couldn't think of anything more to say. I looked out the window and sucked my cheeks. You always see yourself getting picked up by this woman. You know you'll fall for each other and that she'll take you home with her and let you screw her all over the house. I began to get a boner thinking about it. I moved the cap over my lap and closed my eyes and tried to think about baseball.

"I keep saying that one of these days I'll take up fishing," she said. "They say it's very relaxing. I'm a nervous person."

I opened my eyes. We were stopped at the crossroads. I wanted to say, *Are you real busy? Would you like to start this morning?* But I was afraid to look at her.

"Will this help you? I have to turn here. I'm sorry I'm in a hurry this morning," she said.

"That's okay. This is fine." I took my stuff out. Then I put my cap on and took it off again while I talked. "Goodbye. Thanks. Maybe next summer," but I couldn't finish.

"You mean fishing? Sure thing." She waved with a couple of fingers the way women do.

I started walking, going over what I should have said. I could think of a lot of things. What was wrong with me? I cut the air with the fly rod and hollered two or three times. What I should have done to start things off was ask if we could have lunch together. No one was home at my house. Suddenly we are in my bedroom under the covers. She asks me if she can keep her sweater on and I say it's okay with me. She keeps her pants on too. That's all right, I say. I don't mind.

A Piper Cub dipped low over my head as it came in for a landing. I was a few feet from the bridge. I could hear the water running. I hurried down the embankment, unzipped, and shot off five feet over the creek. It must have been a record. I took a while eating the other sandwich and the peanut-butter crackers. I drank up half the water in the canteen. Then I was ready to fish.

I tried to think where to start. I had fished here for three years, ever since we had moved. Dad used to bring George and me in the car and wait for us, smoking, baiting our hooks, tying up new rigs for us if we snagged. We always started at the bridge and moved down, and we always caught a few. Once in a while, at the first of the season, we caught the limit. I rigged up and tried a few casts under the bridge first.

Now and then I cast under a bank or else in behind a big rock. But nothing happened. One place where the water was still and the bottom full of yellow leaves, I looked over and saw a few crawdads crawling there with their big ugly pinchers raised. Some quail flushed out of a brush pile. When I threw a stick, a rooster pheasant jumped up cackling about ten feet away and I almost dropped the rod.

The creek was slow and not very wide. I could walk across almost anywhere without it going over my boots. I crossed a pasture full of cow pads and came to where the water flowed out of a big pipe. I knew there was a little hole below the pipe, so I was careful. I got down on my knees when I was close enough to drop the line. It had just touched the water when I got a strike, but I missed him. I felt him roll with it. Then he was gone and the line flew back. I put another salmon egg on and tried a few more casts. But I knew I had jinxed it.

I went up the embankment and climbed under a fence that had a KEEP OUT sign on the post. One of the airport runways started here. I stopped to look at some flowers growing in the cracks in the pavement. You could see where the tires had smacked down on the pavement and left oily skid marks all around the flowers. I hit the creek again on the other side and fished along for a little way until I came to the hole. I thought this was as far as I would go. When I had first been up here three years ago, the water was roaring right up to the top of the banks. It was so swift then that I couldn't fish. Now the creek was about six feet below the bank. It bubbled and hopped through this little run at the head of the pool where you could hardly see bottom. A little farther down, the bottom sloped up and got shallow again as if nothing had happened. The last time I was up here I caught two fish about ten inches long and turned one that looked twice as big—a summer steelhead, Dad said when I told him about it. He said they come up during the high water in early spring but that most of them return to the river before the water gets low.

I put two more shot on the line and closed them with my teeth. Then I put a fresh salmon egg on and cast out where the water dropped over a shelf into the pool. I let the current take it down. I could feel the sinkers tap-tapping on rocks, a different kind of tapping than when you are getting a bite. Then the line tightened and the current carried the egg into sight at the end of the pool.

I felt lousy to have come this far up for nothing. I pulled out all kinds of line this time and made another cast. I laid the fly rod over a limb and lit the next to last weed. I looked up the valley and began to think about the woman. We were going to her house because she wanted help carrying in the groceries. Her husband was overseas. I touched her and she started shaking. We were French-kissing on the couch when she excused herself to go to the bathroom. I followed her. I watched as she pulled down her pants and sat on the toilet. I had a big boner and she waved me over with her hand. Just as I was going to unzip, I heard a plop in the creek. I looked and saw the tip of my fly rod jiggling.

He wasn't very big and didn't fight much. But I played him as long as I could. He turned on his side and lay in the current down below. I didn't know what he was. He looked strange. I tightened the line and lifted him over the bank into the grass, where he stared wiggling. He was a trout. But he was green. I never saw one like him before. He had green sides with black trout spots, a greenish head, and like a green stomach. He was the color of moss, that color green. It was as if he had been wrapped up in moss a long time, and the color had come off all over him. He was fat, and I wondered why he hadn't put up more of a fight. I wondered if he was all right. I looked at him for a time longer, then I put him out of his pain.

I pulled some grass and put it in the creel and laid him in there on the grass.

I made some more casts, and then I guessed it must be two or three o'clock. I thought I had better move down to the bridge. I thought I would fish below the bridge awhile before I started home. And I decided I would wait until night before I thought about the woman again. But right away I got a boner thinking about the boner I would get that night. Then I thought I had better stop doing it so much. About a month back, a Saturday when they were all gone, I had picked up the

Bible right after and promised and swore I wouldn't do it again. But I got jism on the Bible, and the promising and swearing lasted only a day or two, until I was by myself again.

I didn't fish on the way down. When I got to the bridge, I saw a bicycle in the grass. I looked and saw a kid about George's size running down the bank. I started in his direction. Then he turned and started toward me, looking in the water.

"Hey, what is it!" I hollered. "What's wrong?" I guessed he didn't hear me. I saw his pole and fishing bag on the bank, and I dropped my stuff. I ran over to where he was. He looked like a rat or something. I mean, he had buck teeth and skinny arms and this ragged longsleeved shirt that was too small for him.

"God, I swear there's the biggest fish here I ever saw!" he called. "Hurry! Look! Look here! Here he is!"

I looked where he pointed and my heart jumped.

It was as long as my arm.

"God, oh God, will you look at him!" the boy said.

I kept looking. It was resting in a shadow under a limb that hung over the water. "God almighty," I said to the fish, "where did you come from?"

"What'll we do?" the boy said. "I wish I had my gun."

"We're going to get him," I said. "God, look at him! Let's get him into the riffle."

"You want to help me, then? We'll work it together!" the kid said.

The big fish had drifted a few feet downstream and lay there finning slowly in the clear water.

"Okay, what do we do?" the kid said.

"I can go up and walk down the creek and start him moving," I said. "You stand in the riffle, and when he tries to come through, you kick the living shit out of him. Get him onto the bank someway, I don't care how. Then get a good hold of him and hang on."

"Okay. Oh shit, look at him! Look, he's going! Where's he going?" the boy screamed.

I watched the fish move up the creek again and stop close to the bank. "He's not going anyplace. There's no place for him to go. See him? He's scared shitless. He knows we're here.

He's just cruising around now looking for someplace to go. See, he stopped again. He can't go anyplace. He knows that. He knows we're going to nail him. He knows it's tough shit. I'll go up and scare him down. You get him when he comes through."

"I wish I had my gun," the boy said. "That would take care of him," the boy said.

I went up a little way, then started wading down the creek. I watched ahead of me as I went. Suddenly the fish darted away from the bank, turned right in front of me in a big cloudy swirl, and barrel-assed downstream.

"Here he comes!" I hollered. "Hey, hey, here he comes!" But the fish spun around before it reached the riffle and headed back. I splashed and hollered, and it turned again. "He's coming! Get him, get him! Here he comes!"

But the dumb idiot had himself a club, the asshole, and when the fish hit the riffle, the boy drove at him with the club instead of trying to kick the sonofabitch out like he should have. The fish veered off, going crazy, shooting on his side through the shallow water. He made it. The asshole idiot kid lunged for him and fell flat.

He dragged up onto the bank sopping wet. "I hit him!" the boy hollered. "I think he's hurt, too. I had my hands on him, but I couldn't hold him."

"You didn't have anything!" I was out of breath. I was glad the kid fell in. "You didn't even come close, asshole. What were you doing with that club? You should have kicked him. He's probably a mile away by now." I tried to spit. I shook my head. "I don't know. We haven't got him yet. We just may not get him," I said.

"Goddamn it, I hit him!" the boy screamed. "Didn't you see? I hit him, and I had my hands on him too. How close did you get? Besides, whose fish is it?" He looked at me. Water ran down his trousers over his shoes.

I didn't say anything else, but I wondered about that myself. I shrugged. "Well, okay. I thought it was both ours. Let's get him this time. No goof-ups, either one of us," I said.

We waded downstream. I had water in my boots, but the kid was wet up to his collar. He closed his buck teeth over his lip to keep his teeth from chattering.

—

The fish wasn't in the run below the riffle, and we couldn't see him in the next stretch, either. We looked at each other and began to worry that the fish really had gone far enough downstream to reach one of the deep holes. But then the goddamn thing rolled near the bank, actually knocking dirt into the water with his tail, and took off again. He went through another riffle, his big tail sticking out of the water. I saw him cruise over near the bank and stop, his tail half out of the water, finning just enough to hold against the current.

"Do you see him?" I said. The boy looked. I took his arm and pointed his finger. "Right *there*. Okay now, listen. I'll go down to that little run between those banks. See where I mean? You wait here until I give you a signal. Then you start down. Okay? And this time don't let him get by you if he heads back."

"Yeah," the boy said and worked his lip with those teeth. "Let's get him this time," the boy said, a terrible look of cold in his face.

I got up on the bank and walked down, making sure I moved quiet. I slid off the bank and waded in again. But I couldn't see the great big sonofabitch and my heart turned. I thought it might have taken off already. A little farther downstream and it would get to one of the holes. We would never get him then.

"He still there?" I hollered. I held my breath.

The kid waved.

"Ready!" I hollered again.

"Here goes!" the kid hollered back.

My hands shook. The creek was about three feet wide and ran between dirt banks. The water was low but fast. The kid was moving down the creek now, water up to his knees, throwing rocks ahead of him, splashing and shouting.

"Here he comes!" The kid waved his arms. I saw the fish now; it was coming right at me. He tried to turn when he saw me, but it was too late. I went down on my knees, grasping in the cold water. I scooped him with my hands and arms, up, up, raising him, throwing him out of the water, both of us falling onto the bank. I held him against my shirt, him flopping and twisting, until I could get my hands up his slippery sides to his gills. I ran one hand in and clawed through to his mouth and locked around his jaw. I knew I had him. He was still flopping and hard to hold, but I had him and I wasn't going to let go.

"We got him!" the boy hollered as he splashed up. "We got him, by God! Ain't he something! Look at him! Oh God, let me hold him," the boy hollered.

"We got to kill him first," I said. I ran my other hand down the throat. I pulled back on the head as hard as I could, trying to watch out for the teeth, and felt the heavy crunching. He gave a long slow tremble and was still. I laid him on the bank and we looked at him. He was at least two feet long, queerly skinny, but bigger than anything I had ever caught. I took hold of his jaw again.

"Hey," the kid said but didn't say any more when he saw what I was going to do. I washed off the blood and laid the fish back on the bank.

"I want to show him to my dad so bad," the kid said.

We were wet and shivering. We looked at him, kept touching him. We pried open his big mough and felt his rows of teeth. His sides were scarred, whitish welts as big as quarters and kind of puffy. There were nicks out of his head around his eyes and on his snout where I guess he had banged into the rocks and been in fights. But he was so skinny, too skinny for how long he was, and you could hardly see the pink stripe down his sides, and his belly was gray and slack instead of white and solid like it should have been. But I thought he was something.

"I guess I'd better go pretty soon," I said. I looked at the clouds over the hills where the sun was going down. "I better get home."

"I guess so. Me too. I'm freezing," the kid said. "Hey, I want to carry him," the kid said.

"Let's get a stick. We'll put it through his mouth and both carry him," I said.

The kid found a stick. We put it through the gills and pushed until the fish was in the middle of the stick. Then we each took an end and started back, watching the fish as he swung on the stick.

"What are we going to do with him?" the kid said.

"I don't know," I said. "I guess I caught him," I said.

"We both did. Besides, I saw him first."

"That's true," I said. "Well, you want to flip for him or what?" I felt with my free hand, but I didn't have any money. And what would I have done if I had lost?

Anyway, the kid said, "No, let's not flip."

I said, "All right. It's okay with me." I looked at that boy, his hair standing up, his lips gray. I could have taken him if it came to that. But I didn't want to fight.

We got to where we had left our things and picked up our stuff with one hand, neither of us letting go of his end of the stick. Then we walked up to where his bicycle was. I got a good hold on the stick in case the kid tried something.

Then I had an idea. "We could half him," I said.

"What do you mean?" the boy said, his teeth chattering again. I could feel him tighten his hold on the stick.

"Half him. I got a knife. We cut him in two and each take half. I don't know, but I guess we could do that."

He pulled at a piece of his hair and looked at the fish. "You going to use that knife?"

"You got one?" I said.

The boy shook his head.

"Okay," I said.

I pulled the stick out and laid the fish in the grass beside the kid's bicycle. I took out the knife. A plane taxied down the runway as I measured a line. "Right here?" I said. The kid nodded. The plane roared down the runway and lifted up right over our heads. I started cutting down into him. I came to his guts and turned him over and stripped everything out. I kept cutting until there was only a flap of skin on his belly holding him together. I took the halves and worked them in my hands and I tore him in two.

I handed the kid the tail part.

"No," he said, shaking his head. "I want that half."

I said, "They're both the same! Now goddamn, watch it, I'm going to get mad in a minute."

"I don't care," the boy said. "If they're both the same, I'll take that one. They're both the same, right?"

"They're both the same," I said. "But I think I'm keeping this half here. I did the cutting."

"I want it," the kid said. "I saw him first."

"Whose knife did we use?" I said.

"I don't want the tail," the kid said.

I looked around. There were no cars on the road and nobody else fishing. There was an airplane droning, and the sun was going down. I was cold all the way through. The kid was shivering hard, waiting.

"I got an idea," I said. I opened the creel and showed him the trout. "See? It's a green one. It's the only green one I ever saw. So whoever takes the head, the other guy gets the green trout and the tail part. Is that fair?"

The kid looked at the green trout and took it out of the creel and held it. He studied the halves of the fish.

"I guess so," he said. "Okay, I guess so. You take that half. I got more meat on mine."

"I don't care," I said. "I'm going to wash him off. Which way do you live?" I said.

"Down on Arthur Avenue." He put the green trout and his half of the fish into a dirty canvas bag. "Why?"

"Where's that? Is that down by the ball park?" I said.

"Yeah, but why, I said." That kid looked scared.

"I live close to there," I said. "So I guess I could ride on the handlebars. We could take turns pumping. I got a weed we could smoke, if it didn't get wet on me."

But the kid only said, "I'm freezing."

I washed my half in the creek. I held his big head under water and opened his mouth. The stream poured into his mouth and out the other end of what was left of him.

"I'm freezing," the kid said.

I saw George riding his bicycle at the other end of the street. He didn't see me. I went around to the back to take off my boots. I unslung the creel so I could raise the lid and get set to march into the house, grinning.

I heard their voices and looked through the window. They were sitting at the table. Smoke was all over the kitchen. I saw it was coming from a pan on the burner. But neither of them paid any attention.

"What I'm telling you is the gospel truth," he said. "What do kids know? You'll see."

She said, "I'll see nothing. If I thought that, I'd rather see them dead first."

He said, "What's the matter with you? You better be careful what you say!"

She started to cry. He smashed out a cigaret in the ashtray and stood up.

"Edna, do you know this pan is burning up?" he said.

She looked at the pan. She pushed her chair back and grabbed the pan by its handle and threw it against the wall over the sink.

He said, "Have you lost your mind? Look what you've done!" He took a dish cloth and began to wipe up stuff from the pan.

I opened the back door. I started grinning. I said, "You won't believe what I caught at Birch Creek. Just look. Look here. Look at this. Look what I caught."

My legs shook. I could hardly stand. I held the creel out to her, and she finally looked in. "Oh, oh, my God! What is it? A snake! What is it? Please, please take it out before I throw up."

"Take it out!" he screamed. "Didn't you hear what she said? Take it out of here!" he screamed.

I said, "But look, Dad. Look what it is."

He said, "I don't want to look."

I said, "It's a gigantic summer steelhead from Birch Creek. Look! Isn't he something? It's a monster! I chased him up and down the creek like a madman!" My voice was crazy. But I could not stop. "There was another one, too," I hurried on. "A green one. I swear! It was green! Have you ever seen a green one?"

He looked into the creel and his mouth fell open.

He screamed, "Take that goddamn thing out of here! What in the hell is the matter with you? Take it the hell out of the kitchen and throw it in the goddamn garbage!"

I went back outside. I looked into the creel. What was there looked silver under the porch light. What was there filled the creel.

I lifted him out. I held him. I held that half of him.

Sixty Acres

THE call had come an hour ago, when they were eating. Two men were shooting on Lee Waite's part of Toppenish Creek, down below the bridge on the Cowiche Road. It was the third or fourth time this winter someone had been in there, Joseph Eagle reminded Lee Waite. Joseph Eagle was an old Indian who lived on his government allotment in a little place off the Cowiche Road, with a radio he listened to day and night and a telephone in case he got sick. Lee Waite wished the old Indian would let him be about that land, that Joseph Eagle would do something else about it, if he wanted, besides call.

Out on the porch, Lee Waite leaned on one leg and picked at a string of meat between his teeth. He was a small thin man with a thin face and long black hair. If it had not been for the phone call, he would have slept awhile this afternoon. He frowned and took his time pulling into his coat; they would be gone anyway when he got there. That was usually the way. The hunters from Toppenish or Yakima could drive the reservation roads like anyone else; they just weren't allowed to hunt. But they would cruise by that untenanted and irresistible sixty acres of his, two, maybe three times, then, if they were feeling reckless, park down off the road in the trees and hurry through the knee-deep barley and wild oats, down to the creek —maybe getting some ducks, maybe not, but always doing a lot of shooting in the little time before they cleared out. Joseph Eagle sat crippled in his house and watched them plenty of times. Or so he told Lee Waite.

He cleaned his teeth with his tongue and squinted in the late-afternoon winter half-light. He wasn't afraid; it wasn't that, he told himself. He just didn't want trouble.

The porch, small and built on just before the war, was almost dark. The one window glass had been knocked out years before, and Waite had nailed a beet sack over the opening. It hung there next to the cabinet, matted-thick and frozen, moving slightly as the cold air from outside came in around the edges. The walls were crowded with old yokes and harnesses, and up

49

on one side, above the window, was a row of rusted hand tools. He made a last sweep with his tongue, tightened the light bulb into the overhead socket, and opened the cabinet. He took out the old double-barrel from in back and reached into the box on the top shelf for a handful of shells. The brass ends of the shells felt cold, and he rolled them in his hand before dropping them into a pocket of the old coat he was wearing.

"Aren't you going to load it, Papa?" the boy Benny asked from behind.

Waite turned, saw Benny and little Jack standing in the kitchen doorway. Ever since the call they had been after him— had wanted to know if this time he was going to shoot somebody. It bothered him, kids talking like that, like they would enjoy it, and now they stood at the door, letting all the cold air in the house and looking at the large gun up under his arm.

"Get back in that house where the hell you belong," he said.

They left the door open and ran back in where his mother and Nina were and on through to the bedroom. He could see Nina at the table trying to coax bites of squash into the baby, who was pulling back and shaking her head. Nina looked up, tried to smile.

Waite stepped into the kitchen and shut the door, leaned against it. She was plenty tired, he could tell. A beaded line of moisture glistened over her lip, and, as he watched, she stopped to move the hair away from her forehead. She looked up at him again, then back at the baby. It had never bothered her like this when she was carrying before. The other times she could hardly sit still and used to jump up and walk around, even if there wasn't much to do except cook a meal or sew. He fingered the loose skin around his neck and glanced covertly at his mother, dozing since the meal in a chair by the stove. She squinted her eyes at him and nodded. She was seventy and shriveled, but her hair was still crow-black and hung down in front over her shoulders in two long tight braids. Lee Waite was sure she had something wrong with her because sometimes she went two days without saying something, just sitting in the other room by the window and staring off up the valley. It made him shiver when she did that, and he didn't know any more what her little signs and signals, her silences, were supposed to mean.

"Why don't you say something?" he asked, shaking his

head. "How do I know what you mean, Mama, if you don't say?" Waite looked at her for a minute and watched her tug at the ends of her braids, waited for her to say something. Then he grunted and crossed by in front of her, took his hat off a nail, and went out.

It was cold. An inch or two of grainy snow from three days past covered everything, made the ground lumpy, and gave a foolish look to the stripped rows of beanpoles in front of the house. The dog came scrabbling out from under the house when it heard the door, started off for the truck without looking back. "Come here!" Waite called sharply, his voice looping in the thin air.

Leaning over, he took the dog's cold, dry muzzle in his hand. "You better stay here this time. Yes, yes." He flapped the dog's ear back and forth and looked around. He could not see the Satus Hills across the valley because of the heavy overcast, just the wavy flatness of sugar-beet fields—white, except for black places here and there where the snow had not gotten. One place in sight—Charley Treadwell's, a long way off—but no lights lit that he could tell. Not a sound anywhere, just the low ceiling of heavy clouds pressing down on everything. He'd thought there was a wind, but it was still.

"Stay here now. You hear?"

He started for the truck, wishing again he did not have to go. He had dreamed last night, again—about what he could not remember—but he'd had an uneasy feeling ever since he woke up. He drove in low gear down to the gate, got out and unhooked it, drove past, got out again and hooked it. He did not keep horses any more—but it was a habit he had gotten into, keeping the gate shut.

Down the road, the grader was scraping toward him, the blade shrieking fiercely every time the metal hit the frozen gravel. He was in no hurry, and he waited the long minutes it took the grader to come up. One of the men in the cab leaned out with a cigaret in his hand and waved as they went by. But Waite looked off. He pulled out onto the road after they passed. He looked over at Charley Treadwell's when he went by, but there were still no lights, and the car was gone. He remembered what Charley had told him a few days ago, about a fight Charley had had last Sunday with some kid who came over his fence in the afternoon and shot into a pond of ducks, right down by the barn. The ducks came in there every afternoon, Charley said. They *trusted* him, he said, as if that mattered. He'd run down from the barn where he was milking, waving his arms and shouting, and the kid had pointed the gun at him. If I could've just got that gun away from him, Charley had said, staring hard at Waite with his one good eye and nodding slowly. Waite hitched a little in the seat. He did not want any trouble like that. He hoped whoever it was would be gone when he got there, like the other times.

Out to the left he passed Fort Simcoe, the white-painted tops of the old buildings standing behind the reconstructed palisade. The gates of the place were open, and Lee Waite could see cars parked around inside and a few people in coats, walking. He never bothered to stop. Once the teacher had brought all the kids out here—a field trip, she called it—but Waite had stayed home from school that day. He rolled down the window and cleared his throat, hawked it at the gate as he passed.

He turned onto Lateral B and then came to Joseph Eagle's place—all the lights on, even the porch light. Waite drove past, down to where the Cowiche Road came in, and got out of the truck and listened. He had begun to think they might be gone and he could turn around and go on back when he heard a grouping of dull far-off shots come across the fields. He waited awhile, then took a rag and went around the truck and tried to wipe off some of the snow and ice in the window edges. He kicked the snow off his shoes before getting in, drove a little farther until he could see the bridge, then looked for the tracks that turned off into the trees, where he knew he would find their car. He pulled in behind the gray sedan and switched the ignition off.

He sat in the truck and waited, squeaking his foot back and forth on the brake and hearing them shoot every now and then. After a few minutes he couldn't sit still any longer and got out, walked slowly around to the front. He had not been down there to do anything in four or five years. He leaned against the fender and looked out over the land. He could not understand where all the time had gone.

He remembered when he was little, wanting to grow up. He

used to come down here often then and trap this part of the creek for muskrat and set night-lines for German brown. Waite looked around, moved his feet inside his shoes. All that was a long time ago. Growing up, he had heard his father say he intended this land for the three boys. But both brothers had been killed. Lee Waite was the one it came down to, all of it.

He remembered: deaths. Jimmy first. He remembered waking to the tremendous pounding on the door—dark, the smell of wood pitch from the stove, an automobile outside with the lights on and the motor running, and a crackling voice coming from a speaker inside. His father throws open the door, and the enormous figure of a man in a cowboy hat and wearing a gun—the deputy sheriff—fills the doorway. *Waite? Your boy Jimmy been stabbed at a dance in Wapato.* Everyone had gone away in the truck and Lee was left by himself. He had crouched, alone the rest of the night, in front of the wood stove, watching the shadows jump across the wall. Later, when he was twelve, another one came, a different sheriff, and only said they'd better come along.

He pushed off from the truck and walked the few feet over to the edge of the field. Things were different now, that's all there was to it. He was thirty-two, and Benny and little Jack were growing up. And there was the baby. Waite shook his head. He closed his hand around one of the tall stalks of milkweed. He snapped its neck and looked up when he heard the soft chuckling of ducks overhead. He wiped his hand on his pants and followed them for a moment, watched them set their wings at the same instant and circle once over the creek. Then they flared. He saw three ducks fall before he heard the shots.

He turned abruptly and started back for the truck.

He took out his gun, careful not to slam the door. He moved into the trees. It was almost dark. He coughed once and then stood with his lips pressed together.

They came thrashing through the brush, two of them. Then, jiggling and squeaking the fence, they climbed over into the field and crunched through the snow. They were breathing hard by the time they got up close to the car.

"My God, there's a truck there!" one of them said and dropped the ducks he was carrying.

It was a boy's voice. He had on a heavy hunting coat, and in the game pockets Waite could dimly make out the enormous padding of ducks.

"Take it easy, will you!" The other boy stood craning his head around, trying to see. "Hurry up! There's nobody inside. Get the hell in the car!"

Not moving, trying to keep his voice steady, Waite said, "Stand there. Put your guns right there on the ground." He edged out of the trees and faced them, raised and lowered his gun barrels. "Take off them coats now and empty them out."

"O God! *God* almighty!" one of them said.

The other did not say anything but took off his coat and began pulling out the ducks, still looking around.

Waite opened the door of their car, fumbled an arm around inside until he found the headlights. The boys put a hand up to shield their eyes, then turned their backs to the light.

"Whose land do you think this is?" Waite said. "What do you mean, shooting ducks on my land!"

One boy turned around cautiously, his hand still in front of his eyes. "What are you going to do?"

"What do you think I'm going to do?" Waite said. His voice sounded strange to him, light, insubstantial. He could hear the ducks settling on the creek, chattering to other ducks still in the air. "What do you think I'm going to do with you?" he said. "What would you do if you caught boys trespassing on your land?"

"If they said they was sorry and it was the first time, I'd let them go," the boy answered.

"I would too, sir, if they said they was sorry," the other boy said.

"You would? You really think that's what you'd do?" Waite knew he was stalling for time.

They did not answer. They stood in the glare of the head-lights and then turned their backs again.

"How do I know you wasn't here before?" Waite said. "The other times I had to come down here?"

"Word of honor, sir, we never been here before. We just drove by. For godsake," the boy sobbed.

"That's the whole truth," the other boy said. "Anybody can make a mistake once in his life."

It was dark now, and a thin drizzle was coming down in front of the lights. Waite turned up his collar and stared at the boys. From down on the creek the strident quacking of a drake carried up to him. He glanced around at the awful shapes of the trees, then back at the boys again.

"Maybe so," he said and moved his feet. He knew he would let them go in a minute. There wasn't much else he could do. He was putting them off the land; that was what mattered. "What's your names, anyway? What's yours? You. Is this here your car or not? What's your name?"

"Bob Roberts," the one boy answered quickly and looked sideways at the other.

"Williams, sir," the other boy said. "Bill Williams, sir."

Waite was willing to understand that they were kids, that they were lying to him because they were afraid. They stood with their backs to him, and Waite stood looking at them.

"You're lying!" he said, shocking himself. "Why you lying to me? You come onto my land and shoot my ducks and then you lie like hell to me!" He laid the gun over the car door to steady the barrels. He could hear branches rubbing in the tree-tops. He thought of Joseph Eagle sitting up there in his lighted house, his feet on a box, listening to the radio.

"All right, all right," Waite said. "Liars! Just stand there, liars." He walked stiffly around to his truck and got out an old beet sack, shook it open, had them put all the ducks in that. When he stood still, waiting, his knees unaccountably began to shake.

"Go ahead and go. Go on!"

He stepped back as they came up to the car. "I'll back up to the road. You back up along with me."

"Yes, sir," the one boy said as he slid in behind the wheel. "But what if I can't get this thing started now? The battery might be dead, you know. It wasn't very strong to begin with."

"I don't know," Waite said. He looked around. "I guess I'd have to push you out."

The boy shut off the lights, stamped on the accelerator, and hit the starter. The engine turned over slowly but caught, and the boy held his foot down on the pedal and raced the engine before firing up the lights again. Waite studied their pale cold faces staring out at him, looking for a sign from him.

He slung the bag of ducks into his truck and slid the double-barrel across the seat. He got in and backed out carefully onto the road. He waited until they were out, then followed them down to Lateral B and stopped with his motor running, watching their taillights disappear toward Toppenish. He had put them off the land. That was all that mattered. Yet he could not understand why he felt something crucial had happened, a failure.

But nothing had happened.

Patches of fog had blown in from down the valley. He couldn't see much over toward Charley's when he stopped to open the gate, only a faint light burning out on the porch that Waite did not remember seeing that afternoon. The dog waited on its belly by the barn, jumped up and began snuffling the ducks as Waite swung them over his shoulder and started up to the house. He stopped on the porch long enough to put the gun away. The ducks he left on the floor beside the cabinet. He would clean them tomorrow or the next day.

"Lee?" Nina called.

Waite took off his hat, loosened the light bulb, and before opening the door he paused a moment in the quiet dark.

Nina was at the kitchen table, the little box with her sewing things beside her on another chair. She held a piece of denim in her hand. Two or three of his shirts were on the table, along with a pair of scissors. He pumped a cup of water and picked up from a shelf over the sink some of the colored rocks the kids were always bringing home. There was a dry pine cone there too and a few big papery maple leaves from the summer. He glanced in the pantry. But he was not hungry. Then he walked over to the doorway and leaned against the jamb.

It was a small house. There was no place to go.

In the back, in one room, all of the children slept, and in the room off from this, Waite and Nina and his mother slept, though sometimes, in the summer, Waite and Nina slept outside. There was never a place to go. His mother was still sitting beside the stove, a blanket over her legs now and her tiny eyes open, watching him.

"The boys wanted to stay up until you came back," Nina said, "but I told them you said they had to go to bed."

"Yes, that's right," he said. "They had to go to bed, all right."

"I was afraid," she said.

"Afraid?" He tried to make it sound as if this surprised him. "Were you afraid too, Mama?"

The old woman did not answer. Her fingers fiddled around the sides of the blanket, tucking and pulling, covering against draft.

"How do you feel, Nina? Feel any better tonight?" He pulled out a chair and sat down by the table.

His wife nodded. He said nothing more, only looked down and began scoring his thumbnail into the table.

"Did you catch who it was?" she said.

"It was two kids," he said. "I let them go."

He got up and walked to the other side of the stove, spat into the woodbox, and stood with his fingers hooked into his back pockets. Behind the stove the wood was black and peeling, and overhead he could see, sticking out from a shelf, the brown mesh of a gill net wrapped around the prongs of a salmon spear. But what was it? He squinted at it.

"I let them go," he said. "Maybe I was easy on them."

"You did what was right," Nina said.

He glanced over the stove at his mother. But there was no sign from her, only the black eyes staring at him.

"I don't know," he said. He tried to think about it, but already it seemed as if it had happened, whatever it was, long ago. "I should've given them more of a scare, I guess." He looked at Nina. "My land," he added. "I could've killed them."

"Kill who?" his mother said.

"Them kids down on the Cowiche Road land. What Joseph Eagle called about."

From where he stood he could see his mother's fingers working in her lap, tracing the raised design in the blanket. He leaned over the stove, wanting to say something else. But he did not know what.

He wandered to the table and sat down again. Then he realized he still had on his coat, and he got up, took a while unfastening it, and then laid it across the table. He pulled up the chair close to his wife's knees, crossed his arms limply, and took his shirt sleeves between his fingers.

"I was thinking maybe I'll lease out that land down there to the hunting clubs. No good to us down there like that. Is it? Our house was down there or it was our land right out here in front would be something different, right?"

In the silence he could hear only the wood snapping in the stove. He laid his hands flat on the table and could feel the pulse jumping in his arms. "I can lease it out to one of the duck clubs from Toppenish. Or Yakima. Any of them would be glad to get hold of land like that, right on the flyway. That's some of the best hunting land in the valley. . . . If I could put it to some use someway, it would be different then." His voice trailed off.

She moved in the chair. She said, "If you think we should do it. It's whatever you think. I don't know."

"I don't know, either," he said. His eyes crossed the floor, raised past his mother, and again came to rest on the salmon spear. He got up, shaking his head. As he moved across the little room, the old woman crooked her head and laid her cheek on the chairback, eyes narrowed and following him. He reached up, worked the spear and the mass of netting off the splintery shelf, and turned around behind her chair. He looked at the tiny dark head, at the brown woolen shawl shaped smooth over the hunched shoulders. He turned the spear in his hands and began to unwrap the netting.

"How much would you get?" Nina said.

He knew he didn't know. It even confused him a little. He plucked at the netting, then placed the spear back on the shelf. Outside, a branch scraped roughly against the house.

"Lee?"

He was not sure. He would have to ask around. Mike Chuck had leased out thirty acres last fall for five hundred dollars. Jerome Shinpa leased some of his land every year, but Waite had never asked how much he got.

"Maybe a thousand dollars," he said.

"A thousand dollars?" she said.

He nodded, felt relief at her amazement. "Maybe so. Maybe more. I will have to see. I will have to ask somebody how much." It was a lot of money. He tried to think about having a thousand dollars. He closed his eyes and tried to think.

"That wouldn't be selling it, would it?" Nina asked. "If you lease it to them, that means it's still your land?"

"Yes, yes, it's still my land!" He went over to her and leaned across the table. "Don't you know the difference, Nina? They can't *buy* land on the reservation. Don't you know that? I will lease it to them for them to use."

"I see," she said. She looked down and picked at the sleeve of one of his shirts. "They will have to give it back? It will still belong to you?"

"Don't you understand?" he said. He gripped the table edge. "It is a lease!"

"What will Mama say?" Nina asked. "Will it be all right?"

They both looked over at the old woman. But her eyes were closed and she seemed to be sleeping.

"A thousand dollars," Nina said and shook her head.

A thousand dollars. Maybe more. He didn't know. But even a thousand dollars! He wondered how he would go about it, letting people know he had land to lease. It was too late now for this year—but he could start asking around in the spring. He crossed his arms and tried to think. His legs began to tremble, and he leaned against the wall. He rested there and then let his weight slide gently down the wall until he was squatting.

"It's just a lease," he said.

He stared at the floor. It seemed to slant in his direction; it seemed to move. He shut his eyes and brought his hands against his ears to steady himself. And then he thought to cup his palms, so that there would come that roaring, like the wind howling up from a seashell.

What's in Alaska?

CARL got off work at three. He left the station and drove to a shoe store near his apartment. He put his foot up on the stool and let the clerk unlace his work boot.

"Something comfortable," Carl said. "For casual wear."

"I have something," the clerk said.

The clerk brought out three pairs of shoes and Carl said he would take the soft beige-colored shoes that made his feet feel free and springy. He paid the clerk and put the box with his boots under his arm. He looked down at his new shoes as he walked. Driving home, he felt that his foot moved freely from pedal to pedal.

"You bought some new shoes," Mary said. "Let me see."

"Do you like them?" Carl said.

"I don't like the color, but I'll bet they're comfortable. You needed new shoes."

He looked at the shoes again. "I've got to take a bath," he said.

"We'll have an early dinner," she said. "Helen and Jack asked us over tonight. Helen got Jack a water pipe for his birthday and they're anxious to try it out." Mary looked at him. "Is it all right with you?"

"What time?"

"Around seven."

"It's all right," he said.

She looked at his shoes again and sucked her cheeks. "Take your bath," she said.

Carl ran the water and took off his shoes and clothes. He lay in the tub for a while and then used a brush to get at the lube grease under his nails. He dropped his hands and then raised them to his eyes.

She opened the bathroom door. "I brought you a beer," she said. Steam drifted around her and out into the living room.

"I'll be out in a minute," he said. He drank some of the beer.

She sat on the edge of the tub and put her hand on his thigh. "Home from the wars," she said.

"Home from the wars," he said.

She moved her hand through the wet hair on his thigh. Then she clapped her hands. "Hey, I have something to tell you! I had an interview today, and I think they're going to offer me a job—in *Fairbanks*."

"Alaska?" he said.

She nodded. "What do you think of that?"

"I've always wanted to go to Alaska. Does it look pretty definite?"

She nodded again. "They liked me. They said I'd hear next week."

"That's great. Hand me a towel, will you? I'm getting out."

"I'll go and set the table," she said.

His fingertips and toes were pale and wrinkled. He dried slowly and put on clean clothes and the new shoes. He combed his hair and went out to the kitchen. He drank another beer while she put dinner on the table.

"We're supposed to bring some cream soda and something to munch on," she said. "We'll have to go by the store."

"Cream soda and munchies. Okay," he said.

When they had eaten, he helped her clear the table. Then they drove to the market and bought cream soda and potato chips and corn chips and onion-flavored snack crackers. At the checkout counter he added a handful of U-No bars to the order.

"Hey, yeah," she said when she saw them.

They drove home again and parked, and then they walked the block to Helen and Jack's.

Helen opened the door. Carl put the sack on the dining-room table. Mary sat down in the rocking chair and sniffed.

"We're late," she said. "They started without us, Carl."

Helen laughed. "We had one when Jack came in. We haven't lighted the water pipe yet. We were waiting until you got here." She stood in the middle of the room, looking at them and grinning. "Let's see what's in the sack," she said. "Oh, wow! Say, I think I'll have one of these corn chips right now. You guys want some?"

"We just ate dinner," Carl said. "We'll have some pretty soon." Water had stopped running and Carl could hear Jack whistling in the bathroom.

"We have some Popsicles and some M and M's," Helen said. She stood beside the table and dug into the potato-chip bag. "If Jack ever gets out of the shower, he'll get the water pipe going." She opened the box of snack crackers and put one in her mouth. "Say, these are really good," she said.

"I don't know what Emily Post would say about you," Mary said.

Helen laughed. She shook her head.

Jack came out of the bathroom. "Hi, everybody. Hi, Carl. What's so funny?" he said, grinning. "I could hear you laughing."

"We were laughing at Helen," Mary said.

"Helen was just laughing," Carl said.

"She's funny," Jack said. "Look at the goodies! Hey, you guys ready for a glass of cream soda? I'll get the pipe going."

"I'll have a glass," Mary said. "What about you, Carl?"

"I'll have some," Carl said.

"Carl's on a little bummer tonight," Mary said.

"Why do you say that?" Carl asked. He looked at her. "That's a good way to put me on one."

"I was just teasing," Mary said. She came over and sat beside him on the sofa. "I was just teasing, honey."

"Hey, Carl, don't get on a bummer," Jack said. "Let me show you what I got for my birthday. Helen, open one of those bottles of cream soda while I get the pipe going. I'm real dry."

Helen carried the chips and crackers to the coffee table. Then she produced a bottle of cream soda and four glasses.

"Looks like we're going to have a party," Mary said.

"If I didn't starve myself all day, I'd put on ten pounds a week," Helen said.

"I know what you mean," Mary said.

Jack came out of the bedroom with the water pipe. "What do you think of this?" he said to Carl. He put the water pipe on the coffee table.

"That's really something," Carl said. He picked it up and looked at it.

"It's called a hookah," Helen said. "That's what they called it where I bought it. It's just a little one, but it does the job." She laughed.

"Where did you get it?" Mary said.

"What? That little place on Fourth Street. You know," Helen said.

"Sure. I know," Mary said. "I'll have to go in there some day," Mary said. She folded her hands and watched Jack.

"How does it work?" Carl said.

"You put the stuff here," Jack said. "And you light this. Then you inhale through this here and the smoke is filtered through the water. It has a good taste to it and it really hits you."

"I'd like to get Carl one for Christmas," Mary said. She looked at Carl and grinned and touched his arm.

"I'd like to have one," Carl said. He stretched his legs and looked at his shoes under the light.

"Here, try this," Jack said, letting out a thin stream of smoke and passing the tube to Carl. "See if this isn't okay."

Carl drew on the tube, held the smoke, and passed the tube to Helen.

"Mary first," Helen said. "I'll go after Mary. You guys have to catch up."

"I won't argue," Mary said. She slipped the tube in her mouth and drew rapidly, twice, and Carl watched the bubbles she made.

"That's really okay," Mary said. She passed the tube to Helen.

"We broke it in last night." Helen said, and laughed loudly.

"She was still stoned when she got up with the kids this morning," Jack said, and he laughed. He watched Helen pull on the tube.

"How are the kids?" Mary asked.

"They're fine," Jack said and put the tube in his mouth.

Carl sipped the cream soda and watched the bubbles in the pipe. They reminded him of bubbles rising from a diving helmet. He imagined a lagoon and schools of remarkable fish.

Jack passed the tube.

Carl stood up and stretched.

"Where are you going, honey?" Mary asked.

"No place," Carl said. He sat down and shook his head and grinned. "Jesus."

Helen laughed.

"What's funny?" Carl said after a long, long time.

"God, I don't know," Helen said. She wiped her eyes and laughed again, and Mary and Jack laughed.

After a time Jack unscrewed the top of the water pipe and blew through one of the tubes. "It gets plugged sometimes."

"What did you mean when you said I was on a bummer?" Carl said to Mary.

"What?" Mary said.

Carl stared at her and blinked. "You said something about me being on a bummer. What made you say that?"

"I don't remember now, but I can tell when you are," she said. "But please don't bring up anything negative, okay?"

"Okay," Carl said. "All I'm saying is I don't know why you said that. If I wasn't on a bummer before you said it, it's enough when you say it to put me on one."

"If the shoe fits," Mary said. She leaned on the arm of the sofa and laughed until tears came.

"What was that?" Jack said. He looked at Carl and then at Mary. "I missed that one," Jack said.

"I should have made some dip for these chips," Helen said.

"Wasn't there another bottle of that cream soda?" Jack said.

"We bought two bottles," Carl said.

"Did we drink them both?" Jack said.

"Did we drink any?" Helen said and laughed. "No, I only opened one. I think I only opened one. I don't remember opening more than one," Helen said and laughed.

Carl passed the tube to Mary. She took his hand and guided the tube into her mouth. He watched the smoke flow over her lips a long time later.

"What about some cream soda?" Jack said.

Mary and Helen laughed.

"What about it?" Mary said.

"Well, I thought we were going to have us a glass," Jack said. He looked at Mary and grinned.

Mary and Helen laughed.

"What's funny?" Jack said. He looked at Helen and then at Mary. He shook his head. "I don't know about you guys," he said.

"We might go to Alaska," Carl said.

"Alaska?" Jack said. "What's in Alaska? What would you do up there?"

"I wish we could go someplace," Helen said.

"What's wrong with here?" Jack said. "What would you guys do in Alaska? I'm serious. I'd like to know."

Carl put a potato chip in his mouth and sipped his cream soda. "I don't know. What did you say?"

After a while Jack said, "What's in Alaska?"

"I don't know," Carl said. "Ask Mary. Mary knows. Mary, what am I going to do up there? Maybe I'll grow those giant cabbages you read about."

"Or pumpkins," Helen said. "Grow pumpkins."

"You'd clean up," Jack said. "Ship the pumpkins down here for Halloween. I'll be your distributor."

"Jack will be your distributor," Helen said.

"That's right," Jack said. "We'll clean up."

"Get rich," Mary said.

In a while Jack stood up. "I know what would taste good and that's some cream soda," Jack said.

Mary and Helen laughed.

"Go ahead and laugh," Jack said, grinning. "Who wants some cream soda?"

"Some what?" Mary said.

"Some cream soda," Jack said.

"You stood up like you were going to make a speech," Mary said.

"I hadn't thought of that," Jack said. He shook his head and laughed. He sat down. "That's good stuff," he said.

"We should have got more," Helen said.

"More what?" Mary said.

"More money," Jack said.

"No money," Carl said.

"Did I see some U-No bars in that sack?" Helen said.

"I bought some," Carl said. "I spotted them the last minute."

"U-No bars are good," Jack said.

"They're creamy," Mary said. "They melt in your mouth."

"We have some M and M's and Popsicles if anybody wants any," Jack said.

Mary said, "I'll have a Popsicle. Are you going to the kitchen?"

"Yeah, and I'm going to get the cream soda, too," Jack said. "I just remembered. You guys want a glass?"

"Just bring it all in and we'll decide," Helen said. "The M and M's too."

"Might be easier to move the kitchen out here," Jack said.

"When we lived in the city," Mary said, "people said you could see who'd turned on the night before by looking at their kitchen in the morning. We had a tiny kitchen when we lived in the city," she said.

"We had a tiny kitchen too," Carl said.

"I'm going out to see what I can find," Jack said.

"I'll come with you," Mary said.

Carl watched them walk to the kitchen. He settled back against the cushion and watched them walk. Then he leaned forward very slowly. He squinted. He saw Jack reach up to a shelf in the cupboard. He saw Mary move against Jack from behind and put her arms around his waist.

"Are you guys serious?" Helen said.

"Very serious," Carl said.

"About Alaska," Helen said.

He stared at her.

"I thought you said something," Helen said.

Jack and Mary came back. Jack carried a large bag of M and M's and a bottle of cream soda. Mary sucked on an orange Popsicle.

"Anybody want a sandwich?" Helen said. "We have sandwich stuff."

"Isn't it funny," Mary said. "You start with the desserts first and then you move on to the main course."

"It's funny," Carl said.

"Are you being sarcastic, honey?" Mary said.

"Who wants cream soda?" Jack said. "A round of cream soda coming up."

Carl held his glass out and Jack poured it full. Carl set the glass on the coffee table, but the coffee table smacked it off and the soda poured onto his shoe.

"Goddamn it," Carl said. "How do you like that? I spilled it on my shoe."

"Helen, do we have a towel? Get Carl a towel," Jack said.

"Those were new shoes," Mary said. "He just got them."

"They look comfortable," Helen said a long time later and handed Carl a towel.

"That's what I told him," Mary said.

Carl took the shoe off and rubbed the leather with the towel.

"It's done for," he said. "That cream soda will never come out."

Mary and Jack and Helen laughed.

"That reminds me, I read something in the paper," Helen said. She pushed on the tip of her nose with a finger and narrowed her eyes. "I can't remember what it was now," she said.

Carl worked the shoe back on. He put both feet under the lamp and looked at the shoes together.

"What did you read?" Jack said.

"What?" Helen said.

"You said you read something in the paper," Jack said.

Helen laughed. "I was just thinking about Alaska, and I remembered them finding a prehistoric man in a block of ice. Something reminded me."

"That wasn't in Alaska," Jack said.

"Maybe it wasn't, but it reminded me of it," Helen said.

"What *about* Alaska, you guys?" Jack said.

"There's nothing in Alaska," Carl said.

"He's on a bummer," Mary said.

"What'll you guys *do* in Alaska?" Jack said.

"There's nothing to do in Alaska," Carl said. He put his feet under the coffee table. Then he moved them out under the light once more. "Who wants a new pair of shoes?" Carl said.

"What's that noise?" Helen said.

They listened. Something scratched at the door.

"It sounds like Cindy," Jack said. "I'd better let her in."

"While you're up, get me a Popsicle," Helen said. She put her head back and laughed.

"I'll have another one too, honey," Mary said. "What did I say? I mean *Jack*," Mary said. "Excuse me. I thought I was talking to Carl."

"Popsicles all around," Jack said. "You want a Popsicle, Carl?"

"What?"

"You want an orange Popsicle?"

"An orange one," Carl said.

"Four Popsicles coming up," Jack said.

In a while he came back with the Popsicles and handed them around. He sat down and they heard the scratching again.

"I knew I was forgetting something," Jack said. He got up and opened the front door.

"Good Christ," he said, "if this isn't something. I guess Cindy went out for dinner tonight. Hey, you guys, look at this."

The cat carried a mouse into the living room, stopped to look at them, then carried the mouse down the hall.

"Did you see what I just saw?" Mary said. "Talk about a bummer."

Jack turned the hall light on. The cat carried the mouse out of the hall and into the bathroom.

"She's eating this mouse," Jack said.

"I don't think I want her eating a mouse in my bathroom," Helen said. "Make her get out of there. Some of the children's things are in there."

"She's not going to get out of here," Jack said.

"What about the mouse?" Mary said.

"What the hell," Jack said. "Cindy's got to learn to hunt if we're going to Alaska."

"Alaska?" Helen said. "What's all this about Alaska?"

"Don't ask me," Jack said. He stood near the bathroom door and watched the cat. "Mary and Carl said they're going to Alaska. Cindy's got to learn to hunt."

Mary put her chin in her hands and stared into the hall.

"She's eating the mouse," Jack said.

Helen finished the last of the corn chips. "I told him I didn't want Cindy eating a mouse in the bathroom. Jack?" Helen said.

"What?"

"Make her get out of the bathroom, I said," Helen said.

"For Christ's sake," Jack said.

"Look," Mary said. "Ugh," Mary said. "The goddamn cat is coming in here," Mary said.

"What's she doing?" Carl said.

The cat dragged the mouse under the coffee table. She lay down under the table and licked the mouse. She held the mouse in her paws and licked slowly, from head to tail.

"The cat's high," Jack said.
"It gives you the shivers," Mary said.
"It's just nature," Jack said.

"Look at her eyes," Mary said. "Look at the way she looks at us. She's high, all right."

Jack came over to the sofa and sat beside Mary. Mary inched toward Carl to give Jack room. She rested her hand on Carl's knee.

They watched the cat eat the mouse.

"Don't you ever feed that cat?" Mary said to Helen.

Helen laughed.

"You guys ready for another smoke?" Jack said.

"We have to go," Carl said.

"What's your hurry?" Jack said.

"Stay a little longer," Helen said. "You don't have to go yet."

Carl stared at Mary, who was staring at Jack. Jack stared at something on the rug near his feet.

Helen picked through the M and M's in her hand.

"I like the green ones best," Helen said.

"I have to work in the morning," Carl said.

"What a bummer he's on," Mary said. "You want to hear a bummer, folks? *There's* a bummer."

"Are you coming?" Carl said.

"Anybody want a glass of milk?" Jack said. "We've got some milk out there."

"I'm too full of cream soda," Mary said.

"There's no more cream soda," Jack said.

Helen laughed. She closed her eyes and then opened them and then laughed again.

"We have to go home," Carl said. In a while he stood up and said, "Did we have coats? I don't think we had coats."

"What? I don't think we had coats," Mary said. She stayed seated.

"We'd better go," Carl said.

"They have to go," Helen said.

Carl put his hands under Mary's shoulders and pulled her up.

"Goodbye, you guys," Mary said. She embraced Carl. "I'm so full I can hardly move," Mary said.

Helen laughed.

"Helen's always finding something to laugh at," Jack said, and Jack grinned. "What are you laughing at, Helen?"

"I don't know. Something Mary said," Helen said.

"What did I say?" Mary said.

"I can't remember," Helen said.

"We have to go," Carl said.

"So long," Jack said. "Take it easy."

Mary tried to laugh.

"Let's go," Carl said.

"Night, everybody," Jack said. "Night, Carl," Carl heard Jack say very, very slowly.

Outside, Mary held Carl's arm and walked with her head down. They moved slowly on the sidewalk. He listened to the scuffing sounds her shoes made. He heard the sharp and separate sound of a dog barking and above that a murmuring of very distant traffic.

She raised her head. "When we get home, Carl, I want to be fucked, talked to, diverted. Divert me, Carl. I need to be diverted tonight." She tightened her hold on his arm.

He could feel the dampness in that shoe. He unlocked the door and flipped the light.

"Come to bed," she said.

"I'm coming," he said.

He went to the kitchen and drank two glasses of water. He turned off the living-room light and felt his way along the wall into the bedroom.

"Carl!" she yelled. "Carl!"

"Jesus Christ, it's me!" he said. "I'm trying to get the light on."

He found the lamp, and she sat up in bed. Her eyes were bright. He pulled the stem on the alarm and began taking off his clothes. His knees trembled.

"Is there anything else to smoke?" she said.

"We don't have anything," he said.

"Then fix me a drink. We have something to drink. Don't tell me we don't have something to drink," she said.

"Just some beer."

They stared at each other.

"I'll have a beer," she said.

"You really want a beer?"

She nodded slowly and chewed her lip.

He came back with the beer. She was sitting with his pillow

on her lap. He gave her the can of beer and then crawled into
bed and pulled the covers up.

"I forgot to take my pill," she said.

"What?"

"I forgot my pill."

He got out of bed and brought her the pill. She opened her
eyes and he dropped the pill onto her outstretched tongue.
She swallowed some beer with the pill and he got back in bed.

"Take this. I can't keep my eyes open," she said.

He set the can on the floor and then stayed on his side and
stared into the dark hallway. She put her arm over his ribs and
her fingers crept across his chest.

"What's in Alaska?" she said.

He turned on his stomach and eased all the way to his side
of the bed. In a moment she was snoring.

Just as he started to turn off the lamp, he thought he saw
something in the hall. He kept staring and thought he saw it
again, a pair of small eyes. His heart turned. He blinked and
kept staring. He leaned over to look for something to throw.
He picked up one of his shoes. He sat up straight and held the
shoe with both hands. He heard her snoring and set his teeth.
He waited. He waited for it to move once more, to make the
slightest noise.

Night School

M Y marriage had just fallen apart. I couldn't find a job. I had another girl. But she wasn't in town. So I was at a bar having a glass of beer, and two women were sitting a few stools down, and one of them began to talk to me.

"You have a car?"

"I do, but it's not here," I said.

My wife had the car. I was staying at my parents' place. I used their car sometimes. But tonight I was walking.

The other woman looked at me. They were both about forty, maybe older.

"What'd you ask him?" the other woman said to the first woman.

"I said did he have a car."

"So do you have a car?" the second woman said to me.

"I was telling her. I have a car. But I don't have it with me," I said.

"That doesn't do us much good, does it?" she said.

The first woman laughed. "We had a brainstorm and we need a car to go through with it. Too bad." She turned to the bartender and asked for two more beers.

I'd been nursing my beer along, and now I drank it off and thought they might buy me a round. They didn't.

"What do you do?" the first woman asked me.

"Right now, nothing," I said. "Sometimes, when I can, I go to school."

"He goes to school," she said to the other woman. "He's a student. Where do you go to school?"

"Around," I said.

"I told you," the woman said. "Doesn't he look like a student?"

"What are they teaching you?" the second woman said.

"Everything," I said.

"I mean," she said, "what do you plan to do? What's your big goal in life? Everybody has a big goal in life."

I raised my empty glass to the bartender. He took it and drew me another beer. I counted out some change, which left

me with thirty cents from the two dollars I'd started out with
a couple of hours ago. She was waiting.

"Teach. Teach school," I said.

"He wants to be a teacher," she said.

I sipped my beer. Someone put a coin in the jukebox and a
song that my wife liked began to play. I looked around. Two
men near the front were at the shuffleboard. The door was
open and it was dark outside.

"We're students too, you know," the first woman said. "We
go to school."

"We take a night class," the other one said. "We take this
reading class on Monday nights."

The first woman said, "Why don't you move down here,
teacher, so we don't have to yell?"

I picked up my beer and my cigarets and moved down two
stools.

"That's better," she said. "Now, did you say you were a
student?"

"Sometimes, yes, but not now," I said.

"Where?"

"State College."

"That's right," she said. "I remember now." She looked at
the other woman. "You ever hear of a teacher over there name
of Patterson? He teaches adult-education classes. He teaches
this class we take on Monday nights. You remind me a lot of
Patterson."

They looked at each other and laughed.

"Don't bother about us," the first woman said. "It's a private joke. Shall we tell him what we thought about doing,
Edith? *Shall* we?"

Edith didn't answer. She took a drink of beer and she narrowed her eyes as she looked at herself, at the three of us, in
the mirror behind the bar.

"We were thinking," the first woman went on, "if we had a
car tonight we'd go over and see him. Patterson. Right, Edith?"

Edith laughed to herself. She finished her beer and asked for
a round, one for me included. She paid for the beers with a
five-dollar bill.

"Patterson likes to take a drink," Edith said.

"You can say that again," the other woman said. She turned

to me. "We talked about it in class one night. Patterson says he always has wine with his meals and a highball or two before dinner."

"What class is this?" I said.

"This reading class Patterson teaches. Patterson likes to talk about different things."

"We're learning to read," Edith said. "Can you believe it?"

"I'd like to read Hemingway and things like that," the other woman said. "But Patterson has us reading stories like in *Reader's Digest*."

"We take a test every Monday night," Edith said. "But Patterson's okay. He wouldn't care if we came over for a highball. Wouldn't be much he could do, anyway. We have something on him. On Patterson," she said.

"We're on the loose tonight," the other woman said. "But Edith's car is in the garage."

"If you had a car now, we'd go over and see him," Edith said. She looked at me. "You could tell Patterson you wanted to be a teacher. You'd have something in common."

I finished my beer. I hadn't eaten anything all day except some peanuts. It was hard to keep listening and talking.

"Let's have three more, please, Jerry," the first woman said to the bartender.

"Thank you," I said.

"You'd get along with Patterson," Edith said.

"So call him," I said. I thought it was just talk.

"I wouldn't do that," she said. "He could make an excuse. We just show up on his porch, he'll have to let us in." She sipped her beer.

"So let's go!" the first woman said. "What're we waiting for? Where'd you say the car is?"

"There's a car a few blocks from here," I said. "But I don't know."

"Do you want to go or don't you?" Edith said.

"He said he does," the first woman said. "We'll get a six-pack to take with us."

"I only have thirty cents," I said.

"Who needs your goddamn money?" Edith said. "We need your goddamn car. Jerry, let's have three more. And a six-pack to go."

"Here's to Patterson," the first woman said when the beer came. "To Patterson and his highballs."

"He'll drop his cookies," Edith said.

"Drink up," the first woman said.

On the sidewalk we headed south, away from town. I walked between the two women. It was about ten o'clock.

"I could drink one of those beers now," I said.

"Help yourself," Edith said.

She opened the sack and I reached in and tore a can loose.

"We think he's home," Edith said.

"Patterson," the other woman said. "We don't know for sure. But we think so."

"How much farther?" Edith said.

I stopped, raised the beer, and drained half the can. "The next block," I said. "I'm staying with my parents. It's their place."

"I guess there's nothing wrong with it," Edith said. "But I'd say you're kind of old for that."

"That's not polite, Edith," the other woman said.

"Well, that's the way I am," Edith said. "He'll have to get used to it, that's all. That's the way I am."

"That's the way she is," the other woman said.

I finished the beer and tossed the can into some weeds.

"Now how far?" Edith said.

"This is it. Right here. I'll try and get the car key," I said.

"Well, hurry up," Edith said.

"We'll wait outside," the other woman said.

"Jesus!" Edith said.

I unlocked the door and went downstairs. My father was in his pajamas, watching television. It was warm in the apartment and I leaned against the jamb for a minute and ran a hand over my eyes.

"I had a couple of beers," I said. "What are you watching?"

"John Wayne," he said. "It's pretty good. Sit down and watch it. Your mother hasn't come in yet."

My mother worked the swing shift at Paul's, a *hofbrau* restaurant. My father didn't have a job. He used to work in the woods, and then he got hurt. He'd had a settlement, but most of that was gone now. I asked him for a loan of two hundred dollars when my wife left me, but he refused. He had tears in his eyes when he said no and said he hoped I wouldn't hold it against him. I'd said it was all right, I wouldn't hold it against him.

I knew he was going to say no this time too. But I sat down on the other end of the couch and said, "I met a couple of women who asked me if I'd give them a ride home."

"What'd you tell them?" he said.

"They're waiting for me upstairs," I said.

"Just let them wait," he said. "Somebody'll come along. You don't want to get mixed up with that." He shook his head. "You really didn't show them where we live, did you? They're not really upstairs?" He moved on the couch and looked again at the television. "Anyway, your mother took the keys with her." He nodded slowly, still looking at the television.

"That's okay," I said. "I don't need the car. I'm not going anywhere."

I got up and looked into the hallway, where I slept on a cot. There was an ashtray, a Lux clock, and a few old paperbacks on a table beside the cot. I usually went to bed at midnight and read until the lines of print went fuzzy and I fell asleep with the light on and the book in my hands. In one of the paperbacks I was reading there was something I remembered telling my wife. It made a terrific impression on me. There's a man who has a nightmare and in the nightmare he dreams he's dreaming and wakes to see a man standing at his bedroom window. The dreamer is so terrified he can't move, can hardly breathe. The man at the window stares into the room and then begins to pry off the screen. The dreamer can't move. He'd like to scream, but he can't get his breath. But the moon appears from behind a cloud, and the dreamer in the nightmare recognizes the man outside. It is his best friend, the best friend of the dreamer but no one the man having the nightmare knows.

Telling it to my wife, I'd felt the blood come to my face and my scalp prickle. But she wasn't interested.

"That's only writing," she said. "Being betrayed by somebody in your own family, *there's* a real nightmare for you."

I could hear them shaking the outside door. I could hear footsteps on the sidewalk over my window.

"Goddamn that bastard!" I heard Edith say.

I went into the bathroom for a long time and then I went upstairs and let myself out. It was cooler, and I did up the zipper on my jacket. I started walking to Paul's. If I got there before my mother went off duty, I could have a turkey sandwich. After that I could go to Kirby's newsstand and look through the magazines. Then I could go to the apartment to bed and read the books until I read enough and I slept.

The women, they weren't there when I left, and they wouldn't be there when I got back.

Collectors

I WAS out of work. But any day I expected to hear from up north. I lay on the sofa and listened to the rain. Now and then I'd lift up and look through the curtain for the mailman.

There was no one on the street, nothing.

I hadn't been down again five minutes when I heard someone walk onto the porch, wait, and then knock. I lay still. I knew it wasn't the mailman. I knew his steps. You can't be too careful if you're out of work and you get notices in the mail or else pushed under your door. They come around wanting to talk, too, especially if you don't have a telephone.

The knock sounded again, louder, a bad sign. I eased up and tried to see onto the porch. But whoever was there was standing against the door, another bad sign. I knew the floor creaked, so there was no chance of slipping into the other room and looking out that window.

Another knock, and I said, Who's there?

This is Aubrey Bell, a man said. Are you Mr. Slater?

What is it you want? I called from the sofa.

I have something for Mrs. Slater. She's won something. Is Mrs. Slater home?

Mrs. Slater doesn't live here, I said.

Well, then, are you Mr. Slater? the man said. Mr. Slater . . . and the man sneezed.

I got off the sofa. I unlocked the door and opened it a little. He was an old guy, fat and bulky under his raincoat. Water ran off the coat and dripped onto the big suitcase contraption thing he carried.

He grinned and set down the big case. He put out his hand. Aubrey Bell, he said.

I don't know you, I said.

Mrs. Slater, he began. Mrs. Slater filled out a card. He took cards from an inside pocket and shuffled them a minute. Mrs. Slater, he read. Two-fifty-five South Sixth East? Mrs. Slater is a winner.

He took off his hat and nodded solemnly, slapped the hat

against his coat as if that were it, everything had been settled, the drive finished, the railhead reached.

He waited.

Mrs. Slater doesn't live here, I said. What'd she win?

I have to show you, he said. May I come in?

I don't know. If it won't take long, I said. I'm pretty busy.

Fine, he said. I'll just slide out of this coat first. And the galoshes. Wouldn't want to track up your carpet. I see you do have a carpet, Mr. . . .

His eyes had lighted and then dimmed at the sight of the carpet. He shuddered. Then he took off his coat. He shook it out and hung it by the collar over the doorknob. That's a good place for it, he said. Damn weather, anyway. He bent over and unfastened his galoshes. He set his case inside the room. He stepped out of the galoshes and into the room in a pair of slippers.

I closed the door. He saw me staring at the slippers and said, W. H. Auden wore slippers all through China on his first visit there. Never took them off. Corns.

I shrugged. I took one more look down the street for the mailman and shut the door again.

Aubrey Bell stared at the carpet. He pulled his lips. Then he laughed. He laughed and shook his head.

What's so funny? I said.

Nothing. Lord, he said. He laughed again. I think I'm losing my mind. I think I have a fever. He reached a hand to his forehead. His hair was matted and there was a ring around his scalp where the hat had been.

Do I feel hot to you? he said. I don't know, I think I might have a fever. He was still staring at the carpet. You have any aspirin?

What's the matter with you? I said. I hope you're not getting sick on me. I got things I have to do.

He shook his head. He sat down on the sofa. He stirred at the carpet with his slippered foot.

I went to the kitchen, rinsed a cup, shook two aspirin out of a bottle.

Here, I said. Then I think you ought to leave.

Are you speaking for Mrs. Slater? he hissed. No, no, forget I said that, forget I said that. He wiped his face. He swallowed the aspirin. His eyes skipped around the bare room. Then he leaned forward with some effort and unsnapped the buckles on his case. The case flopped open, revealing compartments filled with an array of hoses, brushes, shiny pipes, and some kind of heavy-looking blue thing mounted on little wheels. He stared at these things as if surprised. Quietly, in a churchly voice, he said, Do you know what this is?

I moved closer. I'd say it was a vacuum cleaner. I'm not in the market, I said. No way am I in the market for a vacuum cleaner.

I want to show you something, he said. He took a card out of his jacket pocket. Look at this, he said. He handed me the card. Nobody said you were in the market. But look at the signature. Is that Mrs. Slater's signature or not?

I looked at the card. I held it up to the light. I turned it over, but the other side was blank. So what? I said.

Mrs. Slater's card was pulled at random out of a basket of cards. Hundreds of cards just like this little card. She has won a free vacuuming and carpet shampoo. Mrs. Slater is a winner. No strings. I am here even to do your mattress, Mr. . . . You'll be surprised to see what can collect in a mattress over the months, over the years. Every day, every night of our lives, we're leaving little bits of ourselves, flakes of this and that, behind. Where do they go, these bits and pieces of ourselves? Right through the sheets and into the mattress, *that's* where! Pillows, too. It's all the same.

He had been removing lengths of the shiny pipe and joining the parts together. Now he inserted the fitted pipes into the hose. He was on his knees, grunting. He attached some sort of scoop to the hose and lifted out the blue thing with wheels.

He let me examine the filter he intended to use.

Do you have a car? he asked.

No car, I said. I don't have a car. If I had a car I would drive you someplace.

Too bad, he said. This little vacuum comes equipped with a sixty-foot extension cord. If you had a car, you could wheel this little vacuum right up to your car door and vacuum the plush carpeting and the luxurious reclining seats as well. You would be surprised how much of us gets lost, how much of us gathers, in those fine seats over the years.

Mr. Bell, I said, I think you better pack up your things and go. I say this without any malice whatsoever.

But he was looking around the room for a plug-in. He found one at the end of the sofa. The machine rattled as if there were a marble inside, anyway something loose inside, then settled to a hum.

Rilke lived in one castle after another, all of his adult life. Benefactors, he said loudly over the hum of the vacuum. He seldom rode in motorcars; he preferred trains. Then look at Voltaire at Cirey with Madame Châtelet. His death mask. Such serenity. He raised his right hand as if I were about to disagree. No, no, it isn't right, is it? Don't say it. But who knows? With that he turned and began to pull the vacuum into the other room.

There was a bed, a window. The covers were heaped on the floor. One pillow, one sheet over the mattress. He slipped the case from the pillow and then quickly stripped the sheet from the mattress. He stared at the mattress and gave me a look out of the corner of his eye. I went to the kitchen and got the chair. I sat down in the doorway and watched. First he tested the suction by putting the scoop against the palm of his hand. He bent and turned a dial on the vacuum. You have to turn it up full strength for a job like this one, he said. He checked the suction again, then extended the hose to the head of the bed and began to move the scoop down the mattress. The scoop tugged at the mattress. The vacuum whirred louder. He made three passes over the mattress, then switched off the machine. He pressed a lever and the lid popped open. He took out the filter. This filter is just for demonstration purposes. In normal use, all of this, this *material*, would go into your bag, here, he said. He pinched some of the dusty stuff between his fingers. There must have been a cup of it.

He had this look to his face.

It's not my mattress, I said. I leaned forward in the chair and tried to show an interest.

Now the pillow, he said. He put the used filter on the sill

and looked out the window for a minute. He turned. I want you to hold onto this end of the pillow, he said.

I got up and took hold of two corners of the pillow. I felt I was holding something by the ears.

Like this? I said.

He nodded. He went into the other room and came back with another filter.

How much do those things cost? I said.

Next to nothing, he said. They're only made out of paper and a little bit of plastic. Couldn't cost much.

He kicked on the vacuum and I held tight as the scoop sank into the pillow and moved down its length—once, twice, three times. He switched off the vacuum, removed the filter, and held it up without a word. He put it on the sill beside the other filter. Then he opened the closet door. He looked inside, but there was only a box of Mouse-Be-Gone.

I heard steps on the porch, the mail slot opened and clinked shut. We looked at each other.

He pulled on the vacuum and I followed him into the other room. We looked at the letter lying face down on the carpet near the front door.

I started toward the letter, turned and said, What else? It's getting late. This carpet's not worth fooling with. It's only a twelve-by-fifteen cotton carpet with no-skid backing from Rug City. It's not worth fooling with.

Do you have a full ashtray? he said. Or a potted plant or something like that? A handful of dirt would be fine.

I found the ashtray. He took it, dumped the contents onto the carpet, ground the ashes and cigarets under his slipper. He got down on his knees again and inserted a new filter. He took off his jacket and threw it onto the sofa. He was sweating under the arms. Fat hung over his belt. He twisted off the scoop and attached another device to the hose. He adjusted his dial. He kicked on the machine and began to move back and forth, back and forth over the worn carpet. Twice I started for the letter. But he seemed to anticipate me, cut me off, so to speak, with his hose and his pipes and his sweeping and his sweeping. . . .

I took the chair back to the kitchen and sat there and watched him work. After a time he shut off the machine, opened the lid, and silently brought me the filter, alive with dust, hair, small grainy things. I looked at the filter, and then I got up and put it in the garbage.

He worked steadily now. No more explanations. He came out to the kitchen with a bottle that held a few ounces of green liquid. He put the bottle under the tap and filled it.

You know I can't pay anything, I said. I couldn't pay you a dollar if my life depended on it. You're going to have to write me off as a dead loss, that's all. You're wasting your time on me, I said.

I wanted it out in the open, no misunderstanding.

He went about his business. He put another attachment on the hose, in some complicated way hooked his bottle to the new attachment. He moved slowly over the carpet, now and then releasing little streams of emerald, moving the brush back and forth over the carpet, working up patches of foam.

I had said all that was on my mind. I sat on the chair in the kitchen, relaxed now, and watched him work. Once in a while I looked out the window at the rain. It had begun to get dark. He switched off the vacuum. He was in a corner near the front door.

You want coffee? I said.

He was breathing hard. He wiped his face.

I put on water and by the time it had boiled and I'd fixed up two cups he had everything dismantled and back in the case. Then he picked up the letter. He read the name on the letter and looked closely at the return address. He folded the letter in half and put it in his hip pocket. I kept watching him. That's all I did. The coffee began to cool.

It's for a Mr. Slater, he said. I'll see to it. He said, Maybe I will skip the coffee. I better not walk across this carpet. I just shampooed it.

That's true, I said. Then I said, You're sure that's who the letter's for?

He reached to the sofa for his jacket, put it on, and opened the front door. It was still raining. He stepped into his galoshes, fastened them, and then pulled on the raincoat and looked back inside.

You want to see it? he said. You don't believe me?

It just seems strange, I said.

Well, I'd better be off, he said. But he kept standing there. You want the vacuum or not?

I looked at the big case, closed now and ready to move on.

No, I said, I guess not. I'm going to be leaving here soon. It would just be in the way.

All right, he said, and he shut the door.

What Do You Do in San Francisco?

THIS has nothing to do with me. It's about a young couple with three children who moved into a house on my route the first of last summer. I got to thinking about them again when I picked up last Sunday's newspaper and found a picture of a young man who'd been arrested down in San Francisco for killing his wife and her boyfriend with a baseball bat. It wasn't the same man, of course, though there was a likeness because of the beard. But the situation was close enough to get me thinking.

Henry Robinson is the name. I'm a postman, a federal civil servant, and have been since 1947. I've lived in the West all my life, except for a three-year stint in the Army during the war. I've been divorced twenty years, have two children I haven't seen in almost that long. I'm not a frivolous man, nor am I, in my opinion, a serious man. It's my belief a man has to be a little of both these days. I believe, too, in the value of work—the harder the better. A man who isn't working has got too much time on his hands, too much time to dwell on himself and his problems.

I'm convinced that was partly the trouble with the young man who lived here—his not working. But I'd lay that at her doorstep, too. The woman. She encouraged it.

Beatniks, I guess you'd have called them if you'd seen them. The man wore a pointed brown beard on his chin and looked like he needed to sit down to a good dinner and a cigar afterwards. The woman was attractive, with her long dark hair and her fair complexion, there's no getting around that. But put me down for saying she wasn't a good wife and mother. She was a painter. The young man, I don't know what he did—probably something along the same line. Neither of them worked. But they paid their rent and got by somehow—at least for the summer.

The first time I saw them it was around eleven, eleven-fifteen, a Saturday morning. I was about two-thirds through my route when I turned onto their block and noticed a '56 Ford sedan

85

pulled up in the yard with a big open U-Haul behind. There are only three houses on Pine, and theirs was the last house, the others being the Murchisons, who'd been in Arcata a little less than a year, and the Grants, who'd been here about two years. Murchison worked at Simpson Redwood, and Gene Grant was a cook on the morning shift at Denny's. Those two, then a vacant lot, then the house on the end that used to belong to the Coles.

The young man was out in the yard behind the trailer and she was just coming out the front door with a cigaret in her mouth, wearing a tight pair of white jeans and a man's white undershirt. She stopped when she saw me and she stood watching me come down the walk. I slowed up when I came even with their box and nodded in her direction.

"Getting settled all right?" I asked.

"It'll be a little while," she said and moved a handful of hair away from her forehead while she continued to smoke.

"That's good," I said. "Welcome to Arcata."

I felt a little awkward after saying it. I don't know why, but I always found myself feeling awkward the few times I was around this woman. It was one of the things helped turn me against her from the first.

She gave me a thin smile and I started to move on when the young man—Marston was his name—came around from behind the trailer carrying a big carton of toys. Now, Arcata is not a small town and it's not a big town, though I guess you'd have to say it's more on the small side. It's not the end of the world, Arcata, by any means, but most of the people who live here work either in the lumber mills or have something to do with the fishing industry, or else work in one of the downtown stores. People here aren't used to seeing men wear beards—or men who don't work, for that matter.

"Hello," I said. I put out my hand when he set the carton down on the front fender. "The name's Henry Robinson. You folks just arrive?"

"Yesterday afternoon," he said.

"Some trip! It took us fourteen hours just to come from San Francisco," the woman spoke up from the porch. "Pulling that damn trailer."

"My, my," I said and shook my head. "San Francisco? I was just down in San Francisco, let me see, last April or March."

"You were, were you?" she said. "What did you do in San Francisco?"

"Oh, nothing, really. I go down about once or twice a year. Out to Fisherman's Wharf and to see the Giants play. That's about all."

There was a little pause and Marston examined something in the grass with his toe. I started to move on. The kids picked that moment to come flying out the front door, yelling and tearing for the end of the porch. When that screen door banged open, I thought Marston was going to jump out of his skin. But she just stood there with her arms crossed, cool as a cucumber, and never batted an eye. He didn't look good at all. Quick, jerky little movements every time he made to do something. And his eyes—they'd land on you and then slip off somewheres else, then land on you again.

There were three kids, two little curly-headed girls about four or five, and a little bit of a boy tagging after.

"Cute kids," I said. "Well, I got to get under way. You might want to change the name on the box."

"Sure," he said. "Sure. I'll see about it in a day or two. But we don't expect to get any mail for a while yet, in any case."

"You never know," I said. "You never know what'll turn up in this old mail pouch. Wouldn't hurt to be prepared." I started to go. "By the way, if you're looking for a job in the mills, I can tell you who to see at Simpson Redwood. A friend of mine's a foreman there. He'd probably have something . . ." I tapered off, seeing how they didn't look interested.

"No, thanks," he said.

"He's not looking for a job," she put in.

"Well, goodbye, then."

"So long," Marston said.

Not another word from her.

That was on a Saturday, as I said, the day before Memorial Day. We took Monday as a holiday and I wasn't by there again until Tuesday. I can't say I was surprised to see the U-Haul still there in the front yard. But it did surprise me to see he still hadn't unloaded it. I'd say about a quarter of the stuff had made its way to the front porch—a covered chair and a chrome kitchen chair and a big carton of clothes that had the flaps pulled off the top. Another quarter must have gotten inside the house, and the rest of the stuff was still in the trailer. The kids were carrying little sticks and hammering on the sides of the trailer as they climbed in and out over the tailgate. Their mama and daddy were nowheres to be seen.

On Thursday I saw him out in the yard again and reminded him about changing the name on the box.

"That's something I've got to get around to doing," he said.

"Takes time," I said. "There's lots of things to take care of when you're moving into a new place. People that lived here, the Coles, just moved out two days before you came. He was going to work in Eureka. With the Fish and Game Department."

Marston stroked his beard and looked off as if thinking of something else.

"I'll be seeing you," I said.

"So long," he said.

Well, the long and the short of it was he never did change the name on the box. I'd come along a bit later with a piece of mail for that address and he'd say something like, "Marston? Yes, that's for us, Marston . . . . I'll have to change the name on that box one of these days. I'll get myself a can of paint and just paint over that other name . . . Cole," all the time his eyes drifting here and there. Then he'd look at me kind of out the corners and bob his chin once or twice. But he never did change the name on the box, and after a time I shrugged and forgot about it.

You hear rumors. At different times I heard that he was an ex-con on parole who come to Arcata to get out of the unhealthy San Francisco environment. According to this story, the woman was his wife, but none of the kids belonged to him. Another story was that he had committed a crime and was hiding out here. But not many people subscribed to that. He just didn't look the sort who'd do something really *criminal.* The story most folks seemed to believe, at least the one that got around most, was the most horrible. The woman was a

dope addict, so this story went, and the husband had brought
her up here to help her get rid of the habit. As evidence, the
fact of Sallie Wilson's visit was always brought up—Sallie Wilson from the Welcome Wagon. She dropped in on them one
afternoon and said later that, no lie, there was something
funny about them—the woman, particular. One minute the
woman would be sitting and listening to Sallie run on—all
ears, it seemed—and the next she'd get up while Sallie was still
talking and start to work on her painting as if Sallie wasn't
there. Also the way she'd be fondling and kissing the kids,
then suddenly start screeching at them for no apparent reason.
Well, just the way her *eyes* looked if you came up close to her,
Sallie said. But Sallie Wilson has been snooping and prying for
years under cover of the Welcome Wagon.

"You don't know," I'd say when someone would bring it
up. "Who can say? If he'd just go to work now."

All the same, the way it looked to me was that they had their
fair share of trouble down there in San Francisco, whatever
was the nature of the trouble, and they decided to get clear
away from it. Though why they ever picked Arcata to settle in,
it's hard to say, since they surely didn't come looking for work.

The first few weeks there was no mail to speak of, just a few
circulars, from Sears and Western Auto and the like. Then a
few letters began to come in, maybe one or two a week. Sometimes I'd see one or the other of them out around the house
when I came by and sometimes not. But the kids were always
there, running in and out of the house or playing in the vacant
lot next door. Of course, it wasn't a model home to begin
with, but after they'd been there a while the weeds sprouted
up and what grass there was yellowed and died. You hate to
see something like that. I understand Old Man Jessup came
out once or twice to get them to turn the water on, but they
claimed they couldn't buy hose. So he left them a hose. Then
I noticed the kids playing with it over in the field, and that was
the end of that. Twice I saw a little white sports car in front, a
car that hadn't come from around here.

One time only I had anything to do with the woman direct.
There was a letter with five cents postage due, and I went up
to the door with it. One of the little girls let me in and ran off

to fetch her mama. The place was cluttered with odds and ends of old furniture and with clothing tossed just anywhere. But it wasn't what you'd call dirty. Not tidy maybe, but not dirty either. An old couch and chair stood along one wall in the living room. Under the window was a bookcase made out of bricks and boards, crammed full of little paperback books. In the corner there was a stack of paintings with their faces turned away, and to one side another painting stood on an easel covered over with a sheet.

I shifted my mail pouch and stood my ground, but starting to wish I'd paid the nickel myself. I eyed the easel as I waited, about to sidle over and raise the sheet when I heard steps.

"What can I do for you?" she said, appearing in the hallway and not at all friendly.

I touched the brim of my cap and said, "A letter here with five cents postage due, if you don't mind."

"Let me see. Who's it from? Why it's from Jer! That kook. Sending us a letter without a stamp. Lee!" she called out. "Here's a letter from Jerry." Marston came in, but he didn't look too happy. I leaned on first one leg, then the other, waiting.

"Five cents," she said. "I'll pay it, seeing as it's from old Jerry. Here. Now goodbye."

Things went on in this fashion—which is to say no fashion at all. I won't say the people hereabouts got used to them— they weren't the sort you'd ever really get used to. But after a bit no one seemed to pay them much mind any more. People might stare at his beard if they met him pushing the grocery cart in Safeway, but that's about all. You didn't hear any more stories.

Then one day they disappeared. In two different directions. I found out later she'd taken off the week before with some- body—a man—and that after a few days he'd taken the kids to his mother's over to Redding. For six days running, from one Thursday to the following Wednesday, their mail stayed in the box. The shades were all pulled and nobody knew for certain whether or not they'd lit out for good. But that Wednesday I noticed the Ford parked in the yard again, all the shades still down but the mail gone.

Beginning the next day he was out there at the box every

day waiting for me to hand over the mail, or else he was sitting on the porch steps smoking a cigaret, waiting, it was plain to see. When he saw me coming, he'd stand up, brush the seat of his trousers, and walk over by the box. If it happened that I had any mail for him, I'd see him start scanning the return addresses even before I could get it handed over. We seldom exchanged a word, just nodded at each other if our eyes happened to meet, which wasn't often. He was suffering, though —anybody could see that—and I wanted to help the boy somehow, if I could. But I didn't know what to say exactly.

It was one morning a week or so after his return that I saw him walking up and down in front of the box with his hands in his back pockets, and I made up my mind to say something. What, I didn't know yet, but I was going to say something, sure. His back was to me as I came up the walk. When I got to him, he suddenly turned on me and there was such a look on his face it froze the words in my mouth. I stopped in my tracks with his article of mail. He took a couple of steps toward me and I handed it over without a peep. He stared at it as if dumbfounded.

"Occupant," he said.

It was a circular from L.A. advertising a hospital-insurance plan. I'd dropped off at least seventy-five that morning. He folded it in two and went back to the house.

Next day he was out there same as always. He had his old look to his face, seemed more in control of himself than the day before. This time I had a hunch I had what it was he'd been waiting for. I'd looked at it down at the station that morning when I was arranging the mail into packets. It was a plain white envelope addressed in a woman's curlicue handwriting that took up most of the space. It had a Portland postmark, and the return address showed the initials JD and a Portland street address.

"Morning," I said, offering the letter.

He took it from me without a word and went absolutely pale. He tottered a minute and then started back for the house, holding the letter up to the light.

I called out, "She's no good, boy. I could tell that the minute I saw her. Why don't you forget her? Why don't you go to work and forget her? What have you got against work? It was work, day and night, work that gave me oblivion when I was in your shoes and there was a war on where I was. . . ."

After that he didn't wait outside for me any more, and he was only there another five days. I'd catch a glimpse of him, though, each day, waiting for me just the same, but standing behind the window and looking out at me through the curtain. He wouldn't come out until I'd gone by, and then I'd hear the screen door. If I looked back, he'd seem to be in no hurry at all to reach the box.

The last time I saw him he was standing at the window and looked calm and rested. The curtains were down, all the shades were raised, and I figured at the time he was getting his things together to leave. But I could tell by the look on his face he wasn't watching for me this time. He was staring past me, over me, you might say, over the rooftops and the trees, south. He kept staring even after I'd come even with the house and moved on down the sidewalk. I looked back. I could see him still there at the window. The feeling was so strong, I had to turn around and look for myself in the same direction he was. But, as you might guess, I didn't see anything except the same old timber, mountains, sky.

The next day he was gone. He didn't leave any forwarding. Sometimes mail of some kind or other shows up for him or his wife or for the both of them. If it's first-class, we hold it a day, then send it back to where it came from. There isn't much. And I don't mind. It's all work, one way or the other, and I'm always glad to have it.

The Student's Wife

H E had been reading to her from Rilke, a poet he admired, when she fell asleep with her head on his pillow. He liked reading aloud, and he read well—a confident sonorous voice, now pitched low and somber, now rising, now thrilling. He never looked away from the page when he read and stopped only to reach to the nightstand for a cigaret. It was a rich voice that spilled her into a dream of caravans just setting out from walled cities and bearded men in robes. She had listened to him for a few minutes, then she had closed her eyes and drifted off.

He went on reading aloud. The children had been asleep for hours, and outside a car rubbered by now and then on the wet pavement. After a while he put down the book and turned in the bed to reach for the lamp. She opened her eyes suddenly, as if frightened, and blinked two or three times. Her eyelids looked oddly dark and fleshy to him as they flicked up and down over her fixed glassy eyes. He stared at her.

"Are you dreaming?" he asked.

She nodded and brought her hand up and touched her fingers to the plastic curlers at each side of her head. Tomorrow would be Friday, her day for all the four-to-seven-year-olds in the Woodlawn Apartments. He kept looking at her, leaning on his elbow, at the same time trying to straighten the spread with his free hand. She had a smooth-skinned face with prominent cheekbones; the cheekbones, she sometimes insisted to friends, were from her father, who had been one-quarter Nez Perce.

Then: "Make me a little sandwich of something, Mike. With butter and lettuce and salt on the bread."

He did nothing and he said nothing because he wanted to go to sleep. But when he opened his eyes she was still awake, watching him.

"Can't you go to sleep, Nan?" he said, very solemnly. "It's late."

"I'd like something to eat first," she said. "My legs and arms hurt for some reason, and I'm hungry."

He groaned extravagantly as he rolled out of bed.

He fixed her the sandwich and brought it in on a saucer. She sat up in bed and smiled when he came into the bedroom, then slipped a pillow behind her back as she took the saucer. He thought she looked like a hospital patient in her white night-gown.

"What a funny little dream I had."

"What were you dreaming?" he said, getting into bed and turning over onto his side away from her. He stared at the nightstand waiting. Then he closed his eyes slowly.

"Do you really want to hear it?" she said.

"Sure," he said.

She settled back comfortably on the pillow and picked a crumb from her lip.

"Well. It seemed like a real long drawn-out kind of dream, you know, with all kinds of relationships going on, but I can't remember everything now. It was all very clear when I woke up, but it's beginning to fade now. How long have I been asleep, Mike? It doesn't really matter, I guess. Anyway, I think it was that we were staying someplace overnight. I don't know where the kids were, but it was just the two of us at some little hotel or something. It was on some lake that wasn't familiar. There was another, older, couple there and they wanted to take us for a ride in their motorboat." She laughed, remembering, and leaned forward off the pillow. "The next thing I recall is we were down at the boat landing. Only the way it turned out, they had just one seat in the boat, a kind of bench up in the front, and it was only big enough for three. You and I started arguing about who was going to sacrifice and sit all cooped up in the back. You said you were, and I said I was. But I finally squeezed in the back of the boat. It was so narrow it hurt my legs, and I was afraid the water was going to come in over the sides. Then I woke up."

"That's some dream," he managed to say and felt drowsily that he should say something more. "You remember Bonnie Travis? Fred Travis' wife? She used to have *color* dreams, she said."

She looked at the sandwich in her hand and took a bite. When she had swallowed, she ran her tongue in behind her lips and balanced the saucer on her lap as she reached behind and plumped up the pillow. Then she smiled and leaned back against the pillow again.

"Do you remember that time we stayed overnight on the Tilton River, Mike? When you caught that big fish the next morning?" She placed her hand on his shoulder. "Do you remember that?" she said.

She did. After scarcely thinking about it these last years, it had begun coming back to her lately. It was a month or two after they'd married and gone away for a weekend. They had sat by a little campfire that night, a watermelon in the snow-cold river, and she'd fried Spam and eggs and canned beans for supper and pancakes and Spam and eggs in the same blackened pan the next morning. She had burned the pan both times she cooked, and they could never get the coffee to boil, but it was one of the best times they'd ever had. She remembered he had read to her that night as well: Elizabeth Browning and a few poems from the *Rubáiyát*. They had had so many covers over them that she could hardly turn her feet under all the weight. The next morning he had hooked a big trout, and people stopped their cars on the road across the river to watch him play it in.

"Well? Do you remember or not?" she said, patting him on the shoulder. "Mike?"

"I remember," he said. He shifted a little on his side, opened his eyes. He did not remember very well, he thought. What he did remember was very carefully combed hair and loud half-baked ideas about life and art, and he did not want to remember that.

"That was a long time ago, Nan," he said.

"We'd just got out of high school. You hadn't started to college," she said.

He waited, and then he raised up onto his arm and turned his head to look at her over his shoulder. "You about finished with that sandwich, Nan?" She was still sitting up in the bed.

She nodded and gave him the saucer.

"I'll turn off the light," he said.

"If you want," she said.

Then he pulled down into the bed again and extended his foot until it touched against hers. He lay still for a minute and then tried to relax.

"Mike, you're not asleep, are you?"

"No," he said. "Nothing like that."

"Well, don't go to sleep before me," she said. "I don't want to be awake by myself."

He didn't answer, but he inched a little closer to her on his side. When she put her arm over him and planted her hand flat against his chest, he took her fingers and squeezed them lightly. But in moments his hand dropped away to the bed, and he sighed.

"Mike? Honey? I wish you'd rub my legs. My legs hurt," she said.

"God," he said softly. "I was sound asleep."

"Well, I wish you'd rub my legs and talk to me. My shoulders hurt, too. But my legs especially."

He turned over and began rubbing her legs, then fell asleep again with his hand on her hip.

"Mike?"

"What is it, Nan? Tell me what it *is*."

"I wish you'd rub me all over," she said, turning onto her back. "My legs and arms both hurt tonight." She raised her knees to make a tower with the covers.

He opened his eyes briefly in the dark and then shut them. "Growing pains, huh?"

"O God, yes," she said, wiggling her toes, glad she had drawn him out. "When I was ten or eleven years old I was as big then as I am now. You should've seen me! I grew so fast in those days my legs and arms hurt me all the time. Didn't you?"

"Didn't I what?"

"Didn't you ever feel yourself growing?"

"Not that I remember," he said.

At last he raised up on his elbow, struck a match, and looked at the clock. He turned his pillow over to the cooler side and lay down again.

She said, "You're asleep, Mike. I wish you'd want to talk."

"All right," he said, not moving.

"Just hold me and get me off to sleep. I can't go to sleep," she said.

He turned over and put his arm over her shoulder as she turned onto her side to face the wall.

"Mike?"

He tapped his toes against her foot.

"Why don't you tell me all the things you like and the things you don't like."

"Don't know any right now," he said. "Tell me if you want," he said.

"If you promise to tell *me*. Is that a promise?"

He tapped her foot again.

"Well . . ." she said and turned onto her back, pleased. "I like good foods, steaks and hash-brown potatoes, things like that. I like good books and magazines, riding on trains at night, and those times I flew in an airplane." She stopped. "Of course none of this is in order of preference. I'd have to think about it if it was in the order of preference. But I like that, flying in airplanes. There's a moment as you leave the ground you feel whatever happens is all right." She put her leg across his ankle. "I like staying up late at night and then staying in bed the next morning. I wish we could do that all the time, not just once in a while. And I like sex. I like to be touched now and then when I'm not expecting it. I like going to movies and drinking beer with friends afterwards. I like to have friends. I like Janice Hendricks very much. I'd like to go dancing at least once a week. I'd like to have nice clothes all the time. I'd like to be able to buy the kids nice clothes every time they need it without having to wait. Laurie needs a new little outfit right now for Easter. And I'd like to get Gary a little suit or something. He's old enough. I'd like you to have a new suit, too. You really need a new suit more than he does. And I'd like us to have a place of our own. I'd like to stop moving around every year, or every other year. Most of all," she said, "I'd like us both just to live a good honest life without having to worry about money and bills and things like that. You're asleep," she said.

"I'm not," he said.

"I can't think of anything else. You go now. Tell me what you'd like."

"I don't know. Lots of things," he mumbled.

"Well, tell me. We're just talking, aren't we?"

"I wish you'd leave me alone, Nan." He turned over to his side of the bed again and let his arm rest off the edge. She turned too and pressed against him.

"Mike?"

"Jesus," he said. Then: "All right. Let me stretch my legs a minute, then I'll wake up."

In a while she said, "Mike? Are you asleep?" She shook his shoulder gently, but there was no response. She lay there for a time huddled against his body, trying to sleep. She lay quietly at first, without moving, crowded against him and taking only very small, very even breaths. But she could not sleep.

She tried not to listen to his breathing, but it began to make her uncomfortable. There was a sound coming from inside his nose when he breathed. She tried to regulate her breathing so that she could breathe in and out at the same rhythm he did. It was no use. The little sound in his nose made everything no use. There was a webby squeak in his chest too. She turned again and nestled her bottom against his, stretched her arm over to the edge and cautiously put her fingertips against the cold wall. The covers had pulled up at the foot of the bed, and she could feel a draft when she moved her legs. She heard two people coming up the stairs to the apartment next door. Someone gave a throaty laugh before opening the door. Then she heard a chair drag on the floor. She turned again. The toilet flushed next door, and then it flushed again. Again she turned, onto her back this time, and tried to relax. She remembered an article she'd once read in a magazine: If all the bones and muscles and joints in the body could join together in perfect relaxation, sleep would almost certainly come. She took a long breath, closed her eyes, and lay perfectly still, arms straight along her sides. She tried to relax. She tried to imagine her legs suspended, bathed in something gauze-like. She turned onto her stomach. She closed her eyes, then she opened them. She thought of the fingers of her hand lying curled on the sheet in front of her lips. She raised a finger and lowered it to the sheet. She touched the wedding band on her ring finger with her thumb. She turned onto her side and then onto her back again. And then she began to feel afraid, and in one unreasoning moment of longing she prayed to go to sleep.

Please, God, let me go to sleep.

She tried to sleep.

"Mike," she whispered.

There was no answer.

She heard one of the children turn over in the bed and bump against the wall in the next room. She listened and listened but there was no other sound. She laid her hand under her left breast and felt the beat of her heart rising into her fingers. She turned onto her stomach and began to cry, her head off the pillow, her mouth against the sheet. She cried. And then she climbed out over the foot of the bed.

She washed her hands and face in the bathroom. She brushed her teeth. She brushed her teeth and watched her face in the mirror. In the living room she turned up the heat. Then she sat down at the kitchen table, drawing her feet up underneath the nightgown. She cried again. She lit a cigaret from the pack on the table. After a time she walked back to the bedroom and got her robe.

She looked in on the children. She pulled the covers up over her son's shoulders. She went back to the living room and sat in the big chair. She paged through a magazine and tried to read. She gazed at the photographs and then she tried to read again. Now and then a car went by on the street outside and she looked up. As each car passed she waited, listening. And then she looked down at the magazine again. There was a stack of magazines in the rack by the big chair. She paged through them all.

When it began to be light outside she got up. She walked to the window. The cloudless sky over the hills was beginning to turn white. The trees and the row of two-story apartment houses across the street were beginning to take shape as she watched. The sky grew whiter, the light expanding rapidly up from behind the hills. Except for the times she had been up with one or another of the children (which she did not count because she had never looked outside, only hurried back to bed or to the kitchen), she had seen few sunrises in her life and those when she was little. She knew that none of them had been like this. Not in pictures she had seen nor in any book she had read had she learned a sunrise was so terrible as this.

She waited and then she moved over to the door and turned the lock and stepped out onto the porch. She closed the robe at her throat. The air was wet and cold. By stages things were becoming very visible. She let her eyes see everything until they fastened on the red winking light atop the radio tower atop the opposite hill.

She went through the dim apartment, back into the bedroom. He was knotted up in the center of the bed, the covers bunched over his shoulders, his head half under the pillow. He looked desperate in his heavy sleep, his arm flung out across her side of the bed, his jaws clenched. As she looked, the room grew very light and the pale sheets whitened grossly before her eyes.

She wet her lips with a sticking sound and got down on her knees. She put her hands out on the bed.

"God," she said. "God, will you help us, God?" she said.

Put Yourself in My Shoes

THE telephone rang while he was running the vacuum cleaner. He had worked his way through the apartment and was doing the living room, using the nozzle attachment to get at the cat hairs between the cushions. He stopped and listened and then switched off the vacuum. He went to answer the telephone.

"Hello," he said. "Myers here."

"Myers," she said. "How are you? What are you doing?"

"Nothing," he said. "Hello, Paula."

"There's an office party this afternoon," she said. "You're invited. Carl invited you."

"I don't think I can come," Myers said.

"Carl just this minute said get that old man of yours on the phone. Get him down here for a drink. Get him out of his ivory tower and back into the real world for a while. Carl's funny when he's drinking. Myers?"

"I heard you," Myers said.

Myers used to work for Carl. Carl always talked of going to Paris to write a novel, and when Myers had quit to write a novel, Carl had said he would watch for Myers' name on the best-seller list.

"I can't come now," Myers said.

"We found out some horrible news this morning," Paula continued, as if she had not heard him. "You remember Larry Gudinas. He was still here when you came to work. He helped out on science books for a while, and then they put him in the field, and then they canned him? We heard this morning he committed suicide. He shot himself in the mouth. Can you imagine? Myers?"

"I heard you," Myers said. He tried to remember Larry Gudinas and recalled a tall, stooped man with wire-frame glasses, bright ties, and a receding hairline. He could imagine the jolt, the head snapping back. "Jesus," Myers said. "Well, I'm sorry to hear that."

"Come down to the office, honey, all right?" Paula said.

"Everybody is just talking and having some drinks and listening to Christmas music. Come down," she said.

Myers could hear it all at the other end of the line. "I don't want to come down," he said. "Paula?" A few snowflakes drifted past the window as he watched. He rubbed his fingers across the glass and then began to write his name on the glass as he waited.

"What? I heard," she said. "All right," Paula said. "Well, then, why don't we meet at Voyles for a drink? Myers?"

"Okay," he said. "Voyles. All right."

"Everybody here will be disappointed you didn't come," she said. "Carl especially. Carl admires you, you know. He does. He's told me so. He admires your nerve. He said if he had your nerve he would have quit years ago. Carl said it takes nerve to do what you did. Myers?"

"I'm right here," Myers said. "I think I can get my car started. If I can't start it, I'll call you back."

"All right," she said. "I'll see you at Voyles. I'll leave here in five minutes if I don't hear from you."

"Say hello to Carl for me," Myers said.

"I will," Paula said. "He's talking about you."

Myers put the vacuum cleaner away. He walked down the two flights and went to his car, which was in the last stall and covered with snow. He got in, worked the pedal a number of times, and tried the starter. It turned over. He kept the pedal down.

As he drove, he looked at the people who hurried along the sidewalks with shopping bags. He glanced at the gray sky, filled with flakes, and at the tall buildings with snow in the crevices and on the window ledges. He tried to see everything, save it for later. He was between stories, and he felt despicable. He found Voyles, a small bar on a corner next to a men's clothing store. He parked in back and went inside. He sat at the bar for a time and then carried a drink over to a little table near the door.

When Paula came in she said, "Merry Christmas," and he got up and gave her a kiss on the cheek. He held a chair for her.

He said, "Scotch?"

"Scotch," she said, then "Scotch over ice" to the girl who came for her order.

Paula picked up his drink and drained the glass.

"I'll have another one, too," Myers said to the girl. "I don't like this place," he said after the girl had moved away.

"What's wrong with this place?" Paula said. "We always come here."

"I just don't like it," he said. "Let's have a drink and then go someplace else."

"Whatever you want," she said.

The girl arrived with the drinks. Myers paid her, and he and Paula touched glasses.

Myers stared at her.

"Carl says hello," she said.

Myers nodded.

Paula sipped her drink. "How was your day today?"

Myers shrugged.

"What'd you do?" she said.

"Nothing," he said. "I vacuumed."

She touched his hand. "Everybody said to tell you hi."

They finished their drinks.

"I have an idea," she said. "Why don't we stop and visit the Morgans for a few minutes. We've never met them, for God's sake, and they've been back for months. We could just drop by and say hello, we're the Myerses. Besides, they sent us a card. They asked us to stop during the holidays. They *invited* us. I don't want to go home," she finally said and fished in her purse for a cigaret.

Myers recalled setting the furnace and turning out all the lights before he had left. And then he thought of the snow drifting past the window.

"What about that insulting letter they sent telling us they heard we were keeping a cat in the house?" he said.

"They've forgotten about that by now," she said. "That wasn't anything serious, anyway. Oh, let's do it, Myers! Let's go by."

"We should call first if we're going to do anything like that," he said.

"No," she said. "That's part of it. Let's not call. Let's just go knock on the door and say hello, we used to live here. All right? Myers?"

"I think we should call first," he said.

"It's the holidays," she said, getting up from her chair. "Come on, baby."

She took his arm and they went out into the snow. She suggested they take her car and pick up his car later. He opened the door for her and then went around to the passenger's side.

Something took him when he saw the lighted windows, saw snow on the roof, saw the station wagon in the driveway. The curtains were open and Christmas-tree lights blinked at them from the window.

They got out of the car. He took her elbow as they stepped over a pile of snow and started up the walk to the front porch. They had gone a few steps when a large bushy dog hurtled around the corner of the garage and headed straight for Myers.

"Oh, God," he said, hunching, stepping back, bringing his hands up. He slipped on the walk, his coat flapped, and he fell onto the frozen grass with the dread certainty that the dog would go for his throat. The dog growled once and then began to sniff Myers' coat.

Paula picked up a handful of snow and threw it at the dog. The porch light came on, the door opened, and a man called, "Buzzy!" Myers got to his feet and brushed himself off.

"What's going on?" the man in the doorway said. "Who is it? Buzzy, come here, fellow. Come here!"

"We're the Myerses," Paula said. "We came to wish you a Merry Christmas."

"The Myerses?" the man in the doorway said. "Get out! Get in the garage, Buzzy. Get, get! It's the Myerses," the man said to the woman who stood behind him trying to look past his shoulder.

"The Myerses," she said. "Well, ask them in, ask them in, for heaven's sake." She stepped onto the porch and said, "Come in, please, it's freezing. I'm Hilda Morgan and this is Edgar. We're happy to meet you. Please come in."

They all shook hands quickly on the front porch. Myers and Paula stepped inside and Edgar Morgan shut the door.

"Let me have your coats. Take off your coats," Edgar Morgan said. "You're all right?" he said to Myers, observing him closely, and Myers nodded. "I knew that dog was crazy, but he's never pulled anything like this. I saw it. I was looking out the window when it happened."

This remark seemed odd to Myers, and he looked at the man. Edgar Morgan was in his forties, nearly bald, and was dressed in slacks and a sweater and was wearing leather slippers.

"His name is Buzzy," Hilda Morgan announced and made a face. "It's Edgar's dog. I can't have an animal in the house myself, but Edgar bought this dog and promised to keep him outside."

"He sleeps in the garage," Edgar Morgan said. "He begs to come in the house, but we can't allow it, you know." Morgan chuckled. "But sit down, sit down, if you can find a place with this clutter. Hilda, dear, move some of those things off the couch so Mr. and Mrs. Myers can sit down."

Hilda Morgan cleared the couch of packages, wrapping paper, scissors, a box of ribbons, bows. She put everything on the floor.

Myers noticed Morgan staring at him again, not smiling now.

Paula said, "Myers, there's something in your hair, dearest."

Myers put a hand up to the back of his head and found a twig and put it in his pocket.

"That dog," Morgan said and chuckled again. "We were just having a hot drink and wrapping some last-minute gifts. Will you join us in a cup of holiday cheer? What would you like?"

"Anything is fine," Paula said.

"Anything," Myers said. "We wouldn't have interrupted."

"Nonsense," Morgan said. "We've been . . . very curious about the Myerses. You'll have a hot drink, sir?"

"That's fine," Myers said.

"Mrs. Myers?" Morgan said.

Paula nodded.

"Two hot drinks coming up," Morgan said. "Dear, I think we're ready too, aren't we?" he said to his wife. "This is certainly an occasion."

He took her cup and went out to the kitchen. Myers heard

the cupboard door bang and heard a muffled word that sounded like a curse. Myers blinked. He looked at Hilda Morgan, who was settling herself into a chair at the end of the couch.

"Sit down over here, you two," Hilda Morgan said. She patted the arm of the couch. "Over here, by the fire. We'll have Mr. Morgan build it up again when he returns." They sat. Hilda Morgan clasped her hands in her lap and leaned forward slightly, examining Myers' face.

The living room was as he remembered it, except that on the wall behind Hilda Morgan's chair he saw three small framed prints. In one print a man in a vest and frock coat was tipping his hat to two ladies who held parasols. All this was happening on a broad concourse with horses and carriages.

"How was Germany?" Paula said. She sat on the edge of the cushion and held her purse on her knees.

"We loved Germany," Edgar Morgan said, coming in from the kitchen with a tray and four large cups. Myers recognized the cups.

"Have you been to Germany, Mrs. Myers?" Morgan asked.

"We want to go," Paula said. "Don't we, Myers? Maybe next year, next summer. Or else the year after. As soon as we can afford it. Maybe as soon as Myers sells something. Myers writes."

"I should think a trip to Europe would be very beneficial to a writer," Edgar Morgan said. He put the cups into coasters. "Please help yourselves." He sat down in a chair across from his wife and gazed at Myers. "You said in your letter you were taking off work to write."

"That's true," Myers said and sipped his drink.

"He writes something almost every day," Paula said.

"Is that a fact?" Morgan said. "That's impressive. What did you write today, may I ask?"

"Nothing," Myers said.

"It's the holidays," Paula said.

"You must be proud of him, Mrs. Myers," Hilda Morgan said.

"I am," Paula said.

"I'm happy for you," Hilda Morgan said.

"I heard something the other day that might interest you," Edgar Morgan said. He took out some tobacco and began to fill a pipe. Myers lighted a cigaret and looked around for an ashtray, then dropped the match behind the couch.

"It's a horrible story, really. But maybe you could use it, Mr. Myers." Morgan struck a flame and drew on the pipe. "Grist for the mill, you know, and all that," Morgan said and laughed and shook the match. "This fellow was about my age or so. He was a colleague for a couple of years. We knew each other a little, and we had good friends in common. Then he moved out, accepted a position at the university down the way. Well, you know how these things go sometimes—the fellow had an affair with one of his students."

Mrs. Morgan made a disapproving noise with her tongue. She reached down for a small package that was wrapped in green paper and began to affix a red bow to the paper.

"According to all accounts, it was a torrid affair that lasted for some months," Morgan continued. "Right up until a short time ago, in fact. A week ago, to be exact. On that day—it was in the evening—he announced to his wife—they'd been married for twenty years—he announced to his wife that he wanted a divorce. You can imagine how the fool woman took it, coming out of the blue like that, so to speak. There was quite a row. The whole family got into it. She ordered him out of the house then and there. But just as the fellow was leaving, his son threw a can of tomato soup at him and hit him in the forehead. It caused a concussion that sent the man to the hospital. His condition is quite serious."

Morgan drew on his pipe and gazed at Myers.

"I've never heard such a story," Mrs. Morgan said. "Edgar, that's disgusting."

"Horrible," Paula said.

Myers grinned.

"Now *there's* a tale for you, Mr. Myers," Morgan said, catching the grin and narrowing his eyes. "Think of the story you'd have if you could get inside that man's head."

"Or her head," Mrs. Morgan said. "The wife's. Think of *her* story. To be betrayed in such fashion after twenty years. Think how she must feel."

"But imagine what the poor *boy* must be going through," Paula said. "Imagine, having almost killed his father."

"Yes, that's all true," Morgan said. "But here's something I don't think any of you has thought about. Think about *this* for a moment. Mr. Myers, are you listening? Tell me what you think of this. Put yourself in the shoes of that eighteen-year-old coed who fell in love with a married man. Think about *her* for a moment, and then you see the possibilities for your story."

Morgan nodded and leaned back in the chair with a satisfied expression.

"I'm afraid I don't have any sympathy for her," Mrs. Morgan said. "I can imagine the sort she is. We all know what she's like, that kind preys on older men. I don't have any sympathy for him, either—the man, the chaser, no, I don't. I'm afraid my sympathies in this case are entirely with the wife and son."

"It would take a Tolstoy to tell it and tell it *right*," Morgan said. "No less than a Tolstoy. Mr. Myers, the water is still hot."

"Time to go," Myers said.

He stood up and threw his cigaret into the fire.

"Stay," Mrs. Morgan said. "We haven't gotten acquainted yet. You don't know how we have . . . speculated about you. Now that we're together at last, stay a little while. It's such a pleasant surprise."

"We appreciated the card and your note," Paula said.

"The card?" Mrs. Morgan said.

Myers sat down.

"We decided not to mail any cards this year," Paula said. "I didn't get around to it when I should have, and it seemed futile to do it at the last minute."

"You'll have another one, Mrs. Myers?" Morgan said, standing in front of her now with his hand on her cup. "You'll set an example for your husband."

"It *was* good," Paula said. "It warms you."

"Right," Morgan said. "It warms you. That's right. Dear, did you hear Mrs. Myers? It warms you. That's very good. Mr. Myers?" Morgan said and waited. "You'll join us?"

"All right," Myers said and let Morgan take the cup.

The dog began to whine and scratch at the door.

"That dog. I don't know what's gotten into that dog," Morgan said. He went to the kitchen and this time Myers distinctly heard Morgan curse as he slammed the kettle onto a burner.

—

Mrs. Morgan began to hum. She picked up a half-wrapped package, cut a piece of tape, and began sealing the paper.

Myers lighted a cigaret. He dropped the match in his coaster. He looked at his watch.

Mrs. Morgan raised her head. "I believe I hear singing," she said. She listened. She rose from her chair and went to the front window. "It *is* singing. Edgar!" she called.

Myers and Paula went to the window.

"I haven't seen carolers in years," Mrs. Morgan said.

"What is it?" Morgan said. He had the tray and cups. "What is it? What's wrong?"

"Nothing's wrong, dear. It's carolers. There they are over there, across the street," Mrs. Morgan said.

"Mrs. Myers," Morgan said, extending the tray. "Mr. Myers. Dear."

"Thank you," Paula said.

"*Muchas gracias*," Myers said.

Morgan put the tray down and came back to the window with his cup. Young people were gathered on the walk in front of the house across the street, boys and girls with an older, taller boy who wore a muffler and a topcoat. Myers could see the faces at the window across the way—the Ardreys—and when the carolers had finished, Jack Ardrey came to the door and gave something to the older boy. The group moved on down the walk, flashlights bobbing, and stopped in front of another house.

"They won't come here," Mrs. Morgan said after a time.

"What? Why won't they come here?" Morgan said and turned to his wife. "What a goddamned silly thing to say! Why won't they come here?"

"I just know they won't," Mrs. Morgan said.

"And I say they will," Morgan said. "Mrs. Myers, are those carolers going to come here or not? What do you think? Will they return to bless this house? We'll leave it up to you."

Paula pressed closer to the window. But the carolers were far down the street now. She did not answer.

"Well, now that all the excitement is over," Morgan said and went over to his chair. He sat down, frowned, and began to fill his pipe.

Myers and Paula went back to the couch. Mrs. Morgan moved away from the window at last. She sat down. She smiled and gazed into her cup. Then she put the cup down and began to weep.

Morgan gave his handkerchief to his wife. He looked at Myers. Presently Morgan began to drum on the arm of his chair. Myers moved his feet. Paula looked into her purse for a cigaret. "See what you've caused?" Morgan said as he stared at something on the carpet near Myers' shoes.

Myers gathered himself to stand.

"Edgar, get them another drink," Mrs. Morgan said as she dabbed at her eyes. She used the handkerchief on her nose. "I want them to hear about Mrs. Attenborough. Mr. Myers writes. I think he might appreciate this. We'll wait until you come back before we begin the story."

Morgan collected the cups. He carried them into the kitchen. Myers heard dishes clatter, cupboard doors bang. Mrs. Morgan looked at Myers and smiled faintly.

"We have to go," Myers said. "We have to go. Paula, get your coat."

"No, no, we insist, Mr. Myers," Mrs. Morgan said. "We want you to hear about Mrs. Attenborough, poor Mrs. Attenborough. You might appreciate this story, too, Mrs. Myers. This is your chance to see how your husband's mind goes to work on raw material."

Morgan came back and passed out the hot drinks. He sat down quickly.

"Tell them about Mrs. Attenborough, dear," Mrs. Morgan said.

"That dog almost tore my leg off," Myers said and was at once surprised at his words. He put his cup down.

"Oh, come, it wasn't that bad," Morgan said. "I saw it."

"You know writers," Mrs. Morgan said to Paula. "They like to exaggerate."

"The power of the pen and all that," Morgan said.

"That's it," Mrs. Morgan said. "Bend your pen into a plowshare, Mr. Myers."

"We'll let Mrs. Morgan tell the story of Mrs. Attenborough," Morgan said, ignoring Myers, who stood up at that moment.

"Mrs. Morgan was intimately connected with the affair. I've already told you of the fellow who was knocked for a loop by a can of soup." Morgan chuckled. "We'll let Mrs. Morgan tell this one."

"You tell it, dear. And Mr. Myers, you listen closely," Mrs. Morgan said.

"We have to go," Myers said. "Paula, let's go."

"Talk about honesty," Mrs. Morgan said.

"Let's talk about it," Myers said. Then he said, "Paula, are you coming?"

"I want you to hear this story," Morgan said, raising his voice. "You will insult Mrs. Morgan, you will insult us both, if you don't listen to this story." Morgan clenched his pipe.

"Myers, please," Paula said anxiously. "I want to hear it. Then we'll go. Myers? Please, honey, sit down for another minute."

Myers looked at her. She moved her fingers, as if signaling him. He hesitated, and then he sat next to her.

Mrs. Morgan began. "One afternoon in Munich, Edgar and I went to the Dortmunder Museum. There was a *Bauhaus* exhibit that fall, and Edgar said the heck with it, let's take a day off —he was doing his research, you see—the heck with it, let's take a day off. We caught a tram and rode across Munich to the museum. We spent several hours viewing the exhibit and revisiting some of the galleries to pay homage to a few of our favorites amongst the old masters. Just as we were to leave, I stepped into the ladies' room. I left my purse. In the purse was Edgar's monthly check from home that had come the day before and a hundred and twenty dollars cash that I was going to deposit along with the check. I also had my identification cards in the purse. I did not miss my purse until we arrived home. Edgar immediately telephoned the museum authorities. But while he was talking I saw a taxi out front. A well-dressed woman with white hair got out. She was a stout woman and she was carrying two purses. I called for Edgar and went to the door. The woman introduced herself as Mrs. Attenborough, gave me my purse, and explained that she too had visited the museum that afternoon and while in the ladies' room had noticed a purse in the trash can. She of course had opened the purse in an effort to trace the owner. There were the identification cards and such giving our local address. She immediately left the museum and took a taxi in order to deliver the purse herself. Edgar's check was there, but the money, the one hundred twenty dollars, was gone. Nevertheless, I was grateful the other things were intact. It was nearly four o'clock and we asked the woman to stay for tea. She sat down, and after a little while she began to tell us about herself. She had been born and reared in Australia, had married young, had had three children, all sons, been widowed, and still lived in Australia with two of her sons. They raised sheep and had more than twenty thousand acres of land for the sheep to run in, and many drovers and shearers and such who worked for them at certain times of the year. When she came to our home in Munich, she was then on her way to Australia from England, where she had been to visit her youngest son, who was a barrister. She was returning to Australia when we met her," Mrs. Morgan said. "She was seeing some of the world in the process. She had many places yet to visit on her itinerary."

"Come to the point, dear," Morgan said.

"Yes. Here is what happened, then. Mr. Myers, I'll go right to the climax, as you writers say. Suddenly, after we had had a very pleasant conversation for an hour, after this woman had told about herself and her adventurous life Down Under, she stood up to go. As she started to pass me her cup, her mouth flew open, the cup dropped, and she fell across our couch and died. Died. Right in our living room. It was the most shocking moment in our lives."

Morgan nodded solemnly.

"God," Paula said.

"Fate sent her to die on the couch in our living room in Germany," Mrs. Morgan said.

Myers began to laugh. "Fate . . . sent . . . her . . . to . . . die . . . in . . . your . . . living . . . room?" he said between gasps.

"Is that funny, sir?" Morgan said. "Do you find that amusing?"

Myers nodded. He kept laughing. He wiped his eyes on his shirt sleeve. "I'm really sorry," he said. "I can't help it. That line '*Fate sent her to die on the couch in our living room in*

Germany.' I'm sorry. Then what happened?" he managed to say. "I'd like to know what happened then."

"Mr. Myers, we didn't know what to do," Mrs. Morgan said. "The shock was terrible. Edgar felt for her pulse, but there was no sign of life. And she had begun to change color. Her face and hands were turning *gray.* Edgar went to the phone to call someone. Then he said, 'Open her purse, see if you can find where she's staying.' All the time averting my eyes from the poor thing there on the couch, I took up her purse. Imagine my complete surprise and bewilderment, my utter bewilderment, when the first thing I saw inside was my hundred twenty dollars, still fastened with the paper clip. I was never so astonished."

"And disappointed," Morgan said. "Don't forget that. It was a keen disappointment."

Myers giggled.

"If you were a real writer, as you say you are, Mr. Myers, you would not laugh," Morgan said as he got to his feet. "You would not dare laugh! You would try to understand. You would plumb the depths of that poor soul's heart and try to understand. But you are no writer, sir!"

Myers kept on giggling.

Morgan slammed his fist on the coffee table and the cups rattled in the coasters. "The real story lies right here, in this house, this very living room, and it's time it was told! The real story is *here*, Mr. Myers," Morgan said. He walked up and down over the brilliant wrapping paper that had unrolled and now lay spread across the carpet. He stopped to glare at Myers, who was holding his forehead and shaking with laughter.

"Consider *this* for a possibility, Mr. Myers!" Morgan screamed. "*Consider!* A friend—let's call him Mr. X—is friends with . . . with Mr. and Mrs. Y, *as well as* Mr. and Mrs. Z. Mr. and Mrs. Y and Mr. and Mrs. Z do not know each other, unfortunately. I say *unfortunately* because if they *had* known each other this story would not exist because it would never have taken place. Now, Mr. X learns that Mr. and Mrs. Y are going to Germany for a year and need someone to occupy their house during the time they are gone. Mr. and Mrs. Z are looking for suitable accommodations, and Mr. X tells them he knows of just the place. But before Mr. X can put Mr. and Mrs. Z in touch with Mr. and Mrs. Y, the Ys have to leave sooner than expected. Mr. X, being a friend, is left to rent the house at his discretion to anyone, including Mr. and Mrs. Y—I mean Z. Now, Mr. and Mrs. . . . Z move into the house and bring a cat with them that Mr. and Mrs. Y hear about later in a letter from Mr. X. Mr. and Mrs. Z bring a cat into the house *even though* the terms of the lease have expressly forbidden cats or other animals in the house because of Mrs. Y's asthma. The *real* story, Mr. Myers, lies in the situation I've just described. Mr. and Mrs. Z—I mean Mr. and Mrs. *Y*'s moving into the Zs' house, *invading* the Zs' house, if the truth is to be told. Sleeping in the Zs' bed is one thing, but unlocking the Zs' private closet and using their linen, vandalizing the things found there, that was against the spirit and letter of the lease. And this *same* couple, the *Zs*, opened boxes of kitchen utensils marked 'Don't Open.' And broke dishes when it was spelled out, *spelled out* in that same lease, that they were not to use the owners', the Zs' *personal*, I emphasize *personal*, possessions."

Morgan's lips were white. He continued to walk up and down on the paper, stopping every now and then to look at Myers and emit little puffing noises from his lips.

"And the bathroom things, dear—don't forget the bathroom things," Mrs. Morgan said. "It's bad enough using the Zs' blankets and sheets, but when they also get into their *bathroom* things and go through the little private things stored in the *attic*, a line has to be drawn."

"That's the *real* story, Mr. Myers," Morgan said. He tried to fill his pipe. His hands trembled and tobacco spilled onto the carpet. "That's the real story that is waiting to be written."

"And it doesn't need Tolstoy to tell it," Mrs. Morgan said.

"It doesn't need Tolstoy," Morgan said.

Myers laughed. He and Paula got up from the couch at the same time and moved toward the door. "Good night," Myers said merrily.

Morgan was behind him. "If you were a real writer, sir, you would put that story into words and not pussyfoot around with it, either."

Myers just laughed. He touched the doorknob.

"One other thing," Morgan said. "I didn't intend to bring this up, but in light of your behavior here tonight, I want to tell you that I'm missing my two-volume set of 'Jazz at the Philharmonic.' Those records are of great sentimental value. I bought them in 1955. And now I insist you tell me what happened to them!"

"In all fairness, Edgar," Mrs. Morgan said as she helped Paula on with her coat, "after you took inventory of the records, you admitted you couldn't recall the last time you had seen those records."

"But I am sure of it now," Morgan said. "I am positive I saw those records just before we left, and now, now I'd like this *writer* to tell me exactly what he knows of their whereabouts. Mr. Myers?"

But Myers was already outdoors, and, taking his wife by the hand, he hurried her down the walk to the car. They surprised Buzzy. The dog yelped in what seemed fear and then jumped to the side.

"I insist on *knowing!*" Morgan called. "I am waiting, sir!"

Myers got Paula into the car and started the engine. He looked again at the couple on the porch. Mrs. Morgan waved, and then she and Edgar Morgan went back inside and shut the door.

Myers pulled away from the curb.

"Those people are crazy," Paula said.

Myers patted her hand.

"They were scary," she said.

He did not answer. Her voice seemed to come to him from a great distance. He kept driving. Snow rushed at the windshield. He was silent and watched the road. He was at the very end of a story.

Jerry and Molly and Sam

As Al saw it, there was only one solution. He had to get rid of the dog without Betty or the kids finding out about it. At night. It would have to be done at night. He would simply drive Suzy—well, someplace, later he'd decide where—open the door, push her out, drive away. The sooner the better. He felt relieved making the decision. Any action was better than no action at all, he was becoming convinced.

It was Sunday. He got up from the kitchen table where he had been eating a late breakfast by himself and stood by the sink, hands in his pockets. Nothing was going right lately. He had enough to contend with without having to worry about a stinking dog. They were laying off at Aerojet when they should be hiring. The middle of the summer, defense contracts let all over the country and Aerojet was talking of cutting back. *Was* cutting back, in fact, a little more every day. He was no safer than anyone else even though he'd been there two years going on three. He got along with the right people, all right, but seniority or friendship, either one, didn't mean a damn these days. If your number was up, that was that—and there was nothing anybody could do. They got ready to lay off, they laid off. Fifty, a hundred men at a time.

No one was safe, from the foreman and supers right on down to the man on the line. And three months ago, just before all the layoffs began, he'd let Betty talk him into moving into this cushy two-hundred-a-month place. Lease, with an option to buy. Shit!

Al hadn't really wanted to leave the other place. He had been comfortable enough. Who could know that two weeks after he'd move they'd start laying off? But who could know anything these days? For example, there was Jill. Jill worked in bookkeeping at Weinstock's. She was a nice girl, said she loved Al. She was just lonely, that's what she told him the first night. She didn't make it a habit, letting herself be picked up by married men, she also told him the first night. He'd met Jill about three months ago, when he was feeling depressed and jittery with all the talk of layoffs just beginning. He met her at the Town and Country, a bar not too far from his new place. They danced a little and he drove her home and they necked in the car in front of her apartment. He had not gone upstairs with her that night, though he was sure he could have. He went upstairs with her the next night.

Now he was having an *affair*, for Christ's sake, and he didn't know what to do about it. He did not want it to go on, and he did not want to break it off: you don't throw everything overboard in a storm. Al was drifting, and he knew he was drifting, and where it was all going to end he could not guess at. But he was beginning to feel he was losing control over everything. Everything. Recently, too, he had caught himself thinking about old age after he'd been constipated a few days—an affliction he had always associated with the elderly. Then there was the matter of the tiny bald spot and of his having just begun to wonder how he would comb his hair a different way. What was he going to do with his life? he wanted to know.

He was thirty-one.

All these things to contend with and then *Sandy*, his wife's younger sister, giving the kids, Alex and Mary, that mongrel dog about four months ago. He wished he'd never seen that dog. Or Sandy, either, for that matter. That bitch! She was always turning up with some shit or other that wound up costing him money, some little flimflam that went haywire after a day or two and *had* to be repaired, something the kids could scream over and fight over and beat the shit out of each other about. God! And then turning right around to touch him, through *Betty*, for twenty-five bucks. The mere thought of all the twenty-five- or fifty-buck checks, and the one just a few months ago for eighty-five to make her car payment—her *car* payment, for God's sake, when he didn't even know if he was going to have a roof over his head—made him want to *kill* the goddamn dog.

Sandy! Betty and Alex and Mary! Jill! And Suzy the goddamn dog!

This was Al.

—

He had to start someplace—setting things in order, sorting all this out. It was time to *do* something, time for some straight thinking for a change. And he intended to start tonight.

He would coax the dog into the car undetected and, on some pretext or another, go out. Yet he hated to think of the way Betty would lower her eyes as she watched him dress, and then, later, just before he went out the door, ask him where, how long, etc., in a resigned voice that made him feel all the worse. He could never get used to the lying. Besides, he hated to use what little reserve he might have left with Betty by telling her a lie for something different from what she suspected. A wasted lie, so to speak. But he could not tell her the truth, could not say he was *not* going drinking, was *not* going calling on somebody, was instead going to do away with the goddamn dog and thus take the first step toward setting his house in order.

He ran his hand over his face, tried to put it all out of his mind for a minute. He took out a cold half quart of Lucky from the fridge and popped the aluminum top. His life had become a maze, one lie overlaid upon another until he was not sure he could untangle them if he had to.

"The goddamn dog," he said out loud.

"She doesn't have good sense!" was how Al put it. She was a sneak, besides. The moment the back door was left open and everyone gone, she'd pry open the screen, come through to the living room, and urinate on the carpet. There were at least a half dozen map-shaped stains on it right now. But her favorite place was the utility room, where she could root in the dirty clothes, so that all of the shorts and panties now had crotch or seat chewed away. And she chewed through the antenna wires on the outside of the house, and once Al pulled into the drive and found her lying in the front yard with one of his Florsheims in her mouth.

"She's crazy," he'd say. "And she's driving me crazy. I can't make it fast enough to replace it. The sonofabitch, I'm going to kill her one of these days!"

Betty tolerated the dog at greater durations, would go along apparently unruffled for a time, but suddenly she would come upon it, with fists clenched, call it a bastard, a bitch, shriek at the kids about keeping it out of their room, the living room, etc. Betty was that way with the children, too. She could go along with them just so far, let them get away with just so much, and then she would turn on them savagely and slap their faces, screaming, "Stop it! Stop it! I can't stand any more of it!"

But then Betty would say, "It's their first dog. You remember how fond you must have been of your first dog."

"My dog had brains," he would say. "It was an Irish setter!"

The afternoon passed. Betty and the kids returned from someplace or another in the car, and they all had sandwiches and potato chips on the patio. He fell asleep on the grass, and when he woke it was nearly evening.

He showered, shaved, put on slacks and a clean shirt. He felt rested but sluggish. He dressed and he thought of Jill. He thought of Betty and Alex and Mary and Sandy and Suzy. He felt drugged.

"We'll have supper pretty soon," Betty said, coming to the bathroom door and staring at him.

"That's all right. I'm not hungry. Too hot to eat," he said fiddling with his shirt collar. "I might drive over to Carl's, shoot a few games of pool, have a couple of beers."

She said, "I see."

He said, "Jesus!"

She said, "Go ahead, I don't care."

He said, "I won't be gone long."

She said, "Go ahead, I said. I said I don't care."

In the garage, he said, "Goddamn you all!" and kicked the rake across the cement floor. Then he lit a cigaret and tried to get hold of himself. He picked up the rake and put it away where it belonged. He was muttering to himself, saying, "Order, order," when the dog came up to the garage, sniffed around the door, and looked in.

"Here. Come here, Suzy. Here, girl," he called.

The dog wagged her tail but stayed where she was.

He went over to the cupboard above the lawn mower and took down one, then two, and finally three cans of food.

"All you want tonight, Suzy, old girl. All you can eat," he coaxed, opening up both ends of the first can and sliding the mess into the dog's dish.

—

He drove around for nearly an hour, not able to decide on a place. If he dropped her off in just any neighborhood and the pound were called, the dog would be back at the house in a day or two. The county pound was the first place Betty would call. He remembered reading stories about lost dogs finding their way hundreds of miles back home again. He remembered crime programs where someone saw a license number, and the thought made his heart jump. Held up to public view, without all the facts being in, it'd be a shameful thing to be caught abandoning a dog. He would have to find the right place.

He drove over near the American River. The dog needed to get out more anyway, get the feel of the wind on its back, be able to swim and wade in the river when it wanted; it was a pity to keep a dog fenced in all the time. But the fields near the levee seemed too desolate, no houses around at all. After all, he did want the dog to be found and cared for. A large old two-story house was what he had in mind, with happy, well-behaved reasonable children who needed a dog, who desperately needed a dog. But there were no old two-story houses here, not a one.

He drove back onto the highway. He had not been able to look at the dog since he'd managed to get her into the car. She lay quietly on the back seat now. But when he pulled off the road and stopped the car, she sat up and whined, looking around.

He stopped at a bar, rolled all the car windows down before he went inside. He stayed nearly an hour, drinking beer and playing the shuffleboard. He kept wondering if he should have left all the doors ajar too. When he went back outside, Suzy sat up in the seat and rolled her lips back, showing her teeth.

He got in and started off again.

Then he thought of the place. The neighborhood where they used to live, swarming with kids and just across the line in Yolo County, that would be just the right place. If the dog were picked up, it would be taken to the Woodland Pound, not the pound in Sacramento. Just drive onto one of the streets in the old neighborhood, stop, throw out a handful of the shit she ate, open the door, a little assistance in the way of a push, and out she'd go while he took off. Done! It would be done.

He stepped on it getting out there.

There were porch lights on and at three or four houses he saw men and women sitting on the front steps as he drove by. He cruised along, and when he came to his old house he slowed down almost to a stop and stared at the front door, the porch, the lighted windows. He felt even more insubstantial, looking at the house. He had lived there—how long? A year, sixteen months? Before that, Chico, Red Bluff, Tacoma, Portland— where he'd met Betty—Yakima . . . Toppenish, where he was born and went to high school. Not since he was a kid, it seemed to him, had he known what it was to be free from worry and worse. He thought of summers fishing and camping in the Cascades, autumns when he'd hunt pheasants behind Sam, the setter's flashing red coat a beacon through cornfields and alfalfa meadows where the boy that he was and the dog that he had would both run like mad. He wished he could keep driving and driving tonight until he was driving onto the old bricked main street of Toppenish, turning left at the first light, then left again, stopping when he came to where his mother lived, and never, never, for any reason ever, ever leave again.

He came to the darkened end of the street. There was a large empty field straight ahead and the street turned to the right, skirting it. For almost a block there were no houses on the side nearer the field and only one house, completely dark, on the other side. He stopped the car and, without thinking any longer about what he was doing, scooped a handful of dog food up, leaned over the seat, opened the back door nearer the field, threw the stuff out, and said, "Go on, Suzy." He pushed her until she jumped down reluctantly. He leaned over farther, pulled the door shut, and drove off, slowly. Then he drove faster and faster.

He stopped at Dupee's, the first bar he came to on the way back to Sacramento. He was jumpy and perspiring. He didn't feel exactly unburdened or relieved, as he had thought he would feel. But he kept assuring himself it was a step in the right direction, that the good feeling would settle on him to-morrow. The thing to do was to wait it out.

After four beers a girl in a turtleneck sweater and sandals

and carrying a suitcase sat down beside him. She set the suitcase between the stools. She seemed to know the bartender, and the bartender had something to say to her whenever he came by, once or twice stopping briefly to talk. She told Al her name was Molly, but she wouldn't let him buy her a beer. Instead, she offered to eat half a pizza.

He smiled at her, and she smiled back. He took out his cigarets and his lighter and put them on the bar.

"Pizza it is!" he said.

Later, he said, "Can I give you a lift somewhere?"

"No, thanks. I'm waiting for someone," she said.

He said, "Where you heading for?"

She said, "No place. Oh," she said, touching the suitcase with her toe, "you mean that?" laughing. "I live here in West Sac. I'm not going anyplace. It's just a washing-machine motor inside belongs to my mother. Jerry—that's the bartender—he's good at fixing things. Jerry said he'd fix it for nothing."

Al got up. He weaved a little as he leaned over her. He said, "Well, goodbye, honey. I'll see you around."

"You bet!" she said. "And thanks for the pizza. Hadn't eaten since lunch. Been trying to take some of this off." She raised her sweater, gathered a handful of flesh at the waist.

"Sure I can't give you a lift someplace?" he said.

The woman shook her head.

In the car again, driving, he reached for his cigarets and then, frantically, for his lighter, remembering leaving everything on the bar. The hell with it, he thought, let her have it. Let her put the lighter and the cigarets in the suitcase along with the washing machine. He chalked it up against the dog, one more expense. But the last, by God! It angered him now, now that he was getting things in order, that the girl hadn't been more friendly. If he'd been in a different frame of mind, he could have picked her up. But when you're depressed, it shows all over you, even the way you light a cigaret.

He decided to go see Jill. He stopped at a liquor store and bought a pint of whiskey and climbed the stairs to her apartment and he stopped at the landing to catch his breath and to clean his teeth with his tongue. He could still taste the mushrooms from the pizza, and his mouth and throat were seared from the whiskey. He realized that what he wanted to do was to go right to Jill's bathroom and use her toothbrush.

He knocked. "It's me, Al," he whispered. "Al," he said louder. He heard her feet hit the floor. She threw the lock and then tried to undo the chain as he leaned heavily against the door.

"Just a minute, honey. Al, you'll have to quit pushing—I can't unhook it. There," she said and opened the door, scanning his face as she took him by the hand.

They embraced clumsily, and he kissed her on the cheek.

"Sit down, honey. Here." She switched on a lamp and helped him to the couch. Then she touched her fingers to her curlers and said, "I'll put on some lipstick. What would you like in the meantime? Coffee? Juice? A beer? I think I have some beer. What do you have there . . . whiskey? What would you like, honey?" She stroked his hair with one hand and leaned over him, gazing into his eyes. "Poor baby, what would you like?" she said.

"Just want you hold me," he said. "Here. Sit down. No lipstick," he said, pulling her onto his lap. "Hold. I'm falling," he said.

She put an arm around his shoulders. She said, "You come on over to the bed, baby, I'll give you what you like."

"Tell you, Jill," he said, "skating on thin ice. Crash through any minute . . . I don't know." He stared at her with a fixed, puffy expression that he could feel but not correct. "Serious," he said.

She nodded. "Don't think about anything, baby. Just relax," she said. She pulled his face to hers and kissed him on the forehead and then the lips. She turned slightly on his lap and said, "No, don't move, Al," the fingers of both hands suddenly slipping around the back of his neck and gripping his face at the same time. His eyes wobbled around the room an instant, then tried to focus on what she was doing. She held his head in place in her strong fingers. With her thumbnails she was squeezing out a blackhead to the side of his nose.

"Sit still!" she said.

"No," he said. "Don't! Stop! Not in the mood for that."

"I almost have it. Sit still, I said! . . . There, look at that.

What do you think of that? Didn't know that was there, did you? Now just one more, a big one, baby. The last one," she said.

"Bathroom," he said, forcing her off, freeing his way.

At home it was all tears, confusion. Mary ran out to the car, crying, before he could get parked.

"Suzy's gone," she sobbed. "Suzy's gone. She's never coming back, Daddy, I know it. She's gone!"

My God, heart lurching. *What have I done?*

"Now don't worry, sweetheart. She's probably just off running around somewhere. She'll be back," he said.

"She isn't, Daddy, I know she isn't. Mama said we may have to get another dog."

"Wouldn't that be all right, honey?" he said. "Another dog, if Suzy doesn't come back? We'll go to the pet store—"

"I don't want another dog!" the child cried, holding onto his leg.

"Can we have a monkey, Daddy, instead of a dog?" Alex asked. "If we go to the pet store to look for a dog, can we have a monkey instead?"

"I don't want a monkey!" Mary cried. "I want Suzy."

"Everybody let go now, let Daddy in the house. Daddy has a terrible, terrible headache," he said.

Betty lifted a casserole dish from the oven. She looked tired, irritable . . . older. She didn't look at him. "The kids tell you? Suzy's gone? I've combed the neighborhood. Everywhere, I swear."

"That dog'll turn up," he said. "Probably just running around somewhere. That dog'll come back," he said.

"Seriously," she said, turning to him with her hands on her hips, "I think it's something else. I think she might have got hit by a car. I want you to drive around. The kids called her last night, and she was gone then. That's the last's been seen of her. I called the pound and described her to them, but they said all their trucks aren't in yet. I'm supposed to call again in the morning."

He went into the bathroom and could hear her still going on. He began to run the water in the sink, wondering, with a fluttery sensation in his stomach, how grave exactly was his mistake. When he turned off the faucets, he could still hear her. He kept staring at the sink.

"Did you hear me?" she called. "I want you to drive around and look for her after supper. The kids can go with you and look too . . . Al?"

"Yes, yes," he answered.

"What?" she said. "What'd you say?"

"I said yes. Yes! All right. Anything! Just let me wash up first, will you?"

She looked through from the kitchen. "Well, what in the hell is eating you? I didn't ask you to get drunk last night, did I? I've had enough of it, I can tell you! I've had a hell of a day, if you want to know. Alex waking me up at five this morning getting in with me, telling me his daddy was snoring so loud that . . . that you *scared* him! *I* saw you out there with your clothes on passed out and the room smelling to high heaven. I tell you, I've had enough of it!" She looked around the kitchen quickly, as if to seize something.

He kicked the door shut. Everything was going to hell. While he was shaving, he stopped once and held the razor in his hand and looked at himself in the mirror: his face doughy, characterless—*immoral*, that was the word. He laid the razor down. *I believe I have made the gravest mistake this time. I believe I have made the gravest mistake of all.* He brought the razor up to his throat and finished.

He did not shower, did not change clothes. "Put my supper in the oven for me," he said. "Or in the refrigerator. I'm going out. Right now," he said.

"You can wait till after supper. The kids can go with you."

"No, the hell with that. Let the kids eat supper, look around here if they want. I'm not hungry, and it'll be dark soon."

"Is everybody going crazy?" she said. "I don't know what's going to happen to us. I'm ready for a nervous breakdown. I'm ready to lose my mind. What's going to happen to the kids if I lose my mind?" She slumped against the draining board, her face crumpled, tears rolling off her cheeks. "You don't love them, anyway! You never have. It isn't the dog I'm worried about. It's us! It's us! I know you don't love me any more— goddamn you!—but you don't even love the kids!"

"Betty, Betty!" he said. "My God!" he said. "Everything's going to be all right. I promise you," he said. "Don't worry," he said. "I promise you, things'll be all right. I'll find the dog and then things will be all right," he said.

He bounded out of the house, ducked into the bushes as he heard his children coming: the girl crying, saying, "Suzy, Suzy"; the boy saying maybe a train ran over her. When they were inside the house, he made a break for the car.

He fretted at all the lights he had to wait for, bitterly resented the time lost when he stopped for gas. The sun was low and heavy, just over the squat range of hills at the far end of the valley. At best, he had an hour of daylight.

He saw his whole life a ruin from here on in. If he lived another fifty years—hardly likely—he felt he'd never get over it, abandoning the dog. He felt he was finished if he didn't find the dog. A man who would get rid of a little dog wasn't worth a damn. That kind of man would do anything, would stop at nothing.

He squirmed in the seat, kept staring into the swollen face of the sun as it moved lower into the hills. He knew the situation was all out of proportion now, but he couldn't help it. He knew he must somehow retrieve the dog, as the night before he had known he must lose it.

"I'm the one going crazy," he said and then nodded his head in agreement.

He came in the other way this time, by the field where he had let her off, alert for any sign of movement.

"Let her be there," he said.

He stopped the car and searched the field. Then he drove on, slowly. A station wagon with the motor idling was parked in the drive of the lone house, and he saw a well-dressed woman in heels come out the front door with a little girl. They stared at him as he passed. Farther on he turned left, his eyes taking in the street and the yards on each side as far down as he could see. Nothing. Two kids with bicycles a block away stood beside a parked car.

"Hi," he said to the two boys as he pulled up alongside. "You fellows see anything of a little white dog around today? A kind of white shaggy dog? I lost one."

One boy just gazed at him. The other said, "I saw a lot of little kids playing with a dog over there this afternoon. The street the other side of this one. I don't know what kind of dog it was. It was white maybe. There was a lot of kids."

"Okay, good. Thanks," Al said. "Thank you very very much," he said.

He turned right at the end of the street. He concentrated on the street ahead. The sun had gone down now. It was nearly dark. Houses pitched side by side, trees, lawns, telephone poles, parked cars, it struck him as serene, untroubled. He could hear a man calling his children; he saw a woman in an apron step to the lighted door of her house.

"Is there still a chance for me?" Al said. He felt tears spring to his eyes. He was amazed. He couldn't help but grin at himself and shake his head as he got out his handkerchief. Then he saw a group of children coming down the street. He waved to get their attention.

"You kids see anything of a little white dog?" Al said to them.

"Oh sure," one boy said. "Is it your dog?"

Al nodded.

"We were just playing with him about a minute ago, down the street. In Terry's yard." The boy pointed. "Down the street."

"You got kids?" one of the little girls spoke up.

"I do," Al said.

"Terry said he's going to keep him. He don't have a dog," the boy said.

"I don't know," Al said. "I don't think my kids would like that. It belongs to them. It's just lost," Al said.

He drove on down the street. It was dark now, hard to see, and he began to panic again, cursing silently. He swore at what a weathervane he was, changing this way and that, one moment this, the next moment that.

He saw the dog then. He understood he had been looking at it for a time. The dog moved slowly, nosing the grass along a fence. Al got out of the car, started across the lawn, crouching forward as he walked, calling, "Suzy, Suzy, Suzy."

The dog stopped when she saw him. She raised her head. He sat down on his heels, reached out his arm, waiting. They looked at each other. She moved her tail in greeting. She lay down with her head between her front legs and regarded him. He waited. She got up. She went around the fence and out of sight.

He sat there. He thought he didn't feel so bad, all things considered. The world was full of dogs. There were dogs and there were dogs. Some dogs you just couldn't do anything with.

Why, Honey?

DEAR SIR:
    I was so surprised to receive your letter asking about my son, how did you know I was here? I moved here years ago right after it started to happen. No one knows who I am here but I'm afraid all the same. Who I am afraid of is him. When I look at the paper I shake my head and wonder. I read what they write about him and I ask myself is that man really my son, is he really doing these things?

He was a good boy except for his outbursts and that he could not tell the truth. I can't give you any reasons. It started one summer over the Fourth of July, he would have been about fifteen. Our cat Trudy disappeared and was gone all night and the next day. Mrs. Cooper who lives behind us came the next evening to tell me Trudy crawled into her backyard that afternoon to die. Trudy was cut up she said but she recognized Trudy. Mr. Cooper buried the remains.

Cut up? I said. What do you mean cut up?

Mr. Cooper saw two boys in the field putting firecrackers in Trudy's ears and in her you know what. He tried to stop them but they ran.

Who, who would do such a thing, did he see who it was?

He didn't know the other boy but one of them ran this way. Mr. Cooper thought it was your son.

I shook my head. No, that's just not so, he wouldn't do a thing like that, he loved Trudy, Trudy has been in the family for years, no, it wasn't my son.

That evening I told him about Trudy and he acted surprised and shocked and said we should offer a reward. He typed something up and promised to post it at school. But just as he was going to his room that night he said don't take it too hard, mom, she was old, in cat years she was 65 or 70, she lived a long time.

He went to work afternoons and Saturdays as a stockboy at Hartley's. A friend of mine who worked there, Betty Wilks, told me about the job and said she would put in a word for him. I mentioned it to him that evening and he said good, jobs for young people are hard to find.

The night he was to draw his first check I cooked his favorite supper and had everything on the table when he walked in. Here's the man of the house, I said, hugging him. I am so proud, how much did you draw, honey? Eighty dollars, he said. I was flabbergasted. That's wonderful, honey, I just cannot believe it. I'm starved, he said, let's eat.

I was happy, but I couldn't understand it, it was more than I was making.

When I did the laundry I found the stub from Hartley's in his pocket, it was for 28 dollars, he said 80. Why didn't he just tell the truth? I couldn't understand.

I would ask him where did you go last night, honey? To the show he would answer. Then I would find out he went to the school dance or spent the evening riding around with somebody in a car. I would think what difference could it make, why doesn't he just be truthful, there is no reason to lie to his mother.

I remember once he was supposed to have gone on a field trip, so I asked him what did you see on the field trip, honey? And he shrugged and said land formations, volcanic rock, ash, they showed us where there used to be a big lake a million years ago, now it's just a desert. He looked me in the eyes and went on talking. Then I got a note from the school the next day saying they wanted permission for a field trip, could he have permission to go.

Near the end of his senior year he bought a car and was always gone. I was concerned about his grades but he only laughed. You know he was an excellent student, you know that about him if you know anything. After that he bought a shotgun and a hunting knife.

I hated to see those things in the house and I told him so. He laughed, he always had a laugh for you. He said he would keep the gun and the knife in the trunk of his car, he said they would be easier to get there anyway.

One Saturday night he did not come home. I worried myself into a terrible state. About ten o'clock the next morning he came in and asked me to cook him breakfast, he said he had worked up an appetite out hunting, he said he was sorry for being gone all night, he said they had driven a long way to get to this place. It sounded strange. He was nervous.

Where did you go?

Up to the Wenas. We got a few shots.

Who did you go with, honey?

Fred.

Fred?

He stared and I didn't say anything else.

On the Sunday right after I tiptoed into his room for his car keys. He had promised to pick up some breakfast items on his way home from work the night before and I thought he might have left the things in his car. I saw his new shoes sitting half under his bed and covered with mud and sand. He opened his eyes.

Honey, what happened to your shoes? Look at your shoes.

I ran out of gas, I had to walk for gas. He sat up. What do you care?

I am your mother.

While he was in the shower I took the keys and went out to his car. I opened the trunk. I didn't find the groceries. I saw the shotgun lying on a quilt and the knife too and I saw a shirt of his rolled in a ball and I shook it out and it was full of blood. It was wet. I dropped it. I closed the trunk and started back for the house and I saw him watching at the window and he opened the door.

I forgot to tell you, he said, I had a bad bloody nose, I don't know if that shirt can be washed, throw it away. He smiled.

A few days later I asked how he was getting along at work. Fine, he said, he said he had gotten a raise. But I met Betty Wilks on the street and she said they were all sorry at Hartley's that he had quit, he was so well liked, she said, Betty Wilks.

Two nights after that I was in bed but I couldn't sleep, I stared at the ceiling. I heard his car pull up out front and I listened as he put the key in the lock and he came through the kitchen and down the hall to his room and he shut the door after him. I got up. I could see light under his door, I knocked and pushed on the door and said would you like a hot cup of tea, honey, I can't sleep. He was bent over by the dresser and slammed a drawer and turned on me, get out he screamed, get out of here, I'm sick of you spying he screamed. I went to my room and cried myself to sleep. He broke my heart that night.

The next morning he was up and out before I could see him, but that was all right with me. From then on I was going to treat him like a lodger unless he wanted to mend his ways, I was at my limit. He would have to apologize if he wanted us to be more than just strangers living together under the same roof.

When I came in that evening he had supper ready. How are you? he said, he took my coat. How was your day?

I said I didn't sleep last night, honey. I promised myself I wouldn't bring it up and I'm not trying to make you feel guilty but I'm not used to being talked to like that by my son.

I want to show you something, he said, and he showed me this essay he was writing for his civics class. I believe it was on relations between the congress and the supreme court. (It was the paper that won a prize for him at graduation!) I tried to read it and then I decided, this was the time. Honey, I'd like to have a talk with you, it's hard to raise a child with things the way they are these days, it's especially hard for us having no father in the house, no man to turn to when we need him. You are nearly grown now but I am still responsible and I feel I am entitled to some respect and consideration and have tried to be fair and honest with you. I want the truth, honey, that's all I've ever asked from you, the truth. Honey, I took a breath, suppose you had a child who when you asked him something, anything, where he's been or where he's going, what he's doing with his time, anything, never, he never once told you the truth? Who if asked him is it raining outside, would answer no, it is nice and sunny, and I guess laugh to himself and think you were too old or too stupid to see his clothes are wet. Why should he lie, you ask yourself, what does he gain I don't understand. I keep asking myself why but I don't have the answer. Why, honey?

He didn't say anything, he kept staring, then he moved over alongside me and said I'll show you. Kneel is what I say, kneel down is what I say, he said, that's the first reason why.

I ran to my room and locked the door. He left that night, he took his things, what he wanted, and he left. Believe it or not I never saw him again. I saw him at his graduation but that was with a lot of people around. I sat in the audience and watched him get his diploma and a prize for his essay, then I heard him give the speech and then I clapped right along with the rest.

I went home after that.

I have never seen him again. Oh sure I have seen him on the TV and I have seen his pictures in the paper.

I found out he joined the marines and then I heard from someone he was out of the marines and going to college back east and then he married that girl and got himself in politics. I began to see his name in the paper. I found out his address and wrote to him, I wrote a letter every few months, there never was an answer. He ran for governor and was elected, and was famous now. That's when I began to worry.

I built up all these fears, I became afraid, I stopped writing him of course and then I hoped he would think I was dead. I moved here. I had them give me an unlisted number. And then I had to change my name. If you are a powerful man and want to find somebody, you can find them, it wouldn't be that hard.

I should be so proud but I am afraid. Last week I saw a car on the street with a man inside I know was watching me, I came straight back and locked the door. A few days ago the phone rang and rang, I was lying down. I picked up the receiver but there was nothing there.

I am old. I am his mother. I should be the proudest mother in all the land but I am only afraid.

Thank you for writing. I wanted someone to know. I am very ashamed.

I also wanted to ask how you got my name and knew where to write, I have been praying no one knew. But you did. Why did you? Please tell me why?

Yours truly,

The Ducks

A WIND came up that afternoon, bringing gusts of rain and sending the ducks up off the lake in black explosions looking for the quiet potholes out in the timber. He was at the back of the house splitting firewood and saw the ducks cutting over the highway and dropping into the marsh behind the trees. He watched, groups of half a dozen, but mostly doubles, one bunch behind the other. Out over the lake it was already dark and misty and he could not see the other side, where the mill was. He worked faster, driving the iron wedge down harder into the big dry chunks, splitting them so far down that the rotten ones flew apart. On his wife's clothesline, strung up between the two sugar pines, sheets and blankets popped shot-like in the wind. He made two trips and carried all the wood onto the porch before it started to rain.

"Supper's ready!" she called from the kitchen.

He went inside and washed up. They talked a little while they ate, mostly about the trip to Reno. Three more days of work, then payday, then the weekend in Reno. After supper he went out onto the porch and began sacking up his decoys. He stopped when she came out. She stood there in the doorway watching him.

"You going hunting again in the morning?"

He looked away from her and out toward the lake. "Look at the weather. I think it's going to be good in the morning." Her sheets were snapping in the wind and there was a blanket down on the ground. He nodded at it. "Your things are going to get wet."

"They weren't dry, anyway. They've been out there two days and they're not dry yet."

"What's the matter? Don't you feel good?" he said.

"I feel all right." She went back into the kitchen and shut the door and looked at him through the window. "I just hate to have you gone all the time. It seems like you're gone all the time," she said to the window. Her breath produced itself on the glass, then went away. When he came inside, he put the decoys in the corner and went to get his lunch pail. She was leaning against the cupboard, her hands on the edge of the draining board. He touched her hip, pinched her dress.

"You wait'll we get to Reno. We're going to have some fun," he said.

She nodded. It was hot in the kitchen and there were little drops of sweat over her eyes. "I'll get up when you come in and fix you some breakfast."

"You sleep. I'd rather have you sleep." He reached around behind her for his lunch pail.

"Kiss me bye," she said.

He hugged her. She fastened her arms around his neck and held him. "I love you. Be careful driving."

She went to the kitchen window and watched him running, jumping over the puddles until he got to the pickup. She waved when he looked back from inside the cab. It was almost dark and it was raining hard.

She was sitting in a chair by the living-room window listening to the radio and the rain when she saw the pickup lights turn into the drive. She got up quickly and hurried to the back door. He stood there in the doorway, and she touched his wet, rubbery coat with her fingers.

"They told everybody to go home. The mill boss had a heart attack. He fell right down on the floor up in the mill and died."

"You scared me." She took his lunch pail and shut the door. "Who was it? Was it that foreman named Mel?"

"No, his name was Jack Granger. He was about fifty years old, I guess." He walked over close to the oil stove and stood there warming his hands. "Jesus, it's so funny! He'd come through where I work and asked me how I was doing and probably wasn't gone five minutes when Bill Bessie come through and told me Jack Granger had just died right up in the mill." He shook his head. "Just like that."

"Don't think about it," she said and took his hands between hers and rubbed his fingers.

"I'm not. Just one of them things, I guess. You never know."

The rain rushed against the house and slashed across the windows.

"God, it's hot in here! There any beer?" he said.

"I think there's some left," she said and followed him out to the kitchen. His hair was still wet and she ran her fingers through it when he sat down. She opened a beer for him and poured some into a cup for herself. He sat drinking it in little sips, looking out the window toward the dark woods.

He said, "One of the guys said he had a wife and two grown kids."

She said, "That Granger man, that's a shame. It's nice to have you home, but I hate for something like that to happen."

"That's what I told some of the boys. I said it's nice to get on to home, but Christ, I hate to have it like this." He edged a little in the chair. "You know, I think most of the men would've gone ahead and worked, but some of the boys up in the mill said they wouldn't work, him laying there like that." He finished off the beer and got up. "I'll tell you—I'm glad they didn't work," he said.

She said, "I'm glad you didn't, either. I had a really funny feeling when you left tonight. I was thinking about it, the funny feeling I had, when I saw the lights."

"He was just in the lunch room last night telling jokes. Granger was a good boy. Always laughing."

She nodded. "I'll fix us something to eat if you'll eat something."

"I'm not hungry, but I'll eat something," he said.

They sat in the living room and held hands and watched television.

"I've never seen any of these programs before," he said.

She said, "I don't much care about watching any more. You can hardly get anything worth watching. Saturday and Sunday it's all right. But there's nothing weeknights."

He stretched his legs and leaned back. He said, "I'm kind of tired. I think I'll go to bed."

She said, "I think I'll take a bath and go to bed, too." She moved her fingers through his hair and dropped her hand and smoothed his neck. "Maybe we'll have a little tonight. We never hardly get a chance to have a little." She touched her other hand to his thigh, leaned over and kissed him. "What do you think about that?"

"That sounds all right," he said. He got up and walked over to the window. Against the trees outside he could see her reflection standing behind him and a little to the side. "Hon, why don't you go ahead and take your bath and we'll turn in," he said. He stood there for a while longer watching the rain beat against the window. He looked at his watch. If he were working, it would be the lunch hour now. He went into the bedroom and began getting undressed.

In his shorts, he walked back into the living room and picked up a book off the floor—*Best-Loved Poems of the American People*. He guessed it had come in the mail from the club she belonged to. He went through the house and turned off the lights. Then he went back into the bedroom. He got under the covers, put her pillow on top of his, and twisted the goose-neck lamp around so that the light fell on the pages. He opened the book to the middle and began to look at some of the poems. Then he laid the book on the bedstand and bent the lamp away toward the wall. He lit a cigaret. He put his arms behind his head and lay there smoking. He looked straight ahead at the wall. The lamplight picked up all of the tiny cracks and swells in the plaster. In a corner, up near the ceiling, there was a cobweb. He could hear the rain washing down off the roof.

She stood up in the tub and began drying herself. When she noticed him watching, she smiled and draped the towel over her shoulder and made a little step in the tub and posed.

"How does it look?"

"All right," he said.

"Okay," she said.

"I thought you were still . . . you know," he said.

"I am." She finished drying and dropped the towel on the floor beside the tub and stepped daintily onto it. The mirror beside her was steamy and the odor of her body carried to him. She turned around and reached up to a shelf for the box. Then she slipped into her belt and adjusted the white pad. She tried to look at him, she tried to smile. He crushed out the cigaret and picked up the book again.

"What are you reading?" she called.

"I don't know. Crap," he said. He turned to the back of the book and began looking through the biographies.

She turned off the light and came out of the bathroom brushing her hair. "You still going in the morning?" she said.

"Guess not," he said.

She said, "I'm glad. We'll sleep in late, then get up and have a big breakfast."

He reached over and got another cigaret.

She put the brush in a drawer, opened another drawer and took out a nightgown.

"Do you remember when you got me this?" she said.

He looked at her in reply.

She came around to his side of the bed. They lay quietly for a time, smoking his cigaret until he nodded he was finished, and then she put it out. He reached over her, kissed her on the shoulder, and switched off the light. "You know," he said, lying back down, "I think I want to get out of here. Go someplace else." She moved over to him and put her leg between his. They lay on their sides facing each other, lips almost touching. He wondered if his breath smelled as clean as hers. He said, "I just want to leave. We been here a long time. I'd like to go back home and see my folks. Or maybe go on up to Oregon. That's good country."

"If that's what you want," she said.

"I think so," he said. "There's a lot of places to go."

She moved a little and took his hand and put it on her breast. Then she opened her mouth and kissed him, pulling his head down with her other hand. Slowly she inched up in the bed, gently moving his head down to her breast. He took the nipple and began working it in his mouth. He tried to think how much he loved her or if he loved her. He could hear her breathing but he could also hear the rain. They lay like this.

She said, "If you don't want to, it's all right."

"It's not that," he said, not knowing what he meant.

He let her go when he could tell she was asleep and turned over to his own side. He tried to think of Reno. He tried to think of the slots and the way the dice clicked and how they looked turning over under the lights. He tried to hear the sound the roulette ball made as it skimmed around the gleaming wheel. He tried to concentrate on the wheel. He looked and looked and listened and listened and heard the saws and the machinery slowing down, coming to a stop.

He got out of bed and went to the window. It was black

outside and he could see nothing, not even the rain. But he could hear it, cascading off the roof and into a puddle under the window. He could hear it all over the house. He ran his finger across the drool on the glass.

When he got back into bed, he moved close to her and put his hand on her hip. "Hon, wake up," he whispered. But she only shuddered and moved over farther to her own side. She kept on sleeping. "Wake up," he whispered. "I hear something outside."

How About This?

ALL the optimism that had colored his flight from the city was gone now, had vanished the evening of the first day, as they drove north through the dark stands of redwood. Now, the rolling pasture land, the cows, the isolated farmhouses of western Washington seemed to hold out nothing for him, nothing he really wanted. He had expected something different. He drove on and on with a rising sense of hopelessness and outrage.

He kept the car at fifty, all that the road allowed. Sweat stood on his forehead and over his upper lip, and there was a sharp heady odor of clover in the air all around them. The land began to change; the highway dipped suddenly, crossed a culvert, rose again, and then the asphalt ran out and he was holding the car on a country dirt road, an astonishing trail of dust rising behind them. As they passed the ancient burned-out foundation of a house set back among some maple trees, Emily removed her dark glasses and leaned forward, staring.

"That *is* the old Owens place," she said. "He and Dad were friends. He kept a still in his attic and had a big team of dray horses he used to enter in all the fairs. He died with a ruptured appendix when I was about ten years old. The house burned down a year later at Christmas. They moved to Bremerton after that."

"Is that so?" he said. "Christmas." Then: "Do I turn right or left here? Emily? Right or left?"

"Left," she said. "Left."

She put on her glasses again, only to take them off a moment later. "Stay on this road, Harry, until you come to another crossroad. Then right. Only a little farther then." She smoked steadily, one cigaret after the other, was silent now as she looked out at the cleared fields, at the isolated stands of fir trees, at the occasional weathered house.

He shifted down, turned right. The road began to drop gradually into a lightly wooded valley. Far ahead—Canada, he supposed—he could see a range of mountains and behind those mountains a darker, still higher range.

"There's a little road," she said, "at the bottom. That's the road."

He turned carefully and drove down the rutted track road slowly, waiting for the first sign of the house. Emily sat next to him, edgy, he could see, smoking again, also waiting for the first glimpse. He blinked his eyes as low shaggy branches slapped the windshield. She leaned forward slightly and touched her hand to his leg. "Now," she said. He slowed almost to a stop, drove through a tiny clear puddle of a stream that came out of the high grass on his left, then into a mass of dogwood that fingered and scraped the length of the car as the little road climbed. "There it is," she said, moving her hand from his leg.

After the first unsettling glance, he kept his eyes on the road. He looked at the house again after he had brought the car to a stop near the front door. Then he licked his lips, turned to her, and tried to smile.

"Well, we're here," he said.

She was looking at him, not looking at the house at all.

Harry had always lived in cities—San Francisco for the last three years, and, before that, Los Angeles, Chicago, and New York. But for a long time he had wanted to move to the country, somewhere in the country. At first he wasn't too clear about where he wanted to go; he just knew he wanted to leave the city to try to start over again. A simpler life was what he had in mind, just the essentials, he said. He was thirty-two years old and was a writer in a way, but he was also an actor and a musician. He played the saxophone, performed occasionally with the Bay City Players, and was writing a first novel. He had been writing the novel since the time he lived in New York. One bleak Sunday afternoon in March, when he had again started talking about a change, a more honest life somewhere in the country, she'd mentioned, jokingly at first, her father's deserted place in the northwestern part of Washington.

"My God," Harry had said, "you wouldn't mind? Roughing it, I mean? Living in the country like that?"

"I was born there," she said, laughing. "Remember? I've lived in the country. It's all right. It has advantages. I could live there again. I don't know about you, though, Harry. If it'd be good for you."

She kept looking at him, serious now. He felt lately that she was always looking at him.

"You wouldn't regret it?" he said. "Giving up things here?"

"I wouldn't be giving up much, would I, Harry?" She shrugged. "But I'm not going to encourage the idea, Harry."

"Could you paint up there?" he asked.

"I can paint anywhere," she said. "And there's Bellingham," she said. "There's a college there. Or else Vancouver or Seattle." She kept watching him. She sat on a stool in front of a shadowy half-finished portrait of a man and woman and rolled two paintbrushes back and forth in her hand.

That was three months ago. They had talked about it and talked about it and now they were here.

He rapped on the walls near the front door. "Solid. A solid foundation. If you have a solid foundation, that's the main thing." He avoided looking at her. She was shrewd and might have read something from his eyes.

"I told you not to expect too much," she said.

"Yes, you did. I distinctly remember," he said, still not looking at her. He gave the bare board another rap with his knuckles and moved over beside her. His sleeves were rolled in the damp afternoon heat, and he was wearing white jeans and sandals. "Quiet, isn't it?"

"A lot different from the city."

"God, yes . . . Pretty up here, too." He tried to smile. "Needs a little work, that's all. A little work. It'll be a good place if we want to stay. Neighbors won't bother us, anyway."

"We had neighbors here when I was a little girl," she said. "You had to drive to see them, but they were neighbors."

The door opened at an angle. The top hinge was loose: nothing much, Harry judged. They moved slowly from room to room. He tried to cover his disappointment. Twice he knocked on the walls and said, "Solid." Or, "They don't make houses like this any more. You can do a lot with a house like this."

She stopped in front of a large room and drew a long breath.

"Yours?"

She shook her head.

"And we could get the necessary furniture we need from your Aunt Elsie?"

"Yes, whatever we need," she said. "That is, if it's what we want, to stay here. I'm not pushing. It's not too late to go back. There's nothing lost."

In the kitchen they found a wood stove and a mattress pushed against one wall. In the living room again, he looked around and said, "I thought it'd have a fireplace."

"I never said it had a fireplace."

"I just had the impression for some reason it would have one . . . No outlets, either," he said a moment later. Then: "No electricity!"

"Toilet, either," she said.

He wet his lips. "Well," he said, turning away to examine something in the corner, "I guess we could fix up one of these rooms with a tub and all, and get someone to do the plumbing work. But electricity is something else, isn't it? I mean, let's face all these things when we come to them. One thing at a time, right? Don't you think? Let's . . . let's not let any of it get us down, okay?"

"I wish you'd just be quiet," she said.

She turned and went outside.

He jumped down the steps a minute later and drew a breath of air and they both lighted cigarets. A flock of crows got up at the far end of the meadow and flew slowly and silently into the woods.

They walked toward the barn, stopping to inspect the withered apple trees. He broke off one of the small dry branches, turned it over and over in his hands while she stood beside him and smoked a cigaret. It *was* peaceful, more or less appealing country, and he thought it pleasant to feel that something permanent, really permanent, might belong to him. He was taken by a sudden affection for the little orchard.

"Get these bearing again," he said. "Just need water and some looking after's all." He could see himself coming out of the house with a wicker basket and pulling down large red apples, still wet with the morning's dew, and he understood that the idea was attractive to him.

He felt a little cheered as they approached the barn. He examined briefly the old license plates nailed to the door. Green, yellow, white plates from the state of Washington, rusted now,

1922-23-24-25-26-27-28-29-34-36-37-40-41-1949; he studied the dates as if he thought their sequence might disclose a code. He threw the wooden latch and pulled and pushed at the heavy door until it swung open. The air inside smelled unused. But he believed it was not an unpleasant smell.

"It rains a lot here in the winter," she said. "I don't remember it ever being this hot in June." Sunlight stuck down through the splits in the roof. "Once Dad shot a deer out of season. I was about—I don't know—eight or nine, around in there." She turned to him as he stood stopped near the door to look at an old harness that hung from a nail. "Dad was down here in the barn with the deer when the game warden drove into the yard. It was dark. Mother sent me down here for Dad, and the game warden, a big heavyset man with a hat, followed me. Dad was carrying a lamp, just coming down from the loft. He and the game warden talked a few minutes. The deer was hanging there, but the game warden didn't say anything. He offered Dad a chew of tobacco, but Dad refused —he never had liked it and wouldn't take any even then. Then the game warden pulled my ear and left. But I don't want to think about any of that," she added quickly. "I haven't thought about things like that in years. I don't want to make comparisons," she said. "No," she said. She stepped back, shaking her head. "I'm not going to cry. I know that sounds melodramatic and just plain stupid, and I'm sorry for sounding melodramatic and stupid. But the truth is, Harry . . ." She shook her head again. "I don't know. Maybe coming back here was a mistake. I can feel your disappointment."

"You don't know," he said.

"No, that's right, I don't know," she said. "And I'm sorry, I'm really not meaning to try to influence you one way or the other. But I don't think you want to stay. Do you?"

He shrugged.

He took out a cigaret. She took it from him and held it, waiting for a match, waiting for his eyes to meet hers over the match.

"When I was little," she went on, "I wanted to be in a circus when I grew up. I didn't want to be a nurse or a teacher. Or a painter. I didn't want to be a painter then. I wanted to be Emily Horner, High-Wire Artist. It was a big thing with me. I used to practice down here in the barn, walking the rafters. That big rafter up there, I walked that hundreds of times." She started to say something else, but puffed her cigaret and put it out under her heel, tamping it down carefully into the dirt.

Outside the barn he could hear a bird calling, and then he heard a scurrying sound over the boards up in the loft. She walked past him, out into the light, and started slowly through the deep grass toward the house.

"What are we going to do, Emily?" he called after her.

She stopped, and he came up beside her.

"Stay alive," she said. Then she shook her head and smiled faintly. She touched his arm. "Jesus, I guess we are in kind of a spot, aren't we? But that's all I can say, Harry."

"We've got to decide," he said, not really knowing what he meant.

"You decide, Harry, if you haven't already. It's your decision. I'd just as soon go back if that makes it any easier for you. We'll stay with Aunt Elsie a day or two and then go back. All right? But give me a cigaret, will you? I'm going up to the house."

He moved closer to her then and thought they might embrace. He wanted to. But she did not move; she only looked at him steadily, and so he touched her on the nose with his forefinger and said, "I'll see you in a little while."

He watched her go. He looked at his watch, turned, and walked slowly down the pasture toward the woods. The grass came up to his knees. Just before he entered the woods, as the grass began to thin out, he found a sort of path. He rubbed the bridge of his nose under his dark glasses, looked back at the house and the barn, and continued on, slowly. A cloud of mosquitoes moved with his head as he walked. He stopped to light a cigaret. He brushed at the mosquitoes. He looked back again, but now he could not see the house or barn. He stood there smoking, beginning to feel the silence that lay in the grass and in the trees and in the shadows farther back in the trees. Wasn't this what he'd longed for? He walked on, looking for a place to sit.

He lighted another cigaret and leaned against a tree. He picked up some wood chips from the soft dirt between his legs. He smoked. He remembered a volume of plays by Ghelderode lying on top of the things in the back seat of the car, and then he recalled some of the little towns they had driven through that morning—Ferndale, Lynden, Custer, Nooksack. He suddenly recalled the mattress in the kitchen. He understood that it made him afraid. He tried to imagine Emily walking the big rafter in the barn. But that made him afraid too. He smoked. He felt very calm really, all things considered. He wasn't going to stay here, he knew that, but it didn't upset him to know that now. He was pleased he knew himself so well. He would be all right, he decided. He was only thirty-two. Not so old. He was, for the moment, in a spot. He could admit that. After all, he considered, that was life, wasn't it? He put out the cigaret. In a little while he lit another one.

As he rounded a corner of the house, he saw her completing a cartwheel. She landed with a light thump, slightly crouched, and then she saw him.

"Hey!" she yelled, grinning gravely.

She raised herself onto the balls of her feet, arms out to the sides over her head, and then pitched forward. She turned two more cartwheels while he watched, and then she called, "How about *this*!" She dropped lightly onto her hands and, getting her balance, began a shaky hesitant movement in his direction. Face flushed, blouse hanging over her chin, legs waving insanely, she advanced on him.

"Have you decided?" she said, quite breathless.

He nodded.

"So?" she said. She let herself fall against her shoulder and rolled onto her back, covering her eyes from the sun with an arm as if to uncover her breasts.

She said, "Harry."

He was reaching to light a cigaret with his last match when his hands began to tremble. The match went out, and he stood there holding the empty matchbook and the cigaret, staring at the vast expanse of trees at the end of the bright meadow.

"Harry, we have to love each other," she said. "We'll just have to love each other," she said.

Bicycles, Muscles, Cigarets

IT had been two days since Evan Hamilton had stopped
smoking, and it seemed to him everything he'd said and
thought for the two days somehow suggested cigarets. He
looked at his hands under the kitchen light. He sniffed his
knuckles and his fingers.

"I can smell it," he said.

"I know. It's as if it sweats out of you," Ann Hamilton said.
"For three days after I stopped I could smell it on me. Even
when I got out of the bath. It was disgusting." She was putting plates on the table for dinner. "I'm so sorry, dear. I know
what you're going through. But, if it's any consolation, the
second day is always the hardest. The third day is hard, too, of
course, but from then on, if you can stay with it that long,
you're over the hump. But I'm so happy you're serious about
quitting, I can't tell you." She touched his arm. "Now, if you'll
just call Roger, we'll eat."

Hamilton opened the front door. It was already dark. It was
early in November and the days were short and cool. An older
boy he had never seen before was sitting on a small, well-
equipped bicycle in the driveway. The boy leaned forward just
off the seat, the toes of his shoes touching the pavement and
keeping him upright.

"You Mr. Hamilton?" the boy said.

"Yes, I am," Hamilton said. "What is it? Is it Roger?"

"I guess Roger is down at my house talking to my mother.
Kip is there and this boy named Gary Berman. It is about my
brother's bike. I don't know for sure," the boy said, twisting
the handle grips, "but my mother asked me to come and get
you. One of Roger's parents."

"But he's all right?" Hamilton said. "Yes, of course, I'll be
right with you."

He went into the house to put his shoes on.

"Did you find him?" Ann Hamilton said.

"He's in some kind of jam," Hamilton answered. "Over a
bicycle. Some boy—I didn't catch his name—is outside. He
wants one of us to go back with him to his house."

"Is he all right?" Ann Hamilton said and took her apron off.

"Sure, he's all right." Hamilton looked at her and shook his head. "It sounds like it's just a childish argument, and the boy's mother is getting herself involved."

"Do you want me to go?" Ann Hamilton asked.

He thought for a minute. "Yes, I'd rather you went, but I'll go. Just hold dinner until we're back. We shouldn't be long."

"I don't like his being out after dark," Ann Hamilton said. "I don't like it."

The boy was sitting on his bicycle and working the hand-brake now.

"How far?" Hamilton said as they started down the sidewalk.

"Over in Arbuckle Court," the boy answered, and when Hamilton looked at him, the boy added, "Not far. About two blocks from here."

"What seems to be the trouble?" Hamilton asked.

"I don't know for sure. I don't understand all of it. He and Kip and this Gary Berman are supposed to have used my brother's bike while we were on vacation, and I guess they wrecked it. On purpose. But I don't know. Anyway, that's what they're talking about. My brother can't find his bike and they had it last, Kip and Roger. My mom is trying to find out where it's at."

"I know Kip," Hamilton said. "Who's this other boy?"

"Gary Berman. I guess he's new in the neighborhood. His dad is coming as soon as he gets home."

They turned a corner. The boy pushed himself along, keeping just slightly ahead. Hamilton saw an orchard, and then they turned another corner onto a dead-end street. He hadn't known of the existence of this street and was sure he would not recognize any of the people who lived here. He looked around him at the unfamiliar houses and was struck with the range of his son's personal life.

The boy turned into a driveway and got off the bicycle and leaned it against the house. When the boy opened the front door, Hamilton followed him through the living room and into the kitchen, where he saw his son sitting on one side of a table along with Kip Hollister and another boy. Hamilton looked closely at Roger and then he turned to the stout, dark-haired woman at the head of the table.

"You're Roger's father?" the woman said to him.

"Yes, my name is Evan Hamilton. Good evening."

"I'm Mrs. Miller, Gilbert's mother," she said. "Sorry to ask you over here, but we have a problem."

Hamilton sat down in a chair at the other end of the table and looked around. A boy of nine or ten, the boy whose bicycle was missing, Hamilton supposed, sat next to the woman. Another boy, fourteen or so, sat on the draining board, legs dangling, and watched another boy who was talking on the telephone. Grinning slyly at something that had just been said to him over the line, the boy reached over to the sink with a cigaret. Hamilton heard the sound of the cigaret sputting out in a glass of water. The boy who had brought him leaned against the refrigerator and crossed his arms.

"Did you get one of Kip's parents?" the woman said to the boy.

"His sister said they were shopping. I went to Gary Berman's and his father will be here in a few minutes. I left the address."

"Mr. Hamilton," the woman said, "I'll tell you what happened. We were on vacation last month and Kip wanted to borrow Gilbert's bike so that Roger could help him with Kip's paper route. I guess Roger's bike had a flat tire or something. Well, as it turns out—"

"Gary was choking me, Dad," Roger said.

"What?" Hamilton said, looking at his son carefully.

"He was choking me. I got the marks." His son pulled down the collar of his T-shirt to show his neck.

"They were out in the garage," the woman continued. "I didn't know what they were doing until Curt, my oldest, went out to see."

"He started it!" Gary Berman said to Hamilton. "He called me a jerk." Gary Berman looked toward the front door.

"I think my bike cost about sixty dollars, you guys," the boy named Gilbert said. "You can pay me for it."

"You keep out of this, Gilbert," the woman said to him.

Hamilton took a breath. "Go on," he said.

"Well, as it turns out, Kip and Roger used Gilbert's bike to help Kip deliver his papers, and then the two of them, and Gary too, they say, took turns rolling it."

"What do you mean 'rolling it'?" Hamilton said.

"Rolling it," the woman said. "Sending it down the street with a push and letting it fall over. Then, mind you—and they just admitted this a few minutes ago—Kip and Roger took it up to the school and threw it against a goalpost."

"Is that true, Roger?" Hamilton said, looking at his son again.

"Part of it's true, Dad," Roger said, looking down and rubbing his finger over the table. "But we only rolled it once. Kip did it, then Gary, and then I did it."

"Once is too much," Hamilton said. "Once is one too many times, Roger. I'm surprised and disappointed in you. And you too, Kip," Hamilton said.

"But you see," the woman said, "someone's fibbing tonight or else not telling all he knows, for the fact is the bike's still missing."

The older boys in the kitchen laughed and kidded with the boy who still talked on the telephone.

"We don't know where the bike is, Mrs. Miller," the boy named Kip said. "We told you already. The last time we saw it was when me and Roger took it to my house after we had it at school. I mean, that was the next to last time. The very last time was when I took it back here the next morning and parked it behind the house." He shook his head. "We don't know where it is," the boy said.

"Sixty dollars," the boy named Gilbert said to the boy named Kip. "You can pay me off like five dollars a week."

"Gilbert, I'm warning you," the woman said. "You see, *they* claim," the woman went on, frowning now, "it disappeared from *here*, from behind the house. But how can we believe them when they haven't been all that truthful this evening?"

"We've told the truth," Roger said. "Everything."

Gilbert leaned back in his chair and shook his head at Hamilton's son.

The doorbell sounded and the boy on the draining board jumped down and went into the living room.

A stiff-shouldered man with a crew haircut and sharp gray eyes entered the kitchen without speaking. He glanced at the woman and moved over behind Gary Berman's chair.

"You must be Mr. Berman?" the woman said. "Happy to meet you. I'm Gilbert's mother, and this is Mr. Hamilton, Roger's father."

The man inclined his head at Hamilton but did not offer his hand.

"What's all this about?" Berman said to his son.

The boys at the table began to speak at once.

"Quiet down!" Berman said. "I'm talking to Gary. You'll get your turn."

The boy began his account of the affair. His father listened closely, now and then narrowing his eyes to study the other two boys.

When Gary Berman had finished, the woman said, "I'd like to get to the bottom of this. I'm not accusing any one of them, you understand, Mr. Hamilton, Mr. Berman—I'd just like to get to the bottom of this." She looked steadily at Roger and Kip, who were shaking their heads at Gary Berman.

"It's not true, Gary," Roger said.

"Dad, can I talk to you in private?" Gary Berman said.

"Let's go," the man said, and they walked into the living room.

Hamilton watched them go. He had the feeling he should stop them, this secrecy. His palms were wet, and he reached to his shirt pocket for a cigaret. Then, breathing deeply, he passed the back of his hand under his nose and said, "Roger, do you know any more about this, other than what you've already said? Do you know where Gilbert's bike is?"

"No, I don't," the boy said. "I swear it."

"When was the last time you saw the bicycle?" Hamilton said.

"When we brought it home from school and left it at Kip's house."

"Kip," Hamilton said, "do you know where Gilbert's bicycle is now?"

"I swear I don't, either," the boy answered. "I brought it back the next morning after we had it at school and I parked it behind the garage."

"I thought you said you left it behind the *house*," the woman said quickly.

"I mean the house! That's what I meant," the boy said.

"Did you come back here some other day to ride it?" she asked, leaning forward.

"No, I didn't," Kip answered.

"Kip?" she said.

"I didn't! I don't know where it is!" the boy shouted.

The woman raised her shoulders and let them drop. "How do you know who or what to believe?" she said to Hamilton. "All I know is, Gilbert's missing a bicycle."

Gary Berman and his father returned to the kitchen.

"It was Roger's idea to roll it," Gary Berman said.

"It was yours!" Roger said, coming out of his chair. "You wanted to! Then you wanted to take it to the orchard and strip it!"

"You shut up!" Berman said to Roger. "You can speak when spoken to, young man, not before. Gary, I'll handle this— dragged out at night because of a couple of roughnecks! Now if either of you," Berman said, looking first at Kip and then Roger, "know where this kid's bicycle is, I'd advise you to start talking."

"I think you're getting out of line," Hamilton said.

"What?" Berman said, his forehead darkening. "And I think you'd do better to mind your own business!"

"Let's go, Roger," Hamilton said, standing up. "Kip, you come now or stay." He turned to the woman. "I don't know what else we can do tonight. I intend to talk this over more with Roger, but if there is a question of restitution I feel since Roger did help manhandle the bike, he can pay a third if it comes to that."

"I don't know what to say," the woman replied, following Hamilton through the living room. "I'll talk to Gilbert's father —he's out of town now. We'll see. It's probably one of those things finally, but I'll talk to his father."

Hamilton moved to one side so that the boys could pass ahead of him onto the porch, and from behind him he heard Gary Berman say, "He called me a jerk, Dad."

"He did, did he?" Hamilton heard Berman say. "Well, he's the jerk. He looks like a jerk."

Hamilton turned and said, "I think you're seriously out of

line here tonight, Mr. Berman. Why don't you get control of yourself?"

"And I told you I think you should keep out of it!" Berman said.

"You get home, Roger," Hamilton said, moistening his lips. "I mean it," he said, "get going!" Roger and Kip moved out to the sidewalk. Hamilton stood in the doorway and looked at Berman, who was crossing the living room with his son.

"Mr. Hamilton," the woman began nervously but did not finish.

"What do you want?" Berman said to him. "Watch out now, get out of my way!" Berman brushed Hamilton's shoulder and Hamilton stepped off the porch into some prickly cracking bushes. He couldn't believe it was happening. He moved out of the bushes and lunged at the man where he stood on the porch. They fell heavily onto the lawn. They rolled on the lawn, Hamilton wrestling Berman onto his back and coming down hard with his knees on the man's biceps. He had Berman by the collar now and began to pound his head against the lawn while the woman cried, "God almighty, someone stop them! For God's sake, someone call the police!"

Hamilton stopped.

Berman looked up at him and said, "Get off me."

"Are you all right?" the woman called to the men as they separated. "For God's sake," she said. She looked at the men, who stood a few feet apart, backs to each other, breathing hard. The older boys had crowded onto the porch to watch; now that it was over, they waited, watching the men, and then they began feinting and punching each other on the arms and ribs.

"You boys get back in the house," the woman said. "I never thought I'd see," she said and put her hand on her breast.

Hamilton was sweating and his lungs burned when he tried to take a deep breath. There was a ball of something in his throat so that he couldn't swallow for a minute. He started walking, his son and the boy named Kip at his sides. He heard car doors slam, an engine start. Headlights swept over him as he walked.

Roger sobbed once, and Hamilton put his arm around the boy's shoulders.

"I better get home," Kip said and began to cry. "My dad'll be looking for me," and the boy ran.

"I'm sorry," Hamilton said. "I'm sorry you had to see something like that," Hamilton said to his son.

They kept walking and when they reached their block, Hamilton took his arm away.

"What if he'd picked up a knife, Dad? Or a club?"

"He wouldn't have done anything like that," Hamilton said.

"But what if he had?" his son said.

"It's hard to say what people will do when they're angry," Hamilton said.

They started up the walk to their door. His heart moved when Hamilton saw the lighted windows.

"Let me feel your muscle," his son said.

"Not now," Hamilton said. "You just go in now and have your dinner and hurry up to bed. Tell your mother I'm all right and I'm going to sit on the porch for a few minutes."

The boy rocked from one foot to the other and looked at his father, and then he dashed into the house and began calling, "Mom! Mom!"

He sat on the porch and leaned against the garage wall and stretched his legs. The sweat had dried on his forehead. He felt clammy under his clothes.

He had once seen his father—a pale, slow-talking man with slumped shoulders —in something like this. It was a bad one, and both men had been hurt. It had happened in a café. The other man was a farmhand. Hamilton had loved his father and could recall many things about him. But now he recalled his father's one fistfight as if it were all there was to the man.

He was still sitting on the porch when his wife came out.

"Dear God," she said and took his head in her hands. "Come in and shower and then have something to eat and tell me about it. Everything is still warm. Roger has gone to bed."

But he heard his son calling him.

"He's still awake," she said.

"I'll be down in a minute," Hamilton said. "Then maybe we should have a drink."

She shook her head. "I really don't believe any of this yet."

He went into the boy's room and sat down at the foot of the bed.

"It's pretty late and you're still up, so I'll say good night," Hamilton said.

"Good night," the boy said, hands behind his neck, elbows jutting.

He was in his pajamas and had a warm fresh smell about him that Hamilton breathed deeply. He patted his son through the covers.

"You take it easy from now on. Stay away from that part of the neighborhood, and don't let me ever hear of you damaging a bicycle or any other personal property. Is that clear?" Hamilton said.

The boy nodded. He took his hands from behind his neck and began picking at something on the bedspread.

"Okay, then," Hamilton said, "I'll say good night."

He moved to kiss his son, but the boy began talking.

"Dad, was Grandfather strong like you? When he was your age, I mean, you know, and you—"

"And I was nine years old? Is that what you mean? Yes, I guess he was," Hamilton said.

"Sometimes I can hardly remember him," the boy said. "I don't want to forget him or anything, you know? You know what I mean, Dad?"

When Hamilton did not answer at once, the boy went on. "When you were young, was it like it is with you and me? Did you love him more than me? Or just the same?" The boy said this abruptly. He moved his feet under the covers and looked away. When Hamilton still did not answer, the boy said, "Did he smoke? I think I remember a pipe or something."

"He started smoking a pipe before he died, that's true," Hamilton said. "He used to smoke cigarets a long time ago and then he'd get depressed with something or other and quit, but later he'd change brands and start in again. Let me show you something," Hamilton said. "Smell the back of my hand."

The boy took the hand in his, sniffed it, and said, "I guess I don't smell anything, Dad. What is it?"

Hamilton sniffed the hand and then the fingers. "Now I can't smell anything, either," he said. "It was there before, but now it's gone." Maybe it was scared out of me, he thought. "I wanted to show you something. All right, it's late now. You better go to sleep," Hamilton said.

The boy rolled onto his side and watched his father walk to the door and watched him put his hand to the switch. And then the boy said, "Dad? You'll think I'm pretty crazy, but I wish I'd known you when you were little. I mean, about as old as I am right now. I don't know how to say it, but I'm lonesome about it. It's like—it's like I miss you already if I think about it now. That's pretty crazy, isn't it? Anyway, please leave the door open."

Hamilton left the door open, and then he thought better of it and closed it halfway.

What Is It?

FACT is the car needs to be sold in a hurry, and Leo sends Toni out to do it. Toni is smart and has personality. She used to sell children's encyclopedias door to door. She signed him up, even though he didn't have kids. Afterward, Leo asked her for a date, and the date led to this. This deal has to be cash, and it has to be done tonight. Tomorrow somebody they owe might slap a lien on the car. Monday they'll be in court, home free—but word on them went out yesterday, when their lawyer mailed the letters of intention. The hearing on Monday is nothing to worry about, the lawyer has said. They'll be asked some questions, and they'll sign some papers, and that's it. But sell the convertible, he said—today, *tonight*. They can hold onto the little car, Leo's car, no problem. But they go into court with that big convertible, the court will take it, and that's that.

Toni dresses up. It's four o'clock in the afternoon. Leo worries the lots will close. But Toni takes her time dressing. She puts on a new white blouse, wide lacy cuffs, the new two-piece suit, new heels. She transfers the stuff from her straw purse into the new patent-leather handbag. She studies the lizard makeup pouch and puts that in too. Toni has been two hours on her hair and face. Leo stands in the bedroom doorway and taps his lips with his knuckles, watching.

"You're making me nervous," she says. "I wish you wouldn't just stand," she says. "So tell me how I look."

"You look fine," he says. "You look great. I'd buy a car from you anytime."

"But you don't have money," she says, peering into the mirror. She pats her hair, frowns. "And your credit's lousy. You're nothing," she says. "Teasing," she says and looks at him in the mirror. "Don't be serious," she says. "It has to be done, so I'll do it. You take it out, you'd be lucky to get three, four hundred and we both know it. Honey, you'd be lucky if you didn't have to pay *them*." She gives her hair a final pat, gums her lips, blots the lipstick with a tissue. She turns away from the mirror and picks up her purse. "I'll have to have dinner or something,

I told you that already, that's the way they work, I know them. But don't worry, I'll get out of it," she says. "I can handle it."

"Jesus," Leo says, "did you have to say that?"

She looks at him steadily. "Wish me luck," she says.

"Luck," he says. "You have the pink slip?" he says.

She nods. He follows her through the house, a tall woman with a small high bust, broad hips and thighs. He scratches a pimple on his neck. "You're sure?" he says. "Make sure. You have to have the pink slip."

"I have the pink slip," she says.

"Make sure."

She starts to say something, instead looks at herself in the front window and then shakes her head.

"At least call," he says. "Let me know what's going on."

"I'll call," she says. "Kiss, kiss. Here," she says and points to the corner of her mouth. "Careful," she says.

He holds the door for her. "Where are you going to try first?" he says. She moves past him and onto the porch.

Ernest Williams looks from across the street. In his Bermuda shorts, stomach hanging, he looks at Leo and Toni as he directs a spray onto his begonias. Once, last winter, during the holidays, when Toni and the kids were visiting his mother's, Leo brought a woman home. Nine o'clock the next morning, a cold foggy Saturday, Leo walked the woman to the car, surprised Ernest Williams on the sidewalk with a newspaper in his hand. Fog drifted, Ernest Williams stared, then slapped the paper against his leg, hard.

Leo recalls that slap, hunches his shoulders, says, "You have someplace in mind first?"

"I'll just go down the line," she says. "The first lot, then I'll just go down the line."

"Open at nine hundred," he says. "Then come down. Nine hundred is low bluebook, even on a cash deal."

"I know where to start," she says.

Ernest Williams turns the hose in their direction. He stares at them through the spray of water. Leo has an urge to cry out a confession.

"Just making sure," he says.

"Okay, okay," she says. "I'm off."

It's her car, they call it her car, and that makes it all the worse. They bought it new that summer three years ago. She wanted something to do after the kids started school, so she went back selling. He was working six days a week in the fiberglass plant. For a while they didn't know how to spend the money. Then they put a thousand on the convertible and doubled and tripled the payments until in a year they had it paid. Earlier, while she was dressing, he took the jack and spare from the trunk and emptied the glove compartment of pencils, matchbooks, Blue Chip stamps. Then he washed it and vacuumed inside. The red hood and fenders shine.

"Good luck," he says and touches her elbow.

She nods. He sees she is already gone, already negotiating.

"Things are going to be different!" he calls to her as she reaches the driveway. "We start over Monday. I mean it."

Ernest Williams looks at them and turns his head and spits. She gets into the car and lights a cigaret.

"This time next week!" Leo calls again. "Ancient history!"

He waves as she backs into the street. She changes gear and starts ahead. She accelerates and the tires give a little scream.

In the kitchen Leo pours Scotch and carries the drink to the backyard. The kids are at his mother's. There was a letter three days ago, his name penciled on the outside of the dirty envelope, the only letter all summer not demanding payment in full. We are having fun, the letter said. We like Grandma. We have a new dog called Mr. Six. He is nice. We love him. Goodbye.

He goes for another drink. He adds ice and sees that his hand trembles. He holds the hand over the sink. He looks at the hand for a while, sets down the glass, and holds out the other hand. Then he picks up the glass and goes back outside to sit on the steps. He recalls when he was a kid his dad pointing at a fine house, a tall white house surrounded by apple trees and a high white rail fence. "That's Finch," his dad said admiringly. "He's been in bankruptcy at least twice. Look at that house." But bankruptcy is a company collapsing utterly, executives cutting their wrists and throwing themselves from windows, thousands of men on the street.

Leo and Toni still had furniture. Leo and Toni had furniture and Toni and the kids had clothes. Those things were exempt. What else? Bicycles for the kids, but these he had sent to his mother's for safekeeping. The portable air-conditioner and the appliances, new washer and dryer, trucks came for those things weeks ago. What else did they have? This and that, nothing mainly, stuff that wore out or fell to pieces long ago. But there were some big parties back there, some fine travel. To Reno and Tahoe, at eighty with the top down and the radio playing. Food, that was one of the big items. They gorged on food. He figures thousands on luxury items alone. Toni would go to the grocery and put in everything she saw. "I had to do without when I was a kid," she says. "These kids are not going to do without," as if he'd been insisting they should. She joins all the book clubs. "We never had books around when I was a kid," she says as she tears open the heavy packages. They enroll in the record clubs for something to play on the new stereo. They sign up for it all. Even a pedigreed terrier named Ginger. He paid two hundred and found her run over in the street a week later. They buy what they want. If they can't pay, they charge. They sign up.

His undershirt is wet; he can feel the sweat rolling from his underarms. He sits on the step with the empty glass in his hand and watches the shadows fill up the yard. He stretches, wipes his face. He listens to the traffic on the highway and considers whether he should go to the basement, stand on the utility sink, and hang himself with his belt. He understands he is willing to be dead.

Inside he makes a large drink and he turns the TV on and he fixes something to eat. He sits at the table with chili and crackers and watches something about a blind detective. He clears the table. He washes the pan and the bowl, dries these things and puts them away, then allows himself a look at the clock.

It's after nine. She's been gone nearly five hours.

He pours Scotch, adds water, carries the drink to the living room. He sits on the couch but finds his shoulders so stiff they won't let him lean back. He stares at the screen and sips, and soon he goes for another drink. He sits again. A news program begins—it's ten o'clock—and he says, "God, what in God's name has gone wrong?" and goes to the kitchen to return with more Scotch. He sits, he closes his eyes, and opens them when he hears the telephone ringing.

"I wanted to call," she says.

"Where are you?" he says. He hears piano music, and his heart moves.

"I don't know," she says. "Someplace. We're having a drink, then we're going someplace else for dinner. I'm with the sales manager. He's crude, but he's all right. He bought the car. I have to go now. I was on my way to the ladies and saw the phone."

"Did somebody buy the car?" Leo says. He looks out the kitchen window to the place in the drive where she always parks.

"I told you," she says. "I have to go now."

"Wait, wait a minute, for Christ's sake," he says. "Did somebody buy the car or not?"

"He had his checkbook out when I left," she says. "I have to go now. I have to go to the bathroom."

"Wait!" he yells. The line goes dead. He listens to the dial tone. "Jesus Christ," he says as he stands with the receiver in his hand.

He circles the kitchen and goes back to the living room. He sits. He gets up. In the bathroom he brushes his teeth very carefully. Then he uses dental floss. He washes his face and goes back to the kitchen. He looks at the clock and takes a clean glass from a set that has a hand of playing cards painted on each glass. He fills the glass with ice. He stares for a while at the glass he left in the sink.

He sits against one end of the couch and puts his legs up at the other end. He looks at the screen, realizes he can't make out what the people are saying. He turns the empty glass in his hand and considers biting off the rim. He shivers for a time and thinks of going to bed, though he knows he will dream of a large woman with gray hair. In the dream he is always leaning over tying his shoelaces. When he straightens up, she looks at him, and he bends to tie again. He looks at his hand. It makes a fist as he watches. The telephone is ringing.

"Where are you, honey?" he says slowly, gently.

"We're at this restaurant," she says, her voice strong, bright.

"Honey, which restaurant?" he says. He puts the heel of his hand against his eye and pushes.

"Downtown someplace," she says. "I think it's New Jimmy's. Excuse me," she says to someone off the line, "is this place New Jimmy's? This is New Jimmy's, Leo," she says to him.

"Everything is all right, we're almost finished, then he's going to bring me home."

"Honey?" he says. He holds the receiver against his ear and rocks back and forth, eyes closed. "Honey?"

"I have to go," she says. "I wanted to call. Anyway, guess how much?"

"Honey," he says.

"Six and a quarter," she says. "I have it in my purse. He said there's no market for convertibles. I guess we're born lucky," she says and laughs. "I told him everything. I think I had to."

"Honey," Leo says.

"What?" she says.

"Please, honey," Leo says.

"He said he sympathizes," she says. "But he would have said anything." She laughs again. "He said personally he'd rather be classified a robber or a rapist than a bankrupt. He's nice enough, though," she says.

"Come home," Leo says. "Take a cab and come home."

"I can't," she says. "I told you, we're halfway through dinner."

"I'll come for you," he says.

"No," she says. "I said we're just finishing. I told you, it's part of the deal. They're out for all they can get. But don't worry, we're about to leave. I'll be home in a little while." She hangs up.

In a few minutes he calls New Jimmy's. A man answers. "New Jimmy's has closed for the evening," the man says.

"I'd like to talk to my wife," Leo says.

"Does she work here?" the man asks. "Who is she?"

"She's a customer," Leo says. "She's with someone. A business person."

"Would I know her?" the man says. "What is her name?"

"I don't think you know her," Leo says.

"That's all right," Leo says. "That's all right. I see her now."

"Thank you for calling New Jimmy's," the man says.

Leo hurries to the window. A car he doesn't recognize slows in front of the house, then picks up speed. He waits. Two, three hours later, the telephone rings again. There is no one at the other end when he picks up the receiver. There is only a dial tone.

"I'm right here!" Leo screams into the receiver.

—

Near dawn he hears footsteps on the porch. He gets up from the couch. The set hums, the screen glows. He opens the door. She bumps the wall coming in. She grins. Her face is puffy, as if she's been sleeping under sedation. She works her lips, ducks heavily and sways as he cocks his fist.

"Go ahead," she says thickly. She stands there swaying. Then she makes a noise and lunges, catches his shirt, tears it down the front. "Bankrupt!" she screams. She twists loose, grabs and tears his undershirt at the neck. "You son of a bitch," she says, clawing.

He squeezes her wrists, then lets go, steps back, looking for something heavy. She stumbles as she heads for the bedroom. "Bankrupt," she mutters. He hears her fall on the bed and groan.

He waits awhile, then splashes water on his face and goes to the bedroom. He turns the lights on, looks at her, and begins to take her clothes off. He pulls and pushes her from side to side undressing her. She says something in her sleep and moves her hand. He takes off her underpants, looks at them closely under the light, and throws them into a corner. He turns back the covers and rolls her in, naked. Then he opens her purse. He is reading the check when he hears the car come into the drive.

He looks through the front curtain and sees the convertible in the drive, its motor running smoothly, the headlamps burning, and he closes and opens his eyes. He sees a tall man come around in front of the car and up to the front porch. The man lays something on the porch and starts back to the car. He wears a white linen suit.

Leo turns on the porch light and opens the door cautiously. Her makeup pouch lies on the top step. The man looks at Leo across the front of the car, and then gets back inside and releases the handbrake.

"Wait!" Leo calls and starts down the steps. The man brakes the car as Leo walks in front of the lights. The car creaks against the brake. Leo tries to pull the two pieces of his shirt together, tries to bunch it all into his trousers.

"What is it you want?" the man says. "Look," the man says, "I have to go. No offense. I buy and sell cars, right? The lady left her makeup. She's a fine lady, very refined. What is it?"

Leo leans against the door and looks at the man. The man takes his hands off the wheel and puts them back. He drops the gear into reverse and the car moves backward a little.

"I want to tell you," Leo says and wets his lips.

The light in Ernest Williams' bedroom goes on. The shade rolls up.

Leo shakes his head, tucks in his shirt again. He steps back from the car. "Monday," he says.

"Monday," the man says and watches for sudden movement.

Leo nods slowly.

"Well, goodnight," the man says and coughs. "Take it easy, hear? Monday, that's right. Okay, then." He takes his foot off the brake, puts it on again after he has rolled back two or three feet. "Hey, one question. Between friends, are these actual miles?" The man waits, then clears his throat. "Okay, look, it doesn't matter either way," the man says. "I have to go. Take it easy." He backs into the street, pulls away quickly, and turns the corner without stopping.

Leo tucks at his shirt and goes back in the house. He locks the front door and checks it. Then he goes to the bedroom and locks that door and turns back the covers. He looks at her before he flicks the light. He takes off his clothes, folds them carefully on the floor, and gets in beside her. He lies on his back for a time and pulls the hair on his stomach, considering. He looks at the bedroom door, outlined now in the faint outside light. Presently he reaches out his hand and touches her hip. She does not move. He turns on his side and puts his hand on her hip. He runs his fingers over her hip and feels the stretch marks there. They are like roads, and he traces them in her flesh. He runs his fingers back and forth, first one, then another. They run everywhere in her flesh, dozens, perhaps hundreds of them. He remembers waking up the morning after they bought the car, seeing it, there in the drive, in the sun, gleaming.

Signals

As their first of the extravagances they had planned for that evening, Wayne and Caroline went to Aldo's, an elegant new restaurant north a good distance. They passed through a tiny walled garden with small pieces of statuary and were met by a tall graying man in a dark suit who said, "Good evening, sir. Madam," and who swung open the heavy door for them.

Inside, Aldo himself showed them the aviary—a peacock, a pair of Golden pheasants, a Chinese ring-necked pheasant, and a number of unannounced birds that flew around or sat perched. Aldo personally conducted them to a table, seated Caroline, and then turned to Wayne and said, "A lovely lady," before moving off—a dark, small, impeccable man with a soft accent.

They were pleased with his attention.

"I read in the paper," Wayne said, "that he has an uncle who has some kind of position in the Vatican. That's how he was able to get copies of some of these paintings." Wayne nodded at a Velasquez reproduction on the nearest wall. "His uncle in the Vatican," Wayne said.

"He used to be *maître d'* at the Copacabana in Rio," Caroline said. "He knew Frank Sinatra, and Lana Turner was a good friend of his."

"Is that so?" Wayne said. "I didn't know that. I read that he was at the Victoria Hotel in Switzerland and at some big hotel in Paris. I didn't know he was at the Copacabana in Rio."

Caroline moved her handbag slightly as the waiter set down the heavy goblets. He poured water and then moved to Wayne's side of the table.

"Did you see the suit he was wearing?" Wayne said. "You seldom see a suit like that. That's a three-hundred-dollar suit." He picked up his menu. In a while, he said, "Well, what are you going to have?"

"I don't know," she said. "I haven't decided. What are you going to have?"

"I don't know," he said. "I haven't decided, either."

"What about one of these French dishes, Wayne? Or else

this? Over here on this side." She placed her finger in instruction, and then she narrowed her eyes at him as he located the language, pursed his lips, frowned, and shook his head.

"I don't know," he said. "I'd kind of like to know what I'm getting. I just don't really know."

The waiter returned with card and pencil and said something Wayne couldn't quite catch.

"We haven't decided yet," Wayne said. He shook his head as the waiter continued to stand beside the table. "I'll signal you when we're ready."

"I think I'll just have a sirloin. You order what you want," he said to Caroline when the waiter had moved off. He closed the menu and raised his goblet. Over the muted voices coming from the other tables Wayne could hear a warbling call from the aviary. He saw Aldo greet a party of four, chat with them as he smiled and nodded and led them to a table.

"We could have had a better table," Wayne said. "Instead of right here in the center where everyone can walk by and watch you eat. We could have had a table against the wall. Or over there by the fountain."

"I think I'll have the beef Tournedos," Caroline said.

She kept looking at her menu. He tapped out a cigaret, lighted it, and then glanced around at the other diners. Caroline still stared at her menu.

"Well, for God's sake, if that's what you're going to have, close your menu so he can take our order." Wayne raised his arm for the waiter, who lingered near the back talking with another waiter.

"Nothing else to do but gas around with the other waiters," Wayne said.

"He's coming," Caroline said.

"Sir?" The waiter was a thin pock-faced man in a loose black suit and a black bow tie.

". . . And we'll have a bottle of champagne, I believe. A small bottle. Something, you know, domestic," Wayne said.

"Yes, sir," the waiter said.

"And we'll have that right away. Before the salad or the relish plate," Wayne said.

"Oh, bring the relish *tray*, anyway," Caroline said. "Please."

"Yes, madam," the waiter said.

"They're a slippery bunch," Wayne said. "Do you remember that guy named Bruno who used to work at the office during the week and wait tables on weekends? Fred caught him stealing out of the petty-cash box. We fired him."

"Let's talk about something pleasant," Caroline said.

"All right, sure," Wayne said.

The waiter poured a little champagne into Wayne's glass, and Wayne took the glass, tasted, and said, "Fine, that will do nicely." Then he said, "Here's to you, baby," and raised his glass high. "Happy birthday."

They clinked glasses.

"I like champagne," Caroline said.

"I like champagne," Wayne said.

"We could have had a bottle of Lancer's," Caroline said.

"Well, why didn't you say something, if that's what you wanted?" Wayne said.

"I don't know," Caroline said. "I just didn't think about it. This is fine, though."

"I don't know too much about champagnes. I don't mind admitting I'm not much of a . . . connoisseur. I don't mind admitting I'm just a lowbrow." He laughed and tried to catch her eye, but she was busy selecting an olive from the relish dish. "Not like the group you've been keeping company with lately. But if you wanted Lancer's," he went on, "you should have ordered Lancer's."

"Oh, shut up!" she said. "Can't you talk about something else?" She looked up at him then and he had to look away. He moved his feet under the table.

He said, "Would you care for some more champagne, dear?"

"Yes, thank you," she said quietly.

"Here's to us," he said.

"To us, my darling," she said.

They looked steadily at each other as they drank.

"We ought to do this more often," he said.

She nodded.

"It's good to get out now and then. I'll make more of an effort, if you want me to."

She reached for celery. "That's up to you."

"That's not true! It's not me who's . . . who's . . ."

"Who's what?" she said.

"I don't care what you do," he said, dropping his eyes.

"Is that true?"

"I don't know why I said that," he said.

The waiter brought the soup and took away the bottle and the wineglasses and refilled their goblets with water.

"Could I have a soup spoon?" Wayne asked.

"Sir?"

"A soup spoon," Wayne repeated.

The waiter looked amazed and then perplexed. He glanced around at the other tables. Wayne made a shoveling motion over his soup. Aldo appeared beside the table.

"Is everything all right? Is there anything wrong?"

"My husband doesn't seem to have a soup spoon," Caroline said. "I'm sorry for the disturbance," she said.

"Certainly. *Une cuiller, s'il vous plaît*," Aldo said to the waiter in an even voice. He looked once at Wayne and then explained to Caroline. "This is Paul's first night. He speaks little English, yet I trust you will agree he is an excellent waiter. The boy who set the table forgot the spoon." Aldo smiled. "It no doubt took Paul by surprise."

"This is a beautiful place," Caroline said.

"Thank you," Aldo said. "I'm delighted you could come tonight. Would you like to see the wine cellar and the private dining rooms?"

"Very much," Caroline said.

"I will have someone show you around when you have finished dining," Aldo said.

"We'll be looking forward to it," Caroline said.

Aldo bowed slightly and looked again at Wayne. "I hope you enjoy your dinner," he said to them.

"That jerk," Wayne said.

"Who?" she said. "Who are you talking about?" she said, laying down her spoon.

"The waiter," Wayne said. "The waiter. The newest and the dumbest waiter in the house, and we got him."

"Eat your soup," she said. "Don't blow a gasket."

Wayne lighted a cigaret. The waiter arrived with salads and took away the soup bowls.

When they had started on the main course, Wayne said, "Well, what do you think? Is there a chance for us or not?" He looked down and arranged the napkin on his lap.

"Maybe so," she said. "There's always a chance."

"Don't give me that kind of crap," he said. "Answer me straight for a change."

"Don't snap at me," she said.

"I'm asking you," he said. "Give me a straight answer," he said.

She said, "You want something signed in blood?"

He said, "That wouldn't be such a bad idea."

She said, "You listen to me! I've given you the best years of my life. The best years of my life!"

"The best years of *your* life?" he said.

"I'm thirty-six years old," she said. "Thirty-seven tonight. Tonight, right now, at this minute, I just can't say what I'm going to do. I'll just have to see," she said.

"I don't care what you do," he said.

"Is that true?" she said.

He threw down his fork and tossed his napkin on the table.

"Are you finished?" she asked pleasantly. "Let's have coffee and dessert. We'll have a nice dessert. Something good."

She finished everything on her plate.

"Two coffees," Wayne said to the waiter. He looked at her and then back to the waiter. "What do you have for dessert?" he said.

"Sir?" the waiter said.

"Dessert!" Wayne said.

The waiter gazed at Caroline and then at Wayne.

"No dessert," she said. "Let's not have any dessert."

"Chocolate mousse," the waiter said. "Orange sherbet," the waiter said. He smiled, showing his bad teeth. "Sir?"

"And I don't want any guided tour of this place," Wayne said when the waiter had moved off.

—

When they rose from the table, Wayne dropped a dollar bill near his coffee cup. Caroline took two dollars from her handbag, smoothed the bills out, and placed them alongside the other dollar, the three bills lined up in a row.

She waited with Wayne while he paid the check. Out of the corner of his eye, Wayne could see Aldo standing near the door dropping grains of seed into the aviary. Aldo looked in their direction, smiled, and went on rubbing the seeds from between his fingers as birds collected in front of him. Then he briskly brushed his hands together and started moving toward Wayne, who looked away, who turned slightly but significantly as Aldo neared him. But when Wayne looked back, he saw Aldo take Caroline's waiting hand, saw Aldo draw his heels smartly together, saw Aldo kiss her wrist.

"Did madam enjoy her dinner?" Aldo said.

"It was marvelous," Caroline said.

"You will come back from time to time?" Aldo said.

"I shall," Caroline said. "As often as I may. Next time, I should like to have your permission to check things out a little, but this time we simply must go."

"Dear lady," Aldo said. "I have something for you. One moment, please." He reached to a vase on a table near the door and swung gracefully back with a long-stemmed rose.

"For you, dear lady," Aldo said. "But caution, please. The thorns. A very lovely lady," he said to Wayne and smiled at him and turned to welcome another couple.

Caroline stood there.

"Let's get out of here," Wayne said.

"You can see how he could be friends with Lana Turner," Caroline said. She held the rose and turned it between her fingers.

"Good night!" she called out to Aldo's back.

But Aldo was occupied selecting another rose.

"I don't think he ever knew her," Wayne said.

Will You Please Be Quiet, Please?

W HEN he was eighteen and was leaving home for the first time, Ralph Wyman was counseled by his father, principal of Jefferson Elementary School and trumpet soloist in the Weaverville Elks Club Auxiliary Band, that life was a very serious matter, an enterprise insisting on strength and purpose in a young person just setting out, an arduous undertaking, everyone knew that, but nevertheless a rewarding one, Ralph Wyman's father believed and said.

But in college Ralph's goals were hazy. He thought he wanted to be a doctor and he thought he wanted to be a lawyer, and he took pre-medical courses and courses in the history of jurisprudence and business law before he decided he had neither the emotional detachment necessary for medicine nor the ability for sustained reading required in law, especially as such reading might concern property and inheritance. Though he continued to take classes here and there in the sciences and in business, Ralph also took some classes in philosophy and literature and felt himself on the brink of some kind of huge discovery about himself. But it never came. It was during this time—his lowest ebb, as he referred to it later—that Ralph believed he almost had a breakdown; he was in a fraternity and he got drunk every night. He drank so much that he acquired a reputation and was called "Jackson," after the bartender at The Keg.

Then, in his third year, Ralph came under the influence of a particularly persuasive teacher. Dr. Maxwell was his name; Ralph would never forget him. He was a handsome, graceful man in his early forties, with exquisite manners and with just the trace of the South in his voice. He had been educated at Vanderbilt, had studied in Europe, and had later had something to do with one or two literary magazines back East. Almost overnight, Ralph would later say, he decided on teaching as a career. He stopped drinking quite so much, began to bear down on his studies, and within a year was elected to Omega Psi, the national journalism fraternity; he became a member of the English Club; was invited to come with his cello, which he hadn't played in three years, and join in a student chamber-music group just forming; and he even ran successfully for secretary of the senior class. It was then that he met Marian Ross —a handsomely pale and slender girl who took a seat beside him in a Chaucer class.

Marian Ross wore her hair long and favored high-necked sweaters and always went around with a leather purse on a long strap swinging from her shoulder. Her eyes were large and seemed to take in everything at a glance. Ralph liked going out with Marian Ross. They went to The Keg and to a few other spots where everyone went, but they never let their going together or their subsequent engagement the next summer interfere with their studies. They were solemn students, and both sets of parents eventually gave approval to the match. Ralph and Marian did their student teaching at the same high school in Chico in the spring and went through graduation exercises together in June. They married in St. James Episcopal Church two weeks later.

They had held hands the night before their wedding and pledged to preserve forever the excitement and the mystery of marriage.

For their honeymoon they drove to Guadalajara, and while they both enjoyed visiting the decayed churches and the poorly lighted museums and the afternoons they spent shopping and exploring in the marketplace, Ralph was secretly appalled by the squalor and open lust he saw and was anxious to return to the safety of California. But the one vision he would always remember and which disturbed him most of all had nothing to do with Mexico. It was late afternoon, almost evening, and Marian was leaning motionless on her arms over the ironwork balustrade of their rented *casita* as Ralph came up the dusty road below. Her hair was long and hung down in front over her shoulders, and she was looking away from him, staring at something in the distance. She wore a white blouse with a bright red scarf at her throat, and he could see her breasts pushing against the white cloth. He had a bottle of dark, unlabeled wine under his arm, and the whole incident put Ralph in mind of something from a film, an intensely dramatic moment into which Marian could be fitted but he could not.

Before they left for their honeymoon they had accepted positions at a high school in Eureka, a town in the lumbering region in the northern part of the state. After a year, when they were sure the school and the town were exactly what they wanted to settle down to, they made a payment on a house in the Fire Hill district. Ralph felt, without really thinking about it, that he and Marian understood each other perfectly—as well, at least, as any two people might. Moreover, Ralph felt he understood himself—what he could do, what he could not do, and where he was headed with the prudent measure of himself that he made.

Their two children, Dorothea and Robert, were now five and four years old. A few months after Robert was born, Marian was offered a post as a French and English instructor at the junior college at the edge of town, and Ralph had stayed on at the high school. They considered themselves a happy couple, with only a single injury to their marriage, and that was well in the past, two years ago this winter. It was something they had never talked about since. But Ralph thought about it sometimes—indeed, he was willing to admit he thought about it more and more. Increasingly, ghastly images would be projected on his eyes, certain unthinkable particularities. For he had taken it into his head that his wife had once betrayed him with a man named Mitchell Anderson.

But now it was a Sunday night in November and the children were asleep and Ralph was sleepy and he sat on the couch grading papers and could hear the radio playing softly in the kitchen, where Marian was ironing, and he felt enormously happy. He stared a while longer at the papers in front of him, then gathered them all up and turned off the lamp.

"Finished, love?" Marian said with a smile when he appeared in the doorway. She was sitting on a tall stool, and she stood the iron up on its end as if she had been waiting for him.

"Damn it, no," he said with an exaggerated grimace, tossing the papers on the kitchen table.

She laughed—bright, pleasant—and held up her face to be kissed, and he gave her a little peck on the cheek. He pulled out a chair from the table and sat down, leaned back on the legs and looked at her. She smiled again and then lowered her eyes.

"I'm already half asleep," he said.

"Coffee?" she said, reaching over and laying the back of her hand against the percolator.

He shook his head.

She took up the cigaret she had burning in the ashtray, smoked it while she stared at the floor, and then put it back in the ashtray. She looked at him, and a warm expression moved across her face. She was tall and limber, with a good bust, narrow hips, and wide wonderful eyes.

"Do you ever think about that party?" she asked, still looking at him.

He was stunned and shifted in the chair, and he said, "Which party? You mean the one two or three years ago?"

She nodded.

He waited, and when she offered no further comment, he said, "What about it? Now that you brought it up, what about it?" Then: "He kissed you, after all, that night, didn't he? I mean, I knew he did. He did try to kiss you, or didn't he?"

"I was just thinking about it and I asked you, that's all," she said. "Sometimes I think about it," she said.

"Well, he did, didn't he? Come on, Marian," he said.

"Do you ever think about that night?" she said.

He said, "Not really. It was a long time ago, wasn't it? Three or four years ago. You can tell me now," he said. "This is still old Jackson you're talking to, remember?" And they both laughed abruptly together and abruptly she said, "Yes." She said, "He did kiss me a few times." She smiled.

He knew he should try to match her smile, but he could not. He said, "You told me before he didn't. You said he only put his arm around you while he was driving. So which is it?"

"What did you do that for?" she was saying dreamily. "Where were you all night?" he was screaming, standing over her, legs watery, fist drawn back to hit again. Then she said, "I didn't do anything. Why did you hit me?" she said.

"How did we ever get onto this?" she said.

"You brought it up," he said.

She shook her head. "I don't know what made me think of it." She pulled in her upper lip and stared at the floor. Then she straightened her shoulders and looked up. "If you'll move this ironing board for me, love, I'll make us a hot drink. A buttered rum. How does that sound?"

"Good," he said.

She went into the living room and turned on the lamp and bent to pick up a magazine from the floor. He watched her hips under the plaid woolen skirt. She moved in front of the window and stood looking out at the streetlight. She smoothed her palm down over her skirt, then began tucking in her blouse. He wondered if she wondered if he were watching her.

After he stood the ironing board in its alcove on the porch, he sat down again and, when she came into the kitchen, he said, "Well, what else went on between you and Mitchell Anderson that night?"

"Nothing," she said. "I was thinking about something else."

"What?"

"About the children, the dress I want Dorothea to have for next Easter. And about the class I'm going to have tomorrow. I was thinking of seeing how they'd go for a little Rimbaud," and she laughed. "I didn't mean to rhyme—really, Ralph, and really, nothing else happened. I'm sorry I ever said anything about it."

"Okay," he said.

He stood up and leaned against the wall by the refrigerator and watched her as she spooned out sugar into two cups and then stirred in the rum. The water was beginning to boil.

"Look, honey, it *has* been brought up now," he said, "and it *was* four years ago, so there's no reason at all I can think of that we *can't* talk about it now if we *want* to. Is there?"

She said, "There's really nothing to talk about."

He said, "I'd like to know."

She said, "Know what?"

"Whatever else he did besides kiss you. We're adults. We haven't seen the Andersons in literally years and we'll probably never see them again and it happened a *long* time ago, so what reason could there possibly be that we can't talk about it?" He was a little surprised at the reasoning quality in his voice. He sat down and looked at the tablecloth and then looked up at her again. "Well?" he said.

"Well," she said, with an impish grin, tilting her head to one side girlishly, remembering. "No, Ralph, really. I'd really just rather not."

"For Christ's sake, Marian! *Now* I mean it," he said, and he suddenly understood that he did.

She turned off the gas under the water and put her hand out on the stool; then she sat down again, hooking her heels over the bottom step. She sat forward, resting her arms across her knees, her breasts pushing at her blouse. She picked at something on her skirt and then looked up.

"You remember Emily'd already gone home with the Beattys, and for some reason Mitchell had stayed on. He looked a little out of sorts that night, to begin with. I don't know, maybe they weren't getting along, Emily and him, but I don't know that. And there were you and I, the Franklins, and Mitchell Anderson still there. All of us a little drunk. I'm not sure how it happened, Ralph, but Mitchell and I just happened to find ourselves alone together in the kitchen for a minute, and there was no whiskey left, only a part of a bottle of that white wine we had. It must've been close to one o'clock, because Mitchell said, 'If we ride on giant wings we can make it before the liquor store closes.' You know how he could be so theatrical when he wanted? Soft-shoe stuff, facial expressions? Anyway, he was very witty about it all. At least it seemed that way at the time. And very drunk, too, I might add. So was I, for that matter. It was an impulse, Ralph. I don't know why I did it, don't ask me, but when he said let's go—I agreed. We went out the back, where his car was parked. We went just as . . . we were . . . didn't even get our coats out of the closet, thought we'd just be gone a few minutes. I don't know what we thought, *I* thought. I don't know *why* I went, Ralph. It was an impulse, that's all I can say. It was the wrong impulse." She paused. "It was my fault that night, Ralph, and I'm sorry. I shouldn't have done anything like that—I *know* that."

"Christ!" The word leaped out of him. "But you've always been that way, Marian!" And he knew at once that he had uttered a new and profound truth.

His mind filled with a swarm of accusations, and he tried to focus on one in particular. He looked down at his hands and noticed they had the same lifeless feeling they had had when he had seen her on the balcony. He picked up the red grading pencil lying on the table and then he put it down again.

"I'm listening," he said.

"Listening to what?" she said. "You're swearing and getting upset, Ralph. For nothing—nothing, honey! . . . there's nothing *else*," she said.

"Go on," he said.

She said, "*What* is the matter with us, anyway? Do you know how this started? Because I don't know how this started."

He said, "Go on, Marian."

"That's *all*, Ralph," she said. "I've told you. We went for a ride. We talked. He kissed me. I still don't see how we could've been gone three hours—or whatever it was you said we were."

"Tell me, Marian," he said, and he knew there was more and knew he had always known. He felt a fluttering in his stomach, and then he said, "No. If you don't want to tell me, that's all right. Actually, I guess I'd just as soon leave it at that," he said. He thought fleetingly that he would be someplace else tonight doing something else, that it would be silent somewhere if he had not married.

"Ralph," she said, "you won't be angry, will you? Ralph? We're just talking. You won't, will you?" She had moved over to a chair at the table.

He said, "I won't."

She said, "Promise?"

He said, "Promise."

She lit a cigaret. He had suddenly a great desire to see the children, to get them up and out of bed, heavy and turning in their sleep, and to hold each of them on a knee, to jog them until they woke up. He moved all his attention into one of the tiny black coaches in the tablecloth. Four tiny white prancing horses pulled each of the black coaches and the figure driving the horses had his arms up and wore a tall hat, and suitcases were strapped down atop the coach, and what looked like a kerosene lamp hung from the side, and if he were listening at all it was from inside the black coach.

". . . We went straight to the liquor store, and I waited in the car until he came out. He had a sack in one hand and one

of those plastic bags of ice in the other. He weaved a little getting into the car. I hadn't realized he was so drunk until we
started driving again. I noticed the way he was driving. It was terribly slow. He was all hunched over the wheel. His eyes staring.
We were talking about a lot of things that didn't make sense. I
can't remember. We were talking about Nietzsche. Strindberg.
He was directing *Miss Julie* second semester. And then something about Norman Mailer stabbing his wife in the breast.
And then he stopped for a minute in the middle of the road.
And we each took a drink out of the bottle. He said he'd hate
to think of me being stabbed in the breast. He said he'd like to
kiss my breast. He drove the car off the road. He put his head
on my lap. . . ."

She hurried on, and he sat with his hands folded on the
table and watched her lips. His eyes skipped around the
kitchen—stove, napkin-holder, stove, cupboards, toaster, back
to her lips, back to the coach in the tablecloth. He felt a peculiar desire for her flicker through his groin, and then he felt the
steady rocking of the coach and he wanted to call *stop* and then
he heard her say, "He said shall we have a go at it?" And then
she was saying, "I'm to blame. I'm the one to blame. He said
he'd leave it all up to me, I could do whatever I want."

He shut his eyes. He shook his head, tried to create possibilities, other conclusions. He actually wondered if he could re-
store that night two years ago and imagined himself coming
into the kitchen just as they were at the door, heard himself
telling her in a hearty voice, oh no, no, you're not going out
for anything with that Mitchell Anderson! The fellow is drunk
and he's a bad driver to boot and you have to go to bed now
and get up with little Robert and Dorothea in the morning and
stop! Thou shalt stop!

He opened his eyes. She had a hand up over her face and
was crying noisily.

"Why did you, Marian?" he asked.

She shook her head without looking up.

Then suddenly he knew! His mind buckled. For a minute he
could only stare dumbly at his hands. He knew! His mind
roared with the knowing.

"Christ! No! Marian! *Jesus Christ!*" he said, springing back
from the table. "Christ! *No*, Marian!"

"No, no," she said, throwing her head back.

"You let him!" he screamed.

"No, no," she pleaded.

"You let him! A go at it! Didn't you? Didn't you? A *go* at it! Is that what he said? Answer me!" he screamed. "Did he come in you? Did you let him come in you when you were having your go at it?"

"Listen, listen to me, Ralph," she whimpered, "I swear to you he didn't. He didn't come. He didn't come in me." She rocked from side to side in the chair.

"Oh God! God *damn* you!" he shrieked.

"God!" she said, getting up, holding out her hands, "Are we crazy, Ralph? Have we lost our minds? Ralph? Forgive me, Ralph. Forgive—"

"Don't touch me! Get away from me!" he screamed. He was screaming.

She began to pant in her fright. She tried to head him off. But he took her by the shoulder and pushed her out of the way.

"Forgive me, Ralph! *Please*. Ralph!" she screamed.

2

He had to stop and lean against a car before going on. Two couples in evening clothes were coming down the sidewalk toward him, and one of the men was telling a story in a loud voice. The others were already laughing. Ralph pushed off from the car and crossed the street. In a few minutes he came to Blake's, where he stopped some afternoons for a beer with Dick Koenig before picking up the children from nursery school.

It was dark inside. Candles flamed in long-necked bottles at the tables along one wall. Ralph glimpsed shadowy figures of men and women talking, their heads close together. One of the couples, near the door, stopped talking and looked up at him. A boxlike fixture in the ceiling revolved overhead, throwing out pins of light. Two men sat at the end of the bar, and a dark cutout of a man leaned over the jukebox in the corner, his hands splayed on each side of the glass. That man is going to play something, Ralph thought as if making a momentous discovery, and he stood in the center of the floor, watching the man.

"Ralph! Mr. Wyman, sir!"

He looked around. It was David Parks calling to him from behind the bar. Ralph walked over, leaned heavily against the bar before sliding onto a stool.

"Should I draw one, Mr. Wyman?" Parks held a glass in his hand, smiling. Ralph nodded, watched Parks fill the glass, watched Parks hold the glass at an angle under the tap, smoothly straighten the glass as it filled.

"How's it going, Mr. Wyman?" Parks put his foot up on a shelf under the bar. "Who's going to win the game next week, Mr. Wyman?" Ralph shook his head, brought the beer to his lips. Parks coughed faintly. "I'll buy you one, Mr. Wyman. This one's on me." He put his leg down, nodded assurance, and reached under his apron into his pocket. "Here. I have it right here," Ralph said and pulled out some change, examined it in his hand. A quarter, nickel, two dimes, two pennies. He counted as if there were a code to be uncovered. He laid down the quarter and stood up, pushing the change back into his pocket. The man was still in front of the jukebox, his hands still out to its sides.

Outside, Ralph turned around, trying to decide what to do. His heart was jumping as if he'd been running. The door opened behind him and a man and woman came out. Ralph stepped out of the way and they got into a car parked at the curb and Ralph saw the woman toss her hair as she got into the car: He had never seen anything so frightening.

He walked to the end of the block, crossed the street, and walked another block before he decided to head downtown. He walked hurriedly, his hands balled into his pockets, his shoes smacking the pavement. He kept blinking his eyes and thought it incredible that this was where he lived. He shook his head. He would have liked to sit someplace for a while and think about it, but he knew he could not sit, could not think about it. He remembered a man he saw once sitting on a curb in Arcata, an old man with a growth of beard and a brown wool cap who just sat there with his arms between his legs. And then Ralph thought: Marian! Dorothea! Robert! It was impossible. He tried to imagine how all this would seem twenty years from now. But he could not imagine anything. And then he imagined snatching up a note being passed among his students and it said *Shall we have a go at it?* Then he could not think. Then he felt profoundly indifferent. Then he thought of Marian. He thought of Marian as he had seen her a little while ago, face crumpled. Then Marian on the floor, blood on her teeth: "Why did you hit me?" Then Marian reaching under her dress to unfasten her garter belt! Then Marian lifting her dress as she arched back! Then Marian ablaze, Marian crying out, *Go! Go! Go!*

He stopped. He believed he was going to vomit. He moved to the curb. He kept swallowing, looked up as a car of yelling teenagers went by and gave him a long blast on their musical horn. Yes, there was a great evil pushing at the world, he thought, and it only needed a little slipway, a little opening.

He came to Second Street, the part of town people called "Two Street." It started here at Shelton, under the streetlight where the old roominghouses ended, and ran for four or five blocks on down to the pier, where fishing boats tied up. He had been down here once, six years ago, to a secondhand shop to finger through the dusty shelves of old books. There was a liquor store across the street, and he could see a man standing just inside the glass door, looking at a newspaper.

A bell over the door tinkled. Ralph almost wept from the sound of it. He bought some cigarets and went out again, continuing along the street, looking in windows, some with signs taped up: a dance, the Shrine circus that had come and gone last summer, an election—*Fred C. Walters for Councilman.* One of the windows he looked through had sinks and pipe joints scattered around on a table, and this too brought tears to his eyes. He came to a Vic Tanney gym where he could see light sneaking under the curtains pulled across a big window and could hear water splashing in the pool inside and the echo of exhilarated voices calling across water. There was more light now, coming from bars and cafés on both sides of the street, and more people, groups of three or four, but now and then a man by himself or a woman in bright slacks walking rapidly. He stopped in front of a window and watched some Negroes shooting pool, smoke drifting in the light burning above the table. One of the men, chalking his cue, hat on, cigaret in his mouth, said something to another man and both men grinned, and then the first man looked intently at the balls and lowered himself over the table.

Ralph stopped in front of Jim's Oyster House. He had never been here before, had never been to any of these places before. Above the door the name was spelled out in yellow lightbulbs: JIM'S OYSTER HOUSE. Above this, fixed to an iron grill, there was a huge neon-lighted clam shell with a man's legs sticking out. The torso was hidden in the shell and the legs flashed red, on and off, up and down, so that they seemed to be kicking. Ralph lit another cigaret from the one he had and pushed the door open.

It was crowded, people bunched on the dance floor, their arms laced around each other, waiting in positions for the band to begin again. Ralph pushed his way to the bar, and once a drunken woman took hold of his coat. There were no stools and he had to stand at the end of the bar between a Coast Guardsman and a shriveled man in denims. In the mirror he could see the men in the band getting up from the table where they had been sitting. They wore white shirts and dark slacks with little red string ties around their necks. There was a fireplace with gas flames behind a stack of metal logs, and the band platform was to the side of this. One of the musicians plucked the strings of his electric guitar, said something to the others with a knowing grin. The band began to play.

Ralph raised his glass and drained it. Down the bar he could hear a woman say angrily, "Well, there's going to be trouble, that's all I've got to say." The musicians came to the end of their number and started another. One of the men, the bass player, moved to the microphone and began to sing. But Ralph could not understand the words. When the band took another break, Ralph looked around for the toilet. He could make out doors opening and closing at the far end of the bar and headed in that direction. He staggered a little and knew he was drunk now. Over one of the doors was a rack of antlers. He saw a man go in and he saw another man catch the door and come out. Inside, in line behind three other men, he found himself staring at opened thighs and vulva drawn on the wall over a pocket-comb machine. Beneath was scrawled EAT ME, and lower down someone had added *Betty M. Eats It—*

RA 5227. The man ahead moved up, and Ralph took a step forward, his heart squeezed in the weight of Betty. Finally, he moved to the bowl and urinated. It was a bolt of lightning cracking. He sighed, leaned forward, and let his head rest against the wall. Oh, Betty, he thought. His life had changed, he was willing to understand. Were there other men, he wondered drunkenly, who could look at one event in their lives and perceive in it the tiny makings of the catastrophe that thereafter set their lives on a different course? He stood there a while longer, and then he looked down: he had urinated on his fingers. He moved to the wash basin, ran water over his hands after deciding against the dirty bar of soap. As he was unrolling the towel, he put his face up close to the pitted mirror and looked into his eyes. A face: nothing out of the ordinary. He touched the glass, and then he moved away as a man tried to get past him to the sink.

When he came out the door, he noticed another door at the other end of the corridor. He went to it and looked through the glass panel in the door at four card players around a green felt table. It seemed to Ralph immensely still and restful inside, the silent movements of the men languorous and heavy with meaning. He leaned against the glass and watched until he felt the men watching him.

Back at the bar there was a flourish of guitars and people began whistling and clapping. A fat middle-aged woman in a white evening dress was being helped onto the platform. She kept trying to pull back but Ralph could see that it was a mock effort, and finally she accepted the mike and made a little curtsy. The people whistled and stamped their feet. Suddenly he knew that nothing could save him but to be in the same room with the card players, watching. He took out his wallet, keeping his hands up over the sides as he looked to see how much he had. Behind him the woman began to sing in a low drowsy voice.

The man dealing looked up.

"Decided to join us?" he said, sweeping Ralph with his eyes and checking the table again. The others raised their eyes for an instant and then looked back at the cards skimming around the table. The men picked up their cards, and the man sitting with his back to Ralph breathed impressively out his nose, turned around in his chair and glared.

"Benny, bring another chair!" the dealer called to an old man sweeping under a table that had chairs turned up on the top. The dealer was a large man; he wore a white shirt, open at the collar, the sleeves rolled back once to expose forearms thick with black curling hair. Ralph drew a long breath.

"Want anything to drink?" Benny asked, carrying a chair to the table.

Ralph gave the old man a dollar and pulled out of his coat. The old man took the coat and hung it up by the door as he went out. Two of the men moved their chairs and Ralph sat down across from the dealer.

"How's it going?" the dealer said to Ralph, not looking up.

"All right," Ralph said.

The dealer said gently, still not looking up, "Low ball or five card. Table stakes, five-dollar limit on raises."

Ralph nodded, and when the hand was finished he bought fifteen dollars' worth of chips. He watched the cards as they flashed around the table, picked up his as he had seen his father do, sliding one card under the corner of another as each card fell in front of him. He raised his eyes once and looked at the faces of the others. He wondered if it had ever happened to any of them.

In half an hour he had won two hands, and, without counting the small pile of chips in front of him, he thought he must still have fifteen or even twenty dollars. He paid for another drink with a chip and was suddenly aware that he had come a long way that evening, a long way in his life. *Jackson*, he thought. He could be Jackson.

"You in or out?" one man asked. "Clyde, what's the bid, for Christ's sake?" the man said to the dealer.

"Three dollars," the dealer said.

"In," Ralph said. "I'm in." He put three chips into the pot.

The dealer looked up and then back at his cards. "You really want some action, we can go to my place when we finish here," the dealer said.

"No, that's all right," Ralph said. "Enough action tonight. I just found out tonight. My wife played around with another guy two years ago. I found out tonight." He cleared his throat.

One man laid down his cards and lit his cigar. He stared at Ralph as he puffed, then shook out the match and picked up his cards again. The dealer looked up, resting his open hands on the table, the black hair very crisp on his dark hands.

"You work here in town?" he said to Ralph.

"I live here," Ralph said. He felt drained, splendidly empty.

"We playing or not?" a man said. "Clyde?"

"Hold your water," the dealer said.

"For Christ's sake," the man said quietly.

"What did you find out tonight?" the dealer said.

"My wife," Ralph said. "I found out."

In the alley, he took out his wallet again, let his fingers number the bills he had left: two dollars—and he thought there was some change in his pocket. Enough for something to eat. But he was not hungry, and he sagged against the building trying to think. A car turned into the alley, stopped, backed out again. He started walking. He went the way he'd come. He stayed close to the buildings, out of the path of the loud groups of men and women streaming up and down the sidewalk. He heard a woman in a long coat say to the man she was with, "It isn't that way at all, Bruce. You don't understand."

He stopped when he came to the liquor store. Inside he moved up to the counter and studied the long orderly rows of bottles. He bought a half pint of rum and some more cigarets. The palm trees on the label of the bottle, the large drooping fronds with the lagoon in the background, had caught his eye, and then he realized *rum!* And he thought he would faint. The clerk, a thin bald man wearing suspenders, put the bottle in a paper sack and rang up the sale and winked. "Got you a little something tonight?" he said.

Outside, Ralph started toward the pier; he thought he'd like to see the water with the lights reflected on it. He thought how Dr. Maxwell would handle a thing like this, and he reached into the sack as he walked, broke the seal on the little bottle and stopped in a doorway to take a long drink and thought Dr. Maxwell would sit handsomely at the water's edge. He crossed some old streetcar tracks and turned onto another, darker, street. He could already hear the waves splashing under the pier, and then he heard someone move up behind him. A small Negro in a leather jacket stepped out in front of him and said, "Just a minute there, man." Ralph tried to move around. The man said, "Christ, baby, that's my feet you're steppin on!" Before Ralph could run the Negro hit him hard in the stomach, and when Ralph groaned and tried to fall, the man hit him in the nose with his open hand, knocking him back against the wall, where he sat down with one leg turned under him and was learning how to raise himself up when the Negro slapped him on the cheek and knocked him sprawling onto the pavement.

3

He kept his eyes fixed in one place and saw them, dozens of them, wheeling and darting just under the overcast, seabirds, birds that came in off the ocean this time of morning. The street was black with the mist that was still falling, and he had to be careful not to step on the snails that trailed across the wet sidewalk. A car with its lights on slowed as it went past. Another car passed. Then another. He looked: mill workers, he whispered to himself. It was Monday morning. He turned a corner, walked past Blake's: blinds pulled, empty bottles standing like sentinels beside the door. It was cold. He walked as fast as he could, crossing his arms now and then and rubbing his shoulders. He came at last to his house, porch light on, windows dark. He crossed the lawn and went around to the back. He turned the knob, and the door opened quietly and the house was quiet. There was the tall stool beside the draining board. There was the table where they had sat. He had gotten up from the couch, come into the kitchen, sat down. What more had he done? He had done nothing more. He looked at the clock over the stove. He could see into the dining room, the table with the lace cloth, the heavy glass centerpiece of red flamingos, their wings opened, the draperies beyond the table open. Had she stood at that window watching for him? He stepped onto the living-room carpet. Her coat was thrown over the couch, and in the pale light he could make out a large ashtray full of her cork cigaret ends. He noticed the phone directory open on the coffee table as he went by. He stopped at the partially open door to their bedroom. Everything seemed to him open. For an instant he resisted the wish to look in at her, and then with his finger he pushed the door open a little bit more. She was sleeping, her head off the pillow, turned toward the wall, her hair black against the sheet, the covers bunched around her shoulders, covers pulled up from the foot of the bed. She was on her side, her secret body angled at the hips. He stared. What, after all, should he do? Take his things and leave? Go to a hotel? Make certain arrangements? How should a man act, given these circumstances? He understood things had been done. He did not understand what things now were to be done. The house was very quiet.

In the kitchen he let his head down onto his arms as he sat at the table. He did not know what to do. Not just now, he thought, not just in this, not just about this, today and tomorrow, but every day on earth. Then he heard the children stirring. He sat up and tried to smile as they came into the kitchen.

"Daddy, Daddy," they said, running to him with their little bodies.

"Tell us a story, Daddy," his son said, getting onto his lap.

"He can't tell us a story," his daughter said. "It's too early for a story. Isn't it, Daddy?"

"What's that on your face, Daddy?" his son said, pointing.

"Let me see!" his daughter said. "Let me see, Daddy."

"Poor Daddy," his son said.

"What did you do to your face, Daddy?" his daughter said.

"It's nothing," Ralph said. "It's all right, sweetheart. Now get down now, Robert, I hear your mother."

Ralph stepped quickly into the bathroom and locked the door.

"Is your father here?" he heard Marian calling. "Where is he, in the bathroom? Ralph?"

"Mama, Mama!" his daughter cried. "Daddy's face is hurt!"

"Ralph!" She turned the knob. "Ralph, let me in, please, darling. Ralph? Please let me in, darling. I want to see you. Ralph? Please!"

He said, "Go away, Marian."

She said, "I can't go away. Please, Ralph, open the door for

a minute, darling. I just want to see you. Ralph. Ralph? The
children said you were hurt. What's wrong, darling? Ralph?"

He said, "Go away."

She said, "Ralph, open up, please."

He said, "Will you please be quiet, please?"

He heard her waiting at the door, he saw the knob turn
again, and then he could hear her moving around the kitchen,
getting the children breakfast, trying to answer their questions. He looked at himself in the mirror a long time. He made
faces at himself. He tried many expressions. Then he gave it
up. He turned away from the mirror and sat down on the edge
of the bathtub, began unlacing his shoes. He sat there with a
shoe in his hand and looked at the clipper ships making their
way across the wide blue sea of the plastic shower curtain. He
thought of the little black coaches in the tablecloth and almost
cried out *Stop!* He unbuttoned his shirt, leaned over the bathtub with a sigh, and pressed the plug into the drain. He ran
hot water, and presently steam rose.

He stood naked on the tiles before getting into the water.
He gathered in his fingers the slack flesh over his ribs. He studied
his face again in the clouded mirror. He started in fear when
Marian called his name.

"Ralph. The children are in their room playing. I called Von
Williams and said you wouldn't be in today, and I'm going to
stay home." Then she said, "I have a nice breakfast on the
stove for you, darling, when you're through with your bath.
Ralph?"

"Just be quiet, please," he said.

He stayed in the bathroom until he heard her in the children's room. She was dressing them, asking didn't they want
to play with Warren and Roy? He went through the house and
into the bedroom, where he shut the door. He looked at the bed
before he crawled in. He lay on his back and stared at the ceiling.
He had gotten up from the couch, had come into the kitchen,
had . . . *sat* . . . *down*. He snapped shut his eyes and turned
onto his side as Marian came into the room. She took off her
robe and sat down on the bed. She put her hand under the
covers and began stroking the lower part of his back.

"Ralph," she said.

He tensed at her fingers, and then he let go a little. It was easier to let go a little. Her hand moved over his hip and over his stomach and she was pressing her body over his now and moving over him and back and forth over him. He held himself, he later considered, as long as he could. And then he turned to her. He turned and turned in what might have been a stupendous sleep, and he was still turning, marveling at the impossible changes he felt moving over him.

FURIOUS SEASONS AND OTHER STORIES

For Maryann, again; and for Curt Johnson; and Max Crawford, Dick Day, Bill Kittredge, Chuck Kinder, and Diane Cecily; creditors.

We're none of us the same. We're moving on. The story continues, but we're no longer the main characters.
James Salter, *Light Years*

Pastoral

WHEN he came out of the cafe it had stopped snowing and the sky was clearing over behind the hills on the other side of the river. He stopped beside the car for a minute and stretched, holding the door half open, yawning a big mouthful of cold air. He'd swear he could almost taste it. He eased in behind the steering wheel and got back on the highway. It was only about an hour's drive from here and he would still have a couple of good hours this afternoon. Then there was tomorrow. All day tomorrow. Just thinking about it was something.

At Parke Junction he crossed the river and turned off the highway up the road to the lodge. The furry, snow-heavy trees came right up beside the road. Clouds mantled the steep white hills that started up on either side so that it was hard to tell where the hills ended and the sky began. A little like some of those Chinese landscapes they'd looked at that time in Portland. He liked them. Something different. Said as much to Frances, but, of course, she wasn't sure. It was a shame she hadn't decided to come along. Thinking about it, he edged a little in the seat, stroked his chin.

It was going on noon when he got there. He saw the cabins first up on the hill and then, as the road straightened out, the lodge itself. He slowed, bumped off the road onto the dirty sand-covered parking lot, and stopped up close to the front door. He rolled down the window and rested for a minute, working his shoulders back and forth into the seat. He closed his eyes then opened them. A pale-red, flickering neon sign said *Castle-rock* and below that a neat, hand painted sign, Deluxe Cabins → OFFICE. The last time he'd been here, Frances and he, three years ago that fall, they'd stayed for three days and he'd landed five nice fish in the hole downriver. They used to come often, two or three times a year. He opened the door and got out slowly, feeling the stiffness in his back and neck. He walked heavily across the bright frozen snow and stuck his hands in his coat pockets as he started up the planked stairs. At the top he scraped the snow and grit off his shoes and nodded to a young couple coming out. He noticed the way the man held her arm as they went down the stairs. He zipped up his coat and pulled it down as far as he could over his pants before opening the door.

It seemed dark inside and there was a smell of wood smoke and fried ham, somewhere a clatter of dishes. He leaned against the door and let his eyes adjust to the light. They had made some changes. Down the wall on his right, the counter and the little tables, they were there before, but not the postcard rack and the colored gum ball machine beside the door. He reached out and laid his hand over the glass top, blotting out the Lion's Club sticker. On his left was a glass case with leather purses and high-heeled shoes inside, leather wallets and pairs of moccasins. Scattered around on top, Indian bead necklaces and bracelets, pieces of petrified wood. He remembered a fireplace from before but they must have covered it up or something. He pushed away from the door, past all of the stuff without looking again, over to the counter. He climbed onto the stool the way somebody might climb onto a horse, swinging his leg over and settling down until his cheeks hung over the sides. He never thought about how it might look until after he'd done it. Carefully, he looked around. Two men sitting a few stools down had stopped talking to look at him. They were hunters, red hats and coats lying on an empty table behind them. He waited, pulling at his fingers, sliding the gold wedding ring up to his knuckle and back again, noticing how loose it was.

"How long you been here?" the girl asked, frowning. She'd come on him soundlessly, from the kitchen.

"Not long."

"You should've rung the bell. I didn't even know you were here!" Silver braces upper and lower glittered as she opened and closed at him.

"I'm supposed to have a cabin. I wrote you a card last week or so."

"I'll have to get Mrs. Maye. She's cooking. She's the one looks after the cabins." She took a step toward the kitchen. "I don't know. She didn't say anything. We don't usually keep them open in the winter, you know."

"But I wrote you a card." He creaked the stool around facing her. The two men turned on their stools to look at him again.

"I'll get Mrs. Maye," she said.

Flushed, he rubbed his hands together. A big Frederic Remington reproduction hung over the counter and he watched
the lurching, frightened buffalo, and the Indians with the
drawn bows fixed at their shoulders.

"Mr. Harold!" the old lady called, coming toward him. A
short gray-haired woman with heavy breasts and a fat throat,
underwear showing through beneath her white uniform. She
undid her apron and held out a white, water-drawn hand.

"Glad to see you, Mrs. Maye."

"My, I hardly recognized you, Mr. Harold. I don't know
what's the matter with the girl sometimes . . . Edith . . .
she's my granddaughter. My daughter and her husband are
looking after the place now." She took off her glasses and
began wiping away the steam, smiling.

He looked down at the polished counter, smoothed his fingers over the cool, grainy wood.

"Where's the missus?"

"Didn't feel too well this week. I don't know." He shifted
his weight to the other leg and raised his eyes to her chin.

"Now I'm sorry to hear that! I had the place fixed up nice
for the two of you. It might have done her good to get out.
It's funny how much better you feel sometimes, just getting
out." She laid the apron behind the cash register. "Edith! I'm
taking Mr. Harold to his cabin! I'll have to get my coat, Mr.
Harold." There was no answer, but the girl came to the
kitchen door and watched them leave.

Outside the sun had come out and the glare hurt his eyes.
He held onto the banister and went slowly down the stairs,
following.

"Sun's bad, isn't it? The first time it's been out all week
though." She waved at some people going by in a car.

They went past a gasoline pump, locked and covered with
snow, and past a little shed with a TIRES sign hung over the
door. He looked through the broken windows at the heaps of
burlap sacks, the old tires, and the barrels. The room was
damp and cold looking with the snow drifted inside and sprinkled on the sill around the broken glass.

"Kids have done that," she said, stopping for a minute and
putting her hand up to the broken window. "They don't miss

a chance to do us dirt. A whole pack of them all the time running wild from down at the construction camp." She shook
her head. "Poor little devils. Sorry home life for kids anyway,
always on the move like that. Their daddies are building on
that dam." She unlocked the cabin door and pushed on it. "I
made a fire this morning so it would be nice for you."

"I appreciate that, Mrs. Maye."

There was a big double bed covered with a plain bedspread,
a bureau, and a writing desk in the front room which was divided from the kitchen by a waist-high, wood partition. A sink,
wood stove, woodbox, an old ice-box, an oilcloth covered
table and two wooden chairs. The other two doors opened to
the toilet and to a little porch where there was a place he could
hang his clothes.

"Looks fine," he said.

"I tried to fix it up a little. Do you need anything, Mr.
Harold?"

"Not now anyway, but I'll see when I come down."

"I'll let you go then. You're probably tired, driving all that
way."

"I guess I should bring up my things." He shut the door
behind them and they stood on the porch looking down the
hill. He fingered a cigarette out, licked the end before putting
it in his mouth.

"I'm just sorry the missus couldn't come," she said. "Doesn't
seem right."

From where they stood they were almost on a level with the
huge, snowy-black rock protruding from the hillside behind
the road. Some people said it looked like a castle. He took the
cigarette out of his mouth as she started to move away.
"How's the fishing?"

"Some of them are getting them, but most of the boys are
out hunting. Deer season, you know."

He drove the car up as far as he could and started to unload.
The last thing he took out of the car was a pint of Scotch from
the glove compartment. He set the bottle on the table, and
later, as he spread out the boxes of weights and the silver
hooks and thick-bodied red and white flies, he moved it to the
drainboard. Sitting there at the table smoking a cigarette with

his tackle box open and everything in place, his flies and the weights spread out, testing leader strength between his hands and tying up outfits for that afternoon, he was glad he'd come. And he still had a couple of good hours left this afternoon. Then tomorrow. He'd already decided he would save the bottle for when he came back tonight and the rest for tomorrow. Once he thought he heard a scratching at the door and got up from the table to look, but there was nothing. Only the steep shiny white hills and dead-looking pines under the overcast sky, and down below, the few buildings and cars drawn up beside the highway. He still had plenty of time. Why not stretch out for a few minutes? It would be better just before dark anyway. He could go down in an hour or so. He shut the door and checked the stove before he began to undress. Then, in his shorts, padding on the cold floor, he cleaned off the table and got in between the cold sheets, trembling. For a while he lay on his side, eyes closed, knees drawn up for warmth, then turned onto his back and wiggled his toes against the sheet. He wished Frances were here—somebody to talk to.

He opened his eyes. The room was dark. The stove gave off little crackling noises and there was a red glow shadowing on the wall behind it. He lay there trying to focus his eyes on the window, not able to believe it was really dark outside. He shut his eyes again and turned over, stretching his legs slowly. He'd only wanted to sleep maybe an hour. He opened his eyes and sat up heavily on the side of the bed. He got on his shirt and reached for his pants. The floor was still cold. He went into the bathroom and pissed, then washed his hands and face with cold water. He walked back into the kitchen turning his head back and forth, trying to get rid of the thick, dull feeling. "Goddamn it!" he said, banging things around in the cupboard and taking down some cans and putting them back again. He heated up a pot of coffee and drank two cups before deciding to go down to the cafe for something solid. He put on wool slippers and a coat, hunted around until he found his flashlight, and went out.

The cold air stung his cheeks and pinched his nostrils together, but it felt good. The trail was slippery but the lights from the cafe showed him where he was walking, and he was careful. He nodded to the girl, Edith, and sat down in a booth near the end of the counter. The cafe was empty now and he could hear a radio playing back in the kitchen.

"Are you closed?"

"Kind of. I'm cleaning up for in the morning."

"Too late for something to eat then."

"I guess I can get you something." She came over with the menu and a glass of water.

"Mrs. Maye around, Edith?"

"She's up in her room. Did you want something?"

"I need more wood. For in the morning."

"That's out in back."

He pointed on the menu to a ham sandwich with potato salad. "I guess I'll have this."

Waiting, he began moving the salt and pepper shakers around in a little circle in front of him. He should have just gotten a milk shake and a sandwich to take back to the cabin. After she brought the plate over she hung around out in front, filling sugar bowls and napkin holders, looking up at him sometimes. The bitch. She came over then with a wet rag and began wiping the crumbs off the table in front of him. He sat with his hands folded across his stomach, looking down at the rag sliding back and forth across the table leaving the little streaks.

He left money and went out through a door on the side, around to the back where he picked up an armload of the frozen blocks. Then the snail's pace up to the cabin. He looked back once and saw her watching him from the kitchen window. By the time he got to his door and dropped the wood, he hated her.

He lay on the bed for a long time and read *Life* magazines that Mrs. Maye had left. When he felt sleepy he got up and cleared off his bed and the table and arranged his things for in the morning in a corner. He looked through the pile of stuff again to make sure he had everything. He liked things in order and didn't want to get up in the morning and have to look all over for something. He picked up the bottle, held it up to the light, and poured some into a cup. He carried it over to the bed and set it on the nightstand. He turned off the light and stood beside the window for a minute scratching himself before getting into bed. He still had tomorrow. Or was it today?

—

He got up so early it was still almost dark in the cabin. The stove had gone down to coals during the night and he could see his breath. He adjusted the grate and pushed in some blocks. He fixed three peanut butter sandwiches, wrapped them in wax paper, and slipped these and some cookies into a coat pocket. He couldn't remember the last time he'd gotten up so early. For breakfast he drank almost a quart of chocolate milk, standing at the drainboard in his wool stocking feet. At the door he pulled on his waders.

Outside it was that vague, gray half-light just before full morning. Clouds lay fastened to the tops of the mountains and filled the long valleys and hung in patches over the trees. Down the hill the lodge was dark and there were no cars, only the pickup with the advertising printed on the side. He moved out slowly down the packed, slippery trail toward the river. Likely there was no one up at this hour and it pleased him. Somewhere in one of the valleys off behind the river he heard the pop-pop of shots and counted them. Seven. Eight. The hunters were awake. And the deer. He wondered if the shots came from the two hunters he'd seen in the lodge yesterday. Deer didn't have much of a chance in snow like this. He kept his eyes down watching the trail. It kept dropping downhill and soon he was in heavy timber, snow up to his ankles.

Under the trees the snow lay drifted around grotesque, frozen bushes, but wasn't too deep where he walked. It was thick with pine needles that crunched into the snow under his boots. He could still see his breath, fogging out in front of him. He held the heavy rod straight ahead of him when he had to push through the bushes or go under the trees with low limbs. He held it under his arm like it was a lance. And sometimes, when he was a kid and had gone fishing for two or three days at a time, hiking in by himself, he'd carried his rod like this even when there was no brush or trees, maybe just a big green meadow and he'd imagine himself in the lists coming down on his opponent. The jays at the crowded edge of the woods screaming for him. Then, when it was over, he would sing something as loud as he could. Yell defiance until his chest hurt, at the hawks that circled and circled over the meadow. The sun and the lace sky, and the back lake with the lean-to.

The water was clear and green you could see fifteen, twenty feet down to where it shelved off. Behind the trees he could hear the fall of the river. The trail was gone and just before he started down the bank to the river, he stepped into a snow drift up over his knees and panicked, clawing up handfuls of snow and vines to get out.

The river looked impossibly cold. Silver-green with ice on the little pools in the rocks along the edge. Before, he'd caught his fish a lot farther downriver, but then it was different, and now the rocks were sharp and slippery to walk on. Here the water was fast and broken and he walked down a little to where it smoothed out. The water ran slower and was deeper here and maybe he just might pick up something, if he were lucky. There was a stiff, yellow beach thirty yards across on the other side, but there was no way of getting over. He lifted up onto a frost-covered black log and looked around. The big trees all around him and the high cloud-cowled white mountains. Pretty as a picture the way the steam lay over the river. It made him feel like he didn't even want to smoke, and he sat there on the log swinging his legs back and forth while he threaded the line through his guides. He tied on one of the outfits he'd made up last night. When everything was ready he slipped down off the log. He pulled the new rubber boots up over his legs as high as they would go and fastened the buckle tops of the waders to his belt. Slowly he waded into the river, holding his breath for the cold water shock. The water hit and swirling embraced his legs, sucking his boots tight. He stopped. Then edged out a little farther. He took the brake off his reel and made a nice cast upstream.

By the time he'd fished out the hole, staying longer than he ever would have before without a strike, he began to feel some of the old excitement coming back. In a few minutes he came out of the water and sat down on a rock with his back against a log. The water drops glistened on his boots. He took out the cookies. He wasn't going to hurry. Not today. Some tiny birds came from somewhere and perched on the rocks beside the water. They began bobbing back and forth, tipping their beaks down toward the water but not quite touching it, then straightening up with a nervous flutter and beginning over. It must be some kind of game, he thought after a while. He almost felt sorry for them, tipping back and forth, over and over, but never quite touching the water. They flew when he scattered a handful of crumbs toward them. The tops of the trees creaked and the wind was drawing the clouds up out of the valleys and over the hills. The silver sound of the never-ending river run. Then he heard a spatter of shots somewhere across the river, but they came too fast for him to count.

He'd just changed flies and made the first cast when he saw the deer. It stumbled out of the brush upriver and onto the little beach, nodding and twisting its head, streaming long ropes of white mucus. Its left hind leg was broken and dragged behind and for an instant the deer stopped and turned her head back to look at it. Then into the water, slipping and almost falling, out into the current until only her back and head were showing. She reached the shallow water on his side and came out clumsily, twisting her head and shaking. He stood very still and watched her go into the trees.

"Dirty bastards."

He had a kind of bad taste in his stomach. He tried to make another cast, then reeled in and went back to the shore. He sat down and ate the sandwich slowly. It was dry and didn't have any taste to it, but he ate it anyway and tried not to think about the deer. Frances would be up now, doing things around the house. But he didn't want to think about Frances either. He remembered that morning when he caught the three steelhead and it was all he could do to carry them up the hill in the gunny sack. But he did, and poured them out on the steps in front of the cabin. She'd whistled, touching her finger on the black spots along their backs. And he'd gone back that after-noon and caught two more.

Now it was colder and the wind was down from the trees, blowing across the river. He got up stiffly and hobbled around over the rocks trying to loosen up. He thought about building a fire but then decided he wouldn't stay much longer. Some crows flapped by overhead coming from across the river. When they were over him he yelled, but they didn't even look down. They weren't like hawks, and he hated their black, awkward flight. He changed flies again, added more weight and cast up-stream. He let the current take the line through his fingers until he saw the slack belly out on the water. He set the brake.

The pencil-lead weight bouncing against the rocks under the water and the gentle throb under his hand running down to the butt of the rod stuck against his stomach. He wondered how the fly looked down there, if it were light enough for a fish to see.

The boys came out of the trees and onto the beach upriver, shifting around, looking at him and then looking up and down the river. Some of them got down on their hands and knees and looked for tracks and then looked up at him again. When they began coming down the beach toward him he looked up at the hills and then down the river where the best water was and where he should have gone. He turned a little in the water until he was facing downriver and began to reel in, catching his fly and setting the hook into the cork above the reel. Then he started easing sideways back toward the shore, thinking only of the shore and that each careful step brought him one step closer.

"Hey!"

He turned slowly around, wishing it could have been when he was on the shore, not here with the water pushing against his legs, off balance on the slippery rocks. His feet moved almost instinctively, wedging themselves into cracks or down between rocks while his eyes picked out the leader. All of them wore what looked like holsters or knife sheaths on their sides, only the one boy had a rifle. Gaunt and thin-faced, wearing a brown duck-billed cap, he said:

"You see a deer come out up there?" He held the gun in his right hand like a pistol, pointing the barrel up the beach.

One of the boys said, "Sure he did, Jule, it ain't been very long," and looked around at the four others. They nodded, passing round a cigarette, watching him.

"I said—you see him?"

"It wasn't a him, it was a her," Harold said. "And her back leg was almost shot off, for Christ's sake."

"What's that to you?" the one with the gun said.

"He's pretty smart, ain't he, Jule? Tell us where it went, you sonofabitch!"

"Where'd he go?" the boy asked, and raised the gun to his hip, half pointing it across at Harold.

"Who wants to know?" Harold dropped the cigarette and it

gave a little *spurt* sound as it hit the water. He held the rod straight ahead, tight up under his arm and with his other hand pulled down his hat. "You little bastards are from that trailer camp downriver, aren't you?"

"You think you know a lot, don't you?" the boy said, looking around at the others, nodding at them, raising up one foot and setting it down slowly, then the other, like some terrible pantomime of chill, or anger. Then the boy raised the rifle to his shoulder and pulled back the hammer.

The barrel pointed somewhere at his stomach, or lower down maybe, his groin, or his balls. He felt them contract. The water swirled and foamed around his boots and made a little trail of white before smoothing out. He swayed, working his mouth at the phlegm pulling in his dry throat but not able to move his tongue, looking down into the clear water at the rocks and the little spaces of sand. He wondered what it would be if his boots tipped water and he went down, rolling like a chunk.

"What's the matter with you?" he asked. The ice water came up through his legs then, poured into his chest.

The boy didn't say anything, just stood there. All of them just stood there looking at him.

"Don't shoot," he said.

The boy held the gun on him for another minute, then lowered it. "Scared, wasn't you?"

Harold nodded his head dreamily. He kept feeling like he wanted to yawn, opening and closing his mouth.

One of them pried loose a rock from the edge of the water and threw it. Harold turned his back and it hit a little behind and below him. The others began throwing, and he stood there looking at the shore, hearing the rocks splash around him.

"You didn't want to fish here anyway, did you? I could've got you, but I didn't. Now you see that deer, remember how lucky you was. Hear?"

One of the boys made an obscene gesture with his hand, and the rest of them grinned. Then they moved in a pack back into the trees. He watched them go, then turned and worked his way back to the shore and dropped down against a log. After a few minutes he got up and started to walk back to the cabin.

The snow had held back all day, and now, as he was in sight

of the clearing, the light sticky flakes began falling. Somewhere he'd lost his rod, maybe when he stopped that one time—he could remember laying it on the snow. Anyway it didn't matter. It was a good rod, one that he'd paid over forty dollars for one summer five or six years ago, but even if it were nice tomorrow, he wouldn't go back for it. But what was tomorrow? He had to be back tomorrow. A jay cried up in a tree over him and another answered across the clearing up by his cabin. He was tired and walked slowly. Each step a conscious raising of one leg and then setting it down again in front of the other.

He came out of the trees and stopped. Down below at the lodge they'd turned on the lights although it still wasn't dark. Somehow he had missed it and it was gone. Something heroic. He didn't know what he was going to do. He couldn't very well go home. Slow, thick flakes sifted down through the freezing air, sticking on his coat collar, melting cold and wet against his face. He stared at the wordless, distorted things around him.

Furious Seasons

That duration which maketh Pyramids
pillars of snow, and all that's past a moment.
Sir Thomas Browne

RAIN threatens. Already the tops of the hills across the valley are obscured by the heavy gray mist. Quick shifting black clouds with white furls and caps are coming from the hills, moving down the valley and passing over the fields and vacant lots in front of the apartment house. If Farrell lets go his imagination he can see the clouds as black horses with flared white manes and, turning behind, slowly, inexorably, black chariots, here and there a white-plumed driver. He shuts the screen door now and watches his wife step slowly down the stairs. She turns at the bottom and smiles, and he opens the screen and waves. In another moment she drives off. He goes back into the room and sits down in the big leather chair under the brass lamp, laying his arms straight out along the sides of the chair.

It is a little darker in the room when Iris comes out of her bath wrapped in a loose white dressing gown. She pulls the stool out from under the dresser and sits down in front of the mirror. With her right hand she takes up a white plastic brush, the handle inset with imitation pearl, and begins combing out her hair in long, sweeping, rhythmical movements, the brush passing down through the length of the hair with a faint squeaking noise. She holds her hair down over the one shoulder with her left hand and makes the long, sweeping, rhythmical movements with the right. She stops once and switches on the lamp over the mirror. Farrell takes up a glossy picture magazine from the stand beside the chair and reaches up to turn on the lamp, fumbling against the parchment-like shade in his hunt for the chain. The lamp is two feet over his right shoulder and the brown shade crackles as he touches it.

It is dark outside and the air smells of rain. Iris asks if he will close the window. He looks up at the window, now a mirror, seeing himself and, behind, Iris sitting at the dresser watching him, with another, darker Farrell staring into another window beside her. He has yet to call Frank and confirm the hunting trip for the next morning. He turns the pages. Iris takes down the brush from her hair and taps it on the dresser edge.

"Lew," she says, "you know I'm pregnant?"

Under the lamp light the glossy pages are open now to a halftone, two page picture of a disaster scene, an earthquake, somewhere in the Near East. There are five almost fat men dressed in white, baggy pants standing in front of a flattened house. One of the men, probably the leader, is wearing a dirty white hat that hangs down over one eye giving him a secret, malevolent look. He is looking sideways at the camera, pointing across the mess of blocks to a river or a neck of the sea on the far side of the rubble. Farrell closes the magazine and lets it slide out of his lap as he stands. He turns out the light and then, before going on through to the bathroom, asks: "What are you going to do?" The words are dry, hurrying like old leaves into the dark corners of the room and Farrell feels at the same instant the words are out that the question has already been asked by someone else, a long time ago. He turns and goes into the bathroom.

It smells of Iris; a warm, moist odor, slightly sticky; New Spring talc and King's Idyll cologne. Her towel lies across the back of the toilet. In the sink she has spilled talcum. It is wet now and pasty and makes a thick yellow ring around the white sides. He rubs it out and washes it into the drain.

He is shaving. By turning his head, he can see into the living room. Iris in profile sitting on the stool in front of the old dresser. He lays down the razor and washes his face, then picks up the razor again. At this moment he hears the first few drops of rain spatter against the roof . . . .

After a while he turns out the light over the dresser and sits down again in the big leather chair, listening to the rain. The rain comes in short, fluttery swishes against his window. The soft fluttering of a white bird.

His sister has caught it. She keeps it in a box, dropping in flowers for it through the top, sometimes shaking the box so they can hear it fluttering its wings against the sides until one morning she shows him, holding out the box, there is no fluttering inside. Only a lumpy, scraping sound the bird makes as she tilts the box from one side to the other. When she gives it to him to get rid of he throws box and all into the river, not wanting to open it for it has started to smell funny. The cardboard box is eighteen inches long and six inches wide and four inches deep, and he is sure it is a Snowflake cracker box because this is what she used for the first few birds.

He runs along the squashy bank following. It is a funeral boat and the muddy river is the Nile and it will soon run into the ocean but before that the boat will burn up and the white bird will fly out and into his father's fields someplace where he will hunt out the bird in some thick growth of green meadow grass, eggs and all. He runs along the bank, the brush whipping his pants, and once a limb hits him on the ear, and it still hasn't burned. He pulls loose some rocks from the bank and begins throwing them at the boat. And then the rain begins; huge, gusty, spattering drops that belt the water, sweeping across the river from one shore to the other.

Farrell had been in bed for a number of hours now, how long he could not be sure. Every so often he raised up on one shoulder, careful not to disturb his wife, and peered across to her nightstand trying for a look at the clock. Its side was turned a little too much in his direction and raising as he does on one shoulder, being as careful as possible, he could see only that the yellow hands say 3:15 or 2:45. Outside the rain came against his window. He turned on his back, his legs spread wide under the sheet barely touching his wife's left foot, listening to the clock on the nightstand. He pulled down into the quilts again and then because it was too hot and his hands were sweating, he threw back the close covers, twisting his fingers into the sheet, crushing it between his fingers and knotting it against his palms until they felt dry.

Outside the rain came in clouds, lifting up in swells against the faint yellow outside light like myriads of tiny yellow insects coming furiously against his window, spitting and rippling. He turned over and slowly began working himself closer to Lorraine until her smooth back touched his chest. For a moment he held her gently, carefully, his hand lying in the hollow of her stomach, his fingers slipped under the elastic band of her underpants, the fingertips barely touching the stiff, brush-like hair below. An odd sensation then, like slipping into a warm bath and feeling himself a child again, the memories flooding back.

He moved his hand and pulled away, then eased out of bed and walked to the streaming window.

It was a huge, foreign dream night outside. The street lamp a gaunt, scarred obelisk running up into the rain with a faint yellow light holding to its point. At its base the street was black, shiny. Darkness swirled and pulled at the edges of the light. He could not see the other apartments and for a moment it was as if they'd been destroyed, like the houses in the picture he'd been looking at a few hours ago. The rain appeared and disappeared against the window like a dark veil opened and closed. Down below it flooded at the curbs. Leaning closer until he could feel the cold drafts of air on his forehead from the bottom of the window, he watched his breath make a fog. He had read some place and it seemed he could remember looking at some picture once, perhaps *National Geographic*, where groups of brown-skinned people stood around their huts watching the frosted sun come up. The caption said they believed the soul was visible in the breath, that they were spitting and blowing into the palms of their hands, offering their souls to God. His breath disappeared while he watched until only a tiny circle, a dot remained, then nothing. He turned away from the window for his things.

He fumbled in the closet for his insulated boots, his hands tracing the sleeves of each coat until he found the rubber slick waterproof. He went to the drawer for socks and long underwear, then picked up his shirt and pants and carried the armload through the hallway into the kitchen before turning on the light. He dressed and pulled on his boots before starting the coffee. He would have liked to turn on the porchlight for Frank but somehow it didn't seem good with Iris out there in bed. While the coffee perked he made sandwiches and when it had finished he filled a thermos, took a cup down from the cupboard, filled it, and sat down near the window where he could watch the street. He smoked and drank the coffee and listened to the clock on the stove, squeaking. The coffee slopped over the cup and the brown drops ran slowly down the side onto the table. He rubbed his fingers through the wet circle across the rough table top.

He is sitting at the desk in his sister's room. He sits in the straightbacked chair on a thick dictionary, his feet curled up beneath the seat of the chair, the heels of his shoes hooked on the rung. When he leans too heavily on the table one of the legs picks up from the floor and so he has had to put a magazine under the leg. He is drawing a picture of the valley he lives in. At first he meant to trace a picture from one of his sister's schoolbooks, but after using three sheets of paper and having it still not turn out right, he has decided to draw his valley and his house. Occasionally he stops drawing and rubs his fingers across the grainy surface of the table.

Outside the April air is still damp and cool, the coolness that comes after the rain in the afternoon. The ground and the trees and the mountains are green and steam is everywhere, coming off the troughs in the corral, from the pond his father made, and out of the meadow in slow, pencil-like columns, rising off the river and going up over the mountains like smoke. He can hear his father shouting to one of the men and he hears the man swear and shout back. He puts his drawing pencil down and slips off the chair. Down below in front of the smokehouse he sees his father working with the pulley. At his feet there is a coil of brown rope and his father is hitting and pulling on the pulley bar trying to swing it out and away from the barn. On his head he wears a brown wool army cap and the collar of his scarred leather jacket is turned up exposing the dirty white lining. With a final blow at the pulley he turns around facing the men. Two of them, big, red-faced Canadians with greasy flannel hats, dragging the sheep toward his father. Their fists are balled deep into the wool and one of them has his arms wrapped around the front legs of the sheep. They go toward the barn, half dragging, half walking the sheep on its hind legs like some wild dance. His father calls out again and they pin the sheep against the barn wall one of the men straddling the sheep, forcing its head back and up toward his window. Its nostrils are dark slits with little streams of mucus running down into its mouth. The ancient, glazed eyes stare up at him for a moment before it tries to bleat, but the sound comes out a sharp squeaking noise as his father cuts it off with a quick, sweeping thrust of the knife. The blood gushes out over the man's hands before he can move. In a few moments they have the animal up on the pulley. He can hear the dull crank-crank-crank of the pulley as his father winds it even higher. The men are sweating now but they keep their jackets fastened up tight.

Starting right below the gaping throat his father opens up the brisket and belly while the men take the smaller knives and begin cutting the pelt away from the legs. The gray guts slide out of the steaming belly and tumble onto the ground in a thick coil. His father grunts and scoops them into a box saying something about bear. The red-faced men laugh. He hears the chain in the bathroom rattle and then the water gurgling into the toilet. A moment later he turns toward the door as footsteps approach. His sister comes into the room, her body faintly steaming. For an instant she is frozen there in the doorway with the towel around her hair one hand holding the ends together and the other on the doorknob. Her breasts are round and smooth-looking, the nipples like the stems of the warm porcelain fruit on the living room table. She drops the towel and it slides down pulling at her neck, touching across her breasts and then heaping up at her feet. She smiles, slowly puts the hand to her mouth and pulls the door shut. He turns back to the window, his toes curling up in his shoes.

Farrell sat at the table sipping his coffee, smoking again on an empty stomach. Once he heard a car in the street and got up quickly out of the chair, walking to the porch window to see. It started up the street in second then slowed in front of his house, taking the corner carefully, water churning half up to its hubs, but it went on. He sat down at the table again and listened to the electric clock on the stove, squeaking. His fingers tightened around the cup. Then he saw the lights. They came bobbing down the street out of the darkness; two close-set signal lanterns on a narrow prow, the heavy white rain falling across the lights, pelting the street ahead. It splashed down the street, slowed, then eased in under his window.

He picked up his things and went out on the porch. Iris was there, stretched out under the twisted pile of heavy quilts. Even as he hunted for a reason for the action, as if he were de-tached somehow, crouched on the other side of her bed watching himself go through this, at the same time knowing it was over, he moved toward her bed. Irresistibly he bent down over her figure, as if he hung suspended, all senses released except that of smell, he breathed deeply for the fleeting scent of her body, bending until his face was against her covers he experienced the scent again, for just an instant, and then it was gone. He backed away, remembered his gun, then pulled the door shut behind him. The rain whipped into his face. He felt almost giddy clutching his gun and holding onto the banister, steadying himself. For a minute, looking down over the porch to the black, ripply sidewalk, it was as though he were standing alone on a bridge someplace, and again the feeling came, as it had last night, that this had already happened, knowing then that it would happen again, just as he somehow knew now. "Christ!" The rain cut at his face, ran down his nose and onto his lips. Frank tapped the horn twice and Farrell went carefully down the wet, slippery stairs to the car.

"Regular downpour, by God!" Frank said. A big man, with a thick quilted jacket zipped up to his chin and a brown duck-bill cap that made him look like a grim umpire. He helped move things around in the back seat so Farrell could put his things in.

Water ran up against the gutters, backed up at the drains on the corners and now and then they could see where it had flooded over the curbs and into a yard. They followed the street to its end and then turned right onto another street that would take them to the highway.

"This is going to slow us down some, but Jesus think what it's going to do to them geese!"

Once again Farrell let go and saw them, pulling them back from that one moment when even the fog had frozen to the rocks and so dark it could as well have been midnight as late afternoon when they started. They come over the bluff, flying low and savage and silent, coming out of the fog suddenly, spectrally, in a swishing of wings over his head and he is jumping up trying to single out the closest, at the same moment pushing forward his safety, but it is jammed and his stiff, gloved finger stays hooked into the guard, pulling against the locked trigger. They all come over him, flying out of the fog across the bluff and over his head. Great strings of them calling down to him. This was the way it happened three years ago.

He watched the wet fields fall under their lights and then sweep beside and then behind the car. The windshield wipers squeaked back and forth.

Iris pulls her hair down over the one shoulder with her left hand while the other wields the brush. Rhythmically the brush makes its sweeping movement through the length of the hair with a faint squeaking noise. The brush rises quickly again to the side of the head and repeats the movement and the sound. She has just told him she is pregnant.

Lorraine has gone to a shower. He has still to call Frank and confirm the hunting trip. The glossy picture of the magazine he holds in his lap is open to the scene of a disaster. One of the men in the picture, evidently the leader, is pointing over the disaster scene to a body of water.

"What are you going to do?" He turns and goes on through to the bathroom. Her towel hangs over the back of the toilet and the bathroom smells of New Spring talc and King's Idyll cologne. There is a yellow pasty ring of talcum powder in the sink that he must rub out with water before he shaves. He can look through to the living room where she sits combing her hair. When he has washed his face and dried, just after he has picked up the razor again, the first raindrops strike the roof.

He looked at the clock on the dashboard but it had stopped. "What time is it?"

"Don't pay any attention to that clock there," Frank said, lifting his thumb off the wheel to indicate the big glowing yellow clock protruding from the dash. "It's stopped. It's six-thirty. Did your wife say you had to be home at a certain time?" He smiled.

Farrell shook his head but Frank would not be able to see this. "No. Just wondered what time it was." He lit a cigarette and slumped back in his seat, watching the rain sweep into the car lights and splash against the window.

They are driving down from Yakima to get Iris. It started to rain when they hit the Columbia River highway and by the time they got through Arlington, it was a torrent.

It is like a long sloping tunnel, and they are speeding down the black road with the thick matted trees close overhead and the water cascading against the front of the car. Lorraine's arm extends along the back of the seat, her hand resting lightly on his left shoulder. She is sitting so close that he can feel her left breast rise and fall with her breathing. She has just tried to dial something on the radio, but there is too much static.

"She can fix up the porch for a place to sleep and keep her things," Farrell says, not taking his eyes off the road. "It won't be for long."

Lorraine turns toward him for a moment leaning forward a little in the seat, placing her free hand on his thigh. With her left hand she squeezes her fingers into his shoulder then leans her head against him. After a while she says: "You're all mine, Lew. I hate to think of sharing you even for a little while with anybody. Even your own sister."

The rain lets up gradually and often there are no trees at all over their heads. Once Farrell sees the moon, a sharp, stark yellow crescent, shining through the mist of gray clouds. They leave the woods and the road curves and they follow it into a valley that opens onto the river below. It has stopped raining and the sky is a black rug with handfuls of glistening stars strewn about.

"How long will she stay?" Lorraine asks.

"A couple of months. Three at the most. The Seattle job will be open for her before Christmas." The ride has made his stomach a little fluttery. He lights a cigarette. The gray smoke streams out of his nose and is immediately pulled out through the wing window.

The cigarette began to bite the tip of his tongue and he cracked the window and dropped it out. Frank turned off the highway and onto a slick blacktop that would take them to the river. They were in the wheat country now, the great fields of harvested wheat rolling out toward the dimly outlined hills beyond and broken every so often by a muddy, churned-looking field glimmering with little pockets of water. Next year they would be in plant and in the summer the wheat would stand as high as a man's waist, hissing and bending when the wind blew.

"It's a shame," Frank said, "all this land without grain half the time with half the people in the world starving." He shook his head. "If the government would keep its fingers off the farm we'd be a damn sight better off."

The pavement ended in a jag of cracks and chuckholes and

the car bounced onto the rubbery, black pitted road that stretched like a long black avenue toward the hills.

"Have you ever seen them when they harvest, Lew?"

"No."

The morning grayed. Farrell saw the stubble fields turned into a cheat-yellow as he watched. He looked out the window at the sky where gray clouds rolled and broke into massive, clumsy chunks. "The rain's going to quit."

They came to the foot of the hills where the fields ended, then turned and drove along at the edge of the fields following the hills until they came to the head of the canyon. Far below at the very bottom of the stone-ribbed canyon lay the river, its far side covered by a bank of fog.

"It's stopped raining," Farrell said.

Frank backed the car into a small, rocky ravine and said it was a good enough place. Farrell took out his shotgun and leaned it against the rear fender before taking out his shell bag and extra coat. Then he lifted out the paper sack with the sandwiches and his hand closed tightly around the warm, hard thermos. They walked away from the car without talking and along the ridge before starting to drop down into one of the small valleys that opened into the canyon. The earth was studded here and there with sharp rocks or a black, dripping bush.

The ground sogged under his feet, pulled at his boots with every step, and made a sucking noise when he released them. He carried the shell bag in his right hand, swinging it like a sling, letting it hang down by its strap from his hand. A wet breeze off the river blew against his face. The sides of the low bluffs overlooking the river down below were deeply grooved and cut back into the rock, leaving table-like projections jutting out, marking the high water lines for thousands of years past. Piles of naked white logs and countless pieces of driftwood lay jammed onto the ledge like cairns of bones dragged up onto the cliffs by some giant bird. Farrell tried to remember where the geese came over three years ago. He stopped on the side of a hill just where it sloped into the canyon and leaned his gun on a rock. He pulled bushes and gathered rocks from nearby and walked down toward the river after some of the driftwood to make a blind.

He sat on his raincoat with his back against a hard shrub, his knees drawn up to his chin, watching the sky whiten and then blue a little and the clouds run with the wind. Geese were gabbling somewhere in the fog on the other side of the river. He rested and smoked and watched the smoke whip out of his mouth. He waited for the sun.

It is four in the afternoon. The sun has just gone behind the gray, late afternoon clouds leaving a dwarfed half-shadow that falls across the car following him as he walks around to open the door for his wife. They kiss.

Iris and he will be back for her in an hour and forty-five minutes, exactly. They are going by the hardware store and then to the grocery. They will be back for her at 5:45. He slides in behind the wheel again and in a moment, seeing his chance, eases out into the traffic. On the way out of town he must stop and wait for every red light, finally turning left onto the secondary, hitting the gas so hard that they both lean back a little in the seat. It is 4:20. At the forks they turn onto the blacktop, orchards on both sides of the road. Over the tops of the trees, the low brown hills and beyond, the blue-black mountains crowned with white. From the close rows of trees, shadows, blackening into the shoulders, creep across the pavement in front of the car. New boxes are jumbled together in white piles at the end of each orchard row and up against the trees or pushed into the limbs, some leaning in the crotches, are the ladders. He slows the car and stops, pulling off onto the shoulder close enough to one of the trees so that all Iris has to do is open her door and she can reach the limb. It scrapes against the door as she releases it. The apples are heavy and yellow, and sweet juice spurts into his teeth as he bites into one.

The road ends and they follow the dust covered hardtrack right up to the edge of the hills where the orchards stop. He can still go farther, though, by turning onto the bank road that follows the irrigation canal. The canal is empty now and the steep dirt banks are dry and crumbling. He has shifted the car into second. The road is steeper, driving is more difficult and slower. He stops the car under a pine tree outside a water gate where the canal comes down out of the hills to slide into a circular, cement trough. Iris lays her head in his lap. It is nearly dark. The wind is blowing through the car and once he hears the tops of the trees creaking.

He gets out of the car to light a cigarette, walking to the rim of the hill overlooking the valley. The wind has strengthened; the air is colder. The grass is sparse under his feet and there are a few flowers. The cigarette makes a short, twisting red arc as it spins down into the valley. It is six o'clock.

The cold was bad. The dead numbness of the toes, the cold slowly working its way up into the calves of his legs and setting in under his knees. His fingers too, stiff and cold even though they were balled into his pockets. Farrell waited for the sun. The huge clouds over the river turned, breaking up, shaping and reshaping while he watched. At first he barely noticed the black line against the lowest clouds. When it crossed into sight he thought it was mosquitos, close up against his blind, and then it was a far-off dark rent between cloud and sky that moved closer while he watched. The line turned toward him then and spread out over the hills below. He was excited but calm, his heart beating in his ears urging him to run, yet his movements slow and ponderous as if heavy stones hung to his legs. He inched up on his knees until his face pressed into the brush wall and turned his eyes toward the ground. His legs shook and he pushed his knees into the soft earth. The legs grew suddenly numb and he moved his hand and pushed it into the ground up over his fingers, surprised at its warmth. Then the soft gabble of geese over his head and the heavy, whistling push of wings. His finger tightened around the trigger. The quick, rasping calls; the sharp upward jerk of ten feet as they saw him. Farrell was on his feet now, pulling down on one goose before swinging to another, then again quickly onto a closer one, following it as it broke and cut back over his head toward the river. He fired once, twice, and the geese kept flying, clamoring, split up and out of range, their low forms melting into the rolling hills. He fired once more before dropping back to his knees inside the blind. Somewhere on the hill behind him and a little to the left he heard Frank shooting, the reports rolling down through the canyon like sharp whip snaps. He felt confused to see more geese getting off the river, stringing out over the low hills and rising up the canyon, flying in V formations for the top of the canyon and the fields behind. He reloaded carefully, pushing the green, ribbed #2's up into the breech, pumping one of the shells into the chamber with a hollow, cracking sound. Yet six shells would do the job better than three. He quickly loosened the plug from the underbarrel of the gun and dropped the coil spring and the wooden plug into his pocket. He heard Frank shoot again, and suddenly there was a flock gone by he hadn't seen. As he watched them he saw three more coming in low and from the side. He waited until they were even with him, swinging across the side of the hill thirty yards away, their heads swinging slowly, rhythmically, right to left, the eyes black and glistening. He raised to one knee, just as they passed him, giving them a good lead, squeezing off an instant before they flared. The one nearest him crumpled and dived straight into the ground. He fired again as they turned, seeing the goose stop it as if it had run into a wall, flailing against the wall trying to get over it before turning over, head downward, wings out, to slowly spiral down. He emptied his gun at the third goose even when it was probably out of range, seeing it stop the charge on the fifth shot, its tail jerking hard and settling down, but its wings still beating. For a long time he watched it flying closer and closer to the ground before it disappeared into one of the canyons.

Farrell laid the two geese on their backs inside the blind and stoked their smooth white undersides. They were Canadian geese, honkers. After this it didn't matter too much that the geese that flew came over too high or went out someplace else down the river. He sat against the shrub and smoked, watching the sky whirl by over his head. Sometime later, perhaps in the early afternoon, he slept.

When he woke he was stiff, cold and sweating and the sun was gone, the sky a thickening gray pall. Somewhere he could hear geese calling and going out, leaving those strange sharp echoes in the valleys, but he could see nothing but wet, black hills that ended in fog where the river should have been. He wiped his hand over his face and began to shiver. He stood up. He could see the fog rolling up the canyon and over the hills, closing off and hemming in the land, and he felt the breath of the cold damp air around him, touching his forehead and cheeks and lips. He broke through the blind getting out and started running up the hill.

He stood outside the car and pressed the horn in a continual blast until Frank ran up and jerked his arm away from the window.

"What's the matter with you? Are you crazy or something?"

"I have to go home, I tell you!"

"*Jesus* Christ! Well, *Jesus* Christ! Get in then, get in!"

They were quiet then but for Farrell's asking twice the time before they were out of the wheat country. Frank held a cigar between his teeth, never taking his eyes from the road. When they ran into the first drifting patches of fog he switched on the car lights. After they turned onto the highway the fog lifted and layered somewhere in the dark over the car, and the first drops of rain began hitting the windshield. Once three ducks flew in front of the car lights and pitched into a puddle beside the road. Farrell blinked.

"Did you see that?" Frank asked.

Farrell nodded.

"How do you feel now?"

"Okay."

"You get any geese?"

Farrell rubbed the palms of his hands together, interlacing his fingers, finally folding them into his lap. "No, I guess not."

"Too bad. I heard you shooting." He worked the cigar to the other side of his mouth and tried to puff, but it had gone cold. He chewed on it for a minute then laid it in the ashtray and glanced at Farrell.

"Course it's none of my affair, but if it's something you're worried about at home . . . . My advice is not to take it too seriously. You'll live longer. No gray hairs like me." He coughed, laughed. "I know, I used to be the same way. I remember . . . ."

Farrell is sitting in the big leather chair under the brass lamp watching Iris comb out her hair. He is holding a magazine in his lap whose glossy pages are open to the scene of a disaster, an earthquake, somewhere in the Near East. Except for the small light over the dresser it is dark in the room. The brush moves quickly through her hair in long, sweeping, rhythmical movements, causing a faint squeaking noise in the room. He has yet to call Frank and confirm the hunting trip for the next morning. There is a cold, moist air coming in through the window from the outside. She is tapping the brush against the edge of the dresser. "Lew," she says, "you know I'm pregnant?"

Her bathroom smell sickens him. Her towel lies across the back of the toilet. In the sink she has spilled talcum. It is wet now and pasty and makes a thick, yellow ring around the white sides. He rubs it out and washes it into the drain.

He is shaving. By turning his head he can see into the living room. Iris in profile sitting on the stool in front of the old dresser. She is combing her hair. He lays down the razor and washes his face, then picks up the razor again. At this moment he hears the first few drops of rain spatter against the roof . . . .

He carries her out to the porch, turns her face to the wall, and covers her up. He goes back into the bathroom, washes his hands, and stuffs the heavy, blood-soaked towel into the clothes hamper. After a while he turns out the light over the dresser and sits down again in his chair by the window, listening to the rain.

Frank laughed. "So it was nothing, nothing at all. We got along fine after that. Oh, the usual bickering now and then but when she found out just who was running the show, everything was all right." He gave Farrell a friendly rap on the knee.

They drove into the outskirts of town, past the long line of motels with their blazing red, blinking, neon lights, past the cafes with steamy windows the cars clustered in front, and past the small businesses, dark and locked until the next day. Frank turned right at the next light, then left, and now they were on Farrell's street. Frank pulled in behind a black and white car that had SHERIFF'S OFFICE painted in small white letters across the trunk. In the lights of their car they could see another glass inside the car inset with a wire screen making the back seat into a cage. Steam rose from the hood of their car and mixed with the rain.

"Could be he's after you, Lew." He started to open the door, then chuckled. "Maybe they've found out you were hunting with no license. Come on, I'll turn you in myself."

"No. You go on Frank. That's all right. I'll be all right. Wait a minute, let me get out!"

"Christ, you'd really think they were after you! Wait a

minute, get your gun." He rolled down the window and passed out the shotgun to Farrell. "Look's like the rain's never going to let up. See you."

"Yeah."

Upstairs all the lights of his apartment were turned on and blurred figures stood frieze-like at the windows looking down through the rain. Farrell stood behind the sheriff's car holding onto the smooth, wet tail fin. Rain fell on his bare head and worked its way down under his collar. Frank drove a few yards up the street and stopped, looking back. Farrell holding onto the tail fin, swaying a little, with the fine impenetrable rain coming down around him. The gutter water rushed over his feet, swirled frothing into a great whirlpool at the drain on the corner and rushed down to the center of the earth.

WHAT WE TALK ABOUT
WHEN WE TALK ABOUT LOVE

For Tess Gallagher

Why Don't You Dance?

IN the kitchen, he poured another drink and looked at the bedroom suite in his front yard. The mattress was stripped and the candy-striped sheets lay beside two pillows on the chiffonier. Except for that, things looked much the way they had in the bedroom—nightstand and reading lamp on his side of the bed, nightstand and reading lamp on her side.

His side, her side.

He considered this as he sipped the whiskey.

The chiffonier stood a few feet from the foot of the bed. He had emptied the drawers into cartons that morning, and the cartons were in the living room. A portable heater was next to the chiffonier. A rattan chair with a decorator pillow stood at the foot of the bed. The buffed aluminum kitchen set took up a part of the driveway. A yellow muslin cloth, much too large, a gift, covered the table and hung down over the sides. A potted fern was on the table, along with a box of silverware and a record player, also gifts. A big console-model television set rested on a coffee table, and a few feet away from this stood a sofa and chair and a floor lamp. The desk was pushed against the garage door. A few utensils were on the desk, along with a wall clock and two framed prints. There was also in the driveway a carton with cups, glasses, and plates, each object wrapped in newspaper. That morning he had cleared out the closets, and except for the three cartons in the living room, all the stuff was out of the house. He had run an extension cord on out there and everything was connected. Things worked, no different from how it was when they were inside.

Now and then a car slowed and people stared. But no one stopped.

It occurred to him that he wouldn't, either.

"It must be a yard sale," the girl said to the boy.

This girl and this boy were furnishing a little apartment.

"Let's see what they want for the bed," the girl said.

"And for the TV," the boy said.

The boy pulled into the driveway and stopped in front of the kitchen table.

They got out of the car and began to examine things, the girl touching the muslin cloth, the boy plugging in the blender and turning the dial to MINCE, the girl picking up a chafing dish, the boy turning on the television set and making little adjustments.

He sat down on the sofa to watch. He lit a cigarette, looked around, flipped the match into the grass.

The girl sat on the bed. She pushed off her shoes and lay back. She thought she could see a star.

"Come here, Jack. Try this bed. Bring one of those pillows," she said.

"How is it?" he said.

"Try it," she said.

He looked around. The house was dark.

"I feel funny," he said. "Better see if anybody's home."

She bounced on the bed.

"Try it first," she said.

He lay down on the bed and put the pillow under his head.

"How does it feel?" she said.

"It feels firm," he said.

She turned on her side and put her hand to his face.

"Kiss me," she said.

"Let's get up," he said.

"Kiss me," she said.

She closed her eyes. She held him.

He said, "I'll see if anybody's home."

But he just sat up and stayed where he was, making believe he was watching the television.

Lights came on in houses up and down the street.

"Wouldn't it be funny if," the girl said and grinned and didn't finish.

The boy laughed, but for no good reason. For no good reason, he switched the reading lamp on.

The girl brushed away a mosquito, whereupon the boy stood up and tucked in his shirt.

"I'll see if anybody's home," he said. "I don't think anybody's home. But if anybody is, I'll see what things are going for."

"Whatever they ask, offer ten dollars less. It's always a good idea," she said. "And, besides, they must be desperate or something."

"It's a pretty good TV," the boy said.

"Ask them how much," the girl said.

The man came down the sidewalk with a sack from the market. He had sandwiches, beer, whiskey. He saw the car in the driveway and the girl on the bed. He saw the television set going and the boy on the porch.

"Hello," the man said to the girl. "You found the bed. That's good."

"Hello," the girl said, and got up. "I was just trying it out." She patted the bed. "It's a pretty good bed."

"It's a good bed," the man said, and put down the sack and took out the beer and the whiskey.

"We thought nobody was here," the boy said. "We're interested in the bed and maybe in the TV. Also maybe the desk. How much do you want for the bed?"

"I was thinking fifty dollars for the bed," the man said.

"Would you take forty?" the girl asked.

"I'll take forty," the man said.

He took a glass out of the carton. He took the newspaper off the glass. He broke the seal on the whiskey.

"How about the TV?" the boy said.

"Twenty-five."

"Would you take fifteen?" the girl said.

"Fifteen's okay. I could take fifteen," the man said.

The girl looked at the boy.

"You kids, you'll want a drink," the man said. "Glasses in that box. I'm going to sit down. I'm going to sit down on the sofa."

The man sat on the sofa, leaned back, and stared at the boy and the girl.

The boy found two glasses and poured whiskey.

"That's enough," the girl said. "I think I want water in mine."

She pulled out a chair and sat at the kitchen table.

"There's water in that spigot over there," the man said. "Turn on that spigot."

The boy came back with the watered whiskey. He cleared his

throat and sat down at the kitchen table. He grinned. But he didn't drink anything from his glass.

The man gazed at the television. He finished his drink and started another. He reached to turn on the floor lamp. It was then that his cigarette dropped from his fingers and fell between the cushions.

The girl got up to help him find it.

"So what do you want?" the boy said to the girl.

The boy took out the checkbook and held it to his lips as if thinking.

"I want the desk," the girl said. "How much money is the desk?"

The man waved his hand at this preposterous question.

"Name a figure," he said.

He looked at them as they sat at the table. In the lamplight, there was something about their faces. It was nice or it was nasty. There was no telling.

"I'm going to turn off this TV and put on a record," the man said. "This record-player is going, too. Cheap. Make me an offer."

He poured more whiskey and opened a beer.

"Everything goes," said the man.

The girl held out her glass and the man poured.

"Thank you," she said. "You're very nice," she said.

"It goes to your head," the boy said. "I'm getting it in the head." He held up his glass and jiggled it.

The man finished his drink and poured another, and then he found the box with the records.

"Pick something," the man said to the girl, and he held the records out to her.

The boy was writing the check.

"Here," the girl said, picking something, picking anything, for she did not know the names on these labels. She got up from the table and sat down again. She did not want to sit still.

"I'm making it out to cash," the boy said.

"Sure," the man said.

They drank. They listened to the record. And then the man put on another.

Why don't you kids dance? he decided to say, and then he said it. "Why don't you dance?"

"I don't think so," the boy said.

"Go ahead," the man said. "It's my yard. You can dance if you want to."

Arms about each other, their bodies pressed together, the boy and the girl moved up and down the driveway. They were dancing. And when the record was over, they did it again, and when that one ended, the boy said, "I'm drunk."

The girl said, "You're not drunk."

"Well, I'm drunk," the boy said.

The man turned the record over and the boy said, "I am."

"Dance with me," the girl said to the boy and then to the man, and when the man stood up, she came to him with her arms wide open.

"Those people over there, they're watching," she said.

"It's okay," the man said. "It's my place," he said.

"Let them watch," the girl said.

"That's right," the man said. "They thought they'd seen everything over here. But they haven't seen this, have they?" he said.

He felt her breath on his neck.

"I hope you like your bed," he said.

The girl closed and then opened her eyes. She pushed her face into the man's shoulder. She pulled the man closer.

"You must be desperate or something," she said.

Weeks later, she said: "The guy was about middle-aged. All his things right there in his yard. No lie. We got real pissed and danced. In the driveway. Oh, my God. Don't laugh. He played us these records. Look at this record-player. The old guy gave it to us. And all these crappy records. Will you look at this shit?"

She kept talking. She told everyone. There was more to it, and she was trying to get it talked out. After a time, she quit trying.

Viewfinder

A MAN without hands came to the door to sell me a photograph of my house. Except for the chrome hooks, he was an ordinary-looking man of fifty or so.

"How did you lose your hands?" I asked after he'd said what he wanted.

"That's another story," he said. "You want this picture or not?"

"Come in," I said. "I just made coffee."

I'd just made some Jell-O, too. But I didn't tell the man I did.

"I might use your toilet," the man with no hands said.

I wanted to see how he would hold a cup.

I knew how he held the camera. It was an old Polaroid, big and black. He had it fastened to leather straps that looped over his shoulders and went around his back, and it was this that secured the camera to his chest. He would stand on the sidewalk in front of your house, locate your house in the viewfinder, push down the lever with one of his hooks, and out would pop your picture.

I'd been watching from the window, you see.

"Where did you say the toilet was?"

"Down there, turn right."

Bending, hunching, he let himself out of the straps. He put the camera on the sofa and straightened his jacket.

"You can look at this while I'm gone."

I took the picture from him.

There was a little rectangle of lawn, the driveway, the carport, front steps, bay window, and the window I'd been watching from in the kitchen.

So why would I want a photograph of this tragedy?

I looked a little closer and saw my head, *my head*, in there inside the kitchen window.

It made me think, seeing myself like that. I can tell you, it makes a man think.

I heard the toilet flush. He came down the hall, zipping and smiling, one hook holding his belt, the other tucking in his shirt.

"What do you think?" he said. "All right? Personally, I think it turned out fine. Don't I know what I'm doing? Let's face it, it takes a professional."

He plucked at his crotch.

"Here's coffee," I said.

He said, "You're alone, right?"

He looked at the living room. He shook his head.

"Hard, hard," he said.

He sat next to the camera, leaned back with a sigh, and smiled as if he knew something he wasn't going to tell me.

"Drink your coffee," I said.

I was trying to think of something to say.

"Three kids were by here wanting to paint my address on the curb. They wanted a dollar to do it. You wouldn't know anything about that, would you?"

It was a long shot. But I watched him just the same.

He leaned forward importantly, the cup balanced between his hooks. He set it down on the table.

"I work alone," he said. "Always have, always will. What are you saying?" he said.

"I was trying to make a connection," I said.

I had a headache. I know coffee's no good for it, but sometimes Jell-O helps. I picked up the picture.

"I was in the kitchen," I said. "Usually I'm in the back."

"Happens all the time," he said. "So they just up and left you, right? Now you take me, I work alone. So what do you say? You want the picture?"

"I'll take it," I said.

I stood up and picked up the cups.

"Sure you will," he said. "Me, I keep a room downtown. It's okay. I take a bus out, and after I've worked the neighborhoods, I go to another downtown. You see what I'm saying? Hey, I had kids once. Just like you," he said.

I waited with the cups and watched him struggle up from the sofa.

He said, "They're what gave me this."

I took a good look at those hooks.

"Thanks for the coffee and the use of the toilet. I sympathize."
He raised and lowered his hooks.

"Show me," I said. "Show me how much. Take more pictures of me and my house."

"It won't work," the man said. "They're not coming back."
But I helped him get into his straps.

"I can give you a rate," he said. "Three for a dollar." He said, "If I go any lower, I don't come out."

We went outside. He adjusted the shutter. He told me where to stand, and we got down to it.

We moved around the house. Systematic. Sometimes I'd look sideways. Sometimes I'd look straight ahead.

"Good," he'd say. "That's good," he'd say, until we'd circled the house and were back in the front again. "That's twenty. That's enough."

"No," I said. "On the roof," I said.

"Jesus," he said. He checked up and down the block. "Sure," he said. "Now you're talking."

I said, "The whole kit and kaboodle. They cleared right out."

"Look at this!" the man said, and again he held up his hooks.

I went inside and got a chair. I put it up under the carport. But it didn't reach. So I got a crate and put the crate on top of the chair.

It was okay up there on the roof.

I stood up and looked around. I waved, and the man with no hands waved back with his hooks.

It was then I saw them, the rocks. It was like a little rock nest on the screen over the chimney hole. You know kids. You know how they lob them up, thinking to sink one down your chimney.

"Ready?" I called, and I got a rock, and I waited until he had me in his viewfinder.

"Okay!" he called.

I laid back my arm and I hollered, "Now!" I threw that son of a bitch as far as I could throw it.

"I don't know," I heard him shout. "I don't do motion shots."

"Again!" I screamed, and took up another rock.

Mr. Coffee and Mr. Fixit

I'VE seen some things. I was going over to my mother's to stay a few nights. But just as I got to the top of the stairs, I looked and she was on the sofa kissing a man. It was summer. The door was open. The TV was going. That's one of the things I've seen.

My mother is sixty-five. She belongs to a singles club. Even so, it was hard. I stood with my hand on the railing and watched as the man kissed her. She was kissing him back, and the TV was going.

Things are better now. But back in those days, when my mother was putting out, I was out of work. My kids were crazy, and my wife was crazy. She was putting out too. The guy that was getting it was an unemployed aerospace engineer she'd met at AA. He was also crazy.

His name was Ross and he had six kids. He walked with a limp from a gunshot wound his first wife gave him.

I don't know what we were thinking of in those days.

This guy's second wife had come and gone, but it was his first wife who had shot him for not meeting his payments. I wish him well now. Ross. What a name! But it was different then. In those days I mentioned weapons. I'd say to my wife, "I think I'll get a Smith and Wesson." But I never did it.

Ross was a little guy. But not too little. He had a moustache and always wore a button-up sweater.

His one wife jailed him once. The second one did. I found out from my daughter that my wife went bail. My daughter Melody didn't like it any better than I did. About the bail. It wasn't that Melody was looking out for me. She wasn't looking out for either one of us, her mother or me neither. It was just that there was a serious cash thing and if some of it went to Ross, there'd be that much less for Melody. So Ross was on Melody's list. Also, she didn't like his kids, and his having so many of them. But in general Melody said Ross was all right.

He'd even told her fortune once.

—

231

This Ross guy spent his time repairing things, now that he had no regular job. But I'd seen his house from the outside. It was a mess. Junk all around. Two busted Plymouths in the yard.

In the first stages of the thing they had going, my wife claimed the guy collected antique cars. Those were her words, "antique cars." But they were just clunkers.

I had his number. Mr. Fixit.

But we had things in common, Ross and me, which was more than just the same woman. For example, he couldn't fix the TV when it went crazy and we lost the picture. I couldn't fix it either. We had volume, but no picture. If we wanted the news, we had to sit around the screen and listen.

Ross and Myrna met when Myrna was trying to stay sober. She was going to meetings, I'd say, three or four times a week. I had been in and out myself. But when Myrna met Ross, I was out and drinking a fifth a day. Myrna went to the meetings, and then she went over to Mr. Fixit's house to cook for him and clean up. His kids were no help in this regard. Nobody lifted a hand around Mr. Fixit's house, except my wife when she was there.

All this happened not too long ago, three years about. It was something in those days.

I left my mother with the man on her sofa and drove around for a while. When I got home, Myrna made me a coffee.

She went out to the kitchen to do it while I waited until I heard her running water. Then I reached under a cushion for the bottle.

I think maybe Myrna really loved the man. But he also had a little something on the side—a twenty-two-year-old named Beverly. Mr. Fixit did okay for a little guy who wore a button-up sweater.

He was in his mid-thirties when he went under. Lost his job and took up the bottle. I used to make fun of him when I had the chance. But I don't make fun of him anymore.

God bless and keep you, Mr. Fixit.

He told Melody he'd worked on the moon shots. He told my daughter he was close friends with the astronauts. He told her he was going to introduce her to the astronauts as soon as they came to town.

It's a modern operation out there, the aerospace place where Mr. Fixit used to work. I've seen it. Cafeteria lines, executive dining rooms, and the like. Mr. Coffees in every office.

Mr. Coffee and Mr. Fixit.

Myrna says he was interested in astrology, auras, I Ching—that business. I don't doubt that this Ross was bright enough and interesting, like most of our ex-friends. I told Myrna I was sure she wouldn't have cared for him if he wasn't.

My dad died in his sleep, drunk, eight years ago. It was a Friday noon and he was fifty-four. He came home from work at the sawmill, took some sausage out of the freezer for his breakfast, and popped a quart of Four Roses.

My mother was there at the same kitchen table. She was trying to write a letter to her sister in Little Rock. Finally, my dad got up and went to bed. My mother said he never said good night. But it was morning, of course.

"Honey," I said to Myrna the night she came home. "Let's hug awhile and then you fix us a real nice supper."

Myrna said, "Wash your hands."

Gazebo

THAT morning she pours Teacher's over my belly and licks it off. That afternoon she tries to jump out the window.

I go, "Holly, this can't continue. This has got to stop."

We are sitting on the sofa in one of the upstairs suites. There were any number of vacancies to choose from. But we needed a suite, a place to move around in and be able to talk. So we'd locked up the motel office that morning and gone upstairs to a suite.

She goes, "Duane, this is killing me."

We are drinking Teacher's with ice and water. We'd slept awhile between morning and afternoon. Then she was out of bed and threatening to climb out the window in her undergarments. I had to get her in a hold. We were only two floors up. But even so.

"I've had it," she goes. "I can't take it anymore."

She puts her hand to her cheek and closes her eyes. She turns her head back and forth and makes this humming noise.

I could die seeing her like this.

"Take what?" I go, though of course I know.

"I don't have to spell it out for you again," she goes. "I've lost control. I've lost pride. I used to be a proud woman."

She's an attractive woman just past thirty. She is tall and has long black hair and green eyes, the only green-eyed woman I've ever known. In the old days I used to say things about her green eyes, and she'd tell me it was because of them she knew she was meant for something special.

And didn't I know it!

I feel so awful from one thing and the other.

I can hear the telephone ringing downstairs in the office. It has been ringing off and on all day. Even when I was dozing I could hear it. I'd open my eyes and look at the ceiling and listen to it ring and wonder at what was happening to us.

But maybe I should be looking at the floor.

"My heart is broken," she goes. "It's turned to a piece of

stone. I'm no good. That's what's as bad as anything, that I'm no good anymore."

"Holly," I go.

When we'd first moved down here and taken over as managers, we thought we were out of the woods. Free rent and free utilities plus three hundred a month. You couldn't beat it with a stick.

Holly took care of the books. She was good with figures, and she did most of the renting of the units. She liked people, and people liked her back. I saw to the grounds, mowed the grass and cut weeds, kept the swimming pool clean, did the small repairs.

Everything was fine for the first year. I was holding down another job nights, and we were getting ahead. We had plans. Then one morning, I don't know. I'd just laid some bathroom tile in one of the units when this little Mexican maid comes in to clean. It was Holly had hired her. I can't really say I'd noticed the little thing before, though we spoke when we saw each other. She called me, I remember, Mister.

Anyway, one thing and the other.

So after that morning I started paying attention. She was a neat little thing with fine white teeth. I used to watch her mouth.

She started calling me by my name.

One morning I was doing a washer for one of the bathroom faucets, and she comes in and turns on the TV as maids are like to do. While they clean, that is. I stopped what I was doing and stepped outside the bathroom. She was surprised to see me. She smiles and says my name.

It was right after she said it that we got down on the bed.

"Holly, you're still a proud woman," I go. "You're still number one. Come on, Holly."

She shakes her head.

"Something's died in me," she goes. "It took a long time for it to do it, but it's dead. You've killed something, just like you'd took an axe to it. Everything is dirt now."

She finishes her drink. Then she begins to cry. I make to hug her. But it's no good.

I freshen our drinks and look out the window.

Two cars with out-of-state plates are parked in front of the office, and the drivers are standing at the door, talking. One of them finishes saying something to the other, and looks around at the units and pulls his chin. There's a woman there too, and she has her face up to the glass, hand shielding her eyes, peering inside. She tries the door.

The phone downstairs begins to ring.

"Even a while ago when we were doing it, you were thinking of her," Holly goes. "Duane, this is hurtful."

She takes the drink I give her.

"Holly," I go.

"It's true, Duane," she goes. "Just don't argue with me," she goes.

She walks up and down the room in her underpants and her brassiere, her drink in her hand.

Holly goes, "You've gone outside the marriage. It's trust that you killed."

I get down on my knees and I start to beg. But I am thinking of Juanita. This is awful. I don't know what's going to happen to me or to anyone else in the world.

I go, "Holly, honey, I love you."

In the lot someone leans on a horn, stops, and then leans again.

Holly wipes her eyes. She goes, "Fix me a drink. This one's too watery. Let them blow their stinking horns. I don't care. I'm moving to Nevada."

"Don't move to Nevada," I go. "You're talking crazy," I go.

"I'm not talking crazy," she goes. "Nothing's crazy about Nevada. You can stay here with your cleaning woman. I'm moving to Nevada. Either there or kill myself."

"Holly!" I go.

"Holly *nothing*!" she goes.

She sits on the sofa and draws her knees up to under her chin.

"Fix me another pop, you son of a bitch," she goes. She goes, "Fuck those horn-blowers. Let them do their dirt in the Travelodge. Is that where your cleaning woman cleans now? Fix me another, you son of a bitch!"

She sets her lips and gives me her special look.

—

Drinking's funny. When I look back on it, all of our important decisions have been figured out when we were drinking. Even when we talked about having to cut back on our drinking, we'd be sitting at the kitchen table or out at the picnic table with a six-pack or whiskey. When we made up our minds to move down here and take this job as managers, we sat up a couple of nights drinking while we weighed the pros and the cons.

I pour the last of the Teacher's into our glasses and add cubes and a spill of water.

Holly gets off the sofa and stretches on out across the bed.

She goes, "Did you do it to her in this bed?"

I don't have anything to say. I feel all out of words inside. I give her the glass and sit down in the chair. I drink my drink and think it's not ever going to be the same.

"Duane?" she goes.

"Holly?"

My heart has slowed. I wait.

Holly was my own true love.

The thing with Juanita was five days a week between the hours of ten and eleven. It was in whatever unit she was in when she was making her cleaning rounds. I'd just walk in where she was working and shut the door behind me.

But mostly it was in 11. It was 11 that was our lucky room.

We were sweet with each other, but swift. It was fine.

I think Holly could maybe have weathered it out. I think the thing she had to do was really give it a try.

Me, I held on to the night job. A monkey could do that work. But things here were going downhill fast. We just didn't have the heart for it anymore.

I stopped cleaning the pool. It filled up with green gick so that the guests wouldn't use it anymore. I didn't fix any more faucets or lay any more tile or do any of the touch-up painting. Well, the truth is we were both hitting it pretty hard. Booze takes a lot of time and effort if you're going to do a good job with it.

Holly wasn't registering the guests right, either. She was charging too much or else not collecting what she should.

Sometimes she'd put three people to a room with only one bed in it, or else she'd put a single in where the bed was a king-size. I tell you, there were complaints, and sometimes there were words. Folks would load up and go somewhere else.

The next thing, there's a letter from the management people. Then there's another, certified.

There's telephone calls. There's someone coming down from the city.

But we had stopped caring, and that's a fact. We knew our days were numbered. We had fouled our lives and we were getting ready for a shake-up.

Holly's a smart woman. She knew it first.

Then that Saturday morning we woke up after a night of re-hashing the situation. We opened our eyes and turned in bed to take a good look at each other. We both knew it then. We'd reached the end of something, and the thing was to find out where new to start.

We got up and got dressed, had coffee, and decided on this talk. Without nothing interrupting. No calls. No guests.

That's when I got the Teacher's. We locked up and came upstairs here with ice, glasses, bottles. First off, we watched the color TV and frolicked some and let the phone ring away downstairs. For food, we went out and got cheese crisps from the machine.

There was this funny thing of anything could happen now that we realized everything had.

"When we were just kids before we married?" Holly goes. "When we had big plans and hopes? You remember?" She was sitting on the bed, holding her knees and her drink.

"I remember, Holly."

"You weren't my first, you know. My first was Wyatt. Imagine. Wyatt. And your name's Duane. Wyatt and Duane. Who knows what I was missing all those years? You were my everything, just like the song."

I go, "You're a wonderful woman, Holly. I know you've had the opportunities."

"But I didn't take them up on it!" she goes. "I couldn't go outside the marriage."

"Holly, please," I go. "No more now, honey. Let's not torture ourselves. What is it we should do?"

"Listen," she goes. "You remember the time we drove out to that old farm place outside of Yakima, out past Terrace Heights? We were just driving around? We were on this little dirt road and it was hot and dusty? We kept going and came to that old house, and you asked if could we have a drink of water? Can you imagine us doing that now? Going up to a house and asking for a drink of water?

"Those old people must be dead now," she goes, "side by side out there in some cemetery. You remember they asked us in for cake? And later on they showed us around? And there was this gazebo there out back? It was out back under some trees? It had a little peaked roof and the paint was gone and there were these weeds growing up over the steps. And the woman said that years before, I mean a real long time ago, men used to come around and play music out there on a Sunday, and the people would sit and listen. I thought we'd be like that too when we got old enough. Dignified. And in a place. And people would come to our door."

I can't say anything just yet. Then I go, "Holly, these things, we'll look back on them too. We'll go, 'Remember the motel with all the crud in the pool?'" I go, "You see what I'm saying, Holly?"

But Holly just sits there on the bed with her glass.

I can see she doesn't know.

I move over to the window and look out from behind the curtain. Someone says something below and rattles the door to the office. I stay there. I pray for a sign from Holly. I pray for Holly to show me.

I hear a car start. Then another. They turn on their lights against the building and, one after the other, they pull away and go out into the traffic.

"Duane," Holly goes.

In this, too, she was right.

I Could See the Smallest Things

I WAS in bed when I heard the gate. I listened carefully. I
didn't hear anything else. But I heard that. I tried to wake
Cliff. He was passed out. So I got up and went to the window.
A big moon was laid over the mountains that went around the
city. It was a white moon and covered with scars. Any damn
fool could imagine a face there.

There was light enough so that I could see everything in the
yard—lawn chairs, the willow tree, clothesline strung between
the poles, the petunias, the fences, the gate standing wide open.

But nobody was moving around. There were no scary shadows. Everything lay in moonlight, and I could see the smallest
things. The clothespins on the line, for instance.

I put my hands on the glass to block out the moon. I looked
some more. I listened. Then I went back to bed.

But I couldn't get to sleep. I kept turning over. I thought
about the gate standing open. It was like a dare.

Cliff's breathing was awful to listen to. His mouth gaped
open and his arms hugged his pale chest. He was taking up his
side of the bed and most of mine.

I pushed and pushed on him. But he just groaned.

I stayed still awhile longer until I decided it was no use. I
got up and got my slippers. I went to the kitchen and made tea
and sat with it at the kitchen table. I smoked one of Cliff's unfiltereds.

It was late. I didn't want to look at the time. I drank the tea
and smoked another cigarette. After a while I decided I'd go
out and fasten up the gate.

So I got my robe.

The moon lighted up everything—houses and trees, poles
and power lines, the whole world. I peered around the backyard before I stepped off the porch. A little breeze came along
that made me close the robe.

I started for the gate.

There was a noise at the fences that separated our place from
Sam Lawton's place. I took a sharp look. Sam was leaning with

his arms on his fence, there being two fences to lean on. He raised his fist to his mouth and gave a dry cough.

"Evening, Nancy," Sam Lawton said.

I said, "Sam, you scared me." I said, "What are you doing up?" "Did you hear something?" I said. "I heard my gate unlatch."

He said, "I didn't hear anything. Haven't seen anything, either. It might have been the wind."

He was chewing something. He looked at the open gate and shrugged.

His hair was silvery in the moonlight and stood up on his head. I could see his long nose, the lines in his big sad face.

I said, "What are you doing up, Sam?" and moved closer to the fence.

"Want to see something?" he said.

"I'll come around," I said.

I let myself out and went along the walk. It felt funny walking around outside in my nightgown and my robe. I thought to myself that I should try to remember this, walking around outside like this.

Sam was standing over by the side of his house, his pajamas way up high over his tan-and-white shoes. He was holding a flashlight in one hand and a can of something in the other.

Sam and Cliff used to be friends. Then one night they got to drinking. They had words. The next thing, Sam had built a fence and then Cliff built one too.

That was after Sam had lost Millie, gotten married again, and become a father again all in the space of no time at all. Millie had been a good friend to me up until she died. She was only forty-five when she did it. Heart failure. It hit her just as she was coming into their drive. The car kept going and went on through the back of the carport.

"Look at this," Sam said, hitching his pajama trousers and squatting down. He pointed his light at the ground.

I looked and saw some wormy things curled on a patch of dirt.

"Slugs," he said. "I just gave them a dose of this," he said, raising a can of something that looked like Ajax. "They're taking over," he said, and worked whatever it was that he had in his mouth. He turned his head to one side and spit what could have been tobacco. "I have to keep at this to just come close to staying up with them." He turned his light on a jar that was filled with the things. "I put bait out, and then every chance I get I come out here with this stuff. Bastards are all over. A crime what they can do. Look here," he said.

He got up. He took my arm and moved me over to his rosebushes. He showed me the little holes in the leaves.

"Slugs," he said. "Everywhere you look around here at night. I lay out bait and then I come out and get them," he said. "An awful invention, the slug. I save them up in that jar there." He moved his light to under the rosebush.

A plane passed overhead. I imagined the people on it sitting belted in their seats, some of them reading, some of them staring down at the ground.

"Sam," I said, "how's everybody?"

"They're fine," he said, and shrugged.

He chewed on whatever it was he was chewing. "How's Clifford?" he said.

I said, "Same as ever."

Sam said, "Sometimes when I'm out here after the slugs, I'll look over in your direction." He said, "I wish me and Cliff was friends again. Look there now," he said, and drew a sharp breath. "There's one there. See him? Right there where my light is." He had the beam directed onto the dirt under the rosebush. "Watch this," Sam said.

I closed my arms under my breasts and bent over to where he was shining his light. The thing stopped moving and turned its head from side to side. Then Sam was over it with his can of powder, sprinkling the powder down.

"Slimy things," he said.

The slug was twisting this way and that. Then it curled and straightened out.

Sam picked up a toy shovel, and scooped the slug into it, and dumped it out in the jar.

"I quit, you know," Sam said. "Had to. For a while it was getting so I didn't know up from down. We still keep it around the house, but I don't have much to do with it anymore."

I nodded. He looked at me and he kept looking.

"I'd better get back," I said.

"Sure," he said. "I'll continue with what I'm doing and then when I'm finished, I'll head in too."

I said, "Good night, Sam."

He said, "Listen." He stopped chewing. With his tongue, he pushed whatever it was behind his lower lip. "Tell Cliff I said hello."

I said, "I'll tell him you said so, Sam."

Sam ran his hand through his silvery hair as if he was going to make it sit down once and for all, and then he used his hand to wave.

In the bedroom, I took off the robe, folded it, put it within reach. Without looking at the time, I checked to make sure the stem was out on the clock. Then I got into the bed, pulled the covers up, and closed my eyes.

It was then that I remembered I'd forgotten to latch the gate.

I opened my eyes and lay there. I gave Cliff a little shake. He cleared his throat. He swallowed. Something caught and dribbled in his chest.

I don't know. It made me think of those things that Sam Lawton was dumping powder on.

I thought for a minute of the world outside my house, and then I didn't have any more thoughts except the thought that I had to hurry up and sleep.

Sacks

IT's October, a damp day. From my hotel window I can see too much of this Midwestern city. I can see lights coming on in some of the buildings, smoke from the tall stacks rising in a thick climb. I wish I didn't have to look.

I want to pass along to you a story my father told me when I stopped over in Sacramento last year. It concerns some events that involved him two years before that time, that time being before he and my mother were divorced.

I'm a book salesman. I represent a well-known organization. We put out textbooks, and the home base is Chicago. My territory is Illinois, parts of Iowa and Wisconsin. I had been attending the Western Book Publishers Association convention in Los Angeles when it occurred to me to visit a few hours with my father. I had not seen him since the divorce, you understand. So I got his address out of my wallet and sent him a wire. The next morning I sent my things on to Chicago and boarded a plane for Sacramento.

It took me a minute to pick him out. He was standing where everyone else was—behind the gate, that is—white hair, glasses, brown Sta-Prest pants.

"Dad, how are you?" I said.

He said, "Les."

We shook hands and moved toward the terminal.

"How's Mary and the kids?" he said.

"Everyone's fine," I said, which was not the truth.

He opened a white confectionary sack. He said, "I picked up a little something you could maybe take back with you. Not much. Some Almond Roca for Mary, and some jellybeans for the kids."

"Thanks," I said.

"Don't forget this when you leave," he said.

We moved out of the way as some nuns came running for the boarding area.

"A drink or a cup of coffee?" I said.

"Anything you say," he said. "But I don't have a car," he said.

244

We located the lounge, got drinks, lit cigarettes.

"Here we are," I said.

"Well, yes," he said.

I shrugged and said, "Yes."

I leaned back in the seat and drew a long breath, inhaling from what I took to be the air of woe that circled his head.

He said, "I guess the Chicago airport would make four of this one."

"More than that," I said.

"Thought it was big," he said.

"When did you start wearing glasses?" I said.

"A while ago," he said.

He took a good swallow, and then he got right down to it.

"I liked to have died over it," he said. He rested his heavy arms on either side of his glass. "You're an educated man, Les. You'll be the one to figure it out."

I turned the ashtray on its edge to read what was on the bottom: HARRAH'S CLUB/RENO AND LAKE TAHOE/GOOD PLACES TO HAVE FUN.

"She was a Stanley Products woman. A little woman, small feet and hands and coal-black hair. She wasn't the most beautiful thing in the world. But she had these nice ways about her. She was thirty and had kids. But she was a decent woman, whatever happened.

"Your mother was always buying from her, a broom, a mop, some kind of pie filling. You know your mother. It was a Saturday, and I was home. Your mother was gone someplace. I don't know where she was. She wasn't working. I was in the front room reading the paper and having a cup of coffee when there was this knock on the door and it was this little woman. Sally Wain. She said she had some things for Mrs. Palmer. 'I'm Mr. Palmer,' I says. 'Mrs. Palmer is not here now,' I says. I ask her just to step in, you know, and I'd pay her for the things. She didn't know whether she should or not. Just stands there holding this little paper sack and the receipt with it.

"'Here, I'll take that,' I says. 'Why don't you come in and sit down a minute till I see if I can find some money.'

"'That's all right,' she says. 'You can owe it. I have lots of people do that. It's all right.' She smiles to let me know it was all right, you see.

" 'No, no,' I says. 'I've got it. I'd sooner pay it now. Save you a trip back and save me owing. Come in,' I said, and I hold the screen door open. It wasn't polite to have her standing out there."

He coughed and took one of my cigarettes. From down the bar a woman laughed. I looked at her and then I read from the ashtray again.

"She steps in, and I says, 'Just a minute, please,' and I go into the bedroom to look for my wallet. I look around on the dresser, but I can't find it. I find some change and matches and my comb, but I can't find my wallet. Your mother has gone through that morning cleaning up, you see. So I go back to the front room and says, 'Well, I'll turn up some money yet.'

" 'Please, don't bother,' she says.

" 'No bother,' I says. 'Have to find my wallet, anyway. Make yourself at home.'

" 'Oh, I'm fine,' she says.

" 'Look here,' I says. 'You hear about that big holdup back East? I was just reading about it.'

" 'I saw it on the TV last night,' she says.

" 'They got away clean,' I says.

" 'Pretty slick,' she says.

" 'The perfect crime,' I says.

" 'Not many people get away with it,' she says.

"I didn't know what else to say. We were just standing there looking at each other. So I went on out to the porch and looked for my pants in the hamper, where I figured your mother had put them. I found the wallet in my back pocket and went back to the other room and asked how much I owed.

"It was three or four dollars, and I paid her. Then, I don't know why, I asked her what she'd do with it if she had it, all the money those robbers got away with.

"She laughed and I saw her teeth.

"I don't know what came over me then, Les. Fifty-five years old. Grown kids. I knew better than that. This woman was half my age with little kids in school. She did this Stanley job just the hours they were in school, just to give her something to keep busy. She didn't have to work. They had enough to get by on. Her husband, Larry, he was a driver for Consolidated Freight. Made good money. Teamster, you know."

He stopped and wiped his face.

"Anybody can make a mistake," I said.

He shook his head.

"She had these two boys, Hank and Freddy. About a year apart. She showed me some pictures. Anyway, she laughs when I say that about the money, says she guessed she'd quit selling Stanley Products and move to Dago and buy a house. She said she had relations in Dago."

I lit another cigarette. I looked at my watch. The bartender raised his eyebrows and I raised my glass.

"So she's sitting down on the sofa now and she asks me do I have a cigarette. Said she'd left hers in her other purse, and how she hadn't had a smoke since she left home. Says she hated to buy from a machine when she had a carton at home. I gave her a cigarette and I hold a match for her. But I can tell you, Les, my fingers were shaking."

He stopped and studied the bottles for a minute. The woman who'd done the laughing had her arms locked through the arms of the men on either side of her.

"It's fuzzy after that. I remember I asked her if she wanted coffee. Said I'd just made a fresh pot. She said she had to be going. She said maybe she had time for one cup. I went out to the kitchen and waited for the coffee to heat. I tell you, Les, I'll swear before God, I never once stepped out on your mother the whole time we were man and wife. Not once. There were times when I felt like it and had the chance. I tell you, you don't know your mother like I do."

I said, "You don't have to say anything in that direction."

"I took her her coffee, and she's taken off her coat by now. I sit down on the other end of the sofa from her and we get to talking more personal. She says she's got two kids in Roosevelt grade school, and Larry, he was a driver and was sometimes gone for a week or two. Up to Seattle, or down to L.A., or maybe to Phoenix. Always someplace. She says she met Larry when they were going to high school. Said she was proud of the fact she'd gone all the way through. Well, pretty soon she gives a little laugh at something I'd said. It was a thing that could maybe be taken two ways. Then she asks if I'd heard the one about the traveling shoe-salesman who called on the widow woman. We laughed over that one, and then I told her one a little worse. So then she laughs hard at that and smokes another cigarette. One thing's leading to another, is what's happening, don't you see.

"Well, I kissed her then. I put her head back on the sofa and I kissed her, and I can feel her tongue out there rushing to get in my mouth. You see what I'm saying? A man can go along obeying all the rules and then it don't matter a damn anymore. His luck just goes, you know?

"But it was all over in no time at all. And afterwards she says, 'You must think I'm a whore or something,' and then she just goes.

"I was so excited, you know? I fixed up the sofa and turned over the cushions. I folded all the newspapers and even washed the cups we'd used. I cleaned out the coffee pot. All the time what I was thinking about was how I was going to have to face your mother. I was scared.

"Well, that's how it started. Your mother and I went along the same as usual. But I took to seeing that woman regular."

The woman down the bar got off her stool. She took some steps toward the center of the floor and commenced to dance. She tossed her head from side to side and snapped her fingers. The bartender stopped doing drinks. The woman raised her arms above her head and moved in a small circle in the middle of the floor. But then she stopped doing it and the bartender went back to work.

"Did you see that?" my father said.

But I didn't say anything at all.

"So that's the way it went," he said. "Larry has this schedule, and I'd be over there every time I had the chance. I'd tell your mother I was going here or going there."

He took off his glasses and shut his eyes. "I haven't told this to nobody."

There was nothing to say to that. I looked out at the field and then at my watch.

"Listen," he said. "What time does your plane leave? Can you take a different plane? Let me buy us another drink, Les. Order us two more. I'll speed it up. I'll be through with this in a minute. *Listen*," he said.

"She kept his picture in the bedroom by the bed. First it bothered me, seeing his picture there and all. But after a while I got used to it. You see how a man gets used to things?" He shook his head. "Hard to believe. Well, it all come to a bad end. You know that. You know all about that."

"I only know what you tell me," I said.

"I'll tell you, Les. I'll tell you what's the most important thing involved here. You see, there are things. More important things than your mother leaving me. Now, you listen to this. We were in bed one time. It must have been around lunch-time. We were just laying there talking. I was dozing maybe. It's that funny kind of dreaming dozing, you know. But at the same time, I'm telling myself I better remember that pretty soon I got to get up and go. So it's like this when this car pulls into the driveway and somebody gets out and slams the door.

" 'My God,' she screams. 'It's Larry!'

"I must have gone crazy. I seem to remember thinking that if I run out the back door he's going to pin me up against this big fence in the yard and maybe kill me. Sally is making a funny kind of sound. Like she couldn't get her breath. She has her robe on, but it's not closed up, and she's standing in the kitchen shaking her head. All this is happening all at once, you understand. So there I am, almost naked with my clothes in my hand, and Larry is opening the front door. Well, I jump. I just jump right into their picture window, right in there through the glass."

"You got away?" I said. "He didn't come after you?"

My father looked at me as if I were crazy. He stared at his empty glass. I looked at my watch, stretched. I had a small headache behind my eyes.

I said, "I guess I better be getting out there soon." I ran my hand over my chin and straightened my collar. "She still in Redding, that woman?"

"You don't know anything, do you?" my father said. "You don't know anything at all. You don't know anything except how to sell books."

It was almost time to go.

"Ah, God, I'm sorry," he said. "The man went all to pieces, is what. He got down on the floor and cried. She stayed out in the kitchen. She did her crying out there. She got down on her knees and she prayed to God, good and loud so the man would hear."

My father started to say something more. But instead he shook his head. Maybe he wanted me to say something.

But then he said, "No, you got to catch a plane."

I helped him into his coat and we started out, my hand guiding him by the elbow.

"I'll put you in a cab," I said.

He said, "I'll see you off."

"That's all right," I said. "Next time maybe."

We shook hands. That was the last I've seen of him. On the way to Chicago, I remembered how I'd left his sack of gifts on the bar. Just as well. Mary didn't need candy, Almond Roca or anything else.

That was last year. She needs it now even less.

The Bath

SATURDAY afternoon the mother drove to the bakery in the shopping center. After looking through a loose-leaf binder with photographs of cakes taped onto the pages, she ordered chocolate, the child's favorite. The cake she chose was decorated with a spaceship and a launching pad under a sprinkling of white stars. The name SCOTTY would be iced on in green as if it were the name of the spaceship.

The baker listened thoughtfully when the mother told him Scotty would be eight years old. He was an older man, this baker, and he wore a curious apron, a heavy thing with loops that went under his arms and around his back and then crossed in front again where they were tied in a very thick knot. He kept wiping his hands on the front of the apron as he listened to the woman, his wet eyes examining her lips as she studied the samples and talked.

He let her take her time. He was in no hurry.

The mother decided on the spaceship cake, and then she gave the baker her name and her telephone number. The cake would be ready Monday morning, in plenty of time for the party Monday afternoon. This was all the baker was willing to say. No pleasantries, just this small exchange, the barest information, nothing that was not necessary.

Monday morning, the boy was walking to school. He was in the company of another boy, the two boys passing a bag of potato chips back and forth between them. The birthday boy was trying to trick the other boy into telling what he was going to give in the way of a present.

At an intersection, without looking, the birthday boy stepped off the curb, and was promptly knocked down by a car. He fell on his side, his head in the gutter, his legs in the road moving as if he were climbing a wall.

The other boy stood holding the potato chips. He was wondering if he should finish the rest or continue on to school.

The birthday boy did not cry. But neither did he wish to talk anymore. He would not answer when the other boy asked what it felt like to be hit by a car. The birthday boy got up and turned back for home, at which time the other boy waved good-bye and headed off for school.

The birthday boy told his mother what had happened. They sat together on the sofa. She held his hands in her lap. This is what she was doing when the boy pulled his hands away and lay down on his back.

Of course, the birthday party never happened. The birthday boy was in the hospital instead. The mother sat by the bed. She was waiting for the boy to wake up. The father hurried over from his office. He sat next to the mother. So now the both of them waited for the boy to wake up. They waited for hours, and then the father went home to take a bath.

The man drove home from the hospital. He drove the streets faster than he should. It had been a good life till now. There had been work, fatherhood, family. The man had been lucky and happy. But fear made him want a bath.

He pulled into the driveway. He sat in the car trying to make his legs work. The child had been hit by a car and he was in the hospital, but he was going to be all right. The man got out of the car and went up to the door. The dog was barking and the telephone was ringing. It kept ringing while the man unlocked the door and felt the wall for the light switch.

He picked up the receiver. He said, "I just got in the door!"

"There's a cake that wasn't picked up."

This is what the voice on the other end said.

"What are you saying?" the father said.

"The cake," the voice said. "Sixteen dollars."

The husband held the receiver against his ear, trying to understand. He said, "I don't know anything about it."

"Don't hand me that," the voice said.

The husband hung up the telephone. He went into the kitchen and poured himself some whiskey. He called the hospital.

The child's condition remained the same.

While the water ran into the tub, the man lathered his face and shaved. He was in the tub when he heard the telephone again. He got himself out and hurried through the house, saying, "Stupid, stupid," because he wouldn't be doing this if he'd stayed where he was in the hospital. He picked up the receiver and shouted, "Hello!"

The voice said, "It's ready."

The father got back to the hospital after midnight. The wife was sitting in the chair by the bed. She looked up at the husband and then she looked back at the child. From an apparatus over the bed hung a bottle with a tube running from the bottle to the child.

"What's this?" the father said.

"Glucose," the mother said.

The husband put his hand to the back of the woman's head. "He's going to wake up," the man said.

"I know," the woman said.

In a little while the man said, "Go home and let me take over." She shook her head. "No," she said.

"Really," he said. "Go home for a while. You don't have to worry. He's sleeping, is all."

A nurse pushed open the door. She nodded to them as she went to the bed. She took the left arm out from under the covers and put her fingers on the wrist. She put the arm back under the covers and wrote on the clipboard attached to the bed.

"How is he?" the mother said.

"Stable," the nurse said. Then she said, "Doctor will be in again shortly."

"I was saying maybe she'd want to go home and get a little rest," the man said. "After the doctor comes."

"She could do that," the nurse said.

The woman said, "We'll see what the doctor says." She brought her hand up to her eyes and leaned her head forward.

The nurse said, "Of course."

The father gazed at his son, the small chest inflating and deflating under the covers. He felt more fear now. He began shaking his head. He talked to himself like this. The child is fine. Instead of sleeping at home, he's doing it here. Sleep is the same wherever you do it.

The doctor came in. He shook hands with the man. The woman got up from the chair.

"Ann," the doctor said and nodded. The doctor said, "Let's just see how he's doing." He moved to the bed and touched the boy's wrist. He peeled back an eyelid and then the other. He turned back the covers and listened to the heart. He pressed his fingers here and there on the body. He went to the end of the bed and studied the chart. He noted the time, scribbled on the chart, and then he considered the mother and the father.

This doctor was a handsome man. His skin was moist and tan. He wore a three-piece suit, a vivid tie, and on his shirt were cufflinks.

The mother was talking to herself like this. He has just come from somewhere with an audience. They gave him a special medal.

The doctor said, "Nothing to shout about, but nothing to worry about. He should wake up pretty soon." The doctor looked at the boy again. "We'll know more after the tests are in."

"Oh, no," the mother said.

The doctor said, "Sometimes you see this."

The father said, "You wouldn't call this a coma, then?"

The father waited and looked at the doctor.

"No, I don't want to call it that," the doctor said. "He's sleeping. It's restorative. The body is doing what it has to do."

"It's a coma," the mother said. "A kind of coma."

The doctor said, "I wouldn't call it that."

He took the woman's hands and patted them. He shook hands with the husband.

The woman put her fingers on the child's forehead and kept them there for a while. "At least he doesn't have a fever," she said. Then she said, "I don't know. Feel his head."

The man put his fingers on the boy's forehead. The man said, "I think he's supposed to feel this way."

The woman stood there awhile longer, working her lip with her teeth. Then she moved to her chair and sat down.

The husband sat in the chair beside her. He wanted to say something else. But there was no saying what it should be. He took her hand and put it in his lap. This made him feel better. It made him feel he was saying something. They sat like that for a while, watching the boy, not talking. From time to time he squeezed her hand until she took it away.

"I've been praying," she said.

"Me too," the father said. "I've been praying too."

A nurse came back in and checked the flow from the bottle.

A doctor came in and said what his name was. This doctor was wearing loafers.

"We're going to take him downstairs for more pictures," he said. "And we want to do a scan."

"A scan?" the mother said. She stood between this new doctor and the bed.

"It's nothing," he said.

"My God," she said.

Two orderlies came in. They wheeled a thing like a bed. They unhooked the boy from the tube and slid him over onto the thing with wheels.

It was after sunup when they brought the birthday boy back out. The mother and father followed the orderlies into the elevator and up to the room. Once more the parents took up their places next to the bed.

They waited all day. The boy did not wake up. The doctor came again and examined the boy again and left after saying the same things again. Nurses came in. Doctors came in. A technician came in and took blood.

"I don't understand this," the mother said to the technician.

"Doctor's orders," the technician said.

The mother went to the window and looked out at the parking lot. Cars with their lights on were driving in and out. She stood at the window with her hands on the sill. She was talking to herself like this. We're into something now, something hard.

She was afraid.

She saw a car stop and a woman in a long coat get into it. She made believe she was that woman. She made believe she was driving away from here to someplace else.

—

The doctor came in. He looked tanned and healthier than ever. He went to the bed and examined the boy. He said, "His signs are fine. Everything's good."

The mother said, "But he's sleeping."

"Yes," the doctor said.

The husband said, "She's tired. She's starved."

The doctor said, "She should rest. She should eat. Ann," the doctor said.

"Thank you," the husband said.

He shook hands with the doctor and the doctor patted their shoulders and left.

"I suppose one of us should go home and check on things," the man said. "The dog needs to be fed."

"Call the neighbors," the wife said. "Someone will feed him if you ask them to."

She tried to think who. She closed her eyes and tried to think anything at all. After a time she said, "Maybe I'll do it. Maybe if I'm not here watching, he'll wake up. Maybe it's because I'm watching that he won't."

"That could be it," the husband said.

"I'll go home and take a bath and put on something clean," the woman said.

"I think you should do that," the man said.

She picked up her purse. He helped her into her coat. She moved to the door, and looked back. She looked at the child, and then she looked at the father. The husband nodded and smiled.

She went past the nurses' station and down to the end of the corridor, where she turned and saw a little waiting room, a family in there, all sitting in wicker chairs, a man in a khaki shirt, a baseball cap pushed back on his head, a large woman wearing a housedress, slippers, a girl in jeans, hair in dozens of kinky braids, the table littered with flimsy wrappers and styrofoam and coffee sticks and packets of salt and pepper.

"Nelson," the woman said. "Is it about Nelson?"

The woman's eyes widened.

"Tell me now, lady," the woman said. "Is it about Nelson?"

The woman was trying to get up from her chair. But the man had his hand closed over her arm.

"Here, here," the man said.

"I'm sorry," the mother said. "I'm looking for the elevator. My son is in the hospital. I can't find the elevator."

"Elevator is down that way," the man said, and he aimed a finger in the right direction.

"My son was hit by a car," the mother said. "But he's going to be all right. He's in shock now, but it might be some kind of coma too. That's what worries us, the coma part. I'm going out for a little while. Maybe I'll take a bath. But my husband is with him. He's watching. There's a chance everything will change when I'm gone. My name is Ann Weiss."

The man shifted in his chair. He shook his head.

He said, "Our Nelson."

She pulled into the driveway. The dog ran out from behind the house. He ran in circles on the grass. She closed her eyes and leaned her head against the wheel. She listened to the ticking of the engine.

She got out of the car and went to the door. She turned on lights and put on water for tea. She opened a can and fed the dog. She sat down on the sofa with her tea.

The telephone rang.

"Yes!" she said. "Hello!" she said.

"Mrs. Weiss," a man's voice said.

"Yes," she said. "This is Mrs. Weiss. Is it about Scotty?" she said.

"Scotty," the voice said. "It is about Scotty," the voice said. "It has to do with Scotty, yes."

Tell the Women We're Going

BILL JAMISON had always been best friends with Jerry Roberts. The two grew up in the south area, near the old fairgrounds, went through grade school and junior high together, and then on to Eisenhower, where they took as many of the same teachers as they could manage, wore each other's shirts and sweaters and pegged pants, and dated and banged the same girls—whichever came up as a matter of course.

Summers they took jobs together—swamping peaches, picking cherries, stringing hops, anything they could do that paid a little and where there was no boss to get on your ass. And then they bought a car together. The summer before their senior year, they chipped in and bought a red '54 Plymouth for $325.

They shared it. It worked out fine.

But Jerry got married before the end of the first semester and dropped out of school to work steady at Robby's Mart.

As for Bill, he'd dated the girl too. Carol was her name, and she went just fine with Jerry, and Bill went over there every chance he got. It made him feel older, having married friends. He'd go over there for lunch or for supper, and they'd listen to Elvis or to Bill Haley and the Comets.

But sometimes Carol and Jerry would start making out right with Bill still there, and he'd have to get up and excuse himself and take a walk to Dezorn's Service Station to get some Coke because there was only the one bed in the apartment, a hideaway that came down in the living room. Or sometimes Jerry and Carol would head off to the bathroom, and Bill would have to move to the kitchen and pretend to be interested in the cupboards and the refrigerator and not trying to listen.

So he stopped going over so much; and then June he graduated, took a job at the Darigold plant, and joined the National Guard. In a year he had a milk route of his own and was going steady with Linda. So Bill and Linda would go over to Jerry and Carol's, drink beer, and listen to records.

Carol and Linda got along fine, and Bill was flattered when Carol said that, confidentially, Linda was "a real person."

Jerry liked Linda too. "She's great," Jerry said.

When Bill and Linda got married, Jerry was best man. The reception, of course, was at the Donnelly Hotel, Jerry and Bill cutting up together and linking arms and tossing off glasses of spiked punch. But once, in the middle of all this happiness, Bill looked at Jerry and thought how much older Jerry looked, a lot older than twenty-two. By then Jerry was the happy father of two kids and had moved up to assistant manager at Robby's, and Carol had one in the oven again.

They saw each other every Saturday and Sunday, sometimes oftener if it was a holiday. If the weather was good, they'd be over at Jerry's to barbecue hot dogs and turn the kids loose in the wading pool Jerry had got for next to nothing, like a lot of other things he got from the Mart.

Jerry had a nice house. It was up on a hill overlooking the Naches. There were other houses around, but not too close. Jerry was doing all right. When Bill and Linda and Jerry and Carol got together, it was always at Jerry's place because Jerry had the barbecue and the records and too many kids to drag around.

It was a Sunday at Jerry's place the time it happened.

The women were in the kitchen straightening up. Jerry's girls were out in the yard throwing a plastic ball into the wading pool, yelling, and splashing after it.

Jerry and Bill were sitting in the reclining chairs on the patio, drinking beer and just relaxing.

Bill was doing most of the talking—things about people they knew, about Darigold, about the four-door Pontiac Catalina he was thinking of buying.

Jerry was staring at the clothesline, or at the '68 Chevy hardtop that stood in the garage. Bill was thinking how Jerry was getting to be deep, the way he stared all the time and hardly did any talking at all.

Bill moved in his chair and lighted a cigarette.

He said, "Anything wrong, man? I mean, you know."

Jerry finished his beer and then mashed the can. He shrugged.

"You know," he said.

Bill nodded.

Then Jerry said, "How about a little run?"

"Sounds good to me," Bill said. "I'll tell the women we're going."

They took the Naches River highway out to Gleed, Jerry driving. The day was sunny and warm, and air blew through the car.

"Where we headed?" Bill said.

"Let's shoot a few balls."

"Fine with me," Bill said. He felt a whole lot better just seeing Jerry brighten up.

"Guy's got to get out," Jerry said. He looked at Bill. "You know what I mean?"

Bill understood. He liked to get out with the guys from the plant for the Friday-night bowling league. He liked to stop off twice a week after work to have a few beers with Jack Broderick. He knew a guy's got to get out.

"Still standing," Jerry said, as they pulled up onto the gravel in front of the Rec Center.

They went inside, Bill holding the door for Jerry, Jerry punching Bill lightly in the stomach as he went on by.

"Hey there!"

It was Riley.

"Hey, how you boys keeping?"

It was Riley coming around from behind the counter, grinning. He was a heavy man. He had on a short-sleeved Hawaiian shirt that hung outside his jeans. Riley said, "So how you boys been keeping?"

"Ah, dry up and give us a couple of Olys," Jerry said, winking at Bill. "So how you been, Riley?" Jerry said.

Riley said, "So how you boys doing? Where you been keeping yourselves? You boys getting any on the side? Jerry, the last time I seen you, your old lady was six months gone."

Jerry stood a minute and blinked his eyes.

"So how about the Olys?" Bill said.

They took stools near the window. Jerry said, "What kind of place is this, Riley, that it don't have any girls on a Sunday afternoon?"

Riley laughed. He said, "I guess they're all in church praying for it."

They each had five cans of beer and took two hours to play three racks of rotation and two racks of snooker, Riley sitting on a stool and talking and watching them play, Bill always looking at his watch and then looking at Jerry.

Bill said, "So what do you think, Jerry? I mean, what do you think?" Bill said.

Jerry drained his can, mashed it, then stood for a time turning the can in his hand.

Back on the highway, Jerry opened it up—little jumps of eighty-five and ninety. They'd just passed an old pickup loaded with furniture when they saw the two girls.

"Look at that!" Jerry said, slowing. "I could use some of that."

Jerry drove another mile or so and then pulled off the road. "Let's go back," Jerry said. "Let's try it."

"Jesus," Bill said. "I don't know."

"I could use some," Jerry said.

Bill said, "Yeah, but I don't know."

"For Christ's sake," Jerry said.

Bill glanced at his watch and then looked all around. He said, "You do the talking. I'm rusty."

Jerry hooted as he whipped the car around.

He slowed when he came nearly even with the girls. He pulled the Chevy onto the shoulder across from them. The girls kept on going on their bicycles, but they looked at each other and laughed. The one on the inside was dark-haired, tall, and willowy. The other was light-haired and smaller. They both wore shorts and halters.

"Bitches," Jerry said. He waited for the cars to pass so he could pull a U.

"I'll take the brunette," he said. He said, "The little one's yours."

Bill moved his back against the front seat and touched the bridge of his sunglasses. "They're not going to do anything," Bill said.

"They're going to be on your side," Jerry said.

He pulled across the road and drove back. "Get ready," Jerry said.

"Hi," Bill said as the girls bicycled up. "My name's Bill," Bill said.

"That's nice," the brunette said.

"Where are you going?" Bill said.

The girls didn't answer. The little one laughed. They kept bicycling and Jerry kept driving.

"Oh, come on now. Where you going?" Bill said.

"No place," the little one said.

"Where's no place?" Bill said.

"Wouldn't you like to know," the little one said.

"I told you my name," Bill said. "What's yours? My friend's Jerry," Bill said.

The girls looked at each other and laughed.

A car came up from behind. The driver hit his horn.

"Cram it!" Jerry shouted.

He pulled off a little and let the car go around. Then he pulled back up alongside the girls.

Bill said, "We'll give you a lift. We'll take you where you want. That's a promise. You must be tired riding those bicycles. You look tired. Too much exercise isn't good for a person. Especially for girls."

The girls laughed.

"You see?" Bill said. "Now tell us your names."

"I'm Barbara, she's Sharon," the little one said.

"All right!" Jerry said. "Now find out where they're going."

"Where you girls going?" Bill said. "Barb?"

She laughed. "No place," she said. "Just down the road."

"Where down the road?"

"Do you want me to tell them?" she said to the other girl.

"I don't care," the other girl said. "It doesn't make any difference," she said. "I'm not going to go anyplace with anybody anyway," the one named Sharon said.

"Where you going?" Bill said. "Are you going to Picture Rock?"

The girls laughed.

"That's where they're going," Jerry said.

He fed the Chevy gas and pulled up off onto the shoulder so that the girls had to come by on his side.

"Don't be that way," Jerry said. He said, "Come on." He said, "We're all introduced."

The girls just rode on by.

"I won't bite you!" Jerry shouted.

The brunette glanced back. It seemed to Jerry she was looking at him in the right kind of way. But with a girl you could never be sure.

Jerry gunned it back onto the highway, dirt and pebbles flying from under the tires.

"We'll be seeing you!" Bill called as they went speeding by.

"It's in the bag," Jerry said. "You see the look that cunt gave me?"

"I don't know," Bill said. "Maybe we should cut for home."

"We got it made!" Jerry said.

He pulled off the road under some trees. The highway forked here at Picture Rock, one road going on to Yakima, the other heading for Naches, Enumclaw, the Chinook Pass, Seattle.

A hundred yards off the road was a high, sloping, black mound of rock, part of a low range of hills, honeycombed with footpaths and small caves, Indian sign-painting here and there on the cave walls. The cliff side of the rock faced the highway and all over it there were things like this: NACHES 67—GLEED WILDCATS—JESUS SAVES—BEAT YAKIMA—REPENT NOW.

They sat in the car, smoking cigarettes. Mosquitoes came in and tried to get at their hands.

"Wish we had a beer now," Jerry said. "I sure could go for a beer," he said.

Bill said, "Me too," and looked at his watch.

When the girls came into view, Jerry and Bill got out of the car. They leaned against the fender in front.

"Remember," Jerry said, starting away from the car, "the dark one's mine. You got the other one."

The girls dropped their bicycles and started up one of the paths. They disappeared around a bend and then reappeared again, a little higher up. They were standing there and looking down.

"What're you guys following us for?" the brunette called down.

Jerry just started up the path.

The girls turned away and went off again at a trot.

Jerry and Bill kept climbing at a walking pace. Bill was smoking a cigarette, stopping every so often to get a good drag. When the path turned, he looked back and caught a glimpse of the car.

"Move it!" Jerry said.

"I'm coming," Bill said.

They kept climbing. But then Bill had to catch his breath. He couldn't see the car now. He couldn't see the highway, either. To his left and all the way down, he could see a strip of the Naches like a strip of aluminum foil.

Jerry said, "You go right and I'll go straight. We'll cut the cockteasers off."

Bill nodded. He was too winded to speak.

He went higher for a while, and then the path began to drop, turning toward the valley. He looked and saw the girls. He saw them crouched behind an outcrop. Maybe they were smiling.

Bill took out a cigarette. But he could not get it lit. Then Jerry showed up. It did not matter after that.

Bill had just wanted to fuck. Or even to see them naked. On the other hand, it was okay with him if it didn't work out.

He never knew what Jerry wanted. But it started and ended with a rock. Jerry used the same rock on both girls, first on the girl called Sharon and then on the one that was supposed to be Bill's.

After the Denim

EDITH PACKER had the tape cassette plugged into her ear, and she was smoking one of his cigarettes. The TV played without any volume as she sat on the sofa with her legs tucked under her and turned the pages of a magazine. James Packer came out of the guest room, which was the room he had fixed up as an office, and Edith Packer took the cord from her ear. She put the cigarette in the ashtray and pointed her foot and wiggled her toes in greeting.

He said, "Are we going or not?"

"I'm going," she said.

Edith Packer liked classical music. James Packer did not. He was a retired accountant. But he still did returns for some old clients, and he didn't like to hear music when he did it.

"If we're going, let's go."

He looked at the TV, and then went to turn it off.

"I'm going," she said.

She closed the magazine and got up. She left the room and went to the back.

He followed her to make sure the back door was locked and also that the porch light was on. Then he stood waiting and waiting in the living room.

It was a ten-minute drive to the community center, which meant they were going to miss the first game.

In the place where James always parked, there was an old van with markings on it, so he had to keep going to the end of the block.

"Lots of cars tonight," Edith said.

He said, "There wouldn't be so many if we'd been on time."

"There'd still be as many. It's just we wouldn't have seen them." She pinched his sleeve, teasing.

He said, "Edith, if we're going to play bingo, we ought to be here on time."

"Hush," Edith Packer said.

He found a parking space and turned into it. He switched off the engine and cut the lights. He said, "I don't know if I feel lucky tonight. I think I felt lucky when I was doing Howard's taxes. But I don't think I feel lucky now. It's not lucky if you have to start out walking half a mile just to play."

"You stick to me," Edith Packer said. "You'll feel lucky."

"I don't feel lucky yet," James said. "Lock your door."

There was a cold breeze. He zipped the windbreaker to his neck, and she pulled her coat closed. They could hear the surf breaking on the rocks at the bottom of the cliff behind the building.

She said, "I'll take one of your cigarettes first."

They stopped under the street lamp at the corner. It was a damaged street lamp, and wires had been added to support it. The wires moved in the wind, made shadows on the pavement.

"When are you going to stop?" he said, lighting his cigarette after he'd lighted hers.

"When you stop," she said. "I'll stop when you stop. Just like it was when you stopped drinking. Like that. Like you."

"I can teach you to do needlework," he said.

"One needleworker in the house is enough," she said.

He took her arm and they kept on walking.

When they reached the entrance, she dropped her cigarette and stepped on it. They went up the steps and into the foyer. There was a sofa in the room, a wooden table, folding chairs stacked up. On the walls were hung photographs of fishing boats and naval vessels, one showing a boat that had turned over, a man standing on the keel and waving.

The Packers passed through the foyer, James taking Edith's arm as they entered the corridor.

Some clubwomen sat to the side of the far doorway signing people in as they entered the assembly hall, where a game was already in progress, the numbers being called by a woman who stood on the stage.

The Packers hurried to their regular table. But a young couple occupied the Packers' usual places. The girl wore denims, and so did the long-haired man with her. She had rings and bracelets and earrings that made her shiny in the milky light. Just as the Packers came up, the girl turned to the fellow with her and poked her finger at a number on his card. Then she pinched his arm. The fellow had his hair pulled back and tied behind his head, and something else the Packers saw—a tiny gold loop through his earlobe.

James guided Edith to another table, turning to look again before sitting down. First he took off his windbreaker and helped Edith with her coat, and then he stared at the couple who had taken their places. The girl was scanning her cards as the numbers were called, leaning over to check the man's cards too—as if, James thought, the fellow did not have sense enough to look after his own numbers.

James picked up the stack of bingo cards that had been set out on the table. He gave half to Edith. "Pick some winners," he said. "Because I'm taking these three on top. It doesn't matter which ones I pick. Edith, I don't feel lucky tonight."

"Don't you pay it any attention," she said. "They're not hurting anybody. They're just young, that's all."

He said, "This is regular Friday night bingo for the people of this community."

She said, "It's a free country."

She handed back the stack of cards. He put them on the other side of the table. Then they served themselves from the bowl of beans.

James peeled a dollar bill from the roll of bills he kept for bingo nights. He put the dollar next to his cards. One of the club-women, a thin woman with bluish hair and a spot on her neck—the Packers knew her only as Alice—would presently come by with a coffee can. She would collect the coins and bills, making change from the can. It was this woman or another woman who paid off the wins.

The woman on the stage called "I–25," and someone in the hall yelled, "Bingo!"

Alice made her way between the tables. She took up the winning card and held it in her hand as the woman on the stage read out the winning numbers.

"It's a bingo," Alice confirmed.

"That bingo, ladies and gentlemen, is worth twelve dollars!" the woman on the stage announced. "Congratulations to the winner!"

—

The Packers played another five games to no effect. James came close once on one of his cards. But then five numbers were called in succession, none of them his, the fifth a number that produced a bingo on somebody else's card.

"You almost had it that time," Edith said. "I was watching your card."

"She was teasing me," James said.

He tilted the card and let the beans slide into his hand. He closed his hand and made a fist. He shook the beans in his fist. Something came to him about a boy who'd thrown some beans out a window. The memory reached to him from a long way off, and it made him feel lonely.

"Change cards, maybe," Edith said.

"It isn't my night," James said.

He looked over at the young couple again. They were laughing at something the fellow had said. James could see they weren't paying attention to anyone else in the hall.

Alice came around collecting money for the next game, and just after the first number had been called, James saw the fellow in the denims put down a bean on a card he hadn't paid for. Another number was called, and James saw the fellow do it again. James was amazed. He could not concentrate on his own cards. He kept looking up to see what the fellow in denim was doing.

"James, look at your cards," Edith said. "You missed N–34. Pay attention."

"That fellow over there who has our place is cheating. I can't believe my eyes," James said.

"How is he cheating?" Edith said.

"He's playing a card that he hasn't paid for," James said. "Somebody ought to report him."

"Not you, dear," Edith said. She spoke slowly and tried to keep her eyes on her cards. She dropped a bean on a number.

"The fellow is cheating," James said.

She extracted a bean from her palm and placed it on a number. "Play your cards," Edith said.

He looked back at his cards. But he knew he might as well write this game off. There was no telling how many numbers he had missed, how far behind he had fallen. He squeezed the beans in his fist.

The woman on the stage called, "G–60."

Someone yelled, "Bingo!"

"Christ," James Packer said.

A ten-minute break was announced. The game after the break would be a Blackout, one dollar a card, winner takes all, this week's jackpot ninety-eight dollars.

There was whistling and clapping.

James looked at the couple. The fellow was touching the ring in his ear and staring up at the ceiling. The girl had her hand on his leg.

"I have to go to the bathroom," Edith said. "Give me your cigarettes."

James said, "And I'll get us some raisin cookies and coffee."

"I'll go to the bathroom," Edith said.

But James Packer did not go to get cookies and coffee. Instead, he went to stand behind the chair of the fellow in denim.

"I see what you're doing," James said.

The man turned around. "Pardon me?" he said and stared. "What am I doing?"

"You know," James said.

The girl held her cookie in mid-bite.

"A word to the wise," James said.

He walked back to his table. He was trembling.

When Edith came back, she handed him the cigarettes and sat down, not talking, not being her jovial self.

James looked at her closely. He said, "Edith, has something happened?"

"I'm spotting again," she said.

"Spotting?" he said. But he knew what she meant. "Spotting," he said again, very quietly.

"Oh, dear," Edith Packer said, picking up some cards and sorting through them.

"I think we should go home," he said.

She kept sorting through the cards. "No, let's stay," she said. "It's just the spotting, is all."

He touched her hand.

"We'll stay," she said. "It'll be all right."

"This is the worst bingo night in history," James Packer said.

They played the Blackout game, James watching the man in denim. The fellow was still at it, still playing a card he hadn't paid for. From time to time, James checked how Edith was doing. But there was no way of telling. She held her lips pursed together. It could mean anything—resolve, worry, pain. Or maybe she just liked having her lips that way for this particular game.

He had three numbers to go on one card and five numbers on another, and no chance at all on a third card when the girl with the man in denim began shrieking: "Bingo! Bingo! Bingo! I have a bingo!"

The fellow clapped and shouted with her. "She's got a bingo! She's got a bingo, folks! A bingo!"

The fellow in denim kept clapping.

It was the woman on the stage herself who went to the girl's table to check her card against the master list. She said, "This young woman has a bingo, and that's a ninety-eight-dollar jackpot! Let's give her a round of applause, people! It's a bingo here! A Blackout!"

Edith clapped along with the rest. But James kept his hands on the table.

The fellow in denim hugged the girl when the woman from the stage handed over the cash.

"They'll use it to buy drugs," James said.

They stayed for the rest of the games. They stayed until the last game was played. It was a game called the Progressive, the jackpot increasing from week to week if no one bingoed before so many numbers were called.

James put his money down and played his cards with no hope of winning. He waited for the fellow in denim to call "Bingo!"

But no one won, and the jackpot would be carried over to the following week, the prize bigger than ever.

"That's bingo for tonight!" the woman on the stage proclaimed. "Thank you all for coming. God bless you and good night."

The Packers filed out of the assembly hall along with the rest, somehow managing to fall in behind the fellow in denim and his girl. They saw the girl pat her pocket. They saw the girl put her arm around the fellow's waist.

"Let those people get ahead of us," James said into Edith's ear. "I can't stand to look at them."

Edith said nothing in reply. But she hung back a little to give the couple time to move ahead.

Outside, the wind was up. James thought sure he could hear the surf over the sound of engines starting.

He saw the couple stop at the van. Of course. He should have put two and two together.

"The dumbbell," James Packer said.

Edith went into the bathroom and shut the door. James took off his windbreaker and put it down on the back of the sofa. He turned on the TV and took up his place and waited.

After a time, Edith came out of the bathroom. James concentrated his attention on the TV. Edith went to the kitchen and ran water. James heard her turn off the faucet. Edith came to the room and said, "I guess I'll have to see Dr. Crawford in the morning. I guess there really is something happening down there."

"The lousy luck," James said.

She stood there shaking her head. She covered her eyes and leaned into him when he came to put his arms around her.

"Edith, dearest Edith," James Packer said.

He felt awkward and terrified. He stood with his arms more or less holding his wife.

She reached for his face and kissed his lips, and then she said good night.

He went to the refrigerator. He stood in front of the open door and drank tomato juice while he studied everything inside. Cold air blew out at him. He looked at the little packages and the containers of foodstuffs on the shelves, a chicken covered in plastic wrap, the neat, protected exhibits.

He shut the door and spit the last of the juice into the sink. Then he rinsed his mouth and made himself a cup of instant coffee. He carried it into the living room. He sat down in front of the TV and lit a cigarette. He understood that it took only one lunatic and a torch to bring everything to ruin.

He smoked and finished the coffee, and then he turned the TV off. He went to the bedroom door and listened for a time. He felt unworthy to be listening, to be standing.

Why not someone else? Why not those people tonight? Why not all those people who sail through life free as birds? Why not them instead of Edith?

He moved away from the bedroom door. He thought about going for a walk. But the wind was wild now, and he could hear the branches whining in the birch tree behind the house.

He sat in front of the TV again. But he did not turn it on. He smoked and thought of that sauntering, arrogant gait as the two of them moved just ahead. If only they knew. If only someone would tell them. Just once!

He closed his eyes. He would get up early and fix breakfast. He would go with her to see Crawford. If only they had to sit with him in the waiting room! He'd tell them what to expect! He'd set those floozies straight! He'd tell them what was waiting for you after the denim and the earrings, after touching each other and cheating at games.

He got up and went into the guest room and turned on the lamp over the bed. He glanced at his papers and at his account books and at the adding machine on his desk. He found a pair of pajamas in one of the drawers. He turned down the covers on the bed. Then he walked back through the house, snapping off lights and checking doors. For a while he stood looking out the kitchen window at the tree shaking under the force of the wind.

He left the porch light on and went back to the guest room. He pushed aside his knitting basket, took up his basket of embroidery, and then settled himself in the chair. He raised the lid of the basket and got out the metal hoop. There was fresh white linen stretched across it. Holding the tiny needle to the light, James Packer stabbed at the eye with a length of blue silk thread. Then he set to work—stitch after stitch—making believe he was waving like the man on the keel.

So Much Water
So Close to Home

M Y husband eats with a good appetite. But I don't think he's really hungry. He chews, arms on the table, and stares at something across the room. He looks at me and looks away. He wipes his mouth on the napkin. He shrugs, and goes on eating.

"What are you staring at me for?" he says. "What is it?" he says and lays down his fork.

"Was I staring?" I say, and shake my head.

The telephone rings.

"Don't answer it," he says.

"It might be your mother," I say.

"Watch and see," he says.

I pick up the receiver and listen. My husband stops eating.

"What did I tell you?" he says when I hang up. He starts to eat again. Then throws his napkin on his plate. He says, "Goddamn it, why can't people mind their own business? Tell me what I did wrong and I'll listen! I wasn't the only man there. We talked it over and we all decided. We couldn't just turn around. We were five miles from the car. I won't have you passing judgment. Do you hear?"

"You know," I say.

He says, "What do I know, Claire? Tell me what I'm supposed to know. I don't know anything except one thing." He gives me what he thinks is a meaningful look. "She was dead," he says. "And I'm as sorry as anyone else. But she was dead."

"That's the point," I say.

He raises his hands. He pushes his chair away from the table. He takes out his cigarettes and goes out to the back with a can of beer. I see him sit in the lawn chair and pick up the newspaper again.

His name is in there on the first page. Along with the names of his friends.

I close my eyes and hold on to the sink. Then I rake my arm across the drainboard and send the dishes to the floor.

He doesn't move. I know he's heard. He lifts his head as if still listening. But he doesn't move otherwise. He doesn't turn around.

He and Gordon Johnson and Mel Dorn and Vern Williams, they play poker and bowl and fish. They fish every spring and early summer before visiting relatives can get in the way. They are decent men, family men, men who take care of their jobs. They have sons and daughters who go to school with our son, Dean.

Last Friday these family men left for the Naches River. They parked the car in the mountains and hiked to where they wanted to fish. They carried their bedrolls, their food, their playing cards, their whiskey.

They saw the girl before they set up camp. Mel Dorn found her. No clothes on her at all. She was wedged into some branches that stuck out over the water.

He called the others and they came to look. They talked about what to do. One of the men—my Stuart didn't say which—said they should start back at once. The others stirred the sand with their shoes, said they didn't feel inclined that way. They pleaded fatigue, the late hour, the fact that the girl wasn't going anywhere.

In the end they went ahead and set up the camp. They built a fire and drank their whiskey. When the moon came up, they talked about the girl. Someone said they should keep the body from drifting away. They took their flashlights and went back to the river. One of the men—it might have been Stuart— waded in and got her. He took her by the fingers and pulled her into shore. He got some nylon cord and tied it to her wrist and then looped the rest around a tree.

The next morning they cooked breakfast, drank coffee, and drank whiskey, and then split up to fish. That night they cooked fish, cooked potatoes, drank coffee, drank whiskey, then took their cooking things and eating things back down to the river and washed them where the girl was.

They played some cards later on. Maybe they played until they couldn't see them anymore. Vern Williams went to sleep. But the others told stories. Gordon Johnson said the trout they'd caught were hard because of the terrible coldness of the water.

The next morning they got up late, drank whiskey, fished a little, took down their tents, rolled their sleeping bags, gathered their stuff, and hiked out. They drove until they got to a telephone. It was Stuart who made the call while the others stood around in the sun and listened. He gave the sheriff their names. They had nothing to hide. They weren't ashamed. They said they'd wait until someone could come for better directions and take down their statements.

I was asleep when he got home. But I woke up when I heard him in the kitchen. I found him leaning against the refrigerator with a can of beer. He put his heavy arms around me and rubbed his big hands on my back. In bed he put his hands on me again and then waited as if thinking of something else. I turned and opened my legs. Afterwards, I think he stayed awake.

He was up that morning before I could get out of bed. To see if there was something in the paper, I suppose.

The telephone began ringing right after eight.

"Go to hell!" I heard him shout.

The telephone rang right again.

"I have nothing to add to what I already said to the sheriff!" He slammed the receiver down.

"What is going on?" I said.

It was then that he told me what I just told you.

I sweep up the broken dishes and go outside. He is lying on his back on the grass now, the newspaper and can of beer within reach.

"Stuart, could we go for a drive?" I say.

He rolls over and looks at me. "We'll pick up some beer," he says. He gets to his feet and touches me on the hip as he goes past. "Give me a minute," he says.

We drive through town without speaking. He stops at a roadside market for beer. I notice a great stack of papers just inside the door. On the top step a fat woman in a print dress holds out a licorice stick to a little girl. Later on, we cross Everson Creek and turn into the picnic grounds. The creek runs under the bridge and into a large pond a few hundred yards away. I can see the men out there. I can see them out there fishing.

So much water so close to home.

I say, "Why did you have to go miles away?"

"Don't rile me," he says.

We sit on a bench in the sun. He opens us cans of beer. He says, "Relax, Claire."

"They said they were innocent. They said they were crazy."

He says, "Who?" He says, "What are you talking about?"

"The Maddox brothers. They killed a girl named Arlene Hubly where I grew up. They cut off her head and threw her into the Cle Elum River. It happened when I was a girl."

"You're going to get me riled," he says.

I look at the creek. I'm right in it, eyes open, face down, staring at the moss on the bottom, dead.

"I don't know what's wrong with you," he says on the way home. "You're getting me more riled by the minute."

There is nothing I can say to him.

He tries to concentrate on the road. But he keeps looking into the rear-view mirror.

He knows.

Stuart believes he is letting me sleep this morning. But I was awake long before the alarm went off. I was thinking, lying on the far side of the bed away from his hairy legs.

He gets Dean off for school, and then he shaves, dresses, and leaves for work. Twice he looks in and clears his throat. But I keep my eyes closed.

In the kitchen I find a note from him. It's signed "Love."

I sit in the breakfast nook and drink coffee and leave a ring on the note. I look at the newspaper and turn it this way and that on the table. Then I skid it close and read what it says. The body has been identified, claimed. But it took some examining it, some putting things into it, some cutting, some weighing, some measuring, some putting things back again and sewing them in.

I sit for a long time holding the newspaper and thinking. Then I call up to get a chair at the hairdresser's.

—

I sit under the dryer with a magazine on my lap and let Marnie do my nails.

"I am going to a funeral tomorrow," I say.

"I'm sorry to hear that," Marnie says.

"It was a murder," I say.

"That's the worst kind," Marnie says.

"We weren't all that close," I say. "But you know."

"We'll get you fixed up for it," Marnie says.

That night I make my bed on the sofa, and in the morning I get up first. I put on coffee and fix breakfast while he shaves.

He appears in the kitchen doorway, towel over his bare shoulder, appraising.

"Here's coffee," I say. "Eggs'll be ready in a minute."

I wake Dean, and the three of us eat. Whenever Stuart looks at me, I ask Dean if he wants more milk, more toast, etc.

"I'll call you today," Stuart says as he opens the door.

I say, "I don't think I'll be home today."

"All right," he says. "Sure."

I dress carefully. I try on a hat and look at myself in the mirror. I write out a note for Dean.

> *Honey, Mommy has things to do this afternoon,*
> *but will be back later. You stay in or be in the*
> *backyard until one of us comes home.*
>
> *Love, Mommy*

I look at the word *Love* and then I underline it. Then I see the word *backyard*. Is it one word or two?

I drive through farm country, through fields of oats and sugar beets and past apple orchards, cattle grazing in pastures. Then everything changes, more like shacks than farmhouses and stands of timber instead of orchards. Then mountains, and on the right, far below, I sometimes see the Naches River.

A green pickup comes up behind me and stays behind me for miles. I keep slowing at the wrong times, hoping he will pass. Then I speed up. But this is at the wrong times, too. I grip the wheel until my fingers hurt.

On a long clear stretch he goes past. But he drives along

beside for a bit, a crewcut man in a blue workshirt. We look each other over. Then he waves, toots his horn, and pulls on up ahead.

I slow down and find a place. I pull over and shut off the motor. I can hear the river down below the trees. Then I hear the pickup coming back.

I lock the doors and roll up the windows.

"You all right?" the man says. He raps on the glass. "You okay?" He leans his arms on the door and brings his face to the window.

I stare at him. I can't think what else to do.

"Is everything all right in there? How come you're all locked up?"

I shake my head.

"Roll down your window." He shakes his head and looks at the highway and then back at me. "Roll it down now."

"Please," I say, "I have to go."

"Open the door," he says as if he isn't listening. "You're going to choke in there."

He looks at my breasts, my legs. I can tell that's what he's doing.

"Hey, sugar," he says. "I'm just here to help is all."

The casket is closed and covered with floral sprays. The organ starts up the minute I take a seat. People are coming in and finding chairs. There's a boy in flared pants and a yellow short-sleeved shirt. A door opens and the family comes in in a group and moves over to a curtained place off to one side. Chairs creak as everybody gets settled. Directly, a nice blond man in a nice dark suit stands and asks us to bow our heads. He says a prayer for us, the living, and when he finishes, he says a prayer for the soul of the departed.

Along with the others I go past the casket. Then I move out onto the front steps and into the afternoon light. There's a woman who limps as she goes down the stairs ahead of me. On the sidewalk she looks around. "Well, they got him," she says. "If that's any consolation. They arrested him this morning. I heard it on the radio before I come. A boy right here in town."

We move a few steps down the hot sidewalk. People are

starting cars. I put out my hand and hold on to a parking meter. Polished hoods and polished fenders. My head swims.

I say, "They have friends, these killers. You can't tell."

"I have known that child since she was a little girl," the woman says. "She used to come over and I'd bake cookies for her and let her eat them in front of the TV."

Back home, Stuart sits at the table with a drink of whiskey in front of him. For a crazy instant I think something's happened to Dean.

"Where is he?" I say. "Where is Dean?"

"Outside," my husband says.

He drains his glass and stands up. He says, "I think I know what you need."

He reaches an arm around my waist and with his other hand he begins to unbutton my jacket and then he goes on to the buttons of my blouse.

"First things first," he says.

He says something else. But I don't need to listen. I can't hear a thing with so much water going.

"That's right," I say, finishing the buttons myself. "Before Dean comes. Hurry."

The Third Thing That Killed My Father Off

I 'LL tell you what did my father in. The third thing was Dummy, that Dummy died. The first thing was Pearl Harbor. And the second thing was moving to my grandfather's farm near Wenatchee. That's where my father finished out his days, except they were probably finished before that.

My father blamed Dummy's death on Dummy's wife. Then he blamed it on the fish. And finally he blamed himself—because he was the one that showed Dummy the ad in the back of *Field and Stream* for live black bass shipped anywhere in the U.S.

It was after he got the fish that Dummy started acting peculiar. The fish changed Dummy's whole personality. That's what my father said.

I never knew Dummy's real name. If anyone did, I never heard it. Dummy it was then, and it's Dummy I remember him by now. He was a little wrinkled man, bald-headed, short but very powerful in the arms and legs. If he grinned, which was seldom, his lips folded back over brown, broken teeth. It gave him a crafty expression. His watery eyes stayed fastened on your mouth when you were talking—and if you weren't, they'd go to someplace queer on your body.

I don't think he was really deaf. At least not as deaf as he made out. But he sure couldn't talk. That was for certain.

Deaf or no, Dummy'd been on as a common laborer out at the sawmill since the 1920s. This was the Cascade Lumber Company in Yakima, Washington. The years I knew him, Dummy was working as a cleanup man. And all those years I never saw him with anything different on. Meaning a felt hat, a khaki workshirt, a denim jacket over a pair of coveralls. In his top pockets he carried rolls of toilet paper, as one of his jobs was to clean and supply the toilets. It kept him busy, seeing as how the men on nights used to walk off after their tours with a roll or two in their lunchboxes.

Dummy carried a flashlight, even though he worked days. He also carried wrenches, pliers, screwdrivers, friction tape, all the same things the millwrights carried. Well, it made them kid Dummy, the way he was, always carrying everything. Carl Lowe, Ted Slade, Johnny Wait, they were the worst kidders of the ones that kidded Dummy. But Dummy took it all in stride. I think he'd gotten used to it.

My father never kidded Dummy. Not to my knowledge, anyway. Dad was a big, heavy-shouldered man with a crew-haircut, double chin, and a belly of real size. Dummy was always staring at that belly. He'd come to the filing room where my father worked, and he'd sit on a stool and watch my dad's belly while he used the big emery wheels on the saws.

Dummy had a house as good as anyone's.

It was a tarpaper-covered affair near the river, five or six miles from town. Half a mile behind the house, at the end of a pasture, there lay a big gravel pit that the state had dug when they were paving the roads around there. Three good-sized holes had been scooped out, and over the years they'd filled with water. By and by, the three ponds came together to make one.

It was deep. It had a darkish look to it.

Dummy had a wife as well as a house. She was a woman years younger and said to go around with Mexicans. Father said it was busybodies that said that, men like Lowe and Wait and Slade.

She was a small stout woman with glittery little eyes. The first time I saw her, I saw those eyes. It was when I was with Pete Jensen and we were on our bicycles and we stopped at Dummy's to get a glass of water.

When she opened the door, I told her I was Del Fraser's son. I said, "He works with—" And then I realized. "You know, your husband. We were on our bicycles and thought we could get a drink."

"Wait here," she said.

She came back with a little tin cup of water in each hand. I downed mine in a single gulp.

But she didn't offer us more. She watched us without saying anything. When we started to get on our bicycles, she came over to the edge of the porch.

"You little fellas had a car now, I might catch a ride with you."

She grinned. Her teeth looked too big for her mouth.

"Let's go," Pete said, and we went.

There weren't many places you could fish for bass in our part of the state. There was rainbow mostly, a few brook and Dolly Varden in some of the high mountain streams, and silvers in Blue Lake and Lake Rimrock. That was mostly it, except for the runs of steelhead and salmon in some of the freshwater rivers in late fall. But if you were a fisherman, it was enough to keep you busy. No one fished for bass. A lot of people I knew had never seen a bass except for pictures. But my father had seen plenty of them when he was growing up in Arkansas and Georgia, and he had high hopes to do with Dummy's bass, Dummy being a friend.

The day the fish arrived, I'd gone swimming at the city pool. I remember coming home and going out again to get them since Dad was going to give Dummy a hand—three tanks Parcel Post from Baton Rouge, Louisiana.

We went in Dummy's pickup, Dad and Dummy and me.

These tanks turned out to be barrels, really, the three of them crated in pine lath. They were standing in the shade out back of the train depot, and it took my dad and Dummy both to lift each crate into the truck.

Dummy drove very carefully through town and just as carefully all the way to his house. He went right through his yard without stopping. He went on down to within feet of the pond. By that time it was nearly dark, so he kept his headlights on and took out a hammer and a tire iron from under the seat, and then the two of them lugged the crates up close to the water and started tearing open the first one.

The barrel inside was wrapped in burlap, and there were these nickel-sized holes in the lid. They raised it off and Dummy aimed his flashlight in.

It looked like a million bass fingerlings were finning inside. It was the strangest sight, all those live things busy in there, like a little ocean that had come on the train.

Dummy scooted the barrel to the edge of the water and

poured it out. He took his flashlight and shined it into the pond. But there was nothing to be seen anymore. You could hear the frogs going, but you could hear them going anytime it newly got dark.

"Let me get the other crates," my father said, and he reached over as if to take the hammer from Dummy's coveralls. But Dummy pulled back and shook his head.

He undid the other two crates himself, leaving dark drops of blood on the lath where he ripped his hand doing it.

From that night on, Dummy was different.

Dummy wouldn't let anyone come around now anymore. He put up fencing all around the pasture, and then he fenced off the pond with electrical barbed wire. They said it cost him all his savings for that fence.

Of course, my father wouldn't have anything to do with Dummy after that. Not since Dummy ran him off. Not from fishing, mind you, because the bass were just babies still. But even from trying to get a look.

One evening two years after, when Dad was working late and I took him his food and a jar of iced tea, I found him standing talking with Syd Glover, the millwright. Just as I came in, I heard Dad saying, "You'd reckon the fool was married to them fish, the way he acts."

"From what I hear," Syd said, "he'd do better to put that fence round his house."

My father saw me then, and I saw him signal Syd Glover with his eyes.

But a month later my dad finally made Dummy do it. What he did was, he told Dummy how you had to thin out the weak ones on account of keeping things fit for the rest of them. Dummy stood there pulling at his ear and staring at the floor. Dad said, Yeah, he'd be down to do it tomorrow because it had to be done. Dummy never said yes, actually. He just never said no, is all. All he did was pull on his ear some more.

When Dad got home that day, I was ready and waiting. I had his old bass plugs out and was testing the treble hooks with my finger.

"You set?" he called to me, jumping out of the car. "I'll go to the toilet, you put the stuff in. You can drive us out there if you want."

I'd stowed everything in the back seat and was trying out the wheel when he came back out wearing his fishing hat and eating a wedge of cake with both hands.

Mother was standing in the door watching. She was a fair-skinned woman, her blonde hair pulled back in a tight bun and fastened down with a rhinestone clip. I wonder if she ever went around back in those happy days, or what she ever really did.

I let out the handbrake. Mother watched until I'd shifted gears, and then, still unsmiling, she went back inside.

It was a fine afternoon. We had all the windows down to let the air in. We crossed the Moxee Bridge and swung west onto Slater Road. Alfalfa fields stood off to either side, and farther on it was cornfields.

Dad had his hand out the window. He was letting the wind carry it back. He was restless, I could see.

It wasn't long before we pulled up at Dummy's. He came out of the house wearing his hat. His wife was looking out the window.

"You got your frying pan ready?" Dad hollered out to Dummy, but Dummy just stood there eyeing the car. "Hey, Dummy!" Dad yelled. "Hey, Dummy, where's your pole, Dummy?"

Dummy jerked his head back and forth. He moved his weight from one leg to the other and looked at the ground and then at us. His tongue rested on his lower lip, and he began working his foot into the dirt.

I shouldered the creel. I handed Dad his pole and picked up my own.

"We set to go?" Dad said. "Hey, Dummy, we set to go?"

Dummy took off his hat and, with the same hand, he wiped his wrist over his head. He turned abruptly, and we followed him across the spongy pasture. Every twenty feet or so a snipe sprang up from the clumps of grass at the edge of the old furrows.

At the end of the pasture, the ground sloped gently and became dry and rocky, nettle bushes and scrub oaks scattered here and there. We cut to the right, following an old set of car tracks, going through a field of milkweed that came up to our waists, the dry pods at the tops of the stalks rattling angrily as we pushed through. Presently, I saw the sheen of water over Dummy's shoulder, and I heard Dad shout, "Oh, Lord, look at that!"

But Dummy slowed down and kept bringing his hand up and moving his hat back and forth over his head, and then he just stopped flat.

Dad said, "Well, what do you think, Dummy? One place good as another? Where do you say we should come onto it?"

Dummy wet his lower lip.

"What's the matter with you, Dummy?" Dad said. "This your pond, ain't it?"

Dummy looked down and picked an ant off his coveralls.

"Well, hell," Dad said, letting out his breath. He took out his watch. "If it's still all right with you, we'll get to it before it gets too dark."

Dummy stuck his hands in his pockets and turned back to the pond. He started walking again. We trailed along behind. We could see the whole pond now, the water dimpled with rising fish. Every so often a bass would leap clear and come down in a splash.

"Great God," I heard my father say.

We came up to the pond at an open place, a gravel beach kind of.

Dad motioned to me and dropped into a crouch. I dropped too. He was peering into the water in front of us, and when I looked, I saw what had taken him so.

"Honest to God," he whispered.

A school of bass was cruising, twenty, thirty, not one of them under two pounds. They veered off, and then they shifted and came back, so densely spaced they looked like they were bumping up against each other. I could see their big, heavy-lidded eyes watching us as they went by. They flashed away again, and again they came back.

They were asking for it. It didn't make any difference if we stayed squatted or stood up. The fish just didn't think a thing about us. I tell you, it was a sight to behold.

We sat there for quite a while, watching that school of bass go so innocently about their business, Dummy the whole time pulling at his fingers and looking around as if he expected someone to show up. All over the pond the bass were coming up to nuzzle the water, or jumping clear and falling back, or coming up to the surface to swim along with their dorsals sticking out.

Dad signaled, and we got up to cast. I tell you, I was shaky with excitement. I could hardly get the plug loose from the cork handle of my pole. It was while I was trying to get the hooks out that I felt Dummy seize my shoulder with his big fingers. I looked, and in answer Dummy worked his chin in Dad's direction. What he wanted was clear enough, no more than one pole.

Dad took off his hat and then put it back on and then he moved over to where I stood.

"You go on, Jack," he said. "That's all right, son—you do it now."

I looked at Dummy just before I laid out my cast. His face had gone rigid, and there was a thin line of drool on his chin.

"Come back stout on the sucker when he strikes," Dad said. "Sons of bitches got mouths hard as doorknobs."

I flipped off the drag lever and threw back my arm. I sent her out a good forty feet. The water was boiling even before I had time to take up the slack.

"Hit him!" Dad yelled. "Hit the son of a bitch! Hit him good!"

I came back hard, twice. I had him, all right. The rod bowed over and jerked back and forth. Dad kept yelling what to do.

"Let him go, let him go! Let him run! Give him more line! Now wind in! Wind in! No, let him run! Woo-ee! Will you look at that!"

The bass danced around the pond. Every time it came up out of the water, it shook its head so hard you could hear the plug rattle. And then he'd take off again. But by and by I wore him out and had him in up close. He looked enormous, six or seven pounds maybe. He lay on his side, whipped, mouth open, gills working. My knees felt so weak I could hardly stand. But I held the rod up, the line tight.

Dad waded out over his shoes. But when he reached for the fish, Dummy started sputtering, shaking his head, waving his arms.

"Now what the hell's the matter with you, Dummy? The boy's got hold of the biggest bass I ever seen, and he ain't going to throw him back, by God!"

Dummy kept carrying on and gesturing toward the pond.

"I ain't about to let this boy's fish go. You hear me, Dummy? You got another think coming if you think I'm going to do that."

Dummy reached for my line. Meanwhile, the bass had gained some strength back. He turned himself over and started swimming again. I yelled and then I lost my head and slammed down the brake on the reel and started winding. The bass made a last, furious run.

That was that. The line broke. I almost fell over on my back.

"Come on, Jack," Dad said, and I saw him grabbing up his pole. "Come on, goddamn the fool, before I knock the man down."

That February the river flooded.

It had snowed pretty heavy the first weeks of December, and turned real cold before Christmas. The ground froze. The snow stayed where it was. But toward the end of January, the Chinook wind struck. I woke up one morning to hear the house getting buffeted and the steady drizzle of water running off the roof.

It blew for five days, and on the third day the river began to rise.

"She's up to fifteen feet," my father said one evening, looking over his newspaper. "Which is three feet over what you need to flood. Old Dummy going to lose his darlings."

I wanted to go down to the Moxee Bridge to see how high the water was running. But my dad wouldn't let me. He said a flood was nothing to see.

Two days later the river crested, and after that the water began to subside.

Orin Marshall and Danny Owens and I bicycled out to Dummy's one morning a week after. We parked our bicycles and walked across the pasture that bordered Dummy's property.

It was a wet, blustery day, the clouds dark and broken, moving fast across the sky. The ground was soppy wet and we kept coming to puddles in the thick grass. Danny was just learning how to cuss, and he filled the air with the best he had every time he stepped in over his shoes. We could see the swollen river at the end of the pasture. The water was still high and out of its channel, surging around the trunks of trees and eating away at the edge of the land. Out toward the middle, the current moved heavy and swift, and now and then a bush floated by, or a tree with its branches sticking up.

We came to Dummy's fence and found a cow wedged in up against the wire. She was bloated and her skin was shiny-looking and gray. It was the first dead thing of any size I'd ever seen. I remember Orin took a stick and touched the open eyes.

We moved on down the fence, toward the river. We were afraid to go near the wire because we thought it might still have electricity in it. But at the edge of what looked like a deep canal, the fence came to an end. The ground had simply dropped into the water here, and the fence along with it.

We crossed over and followed the new channel that cut directly into Dummy's land and headed straight for his pond, going into it lengthwise and forcing an outlet for itself at the other end, then twisting off until it joined up with the river farther on.

You didn't doubt that most of Dummy's fish had been carried off. But those that hadn't been were free to come and go.

Then I caught sight of Dummy. It scared me, seeing him. I motioned to the other fellows, and we all got down.

Dummy was standing at the far side of the pond near where the water was rushing out. He was just standing there, the saddest man I ever saw.

"I sure do feel sorry for old Dummy, though," my father said at supper a few weeks after. "Mind, the poor devil brought it on himself. But you can't help but be troubled for him."

Dad went on to say George Laycock saw Dummy's wife sitting in the Sportsman's Club with a big Mexican fellow.

"And that ain't the half of it—"

Mother looked up at him sharply and then at me. But I just went on eating like I hadn't heard a thing.

Dad said, "Damn it to hell, Bea, the boy's old enough!"

He'd changed a lot, Dummy had. He was never around any

of the men anymore, not if he could help it. No one felt like joking with him either, not since he'd chased Carl Lowe with a two-by-four stud after Carl tipped Dummy's hat off. But the worst of it was that Dummy was missing from work a day or two a week on the average now, and there was some talk of his being laid off.

"The man's going off the deep end," Dad said. "Clear crazy if he don't watch out."

Then on a Sunday afternoon just before my birthday, Dad and I were cleaning the garage. It was a warm, drifty day. You could see the dust hanging in the air. Mother came to the back door and said, "Del, it's for you. I think it's Vern."

I followed Dad in to wash up. When he was through talking, he put the phone down and turned to us.

"It's Dummy," he said. "Did in his wife with a hammer and drowned himself. Vern just heard it in town."

When we got out there, cars were parked all around. The gate to the pasture stood open, and I could see tire marks that led on to the pond.

The screen door was propped ajar with a box, and there was this lean, pock-faced man in slacks and sports shirt and wearing a shoulder holster. He watched Dad and me get out of the car.

"I was his friend," Dad said to the man.

The man shook his head. "Don't care who you are. Clear off unless you got business here."

"Did they find him?" Dad said.

"They're dragging," the man said, and adjusted the fit of his gun.

"All right if we walk down? I knew him pretty well."

The man said, "Take your chances. They chase you off, don't say you wasn't warned."

We went on across the pasture, taking pretty much the same route we had the day we tried fishing. There were motorboats going on the pond, dirty fluffs of exhaust hanging over it. You could see where the high water had cut away the ground and carried off trees and rocks. The two boats had uniformed men in them, and they were going back and forth, one man steering and the other man handling the rope and hooks.

An ambulance waited on the gravel beach where we'd set ourselves to cast for Dummy's bass. Two men in white lounged against the back, smoking cigarettes.

One of the motorboats cut off. We all looked up. The man in back stood up and started heaving on his rope. After a time, an arm came out of the water. It looked like the hooks had gotten Dummy in the side. The arm went back down and then it came out again, along with a bundle of something.

It's not him, I thought. It's something else that has been in there for years.

The man in the front of the boat moved to the back, and together the two men hauled the dripping thing over the side.

I looked at Dad. His face was funny the way it was set.

"Women," he said. He said, "That's what the wrong kind of woman can do to you, Jack."

But I don't think Dad really believed it. I think he just didn't know who to blame or what to say.

It seemed to me everything took a bad turn for my father after that. Just like Dummy, he wasn't the same man anymore. That arm coming up and going back down in the water, it was like so long to good times and hello to bad. Because it was nothing but that all the years after Dummy drowned himself in that dark water.

Is that what happens when a friend dies? Bad luck for the pals he left behind?

But as I said, Pearl Harbor and having to move back to his dad's place didn't do my dad one bit of good, either.

A Serious Talk

VERA'S car was there, no others, and Burt gave thanks for that. He pulled into the drive and stopped beside the pie he'd dropped the night before. It was still there, the aluminum pan upside down, a halo of pumpkin filling on the pavement. It was the day after Christmas.

He'd come on Christmas day to visit his wife and children. Vera had warned him beforehand. She'd told him the score. She'd said he had to be out by six o'clock because her friend and his children were coming for dinner.

They had sat in the living room and solemnly opened the presents Burt had brought over. They had opened his packages while other packages wrapped in festive paper lay piled under the tree waiting for after six o'clock.

He had watched the children open their gifts, waited while Vera undid the ribbon on hers. He saw her slip off the paper, lift the lid, take out the cashmere sweater.

"It's nice," she said. "Thank you, Burt."

"Try it on," his daughter said.

"Put it on," his son said.

Burt looked at his son, grateful for his backing him up.

She did try it on. Vera went into the bedroom and came out with it on.

"It's nice," she said.

"It's nice on *you*," Burt said, and felt a welling in his chest.

He opened his gifts. From Vera, a gift certificate at Sondheim's men's store. From his daughter, a matching comb and brush. From his son, a ballpoint pen.

Vera served sodas, and they did a little talking. But mostly they looked at the tree. Then his daughter got up and began setting the dining-room table, and his son went off to his room.

But Burt liked it where he was. He liked it in front of the fireplace, a glass in his hand, his house, his home.

Then Vera went into the kitchen.

From time to time his daughter walked into the dining room with something for the table. Burt watched her. He watched

291

her fold the linen napkins into the wine glasses. He watched her put a slender vase in the middle of the table. He watched her lower a flower into the vase, doing it ever so carefully.

A small wax and sawdust log burned on the grate. A carton of five more sat ready on the hearth. He got up from the sofa and put them all in the fireplace. He watched until they flamed. Then he finished his soda and made for the patio door. On the way, he saw the pies lined up on the sideboard. He stacked them in his arms, all six, one for every ten times she had ever betrayed him.

In the driveway in the dark, he'd let one fall as he fumbled with the door.

The front door was permanently locked since the night his key had broken off inside it. He went around to the back. There was a wreath on the patio door. He rapped on the glass. Vera was in her bathrobe. She looked out at him and frowned. She opened the door a little.

Burt said, "I want to apologize to you for last night. I want to apologize to the kids, too."

Vera said, "They're not here."

She stood in the doorway and he stood on the patio next to the philodendron plant. He pulled at some lint on his sleeve.

She said, "I can't take any more. You tried to burn the house down."

"I did not."

"You did. Everybody here was a witness."

He said, "Can I come in and talk about it?"

She drew the robe together at her throat and moved back inside.

She said, "I have to go somewhere in an hour."

He looked around. The tree blinked on and off. There was a pile of colored tissue paper and shiny boxes at one end of the sofa. A turkey carcass sat on a platter in the center of the dining-room table, the leathery remains in a bed of parsley as if in a horrible nest. A cone of ash filled the fireplace. There were some empty Shasta cola cans in there too. A trail of smoke stains rose up the bricks to the mantel, where the wood that stopped them was scorched black.

He turned around and went back to the kitchen.

He said, "What time did your friend leave last night?"

She said, "If you're going to start that, you can go right now."

He pulled a chair out and sat down at the kitchen table in front of the big ashtray. He closed his eyes and opened them. He moved the curtain aside and looked out at the backyard. He saw a bicycle without a front wheel standing upside down. He saw weeds growing along the redwood fence.

She ran water into a saucepan. "Do you remember Thanksgiving?" she said. "I said then that was the last holiday you were going to wreck for us. Eating bacon and eggs instead of turkey at ten o'clock at night."

"I know it," he said. "I said I'm sorry."

"Sorry isn't good enough."

The pilot light was out again. She was at the stove trying to get the gas going under the pan of water.

"Don't burn yourself," he said. "Don't catch yourself on fire."

He considered her robe catching fire, him jumping up from the table, throwing her down onto the floor and rolling her over and over into the living room, where he would cover her with his body. Or should he run to the bedroom for a blanket?

"Vera?"

She looked at him.

"Do you have anything to drink? I could use a drink this morning."

"There's some vodka in the freezer."

"When did you start keeping vodka in the freezer?"

"Don't ask."

"Okay," he said, "I won't ask."

He got out the vodka and poured some into a cup he found on the counter.

She said, "Are you just going to drink it like that, out of a cup?" She said, "Jesus, Burt. What'd you want to talk about, anyway? I told you I have someplace to go. I have a flute lesson at one o'clock."

"Are you still taking flute?"

"I just said so. What is it? Tell me what's on your mind, and then I have to get ready."

"I wanted to say I was sorry."

She said, "You said that."

He said, "If you have any juice, I'll mix it with this vodka."

She opened the refrigerator and moved things around.

"There's cranapple juice," she said.

"That's fine," he said.

"I'm going to the bathroom," she said.

He drank the cup of cranapple juice and vodka. He lit a cig- arette and tossed the match into the big ashtray that always sat on the kitchen table. He studied the butts in it. Some of them were Vera's brand, and some of them weren't. Some even were lavender-colored. He got up and dumped it all under the sink.

The ashtray was not really an ashtray. It was a big dish of stoneware they'd bought from a bearded potter on the mall in Santa Clara. He rinsed it out and dried it. He put it back on the table. And then he ground out his cigarette in it.

The water on the stove began to bubble just as the phone began to ring.

He heard her open the bathroom door and call to him through the living room. "Answer that! I'm about to get into the shower."

The kitchen phone was on the counter in a corner behind the roasting pan. He moved the roasting pan and picked up the receiver.

"Is Charlie there?" the voice said.

"No," Burt said.

"Okay," the voice said.

While he was seeing to the coffee, the phone rang again.

"Charlie?"

"Not here," Burt said.

This time he left the receiver off the hook.

Vera came back into the kitchen wearing jeans and a sweater and brushing her hair.

He spooned the instant into the cups of hot water and then spilled some vodka into his. He carried the cups over to the table.

She picked up the receiver, listened. She said, "What's this? Who was on the phone?"

"Nobody," he said. "Who smokes colored cigarettes?"

"I do."

"I didn't know you did that."

"Well, I do."

She sat across from him and drank her coffee. They smoked and used the ashtray.

There were things he wanted to say, grieving things, consoling things, things like that.

"I'm smoking three packs a day," Vera said. "I mean, if you really want to know what goes on around here."

"God almighty," Burt said.

Vera nodded.

"I didn't come over here to hear that," he said.

"What did you come over here to hear, then? You want to hear the house burned down?"

"Vera," he said. "It's Christmas. That's why I came."

"It's the day after Christmas," she said. "Christmas has come and gone," she said. "I don't ever want to see another one."

"What about me?" he said. "You think I look forward to holidays?"

The phone rang again. Burt picked it up.

"It's someone wanting Charlie," he said.

"What?"

"Charlie," Burt said.

Vera took the phone. She kept her back to him as she talked. Then she turned to him and said, "I'll take this call in the bedroom. So would you please hang up after I've picked it up in there? I can tell, so hang it up when I say."

He took the receiver. She left the kitchen. He held the receiver to his ear and listened. He heard nothing. Then he heard a man clear his throat. Then he heard Vera pick up the other phone. She shouted, "Okay, Burt! I have it now, Burt!"

He put down the receiver and stood looking at it. He opened the silverware drawer and pushed things around inside. He opened another drawer. He looked in the sink. He went into the dining room and got the carving knife. He held it under hot water until the grease broke and ran off. He wiped the blade on his sleeve. He moved to the phone, doubled the cord, and sawed through without any trouble at all. He examined the ends of the cord. Then he shoved the phone back into its corner behind the roasting pan.

She came in. She said, "The phone went dead. Did you do anything to the telephone?" She looked at the phone and then picked it up from the counter.

"Son of a bitch!" she screamed. She screamed, "Out, out, where you belong!" She was shaking the phone at him. "That's it! I'm going to get a restraining order, that's what I'm going to get!"

The phone made a *ding* when she banged it down on the counter.

"I'm going next door to call the police if you don't get out of here now!"

He picked up the ashtray. He held it by its edge. He posed with it like a man preparing to hurl the discus.

"Please," she said. "That's our ashtray."

He left through the patio door. He was not certain, but he thought he had proved something. He hoped he had made something clear. The thing was, they had to have a serious talk soon. There were things that needed talking about, important things that had to be discussed. They'd talk again. Maybe after the holidays were over and things got back to normal. He'd tell her the goddamn ashtray was a goddamn dish, for example.

He stepped around the pie in the driveway and got back into his car. He started the car and put it into reverse. It was hard managing until he put the ashtray down.

The Calm

I WAS getting a haircut. I was in the chair and three men were sitting along the wall across from me. Two of the men waiting I'd never seen before. But one of them I recognized, though I couldn't exactly place him. I kept looking at him as the barber worked on my hair. The man was moving a toothpick around in his mouth, a heavyset man, short wavy hair. And then I saw him in a cap and uniform, little eyes watchful in the lobby of a bank.

Of the other two, one was considerably the older, with a full head of curly gray hair. He was smoking. The third, though not so old, was nearly bald on top, but the hair at the sides hung over his ears. He had on logging boots, pants shiny with machine oil.

The barber put a hand on top of my head to turn me for a better look. Then he said to the guard, "Did you get your deer, Charles?"

I liked this barber. We weren't acquainted well enough to call each other by name. But when I came in for a haircut, he knew me. He knew I used to fish. So we'd talk fishing. I don't think he hunted. But he could talk on any subject. In this regard, he was a good barber.

"Bill, it's a funny story. The damnedest thing," the guard said. He took out the toothpick and laid it in the ashtray. He shook his head. "I did and I didn't. So yes and no to your question."

I didn't like the man's voice. For a guard, the voice didn't fit. It wasn't the voice you'd expect.

The two other men looked up. The older man was turning the pages of a magazine, smoking, and the other fellow was holding a newspaper. They put down what they were looking at and turned to listen to the guard.

"Go on, Charles," the barber said. "Let's hear it."

The barber turned my head again, and went back to work with his clippers.

—

"We were up on Fikle Ridge. My old man and me and the kid. We were hunting those draws. My old man was stationed at the head of one, and me and the kid were at the head of another. The kid had a hangover, goddamn his hide. The kid, he was green around the gills and drank water all day, mine and his both. It was in the afternoon and we'd been out since daybreak. But we had our hopes. We figured the hunters down below would move a deer in our direction. So we were sitting behind a log and watching the draw when we heard this shooting down in the valley."

"There's orchards down there," said the fellow with the newspaper. He was fidgeting a lot and kept crossing a leg, swinging his boot for a time, and then crossing his legs the other way. "Those deer hang out around those orchards."

"That's right," said the guard. "They'll go in there at night, the bastards, and eat those little green apples. Well, we heard this shooting and we're just sitting there on our hands when this big old buck comes up out of the underbrush not a hundred feet away. The kid sees him the same time I do, of course, and he throws down and starts banging. The knothead. That old buck wasn't in any danger. Not from the kid, as it turns out. But he can't tell where the shots are coming from. He doesn't know which way to jump. Then I get off a shot. But in all the commotion, I just stun him."

"Stunned him?" the barber said.

"You know, stun him," the guard said. "It was a gut shot. It just like stuns him. So he drops his head and begins this trembling. He trembles all over. The kid's still shooting. Me, I felt like I was back in Korea. So I shot again but missed. Then old Mr. Buck moves back into the brush. But now, by God, he doesn't have any oomph left in him. The kid has emptied his goddamn gun all to no purpose. But I hit solid. I'd rammed one right in his guts. That's what I meant by stunned him."

"Then what?" said the fellow with the newspaper, who had rolled it and was tapping it against his knee. "Then what? You must have trailed him. They find a hard place to die every time."

"But you trailed him?" the older man asked, though it wasn't really a question.

"I did. Me and the kid, we trailed him. But the kid wasn't good for much. He gets sick on the trail, slows us down. That chucklehead." The guard had to laugh now, thinking about that situation. "Drinking beer and chasing all night, then saying he can hunt deer. He knows better now, by God. But, sure, we trailed him. A good trail, too. Blood on the ground and blood on the leaves. Blood everywhere. Never seen a buck with so much blood. I don't know how the sucker kept going."

"Sometimes they'll go forever," the fellow with the newspaper said. "They find them a hard place to die every time."

"I chewed the kid out for missing his shot, and when he smarted off at me, I cuffed him a good one. Right here." The guard pointed to the side of his head and grinned. "I boxed his goddamn ears for him, that goddamn kid. He's not too old. He needed it. So the point is, it got too dark to trail, what with the kid laying back to vomit and all."

"Well, the coyotes will have that deer by now," the fellow with the newspaper said. "Them and the crows and the buzzards."

He unrolled the newspaper, smoothed it all the way out, and put it off to one side. He crossed a leg again. He looked around at the rest of us and shook his head.

The older man had turned in his chair and was looking out the window. He lit a cigarette.

"I figure so," the guard said. "Pity too. He was a big old son of a bitch. So in answer to your question, Bill, I both got my deer and I didn't. But we had venison on the table anyway. Because it turns out the old man has got himself a little spike in the meantime. Already has him back to camp, hanging up and gutted slick as a whistle, liver, heart, and kidneys wrapped in waxed paper and already setting in the cooler. A spike. Just a little bastard. But the old man, he was tickled."

The guard looked around the shop as if remembering. Then he picked up his toothpick and stuck it back in his mouth.

The older man put his cigarette out and turned to the guard. He drew a breath and said, "You ought to be out there right now looking for that deer instead of in here getting a haircut."

"You can't talk like that," the guard said. "You old fart. I've seen you someplace."

"I've seen you too," the old fellow said.

"Boys, that's enough. This is my barbershop," the barber said.

"I ought to box *your* ears," the old fellow said.

"You ought to try it," the guard said.

"Charles," the barber said.

The barber put his comb and scissors on the counter and his hands on my shoulders, as if he thought I was thinking to spring from the chair into the middle of it. "Albert, I've been cutting Charles's head of hair, and his boy's too, for years now. I wish you wouldn't pursue this."

The barber looked from one man to the other and kept his hands on my shoulders.

"Take it outside," the fellow with the newspaper said, flushed and hoping for something.

"That'll be enough," the barber said. "Charles, I don't want to hear anything more on the subject. Albert, you're next in line. Now." The barber turned to the fellow with the newspaper. "I don't know you from Adam, mister, but I'd appreciate if you wouldn't put your oar in."

The guard got up. He said, "I think I'll come back for my cut later. Right now the company leaves something to be desired."

The guard went out and pulled the door closed, hard.

The old fellow sat smoking his cigarette. He looked out the window. He examined something on the back of his hand. He got up and put on his hat.

"I'm sorry, Bill," the old fellow said. "I can go a few more days."

"That's all right, Albert," the barber said.

When the old fellow went out, the barber stepped over to the window to watch him go.

"Albert's about dead from emphysema," the barber said from the window. "We used to fish together. He taught me salmon inside out. The women. They used to crawl all over that old boy. He's picked up a temper, though. But in all honesty, there was provocation."

The man with the newspaper couldn't sit still. He was on his feet and moving around, stopping to examine everything, the hat rack, the photos of Bill and his friends, the calendar from the hardware showing scenes for each month of the year. He flipped every page. He even went so far as to stand and scrutinize Bill's barbering license, which was up on the wall in a frame. Then he turned and said, "I'm going too," and out he went just like he said.

"Well, do you want me to finish barbering this hair or not?" the barber said to me as if I was the cause of everything.

The barber turned me in the chair to face the mirror. He put a hand to either side of my head. He positioned me a last time, and then he brought his head down next to mine.

We looked into the mirror together, his hands still framing my head.

I was looking at myself, and he was looking at me too. But if the barber saw something, he didn't offer comment.

He ran his fingers through my hair. He did it slowly, as if thinking about something else. He ran his fingers through my hair. He did it tenderly, as a lover would.

That was in Crescent City, California, up near the Oregon border. I left soon after. But today I was thinking of that place, of Crescent City, and of how I was trying out a new life there with my wife, and how, in the barber's chair that morning, I had made up my mind to go. I was thinking today about the calm I felt when I closed my eyes and let the barber's fingers move through my hair, the sweetness of those fingers, the hair already starting to grow.

Popular Mechanics

EARLY that day the weather turned and the snow was melting into dirty water. Streaks of it ran down from the little shoulder-high window that faced the backyard. Cars slushed by on the street outside, where it was getting dark. But it was getting dark on the inside too.

He was in the bedroom pushing clothes into a suitcase when she came to the door.

I'm glad you're leaving! I'm glad you're leaving! she said. Do you hear?

He kept on putting his things into the suitcase.

Son of a bitch! I'm so glad you're leaving! She began to cry. You can't even look me in the face, can you?

Then she noticed the baby's picture on the bed and picked it up.

He looked at her and she wiped her eyes and stared at him before turning and going back to the living room.

Bring that back, he said.

Just get your things and get out, she said.

He did not answer. He fastened the suitcase, put on his coat, looked around the bedroom before turning off the light. Then he went out to the living room.

She stood in the doorway of the little kitchen, holding the baby.

I want the baby, he said.

Are you crazy?

No, but I want the baby. I'll get someone to come by for his things.

You're not touching this baby, she said.

The baby had begun to cry and she uncovered the blanket from around his head.

Oh, oh, she said, looking at the baby.

He moved toward her.

For God's sake! she said. She took a step back into the kitchen.

I want the baby.

Get out of here!

She turned and tried to hold the baby over in a corner behind the stove.

But he came up. He reached across the stove and tightened his hands on the baby.

Let go of him, he said.

Get away, get away! she cried.

The baby was red-faced and screaming. In the scuffle they knocked down a flowerpot that hung behind the stove.

He crowded her into the wall then, trying to break her grip. He held on to the baby and pushed with all his weight.

Let go of him, he said.

Don't, she said. You're hurting the baby, she said.

I'm not hurting the baby, he said.

The kitchen window gave no light. In the near-dark he worked on her fisted fingers with one hand and with the other hand he gripped the screaming baby up under an arm near the shoulder.

She felt her fingers being forced open. She felt the baby going from her.

No! she screamed just as her hands came loose.

She would have it, this baby. She grabbed for the baby's other arm. She caught the baby around the wrist and leaned back.

But he would not let go. He felt the baby slipping out of his hands and he pulled back very hard.

In this manner, the issue was decided.

Everything Stuck to Him

SHE'S in Milan for Christmas and wants to know what it was like when she was a kid.

Tell me, she says. Tell me what it was like when I was a kid. She sips Strega, waits, eyes him closely.

She is a cool, slim, attractive girl, a survivor from top to bottom.

That was a long time ago. That was twenty years ago, he says.

You can remember, she says. Go on.

What do you want to hear? he says. What else can I tell you? I could tell you about something that happened when you were a baby. It involves you, he says. But only in a minor way.

Tell me, she says. But first fix us another so you won't have to stop in the middle.

He comes back from the kitchen with drinks, settles into his chair, begins.

They were kids themselves, but they were crazy in love, this eighteen-year-old boy and this seventeen-year-old girl when they married. Not all that long afterwards they had a daughter.

The baby came along in late November during a cold spell that just happened to coincide with the peak of the waterfowl season. The boy loved to hunt, you see. That's part of it.

The boy and girl, husband and wife, father and mother, they lived in a little apartment under a dentist's office. Each night they cleaned the dentist's place upstairs in exchange for rent and utilities. In summer they were expected to maintain the lawn and the flowers. In winter the boy shoveled snow and spread rock salt on the walks. Are you still with me? Are you getting the picture?

I am, she says.

That's good, he says. So one day the dentist finds out they were using his letterhead for their personal correspondence. But that's another story.

He gets up from his chair and looks out the window. He

sees the tile rooftops and the snow that is falling steadily on them.

Tell the story, she says.

The two kids were very much in love. On top of this they had great ambitions. They were always talking about the things they were going to do and the places they were going to go.

Now the boy and girl slept in the bedroom, and the baby slept in the living room. Let's say the baby was about three months old and had only just begun to sleep through the night.

On this one Saturday night after finishing his work upstairs, the boy stayed in the dentist's office and called an old hunting friend of his father's.

Carl, he said when the man picked up the receiver, believe it or not, I'm a father.

Congratulations, Carl said. How is the wife?

She's fine, Carl. Everybody's fine.

That's good, Carl said, I'm glad to hear it. But if you called about going hunting, I'll tell you something. The geese are flying to beat the band. I don't think I've ever seen so many. Got five today. Going back in the morning, so come along if you want to.

I want to, the boy said.

The boy hung up the telephone and went downstairs to tell the girl. She watched while he laid out his things. Hunting coat, shell bag, boots, socks, hunting cap, long underwear, pump gun.

What time will you be back? the girl said.

Probably around noon, the boy said. But maybe as late as six o'clock. Would that be too late?

It's fine, she said. The baby and I will get along fine. You go and have some fun. When you get back, we'll dress the baby up and go visit Sally.

The boy said, Sounds like a good idea.

Sally was the girl's sister. She was striking. I don't know if you've seen pictures of her. The boy was a little in love with Sally, just as he was a little in love with Betsy, who was another sister the girl had. The boy used to say to the girl, If we weren't married, I could go for Sally.

What about Betsy? the girl used to say. I hate to admit it,

but I truly feel she's better looking than Sally and me. What about Betsy?

Betsy too, the boy used to say.

After dinner he turned up the furnace and helped her bathe the baby. He marveled again at the infant who had half his features and half the girl's. He powdered the tiny body. He powdered between fingers and toes.

He emptied the bath into the sink and went upstairs to check the air. It was overcast and cold. The grass, what there was of it, looked like canvas, stiff and gray under the street light.

Snow lay in piles beside the walk. A car went by. He heard sand under the tires. He let himself imagine what it might be like tomorrow, geese beating the air over his head, shotgun plunging against his shoulder.

Then he locked the door and went downstairs.

In bed they tried to read. But both of them fell asleep, she first, letting the magazine sink to the quilt.

It was the baby's cries that woke him up.

The light was on out there, and the girl was standing next to the crib rocking the baby in her arms. She put the baby down, turned out the light, and came back to the bed.

He heard the baby cry. This time the girl stayed where she was. The baby cried fitfully and stopped. The boy listened, then dozed. But the baby's cries woke him again. The living room light was burning. He sat up and turned on the lamp.

I don't know what's wrong, the girl said, walking back and forth with the baby. I've changed her and fed her, but she keeps on crying. I'm so tired I'm afraid I might drop her.

You come back to bed, the boy said. I'll hold her for a while.

He got up and took the baby, and the girl went to lie down again.

Just rock her for a few minutes, the girl said from the bedroom. Maybe she'll go back to sleep.

The boy sat on the sofa and held the baby. He jiggled it in his lap until he got its eyes to close, his own eyes closing right along. He rose carefully and put the baby back in the crib.

It was a quarter to four, which gave him forty-five minutes.

He crawled into bed and dropped off. But a few minutes later the baby was crying again, and this time they both got up.

The boy did a terrible thing. He swore.

For God's sake, what's the matter with you? the girl said to the boy. Maybe she's sick or something. Maybe we shouldn't have given her the bath.

The boy picked up the baby. The baby kicked its feet and smiled.

Look, the boy said, I really don't think there's anything wrong with her.

How do you know that? the girl said. Here, let me have her. I know I ought to give her something, but I don't know what it's supposed to be.

The girl put the baby down again. The boy and the girl looked at the baby, and the baby began to cry.

The girl took the baby. Baby, baby, the girl said with tears in her eyes.

Probably it's something on her stomach, the boy said.

The girl didn't answer. She went on rocking the baby, paying no attention to the boy.

The boy waited. He went to the kitchen and put on water for coffee. He drew his woolen underwear on over his shorts and T-shirt, buttoned up, then got into his clothes.

What are you doing? the girl said.

Going hunting, the boy said.

I don't think you should, she said. I don't want to be left alone with her like this.

Carl's planning on me going, the boy said. We've planned it.

I don't care about what you and Carl planned, she said. And I don't care about Carl, either. I don't even know Carl.

You've met Carl before. You know him, the boy said. What do you mean you don't know him?

That's not the point and you know it, the girl said.

What is the point? the boy said. The point is we planned it.

The girl said, I'm your wife. This is your baby. She's sick or something. Look at her. Why else is she crying?

I know you're my wife, the boy said.

The girl began to cry. She put the baby back in the crib. But the baby started up again. The girl dried her eyes on the sleeve of her nightgown and picked the baby up.

The boy laced up his boots. He put on his shirt, his sweater, his coat. The kettle whistled on the stove in the kitchen.

You're going to have to choose, the girl said. Carl or us. I mean it.

What do you mean? the boy said.

You heard what I said, the girl said. If you want a family, you're going to have to choose.

They stared at each other. Then the boy took up his hunting gear and went outside. He started the car. He went around to the car windows and, making a job of it, scraped away the ice.

He turned off the motor and sat awhile. And then he got out and went back inside.

The living-room light was on. The girl was asleep on the bed. The baby was asleep beside her.

The boy took off his boots. Then he took off everything else. In his socks and his long underwear, he sat on the sofa and read the Sunday paper.

The girl and the baby slept on. After a while, the boy went to the kitchen and started frying bacon.

The girl came out in her robe and put her arms around the boy.

Hey, the boy said.

I'm sorry, the girl said.

It's all right, the boy said.

I didn't mean to snap like that.

It was my fault, he said.

You sit down, the girl said. How does a waffle sound with bacon?

Sounds great, the boy said.

She took the bacon out of the pan and made waffle batter. He sat at the table and watched her move around the kitchen.

She put a plate in front of him with bacon, a waffle. He spread butter and poured syrup. But when he started to cut, he turned the plate into his lap.

I don't believe it, he said, jumping up from the table.

If you could see yourself, the girl said.

The boy looked down at himself, at everything stuck to his underwear.

I was starved, he said, shaking his head.

You were starved, she said, laughing.

He peeled off the woolen underwear and threw it at the bathroom door. Then he opened his arms and the girl moved into them.

We won't fight anymore, she said.

The boy said, We won't.

He gets up from his chair and refills their glasses.

That's it, he says. End of story. I admit it's not much of a story.

I was interested, she says.

He shrugs and carries his drink over to the window. It's dark now but still snowing.

Things change, he says. I don't know how they do. But they do without your realizing it or wanting them to.

Yes, that's true, only— But she does not finish what she started.

She drops the subject. In the window's reflection he sees her study her nails. Then she raises her head. Speaking brightly, she asks if he is going to show her the city, after all.

He says, Put your boots on and let's go.

But he stays by the window, remembering. They had laughed. They had leaned on each other and laughed until the tears had come, while everything else—the cold, and where he'd go in it—was outside, for a while anyway.

What We Talk About
When We Talk About Love

M Y friend Mel McGinnis was talking. Mel McGinnis is a cardiologist, and sometimes that gives him the right.

The four of us were sitting around his kitchen table drinking gin. Sunlight filled the kitchen from the big window behind the sink. There were Mel and me and his second wife, Teresa —Terri, we called her—and my wife, Laura. We lived in Albuquerque then. But we were all from somewhere else.

There was an ice bucket on the table. The gin and the tonic water kept going around, and we somehow got on the subject of love. Mel thought real love was nothing less than spiritual love. He said he'd spent five years in a seminary before quitting to go to medical school. He said he still looked back on those years in the seminary as the most important years in his life.

Terri said the man she lived with before she lived with Mel loved her so much he tried to kill her. Then Terri said, "He beat me up one night. He dragged me around the living room by my ankles. He kept saying, 'I love you, I love you, you bitch.' He went on dragging me around the living room. My head kept knocking on things." Terri looked around the table. "What do you do with love like that?"

She was a bone-thin woman with a pretty face, dark eyes, and brown hair that hung down her back. She liked necklaces made of turquoise, and long pendant earrings.

"My God, don't be silly. That's not love, and you know it," Mel said. "I don't know what you'd call it, but I sure know you wouldn't call it love."

"Say what you want to, but I know it was," Terri said. "It may sound crazy to you, but it's true just the same. People are different, Mel. Sure, sometimes he may have acted crazy. Okay. But he loved me. In his own way maybe, but he loved me. There was love there, Mel. Don't say there wasn't."

Mel let out his breath. He held his glass and turned to Laura and me. "The man threatened to kill me," Mel said. He finished his drink and reached for the gin bottle. "Terri's a romantic.

Terri's of the kick-me-so-I'll-know-you-love-me school. Terri, hon, don't look that way." Mel reached across the table and touched Terri's cheek with his fingers. He grinned at her.

"Now he wants to make up," Terri said.

"Make up what?" Mel said. "What is there to make up? I know what I know. That's all."

"How'd we get started on this subject, anyway?" Terri said. She raised her glass and drank from it. "Mel always has love on his mind," she said. "Don't you, honey?" She smiled, and I thought that was the last of it.

"I just wouldn't call Ed's behavior love. That's all I'm saying, honey," Mel said. "What about you guys?" Mel said to Laura and me. "Does that sound like love to you?"

"I'm the wrong person to ask," I said. "I didn't even know the man. I've only heard his name mentioned in passing. I wouldn't know. You'd have to know the particulars. But I think what you're saying is that love is an absolute."

Mel said, "The kind of love I'm talking about is. The kind of love I'm talking about, you don't try to kill people."

Laura said, "I don't know anything about Ed, or anything about the situation. But who can judge anyone else's situation?"

I touched the back of Laura's hand. She gave me a quick smile. I picked up Laura's hand. It was warm, the nails polished, perfectly manicured. I encircled the broad wrist with my fingers, and I held her.

"When I left, he drank rat poison," Terri said. She clasped her arms with her hands. "They took him to the hospital in Santa Fe. That's where we lived then, about ten miles out. They saved his life. But his gums went crazy from it. I mean they pulled away from his teeth. After that, his teeth stood out like fangs. My God," Terri said. She waited a minute, then let go of her arms and picked up her glass.

"What people won't do!" Laura said.

"He's out of the action now," Mel said. "He's dead."

Mel handed me the saucer of limes. I took a section, squeezed it over my drink, and stirred the ice cubes with my finger.

"It gets worse," Terri said. "He shot himself in the mouth. But he bungled that too. Poor Ed," she said. Terri shook her head.

"Poor Ed nothing," Mel said. "He was dangerous."

Mel was forty-five years old. He was tall and rangy with curly soft hair. His face and arms were brown from the tennis he played. When he was sober, his gestures, all his movements, were precise, very careful.

"He did love me though, Mel. Grant me that," Terri said. "That's all I'm asking. He didn't love me the way you love me. I'm not saying that. But he loved me. You can grant me that, can't you?"

"What do you mean, he bungled it?" I said.

Laura leaned forward with her glass. She put her elbows on the table and held her glass in both hands. She glanced from Mel to Terri and waited with a look of bewilderment on her open face, as if amazed that such things happened to people you were friendly with.

"How'd he bungle it when he killed himself?" I said.

"I'll tell you what happened," Mel said. "He took this twenty-two pistol he'd bought to threaten Terri and me with. Oh, I'm serious, the man was always threatening. You should have seen the way we lived in those days. Like fugitives. I even bought a gun myself. Can you believe it? A guy like me? But I did. I bought one for self-defense and carried it in the glove compartment. Sometimes I'd have to leave the apartment in the middle of the night. To go to the hospital, you know? Terri and I weren't married then, and my first wife had the house and kids, the dog, everything, and Terri and I were living in this apartment here. Sometimes, as I say, I'd get a call in the middle of the night and have to go in to the hospital at two or three in the morning. It'd be dark out there in the parking lot, and I'd break into a sweat before I could even get to my car. I never knew if he was going to come up out of the shrubbery or from behind a car and start shooting. I mean, the man was crazy. He was capable of wiring a bomb, anything. He used to call my service at all hours and say he needed to talk to the doctor, and when I'd return the call, he'd say, 'Son of a bitch, your days are numbered.' Little things like that. It was scary, I'm telling you."

"I still feel sorry for him," Terri said.

"It sounds like a nightmare," Laura said. "But what exactly happened after he shot himself?"

Laura is a legal secretary. We'd met in a professional capacity. Before we knew it, it was a courtship. She's thirty-five, three years younger than I am. In addition to being in love, we like each other and enjoy one another's company. She's easy to be with.

"What happened?" Laura said.

Mel said, "He shot himself in the mouth in his room. Someone heard the shot and told the manager. They came in with a passkey, saw what had happened, and called an ambulance. I happened to be there when they brought him in, alive but past recall. The man lived for three days. His head swelled up to twice the size of a normal head. I'd never seen anything like it, and I hope I never do again. Terri wanted to go in and sit with him when she found out about it. We had a fight over it. I didn't think she should see him like that. I didn't think she should see him, and I still don't."

"Who won the fight?" Laura said.

"I was in the room with him when he died," Terri said. "He never came up out of it. But I sat with him. He didn't have anyone else."

"He was dangerous," Mel said. "If you call that love, you can have it."

"It was love," Terri said. "Sure, it's abnormal in most people's eyes. But he was willing to die for it. He did die for it."

"I sure as hell wouldn't call it love," Mel said. "I mean, no one knows what he did it for. I've seen a lot of suicides, and I couldn't say anyone ever knew what they did it for."

Mel put his hands behind his neck and tilted his chair back. "I'm not interested in that kind of love," he said. "If that's love, you can have it."

Terri said, "We were afraid. Mel even made a will out and wrote to his brother in California who used to be a Green Beret. Mel told him who to look for if something happened to him."

Terri drank from her glass. She said, "But Mel's right—we lived like fugitives. We were afraid. Mel was, weren't you, honey? I even called the police at one point, but they were no help. They said they couldn't do anything until Ed actually did something. Isn't that a laugh?" Terri said.

She poured the last of the gin into her glass and waggled the bottle. Mel got up from the table and went to the cupboard. He took down another bottle.

"Well, Nick and I know what love is," Laura said. "For us, I mean," Laura said. She bumped my knee with her knee. "You're supposed to say something now," Laura said, and turned her smile on me.

For an answer, I took Laura's hand and raised it to my lips. I made a big production out of kissing her hand. Everyone was amused.

"We're lucky," I said.

"You guys," Terri said. "Stop that now. You're making me sick. You're still on the honeymoon, for God's sake. You're still gaga, for crying out loud. Just wait. How long have you been together now? How long has it been? A year? Longer than a year?"

"Going on a year and a half," Laura said, flushed and smiling.

"Oh, now," Terri said. "Wait awhile."

She held her drink and gazed at Laura.

"I'm only kidding," Terri said.

Mel opened the gin and went around the table with the bottle.

"Here, you guys," he said. "Let's have a toast. I want to propose a toast. A toast to love. To true love," Mel said.

We touched glasses.

"To love," we said.

Outside in the backyard, one of the dogs began to bark. The leaves of the aspen that leaned past the window ticked against the glass. The afternoon sun was like a presence in this room, the spacious light of ease and generosity. We could have been anywhere, somewhere enchanted. We raised our glasses again and grinned at each other like children who had agreed on something forbidden.

"I'll tell you what real love is," Mel said. "I mean, I'll give you a good example. And then you can draw your own conclusions." He poured more gin into his glass. He added an ice cube and a sliver of lime. We waited and sipped our drinks. Laura and I touched knees again. I put a hand on her warm thigh and left it there.

"What do any of us really know about love?" Mel said. "It

seems to me we're just beginners at love. We say we love each other and we do, I don't doubt it. I love Terri and Terri loves me, and you guys love each other too. You know the kind of love I'm talking about now. Physical love, that impulse that drives you to someone special, as well as love of the other person's being, his or her essence, as it were. Carnal love and, well, call it sentimental love, the day-to-day caring about the other person. But sometimes I have a hard time accounting for the fact that I must have loved my first wife too. But I did, I know I did. So I suppose I am like Terri in that regard. Terri and Ed." He thought about it and then he went on. "There was a time when I thought I loved my first wife more than life itself. But now I hate her guts. I do. How do you explain that? What happened to that love? What happened to it, is what I'd like to know. I wish someone could tell me. Then there's Ed. Okay, we're back to Ed. He loves Terri so much he tries to kill her and he winds up killing himself." Mel stopped talking and swallowed from his glass. "You guys have been together eighteen months and you love each other. It shows all over you. You glow with it. But you both loved other people before you met each other. You've both been married before, just like us. And you probably loved other people before that too, even. Terri and I have been together five years, been married for four. And the terrible thing, the terrible thing is, but the good thing too, the saving grace, you might say, is that if something happened to one of us—excuse me for saying this—but if something happened to one of us tomorrow, I think the other one, the other person, would grieve for a while, you know, but then the surviving party would go out and love again, have someone else soon enough. All this, all of this love we're talking about, it would just be a memory. Maybe not even a memory. Am I wrong? Am I way off base? Because I want you to set me straight if you think I'm wrong. I want to know. I mean, I don't know anything, and I'm the first one to admit it."

"Mel, for God's sake," Terri said. She reached out and took hold of his wrist. "Are you getting drunk? Honey? Are you drunk?"

"Honey, I'm just talking," Mel said. "All right? I don't have to be drunk to say what I think. I mean, we're all just talking, right?" Mel said. He fixed his eyes on her.

"Sweetie, I'm not criticizing," Terri said.

She picked up her glass.

"I'm not on call today," Mel said. "Let me remind you of that. I am not on call," he said.

"Mel, we love you," Laura said.

Mel looked at Laura. He looked at her as if he could not place her, as if she was not the woman she was.

"Love you too, Laura," Mel said. "And you, Nick, love you too. You know something?" Mel said. "You guys are our pals," Mel said.

He picked up his glass.

Mel said, "I was going to tell you about something. I mean, I was going to prove a point. You see, this happened a few months ago, but it's still going on right now, and it ought to make us feel ashamed when we talk like we know what we're talking about when we talk about love."

"Come on now," Terri said. "Don't talk like you're drunk if you're not drunk."

"Just shut up for once in your life," Mel said very quietly. "Will you do me a favor and do that for a minute? So as I was saying, there's this old couple who had this car wreck out on the interstate. A kid hit them and they were all torn to shit and nobody was giving them much chance to pull through."

Terri looked at us and then back at Mel. She seemed anxious, or maybe that's too strong a word.

Mel was handing the bottle around the table.

"I was on call that night," Mel said. "It was May or maybe it was June. Terri and I had just sat down to dinner when the hospital called. There'd been this thing out on the interstate. Drunk kid, teenager, plowed his dad's pickup into this camper with this old couple in it. They were up in their mid-seventies, that couple. The kid—eighteen, nineteen, something—he was DOA. Taken the steering wheel through his sternum. The old couple, they were alive, you understand. I mean, just barely. But they had everything. Multiple fractures, internal injuries, hemorrhaging, contusions, lacerations, the works, and they each of them had themselves concussions. They were in a bad way, believe me. And, of course, their age was two strikes against them. I'd say she was worse off than he was. Ruptured spleen along with everything else. Both kneecaps broken. But they'd been wearing their seatbelts and, God knows, that's what saved them for the time being."

"Folks, this is an advertisement for the National Safety Council," Terri said. "This is your spokesman, Dr. Melvin R. McGinnis, talking." Terri laughed. "Mel," she said, "sometimes you're just too much. But I love you, hon," she said.

"Honey, I love you," Mel said.

He leaned across the table. Terri met him halfway. They kissed.

"Terri's right," Mel said as he settled himself again. "Get those seatbelts on. But seriously, they were in some shape, those oldsters. By the time I got down there, the kid was dead, as I said. He was off in a corner, laid out on a gurney. I took one look at the old couple and told the ER nurse to get me a neurologist and an orthopedic man and a couple of surgeons down there right away."

He drank from his glass. "I'll try to keep this short," he said. "So we took the two of them up to the OR and worked like fuck on them most of the night. They had these incredible reserves, those two. You see that once in a while. So we did everything that could be done, and toward morning we're giving them a fifty-fifty chance, maybe less than that for her. So here they are, still alive the next morning. So, okay, we move them into the ICU, which is where they both kept plugging away at it for two weeks, hitting it better and better on all the scopes. So we transfer them out to their own room."

Mel stopped talking. "Here," he said, "let's drink this cheapo gin the hell up. Then we're going to dinner, right? Terri and I know a new place. That's where we'll go, to this new place we know about. But we're not going until we finish up this cut-rate, lousy gin."

Terri said, "We haven't actually eaten there yet. But it looks good. From the outside, you know."

"I like food," Mel said. "If I had it to do all over again, I'd be a chef, you know? Right, Terri?" Mel said.

He laughed. He fingered the ice in his glass.

"Terri knows," he said. "Terri can tell you. But let me say

this. If I could come back again in a different life, a different time and all, you know what? I'd like to come back as a knight. You were pretty safe wearing all that armor. It was all right being a knight until gunpowder and muskets and pistols came along."

"Mel would like to ride a horse and carry a lance," Terri said.

"Carry a woman's scarf with you everywhere," Laura said.

"Or just a woman," Mel said.

"Shame on you," Laura said.

Terri said, "Suppose you came back as a serf. The serfs didn't have it so good in those days," Terri said.

"The serfs never had it good," Mel said. "But I guess even the knights were vessels to someone. Isn't that the way it worked? But then everyone is always a vessel to someone. Isn't that right? Terri? But what I liked about knights, besides their ladies, was that they had that suit of armor, you know, and they couldn't get hurt very easy. No cars in those days, you know? No drunk teenagers to tear into your ass."

"Vassals," Terri said.

"What?" Mel said.

"Vassals," Terri said. "They were called vassals, not vessels."

"Vassals, vessels," Mel said, "what the fuck's the difference? You knew what I meant anyway. All right," Mel said. "So I'm not educated. I learned my stuff. I'm a heart surgeon, sure, but I'm just a mechanic. I go in and I fuck around and I fix things. Shit," Mel said.

"Modesty doesn't become you," Terri said.

"He's just a humble sawbones," I said. "But sometimes they suffocated in all that armor, Mel. They'd even have heart attacks if it got too hot and they were too tired and worn out. I read somewhere that they'd fall off their horses and not be able to get up because they were too tired to stand with all that armor on them. They got trampled by their own horses sometimes."

"That's terrible," Mel said. "That's a terrible thing, Nicky. I guess they'd just lay there and wait until somebody came along and made a shish kebab out of them."

"Some other vessel," Terri said.

"That's right," Mel said. "Some vassal would come along

and spear the bastard in the name of love. Or whatever the fuck it was they fought over in those days."

"Same things we fight over these days," Terri said.

Laura said, "Nothing's changed."

The color was still high in Laura's cheeks. Her eyes were bright. She brought her glass to her lips.

Mel poured himself another drink. He looked at the label closely as if studying a long row of numbers. Then he slowly put the bottle down on the table and slowly reached for the tonic water.

"What about the old couple?" Laura said. "You didn't finish that story you started."

Laura was having a hard time lighting her cigarette. Her matches kept going out.

The sunshine inside the room was different now, changing, getting thinner. But the leaves outside the window were still shimmering, and I stared at the pattern they made on the panes and on the Formica counter. They weren't the same patterns, of course.

"What about the old couple?" I said.

"Older but wiser," Terri said.

Mel stared at her.

Terri said, "Go on with your story, hon. I was only kidding. Then what happened?"

"Terri, sometimes," Mel said.

"Please, Mel," Terri said. "Don't always be so serious, sweetie. Can't you take a joke?"

"Where's the joke?" Mel said.

He held his glass and gazed steadily at his wife.

"What happened?" Laura said.

Mel fastened his eyes on Laura. He said, "Laura, if I didn't have Terri and if I didn't love her so much, and if Nick wasn't my best friend, I'd fall in love with you. I'd carry you off, honey," he said.

"Tell your story," Terri said. "Then we'll go to that new place, okay?"

"Okay," Mel said. "Where was I?" he said. He stared at the table and then he began again.

"I dropped in to see each of them every day, sometimes twice a day if I was up doing other calls anyway. Casts and bandages, head to foot, the both of them. You know, you've seen it in the movies. That's just the way they looked, just like in the movies. Little eye-holes and nose-holes and mouth-holes. And she had to have her legs slung up on top of it. Well, the husband was very depressed for the longest while. Even after he found out that his wife was going to pull through, he was still very depressed. Not about the accident, though. I mean, the accident was one thing, but it wasn't everything. I'd get up to his mouth-hole, you know, and he'd say no, it wasn't the accident exactly but it was because he couldn't see her through his eye-holes. He said that was what was making him feel so bad. Can you imagine? I'm telling you, the man's heart was breaking because he couldn't turn his goddamn head and *see* his goddamn wife."

Mel looked around the table and shook his head at what he was going to say.

"I mean, it was killing the old fart just because he couldn't *look* at the fucking woman."

We all looked at Mel.

"Do you see what I'm saying?" he said.

Maybe we were a little drunk by then. I know it was hard keeping things in focus. The light was draining out of the room, going back through the window where it had come from. Yet nobody made a move to get up from the table to turn on the overhead light.

"Listen," Mel said. "Let's finish this fucking gin. There's about enough left here for one shooter all around. Then let's go eat. Let's go to the new place."

"He's depressed," Terri said. "Mel, why don't you take a pill?"

Mel shook his head. "I've taken everything there is."

"We all need a pill now and then," I said.

"Some people are born needing them," Terri said.

She was using her finger to rub at something on the table. Then she stopped rubbing.

"I think I want to call my kids," Mel said. "Is that all right with everybody? I'll call my kids," he said.

Terri said, "What if Marjorie answers the phone? You guys, you've heard us on the subject of Marjorie? Honey, you know you don't want to talk to Marjorie. It'll make you feel even worse."

"I don't want to talk to Marjorie," Mel said. "But I want to talk to my kids."

"There isn't a day goes by that Mel doesn't say he wishes she'd get married again. Or else die," Terri said. "For one thing," Terri said, "she's bankrupting us. Mel says it's just to spite him that she won't get married again. She has a boyfriend who lives with her and the kids, so Mel is supporting the boyfriend too."

"She's allergic to bees," Mel said. "If I'm not praying she'll get married again, I'm praying she'll get herself stung to death by a swarm of fucking bees."

"Shame on you," Laura said.

"Bzzzzzzz," Mel said, turning his fingers into bees and buzzing them at Terri's throat. Then he let his hands drop all the way to his sides.

"She's vicious," Mel said. "Sometimes I think I'll go up there dressed like a beekeeper. You know, that hat that's like a helmet with the plate that comes down over your face, the big gloves, and the padded coat? I'll knock on the door and let loose a hive of bees in the house. But first I'd make sure the kids were out, of course."

He crossed one leg over the other. It seemed to take him a lot of time to do it. Then he put both feet on the floor and leaned forward, elbows on the table, his chin cupped in his hands.

"Maybe I won't call the kids, after all. Maybe it isn't such a hot idea. Maybe we'll just go eat. How does that sound?"

"Sounds fine to me," I said. "Eat or not eat. Or keep drinking. I could head right out into the sunset."

"What does that mean, honey?" Laura said.

"It just means what I said," I said. "It means I could just keep going. That's all it means."

"I could eat something myself," Laura said. "I don't think I've ever been so hungry in my life. Is there something to nibble on?"

"I'll put out some cheese and crackers," Terri said.

But Terri just sat there. She did not get up to get anything.

Mel turned his glass over. He spilled it out on the table.

"Gin's gone," Mel said.

Terri said, "Now what?"

I could hear my heart beating. I could hear everyone's heart. I could hear the human noise we sat there making, not one of us moving, not even when the room went dark.

One More Thing

L.D.'s wife, Maxine, told him to get out the night she came home from work and found L.D. drunk again and being abusive to Rae, their fifteen-year-old. L.D. and Rae were at the kitchen table, arguing. Maxine didn't have time to put her purse away or take off her coat.

Rae said, "Tell him, Mom. Tell him what we talked about."

L.D. turned the glass in his hand, but he didn't drink from it. Maxine had him in a fierce and disquieting gaze.

"Keep your nose out of things you don't know anything about," L.D. said. L.D. said, "I can't take anybody seriously who sits around all day reading astrology magazines."

"This has nothing to do with astrology," Rae said. "You don't have to insult me."

As for Rae, she hadn't been to school for weeks. She said no one could make her go. Maxine said it was another tragedy in a long line of low-rent tragedies.

"Why don't you both shut up!" Maxine said. "My God, I already have a headache."

"Tell him, Mom," Rae said. "Tell him it's all in his head. Anybody who knows anything about it will tell you that's where it is!"

"How about sugar diabetes?" L.D. said. "What about epilepsy? Can the brain control that?"

He raised the glass right under Maxine's eyes and finished his drink.

"Diabetes, too," Rae said. "Epilepsy. Anything! The brain is the most powerful organ in the body, for your information."

She picked up his cigarettes and lit one for herself.

"Cancer. What about cancer?" L.D. said.

He thought he might have her there. He looked at Maxine.

"I don't know how we got started on this," L.D. said to Maxine.

"Cancer," Rae said, and shook her head at his simplicity. "Cancer, too. Cancer *starts* in the brain."

"That's crazy!" L.D. said. He hit the table with the flat of his hand. The ashtray jumped. His glass fell on its side and rolled off. "You're crazy, Rae! Do you know that?"

"Shut up!" Maxine said.

She unbuttoned her coat and put her purse down on the counter. She looked at L.D. and said, "L.D., I've had it. So has Rae. So has everyone who knows you. I've been thinking it over. I want you out of here. Tonight. This minute. Now. Get the hell out of here right now."

L.D. had no intention of going anywhere. He looked from Maxine to the jar of pickles that had been on the table since lunch. He picked up the jar and pitched it through the kitchen window.

Rae jumped away from her chair. "God! He's crazy!"

She went to stand next to her mother. She took in little breaths through her mouth.

"Call the police," Maxine said. "He's violent. Get out of the kitchen before he hurts you. Call the police," Maxine said.

They started backing out of the kitchen.

"I'm going," L.D. said. "All right, I'm going right now," he said. "It suits me to a tee. You're nuts here, anyway. This is a nuthouse. There's another life out there. Believe me, this is no picnic, this nuthouse."

He could feel air from the hole in the window on his face.

"That's where I'm going," he said. "Out there," he said and pointed.

"Good," Maxine said.

"All right, I'm going," L.D. said.

He slammed down his hand on the table. He kicked back his chair. He stood up.

"You won't ever see me again," L.D. said.

"You've given me plenty to remember you by," Maxine said.

"Okay," L.D. said.

"Go on, get out," Maxine said. "I'm paying the rent here, and I'm saying go. Now."

"I'm going," he said. "Don't push me," he said. "I'm going."

"Just go," Maxine said.

"I'm leaving this nuthouse," L.D. said.

He made his way into the bedroom and took one of her suitcases from the closet. It was an old white Naugahyde suitcase with a broken clasp. She'd used to pack it full of sweater sets and carry it with her to college. He had gone to college too. He threw the suitcase onto the bed and began putting in his underwear, his trousers, his shirts, his sweaters, his old leather belt with the brass buckle, his socks, and everything else he had. From the nightstand he took magazines for reading material. He took the ashtray. He put everything he could into the suitcase, everything it could hold. He fastened the one good side, secured the strap, and then he remembered his bathroom things. He found the vinyl shaving bag up on the closet shelf behind her hats. Into it went his razor and his shaving cream, his talcum powder and his stick deodorant and his toothbrush. He took the toothpaste, too. And then he got the dental floss.

He could hear them in the living room talking in their low voices.

He washed his face. He put the soap and towel into the shaving bag. Then he put in the soap dish and the glass from over the sink and the fingernail clippers and her eyelash curlers.

He couldn't get the shaving bag closed, but that was okay. He put on his coat and picked up the suitcase. He went into the living room.

When she saw him, Maxine put her arm around Rae's shoulders.

"This is it," L.D. said. "This is good-bye," he said. "I don't know what else to say except I guess I'll never see you again. You too," L.D. said to Rae. "You and your crackpot ideas."

"Go," Maxine said. She took Rae's hand. "Haven't you done enough damage in this house already? Go on, L.D. Get out of here and leave us in peace."

"Just remember," Rae said. "It's in your head."

"I'm going, that's all I can say," L.D. said. "Anyplace. Away from this nuthouse," he said. "That's the main thing."

He took a last look around the living room and then he moved the suitcase from one hand to the other and put the shaving bag under his arm. "I'll be in touch, Rae. Maxine, you're better off out of this nuthouse yourself."

"You made it into a nuthouse," Maxine said. "If it's a nuthouse, then that's what you made it."

He put the suitcase down and the shaving bag on top of the suitcase. He drew himself up and faced them.

They moved back.

"Watch it, Mom," Rae said.

"I'm not afraid of him," Maxine said.

L.D. put the shaving bag under his arm and picked up the suitcase.

He said, "I just want to say one more thing."

But then he could not think what it could possibly be.

STORIES FROM

FIRES

For Tess Gallagher

And isn't the past inevitable,
now that we call the little
we remember of it "the past"?

William Matthews, "Flood"

The Lie

I T'S a lie," my wife said. "How could you believe such a thing? She's jealous, that's all." She tossed her head and kept staring at me. She hadn't yet taken off her hat and coat. Her face was flushed from the accusation. "You believe me, don't you? Surely you don't believe that?"

I shrugged. Then I said, "Why should she lie? Where would it get her? What would she have to gain by lying?" I was uncomfortable. I stood there in my slippers opening and closing my hands, feeling a little ridiculous and on display in spite of the circumstances. I'm not cut out to play the inquisitor. I wish now it had never reached my ears, that everything could have been as before. "She's supposed to be a friend," I said. "A friend to both of us."

"She's a bitch, is what she is! You don't think a friend, however poor a friend, even a chance acquaintance, would tell a thing like that, such an outright lie, do you? You simply can't believe it." She shook her head at my folly. Then she unpinned her hat, pulled off her gloves, laid everything on the table. She removed her coat and dropped it over the back of a chair.

"I don't know what to believe any more," I said. "I want to believe you."

"Then do!" she said. "Believe me—that's all I'm asking. I'm telling you the truth. I wouldn't lie about something like that. There now. Say it isn't true, darling. Say you don't believe it."

I love her. I wanted to take her in my arms, hold her, tell her I believed her. But the lie, if it was a lie, had come between us. I moved over to the window.

"You must believe me," she said. "You know this is stupid. You know I'm telling you the truth."

I stood at the window and looked down at the traffic moving slowly below. If I raised my eyes, I could see my wife's reflection in the window. I'm a broad-minded man, I told myself. I can work this through. I began to think about my wife, about our life together, about truth versus fiction, honesty opposed to falsehood, illusion and reality. I thought about that movie *Blow-up* we'd recently seen. I remembered the biography of Leo Tolstoy that lay on the coffee table, the things he says about truth, the splash he'd made in old Russia. Then I recalled a friend from long ago, a friend I'd had in my junior and senior years of high school. A friend who could never tell the truth, a chronic, unmitigated liar, yet a pleasant, well-meaning person and a true friend for two or three years during a difficult period in my life. I was overjoyed with my discovery of this habitual liar from out of my past, this precedent to draw upon for aid in the present crisis in our—up to now—happy marriage. This person, this spirited liar, could indeed bear out my wife's theory that there were such people in the world. I was happy again. I turned around to speak. I knew what I wanted to say: Yes, indeed, it could be true, it *is* true—people can and do lie, uncontrollably, perhaps unconsciously, pathologically at times, without thought to the consequences. Surely my informant was such a person. But just at that moment my wife sat down on the sofa, covered her face with her hands and said, "It's true, God forgive me. Everything she told you is true. It was a lie when I said I didn't know anything about it."

"Is that true?" I said. I sat down in one of the chairs near the window.

She nodded. She kept her hands over her face.

I said, "Why did you deny it, then? We never lie to one another. Haven't we always told each other the truth?"

"I was sorry," she said. She looked at me and shook her head. "I was ashamed. You don't know how ashamed I was. I didn't want you to believe it."

"I think I understand," I said.

She kicked off her shoes and leaned back on the sofa. Then she sat up and tugged her sweater over her head. She patted her hair into place. She took one of the cigarettes from the tray. I held the lighter for her and was momentarily astonished by the sight of her slim, pale fingers and her well-manicured nails. It was as if I were seeing them in a new and somehow revealing way.

She drew on the cigarette and said, after a minute, "And how was your day today, sweet? Generally speaking, that is. You know what I mean." She held the cigarette between her lips and stood up for a minute to step out of her skirt. "There," she said.

"It was so-so," I answered. "There was a policeman here in the afternoon, with a warrant, believe it or not, looking for someone who used to live down the hall. And the apartment manager himself called to say the water would be shut off for a half-hour between three and three-thirty while they made repairs. In fact, come to think of it, it was just during the time the policeman was here that they had to shut off the water."

"Is that so?" she said. She put her hands on her hips and stretched. Then she closed her eyes, yawned, and shook her long hair.

"And I read a good portion of the Tolstoy book today," I said.

"Marvelous." She began to eat cocktail nuts, tossing them one after the other with her right hand into her open mouth, while still holding the cigarette between the fingers of her left hand. From time to time she stopped eating long enough to wipe her lips with the back of her hand and draw on the cigarette. She'd slipped out of her underthings by now. She doubled her legs under her and settled into the sofa. "How is it?" she said.

"He had some interesting ideas," I said. "He was quite a character." My fingers tingled and the blood was beginning to move faster. But I felt weak, too.

"Come here my little muzhik," she said.

"I want the truth," I said faintly, on my hands and knees now. The plush, springy softness of the carpet excited me. Slowly I crawled over to the sofa and rested my chin on one of the cushions. She ran her hand through my hair. She was still smiling. Grains of salt glimmered on her full lips. But as I watched, her eyes filled with a look of inexpressible sadness, though she continued smiling and stroking my hair.

"Little Pasha," she said. "Come up here, dumpling. Did it really believe that nasty lady, that nasty lie? Here, put your head on mommy's breast. That's it. Now close your eyes. There. How could it believe such a thing? I'm disappointed in you. Really, you know me better than that. Lying is just a sport for some people."

The Cabin

M R. HARROLD came out of the cafe to find it'd stopped snowing. The sky was clearing behind the hills on the other side of the river. He stopped beside the car for a minute and stretched, holding the car door open while he drew a big mouthful of cold air. He'd swear he could almost taste this air. He eased in behind the steering wheel and got back on the highway. It was only an hour's drive to the lodge. He could get in a couple of hours of fishing this afternoon. Then there was tomorrow. All day tomorrow.

At Parke Junction he took the bridge over the river and turned off onto the road that would take him to the lodge. Pine trees whose branches were heavy with snow stood on either side of the road. Clouds mantled the white hills so that it was hard to tell where the hills ended and the sky began. It reminded him of those Chinese landscapes they'd looked at that time in the museum in Portland. He liked them. He'd said as much to Frances, but she didn't say anything back. She'd spent a few minutes with him in that wing of the gallery and then moved on to the next exhibit.

It was going on noon when he reached the lodge. He saw the cabins up on the hill and then, as the road straightened out, the lodge itself. He slowed, bumped off the road onto the dirty, sand-covered parking lot, and stopped the car up close to the front door. He rolled down the window and rested for a minute, working his shoulders back and forth into the seat. He closed and then opened his eyes. A flickering neon sign said Castlerock and below that, on a neat, hand-painted sign, Deluxe Cabins—OFFICE. The last time he'd been here—Frances had been with him that time—they'd stayed for four days, and he'd landed five nice fish downriver. That had been three years ago. They used to come here often, two or three times a year. He opened the door and got out of the car slowly, feeling the stiffness in his back and neck. He walked heavily across the frozen snow and stuck his hands in his coat pockets as he started up the planked steps. At the top he scraped the snow and grit off

his shoes and nodded to a young couple coming out. He
noticed the way the man held the woman's arm as they went
down the steps.

Inside the lodge there was the smell of wood smoke and
fried ham. He heard the clatter of dishes. He looked at the big
Brown trout mounted over the fireplace in the dining room,
and he felt glad to be back. Near the cash register, where he
stood, was a display case with leather purses, wallets, and pairs
of moccasins arranged behind the glass. Scattered around on
top of the case were Indian bead necklaces and bracelets and
pieces of petrified wood. He moved over to the horseshoe-
shaped counter and took a stool. Two men sitting a few stools
down stopped talking and turned their heads to look at him.
They were hunters, and their red hats and coats lay on an
empty table behind them. Mr. Harrold waited and pulled at
his fingers.

"How long you been here?" the girl asked, frowning. She'd
come on him soundlessly, from the kitchen. She put down a
glass of water in front of him.

"Not long," Mr. Harrold said.

"You should've rung the bell," she said. Her braces glittered
as she opened and closed her mouth.

"I'm supposed to have a cabin," he said. "I wrote you a card
and made a reservation a week or so ago."

"I'll have to get Mrs. Maye," the girl said. "She's cooking.
She's the one who looks after the cabins. She didn't say anything to me about it. We don't usually keep them open in the
winter, you know."

"I wrote you a card," he said. "You check with Mrs. Maye.
You ask her about it." The two men had turned on their stools
to look at him again.

"I'll get Mrs. Maye," the girl said.

Flushed, he closed his hands together on the counter in
front of him. A big Frederic Remington reproduction hung on
the wall at the far end of the room. He watched the lurching,
frightened buffalo, and the Indians with the drawn bows fixed
at their shoulders.

"Mr. Harrold!" the old woman called, hobbling toward
him. She was a small gray-haired woman with heavy breasts

and a fat throat. The straps to her underwear showed through her white uniform. She undid her apron and held out her hand.

"Glad to see you, Mrs. Maye," he said as he got up off the stool.

"I hardly recognized you," the old woman said. "I don't know what's the matter with the girl sometimes . . . Edith . . . she's my granddaughter. My daughter and her husband are looking after the place now." She took her glasses off and began wiping away the steam from the lenses.

He looked down at the polished counter. He smoothed his fingers over the grainy wood.

"Where's the Missus?" she asked.

"She didn't feel too well this week," Mr. Harrold said. He started to say something else, but there was nothing else to say.

"I'm sorry to hear that! I had the cabin fixed up nice for the two of you," Mrs. Maye said. She took off the apron and put it behind the cash register. "Edith! I'm taking Mr. Harrold to his cabin! I'll have to get my coat, Mr. Harrold." The girl didn't answer. But she came to the kitchen door with a coffee pot in her hand and stared at them.

Outside the sun had come out and the glare hurt his eyes. He held onto the banister and went slowly down the stairs, following Mrs. Maye, who limped.

"Sun's bad, isn't it?" she said, moving carefully over the packed snow. He felt she ought to be using a cane. "The first time it's been out all week," she said. She waved at some people going by in a car.

They went past a gasoline pump, locked and covered with snow, and past a little shed with a TIRES sign hung over the door. He looked through the broken windows at the heaps of burlap sacks inside, the old tires, and the barrels. The room was damp and cold-looking. Snow had drifted inside and lay sprinkled on the sill around the broken glass.

"Kids have done that," Mrs. Maye said, stopping for a minute and putting her hand up to the broken window. "They don't miss a chance to do us dirt. A whole pack of them are all the time running wild from down at the construction camp." She shook her head. "Poor little devils. Sorry home life for kids anyway, always on the move like that. Their daddies are building on that dam." She unlocked the cabin door and pushed on it. "I laid a little fire this morning so it would be nice for you," she said.

"I appreciate that, Mrs. Maye," he said.

There was a big double bed covered with a plain bedspread, a bureau, and a desk in the front room which was divided from the kitchen by a little plywood partition. There was also a sink, wood stove, woodbox, an old ice-box, an oilcloth covered table and two wooden chairs. A door opened to a bathroom. He saw a little porch to one side where he could hang his clothes.

"Looks fine," he said.

"I tried to make it as nice as I could," she said. "Do you need anything now, Mr. Harrold?"

"Not now anyway, thanks," he said.

"I'll let you rest then. You're probably tired, driving all that way," she said.

"I should bring in my things," Mr. Harrold said, following her out. He shut the door behind them and they stood on the porch looking down the hill.

"I'm just sorry your wife couldn't come," the old woman said.

He didn't answer.

From where they stood they were almost on a level with the huge rock protruding from the hillside behind the road. Some people said it looked like a petrified castle. "How's the fishing?" he said.

"Some of them are getting fish, but most of the men are out hunting," she said. "Deer season, you know."

He drove the car as close as he could to the cabin and started to unload. The last thing he took out of the car was a pint of Scotch from the glove compartment. He set the bottle on the table. Later, as he spread out the boxes of weights and hooks and thick-bodied red and white flies, he moved the bottle to the drainboard. Sitting there at the table smoking a cigarette with his tackle box open and everything in its place, his flies and the weights spread out, testing leader strength between his hands and tying up outfits for that afternoon, he was glad he'd come after all. And he'd still be able to get in a couple of hours fishing this afternoon. Then there was tomorrow. He'd already decided he would save some of the bottle for when he came back from fishing that afternoon and have the rest for tomorrow.

As he sat at the table tying up outfits, he thought he heard something digging out on the porch. He got up from the table and opened the door. But there was nothing there. There were only the white hills and the dead-looking pines under the overcast sky and, down below, the few buildings and some cars drawn up beside the highway. He was all at once very tired and thought he would lie down on the bed for a few minutes. He didn't want to sleep. He'd just lie down and rest, and then he'd get up, dress, take his things, and walk down to the river. He cleaned off the table, undressed, and then got in between the cold sheets. For a while he lay on his side, eyes closed, knees drawn up for warmth, then he turned onto his back and wiggled his toes against the sheet. He wished Frances were here. He wished there were somebody to talk to.

He opened his eyes. The room was dark. The stove gave off little crackling noises, and there was a red glow on the wall behind the stove. He lay in bed and stared at the window, not able to believe it was really dark outside. He shut his eyes again and then opened them. He'd only wanted to rest. He hadn't intended to fall asleep. He opened his eyes and sat up heavily on the side of the bed. He got on his shirt and reached for his pants. He went into the bathroom and threw water on his face.

"Goddamn it!" he said, banging things around in the kitchen cupboard, taking down some cans and putting them back again. He made a pot of coffee and drank two cups before deciding to go down to the cafe for something to eat. He put on wool slippers and a coat and hunted around until he found his flashlight. Then he went outside.

The cold air stung his cheeks and pinched his nostrils together. But the air felt good to him. It cleared his head. The lights from the lodge showed him where he was walking, and he was careful. Inside the cafe, he nodded to the girl, Edith, and sat down in a booth near the end of the counter. He could hear a radio playing back in the kitchen. The girl made no effort to wait on him.

"Are you closed?" Mr. Harrold said.

"Kind of. I'm cleaning up for the morning," she said.

"Too late for something to eat then," he said.

"I guess I can get you something," she said. She came over with a menu.

"Mrs. Maye around, Edith?"

"She's up in her room. Did you need her for something?"

"I need more wood. For in the morning."

"It's out in back," she said. "Right here behind the kitchen."

He pointed to something simple on the menu—a ham sandwich with potato salad. "I'll have this," he said.

As he waited, he began moving the salt and pepper shakers around in a little circle in front of him. After she brought his plate to him, she hung around out in front, filling sugar bowls and napkin holders, looking up at him from time to time. Pretty soon, before he'd finished, she came over with a wet rag and began wiping off his table.

He left some money, considerably more than the bill, and went out through a door at the side of the lodge. He went around back where he picked up an armload of wood. Then the snail's pace climb up to the cabin. He looked back once and saw the girl watching him from the kitchen window. By the time he got to his door and dropped the wood, he hated her.

He lay on the bed for a long time and read old *Life* magazines that he'd found on the porch. When the heat from the fire finally made him sleepy, he got up and cleared off his bed, then arranged his things for the next morning. He looked through the pile of stuff again to make sure he had everything. He liked things in order and didn't want to get up the next morning and have to look for something. He picked up the Scotch and held the bottle up to the light. Then he poured some into a cup. He carried the cup over to the bed and set it on the nightstand. He turned off the light and stood looking out the window for a minute before getting into bed.

He got up so early it was still almost dark in the cabin. The fire had gone down to coals during the night. He could see his breath in the cabin. He adjusted the grate and pushed in some wood. He couldn't remember the last time he'd gotten up so early. He fixed peanut butter sandwiches and wrapped them in waxed paper. He put the sandwiches and some oatmeal cookies into a coat pocket. At the door he pulled on his waders.

The light outside was vague and gray. Clouds filled the long valleys and hung in patches over the trees and mountains. The lodge was dark. He moved out slowly down the packed, slippery trail toward the river. It pleased him to be up this early and to be going fishing. Somewhere in one of the valleys off behind the river he heard the pop-pop of shots and counted them. Seven. Eight. The hunters were awake. And the deer. He wondered if the shots came from the two hunters he'd seen in the lodge yesterday. Deer didn't have much of a chance in snow like this. He kept his eyes down, watching the trail. It kept dropping downhill and soon he was in heavy timber with snow up to his ankles.

Snow lay in drifts under the trees, but it wasn't too deep where he walked. It was a good trail, packed solid, thick with pine needles that crunched into the snow under his boots. He could see his breath streaming out in front of him. He held the fishing rod straight ahead of him when he had to push through the bushes or go under trees with low limbs. He held the rod by its big reel, tucked up under his arm like a lance. Sometimes, back when he was a kid and had gone into a remote area to fish for two or three days at a time, hiking in by himself, he'd carried his rod like this, even when there was no brush or trees, maybe just a big green meadow. Those times he would imagine himself waiting for his opponent to ride out of the trees on a horse. The jays at the crowded edge of the woods would scream. Then he'd sing something as loud as he could. Yell defiance until his chest hurt, at the hawks that circled and circled over the meadow. The sun and the sky came back to him now, and the lake with the lean-to. The water so clear and green you could see fifteen or twenty feet down to where it shelved off into deeper water. He could hear the river. But the trail was gone now and just before he started down the bank to the river, he stepped into a snowdrift up over his knees and panicked, clawing up handfuls of snow and vines to get out.

The river looked impossibly cold. It was silver-green in color and there was ice on the little pools in the rocks along the edge. Before, in the summer, he'd caught his fish further downriver. But he couldn't go downriver this morning. This morning he was simply glad to be where he was. A hundred feet away, on the other side of the river, lay a beach with a nice riffle running just in front of the beach. But of course there was no way of getting over there. He decided he was just fine where he was. He lifted up onto a log, positioned himself there, and looked around. He saw tall trees and snow-covered mountains. He thought it was pretty as a picture, the way the steam lay over the river. He sat there on the log swinging his legs back and forth while he threaded the line through the guides of his rod. He tied on one of the outfits he'd made up last night. When everything was ready he slipped down off the log, pulled the rubber boots up over his legs as high as they'd go, and fastened the buckle tops of the waders to his belt. He waded slowly into the river, holding his breath for the cold water shock. The water hit and, swirling, braced against him up to his knees. He stopped, then he moved out a little further. He took the brake off his reel and made a nice cast upstream.

As he fished, he began to feel some of the old excitement coming back. He kept on fishing. After a time he waded out and sat down on a rock with his back against a log. He took out the cookies. He wasn't going to hurry anything. Not today. A flock of small birds flew from across the river and perched on some rocks close to where he was sitting. They rose when he scattered a handful of crumbs toward them. The tops of the trees creaked and the wind was drawing the clouds up out of the valley and over the hills. Then he heard a spatter of shots from somewhere in the forest across the river.

He'd just changed flies and made his cast when he saw the deer. It stumbled out of the brush upriver and ran onto the little beach, shaking and twisting its head, ropes of white mucous hanging from its nostrils. Its left hind leg was broken and dragged behind as, for an instant, the deer stopped, and turned her head back to look at it. Then she went into the river and out into the current until only her back and head were visible. She reached the shallow water on his side and came out clumsily, moving her head from side to side. He stood very still and watched her plunge into the trees.

"Dirty bastards," he said.

He made another cast. Then he reeled in and made his way

back to the shore. He sat down in the same place on the log and ate his sandwich. It was dry and it didn't have any taste to it, but he ate it anyway and tried not to think about the deer. Frances would be up now, doing things around the house. He didn't want to think about Frances, either. But he remembered that morning when he'd caught the three steelhead. It was all he could do to carry them up the hill to their cabin. But he had, and when she came to the door, he'd emptied them out of the sack onto the steps in front of her. She'd whistled and bent down to touch the black spots that ran along their backs. And he'd gone back that afternoon and caught two more.

It had turned colder. The wind was blowing down the river. He got up stiffly and hobbled over the rocks trying to loosen up. He thought about building a fire, but then decided he wouldn't stay much longer. Some crows flapped by overhead coming from across the river. When they were over him he yelled, but they didn't even look down.

He changed flies again, added more weight and cast upstream. He let the current draw the line through his fingers until he saw it go slack. Then he set the brake on his reel. The pencil-lead weight bounced against the rocks under the water. He held the butt of the rod against his stomach and wondered how the fly might look to a fish.

Several boys came out of the trees upriver and walked onto the beach. Some of them were wearing red hats and down vests. They moved around on the beach, looking at Mr. Harrold and then looking up and down the river. When they began moving down the beach in his direction, Mr. Harrold looked up at the hills, then downriver to where the best water was. He began to reel in. He caught his fly and set the hook into the cork above the reel. Then he started easing his way back toward the shore, thinking only of the shore and that each careful step brought him one step closer.

"Hey!"

He stopped and turned slowly around in the water, wishing this thing had happened when he was on the shore and not out here with the water pushing against his legs and him off balance on the slippery rocks. His feet wedged themselves down between rocks while he kept his eyes on them until he'd picked out the leader. All of them wore what looked like holsters or knife sheaths on their belts. But only one boy had a rifle. It was, he knew, the boy who'd called to him. Gaunt and thin-faced, wearing a brown duck-billed cap, the boy said:

"You see a deer come out up there?" The boy held the gun in his right hand, as if it were a pistol, and pointed the barrel up the beach.

One of the boys said, "Sure he did, Earl, it ain't been very long," and looked around at the four others. They nodded. They passed round a cigarette and kept their eyes on him.

"I said—Hey you deaf? I said did you see him?"

"It wasn't a him, it was a her," Mr. Harrold said. "And her back leg was almost shot off, for Christ's sake."

"What's that to you?" the one with the gun said.

"He's pretty smart, ain't he, Earl? Tell us where it went, you old son of a bitch!" one of the boys said.

"Where'd he go?" the boy asked, and raised the gun to his hip, half pointing it across at Mr. Harrold.

"Who wants to know?" He held the rod straight ahead, tight up under his arm and with his other hand he pulled down his hat. "You little bastards are from that trailer camp up the river, aren't you?"

"You think you know a lot, don't you?" the boy said, looking around him at the others, nodding at them. He raised up one foot and set it down slowly, then the other. In a moment, he raised the rifle to his shoulder and pulled back the hammer.

The barrel was pointed at Mr. Harrold's stomach, or else a little lower down. The water swirled and foamed around his boots. He opened and closed his mouth. But he was not able to move his tongue. He looked down into the clear water at the rocks and the little spaces of sand. He wondered what it would be like if his boots tipped water and he went down, rolling like a chunk.

"What's the matter with you?" he asked the boy. The ice water came up through his legs then and poured into his chest.

The boy didn't say anything. He just stood there. All of them just stood there looking at him.

"Don't shoot," Mr. Harrold said.

The boy held the gun on him for another minute, then he lowered it. "Scared, wasn't you?"

Mr. Harrold nodded his head dreamily. He felt as if he wanted to yawn. He kept opening and closing his mouth.

One of the boys pried loose a rock from the edge of the water and threw it. Mr. Harrold turned his back and the rock hit the water two feet away from him. The others began throwing. He stood there looking at the shore, hearing the rocks splash around him.

"You didn't want to fish here anyway, did you?" the boy said. "I could've got you, but I didn't. You see that deer, you remember how lucky you was."

Mr. Harrold stood there a minute longer. Then he looked over his shoulder. One of the boys gave him the finger, and the rest of them grinned. Then they moved together back into the trees. He watched them go. He turned and worked his way back to the shore and dropped down against the log. After a few minutes he got up and started the walk back to the cabin.

The snow had held back all morning and now, just as he was in sight of the clearing, light flakes began falling. His rod was back there somewhere. Maybe he'd left it when he stopped that one time after he turned his ankle. He could remember laying the rod on the snow as he tried to undo his boot, but he didn't recall picking it up. Anyway, it didn't matter to him now. It was a good rod and one that he'd paid over ninety dollars for one summer five or six years ago. But even if it were nice tomorrow, he wouldn't go back for it. Tomorrow? He had to be back home and at work tomorrow. A jay cried from a nearby tree, and another answered from across the clearing by his cabin. He was tired and walking slowly by now, trying to keep weight off his foot.

He came out of the trees and stopped. Lights were on down at the lodge. Even the lights in the parking area were on. There were still many hours of daylight left, but they had turned on all the lights down there. This seemed mysterious and impenetrable to him. Had something happened? He shook his head. Then he went up the steps to his cabin. He stopped on the porch. He didn't want to go inside. But he understood he had to open the door and enter the room. He didn't know if he could do that. He thought for a minute of just getting into his car and driving away. He looked once more down the hill at the lights. Then he grasped the door knob and opened the door to his cabin.

Someone, Mrs. Maye, he supposed, had built a little fire in the stove. Still, he looked around cautiously. It was quiet, except for the sizzling of the fire. He sat down on the bed and began to work off his boots. Then he sat there in his stocking feet, thinking of the river and of the large fish that must even now be moving upriver in that heart-stopping cold water. He shook his head, got up, and held his hands a few inches from the stove, opening and closing his fingers until they tingled. He let the warmth gradually come back into his body. He began to think of home, of getting back there before dark.

Harry's Death

EVERYTHING has changed since Harry's death. Being down here, for instance. Who'd have thought it, only three short months ago, that I'd be down here in Mexico and poor Harry dead and buried? Harry! Dead and buried—but not forgotten.

I couldn't go to work that day when I got the news. I was just too torn up. Jack Berger, who is the fender-and-body man at Frank's Custom Repair where we all work, called me at 6:30 a.m. as I was having a cup of coffee and a cigarette before sitting down to breakfast.

"Harry's dead," he said just like that, dropping the bomb. "Turn on your radio," he said. "Turn on your TV."

The police had just left his house after asking Jack a lot of questions about Harry. They'd told him to come down right away and identify the body. Jack said they'd probably come to my place next. Why they went to Jack Berger's place first is a mystery to me since he and Harry weren't what you'd say close. Not as close anyway as Harry and me.

I couldn't believe it, but I knew it must be true for Jack to call. I felt like I was in shock and forgot all about breakfast. I turned from one news broadcast to another until I had the story. I must have hung around an hour or so listening to the radio and getting more and more upset as I thought about Harry and what the radio was saying. There would be a lot of crummy people who wouldn't be sorry to see Harry dead, would be glad he'd bought it in fact. His wife for one would be glad, though she lived in San Diego and they hadn't seen each other for two or three years. She'd be glad. She's that kind of person, from what Harry had said. She didn't want to give him the divorce for another woman. No divorce, nothing. Now she wouldn't have to worry about it any more. No, she wouldn't be sorry to see Harry dead. But Little Judith, that's another story.

I left the house after calling in at work to report off. Frank didn't say much, he said he could understand. He felt the same

way, he said, but he had to keep the shop open. Harry would
have wanted it that way, he said. Frank Klovee. He's the owner
and shop foreman rolled into one, and the best man I ever
worked for.

I got in the car and started off in the general direction of the
Red Fox, a place where Harry and myself and Gene Smith and
Rod Williams and Ned Clark and some of the rest of the gang
hung out nights after work. It was 8:30 in the morning by then
and the traffic was heavy, so I had to keep my mind on my
driving. Still, I couldn't help thinking now and then about
poor Harry.

Harry was an operator. That is to say he always had something going. It was never a drag being around Harry. He was
good with women, if you know what I mean, always had
money and lived high. He was sharp too and somehow he
could always work it around so that in any deal he came out
smelling like a rose. The Jag he drove, for instance. It was
nearly new, a twenty-thousand-dollar car, but it had been
wrecked in a big pileup on 101. Harry bought it for a song
from the insurance company and fixed it up himself till it was
like new. That's the kind of guy Harry was. Then there's this
thirty-two-foot Chris Craft cabin cruiser that Harry's uncle in
L.A. had left Harry in his will. Harry'd only had the boat
about a month. He'd just gone down to look it over and take
it out for a little spin a couple of weeks ago. But there was the
problem of Harry's wife who was legally entitled to her share.
To keep her from somehow getting her hands on it if she got
wind of it—before he'd even laid eyes on the boat in fact—
Harry had gone to a lawyer and worked something out so that
he signed the thing over lock, stock, and pickle barrel to Little
Judith. The two of them had been planning to take it for a trip
someplace on Harry's vacation in August. Harry had been all
over, I might add. He'd been to Europe when he was in the
service and had been to all the capitals and big resort cities.
He'd been in a crowd once when someone took a shot at General de Gaulle. He'd been places and done things, Harry had.
Now he was dead.

At the Red Fox, which opens early, there was only one guy
in the place. He was sitting at the other end of the bar, and he
was no one I knew. Jimmy, the bartender, had the television

on and nodded at me as I came in. His eyes were red and it came home to me hard, Harry's death, when I saw Jimmy. There was an old Lucille Ball–Desi Arnaz show just starting and Jimmy took a long stick and turned the channel selector to another station, but there was nothing on right now about Harry.

"I can't believe it," Jimmy said, shaking his head. "Anybody but Harry."

"I feel the same way, Jimmy," I said. "Anybody but Harry."

Jimmy poured us two stiff ones and threw his off without batting an eye. "It hurts as bad as if Harry'd been my own brother. It couldn't hurt any worse." He shook his head again and stared a while at his glass. He was pretty far gone already.

"We'd better have another one," he said.

"Put a little water in mine this time," I said.

A few guys, friends of Harry's, drifted in from time to time that morning. Once I saw Jimmy get out a handkerchief and blow his nose. The guy at the other end of the bar, the stranger, made a move as if to play something on the juke box. But Jimmy went over and pulled the plug with a wild jerk and glared at the guy till he left. None of us had much to say to each other. What could we say? We were still too numb. Finally Jimmy brought out an empty cigar box and put it on the bar. He said we'd better start a collection for a wreath. We all put in a dollar or two to get things going. Jimmy took a grease pencil and marked HARRY FUND on the box.

Mike Demarest came in and took the stool next to mine. He's a bartender at the T-'N-T Club. "Cripes!" he said. "I heard it on the clock radio. The wife was getting dressed for work and woke me up and said, 'Is that the Harry you know?' Sure as hell. Give me a double and a beer chaser, Jimmy."

In a few minutes he said, "How's Little Judith taking it? Has anybody seen Little Judith?" I could see he was watching me out of the corner of his eye. I didn't have anything to say to him. Jimmy said, "She called here this morning and sounded pretty hysterical, poor kid."

After another drink or two, Mike turned to me and said, "You going down to view him?"

I waited for a minute before answering. "I don't care much for that sort of thing. I doubt it."

Mike nodded as if he understood. But a minute later I caught him watching me in the mirror behind the bar. I might put in here that I don't like Mike Demarest, if you haven't already guessed. I have never liked him. Harry didn't like him either. We'd talked about it. But that's the way it always is— the good guys get it and the others go about their business.

About then I noticed my palms were getting clammy and my insides felt like lead. At the same time I could feel the blood pounding hard in my temples. For a minute I thought I was going to faint. I slid off the stool, nodded at Mike and said, "Take it easy, Jimmy."

"Yeah, you too," he said.

Outside I leaned against the wall for a minute, trying to get my bearings. I remembered I hadn't had any breakfast. What with the anxiety and depression and the drinks I'd had, it was no wonder my head was spinning. But I didn't want anything to eat. I couldn't have eaten a bite for anything. A clock over a jewelry store window across the street said ten to eleven. It seemed like it should be late afternoon at least, so much had happened.

It was at that moment I saw Little Judith. She came around the corner walking slowly, her shoulders hunched and drawn, a pinched look to her face. A pitiful sight. She had a big wad of Kleenex in her hand. She stopped once and blew her nose.

"Judith," I said.

She made a sound that went to my heart like a bullet. We put our arms around each other right there on the sidewalk.

I said, "Judith, I'm so sorry. What can I do? I'd give my right arm, you know that."

She nodded. She couldn't say anything. We stood there patting and rubbing each other, me trying to console her, saying whatever came to mind, both of us sniffling. She let go for a minute and looked at me with a dazed look, then she threw her arms around me again.

"I can't, I can't believe it, that's all," she said. "I just can't." She kept squeezing my shoulder with one hand and patting my back with the other.

"It's true, Judith," I said. "It's on the radio and TV news, and it'll be in all the papers tonight."

"No, no," she said, squeezing me all the harder.

I was beginning to get woozy again. I could feel the sun burning down on my head. She still had her arms around me. I moved just enough so that we had to pull apart. But I kept my arm around her waist to give her support.

"We were going away next month," she said. "Last night we sat at our table in the Red Fox for three or four hours, making plans."

"Judith," I said, "let's go someplace and have a cup of coffee or a drink."

"Let's go inside," she said.

"No, someplace else," I said. "We can come back here later."

"I think if I ate something I might feel better," she said.

"That's a good idea," I said. "I could eat something."

The next three days passed in a whirl. I went to work each day, but it was a sad and depressing place without Harry. I saw a lot of Little Judith after work. I sat with her in the evenings and tried to keep her from dwelling on too many unpleasant aspects of the thing. I also took her around here and there for things she had to attend to. Twice I took her to the funeral parlor. She collapsed the first time. I wouldn't go inside the place myself. I wanted to remember poor Harry as he used to be.

The day before the service all of us at the shop chipped in thirty-eight bucks for a funeral spray. I was delegated to go and pick it out since I'd been close to Harry. I remembered a florist's not too far from my place. So I drove home, fixed some lunch, then drove to Howard's House of Flowers. It was in this shopping center along with a pharmacy, a barber shop, a bank and a travel agency. I parked the car and hadn't taken more than a couple of steps when my eye was caught by this big poster in the travel agency window. I went over to the window and stood for a while. Mexico. There was this giant stone face grinning down like the sun over a blue sea filled with little sailboats that looked like white paper napkins. On the beach, women in bikinis lounged around in sun glasses, or else played badminton. I looked at all the posters in the window, including those for Germany and Merrie England, but I kept going back to that grinning sun, the beach, the women, and the little boats. Finally I combed my hair in the reflection from the window, straightened my shoulders, and went on to the florist's.

The next morning Frank Klovee came to work wearing slacks, white shirt and tie. He said if any of us wanted to go see Harry off it was all right with him. Most of the guys went home to change, took in the funeral, and then took the rest of the afternoon off. Jimmy had set up a little buffet at the Red Fox in honor of Harry. He had different kinds of dip, potato chips and sandwiches. I didn't go to the funeral but I did drop by the Red Fox later in the afternoon. Little Judith was there, sure. She was dressed up and moving around the place like she'd had a heavy dose of shell shock. Mike Demarest was there too, and I could see him looking her over from time to time. She went from one guy to another talking about Harry and saying things like, "Harry thought the world of you, Gus." Or, "Harry would have wanted it that way." Or, "Harry would have liked that part best. Harry was just that sort." Two or three guys hugged her and patted her on the hips and carried on so that I almost asked them to leave off. A few old pods drifted in, guys that Harry probably hadn't exchanged a dozen words with in his life—if he'd ever even laid eyes on them—and said what a tragedy it was, and threw down beer and sandwiches. Little Judith and I stayed around till the place emptied out around seven. Then I took her home.

You've probably guessed some of the rest of the story by now. Little Judith and I started keeping company after Harry's death. We went to the movies nearly every night and then to a bar or else to her place. We only went back to the Red Fox once, and then we decided not to go there any more, but to go to new places instead—places where she and Harry had never been. One Sunday not long after the funeral the two of us went out to Golden Gate Cemetery to put a pot of flowers on Harry's grave. But they hadn't put his marker in yet, so we spent an hour looking for it and were still not able to find the goddamn grave. Little Judith kept running around from one spot to another calling, "Here it is! Here it is!" But the plot always turned out to belong to somebody else. We finally left, both of us feeling depressed.

In August we drove down to L.A. to have a look at the boat.

It was a fine piece of work. Harry's uncle had kept it in prime shape and Tomás, the Mexican boy who looked after it, said he wouldn't be afraid to take it around the world. Little Judith and I just looked at it and then looked at each other. It's seldom anything turns out to be better than you expected it to be. Usually it's the other way around. But that's the way it was with this boat—better than anything we'd dreamed. On our way back to San Francisco we decided to take it on a little cruise the next month. And so we set out on our trip in September, just before the Labor Day weekend.

As I said, a lot of things have changed since Harry's death. Even Little Judith is out of the picture now, gone in a way that is tragic and still has me wondering. It was somewhere off the Baja coast that it happened: Little Judith, who couldn't swim a stroke, came up missing. We figured she fell overboard during the night. What she was doing up on deck so late, or what caused her to fall overboard, neither Tomás nor I know. All we know is that the next morning she was gone and neither of us saw anything or heard her cry out. She simply disappeared. That is the truth, so help me, and what I told the police when we put in at Guaymas a few days later. My wife, I told them— for luckily we'd married just before leaving San Francisco. It was to have been our honeymoon trip.

I said things have changed since Harry's death. Now here I am in Mazatlan and Tomás is showing me some of the sights. Things you never thought existed back in the States. Our next stop is Manzanillo, Tomás's home town. Then Acapulco. We intend to keep going until the money runs out, then put in and work for a while, then set out again. It occurs to me that I'm doing things the way Harry would have wanted. But who can tell about that now?

Sometimes I think I was born to be a rover.

The Pheasant

GERALD WEBER didn't have any words left in him. He kept quiet and drove the car. Shirley Lennart had stayed awake at first, for the novelty of it more than anything, the fact of being alone with him for any length of time. She'd put several cassettes on to play—Crystal Gayle, Chuck Mangione, Willie Nelson—and then later, toward morning, had begun dialing the radio from one station to another, picking up world and local news, brief weather and farm reports, even an early morning question-and-answer program on the effects of marijuana smoking on nursing mothers, anything to fill in the long silences. From time to time, smoking, she looked across at him through the dark gloom of the big car. Somewhere between San Luis Obispo and Potter, California, a hundred and fifty miles or so from her summer house at Carmel, she gave up Gerald Weber as a bad investment—she'd made others, she reflected wearily—and fell asleep on the seat.

He could hear her ragged breathing over the sound of the air that rushed by outside. He turned off the radio and was glad for the privacy. It had been a mistake to leave Hollywood in the middle of the night for a three-hundred-mile drive, but that night, two days before his thirtieth birthday, he'd felt at loose ends and suggested that they drive up to her beach house for a few days. It was ten o'clock and they were still drinking martinis, though they'd moved out to the patio that overlooked the city. "Why not?" she'd said, stirring the drink with her finger and looking at him where he stood against the balcony railing. "Let's. I think it's the best idea you've had all week," licking the gin off her finger.

He took his eyes off the road. She didn't look asleep, she looked unconscious, or seriously injured—as if she'd fallen out of a building. She lay twisted in the seat, one leg doubled under and the other hanging over the seat almost to the floor. The skirt was pulled above her thighs, exposing the tops of the nylons, the garter belt, and the flesh in between. Her head lay on the arm rest and her mouth was open.

It had rained off and on through the night. Now, just as it

began to turn light, the rain stopped, although the highway was still damp and black and he could see small puddles of water lying in the depressions in the open fields on either side of the road. He wasn't tired yet. He felt all right, considering. He was glad to be doing something. It felt good to sit there behind the wheel, driving, not having to think.

He had just turned off the headlights and decreased his speed a little when he saw the pheasant out of the corner of his eye. It was flying low and fast and at an angle that might take it into the path of the car. He touched the brake, then increased his speed and tightened his grip on the wheel. The bird struck the left headlamp with a loud *thunk*. It spun up past the windshield, trailing feathers and a stream of shit.

"Oh my God," he said, appalled at what he'd done.

"What's happened?" she said, sitting up heavily, wide-eyed and startled.

"I hit something . . . a pheasant." He could hear the glass from the broken headlamp tinkling on the pavement as he braked the car.

He pulled onto the shoulder and got out. The air was damp and cold and he buttoned his sweater as he bent over to inspect the damage. Except for a few jagged pieces of glass which he tried for a minute with trembling fingers to loosen and work out, the headlamp was gone. There was also a small dent in the left front fender. In the dent, a smear of blood coated the metal and several dun-colored feathers were pressed into the blood. It was a hen pheasant, he'd seen that the moment before the impact.

Shirley leaned over to his side of the car and pressed the button for the window. She was still half-asleep. "Gerry?" she called to him.

"Just a minute. Just stay in the car," he said.

"I wasn't about to get out," she said. "Just hurry, I mean."

He walked back along the shoulder. A truck went by throwing up a mist of spray, and the driver looked out of the cab at him as he roared past. Gerry hunched his shoulders against the cold and kept walking until he came to the sprinkling of broken glass in the road. He walked further, looking closely into the wet grass beside the road, until he found the bird. He couldn't bring himself to touch it, but he looked at it for a minute; crumpled, its eyes open, a bright spot of blood on its beak.

When he was back in the car, Shirley said, "I didn't know what had happened. Did it do much damage?"

"It knocked out a headlight and made a little dent in the fender," he said. He looked back the way they'd come, and then pulled out onto the road.

"Did it kill it?" she said. "I mean, it must have, of course. I suppose it didn't have a chance."

He looked at her and then back at the road. "We were going seventy miles an hour."

"How long have I been asleep?"

When he didn't answer, she said, "I have a headache. I have a bad headache. How far are we from Carmel?"

"A couple of hours," he said.

"I'd like something to eat and some coffee. Maybe that'll make my head feel better," she said.

"We'll stop in the next town," he said.

She turned the rearview mirror and studied her face. She touched here and there under her eyes with her finger. Then she yawned and turned on the radio. She began to spin the knob.

He thought about the pheasant. It had happened very fast, but it was clear to him he'd hit the bird deliberately. "How well do you really know me?" he said.

"What do you mean?" she said. She let the radio alone for a minute and leaned back against the seat.

"I just said, How well do you know me?"

"I don't have any idea what you mean."

He said, "Just how well do you know me? That's all I'm asking."

"Why do you ask me that at this time of the morning?"

"We're just talking. I just asked you how well you knew me. Would I"—how should he put it?—"am I trustworthy, for instance? Do you trust me?" It wasn't clear to him what he was asking, but he felt on the edge of something.

"Is it important?" she said. She looked at him steadily.

He shrugged. "If you don't think it is, then I guess it isn't." He gave his attention back to the road. At least in the beginning, he thought, there'd been some affection. They began living together because she had suggested it for one thing, and because at the time he'd met her, at the party of a friend in a Pacific Palisades apartment, he'd wanted the kind of life he imagined she could give him. She had money and she had connections. Connections were more important than money. But money and connections both—that was unbeatable. As for him, he was just out of graduate studies at UCLA, a drama major—wasn't the city filled with them though—and, except for university theater productions, an actor without a salaried role to his credit. He was also broke. She was older by twelve years, had been married and divorced twice, but she had some money and she took him to parties where he met people. As a result, he'd landed a few minor roles. He could call himself an actor at long last, even if he didn't have more than a month or two month's work each year. The rest of the time, these last three years, he'd spent lying in the sun near her pool, or at parties, or else running here and there with Shirley.

"Let me ask you this then," he went on. "Do you think I'd act, that I'd ever do something against my own best interests?"

She looked at him and tapped a tooth with her thumbnail.

"Well?" he said. It still wasn't clear to him where this might lead. But he intended to keep on with it.

"Well, what?" she said.

"You heard me."

"I think you would, Gerald. I think you would if you thought it was important enough at the time. Now don't ask me any more questions, okay?"

The sun was out now. The clouds had broken up. He began to see signs announcing various services in the next town. There was more traffic on the road. The wet fields on either side looked freshly green and sparkled in the early morning sun.

She smoked her cigarette and stared out the window. She wondered if she should spend the energy to change the subject. But she was becoming irritated too. She was sick of this whole thing. It was too bad she'd agreed to come with him. She should've stayed in Hollywood. She didn't like people who were forever trying to find themselves, the brooding, introspective bit.

Then she said, "Look! Look at those places," she exclaimed. Out in the fields on their left were sections of portable barracks, housing for the farmworkers. The barracks stood on blocks two or three feet off the ground, waiting to be trucked to another location. There were twenty-five or thirty such barracks. They had been raised off the ground and left standing so that some of the barracks faced the road and some of them were facing in other directions. It looked as if an upheaval had taken place.

"Look at that," she said as they sped past.

"John Steinbeck," he said. "Something out of Steinbeck."

"What?" she said. "Oh, Steinbeck. Yes, that's right. Steinbeck."

He blinked his eyes and imagined he saw the pheasant. He remembered his foot punching down on the accelerator as he tried to hit the bird. He opened his mouth to say something. But he couldn't find any words. He was amazed, and at the same time deeply moved and ashamed, at the sudden impulse —which he'd acted upon—to kill the pheasant. His fingers stiffened on the wheel.

"What would you say if I told you I killed that pheasant intentionally? That I tried to hit it?"

She gazed at him for a minute without any interest. She didn't say anything. Something became clear to him then. Partly, he supposed later, it was a result of the look of bored indifference she turned on him, and partly it was a consequence of his own state of mind. But he suddenly understood that he no longer had any values. No frame of reference, was the phrase that ran through his mind.

"Is it true?" she said.

He nodded. "It could have been dangerous. It could have gone through the windshield. But it's more than that," he said.

"I'm sure it's more than that. If you say so, Gerry. But it doesn't surprise me, if that's what you think. I'm not surprised," she said. "Nothing about you surprises me any more. You get your kicks, don't you?"

They were entering Potter. He cut his speed and began looking for the restaurant he'd seen advertised on the billboard. He located it a few blocks into the downtown area and pulled up in front onto the gravelled parking area. It was still early in the morning. Inside the restaurant, heads turned in their direction as he eased the big car to a stop and set the brake. He took the key from the ignition. They turned in the seat and looked at each other.

"I'm not hungry any more," she said. "You know something? You take away my appetite."

"I take away my own appetite," he said.

She continued to stare at him. "Do you know what you'd better do, Gerald? You'd better do something."

"I'll think of something." He opened the car door and got out. He bent down in front of the car and examined the smashed headlamp and the dented fender. Then he went around to her side of the car and opened the door for her. She hesitated, then got out of the car.

"Keys," she said. "The car keys, please."

He felt as if they were doing a scene and this was the fifth or sixth take. But it still wasn't clear what was going to happen next. He was suddenly tired through to his bones, but he felt high too and on the edge of something. He gave her the keys. She closed her hand and made a fist.

He said, "I suppose I'll say goodbye then, Shirley. If that isn't too melodramatic." They stood there in front of the restaurant. "I'm going to try and get my life in order," he said. "For one thing, find a job, a real job. Just not see anybody for a while. Okay? No tears, okay? We'll stay friends, if you want. We had some good times, right?"

"Gerald, you are nothing to me," Shirley said. "You're an ass. You can go to hell, you son of a bitch."

Inside the restaurant, two waitresses and a few men in coveralls all moved to the front window to watch after the woman outside slapped the man on his cheek with the back of her hand. The people inside were at first shocked and then amused with the scene. Now the woman in the parking area was pointing down the road and shaking her finger. Very dramatic. But the man had already started walking. He didn't look back, either. The people inside couldn't hear what the woman was saying, but they thought they had the picture since the man kept walking.

"God, she let him have it, didn't she?" one of the waitresses spoke up. "He got the boot and no mistake."

"He don't know how to treat them," said a trucker who had watched everything. "He should turn around and just knock hell out of her."

CATHEDRAL

For Tess Gallagher
and in memory of John Gardner

Feathers

THIS friend of mine from work, Bud, he asked Fran and
me to supper. I didn't know his wife and he didn't know
Fran. That made us even. But Bud and I were friends. And I
knew there was a little baby at Bud's house. That baby must
have been eight months old when Bud asked us to supper.
Where'd those eight months go? Hell, where's the time gone
since? I remember the day Bud came to work with a box of cigars. He handed them out in the lunchroom. They were drugstore cigars. Dutch Masters. But each cigar had a red sticker on
it and a wrapper that said IT'S A BOY! I didn't smoke cigars, but
I took one anyway. "Take a couple," Bud said. He shook the
box. "I don't like cigars either. This is her idea." He was talking
about his wife. Olla.

I'd never met Bud's wife, but once I'd heard her voice over
the telephone. It was a Saturday afternoon, and I didn't have
anything I wanted to do. So I called Bud to see if he wanted to
do anything. This woman picked up the phone and said,
"Hello." I blanked and couldn't remember her name. Bud's
wife. Bud had said her name to me any number of times. But it
went in one ear and out the other. "Hello!" the woman said
again. I could hear a TV going. Then the woman said, "Who is
this?" I heard a baby start up. "Bud!" the woman called.
"What?" I heard Bud say. I still couldn't remember her name.
So I hung up. The next time I saw Bud at work I sure as hell
didn't tell him I'd called. But I made a point of getting him to
mention his wife's name. "Olla," he said. Olla, I said to myself.
Olla.

"No big deal," Bud said. We were in the lunchroom drinking coffee. "Just the four of us. You and your missus, and me
and Olla. Nothing fancy. Come around seven. She feeds the
baby at six. She'll put him down after that, and then we'll eat.
Our place isn't hard to find. But here's a map." He gave me a
sheet of paper with all kinds of lines indicating major and minor roads, lanes and such, with arrows pointing to the four
poles of the compass. A large X marked the location of his

house. I said, "We're looking forward to it." But Fran wasn't too thrilled.

That evening, watching TV, I asked her if we should take anything to Bud's.

"Like what?" Fran said. "Did he say to bring something? How should I know? I don't have any idea." She shrugged and gave me this look. She'd heard me before on the subject of Bud. But she didn't know him and she wasn't interested in knowing him. "We could take a bottle of wine," she said. "But I don't care. Why don't you take some wine?" She shook her head. Her long hair swung back and forth over her shoulders. Why do we need other people? she seemed to be saying. We have each other. "Come here," I said. She moved a little closer so I could hug her. Fran's a big tall drink of water. She has this blond hair that hangs down her back. I picked up some of her hair and sniffed it. I wound my hand in her hair. She let me hug her. I put my face right up in her hair and hugged her some more.

Sometimes when her hair gets in her way she has to pick it up and push it over her shoulder. She gets mad at it. "This hair," she says. "Nothing but trouble." Fran works in a creamery and has to wear her hair up when she goes to work. She has to wash it every night and take a brush to it when we're sitting in front of the TV. Now and then she threatens to cut it off. But I don't think she'd do that. She knows I like it too much. She knows I'm crazy about it. I tell her I fell in love with her because of her hair. I tell her I might stop loving her if she cut it. Sometimes I call her "Swede." She could pass for a Swede. Those times together in the evening she'd brush her hair and we'd wish out loud for things we didn't have. We wished for a new car, that's one of the things we wished for. And we wished we could spend a couple of weeks in Canada. But one thing we didn't wish for was kids. The reason we didn't have kids was that we didn't want kids. Maybe sometime, we said to each other. But right then, we were waiting. We thought we might keep on waiting. Some nights we went to a movie. Other nights we just stayed in and watched TV. Sometimes Fran baked things for me and we'd eat whatever it was all in a sitting.

"Maybe they don't drink wine," I said.

"Take some wine anyway," Fran said. "If they don't drink it, we'll drink it."

"White or red?" I said.

"We'll take something sweet," she said, not paying me any attention. "But I don't care if we take anything. This is your show. Let's not make a production out of it, or else I don't want to go. I can make a raspberry coffee ring. Or else some cupcakes."

"They'll have dessert," I said. "You don't invite people to supper without fixing a dessert."

"They might have rice pudding. Or Jell-O! Something we don't like," she said. "I don't know anything about the woman. How do we know what she'll have? What if she gives us Jell-O?" Fran shook her head. I shrugged. But she was right. "Those old cigars he gave you," she said. "Take them. Then you and him can go off to the parlor after supper and smoke cigars and drink port wine, or whatever those people in movies drink."

"Okay, we'll just take ourselves," I said.

Fran said, "We'll take a loaf of my bread."

Bud and Olla lived twenty miles or so from town. We'd lived in that town for three years, but, damn it, Fran and I hadn't so much as taken a spin in the country. It felt good driving those winding little roads. It was early evening, nice and warm, and we saw pastures, rail fences, milk cows moving slowly toward old barns. We saw red-winged blackbirds on the fences, and pigeons circling around haylofts. There were gardens and such, wildflowers in bloom, and little houses set back from the road. I said, "I wish we had us a place out here." It was just an idle thought, another wish that wouldn't amount to anything. Fran didn't answer. She was busy looking at Bud's map. We came to the four-way stop he'd marked. We turned right like the map said and drove exactly three and three-tenths miles. On the left side of the road, I saw a field of corn, a mailbox, and a long, graveled driveway. At the end of the driveway, back in some trees, stood a house with a front porch. There was a chimney on the house. But it was summer, so, of course, no smoke rose from the chimney. But I thought it was a pretty picture, and I said so to Fran.

"It's the sticks out here," she said.

I turned into the drive. Corn rose up on both sides of the drive. Corn stood higher than the car. I could hear gravel crunching under the tires. As we got up close to the house, we could see a garden with green things the size of baseballs hanging from the vines.

"What's that?" I said.

"How should I know?" she said. "Squash, maybe. I don't have a clue."

"Hey, Fran," I said. "Take it easy."

She didn't say anything. She drew in her lower lip and let it go. She turned off the radio as we got close to the house.

A baby's swing-set stood in the front yard and some toys lay on the porch. I pulled up in front and stopped the car. It was then that we heard this awful squall. There was a baby in the house, right, but this cry was too loud for a baby.

"What's that sound?" Fran said.

Then something as big as a vulture flapped heavily down from one of the trees and landed just in front of the car. It shook itself. It turned its long neck toward the car, raised its head, and regarded us.

"Goddamn it," I said. I sat there with my hands on the wheel and stared at the thing.

"Can you believe it?" Fran said. "I never saw a real one before."

We both knew it was a peacock, sure, but we didn't say the word out loud. We just watched it. The bird turned its head up in the air and made this harsh cry again. It had fluffed itself out and looked about twice the size it'd been when it landed.

"Goddamn," I said again. We stayed where we were in the front seat.

The bird moved forward a little. Then it turned its head to the side and braced itself. It kept its bright, wild eye right on us. Its tail was raised, and it was like a big fan folding in and out. There was every color in the rainbow shining from that tail.

"My God," Fran said quietly. She moved her hand over to my knee.

"Goddamn," I said. There was nothing else to say.

The bird made this strange wailing sound once more. "*May-awe, may-awe!*" it went. If it'd been something I was hearing late at night and for the first time, I'd have thought it was somebody dying, or else something wild and dangerous.

The front door opened and Bud came out on the porch. He was buttoning his shirt. His hair was wet. It looked like he'd just come from the shower.

"Shut yourself up, Joey!" he said to the peacock. He clapped his hands at the bird, and the thing moved back a little. "That's enough now. That's right, shut up! You shut up, you old devil!" Bud came down the steps. He tucked in his shirt as he came over to the car. He was wearing what he always wore to work—blue jeans and a denim shirt. I had on my slacks and a short-sleeved sport shirt. My good loafers. When I saw what Bud was wearing, I didn't like it that I was dressed up.

"Glad you could make it," Bud said as he came over beside the car. "Come on inside."

"Hey, Bud," I said.

Fran and I got out of the car. The peacock stood off a little to one side, dodging its mean-looking head this way and that. We were careful to keep some distance between it and us.

"Any trouble finding the place?" Bud said to me. He hadn't looked at Fran. He was waiting to be introduced.

"Good directions," I said. "Hey, Bud, this is Fran. Fran, Bud. She's got the word on you, Bud."

He laughed and they shook hands. Fran was taller than Bud. Bud had to look up.

"He talks about you," Fran said. She took her hand back. "Bud this, Bud that. You're about the only person down there he talks about. I feel like I know you." She was keeping an eye on the peacock. It had moved over near the porch.

"This here's my friend," Bud said. "He *ought* to talk about me." Bud said this and then he grinned and gave me a little punch on the arm.

Fran went on holding her loaf of bread. She didn't know what to do with it. She gave it to Bud. "We brought you something."

Bud took the loaf. He turned it over and looked at it as if it was the first loaf of bread he'd ever seen. "This is real nice of you." He brought the loaf up to his face and sniffed it.

"Fran baked that bread," I told Bud.

Bud nodded. Then he said, "Let's go inside and meet the wife and mother."

He was talking about Olla, sure. Olla was the only mother around. Bud had told me his own mother was dead and that his dad had pulled out when Bud was a kid.

The peacock scuttled ahead of us, then hopped onto the porch when Bud opened the door. It was trying to get inside the house.

"Oh," said Fran as the peacock pressed itself against her leg.

"Joey, goddamn it," Bud said. He thumped the bird on the top of its head. The peacock backed up on the porch and shook itself. The quills in its train rattled as it shook. Bud made as if to kick it, and the peacock backed up some more. Then Bud held the door for us. "She lets the goddamn thing in the house. Before long, it'll be wanting to eat at the goddamn table and sleep in the goddamn bed."

Fran stopped just inside the door. She looked back at the cornfield. "You have a nice place," she said. Bud was still holding the door. "Don't they, Jack?"

"You bet," I said. I was surprised to hear her say it.

"A place like this is not all it's cracked up to be," Bud said, still holding the door. He made a threatening move toward the peacock. "Keeps you going. Never a dull moment." Then he said, "Step on inside, folks."

I said, "Hey, Bud, what's that growing there?"

"Them's tomatoes," Bud said.

"Some farmer I got," Fran said, and shook her head.

Bud laughed. We went inside. This plump little woman with her hair done up in a bun was waiting for us in the living room. She had her hands rolled up in her apron. The cheeks of her face were bright red. I thought at first she might be out of breath, or else mad at something. She gave me the once-over, and then her eyes went to Fran. Not unfriendly, just looking. She stared at Fran and continued to blush.

Bud said, "Olla, this is Fran. And this is my friend Jack. You know all about Jack. Folks, this is Olla." He handed Olla the bread.

"What's this?" she said. "Oh, it's homemade bread. Well, thanks. Sit down anywhere. Make yourselves at home. Bud, why don't you ask them what they'd like to drink. I've got something on the stove." Olla said that and went back into the kitchen with the bread.

"Have a seat," Bud said. Fran and I plunked ourselves down on the sofa. I reached for my cigarettes. Bud said, "Here's an ashtray." He picked up something heavy from the top of the TV. "Use this," he said, and he put the thing down on the coffee table in front of me. It was one of those glass ashtrays made to look like a swan. I lit up and dropped the match into the opening in the swan's back. I watched a little wisp of smoke drift out of the swan.

The color TV was going, so we looked at that for a minute. On the screen, stock cars were tearing around a track. The announcer talked in a grave voice. But it was like he was holding back some excitement, too. "We're still waiting to have official confirmation," the announcer said.

"You want to watch this?" Bud said. He was still standing.

I said I didn't care. And I didn't. Fran shrugged. What difference could it make to her? she seemed to say. The day was shot anyway.

"There's only about twenty laps left," Bud said. "It's close now. There was a big pile-up earlier. Knocked out half-a-dozen cars. Some drivers got hurt. They haven't said yet how bad."

"Leave it on," I said. "Let's watch it."

"Maybe one of those damn cars will explode right in front of us," Fran said. "Or else maybe one'll run up into the grandstand and smash the guy selling the crummy hot dogs." She took a strand of hair between her fingers and kept her eyes fixed on the TV.

Bud looked at Fran to see if she was kidding. "That other business, that pile-up, was something. One thing led to another. Cars, parts of cars, people all over the place. Well, what can I get you? We have ale, and there's a bottle of Old Crow."

"What are you drinking?" I said to Bud.

"Ale," Bud said. "It's good and cold."

"I'll have ale," I said.

"I'll have some of that Old Crow and a little water," Fran said. "In a tall glass, please. With some ice. Thank you, Bud."

"Can do," Bud said. He threw another look at the TV and moved off to the kitchen.

—

Fran nudged me and nodded in the direction of the TV. "Look up on top," she whispered. "Do you see what I see?" I looked at where she was looking. There was a slender red vase into which somebody had stuck a few garden daisies. Next to the vase, on the doily, sat an old plaster-of-Paris cast of the most crooked, jaggedy teeth in the world. There were no lips to the awful-looking thing, and no jaw either, just these old plaster teeth packed into something that resembled thick yellow gums.

Just then Olla came back with a can of mixed nuts and a bottle of root beer. She had her apron off now. She put the can of nuts onto the coffee table next to the swan. She said, "Help yourselves. Bud's getting your drinks." Olla's face came on red again as she said this. She sat down in an old cane rocking chair and set it in motion. She drank from her root beer and looked at the TV. Bud came back carrying a little wooden tray with Fran's glass of whiskey and water and my bottle of ale. He had a bottle of ale on the tray for himself.

"You want a glass?" he asked me.

I shook my head. He tapped me on the knee and turned to Fran.

She took her glass from Bud and said, "Thanks." Her eyes went to the teeth again. Bud saw where she was looking. The cars screamed around the track. I took the ale and gave my attention to the screen. The teeth were none of my business. "Them's what Olla's teeth looked like before she had her braces put on," Bud said to Fran. "I've got used to them. But I guess they look funny up there. For the life of me, I don't know why she keeps them around." He looked over at Olla. Then he looked at me and winked. He sat down in his La-Z-Boy and crossed one leg over the other. He drank from his ale and gazed at Olla.

Olla turned red once more. She was holding her bottle of root beer. She took a drink of it. Then she said, "They're to remind me how much I owe Bud."

"What was that?" Fran said. She was picking through the can of nuts, helping herself to the cashews. Fran stopped what she was doing and looked at Olla. "Sorry, but I missed that."

Fran stared at the woman and waited for whatever thing it was she'd say next.

Olla's face turned red again. "I've got lots of things to be thankful for," she said. "That's one of the things I'm thankful for. I keep them around to remind me how much I owe Bud." She drank from her root beer. Then she lowered the bottle and said, "You've got pretty teeth, Fran. I noticed right away. But these teeth of mine, they came in crooked when I was a kid." With her fingernail, she tapped a couple of her front teeth. She said, "My folks couldn't afford to fix teeth. These teeth of mine came in just any which way. My first husband didn't care what I looked like. No, he didn't! He didn't care about any-thing except where his next drink was coming from. He had one friend only in this world, and that was his bottle." She shook her head. "Then Bud come along and got me out of that mess. After we were together, the first thing Bud said was, 'We're going to have them teeth fixed.' That mold was made right after Bud and I met, on the occasion of my second visit to the orthodontist. Right before the braces went on."

Olla's face stayed red. She looked at the picture on the screen. She drank from her root beer and didn't seem to have any more to say.

"That orthodontist must have been a whiz," Fran said. She looked back at the horror-show teeth on top of the TV.

"He was great," Olla said. She turned in her chair and said, "See?" She opened her mouth and showed us her teeth once more, not a bit shy now.

Bud had gone to the TV and picked up the teeth. He walked over to Olla and held them up against Olla's cheek. "Before and after," Bud said.

Olla reached up and took the mold from Bud. "You know something? That orthodontist wanted to keep this." She was holding it in her lap while she talked. "I said nothing doing. I pointed out to him they were *my* teeth. So he took pictures of the mold instead. He told me he was going to put the pictures in a magazine."

Bud said, "Imagine what kind of magazine that'd be. Not much call for that kind of publication, I don't think," he said, and we all laughed.

"After I got the braces off, I kept putting my hand up to my mouth when I laughed. Like this," she said. "Sometimes I still do it. Habit. One day Bud said, 'You can stop doing that anytime, Olla. You don't have to hide teeth as pretty as that. You have nice teeth now.'" Olla looked over at Bud. Bud winked at her. She grinned and lowered her eyes.

Fran drank from her glass. I took some of my ale. I didn't know what to say to this. Neither did Fran. But I knew Fran would have plenty to say about it later.

I said, "Olla, I called here once. You answered the phone. But I hung up. I don't know why I hung up." I said that and then sipped my ale. I didn't know why I'd brought it up now.

"I don't remember," Olla said. "When was that?"

"A while back."

"I don't remember," she said and shook her head. She fingered the plaster teeth in her lap. She looked at the race and went back to rocking.

Fran turned her eyes to me. She drew her lip under. But she didn't say anything.

Bud said, "Well, what else is new?"

"Have some more nuts," Olla said. "Supper'll be ready in a little while."

There was a cry from a room in the back of the house.

"Not him," Olla said to Bud, and made a face.

"Old Junior boy," Bud said. He leaned back in his chair, and we watched the rest of the race, three or four laps, no sound.

Once or twice we heard the baby again, little fretful cries coming from the room in the back of the house.

"I don't know," Olla said. She got up from her chair. "Everything's about ready for us to sit down. I just have to take up the gravy. But I'd better look in on him first. Why don't you folks go out and sit down at the table? I'll just be a minute."

"I'd like to see the baby," Fran said.

Olla was still holding the teeth. She went over and put them back on top of the TV. "It might upset him just now," she said. "He's not used to strangers. Wait and see if I can get him back to sleep. Then you can peek in. While he's asleep." She said this and then she went down the hall to a room, where she opened a door. She eased in and shut the door behind her. The baby stopped crying.

—

Bud killed the picture and we went in to sit at the table. Bud and I talked about things at work. Fran listened. Now and then she even asked a question. But I could tell she was bored, and maybe feeling put out with Olla for not letting her see the baby. She looked around Olla's kitchen. She wrapped a strand of hair around her fingers and checked out Olla's things.

Olla came back into the kitchen and said, "I changed him and gave him his rubber duck. Maybe he'll let us eat now. But don't bet on it." She raised a lid and took a pan off the stove. She poured red gravy into a bowl and put the bowl on the table. She took lids off some other pots and looked to see that everything was ready. On the table were baked ham, sweet potatoes, mashed potatoes, lima beans, corn on the cob, salad greens. Fran's loaf of bread was in a prominent place next to the ham.

"I forgot the napkins," Olla said. "You all get started. Who wants what to drink? Bud drinks milk with all of his meals."

"Milk's fine," I said.

"Water for me," Fran said. "But I can get it. I don't want you waiting on me. You have enough to do." She made as if to get up from her chair.

Olla said, "Please. You're company. Sit still. Let me get it." She was blushing again.

We sat with our hands in our laps and waited. I thought about those plaster teeth. Olla came back with napkins, big glasses of milk for Bud and me, and a glass of ice water for Fran. Fran said, "Thanks."

"You're welcome," Olla said. Then she seated herself. Bud cleared his throat. He bowed his head and said a few words of grace. He talked in a voice so low I could hardly make out the words. But I got the drift of things—he was thanking the Higher Power for the food we were about to put away.

"Amen," Olla said when he'd finished.

Bud passed me the platter of ham and helped himself to some mashed potatoes. We got down to it then. We didn't say much except now and then Bud or I would say, "This is real good ham." Or, "This sweet corn is the best sweet corn I ever ate."

"This bread is what's special," Olla said.

"I'll have some more salad, please, Olla," Fran said, softening up maybe a little.

"Have more of this," Bud would say as he passed me the platter of ham, or else the bowl of red gravy.

From time to time, we heard the baby make its noise. Olla would turn her head to listen, then, satisfied it was just fussing, she would give her attention back to her food.

"The baby's out of sorts tonight," Olla said to Bud.

"I'd still like to see him," Fran said. "My sister has a little baby. But she and the baby live in Denver. When will I ever get to Denver? I have a niece I haven't even seen." Fran thought about this for a minute, and then she went back to eating.

Olla forked some ham into her mouth. "Let's hope he'll drop off to sleep," she said.

Bud said, "There's a lot more of everything. Have some more ham and sweet potatoes, everybody."

"I can't eat another bite," Fran said. She laid her fork on her plate. "It's great, but I can't eat any more."

"Save room," Bud said. "Olla's made rhubarb pie."

Fran said, "I guess I could eat a little piece of that. When everybody else is ready."

"Me, too," I said. But I said it to be polite. I'd hated rhubarb pie since I was thirteen years old and had got sick on it, eating it with strawberry ice cream.

We finished what was on our plates. Then we heard that damn peacock again. The thing was on the roof this time. We could hear it over our heads. It made a ticking sound as it walked back and forth on the shingles.

Bud shook his head. "Joey will knock it off in a minute. He'll get tired and turn in pretty soon," Bud said. "He sleeps in one of them trees."

The bird let go with its cry once more. "*May-awe!*" it went. Nobody said anything. What was there to say?

Then Olla said, "He wants in, Bud."

"Well, he can't come in," Bud said. "We got company, in case you hadn't noticed. These people don't want a goddamn old bird in the house. That dirty bird and your old pair of teeth! What're people going to think?" He shook his head. He laughed. We all laughed. Fran laughed along with the rest of us.

"He's not *dirty*, Bud," Olla said. "What's gotten into you? You like Joey. Since when did you start calling him dirty?"

"Since he shit on the rug that time," Bud said. "Pardon the French," he said to Fran. "But, I'll tell you, sometimes I could wring that old bird's neck for him. He's not even worth killing, is he, Olla? Sometimes, in the middle of the night, he'll bring me up out of bed with that cry of his. He's not worth a nickel—right, Olla?"

Olla shook her head at Bud's nonsense. She moved a few lima beans around on her plate.

"How'd you get a peacock in the first place?" Fran wanted to know.

Olla looked up from her plate. She said, "I always dreamed of having me a peacock. Since I was a girl and found a picture of one in a magazine. I thought it was the most beautiful thing I ever saw. I cut the picture out and put it over my bed. I kept that picture for the longest time. Then when Bud and I got this place, I saw my chance. I said, 'Bud, I want a peacock.' Bud laughed at the idea."

"I finally asked around," Bud said. "I heard tell of an old boy who raised them over in the next county. Birds of paradise, he called them. We paid a hundred bucks for that bird of paradise," he said. He smacked his forehead. "God Almighty, I got me a woman with expensive tastes." He grinned at Olla.

"Bud," Olla said, "you know that isn't true. Besides everything else, Joey's a good watchdog," she said to Fran. "We don't need a watchdog with Joey. He can hear just about anything."

"If times get tough, as they might, I'll put Joey in a pot," Bud said. "Feathers and all."

"Bud! That's not funny," Olla said. But she laughed and we got a good look at her teeth again.

The baby started up once more. It was serious crying this time. Olla put down her napkin and got up from the table.

Bud said, "If it's not one thing, it's another. Bring him on out here, Olla."

"I'm going to," Olla said, and went to get the baby.

—

The peacock wailed again, and I could feel the hair on the back of my neck. I looked at Fran. She picked up her napkin and then put it down. I looked toward the kitchen window. It was dark outside. The window was raised, and there was a screen in the frame. I thought I heard the bird on the front porch.

Fran turned her eyes to look down the hall. She was watching for Olla and the baby.

After a time, Olla came back with it. I looked at the baby and drew a breath. Olla sat down at the table with the baby. She held it up under its arms so it could stand on her lap and face us. She looked at Fran and then at me. She wasn't blushing now. She waited for one of us to comment.

"Ah!" said Fran.

"What is it?" Olla said quickly.

"Nothing," Fran said. "I thought I saw something at the window. I thought I saw a bat."

"We don't have any bats around here," Olla said.

"Maybe it was a moth," Fran said. "It was something. Well," she said, "isn't that some baby."

Bud was looking at the baby. Then he looked over at Fran. He tipped his chair onto its back legs and nodded. He nodded again, and said, "That's all right, don't worry any. We know he wouldn't win no beauty contests right now. He's no Clark Gable. But give him time. With any luck, you know, he'll grow up to look like his old man."

The baby stood in Olla's lap, looking around the table at us. Olla had moved her hands down to its middle so that the baby could rock back and forth on its fat legs. Bar none, it was the ugliest baby I'd ever seen. It was so ugly I couldn't say anything. No words would come out of my mouth. I don't mean it was diseased or disfigured. Nothing like that. It was just ugly. It had a big red face, pop eyes, a broad forehead, and these big fat lips. It had no neck to speak of, and it had three or four fat chins. Its chins rolled right up under its ears, and its ears stuck out from its bald head. Fat hung over its wrists. Its arms and fingers were fat. Even calling it ugly does it credit.

The ugly baby made its noise and jumped up and down on its mother's lap. Then it stopped jumping. It leaned forward and tried to reach its fat hand into Olla's plate.

I've seen babies. When I was growing up, my two sisters had a total of six babies. I was around babies a lot when I was a kid. I've seen babies in stores and so on. But this baby beat anything. Fran stared at it, too. I guess she didn't know what to say either.

"He's a big fellow, isn't he?" I said.

Bud said, "He'll by God be turning out for football before long. He sure as hell won't go without meals around this house."

As if to make sure of this, Olla plunged her fork into some sweet potatoes and brought the fork up to the baby's mouth. "He's my baby, isn't he?" she said to the fat thing, ignoring us.

The baby leaned forward and opened up for the sweet potatoes. It reached for Olla's fork as she guided the sweet potatoes into its mouth, then clamped down. The baby chewed the stuff and rocked some more on Olla's lap. It was so pop-eyed, it was like it was plugged into something.

Fran said, "He's some baby, Olla."

The baby's face screwed up. It began to fuss all over again.

"Let Joey in," Olla said to Bud.

Bud let the legs of his chair come down on the floor. "I think we should at least ask these people if they mind," Bud said.

Olla looked at Fran and then she looked at me. Her face had gone red again. The baby kept prancing in her lap, squirming to get down.

"We're friends here," I said. "Do whatever you want."

Bud said, "Maybe they don't want a big old bird like Joey in the house. Did you ever think of that, Olla?"

"Do you folks mind?" Olla said to us. "If Joey comes inside? Things got headed in the wrong direction with that bird tonight. The baby, too, I think. He's used to having Joey come in and fool around with him a little before his bedtime. Neither of them can settle down tonight."

"Don't ask us," Fran said. "I don't mind if he comes in. I've never been up close to one before. But I don't mind." She looked at me. I suppose I could tell she wanted me to say something.

"Hell, no," I said. "Let him in." I picked up my glass and finished the milk.

Bud got up from his chair. He went to the front door and opened it. He flicked on the yard lights.

"What's your baby's name?" Fran wanted to know.

"Harold," Olla said. She gave Harold some more sweet potatoes from her plate. "He's real smart. Sharp as a tack. Always knows what you're saying to him. Don't you, Harold? You wait until you get your own baby, Fran. You'll see."

Fran just looked at her. I heard the front door open and then close.

"He's smart, all right," Bud said as he came back into the kitchen. "He takes after Olla's dad. Now there was one smart old boy for you."

I looked around behind Bud and could see that peacock hanging back in the living room, turning its head this way and that, like you'd turn a hand mirror. It shook itself, and the sound was like a deck of cards being shuffled in the other room.

It moved forward a step. Then another step.

"Can I hold the baby?" Fran said. She said it like it would be a favor if Olla would let her.

Olla handed the baby across the table to her.

Fran tried to get the baby settled in her lap. But the baby began to squirm and make its noises.

"Harold," Fran said.

Olla watched Fran with the baby. She said, "When Harold's grandpa was sixteen years old, he set out to read the encyclopedia from A to Z. He did it, too. He finished when he was twenty. Just before he met my mama."

"Where's he now?" I asked. "What's he do?" I wanted to know what had become of a man who'd set himself a goal like that.

"He's dead," Olla said. She was watching Fran, who by now had the baby down on its back and across her knees. Fran chucked the baby under one of its chins. She started to talk baby talk to it.

"He worked in the woods," Bud said. "Loggers dropped a tree on him."

"Mama got some insurance money," Olla said. "But she spent that. Bud sends her something every month."

"Not much," Bud said. "Don't have much ourselves. But she's Olla's mother."

By this time, the peacock had gathered its courage and was beginning to move slowly, with little swaying and jerking motions, into the kitchen. Its head was erect but at an angle, its red eyes fixed on us. Its crest, a little sprig of feathers, stood a few inches over its head. Plumes rose from its tail. The bird stopped a few feet away from the table and looked us over.

"They don't call them birds of paradise for nothing," Bud said.

Fran didn't look up. She was giving all her attention to the baby. She'd begun to patty-cake with it, which pleased the baby somewhat. I mean, at least the thing had stopped fussing. She brought it up to her neck and whispered something into its ear.

"Now," she said, "don't tell anyone what I said."

The baby stared at her with its pop eyes. Then it reached and got itself a baby handful of Fran's blond hair. The peacock stepped closer to the table. None of us said anything. We just sat still. Baby Harold saw the bird. It let go of Fran's hair and stood up on her lap. It pointed its fat fingers at the bird. It jumped up and down and made noises.

The peacock walked quickly around the table and went for the baby. It ran its long neck across the baby's legs. It pushed its beak in under the baby's pajama top and shook its stiff head back and forth. The baby laughed and kicked its feet. Scooting onto its back, the baby worked its way over Fran's knees and down onto the floor. The peacock kept pushing against the baby, as if it was a game they were playing. Fran held the baby against her legs while the baby strained forward.

"I just don't believe this," she said.

"That peacock is crazy, that's what," Bud said. "Damn bird doesn't know it's a bird, that's its major trouble."

Olla grinned and showed her teeth again. She looked over at Bud. Bud pushed his chair away from the table and nodded.

It *was* an ugly baby. But, for all I know, I guess it didn't matter that much to Bud and Olla. Or if it did, maybe they simply thought, So okay if it's ugly. It's our baby. And this is just a stage. Pretty soon there'll be another stage. There is this stage and then there is the next stage. Things will be okay in the long run, once all the stages have been gone through. They might have thought something like that.

Bud picked up the baby and swung him over his head until Harold shrieked. The peacock ruffled its feathers and watched.

Fran shook her head again. She smoothed out her dress where the baby had been. Olla picked up her fork and was working at some lima beans on her plate.

Bud shifted the baby onto his hip and said, "There's pie and coffee yet."

That evening at Bud and Olla's was special. I knew it was special. That evening I felt good about almost everything in my life. I couldn't wait to be alone with Fran to talk to her about what I was feeling. I made a wish that evening. Sitting there at the table, I closed my eyes for a minute and thought hard. What I wished for was that I'd never forget or otherwise let go of that evening. That's one wish of mine that came true. And it was bad luck for me that it did. But, of course, I couldn't know that then.

"What are you thinking about, Jack?" Bud said to me.

"I'm just thinking," I said. I grinned at him.

"A penny," Olla said.

I just grinned some more and shook my head.

After we got home from Bud and Olla's that night, and we were under the covers, Fran said, "Honey, fill me up with your seed!" When she said that, I heard her all the way down to my toes, and I hollered and let go.

Later, after things had changed for us, and the kid had come along, all of that, Fran would look back on that evening at Bud's place as the beginning of the change. But she's wrong. The change came later—and when it came, it was like something that happened to other people, not something that could have happened to us.

"Goddamn those people and their ugly baby," Fran will say, for no apparent reason, while we're watching TV late at night. "And that smelly bird," she'll say. "Christ, who needs it!" Fran will say. She says this kind of stuff a lot, even though she hasn't seen Bud and Olla since that one time.

Fran doesn't work at the creamery anymore, and she cut her

hair a long time ago. She's gotten fat on me, too. We don't talk about it. What's to say?

I still see Bud at the plant. We work together and we open our lunch pails together. If I ask, he tells me about Olla and Harold. Joey's out of the picture. He flew into his tree one night and that was it for him. He didn't come down. Old age, maybe, Bud says. Then the owls took over. Bud shrugs. He eats his sandwich and says Harold's going to be a linebacker someday. "You ought to see that kid," Bud says. I nod. We're still friends. That hasn't changed any. But I've gotten careful with what I say to him. And I know he feels that and wishes it could be different. I wish it could be, too.

Once in a blue moon, he asks about my family. When he does, I tell him everybody's fine. "Everybody's fine," I say. I close the lunch pail and take out my cigarettes. Bud nods and sips his coffee. The truth is, my kid has a conniving streak in him. But I don't talk about it. Not even with his mother. Especially her. She and I talk less and less as it is. Mostly it's just the TV. But I remember that night. I recall the way the peacock picked up its gray feet and inched around the table. And then my friend and his wife saying goodnight to us on the porch. Olla giving Fran some peacock feathers to take home. I remember all of us shaking hands, hugging each other, saying things. In the car, Fran sat close to me as we drove away. She kept her hand on my leg. We drove home like that from my friend's house.

Chef's House

THAT summer Wes rented a furnished house north of Eureka from a recovered alcoholic named Chef. Then he called to ask me to forget what I had going and to move up there and live with him. He said he was on the wagon. I knew about that wagon. But he wouldn't take no for an answer. He called again and said, Edna, you can see the ocean from the front window. You can smell salt in the air. I listened to him talk. He didn't slur his words. I said, I'll think about it. And I did. A week later he called again and said, Are you coming? I said I was still thinking. He said, We'll start over. I said, If I come up there, I want you to do something for me. Name it, Wes said. I said, I want you to try and be the Wes I used to know. The old Wes. The Wes I married. Wes began to cry, but I took it as a sign of his good intentions. So I said, All right, I'll come up.

Wes had quit his girlfriend, or she'd quit him—I didn't know, didn't care. When I made up my mind to go with Wes, I had to say goodbye to my friend. My friend said, You're making a mistake. He said, Don't do this to me. What about us? he said. I said, I have to do it for Wes's sake. He's trying to stay sober. You remember what that's like. I remember, my friend said, but I don't want you to go. I said, I'll go for the summer. Then I'll see. I'll come back, I said. He said, What about me? What about *my* sake? Don't come back, he said.

We drank coffee, pop, and all kinds of fruit juice that summer. The whole summer, that's what we had to drink. I found myself wishing the summer wouldn't end. I knew better, but after a month of being with Wes in Chef's house, I put my wedding ring back on. I hadn't worn the ring in two years. Not since the night Wes was drunk and threw his ring into a peach orchard.

Wes had a little money, so I didn't have to work. And it turned out Chef was letting us have the house for almost nothing. We didn't have a telephone. We paid the gas and light and shopped for specials at the Safeway. One Sunday afternoon

Wes went out to get a sprinkler and came back with something for me. He came back with a nice bunch of daisies and a straw hat. Tuesday evenings we'd go to a movie. Other nights Wes would go to what he called his Don't Drink meetings. Chef would pick him up in his car at the door and drive him home again afterward. Some days Wes and I would go fishing for trout in one of the freshwater lagoons nearby. We'd fish off the bank and take all day to catch a few little ones. They'll do fine, I'd say, and that night I'd fry them for supper. Sometimes I'd take off my hat and fall asleep on a blanket next to my fishing pole. The last thing I'd remember would be clouds passing overhead toward the central valley. At night, Wes would take me in his arms and ask me if I was still his girl.

Our kids kept their distance. Cheryl lived with some people on a farm in Oregon. She looked after a herd of goats and sold the milk. She kept bees and put up jars of honey. She had her own life, and I didn't blame her. She didn't care one way or the other about what her dad and I did so long as we didn't get her into it. Bobby was in Washington working in the hay. After the haying season, he planned to work in the apples. He had a girl and was saving his money. I wrote letters and signed them, "Love always."

One afternoon Wes was in the yard pulling weeds when Chef drove up in front of the house. I was working at the sink. I looked and saw Chef's big car pull in. I could see his car, the access road and the freeway, and, behind the freeway, the dunes and the ocean. Clouds hung over the water. Chef got out of his car and hitched his pants. I knew there was something. Wes stopped what he was doing and stood up. He was wearing his gloves and a canvas hat. He took off the hat and wiped his face with the back of his hand. Chef walked over and put his arm around Wes's shoulders. Wes took off one of his gloves. I went to the door. I heard Chef say to Wes God knows he was sorry but he was going to have to ask us to leave at the end of the month. Wes pulled off his other glove. Why's that, Chef? Chef said his daughter, Linda, the woman Wes used to call Fat Linda from the time of his drinking days, needed a place to live and this place was it. Chef told Wes that Linda's husband had taken his fishing boat out a few weeks back and nobody had heard from him since. She's my own blood, Chef said to Wes. She's lost her husband. She's lost her baby's father. I can help. I'm glad I'm in a position to help, Chef said. I'm sorry, Wes, but you'll have to look for another house. Then Chef hugged Wes again, hitched his pants, and got in his big car and drove away.

Wes came inside the house. He dropped his hat and gloves on the carpet and sat down in the big chair. Chef's chair, it occurred to me. Chef's carpet, even. Wes looked pale. I poured two cups of coffee and gave one to him.

It's all right, I said. Wes, don't worry about it, I said. I sat down on Chef's sofa with my coffee.

Fat Linda's going to live here now instead of us, Wes said. He held his cup, but he didn't drink from it.

Wes, don't get stirred up, I said.

Her man will turn up in Ketchikan, Wes said. Fat Linda's husband has simply pulled out on them. And who could blame him? Wes said. Wes said if it came to that, he'd go down with his ship, too, rather than live the rest of his days with Fat Linda and her kid. Then Wes put his cup down next to his gloves. This has been a happy house up to now, he said.

We'll get another house, I said.

Not like this one, Wes said. It wouldn't be the same, anyway. This house has been a good house for us. This house has good memories to it. Now Fat Linda and her kid will be in here, Wes said. He picked up his cup and tasted from it.

It's Chef's house, I said. He has to do what he has to do.

I know that, Wes said. But I don't have to like it.

Wes had this look about him. I knew that look. He kept touching his lips with his tongue. He kept thumbing his shirt under his waistband. He got up from the chair and went to the window. He stood looking out at the ocean and at the clouds, which were building up. He patted his chin with his fingers like he was thinking about something. And he *was* thinking.

Go easy, Wes, I said.

She wants me to go easy, Wes said. He kept standing there.

But in a minute he came over and sat next to me on the sofa. He crossed one leg over the other and began fooling with the buttons on his shirt. I took his hand. I started to talk. I talked about the summer. But I caught myself talking like it was something that had happened in the past. Maybe years back. At any rate, like something that was over. Then I started talking about the kids. Wes said he wished he could do it over again and do it right this time.

They love you, I said.

No, they don't, he said.

I said, Someday, they'll understand things.

Maybe, Wes said. But it won't matter then.

You don't know, I said.

I know a few things, Wes said, and looked at me. I know I'm glad you came up here. I won't forget you did it, Wes said.

I'm glad, too, I said. I'm glad you found this house, I said.

Wes snorted. Then he laughed. We both laughed. That Chef, Wes said, and shook his head. He threw us a knuckle-ball, that son of a bitch. But I'm glad you wore your ring. I'm glad we had us this time together, Wes said.

Then I said something. I said, Suppose, just suppose, nothing had ever happened. Suppose this was for the first time. Just suppose. It doesn't hurt to suppose. Say none of the other had ever happened. You know what I mean? Then what? I said.

Wes fixed his eyes on me. He said, Then I suppose we'd have to be somebody else if that was the case. Somebody we're not. I don't have that kind of supposing left in me. We were born who we are. Don't you see what I'm saying?

I said I hadn't thrown away a good thing and come six hundred miles to hear him talk like this.

He said, I'm sorry, but I can't talk like somebody I'm not. I'm not somebody else. If I was somebody else, I sure as hell wouldn't be here. If I was somebody else, I wouldn't be me. But I'm who I am. Don't you see?

Wes, it's all right, I said. I brought his hand to my cheek. Then, I don't know, I remembered how he was when he was nineteen, the way he looked running across this field to where his dad sat on a tractor, hand over his eyes, watching Wes run toward him. We'd just driven up from California. I got out with Cheryl and Bobby and said, There's Grandpa. But they were just babies.

Wes sat next to me patting his chin, like he was trying to fig-ure out the next thing. Wes's dad was gone and our kids were grown up. I looked at Wes and then I looked around Chef's living room at Chef's things, and I thought, We have to do something now and do it quick.

Hon, I said. Wes, listen to me.

What do you want? he said. But that's all he said. He seemed to have made up his mind. But, having made up his mind, he was in no hurry. He leaned back on the sofa, folded his hands in his lap, and closed his eyes. He didn't say anything else. He didn't have to.

I said his name to myself. It was an easy name to say, and I'd been used to saying it for a long time. Then I said it once more. This time I said it out loud. Wes, I said.

He opened his eyes. But he didn't look at me. He just sat where he was and looked toward the window. Fat Linda, he said. But I knew it wasn't her. She was nothing. Just a name. Wes got up and pulled the drapes and the ocean was gone just like that. I went in to start supper. We still had some fish in the icebox. There wasn't much else. We'll clean it up tonight, I thought, and that will be the end of it.

Preservation

S ANDY'S husband had been on the sofa ever since he'd been
terminated three months ago. That day, three months ago,
he'd come home looking pale and scared and with all of his
work things in a box. "Happy Valentine's Day," he said to
Sandy and put a heart-shaped box of candy and a bottle of Jim
Beam on the kitchen table. He took off his cap and laid that
on the table, too. "I got canned today. Hey, what do you
think's going to happen to us now?"

Sandy and her husband sat at the table and drank whiskey
and ate the chocolates. They talked about what he might be
able to do instead of putting roofs on new houses. But they
couldn't think of anything. "Something will turn up," Sandy
said. She wanted to be encouraging. But she was scared, too.
Finally, he said he'd sleep on it. And he did. He made his bed
on the sofa that night, and that's where he'd slept every night
since it had happened.

The day after his termination there were unemployment
benefits to see about. He went downtown to the state office to
fill out papers and look for another job. But there were no jobs
in his line of work, or in any other line of work. His face began
to sweat as he tried to describe to Sandy the milling crowd of
men and women down there. That evening he got back on the
sofa. He began spending all of his time there, as if, she
thought, it was the thing he was supposed to do now that he
no longer had any work. Once in a while he had to go talk to
somebody about a job possibility, and every two weeks he had
to go sign something to collect his unemployment compensa-
tion. But the rest of the time he stayed on the sofa. It's like he
lives there, Sandy thought. He *lives* in the living room. Now
and then he looked through magazines she brought home
from the grocery store; and every so often she came in to find
him looking at this big book she'd got as a bonus for joining a
book club—something called *Mysteries of the Past*. He held the
book in front of him with both hands, his head inclined over
the pages, as if he were being drawn in by what he was reading.
But after a while she noticed that he didn't seem to be making

any progress in it; he still seemed to be at about the same place—somewhere around chapter two, she guessed. Sandy picked it up once and opened it to his place. There she read about a man who had been discovered after spending two thousand years in a peat bog in the Netherlands. A photograph appeared on one page. The man's brow was furrowed, but there was a serene expression to his face. He wore a leather cap and lay on his side. The man's hands and feet had shriveled, but otherwise he didn't look so awful. She read in the book a little further, then put it back where she'd gotten it. Her husband kept it within easy reach on the coffee table that stood in front of the sofa. That goddamn sofa! As far as she was concerned, she didn't even want to sit on it again. She couldn't imagine them ever having lain down there in the past to make love.

The newspaper came to the house every day. He read it from the first page to the last. She saw him read everything, right down to the obituary section, and the part showing the temperatures of the major cities, as well as the Business News section which told about mergers and interest rates. Mornings, he got up before she did and used the bathroom. Then he turned the TV on and made coffee. She thought he seemed upbeat and cheerful at that hour of the day. But by the time she left for work, he'd made his place on the sofa and the TV was going. Most often it would still be going when she came in again that afternoon. He'd be sitting up on the sofa, or else lying down on it, dressed in what he used to wear to work— jeans and a flannel shirt. But sometimes the TV would be off and he'd be sitting there holding his book.

"How's it going?" he'd say when she looked in on him.

"Okay," she'd say. "How's it with you?"

"Okay."

He always had a pot of coffee warming on the stove for her. In the living room, she'd sit in the big chair and he'd sit on the sofa while they talked about her day. They'd hold their cups and drink their coffee as if they were normal people, Sandy thought.

Sandy still loved him, even though she knew things were getting weird. She was thankful to have her job, but she didn't know what was going to happen to them or to anybody else in the world. She had a girlfriend at work she confided in one time about her husband—about his being on the sofa all the time. For some reason, her friend didn't seem to think it was anything very strange, which both surprised and depressed Sandy. Her friend told her about her uncle in Tennessee— when her uncle had turned forty, he got into his bed and wouldn't get up anymore. And he cried a lot—he cried at least once every day. She told Sandy she guessed her uncle was afraid of getting old. She guessed maybe he was afraid of a heart attack or something. But the man was sixty-three now and still breathing, she said. When Sandy heard this, she was stunned. If this woman was telling the truth, she thought, the man has been in bed for twenty-three years. Sandy's husband was only thirty-one. Thirty-one and twenty-three is fifty-four. That'd put her in her fifties then, too. My God, a person couldn't live the whole rest of his life in bed, or else on the sofa. If her husband had been wounded or was ill, or had been hurt in a car accident, that'd be different. She could under- stand that. If something like that was the case, she knew she could bear it. Then if he had to live on the sofa, and she had to bring him his food out there, maybe carry the spoon up to his mouth—there was even something like romance in that kind of thing. But for her husband, a young and otherwise healthy man, to take to the sofa in this way and not want to get up except to go to the bathroom or to turn the TV on in the morning or off at night, this was different. It made her ashamed; and except for that one time, she didn't talk about it to any- body. She didn't say any more about it to her friend, whose uncle had gotten into bed twenty-three years ago and was still there, as far as Sandy knew.

Late one afternoon she came home from work, parked the car, and went inside the house. She could hear the TV going in the living room as she let herself in the door to the kitchen. The coffee pot was on the stove, and the burner was on low. From where she stood in the kitchen, holding her purse, she could look into the living room and see the back of the sofa and the TV screen. Figures moved across the screen. Her husband's bare feet stuck out from one end of the sofa. At the other end, on a pillow which lay across the arm of the sofa, she could see the crown of his head. He didn't stir. He may or may not have been asleep, and he may or may not have heard her come in. But she decided it didn't make any difference one way or the other. She put her purse on the table and went over to the fridge to get herself some yogurt. But when she opened the door, warm, boxed-in air came out at her. She couldn't believe the mess inside. The ice cream from the freezer had melted and run down into the leftover fish sticks and cole slaw. Ice cream had gotten into the bowl of Spanish rice and pooled on the bottom of the fridge. Ice cream was everywhere. She opened the door to the freezer compartment. An awful smell puffed out at her that made her want to gag. Ice cream covered the bottom of the compartment and puddled around a three-pound package of hamburger. She pressed her finger into the cellophane wrapper covering the meat, and her finger sank into the package. The pork chops had thawed, too. Everything had thawed, including some more fish sticks, a package of Steak-ums, and two Chef Sammy Chinese food dinners. The hot dogs and homemade spaghetti sauce had thawed. She closed the door to the freezer and reached into the fridge for her carton of yogurt. She raised the lid on the yogurt and sniffed. That's when she yelled at her husband.

"What is it?" he said, sitting up and looking over the back of the sofa. "Hey, what's wrong?" He pushed his hand through his hair a couple of times. She couldn't tell if he'd been asleep all this time or what.

"This goddamn fridge has gone out," Sandy said. "That's what."

Her husband got up off the sofa and lowered the volume on the TV. Then he turned it off and came out to the kitchen. "Let me see this," he said. "Hey, I don't believe this."

"See for yourself," she said. "Everything's going to spoil."

Her husband looked inside the fridge, and his face assumed a very grave expression. Then he poked around in the freezer and saw what things were like in there.

"Tell me what next," he said.

A bunch of things suddenly flew into her head, but she didn't say anything.

"Goddamn it," he said, "when it rains, it pours. Hey, this

fridge can't be more than ten years old. It was nearly new when we bought it. Listen, my folks had a fridge that lasted them twenty-five years. They gave it to my brother when he got married. It was working fine. Hey, what's going on?" He moved over so that he could see into the narrow space between the fridge and the wall. "I don't get it," he said and shook his head. "It's plugged in." Then he took hold of the fridge and rocked it back and forth. He put his shoulder against it and pushed and jerked the appliance a few inches out into the kitchen. Something inside the fridge fell off a shelf and broke. "Hell's bells," he said.

Sandy realized she was still holding the yogurt. She went over to the garbage can, raised the lid, and dropped the carton inside. "I have to cook everything tonight," she said. She saw herself at the stove frying meat, fixing things in pans on the stove and in the oven. "We need a new fridge," she said.

He didn't say anything. He looked into the freezer compartment once more and turned his head back and forth.

She moved in front of him and started taking things off the shelves and putting stuff on the table. He helped. He took the meat out of the freezer and put the packages on the table. Then he took the other things out of the freezer and put them in a different place on the table. He took everything out and then found the paper towels and the dishcloth and started wiping up inside.

"We lost our Freon," he said and stopped wiping. "That's what happened. I can smell it. The Freon leaked out. Something happened and the Freon went. Hey, I saw this happen to somebody else's box once." He was calm now. He started wiping again. "It's the Freon," he said.

She stopped what she was doing and looked at him. "We need another fridge," she said.

"You said that. Hey, where are we going to get one? They don't grow on trees."

"We have to have one," she said. "Don't we need a fridge? Maybe we don't. Maybe we can keep our perishables on the window sill like those people in tenements do. Or else we could get one of those little Styrofoam coolers and buy some ice every day." She put a head of lettuce and some tomatoes on the table next to the packages of meat. Then she sat down on one of the dinette chairs and brought her hands up to her face.

"We'll get us another fridge," her husband said. "Hell, yes. We need one, don't we? We can't get along without one. The question is, where do we get one and how much can we pay for it? There must be zillions of used ones in the classifieds. Just hold on and we'll see what's in the paper. Hey, I'm an expert on the classifieds," he said.

She brought her hands down from her face and looked at him.

"Sandy, we'll find us a good used box out of the paper," he went on. "Most of your fridges are built to last a lifetime. This one of ours, Jesus, I don't know what happened to it. It's only the second one in my life I ever heard about going on the fritz like this." He switched his gaze to the fridge again. "Goddamn lousy luck," he said.

"Bring the paper out here," she said. "Let's see what there is."

"Don't worry," he said. He went out to the coffee table, sorted through the stack of newspapers, and came back to the kitchen with the classified section. She pushed the food to one side so that he could spread the pages out. He took one of the chairs.

She glanced down at the paper, then at the food that had thawed. "I've got to fry pork chops tonight," she said. "And I have to cook up that hamburger. And those sandwich steaks and the fish sticks. Don't forget the TV dinners, either."

"That goddamned Freon," he said. "You can smell it."

They began to go through the classifieds. He ran his finger down one column and then another. He passed quickly over the JOBS AVAILABLE section. She saw checks beside a couple of things, but she didn't look to see what he'd marked. It didn't matter. There was a column headlined OUTDOOR CAMPING SUPPLIES. Then they found it—APPLIANCES NEW AND USED.

"Here," she said, and put her finger down on the paper.

He moved her finger. "Let me see," he said.

She put her finger back where it'd been. "'Refrigerators, Ranges, Washers, Dryers, etc.,'" she said, reading from the ad boxed in the column. "'Auction Barn.' What's that? Auction Barn." She went on reading. "'New and used appliances and more every Thursday night. Auction at seven o'clock.' That's today. Today's Thursday," she said. "This auction's tonight. And this place is not very far away. It's down on Pine Street. I must have driven by there a hundred times. You, too. You know where it is. It's down there close to that Baskin-Robbins."

Her husband didn't say anything. He stared at the ad. He brought his hand up and pulled at his lower lip with two of his fingers. "Auction Barn," he said.

She fixed her eyes on him. "Let's go to it. What do you say? It'll do you good to get out, and we'll see if we can't find us a fridge. Two birds with one stone," she said.

"I've never been to an auction in my life," he said. "I don't believe I want to go to one now."

"Come *on*," Sandy said. "What's the matter with you? They're fun. I haven't been to one in years, not since I was a kid. I used to go to them with my dad." She suddenly wanted to go to this auction very much.

"Your dad," he said.

"Yeah, my dad." She looked at her husband, waiting for him to say something else. The least thing. But he didn't.

"Auctions are fun," she said.

"They probably are, but I don't want to go."

"I need a bed lamp, too," she went on. "They'll have bed lamps."

"Hey, we need lots of things. But I don't have a job, remember?"

"I'm going to this auction," she said. "Whether you go or not. You might as well come along. But I don't care. If you want the truth, it's immaterial to me. But I'm going."

"I'll go with you. Who said I wouldn't go?" He looked at her and then looked away. He picked up the paper and read the ad again. "I don't know the first thing about auctions. But, sure, I'll try anything once. Whoever said anything about us buying an icebox at an auction?"

"Nobody," she said. "But we'll do it anyway."

"Okay," he said.

"Good," she said. "But only if you really want to."

He nodded.

She said, "I guess I'd better start cooking. I'll cook the

goddamn pork chops now, and we'll eat. The rest of this stuff can wait. I'll cook everything else later. After we go to this auction. But we have to get moving. The paper said seven o'clock."

"Seven o'clock," he said. He got up from the table and made his way into the living room, where he looked out the bay window for a minute. A car passed on the street outside. He brought his fingers up to his lip. She watched him sit down on the sofa and take up his book. He opened it to his place. But in a minute he put it down and lay back on the sofa. She saw his head come down on the pillow that lay across the arm of the sofa. He adjusted the pillow under his head and put his hands behind his neck. Then he lay still. Pretty soon she saw his arms move down to his sides.

She folded the paper. She got up from the chair and went quietly out to the living room, where she looked over the back of the sofa. His eyes were shut. His chest seemed to barely rise and then fall. She went back to the kitchen and put a frying pan on the burner. She turned the burner on and poured oil into the pan. She started frying pork chops. She'd gone to auctions with her dad. Most of those auctions had to do with farm animals. She seemed to remember her dad was always trying to sell a calf, or else buy one. Sometimes there'd be farm equipment and household items at the auctions. But mostly it was farm animals. Then, after her dad and mom had divorced, and she'd gone away to live with her mom, her dad wrote to say he missed going to auctions with her. The last letter he wrote to her, after she'd grown up and was living with her husband, he said he'd bought a peach of a car at this auction for two hundred dollars. If she'd been there, he said, he'd have bought one for her, too. Three weeks later, in the middle of the night, a telephone call told her that he was dead. The car he'd bought leaked carbon monoxide up through the floorboards and caused him to pass out behind the wheel. He lived in the country. The motor went on running until there was no more gas in the tank. He stayed in the car until somebody found him a few days later.

The pan was starting to smoke. She poured in more oil and turned on the fan. She hadn't been to an auction in twenty years, and now she was getting ready to go to one tonight. But first she had to fry these pork chops. It was bad luck their fridge had gone flooey, but she found herself looking forward to this auction. She began missing her dad. She even missed her mom now, though the two of them used to argue all the time before she met her husband and began living with him. She stood at the stove, turning the meat, and missing both her dad and her mom.

Still missing them, she took a pot holder and moved the pan off the stove. Smoke was being drawn up through the vent over the stove. She stepped to the doorway with the pan and looked into the living room. The pan was still smoking and drops of oil and grease jumped over the sides as she held it. In the darkened room, she could just make out her husband's head, and his bare feet. "Come on out here," she said. "It's ready."

"Okay," he said.

She saw his head come up from the end of the sofa. She put the pan back on the stove and turned to the cupboard. She took down a couple of plates and put them on the counter. She used her spatula to raise one of the pork chops. Then she lifted it onto a plate. The meat didn't look like meat. It looked like part of an old shoulder blade, or a digging instrument. But she knew it was a pork chop, and she took the other one out of the pan and put that on a plate, too.

In a minute, her husband came into the kitchen. He looked at the fridge once more, which was standing there with its door open. And then his eyes took in the pork chops. His mouth dropped open, but he didn't say anything. She waited for him to say something, anything, but he didn't. She put salt and pepper on the table and told him to sit down.

"Sit down," she said and gave him a plate on which lay the remains of a pork chop. "I want you to eat this," she said. He took the plate. But he just stood there and looked at it. Then she turned to get her own plate.

Sandy cleared the newspaper away and shoved the food to the far side of the table. "Sit down," she said to her husband once more. He moved his plate from one hand to the other. But he kept standing there. It was then she saw puddles of water on the table. She heard water, too. It was dripping off the table and onto the linoleum.

She looked down at her husband's bare feet. She stared at
his feet next to the pool of water. She knew she'd never again
in her life see anything so unusual. But she didn't know what
to make of it yet. She thought she'd better put on some lipstick, get her coat, and go ahead to the auction. But she
couldn't take her eyes from her husband's feet. She put her
plate on the table and watched until the feet left the kitchen
and went back into the living room.

The Compartment

MYERS was traveling through France in a first-class rail car on his way to visit his son in Strasbourg, who was a student at the university there. He hadn't seen the boy in eight years. There had been no phone calls between them during this time, not even a postcard since Myers and the boy's mother had gone their separate ways—the boy staying with her. The final break-up was hastened along, Myers always believed, by the boy's malign interference in their personal affairs.

The last time Myers had seen his son, the boy had lunged for him during a violent quarrel. Myers's wife had been standing by the sideboard, dropping one dish of china after the other onto the dining-room floor. Then she'd gone on to the cups. "That's enough," Myers had said, and at that instant the boy charged him. Myers sidestepped and got him in a headlock while the boy wept and pummeled Myers on the back and kidneys. Myers had him, and while he had him, he made the most of it. He slammed him into the wall and threatened to kill him. He meant it. "I gave you life," Myers remembered himself shouting, "and I can take it back!"

Thinking about that horrible scene now, Myers shook his head as if it had happened to someone else. And it had. He was simply not that same person. These days he lived alone and had little to do with anybody outside of his work. At night, he listened to classical music and read books on waterfowl decoys.

He lit a cigarette and continued to gaze out the train window, ignoring the man who sat in the seat next to the door and who slept with a hat pulled over his eyes. It was early in the morning and mist hung over the green fields that passed by outside. Now and then Myers saw a farmhouse and its outbuildings, everything surrounded by a wall. He thought this might be a good way to live—in an old house surrounded by a wall.

It was just past six o'clock. Myers hadn't slept since he'd boarded the train in Milan at eleven the night before. When the train had left Milan, he'd considered himself lucky to have the compartment to himself. He kept the light on and looked

393

at guidebooks. He read things he wished he'd read before he'd been to the place they were about. He discovered much that he should have seen and done. In a way, he was sorry to be finding out certain things about the country now, just as he was leaving Italy behind after his first and, no doubt, last visit.

He put the guidebooks away in his suitcase, put the suitcase in the overhead rack, and took off his coat so he could use it for a blanket. He switched off the light and sat there in the darkened compartment with his eyes closed, hoping sleep would come.

After what seemed a long time, and just when he thought he was going to drop off, the train began to slow. It came to a stop at a little station outside of Basel. There, a middle-aged man in a dark suit, and wearing a hat, entered the compartment. The man said something to Myers in a language Myers didn't understand, and then the man put his leather bag up into the rack. He sat down on the other side of the compartment and straightened his shoulders. Then he pulled his hat over his eyes. By the time the train was moving again, the man was asleep and snoring quietly. Myers envied him. In a few minutes, a Swiss official opened the door of the compartment and turned on the light. In English, and in some other language—German, Myers assumed—the official asked to see their passports. The man in the compartment with Myers pushed the hat back on his head, blinked his eyes, and reached into his coat pocket. The official studied the passport, looked at the man closely, and gave him back the document. Myers handed over his own passport. The official read the data, examined the photograph, and then looked at Myers before nodding and giving it back. He turned off the light as he went out. The man across from Myers pulled the hat over his eyes and put out his legs. Myers supposed he'd go right back to sleep, and once again he felt envy.

He stayed awake after that and began to think of the meeting with his son, which was now only a few hours away. How would he act when he saw the boy at the station? Should he embrace him? He felt uncomfortable with that prospect. Or should he merely offer his hand, smile as if these eight years had never occurred, and then pat the boy on the shoulder? Maybe the boy would say a few words—*I'm glad to see you—how was your trip?* And Myers would say—something. He really didn't know what he was going to say.

The French *contrôleur* walked by the compartment. He looked in on Myers and at the man sleeping across from Myers. This same *contrôleur* had already punched their tickets, so Myers turned his head and went back to looking out the window. More houses began to appear. But now there were no walls, and the houses were smaller and set closer together. Soon, Myers was sure, he'd see a French village. The haze was lifting. The train blew its whistle and sped past a crossing over which a barrier had been lowered. He saw a young woman with her hair pinned up and wearing a sweater, standing with her bicycle as she watched the cars whip past.

How's your mother? he might say to the boy after they had walked a little way from the station. *What do you hear from your mother?* For a wild instant, it occurred to Myers she could be dead. But then he understood that it couldn't be so, he'd have heard something—one way or the other, he'd have heard. He knew if he let himself go on thinking about these things, his heart could break. He closed the top button of his shirt and fixed his tie. He laid his coat across the seat next to him. He laced his shoes, got up, and stepped over the legs of the sleeping man. He let himself out of the compartment.

Myers had to put his hand against the windows along the corridor to steady himself as he moved toward the end of the car. He closed the door to the little toilet and locked it. Then he ran water and splashed his face. The train moved into a curve, still at the same high speed, and Myers had to hold on to the sink for balance.

The boy's letter had come to him a couple of months ago. The letter had been brief. He wrote that he'd been living in France and studying for the past year at the university in Strasbourg. There was no other information about what had possessed him to go to France, or what he'd been doing with himself during those years before France. Appropriately enough, Myers thought, no mention was made in the letter of the boy's mother—not a clue to her condition or whereabouts. But, inexplicably, the boy had closed the letter with the word *Love*, and Myers had pondered this for a long while. Finally, he'd answered the letter. After some deliberation, Myers wrote to say

he had been thinking for some time of making a little trip to
Europe. Would the boy like to meet him at the station in Strasbourg? He signed his letter, "Love, Dad." He'd heard back
from the boy and then he made his arrangements. It struck
him that there was really no one, besides his secretary and a
few business associates, that he felt it was necessary to tell he
was going away. He had accumulated six weeks of vacation at
the engineering firm where he worked, and he decided he
would take all of the time coming to him for this trip. He was
glad he'd done this, even though he now had no intention of
spending all that time in Europe.

He'd gone first to Rome. But after the first few hours, walking
around by himself on the streets, he was sorry he hadn't arranged
to be with a group. He was lonely. He went to Venice, a city he
and his wife had always talked of visiting. But Venice was a disappointment. He saw a man with one arm eating fried squid,
and there were grimy, water-stained buildings everywhere he
looked. He took a train to Milan, where he checked into a
four-star hotel and spent the night watching a soccer match on
a Sony color TV until the station went off the air. He got up
the next morning and wandered around the city until it was
time to go to the station. He'd planned the stopover in Strasbourg as the culmination of his trip. After a day or two, or
three days—he'd see how it went—he would travel to Paris and
fly home. He was tired of trying to make himself understood
to strangers and would be glad to get back.

Someone tried the door to the WC. Myers finished tucking
his shirt. He fastened his belt. Then he unlocked the door and,
swaying with the movement of the train, walked back to his
compartment. As he opened the door, he saw at once that his
coat had been moved. It lay across a different seat from the
one where he'd left it. He felt he had entered into a ludicrous
but potentially serious situation. His heart began to race as he
picked up the coat. He put his hand into the inside pocket and
took out his passport. He carried his wallet in his hip pocket.
So he still had his wallet and the passport. He went through
the other coat pockets. What was missing was the gift he'd
bought for the boy—an expensive Japanese wristwatch purchased at a shop in Rome. He had carried the watch in his inside coat pocket for safekeeping. Now the watch was gone.

"Pardon," he said to the man who slumped in the seat, legs out, the hat over his eyes. "Pardon." The man pushed the hat back and opened his eyes. He pulled himself up and looked at Myers. His eyes were large. He might have been dreaming. But he might not.

Myers said, "Did you see somebody come in here?"

But it was clear the man didn't know what Myers was saying. He continued to stare at him with what Myers took to be a look of total incomprehension. But maybe it was something else, Myers thought. Maybe the look masked slyness and deceit. Myers shook his coat to focus the man's attention. Then he put his hand into the pocket and rummaged. He pulled his sleeve back and showed the man his own wristwatch. The man looked at Myers and then at Myers's watch. He seemed mystified. Myers tapped the face of his watch. He put his other hand back into his coat pocket and made a gesture as if he were fishing for something. Myers pointed at the watch once more and waggled his fingers, hoping to signify the wristwatch taking flight out the door.

The man shrugged and shook his head.

"Goddamn it," Myers said in frustration. He put his coat on and went out into the corridor. He couldn't stay in the compartment another minute. He was afraid he might strike the man. He looked up and down the corridor, as if hoping he could see and recognize the thief. But there was no one around. Maybe the man who shared his compartment hadn't taken the watch. Maybe someone else, the person who tried the door to the WC, had walked past the compartment, spotted the coat and the sleeping man, and simply opened the door, gone through the pockets, closed the door, and gone away again.

Myers walked slowly to the end of the car, peering into the other compartments. It was not crowded in this first-class car, but there were one or two people in each compartment. Most of them were asleep, or seemed to be. Their eyes were closed, and their heads were thrown back against the seats. In one compartment, a man about his own age sat by the window looking out at the countryside. When Myers stopped at the glass and looked in at him, the man turned and regarded him fiercely.

Myers crossed into the second-class car. The compartments
in this car were crowded—sometimes five or six passengers in
each, and the people, he could tell at a glance, were more desperate. Many of them were awake—it was too uncomfortable
to sleep—and they turned their eyes on him as he passed. For-
eigners, he thought. It was clear to him that if the man in his
compartment hadn't taken the watch, then the thief was from
one of these compartments. But what could he do? It was
hopeless. The watch was gone. It was in someone else's pocket
now. He couldn't hope to make the *contrôleur* understand
what had happened. And even if he could, then what? He
made his way back to his own compartment. He looked in and
saw that the man had stretched out again with his hat over his
eyes.

Myers stepped over the man's legs and sat down in his seat
by the window. He felt dazed with anger. They were on the
outskirts of the city now. Farms and grazing land had given
over to industrial plants with unpronounceable names on the
fronts of the buildings. The train began slowing. Myers could
see automobiles on city streets, and others waiting in line at
the crossings for the train to pass. He got up and took his suitcase down. He held it on his lap while he looked out the
window at this hateful place.

It came to him that he didn't want to see the boy after all.
He was shocked by this realization and for a moment felt diminished by the meanness of it. He shook his head. In a lifetime of foolish actions, this trip was possibly the most foolish
thing he'd ever done. But the fact was, he really had no desire
to see this boy whose behavior had long ago isolated him from
Myers's affections. He suddenly, and with great clarity, recalled the boy's face when he had lunged that time, and a wave
of bitterness passed over Myers. This boy had devoured Myers's
youth, had turned the young girl he had courted and wed into
a nervous, alcoholic woman whom the boy alternately pitied
and bullied. Why on earth, Myers asked himself, would he
come all this way to see someone he disliked? He didn't want
to shake the boy's hand, the hand of his enemy, nor have to
clap him on the shoulder and make small-talk. He didn't want
to have to ask him about his mother.

He sat forward in the seat as the train pulled into the sta-

tion. An announcement was called out in French over the
train's intercom. The man across from Myers began to stir. He
adjusted his hat and sat up in the seat as something else in
French came over the speaker. Myers didn't understand anything that was said. He grew more agitated as the train slowed
and then came to a stop. He decided he wasn't going to leave
the compartment. He was going to sit where he was until the
train pulled away. When it did, he'd be on it, going on with
the train to Paris, and that would be that. He looked out the
window cautiously, afraid he'd see the boy's face at the glass.
He didn't know what he'd do if that happened. He was afraid
he might shake his fist. He saw a few people on the platform
wearing coats and scarves who stood next to their suitcases,
waiting to board the train. A few other people waited, without
luggage, hands in their pockets, obviously expecting to meet
someone. His son was not one of those waiting, but, of course,
that didn't mean he wasn't out there somewhere. Myers
moved the suitcase off his lap onto the floor and inched down
in his seat.

The man across from him was yawning and looking out the
window. Now he turned his gaze on Myers. He took off his
hat and ran his hand through his hair. Then he put the hat
back on, got to his feet, and pulled his bag down from the rack.
He opened the compartment door. But before he went out, he
turned around and gestured in the direction of the station.

"Strasbourg," the man said.

Myers turned away.

The man waited an instant longer, and then went out into
the corridor with his bag and, Myers felt certain, with the
wristwatch. But that was the least of his concerns now. He
looked out the train window once again. He saw a man in an
apron standing in the door of the station, smoking a cigarette.
The man was watching two trainmen explaining something to
a woman in a long skirt who held a baby in her arms. The
woman listened and then nodded and listened some more. She
moved the baby from one arm to the other. The men kept
talking. She listened. One of the men chucked the baby under
its chin. The woman looked down and smiled. She moved the
baby again and listened some more. Myers saw a young couple
embracing on the platform a little distance from his car. Then

the young man let go of the young woman. He said something, picked up his valise, and moved to board the train. The
woman watched him go. She brought a hand up to her face,
touched one eye and then the other with the heel of her hand.
In a minute, Myers saw her moving down the platform, her
eyes fixed on his car, as if following someone. He glanced away
from the woman and looked at the big clock over the station's
waiting room. He looked up and down the platform. The boy
was nowhere in sight. It was possible he had overslept or it might
be that he, too, had changed his mind. In any case, Myers felt
relieved. He looked at the clock again, then at the young
woman who was hurrying up to the window where he sat.
Myers drew back as if she were going to strike the glass.

The door to the compartment opened. The young man
he'd seen outside closed the door behind him and said, "*Bon-
jour.*" Without waiting for a reply, he threw his valise into the
overhead rack and stepped over to the window. "*Pardonnez-
moi.*" He pulled the window down. "Marie," he said. The
young woman began to smile and cry at the same time. The
young man brought her hands up and began kissing her fingers.

Myers looked away and clamped his teeth. He heard the
final shouts of the trainmen. Someone blew a whistle. Presently,
the train began to move away from the platform. The young
man had let go of the woman's hands, but he continued to
wave at her as the train rolled forward.

But the train went only a short distance, into the open air of
the railyard, and then Myers felt it come to an abrupt stop.
The young man closed the window and moved over to the seat
by the door. He took a newspaper from his coat and began to
read. Myers got up and opened the door. He went to the end
of the corridor, where the cars were coupled together. He didn't
know why they had stopped. Maybe something was wrong.
He moved to the window. But all he could see was an intricate
system of tracks where trains were being made up, cars taken
off or switched from one train to another. He stepped back
from the window. The sign on the door to the next car said,
POUSSEZ. Myers struck the sign with his fist, and the door slid
open. He was in the second-class car again. He passed along a
row of compartments filled with people settling down, as if
making ready for a long trip. He needed to find out from

someone where this train was going. He had understood, at the time he purchased the ticket, that the train to Strasbourg went on to Paris. But he felt it would be humiliating to put his head into one of the compartments and say, "Paree?" or however they said it—as if asking if they'd arrived at a destination. He heard a loud clanking, and the train backed up a little. He could see the station again, and once more he thought of his son. Maybe he was standing back there, breathless from having rushed to get to the station, wondering what had happened to his father. Myers shook his head.

The car he was in creaked and groaned under him, then something caught and fell heavily into place. Myers looked out at the maze of tracks and realized that the train had begun to move again. He turned and hurried back to the end of the car and crossed back into the car he'd been traveling in. He walked down the corridor to his compartment. But the young man with the newspaper was gone. And Myers's suitcase was gone. It was not his compartment after all. He realized with a start they must have uncoupled his car while the train was in the yard and attached another second-class car to the train. The compartment he stood in front of was nearly filled with small, dark-skinned men who spoke rapidly in a language Myers had never heard before. One of the men signaled him to come inside. Myers moved into the compartment, and the men made room for him. There seemed to be a jovial air in the compartment. The man who'd signaled him laughed and patted the space next to him. Myers sat down with his back to the front of the train. The countryside out the window began to pass faster and faster. For a moment, Myers had the impression of the landscape shooting away from him. He was going somewhere, he knew that. And if it was the wrong direction, sooner or later he'd find it out.

He leaned against the seat and closed his eyes. The men went on talking and laughing. Their voices came to him as if from a distance. Soon the voices became part of the train's movements—and gradually Myers felt himself being carried, then pulled back, into sleep.

A Small, Good Thing

SATURDAY afternoon she drove to the bakery in the shopping center. After looking through a loose-leaf binder with photographs of cakes taped onto the pages, she ordered chocolate, the child's favorite. The cake she chose was decorated with a space ship and launching pad under a sprinkling of white stars, and a planet made of red frosting at the other end. His name, SCOTTY, would be in green letters beneath the planet. The baker, who was an older man with a thick neck, listened without saying anything when she told him the child would be eight years old next Monday. The baker wore a white apron that looked like a smock. Straps cut under his arms, went around in back and then to the front again, where they were secured under his heavy waist. He wiped his hands on his apron as he listened to her. He kept his eyes down on the photographs and let her talk. He let her take her time. He'd just come to work and he'd be there all night, baking, and he was in no real hurry.

She gave the baker her name, Ann Weiss, and her telephone number. The cake would be ready on Monday morning, just out of the oven, in plenty of time for the child's party that afternoon. The baker was not jolly. There were no pleasantries between them, just the minimum exchange of words, the necessary information. He made her feel uncomfortable, and she didn't like that. While he was bent over the counter with the pencil in his hand, she studied his coarse features and wondered if he'd ever done anything else with his life besides be a baker. She was a mother and thirty-three years old, and it seemed to her that everyone, especially someone the baker's age—a man old enough to be her father—must have children who'd gone through this special time of cakes and birthday parties. There must be that between them, she thought. But he was abrupt with her—not rude, just abrupt. She gave up trying to make friends with him. She looked into the back of the bakery and could see a long, heavy wooden table with aluminum pie pans stacked at one end; and beside the table a

metal container filled with empty racks. There was an enormous oven. A radio was playing country-Western music.

The baker finished printing the information on the special
order card and closed up the binder. He looked at her and
said, "Monday morning." She thanked him and drove home.

On Monday morning, the birthday boy was walking to school
with another boy. They were passing a bag of potato chips
back and forth and the birthday boy was trying to find out
what his friend intended to give him for his birthday that
afternoon. Without looking, the birthday boy stepped off the
curb at an intersection and was immediately knocked down by
a car. He fell on his side with his head in the gutter and his legs
out in the road. His eyes were closed, but his legs moved back
and forth as if he were trying to climb over something. His
friend dropped the potato chips and started to cry. The car had
gone a hundred feet or so and stopped in the middle of the
road. The man in the driver's seat looked back over his shoulder. He waited until the boy got unsteadily to his feet. The boy
wobbled a little. He looked dazed, but okay. The driver put
the car into gear and drove away.

The birthday boy didn't cry, but he didn't have anything to
say about anything either. He wouldn't answer when his friend
asked him what it felt like to be hit by a car. He walked home,
and his friend went on to school. But after the birthday boy
was inside his house and was telling his mother about it—she
sitting beside him on the sofa, holding his hands in her lap,
saying, "Scotty, honey, are you sure you feel all right, baby?"
thinking she would call the doctor anyway—he suddenly lay
back on the sofa, closed his eyes, and went limp. When she
couldn't wake him up, she hurried to the telephone and called
her husband at work. Howard told her to remain calm, remain
calm, and then he called an ambulance for the child and left for
the hospital himself.

Of course, the birthday party was canceled. The child was in
the hospital with a mild concussion and suffering from shock.
There'd been vomiting, and his lungs had taken in fluid which
needed pumping out that afternoon. Now he simply seemed
to be in a very deep sleep—but no coma, Dr. Francis had

emphasized, no coma, when he saw the alarm in the parents' eyes. At eleven o'clock that night, when the boy seemed to be resting comfortably enough after the many X-rays and the lab work, and it was just a matter of his waking up and coming around, Howard left the hospital. He and Ann had been at the hospital with the child since that afternoon, and he was going home for a short while to bathe and change clothes. "I'll be back in an hour," he said. She nodded. "It's fine," she said. "I'll be right here." He kissed her on the forehead, and they touched hands. She sat in the chair beside the bed and looked at the child. She was waiting for him to wake up and be all right. Then she could begin to relax.

Howard drove home from the hospital. He took the wet, dark streets very fast, then caught himself and slowed down. Until now, his life had gone smoothly and to his satisfaction—college, marriage, another year of college for the advanced degree in business, a junior partnership in an investment firm. Fatherhood. He was happy and, so far, lucky—he knew that. His parents were still living, his brothers and his sister were established, his friends from college had gone out to take their places in the world. So far, he had kept away from any real harm, from those forces he knew existed and that could cripple or bring down a man if the luck went bad, if things suddenly turned. He pulled into the driveway and parked. His left leg began to tremble. He sat in the car for a minute and tried to deal with the present situation in a rational manner. Scotty had been hit by a car and was in the hospital, but he was going to be all right. Howard closed his eyes and ran his hand over his face. He got out of the car and went up to the front door. The dog was barking inside the house. The telephone rang and rang while he unlocked the door and fumbled for the light switch. He shouldn't have left the hospital, he shouldn't have. "Goddamn it!" he said. He picked up the receiver and said, "I just walked in the door!"

"There's a cake here that wasn't picked up," the voice on the other end of the line said.

"What are you saying?" Howard asked.

"A cake," the voice said. "A sixteen-dollar cake."

Howard held the receiver against his ear, trying to understand. "I don't know anything about a cake," he said. "Jesus, what are you talking about?"

"Don't hand me that," the voice said.

Howard hung up the telephone. He went into the kitchen and poured himself some whiskey. He called the hospital. But the child's condition remained the same; he was still sleeping and nothing had changed there. While water poured into the tub, Howard lathered his face and shaved. He'd just stretched out in the tub and closed his eyes when the telephone rang again. He hauled himself out, grabbed a towel, and hurried through the house, saying, "Stupid, stupid," for having left the hospital. But when he picked up the receiver and shouted, "Hello!" there was no sound at the other end of the line. Then the caller hung up.

He arrived back at the hospital a little after midnight. Ann still sat in the chair beside the bed. She looked up at Howard, and then she looked back at the child. The child's eyes stayed closed, the head was still wrapped in bandages. His breathing was quiet and regular. From an apparatus over the bed hung a bottle of glucose with a tube running from the bottle to the boy's arm.

"How is he?" Howard said. "What's all this?" waving at the glucose and the tube.

"Dr. Francis's orders," she said. "He needs nourishment. He needs to keep up his strength. Why doesn't he wake up, Howard? I don't understand, if he's all right."

Howard put his hand against the back of her head. He ran his fingers through her hair. "He's going to be all right. He'll wake up in a little while. Dr. Francis knows what's what."

After a time, he said, "Maybe you should go home and get some rest. I'll stay here. Just don't put up with this creep who keeps calling. Hang up right away."

"Who's calling?" she asked.

"I don't know who, just somebody with nothing better to do than call up people. You go on now."

She shook her head. "No," she said, "I'm fine."

"Really," he said. "Go home for a while, and then come back and spell me in the morning. It'll be all right. What did

Dr. Francis say? He said Scotty's going to be all right. We don't have to worry. He's just sleeping now, that's all."

A nurse pushed the door open. She nodded at them as she went to the bedside. She took the left arm out from under the covers and put her fingers on the wrist, found the pulse, then consulted her watch. In a little while, she put the arm back under the covers and moved to the foot of the bed, where she wrote something on a clipboard attached to the bed.

"How is he?" Ann said. Howard's hand was a weight on her shoulder. She was aware of the pressure from his fingers.

"He's stable," the nurse said. Then she said, "Doctor will be in again shortly. Doctor's back in the hospital. He's making rounds right now."

"I was saying maybe she'd want to go home and get a little rest," Howard said. "After the doctor comes," he said.

"She could do that," the nurse said. "I think you should both feel free to do that, if you wish." The nurse was a big Scandinavian woman with blond hair. There was the trace of an accent in her speech.

"We'll see what the doctor says," Ann said. "I want to talk to the doctor. I don't think he should keep sleeping like this. I don't think that's a good sign." She brought her hand up to her eyes and let her head come forward a little. Howard's grip tightened on her shoulder, and then his hand moved up to her neck, where his fingers began to knead the muscles there.

"Dr. Francis will be here in a few minutes," the nurse said. Then she left the room.

Howard gazed at his son for a time, the small chest quietly rising and falling under the covers. For the first time since the terrible minutes after Ann's telephone call to him at his office, he felt a genuine fear starting in his limbs. He began shaking his head. Scotty was fine, but instead of sleeping at home in his own bed, he was in a hospital bed with bandages around his head and a tube in his arm. But this help was what he needed right now.

Dr. Francis came in and shook hands with Howard, though they'd just seen each other a few hours before. Ann got up from the chair. "Doctor?"

"Ann," he said and nodded. "Let's just first see how he's doing," the doctor said. He moved to the side of the bed and took the boy's pulse. He peeled back one eyelid and then the other. Howard and Ann stood beside the doctor and watched. Then the doctor turned back the covers and listened to the boy's heart and lungs with his stethoscope. He pressed his fingers here and there on the abdomen. When he was finished, he went to the end of the bed and studied the chart. He noted the time, scribbled something on the chart, and then looked at Howard and Ann.

"Doctor, how is he?" Howard said. "What's the matter with him exactly?"

"Why doesn't he wake up?" Ann said.

The doctor was a handsome, big-shouldered man with a tanned face. He wore a three-piece blue suit, a striped tie, and ivory cufflinks. His gray hair was combed along the sides of his head, and he looked as if he had just come from a concert. "He's all right," the doctor said. "Nothing to shout about, he could be better, I think. But he's all right. Still, I wish he'd wake up. He should wake up pretty soon." The doctor looked at the boy again. "We'll know some more in a couple of hours, after the results of a few more tests are in. But he's all right, believe me, except for the hairline fracture of the skull. He does have that."

"Oh, no," Ann said.

"And a bit of a concussion, as I said before. Of course, you know he's in shock," the doctor said. "Sometimes you see this in shock cases. This sleeping."

"But he's out of any real danger?" Howard said. "You said before he's not in a coma. You wouldn't call this a coma, then —would you, doctor?" Howard waited. He looked at the doctor.

"No, I don't want to call it a coma," the doctor said and glanced over at the boy once more. "He's just in a very deep sleep. It's a restorative measure the body is taking on its own. He's out of any real danger, I'd say that for certain, yes. But we'll know more when he wakes up and the other tests are in," the doctor said.

"It's a coma," Ann said. "Of sorts."

"It's not a coma yet, not exactly," the doctor said. "I wouldn't want to call it coma. Not yet, anyway. He's suffered shock. In shock cases, this kind of reaction is common enough;

it's a temporary reaction to bodily trauma. Coma. Well, coma is a deep, prolonged unconsciousness, something that could go on for days, or weeks even. Scotty's not in that area, not as far as we can tell. I'm certain his condition will show improvement by morning. I'm betting that it will. We'll know more when he wakes up, which shouldn't be long now. Of course, you may do as you like, stay here or go home for a time. But by all means feel free to leave the hospital for a while if you want. This is not easy, I know." The doctor gazed at the boy again, watching him, and then he turned to Ann and said, "You try not to worry, little mother. Believe me, we're doing all that can be done. It's just a question of a little more time now." He nodded at her, shook hands with Howard again, and then he left the room.

Ann put her hand over the child's forehead. "At least he doesn't have a fever," she said. Then she said, "My God, he feels so cold, though. Howard? Is he supposed to feel like this? Feel his head."

Howard touched the child's temples. His own breathing had slowed. "I think he's supposed to feel this way right now," he said. "He's in shock, remember? That's what the doctor said. The doctor was just in here. He would have said something if Scotty wasn't okay."

Ann stood there a while longer, working her lip with her teeth. Then she moved over to her chair and sat down.

Howard sat in the chair next to her chair. They looked at each other. He wanted to say something else and reassure her, but he was afraid, too. He took her hand and put it in his lap, and this made him feel better, her hand being there. He picked up her hand and squeezed it. Then he just held her hand. They sat like that for a while, watching the boy and not talking. From time to time, he squeezed her hand. Finally, she took her hand away.

"I've been praying," she said.

He nodded.

She said, "I almost thought I'd forgotten how, but it came back to me. All I had to do was close my eyes and say, 'Please God, help us—help Scotty,' and then the rest was easy. The words were right there. Maybe if you prayed, too," she said to him.

"I've already prayed," he said. "I prayed this afternoon—yesterday afternoon, I mean—after you called, while I was driving to the hospital. I've been praying," he said.

"That's good," she said. For the first time, she felt they were together in it, this trouble. She realized with a start that, until now, it had only been happening to her and to Scotty. She hadn't let Howard into it, though he was there and needed all along. She felt glad to be his wife.

The same nurse came in and took the boy's pulse again and checked the flow from the bottle hanging above the bed.

In an hour, another doctor came in. He said his name was Parsons, from Radiology. He had a bushy mustache. He was wearing loafers, a Western shirt, and a pair of jeans.

"We're going to take him downstairs for more pictures," he told them. "We need to do some more pictures, and we want to do a scan."

"What's that?" Ann said. "A scan?" She stood between this new doctor and the bed. "I thought you'd already taken all your X-rays."

"I'm afraid we need some more," he said. "Nothing to be alarmed about. We just need some more pictures, and we want to do a brain scan on him."

"My God," Ann said.

"It's perfectly normal procedure in cases like this," this new doctor said. "We just need to find out for sure why he isn't back awake yet. It's normal medical procedure, and nothing to be alarmed about. We'll be taking him down in a few minutes," this doctor said.

In a little while, two orderlies came into the room with a gurney. They were black-haired, dark-complexioned men in white uniforms, and they said a few words to each other in a foreign tongue as they unhooked the boy from the tube and moved him from his bed to the gurney. Then they wheeled him from the room. Howard and Ann got on the same elevator. Ann gazed at the child. She closed her eyes as the elevator began its descent. The orderlies stood at either end of the gurney without saying anything, though once one of the men made a comment to the other in their own language, and the other man nodded slowly in response.

Later that morning, just as the sun was beginning to lighten the windows in the waiting room outside the X-ray department, they brought the boy out and moved him back up to his room. Howard and Ann rode up on the elevator with him once more, and once more they took up their places beside the bed.

They waited all day, but still the boy did not wake up. Occasionally, one of them would leave the room to go downstairs to the cafeteria to drink coffee and then, as if suddenly remembering and feeling guilty, get up from the table and hurry back to the room. Dr. Francis came again that afternoon and examined the boy once more and then left after telling them he was coming along and could wake up at any minute now. Nurses, different nurses from the night before, came in from time to time. Then a young woman from the lab knocked and entered the room. She wore white slacks and a white blouse and carried a little tray of things which she put on the stand beside the bed. Without a word to them, she took blood from the boy's arm. Howard closed his eyes as the woman found the right place on the boy's arm and pushed the needle in.

"I don't understand this," Ann said to the woman.

"Doctor's orders," the young woman said. "I do what I'm told. They say draw that one, I draw. What's wrong with him, anyway?" she said. "He's a sweetie."

"He was hit by a car," Howard said. "A hit-and-run."

The young woman shook her head and looked again at the boy. Then she took her tray and left the room.

"Why won't he wake up?" Ann said. "Howard? I want some answers from these people."

Howard didn't say anything. He sat down again in the chair and crossed one leg over the other. He rubbed his face. He looked at his son and then he settled back in the chair, closed his eyes, and went to sleep.

Ann walked to the window and looked out at the parking lot. It was night, and cars were driving into and out of the parking lot with their lights on. She stood at the window with her hands gripping the sill, and knew in her heart that they were into something now, something hard. She was afraid, and her teeth began to chatter until she tightened her jaws. She saw a big car stop in front of the hospital and someone, a woman in a long coat, get into the car. She wished she were that woman and somebody, anybody, was driving her away from here to somewhere else, a place where she would find Scotty waiting for her when she stepped out of the car, ready to say *Mom* and let her gather him in her arms.

In a little while, Howard woke up. He looked at the boy again. Then he got up from the chair, stretched, and went over to stand beside her at the window. They both stared out at the parking lot. They didn't say anything. But they seemed to feel each other's insides now, as though the worry had made them transparent in a perfectly natural way.

The door opened and Dr. Francis came in. He was wearing a different suit and tie this time. His gray hair was combed along the sides of his head, and he looked as if he had just shaved. He went straight to the bed and examined the boy. "He ought to have come around by now. There's just no good reason for this," he said. "But I can tell you we're all convinced he's out of any danger. We'll just feel better when he wakes up. There's no reason, absolutely none, why he shouldn't come around. Very soon. Oh, he'll have himself a dilly of a headache when he does, you can count on that. But all of his signs are fine. They're as normal as can be."

"It is a coma, then?" Ann said.

The doctor rubbed his smooth cheek. "We'll call it that for the time being, until he wakes up. But you must be worn out. This is hard. I know this is hard. Feel free to go out for a bite," he said. "It would do you good. I'll put a nurse in here while you're gone if you'll feel better about going. Go and have yourselves something to eat."

"I couldn't eat anything," Ann said.

"Do what you need to do, of course," the doctor said. "Anyway, I wanted to tell you that all the signs are good, the tests are negative, nothing showed up at all, and just as soon as he wakes up he'll be over the hill."

"Thank you, doctor," Howard said. He shook hands with the doctor again. The doctor patted Howard's shoulder and went out.

"I suppose one of us should go home and check on things," Howard said. "Slug needs to be fed, for one thing."

"Call one of the neighbors," Ann said. "Call the Morgans. Anyone will feed a dog if you ask them to."

"All right," Howard said. After a while, he said, "Honey, why don't *you* do it? Why don't you go home and check on things, and then come back? It'll do you good. I'll be right here with him. Seriously," he said. "We need to keep up our strength on this. We'll want to be here for a while even after he wakes up."

"Why don't *you* go?" she said. "Feed Slug. Feed yourself."

"I already went," he said. "I was gone for exactly an hour and fifteen minutes. You go home for an hour and freshen up. Then come back."

She tried to think about it, but she was too tired. She closed her eyes and tried to think about it again. After a time, she said, "Maybe I *will* go home for a few minutes. Maybe if I'm not just sitting right here watching him every second, he'll wake up and be all right. You know? Maybe he'll wake up if I'm not here. I'll go home and take a bath and put on clean clothes. I'll feed Slug. Then I'll come back."

"I'll be right here," he said. "You go on home, honey. I'll keep an eye on things here." His eyes were bloodshot and small, as if he'd been drinking for a long time. His clothes were rumpled. His beard had come out again. She touched his face, and then she took her hand back. She understood he wanted to be by himself for a while, not have to talk or share his worry for a time. She picked her purse up from the night-stand, and he helped her into her coat.

"I won't be gone long," she said.

"Just sit and rest for a little while when you get home," he said. "Eat something. Take a bath. After you get out of the bath, just sit for a while and rest. It'll do you a world of good, you'll see. Then come back," he said. "Let's try not to worry. You heard what Dr. Francis said."

She stood in her coat for a minute trying to recall the doc-tor's exact words, looking for any nuances, any hint of some-thing behind his words other than what he had said. She tried to remember if his expression had changed any when he bent over to examine the child. She remembered the way his fea-tures had composed themselves as he rolled back the child's eyelids and then listened to his breathing.

She went to the door, where she turned and looked back. She looked at the child, and then she looked at the father.

Howard nodded. She stepped out of the room and pulled the door closed behind her.

She went past the nurses' station and down to the end of the corridor, looking for the elevator. At the end of the corridor, she turned to her right and entered a little waiting room where a Negro family sat in wicker chairs. There was a middle-aged man in a khaki shirt and pants, a baseball cap pushed back on his head. A large woman wearing a housedress and slippers was slumped in one of the chairs. A teenaged girl in jeans, hair done in dozens of little braids, lay stretched out in one of the chairs smoking a cigarette, her legs crossed at the ankles. The family swung their eyes to Ann as she entered the room. The little table was littered with hamburger wrappers and Styrofoam cups.

"Franklin," the large woman said as she roused herself. "Is it about Franklin?" Her eyes widened. "Tell me now, lady," the woman said. "Is it about Franklin?" She was trying to rise from her chair, but the man had closed his hand over her arm.

"Here, here," he said. "Evelyn."

"I'm sorry," Ann said. "I'm looking for the elevator. My son is in the hospital, and now I can't find the elevator."

"Elevator is down that way, turn left," the man said as he aimed a finger.

The girl drew on her cigarette and stared at Ann. Her eyes were narrowed to slits, and her broad lips parted slowly as she let the smoke escape. The Negro woman let her head fall on her shoulder and looked away from Ann, no longer interested.

"My son was hit by a car," Ann said to the man. She seemed to need to explain herself. "He has a concussion and a little skull fracture, but he's going to be all right. He's in shock now, but it might be some kind of coma, too. That's what really worries us, the coma part. I'm going out for a little while, but my husband is with him. Maybe he'll wake up while I'm gone."

"That's too bad," the man said and shifted in the chair. He shook his head. He looked down at the table, and then he looked back at Ann. She was still standing there. He said, "Our Franklin, he's on the operating table. Somebody cut him. Tried to kill him. There was a fight where he was at. At this party. They say he was just standing and watching. Not bothering nobody. But that don't mean nothing these days.

Now he's on the operating table. We're just hoping and praying, that's all we can do now." He gazed at her steadily.

Ann looked at the girl again, who was still watching her, and at the older woman, who kept her head down, but whose eyes were now closed. Ann saw the lips moving silently, making words. She had an urge to ask what those words were. She wanted to talk more with these people who were in the same kind of waiting she was in. She was afraid, and they were afraid. They had that in common. She would have liked to have said something else about the accident, told them more about Scotty, that it had happened on the day of his birthday, Monday, and that he was still unconscious. Yet she didn't know how to begin. She stood looking at them without saying anything more.

She went down the corridor the man had indicated and found the elevator. She waited a minute in front of the closed doors, still wondering if she was doing the right thing. Then she put out her finger and touched the button.

She pulled into the driveway and cut the engine. She closed her eyes and leaned her head against the wheel for a minute. She listened to the ticking sounds the engine made as it began to cool. Then she got out of the car. She could hear the dog barking inside the house. She went to the front door, which was unlocked. She went inside and turned on lights and put on a kettle of water for tea. She opened some dogfood and fed Slug on the back porch. The dog ate in hungry little smacks. It kept running into the kitchen to see that she was going to stay. As she sat down on the sofa with her tea, the telephone rang.

"Yes!" she said as she answered. "Hello!"

"Mrs. Weiss," a man's voice said. It was five o'clock in the morning, and she thought she could hear machinery or equipment of some kind in the background.

"Yes, yes! What is it?" she said. "This is Mrs. Weiss. This is she. What is it, please?" She listened to whatever it was in the background. "Is it Scotty, for Christ's sake?"

"Scotty," the man's voice said. "It's about Scotty, yes. It has to do with Scotty, that problem. Have you forgotten about Scotty?" the man said. Then he hung up.

She dialed the hospital's number and asked for the third

floor. She demanded information about her son from the nurse who answered the telephone. Then she asked to speak to her husband. It was, she said, an emergency.

She waited, turning the telephone cord in her fingers. She closed her eyes and felt sick at her stomach. She would have to make herself eat. Slug came in from the back porch and lay down near her feet. He wagged his tail. She pulled at his ear while he licked her fingers. Howard was on the line.

"Somebody just called here," she said. She twisted the telephone cord. "He said it was about Scotty," she cried.

"Scotty's fine," Howard told her. "I mean, he's still sleeping. There's been no change. The nurse has been in twice since you've been gone. A nurse or else a doctor. He's all right."

"This man called. He said it was about Scotty," she told him.

"Honey, you rest for a little while, you need the rest. It must be that same caller I had. Just forget it. Come back down here after you've rested. Then we'll have breakfast or something."

"Breakfast," she said. "I don't want any breakfast."

"You know what I mean," he said. "Juice, something. I don't know. I don't know anything, Ann. Jesus, I'm not hungry, either. Ann, it's hard to talk now. I'm standing here at the desk. Dr. Francis is coming again at eight o'clock this morning. He's going to have something to tell us then, something more definite. That's what one of the nurses said. She didn't know any more than that. Ann? Honey, maybe we'll know something more then. At eight o'clock. Come back here before eight. Meanwhile, I'm right here and Scotty's all right. He's still the same," he added.

"I was drinking a cup of tea," she said, "when the telephone rang. They said it was about Scotty. There was a noise in the background. Was there a noise in the background on that call you had, Howard?"

"I don't remember," he said. "Maybe the driver of the car, maybe he's a psychopath and found out about Scotty somehow. But I'm here with him. Just rest like you were going to do. Take a bath and come back by seven or so, and we'll talk to the doctor together when he gets here. It's going to be all right, honey. I'm here, and there are doctors and nurses around. They say his condition is stable."

"I'm scared to death," she said.

She ran water, undressed, and got into the tub. She washed and dried quickly, not taking the time to wash her hair. She put on clean underwear, wool slacks, and a sweater. She went into the living room, where the dog looked up at her and let its tail thump once against the floor. It was just starting to get light outside when she went out to the car.

She drove into the parking lot of the hospital and found a space close to the front door. She felt she was in some obscure way responsible for what had happened to the child. She let her thoughts move to the Negro family. She remembered the name Franklin and the table that was covered with hamburger papers, and the teenaged girl staring at her as she drew on her cigarette. "Don't have children," she told the girl's image as she entered the front door of the hospital. "For God's sake, don't."

She took the elevator up to the third floor with two nurses who were just going on duty. It was Wednesday morning, a few minutes before seven. There was a page for a Dr. Madison as the elevator doors slid open on the third floor. She got off behind the nurses, who turned in the other direction and continued the conversation she had interrupted when she'd gotten into the elevator. She walked down the corridor to the little alcove where the Negro family had been waiting. They were gone now, but the chairs were scattered in such a way that it looked as if people had just jumped up from them the minute before. The tabletop was cluttered with the same cups and papers, the ashtray was filled with cigarette butts.

She stopped at the nurses' station. A nurse was standing behind the counter, brushing her hair and yawning.

"There was a Negro boy in surgery last night," Ann said. "Franklin was his name. His family was in the waiting room. I'd like to inquire about his condition."

A nurse who was sitting at a desk behind the counter looked up from a chart in front of her. The telephone buzzed and she picked up the receiver, but she kept her eyes on Ann.

"He passed away," said the nurse at the counter. The nurse held the hairbrush and kept looking at her. "Are you a friend of the family or what?"

"I met the family last night," Ann said. "My own son is in the hospital. I guess he's in shock. We don't know for sure what's wrong. I just wondered about Franklin, that's all. Thank you." She moved down the corridor. Elevator doors the same color as the walls slid open and a gaunt, bald man in white pants and white canvas shoes pulled a heavy cart off the elevator. She hadn't noticed these doors last night. The man wheeled the cart out into the corridor and stopped in front of the room nearest the elevator and consulted a clipboard. Then he reached down and slid a tray out of the cart. He rapped lightly on the door and entered the room. She could smell the unpleasant odors of warm food as she passed the cart. She hurried on without looking at any of the nurses and pushed open the door to the child's room.

Howard was standing at the window with his hands behind his back. He turned around as she came in.

"How is he?" she said. She went over to the bed. She dropped her purse on the floor beside the nightstand. It seemed to her she had been gone a long time. She touched the child's face. "Howard?"

"Dr. Francis was here a little while ago," Howard said. She looked at him closely and thought his shoulders were bunched a little.

"I thought he wasn't coming until eight o'clock this morning," she said quickly.

"There was another doctor with him. A neurologist."

"A neurologist," she said.

Howard nodded. His shoulders were bunching, she could see that. "What'd they say, Howard? For Christ's sake, what'd they say? What is it?"

"They said they're going to take him down and run more tests on him, Ann. They think they're going to operate, honey. Honey, they *are* going to operate. They can't figure out why he won't wake up. It's more than just shock or concussion, they know that much now. It's in his skull, the fracture, it has something, something to do with that, they think. So they're going to operate. I tried to call you, but I guess you'd already left the house."

"Oh, God," she said. "Oh, please, Howard, please," she said, taking his arms.

"Look!" Howard said. "Scotty! Look, Ann!" He turned her toward the bed.

The boy had opened his eyes, then closed them. He opened them again now. The eyes stared straight ahead for a minute, then moved slowly in his head until they rested on Howard and Ann, then traveled away again.

"Scotty," his mother said, moving to the bed.

"Hey, Scott," his father said. "Hey, son."

They leaned over the bed. Howard took the child's hand in his hands and began to pat and squeeze the hand. Ann bent over the boy and kissed his forehead again and again. She put her hands on either side of his face. "Scotty, honey, it's Mommy and Daddy," she said. "Scotty?"

The boy looked at them, but without any sign of recognition. Then his mouth opened, his eyes scrunched closed, and he howled until he had no more air in his lungs. His face seemed to relax and soften then. His lips parted as his last breath was puffed through his throat and exhaled gently through the clenched teeth.

The doctors called it a hidden occlusion and said it was a one-in-a-million circumstance. Maybe if it could have been detected somehow and surgery undertaken immediately, they could have saved him. But more than likely not. In any case, what would they have been looking for? Nothing had shown up in the tests or in the X-rays.

Dr. Francis was shaken. "I can't tell you how badly I feel. I'm so very sorry, I can't tell you," he said as he led them into the doctors' lounge. There was a doctor sitting in a chair with his legs hooked over the back of another chair, watching an early-morning TV show. He was wearing a green delivery-room outfit, loose green pants and green blouse, and a green cap that covered his hair. He looked at Howard and Ann and then looked at Dr. Francis. He got to his feet and turned off the set and went out of the room. Dr. Francis guided Ann to the sofa, sat down beside her, and began to talk in a low, consoling voice. At one point, he leaned over and embraced her. She could feel his chest rising and falling evenly against her shoulder. She kept her eyes open and let him hold her. Howard went into the bathroom, but he left the door open. After a violent fit of weeping, he ran water and washed his face. Then he came out and sat down at the little table that held a telephone.

He looked at the telephone as though deciding what to do first. He made some calls. After a time, Dr. Francis used the telephone.

"Is there anything else I can do for the moment?" he asked them.

Howard shook his head. Ann stared at Dr. Francis as if unable to comprehend his words.

The doctor walked them to the hospital's front door. People were entering and leaving the hospital. It was eleven o'clock in the morning. Ann was aware of how slowly, almost reluctantly, she moved her feet. It seemed to her that Dr. Francis was making them leave when she felt they should stay, when it would be more the right thing to do to stay. She gazed out into the parking lot and then turned around and looked back at the front of the hospital. She began shaking her head. "No, no," she said. "I can't leave him here, no." She heard herself say that and thought how unfair it was that the only words that came out were the sort of words used on TV shows where people were stunned by violent or sudden deaths. She wanted her words to be her own. "No," she said, and for some reason the memory of the Negro woman's head lolling on the woman's shoulder came to her. "No," she said again.

"I'll be talking to you later in the day," the doctor was saying to Howard. "There are still some things that have to be done, things that have to be cleared up to our satisfaction. Some things that need explaining."

"An autopsy," Howard said.

Dr. Francis nodded.

"I understand," Howard said. Then he said, "Oh, Jesus. No, I don't understand, doctor. I can't, I can't. I just can't."

Dr. Francis put his arm around Howard's shoulders. "I'm sorry. God, how I'm sorry." He let go of Howard's shoulders and held out his hand. Howard looked at the hand, and then he took it. Dr. Francis put his arms around Ann once more. He seemed full of some goodness she didn't understand. She let her head rest on his shoulder, but her eyes stayed open. She kept looking at the hospital. As they drove out of the parking lot, she looked back at the hospital.

—

At home, she sat on the sofa with her hands in her coat pockets. Howard closed the door to the child's room. He got the coffee-maker going and then he found an empty box. He had thought to pick up some of the child's things that were scattered around the living room. But instead he sat down beside her on the sofa, pushed the box to one side, and leaned forward, arms between his knees. He began to weep. She pulled his head over into her lap and patted his shoulder. "He's gone," she said. She kept patting his shoulder. Over his sobs, she could hear the coffee-maker hissing in the kitchen. "There, there," she said tenderly. "Howard, he's gone. He's gone and now we'll have to get used to that. To being alone."

In a little while, Howard got up and began moving aimlessly around the room with the box, not putting anything into it, but collecting some things together on the floor at one end of the sofa. She continued to sit with her hands in her coat pockets. Howard put the box down and brought coffee into the living room. Later, Ann made calls to relatives. After each call had been placed and the party had answered, Ann would blurt out a few words and cry for a minute. Then she would quietly explain, in a measured voice, what had happened and tell them about arrangements. Howard took the box out to the garage, where he saw the child's bicycle. He dropped the box and sat down on the pavement beside the bicycle. He took hold of the bicycle awkwardly so that it leaned against his chest. He held it, the rubber pedal sticking into his chest. He gave the wheel a turn.

Ann hung up the telephone after talking to her sister. She was looking up another number when the telephone rang. She picked it up on the first ring.

"Hello," she said, and she heard something in the background, a humming noise. "Hello!" she said. "For God's sake," she said. "Who is this? What is it you want?"

"Your Scotty, I got him ready for you," the man's voice said. "Did you forget him?"

"You evil bastard!" she shouted into the receiver. "How can you do this, you evil son of a bitch?"

"Scotty," the man said. "Have you forgotten about Scotty?" Then the man hung up on her.

Howard heard the shouting and came in to find her with her

head on her arms over the table, weeping. He picked up the receiver and listened to the dial tone.

Much later, just before midnight, after they had dealt with many things, the telephone rang again.

"You answer it," she said. "Howard, it's him, I know." They were sitting at the kitchen table with coffee in front of them. Howard had a small glass of whiskey beside his cup. He answered on the third ring.

"Hello," he said. "Who is this? Hello! Hello!" The line went dead. "He hung up," Howard said. "Whoever it was."

"It was him," she said. "That bastard. I'd like to kill him," she said. "I'd like to shoot him and watch him kick," she said.

"Ann, my God," he said.

"Could you hear anything?" she said. "In the background? A noise, machinery, something humming?"

"Nothing, really. Nothing like that," he said. "There wasn't much time. I think there was some radio music. Yes, there was a radio going, that's all I could tell. I don't know what in God's name is going on," he said.

She shook her head. "If I could, could get my hands on him." It came to her then. She knew who it was. Scotty, the cake, the telephone number. She pushed the chair away from the table and got up. "Drive me down to the shopping center," she said. "Howard."

"What are you saying?"

"The shopping center. I know who it is who's calling. I know who it is. It's the baker, the son-of-a-bitching baker, Howard. I had him bake a cake for Scotty's birthday. That's who's calling. That's who has the number and keeps calling us. To harass us about that cake. The baker, that bastard."

They drove down to the shopping center. The sky was clear and stars were out. It was cold, and they ran the heater in the car. They parked in front of the bakery. All of the shops and stores were closed, but there were cars at the far end of the lot in front of the movie theater. The bakery windows were dark, but when they looked through the glass they could see a light in the back room and, now and then, a big man in an apron moving in and out of the white, even light. Through the glass, she could see the display cases and some little tables with chairs. She tried the door. She rapped on the glass. But if the baker heard them, he gave no sign. He didn't look in their direction.

They drove around behind the bakery and parked. They got out of the car. There was a lighted window too high up for them to see inside. A sign near the back door said THE PANTRY BAKERY, SPECIAL ORDERS. She could hear faintly a radio playing inside and something creak—an oven door as it was pulled down? She knocked on the door and waited. Then she knocked again, louder. The radio was turned down and there was a scraping sound now, the distinct sound of something, a drawer, being pulled open and then closed.

Someone unlocked the door and opened it. The baker stood in the light and peered out at them. "I'm closed for business," he said. "What do you want at this hour? It's midnight. Are you drunk or something?"

She stepped into the light that fell through the open door. He blinked his heavy eyelids as he recognized her. "It's you," he said.

"It's me," she said. "Scotty's mother. This is Scotty's father. We'd like to come in."

The baker said, "I'm busy now. I have work to do."

She had stepped inside the doorway anyway. Howard came in behind her. The baker moved back. "It smells like a bakery in here. Doesn't it smell like a bakery in here, Howard?"

"What do you want?" the baker said. "Maybe you want your cake? That's it, you decided you want your cake. You ordered a cake, didn't you?"

"You're pretty smart for a baker," she said. "Howard, this is the man who's been calling us." She clenched her fists. She stared at him fiercely. There was a deep burning inside her, an anger that made her feel larger than herself, larger than either of these men.

"Just a minute here," the baker said. "You want to pick up your three-day-old cake? That it? I don't want to argue with you, lady. There it sits over there, getting stale. I'll give it to you for half of what I quoted you. No. You want it? You can have it. It's no good to me, no good to anyone now. It cost me time and money to make that cake. If you want it, okay, if you don't, that's okay, too. I have to get back to work." He looked at them and rolled his tongue behind his teeth.

"More cakes," she said. She knew she was in control of it, of what was increasing in her. She was calm.

"Lady, I work sixteen hours a day in this place to earn a living," the baker said. He wiped his hands on his apron. "I work night and day in here, trying to make ends meet." A look crossed Ann's face that made the baker move back and say, "No trouble, now." He reached to the counter and picked up a rolling pin with his right hand and began to tap it against the palm of his other hand. "You want the cake or not? I have to get back to work. Bakers work at night," he said again. His eyes were small, mean-looking, she thought, nearly lost in the bristly flesh around his cheeks. His neck was thick with fat.

"I know bakers work at night," Ann said. "They make phone calls at night, too. You bastard," she said.

The baker continued to tap the rolling pin against his hand. He glanced at Howard. "Careful, careful," he said to Howard.

"My son's dead," she said with a cold, even finality. "He was hit by a car Monday morning. We've been waiting with him until he died. But, of course, you couldn't be expected to know that, could you? Bakers can't know everything—can they, Mr. Baker? But he's dead. He's dead, you bastard!" Just as suddenly as it had welled in her, the anger dwindled, gave way to something else, a dizzy feeling of nausea. She leaned against the wooden table that was sprinkled with flour, put her hands over her face, and began to cry, her shoulders rocking back and forth. "It isn't fair," she said. "It isn't, isn't fair."

Howard put his hand at the small of her back and looked at the baker. "Shame on you," Howard said to him. "Shame."

The baker put the rolling pin back on the counter. He undid his apron and threw it on the counter. He looked at them, and then he shook his head slowly. He pulled a chair out from under the card table that held papers and receipts, an adding machine, and a telephone directory. "Please sit down," he said. "Let me get you a chair," he said to Howard. "Sit down now, please." The baker went into the front of the shop and returned with two little wrought-iron chairs. "Please sit down, you people."

Ann wiped her eyes and looked at the baker. "I wanted to kill you," she said. "I wanted you dead."

The baker had cleared a space for them at the table. He shoved the adding machine to one side, along with the stacks of notepaper and receipts. He pushed the telephone directory onto the floor, where it landed with a thud. Howard and Ann sat down and pulled their chairs up to the table. The baker sat down, too.

"Let me say how sorry I am," the baker said, putting his elbows on the table. "God alone knows how sorry. Listen to me. I'm just a baker. I don't claim to be anything else. Maybe once, maybe years ago, I was a different kind of human being. I've forgotten, I don't know for sure. But I'm not any longer, if I ever was. Now I'm just a baker. That don't excuse my doing what I did, I know. But I'm deeply sorry. I'm sorry for your son, and sorry for my part in this," the baker said. He spread his hands out on the table and turned them over to reveal his palms. "I don't have any children myself, so I can only imagine what you must be feeling. All I can say to you now is that I'm sorry. Forgive me, if you can," the baker said. "I'm not an evil man, I don't think. Not evil, like you said on the phone. You got to understand what it comes down to is I don't know how to act anymore, it would seem. Please," the man said, "let me ask you if you can find it in your hearts to forgive me?"

It was warm inside the bakery. Howard stood up from the table and took off his coat. He helped Ann from her coat. The baker looked at them for a minute and then nodded and got up from the table. He went to the oven and turned off some switches. He found cups and poured coffee from an electric coffee-maker. He put a carton of cream on the table, and a bowl of sugar.

"You probably need to eat something," the baker said. "I hope you'll eat some of my hot rolls. You have to eat and keep going. Eating is a small, good thing in a time like this," he said.

He served them warm cinnamon rolls just out of the oven, the icing still runny. He put butter on the table and knives to spread the butter. Then the baker sat down at the table with them. He waited. He waited until they each took a roll from the platter and began to eat. "It's good to eat something," he said, watching them. "There's more. Eat up. Eat all you want. There's all the rolls in the world in here."

They ate rolls and drank coffee. Ann was suddenly hungry,

and the rolls were warm and sweet. She ate three of them, which pleased the baker. Then he began to talk. They listened carefully. Although they were tired and in anguish, they listened to what the baker had to say. They nodded when the baker began to speak of loneliness, and of the sense of doubt and limitation that had come to him in his middle years. He told them what it was like to be childless all these years. To repeat the days with the ovens endlessly full and endlessly empty. The party food, the celebrations he'd worked over. Icing knuckle-deep. The tiny wedding couples stuck into cakes. Hundreds of them, no, thousands by now. Birthdays. Just imagine all those candles burning. He had a necessary trade. He was a baker. He was glad he wasn't a florist. It was better to be feeding people. This was a better smell anytime than flowers.

"Smell this," the baker said, breaking open a dark loaf. "It's a heavy bread, but rich." They smelled it, then he had them taste it. It had the taste of molasses and coarse grains. They listened to him. They ate what they could. They swallowed the dark bread. It was like daylight under the fluorescent trays of light. They talked on into the early morning, the high, pale cast of light in the windows, and they did not think of leaving.

Vitamins

I HAD a job and Patti didn't. I worked a few hours a night for the hospital. It was a nothing job. I did some work, signed the card for eight hours, went drinking with the nurses. After a while, Patti wanted a job. She said she needed a job for her self-respect. So she started selling multiple vitamins door to door.

For a while, she was just another girl who went up and down blocks in strange neighborhoods, knocking on doors. But she learned the ropes. She was quick and had excelled at things in school. She had personality. Pretty soon the company gave her a promotion. Some of the girls who weren't doing so hot were put to work under her. Before long, she had herself a crew and a little office out in the mall. But the girls who worked for her were always changing. Some would quit after a couple of days —after a couple of hours, sometimes. But sometimes there were girls who were good at it. They could sell vitamins. These were the girls that stuck with Patti. They formed the core of the crew. But there were girls who couldn't give away vitamins.

The girls who couldn't cut it would just quit. Just not show up for work. If they had a phone, they'd take it off the hook. They wouldn't answer the door. Patti took these losses to heart, like the girls were new converts who had lost their way. She blamed herself. But she got over it. There were too many not to get over it.

Once in a while a girl would freeze and not be able to push the doorbell. Or maybe she'd get to the door and something would happen to her voice. Or she'd get the greeting mixed up with something she shouldn't be saying until she got inside. A girl like this, she'd decide to pack it in, take the sample case, head for the car, hang around until Patti and the others finished. There'd be a conference. Then they'd all ride back to the office. They'd say things to buck themselves up. "When the going gets tough, the tough get going." And, "Do the right things and the right things will happen." Things like that.

Sometimes a girl just disappeared in the field, sample case and all. She'd hitch a ride into town, then beat it. But there

were always girls to take her place. Girls were coming and
going in those days. Patti had a list. Every few weeks she'd run
a little ad in *The Pennysaver*. There'd be more girls and more
training. There was no end of girls.

The core group was made up of Patti, Donna, and Sheila.
Patti was a looker. Donna and Sheila were only medium-
pretty. One night this Sheila said to Patti that she loved her
more than anything on earth. Patti told me these were the
words. Patti had driven Sheila home and they were sitting in
front of Sheila's place. Patti said to Sheila she loved her, too.
Patti said to Sheila she loved all her girls. But not in the way
Sheila had in mind. Then Sheila touched Patti's breast. Patti
said she took Sheila's hand and held it. She said she told her
she didn't swing that way. She said Sheila didn't bat an eye,
that she only nodded, held on to Patti's hand, kissed it, and
got out of the car.

That was around Christmas. The vitamin business was pretty
bad off back then, so we thought we'd have a party to cheer
everybody up. It seemed like a good idea at the time. Sheila
was the first to get drunk and pass out. She passed out on her
feet, fell over, and didn't wake up for hours. One minute she
was standing in the middle of the living room, then her eyes
closed, the legs buckled, and she went down with a glass in her
hand. The hand holding the drink smacked the coffee table
when she fell. She didn't make a sound otherwise. The drink
poured out onto the rug. Patti and I and somebody else lugged
her out to the back porch and put her down on a cot and did
what we could to forget about her.

Everybody got drunk and went home. Patti went to bed. I
wanted to keep on, so I sat at the table with a drink until it
began to get light out. Then Sheila came in from the porch
and started up. She said she had this headache that was so bad
it was like somebody was sticking wires in her brain. She said it
was such a bad headache she was afraid it was going to leave
her with a permanent squint. And she was sure her little finger
was broken. She showed it to me. It looked purple. She
bitched about us letting her sleep all night with her contacts
in. She wanted to know didn't anybody give a shit. She brought
the finger up close and looked at it. She shook her head. She

held the finger as far away as she could and looked some more. It was like she couldn't believe the things that must have happened to her that night. Her face was puffy, and her hair was all over. She ran cold water on her finger. "God. Oh, God," she said and cried some over the sink. But she'd made a serious pass at Patti, a declaration of love, and I didn't have any sympathy.

I was drinking Scotch and milk with a sliver of ice. Sheila was leaning on the drainboard. She watched me from her little slits of eyes. I took some of my drink. I didn't say anything. She went back to telling me how bad she felt. She said she needed to see a doctor. She said she was going to wake Patti. She said she was quitting, leaving the state, going to Portland. That she had to say goodbye to Patti first. She kept on. She wanted Patti to drive her to the hospital for her finger and her eyes.

"I'll drive you," I said. I didn't want to do it, but I would.

"I want Patti to drive me," Sheila said.

She was holding the wrist of her bad hand with her good hand, the little finger as big as a pocket flashlight. "Besides, we need to talk. I need to tell her I'm going to Portland. I need to say goodbye."

I said, "I guess I'll have to tell her for you. She's asleep."

Sheila turned mean. "We're *friends*," she said. "I have to talk to her. I have to tell her myself."

I shook my head. "She's asleep. I just said so."

"We're friends and we love each other," Sheila said. "I have to say goodbye to her."

Sheila made to leave the kitchen.

I started to get up. I said, "I said I'll drive you."

"You're drunk! You haven't even been to bed yet." She looked at her finger again and said, "Goddamn, why'd this have to happen?"

"Not too drunk to drive you to the hospital," I said.

"I won't ride with you!" Sheila yelled.

"Suit yourself. But you're not going to wake Patti. Lesbo bitch," I said.

"Bastard," she said.

That's what she said, and then she went out of the kitchen and out the front door without using the bathroom or even washing her face. I got up and looked through the window.

She was walking down the road toward Euclid. Nobody else was up. It was too early.

I finished my drink and thought about fixing another one.

I fixed it.

Nobody saw any more of Sheila after that. None of us vitamin-related people, anyway. She walked to Euclid Avenue and out of our lives.

Later on Patti said, "What happened to Sheila?" and I said, "She went to Portland."

I had the hots for Donna, the other member of the core group. We'd danced to some Duke Ellington records that night of the party. I'd held her pretty tight, smelled her hair, kept a hand low on her back as I moved her over the rug. It was great dancing with her. I was the only fellow at the party, and there were seven girls, six of them dancing with each other. It was great just looking around the living room.

I was in the kitchen when Donna came in with her empty glass. We were alone for a bit. I got her into a little embrace. She hugged me back. We stood there and hugged.

Then she said, "Don't. Not now."

When I heard that "Not now," I let go. I figured it was money in the bank.

I'd been at the table thinking about that hug when Sheila came in with her finger.

I thought some more about Donna. I finished the drink. I took the phone off the hook and headed for the bedroom. I took off my clothes and got in next to Patti. I lay for a while, winding down. Then I started in. But she didn't wake up. Afterwards, I closed my eyes.

It was the afternoon when I opened them again. I was in bed alone. Rain was blowing against the window. A sugar doughnut was lying on Patti's pillow, and a glass of old water was on the nightstand. I was still drunk and couldn't figure anything out. I knew it was Sunday and close to Christmas. I ate the doughnut and drank the water. I went back to sleep until I heard Patti running the vacuum. She came into the bedroom and asked about Sheila. That's when I told her, said she'd gone to Portland.

—

A week or so into the new year, Patti and I were having a drink. She'd just come home from work. It wasn't so late, but it was dark and rainy. I was going to work in a couple of hours. But first we were having us some Scotch and talking. Patti was tired. She was down in the dumps and into her third drink. Nobody was buying vitamins. All she had was Donna and Pam, a semi-new girl who was a klepto. We were talking about things like negative weather and the number of parking tickets you could get away with. Then we got to talking about how we'd be better off if we moved to Arizona, someplace like that.

I fixed us another one. I looked out the window. Arizona wasn't a bad idea.

Patti said, "Vitamins." She picked up her glass and spun the ice. "For shit's sake!" she said. "I mean, when I was a girl, this is the last thing I ever saw myself doing. Jesus, I never thought I'd grow up to sell vitamins. Door-to-door vitamins. This beats all. This really blows my mind."

"I never thought so either, honey," I said.

"That's right," she said. "You said it in a nutshell."

"Honey."

"Don't honey me," she said. "This is hard, brother. This life is not easy, any way you cut it."

She seemed to think things over for a bit. She shook her head. Then she finished her drink. She said, "I even dream of vitamins when I'm asleep. I don't have any relief. There's no relief! At least you can walk away from your job and leave it behind. I'll bet you haven't had one dream about it. I'll bet you don't dream about waxing floors or whatever you do down there. After you've left the goddamn place, you don't come home and dream about it, do you?" she screamed.

I said, "I can't remember what I dream. Maybe I don't dream. I don't remember anything when I wake up." I shrugged. I didn't keep track of what went on in my head when I was asleep. I didn't care.

"You dream!" Patti said. "Even if you don't remember. Everybody dreams. If you didn't dream, you'd go crazy. I read about it. It's an outlet. People dream when they're asleep. Or else they'd go nuts. But when I dream, I dream of vitamins. Do you see what I'm saying?" She had her eyes fixed on me.

"Yes and no," I said.

It wasn't a simple question.

"I dream I'm pitching vitamins," she said. "I'm selling vitamins day and night. Jesus, what a life," she said.

She finished her drink.

"How's Pam doing?" I said. "She still stealing things?" I wanted to get us off this subject. But there wasn't anything else I could think of.

Patti said, "Shit," and shook her head like I didn't know anything. We listened to it rain.

"Nobody's selling vitamins," Patti said. She picked up her glass. But it was empty. "Nobody's buying vitamins. That's what I'm telling you. Didn't you hear me?"

I got up to fix us another. "Donna doing anything?" I said. I read the label on the bottle and waited.

Patti said, "She made a little sale two days ago. That's all. That's all that any of us has done this week. It wouldn't surprise me if she quit. I wouldn't blame her," Patti said. "If I was in her place, I'd quit. But if she quits, then what? Then I'm back at the start, that's what. Ground zero. Middle of winter, people sick all over the state, people dying, and nobody thinks they need vitamins. I'm sick as hell myself."

"What's wrong, honey?" I put the drinks on the table and sat down. She went on like I hadn't said anything. Maybe I hadn't.

"I'm my only customer," she said. "I think taking all these vitamins is doing something to my skin. Does my skin look okay to you? Can a person get overdosed on vitamins? I'm getting to where I can't even take a crap like a normal person."

"Honey," I said.

Patti said, "You don't care if I take vitamins. That's the point. You don't care about anything. The windshield wiper quit this afternoon in the rain. I almost had a wreck. I came this close."

We went on drinking and talking until it was time for me to go to work. Patti said she was going to soak in a tub if she didn't fall asleep first. "I'm asleep on my feet," she said. She said, "Vitamins. That's all there is anymore." She looked around the kitchen. She looked at her empty glass. She was drunk. But she let me kiss her. Then I left for work.

———

There was a place I went to after work. I'd started going for
the music and because I could get a drink there after closing
hours. It was a place called the Off-Broadway. It was a spade
place in a spade neighborhood. It was run by a spade named
Khaki. People would show up after the other places had
stopped serving. They'd ask for house specials—RC Colas with
a shooter of whiskey—or else they'd bring in their own stuff
under their coats, order RC, and build their own. Musicians
showed up to jam, and the drinkers who wanted to keep drinking
came to drink and listen to the music. Sometimes people
danced. But mainly they sat around and drank and listened.

Now and then a spade hit a spade in the head with a bottle.
A story went around once that somebody had followed somebody into the Gents and cut the man's throat while he had his
hands down pissing. But I never saw any trouble. Nothing that
Khaki couldn't handle. Khaki was a big spade with a bald head
that lit up weird under the fluorescents. He wore Hawaiian shirts
that hung over his pants. I think he carried something inside
his waistband. At least a sap, maybe. If somebody started to
get out of line, Khaki would go over to where it was beginning. He'd rest his big hand on the party's shoulder and say a
few words and that was that. I'd been going there off and on
for months. I was pleased that he'd say things to me, things
like, "How're you doing tonight, friend?" Or, "Friend, I
haven't seen you for a spell."

The Off-Broadway is where I took Donna on our date. It
was the one date we ever had.

I'd walked out of the hospital just after midnight. It'd cleared
up and stars were out. I still had this buzz on from the Scotch
I'd had with Patti. But I was thinking to hit New Jimmy's for
a quick one on the way home. Donna's car was parked in the
space next to my car, and Donna was inside the car. I remembered that hug we'd had in the kitchen. "Not now," she'd said.

She rolled the window down and knocked ashes from her
cigarette.

"I couldn't sleep," she said. "I have some things on my
mind, and I couldn't sleep."

I said, "Donna. Hey, I'm glad to see you, Donna."

"I don't know what's wrong with me," she said.

"You want to go someplace for a drink?" I said.

"Patti's my friend," she said.

"She's my friend, too," I said. Then I said, "Let's go."

"Just so you know," she said.

"There's this place. It's a spade place," I said. "They have music. We can get a drink, listen to some music."

"You want to drive me?" Donna said.

I said, "Scoot over."

She started right in about vitamins. Vitamins were on the skids, vitamins had taken a nosedive. The bottom had fallen out of the vitamin market.

Donna said, "I hate to do this to Patti. She's my best friend, and she's trying to build things up for us. But I may have to quit. This is between us. Swear it! But I have to eat. I have to pay rent. I need new shoes and a new coat. Vitamins can't cut it," Donna said. "I don't think vitamins is where it's at anymore. I haven't said anything to Patti. Like I said, I'm still just thinking about it."

Donna laid her hand next to my leg. I reached down and squeezed her fingers. She squeezed back. Then she took her hand away and pushed in the lighter. After she had her cigarette going, she put the hand back. "Worse than anything, I hate to let Patti down. You know what I'm saying? We were a team." She reached me her cigarette. "I know it's a different brand," she said, "but try it, go ahead."

I pulled into the lot for the Off-Broadway. Three spades were up against an old Chrysler that had a cracked windshield. They were just lounging, passing a bottle in a sack. They looked us over. I got out and went around to open up for Donna. I checked the doors, took her arm, and we headed for the street. The spades just watched us.

I said, "You're not thinking about moving to Portland, are you?"

We were on the sidewalk. I put my arm around her waist.

"I don't know anything about Portland. Portland hasn't crossed my mind once."

The front half of the Off-Broadway was like a regular café and bar. A few spades sat at the counter and a few more worked over plates of food at tables with red oilcloth. We went through the café and into the big room in back. There was a long counter with booths against the wall and farther back a platform where musicians could set up. In front of the platform was what passed for a dance floor. The bars and nightclubs were still serving, so people hadn't turned up in any real numbers yet. I helped Donna take off her coat. We picked a booth and put our cigarettes on the table. The spade waitress named Hannah came over. Hannah and me nodded. She looked at Donna. I ordered us two RC specials and decided to feel good about things.

After the drinks came and I'd paid and we'd each had a sip, we started hugging. We carried on like this for a while, squeezing and patting, kissing each other's face. Every so often Donna would stop and draw back, push me away a little, then hold me by the wrists. She'd gaze into my eyes. Then her lids would close slowly and we'd fall to kissing again. Pretty soon the place began to fill up. We stopped kissing. But I kept my arm around her. She put her fingers on my leg. A couple of spade horn-players and a white drummer began fooling around with something. I figured Donna and me would have another drink and listen to the set. Then we'd leave and go to her place to finish things.

I'd just ordered two more from Hannah when this spade named Benny came over with this other spade—this big, dressed-up spade. This big spade had little red eyes and was wearing a three-piece pinstripe. He had on a rose-colored shirt, a tie, a topcoat, a fedora—all of it.

"How's my man?" said Benny.

Benny stuck out his hand for a brother handshake. Benny and I had talked. He knew I liked the music, and he used to come over to talk whenever we were both in the place. He liked to talk about Johnny Hodges, how he'd played sax backup for Johnny. He'd say things like, "When Johnny and me had this gig in Mason City."

"Hi, Benny," I said.

"I want you to meet Nelson," Benny said. "He just back from Nam today. This morning. He here to listen to some of these good sounds. He got on his dancing shoes in case." Benny looked at Nelson and nodded. "This here is Nelson."

I was looking at Nelson's shiny shoes, and then I looked at Nelson. He seemed to want to place me from somewhere. He studied me. Then he let loose a rolling grin that showed his teeth.

"This is Donna," I said. "Donna, this is Benny, and this is Nelson. Nelson, this is Donna."

"Hello, girl," Nelson said, and Donna said right back, "Hello there, Nelson. Hello, Benny."

"Maybe we'll just slide in and join you folks?" Benny said. "Okay?"

I said, "Sure."

But I was sorry they hadn't found someplace else.

"We're not going to be here long," I said. "Just long enough to finish this drink, is all."

"I know, man, I know," Benny said. He sat across from me after Nelson had let himself down into the booth. "Things to do, places to go. Yes sir, Benny knows," Benny said, and winked.

Nelson looked across the booth to Donna. Then he took off the hat. He seemed to be looking for something on the brim as he turned the hat around in his big hands. He made room for the hat on the table. He looked up at Donna. He grinned and squared his shoulders. He had to square his shoulders every few minutes. It was like he was very tired of carrying them around.

"You real good friends with him, I bet," Nelson said to Donna.

"We're good friends," Donna said.

Hannah came over. Benny asked for RCs. Hannah went away, and Nelson worked a pint of whiskey from his topcoat.

"Good friends," Nelson said. "Real good friends." He unscrewed the cap on his whiskey.

"Watch it, Nelson," Benny said. "Keep that out of sight. Nelson just got off the plane from Nam," Benny said.

Nelson raised the bottle and drank some of his whiskey. He screwed the cap back on, laid the bottle on the table, and put his hat down on top of it. "Real good friends," he said.

Benny looked at me and rolled his eyes. But he was drunk, too. "I got to get into shape," he said to me. He drank RC from both of their glasses and then held the glasses under the table and poured whiskey. He put the bottle in his coat pocket. "Man, I ain't put my lips to a reed for a month now. I got to get with it."

We were bunched in the booth, glasses in front of us, Nelson's hat on the table. "You," Nelson said to me. "You with somebody else, ain't you? This beautiful woman, she ain't your wife. I know that. But you real good friends with this woman. Ain't I right?"

I had some of my drink. I couldn't taste the whiskey. I couldn't taste anything. I said, "Is all that shit about Vietnam true we see on the TV?"

Nelson had his red eyes fixed on me. He said, "What I want to say is, do you know where your wife is? I bet she out with some dude and she be seizing his nipples for him and pulling his pud for him while you setting here big as life with your good friend. I bet she have herself a good friend, too."

"Nelson," Benny said.

"Nelson nothing," Nelson said.

Benny said, "Nelson, let's leave these people be. There's somebody in that other booth. Somebody I told you about. Nelson just this morning got off a plane," Benny said.

"I bet I know what you thinking," Nelson said. "I bet you thinking, 'Now here a big drunk nigger and what am I going to do with him? Maybe I have to whip his ass for him!' That what you thinking?"

I looked around the room. I saw Khaki standing near the platform, the musicians working away behind him. Some dancers were on the floor. I thought Khaki looked right at me —but if he did, he looked away again.

"Ain't it your turn to talk?" Nelson said. "I just teasing you. I ain't done any teasing since I left Nam. I teased the gooks some." He grinned again, his big lips rolling back. Then he stopped grinning and just stared.

"Show them that ear," Benny said. He put his glass on the table. "Nelson got himself an ear off one of them little dudes," Benny said. "He carry it with him. Show them, Nelson."

Nelson sat there. Then he started feeling the pockets of his topcoat. He took things out of one pocket. He took out some keys and a box of cough drops.

Donna said, "I don't want to see an ear. Ugh. Double ugh. Jesus." She looked at me.

"We have to go," I said.

Nelson was still feeling in his pockets. He took a wallet from a pocket inside the suit coat and put it on the table. He patted the wallet. "Five big ones there. Listen here," he said to Donna. "I going to give you two bills. You with me? I give you two big ones, and then you French me. Just like his woman doing some other big fellow. You hear? You know she got her mouth on somebody's hammer right this minute while he here with his hand up your skirt. Fair's fair. Here." He pulled the corners of the bills from his wallet. "Hell, here another hundred for your good friend, so he won't feel left out. He don't have to do nothing. You don't have to do nothing," Nelson said to me. "You just sit there and drink your drink and listen to the music. Good music. Me and this woman walk out together like good friends. And she walk back in by herself. Won't be long, she be back."

"Nelson," Benny said, "this is no way to talk, Nelson."

Nelson grinned. "I finished talking," he said.

He found what he'd been feeling for. It was a silver cigarette case. He opened it up. I looked at the ear inside. It sat on a bed of cotton. It looked like a dried mushroom. But it was a real ear, and it was hooked up to a key chain.

"Jesus," said Donna. "Yuck."

"Ain't that something?" Nelson said. He was watching Donna.

"No way. Fuck off," Donna said.

"Girl," Nelson said.

"Nelson," I said. And then Nelson fixed his red eyes on me. He pushed the hat and wallet and cigarette case out of his way.

"What do you want?" Nelson said. "I give you what you want."

Khaki had a hand on my shoulder and the other one on Benny's shoulder. He leaned over the table, his head shining under the lights. "How you folks? You all having fun?"

"Everything all right, Khaki," Benny said. "Everything A-okay. These people here was just fixing to leave. Me and Nelson going to sit and listen to the music."

"That's good," Khaki said. "Folks be happy is my motto."

He looked around the booth. He looked at Nelson's wallet on the table and at the open cigarette case next to the wallet. He saw the ear.

"That a real ear?" Khaki said.

Benny said, "It is. Show him that ear, Nelson. Nelson just stepped off the plane from Nam with this ear. This ear has traveled halfway around the world to be on this table tonight. Nelson, show him," Benny said.

Nelson picked up the case and handed it to Khaki.

Khaki examined the ear. He took up the chain and dangled the ear in front of his face. He looked at it. He let it swing back and forth on the chain. "I heard about these dried-up ears and dicks and such."

"I took it off one of them gooks," Nelson said. "He couldn't hear nothing with it no more. I wanted me a keepsake."

Khaki turned the ear on its chain.

Donna and I began getting out of the booth.

"Girl, don't go," Nelson said.

"Nelson," Benny said.

Khaki was watching Nelson now. I stood beside the booth with Donna's coat. My legs were crazy.

Nelson raised his voice. He said, "You go with this mother here, you let him put his face in your sweets, you both going to have to deal with me."

We started to move away from the booth. People were looking.

"Nelson just got off the plane from Nam this morning," I heard Benny say. "We been drinking all day. This been the longest day on record. But me and him, we going to be fine, Khaki."

Nelson yelled something over the music. He yelled, "It ain't going to do no good! Whatever you do, it ain't going to help none!" I heard him say that, and then I couldn't hear anymore. The music stopped, and then it started again. We didn't look back. We kept going. We got out to the sidewalk.

I opened the door for her. I started us back to the hospital. Donna stayed over on her side. She'd used the lighter on a cigarette, but she wouldn't talk.

I tried to say something. I said, "Look, Donna, don't get on a downer because of this. I'm sorry it happened," I said.

"I could of used the money," Donna said. "That's what I was thinking."

I kept driving and didn't look at her.

"It's true," she said. "I could of used the money." She shook her head. "I don't know," she said. She put her chin down and cried.

"Don't cry," I said.

"I'm not going in to work tomorrow, today, whenever it is the alarm goes off," she said. "I'm not going in. I'm leaving town. I take what happened back there as a sign." She pushed in the lighter and waited for it to pop out.

I pulled in beside my car and killed the engine. I looked in the rearview, half thinking I'd see that old Chrysler drive into the lot behind me with Nelson in the seat. I kept my hands on the wheel for a minute, and then dropped them to my lap. I didn't want to touch Donna. The hug we'd given each other in my kitchen that night, the kissing we'd done at the Off-Broadway, that was all over.

I said, "What are you going to do?" But I didn't care. Right then she could have died of a heart attack and it wouldn't have meant anything.

"Maybe I could go up to Portland," she said. "There must be something in Portland. Portland's on everybody's mind these days. Portland's a drawing card. Portland this, Portland that. Portland's as good a place as any. It's all the same."

"Donna," I said, "I'd better go."

I started to let myself out. I cracked the door, and the overhead light came on.

"For Christ's sake, turn off that light!"

I got out in a hurry. "'Night, Donna," I said.

I left her staring at the dashboard. I started up my car and turned on the lights. I slipped it in gear and fed it the gas.

I poured Scotch, drank some of it, and took the glass into the bathroom. I brushed my teeth. Then I pulled open a drawer. Patti yelled something from the bedroom. She opened the bathroom door. She was still dressed. She'd been sleeping with her clothes on, I guess.

"What time is it?" she screamed. "I've overslept! Jesus, oh my God! You've let me oversleep, goddamn you!"

She was wild. She stood in the doorway with her clothes on. She could have been fixing to go to work. But there was no sample case, no vitamins. She was having a bad dream, is all. She began shaking her head from side to side.

I couldn't take any more tonight. "Go back to sleep, honey. I'm looking for something," I said. I knocked some stuff out of the medicine chest. Things rolled into the sink. "Where's the aspirin?" I said. I knocked down some more things. I didn't care. Things kept falling.

Careful

AFTER a lot of talking—what his wife, Inez, called *assessment*—Lloyd moved out of the house and into his own place. He had two rooms and a bath on the top floor of a three-story house. Inside the rooms, the roof slanted down sharply. If he walked around, he had to duck his head. He had to stoop to look from his windows and be careful getting in and out of bed. There were two keys. One key let him into the house itself. Then he climbed some stairs that passed through the house to a landing. He went up another flight of stairs to the door of his room and used the other key on that lock.

Once, when he was coming back to his place in the afternoon, carrying a sack with three bottles of André champagne and some lunch meat, he stopped on the landing and looked into his landlady's living room. He saw the old woman lying on her back on the carpet. She seemed to be asleep. Then it occurred to him she might be dead. But the TV was going, so he chose to think she was asleep. He didn't know what to make of it. He moved the sack from one arm to the other. It was then that the woman gave a little cough, brought her hand to her side, and went back to being quiet and still again. Lloyd continued on up the stairs and unlocked his door. Later that day, toward evening, as he looked from his kitchen window, he saw the old woman down in the yard, wearing a straw hat and holding her hand against her side. She was using a little watering can on some pansies.

In his kitchen, he had a combination refrigerator and stove. The refrigerator and stove was a tiny affair wedged into a space between the sink and the wall. He had to bend over, almost get down on his knees, to get anything out of the refrigerator. But it was all right because he didn't keep much in there, anyway—except fruit juice, lunch meat, and champagne. The stove had two burners. Now and then he heated water in a saucepan and made instant coffee. But some days he didn't drink any coffee. He forgot, or else he just didn't feel like coffee. One morning he woke up and promptly fell to eating crumb doughnuts and drinking champagne. There'd been a time, some years back,

441

when he would have laughed at having a breakfast like this. Now, there didn't seem to be anything very unusual about it. In fact, he hadn't thought anything about it until he was in bed and trying to recall the things he'd done that day, starting with when he'd gotten up that morning. At first, he couldn't remember anything noteworthy. Then he remembered eating those doughnuts and drinking champagne. Time was when he would have considered this a mildly crazy thing to do, something to tell friends about. Then, the more he thought about it, the more he could see it didn't matter much one way or the other. He'd had doughnuts and champagne for breakfast. So what?

In his furnished rooms, he also had a dinette set, a little sofa, an old easy chair, and a TV set that stood on a coffee table. He wasn't paying the electricity here, it wasn't even his TV, so sometimes he left the set on all day and all night. But he kept the volume down unless he saw there was something he wanted to watch. He did not have a telephone, which was fine with him. He didn't want a telephone. There was a bedroom with a double bed, a nightstand, a chest of drawers, a bathroom.

The one time Inez came to visit, it was eleven o'clock in the morning. He'd been in his new place for two weeks, and he'd been wondering if she were going to drop by. But he was trying to do something about his drinking, too, so he was glad to be alone. He'd made that much clear—being alone was the thing he needed most. The day she came, he was on the sofa, in his pajamas, hitting his fist against the right side of his head. Just before he could hit himself again, he heard voices downstairs on the landing. He could make out his wife's voice. The sound was like the murmur of voices from a faraway crowd, but he knew it was Inez and somehow knew the visit was an important one. He gave his head another jolt with his fist, then got to his feet.

He'd awakened that morning and found that his ear had stopped up with wax. He couldn't hear anything clearly, and he seemed to have lost his sense of balance, his equilibrium, in the process. For the last hour, he'd been on the sofa, working frustratedly on his ear, now and again slamming his head with his fist. Once in a while he'd massage the gristly underpart of his ear, or else tug at his lobe. Then he'd dig furiously in his ear with his little finger and open his mouth, simulating yawns. But he'd tried everything he could think of, and he was nearing the end of his rope. He could hear the voices below break off their murmuring. He pounded his head a good one and finished the glass of champagne. He turned off the TV and carried the glass to the sink. He picked up the open bottle of champagne from the drainboard and took it into the bathroom, where he put it behind the stool. Then he went to answer the door.

"Hi, Lloyd," Inez said. She didn't smile. She stood in the doorway in a bright spring outfit. He hadn't seen these clothes before. She was holding a canvas handbag that had sunflowers stitched onto its sides. He hadn't seen the handbag before, either.

"I didn't think you heard me," she said. "I thought you might be gone or something. But the woman downstairs—what's her name? Mrs. Matthews—she thought you were up here."

"I heard you," Lloyd said. "But just barely." He hitched his pajamas and ran a hand through his hair. "Actually, I'm in one hell of a shape. Come on in."

"It's eleven o'clock," she said. She came inside and shut the door behind her. She acted as if she hadn't heard him. Maybe she hadn't.

"I know what time it is," he said. "I've been up for a long time. I've been up since eight. I watched part of the *Today* show. But just now I'm about to go crazy with something. My ear's plugged up. You remember that other time it happened? We were living in that place near the Chinese take-out joint. Where the kids found that bulldog dragging its chain? I had to go to the doctor then and have my ears flushed out. I know you remember. You drove me and we had to wait a long time. Well, it's like that now. I mean it's that bad. Only I can't go to a doctor this morning. I don't have a doctor for one thing. I'm about to go nuts, Inez. I feel like I want to cut my head off or something."

He sat down at one end of the sofa, and she sat down at the other end. But it was a small sofa, and they were still sitting close to each other. They were so close he could have put out his hand and touched her knee. But he didn't. She glanced around the room and then fixed her eyes on him again. He knew he hadn't shaved and that his hair stood up. But she was his wife, and she knew everything there was to know about him.

"What have you tried?" she said. She looked in her purse and brought up a cigarette. "I mean, what have you done for it so far?"

"What'd you say?" He turned the left side of his head to her. "Inez, I swear, I'm not exaggerating. This thing is driving me crazy. When I talk, I feel like I'm talking inside a barrel. My head rumbles. And I can't hear good, either. When *you* talk, it sounds like you're talking through a lead pipe."

"Do you have any Q-tips, or else Wesson oil?" Inez said.

"Honey, this is serious," he said. "I don't have any Q-tips or Wesson oil. Are you kidding?"

"If we had some Wesson oil, I could heat it and put some of that in your ear. My mother used to do that," she said. "It might soften things up in there."

He shook his head. His head felt full and like it was awash with fluid. It felt like it had when he used to swim near the bottom of the municipal pool and come up with his ears filled with water. But back then it'd been easy to clear the water out. All he had to do was fill his lungs with air, close his mouth, and clamp down on his nose. Then he'd blow out his cheeks and force air into his head. His ears would pop, and for a few seconds he'd have the pleasant sensation of water running out of his head and dripping onto his shoulders. Then he'd heave himself out of the pool.

Inez finished her cigarette and put it out. "Lloyd, we have things to talk about. But I guess we'll have to take things one at a time. Go sit in the chair. Not *that* chair, the chair in the kitchen! So we can have some light on the situation."

He whacked his head once more. Then he went over to sit on a dinette chair. She moved over and stood behind him. She touched his hair with her fingers. Then she moved the hair away from his ears. He reached for her hand, but she drew it away.

"Which ear did you say it was?" she said.

"The right ear," he said. "The right one."

"First," she said, "you have to sit here and not move. I'll find a hairpin and some tissue paper. I'll try to get in there with that. Maybe it'll do the trick."

He was alarmed at the prospect of her putting a hairpin inside his ear. He said something to that effect.

"What?" she said. "Christ, I can't hear you, either. Maybe this is catching."

"When I was a kid, in school," Lloyd said, "we had this health teacher. She was like a nurse, too. She said we should never put anything smaller than an elbow into our ear." He vaguely remembered a wall chart showing a massive diagram of the ear, along with an intricate system of canals, passageways, and walls.

"Well, your nurse was never faced with this exact problem," Inez said. "Anyway, we need to try *something*. We'll try this first. If it doesn't work, we'll try something else. That's life, isn't it?"

"Does that have a hidden meaning or something?" Lloyd said.

"It means just what I said. But you're free to think as you please. I mean, it's a free country," she said. "Now, let me get fixed up with what I need. You just sit there."

She went through her purse, but she didn't find what she was looking for. Finally, she emptied the purse out onto the sofa. "No hairpins," she said. "Damn." But it was as if she were saying the words from another room. In a way, it was almost as if he'd imagined her saying them. There'd been a time, long ago, when they used to feel they had ESP when it came to what the other one was thinking. They could finish sentences that the other had started.

She picked up some nail clippers, worked for a minute, and then he saw the device separate in her fingers and part of it swing away from the other part. A nail file protruded from the clippers. It looked to him as if she were holding a small dagger.

"You're going to put that in my ear?" he said.

"Maybe you have a better idea," she said. "It's this, or else I don't know what. Maybe you have a pencil? You want me to use that? Or maybe you have a screwdriver around," she said and laughed. "Don't worry. Listen, Lloyd, I won't hurt you. I said I'd be careful. I'll wrap some tissue around the end of this. It'll be all right. I'll be careful, like I said. You just stay where you are, and I'll get some tissue for this. I'll make a swab."

She went into the bathroom. She was gone for a time. He stayed where he was on the dinette chair. He began thinking of things he ought to say to her. He wanted to tell her he was limiting himself to champagne and champagne only. He wanted to tell her he was tapering off the champagne, too. It was only a matter of time now. But when she came back into the room, he couldn't say anything. He didn't know where to start. But she didn't look at him, anyway. She fished a cigarette from the heap of things she'd emptied onto the sofa cushion. She lit the cigarette with her lighter and went to stand by the window that faced onto the street. She said something, but he couldn't make out the words. When she stopped talking, he didn't ask her what it was she'd said. Whatever it was, he knew he didn't want her to say it again. She put out the cigarette. But she went on standing at the window, leaning forward, the slope of the roof just inches from her head.

"Inez," he said.

She turned and came over to him. He could see tissue on the point of the nail file.

"Turn your head to the side and keep it that way," she said. "That's right. Sit still now and don't move. Don't move," she said again.

"Be careful," he said. "For Christ's sake."

She didn't answer him.

"Please, please," he said. Then he didn't say any more. He was afraid. He closed his eyes and held his breath as he felt the nail file turn past the inner part of his ear and begin its probe. He was sure his heart would stop beating. Then she went a little farther and began turning the blade back and forth, working at whatever it was in there. Inside his ear, he heard a squeaking sound.

"Ouch!" he said.

"Did I hurt you?" She took the nail file out of his ear and moved back a step. "Does anything feel different, Lloyd?"

He brought his hands up to his ears and lowered his head.

"It's just the same," he said.

She looked at him and bit her lips.

"Let me go to the bathroom," he said. "Before we go any farther, I have to go to the bathroom."

"Go ahead," Inez said. "I think I'll go downstairs and see if your landlady has any Wesson oil, or anything like that. She might even have some Q-tips. I don't know why I didn't think of that before. Of asking her."

"That's a good idea," he said. "I'll go to the bathroom."

She stopped at the door and looked at him, and then she opened the door and went out. He crossed the living room, went into his bedroom, and opened the bathroom door. He reached down behind the stool and brought up the bottle of champagne. He took a long drink. It was warm but it went right down. He took some more. In the beginning, he'd really thought he could continue drinking if he limited himself to champagne. But in no time he found he was drinking three or four bottles a day. He knew he'd have to deal with this pretty soon. But first, he'd have to get his hearing back. One thing at a time, just like she'd said. He finished off the rest of the champagne and put the empty bottle in its place behind the stool. Then he ran water and brushed his teeth. After he'd used the towel, he went back into the other room.

Inez had returned and was at the stove heating something in a little pan. She glanced in his direction, but didn't say anything at first. He looked past her shoulder and out the window. A bird flew from one tree to another and preened its feathers. But if it made any kind of bird noise, he didn't hear it.

She said something that he didn't catch.

"Say again," he said.

She shook her head and turned back to the stove. But then she turned again and said, loud enough and slow enough so he could hear it: "I found your stash in the bathroom."

"I'm trying to cut back," he said.

She said something else. "What?" he said. "What'd you say?" He really hadn't heard her.

"We'll talk later," she said. "We have things to discuss, Lloyd. Money is one thing. But there are other things, too. First we have to see about this ear." She put her finger into the pan and then took the pan off the stove. "I'll let it cool for a minute," she said. "It's too hot right now. Sit down. Put this towel around your shoulders."

He did as he was told. He sat on a chair and put the towel around his neck and shoulders. Then he hit the side of his head with his fist.

"Goddamn it," he said.

She didn't look up. She put her finger into the pan once more, testing. Then she poured the liquid from the pan into his plastic glass. She picked up the glass and came over to him.

"Don't be scared," she said. "It's just some of your landlady's baby oil, that's all it is. I told her what was wrong, and she thought this might help. No guarantees," Inez said. "But maybe this'll loosen things up in there. She said it used to happen to her husband. She said this one time she saw a piece of wax fall out of his ear, and it was like a big plug of something. It was ear wax, was what it was. She said try this. And she didn't have any Q-tips. I can't understand that, her not having any Q-tips. That part really surprises me."

"Okay," he said. "All right. I'm willing to try anything. Inez, if I had to go on like this, I think I'd rather be dead. You know? I mean it, Inez."

"Tilt your head all the way to the side now," she said. "Don't move. I'll pour this in until your ear fills up, then I'll stopper it with this dishrag. And you just sit there for ten minutes, say. Then we'll see. If this doesn't do it, well, I don't have any other suggestions. I just don't know what to do then."

"This'll work," he said. "If this doesn't work, I'll find a gun and shoot myself. I'm serious. That's what I feel like doing, anyway."

He turned his head to the side and let it hang down. He looked at the things in the room from this new perspective. But it wasn't any different from the old way of looking, except that everything was on its side.

"Farther," she said. He held on to the chair for balance and lowered his head even more. All of the objects in his vision, all of the objects in his life, it seemed, were at the far end of this room. He could feel the warm liquid pour into his ear. Then she brought the dishrag up and held it there. In a little while, she began to massage the area around his ear. She pressed into the soft part of the flesh between his jaw and skull. She moved her fingers to the area over his ear and began to work the tips of her fingers back and forth. After a while, he didn't know how long he'd been sitting there. It could have been ten minutes. It could have been longer. He was still holding on to the chair. Now and then, as her fingers pressed the side of his head, he could feel the warm oil she'd poured in there wash back and forth in the canals inside his ear. When she pressed a certain way, he imagined he could hear, inside his head, a soft, swishing sound.

"Sit up straight," Inez said. He sat up and pressed the heel of his hand against his head while the liquid poured out of his ear. She caught it in the towel. Then she wiped the outside of his ear.

Inez was breathing through her nose. Lloyd heard the sound her breath made as it came and went. He heard a car pass on the street outside the house and, at the back of the house, down below his kitchen window, the clear *snick-snick* of pruning shears.

"Well?" Inez said. She waited with her hands on her hips, frowning.

"I can hear you," he said. "I'm all right! I mean, I can *hear*. It doesn't sound like you're talking underwater anymore. It's fine now. It's okay. God, I thought for a while I was going to go crazy. But I feel fine now. I can hear everything. Listen, honey, I'll make coffee. There's some juice, too."

"I have to go," she said. "I'm late for something. But I'll come back. We'll go out for lunch sometime. We need to talk."

"I just can't sleep on this side of my head, is all," he went on. He followed her into the living room. She lit a cigarette. "That's what happened. I slept all night on this side of my head, and my ear plugged up. I think I'll be all right as long as I don't forget and sleep on this side of my head. If I'm careful. You know what I'm saying? If I can just sleep on my back, or else on my left side."

She didn't look at him.

"Not forever, of course not, I know that. I couldn't do that. I couldn't do it the rest of my life. But for a while, anyway. Just my left side, or else flat on my back."

But even as he said this, he began to feel afraid of the night that was coming. He began to fear the moment he would begin to make his preparations for bed and what might happen afterward. That time was hours away, but already he was afraid. What if, in the middle of the night, he accidentally turned onto his right side, and the weight of his head pressing into the pillow were to seal the wax again into the dark canals of his ear? What if he woke up then, unable to hear, the ceiling inches from his head?

"Good God," he said. "Jesus, this is awful. Inez, I just had something like a terrible nightmare. Inez, where do you have to go?"

"I told you," she said, as she put everything back into her purse and made ready to leave. She looked at her watch. "I'm late for something." She went to the door. But at the door she turned and said something else to him. He didn't listen. He didn't want to. He watched her lips move until she'd said what she had to say. When she'd finished, she said, "Goodbye." Then she opened the door and closed it behind her.

He went into the bedroom to dress. But in a minute he hurried out, wearing only his trousers, and went to the door. He opened it and stood there, listening. On the landing below, he heard Inez thank Mrs. Matthews for the oil. He heard the old woman say, "You're welcome." And then he heard her draw a connection between her late husband and himself. He heard her say, "Leave me your number. I'll call if something happens. You never know."

"I hope you don't have to," Inez said. "But I'll give it to you, anyway. Do you have something to write it down with?"

Lloyd heard Mrs. Matthews open a drawer and rummage through it. Then her old woman's voice said, "Okay."

Inez gave her their telephone number at home. "Thanks," she said.

"It was nice meeting you," Mrs. Matthews said.

He listened as Inez went on down the stairs and opened the front door. Then he heard it close. He waited until he heard her start their car and drive away. Then he shut the door and went back into the bedroom to finish dressing.

After he'd put on his shoes and tied the laces, he lay down on the bed and pulled the covers up to his chin. He let his arms rest under the covers at his sides. He closed his eyes and pretended it was night and pretended he was going to fall asleep. Then he brought his arms up and crossed them over his chest to see how this position would suit him. He kept his eyes closed, trying it out. All right, he thought. Okay. If he didn't want that ear to plug up again, he'd have to sleep on his back, that was all. He knew he could do it. He just couldn't forget, even in his sleep, and turn onto the wrong side. Four or five hours' sleep a night was all he needed, anyway. He'd manage. Worse things could happen to a man. In a way, it was a challenge. But he was up to it. He knew he was. In a minute, he threw back the covers and got up.

He still had the better part of the day ahead of him. He went into the kitchen, bent down in front of the little refrigerator, and took out a fresh bottle of champagne. He worked the plastic cork out of the bottle as carefully as he could, but there was still the festive *pop* of champagne being opened. He rinsed the baby oil out of his glass, then poured it full of champagne. He took the glass over to the sofa and sat down. He put the glass on the coffee table. Up went his feet onto the coffee table, next to the champagne. He leaned back. But after a time he began to worry some more about the night that was coming on. What if, despite all his efforts, the wax decided to plug his other ear? He closed his eyes and shook his head. Pretty soon he got up and went into the bedroom. He undressed and put his pajamas back on. Then he moved back into the living room. He sat down on the sofa once more, and once more put his feet up. He reached over and turned the TV on. He adjusted the volume. He knew he couldn't keep from worrying about what might happen when he went to bed. It was just something he'd have to learn to live with. In a way, this whole business reminded him of the thing with the doughnuts and champagne. It was not that remarkable at all, if you thought about it. He took some champagne. But it didn't taste right. He ran his tongue over his lips, then wiped his mouth on his sleeve. He looked and saw a film of oil on the champagne.

He got up and carried the glass to the sink, where he poured it into the drain. He took the bottle of champagne into the living room and made himself comfortable on the sofa. He held the bottle by its neck as he drank. He wasn't in the habit of drinking from the bottle, but it didn't seem that much out of the ordinary. He decided that even if he were to fall asleep sitting up on the sofa in the middle of the afternoon, it wouldn't be any more strange than somebody having to lie on his back for hours at a time. He lowered his head to peer out the window. Judging from the angle of sunlight, and the shadows that had entered the room, he guessed it was about three o'clock.

Where I'm Calling From

J.P. AND I are on the front porch at Frank Martin's drying-out facility. Like the rest of us at Frank Martin's, J.P. is first and foremost a drunk. But he's also a chimney sweep. It's his first time here, and he's scared. I've been here once before. What's to say? I'm back. J.P.'s real name is Joe Penny, but he says I should call him J.P. He's about thirty years old. Younger than I am. Not much younger, but a little. He's telling me how he decided to go into his line of work, and he wants to use his hands when he talks. But his hands tremble. I mean, they won't keep still. "This has never happened to me before," he says. He means the trembling. I tell him I sympathize. I tell him the shakes will idle down. And they will. But it takes time.

We've only been in here a couple of days. We're not out of the woods yet. J.P. has these shakes, and every so often a nerve —maybe it isn't a nerve, but it's something—begins to jerk in my shoulder. Sometimes it's at the side of my neck. When this happens, my mouth dries up. It's an effort just to swallow then. I know something's about to happen and I want to head it off. I want to hide from it, that's what I want to do. Just close my eyes and let it pass by, let it take the next man. J.P. can wait a minute.

I saw a seizure yesterday morning. A guy they call Tiny. A big fat guy, an electrician from Santa Rosa. They said he'd been in here for nearly two weeks and that he was over the hump. He was going home in a day or two and would spend New Year's Eve with his wife in front of the TV. On New Year's Eve, Tiny planned to drink hot chocolate and eat cookies. Yesterday morning he seemed just fine when he came down for breakfast. He was letting out with quacking noises, showing some guy how he called ducks right down onto his head. "Blam. Blam," said Tiny, picking off a couple. Tiny's hair was damp and was slicked back along the sides of his head. He'd just come out of the shower. He'd also nicked himself on the chin with his razor. But so what? Just about everybody at Frank Martin's has nicks on his face. It's something that happens. Tiny edged in at the head of the table and began telling about something that had happened on one of his drinking bouts. People at the table laughed and shook their heads as they shoveled up their eggs. Tiny would say something, grin, then look around the table for a sign of recognition. We'd all done things just as bad and crazy, so, sure, that's why we laughed. Tiny had scrambled eggs on his plate, and some biscuits and honey. I was at the table, but I wasn't hungry. I had some coffee in front of me. Suddenly, Tiny wasn't there anymore. He'd gone over in his chair with a big clatter. He was on his back on the floor with his eyes closed, his heels drumming the linoleum. People hollered for Frank Martin. But he was right there. A couple of guys got down on the floor beside Tiny. One of the guys put his fingers inside Tiny's mouth and tried to hold his tongue. Frank Martin yelled, "Everybody stand back!" Then I noticed that the bunch of us were leaning over Tiny, just looking at him, not able to take our eyes off him. "Give him air!" Frank Martin said. Then he ran into the office and called the ambulance.

Tiny is on board again today. Talk about bouncing back. This morning Frank Martin drove the station wagon to the hospital to get him. Tiny got back too late for his eggs, but he took some coffee into the dining room and sat down at the table anyway. Somebody in the kitchen made toast for him, but Tiny didn't eat it. He just sat with his coffee and looked into his cup. Every now and then he moved his cup back and forth in front of him.

I'd like to ask him if he had any signal just before it happened. I'd like to know if he felt his ticker skip a beat, or else begin to race. Did his eyelid twitch? But I'm not about to say anything. He doesn't look like he's hot to talk about it, anyway. But what happened to Tiny is something I won't ever forget. Old Tiny flat on the floor, kicking his heels. So every time this little flitter starts up anywhere, I draw some breath and wait to find myself on my back, looking up, somebody's fingers in my mouth.

In his chair on the front porch, J.P. keeps his hands in his lap. I smoke cigarettes and use an old coal bucket for an ashtray. I listen to J.P. ramble on. It's eleven o'clock in the morning—an hour and a half until lunch. Neither one of us is hungry. But just the same we look forward to going inside and sitting down at the table. Maybe we'll get hungry.

What's J.P. talking about, anyway? He's saying how when he was twelve years old he fell into a well in the vicinity of the farm he grew up on. It was a dry well, lucky for him. "Or un-lucky," he says, looking around him and shaking his head. He says how late that afternoon, after he'd been located, his dad hauled him out with a rope. J.P. had wet his pants down there. He'd suffered all kinds of terror in that well, hollering for help, waiting, and then hollering some more. He hollered himself hoarse before it was over. But he told me that being at the bot-tom of that well had made a lasting impression. He'd sat there and looked up at the well mouth. Way up at the top, he could see a circle of blue sky. Every once in a while a white cloud passed over. A flock of birds flew across, and it seemed to J.P. their wingbeats set up this odd commotion. He heard other things. He heard tiny rustlings above him in the well, which made him wonder if things might fall down into his hair. He was thinking of insects. He heard wind blow over the well mouth, and that sound made an impression on him, too. In short, everything about his life was different for him at the bottom of that well. But nothing fell on him and nothing closed off that little circle of blue. Then his dad came along with the rope, and it wasn't long before J.P. was back in the world he'd always lived in.

"Keep talking, J.P. Then what?" I say.

When he was eighteen or nineteen years old and out of high school and had nothing whatsoever he wanted to do with his life, he went across town one afternoon to visit a friend. This friend lived in a house with a fireplace. J.P. and his friend sat around drinking beer and batting the breeze. They played some records. Then the doorbell rings. The friend goes to the door. This young woman chimney sweep is there with her cleaning things. She's wearing a top hat, the sight of which knocked J.P. for a loop. She tells J.P.'s friend that she has an appointment to clean the fireplace. The friend lets her in and bows. The young woman doesn't pay him any mind. She spreads a blanket on the hearth and lays out her gear. She's wearing these black pants, black shirt, black shoes and socks. Of course, by now she's taken her hat off. J.P. says it nearly drove him nuts to look at her. She does the work, she cleans the chimney, while J.P. and his friend play records and drink beer. But they watch her and they watch what she does. Now and then J.P. and his friend look at each other and grin, or else they wink. They raise their eyebrows when the upper half of the young woman disappears into the chimney. She was all-right-looking, too, J.P. said.

When she'd finished her work, she rolled her things up in the blanket. From J.P.'s friend, she took a check that had been made out to her by his parents. And then she asks the friend if he wants to kiss her. "It's supposed to bring good luck," she says. That does it for J.P. The friend rolls his eyes. He clowns some more. Then, probably blushing, he kisses her on the cheek. At this minute, J.P. made his mind up about something. He put his beer down. He got up from the sofa. He went over to the young woman as she was starting to go out the door.

"Me, too?" J.P. said to her.

She swept her eyes over him. J.P. says he could feel his heart knocking. The young woman's name, it turns out, was Roxy.

"Sure," Roxy says. "Why not? I've got some extra kisses." And she kissed him a good one right on the lips and then turned to go.

Like that, quick as a wink, J.P. followed her onto the porch. He held the porch screen door for her. He went down the steps with her and out to the drive, where she'd parked her panel truck. It was something that was out of his hands. Nothing else in the world counted for anything. He knew he'd met some-body who could set his legs atremble. He could feel her kiss still burning on his lips, etc. J.P. couldn't begin to sort any-thing out. He was filled with sensations that were carrying him every which way.

He opened the rear door of the panel truck for her. He helped her store her things inside. "Thanks," she told him. Then he blurted it out—that he'd like to see her again. Would she go to a movie with him sometime? He'd realized, too, what he wanted to do with his life. He wanted to do what she did. He wanted to be a chimney sweep. But he didn't tell her that then.

J.P. says she put her hands on her hips and looked him over. Then she found a business card in the front seat of her truck. She gave it to him. She said, "Call this number after ten tonight. We can talk. I have to go now." She put the top hat on and then took it off. She looked at J.P. once more. She must have liked what she saw, because this time she grinned. He told her there was a smudge near her mouth. Then she got into her truck, tooted the horn, and drove away.

"Then what?" I say. "Don't stop now, J.P."

I was interested. But I would have listened if he'd been going on about how one day he'd decided to start pitching horseshoes.

It rained last night. The clouds are banked up against the hills across the valley. J.P. clears his throat and looks at the hills and the clouds. He pulls his chin. Then he goes on with what he was saying.

Roxy starts going out with him on dates. And little by little he talks her into letting him go along on jobs with her. But Roxy's in business with her father and brother and they've got just the right amount of work. They don't need anybody else. Besides, who was this guy J.P.? J.P. what? Watch out, they warned her.

So she and J.P. saw some movies together. They went to a few dances. But mainly the courtship revolved around their cleaning chimneys together. Before you know it, J.P. says, they're talking about tying the knot. And after a while they do it, they get married. J.P.'s new father-in-law takes him in as a full partner. In a year or so, Roxy has a kid. She's quit being a chimney sweep. At any rate, she's quit doing the work. Pretty soon she has another kid. J.P.'s in his mid-twenties by now. He's buying a house. He says he was happy with his life. "I was happy with the way things were going," he says. "I had everything I wanted. I had a wife and kids I loved, and I was doing what I wanted to do with my life." But for some reason—who knows why we do what we do?—his drinking picks up. For a long time he drinks beer and beer only. Any kind of beer—it didn't matter. He says he could drink beer twenty-four hours a day. He'd drink beer at night while he watched TV. Sure, once in a while he drank hard stuff. But that was only if they went out on the town, which was not often, or else when they had company over. Then a time comes, he doesn't know why, when he makes the switch from beer to gin-and-tonic. And he'd have more gin-and-tonic after dinner, sitting in front of the TV. There was always a glass of gin-and-tonic in his hand. He says he actually liked the taste of it. He began stopping off after work for drinks before he went home to have more drinks. Then he began missing some dinners. He just wouldn't show up. Or else he'd show up, but he wouldn't want anything to eat. He'd filled up on snacks at the bar. Sometimes he'd walk in the door and for no good reason throw his lunch pail across the living room. When Roxy yelled at him, he'd turn around and go out again. He moved his drinking time up to early afternoon, while he was still supposed to be working. He tells me that he was starting off the morning with a couple of drinks. He'd have a belt of the stuff before he brushed his teeth. Then he'd have his coffee. He'd go to work with a thermos bottle of vodka in his lunch pail.

J.P. quits talking. He just clams up. What's going on? I'm listening. It's helping me relax, for one thing. It's taking me away from my own situation. After a minute, I say, "What the hell? Go on, J.P." He's pulling his chin. But pretty soon he starts talking again.

J.P. and Roxy are having some real fights now. I mean *fights*. J.P. says that one time she hit him in the face with her fist and broke his nose. "Look at this," he says. "Right here." He shows me a line across the bridge of his nose. "That's a broken nose." He returned the favor. He dislocated her shoulder for her. Another time he split her lip. They beat on each other in front of the kids. Things got out of hand. But he kept on drinking. He couldn't stop. And nothing could make him stop. Not even with Roxy's dad and her brother threatening to beat the hell out of him. They told Roxy she should take the kids and clear out. But Roxy said it was her problem. She got herself into it, and she'd solve it.

Now J.P. gets real quiet again. He hunches his shoulders and pulls down in his chair. He watches a car driving down the road between this place and the hills.

I say, "I want to hear the rest of this, J.P. You better keep talking."

"I just don't know," he says. He shrugs.

"It's all right," I say. And I mean it's okay for him to tell it. "Go on, J.P."

One way she tried to fix things, J.P. says, was by finding a boyfriend. J.P. would like to know how she found the time with the house and kids.

I look at him and I'm surprised. He's a grown man. "If you want to do that," I say, "you find the time. You make the time."

J.P. shakes his head. "I guess so," he says.

Anyway, he found out about it—about Roxy's boyfriend— and he went wild. He manages to get Roxy's wedding ring off her finger. And when he does, he cuts it into several pieces with a pair of wire-cutters. Good, solid fun. They'd already gone a couple of rounds on this occasion. On his way to work the next morning, he gets arrested on a drunk charge. He loses his driver's license. He can't drive the truck to work anymore. Just as well, he says. He'd already fallen off a roof the week before and broken his thumb. It was just a matter of time until he broke his neck, he says.

He was here at Frank Martin's to dry out and to figure how to get his life back on track. But he wasn't here against his will, any more than I was. We weren't locked up. We could leave any time we wanted. But a minimum stay of a week was recommended, and two weeks or a month was, as they put it, "strongly advised."

As I said, this is my second time at Frank Martin's. When I was trying to sign a check to pay in advance for a week's stay, Frank Martin said, "The holidays are always bad. Maybe you should think of sticking around a little longer this time? Think in terms of a couple of weeks. Can you do a couple of weeks? Think about it, anyway. You don't have to decide anything right now," he said. He held his thumb on the check and I signed my name. Then I walked my girlfriend to the front door and said goodbye. "Goodbye," she said, and she lurched into the doorjamb and then onto the porch. It's late afternoon. It's raining. I go from the door to the window. I move the curtain and watch her drive away. She's in my car. She's drunk. But I'm drunk, too, and there's nothing I can do. I make it to a big chair that's close to the radiator, and I sit down. Some guys look up from their TV. Then they shift back to what they were watching. I just sit there. Now and then I look up at something that's happening on the screen.

Later that afternoon the front door banged open and J.P. was brought in between these two big guys—his father-in-law and brother-in-law, I find out afterward. They steered J.P. across the room. The old guy signed him in and gave Frank Martin a check. Then these two guys helped J.P. upstairs. I guess they put him to bed. Pretty soon the old guy and the other guy came downstairs and headed for the front door. They couldn't seem to get out of this place fast enough. It was like they couldn't wait to wash their hands of all this. I didn't blame them. Hell, no. I don't know how I'd act if I was in their shoes.

A day and a half later J.P. and I meet up on the front porch. We shake hands and comment on the weather. J.P. has a case of the shakes. We sit down and prop our feet up on the railing. We lean back in our chairs like we're just out there taking our ease, like we might be getting ready to talk about our bird dogs. That's when J.P. gets going with his story.

It's cold out, but not too cold. It's a little overcast. Frank Martin comes outside to finish his cigar. He has on a sweater buttoned all the way up. Frank Martin is short and heavy-set. He has curly gray hair and a small head. His head is too small for the rest of his body. Frank Martin puts the cigar in his mouth and stands with his arms crossed over his chest. He works that cigar in his mouth and looks across the valley. He stands there like a prizefighter, like somebody who knows the score.

J.P. gets quiet again. I mean, he's hardly breathing. I toss my cigarette into the coal bucket and look hard at J.P., who scoots farther down in his chair. J.P. pulls up his collar. What the hell's going on? I wonder. Frank Martin uncrosses his arms and takes a puff on the cigar. He lets the smoke carry out of his mouth. Then he raises his chin toward the hills and says, "Jack London used to have a big place on the other side of this valley. Right over there behind that green hill you're looking at. But alcohol killed him. Let that be a lesson to you. He was a better man than any of us. But he couldn't handle the stuff, either." Frank Martin looks at what's left of his cigar. It's gone out. He tosses it into the bucket. "You guys want to read something while you're here, read that book of his, *The Call of the Wild*. You know the one I'm talking about? We have it inside if you want to read something. It's about this animal that's half dog and half wolf. End of sermon," he says, and then hitches his pants up and tugs his sweater down. "I'm going inside," he says. "See you at lunch."

"I feel like a bug when he's around," J.P. says. "He makes me feel like a bug." J.P. shakes his head. Then he says, "Jack London. What a name! I wish I had me a name like that. Instead of the name I got."

My wife brought me up here the first time. That's when we were still together, trying to make things work out. She brought me here and she stayed around for an hour or two, talking to Frank Martin in private. Then she left. The next morning Frank Martin got me aside and said, "We can help you. If you want help and want to listen to what we say." But I didn't know if they could help me or not. Part of me wanted help. But there was another part.

This time around, it was my girlfriend who drove me here. She was driving my car. She drove us through a rainstorm. We drank champagne all the way. We were both drunk when she pulled up in the drive. She intended to drop me off, turn around, and drive home again. She had things to do. One thing she had to do was to go to work the next day. She was a secretary. She had an okay job with this electronic-parts firm. She also had this mouthy teenaged son. I wanted her to get a room in town, spend the night, and then drive home. I don't know if she got the room or not. I haven't heard from her since she led me up the front steps the other day and walked me into Frank Martin's office and said, "Guess who's here."

But I wasn't mad at her. In the first place, she didn't have any idea what she was letting herself in for when she said I could stay with her after my wife asked me to leave. I felt sorry for her. The reason I felt sorry for her was that on the day before Christmas her Pap smear came back, and the news was not cheery. She'd have to go back to the doctor, and real soon. That kind of news was reason enough for both of us to start drinking. So what we did was get ourselves good and drunk. And on Christmas Day we were still drunk. We had to go out to a restaurant to eat, because she didn't feel like cooking. The two of us and her mouthy teenaged son opened some presents, and then we went to this steakhouse near her apartment. I wasn't hungry. I had some soup and a hot roll. I drank a bottle of wine with the soup. She drank some wine, too. Then we started in on Bloody Marys. For the next couple of days, I didn't eat anything except salted nuts. But I drank a lot of bourbon. Then I said to her, "Sugar, I think I'd better pack up. I better go back to Frank Martin's."

She tried to explain to her son that she was going to be gone for a while and he'd have to get his own food. But right as we were going out the door, this mouthy kid screamed at us. He screamed, "The hell with you! I hope you never come back. I hope you kill yourselves!" Imagine this kid!

Before we left town, I had her stop at the package store, where I bought us the champagne. We stopped someplace else for plastic glasses. Then we picked up a bucket of fried chicken. We set out for Frank Martin's in this rainstorm, drinking and listening to music. She drove. I looked after the radio and poured. We tried to make a little party of it. But we were sad, too. There was that fried chicken, but we didn't eat any.

I guess she got home okay. I think I would have heard something if she didn't. But she hasn't called me, and I haven't called her. Maybe she's had some news about herself by now. Then again, maybe she hasn't heard anything. Maybe it was all a mistake. Maybe it was somebody else's smear. But she has my car, and I have things at her house. I know we'll be seeing each other again.

They clang an old farm bell here to call you for mealtime. J.P. and I get out of our chairs and we go inside. It's starting to get too cold on the porch, anyway. We can see our breath drifting out from us as we talk.

New Year's Eve morning I try to call my wife. There's no answer. It's okay. But even if it wasn't okay, what am I supposed to do? The last time we talked on the phone, a couple of weeks ago, we screamed at each other. I hung a few names on her. "Wet brain!" she said, and put the phone back where it belonged.

But I wanted to talk to her now. Something had to be done about my stuff. I still had things at her house, too.

One of the guys here is a guy who travels. He goes to Europe and places. That's what he says, anyway. Business, he says.

He also says he has his drinking under control and he doesn't
have any idea why he's here at Frank Martin's. But he doesn't remember getting here. He laughs about it, about his not remembering. "Anyone can have a blackout," he says. "That doesn't
prove a thing." He's not a drunk—he tells us this and we listen.
"That's a serious charge to make," he says. "That kind of talk
can ruin a good man's prospects." He says that if he'd only
stick to whiskey and water, no ice, he'd never have these black-
outs. It's the ice they put into your drink that does it. "Who
do you know in Egypt?" he asks me. "I can use a few names over
there."

For New Year's Eve dinner Frank Martin serves steak and
baked potato. My appetite's coming back. I clean up everything on my plate and I could eat more. I look over at Tiny's
plate. Hell, he's hardly touched a thing. His steak is just sitting
there. Tiny is not the same old Tiny. The poor bastard had
planned to be at home tonight. He'd planned to be in his robe
and slippers in front of the TV, holding hands with his wife.
Now he's afraid to leave. I can understand. One seizure means
you're ready for another. Tiny hasn't told any more nutty stories on himself since it happened. He's stayed quiet and kept to
himself. I ask him if I can have his steak, and he pushes his
plate over to me.

Some of us are still up, sitting around the TV, watching
Times Square, when Frank Martin comes in to show us his
cake. He brings it around and shows it to each of us. I know he
didn't make it. It's just a bakery cake. But it's still a cake. It's a
big white cake. Across the top there's writing in pink letters.
The writing says, HAPPY NEW YEAR— ONE DAY AT A TIME.

"I don't want any stupid cake," says the guy who goes to Europe and places. "Where's the champagne?" he says, and
laughs.

We all go into the dining room. Frank Martin cuts the cake.
I sit next to J.P. J.P. eats two pieces and drinks a Coke. I eat a
piece and wrap another piece in a napkin, thinking of later.

J.P. lights a cigarette—his hands are steady now—and he
tells me his wife is coming in the morning, the first day of the
new year.

"That's great," I say. I nod. I lick the frosting off my finger.
"That's good news, J.P."

"I'll introduce you," he says.

"I look forward to it," I say.

We say goodnight. We say Happy New Year. I use a napkin on my fingers. We shake hands.

I go to the phone, put in a dime, and call my wife collect. But nobody answers this time, either. I think about calling my girlfriend, and I'm dialing her number when I realize I really don't want to talk to her. She's probably at home watching the same thing on TV that I've been watching. Anyway, I don't want to talk to her. I hope she's okay. But if she has something wrong with her, I don't want to know about it.

After breakfast, J.P. and I take coffee out to the porch. The sky is clear, but it's cold enough for sweaters and jackets.

"She asked me if she should bring the kids," J.P. says. "I told her she should keep the kids at home. Can you imagine? My God, I don't want my kids up here."

We use the coal bucket for an ashtray. We look across the valley to where Jack London used to live. We're drinking more coffee when this car turns off the road and comes down the drive.

"That's her!" J.P. says. He puts his cup next to his chair. He gets up and goes down the steps.

I see this woman stop the car and set the brake. I see J.P. open the door. I watch her get out, and I see them hug each other. I look away. Then I look back. J.P. takes her by the arm and they come up the stairs. This woman broke a man's nose once. She has had two kids, and much trouble, but she loves this man who has her by the arm. I get up from the chair.

"This is my friend," J.P. says to his wife. "Hey, this is Roxy."

Roxy takes my hand. She's a tall, good-looking woman in a knit cap. She has on a coat, a heavy sweater, and slacks. I recall what J.P. told me about the boyfriend and the wire-cutters. I don't see any wedding ring. That's in pieces somewhere, I guess. Her hands are broad and the fingers have these big knuckles. This is a woman who can make fists if she has to.

"I've heard about you," I say. "J.P. told me how you got acquainted. Something about a chimney, J.P. said."

"Yes, a chimney," she says. "There's probably a lot else he didn't tell you," she says. "I bet he didn't tell you everything," she says, and laughs. Then—she can't wait any longer—she slips her arm around J.P. and kisses him on the cheek. They start to move to the door. "Nice meeting you," she says. "Hey, did he tell you he's the best sweep in the business?"

"Come on now, Roxy," J.P. says. He has his hand on the doorknob.

"He told me he learned everything he knew from you," I say.

"Well, that much is sure true," she says. She laughs again. But it's like she's thinking about something else. J.P. turns the doorknob. Roxy lays her hand over his. "Joe, can't we go into town for lunch? Can't I take you someplace?"

J.P. clears his throat. He says, "It hasn't been a week yet." He takes his hand off the doorknob and brings his fingers to his chin. "I think they'd like it if I didn't leave the place for a little while yet. We can have some coffee here," he says.

"That's fine," she says. Her eyes work over to me again. "I'm glad Joe's made a friend. Nice to meet you," she says.

They start to go inside. I know it's a dumb thing to do, but I do it anyway. "Roxy," I say. And they stop in the doorway and look at me. "I need some luck," I say. "No kidding. I could do with a kiss myself."

J.P. looks down. He's still holding the knob, even though the door is open. He turns the knob back and forth. But I keep looking at her. Roxy grins. "I'm not a sweep anymore," she says. "Not for years. Didn't Joe tell you that? But, sure, I'll kiss you, sure."

She moves over. She takes me by the shoulders—I'm a big man—and she plants this kiss on my lips. "How's that?" she says.

"That's fine," I say.

"Nothing to it," she says. She's still holding me by the shoulders. She's looking me right in the eyes. "Good luck," she says, and then she lets go of me.

"See you later, pal," J.P. says. He opens the door all the way, and they go in.

I sit down on the front steps and light a cigarette. I watch what my hand does, then I blow out the match. I've got the shakes. I started out with them this morning. This morning I wanted something to drink. It's depressing, but I didn't say anything about it to J.P. I try to put my mind on something else.

I'm thinking about chimney sweeps—all that stuff I heard

from J.P.—when for some reason I start to think about a house my wife and I once lived in. That house didn't have a chimney, so I don't know what makes me remember it now. But I remember the house and how we'd only been in there a few weeks when I heard a noise outside one morning. It was Sunday morning and it was still dark in the bedroom. But there was this pale light coming in from the bedroom window. I listened. I could hear something scrape against the side of the house. I jumped out of bed and went to look.

"My God!" my wife says, sitting up in bed and shaking the hair away from her face. Then she starts to laugh. "It's Mr. Venturini," she says. "I forgot to tell you. He said he was coming to paint the house today. Early. Before it gets too hot. I forgot all about it," she says, and laughs. "Come on back to bed, honey. It's just him."

"In a minute," I say.

I push the curtain away from the window. Outside, this old guy in white coveralls is standing next to his ladder. The sun is just starting to break above the mountains. The old guy and I look each other over. It's the landlord, all right—this old guy in coveralls. But his coveralls are too big for him. He needs a shave, too. And he's wearing this baseball cap to cover his bald head. Goddamn it, I think, if he isn't a weird old fellow. And a wave of happiness comes over me that I'm not him—that I'm me and that I'm inside this bedroom with my wife.

He jerks his thumb toward the sun. He pretends to wipe his forehead. He's letting me know he doesn't have all that much time. The old fart breaks into a grin. It's then I realize I'm naked. I look down at myself. I look at him again and shrug. What did he expect?

My wife laughs. "Come *on*," she says. "Get back in this bed. Right now. This minute. Come on back to bed."

I let go of the curtain. But I keep standing there at the window. I can see the old fellow nod to himself like he's saying, "Go on, sonny, go back to bed. I understand." He tugs on the bill of his cap. Then he sets about his business. He picks up his bucket. He starts climbing the ladder.

I lean back into the step behind me now and cross one leg over the other. Maybe later this afternoon I'll try calling my wife again. And then I'll call to see what's happening with my girl-friend. But I don't want to get her mouthy kid on the line. If I do call, I hope he'll be out somewhere doing whatever he does when he's not around the house. I try to remember if I ever read any Jack London books. I can't remember. But there was a story of his I read in high school. "To Build a Fire," it was called. This guy in the Yukon is freezing. Imagine it—he's ac-tually going to freeze to death if he can't get a fire going. With a fire, he can dry his socks and things and warm himself.

He gets his fire going, but then something happens to it. A branchful of snow drops on it. It goes out. Meanwhile, it's getting colder. Night is coming on.

I bring some change out of my pocket. I'll try my wife first. If she answers, I'll wish her a Happy New Year. But that's it. I won't bring up business. I won't raise my voice. Not even if she starts something. She'll ask me where I'm calling from, and I'll have to tell her. I won't say anything about New Year's resolutions. There's no way to make a joke out of this. After I talk to her, I'll call my girlfriend. Maybe I'll call her first. I'll just have to hope I don't get her kid on the line. "Hello, sugar," I'll say when she answers. "It's me."

The Train

for John Cheever

THE woman was called Miss Dent, and earlier that evening she'd held a gun on a man. She'd made him get down in the dirt and plead for his life. While the man's eyes welled with tears and his fingers picked at leaves, she pointed the revolver at him and told him things about himself. She tried to make him see that he couldn't keep trampling on people's feelings. "Be still!" she'd said, although the man was only digging his fingers into the dirt and moving his legs a little out of fear. When she had finished talking, when she had said all she could think of to say to him, she put her foot on the back of his head and pushed his face into the dirt. Then she put the revolver into her handbag and walked back to the railway station.

She sat on a bench in the deserted waiting room with the handbag on her lap. The ticket office was closed; no one was around. Even the parking lot outside the station was empty. She let her eyes rest on the big wall clock. She wanted to stop thinking about the man and how he'd acted toward her after taking what he wanted. But she knew she would remember for a long time the sound he made through his nose as he got down on his knees. She took a breath, closed her eyes, and listened for the sound of a train.

The waiting-room door opened. Miss Dent looked in that direction as two people came inside. One person was an old man with white hair and a white silk cravat; the other was a middle-aged woman wearing eye-shadow, lipstick, and a rose-colored knit dress. The evening had turned cool, but neither of the people wore a coat, and the old man was without shoes. They stopped in the doorway, seemingly astounded at finding someone in the waiting room. They tried to act as if her presence there was not a disappointment. The woman said something to the old man, but Miss Dent didn't catch what it was the woman had said. The couple moved on into the room. It seemed to Miss Dent that they gave off an air of agitation, of having just left somewhere in a great hurry and not yet being able to find a way to talk about it. It might be, Miss Dent thought, that they'd had too much to drink as well. The woman and the white-haired old man looked at the clock, as if it might tell them something about their situation and what they were supposed to do next.

Miss Dent also turned her eyes to the clock. There was nothing in the waiting room that announced when trains arrived and departed. But she was prepared to wait for any length of time. She knew if she waited long enough, a train would come along, and she could board it, and it would take her away from this place.

"Good evening," the old man said to Miss Dent. He said this, she thought, as if it had been a normal summer's night and he were an important old man wearing shoes and an evening jacket.

"Good evening," Miss Dent said.

The woman in the knit dress looked at her in a way that was calculated to let Miss Dent know the woman was not happy at finding her in the waiting room.

The old man and the woman seated themselves on a bench directly across the lobby from Miss Dent. She watched as the old man gave the knees of his trousers a little tug and then crossed one leg over the other and began to wag his stockinged foot. He took a pack of cigarettes and a cigarette holder from his shirt pocket. He inserted the cigarette into the holder and brought his hand up to his shirt pocket. Then he reached into his trouser pockets.

"I don't have a light," he said to the woman.

"I don't smoke," the woman said. "I should think if you knew anything about me, you'd know that much. If you really must smoke, *she* may have a match." The woman raised her chin and looked sharply at Miss Dent.

But Miss Dent shook her head. She pulled the handbag closer. She held her knees together, her fingers gripping the bag.

"So on top of everything else, no matches," the white-haired old man said. He checked his pockets once more. Then he sighed and removed the cigarette from the holder. He pushed the cigarette back into the pack. He put the cigarettes and the cigarette holder into his shirt pocket.

The woman began to speak in a language that Miss Dent did not understand. She thought it might be Italian because the rapid-fire words sounded like words she'd heard Sophia Loren use in a film.

The old man shook his head. "I can't follow you, you know. You're going too fast for me. You'll have to slow down. You'll have to speak English. I can't follow you," he said.

Miss Dent released her grasp on the handbag and moved it from her lap to a place next to her on the bench. She stared at the catch on the handbag. She wasn't sure what she should do. It was a small waiting room, and she hated to get up suddenly and move somewhere else to sit. Her eyes traveled to the clock.

"I can't get over that bunch of nuts back there," the woman said. "It's colossal! It's simply too much for words. My God!" The woman said this and shook her head. She slumped against the bench as if exhausted. She raised her eyes and stared briefly at the ceiling.

The old man took the silk cravat between his fingers and began idly to rub the material back and forth. He opened a button on his shirt and tucked the cravat inside. He seemed to be thinking about something else as the woman went on.

"It's that girl I feel sorry for," the woman said. "That poor soul alone in a house filled with simps and vipers. She's the one I feel sorry for. And she'll be the one to pay! None of the rest of them. Certainly not that imbecile they call Captain Nick! He isn't responsible for anything. Not him," the woman said.

The old man raised his eyes and looked around the waiting room. He gazed for a time at Miss Dent.

Miss Dent looked past his shoulder and through the window. There she could see the tall lamp post, its light shining on the empty parking lot. She held her hands together in her lap and tried to keep her attention on her own affairs. But she couldn't help hearing what these people said.

"I can tell you this much," the woman said. "The girl is the extent of my concern. Who cares about the rest of that tribe? Their entire existence is taken up with *café au lait* and cigarettes, their precious Swiss chocolate and those goddamned macaws. Nothing else means anything to them," the woman said. "What do they care? If I never see that outfit again, it'll be too soon. Do you understand me?"

"Sure, I understand," the old man said. "Of course." He put his feet on the floor and then brought his other leg up over his knee. "But don't fret about it now," he said.

"'Don't fret about it,' he says. Why don't you take a look at yourself in the mirror?" the woman said.

"Don't worry about me," the old man said. "Worse things have happened to me, and I'm still here." He laughed quietly and shook his head. "Don't worry about me."

"How can I help not worrying about you?" the woman said. "Who else is going to worry about you? Is this woman with the handbag going to worry about you?" she said, stopping long enough to glare at Miss Dent. "I'm serious, *amico mio.* Just look at yourself! My God, if I didn't already have so many things on my mind, I could have a nervous breakdown right here. Tell me who else there is to worry about you if I don't worry? I'm asking a serious question. You know so much," the woman said, "so answer me that."

The white-haired old man got to his feet and then sat down again. "Just don't worry about me," he said. "Worry about someone else. Worry about the girl and Captain Nick, if you want to worry. You were in another room when he said, 'I'm not serious, but I'm in love with her.' Those were his exact words."

"I knew something like that was coming!" the woman cried. She closed her fingers and brought her hands up to her temples. "I knew you'd tell me something like that! But I'm not surprised, either. No, I'm not. A leopard doesn't change its spots. Truer words were never spoken. Live and learn. But when are you going to wake up, you old fool? Answer me that," she said to him. "Are you like the mule that first has to be hit between the eyes with a two-by-four? *O Dio mio!* Why don't you go look at yourself in the mirror?" the woman said. "Take a good long look while you're at it."

The old man got up from the bench and moved over to the drinking fountain. He put one hand behind his back, turned the knob, and bent over to drink. Then he straightened up and dabbed his chin with the back of his hand. He put both hands behind his back and began to stroll around the waiting room as if he were on a promenade.

But Miss Dent could see his eyes scanning the floor, the

empty benches, the ashtrays. She understood he was looking for matches, and she was sorry she didn't have any.

The woman had turned to follow the old man's progress. She raised her voice and said: "Kentucky Fried Chicken at the North Pole! Colonel Sanders in a parka and boots. That tore it! That was the limit!"

The old man didn't answer. He continued his circumnavigation of the room and came to a stop at the front window. He stood at the window, hands behind his back, and looked out onto the empty parking lot.

The woman turned around to Miss Dent. She pulled at the material under the arm of her dress. "The next time I want to see home movies about Point Barrow, Alaska, and its native American Eskimos, I'll ask for them. My God, it was priceless! Some people will go to any lengths. Some people will try to kill their enemies with boredom. But you'd have needed to be there." The woman stared hotly at Miss Dent as if daring her to contradict.

Miss Dent picked up the handbag and placed it on her lap. She looked at the clock, which seemed to be moving very slowly, if at all.

"You don't say much," the woman said to Miss Dent. "But I'll wager you could say a lot if someone got you started. Couldn't you? But you're a sly boots. You'd rather just sit with your prim little mouth while other people talk their heads off. Am I right? Still waters. Is that your name?" the woman asked. "What *do* they call you?"

"Miss Dent. But I don't know you," Miss Dent said.

"I sure as hell don't know you, either!" the woman said. "Don't know you and don't care to know you. Sit there and think what you want. It won't change anything. But I know what I think, and I think it stinks!"

The old man left his place at the window and went outside. When he came back in a minute later, he had a cigarette burning in his holder and he seemed in better spirits. He carried his shoulders back and his chin out. He sat down beside the woman.

"I found some matches," he said. "There they were, a book of matches right next to the curb. Someone must have dropped them."

"Basically, you're lucky," the woman said. "And that's a plus in your situation. I always knew that about you, even if no one else did. Luck is important." The woman looked over at Miss Dent and said: "Young lady, I'll wager you've had your share of trial and error in this life. I know you have. The expression on your face tells me so. But you aren't going to talk about it. Go ahead then, don't talk. Let us do the talking. But you'll get older. Then you'll have something to talk about. Wait until you're my age. Or his age," the woman said and jerked her thumb at the old man. "God forbid. But it'll all come to you. In its own sweet time, it'll come. You won't have to hunt for it, either. It'll find you."

Miss Dent got up from the bench with her handbag and went over to the water fountain. She drank from the fountain and turned to look at them. The old man had finished smoking. He took what was left of his cigarette from the holder and dropped it under the bench. He tapped the holder against his palm, blew into the mouthpiece, and returned the holder to his shirt pocket. Now he, too, gave his attention to Miss Dent. He fixed his eyes on her and waited along with the woman. Miss Dent gathered herself to speak. She wasn't sure where to begin, but she thought she might start by saying she had a gun in her handbag. She might even tell them she'd nearly killed a man earlier that night.

But at that moment they heard the train. First they heard the whistle, then a clanging sound, an alarm bell, as the guard rails went down at the crossing. The woman and the white-haired old man got up from the bench and moved toward the door. The old man opened the door for his companion, and then he smiled and made a little movement with his fingers for Miss Dent to precede him. She held the handbag against the front of her blouse and followed the older woman outside.

The train tooted its whistle once more as it slowed and then ground to a stop in front of the station. The light on the cab of the engine went back and forth over the track. The two cars that made up this little train were well lighted, so it was easy for the three people on the platform to see that the train was nearly empty. But this didn't surprise them. At this hour, they were surprised to see anyone at all on the train.

The few passengers in the cars looked out through the glass and thought it strange to find these people on the platform, making ready to board a train at this time of night. What business could have taken them out? This was the hour when people should be thinking of going to bed. The kitchens in the houses up on the hills behind the station were clean and orderly; the dishwashers had long ago finished their cycle, all things were in their places. Night-lights burned in children's bedrooms. A few teenaged girls might still be reading novels, their fingers twisting a strand of hair as they did so. But television sets were going off now. Husbands and wives were making their own preparations for the night. The half-dozen or so passengers, sitting by themselves in the two cars, looked through the glass and wondered about the three people on the platform.

They saw a heavily made-up, middle-aged woman wearing a rose-colored knit dress mount the steps and enter the train. Behind her came a younger woman dressed in a summer blouse and skirt who clutched a handbag. They were followed onto the train by an old man who moved slowly and who carried himself in a dignified manner. The old man had white hair and a white silk cravat, but he was without shoes. The passengers naturally assumed that the three people boarding were together; and they felt sure that whatever these people's business had been that night, it had not come to a happy conclusion. But the passengers had seen things more various than this in their lifetime. The world is filled with business of every sort, as they well knew. This still was not as bad, perhaps, as it could be. For this reason, they scarcely gave another thought to these three who moved down the aisle and took up their places—the woman and the white-haired old man next to each other, the young woman with the handbag a few seats behind. Instead, the passengers gazed out at the station and went back to thinking about their own business, those things that had engaged them before the station stop.

The conductor looked up the track. Then he glanced back in the direction the train had come from. He raised his arm and, with his lantern, signaled the engineer. This was what the engineer was waiting for. He turned a dial and pushed down on a lever. The train began to move forward. It went slowly at first, but it began to pick up speed. It moved faster until once more it sped through the dark countryside, its brilliant cars throwing light onto the roadbed.

Fever

CARLYLE was in a spot. He'd been in a spot all summer, since early June when his wife had left him. But up until a little while ago, just a few days before he had to start meeting his classes at the high school, Carlyle hadn't needed a sitter. He'd been the sitter. Every day and every night he'd attended to the children. Their mother, he told them, was away on a long trip.

Debbie, the first sitter he contacted, was a fat girl, nineteen years old, who told Carlyle she came from a big family. Kids loved her, she said. She offered a couple of names for reference. She penciled them on a piece of notebook paper. Carlyle took the names, folded the piece of paper, and put it in his shirt pocket. He told her he had meetings the next day. He said she could start to work for him the next morning. She said, "Okay."

He understood that his life was entering a new period. Eileen had left while Carlyle was still filling out his grade reports. She'd said she was going to Southern California to begin a new life for herself there. She'd gone with Richard Hoopes, one of Carlyle's colleagues at the high school. Hoopes was a drama teacher and glass-blowing instructor who'd apparently turned his grades in on time, taken his things, and left town in a hurry with Eileen. Now, the long and painful summer nearly behind him, and his classes about to resume, Carlyle had finally turned his attention to this matter of finding a baby-sitter. His first efforts had not been successful. In his desperation to find someone—anyone—he'd taken Debbie on.

In the beginning, he was grateful to have this girl turn up in response to his call. He'd yielded up the house and children to her as if she were a relative. So he had no one to blame but himself, his own carelessness, he was convinced, when he came home early from school one day that first week and pulled into the drive next to a car that had a big pair of flannel dice hanging from the rearview mirror. To his astonishment, he saw his children in the front yard, their clothes filthy, playing with a dog big enough to bite off their hands. His son, Keith, had the hiccups and had been crying. Sarah, his daughter, began to cry when she saw him get out of the car. They were sitting on the grass, and the dog was licking their hands and faces. The dog growled at him and then moved off a little as Carlyle made for his children. He picked up Keith and then he picked up Sarah. One child under each arm, he made for his front door. Inside the house, the phonograph was turned up so high the front windows vibrated.

In the living room, three teenaged boys jumped to their feet from where they'd been sitting around the coffee table. Beer bottles stood on the table and cigarettes burned in the ashtray. Rod Stewart screamed from the stereo. On the sofa, Debbie, the fat girl, sat with another teenaged boy. She stared at Carlyle with dumb disbelief as he entered the living room. The fat girl's blouse was unbuttoned. She had her legs drawn under her, and she was smoking a cigarette. The living room was filled with smoke and music. The fat girl and her friend got off the sofa in a hurry.

"Mr. Carlyle, wait a minute," Debbie said. "I can explain."

"Don't explain," Carlyle said. "Get the hell out of here. All of you. Before I throw you out." He tightened his grip on the children.

"You owe me for four days," the fat girl said, as she tried to button her blouse. She still had the cigarette between her fingers. Ashes fell from the cigarette as she tried to button up. "Forget today. You don't owe me for today. Mr. Carlyle, it's not what it looks like. They dropped by to listen to this record."

"I understand, Debbie," he said. He let the children down onto the carpet. But they stayed close to his legs and watched the people in the living room. Debbie looked at them and shook her head slowly, as if she'd never laid eyes on them before. "Goddamn it, get out!" Carlyle said. "Now. Get going. All of you."

He went over and opened the front door. The boys acted as if they were in no real hurry. They picked up their beer and started slowly for the door. The Rod Stewart record was still playing. One of them said, "That's my record."

"Get it," Carlyle said. He took a step toward the boy and then stopped.

"Don't touch me, okay? Just don't touch me," the boy said.

He went over to the phonograph, picked up the arm, swung it back, and took his record off while the turntable was still spinning.

Carlyle's hands were shaking. "If that car's not out of the drive in one minute—one minute—I'm calling the police." He felt sick and dizzy with his anger. He saw, really saw, spots dance in front of his eyes.

"Hey, listen, we're on our way, all right? We're going," the boy said.

They filed out of the house. Outside, the fat girl stumbled a little. She weaved as she moved toward the car. Carlyle saw her stop and bring her hands up to her face. She stood like that in the drive for a minute. Then one of the boys pushed her from behind and said her name. She dropped her hands and got into the back seat of the car.

"Daddy will get you into some clean clothes," Carlyle told his children, trying to keep his voice steady. "I'll give you a bath, and put you into some clean clothes. Then we'll go out for some pizza. How does pizza sound to you?"

"Where's Debbie?" Sarah asked him.

"She's gone," Carlyle said.

That evening, after he'd put the children to bed, he called Carol, the woman from school he'd been seeing for the past month. He told her what had happened with his sitter.

"My kids were out in the yard with this big dog," he said. "The dog was as big as a wolf. The baby-sitter was in the house with a bunch of her hoodlum boyfriends. They had Rod Stewart going full blast, and they were tying one on while my kids were outside playing with this strange dog." He brought his fingers to his temples and held them there while he talked.

"My God," Carol said. "Poor sweetie, I'm so sorry." Her voice sounded indistinct. He pictured her letting the receiver slide down to her chin, as she was in the habit of doing while talking on the phone. He'd seen her do it before. It was a habit of hers he found vaguely irritating. Did he want her to come over to his place? she asked. She would. She thought maybe she'd better do that. She'd call her sitter. Then she'd drive to his place. She wanted to. He shouldn't be afraid to say when he needed affection, she said. Carol was one of the secretaries in the principal's office at the high school where Carlyle taught art classes. She was divorced and had one child, a neurotic ten-year-old the father had named Dodge, after his automobile.

"No, that's all right," Carlyle said. "But thanks. *Thanks*, Carol. The kids are in bed, but I think I'd feel a little funny, you know, having company tonight."

She didn't offer again. "Sweetie, I'm sorry about what happened. But I understand your wanting to be alone tonight. I respect that. I'll see you at school tomorrow."

He could hear her waiting for him to say something else. "That's two baby-sitters in less than a week," he said. "I'm going out of my tree with this."

"Honey, don't let it get you down," she said. "Something will turn up. I'll help you find somebody this weekend. It'll be all right, you'll see."

"Thanks again for being there when I need you," he said. "You're one in a million, you know."

"'Night, Carlyle," she said.

After he'd hung up, he wished he could have thought of something else to say to her instead of what he'd just said. He'd never talked that way before in his life. They weren't having a love affair, he wouldn't call it that, but he liked her. She knew it was a hard time for him, and she didn't make demands.

After Eileen had left for California, Carlyle had spent every waking minute for the first month with his children. He supposed the shock of her going had caused this, but he didn't want to let the children out of his sight. He'd certainly not been interested in seeing other women, and for a time he didn't think he ever would be. He felt as if he were in mourning. His days and nights were passed in the company of his children. He cooked for them—he had no appetite himself—washed and ironed their clothes, drove them into the country, where they picked flowers and ate sandwiches wrapped up in waxed paper. He took them to the supermarket and let them pick out what they liked. And every few days they went to the park, or else to the library, or the zoo. They took old bread to the zoo so they could feed the ducks. At night, before tucking them in, Carlyle read to them—Aesop, Hans Christian Andersen, the Brothers Grimm.

"When is Mama coming back?" one of them might ask him in the middle of a fairy tale.

"Soon," he'd say. "One of these days. Now listen to this." Then he'd read the tale to its conclusion, kiss them, and turn off the light.

And while they'd slept, he had wandered the rooms of his house with a glass in his hand, telling himself that, yes, sooner or later, Eileen would come back. In the next breath, he would say, "I never want to see your face again. I'll never forgive you for this, you crazy bitch." Then, a minute later, "Come back, sweetheart, please. I love you and need you. The kids need you, too." Some nights that summer he fell asleep in front of the TV and woke up with the set still going and the screen filled with snow. This was the period when he didn't think he would be seeing any women for a long time, if ever. At night, sitting in front of the TV with an unopened book or magazine next to him on the sofa, he often thought of Eileen. When he did, he might remember her sweet laugh, or else her hand rubbing his neck if he complained of a soreness there. It was at these times that he thought he could weep. He thought, You hear about stuff like this happening to other people.

Just before the incident with Debbie, when some of the shock and grief had worn off, he'd phoned an employment service to tell them something of his predicament and his requirements. Someone took down the information and said they would get back to him. Not many people wanted to do housework *and* baby-sit, they said, but they'd find somebody. A few days before he had to be at the high school for meetings and registration, he called again and was told there'd be somebody at his house first thing the next morning.

That person was a thirty-five-year-old woman with hairy arms and run-over shoes. She shook hands with him and listened to him talk without asking a single question about the children— not even their names. When he took her into the back of the house where the children were playing, she simply stared at them for a minute without saying anything. When she finally smiled, Carlyle noticed for the first time that she had a tooth missing. Sarah left her crayons and got up to come over and stand next to him. She took Carlyle's hand and stared at the woman. Keith stared at her, too. Then he went back to his coloring. Carlyle thanked the woman for her time and said he would be in touch.

That afternoon he took down a number from an index card tacked to the bulletin board at the supermarket. Someone was offering baby-sitting services. References furnished on request. Carlyle called the number and got Debbie, the fat girl.

Over the summer, Eileen had sent a few cards, letters, and photographs of herself to the children, and some pen-and-ink drawings of her own that she'd done since she'd gone away. She also sent Carlyle long, rambling letters in which she asked for his understanding in this matter—*this matter*—but told him that she was happy. Happy. As if, Carlyle thought, happiness was all there was to life. She told him that if he really loved her, as he said he did, and as she really believed—she loved him, too, don't forget—then he would understand and accept things as they were. She wrote, "That which is truly bonded can never become unbonded." Carlyle didn't know if she was talking about their own relationship or her way of life out in California. He hated the word *bonded*. What did it have to do with the two of them? Did she think they were a corporation? He thought Eileen must be losing her mind to talk like that. He read that part again and then crumpled the letter.

But a few hours later he retrieved the letter from the trash can where he'd thrown it, and put it with her other cards and letters in a box on the shelf in his closet. In one of the envelopes, there was a photograph of her in a big, floppy hat, wearing a bathing suit. And there was a pencil drawing on heavy paper of a woman on a riverbank in a filmy gown, her hands covering her eyes, her shoulders slumped. It was, Carlyle assumed, Eileen showing her heartbreak over the situation. In college, she had majored in art, and even though she'd agreed to marry him, she said she intended to do something with her talent. Carlyle said he wouldn't have it any other way. She owed it to herself, he said. She owed it to both of them. They had loved each other in those days. He knew they had. He couldn't imagine ever loving anyone again the way he'd loved her. And he'd felt loved, too. Then, after eight years of being married to him, Eileen had pulled out. She was, she said in her letter, "going for it."

After talking to Carol, he looked in on the children, who were asleep. Then he went into the kitchen and made himself a drink. He thought of calling Eileen to talk to her about the baby-sitting crisis, but decided against it. He had her phone number and her address out there, of course. But he'd only called once and, so far, had not written a letter. This was partly out of a feeling of bewilderment with the situation, partly out of anger and humiliation. Once, earlier in the summer, after a few drinks, he'd chanced humiliation and called. Richard Hoopes answered the phone. Richard had said, "Hey, Carlyle," as if he were still Carlyle's friend. And then, as if remembering something, he said, "Just a minute, all right?"

Eileen had come on the line and said, "Carlyle, how are you? How are the kids? Tell me about yourself." He told her the kids were fine. But before he could say anything else, she interrupted him to say, "I know *they're* fine. What about *you*?" Then she went on to tell him that her head was in the right place for the first time in a long time. Next she wanted to talk about his head and his karma. She'd looked into his karma. It was going to improve any time now, she said. Carlyle listened, hardly able to believe his ears. Then he said, "I have to go now, Eileen." And he hung up. The phone rang a minute or so later, but he let it ring. When it stopped ringing, he took the phone off the hook and left it off until he was ready for bed.

He wanted to call her now, but he was afraid to call. He still missed her and wanted to confide in her. He longed to hear her voice—sweet, steady, not manic as it had been for months now—but if he dialed her number, Richard Hoopes might answer the telephone. Carlyle knew he didn't want to hear that man's voice again. Richard had been a colleague for three years and, Carlyle supposed, a kind of friend. At least he was someone Carlyle ate lunch with in the faculty dining room, someone who talked about Tennessee Williams and the photographs of Ansel Adams. But even if Eileen answered the telephone, she might launch into something about his karma.

While he was sitting there with the glass in his hand, trying to remember what it had felt like to be married and intimate with someone, the phone rang. He picked up the receiver, heard a trace of static on the line, and knew, even before she'd said his name, that it was Eileen.

"I was just thinking about you," Carlyle said, and at once regretted saying it.

"See! I knew I was on your mind, Carlyle. Well, I was thinking about you, too. That's why I called." He drew a breath. She *was* losing her mind. That much was clear to him. She kept talking. "Now listen," she said. "The big reason I called is that I know things are in kind of a mess out there right now. Don't ask me how, but I know. I'm sorry, Carlyle. But here's the thing. You're still in need of a good housekeeper and sitter combined, right? Well, she's practically right there in the neighborhood! Oh, you may have found someone already, and that's good, if that's the case. If so, it's supposed to be that way. But see, just in case you're having trouble in that area, there's this woman who used to work for Richard's mother. I told Richard about the potential problem, and he put himself to work on it. You want to know what he did? Are you listening? He called his mother, who used to have this woman who kept house for her. The woman's name is Mrs. Webster. She looked after things for Richard's mother before his aunt and her daughter moved in there. Richard was able to get a number through his mother. He talked to Mrs. Webster today. Richard did. Mrs. Webster is going to call you tonight. Or else maybe she'll call you in the morning. One or the other. Anyway, she's going to volunteer her services, if you need her. You might, you never can tell. Even if your situation is okay right now, which I hope it is. But some time or another you might need her. You know what I'm saying? If not this minute, some other time. Okay? How are the kids? What are they up to?"

"The children are fine, Eileen. They're asleep now," he said. Maybe he should tell her they cried themselves to sleep every night. He wondered if he should tell her the truth—that they hadn't asked about her even once in the last couple of weeks. He decided not to say anything.

"I called earlier, but the line was busy. I told Richard you were probably talking to your girlfriend," Eileen said and laughed. "Think positive thoughts. You sound depressed," she said.

"I have to go, Eileen." He started to hang up, and he took the receiver from his ear. But she was still talking.

"Tell Keith and Sarah I love them. Tell them I'm sending some more pictures. Tell them that. I don't want them to forget their mother is an artist. Maybe not a great artist yet, that's not important. But, you know, an artist. It's important they shouldn't forget that."

Carlyle said, "I'll tell them."

"Richard says hello."

Carlyle didn't say anything. He said the word to himself—*hello*. What could the man possibly mean by this? Then he said, "Thanks for calling. Thanks for talking to that woman."

"Mrs. Webster!"

"Yes. I'd better get off the phone now. I don't want to run up your nickel."

Eileen laughed. "It's only money. Money's not important except as a necessary medium of exchange. There are more important things than money. But then you already know that."

He held the receiver out in front of him. He looked at the instrument from which her voice was issuing.

"Carlyle, things are going to get better for you. I *know* they are. You may think I'm crazy or something," she said. "But just remember."

Remember what? Carlyle wondered in alarm, thinking he must have missed something she'd said. He brought the receiver in close. "Eileen, thanks for calling," he said.

"We have to stay in touch," Eileen said. "We have to keep all lines of communication open. I think the worst is over. For both of us. I've suffered, too. But we're going to get what we're supposed to get out of this life, both of us, and we're going to be made *stronger* for it in the long run."

"Goodnight," he said. He put the receiver back. Then he looked at the phone. He waited. It didn't ring again. But an hour later it did ring. He answered it.

"Mr. Carlyle." It was an old woman's voice. "You don't know me, but my name is Mrs. Jim Webster. I was supposed to get in touch."

"Mrs. Webster. Yes," he said. Eileen's mention of the woman came back to him. "Mrs. Webster, can you come to my house in the morning? Early. Say seven o'clock?"

"I can do that easily," the old woman said. "Seven o'clock. Give me your address."

"I'd like to be able to count on you," Carlyle said.

"You can count on me," she said.

"I can't tell you how important it is," Carlyle said.

"Don't you worry," the old woman said.

The next morning, when the alarm went off, he wanted to keep his eyes closed and keep on with the dream he was having. Something about a farmhouse. And there was a waterfall in there, too. Someone, he didn't know who, was walking along the road carrying something. Maybe it was a picnic hamper. He was not made uneasy by the dream. In the dream, there seemed to exist a sense of well-being.

Finally, he rolled over and pushed something to stop the buzzing. He lay in bed awhile longer. Then he got up, put his feet into his slippers, and went out to the kitchen to start the coffee.

He shaved and dressed for the day. Then he sat down at the kitchen table with coffee and a cigarette. The children were still in bed. But in five minutes or so he planned to put boxes of cereal on the table and lay out bowls and spoons, then go in to wake them for breakfast. He really couldn't believe that the old woman who'd phoned him last night would show up this morning, as she'd said she would. He decided he'd wait until five minutes after seven o'clock, and then he'd call in, take the day off, and make every effort in the book to locate someone reliable. He brought the cup of coffee to his lips.

It was then that he heard a rumbling sound out in the street. He left his cup and got up from the table to look out the window. A pickup truck had pulled over to the curb in front of his house. The pickup cab shook as the engine idled. Carlyle went to the front door, opened it, and waved. An old woman waved back and then let herself out of the vehicle. Carlyle saw the driver lean over and disappear under the dash. The truck gasped, shook itself once more, and fell still.

"Mr. Carlyle?" the old woman said, as she came slowly up his walk carrying a large purse.

"Mrs. Webster," he said. "Come on inside. Is that your husband? Ask him in. I just made coffee."

"It's okay," she said. "He has his thermos."

Carlyle shrugged. He held the door for her. She stepped

inside and they shook hands. Mrs. Webster smiled. Carlyle nodded. They moved out to the kitchen. "Did you want me today, then?" she asked.

"Let me get the children up," he said. "I'd like them to meet you before I leave for school."

"That'd be good," she said. She looked around his kitchen. She put her purse on the drainboard.

"Why don't I get the children?" he said. "I'll just be a minute or two."

In a little while, he brought the children out and introduced them. They were still in their pajamas. Sarah was rubbing her eyes. Keith was wide awake. "This is Keith," Carlyle said. "And this one here, this is my Sarah." He held on to Sarah's hand and turned to Mrs. Webster. "They need someone, you see. We need someone we can count on. I guess that's our problem."

Mrs. Webster moved over to the children. She fastened the top button of Keith's pajamas. She moved the hair away from Sarah's face. They let her do it. "Don't you kids worry, now," she said to them. "Mr. Carlyle, it'll be all right. We're going to be fine. Give us a day or two to get to know each other, that's all. But if I'm going to stay, why don't you give Mr. Webster the all-clear sign? Just wave at him through the window," she said, and then she gave her attention back to the children.

Carlyle stepped to the bay window and drew the curtain. An old man was watching the house from the cab of the truck. He was just bringing a thermos cup to his lips. Carlyle waved to him, and with his free hand the man waved back. Carlyle watched him roll down the truck window and throw out what was left in his cup. Then he bent down under the dash again— Carlyle imagined him touching some wires together—and in a minute the truck started and began to shake. The old man put the truck in gear and pulled away from the curb.

Carlyle turned from the window. "Mrs. Webster," he said, "I'm glad you're here."

"Likewise, Mr. Carlyle," she said. "Now you go on about your business before you're late. Don't worry about anything. We're going to be fine. Aren't we, kids?"

The children nodded their heads. Keith held on to her dress with one hand. He put the thumb of his other hand into his mouth.

"Thank you," Carlyle said. "I feel, I really feel a hundred percent better." He shook his head and grinned. He felt a welling in his chest as he kissed each of his children goodbye. He told Mrs. Webster what time she could expect him home, put on his coat, said goodbye once more, and went out of the house. For the first time in months, it seemed, he felt his burden had lifted a little. Driving to school, he listened to some music on the radio.

During first-period art-history class, he lingered over slides of Byzantine paintings. He patiently explained the nuances of detail and motif. He pointed out the emotional power and fitness of the work. But he took so long trying to place the anonymous artists in their social milieu that some of his students began to scrape their shoes on the floor, or else clear their throats. They covered only a third of the lesson plan that day. He was still talking when the bell rang.

In his next class, watercolor painting, he felt unusually calm and insightful. "Like this, like this," he said, guiding their hands. "Delicately. Like a breath of air on the paper. Just a touch. Like so. See?" he'd say and felt on the edge of discovery himself. "*Suggestion* is what it's all about," he said, holding lightly to Sue Colvin's fingers as he guided her brush. "You've got to work with your mistakes until they look intended. Understand?"

As he moved down the lunch line in the faculty dining room, he saw Carol a few places ahead of him. She paid for her food. He waited impatiently while his own bill was being rung up. Carol was halfway across the room by the time he caught up with her. He slipped his hand under her elbow and guided her to an empty table near the window.

"God, Carlyle," she said after they'd seated themselves. She picked up her glass of iced tea. Her face was flushed. "Did you see the look Mrs. Storr gave us? What's wrong with you? Everybody will know." She sipped from her iced tea and put the glass down.

"The hell with Mrs. Storr," Carlyle said. "Hey, let me tell you something. Honey, I feel light-years better than I did this time yesterday. Jesus," he said.

"What's happened?" Carol said. "Carlyle, tell me." She moved her fruit cup to one side of her tray and shook cheese

over her spaghetti. But she didn't eat anything. She waited for
him to go on. "Tell me what it is."

He told her about Mrs. Webster. He even told her about
Mr. Webster. How the man'd had to hot-wire the truck in
order to start it. Carlyle ate his tapioca while he talked. Then
he ate the garlic bread. He drank Carol's iced tea down before
he realized he was doing it.

"You're nuts, Carlyle," she said, nodding at the spaghetti in
his plate that he hadn't touched.

He shook his head. "My *God*, Carol. God, I feel good, you
know? I feel better than I have all summer." He lowered his
voice. "Come over tonight, will you?"

He reached under the table and put his hand on her knee.
She turned red again. She raised her eyes and looked around
the dining room. But no one was paying any attention to
them. She nodded quickly. Then she reached under the table
and touched his hand.

That afternoon he arrived home to find his house neat and
orderly and his children in clean clothes. In the kitchen, Keith
and Sarah stood on chairs, helping Mrs. Webster with ginger-
bread cookies. Sarah's hair was out of her face and held back
with a barrette.

"Daddy!" his children cried, happy, when they saw him.

"Keith, Sarah," he said. "Mrs. Webster, I—" But she didn't
let him finish.

"We've had a fine day, Mr. Carlyle," Mrs. Webster said quickly.
She wiped her fingers on the apron she was wearing. It was an
old apron with blue windmills on it and it had belonged to
Eileen. "Such beautiful children. They're a treasure. Just a
treasure."

"I don't know what to say." Carlyle stood by the drainboard
and watched Sarah press out some dough. He could smell the
spice. He took off his coat and sat down at the kitchen table.
He loosened his tie.

"Today was a get-acquainted day," Mrs. Webster said. "Tomorrow we have some other plans. I thought we'd walk to the
park. We ought to take advantage of this good weather."

"That's a fine idea," Carlyle said. "That's just fine. Good.
Good for you, Mrs. Webster."

"I'll finish putting these cookies in the oven, and by that time Mr. Webster should be here. You said four o'clock? I told him to come at four."

Carlyle nodded, his heart full.

"You had a call today," she said as she went over to the sink with the mixing bowl. "Mrs. Carlyle called."

"Mrs. Carlyle," he said. He waited for whatever it was Mrs. Webster might say next.

"Yes. I identified myself, but she didn't seem surprised to find me here. She said a few words to each of the children."

Carlyle glanced at Keith and Sarah, but they weren't paying any attention. They were lining up cookies on another baking sheet.

Mrs. Webster continued. "She left a message. Let me see, I wrote it down, but I think I can remember it. She said, 'Tell him'—that is, tell you—'what goes around, comes around.' I think that's right. She said you'd understand."

Carlyle stared at her. He heard Mr. Webster's truck outside.

"That's Mr. Webster," she said and took off the apron.

Carlyle nodded.

"Seven o'clock in the morning?" she asked.

"That will be fine," he said. "And thank you again."

That evening he bathed each of the children, got them into their pajamas, and then read to them. He listened to their prayers, tucked in their covers, and turned out the light. It was nearly nine o'clock. He made himself a drink and watched something on TV until he heard Carol's car pull into the drive.

Around ten, while they were in bed together, the phone rang. He swore, but he didn't get up to answer it. It kept ringing.

"It might be important," Carol said, sitting up. "It might be my sitter. She has this number."

"It's my wife," Carlyle said. "I know it's her. She's losing her mind. She's going crazy. I'm not going to answer it."

"I have to go pretty soon anyway," Carol said. "It was real sweet tonight, honey." She touched his face.

It was the middle of the fall term. Mrs. Webster had been with him for nearly six weeks. During this time, Carlyle's life had undergone a number of changes. For one thing, he was becoming reconciled to the fact that Eileen was gone and, as far as he could understand it, had no intention of coming back. He had stopped imagining that this might change. It was only late at night, on the nights he was not with Carol, that he wished for an end to the love he still had for Eileen and felt tormented as to why all of this had happened. But for the most part he and the children were happy; they thrived under Mrs. Webster's attentions. Lately, she'd gotten into the routine of making their dinner and keeping it in the oven, warming, until his arrival home from school. He'd walk in the door to the smell of something good coming from the kitchen and find Keith and Sarah helping to set the dining-room table. Now and again he asked Mrs. Webster if she would care for over-time work on Saturdays. She agreed, as long as it wouldn't en-tail her being at his house before noon. Saturday mornings, she said, she had things to do for Mr. Webster and herself. On these days, Carol would leave Dodge with Carlyle's children, all of them under Mrs. Webster's care, and Carol and he would drive to a restaurant out in the country for dinner. He believed his life was beginning again. Though he hadn't heard from Eileen since that call six weeks ago, he found himself able to think about her now without either being angry or else feeling close to tears.

At school, they were just leaving the medieval period and about to enter the Gothic. The Renaissance was still some time off, at least not until after the Christmas recess. It was during this time that Carlyle got sick. Overnight, it seemed, his chest tightened and his head began to hurt. The joints of his body became stiff. He felt dizzy when he moved around. The head-ache got worse. He woke up with it on a Sunday and thought of calling Mrs. Webster to ask her to come and take the chil-dren somewhere. They'd been sweet to him, bringing him glasses of juice and some soda pop. But he couldn't take care of them. On the second morning of his illness, he was just able to get to the phone to call in sick. He gave his name, his school, department, and the nature of his illness to the person who answered the number. Then he recommended Mel Fisher as his substitute. Fisher was a man who painted abstract oils three or four days a week, sixteen hours a day, but who didn't sell or even show his work. He was a friend of Carlyle's. "Get

Mel Fisher," Carlyle told the woman on the other end of the line. "Fisher," he whispered.

He made it back to his bed, got under the covers, and went to sleep. In his sleep, he heard the pickup engine running outside, and then the backfire it made as the engine was turned off. Sometime later he heard Mrs. Webster's voice outside the bedroom door.

"Mr. Carlyle?"

"Yes, Mrs. Webster." His voice sounded strange to him. He kept his eyes shut. "I'm sick today. I called the school. I'm going to stay in bed today."

"I see. Don't worry, then," she said. "I'll look after things at this end."

He shut his eyes. Directly, still in a state between sleeping and waking, he thought he heard his front door open and close. He listened. Out in the kitchen, he heard a man say something in a low voice, and a chair being pulled away from the table. Pretty soon he heard the voices of the children. Sometime later—he wasn't sure how much time had passed—he heard Mrs. Webster outside his door.

"Mr. Carlyle, should I call the doctor?"

"No, that's all right," he said. "I think it's just a bad cold. But I feel hot all over. I think I have too many covers. And it's too warm in the house. Maybe you'll turn down the furnace." Then he felt himself drift back into sleep.

In a little while, he heard the children talking to Mrs. Webster in the living room. Were they coming inside or going out? Carlyle wondered. Could it be the next day already?

He went back to sleep. But then he was aware of his door opening. Mrs. Webster appeared beside his bed. She put her hand on his forehead.

"You're burning up," she said. "You have a fever."

"I'll be all right," Carlyle said. "I just need to sleep a little longer. And maybe you could turn the furnace down. Please, I'd appreciate it if you could get me some aspirin. I have an awful headache."

Mrs. Webster left the room. But his door stood open. Carlyle could hear the TV going out there. "Keep it down, Jim," he heard her say, and the volume was lowered at once. Carlyle fell asleep again.

But he couldn't have slept more than a minute, because Mrs. Webster was suddenly back in his room with a tray. She sat down on the side of his bed. He roused himself and tried to sit up. She put a pillow behind his back.

"Take these," she said and gave him some tablets. "Drink this." She held a glass of juice for him. "I also brought you some Cream of Wheat. I want you to eat it. It'll be good for you."

He took the aspirin and drank the juice. He nodded. But he shut his eyes once more. He was going back to sleep.

"Mr. Carlyle," she said.

He opened his eyes. "I'm awake," he said. "I'm sorry." He sat up a little. "I'm too warm, that's all. What time is it? Is it eight-thirty yet?"

"It's a little after nine-thirty," she said.

"Nine-thirty," he said.

"Now I'm going to feed this cereal to you. And you're going to open up and eat it. Six bites, that's all. Here, here's the first bite. Open," she said. "You're going to feel better after you eat this. Then I'll let you go back to sleep. You eat this, and then you can sleep all you want."

He ate the cereal she spooned to him and asked for more juice. He drank the juice, and then he pulled down in the bed again. Just as he was going off to sleep, he felt her covering him with another blanket.

The next time he awoke, it was afternoon. He could tell it was afternoon by the pale light that came through his window. He reached up and pulled the curtain back. He could see that it was overcast outside; the wintry sun was behind the clouds. He got out of bed slowly, found his slippers, and put on his robe. He went into the bathroom and looked at himself in the mirror. Then he washed his face and took some more aspirin. He used the towel and then went out to the living room.

On the dining-room table, Mrs. Webster had spread some newspaper, and she and the children were pinching clay figures together. They had already made some things that had long necks and bulging eyes, things that resembled giraffes, or else dinosaurs. Mrs. Webster looked up as he walked by the table.

"How are you feeling?" Mrs. Webster asked him as he settled onto the sofa. He could see into the dining-room area, where Mrs. Webster and the children sat at the table.

"Better, thanks. A little better," he said. "I still have a head-ache, and I feel a little warm." He brought the back of his hand up to his forehead. "But I'm better. Yes, I'm better. Thanks for your help this morning."

"Can I get you anything now?" Mrs. Webster said. "Some more juice or some tea? I don't think coffee would hurt, but I think tea would be better. Some juice would be best of all."

"No, no thanks," he said. "I'll just sit here for a while. It's good to be out of bed. I feel a little weak is all. Mrs. Webster?"

She looked at him and waited.

"Did I hear Mr. Webster in the house this morning? It's fine, of course. I'm just sorry I didn't get a chance to meet him and say hello."

"It was him," she said. "He wanted to meet you, too. I asked him to come in. He just picked the wrong morning, what with you being sick and all. I'd wanted to tell you something about our plans, Mr. Webster's and mine, but this morning wasn't a good time for it."

"Tell me what?" he said, alert, fear plucking at his heart.

She shook her head. "It's all right," she said. "It can wait."

"Tell him what?" Sarah said. "Tell him what?"

"What, what?" Keith picked it up. The children stopped what they were doing.

"Just a minute, you two," Mrs. Webster said as she got to her feet.

"Mrs. Webster, Mrs. Webster!" Keith cried.

"Now see here, little man," Mrs. Webster said. "I need to talk to your father. Your father is sick today. You just take it easy. You go on and play with your clay. If you don't watch it, your sister is going to get ahead of you with these creatures."

Just as she began to move toward the living room, the phone rang. Carlyle reached over to the end table and picked up the receiver.

As before, he heard faint singing in the wire and knew that it was Eileen. "Yes," he said. "What is it?"

"Carlyle," his wife said, "I know, don't ask me how, that things are not going so well right now. You're sick, aren't you? Richard's been sick, too. It's something going around. He can't keep anything on his stomach. He's already missed a week of rehearsal for this play he's doing. I've had to go down myself and help block out scenes with his assistant. But I didn't call to tell you that. Tell me how things are out there."

"Nothing to tell," Carlyle said. "I'm sick, that's all. A touch of the flu. But I'm getting better."

"Are you still writing in your journal?" she asked. It caught him by surprise. Several years before, he'd told her that he was keeping a journal. Not a diary, he'd said, a journal—as if that explained something. But he'd never shown it to her, and he hadn't written in it for over a year. He'd forgotten about it.

"Because," she said, "you ought to write something in the journal during this period. How you feel and what you're thinking. You know, where your head is at during this period of sickness. Remember, sickness is a message about your health and your well-being. It's telling you things. Keep a record. You know what I mean? When you're well, you can look back and see what the message was. You can read it later, after the fact. Colette did that," Eileen said. "When she had a fever this one time."

"Who?" Carlyle said. "What did you say?"

"Colette," Eileen answered. "The French writer. You know who I'm talking about. We had a book of hers around the house. *Gigi* or something. I didn't read *that* book, but I've been reading her since I've been out here. Richard turned me on to her. She wrote a little book about what it was like, about what she was thinking and feeling the whole time she had this fever. Sometimes her temperature was a hundred and two. Sometimes it was lower. Maybe it went higher than a hundred and two. But a hundred and two was the highest she ever took her temperature and wrote, too, when she had the fever. Anyway, she wrote about it. That's what I'm saying. Try writing about what it's like. Something might come of it," Eileen said and, inexplicably, it seemed to Carlyle, she laughed. "At least later on you'd have an hour-by-hour account of your sickness. To look back at. At least you'd have that to show for it. Right now you've just got this discomfort. You've got to translate that into something usable."

He pressed his fingertips against his temple and shut his eyes. But she was still on the line, waiting for him to say something. What could he say? It was clear to him that she was insane.

"Jesus," he said. "Jesus, Eileen. I don't know what to say to that. I really don't. I have to go now. Thanks for calling," he said.

"It's all right," she said. "We have to be able to communicate. Kiss the kids for me. Tell them I love them. And Richard sends his hellos to you. Even though he's flat on his back."

"Goodbye," Carlyle said and hung up. Then he brought his hands to his face. He remembered, for some reason, seeing the fat girl make the same gesture that time as she moved toward the car. He lowered his hands and looked at Mrs. Webster, who was watching him.

"Not bad news, I hope," she said. The old woman had moved a chair near to where he sat on the sofa.

Carlyle shook his head.

"Good," Mrs. Webster said. "That's good. Now, Mr. Carlyle, this may not be the best time in the world to talk about this." She glanced out to the dining room. At the table, the children had their heads bent over the clay. "But since it has to be talked about sometime soon, and since it concerns you and the children, and you're up now, I have something to tell you. Jim and I, we're getting on. The thing is, we need something more than we have at the present. Do you know what I'm saying? This is hard for me," she said and shook her head. Carlyle nodded slowly. He knew that she was going to tell him she had to leave. He wiped his face on his sleeve. "Jim's son by a former marriage, Bob—the man is forty years old—called yesterday to invite us to go out to Oregon and help him with his mink ranch. Jim would be doing whatever they do with minks, and I'd cook, buy the groceries, clean house, and do anything else that needed doing. It's a chance for both of us. And it's board and room and then some. Jim and I won't have to worry anymore about what's going to happen to us. You know what I'm saying. Right now, Jim doesn't have anything," she said. "He was sixty-two last week. He hasn't had anything for some time. He came in this morning to tell you about it himself, because I was going to have to give notice, you see. We thought—*I* thought—it would help if Jim was here when I told you." She waited for Carlyle to say something. When he didn't, she went on. "I'll finish out the week, and I could stay on a couple of days next week, if need be. But then, you know, for sure, we really have to leave, and you'll have to wish us luck. I mean, can you imagine—all the way out there to Oregon in that old rattletrap of ours? But I'm going to miss these little kids. They're so precious."

After a time, when he still hadn't moved to answer her, she got up from her chair and went to sit on the cushion next to his. She touched the sleeve of his robe. "Mr. Carlyle?"

"I understand," he said. "I want you to know your being here has made a big difference to me and the children." His head ached so much that he had to squint his eyes. "This headache," he said. "This headache is killing me."

Mrs. Webster reached over and laid the back of her hand against his forehead. "You still have some fever," she told him. "I'll get more aspirin. That'll help bring it down. I'm still on the case here," she said. "I'm still the doctor."

"My wife thinks I should write down what this feels like," Carlyle said. "She thinks it might be a good idea to describe what the fever is like. So I can look back later and get the message." He laughed. Some tears came to his eyes. He wiped them away with the heel of his hand.

"I think I'll get your aspirin and juice and then go out there with the kids," Mrs. Webster said. "Looks to me like they've about worn out their interest with that clay."

Carlyle was afraid she'd move into the other room and leave him alone. He wanted to talk to her. He cleared his throat. "Mrs. Webster, there's something I want you to know. For a long time, my wife and I loved each other more than anything or anybody in the world. And that includes those children. We thought, well, we *knew* that we'd grow old together. And we knew we'd do all the things in the world that we wanted to do, and do them together." He shook his head. That seemed the saddest thing of all to him now—that whatever they did from now on, each would do it without the other.

"There, it's all right," Mrs. Webster said. She patted his hand. He sat forward and began to talk again. After a time, the children came out to the living room. Mrs. Webster caught their attention and held a finger to her lips. Carlyle looked at them and went on talking. Let them listen, he thought. It concerns them, too. The children seemed to understand they had to remain quiet, even pretend some interest, so they sat down next to Mrs. Webster's legs. Then they got down on their stomachs on the carpet and started to giggle. But Mrs. Webster looked sternly in their direction, and that stopped it.

Carlyle went on talking. At first, his head still ached, and he felt awkward to be in his pajamas on the sofa with this old woman beside him, waiting patiently for him to go on to the next thing. But then his headache went away. And soon he stopped feeling awkward and forgot how he was supposed to feel. He had begun his story somewhere in the middle, after the children were born. But then he backed up and started at the beginning, back when Eileen was eighteen and he was nineteen, a boy and girl in love, burning with it.

He stopped to wipe his forehead. He moistened his lips.

"Go on," Mrs. Webster said. "I know what you're saying. You just keep talking, Mr. Carlyle. Sometimes it's good to talk about it. Sometimes it has to be talked about. Besides, I want to hear it. And you're going to feel better afterwards. Something just like it happened to me once, something like what you're describing. Love. That's what it is."

The children fell asleep on the carpet. Keith had his thumb in his mouth. Carlyle was still talking when Mr. Webster came to the door, knocked, and then stepped inside to collect Mrs. Webster.

"Sit down, Jim," Mrs. Webster said. "There's no hurry. Go on with what you were saying, Mr. Carlyle."

Carlyle nodded at the old man, and the old man nodded back, then got himself one of the dining-room chairs and carried it into the living room. He brought the chair close to the sofa and sat down on it with a sigh. Then he took off his cap and wearily lifted one leg over the other. When Carlyle began talking again, the old man put both feet on the floor. The children woke up. They sat up on the carpet and rolled their heads back and forth. But by then Carlyle had said all he knew to say, so he stopped talking.

"Good. Good for you," Mrs. Webster said when she saw he had finished. "You're made out of good stuff. And so is she—so is Mrs. Carlyle. And don't you forget it. You're both going to be okay after this is over." She got up and took off the apron she'd been wearing. Mr. Webster got up, too, and put his cap back on.

At the door, Carlyle shook hands with both of the Websters.

"So long," Jim Webster said. He touched the bill of his cap.

"Good luck to you," Carlyle said.

Mrs. Webster said she'd see him in the morning then, bright and early as always.

As if something important had been settled, Carlyle said, "Right!"

The old couple went carefully along the walk and got into their truck. Jim Webster bent down under the dashboard. Mrs. Webster looked at Carlyle and waved. It was then, as he stood at the window, that he felt something come to an end. It had to do with Eileen and the life before this. Had he ever waved at her? He must have, of course, he knew he had, yet he could not remember just now. But he understood it was over, and he felt able to let her go. He was sure their life together had happened in the way he said it had. But it was something that had passed. And that passing—though it had seemed impossible and he'd fought against it—would become a part of him now, too, as surely as anything else he'd left behind.

As the pickup lurched forward, he lifted his arm once more. He saw the old couple lean toward him briefly as they drove away. Then he brought his arm down and turned to his children.

The Bridle

THIS old station wagon with Minnesota plates pulls into a parking space in front of the window. There's a man and woman in the front seat, two boys in the back. It's July, temperature's one hundred plus. These people look whipped. There are clothes hanging inside; suitcases, boxes, and such piled in back. From what Harley and I put together later, that's all they had left after the bank in Minnesota took their house, their pickup, their tractor, the farm implements, and a few cows.

The people inside sit for a minute, as if collecting themselves. The air-conditioner in our apartment is going full blast. Harley's around in back cutting grass. There's some discussion in the front seat, and then she and him get out and start for the front door. I pat my hair to make sure that it's in place and wait till they push the doorbell for the second time. Then I go to let them in. "You're looking for an apartment?" I say. "Come on in here where it's cool." I show them into the living room. The living room is where I do business. It's where I collect the rents, write the receipts, and talk to interested parties. I also do hair. I call myself a *stylist*. That's what my cards say. I don't like the word *beautician*. It's an old-time word. I have the chair in a corner of the living room, and a dryer I can pull up to the back of the chair. And there's a sink that Harley put in a few years ago. Alongside the chair, I have a table with some magazines. The magazines are old. The covers are gone from some of them. But people will look at anything while they're under the dryer.

The man says his name.

"My name is Holits."

He tells me she's his wife. But she won't look at me. She looks at her nails instead. She and Holits won't sit down, either. He says they're interested in one of the furnished units.

"How many of you?" But I'm just saying what I always say. I know how many. I saw the two boys in the back seat. Two and two is four.

"Me and her and the boys. The boys are thirteen and four-teen, and they'll share a room, like always."

She has her arms crossed and is holding the sleeves of her blouse. She takes in the chair and the sink as if she's never seen their like before. Maybe she hasn't.

"I do hair," I say.

She nods. Then she gives my prayer plant the once-over. It has exactly five leaves to it.

"That needs watering," I say. I go over and touch one of its leaves. "Everything around here needs water. There's not enough water in the air. It rains three times a year if we're lucky. But you'll get used to it. We had to get used to it. But everything here is air-conditioned."

"How much is the place?" Holits wants to know.

I tell him and he turns to her to see what she thinks. But he may as well have been looking at the wall. She won't give him back his look. "I guess we'll have you show us," he says. So I move to get the key for 17, and we go outside.

I hear Harley before I see him.

Then he comes into sight between the buildings. He's moving along behind the power mower in his Bermudas and T-shirt, wearing the straw hat he bought in Nogales. He spends his time cutting grass and doing the small maintenance work. We work for a corporation, Fulton Terrace, Inc. They own the place. If anything major goes wrong, like air-conditioning trouble or something serious in the plumbing department, we have a list of phone numbers.

I wave. I have to. Harley takes a hand off the mower handle and signals. Then he pulls the hat down over his forehead and gives his attention back to what he's doing. He comes to the end of his cut, makes his turn, and starts back toward the street.

"That's Harley." I have to shout it. We go in at the side of the building and up some stairs. "What kind of work are you in, Mr. Holits?" I ask him.

"He's a farmer," she says.

"No more."

"Not much to farm around here." I say it without thinking.

"We had us a farm in Minnesota. Raised wheat. A few cattle.

And Holits knows horses. He knows everything there is about horses."

"That's all right, Betty."

I get a piece of the picture then. Holits is unemployed. It's not my affair, and I feel sorry if that's the case—it is, it turns out—but as we stop in front of the unit, I have to say something. "If you decide, it's first month, last month, and one-fifty as security deposit." I look down at the pool as I say it. Some people are sitting in deck chairs, and there's somebody in the water.

Holits wipes his face with the back of his hand. Harley's mower is clacking away. Farther off, cars speed by on Calle Verde. The two boys have got out of the station wagon. One of them is standing at military attention, legs together, arms at his sides. But as I watch, I see him begin to flap his arms up and down and jump, like he intends to take off and fly. The other one is squatting down on the driver's side of the station wagon, doing knee bends.

I turn to Holits.

"Let's have a look," he says.

I turn the key and the door opens. It's just a little two-bedroom furnished apartment. Everybody has seen dozens. Holits stops in the bathroom long enough to flush the toilet. He watches till the tank fills. Later, he says, "This could be our room." He's talking about the bedroom that looks out over the pool. In the kitchen, the woman takes hold of the edge of the drainboard and stares out the window.

"That's the swimming pool," I say.

She nods. "We stayed in some motels that had swimming pools. But in one pool they had too much chlorine in the water."

I wait for her to go on. But that's all she says. I can't think of anything else, either.

"I guess we won't waste any more time. I guess we'll take it." Holits looks at her as he says it. This time she meets his eyes. She nods. He lets out breath through his teeth. Then she does something. She begins snapping her fingers. One hand is still holding the edge of the drainboard, but with her other hand she begins snapping her fingers. Snap, snap, snap, like she was calling her dog, or else trying to get somebody's attention. Then she stops and runs her nails across the counter.

I don't know what to make of it. Holits doesn't either. He moves his feet.

"We'll walk back to the office and make things official," I say. "I'm glad."

I *was* glad. We had a lot of empty units for this time of year. And these people seemed like dependable people. Down on their luck, that's all. No disgrace can be attached to that.

Holits pays in cash—first, last, and the one-fifty deposit. He counts out bills of fifty-dollar denomination while I watch. U. S. Grants, Harley calls them, though he's never seen many. I write out the receipt and give him two keys. "You're all set."

He looks at the keys. He hands her one. "So, we're in Arizona. Never thought you'd see Arizona, did you?"

She shakes her head. She's touching one of the prayer-plant leaves.

"Needs water," I say.

She lets go of the leaf and turns to the window. I go over next to her. Harley is still cutting grass. But he's around in front now. There's been this talk of farming, so for a minute I think of Harley moving along behind a plow instead of behind his Black and Decker power mower.

I watch them unload their boxes, suitcases, and clothes. Holits carries in something that has straps hanging from it. It takes a minute, but then I figure out it's a bridle. I don't know what to do next. I don't feel like doing anything. So I take the Grants out of the cashbox. I just put them in there, but I take them out again. The bills have come from Minnesota. Who knows where they'll be this time next week? They could be in Las Vegas. All I know about Las Vegas is what I see on TV—about enough to put into a thimble. I can imagine one of the Grants finding its way out to Waikiki Beach, or else some other place. Miami or New York City. New Orleans. I think about one of those bills changing hands during Mardi Gras. They could go anyplace, and anything could happen because of them. I write my name in ink across Grant's broad old forehead: MARGE. I print it. I do it on every one. Right over his thick brows. People will stop in the midst of their spending and wonder. Who's this Marge? That's what they'll ask themselves, Who's this Marge?

Harley comes in from outside and washes his hands in my

sink. He knows it's something I don't like him to do. But he goes ahead and does it anyway.

"Those people from Minnesota," he says. "The Swedes. They're a long way from home." He dries his hands on a paper towel. He wants me to tell him what I know. But I don't know anything. They don't look like Swedes and they don't talk like Swedes.

"They're not Swedes," I tell him. But he acts like he doesn't hear me.

"So what's he do?"

"He's a farmer."

"What do you know about that?"

Harley takes his hat off and puts it on my chair. He runs a hand through his hair. Then he looks at the hat and puts it on again. He may as well be glued to it. "There's not much to farm around here. Did you tell him that?" He gets a can of soda pop from the fridge and goes to sit in his recliner. He picks up the remote-control, pushes something, and the TV sizzles on. He pushes some more buttons until he finds what he's looking for. It's a hospital show. "What else does the Swede do? Besides farm?"

I don't know, so I don't say anything. But Harley's already taken up with his program. He's probably forgotten he asked me the question. A siren goes off. I hear the screech of tires. On the screen, an ambulance has come to a stop in front of an emergency-room entrance, its red lights flashing. A man jumps out and runs around to open up the back.

The next afternoon the boys borrow the hose and wash the station wagon. They clean the outside and the inside. A little later I notice her drive away. She's wearing high heels and a nice dress. Hunting up a job, I'd say. After a while, I see the boys messing around the pool in their bathing suits. One of them springs off the board and swims all the way to the other end underwater. He comes up blowing water and shaking his head. The other boy, the one who'd been doing knee bends the day before, lies on his stomach on a towel at the far side of the pool. But this one boy keeps swimming back and forth from one end of the pool to the other, touching the wall and turning back with a little kick.

There are two other people out there. They're in lounge chairs, one on either side of the pool. One of them is Irving Cobb, a cook at Denny's. He calls himself Spuds. People have taken to calling him that, Spuds, instead of Irv or some other nickname. Spuds is fifty-five and bald. He already looks like beef jerky, but he wants more sun. Right now, his new wife, Linda Cobb, is at work at the K Mart. Spuds works nights. But him and Linda Cobb have it arranged so they take their Saturdays and Sundays off. Connie Nova is in the other chair. She's sitting up and rubbing lotion on her legs. She's nearly naked— just this little two-piece suit covering her. Connie Nova is a cocktail waitress. She moved in here six months ago with her so-called fiancé, an alcoholic lawyer. But she got rid of him. Now she lives with a long-haired student from the college whose name is Rick. I happen to know he's away right now, visiting his folks. Spuds and Connie are wearing dark glasses. Connie's portable radio is going.

Spuds was a recent widower when he moved in, a year or so back. But after a few months of being a bachelor again, he got married to Linda. She's a red-haired woman in her thirties. I don't know how they met. But one night a couple of months ago Spuds and the new Mrs. Cobb had Harley and me over to a nice dinner that Spuds fixed. After dinner, we sat in their living room drinking sweet drinks out of big glasses. Spuds asked if we wanted to see home movies. We said sure. So Spuds set up his screen and his projector. Linda Cobb poured us more of that sweet drink. Where's the harm? I asked myself. Spuds began to show films of a trip he and his dead wife had made to Alaska. It began with her getting on the plane in Seattle. Spuds talked as he ran the projector. The deceased was in her fifties, good-looking, though maybe a little heavy. Her hair was nice.

"That's Spuds's first wife," Linda Cobb said. "That's the first Mrs. Cobb."

"That's Evelyn," Spuds said.

The first wife stayed on the screen for a long time. It was funny seeing her and hearing them talk about her like that. Harley passed me a look, so I know he was thinking something, too. Linda Cobb asked if we wanted another drink or a macaroon. We didn't. Spuds was saying something about the first Mrs. Cobb again. She was still at the entrance to the plane, smiling and moving her mouth even if all you could hear was the film going through the projector. People had to go around her to get on the plane. She kept waving at the camera, waving at us there in Spuds's living room. She waved and waved. "There's Evelyn again," the new Mrs. Cobb would say each time the first Mrs. Cobb appeared on the screen.

Spuds would have shown films all night, but we said we had to go. Harley made the excuse.

I don't remember what he said.

Connie Nova is lying on her back in the chair, dark glasses covering half of her face. Her legs and stomach shine with oil. One night, not long after she moved in, she had a party. This was before she kicked the lawyer out and took up with the long-hair. She called her party a housewarming. Harley and I were invited, along with a bunch of other people. We went, but we didn't care for the company. We found a place to sit close to the door, and that's where we stayed till we left. It wasn't all that long, either. Connie's boyfriend was giving a door prize. It was the offer of his legal services, without charge, for the handling of a divorce. Anybody's divorce. Anybody who wanted to could draw a card out of the bowl he was passing around. When the bowl came our way, everybody began to laugh. Harley and I swapped glances. I didn't draw. Harley didn't draw, either. But I saw him look in the bowl at the pile of cards. Then he shook his head and handed the bowl to the person next to him. Even Spuds and the new Mrs. Cobb drew cards. The winning card had something written across the back. "Entitles bearer to one free uncontested divorce," and the lawyer's signature and the date. The lawyer was a drunk, but I say this is no way to conduct your life. Everybody but us had put his hand into the bowl, like it was a fun thing to do. The woman who drew the winning card clapped. It was like one of those game shows. "Goddamn, this is the first time I ever won anything!" I was told she had a husband in the military. There's no way of knowing if she still has him, or if she got her divorce, because Connie Nova took up with a different set of friends after she and the lawyer went their separate ways.

We left the party right after the drawing. It made such an impression we couldn't say much, except one of us said, "I don't believe I saw what I think I saw."

Maybe I said it.

A week later Harley asks if the Swede—he means Holits—has found work yet. We've just had lunch, and Harley's in his chair with his can of pop. But he hasn't turned his TV on. I say I don't know. And I don't. I wait to see what else he has to say. But he doesn't say anything else. He shakes his head. He seems to think about something. Then he pushes a button and the TV comes to life.

She finds a job. She starts working as a waitress in an Italian restaurant a few blocks from here. She works a split shift, doing lunches and then going home, then back to work again in time for the dinner shift. She's meeting herself coming and going. The boys swim all day, while Holits stays inside the apartment. I don't know what he does in there. Once, I did her hair and she told me a few things. She told me she did waitressing when she was just out of high school and that's where she met Holits. She served him some pancakes in a place back in Minnesota.

She'd walked down that morning and asked me could I do her a favor. She wanted me to fix her hair after her lunch shift and have her out in time for her dinner shift. Could I do it? I told her I'd check the book. I asked her to step inside. It must have been a hundred degrees already.

"I know it's short notice," she said. "But when I came in from work last night, I looked in the mirror and saw my roots showing. I said to myself, 'I need a treatment.' I don't know where else to go."

I find Friday, August 14. There's nothing on the page.

"I could work you in at two-thirty, or else at three o'clock," I say.

"Three would be better," she says. "I have to run for it now before I'm late. I work for a real bastard. See you later."

At two-thirty, I tell Harley I have a customer, so he'll have to take his baseball game into the bedroom. He grumps, but he winds up the cord and wheels the set out back. He closes the door. I make sure everything I need is ready. I fix up the magazines so they're easy to get to. Then I sit next to the dryer and file my nails. I'm wearing the rose-colored uniform that I put on when I do hair. I go on filing my nails and looking up at the window from time to time.

She walks by the window and then pushes the doorbell. "Come on in," I call. "It's unlocked."

She's wearing the black-and-white uniform from her job. I can see how we're both wearing uniforms. "Sit down, honey, and we'll get started." She looks at the nail file. "I give manicures, too," I say.

She settles into the chair and draws a breath.

I say, "Put your head back. That's it. Close your eyes now, why don't you? Just relax. First I'll shampoo you and touch up these roots here. Then we'll go from there. How much time do you have?"

"I have to be back there at five-thirty."

"We'll get you fixed up."

"I can eat at work. But I don't know what Holits and the boys will do for their supper."

"They'll get along fine without you."

I start the warm water and then notice Harley's left me some dirt and grass. I wipe up his mess and start over.

I say, "If they want, they can just walk down the street to the hamburger place. It won't hurt them."

"They won't do that. Anyway, I don't want them to have to go there."

It's none of my business, so I don't say any more. I make up a nice lather and go to work. After I've done the shampoo, rinse, and set, I put her under the dryer. Her eyes have closed. I think she could be asleep. So I take one of her hands and begin.

"No manicure." She opens her eyes and pulls away her hand.

"It's all right, honey. The first manicure is always no charge."

She gives me back her hand and picks up one of the magazines and rests it in her lap. "They're his boys," she says. "From his first marriage. He was divorced when we met. But I love them like they were my own. I couldn't love them any more if I tried. Not even if I was their natural mother."

I turn the dryer down a notch so that it's making a low, quiet sound. I keep on with her nails. Her hand starts to relax.

"She lit out on them, on Holits and the boys, on New Year's

Day ten years ago. They never heard from her again." I can see she wants to tell me about it. And that's fine with me. They like to talk when they're in the chair. I go on using the file. "Holits got the divorce. Then he and I started going out. Then we got married. For a long time, we had us a life. It had its ups and downs. But we thought we were working toward something." She shakes her head. "But something happened. Something happened to Holits, I mean. One thing happened was he got interested in horses. This one particular race horse, he bought it, you know—something down, something each month. He took it around to the tracks. He was still up before daylight, like always, still doing the chores and such. I thought everything was all right. But I don't know anything. If you want the truth, I'm not so good at waiting tables. I think those wops would fire me at the drop of a hat, if I gave them a reason. Or for no reason. What if I got fired? Then what?"

I say, "Don't worry, honey. They're not going to fire you."

Pretty soon she picks up another magazine. But she doesn't open it. She just holds it and goes on talking. "Anyway, there's this horse of his. Fast Betty. The Betty part is a joke. But he says it can't help but be a winner if he names it after me. A big winner, all right. The fact is, wherever it ran, it lost. Every race. Betty Longshot—that's what it should have been called. In the beginning, I went to a few races. But the horse always ran ninety-nine to one. Odds like that. But Holits is stubborn if he's anything. He wouldn't give up. He'd bet on the horse and bet on the horse. Twenty dollars to win. Fifty dollars to win. Plus all the other things it costs for keeping a horse. I know it don't sound like a large amount. But it adds up. And when the odds were like that—ninety-nine to one, you know —sometimes he'd buy a combination ticket. He'd ask me if I realized how much money we'd make if the horse came in. But it didn't, and I quit going."

I keep on with what I'm doing. I concentrate on her nails. "You have nice cuticles," I say. "Look here at your cuticles. See these little half-moons? Means your blood's good."

She brings her hand up close and looks. "What do you know about that?" She shrugs. She lets me take her hand again. She's still got things to tell. "Once, when I was in high school, a counselor asked me to come to her office. She did it with all the girls, one of us at a time. 'What dreams do you have?' this woman asked me. 'What do you see yourself doing in ten years? Twenty years?' I was sixteen or seventeen. I was just a kid. I couldn't think what to answer. I just sat there like a lump. This counselor was about the age I am now. I thought she was *old*. She's old, I said to myself. I knew *her* life was half over. And I felt like I knew something she didn't. Something she'd never know. A secret. Something nobody's supposed to know, or ever talk about. So I stayed quiet. I just shook my head. She must've written me off as a dope. But I couldn't say anything. You know what I mean? I thought I knew things she couldn't guess at. Now, if anybody asked me that question again, about my dreams and all, I'd tell them."

"What would you tell them, honey?" I have her other hand now. But I'm not doing her nails. I'm just holding it, waiting to hear.

She moves forward in the chair. She tries to take her hand back.

"What would you tell them?"

She sighs and leans back. She lets me keep the hand. "I'd say, 'Dreams, you know, are what you wake up from.' That's what I'd say." She smooths the lap of her skirt. "If anybody asked, that's what I'd say. But they won't ask." She lets out her breath again. "So how much longer?" she says.

"Not long," I say.

"You don't know what it's like."

"Yes, I do," I say. I pull the stool right up next to her legs. I'm starting to tell how it was before we moved here, and how it's still like that. But Harley picks right then to come out of the bedroom. He doesn't look at us. I hear the TV jabbering away in the bedroom. He goes to the sink and draws a glass of water. He tips his head back to drink. His Adam's apple moves up and down in his throat.

I move the dryer away and touch the hair at both sides of her head. I lift one of the curls just a little.

I say, "You look brand-new, honey."

"Don't I wish."

The boys keep on swimming all day, every day, till their school starts. Betty keeps on at her job. But for some reason she doesn't come back to get her hair done. I don't know why this is. Maybe she doesn't think I did a good job. Sometimes I lie awake, Harley sleeping like a grindstone beside me, and try to picture myself in Betty's shoes. I wonder what I'd do then.

Holits sends one of his sons with the rent on the first of September, and on the first of October, too. He still pays in cash. I take the money from the boy, count the bills right there in front of him, and then write out the receipt. Holits has found work of some sort. I think so, anyway. He drives off every day with the station wagon. I see him leave early in the morning and drive back late in the afternoon. She goes past the window at ten-thirty and comes back at three. If she sees me, she gives me a little wave. But she's not smiling. Then I see Betty again at five, walking back to the restaurant. Holits drives in a little later. This goes on till the middle of October.

Meanwhile, the Holits couple acquainted themselves with Connie Nova and her long-hair friend, Rick. And they also met up with Spuds and the new Mrs. Cobb. Sometimes, on a Sunday afternoon, I'd see all of them sitting around the pool, drinks in their hands, listening to Connie's portable radio. One time Harley said he saw them all behind the building, in the barbecue area. They were in their bathing suits then, too. Harley said the Swede had a chest like a bull. Harley said they were eating hot dogs and drinking whiskey. He said they were drunk.

It was Saturday, and it was after eleven at night. Harley was asleep in his chair. Pretty soon I'd have to get up and turn off the set. When I did that, I knew he'd wake up. "Why'd you turn it off? I was watching that show." That's what he'd say. That's what he always said. Anyway, the TV was going, I had the curlers in, and there's a magazine on my lap. Now and then I'd look up. But I couldn't get settled on the show. They were all out there in the pool area—Spuds and Linda Cobb, Connie Nova and the long-hair, Holits and Betty. We have a rule against anyone being out there after ten. But this night they didn't care about rules. If Harley woke up, he'd go out and say something. I felt it was all right for them to have their fun, but it was time for it to stop. I kept getting up and going over to the window. All of them except Betty had on bathing suits.

She was still in her uniform. But she had her shoes off, a glass in her hand, and she was drinking right along with the rest of them. I kept putting off having to turn off the set. Then one of them shouted something, and another one took it up and began to laugh. I looked and saw Holits finish off his drink. He put the glass down on the deck. Then he walked over to the cabana. He dragged up one of the tables and climbed onto that. Then—he seemed to do it without any effort at all—he lifted up onto the roof of the cabana. It's true, I thought; he's strong. The long-hair claps his hands, like he's all for this. The rest of them are hooting Holits on, too. I know I'm going to have to go out there and put a stop to it.

Harley's slumped in his chair. The TV's still going. I ease the door open, step out, and then push it shut behind me. Holits is up on the roof of the cabana. They're egging him on. They're saying, "Go on, you can do it." "Don't belly-flop, now." "I double-dare you." Things like that.

Then I hear Betty's voice. "Holits, think what you're doing." But Holits just stands there at the edge. He looks down at the water. He seems to be figuring how much of a run he's going to have to make to get out there. He backs up to the far side. He spits in his palm and rubs his hands together. Spuds calls out, "That's it, boy! You'll do it now."

I see him hit the deck. I hear him, too.

"Holits!" Betty cries.

They all hurry over to him. By the time I get there, he's sitting up. Rick is holding him by the shoulders and yelling into his face. "Holits! Hey, man!"

Holits has this gash on his forehead, and his eyes are glassy. Spuds and Rick help him into a chair. Somebody gives him a towel. But Holits holds the towel like he doesn't know what he's supposed to do with it. Somebody else hands him a drink. But Holits doesn't know what to do with that, either. People keep saying things to him. Holits brings the towel up to his face. Then he takes it away and looks at the blood. But he just looks at it. He can't seem to understand anything.

"Let me see him." I get around in front of him. It's bad. "Holits, are you all right?" But Holits just looks at me, and then his eyes drift off. "I think he'd best go to the emergency room." Betty looks at me when I say this and begins to shake her head. She looks back at Holits. She gives him another towel. I think she's sober. But the rest of them are drunk. Drunk is the best that can be said for them.

Spuds picks up what I said. "Let's take him to the emergency room."

Rick says, "I'll go, too."

"We'll all go," Connie Nova says.

"We better stick together," Linda Cobb says.

"Holits." I say his name again.

"I can't go it," Holits says.

"What'd he say?" Connie Nova asks me.

"He said he can't go it," I tell her.

"Go what? What's he talking about?" Rick wants to know.

"Say again?" Spuds says. "I didn't hear."

"He says he can't go it. I don't think he knows what he's talking about. You'd best take him to the hospital," I say. Then I remember Harley and the rules. "You shouldn't have been out here. Any of you. We have rules. Now go on and take him to the hospital."

"Let's take him to the hospital," Spuds says like it's something he's just thought of. He might be farther gone than any of them. For one thing, he can't stand still. He weaves. And he keeps picking up his feet and putting them down again. The hair on his chest is snow white under the overhead pool lights.

"I'll get the car." That's what the long-hair says. "Connie, let me have the keys."

"I can't go it," Holits says. The towel has moved down to his chin. But the cut is on his forehead.

"Get him that terry-cloth robe. He can't go to the hospital that way." Linda Cobb says that. "Holits! Holits, it's us." She waits and then she takes the glass of whiskey from Holits's fingers and drinks from it.

I can see people at some of the windows, looking down on the commotion. Lights are going on. "Go to bed!" someone yells.

Finally, the long-hair brings Connie's Datsun from behind the building and drives it up close to the pool. The headlights are on bright. He races the engine.

"For Christ's sake, go to bed!" the same person yells. More people come to their windows. I expect to see Harley come out any minute, wearing his hat, steaming. Then I think, No, he'll sleep through it. Just forget Harley.

Spuds and Connie Nova get on either side of Holits. Holits can't walk straight. He's wobbly. Part of it's because he's drunk. But there's no question he's hurt himself. They get him into the car, and they all crowd inside, too. Betty is the last to get in. She has to sit on somebody's lap. Then they drive off. Whoever it was that has been yelling slams the window shut.

The whole next week Holits doesn't leave the place. And I think Betty must have quit her job, because I don't see her pass the window anymore. When I see the boys go by, I step outside and ask them, point-blank: "How's your dad?"

"He hurt his head," one of them says.

I wait in hopes they'll say some more. But they don't. They shrug and go on to school with their lunch sacks and binders. Later, I was sorry I hadn't asked after their step-mom.

When I see Holits outside, wearing a bandage and standing on his balcony, he doesn't even nod. He acts like I'm a stranger. It's like he doesn't know me or doesn't want to know me. Harley says he's getting the same treatment. He doesn't like it. "What's with him?" Harley wants to know. "Damn Swede. What happened to his head? Somebody belt him or what?" I don't tell Harley anything when he says that. I don't go into it at all.

Then that Sunday afternoon I see one of the boys carry out a box and put it in the station wagon. He goes back upstairs. But pretty soon he comes back down with another box, and he puts that in, too. It's then I know they're making ready to leave. But I don't say what I know to Harley. He'll know everything soon enough.

Next morning, Betty sends one of the boys down. He's got a note that says she's sorry but they have to move. She gives me her sister's address in Indio where she says we can send the deposit to. She points out they're leaving eight days before their rent is up. She hopes there might be something in the way of a refund there, even though they haven't given the thirty days' notice. She says, "Thanks for everything. Thanks for doing my hair that time." She signs the note, "Sincerely, Betty Holits."

"What's your name?" I ask the boy.

"Billy."

"Billy, tell her I said I'm real sorry."

Harley reads what she's written, and he says it will be a cold day in hell before they see any money back from Fulton Terrace. He says he can't understand these people. "People who sail through life like the world owes them a living." He asks me where they're going. But I don't have any idea where they're going. Maybe they're going back to Minnesota. How do I know where they're going? But I don't think they're going back to Minnesota. I think they're going someplace else to try their luck.

Connie Nova and Spuds have their chairs in the usual places, one on either side of the pool. From time to time, they look over at the Holits boys carrying things out to the station wagon. Then Holits himself comes out with some clothes over his arm. Connie Nova and Spuds holler and wave. Holits looks at them like he doesn't know them. But then he raises up his free hand. Just raises it, that's all. They wave. Then Holits is waving. He keeps waving at them, even after they've stopped. Betty comes downstairs and touches his arm. She doesn't wave. She won't even look at these people. She says something to Holits, and he goes on to the car. Connie Nova lies back in her chair and reaches over to turn up her portable radio. Spuds holds his sunglasses and watches Holits and Betty for a while. Then he fixes the glasses over his ears. He settles himself in the lounge chair and goes back to tanning his leathery old self.

Finally, they're all loaded and ready to move on. The boys are in the back, Holits behind the wheel, Betty in the seat right up next to him. It's just like it was when they drove in here.

"What are you looking at?" Harley says.

He's taking a break. He's in his chair, watching the TV. But he gets up and comes over to the window.

"Well, there they go. They don't know where they're going or what they're going to do. Crazy Swede."

I watch them drive out of the lot and turn onto the road that's going to take them to the freeway. Then I look at Harley again. He's settling into his chair. He has his can of pop, and he's wearing his straw hat. He acts like nothing has happened or ever will happen.

"Harley?"

But, of course, he can't hear me. I go over and stand in front of his chair. He's surprised. He doesn't know what to make of it. He leans back, just sits there looking at me.

The phone starts ringing.

"Get that, will you?" he says.

I don't answer him. Why should I?

"Then let it ring," he says.

I go find the mop, some rags, S.O.S. pads, and a bucket. The phone stops ringing. He's still sitting in his chair. But he's turned off the TV. I take the passkey, go outside and up the stairs to 17. I let myself in and walk through the living room to their kitchen—what used to be their kitchen.

The counters have been wiped down, the sink and cupboards are clean. It's not so bad. I leave the cleaning things on the stove and go take a look at the bathroom. Nothing there a little steel wool won't take care of. Then I open the door to the bedroom that looks out over the pool. The blinds are raised, the bed is stripped. The floor shines. "Thanks," I say out loud. Wherever she's going, I wish her luck. "Good luck, Betty." One of the bureau drawers is open and I go to close it. Back in a corner of the drawer I see the bridle he was carrying in when he first came. It must have been passed over in their hurry. But maybe it wasn't. Maybe the man left it on purpose.

"Bridle," I say. I hold it up to the window and look at it in the light. It's not fancy, it's just an old dark leather bridle. I don't know much about them. But I know that one part of it fits in the mouth. That part's called the bit. It's made of steel. Reins go over the head and up to where they're held on the neck between the fingers. The rider pulls the reins this way and that, and the horse turns. It's simple. The bit's heavy and cold. If you had to wear this thing between your teeth, I guess you'd catch on in a hurry. When you felt it pull, you'd know it was time. You'd know you were going somewhere.

Cathedral

THIS blind man, an old friend of my wife's, he was on his way to spend the night. His wife had died. So he was visiting the dead wife's relatives in Connecticut. He called my wife from his in-laws'. Arrangements were made. He would come by train, a five-hour trip, and my wife would meet him at the station. She hadn't seen him since she worked for him one summer in Seattle ten years ago. But she and the blind man had kept in touch. They made tapes and mailed them back and forth. I wasn't enthusiastic about his visit. He was no one I knew. And his being blind bothered me. My idea of blindness came from the movies. In the movies, the blind moved slowly and never laughed. Sometimes they were led by seeing-eye dogs. A blind man in my house was not something I looked forward to.

That summer in Seattle she had needed a job. She didn't have any money. The man she was going to marry at the end of the summer was in officers' training school. He didn't have any money, either. But she was in love with the guy, and he was in love with her, etc. She'd seen something in the paper: HELP WANTED—*Reading to Blind Man*, and a telephone number. She phoned and went over, was hired on the spot. She'd worked with this blind man all summer. She read stuff to him, case studies, reports, that sort of thing. She helped him organize his little office in the county social-service department. They'd become good friends, my wife and the blind man. How do I know these things? She told me. And she told me something else. On her last day in the office, the blind man asked if he could touch her face. She agreed to this. She told me he touched his fingers to every part of her face, her nose— even her neck! She never forgot it. She even tried to write a poem about it. She was always trying to write a poem. She wrote a poem or two every year, usually after something really important had happened to her.

When we first started going out together, she showed me the poem. In the poem, she recalled his fingers and the way they had moved around over her face. In the poem, she talked

514

about what she had felt at the time, about what went through her mind when the blind man touched her nose and lips. I can remember I didn't think much of the poem. Of course, I didn't tell her that. Maybe I just don't understand poetry. I admit it's not the first thing I reach for when I pick up something to read.

Anyway, this man who'd first enjoyed her favors, the officer-to-be, he'd been her childhood sweetheart. So okay. I'm saying that at the end of the summer she let the blind man run his hands over her face, said goodbye to him, married her child-hood etc., who was now a commissioned officer, and she moved away from Seattle. But they'd kept in touch, she and the blind man. She made the first contact after a year or so. She called him up one night from an Air Force base in Al-abama. She wanted to talk. They talked. He asked her to send him a tape and tell him about her life. She did this. She sent the tape. On the tape, she told the blind man about her hus-band and about their life together in the military. She told the blind man she loved her husband but she didn't like it where they lived and she didn't like it that he was a part of the mili-tary-industrial thing. She told the blind man she'd written a poem and he was in it. She told him that she was writing a poem about what it was like to be an Air Force officer's wife. The poem wasn't finished yet. She was still writing it. The blind man made a tape. He sent her the tape. She made a tape. This went on for years. My wife's officer was posted to one base and then another. She sent tapes from Moody AFB, McGuire, McConnell, and finally Travis, near Sacramento, where one night she got to feeling lonely and cut off from people she kept losing in that moving-around life. She got to feeling she couldn't go it another step. She went in and swallowed all the pills and capsules in the medicine chest and washed them down with a bottle of gin. Then she got into a hot bath and passed out.

But instead of dying, she got sick. She threw up. Her officer —why should he have a name? he was the childhood sweet-heart, and what more does he want?—came home from some-where, found her, and called the ambulance. In time, she put it all on a tape and sent the tape to the blind man. Over the years, she put all kinds of stuff on tapes and sent the tapes off lickety-split. Next to writing a poem every year, I think it was her chief means of recreation. On one tape, she told the blind man she'd decided to live away from her officer for a time. On another tape, she told him about her divorce. She and I began going out, and of course she told her blind man about it. She told him everything, or so it seemed to me. Once she asked me if I'd like to hear the latest tape from the blind man. This was a year ago. I was on the tape, she said. So I said okay, I'd listen to it. I got us drinks and we settled down in the living room. We made ready to listen. First she inserted the tape into the player and adjusted a couple of dials. Then she pushed a lever. The tape squeaked and someone began to talk in this loud voice. She lowered the volume. After a few minutes of harmless chitchat, I heard my own name in the mouth of this stranger, this blind man I didn't even know! And then this: "From all you've said about him, I can only conclude—" But we were interrupted, a knock at the door, something, and we didn't ever get back to the tape. Maybe it was just as well. I'd heard all I wanted to.

Now this same blind man was coming to sleep in my house.

"Maybe I could take him bowling," I said to my wife. She was at the draining board doing scalloped potatoes. She put down the knife she was using and turned around.

"If you love me," she said, "you can do this for me. If you don't love me, okay. But if you had a friend, any friend, and the friend came to visit, I'd make him feel comfortable." She wiped her hands with the dish towel.

"I don't have any blind friends," I said.

"You don't have *any* friends," she said. "Period. Besides," she said, "goddamn it, his wife's just died! Don't you understand that? The man's lost his wife!"

I didn't answer. She'd told me a little about the blind man's wife. Her name was Beulah. Beulah! That's a name for a colored woman.

"Was his wife a Negro?" I asked.

"Are you crazy?" my wife said. "Have you just flipped or something?" She picked up a potato. I saw it hit the floor, then roll under the stove. "What's wrong with you?" she said. "Are you drunk?"

"I'm just asking," I said.

Right then my wife filled me in with more detail than I cared to know. I made a drink and sat at the kitchen table to listen. Pieces of the story began to fall into place.

Beulah had gone to work for the blind man the summer after my wife had stopped working for him. Pretty soon Beulah and the blind man had themselves a church wedding. It was a little wedding—who'd want to go to such a wedding in the first place?—just the two of them, plus the minister and the minister's wife. But it was a church wedding just the same. It was what Beulah had wanted, he'd said. But even then Beulah must have been carrying the cancer in her glands. After they had been inseparable for eight years—my wife's word, *inseparable* —Beulah's health went into a rapid decline. She died in a Seattle hospital room, the blind man sitting beside the bed and holding on to her hand. They'd married, lived and worked together, slept together—had sex, sure—and then the blind man had to bury her. All this without his having ever seen what the god-damned woman looked like. It was beyond my understanding. Hearing this, I felt sorry for the blind man for a little bit. And then I found myself thinking what a pitiful life this woman must have led. Imagine a woman who could never see herself as she was seen in the eyes of her loved one. A woman who could go on day after day and never receive the smallest compliment from her beloved. A woman whose husband could never read the expression on her face, be it misery or something better. Someone who could wear makeup or not—what difference to him? She could, if she wanted, wear green eyeshadow around one eye, a straight pin in her nostril, yellow slacks and purple shoes, no matter. And then to slip off into death, the blind man's hand on her hand, his blind eyes streaming tears—I'm imagining now—her last thought maybe this: that he never even knew what she looked like, and she on an express to the grave. Robert was left with a small insurance policy and half of a twenty-peso Mexican coin. The other half of the coin went into the box with her. Pathetic.

So when the time rolled around, my wife went to the depot to pick him up. With nothing to do but wait—sure, I blamed him for that—I was having a drink and watching the TV when I heard the car pull into the drive. I got up from the sofa with my drink and went to the window to have a look.

I saw my wife laughing as she parked the car. I saw her get out of the car and shut the door. She was still wearing a smile. Just amazing. She went around to the other side of the car to where the blind man was already starting to get out. This blind man, feature this, he was wearing a full beard! A beard on a blind man! Too much, I say. The blind man reached into the back seat and dragged out a suitcase. My wife took his arm, shut the car door, and, talking all the way, moved him down the drive and then up the steps to the front porch. I turned off the TV. I finished my drink, rinsed the glass, dried my hands. Then I went to the door.

My wife said, "I want you to meet Robert. Robert, this is my husband. I've told you all about him." She was beaming. She had this blind man by his coat sleeve.

The blind man let go of his suitcase and up came his hand.

I took it. He squeezed hard, held my hand, and then he let it go.

"I feel like we've already met," he boomed.

"Likewise," I said. I didn't know what else to say. Then I said, "Welcome. I've heard a lot about you." We began to move then, a little group, from the porch into the living room, my wife guiding him by the arm. The blind man was carrying his suitcase in his other hand. My wife said things like, "To your left here, Robert. That's right. Now watch it, there's a chair. That's it. Sit down right here. This is the sofa. We just bought this sofa two weeks ago."

I started to say something about the old sofa. I'd liked that old sofa. But I didn't say anything. Then I wanted to say something else, small-talk, about the scenic ride along the Hudson. How going *to* New York, you should sit on the right-hand side of the train, and coming *from* New York, the left-hand side.

"Did you have a good train ride?" I said. "Which side of the train did you sit on, by the way?"

"What a question, which side!" my wife said. "What's it matter which side?" she said.

"I just asked," I said.

"Right side," the blind man said. "I hadn't been on a train in nearly forty years. Not since I was a kid. With my folks. That's been a long time. I'd nearly forgotten the sensation. I have winter in my beard now," he said. "So I've been told, anyway. Do I look distinguished, my dear?" the blind man said to my wife.

"You look distinguished, Robert," she said. "Robert," she said. "Robert, it's just so good to see you."

My wife finally took her eyes off the blind man and looked at me. I had the feeling she didn't like what she saw. I shrugged.

I've never met, or personally known, anyone who was blind. This blind man was late forties, a heavy-set, balding man with stooped shoulders, as if he carried a great weight there. He wore brown slacks, brown shoes, a light-brown shirt, a tie, a sports coat. Spiffy. He also had this full beard. But he didn't use a cane and he didn't wear dark glasses. I'd always thought dark glasses were a must for the blind. Fact was, I wished he had a pair. At first glance, his eyes looked like anyone else's eyes. But if you looked close, there was something different about them. Too much white in the iris, for one thing, and the pupils seemed to move around in the sockets without his knowing it or being able to stop it. Creepy. As I stared at his face, I saw the left pupil turn in toward his nose while the other made an effort to keep in one place. But it was only an effort, for that eye was on the roam without his knowing it or wanting it to be.

I said, "Let me get you a drink. What's your pleasure? We have a little of everything. It's one of our pastimes."

"Bub, I'm a Scotch man myself," he said fast enough in this big voice.

"Right," I said. Bub! "Sure you are. I knew it."

He let his fingers touch his suitcase, which was sitting alongside the sofa. He was taking his bearings. I didn't blame him for that.

"I'll move that up to your room," my wife said.

"No, that's fine," the blind man said loudly. "It can go up when I go up."

"A little water with the Scotch?" I said.

"Very little," he said.

"I knew it," I said.

He said, "Just a tad. The Irish actor, Barry Fitzgerald? I'm like that fellow. When I drink water, Fitzgerald said, I drink water. When I drink whiskey, I drink whiskey." My wife laughed. The blind man brought his hand up under his beard. He lifted his beard slowly and let it drop.

I did the drinks, three big glasses of Scotch with a splash of water in each. Then we made ourselves comfortable and talked about Robert's travels. First the long flight from the West Coast to Connecticut, we covered that. Then from Connecticut up here by train. We had another drink concerning that leg of the trip.

I remembered having read somewhere that the blind didn't smoke because, as speculation had it, they couldn't see the smoke they exhaled. I thought I knew that much and that much only about blind people. But this blind man smoked his cigarette down to the nubbin and then lit another one. This blind man filled his ashtray and my wife emptied it.

When we sat down at the table for dinner, we had another drink. My wife heaped Robert's plate with cube steak, scalloped potatoes, green beans. I buttered him up two slices of bread. I said, "Here's bread and butter for you." I swallowed some of my drink. "Now let us pray," I said, and the blind man lowered his head. My wife looked at me, her mouth agape. "Pray the phone won't ring and the food doesn't get cold," I said.

We dug in. We ate everything there was to eat on the table. We ate like there was no tomorrow. We didn't talk. We ate. We scarfed. We grazed that table. We were into serious eating. The blind man had right away located his foods, he knew just where everything was on his plate. I watched with admiration as he used his knife and fork on the meat. He'd cut two pieces of meat, fork the meat into his mouth, and then go all out for the scalloped potatoes, the beans next, and then he'd tear off a hunk of buttered bread and eat that. He'd follow this up with a big drink of milk. It didn't seem to bother him to use his fingers once in a while, either.

We finished everything, including half a strawberry pie. For a few moments, we sat as if stunned. Sweat beaded on our faces. Finally, we got up from the table and left the dirty plates. We didn't look back. We took ourselves into the living room and sank into our places again. Robert and my wife sat on the sofa. I took the big chair. We had us two or three more drinks while they talked about the major things that had come to pass

for them in the past ten years. For the most part, I just listened. Now and then I joined in. I didn't want him to think
I'd left the room, and I didn't want her to think I was feeling
left out. They talked of things that had happened to them—to
them!—these past ten years. I waited in vain to hear my name
on my wife's sweet lips: "And then my dear husband came into
my life"—something like that. But I heard nothing of the sort.
More talk of Robert. Robert had done a little of everything, it
seemed, a regular blind jack-of-all-trades. But most recently he
and his wife had had an Amway distributorship, from which, I
gathered, they'd earned their living, such as it was. The blind
man was also a ham radio operator. He talked in his loud voice
about conversations he'd had with fellow operators in Guam,
in the Philippines, in Alaska, and even in Tahiti. He said he'd
have a lot of friends there if he ever wanted to go visit those
places. From time to time, he'd turn his blind face toward me,
put his hand under his beard, ask me something. How long
had I been in my present position? (Three years.) Did I like my
work? (I didn't.) Was I going to stay with it? (What were the
options?) Finally, when I thought he was beginning to run
down, I got up and turned on the TV.

My wife looked at me with irritation. She was heading
toward a boil. Then she looked at the blind man and said,
"Robert, do you have a TV?"

The blind man said, "My dear, I have two TVs. I have a
color set and a black-and-white thing, an old relic. It's funny,
but if I turn the TV on, and I'm always turning it on, I turn on
the color set. It's funny, don't you think?"

I didn't know what to say to that. I had absolutely nothing
to say to that. No opinion. So I watched the news program
and tried to listen to what the announcer was saying.

"This is a color TV," the blind man said. "Don't ask me
how, but I can tell."

"We traded up a while ago," I said.

The blind man had another taste of his drink. He lifted his
beard, sniffed it, and let it fall. He leaned forward on the sofa.
He positioned his ashtray on the coffee table, then put the
lighter to his cigarette. He leaned back on the sofa and crossed
his legs at the ankles.

My wife covered her mouth, and then she yawned. She

stretched. She said, "I think I'll go upstairs and put on my robe. I think I'll change into something else. Robert, you make yourself comfortable," she said.

"I'm comfortable," the blind man said.

"I want you to feel comfortable in this house," she said.

"I am comfortable," the blind man said.

After she'd left the room, he and I listened to the weather report and then to the sports roundup. By that time, she'd been gone so long I didn't know if she was going to come back. I thought she might have gone to bed. I wished she'd come back downstairs. I didn't want to be left alone with a blind man. I asked him if he wanted another drink, and he said sure. Then I asked if he wanted to smoke some dope with me. I said I'd just rolled a number. I hadn't, but I planned to do so in about two shakes.

"I'll try some with you," he said.

"Damn right," I said. "That's the stuff."

I got our drinks and sat down on the sofa with him. Then I rolled us two fat numbers. I lit one and passed it. I brought it to his fingers. He took it and inhaled.

"Hold it as long as you can," I said. I could tell he didn't know the first thing.

My wife came back downstairs wearing her pink robe and her pink slippers.

"What do I smell?" she said.

"We thought we'd have us some cannabis," I said.

My wife gave me a savage look. Then she looked at the blind man and said, "Robert, I didn't know you smoked."

He said, "I do now, my dear. There's a first time for everything. But I don't feel anything yet."

"This stuff is pretty mellow," I said. "This stuff is mild. It's dope you can reason with," I said. "It doesn't mess you up."

"Not much it doesn't, bub," he said, and laughed.

My wife sat on the sofa between the blind man and me. I passed her the number. She took it and toked and then passed it back to me. "Which way is this going?" she said. Then she said, "I shouldn't be smoking this. I can hardly keep my eyes open as it is. That dinner did me in. I shouldn't have eaten so much."

"It was the strawberry pie," the blind man said. "That's what did it," he said, and he laughed his big laugh. Then he shook his head.

"There's more strawberry pie," I said.

"Do you want some more, Robert?" my wife said.

"Maybe in a little while," he said.

We gave our attention to the TV. My wife yawned again. She said, "Your bed is made up when you feel like going to bed, Robert. I know you must have had a long day. When you're ready to go to bed, say so." She pulled his arm. "Robert?"

He came to and said, "I've had a real nice time. This beats tapes, doesn't it?"

I said, "Coming at you," and I put the number between his fingers. He inhaled, held the smoke, and then let it go. It was like he'd been doing it since he was nine years old.

"Thanks, bub," he said. "But I think this is all for me. I think I'm beginning to feel it," he said. He held the burning roach out for my wife.

"Same here," she said. "Ditto. Me, too." She took the roach and passed it to me. "I may just sit here for a while between you two guys with my eyes closed. But don't let me bother you, okay? Either one of you. If it bothers you, say so. Otherwise, I may just sit here with my eyes closed until you're ready to go to bed," she said. "Your bed's made up, Robert, when you're ready. It's right next to our room at the top of the stairs. We'll show you up when you're ready. You wake me up now, you guys, if I fall asleep." She said that and then she closed her eyes and went to sleep.

The news program ended. I got up and changed the channel. I sat back down on the sofa. I wished my wife hadn't pooped out. Her head lay across the back of the sofa, her mouth open. She'd turned so that her robe had slipped away from her legs, exposing a juicy thigh. I reached to draw her robe back over her, and it was then that I glanced at the blind man. What the hell! I flipped the robe open again.

"You say when you want some strawberry pie," I said.

"I will," he said.

I said, "Are you tired? Do you want me to take you up to your bed? Are you ready to hit the hay?"

"Not yet," he said. "No, I'll stay up with you, bub. If that's all right. I'll stay up until you're ready to turn in. We haven't had a chance to talk. Know what I mean? I feel like me and her monopolized the evening." He lifted his beard and he let it fall. He picked up his cigarettes and his lighter.

"That's all right," I said. Then I said, "I'm glad for the company."

And I guess I was. Every night I smoked dope and stayed up as long as I could before I fell asleep. My wife and I hardly ever went to bed at the same time. When I did go to sleep, I had these dreams. Sometimes I'd wake up from one of them, my heart going crazy.

Something about the church and the Middle Ages was on the TV. Not your run-of-the-mill TV fare. I wanted to watch something else. I turned to the other channels. But there was nothing on them, either. So I turned back to the first channel and apologized.

"Bub, it's all right," the blind man said. "It's fine with me. Whatever you want to watch is okay. I'm always learning something. Learning never ends. It won't hurt me to learn something tonight. I got ears," he said.

We didn't say anything for a time. He was leaning forward with his head turned at me, his right ear aimed in the direction of the set. Very disconcerting. Now and then his eyelids drooped and then they snapped open again. Now and then he put his fingers into his beard and tugged, like he was thinking about something he was hearing on the television.

On the screen, a group of men wearing cowls was being set upon and tormented by men dressed in skeleton costumes and men dressed as devils. The men dressed as devils wore devil masks, horns, and long tails. This pageant was part of a procession. The Englishman who was narrating the thing said it took place in Spain once a year. I tried to explain to the blind man what was happening.

"Skeletons," he said. "I know about skeletons," he said, and he nodded.

The TV showed this one cathedral. Then there was a long, slow look at another one. Finally, the picture switched to the famous one in Paris, with its flying buttresses and its spires reaching up to the clouds. The camera pulled away to show the whole of the cathedral rising above the skyline.

There were times when the Englishman who was telling the thing would shut up, would simply let the camera move around over the cathedrals. Or else the camera would tour the countryside, men in fields walking behind oxen. I waited as long as I could. Then I felt I had to say something. I said, "They're showing the outside of this cathedral now. Gargoyles. Little statues carved to look like monsters. Now I guess they're in Italy. Yeah, they're in Italy. There's paintings on the walls of this one church."

"Are those fresco paintings, bub?" he asked, and he sipped from his drink.

I reached for my glass. But it was empty. I tried to remember what I could remember. "You're asking me are those frescoes?" I said. "That's a good question. I don't know."

The camera moved to a cathedral outside Lisbon. The differences in the Portuguese cathedral compared with the French and Italian were not that great. But they were there. Mostly the interior stuff. Then something occurred to me, and I said, "Something has occurred to me. Do you have any idea what a cathedral is? What they look like, that is? Do you follow me? If somebody says cathedral to you, do you have any notion what they're talking about? Do you know the difference between that and a Baptist church, say?"

He let the smoke dribble from his mouth. "I know they took hundreds of workers fifty or a hundred years to build," he said. "I just heard the man say that, of course. I know generations of the same families worked on a cathedral. I heard him say that, too. The men who began their life's work on them, they never lived to see the completion of their work. In that wise, bub, they're no different from the rest of us, right?" He laughed. Then his eyelids drooped again. His head nodded. He seemed to be snoozing. Maybe he was imagining himself in Portugal. The TV was showing another cathedral now. This one was in Germany. The Englishman's voice droned on. "Cathedrals," the blind man said. He sat up and rolled his head back and forth. "If you want the truth, bub, that's about all I know. What I just said. What I heard him say. But maybe you could describe one to me? I wish you'd do it. I'd like that. If you want to know, I really don't have a good idea."

I stared hard at the shot of the cathedral on the TV. How could I even begin to describe it? But say my life depended on it. Say my life was being threatened by an insane guy who said I had to do it or else.

I stared some more at the cathedral before the picture flipped off into the countryside. There was no use. I turned to the blind man and said, "To begin with, they're very tall." I was looking around the room for clues. "They reach way up. Up and up. Toward the sky. They're so big, some of them, they have to have these supports. To help hold them up, so to speak. These supports are called buttresses. They remind me of viaducts, for some reason. But maybe you don't know viaducts, either? Sometimes the cathedrals have devils and such carved into the front. Sometimes lords and ladies. Don't ask me why this is," I said.

He was nodding. The whole upper part of his body seemed to be moving back and forth.

"I'm not doing so good, am I?" I said.

He stopped nodding and leaned forward on the edge of the sofa. As he listened to me, he was running his fingers through his beard. I wasn't getting through to him, I could see that. But he waited for me to go on just the same. He nodded, like he was trying to encourage me. I tried to think what else to say. "They're really big," I said. "They're massive. They're built of stone. Marble, too, sometimes. In those olden days, when they built cathedrals, men wanted to be close to God. In those olden days, God was an important part of everyone's life. You could tell this from their cathedral-building. I'm sorry," I said, "but it looks like that's the best I can do for you. I'm just no good at it."

"That's all right, bub," the blind man said. "Hey, listen. I hope you don't mind my asking you. Can I ask you something? Let me ask you a simple question, yes or no. I'm just curious and there's no offense. You're my host. But let me ask if you are in any way religious? You don't mind my asking?"

I shook my head. He couldn't see that, though. A wink is the same as a nod to a blind man. "I guess I don't believe in it. In anything. Sometimes it's hard. You know what I'm saying?"

"Sure, I do," he said.

"Right," I said.

The Englishman was still holding forth. My wife sighed in her sleep. She drew a long breath and went on with her sleeping.

"You'll have to forgive me," I said. "But I can't tell you what a cathedral looks like. It just isn't in me to do it. I can't do any more than I've done."

The blind man sat very still, his head down, as he listened to me.

I said, "The truth is, cathedrals don't mean anything special to me. Nothing. Cathedrals. They're something to look at on late-night TV. That's all they are."

It was then that the blind man cleared his throat. He brought something up. He took a handkerchief from his back pocket. Then he said, "I get it, bub. It's okay. It happens. Don't worry about it," he said. "Hey, listen to me. Will you do me a favor? I got an idea. Why don't you find us some heavy paper? And a pen. We'll do something. We'll draw one together. Get us a pen and some heavy paper. Go on, bub, get the stuff," he said.

So I went upstairs. My legs felt like they didn't have any strength in them. They felt like they did after I'd done some running. In my wife's room, I looked around. I found some ballpoints in a little basket on her table. And then I tried to think where to look for the kind of paper he was talking about.

Downstairs, in the kitchen, I found a shopping bag with onion skins in the bottom of the bag. I emptied the bag and shook it. I brought it into the living room and sat down with it near his legs. I moved some things, smoothed the wrinkles from the bag, spread it out on the coffee table.

The blind man got down from the sofa and sat next to me on the carpet.

He ran his fingers over the paper. He went up and down the sides of the paper. The edges, even the edges. He fingered the corners.

"All right," he said. "All right, let's do her."

He found my hand, the hand with the pen. He closed his hand over my hand. "Go ahead, bub, draw," he said. "Draw. You'll see. I'll follow along with you. It'll be okay. Just begin now like I'm telling you. You'll see. Draw," the blind man said.

So I began. First I drew a box that looked like a house. It could have been the house I lived in. Then I put a roof on it. At either end of the roof, I drew spires. Crazy.

"Swell," he said. "Terrific. You're doing fine," he said. "Never thought anything like this could happen in your life-time, did you, bub? Well, it's a strange life, we all know that. Go on now. Keep it up."

I put in windows with arches. I drew flying buttresses. I hung great doors. I couldn't stop. The TV station went off the air. I put down the pen and closed and opened my fingers. The blind man felt around over the paper. He moved the tips of his fingers over the paper, all over what I had drawn, and he nodded.

"Doing fine," the blind man said.

I took up the pen again, and he found my hand. I kept at it. I'm no artist. But I kept drawing just the same.

My wife opened up her eyes and gazed at us. She sat up on the sofa, her robe hanging open. She said, "What are you doing? Tell me, I want to know."

I didn't answer her.

The blind man said, "We're drawing a cathedral. Me and him are working on it. Press hard," he said to me. "That's right. That's good," he said. "Sure. You got it, bub. I can tell. You didn't think you could. But you can, can't you? You're cooking with gas now. You know what I'm saying? We're going to really have us something here in a minute. How's the old arm?" he said. "Put some people in there now. What's a cathedral without people?"

My wife said, "What's going on? Robert, what are you doing? What's going on?"

"It's all right," he said to her. "Close your eyes now," the blind man said to me.

I did it. I closed them just like he said.

"Are they closed?" he said. "Don't fudge."

"They're closed," I said.

"Keep them that way," he said. He said, "Don't stop now. Draw."

So we kept on with it. His fingers rode my fingers as my hand went over the paper. It was like nothing else in my life up to now.

Then he said, "I think that's it. I think you got it," he said. "Take a look. What do you think?"

But I had my eyes closed. I thought I'd keep them that way for a little longer. I thought it was something I ought to do.

"Well?" he said. "Are you looking?"

My eyes were still closed. I was in my house. I knew that. But I didn't feel like I was inside anything.

"It's really something," I said.

WHERE I'M CALLING FROM

To Tess Gallagher

*We can never know what to want, because, living
only one life, we can neither compare it with our previous lives nor perfect it in our lives to come.*

Milan Kundera,
The Unbearable Lightness of Being

Boxes

M Y mother is packed and ready to move. But Sunday afternoon, at the last minute, she calls and says for us to come eat with her. "My icebox is defrosting," she tells me. "I have to fry up this chicken before it rots." She says we should bring our own plates and some knives and forks. She's packed most of her dishes and kitchen things. "Come on and eat with me one last time," she says. "You and Jill."

I hang up the phone and stand at the window for a minute longer, wishing I could figure this thing out. But I can't. So finally I turn to Jill and say, "Let's go to my mother's for a good-bye meal."

Jill is at the table with a Sears catalogue in front of her, trying to find us some curtains. But she's been listening. She makes a face. "Do we have to?" she says. She bends down the corner of a page and closes the catalogue. She sighs. "God, we been over there to eat two or three times in this last month alone. Is she ever actually going to leave?"

Jill always says what's on her mind. She's thirty-five years old, wears her hair short, and grooms dogs for a living. Before she became a groomer, something she likes, she used to be a housewife and mother. Then all hell broke loose. Her two children were kidnapped by her first husband and taken to live in Australia. Her second husband, who drank, left her with a broken eardrum before he drove their car through a bridge into the Elwha River. He didn't have life insurance, not to mention property-damage insurance. Jill had to borrow money to bury him, and then—can you beat it?—she was presented with a bill for the bridge repair. Plus, she had her own medical bills. She can tell this story now. She's bounced back. But she has run out of patience with my mother. I've run out of patience, too. But I don't see my options.

"She's leaving day after tomorrow," I say. "Hey, Jill, don't do any favors. Do you want to come with me or not?" I tell her it doesn't matter to me one way or the other. I'll say she has a migraine. It's not like I've never told a lie before.

533

"I'm coming," she says. And like that she gets up and goes into the bathroom, where she likes to pout.

We've been together since last August, about the time my mother picked to move up here to Longview from California. Jill tried to make the best of it. But my mother pulling into town just when we were trying to get our act together was nothing either of us had bargained for. Jill said it reminded her of the situation with her first husband's mother. "She was a clinger," Jill said. "You know what I mean? I thought I was going to suffocate."

It's fair to say that my mother sees Jill as an intruder. As far as she's concerned, Jill is just another girl in a series of girls who have appeared in my life since my wife left me. Someone, to her mind, likely to take away affection, attention, maybe even some money that might otherwise come to her. But someone deserving of respect? No way. I remember—how can I forget it?—she called my wife a whore before we were married, and then called her a whore fifteen years later, after she left me for someone else.

Jill and my mother act friendly enough when they find themselves together. They hug each other when they say hello or good-bye. They talk about shopping specials. But Jill dreads the time she has to spend in my mother's company. She claims my mother bums her out. She says my mother is negative about everything and everybody and ought to find an outlet, like other people in her age bracket. Crocheting, maybe, or card games at the Senior Citizens Center, or else going to church. Something, anyway, so that she'll leave us in peace. But my mother had her own way of solving things. She announced she was moving back to California. The hell with everything and everybody in this town. What a place to live! She wouldn't continue to live in this town if they gave her the place and six more like it.

Within a day or two of deciding to move, she'd packed her things into boxes. That was last January. Or maybe it was February. Anyway, last winter sometime. Now it's the end of June. Boxes have been sitting around inside her house for months. You have to walk around them or step over them to get from one room to another. This is no way for anyone's mother to live.

After a while, ten minutes or so, Jill comes out of the bathroom. I've found a roach and am trying to smoke that and drink a bottle of ginger ale while I watch one of the neighbors change the oil in his car. Jill doesn't look at me. Instead, she goes into the kitchen and puts some plates and utensils into a paper sack. But when she comes back through the living room I stand up, and we hug each other. Jill says, "It's okay." What's okay, I wonder. As far as I can see, nothing's okay. But she holds me and keeps patting my shoulder. I can smell the pet shampoo on her. She comes home from work wearing the stuff. It's everywhere. Even when we're in bed together. She gives me a final pat. Then we go out to the car and drive across town to my mother's.

I like where I live. I didn't when I first moved here. There was nothing to do at night, and I was lonely. Then I met Jill. Pretty soon, after a few weeks, she brought her things over and started living with me. We didn't set any long-term goals. We were happy and we had a life together. We told each other we'd finally got lucky. But my mother didn't have anything going in her life. So she wrote me and said she'd decided on moving here. I wrote her back and said I didn't think it was such a good idea. The weather's terrible in the winter, I said. They're building a prison a few miles from town, I told her. The place is bumper-to-bumper tourists all summer, I said. But she acted as if she never got my letters, and came anyway. Then, after she'd been in town a little less than a month, she told me she hated the place. She acted as if it were my fault she'd moved here and my fault she found everything so disagreeable. She started calling me up and telling me how crummy the place was. "Laying guilt trips," Jill called it. She told me the bus service was terrible and the drivers unfriendly. As for the people at the Senior Citizens—well, she didn't want to play casino. "They can go to hell," she said, "and take their card games with them." The clerks at the supermarket were surly, the guys in the service station didn't give a damn about her or her car. And she'd made up her mind about the man she rented from, Larry Hadlock. King Larry, she called him. "He thinks he's *superior* to everyone because he has some shacks for rent and a few dollars. I wish to God I'd never laid eyes on him."

It was too hot for her when she arrived, in August, and in

September it started to rain. It rained almost every day for
weeks. In October it turned cold. There was snow in November and December. But long before that she began to put the
bad mouth on the place and the people to the extent that I
didn't want to hear about it anymore, and I told her so finally.
She cried, and I hugged her and thought that was the end of
it. But a few days later she started in again, same stuff. Just
before Christmas she called to see when I was coming by with
her presents. She hadn't put up a tree and didn't intend to, she
said. Then she said something else. She said if this weather
didn't improve she was going to kill herself.

"Don't talk crazy," I said.

She said, "I mean it, honey. I don't want to see this place
again except from my coffin. I hate this g.d. place. I don't
know why I moved here. I wish I could just die and get it over
with."

I remember hanging on to the phone and watching a man
high up on a pole doing something to a power line. Snow
whirled around his head. As I watched, he leaned out from the
pole, supported only by his safety belt. Suppose he falls, I
thought. I didn't have any idea what I was going to say next. I
had to say something. But I was filled with unworthy feelings,
thoughts no son should admit to. "You're my mother," I said
finally. "What can I do to help?"

"Honey, you can't do anything," she said. "The time for
doing anything has come and gone. It's too late to do anything. I wanted to like it here. I thought we'd go on picnics
and take drives together. But none of that happened. You're
always busy. You're off working, you and Jill. You're never at
home. Or else if you are at home you have the phone off the
hook all day. Anyway, I never see you," she said.

"That's not true," I said. And it wasn't. But she went on as
if she hadn't heard me. Maybe she hadn't.

"Besides," she said, "this weather's killing me. It's too
damned cold here. Why didn't you tell me this was the North
Pole? If you had, I'd never have come. I want to go back to
California, honey. I can get out and go places there. I don't
know anywhere to go here. There are people back in California. I've got friends there who care what happens to me. Nobody gives a damn here. Well, I just pray I can get through to

June. If I can make it that long, if I can last to June, I'm leaving this place forever. This is the worst place I've ever lived in."

What could I say? I didn't know what to say. I couldn't even say anything about the weather. Weather was a real sore point. We said good-bye and hung up.

Other people take vacations in the summer, but my mother moves. She started moving years ago, after my dad lost his job. When that happened, when he was laid off, they sold their home, as if this were what they should do, and went to where they thought things would be better. But things weren't any better there, either. They moved again. They kept on moving. They lived in rented houses, apartments, mobile homes, and motel units even. They kept moving, lightening their load with each move they made. A couple of times they landed in a town where I lived. They'd move in with my wife and me for a while and then they'd move on again. They were like migrating animals in this regard, except there was no pattern to their movement. They moved around for years, sometimes even leaving the state for what they thought would be greener pastures. But mostly they stayed in Northern California and did their moving there. Then my dad died, and I thought my mother would stop moving and stay in one place for a while. But she didn't. She kept moving. I suggested once that she go to a psychiatrist. I even said I'd pay for it. But she wouldn't hear of it. She packed and moved out of town instead. I was desperate about things or I wouldn't have said that about the psychiatrist.

She was always in the process of packing or else unpacking. Sometimes she'd move two or three times in the same year. She talked bitterly about the place she was leaving and optimistically about the place she was going to. Her mail got fouled up, her benefit checks went off somewhere else, and she spent hours writing letters, trying to get it all straightened out. Sometimes she'd move out of an apartment house, move to another one a few blocks away, and then, a month later, move back to the place she'd left, only to a different floor or a different side of the building. That's why when she moved here I rented a house for her and saw to it that it was furnished to her liking. "Moving around keeps her alive," Jill said. "It gives her something to do. She must get some kind of weird enjoyment out of it, I guess." But enjoyment or not, Jill thinks my mother must be losing her mind. I think so, too. But how do you tell your mother this? How do you deal with her if this is the case? Crazy doesn't stop her from planning and getting on with her next move.

She is waiting at the back door for us when we pull in. She's seventy years old, has gray hair, wears glasses with rhinestone frames, and has never been sick a day in her life. She hugs Jill, and then she hugs me. Her eyes are bright, as if she's been drinking. But she doesn't drink. She quit years ago, after my dad went on the wagon. We finish hugging and go inside. It's around five in the afternoon. I smell whatever it is drifting out of her kitchen and remember I haven't eaten since breakfast. My buzz has worn off.

"I'm starved," I say.

"Something smells good," Jill says.

"I hope it tastes good," my mother says. "I hope this chicken's done." She raises the lid on a fry pan and pushes a fork into a chicken breast. "If there's anything I can't stand, it's raw chicken. I think it's done. Why don't you sit down? Sit anyplace. I still can't regulate my stove. The burners heat up too fast. I don't like electric stoves and never have. Move that junk off the chair, Jill. I'm living here like a damned gypsy. But not for much longer, I hope." She sees me looking around for the ashtray. "Behind you," she says. "On the windowsill, honey. Before you sit down, why don't you pour us some of that Pepsi? You'll have to use these paper cups. I should have told you to bring some glasses. Is the Pepsi cold? I don't have any ice. This icebox won't keep anything cold. It isn't worth a damn. My ice cream turns to soup. It's the worst icebox I've ever had."

She forks the chicken onto a plate and puts the plate on the table along with beans and coleslaw and white bread. Then she looks to see if there is anything she's forgetting. Salt and pepper! "Sit down," she says.

We draw our chairs up to the table, and Jill takes the plates out of the sack and hands them around the table to us. "Where are you going to live when you go back?" she says. "Do you have a place lined up?"

My mother passes the chicken to Jill and says, "I wrote that lady I rented from before. She wrote back and said she had a nice first-floor place I could have. It's close to the bus stop and there's lots of stores in the area. There's a bank and a Safeway. It's the nicest place. I don't know why I left there." She says that and helps herself to some coleslaw.

"Why'd you leave then?" Jill says. "If it was so nice and all." She picks up her drumstick, looks at it, and takes a bite of the meat.

"I'll tell you why. There was an old alcoholic woman who lived next door to me. She drank from morning to night. The walls were so thin I could hear her munching ice cubes all day. She had to use a walker to get around, but that still didn't stop her. I'd hear that walker *scrape, scrape* against the floor from morning to night. That and her icebox door closing." She shakes her head at all she had to put up with. "I had to get out of there. *Scrape, scrape* all day. I couldn't stand it. I just couldn't live like that. This time I told the manager I didn't want to be next to any alcoholics. And I didn't want anything on the second floor. The second floor looks out on the parking lot. Nothing to see from there." She waits for Jill to say something more. But Jill doesn't comment. My mother looks over at me.

I'm eating like a wolf and don't say anything, either. In any case, there's nothing more to say on the subject. I keep chewing and look over at the boxes stacked against the fridge. Then I help myself to more coleslaw.

Pretty soon I finish and push my chair back. Larry Hadlock pulls up in back of the house, next to my car, and takes a lawn mower out of his pickup. I watch him through the window behind the table. He doesn't look in our direction.

"What's he want?" my mother says and stops eating.

"He's going to cut your grass, it looks like," I say.

"It doesn't need cutting," she says. "He cut it last week. What's there for him to cut?"

"It's for the new tenant," Jill says. "Whoever that turns out to be."

My mother takes this in and then goes back to eating.

Larry Hadlock starts his mower and begins to cut the grass. I know him a little. He lowered the rent twenty-five a month when I told him it was my mother. He is a widower—a big fellow, mid-sixties. An unhappy man with a good sense of humor. His arms are covered with white hair, and white hair stands out from under his cap. He looks like a magazine illustration of a farmer. But he isn't a farmer. He is a retired construction worker who's saved a little money. For a while, in the beginning, I let myself imagine that he and my mother might take some meals together and become friends.

"There's the king," my mother says. "King Larry. Not everyone has as much money as he does and can live in a big house and charge other people high rents. Well, I hope I never see his cheap old face again once I leave here. Eat the rest of this chicken," she says to me. But I shake my head and light a cigarette. Larry pushes his mower past the window.

"You won't have to look at it much longer," Jill says.

"I'm sure glad of that, Jill. But I know he won't give me my deposit back."

"How do you know that?" I say.

"I just know," she says. "I've had dealings with his kind before. They're out for all they can get."

Jill says, "It won't be long now and you won't have to have anything more to do with him."

"I'll be so glad."

"But it'll be somebody just like him," Jill says.

"I don't want to think that, Jill," my mother says.

She makes coffee while Jill clears the table. I rinse the cups. Then I pour coffee, and we step around a box marked "Knickknacks" and take our cups into the living room.

Larry Hadlock is at the side of the house. Traffic moves slowly on the street out in front, and the sun has started down over the trees. I can hear the commotion the mower makes. Some crows leave the phone line and settle onto the newly cut grass in the front yard.

"I'm going to miss you, honey," my mother says. Then she says, "I'll miss you, too, Jill. I'm going to miss both of you."

Jill sips from her coffee and nods. Then she says, "I hope you have a safe trip back and find the place you're looking for at the end of the road."

"When I get settled—and this is my last move, so help me— I hope you'll come and visit," my mother says. She looks at me and waits to be reassured.

"We will," I say. But even as I say it I know it isn't true. My life caved in on me down there, and I won't be going back.

"I wish you could have been happier here," Jill says. "I wish you'd been able to stick it out or something. You know what? Your son is worried sick about you."

"Jill," I say.

But she gives her head a little shake and goes on. "Sometimes he can't sleep over it. He wakes up sometimes in the night and says, 'I can't sleep. I'm thinking about my mother.' There," she says and looks at me. "I've said it. But it was on my mind."

"How do you think I must feel?" my mother says. Then she says, "Other women my age can be happy. Why can't I be like other women? All I want is a house and a town to live in that will make me happy. That isn't a crime, is it? I hope not. I hope I'm not asking too much out of life." She puts her cup on the floor next to her chair and waits for Jill to tell her she isn't asking for too much. But Jill doesn't say anything, and in a minute my mother begins to outline her plans to be happy.

After a time Jill lowers her eyes to her cup and has some more coffee. I can tell she's stopped listening. But my mother keeps talking anyway. The crows work their way through the grass in the front yard. I hear the mower howl and then thud as it picks up a clump of grass in the blade and comes to a stop. In a minute, after several tries, Larry gets it going again. The crows fly off, back to their wire. Jill picks at a fingernail. My mother is saying that the secondhand-furniture dealer is coming around the next morning to collect the things she isn't going to send on the bus or carry with her in the car. The table and chairs, TV, sofa, and bed are going with the dealer. But he's told her he doesn't have any use for the card table, so my mother is going to throw it out unless we want it.

"We'll take it," I say. Jill looks over. She starts to say something but changes her mind.

I will drive the boxes to the Greyhound station the next afternoon and start them on the way to California. My mother will spend the last night with us, as arranged. And then, early the next morning, two days from now, she'll be on her way.

She continues to talk. She talks on and on as she describes the trip she is about to make. She'll drive until four o'clock in

the afternoon and then take a motel room for the night. She
figures to make Eugene by dark. Eugene is a nice town—she
stayed there once before, on the way up here. When she leaves
the motel, she'll leave at sunrise and should, if God is looking
out for her, be in California that afternoon. And God *is*
looking out for her, she knows he is. How else explain her
being kept around on the face of the earth? He has a plan for
her. She's been praying a lot lately. She's been praying for me,
too.

"Why are you praying for him?" Jill wants to know.

"Because I feel like it. Because he's my son," my mother says.
"Is there anything the matter with that? Don't we all need
praying for sometimes? Maybe some people don't. I don't know.
What do I know anymore?" She brings a hand to her forehead
and rearranges some hair that's come loose from a pin.

The mower sputters off, and pretty soon we see Larry go
around the house pulling the hose. He sets the hose out and
then goes slowly back around the house to turn the water on.
The sprinkler begins to turn.

My mother starts listing the ways she imagines Larry has
wronged her since she's been in the house. But now I'm not
listening, either. I am thinking how she is about to go down
the highway again, and nobody can reason with her or do anything to stop her. What can I do? I can't tie her up, or commit
her, though it may come to that eventually. I worry for her,
and she is a heartache to me. She is all the family I have left.
I'm sorry she didn't like it here and wants to leave. But I'm
never going back to California. And when that's clear to me I
understand something else, too. I understand that after she
leaves I'm probably never going to see her again.

I look over at my mother. She stops talking. Jill raises her
eyes. Both of them look at me.

"What is it, honey?" my mother says.

"What's wrong?" Jill says.

I lean forward in the chair and cover my face with my hands.
I sit like that for a minute, feeling bad and stupid for doing it.
But I can't help it. And the woman who brought me into this
life, and this other woman I picked up with less than a year
ago, they exclaim together and rise and come over to where I

sit with my head in my hands like a fool. I don't open my eyes.
I listen to the sprinkler whipping the grass.

"What's wrong? What's the matter?" they say.

"It's okay," I say. And in a minute it is. I open my eyes and
bring my head up. I reach for a cigarette.

"See what I mean?" Jill says. "You're driving him crazy. He's
going crazy with worry over you." She is on one side of my
chair, and my mother is on the other side. They could tear me
apart in no time at all.

"I wish I could die and get out of everyone's way," my
mother says quietly. "So help me Hannah, I can't take much
more of this."

"How about some more coffee?" I say. "Maybe we ought to
catch the news," I say. "Then I guess Jill and I better head for
home."

Two days later, early in the morning, I say good-bye to my
mother for what may be the last time. I've let Jill sleep. It
won't hurt if she's late to work for a change. The dogs can
wait for their baths and trimmings and such. My mother holds
my arm as I walk her down the steps to the driveway and open
the car door for her. She is wearing white slacks and a white
blouse and white sandals. Her hair is pulled back and tied with
a scarf. That's white, too. It's going to be a nice day, and the
sky is clear and already blue.

On the front seat of the car I see maps and a thermos of coffee. My mother looks at these things as if she can't recall
having come outside with them just a few minutes ago. She
turns to me then and says, "Let me hug you once more. Let
me love your neck. I know I won't see you for a long time."
She puts an arm around my neck, draws me to her, and then
begins to cry. But she stops almost at once and steps back,
pushing the heel of her hand against her eyes. "I said I
wouldn't do that, and I won't. But let me get a last look at you
anyway. I'll miss you, honey," she says. "I'm just going to have
to live through this. I've already lived through things I didn't
think were possible. But I'll live through this, too, I guess."
She gets into the car, starts it, and runs the engine for a
minute. She rolls her window down.

"I'm going to miss you," I say. And I *am* going to miss her. She's my mother, after all, and why shouldn't I miss her? But, God forgive me, I'm glad, too, that it's finally time and that she is leaving.

"Good-bye," she says. "Tell Jill thanks for supper last night. Tell her I said good-bye."

"I will," I say. I stand there wanting to say something else. But I don't know what. We keep looking at each other, trying to smile and reassure each other. Then something comes into her eyes, and I believe she is thinking about the highway and how far she is going to have to drive that day. She takes her eyes off me and looks down the road. Then she rolls her window up, puts the car into gear, and drives to the intersection, where she has to wait for the light to change. When I see she's made it into traffic and headed toward the highway, I go back in the house and drink some coffee. I feel sad for a while, and then the sadness goes away and I start thinking about other things.

A few nights later my mother calls to say she is in her new place. She is busy fixing it up, the way she does when she has a new place. She tells me I'll be happy to know she likes it just fine to be back in sunny California. But she says there's something in the air where she is living, maybe it's pollen, that is causing her to sneeze a lot. And the traffic is heavier than she remembers from before. She doesn't recall there being so much traffic in her neighborhood. Naturally, everyone still drives like crazy down there. "California drivers," she says. "What else can you expect?" She says it's hot for this time of the year. She doesn't think the air-conditioning unit in her apartment is working right. I tell her she should talk to the manager. "She's never around when you need her," my mother says. She hopes she hasn't made a mistake in moving back to California. She waits before she says anything else.

I'm standing at the window with the phone pressed to my ear, looking out at the lights from town and at the lighted houses closer by. Jill is at the table with the catalogue, listening.

"Are you still there?" my mother asks. "I wish you'd say something."

I don't know why, but it's then I recall the affectionate

name my dad used sometimes when he was talking nice to my mother—those times, that is, when he wasn't drunk. It was a long time ago, and I was a kid, but always, hearing it, I felt better, less afraid, more hopeful about the future. "*Dear*," he'd say. He called her "dear" sometimes—a sweet name. "Dear," he'd say, "if you're going to the store, will you bring me some cigarettes?" Or "Dear, is your cold any better?" "Dear, where is my coffee cup?"

The word issues from my lips before I can think what else I want to say to go along with it. "Dear." I say it again. I call her "dear." "Dear, try not to be afraid," I say. I tell my mother I love her and I'll write to her, yes. Then I say good-bye, and I hang up.

For a while I don't move from the window. I keep standing there, looking out at the lighted houses in our neighborhood. As I watch, a car turns off the road and pulls into a driveway. The porch light goes on. The door to the house opens and someone comes out on the porch and stands there waiting.

Jill turns the pages of her catalogue, and then she stops turning them. "This is what we want," she says. "This is more like what I had in mind. Look at this, will you." But I don't look. I don't care five cents for curtains. "What is it you see out there, honey?" Jill says. "Tell me."

What's there to tell? The people over there embrace for a minute, and then they go inside the house together. They leave the light burning. Then they remember, and it goes out.

Whoever Was Using This Bed

T HE call comes in the middle of the night, three in the morning, and it nearly scares us to death.

"Answer it, answer it!" my wife cries. "My God, who is it? Answer it!"

I can't find the light, but I get to the other room, where the phone is, and pick it up after the fourth ring.

"Is Bud there?" this woman says, very drunk.

"Jesus, you have the wrong number," I say, and hang up.

I turn the light on, and go into the bathroom, and that's when I hear the phone start again.

"Answer that!" my wife screams from the bedroom. "What in God's name do they want, Jack? I can't take any more."

I hurry out of the bathroom and pick up the phone.

"Bud?" the woman says. "What are you doing, Bud?"

I say, "Look here. You have a wrong number. Don't ever call this number again."

"I have to talk to Bud," she says.

I hang up, wait until it rings again, and then I take the receiver and lay it on the table beside the phone. But I hear the woman's voice say, "Bud, talk to me, please." I leave the receiver on its side on the table, turn off the light, and close the door to the room.

In the bedroom I find the lamp on and my wife, Iris, sitting against the headboard with her knees drawn up under the covers. She has a pillow behind her back, and she's more on my side than her own side. The covers are up around her shoulders. The blankets and the sheet have been pulled out from the foot of the bed. If we want to go back to sleep—I want to go back to sleep, anyway—we may have to start from scratch and do this bed over again.

"What the hell was that all about?" Iris says. "We should have unplugged the phone. I guess we forgot. Try forgetting one night to unplug the phone and see what happens. I don't believe it."

After Iris and I started living together, my former wife, or else one of my kids, used to call up when we were asleep and want to harangue us. They kept doing it even after Iris and I were married. So we started unplugging our phone before we went to bed. We unplugged the phone every night of the year, just about. It was a habit. This time I slipped up, that's all.

"Some woman wanting *Bud*," I say. I'm standing there in my pajamas, wanting to get into bed, but I can't. "She was drunk. Move over, honey. I took the phone off the hook."

"She can't call again?"

"No," I say. "Why don't you move over a little and give me some of those covers?"

She takes her pillow and puts it on the far side of the bed, against the headboard, scoots over, and then she leans back once more. She doesn't look sleepy. She looks fully awake. I get into bed and take some covers. But the covers don't feel right. I don't have any sheet; all I have is blanket. I look down and see my feet sticking out. I turn onto my side, facing her, and bring my legs up so that my feet are under the blanket. We should make up the bed again. I ought to suggest that. But I'm thinking, too, that if we kill the light now, this minute, we might be able to go right back to sleep.

"How about you turning off your light, honey?" I say, as nice as I can.

"Let's have a cigarette first," she says. "Then we'll go to sleep. Get us the cigarettes and the ashtray, why don't you? We'll have a cigarette."

"Let's go to sleep," I say. "Look at what time it is." The clock radio is right there beside the bed. Anyone can see it says three-thirty.

"Come on," Iris says. "I need a cigarette after all that."

I get out of bed for the cigarettes and ashtray. I have to go into the room where the phone is, but I don't touch the phone. I don't even want to look at the phone, but I do, of course. The receiver is still on its side on the table.

I crawl back in bed and put the ashtray on the quilt between us. I light a cigarette, give it to her, and then light one for myself.

She tries to remember the dream she was having when the phone rang. "I can just about remember it, but I can't remember exactly. Something about, about—no, I don't know what it was about now. I can't be sure. I can't remember it," she says finally. "God damn that woman and her phone call. '*Bud*,'" she says. "I'd like to punch her." She puts out her cigarette and immediately lights another, blows smoke, and lets her eyes take in the chest of drawers and the window curtains. Her hair is undone and around her shoulders. She uses the ashtray and then stares over the foot of the bed, trying to remember.

But, really, I don't care what she's dreamed. I want to go back to sleep is all. I finish my cigarette and put it out and wait for her to finish. I lie still and don't say anything.

Iris is like my former wife in that when she sleeps she sometimes has violent dreams. She thrashes around in bed during the night and wakes in the morning drenched with sweat, the nightgown sticking to her body. And, like my former wife, she wants to tell me her dreams in great detail and speculate as to what this stands for or that portends. My former wife used to kick the covers off in the night and cry out in her sleep, as if someone were laying hands on her. Once, in a particularly violent dream, she hit me on the ear with her fist. I was in a dreamless sleep, but I struck out in the dark and hit her on the forehead. Then we began yelling. We both yelled and yelled. We'd hurt each other, but we were mainly scared. We had no idea what had happened until I turned the lamp on; then we sorted it out. Afterward, we joked about it—fistfighting in our sleep. But then so much else began to happen that was far more serious we tended to forget about that night. We never mentioned it again, even when we teased each other.

Once I woke up in the night to hear Iris grinding her teeth in her sleep. It was such a peculiar thing to have going on right next to my ear that it woke me up. I gave her a little shake, and she stopped. The next morning she told me she'd had a very bad dream, but that's all she'd tell me about it. I didn't press her for details. I guess I really didn't want to know what could have been so bad that she didn't want to say. When I told her she'd been grinding her teeth in her sleep, she frowned and said she was going to have to do something about that. The next night she brought home something called a Niteguard—something she was supposed to wear in her mouth while she slept. She had to do something, she said. She couldn't afford to keep grinding her teeth; pretty soon she wouldn't have any.

So she wore this protective device in her mouth for a week or so, and then she stopped wearing it. She said it was uncomfortable and, anyway, it was not very cosmetic. Who'd want to kiss a woman wearing a thing like that in her mouth, she said. She had something there, of course.

Another time I woke up because she was stroking my face and calling me Earl. I took her hand and squeezed her fingers. "What is it?" I said. "What is it, sweetheart?" But instead of answering she simply squeezed back, sighed, and then lay still again. The next morning, when I asked her what she'd dreamed the night before, she claimed not to have had any dreams.

"So who's Earl?" I said. "Who is this Earl you were talking about in your sleep?" She blushed and said she didn't know anybody named Earl and never had.

The lamp is still on and, because I don't know what else to think about, I think about that phone being off the hook. I ought to hang it up and unplug the cord. Then we have to think about sleep.

"I'll go take care of that phone," I say. "Then let's go to sleep."

Iris uses the ashtray and says, "Make sure it's unplugged this time."

I get up again and go to the other room, open the door, and turn on the light. The receiver is still on its side on the table. I bring it to my ear, expecting to hear the dial tone. But I don't hear anything, not even the tone.

On an impulse, I say something. "Hello," I say.

"Oh, Bud, it's you," the woman says.

I hang up the phone and bend over and unplug it from the wall before it can ring again. This is a new one on me. This deal is a mystery, this woman and her Bud person. I don't know how to tell Iris about this new development, because it'll just lead to more discussion and further speculation. I decide not to say anything for now. Maybe I'll say something over breakfast.

Back in the bedroom I see she is smoking another cigarette. I see, too, that it's nearly four in the morning. I'm starting to worry. When it's four o'clock it'll soon be five o'clock, and then it will be six, then six-thirty, then time to get up for work.

I lie back down, close my eyes, and decide I'll count to sixty, slowly, before I say anything else about the light.

"I'm starting to remember," Iris says. "It's coming back to me. You want to hear it, Jack?"

I stop counting, open my eyes, sit up. The bedroom is filled with smoke. I light one up, too. Why not? The hell with it.

She says, "There was a party going on in my dream."

"Where was I when this was going on?" Usually, for whatever reason, I don't figure in her dreams. It irritates me a little, but I don't let on. My feet are uncovered again. I pull them under the covers, raise myself up on my elbow, and use the ashtray. "Is this another dream that I'm not in? It's okay, if that's the case." I pull on the cigarette, hold the smoke, let it out.

"Honey, you weren't in the dream," Iris says. "I'm sorry, but you weren't. You weren't anywhere around. I *missed* you, though. I did miss you, I'm sure of it. It was like I knew you were somewhere nearby, but you weren't there where I needed you. You know how I get into those anxiety states sometimes? If we go someplace together where there's a group of people and we get separated and I can't find you? It was a little like that. You were there, I think, but I couldn't find you."

"Go ahead and tell me about the dream," I say.

She rearranges the covers around her waist and legs and reaches for a cigarette. I hold the lighter for her. Then she goes on to describe this party where all that was being served was beer. "I don't even like beer," she says. But she drank a large quantity anyway, and just when she went to leave—to go home, she says—this little dog took hold of the hem of her dress and made her stay.

She laughs, and I laugh right along with her, even though, when I look at the clock, I see the hands are close to saying four-thirty.

There was some kind of music being played in her dream—a piano, maybe, or else it was an accordion, who knows? Dreams are that way sometimes, she says. Anyway, she vaguely remembers her former husband putting in an appearance. He might have been the one serving the beer. People were drinking beer from a keg, using plastic cups. She thought she might even have danced with him.

"Why are you telling me this?"

She says, "It was a dream, honey."

"I don't think I like it, knowing you're supposed to be here beside me all night but instead you're dreaming about strange dogs, parties, and ex-husbands. I don't like you dancing with him. What the hell is this? What if I told you I dreamed I danced the night away with Carol? Would you like it?"

"It's just a dream, right?" she says. "Don't get weird on me. I won't say any more. I see I can't. I can see it isn't a good idea." She brings her fingers to her lips slowly, the way she does sometimes when she's thinking. Her face shows how hard she's concentrating; little lines appear on her forehead. "I'm sorry that you weren't in the dream. But if I told you otherwise I'd be lying to you, right?"

I nod. I touch her arm to show her it's okay. I don't really mind. And I don't, I guess. "What happened then, honey? Finish telling the dream," I say. "And maybe we can go to sleep then." I guess I wanted to know the next thing. The last I'd heard, she'd been dancing with Jerry. If there was more, I needed to hear it.

She plumps up the pillow behind her back and says, "That's all I can remember. I can't remember any more about it. That was when the goddamn phone rang."

"Bud," I say. I can see smoke drifting in the light under the lamp, and smoke hangs in the air in the room. "Maybe we should open a window," I say.

"That's a good idea," she says. "Let some of this smoke out. It can't be any good for us."

"Hell no, it isn't," I say.

I get up again and go to the window and raise it a few inches. I can feel the cool air that comes in and from a distance I hear a truck gearing down as it starts up the grade that will take it to the pass and on over into the next state.

"I guess pretty soon we're going to be the last smokers left in America," she says. "Seriously, we should think about quitting." She says this as she puts her cigarette out and reaches for the pack next to the ashtray.

"It's open season on smokers," I say.

I get back in the bed. The covers are turned every which way, and it's five o'clock in the morning. I don't think we're going to sleep any more tonight. But so what if we don't? Is there a law on the books? Is something bad going to happen to us if we don't?

She takes some of her hair between her fingers. Then she pushes it behind her ear, looks at me, and says, "Lately I've been feeling this vein in my forehead. It *pulses* sometimes. It throbs. Do you know what I'm talking about? I don't know if you've ever had anything like that. I hate to think about it, but probably one of these days I'll have a stroke or something. Isn't that how they happen? A vein in your head bursts? That's probably what'll happen to me, eventually. My mother, my grandmother, and one of my aunts died of stroke. There's a history of stroke in my family. It can run in the family, you know. It's hereditary, just like heart disease, or being too fat, or whatever. Anyway," she says, "something's going to happen to me someday, right? So maybe that's what it'll be—a stroke. Maybe that's how I'll go. That's what it feels like it could be the beginning of. First it pulses a little, like it wants my attention, and then it starts to throb. Throb, throb, throb. It scares me silly," she says. "I want us to give up these goddamn cigarettes before it's too late." She looks at what's left of her cigarette, mashes it into the ashtray, and tries to fan the smoke away.

I'm on my back, studying the ceiling, thinking that this is the kind of talk that could only take place at five in the morning. I feel I ought to say something. "I get winded easy," I say. "I found myself out of breath when I ran in there to answer the phone."

"That could have been because of anxiety," Iris says. "Who needs it, anyway! The *idea* of somebody calling at this hour! I could tear that woman limb from limb."

I pull myself up in the bed and lean back against the headboard. I put the pillow behind my back and try to get comfortable, same as Iris. "I'll tell you something I haven't told you," I say. "Once in a while my heart palpitates. It's like it goes crazy." She's watching me closely, listening for whatever it is I'm going to say next. "Sometimes it feels like it's going to jump out of my chest. I don't know what the hell causes it."

"Why didn't you tell me?" she says. She takes my hand and holds it. She squeezes my hand. "You never said anything, honey. Listen, I don't know what I'd *do* if something ever happened to you. I'd fold up. How often does it happen? That's scary, you know." She's still holding my hand. But her fingers slide to my wrist, where my pulse is. She goes on holding my wrist like this.

"I never told you because I didn't want to scare you," I say. "But it happens sometimes. It happened as recently as a week ago. I don't have to be doing anything in particular when it happens, either. I can be sitting in a chair with the paper. Or else driving the car, or pushing a grocery basket. It doesn't matter if I'm exerting myself or not. It just starts—boom, boom, boom. Like that. I'm surprised people can't hear it. It's that loud, I think. *I* can hear it, anyway, and I don't mind telling you it scares me," I say. "So if emphysema doesn't get me, or lung cancer, or maybe a stroke like what you're talking about, then it's going to be a heart attack probably."

I reach for the cigarettes. I give her one. We're through with sleep for the night. Did we sleep? For a minute, I can't remember.

"Who knows what we'll die of?" Iris says. "It could be anything. If we live long enough, maybe it'll be kidney failure, or something like that. A friend of mine at work, her father just died of kidney failure. That's what can happen to you sometimes if you're lucky enough to get really old. When your kidneys fail, the body starts filling up with uric acid then. You finally turn a whole different color before you die."

"Great. That sounds wonderful," I say. "Maybe we should get off this subject. How'd we get onto this stuff, anyway?"

She doesn't answer. She leans forward, away from her pillow, arms clasping her legs. She closes her eyes and lays her head on her knees. Then she begins to rock back and forth, slowly. It's as if she were listening to music. But there isn't any music. None that I can hear, anyway.

"You know what I'd like?" she says. She stops moving, opens her eyes, and tilts her head at me. Then she grins, so I'll know she's all right.

"What would you like, honey?" I've got my leg hooked over her leg, at the ankle.

She says, "I'd like some coffee, that's what. I could go for a nice strong cup of black coffee. We're awake, aren't we? Who's going back to sleep? Let's have some coffee."

"We drink too much coffee," I say. "All that coffee isn't good for us, either. I'm not saying we shouldn't have any, I'm just saying we drink too much of it. It's just an observation," I add. "Actually, I could drink some coffee myself."

"Good," she says.

But neither of us makes a move.

She shakes out her hair and then lights another cigarette. Smoke drifts slowly in the room. Some of it drifts toward the open window. A little rain begins to fall on the patio outside the window. The alarm comes on, and I reach over and shut it off. Then I take the pillow and put it under my head again. I lie back and stare at the ceiling some more. "What happened to that bright idea we had about a girl who could bring us our coffee in bed?" I say.

"I wish *somebody* would bring us coffee," she says. "A girl or a boy, one or the other. I could really go for some coffee right now."

She moves the ashtray to the nightstand, and I think she's going to get up. Somebody has to get up and start the coffee and put a can of frozen juice in the blender. One of us has to make a move. But what she does instead is slide down in the bed until she's sitting somewhere in the middle. The covers are all over the place. She picks at something on the quilt, and then rubs her palm across whatever it is before she looks up. "Did you see in the paper where that guy took a shotgun into an intensive-care unit and made the nurses take his father off the life-support machine? Did you read about that?" Iris says.

"I saw something about it on the news," I say. "But mostly they were talking about this nurse who unplugged six or eight people from their machines. At this point they don't know exactly how many she unplugged. She started off by unplugging her mother, and then she went on from there. It was like a spree, I guess. She said she thought she was doing everybody a favor. She said she hoped somebody'd do it for *her*, if they cared about her."

Iris decides to move on down to the foot of the bed. She positions herself so that she is facing me. Her legs are still under the covers. She puts her legs between my legs and says, "What about that quadriplegic woman on the news who says she wants to die, wants to starve herself to death? Now she's suing her doctor and the hospital because they insist on force-feeding her to keep her alive. Can you believe it? It's insane. They strap her down three times a day so they can run this tube into her throat. They feed her breakfast, lunch, and dinner that way. And they keep her plugged into this machine, too, because her lungs don't want to work on their own. It said in the paper that she's *begging* them to unplug her, or else to just let her starve to death. She's having to plead with them to let her die, but they won't listen. She said she started out wanting to die with some dignity. Now she's just mad and looking to sue everybody. Isn't that amazing? Isn't that one for the books?" she says. "I have these headaches sometimes," she says. "Maybe it has something to do with the vein. Maybe not. Maybe they're not related. But I don't tell you when my head hurts, because I don't want to worry you."

"What are you talking about?" I say. "Look at me. Iris? I have a right to know. I'm your husband, in case you've forgotten. If something's wrong with you, I should know about it."

"But what could you *do*? You'd just worry." She bumps my leg with her leg, then bumps it again. "Right? You'd tell me to take some aspirin. I know you."

I look toward the window, where it's beginning to get light. I can feel a damp breeze from the window. It's stopped raining now, but it's one of those mornings where it could begin to pour. I look at her again. "To tell you the truth, Iris, I get sharp pains in my side from time to time." But the moment I say the words I'm sorry. She'll be concerned, and want to talk about it. We ought to be thinking of showers; we should be sitting down to breakfast.

"Which side?" she says.

"Right side."

"It could be your appendix," she says. "Something fairly simple like that."

I shrug. "Who knows? I don't know. All I know is it happens. Every so often, for just a minute or two, I feel something sharp down there. Very sharp. At first I thought it might be a pulled muscle. Which side's your gallbladder on, by the way? Is it the left or right side? Maybe it's my gallbladder. Or else maybe a gall*stone*, whatever the hell that is."

"It's not really a stone," she says. "A gallstone is like a little granule, or something like that. It's about as big as the tip of a pencil. No, wait, that might be a *kidney* stone I'm talking about. I guess I don't know anything about it." She shakes her head.

"What's the difference between kidney stone and gall-stone?" I say. "Christ, we don't even know which side of the body they're on. You don't know, and I don't know. That's how much we know together. A total of nothing. But I read somewhere that you can pass a kidney stone, if that's what this is, and usually it won't kill you. Painful, yes. I don't know what they say about a gallstone."

"I like that 'usually,'" she says.

"I know," I say. "Listen, we'd better get up. It's getting really late. It's seven o'clock."

"I know," she says. "Okay." But she continues to sit there. Then she says, "My grandma had arthritis so bad toward the end she couldn't get around by herself, or even move her fingers. She had to sit in a chair and wear these mittens all day. Finally, she couldn't even hold a cup of cocoa. That's how bad her arthritis was. Then she had her stroke. And my *grandpa*," she says. "He went into a nursing home not long after Grandma died. It was either that or else somebody had to come in and be with him around the clock, and nobody could do that. Nobody had the money for twenty-four-hour-a-day care, either. So he goes into the nursing home. But he began to deteriorate fast in there. One time, after he'd been in that place for a while, my mom went to visit him and then she came home and said something. I'll never forget what she said." She looks at me as if I'm never going to forget it, either. And I'm not. "She said, 'My dad doesn't recognize me anymore. He doesn't even know who I am. My dad has become a vege-table.' That was my mom who said that."

She leans over and covers her face with her hands and begins to cry. I move down there to the foot of the bed and sit beside her. I take her hand and hold it in my lap. I put my arm around her. We're sitting together looking at the headboard and at the nightstand. The clock's there, too, and beside the clock a few magazines and a paperback. We're sitting on the part of the bed where we keep our feet when we sleep. It looks like who-ever was using this bed left in a hurry. I know I won't ever look at this bed again without remembering it like this. We're into something now, but I don't know what, exactly.

"I don't want anything like that to ever happen to me," she says. "Or to you, either." She wipes her face with a corner of the blanket and takes a deep breath, which comes out as a sob. "I'm sorry. I just can't help it," she says.

"It won't happen to us. It won't," I say. "Don't worry about any of it, okay? We're fine, Iris, and we're going to stay fine. In any case, that time's a long time off. Hey, I love you. We love each other, don't we? That's the important thing. That's what counts. Don't worry, honey."

"I want you to promise me something," she says. She takes her hand back. She moves my arm away from her shoulder. "I want you to promise me you'll pull the plug on me, if and when it's ever necessary. If it ever comes to that, I mean. Do you hear what I'm saying? I'm serious about this, Jack. I want you to pull the plug on me if you ever have to. Will you promise?"

I don't say anything right away. What am I supposed to say? They haven't written the book on this one yet. I need a minute to think. I know it won't cost me anything to tell her I'll do whatever she wants. It's just words, right? Words are easy. But there's more to it than this; she wants an honest response from me. And I don't know what I feel about it yet. I shouldn't be hasty. I can't say something without thinking about what I'm saying, about consequences, about what she's going to feel when I say it—whatever it is I say.

I'm still thinking about it when she says, "What about you?"

"What about me what?"

"Do you want to be unplugged if it comes to that? God forbid it ever does, of course," she says. "But I should have some kind of idea, you know—some word from you now—about what you want me to do if worst comes to worst." She's looking at me closely, waiting for me to say. She wants something she can file away to use later, if and when she ever has to. Sure. Okay. Easy enough for me to say, *Unplug me, honey, if you think it's for the best.* But I need to consider this a little more. I haven't even said yet what I will or won't do for *her.* Now I have to think about me and *my* situation. I don't feel I should jump into this. This is nuts. *We're* nuts. But I realize that whatever I say now might come back to me sometime. It's

important. This is a life-and-death thing we're talking about
here.

She hasn't moved. She's still waiting for her answer. And I
can see we're not going anywhere this morning until she has
an answer. I think about it some more, and then I say what I
mean. "No. Don't unplug me. I don't want to be unplugged.
Leave me hooked up just as long as possible. Who's going to
object? Are you going to object? Will I be offending anybody?
As long as people can stand the sight of me, just so long as
they don't start howling, don't unplug anything. Let me keep
going, okay? Right to the bitter end. Invite my friends in to say
good-bye. Don't do anything rash."

"Be serious," she says. "This is a very serious matter we're
discussing."

"I am serious. Don't unplug me. It's as simple as that."

She nods. "Okay, then. I promise you I won't." She hugs me.
She holds me tight for a minute. Then she lets me go. She looks
at the clock radio and says, "Jesus, we better get moving."

So we get out of bed and start getting dressed. In some ways
it's just like any other morning, except we do things faster. We
drink coffee and juice and we eat English muffins. We remark
on the weather, which is overcast and blustery. We don't talk
anymore about plugs, or about sickness and hospitals and stuff
like that. I kiss her and leave her on the front porch with her
umbrella open, waiting for her ride to work. Then I hurry to
my car and get in. In a minute, after I've run the motor, I wave
and drive off.

But during the day, at work, I think about some of those
things we talked about this morning. I can't help it. For one
thing, I'm bone-tired from lack of sleep. I feel vulnerable and
prey to any random, gruesome thought. Once, when nobody
is around, I put my head on my desk and think I might catch a
few minutes' sleep. But when I close my eyes I find myself
thinking about it again. In my mind I can see a hospital bed.
That's all—just a hospital bed. The bed's in a room, I guess.
Then I see an oxygen tent over the bed, and beside the bed
some of those screens and some big monitors—the kind they
have in movies. I open my eyes and sit up in my chair and light

a cigarette. I drink some coffee while I smoke the cigarette. Then I look at the time and get back to work.

At five o'clock, I'm so tired it's all I can do to drive home. It's raining, and I have to be careful driving. Very careful. There's been an accident, too. Someone has rear-ended someone else at a traffic light, but I don't think anyone has been hurt. The cars are still out in the road, and people are standing around in the rain, talking. Still, traffic moves slowly; the police have set out flares.

When I see my wife, I say, "God, what a day. I'm whipped. How are you doing?" We kiss each other. I take off my coat and hang it up. I take the drink Iris gives me. Then, because it's been on my mind, and because I want to clear the deck, so to speak, I say, "All right, if it's what you want to hear, I'll pull the plug for you. If that's what you want me to do, I'll do it. If it will make you happy, here and now, to hear me say so, I'll say it. I'll do it for you. I'll pull the plug, or have it pulled, if I ever think it's necessary. But what I said about my plug still stands. Now I don't want to have to think about this stuff ever again. I don't even want to have to *talk* about it again. I think we've said all there is to say on the subject. We've exhausted every angle. *I'm* exhausted."

Iris grins. "Okay," she says. "At least I know now, anyway. I didn't before. Maybe I'm crazy, but I feel better somehow, if you want to know. I don't want to think about it anymore, either. But I'm glad we talked it over. I'll never bring it up again, either, and that's a promise."

She takes my drink and puts it on the table, next to the phone. She puts her arms around me and holds me and lets her head rest on my shoulder. But here's the thing. What I've just said to her, what I've been thinking about off and on all day, well, I feel as if I've crossed some kind of invisible line. I feel as if I've come to a place I never thought I'd have to come to. And I don't know how I got here. It's a strange place. It's a place where a little harmless dreaming and then some sleepy, early-morning talk has led me into considerations of death and annihilation.

The phone rings. We let go of each other, and I reach to answer it. "Hello," I say.

"Hello, there," the woman says back.

It's the same woman who called this morning, but she isn't drunk now. At least, I don't think she is; she doesn't sound drunk. She is speaking quietly, reasonably, and she is asking me if I can put her in touch with Bud Roberts. She apologizes. She hates to trouble me, she says, but this is an urgent matter. She's sorry for any trouble she might be giving.

While she talks, I fumble with my cigarettes. I put one in my mouth and use the lighter. Then it's my turn to talk. This is what I say to her: "Bud Roberts doesn't live here. He is not at this number, and I don't expect he ever will be. I will never, never lay eyes on this man you're talking about. Please don't ever call here again. Just don't, okay? Do you hear me? If you're not careful, I'll wring your neck for you."

"The *gall* of that woman," Iris says.

My hands are shaking. I think my voice is doing things. But while I'm trying to tell all this to the woman, while I'm trying to make myself understood, my wife moves quickly and bends over, and that's it. The line goes dead, and I can't hear anything.

Intimacy

I HAVE some business out west anyway, so I stop off in this little town where my former wife lives. We haven't seen each other in four years. But from time to time, when something of mine appeared, or was written about me in the magazines or papers—a profile or an interview—I sent her these things. I don't know what I had in mind except I thought she might be interested. In any case, she never responded.

It is nine in the morning, I haven't called, and it's true I don't know what I am going to find.

But she lets me in. She doesn't seem surprised. We don't shake hands, much less kiss each other. She takes me into the living room. As soon as I sit down she brings me some coffee. Then she comes out with what's on her mind. She says I've caused her anguish, made her feel exposed and humiliated.

Make no mistake, I feel I'm home.

She says, But then you were into betrayal early. You always felt comfortable with betrayal. No, she says, that's not true. Not in the beginning, at any rate. You were different then. But I guess I was different too. Everything was different, she says. No, it was after you turned thirty-five, or thirty-six, whenever it was, around in there anyway, your mid-thirties somewhere, then you started in. You really started in. You turned on me. You did it up pretty then. You must be proud of yourself.

She says, Sometimes I could scream.

She says she wishes I'd forget about the hard times, the bad times, when I talk about back then. Spend some time on the good times, she says. Weren't there some good times? She wishes I'd get off that other subject. She's bored with it. Sick of hearing about it. Your private hobby horse, she says. What's done is done and water under the bridge, she says. A tragedy, yes. God knows it was a tragedy and then some. But why keep it going? Don't you ever get tired of dredging up that old business?

She says, Let go of the past, for Christ's sake. Those old hurts. You must have some other arrows in your quiver, she says.

She says, You know something? I think you're sick. I think

you're crazy as a bedbug. Hey, you don't believe the things they're saying about you, do you? Don't believe them for a minute, she says. Listen, I could tell them a thing or two. Let them talk to me about it, if they want to hear a story.

She says, Are you listening to me?

I'm listening, I say. I'm all ears, I say.

She says, I've really had a bellyful of it, buster! Who asked you here today anyway? I sure as hell didn't. You just show up and walk in. What the hell do you want from me? Blood? You want more blood? I thought you had your fill by now.

She says, Think of me as dead. I want to be left in peace now. That's all I want anymore is to be left in peace and forgotten about. Hey, I'm forty-five years old, she says. Forty-five going on fifty-five, or sixty-five. Lay off, will you.

She says, Why don't you wipe the blackboard clean and see what you have left after that? Why don't you start with a clean slate? See how far that gets you, she says.

She has to laugh at this. I laugh too, but it's nerves.

She says, You know something? I had my chance once, but I let it go. I just let it go. I don't guess I ever told you. But now look at me. Look! Take a good look while you're at it. You threw me away, you son of a bitch.

She says, I was younger then and a better person. Maybe you were too, she says. A better person, I mean. You had to be. You were better then or I wouldn't have had anything to do with you.

She says, I loved you so much once. I loved you to the point of distraction. I did. More than anything in the whole wide world. Imagine that. What a laugh that is now. Can you imagine it? We were so *intimate* once upon a time I can't believe it now. I think that's the strangest thing of all now. The memory of being that intimate with somebody. We were so intimate I could puke. I can't imagine ever being that intimate with somebody else. I haven't been.

She says, Frankly, and I mean this, I want to be kept out of it from here on out. Who do you think you are anyway? You think you're God or somebody? You're not fit to lick God's boots, or anybody else's for that matter. Mister, you've been hanging out with the wrong people. But what do I know? I don't even know what I know any longer. I know I don't like what you've been dishing out. I know that much. You know what I'm talking about, don't you? Am I right?

Right, I say. Right as rain.

She says, You'll agree to anything, won't you? You give in too easy. You always did. You don't have any principles, not one. Anything to avoid a fuss. But that's neither here nor there.

She says, You remember that time I pulled the knife on you?

She says this as if in passing, as if it's not important.

Vaguely, I say. I must have deserved it, but I don't remember much about it. Go ahead, why don't you, and tell me about it.

She says, I'm beginning to understand something now. I think I know why you're here. Yes. I know why you're here, even if you don't. But you're a slyboots. You know why you're here. You're on a fishing expedition. You're hunting for *material*. Am I getting warm? Am I right?

Tell me about the knife, I say.

She says, If you want to know, I'm real sorry I didn't use that knife. I am. I really and truly am. I've thought and thought about it, and I'm sorry I didn't use it. I had the chance. But I hesitated. I hesitated and was lost, as somebody or other said. But I should have used it, the hell with everything and everybody. I should have nicked your arm with it at least. At least that.

Well, you didn't, I say. I thought you were going to cut me with it, but you didn't. I took it away from you.

She says, You were always lucky. You took it away and then you slapped me. Still, I regret I didn't use that knife just a little bit. Even a little would have been something to remember me by.

I remember a lot, I say. I say that, then wish I hadn't.

She says, Amen, brother. That's the bone of contention here, if you hadn't noticed. That's the whole problem. But like I said, in my opinion you remember the wrong things. You remember the low, shameful things. That's why you got interested when I brought up the knife.

She says, I wonder if you ever have any regret. For whatever that's worth on the market these days. Not much, I guess. But you ought to be a specialist in it by now.

Regret, I say. It doesn't interest me much, to tell the truth.

Regret is not a word I use very often. I guess I mainly don't have it. I admit I hold to the dark view of things. Sometimes, anyway. But regret? I don't think so.

She says, You're a real son of a bitch, did you know that? A ruthless, coldhearted son of a bitch. Did anybody ever tell you that?

You did, I say. Plenty of times.

She says, I always speak the truth. Even when it hurts. You'll never catch me in a lie.

She says, My eyes were opened a long time ago, but by then it was too late. I had my chance but I let it slide through my fingers. I even thought for a while you'd come back. Why'd I think that anyway? I must have been out of my mind. I could cry my eyes out now, but I wouldn't give you that satisfaction.

She says, You know what? I think if you were on fire right now, if you suddenly burst into flame this minute, I wouldn't throw a bucket of water on you.

She laughs at this. Then her face closes down again.

She says, Why in hell *are* you here? You want to hear some more? I could go on for days. I think I know why you turned up, but I want to hear it from you.

When I don't answer, when I just keep sitting there, she goes on.

She says, After that time, when you went away, nothing much mattered after that. Not the kids, not God, not anything. It was like I didn't know what hit me. It was like I had *stopped living.* My life had been going along, going along, and then it just stopped. It didn't just come to a stop, it screeched to a stop. I thought, If I'm not worth anything to him, well, I'm not worth anything to myself or anybody else either. That was the worst thing I felt. I thought my heart would break. What am I saying? It did break. Of course it broke. It broke, just like that. It's still broke, if you want to know. And so there you have it in a nutshell. My eggs in one basket, she says. A tisket, a tasket. All my rotten eggs in one basket.

She says, You found somebody else for yourself, didn't you? It didn't take long. And you're happy now. That's what they say about you anyway: "He's happy now." Hey, I read everything you send! You think I don't? Listen, I know your heart, mister. I always did. I knew it back then, and I know it now. I know your heart inside and out, and don't you ever forget it. Your heart is a jungle, a dark forest, it's a garbage pail, if you want to know. Let them talk to me if they want to ask somebody something. I know how you operate. Just let them come around here, and I'll give them an earful. I was there. I served, buddy boy. Then you held me up for display and ridicule in your so-called work. For any Tom or Harry to pity or pass judgment on. Ask me if I cared. Ask me if it embarrassed me. Go ahead, ask.

No, I say, I won't ask that. I don't want to get into that, I say.

Damn straight you don't! she says. And you know *why*, too!

She says, Honey, no offense, but sometimes I think I could shoot you and watch you kick.

She says, You can't look me in the eyes, can you?

She says, and this is exactly what she says, You can't even look me in the eyes when I'm talking to you.

So, okay, I look her in the eyes.

She says, Right. Okay, she says. Now we're getting someplace, maybe. That's better. You can tell a lot about the person you're talking to from his eyes. Everybody knows that. But you know something else? There's nobody in this whole world who would tell you this, but I can tell you. I have the right. I *earned* that right, sonny. You have yourself confused with somebody else. And that's the pure truth of it. But what do I know? they'll say in a hundred years. They'll say, Who was she anyway?

She says, In any case, you sure as hell have *me* confused with somebody else. Hey, I don't even have the same name anymore! Not the name I was born with, not the name I lived with you with, not even the name I had two years ago. What is this? What is this in hell all about anyway? Let me say something. I want to be left alone now. Please. That's not a crime.

She says, Don't you have someplace else you should be? Some plane to catch? Shouldn't you be somewhere far from here at this very minute?

No, I say. I say it again: No. No place, I say. I don't have anyplace I have to be.

And then I do something. I reach over and take the sleeve of her blouse between my thumb and forefinger. That's all. I just touch it that way, and then I just bring my hand back. She doesn't draw away. She doesn't move.

Then here's the thing I do next. I get down on my knees, a big guy like me, and I take the hem of her dress. What am I doing on the floor? I wish I could say. But I know it's where I ought to be, and I'm there on my knees holding on to the hem of her dress.

She is still for a minute. But in a minute she says, Hey, it's all right, stupid. You're so dumb, sometimes. Get up now. I'm telling you to get up. Listen, it's okay. I'm over it now. It took me a while to get over it. What do you think? Did you think it wouldn't? Then you walk in here and suddenly the whole cruddy business is back. I felt a need to ventilate. But you know, and I know, it's over and done with now.

She says, For the longest while, honey, I was inconsolable. *Inconsolable*, she says. Put that word in your little notebook. I can tell you from experience that's the saddest word in the English language. Anyway, I got over it finally. Time is a gentleman, a wise man said. Or else maybe a worn-out old woman, one or the other anyway.

She says, I have a life now. It's a different kind of life than yours, but I guess we don't need to compare. It's my life, and that's the important thing I have to realize as I get older. Don't feel *too* bad, anyway, she says. I mean, it's all right to feel a *little* bad, maybe. That won't hurt you, that's only to be expected after all. Even if you can't move yourself to regret.

She says, Now you have to get up and get out of here. My husband will be along pretty soon for his lunch. How would I explain this kind of thing?

It's crazy, but I'm still on my knees holding the hem of her dress. I won't let it go. I'm like a terrier, and it's like I'm stuck to the floor. It's like I can't move.

She says, Get up now. What is it? You still want something from me. What do you want? Want me to forgive you? Is that why you're doing this? That's it, isn't it? That's the reason you came all this way. The knife thing kind of perked you up, too. I think you'd forgotten about that. But you needed me to remind you. Okay, I'll say something if you'll just go.

She says, I forgive you.

She says, Are you satisfied now? Is that better? Are you happy? He's happy now, she says.

But I'm still there, knees to the floor.

She says, Did you hear what I said? You have to go now. Hey, stupid. Honey, I said I forgive you. And I even reminded you about the knife thing. I can't think what else I can do now. You got it made in the shade, baby. Come *on* now, you have to get out of here. Get up. That's right. You're still a big guy, aren't you. Here's your hat, don't forget your hat. You never used to wear a hat. I never in my life saw you in a hat before.

She says, Listen to me now. Look at me. Listen carefully to what I'm going to tell you.

She moves closer. She's about three inches from my face. We haven't been this close in a long time. I take these little breaths that she can't hear, and I wait. I think my heart slows way down, I think.

She says, You just tell it like you have to, I guess, and forget the rest. Like always. You been doing that for so long now anyway it shouldn't be hard for you.

She says, There, I've done it. You're free, aren't you? At least you think you are anyway. Free at last. That's a joke, but don't laugh. Anyway, you feel better, don't you?

She walks with me down the hall.

She says, I can't imagine how I'd explain this if my husband was to walk in this very minute. But who really cares anymore, right? In the final analysis, nobody gives a damn anymore. Besides which, I think everything that can happen that way has already happened. His name is Fred, by the way. He's a decent guy and works hard for his living. He cares for me.

So she walks me to the front door, which has been standing open all this while. The door that was letting in light and fresh air this morning, and sounds off the street, all of which we had ignored. I look outside and, Jesus, there's this white moon hanging in the morning sky. I can't think when I've ever seen anything so remarkable. But I'm afraid to comment on it. I am. I don't know what might happen. I might break into tears even. I might not understand a word I'd say.

She says, Maybe you'll be back sometime, and maybe you won't. This'll wear off, you know. Pretty soon you'll start feeling bad again. Maybe it'll make a good story, she says. But I don't want to know about it if it does.

I say good-bye. She doesn't say anything more. She looks at her hands, and then she puts them into the pockets of her dress. She shakes her head. She goes back inside, and this time she closes the door.

I move off down the sidewalk. Some kids are tossing a football at the end of the street. But they aren't my kids, and they aren't her kids either. There are these leaves everywhere, even in the gutters. Piles of leaves wherever I look. They're falling off the limbs as I walk. I can't take a step without putting my shoe into leaves. Somebody ought to make an effort here. Somebody ought to get a rake and take care of this.

Menudo

I CAN'T sleep, but when I'm sure my wife Vicky is asleep, I get up and look through our bedroom window, across the street, at Oliver and Amanda's house. Oliver has been gone for three days, but his wife Amanda is awake. She can't sleep either. It's four in the morning, and there's not a sound outside—no wind, no cars, no moon even—just Oliver and Amanda's place with the lights on, leaves heaped up under the front windows.

A couple of days ago, when I couldn't sit still, I raked our yard—Vicky's and mine. I gathered all the leaves into bags, tied off the tops, and put the bags alongside the curb. I had an urge then to cross the street and rake over there, but I didn't follow through. It's my fault things are the way they are across the street.

I've only slept a few hours since Oliver left. Vicky saw me moping around the house, looking anxious, and decided to put two and two together. She's on her side of the bed now, scrunched on to about ten inches of mattress. She got into bed and tried to position herself so she wouldn't accidentally roll into me while she slept. She hasn't moved since she lay down, sobbed, and then dropped into sleep. She's exhausted. I'm exhausted too.

I've taken nearly all of Vicky's pills, but I still can't sleep. I'm keyed up. But maybe if I keep looking I'll catch a glimpse of Amanda moving around inside her house, or else find her peering from behind a curtain, trying to see what she can see over here.

What if I do see her? So what? What then?

Vicky says I'm crazy. She said worse things too last night. But who could blame her? I told her—I had to—but I didn't tell her it was Amanda. When Amanda's name came up, I insisted it wasn't her. Vicky suspects, but I wouldn't name names. I wouldn't say who, even though she kept pressing and then hit me a few times in the head.

"What's it matter *who*?" I said. "You've never met the woman," I lied. "You don't know her." That's when she started hitting me.

I feel *wired*. That's what my painter friend Alfredo used to call it when he talked about friends of his coming down off something. *Wired*. I'm wired.

This thing is nuts. I know it is, but I can't stop thinking about Amanda. Things are so bad just now I even find myself thinking about my first wife, Molly. I loved Molly, I thought, more than my own life.

I keep picturing Amanda in her pink nightgown, the one I like on her so much, along with her pink slippers. And I feel certain she's in the big leather chair right now, under the brass reading lamp. She's smoking cigarettes, one after the other. There are two ashtrays close at hand, and they're both full. To the left of her chair, next to the lamp, there's an end table stacked with magazines—the usual magazines that nice people read. We're nice people, all of us, to a point. Right this minute, Amanda is, I imagine, paging through a magazine, stopping every so often to look at an illustration or a cartoon.

Two days ago, in the afternoon, Amanda said to me, "I can't read books anymore. Who has the time?" It was the day after Oliver had left, and we were in this little café in the industrial part of the city. "Who can concentrate anymore?" she said, stirring her coffee. "Who reads? Do you read?" (I shook my head.) "Somebody must read, I guess. You see all these books around in store windows, and there are those clubs. Somebody's reading," she said. "Who? I don't know anybody who reads."

That's what she said, apropos of nothing—that is, we weren't talking about books, we were talking about our *lives*. Books had nothing to do with it.

"What did Oliver say when you told him?"

Then it struck me that what we were saying—the tense, watchful expressions we wore—belonged to the people on afternoon TV programs that I'd never done more than switch on and then off.

Amanda looked down and shook her head, as if she couldn't bear to remember.

"You didn't admit who it was you were involved with, did you?"

She shook her head again.

"You're sure of that?" I waited until she looked up from her coffee.

"I didn't mention any names, if that's what you mean."

"Did he say where he was going, or how long he'd be away?" I said, wishing I didn't have to hear myself. This was my neighbor I was talking about. Oliver Porter. A man I'd helped drive out of his home.

"He didn't say where. A hotel. He said I should make my arrangements and be gone—*be gone*, he said. It was like biblical the way he said it—out of his house, out of his *life*, in a week's time. I guess he's coming back then. So we have to decide something real important, real soon, honey. You and I have to make up our minds pretty damn quick."

It was her turn to look at me now, and I know she was looking for a sign of life-long commitment. "A week," I said. I looked at my coffee, which had gotten cold. A lot had happened in a little while, and we were trying to take it in. I don't know what long-term things, if any, we'd thought about those months as we moved from flirtation to love, and then afternoon assignations. In any case, we were in a serious fix now. Very serious. We'd never expected—not in a hundred years—to be hiding out in a café, in the middle of the afternoon, trying to decide matters like this.

I raised my eyes, and Amanda began stirring her coffee. She kept stirring it. I touched her hand, and the spoon dropped out of her fingers. She picked it up and began stirring again. We could have been anybody drinking coffee at a table under fluorescent lights in a run-down café. Anybody, just about. I took Amanda's hand and held it, and it seemed to make a difference.

Vicky's still sleeping on her side when I go downstairs. I plan to heat some milk and drink that. I used to drink whiskey when I couldn't sleep, but I gave it up. Now it's strictly hot milk. In the whiskey days I'd wake up with this tremendous thirst in the middle of the night. But, back then, I was always looking ahead: I kept a bottle of water in the fridge, for instance. I'd be dehydrated, sweating from head to toe when I woke, but I'd wander out to the kitchen and could count on finding that bottle of cold water in the fridge. I'd drink it, all of it, down the hatch, an entire quart of water. Once in a while I'd use a glass, but not often. Suddenly I'd be drunk all over again and weaving around the kitchen. I can't begin to account for it—sober one minute, drunk the next.

The drinking was part of my destiny—according to Molly, anyway. She put a lot of stock in destiny.

I feel wild from lack of sleep. I'd give anything, just about, to be able to go to sleep, and sleep the sleep of an honest man.

Why do we have to sleep anyway? And why do we tend to sleep less during some crises and more during others? For instance, that time my dad had his stroke. He woke up after a coma—seven days and nights in a hospital bed—and calmly said "Hello" to the people in his room. Then his eyes picked me out. "Hello, son," he said. Five minutes later, he died. Just like that—he died. But, during that whole crisis, I never took my clothes off and didn't go to bed. I may have catnapped in a waiting-room chair from time to time, but I never went to bed and *slept*.

And then a year or so ago I found out Vicky was seeing somebody else. Instead of confronting *her*, I went to bed when I heard about it, and stayed there. I didn't get up for days, a week maybe—I don't know. I mean, I got up to go to the bathroom, or else to the kitchen to make a sandwich. I even went out to the living room in my pajamas, in the afternoon, and tried to read the papers. But I'd fall asleep sitting up. Then I'd stir, open my eyes and go back to bed and sleep some more. I couldn't get enough sleep.

It passed. We weathered it. Vicky quit her boyfriend, or he quit her, I never found out. I just know she went away from me for a while, and then she came back. But I have the feeling we're not going to weather this business. This thing is different. Oliver has given Amanda that ultimatum.

Still, isn't it possible that Oliver himself is awake at this moment and writing a letter to Amanda, urging reconciliation? Even now he might be scribbling away, trying to persuade her that what she's doing to him and their daughter Beth is foolish, disastrous, and finally a tragic thing for the three of them.

No, that's insane. I know Oliver. He's relentless, unforgiving. He could slam a croquet ball into the next block—and has. He isn't going to write any such letter. He gave her an ultimatum, right?—and that's that. A week. Four days now. Or is it three? Oliver may be awake, but if he is, he's sitting in a chair in his hotel room with a glass of iced vodka in his hand, his feet on the bed, TV turned on low. He's dressed, except for his shoes. He's not wearing shoes—that's the only concession he makes. That and the fact he's loosened his tie.

Oliver is relentless.

I heat the milk, spoon the skin from the surface and pour it up. Then I turn off the kitchen light and take the cup into the living room and sit on the sofa, where I can look across the street at the lighted windows. But I can hardly sit still. I keep fidgeting, crossing one leg and then the other. I feel like I could throw off sparks, or break a window—maybe rearrange all the furniture.

The things that go through your mind when you can't sleep! Earlier, thinking about Molly, for a moment I couldn't even remember what she *looked* like, for Christ's sake, yet we were together for years, more or less continuously, since we were kids. Molly, who said she'd love me forever. The only thing left was the memory of her sitting and weeping at the kitchen table, her shoulders bent forward, and her hands covering her face. *Forever*, she said. But it hadn't worked out that way. Finally, she said, it didn't matter, it was of no real concern to her, if she and I lived together the rest of our lives or not. Our love existed on a "higher plane." That's what she said to Vicky over the phone that time, after Vicky and I had set up housekeeping together. Molly called, got hold of Vicky, and said, "You have your relationship with him, but I'll always have mine. His destiny and mine are linked."

My first wife, Molly, she talked like that. "Our destinies are linked." She didn't talk like that in the beginning. It was only later, after so much had happened, that she started using words like "cosmic" and "empowerment" and so forth. But our destinies are *not* linked—not now, anyway, if they ever were. I don't even know where she is now, not for certain.

I think I could put my finger on the exact time, the real turning point, when it came undone for Molly. It was after I started seeing Vicky, and Molly found out. They called me up one day from the high school where Molly taught and said,

"Please. Your wife is doing handsprings in front of the school. You'd better get down here." It was after I took her home that I began hearing about "higher power" and "going with the flow"—stuff of that sort. Our destiny had been "revised." And if I'd been hesitating before, well, I left her then as fast as I could—this woman I'd known all my life, the one who'd been my best friend for years, my intimate, my confidante. I bailed out on her. For one thing, I was scared. *Scared.*

This girl I'd started out with in life, this sweet thing, this gentle soul, she wound up going to fortune-tellers, palm readers, *crystal ball gazers*, looking for answers, trying to figure out what she should do with her life. She quit her job, drew out her teacher's retirement money, and thereafter never made a decision without consulting the *I Ching*. She began wearing strange clothes—clothes with permanent wrinkles and a lot of burgundy and orange. She even got involved with a group that sat around, I'm not kidding, trying to levitate.

When Molly and I were growing up together, she was a part of me and, sure, I was a part of her, too. We loved each other. It *was* our destiny. I believed in it then myself. But now I don't know what to believe in. I'm not complaining, simply stating a fact. I'm down to nothing. And I have to go on like this. No destiny. Just the next thing meaning whatever you think it does. Compulsion and error, just like everybody else.

Amanda? I'd like to believe in her, bless her heart. But she was looking for somebody when she met me. That's the way with people when they get restless: they start up something, knowing that's going to change things for good.

I'd like to go out in the front yard and shout something. "None of this is worth it!" That's what I'd like people to hear.

"Destiny," Molly said. For all I know she's still talking about it.

All the lights are off over there now, except for that light in the kitchen. I could try calling Amanda on the phone. I could do that and see how far it gets me! What if Vicky heard me dialing or talking on the phone and came downstairs? What if she lifted the receiver upstairs and listened? Besides, there's always the chance Beth might pick up the phone. I don't want to talk to any kids this morning. I don't want to talk to anybody. Ac-

tually, I'd talk to Molly, if I could, but I can't any longer—
she's somebody else now. She isn't *Molly* anymore. But—what
can I say?—I'm somebody else, too.

I wish I could be like everybody else in this neighborhood—
your basic, normal, unaccomplished person—and go up to my
bedroom, and lie down, and sleep. It's going to be a big day
today, and I'd like to be ready for it. I wish I could sleep and
wake up and find everything in my life different. Not necessarily just the big things, like this thing with Amanda or the past
with Molly. But things clearly within my power.

Take the situation with my mother: I used to send money
every month. But then I started sending her the same amount
in twice-yearly sums. I gave her money on her birthday, and
I gave her money at Christmas. I thought: I won't have to
worry about forgetting her birthday, and I won't have to worry
about sending her a Christmas present. I won't have to
worry, period. It went like clockwork for a long time.

Then last year she asked me—it was in between money
times, it was in March, or maybe April—for a radio. A radio,
she said, would make a difference to her.

What she wanted was a little clock radio. She could put it in
her kitchen and have it out there to listen to while she was fixing
something to eat in the evening. And she'd have the clock to
look at too, so she'd know when something was supposed to
come out of the oven, or how long it was until one of her programs started.

A little clock radio.

She hinted around at first. She said, "I'd sure like to have a
radio. But I can't afford one. I guess I'll have to wait for my
birthday. That little radio I had, it fell and broke. I miss a
radio." *I miss a radio.* That's what she said when we talked on
the phone, or else she'd bring it up when she'd write.

Finally—what'd I say? I said to her over the phone that I
couldn't afford any radios. I said it in a letter too, so she'd be
sure and understand. *I can't afford any radios,* is what I wrote.
I can't do any more, I said, than I'm doing. Those were my
very words.

But it wasn't true! I could have done more. I just said I
couldn't. I could have afforded to buy a radio for her. What
would it have cost me? Thirty-five dollars? Forty dollars or less,

including tax. I could have sent her a radio through the mail. I could have had somebody in the store do it, if I didn't want to go to the trouble myself. Or else I could have sent her a forty-dollar check along with a note saying, *This money is for your radio, mother.*

I could have handled it in any case. Forty dollars—are you kidding? But I didn't. I wouldn't part with it. It seemed there was a *principle* involved. That's what I told myself anyway—there's a principle involved here.

Ha.

Then what happened? She died. She *died*. She was walking home from the grocery store, back to her apartment, carrying her sack of groceries, and she fell into somebody's bushes and died.

I took a flight out there to make the arrangements. She was still at the coroner's, and they had her purse and her groceries behind the desk in the office. I didn't bother to look in the purse they handed me. But what she had from the grocery store was a jar of Metamucil, two grapefruits, a carton of cottage cheese, a quart of buttermilk, some potatoes and onions, and a package of ground meat that was beginning to change color.

Boy! I cried when I saw those things. I couldn't stop. I didn't think I'd ever quit crying. The woman who worked at the desk was embarrassed and brought me a glass of water. They gave me a bag for my mother's groceries and another bag for her personal effects—her purse and her dentures. Later, I put the dentures in my coat pocket and drove them down in a rental car and gave them to somebody at the funeral home.

The light in Amanda's kitchen is still on. It's a bright light that spills out on to all those leaves. Maybe she's like I am, and she's scared. Maybe she left that light burning as a night-light. Or maybe she's still awake and is at the kitchen table, under the light, writing me a letter. Amanda is writing me a letter, and somehow she'll get it into my hands later on when the real day starts.

Come to think of it, I've never had a letter from her since we've known each other. All the time we've been involved—

six months, eight months—and I've never once seen a scrap of
her handwriting. I don't even know if she's *literate* that way.

I think she is. Sure, she is. She talks about books, doesn't
she? It doesn't matter of course. Well, a little, I suppose. I love
her in any case, right?

But I've never written anything to her, either. We always
talked on the phone or else face to face.

Molly, she was the letter writer. She used to write me even
after we weren't living together. Vicky would bring her letters
in from the box and leave them on the kitchen table without a
word. Finally the letters dwindled away, became more and
more infrequent and bizarre. When she did write, the letters
gave me a chill. They were full of talk about "auras" and "signs."
Occasionally she reported a voice that was telling her something she ought to do or some place she should go. And once
she told me that no matter what happened, we were still "on
the same frequency." She always knew exactly what I felt, she
said. She "beamed in on me," she said, from time to time.
Reading those letters of hers, the hair on the back of my neck
would tingle. She also had a new word for destiny: *Karma*.
"I'm following out my karma," she wrote. "Your karma has
taken a bad turn."

I'd like to go to sleep, but what's the point? People will be getting up soon. Vicky's alarm will go off before much longer. I
wish I could go upstairs and get back in bed with my wife, tell
her I'm sorry, there's been a mistake, let's forget all this—then
go to sleep and wake up with her in my arms. But I've forfeited
that right. I'm outside all that now, and I can't get back inside!
But say I did that. Say I went upstairs and slid into bed with
Vicky as I'd like to do. She might wake up and say, *You bastard. Don't you dare touch me, son of a bitch.*

What's she talking about, anyway? I wouldn't touch her.
Not in that way, I wouldn't.

After I left Molly, after I'd pulled out on her, about two
months after, then Molly really did it. She had her real collapse
then, the one that'd been coming on. Her sister saw to it that
she got the care she needed. What am I saying? *They put her
away.* They had to, they said. They put my wife away. By then

I was living with Vicky, and trying not to drink whiskey. I couldn't do anything for Molly. I mean, she was there, I was here, and I couldn't have gotten her out of that place if I'd wanted to. But the fact is, I didn't want to. She was in there, they said, because she *needed* to be in there. Nobody said anything about destiny. Things had gone beyond that.

And I didn't even go visit her—not once! At the time, I didn't think I could stand seeing her in there. But, Christ, what was I? A fair-weather friend? We'd been through plenty. But what on earth would I have said to her? *I'm sorry about all this, honey.* I could have said that, I guess. I intended to write, but I didn't. Not a word. Anyway, when you get right down to it, what could I have said in a letter? *How are they treating you, baby? I'm sorry you're where you are, but don't give up. Remember all the good times? Remember when we were happy together? Hey, I'm sorry they've done this to you. I'm sorry it turned out this way. I'm sorry everything is just garbage now.* I'm sorry, Molly.

I didn't write. I think I was trying to forget about her, to pretend she didn't exist. Molly who?

I left my wife and took somebody else's: Vicky. Now I think maybe I've lost Vicky, too. But Vicky won't be going away to any summer camp for the mentally disabled. She's a hard case. She left her former husband, Joe Kraft, and didn't bat an eye; I don't think she ever lost a night's sleep over it.

Vicky Kraft-Hughes. Amanda Porter. This is where my destiny has brought me? To this street in this neighborhood, messing up the lives of these women?

Amanda's kitchen light went off when I wasn't looking. The room that was there is gone now, like the others. Only the porch light is still burning. Amanda must have forgotten it, I guess. Hey, Amanda.

Once, when Molly was away in that place and I wasn't in my right mind—let's face it, I was crazy too—one night I was at my friend Alfredo's house, a bunch of us drinking and listening to records. I didn't care any longer what happened to me. Everything, I thought, that could happen had happened. I felt unbalanced. I felt lost. Anyway, there I was at Alfredo's. His paintings of tropical birds and animals hung on every wall in his house, and there were paintings standing around in the rooms, leaning against things—table-legs, say, or his brick-and-board bookcase, as well as being stacked on his back porch. The kitchen served as his studio, and I was sitting at the kitchen table with a drink in front of me. An easel stood off to one side in front of the window that overlooked the alley, and there were crumpled tubes of paint, a palette, and some brushes lying at one end of the table. Alfredo was making himself a drink at the counter a few feet away. I loved the shabby economy of that little room. The stereo music that came from the living room was turned up, filling the house with so much sound the kitchen windows rattled in their frames. Suddenly I began to shake. First my hands began to shake, and then my arms and shoulders, too. My teeth started to chatter. I couldn't hold the glass.

"What's going on, man?" Alfredo said, when he turned and saw the state I was in. "Hey, what is it? What's going on with you?"

I couldn't tell him. What could I say? I thought I was having some kind of an attack. I managed to raise my shoulders and let them drop.

Then Alfredo came over, took a chair and sat down beside me at the kitchen table. He put his big painter's hand on my shoulder. I went on shaking. He could feel me shaking.

"What's wrong with you, man? I'm real sorry about everything, man. I know it's real hard right now." Then he said he was going to fix *menudo* for me. He said it would be good for what ailed me. "Help your nerves, man," he said. "Calm you right down." He had all the ingredients for *menudo*, he said, and he'd been wanting to make some anyway.

"You listen to me. Listen to what I say, man. I'm your family now," Alfredo said.

It was two in the morning, we were drunk, there were these other drunk people in the house and the stereo was going full blast. But Alfredo went to his fridge and opened it and took some stuff out. He closed the fridge door and looked in his freezer compartment. He found something in a package. Then he looked around in his cupboards. He took a big pan from the cabinet under the sink, and he was ready.

Tripe. He started with tripe and about a gallon of water.

Then he chopped onions and added them to the water, which had started to boil. He put *chorizo* sausage in the pot. After that, he dropped peppercorns into the boiling water and sprinkled in some chili powder. Then came the olive oil. He opened a big can of tomato sauce and poured that in. He added cloves of garlic, some slices of white bread, salt, and lemon juice. He opened another can—it was hominy—and poured that in the pot, too. He put it all in, and then he turned the heat down and put a lid on the pot.

I watched him. I sat there shaking while Alfredo stood at the stove making *menudo*, talking—I didn't have any idea what he was saying—and, from time to time, he'd shake his head, or else start whistling to himself. Now and then people drifted into the kitchen for beer. But all the while Alfredo went on very seriously looking after his *menudo*. He could have been home, in Morelia, making *menudo* for his family on New Year's day.

People hung around in the kitchen for a while, joking, but Alfredo didn't joke back when they kidded him about cooking *menudo* in the middle of the night. Pretty soon they left us alone. Finally, while Alfredo stood at the stove with a spoon in his hand, watching me, I got up slowly from the table. I walked out of the kitchen into the bathroom, and then opened another door off the bathroom to the spare room—where I lay down on the bed and fell asleep. When I woke it was midafternoon. The *menudo* was gone. The pot was in the sink, soaking. Those other people must have eaten it! They must have eaten it and grown calm. Everyone was gone, and the house was quiet.

I never saw Alfredo more than once or twice afterward. After that night, our lives took us in separate directions. And those other people who were there—who knows where they went? I'll probably die without ever tasting *menudo*. But who can say?

Is this what it all comes down to then? A middle-aged man involved with his neighbor's wife, linked to an angry ultimatum? What kind of destiny is that? A week, Oliver said. Three or four days now.

—

A car passes outside with its lights on. The sky is turning gray, and I hear some birds starting up. I decide I can't wait any longer. I can't just sit here, doing nothing—that's all there is to it. I can't keep waiting. I've waited and waited and where's it gotten me? Vicky's alarm will go off soon, Beth will get up and dress for school, Amanda will wake up, too. The entire neighborhood.

On the back porch I find some old jeans and a sweatshirt, and I change out of my pajamas. Then I put on my white canvas shoes—"wino" shoes, Alfredo would have called them. Alfredo, where are you?

I go outside to the garage and find the rake and some lawn bags. By the time I get around to the front of the house with the rake, ready to begin, I feel I don't have a choice in the matter any longer. It's light out—light enough at any rate for what I have to do. And then, without thinking about it any more, I start to rake. I rake our yard, every inch of it. It's important it be done right, too. I set the rake right down into the turf and pull hard. It must feel to the grass like it does whenever someone gives your hair a hard jerk. Now and then a car passes in the street and slows, but I don't look up from my work. I know what the people in the cars must be thinking, but they're dead wrong—they don't know the half of it. How could they? I'm happy, raking.

I finish our yard and put the bag out next to the curb. Then I begin next door on the Baxters' yard. In a few minutes Mrs. Baxter comes out on her porch, wearing her bathrobe. I don't acknowledge her. I'm not embarrassed, and I don't want to appear unfriendly. I just want to keep on with what I'm doing.

She doesn't say anything for a while, and then she says, "Good morning, Mr. Hughes. How are you this morning?"

I stop what I'm doing and run my arm across my forehead. "I'll be through in a little while," I say. "I hope you don't mind."

"We don't mind," Mrs. Baxter says. "Go right ahead, I guess." I see Mr. Baxter standing in the doorway behind her. He's already dressed for work in his slacks and sports coat and tie. But he doesn't venture on to the porch. Then Mrs. Baxter turns and looks at Mr. Baxter, who shrugs.

It's okay, I've finished here anyway. There are other yards, more important yards for that matter. I kneel, and, taking a grip low down on the rake handle, I pull the last of the leaves into my bag and tie off the top. Then, I can't help it, I just stay there, kneeling on the grass with the rake in my hand. When I look up, I see the Baxters come down the porch steps together and move slowly toward me through the wet, sweet-smelling grass. They stop a few feet away and look at me closely.

"There now," I hear Mrs. Baxter say. She's still in her robe and slippers. It's nippy out; she holds her robe at the throat. "You did a real fine job for us, yes, you did."

I don't say anything. I don't even say, "You're welcome."

They stand in front of me a while longer, and none of us says anything more. It's as if we've come to an agreement on something. In a minute, they turn around and go back to their house. High over my head, in the branches of the old maple— the place where these leaves come from—birds call out to each other. At least I think they're calling to each other.

Suddenly a car door slams. Mr. Baxter is in his car in the drive with the window rolled down. Mrs. Baxter says something to him from the front porch which causes Mr. Baxter to nod slowly and turn his head in my direction. He sees me kneeling there with the rake, and a look crosses his face. He frowns. In his better moments, Mr. Baxter is a decent, ordinary guy—a guy you wouldn't mistake for anyone special. But he *is* special. In my book, he is. For one thing he has a full night's sleep behind him, and he's just embraced his wife before leaving for work. But even before he goes, he's already expected home a set number of hours later. True, in the grander scheme of things, his return will be an event of small moment—but an event nonetheless.

Baxter starts his car and races the engine. Then he backs effortlessly out of the drive, brakes, and changes gears. As he passes on the street, he slows and looks briefly in my direction. He lifts his hand off the steering wheel. It could be a salute or a sign of dismissal. It's a sign, in any case. And then he looks away toward the city. I get up and raise my hand, too—not a wave, exactly, but close to it. Some other cars drive past. One of the drivers must think he knows me because he gives his horn a friendly little tap. I look both ways and then cross the street.

Elephant

I KNEW it was a mistake to let my brother have the money. I didn't need anybody else owing me. But when he called and said he couldn't make the payment on his house, what could I do? I'd never been inside his house—he lived a thousand miles away, in California; I'd never even *seen* his house—but I didn't want him to lose it. He cried over the phone and said he was losing everything he'd worked for. He said he'd pay me back. February, he said. Maybe sooner. No later, anyway, than March. He said his income-tax refund was on the way. Plus, he said, he had a little investment that would mature in February. He acted secretive about the investment thing, so I didn't press for details.

"Trust me on this," he said. "I won't let you down."

He'd lost his job last July, when the company he worked for, a fiberglass-insulation plant, decided to lay off two hundred employees. He'd been living on his unemployment since then, but now the unemployment was gone, and his savings were gone, too. And he didn't have health insurance any longer. When his job went, the insurance went. His wife, who was ten years older, was diabetic and needed treatment. He'd had to sell the other car—her car, an old station wagon—and a week ago he'd pawned his TV. He told me he'd hurt his back carrying the TV up and down the street where the pawnshops did business. He went from place to place, he said, trying to get the best offer. Somebody finally gave him a hundred dollars for it, this big Sony TV. He told me about the TV, and then about throwing his back out, as if this ought to cinch it with me, unless I had a stone in place of a heart.

"I've gone belly up," he said. "But you can help me pull out of it."

"How much?" I said.

"Five hundred. I could use more, sure, who couldn't?" he said. "But I want to be realistic. I can pay back five hundred. More than that, I'll tell you the truth, I'm not so sure. Brother, I hate to ask. But you're my last resort. Irma Jean and I are going to be on the street before long. I won't let you

down," he said. That's what he said. Those were his exact
words.

We talked a little more—mostly about our mother and her
problems—but, to make a long story short, I sent him the
money. I had to. I felt I had to, at any rate—which amounts to
the same thing. I wrote him a letter when I sent the check and
said he should pay the money back to our mother, who lived in
the same town he lived in and who was poor and greedy. I'd
been mailing checks to her every month, rain or shine, for
three years. But I was thinking that if he paid her the money he
owed me it might take me off the hook there and let me
breathe for a while. I wouldn't have to worry on that score for
a couple of months, anyway. Also, and this is the truth, I
thought maybe he'd be more likely to pay her, since they lived
right there in the same town and he saw her from time to time.
All I was doing was trying to cover myself some way. The thing
is, he might have the best intentions of paying me back, but
things happen sometimes. Things get in the way of best intentions. Out of sight, out of mind, as they say. But he wouldn't
stiff his own mother. Nobody would do that.

I spent hours writing letters, trying to make sure everybody
knew what could be expected and what was required. I even
phoned out there to my mother several times, trying to explain
it to her. But she was suspicious over the whole deal. I went
through it with her on the phone step by step, but she was still
suspicious. I told her the money that was supposed to come
from me on the first of March and on the first of April would
instead come from Billy, who owed the money to me. She'd
get her money, and she didn't have to worry. The only difference was that Billy would pay it to her those two months instead of me. He'd pay her the money I'd normally be sending
to her, but instead of him mailing it to me and then me having
to turn around and send it to her he'd pay it to her directly.
On any account, she didn't have to worry. She'd get her
money, but for those two months it'd come from him—from
the money he owed me. My God, I don't know how much I
spent on phone calls. And I wish I had fifty cents for every
letter I wrote, telling him what I'd told her and telling her
what to expect from him—that sort of thing.

But my mother didn't trust Billy. "What if he can't come up

with it?" she said to me over the phone. "What then? He's in bad shape, and I'm sorry for him," she said. "But, son, what I want to know is, what if he isn't able to pay me? What if he can't? Then what?"

"Then I'll pay you myself," I said. "Just like always. If he doesn't pay you, I'll pay you. But he'll pay you. Don't worry. He says he will, and he will."

"I don't want to worry," she said. "But I worry anyway. I worry about my boys, and after that I worry about myself. I never thought I'd see one of my boys in this shape. I'm just glad your dad isn't alive to see it."

In three months my brother gave her fifty dollars of what he owed me and was supposed to pay to her. Or maybe it was seventy-five dollars he gave her. There are conflicting stories— two conflicting stories, his and hers. But that's all he paid her of the five hundred—fifty dollars or else seventy-five dollars, according to whose story you want to listen to. I had to make up the rest to her. I had to keep shelling out, same as always. My brother was finished. That's what he told me—that he was finished—when I called to see what was up, after my mother had phoned, looking for her money.

My mother said, "I made the mailman go back and check inside his truck, to see if your letter might have fallen down behind the seat. Then I went around and asked the neighbors did they get any of my mail by mistake. I'm going crazy with worry about this situation, honey." Then she said, "What's a mother supposed to think?" Who was looking out for her best interests in this business? She wanted to know that, and she wanted to know when she could expect her money.

So that's when I got on the phone to my brother to see if this was just a simple delay or a full-fledged collapse. But, according to Billy, he was a goner. He was absolutely done for. He was putting his house on the market immediately. He just hoped he hadn't waited too long to try and move it. And there wasn't anything left inside the house that he could sell. He'd sold off everything except the kitchen table and chairs. "I wish I could sell my blood," he said. "But who'd buy it? With my luck, I probably have an incurable disease." And, naturally, the investment thing hadn't worked out. When I asked him about it over the phone, all he said was that it hadn't materialized.

His tax refund didn't make it, either—the I.R.S. had some kind of lien on his return. "When it rains it pours," he said. "I'm sorry, brother. I didn't mean for this to happen."

"I understand," I said. And I did. But it didn't make it any easier. Anyway, one thing and the other, I didn't get my money from him, and neither did my mother. I had to keep on sending her money every month.

I was sore, yes. Who wouldn't be? My heart went out to him, and I wished trouble hadn't knocked on his door. But my own back was against the wall now. At least, though, whatever happens to him from here on, he won't come back to me for more money—seeing as how he still owes me. Nobody would do that to you. That's how I figured, anyway. But that's how little I knew.

I kept my nose to the grindstone. I got up early every morning and went to work and worked hard all day. When I came home I plopped into the big chair and just sat there. I was so tired it took me a while to get around to unlacing my shoes. Then I just went on sitting there. I was too tired to even get up and turn on the TV.

I was sorry about my brother's troubles. But I had troubles of my own. In addition to my mother, I had several other people on my payroll. I had a former wife I was sending money to every month. I had to do that. I didn't want to, but the court said I had to. And I had a daughter with two kids in Bellingham, and I had to send her something every month. Her kids had to eat, didn't they? She was living with a swine who wouldn't even *look* for work, a guy who couldn't hold a job if they handed him one. The time or two he did find something, he overslept, or his car broke down on the way in to work, or else he'd just be let go, no explanation, and that was that.

Once, long ago, when I used to think like a man about these things, I threatened to kill that guy. But that's neither here nor there. Besides, I was drinking in those days. In any case, the bastard is still hanging around.

My daughter would write these letters and say how they were living on oatmeal, she and her kids. (I guess he was starving, too, but she knew better than to mention that guy's name in her letters to me.) She'd tell me that if I could just carry her until summer things would pick up for her. Things would turn around for her, she was sure, in the summer. If nothing else worked out—but she was sure it would; she had several irons in the fire—she could always get a job in the fish cannery that was not far from where she lived. She'd wear rubber boots and rubber clothes and gloves and pack salmon into cans. Or else she might sell root beer from a vending stand beside the road to people who lined up in their cars at the border, waiting to get into Canada. People sitting in their cars in the middle of summer were going to be thirsty, right? They were going to be crying out for cold drinks. Anyway, one thing or the other, whatever line of work she decided on, she'd do fine in the summer. She just had to make it until then, and that's where I came in.

My daughter said she knew she had to change her life. She wanted to stand on her own two feet like everyone else. She wanted to quit looking at herself as a victim. "I'm not a victim," she said to me over the phone one night. "I'm just a young woman with two kids and a son-of-a-bitch bum who lives with me. No different from lots of other women. I'm not afraid of hard work. Just give me a chance. That's all I ask of the world." She said she could do without for herself. But until her break came, until opportunity knocked, it was the kids she worried about. The kids were always asking her when Grandpop was going to visit, she said. Right this minute they were drawing pictures of the swing sets and swimming pool at the motel I'd stayed in when I'd visited a year ago. But summer was the thing, she said. If she could make it until summer, her troubles would be over. Things would change then—she knew they would. And with a little help from me she could make it. "I don't know what I'd do without you, Dad." That's what she said. It nearly broke my heart. Sure I had to help her. I was glad to be even halfway in a position to help her. I had a job, didn't I? Compared to her and everyone else in my family, I had it made. Compared to the rest, I lived on Easy Street.

I sent the money she asked for. I sent money every time she asked. And then I told her I thought it'd be simpler if I just sent a sum of money, not a whole lot, but money even so, on the first of each month. It would be money she could count on, and it would be *her* money, no one else's—hers and the kids'. That's what I hoped for, anyway. I wished there was some way I could be sure the bastard who lived with her couldn't get his hands on so much as an orange or a piece of bread that my money bought. But I couldn't. I just had to go ahead and send the money and stop worrying about whether he'd soon be tucking into a plate of my eggs and biscuits.

My mother and my daughter and my former wife. That's three people on the payroll right there, not counting my brother. But my son needed money, too. After he graduated from high school, he packed his things, left his mother's house, and went to a college back East. A college in New Hampshire, of all places. Who's ever heard of New Hampshire? But he was the first kid in the family, on either side of the family, to even *want* to go to college, so everybody thought it was a good idea. I thought so, too, at first. How'd I know it was going to wind up costing me an arm and a leg? He borrowed left and right from the banks to keep himself going. He didn't want to have to work a job and go to school at the same time. That's what he said. And, sure, I guess I can understand it. In a way, I can even sympathize. Who likes to work? I don't. But after he'd borrowed everything he could, everything in sight, including enough to finance a junior year in Germany, I had to begin sending him money, and a lot of it. When, finally, I said I couldn't send any more, he wrote back and said if that was the case, if that was really the way I felt, he was going to deal drugs or else rob a bank—whatever he had to do to get money to live on. I'd be lucky if he wasn't shot or sent to prison.

I wrote back and said I'd changed my mind and I could send him a little more after all. What else could I do? I didn't want his blood on my hands. I didn't want to think of my kid being packed off to prison, or something even worse. I had plenty on my conscience as it was.

That's four people, right? Not counting my brother, who wasn't a regular yet. I was going crazy with it. I worried night and day. I couldn't sleep over it. I was paying out nearly as much money every month as I was bringing in. You don't have to be a genius, or know anything about economics, to understand that this state of affairs couldn't keep on. I had to get a loan to keep up my end of things. That was another monthly payment.

So I started cutting back. I had to quit eating out, for instance. Since I lived alone, eating out was something I liked to do, but it became a thing of the past. And I had to watch myself when it came to thinking about movies. I couldn't buy clothes or get my teeth fixed. The car was falling apart. I needed new shoes, but forget it.

Once in a while I'd get fed up with it and write letters to all of them, threatening to change my name and telling them I was going to quit my job. I'd tell them I was planning a move to Australia. And the thing was, I was serious when I'd say that about Australia, even though I didn't know the first thing about Australia. I just knew it was on the other side of the world, and that's where I wanted to be.

But when it came right down to it, none of them really believed I'd go to Australia. They had me, and they knew it. They knew I was desperate, and they were sorry and they said so. But they counted on it all blowing over before the first of the month, when I had to sit down and make out the checks.

After one of my letters where I talked about moving to Australia, my mother wrote that she didn't want to be a burden any longer. Just as soon as the swelling went down in her legs, she said, she was going out to look for work. She was seventy-five years old, but maybe she could go back to waitressing, she said. I wrote her back and told her not to be silly. I said I was glad I could help her. And I was. I was glad I could help. I just needed to win the lottery.

My daughter knew Australia was just a way of saying to everybody that I'd had it. She knew I needed a break and something to cheer me up. So she wrote that she was going to leave her kids with somebody and take the cannery job when the season rolled around. She was young and strong, she said. She thought she could work the twelve-to-fourteen-hour-a-day shifts, seven days a week, no problem. She'd just have to tell herself she could do it, get herself psyched up for it, and her body would listen. She just had to line up the right kind of babysitter. That'd be the big thing. It was going to require a special kind of sitter, seeing as how the hours would be long and the kids were hyper to begin with, because of all the Popsicles and Tootsie Rolls, M&M's, and the like that they put away every day. It's the stuff kids like to eat, right? Anyway, she thought she could find the right person if she kept looking. But she had to buy the boots and clothes for the work, and that's where I could help.

My son wrote that he was sorry for his part in things and thought he and I would both be better off if he ended it once and for all. For one thing, he'd discovered he was allergic to cocaine. It made his eyes stream and affected his breathing, he said. This meant he couldn't test the drugs in the transactions he'd need to make. So, before it could even begin, his career as a drug dealer was over. No, he said, better a bullet in the temple and end it all right here. Or maybe hanging. That would save him the trouble of borrowing a gun. And save us the price of bullets. That's actually what he said in his letter, if you can believe it. He enclosed a picture of himself that somebody had taken last summer when he was in the study-abroad program in Germany. He was standing under a big tree with thick limbs hanging down a few feet over his head. In the picture, he wasn't smiling.

My former wife didn't have anything to say on the matter. She didn't have to. She knew she'd get her money the first of each month, even if it had to come all the way from Sydney. If she didn't get it, she just had to pick up the phone and call her lawyer.

This is where things stood when my brother called one Sunday afternoon in early May. I had the windows open, and a nice breeze moved through the house. The radio was playing. The hillside behind the house was in bloom. But I began to sweat when I heard his voice on the line. I hadn't heard from him since the dispute over the five hundred, so I couldn't believe he was going to try and touch me for more money now. But I began to sweat anyway. He asked how things stood with me, and I launched into the payroll thing and all. I talked about oatmeal, cocaine, fish canneries, suicide, bank jobs, and how I couldn't go to the movies or eat out. I said I had a hole in my shoe. I talked about the payments that went on and on to my former wife. He knew all about this, of course. He knew everything I was telling him. Still, he said he was sorry to hear it. I kept talking. It was his dime. But as he talked I started thinking, *How are you going to pay for this call, Billy?* Then it came to me that *I* was going to pay for it. It was only a matter of minutes, or seconds, until it was all decided.

I looked out the window. The sky was blue, with a few white clouds in it. Some birds clung to a telephone wire. I wiped my face on my sleeve. I didn't know what else I could say. So I suddenly stopped talking and just stared out the window at the mountains, and waited. And that's when my brother said, "I hate to ask you this, but—" When he said that, my heart did this sinking thing. And then he went ahead and asked.

This time it was a thousand. A thousand! He was worse off than when he'd called that other time. He let me have some details. The bill collectors were at the door—the door! he said —and the windows rattled, the house shook, when they hammered with their fists. *Blam, blam, blam*, he said. There was no place to hide from them. His house was about to be pulled out from under him. "Help me, brother," he said.

Where was I going to raise a thousand dollars? I took a good grip on the receiver, turned away from the window, and said, "But you didn't pay me back the last time you borrowed money. What about that?"

"I didn't?" he said, acting surprised. "I guess I thought I had. I wanted to, anyway. I tried to, so help me God."

"You were supposed to pay that money to Mom," I said. "But you didn't. I had to keep giving her money every month, same as always. There's no end to it, Billy. Listen, I take one step forward and I go two steps back. I'm going under. You're all going under, and you're pulling me down with you."

"I paid her *some* of it," he said. "I did pay her a little. Just for the record," he said, "I paid her something."

"She said you gave her fifty dollars and that was all."

"No," he said, "I gave her seventy-five. She forgot about the other twenty-five. I was over there one afternoon, and I gave her two tens and a five. I gave her some cash, and she just forgot about it. Her memory's going. Look," he said, "I promise I'll be good for it this time, I swear to God. Add up what I still owe you and add it to this money here I'm trying to borrow, and I'll send you a check. We'll exchange checks.

Hold on to my check for two months, that's all I'm asking. I'll be out of the woods in two months' time. Then you'll have your money. July 1st, I promise, no later, and this time I *can* swear to it. We're in the process of selling this little piece of property that Irma Jean inherited a while back from her uncle. It's as good as sold. The deal has closed. It's just a question now of working out a couple of minor details and signing the papers. Plus, I've got this job lined up. It's definite. I'll have to drive fifty miles round trip every day, but that's no problem— hell, no. I'd drive a hundred and fifty if I had to, and be glad to do it. I'm saying I'll have money in the bank in two months' time. You'll get your money, all of it, by July 1st, and you can count on it."

"Billy, I love you," I said. "But I've got a load to carry. I'm carrying a very heavy load these days, in case you didn't know."

"That's why I won't let you down on this," he said. "You have my word of honor. You can trust me on this absolutely. I promise you my check will be good in two months, no later. Two months is all I'm asking for. Brother, I don't know where else to turn. You're my last hope."

I did it, sure. To my surprise, I still had some credit with the bank, so I borrowed the money, and I sent it to him. Our checks crossed in the mail. I stuck a thumbtack through his check and put it up on the kitchen wall next to the calendar and the picture of my son standing under that tree. And then I waited.

I kept waiting. My brother wrote and asked me not to cash the check on the day we'd agreed to. Please wait a while longer is what he said. Some things had come up. The job he'd been promised had fallen through at the last minute. That was one thing that came up. And that little piece of property belonging to his wife hadn't sold after all. At the last minute, she'd had a change of heart about selling it. It had been in her family for generations. What could he do? It was her land, and she wouldn't listen to reason, he said.

My daughter telephoned around this time to say that somebody had broken into her trailer and ripped her off. Everything in the trailer. Every stick of furniture was gone when she came home from work after her first night at the cannery. There wasn't even a chair left for her to sit down on. Her bed had been stolen, too. They were going to have to sleep on the floor like Gypsies, she said.

"Where was what's-his-name when this happened?" I said.

She said he'd been out looking for work earlier in the day. She guessed he was with friends. Actually, she didn't know his whereabouts at the time of the crime, or even right now, for that matter. "I hope he's at the bottom of the river," she said. The kids had been with the sitter when the ripoff happened. But, anyway, if she could just borrow enough from me to buy some secondhand furniture she'd pay me back, she said, when she got her first check. If she had some money from me before the end of the week—I could wire it, maybe—she could pick up some essentials. "Somebody's violated my space," she said. "I feel like I've been raped."

My son wrote from New Hampshire that it was essential he go back to Europe. His life hung in the balance, he said. He was graduating at the end of summer session, but he couldn't stand to live in America a day longer after that. This was a materialist society, and he simply couldn't take it anymore. People over here, in the U.S., couldn't hold a conversation unless *money* figured in it some way, and he was sick of it. He wasn't a Yuppie, and didn't want to become a Yuppie. That wasn't his thing. He'd get out of my hair, he said, if he could just borrow enough from me, this one last time, to buy a ticket to Germany.

I didn't hear anything from my former wife. I didn't have to. We both knew how things stood there.

My mother wrote that she was having to do without support hose and wasn't able to have her hair tinted. She'd thought this would be the year she could put some money back for the rainy days ahead, but it wasn't working out that way. She could see it wasn't in the cards. "How are you?" she wanted to know. "How's everybody else? I hope you're okay."

I put more checks in the mail. Then I held my breath and waited.

While I was waiting, I had this dream one night. Two dreams, really. I dreamt them on the same night. In the first dream, my dad was alive once more, and he was giving me a ride on his shoulders. I was this little kid, maybe five or six years old. *Get up here*, he said, and he took me by the hands and swung me onto his shoulders. I was high off the ground, but I wasn't afraid. He was holding on to me. We were holding on to each other. Then he began to move down the sidewalk. I brought my hands up from his shoulders and put them around his fore-head. *Don't muss my hair*, he said. *You can let go*, he said, *I've got you. You won't fall.* When he said that, I became aware of the strong grip of his hands around my ankles. Then I did let go. I turned loose and held my arms out on either side of me. I kept them out there like that for balance. My dad went on walking while I rode on his shoulders. I pretended he was an elephant. I don't know where we were going. Maybe we were going to the store, or else to the park so he could push me in the swing.

I woke up then, got out of bed, and used the bathroom. It was starting to get light out, and it was only an hour or so until I had to get up. I thought about making coffee and getting dressed. But then I decided to go back to bed. I didn't plan to sleep, though. I thought I'd just lie there for a while with my hands behind my neck and watch it turn light out and maybe think about my dad a little, since I hadn't thought about him in a long time. He just wasn't a part of my life any longer, waking or sleeping. Anyway, I got back in bed. But it couldn't have been more than a minute before I fell asleep once more, and when I did I got into this other dream. My former wife was in it, though she wasn't my former wife in the dream. She was still my wife. My kids were in it, too. They were little, and they were eating potato chips. In my dream, I thought I could smell the potato chips and hear them being eaten. We were on a blanket, and we were close to some water. There was a sense of satisfaction and well-being in the dream. Then, suddenly, I found myself in the company of some other people—people I didn't know—and the next thing that happened was that I was kicking the window out of my son's car and threatening his life, as I did once, a long time ago. He was inside the car as my shoe smashed through the glass. That's when my eyes flew open, and I woke up. The alarm was going off. I reached over and pushed the switch and lay there for a few minutes more, my heart racing. In the second dream, somebody had offered me some whiskey, and I drank it. Drinking that whiskey was the thing that scared me. That was the worst thing that could have happened. That was rock bottom. Compared to that, everything else was a picnic. I lay there for a minute longer, trying to calm down. Then I got up.

I made coffee and sat at the kitchen table in front of the window. I pushed my cup back and forth in little circles on the table and began to think seriously about Australia again. And then, all of a sudden, I could imagine how it must have sounded to my family when I'd threatened them with a move to Australia. They would have been shocked at first, and even a little scared. Then, because they knew me, they'd probably started laughing. Now, thinking about their laughter, I had to laugh, too. *Ha, ha, ha.* That was exactly the sound I made there at the table—*ha, ha, ha*—as if I'd read somewhere how to laugh.

What was it I planned to do in Australia, anyway? The truth was, I wouldn't be going there any more than I'd be going to Timbuktu, the moon, or the North Pole. Hell, I didn't want to go to Australia. But once I understood this, once I understood I wouldn't be going there—or anywhere else, for that matter—I began to feel better. I lit another cigarette and poured some more coffee. There wasn't any milk for the coffee, but I didn't care. I could skip having milk in my coffee for a day and it wouldn't kill me. Pretty soon I packed the lunch and filled the thermos and put the thermos in the lunch pail. Then I went outside.

It was a fine morning. The sun lay over the mountains behind the town, and a flock of birds was moving from one part of the valley to another. I didn't bother to lock the door. I remembered what had happened to my daughter, but decided I didn't have anything worth stealing anyway. There was nothing in the house I couldn't live without. I had the TV, but I was sick of watching TV. They'd be doing me a favor if they broke in and took it off my hands.

I felt pretty good, all things considered, and I decided to walk to work. It wasn't all that far, and I had time to spare. I'd save a little gas, sure, but that wasn't the main consideration. It was summer, after all, and before long summer would be over. Summer, I couldn't help thinking, had been the time every-body's luck had been going to change.

I started walking alongside the road, and it was then, for

some reason, I began to think about my son. I wished him well, wherever he was. If he'd made it back to Germany by now—and he should have—I hoped he was happy. He hadn't written yet to give me his address, but I was sure I'd hear something before long. And my daughter, God love her and keep her. I hoped she was doing okay. I decided to write her a letter that evening and tell her I was rooting for her. My mother was alive and more or less in good health, and I felt lucky there, too. If all went well, I'd have her for several more years.

Birds were calling, and some cars passed me on the highway. Good luck to you, too, brother, I thought. I hope your ship comes in. Pay me back when you get it. And my former wife, the woman I used to love so much. She was alive, and she was well, too—so far as I knew, anyway. I wished her happiness. When all was said and done, I decided things could be a lot worse. Just now, of course, things were hard for everyone. People's luck had gone south on them was all. But things were bound to change soon. Things would pick up in the fall maybe. There was lots to hope for.

I kept on walking. Then I began to whistle. I felt I had the right to whistle if I wanted to. I let my arms swing as I walked. But the lunch pail kept throwing me off balance. I had sand-wiches, an apple, and some cookies in there, not to mention the thermos. I stopped in front of Smitty's, an old café that had gravel in the parking area and boards over the windows. The place had been boarded up for as long as I could remem-ber. I decided to put the lunch pail down for a minute. I did that, and then I raised my arms—raised them up level with my shoulders. I was standing there like that, like a goof, when somebody tooted a car horn and pulled off the highway into the parking area. I picked up my lunch pail and went over to the car. It was a guy I knew from work whose name was George. He reached over and opened the door on the passenger's side. "Hey, get in, buddy," he said.

"Hello, George," I said. I got in and shut the door, and the car sped off, throwing gravel from under the tires.

"I saw you," George said. "Yeah, I did, I saw you. You're in training for something, but I don't know what." He looked at me and then looked at the road again. He was going fast. "You always walk down the road with your arms out like that?" He laughed—*ha, ha, ha*—and stepped on the gas.

"Sometimes," I said. "It depends, I guess. Actually, I was standing," I said. I lit a cigarette and leaned back in the seat.

"So what's new?" George said. He put a cigar in his mouth, but he didn't light it.

"Nothing's new," I said. "What's new with you?"

George shrugged. Then he grinned. He was going very fast now. Wind buffeted the car and whistled by outside the windows. He was driving as if we were late for work. But we weren't late. We had lots of time, and I told him so.

Nevertheless, he cranked it up. We passed the turnoff and kept going. We were moving by then, heading straight toward the mountains. He took the cigar out of his mouth and put it in his shirt pocket. "I borrowed some money and had this baby overhauled," he said. Then he said he wanted me to see something. He punched it and gave it everything he could. I fastened my seat belt and held on.

"*Go*," I said. "What are you waiting for, George?" And that's when we really flew. Wind howled outside the windows. He had it floored, and we were going flat out. We streaked down that road in his big unpaid-for car.

Blackbird Pie

I WAS in my room one night when I heard something in the corridor. I looked up from my work and saw an envelope slide under the door. It was a thick envelope, but not so thick it couldn't be pushed under the door. My name was written on the envelope, and what was inside purported to be a letter from my wife. I say "purported" because even though the grievances could only have come from someone who'd spent twenty-three years observing me on an intimate, day-to-day basis, the charges were outrageous and completely out of keeping with my wife's character. Most important, however, the handwriting was not my wife's handwriting. But if it wasn't her handwriting, then whose was it?

I wish now I'd kept the letter, so I could reproduce it down to the last comma, the last uncharitable exclamation point. The tone is what I'm talking about now, not just the content. But I didn't keep it, I'm sorry to say. I lost it, or else misplaced it. Later, after the sorry business I'm about to relate, I was cleaning out my desk and may have accidentally thrown it away—which is uncharacteristic of *me*, since I usually don't throw anything away.

In any case, I have a good memory. I can recall every word of what I read. My memory is such that I used to win prizes in school because of my ability to remember names and dates, inventions, battles, treaties, alliances, and the like. I always scored highest on factual tests, and in later years, in the "real world," as it's called, my memory stood me in good stead. For instance, if I were asked right now to give the details of the Council of Trent or the Treaty of Utrecht, or to talk about Carthage, that city razed by the Romans after Hannibal's defeat (the Roman soldiers plowed salt into the ground so that Carthage could never be called Carthage again), I could do so. If called upon to talk about the Seven Years' War, the Thirty Years', or the Hundred Years' War, or simply the First Silesian War, I could hold forth with the greatest enthusiasm and confidence. Ask me anything about the Tartars, the Renaissance popes, or the rise and fall of the Ottoman Empire. Thermopylae, Shiloh, or the Maxim gun. Easy. Tannenberg? Simple as blackbird pie. The famous four and twenty that were set before the king. At Agincourt, English longbows carried the day. And here's something else. Everyone has heard of the Battle of Lepanto, the last great sea battle fought in ships powered by galley slaves. This fracas took place in 1571 in the eastern Mediterranean, when the combined naval forces of the Christian nations of Europe turned back the Arab hordes under the infamous Ali Muezzin Zade, a man who was fond of personally cutting off the noses of his prisoners before calling in the executioners. But does anyone remember that Cervantes was involved in this affair and had his left hand lopped off in the battle? Something else. The combined French and Russian losses in one day at Borodino were seventy-five thousand men—the equivalent in fatalities of a fully loaded jumbo jet crashing every three minutes from breakfast to sundown. Kutuzov pulled his forces back toward Moscow. Napoleon drew breath, marshaled his troops, and continued his advance. He entered the downtown area of Moscow, where he stayed for a month waiting for Kutuzov, who never showed his face again. The Russian generalissimo was waiting for snow and ice, for Napoleon to begin his retreat to France.

Things stick in my head. I remember. So when I say I can re-create the letter—the portion that I read, which catalogues the charges against me—I mean what I say.

In part, the letter went as follows:

Dear,

Things are not good. Things, in fact, are bad. Things have gone from bad to worse. And you know what I'm talking about. We've come to the end of the line. It's over with us. Still, I find myself wishing we could have talked about it.

It's been such a long time now since we've talked. I mean really *talked*. Even after we were married we used to talk and talk, exchanging news and ideas. When the children were little, or even after they were more grown-up, we still found time to talk. It was more difficult then, naturally, but we managed, we found time. We *made* time. We'd have to wait until after they were asleep, or else when they were playing outside, or with a sitter. But we managed. Sometimes we'd engage a sitter just so we *could* talk. On occasion we talked the night away, talked until the sun came up. Well. Things happen, I know. Things change.

Bill had that trouble with the police, and Linda found herself pregnant, etc. Our quiet time together flew out the window. And gradually your responsibilities backed up on you. Your work became more
important, and our time together was squeezed out. Then, once the
children left home, our time for talking was back. We had each other
again, only we had less and less to talk about. "It happens," I can hear
some wise man saying. And he's right. *It happens.* But it happened to
us. In any case, no blame. *No blame.* That's not what this letter is
about. *I want to talk about us.* I want to talk about *now.* The time has
come, you see, to admit that *the impossible* has happened. To cry
Uncle. To beg off. To—

I read this far and stopped. Something was wrong. Something was fishy in Denmark. The sentiments expressed in the
letter may have belonged to my wife. (Maybe they did. Say
they did, grant that the sentiments expressed *were* hers.) But
the handwriting *was not her handwriting.* And I ought to know.
I consider myself an expert in this matter of her handwriting.
And yet if it wasn't her handwriting, who on earth *had* written
these lines?

I should say a little something about ourselves and our life
here. During the time I'm writing about we were living in a
house we'd taken for the summer. I'd just recovered from an
illness that had set me back in most things I'd hoped to accomplish that spring. We were surrounded on three sides by
meadows, birch woods, and some low, rolling hills—a "territorial view," as the realtor had called it when he described it to us
over the phone. In front of the house was a lawn that had
grown shaggy, owing to lack of interest on my part, and a long
graveled drive that led to the road. Behind the road we could
see the distant peaks of mountains. Thus the phrase "territorial
view"—having to do with a vista appreciated only at a distance.

My wife had no friends here in the country, and no one
came to visit. Frankly, I was glad for the solitude. But she was
a woman who was used to having friends, used to dealing with
shopkeepers and tradesmen. Out here, it was just the two of
us, thrown back on our resources. Once upon a time a house
in the country would have been our ideal—we would have
coveted such an arrangement. Now I can see it wasn't such a
good idea. No, it wasn't.

Both our children had left home long ago. Now and then a

letter came from one of them. And once in a blue moon, on a holiday, say, one of them might telephone—a collect call, naturally, my wife being only too happy to accept the charges. This seeming indifference on their part was, I believe, a major cause of my wife's sadness and general discontent—a discontent, I have to admit, I'd been vaguely aware of before our move to the country. In any case, to find herself in the country after so many years of living close to a shopping mall and bus service, with a taxi no farther away than the telephone in the hall —it must have been hard on her, very hard. I think her *decline*, as a historian might put it, was accelerated by our move to the country. I think she slipped a cog after that. I'm speaking from hindsight, of course, which always tends to confirm the obvious.

I don't know what else to say in regard to this matter of the handwriting. How much more can I say and still retain credibility? We were alone in the house. No one else—to my knowledge, anyway—was in the house and could have penned the letter. Yet I remain convinced to this day that it was not her handwriting that covered the pages of the letter. After all, I'd been reading my wife's handwriting since before she was my wife. As far back as what might be called our pre-history days —the time she went away to school as a girl, wearing a gray-and-white school uniform. She wrote letters to me every day that she was away, and she was away for two years, not counting holidays and summer vacations. Altogether, in the course of our relationship, I would estimate (a conservative estimate, too), counting our separations and the short periods of time I was away on business or in the hospital, etc.—I would estimate, as I say, that I received seventeen hundred or possibly eighteen hundred and fifty handwritten letters from her, not to mention hundreds, maybe thousands, more informal notes ("On your way home, please pick up dry cleaning, and some spinach pasta from Corti Bros"). I could recognize her handwriting anywhere in the world. Give me a few words. I'm confident that if I were in Jaffa, or Marrakech, and picked up a note in the marketplace, I would recognize it if it was my wife's handwriting. A word, even. Take this word "*talked*," for instance. That simply isn't the way she'd write "talked"! Yet I'm the first to admit I don't know *whose* handwriting it is if it isn't hers.

Secondly, my wife *never* underlined her words for emphasis.

Never. I don't recall a single instance of her doing this—not once in our entire married life, not to mention the letters I received from her before we were married. It would be reasonable enough, I suppose, to point out that it could happen to anyone. That is, anyone could find himself in a situation that is completely atypical and, *given the pressure of the moment*, do something totally out of character and draw a line, the merest *line*, under a word, or maybe under an entire sentence.

I would go so far as to say that every word of this entire letter, so-called (though I haven't read it through in its entirety, and won't, since I can't find it now), is utterly false. I don't mean false in the sense of "untrue," necessarily. There is some truth, perhaps, to the charges. I don't want to quibble. I don't want to appear small in this matter; things are bad enough already in this department. No. What I want to say, all I want to say, is that while the sentiments expressed in the letter may be my wife's, may even hold *some* truth—be legitimate, so to speak—the force of the accusations leveled against me is diminished, if not entirely undermined, even discredited, because she *did not* in fact write the letter. Or, if she *did* write it, then discredited by the fact that she didn't write it in her own handwriting! Such evasion is what makes men hunger for facts. As always, there are some.

On the evening in question, we ate dinner rather silently but not unpleasantly, as was our custom. From time to time I looked up and smiled across the table as a way of showing my gratitude for the delicious meal—poached salmon, fresh asparagus, rice pilaf with almonds. The radio played softly in the other room; it was a little suite by Poulenc that I'd first heard on a digital recording five years before in an apartment on Van Ness, in San Francisco, during a thunderstorm.

When we'd finished eating, and after we'd had our coffee and dessert, my wife said something that startled me. "Are you planning to be in your room this evening?" she said.

"I am," I said. "What did you have in mind?"

"I simply wanted to know." She picked up her cup and drank some coffee. But she avoided looking at me, even though I tried to catch her eye.

Are you planning to be in your room this evening? Such a

question was altogether out of character for her. I wonder now why on earth I didn't pursue this at the time. She knows my habits, if anyone does. But I think her mind was made up even then. I think she was concealing something even as she spoke.

"Of course I'll be in my room this evening," I repeated, perhaps a trifle impatiently. She didn't say anything else, and neither did I. I drank the last of my coffee and cleared my throat.

She glanced up and held my eyes a moment. Then she nodded, as if we had agreed on something. (But we hadn't, of course.) She got up and began to clear the table.

I felt as if dinner had somehow ended on an unsatisfactory note. Something else—a few words maybe—was needed to round things off and put the situation right again.

"There's a fog coming in," I said.

"Is there? I hadn't noticed," she said.

She wiped away a place on the window over the sink with a dish towel and looked out. For a minute she didn't say anything. Then she said—again mysteriously, or so it seems to me now—"There is. Yes, it's very foggy. It's a heavy fog, isn't it?" That's all she said. Then she lowered her eyes and began to wash the dishes.

I sat at the table a while longer before I said, "I think I'll go to my room now."

She took her hands out of the water and rested them against the counter. I thought she might proffer a word or two of encouragement for the work I was engaged in, but she didn't. Not a peep. It was as if she were waiting for me to leave the kitchen so she could enjoy her privacy.

Remember, I was at work in my room at the time the letter was slipped under the door. I read enough to question the handwriting and to wonder how it was that my wife had presumably been busy somewhere in the house and writing me a letter at the same time. Before reading further in the letter, I got up and went over to the door, unlocked it, and checked the corridor.

It was dark at this end of the house. But when I cautiously put my head out I could see light from the living room at the end of the hallway. The radio was playing quietly, as usual. Why did I hesitate? Except for the fog, it was a night very much like any other we had spent together in the house. But there was *something else afoot* tonight. At that moment I found myself afraid—afraid, if you can believe it, in my own house!—to walk down the hall and satisfy myself that all was well. Or if something was wrong, if my wife was experiencing—how should I put it?—difficulties of any sort, hadn't I best confront the situation before letting it go any further, before losing any more time on this stupid business of reading her words in somebody else's handwriting!

But I didn't investigate. Perhaps I wanted to avoid a frontal attack. In any case, I drew back and shut and locked the door before returning to the letter. But I was angry now as I saw the evening sliding away in this foolish and incomprehensible business. I was beginning to feel *uneasy*. (No other word will do.) I could feel my gorge rising as I picked up the letter purporting to be from my wife and once more began to read.

The time has come and gone for us—us, you and me—to put all our cards on the table. Thee and me. Lancelot and Guinevere. Abélard and Héloïse. Troilus and Cressida. Pyramus and Thisbe. JAJ and Nora Barnacle, etc. You know what I'm saying, honey. We've been together a long time—thick and thin, illness and health, stomach distress, eye-ear-nose-and-throat trouble, high times and low. Now? Well, I don't know what I can say now except the truth: I can't go it another step.

At this point, I threw down the letter and went to the door again, deciding to settle this once and for all. I wanted an accounting, and I wanted it now. I was, I think, *in a rage*. But at this point, just as I opened the door, I heard a low murmuring from the living room. It was as if somebody were trying to say something over the phone and this somebody were taking pains not to be overheard. Then I heard the receiver being replaced. Just this. Then everything was *as before*—the radio playing softly, the house otherwise quiet. But I had heard a voice.

In place of anger, I began to feel panic. I grew afraid as I looked down the corridor. Things were the same as before—the light was on in the living room, the radio played softly. I took a few steps and listened. I hoped I might hear the comforting, rhythmic clicking of her knitting needles, or the sound of a page being turned, but there was nothing of the sort. I took a few steps toward the living room and then—what should I say?—I lost my nerve, or maybe my curiosity. It was at that moment I heard *the muted sound of a doorknob being turned*, and afterward the unmistakable sound of a door opening and closing quietly.

My impulse was to walk rapidly down the corridor and into the living room and get to the bottom of this thing once and for all. But I didn't want to act impulsively and possibly discredit myself. I'm not impulsive, so I waited. But there *was* activity of some sort in the house—something was afoot, I was sure of it—and of course it was my duty, for my own peace of mind, not to mention the possible safety and well-being of my wife, to act. But I didn't. I couldn't. The moment was there, but I hesitated. Suddenly it was too late for any decisive action. The moment had come and gone, and could not be called back. Just so did Darius hesitate and then fail to act at the Battle of Granicus, and the day was lost, Alexander the Great rolling him up on every side and giving him a real walloping.

I went back to my room and closed the door. But *my heart was racing*. I sat in my chair and, trembling, picked up the pages of the letter once more.

But now here's the curious thing. Instead of beginning to read the letter through, from start to finish, or even starting at the point where I'd stopped earlier, I took pages at random and held them under the table lamp, picking out a line here and a line there. This allowed me to juxtapose the charges made against me until the entire indictment (for that's what it was) took on quite another character—one more acceptable, since it had lost its chronology and, with it, a little of its punch.

So. Well. In this manner, going from page to page, here a line, there a line, I read in snatches the following—which might under different circumstances serve as a kind of abstract:

. . . withdrawing farther into . . . a small enough thing, but . . . talcum powder sprayed over the bathroom, including walls and baseboards . . . a shell . . . not to mention the insane asylum . . . until finally . . . a balanced view . . . the grave. Your "work" . . . Please! Give me a break . . . No one, not even . . .

Not another word on the subject! . . . The children . . . but the
real issue . . . not to mention the loneliness . . . Jesus H. Christ!
Really! I mean . . .

At this point I distinctly heard the front door close. I
dropped the pages of the letter onto the desk and hurried to
the living room. It didn't take long to see that my wife wasn't
in the house. (The house is small—two bedrooms, one of
which we refer to as my room or, on occasion, as my study.)
But let the record show: *every light in the house was burning.*

A heavy fog lay outside the windows, a fog so dense I could
scarcely see the driveway. The porch light was on and a suitcase
stood outside on the porch. It was my wife's suitcase, the one
she'd brought packed full of her things when we moved here.
What on earth was going on? I opened the door. Suddenly—I
don't know how to say this other than how it was—a horse
stepped out of the fog, and then, an instant later, as I watched,
dumbfounded, another horse. These horses were grazing in
our front yard. I saw my wife alongside one of the horses, and
I called her name.

"Come on out here," she said. "Look at this. Doesn't this
beat anything?"

She was standing beside this big horse, patting its flank. She
was dressed in her best clothes and had on heels and was wearing
a hat. (I hadn't seen her in a hat since her mother's funeral,
three years before.) Then she moved forward and put her face
against the horse's mane.

"Where did you come from, you big baby?" she said. "Where
did you come from, sweetheart?" Then, as I watched, she
began to cry into the horse's mane.

"There, there," I said and started down the steps. I went
over and patted the horse, and then I touched my wife's shoulder. She drew back. The horse snorted, raised its head a moment, and then went to cropping the grass once more. "What
is it?" I said to my wife. "For God's sake, what's happening here,
anyway?"

She didn't answer. The horse moved a few steps but continued pulling and eating the grass. The other horse was munching

grass as well. My wife moved with the horse, hanging on to its mane. I put my hand against the horse's neck and felt a surge of power run up my arm to the shoulder. I shivered. My wife was still crying. I felt helpless, but I was scared, too.

"Can you tell me what's going on?" I said. "Why are you dressed like this? What's that suitcase doing on the front porch? Where did these horses come from? For God's sake, can you tell me what's happening?"

My wife began to croon to the horse. Croon! Then she stopped and said, "You didn't read my letter, did you? You might have skimmed it, but you didn't read it. Admit it!"

"I did read it," I said. I was lying, yes, but it was a white lie. A partial untruth. But he who is blameless, let him throw out the first stone. "But tell me what is going on anyway," I said.

My wife turned her head from side to side. She pushed her face into the horse's dark wet mane. I could hear the horse *chomp, chomp, chomp*. Then it snorted as it took in air through its nostrils.

She said, "There was this girl, you see. Are you listening? And this girl loved this boy so much. She loved him even more than herself. But the boy—well, he grew up. I don't know what happened to him. Something, anyway. He got cruel without meaning to be cruel and he—"

I didn't catch the rest, because just then a car appeared out of the fog, in the drive, with its headlights on and a flashing blue light on its roof. It was followed, a minute later, by a pickup truck pulling what looked like a horse trailer, though with the fog it was hard to tell. It could have been anything—a big portable oven, say. The car pulled right up onto the lawn and stopped. Then the pickup drove alongside the car and stopped, too. Both vehicles kept their headlights on and their engines running, which contributed to the eerie, bizarre aspect of things. A man wearing a cowboy hat—a rancher, I supposed—stepped down from the pickup. He raised the collar of his sheepskin coat and whistled to the horses. Then a big man in a raincoat got out of the car. He was a much bigger man than the rancher, and he, too, was wearing a cowboy hat. But his raincoat was open, and I could see a pistol strapped to his waist. He had to be a deputy sheriff. Despite everything that was going on, and the anxiety I felt, I found it *worth noting* that both men were wearing hats. I ran my hand through my hair, and was sorry I wasn't wearing a hat of my own.

"I called the sheriff's department a while ago," my wife said. "When I first saw the horses." She waited a minute and then she said something else. "Now you won't need to give me a ride into town after all. I mentioned that in my letter, the letter you read. I said I'd need a ride into town. I can get a ride—at least, I think I can—with one of these gentlemen. And I'm not changing my mind about anything, either. I'm saying this decision is irrevocable. Look at me!" she said.

I'd been watching them round up the horses. The deputy was holding his flashlight while the rancher walked a horse up a little ramp into the trailer. I turned to look at this woman I didn't know any longer.

"I'm leaving you," she said. "That's what's happening. I'm heading for town tonight. I'm striking out on my own. It's all in the letter you read." Whereas, as I said earlier, my wife never underlined words in her letters, she was now speaking (having dried her tears) as if virtually every other word out of her mouth ought to be emphasized.

"What's gotten *into* you?" I heard myself say. It was almost as if I couldn't help adding pressure to some of my own words. "Why are you *doing* this?"

She shook her head. The rancher was loading the second horse into the trailer now, whistling sharply, clapping his hands and shouting an occasional "Whoa! Whoa, damn you! Back up now. Back up!"

The deputy came over to us with a clipboard under his arm. He was holding a big flashlight. "Who called?" he said.

"I did," my wife said.

The deputy looked her over for a minute. He flashed the light onto her high heels and then up to her hat. "You're all dressed up," he said.

"I'm leaving my husband," she said.

The deputy nodded, as if he understood. (But he didn't, he couldn't!) "He's not going to give you any trouble, is he?" the deputy said, shining his light into my face and moving the light up and down rapidly. "You're not, are you?"

"No," I said. "No trouble. But I resent—"

"Good," the deputy said. "Enough said, then."

The rancher closed and latched the door to his trailer. Then he walked toward us through the wet grass, which, I noticed, reached to the tops of his boots.

"I want to thank you folks for calling," he said. "Much obliged. That's one heavy fog. If they'd wandered onto the main road, they could have raised hob out there."

"The lady placed the call," the deputy said. "Frank, she needs a ride into town. She's leaving home. I don't know who the injured party is here, but she's the one leaving." He turned then to my wife. "You sure about this, are you?" he said to her.

She nodded. "I'm sure."

"Okay," the deputy said. "That's settled, anyway. Frank, you listening? I can't drive her to town. I've got another stop to make. So can you help her out and take her into town? She probably wants to go to the bus station or else to the hotel. That's where they usually go. Is that where you want to go to?" the deputy said to my wife. "Frank needs to know."

"He can drop me off at the bus station," my wife said. "That's my suitcase on the porch."

"What about it, Frank?" the deputy said.

"I guess I can, sure," Frank said, taking off his hat and putting it back on again. "I'd be glad to, I guess. But I don't want to interfere in anything."

"Not in the least," my wife said. "I don't want to be any trouble, but I'm—well, I'm distressed just now. Yes, I'm distressed. But it'll be all right once I'm away from here. Away from this awful place. I'll just check and make doubly sure I haven't left anything behind. Anything *important*," she added. She hesitated and then she said, "This isn't as sudden as it looks. It's been coming for a long, long time. We've been married for a good many years. Good times and bad, up times and down. We've had them all. But it's time I was on my own. Yes, it's time. Do you know what I'm saying, gentlemen?"

Frank took off his hat again and turned it around in his hands as if examining the brim. Then he put it back on his head.

The deputy said, "These things happen. Lord knows none of us is perfect. We weren't made perfect. The only angels is to be found in Heaven."

My wife moved toward the house, picking her way through the wet, shaggy grass in her high heels. She opened the front door and went inside. I could see her moving behind the lighted windows, and something came to me then. *I might never see her again*. That's what crossed my mind, and it staggered me.

The rancher, the deputy, and I stood around waiting, not saying anything. The damp fog drifted between us and the lights from their vehicles. I could hear the horses shifting in the trailer. We were all uncomfortable, I think. But I'm speaking only for myself, of course. I don't know what they felt. Maybe they saw things like this happen every night—saw people's lives flying apart. The deputy did, maybe. But Frank, the rancher, he kept his eyes lowered. He put his hands in his front pockets and then took them out again. He kicked at something in the grass. I folded my arms and went on standing there, not knowing what was going to happen next. The deputy kept turning off his flashlight and then turning it on again. Every so often he'd reach out and swat the fog with it. One of the horses whinnied from the trailer, and then the other horse whinnied, too.

"A fellow can't see anything in this fog," Frank said.

I knew he was saying it to make conversation.

"It's as bad as I've ever seen it," the deputy said. Then he looked over at me. He didn't shine the light in my eyes this time, but he said something. He said, "Why's she leaving you? You hit her or something? Give her a smack, did you?"

"I've never hit her," I said. "Not in all the time we've been married. There was reason enough a few times, but I didn't. She hit me once," I said.

"Now, don't get started," the deputy said. "I don't want to hear any crap tonight. Don't say anything, and there won't be anything. No rough stuff. Don't even think it. There isn't going to be any trouble here tonight, is there?"

The deputy and Frank were watching me. I could tell Frank was embarrassed. He took out his makings and began to roll a cigarette.

"No," I said. "No trouble."

My wife came onto the porch and picked up her suitcase. I had the feeling that not only had she taken a last look around but she'd used the opportunity to freshen herself up, put on new lipstick, etc. The deputy held his flashlight for her as she came down the steps. "Right this way, Ma'am," he said. "Watch your step, now—it's slippery."

"I'm ready to go," she said.

"Right," Frank said. "Well, just to make sure we got this all straight now." He took off his hat once more and held it. "I'll carry you into town and I'll drop you off at the bus station. But, you understand, I don't want to be in the middle of something. You know what I mean." He looked at my wife, and then he looked at me.

"That's right," the deputy said. "You said a mouthful. Statistics show that your domestic dispute is, time and again, potentially the most dangerous situation a person, especially a law-enforcement officer, can get himself involved in. But I think this situation is going to be the shining exception. Right, folks?"

My wife looked at me and said, "I don't think I'll kiss you. No, I won't kiss you good-bye. I'll just say so long. Take care of yourself."

"That's right," the deputy said. "Kissing—who knows what that'll lead to, right?" He laughed.

I had the feeling they were all waiting for me to say something. But for the first time in my life I felt at a loss for words. Then *I took heart* and said to my wife, "The last time you wore that hat, you wore a veil with it and I held your arm. You were in mourning for your mother. And you wore a dark dress, not the dress you're wearing tonight. But those are the same high heels, I remember. Don't leave me like this," I said. "I don't know what I'll do."

"I have to," she said. "It's all in the letter—everything's spelled out in the letter. The rest is in the area of—I don't know. Mystery or speculation, I guess. In any case, there's nothing in the letter you don't already know." Then she turned to Frank and said, "Let's go, Frank. I can call you Frank, can't I?"

"Call him anything you want," the deputy said, "long as you call him in time for supper." He laughed again—a big, hearty laugh.

"Right," Frank said. "Sure you can. Well, okay. Let's go,

then." He took the suitcase from my wife and went over to his pickup and put the suitcase into the cab. Then he stood by the door on the passenger's side, holding it open.

"I'll write after I'm settled," my wife said. "I think I will, anyway. But first things first. We'll have to see."

"Now you're talking," the deputy said. "Keep all lines of communication open. Good luck, pardee," the deputy said to me. Then he went over to his car and got in.

The pickup made a wide, slow turn with the trailer across the lawn. One of the horses whinnied. The last image I have of my wife was when a match flared in the cab of the pickup, and I saw her lean over with a cigarette to accept the light the rancher was offering. Her hands were cupped around the hand that held the match. The deputy waited until the pickup and trailer had gone past him and then he swung his car around, slipping in the wet grass until he found purchase on the drive-way, throwing gravel from under his tires. As he headed for the road, he tooted his horn. *Tooted.* Historians should use more words like "tooted" or "beeped" or "blasted"—especially at serious moments such as after a massacre or when an awful oc-currence has cast a pall on the future of an entire nation. That's when a word like "tooted" is necessary, is gold in a brass age.

I'd like to say it was at this moment, as I stood in the fog watching her drive off, that I remembered a black-and-white photograph of my wife holding her wedding bouquet. She was eighteen years old—*a mere girl*, her mother had shouted at me only a month before the wedding. A few minutes before the photo, she'd got married. She's smiling. She's just finished, or is just about to begin, laughing. In either case, her mouth is open in amazed happiness as she looks into the camera. She is three months pregnant, though the camera doesn't show that, of course. But what if she *is* pregnant? So what? Wasn't every-body pregnant in those days? She's happy, in any case. I was happy, too—I know I was. We were both happy. I'm not in that particular picture, but I was close—only a few steps away, as I remember, shaking hands with someone offering me good wishes. My wife knew Latin and German and chemistry and physics and history and Shakespeare and all those other things they teach you in private school. She knew how to properly hold a teacup. She also knew how to cook and to make love. She was a prize.

But I found this photograph, along with several others, a few days after the horse business, when I was going through my wife's belongings, trying to see what I could throw out and what I should keep. I was packing to move, and I looked at the photograph for a minute and then I threw it away. I was ruthless. I told myself I didn't care. Why should I care?

If I know anything—and I do—if I know the slightest thing about human nature, I know she won't be able to live without me. She'll come back to me. And soon. Let it be soon.

No, I don't know anything about anything, and I never did. She's gone for good. She is. I can feel it. Gone and never coming back. Period. Not ever. I won't see her again, unless we run into each other on the street somewhere.

There's still the question of the handwriting. That's a bewilderment. But the handwriting business isn't the important thing, of course. How could it be after the consequences of the letter? Not the letter itself but the things I can't forget that were *in* the letter. No, the letter is not paramount at all—there's far more to this than somebody's handwriting. The "far more" has to do with subtle things. It could be said, for instance, that to take a wife is to take a history. And if that's so, then I understand that I'm outside history now—like horses and fog. Or you could say that my history has left me. Or that I'm having to go on *without history*. Or that history will now have to do without me—unless my wife writes more letters, or tells a friend who keeps a diary, say. Then, years later, someone can look back on this time, interpret it according to the record, its scraps and tirades, its silences and innuendos. That's when it dawns on me that autobiography is the poor man's history. And that I am saying good-bye to history. Good-bye, my darling.

Errand

C HEKHOV. On the evening of March 22, 1897, he went to dinner in Moscow with his friend and confidant Alexei Suvorin. This Suvorin was a very rich newspaper and book publisher, a reactionary, a self-made man whose father was a private at the battle of Borodino. Like Chekhov, he was the grandson of a serf. They had that in common: each had peasant's blood in his veins. Otherwise, politically and temperamentally, they were miles apart. Nevertheless, Suvorin was one of Chekhov's few intimates, and Chekhov enjoyed his company.

Naturally, they went to the best restaurant in the city, a former town house called the Hermitage—a place where it could take hours, half the night even, to get through a ten-course meal that would, of course, include several wines, liqueurs, and coffee. Chekhov was impeccably dressed, as always—a dark suit and waistcoat, his usual pince-nez. He looked that night very much as he looks in the photographs taken of him during this period. He was relaxed, jovial. He shook hands with the maître d', and with a glance took in the large dining room. It was brilliantly illuminated by ornate chandeliers, the tables occupied by elegantly dressed men and women. Waiters came and went ceaselessly. He had just been seated across the table from Suvorin when suddenly, without warning, blood began gushing from his mouth. Suvorin and two waiters helped him to the gentlemen's room and tried to stanch the flow of blood with ice packs. Suvorin saw him back to his own hotel and had a bed prepared for Chekhov in one of the rooms of the suite. Later, after another hemorrhage, Chekhov allowed himself to be moved to a clinic that specialized in the treatment of tuberculosis and related respiratory infections. When Suvorin visited him there, Chekhov apologized for the "scandal" at the restaurant three nights earlier but continued to insist there was nothing seriously wrong. "He laughed and jested as usual," Suvorin noted in his diary, "while spitting blood into a large vessel."

Maria Chekhov, his younger sister, visited Chekhov in the clinic during the last days of March. The weather was miserable; a sleet storm was in progress, and frozen heaps of snow lay everywhere. It was hard for her to wave down a carriage to take her to the hospital. By the time she arrived she was filled with dread and anxiety.

"Anton Pavlovich lay on his back," Maria wrote in her *Memoirs*. "He was not allowed to speak. After greeting him, I went over to the table to hide my emotions." There, among bottles of champagne, jars of caviar, bouquets of flowers from well-wishers, she saw something that terrified her: a freehand drawing, obviously done by a specialist in these matters, of Chekhov's lungs. It was the kind of sketch a doctor often makes in order to show his patient what he thinks is taking place. The lungs were outlined in blue, but the upper parts were filled in with red. "I realized they were diseased," Maria wrote.

Leo Tolstoy was another visitor. The hospital staff were awed to find themselves in the presence of the country's greatest writer. The most famous man in Russia? Of course they had to let him in to see Chekhov, even though "nonessential" visitors were forbidden. With much obsequiousness on the part of the nurses and resident doctors, the bearded, fierce-looking old man was shown into Chekhov's room. Despite his low opinion of Chekhov's abilities as a playwright (Tolstoy felt the plays were static and lacking in any moral vision. "Where do your characters take you?" he once demanded of Chekhov. "From the sofa to the junk room and back"), Tolstoy liked Chekhov's short stories. Furthermore, and quite simply, he loved the man. He told Gorky, "What a beautiful, magnificent man: modest and quiet, like a girl. He even walks like a girl. He's simply wonderful." And Tolstoy wrote in his journal (everyone kept a journal or a diary in those days), "I am glad I love . . . Chekhov."

Tolstoy removed his woollen scarf and bearskin coat, then lowered himself into a chair next to Chekhov's bed. Never mind that Chekhov was taking medication and not permitted to talk, much less carry on a conversation. He had to listen, amazedly, as the Count began to discourse on his theories of the immortality of the soul. Concerning that visit, Chekhov later wrote, "Tolstoy assumes that all of us (humans and animals alike) will live on in a principle (such as reason or love) the essence and goals of which are a mystery to us. . . . I have no use for that kind of immortality. I don't understand it, and Lev Nikolayevich was astonished I didn't."

Nevertheless, Chekhov was impressed with the solicitude shown by Tolstoy's visit. But, unlike Tolstoy, Chekhov didn't believe in an afterlife and never had. He didn't believe in anything that couldn't be apprehended by one or more of his five senses. And as far as his outlook on life and writing went, he once told someone that he lacked "a political, religious, and philosophical world view. I change it every month, so I'll have to limit myself to the description of how my heroes love, marry, give birth, die, and how they speak."

Earlier, before his t.b. was diagnosed, Chekhov had remarked, "When a peasant has consumption, he says, 'There's nothing I can do. I'll go off in the spring with the melting of the snows.'" (Chekhov himself died in the summer, during a heat wave.) But once Chekhov's own tuberculosis was discovered he continually tried to minimize the seriousness of his condition. To all appearances, it was as if he felt, right up to the end, that he might be able to throw off the disease as he would a lingering catarrh. Well into his final days, he spoke with seeming conviction of the possibility of an improvement. In fact, in a letter written shortly before his end, he went so far as to tell his sister that he was "getting fat" and felt much better now that he was in Badenweiler.

Badenweiler is a spa and resort city in the western area of the Black Forest, not far from Basel. The Vosges are visible from nearly anywhere in the city, and in those days the air was pure and invigorating. Russians had been going there for years to soak in the hot mineral baths and promenade on the boulevards. In June, 1904, Chekhov went there to die.

Earlier that month, he'd made a difficult journey by train from Moscow to Berlin. He traveled with his wife, the actress Olga Knipper, a woman he'd met in 1898 during rehearsals for "The Seagull." Her contemporaries describe her as an excellent actress. She was talented, pretty, and almost ten years younger than the playwright. Chekhov had been immediately attracted to her, but was slow to act on his feelings. As always, he preferred a flirtation to marriage. Finally, after a three-year courtship involving many separations, letters, and the inevitable

misunderstandings, they were at last married, in a private cere-
mony in Moscow, on May 25, 1901. Chekhov was enormously
happy. He called Olga his "pony," and sometimes "dog" or
"puppy." He was also fond of addressing her as "little turkey"
or simply as "my joy."

In Berlin, Chekhov consulted with a renowned specialist in
pulmonary disorders, a Dr. Karl Ewald. But, according to an
eyewitness, after the doctor examined Chekhov he threw up
his hands and left the room without a word. Chekhov was too
far gone for help: this Dr. Ewald was furious with himself for
not being able to work miracles, and with Chekhov for being
so ill.

A Russian journalist happened to visit the Chekhovs at their
hotel and sent back this dispatch to his editor: "Chekhov's
days are numbered. He seems mortally ill, is terribly thin,
coughs all the time, gasps for breath at the slightest movement,
and is running a high temperature." This same journalist saw
the Chekhovs off at Potsdam Station when they boarded their
train for Badenweiler. According to his account, "Chekhov
had trouble making his way up the small staircase at the station.
He had to sit down for several minutes to catch his breath." In
fact, it was painful for Chekhov to move: his legs ached continually and his insides hurt. The disease had attacked his in-
testines and spinal cord. At this point he had less than a month
to live. When Chekhov spoke of his condition now, it was, according to Olga, "with an almost reckless indifference."

Dr. Schwöhrer was one of the many Badenweiler physicians
who earned a good living by treating the well-to-do who came
to the spa seeking relief from various maladies. Some of his patients were ill and infirm, others simply old and hypochondria-
cal. But Chekhov's was a special case: he was clearly beyond
help and in his last days. He was also very famous. Even Dr.
Schwöhrer knew his name: he'd read some of Chekhov's stories in a German magazine. When he examined the writer early
in June, he voiced his appreciation of Chekhov's art but kept
his medical opinions to himself. Instead, he prescribed a diet
of cocoa, oatmeal drenched in butter, and strawberry tea. This
last was supposed to help Chekhov sleep at night.

On June 13, less than three weeks before he died, Chekhov
wrote a letter to his mother in which he told her his health was

on the mend. In it he said, "It's likely that I'll be completely cured in a week." Who knows why he said this? What could he have been thinking? He was a doctor himself, and he knew better. He was dying, it was as simple and as unavoidable as that. Nevertheless, he sat out on the balcony of his hotel room and read railway timetables. He asked for information on sailings of boats bound for Odessa from Marseilles. But he *knew*. At this stage he had to have known. Yet in one of the last letters he ever wrote he told his sister he was growing stronger by the day.

He no longer had any appetite for literary work, and hadn't for a long time. In fact, he had very nearly failed to complete *The Cherry Orchard* the year before. Writing that play was the hardest thing he'd ever done in his life. Toward the end, he was able to manage only six or seven lines a day. "I've started losing heart," he wrote Olga. "I feel I'm finished as a writer, and every sentence strikes me as worthless and of no use whatever." But he didn't stop. He finished his play in October, 1903. It was the last thing he ever wrote, except for letters and a few entries in his notebook.

A little after midnight on July 2, 1904, Olga sent someone to fetch Dr. Schwöhrer. It was an emergency: Chekhov was delirious. Two young Russians on holiday happened to have the adjacent room, and Olga hurried next door to explain what was happening. One of the youths was in his bed asleep, but the other was still awake, smoking and reading. He left the hotel at a run to find Dr. Schwöhrer. "I can still hear the sound of the gravel under his shoes in the silence of that stifling July night," Olga wrote later on in her memoirs. Chekhov was hallucinating, talking about sailors, and there were snatches of something about the Japanese. "You don't put ice on an empty stomach," he said when she tried to place an ice pack on his chest.

Dr. Schwöhrer arrived and unpacked his bag, all the while keeping his gaze fastened on Chekhov, who lay gasping in the bed. The sick man's pupils were dilated and his temples glistened with sweat. Dr. Schwöhrer's face didn't register anything. He was not an emotional man, but he knew Chekhov's end was near. Still, he was a doctor, sworn to do his utmost, and Chekhov held on to life, however tenuously. Dr. Schwöhrer prepared a hypodermic and administered an injection of camphor, something that was supposed to speed up the heart. But the injection didn't help—nothing, of course, could have helped. Nevertheless, the doctor made known to Olga his intention of sending for oxygen. Suddenly, Chekhov roused himself, became lucid, and said quietly, "What's the use? Before it arrives I'll be a corpse."

Dr. Schwöhrer pulled on his big moustache and stared at Chekhov. The writer's cheeks were sunken and gray, his complexion waxen; his breath was raspy. Dr. Schwöhrer knew the time could be reckoned in minutes. Without a word, without conferring with Olga, he went over to an alcove where there was a telephone on the wall. He read the instructions for using the device. If he activated it by holding his finger on a button and turning a handle on the side of the phone, he could reach the lower regions of the hotel—the kitchen. He picked up the receiver, held it to his ear, and did as the instructions told him. When someone finally answered, Dr. Schwöhrer ordered a bottle of the hotel's best champagne. "How many glasses?" he was asked. "Three glasses!" the doctor shouted into the mouthpiece. "And hurry, do you hear?" It was one of those rare moments of inspiration that can easily enough be overlooked later on, because the action is so entirely appropriate it seems inevitable.

The champagne was brought to the door by a tired-looking young man whose blond hair was standing up. The trousers of his uniform were wrinkled, the creases gone, and in his haste he'd missed a loop while buttoning his jacket. His appearance was that of someone who'd been resting (slumped in a chair, say, dozing a little), when off in the distance the phone had clamored in the early-morning hours—great God in Heaven! —and the next thing he knew he was being shaken awake by a superior and told to deliver a bottle of Moët to Room 211. "And hurry, do you hear?"

The young man entered the room carrying a silver ice bucket with the champagne in it and a silver tray with three cut-crystal glasses. He found a place on the table for the bucket and glasses, all the while craning his neck, trying to see into the other room, where someone panted ferociously for breath. It was a dreadful, harrowing sound, and the young man lowered his chin into his collar and turned away as the ratchety breathing worsened. Forgetting himself, he stared out the open window toward the darkened city. Then this big imposing man with a thick moustache pressed some coins into his hand—a large tip, by the feel of it—and suddenly the young man saw the door open. He took some steps and found himself on the landing, where he opened his hand and looked at the coins in amazement.

Methodically, the way he did everything, the doctor went about the business of working the cork out of the bottle. He did it in such a way as to minimize, as much as possible, the festive explosion. He poured three glasses and, out of habit, pushed the cork back into the neck of the bottle. He then took the glasses of champagne over to the bed. Olga momentarily released her grip on Chekhov's hand—a hand, she said later, that burned her fingers. She arranged another pillow behind his head. Then she put the cool glass of champagne against Chekhov's palm and made sure his fingers closed around the stem. They exchanged looks—Chekhov, Olga, Dr. Schwöhrer. They didn't touch glasses. There was no toast. What on earth was there to drink to? To death? Chekhov summoned his remaining strength and said, "It's been so long since I've had champagne." He brought the glass to his lips and drank. In a minute or two Olga took the empty glass from his hand and set it on the nightstand. Then Chekhov turned onto his side. He closed his eyes and sighed. A minute later, his breathing stopped.

Dr. Schwöhrer picked up Chekhov's hand from the bed-sheet. He held his fingers to Chekhov's wrist and drew a gold watch from his vest pocket, opening the lid of the watch as he did so. The second hand on the watch moved slowly, very slowly. He let it move around the face of the watch three times while he waited for signs of a pulse. It was three o'clock in the morning and still sultry in the room. Badenweiler was in the grip of its worst heat wave in years. All the windows in both rooms stood open, but there was no sign of a breeze. A large, black-winged moth flew through a window and banged wildly against the electric lamp. Dr. Schwöhrer let go of Chekhov's wrist. "It's over," he said. He closed the lid of his watch and returned it to his vest pocket.

At once Olga dried her eyes and set about composing herself. She thanked the doctor for coming. He asked if she wanted some medication—laudanum, perhaps, or a few drops of valerian. She shook her head. She did have one request, though: before the authorities were notified and the newspapers found out, before the time came when Chekhov was no longer in her keeping, she wanted to be alone with him for a while. Could the doctor help with this? Could he withhold, for a while anyway, news of what had just occurred?

Dr. Schwöhrer stroked his moustache with the back of a finger. Why not? After all, what difference would it make to anyone whether this matter became known now or a few hours from now? The only detail that remained was to fill out a death certificate, and this could be done at his office later on in the morning, after he'd slept a few hours. Dr. Schwöhrer nodded his agreement and prepared to leave. He murmured a few words of condolence. Olga inclined her head. "An honor," Dr. Schwöhrer said. He picked up his bag and left the room and, for that matter, history.

It was at this moment that the cork popped out of the champagne bottle; foam spilled down onto the table. Olga went back to Chekhov's bedside. She sat on a footstool, holding his hand, from time to time stroking his face. "There were no human voices, no everyday sounds," she wrote. "There was only beauty, peace, and the grandeur of death."

She stayed with Chekhov until daybreak, when thrushes began to call from the garden below. Then came the sound of tables and chairs being moved about down there. Before long, voices carried up to her. It was then a knock sounded at the door. Of course she thought it must be an official of some sort—the medical examiner, say, or someone from the police who had questions to ask and forms for her to fill out, or maybe, just maybe, it could be Dr. Schwöhrer returning with a mortician to render assistance in embalming and transporting Chekhov's remains back to Russia.

But, instead, it was the same blond young man who'd brought the champagne a few hours earlier. This time, however, his uniform trousers were neatly pressed, with stiff creases in front, and every button on his snug green jacket was fastened.

He seemed quite another person. Not only was he wide awake but his plump cheeks were smooth-shaven, his hair was in place, and he appeared anxious to please. He was holding a porcelain vase with three long-stemmed yellow roses. He presented these to Olga with a smart click of his heels. She stepped back and let him into the room. He was there, he said, to collect the glasses, ice bucket, and tray, yes. But he also wanted to say that, because of the extreme heat, breakfast would be served in the garden this morning. He hoped this weather wasn't too bothersome; he apologized for it.

The woman seemed distracted. While he talked, she turned her eyes away and looked down at something in the carpet. She crossed her arms and held her elbows. Meanwhile, still holding his vase, waiting for a sign, the young man took in the details of the room. Bright sunlight flooded through the open windows. The room was tidy and seemed undisturbed, almost untouched. No garments were flung over chairs, no shoes, stockings, braces, or stays were in evidence, no open suitcases. In short, there was no clutter, nothing but the usual heavy pieces of hotel-room furniture. Then, because the woman was still looking down, he looked down, too, and at once spied a cork near the toe of his shoe. The woman did not see it—she was looking somewhere else. The young man wanted to bend over and pick up the cork, but he was still holding the roses and was afraid of seeming to intrude even more by drawing any further attention to himself. Reluctantly, he left the cork where it was and raised his eyes. Everything was in order except for the uncorked, half-empty bottle of champagne that stood alongside two crystal glasses over on the little table. He cast his gaze about once more. Through an open door he saw that the third glass was in the bedroom, on the nightstand. But someone still occupied the bed! He couldn't see a face, but the figure under the covers lay perfectly motionless and quiet. He noted the figure and looked elsewhere. Then, for a reason he couldn't understand, a feeling of uneasiness took hold of him. He cleared his throat and moved his weight to the other leg. The woman still didn't look up or break her silence. The young man felt his cheeks grow warm. It occurred to him, quite without his having thought it through, that he should perhaps suggest an alternative to breakfast in the garden. He coughed, hoping to focus the woman's attention, but she didn't look at him. The distinguished foreign guests could, he said, take breakfast in their rooms this morning if they wished. The young man (his name hasn't survived, and it's likely he perished in the Great War) said he would be happy to bring up a tray. Two trays, he added, glancing uncertainly once again in the direction of the bedroom.

He fell silent and ran a finger around the inside of his collar. He didn't understand. He wasn't even sure the woman had been listening. He didn't know what else to do now; he was still holding the vase. The sweet odor of the roses filled his nostrils and inexplicably caused a pang of regret. The entire time he'd been waiting, the woman had apparently been lost in thought. It was as if all the while he'd been standing there, talking, shifting his weight, holding his flowers, she had been someplace else, somewhere far from Badenweiler. But now she came back to herself, and her face assumed another expression. She raised her eyes, looked at him, and then shook her head. She seemed to be struggling to understand what on earth this young man could be doing there in the room holding a vase with three yellow roses. Flowers? She hadn't ordered flowers.

The moment passed. She went over to her handbag and scooped up some coins. She drew out a number of banknotes as well. The young man touched his lips with his tongue; another large tip was forthcoming, but for what? What did she want him to do? He'd never before waited on such guests. He cleared his throat once more.

No breakfast, the woman said. Not yet, at any rate. Breakfast wasn't the important thing this morning. She required something else. She needed him to go out and bring back a mortician. Did he understand her? Herr Chekhov was dead, you see. *Comprenez-vous?* Young man? Anton Chekhov was dead. Now listen carefully to me, she said. She wanted him to go downstairs and ask someone at the front desk where he could go to find the most respected mortician in the city. Someone reliable, who took great pains in his work and whose manner was appropriately reserved. A mortician, in short, worthy of a great artist. Here, she said, and pressed the money on him. Tell them downstairs that I have specifically requested you to perform this duty for me. Are you listening? Do you understand what I'm saying to you?

The young man grappled to take in what she was saying. He chose not to look again in the direction of the other room. He had sensed that something was not right. He became aware of his heart beating rapidly under his jacket, and he felt perspiration break out on his forehead. He didn't know where he should turn his eyes. He wanted to put the vase down.

Please do this for me, the woman said. I'll remember you with gratitude. Tell them downstairs that I insist. Say that. But don't call any unnecessary attention to yourself or to the situation. Just say that this is necessary, that I request it—and that's all. Do you hear me? Nod if you understand. Above all, don't raise an alarm. Everything else, all the rest, the commotion—that'll come soon enough. The worst is over. Do we understand each other?

The young man's face had grown pale. He stood rigid, clasping the vase. He managed to nod his head.

After securing permission to leave the hotel he was to proceed quietly and resolutely, though without any unbecoming haste, to the mortician's. He was to behave exactly as if he were engaged on a very important errand, nothing more. He *was* engaged on an important errand, she said. And if it would help keep his movements purposeful he should imagine himself as someone moving down the busy sidewalk carrying in his arms a porcelain vase of roses that he had to deliver to an important man. (She spoke quietly, almost confidentially, as if to a relative or a friend.) He could even tell himself that the man he was going to see was expecting him, was perhaps impatient for him to arrive with his flowers. Nevertheless, the young man was not to become excited and run, or otherwise break his stride. Remember the vase he was carrying! He was to walk briskly, comporting himself at all times in as dignified a manner as possible. He should keep walking until he came to the mortician's house and stood before the door. He would then raise the brass knocker and let it fall, once, twice, three times. In a minute the mortician himself would answer.

This mortician would be in his forties, no doubt, or maybe early fifties—bald, solidly built, wearing steel-frame spectacles set very low on his nose. He would be modest, unassuming, a man who would ask only the most direct and necessary questions. An apron. Probably he would be wearing an apron. He might even be wiping his hands on a dark towel while he listened to what was being said. There'd be a faint whiff of formaldehyde on his clothes. But it was all right, and the young man shouldn't worry. He was nearly a grown-up now and shouldn't be frightened or repelled by any of this. The mortician would hear him out. He was a man of restraint and bearing, this mortician, someone who could help allay people's fears in this situation, not increase them. Long ago he'd acquainted himself with death in all its various guises and forms; death held no surprises for him any longer, no hidden secrets. It was this man whose services were required this morning.

The mortician takes the vase of roses. Only once while the young man is speaking does the mortician betray the least flicker of interest, or indicate that he's heard anything out of the ordinary. But the one time the young man mentions the name of the deceased, the mortician's eyebrows rise just a little. Chekhov, you say? Just a minute, and I'll be with you.

Do you understand what I'm saying, Olga said to the young man. Leave the glasses. Don't worry about them. Forget about crystal wine-glasses and such. Leave the room as it is. Everything is ready now. We're ready. Will you go?

But at that moment the young man was thinking of the cork still resting near the toe of his shoe. To retrieve it he would have to bend over, still gripping the vase. He would do this. He leaned over. Without looking down, he reached out and closed it into his hand.

OTHER FICTION

The Hair

H E worked at it with his tongue for a while then sat up in bed and began picking at it with his fingers. Outside it was going to be a nice day and some birds were singing. He tore off a corner of the matchbook and scraped in between his teeth. Nothing. He could still feel it. He ran his tongue over his teeth again from back to front, stopping when he got to the hair. He touched all around it then stroked it with his tongue where it threaded in between two of the front teeth, followed it in an inch or so to the end and smoothed it against the roof of his mouth. He touched it with his finger.

"Uuuk—Christ!"

"What's the matter?" his wife asked, sitting up. "We oversleep? What time is it?"

"I've got something in my teeth. Can't get it out. I don't know . . . feels like a hair."

He went into the bathroom and glanced at the mirror, then washed his hands and face with cold water. He turned on the shaving lamp over the mirror.

"I can't see it but I know it's there. If I could just get hold of it maybe I could pull it out."

His wife came into the bathroom, scratching her head and yawning. "You get it, honey?"

He ground his teeth together, squeezed his lips down against his teeth until his fingernails broke the skin.

"Just a minute. Let me see it," she said, moving closer. He stood under the light, mouth open, twisting his head back and forth, wiping his pajama sleeve over the glass as it fogged up.

"I don't see anything," she said.

"Well, I can feel it." He turned off the light and started running water in the tub. "The hell with it! Forget it. I've got to get ready for work."

He decided to walk downtown since he didn't want any breakfast and still had plenty of time to get to work. Nobody had a key except the boss and if he got there too early he'd only have to wait. He walked by the empty corner where he

usually caught the bus. A dog he'd seen around the neighborhood before had his leg cocked, pissing on the bus stop sign.

"Hey!"

The dog quit pissing and came running over to him. Another dog that he didn't recognize came trotting up, sniffed at
the sign, and pissed. Golden, slightly steaming as it ran down
the sidewalk.

"Hey—get out of here!" The dog squirted a few more drops
then both dogs crossed the street. They almost looked like they
were laughing. He threaded the hair back and forth through
his teeth.

"Nice day now, isn't it, huh?" the boss asked. He opened
the front door, raised the shade.

Everyone turned to look back outside and nodded, smiling.

"Yes it is, sir, just a beautiful day," someone said.

"Too nice to be working," someone else said, laughed with
the others.

"Yes it is. It is at that," the boss said. He went on up the
stairs to open up Boys Clothing, whistling, jingling his keys.

Later on when he came up from the basement and was taking
his break in the lounge, smoking a cigarette, the boss came in
wearing a short-sleeved shirt.

"Hot today, isn't it, huh?"

"Yes it is, sir." He'd never noticed before that the boss had
such hairy arms. He sat picking his teeth, staring at the thick
tufts of black hair that grew in between the boss's fingers.

"Sir, I was wondering—if you don't think I can, that's all
right, naturally, but if you think so, without putting anybody
in a bind, I mean—I'd like to go home. I don't feel so well."

"Mmm. Well, we can make it all right, of course. That's not
the point, of course." He took a long drink of his Coke, kept
looking at him.

"Well then, that's all right then, sir. I'll make it. I was just
wondering."

"No, no, that's all right now. You go on home. Call me up
tonight, let me know how you are." He looked at his watch,
finished his Coke. "Ten twenty-five. Say 10:30. Go on home
now, we'll call it 10:30."

Out in the street he loosened his collar and began to walk.
He felt strange walking around town with a hair in his mouth.

He kept touching it with his tongue. He didn't look at any of the people he met. In a little while he began to sweat under his arms and could feel it dripping through the hair into his undershirt. Sometimes he stopped in front of the showroom windows and stared at the glass, opening and closing his mouth, fishing around with his finger. He took the long way home, down through the Lions Club park where he watched the kids play in the wading pool and paid fifteen cents to an old lady to go through the little zoo and see the birds and animals. Once after he had stood for a long time looking through the glass at the giant Gila monster, the creature opened one of its eyes and looked at him. He backed away from the glass and went on walking around the park until it was time to go home.

He wasn't very hungry and only drank some coffee for supper. After a few swallows he rolled his tongue over the hair again. He got up from the table.

"Honey, what's the matter?" his wife asked. "Where you going?"

"I think I'm going to go to bed. I don't feel so well."

She followed him into the bedroom, watched while he undressed. "Can I get you something? Maybe I should call the doctor? I wish I knew what was the matter."

"That's all right. I'll be all right." He pulled up the covers over his shoulders and turned over, closing his eyes.

She pulled the shade. "I'll straighten up the kitchen a little, then I'll be back."

It felt better just to stretch out. He touched his face and thought he might have a fever. He licked his lips and touched the end of the hair with his tongue. He shivered. After a few minutes, he began to doze but woke suddenly and remembered about calling the boss. He got slowly out of bed and went out to the kitchen.

His wife was at the draining board doing dishes. "I thought you were asleep. Honey? You feel better now?"

He nodded, picked up the phone and got Information. He had a kind of bad taste in his mouth as he dialed.

"Hello. Yes, sir, I think I feel better. Just wanted you to know I'll be at work tomorrow. Right. Eight thirty, sharp."

After he got back in bed he smoothed his tongue over his teeth again. Maybe it was just something he could get used to.

He didn't know. Just before he went to sleep, he'd almost stopped thinking about it. He remembered what a warm day it had been and those kids out wading—how the birds were singing that morning. But once during the night he yelled out and woke up sweating, almost choking. No, no, he kept saying, kicking his feet against the covers. It scared his wife and she didn't know what was the matter.

The Aficionados

THEY are sitting in the shade at a small iron patio table drinking wine out of heavy metal cups.

"Why should you feel this way now?" he asks her.

"I don't know," she says. "It always makes me sad when it comes. It's been such a short year, and I don't even know any of the others." She leans forward and reaches for his hand, but he is too quick for her. "They seem so, so unprofessional." From her lap she takes her napkin and wipes her lips in a way that has become detestable to him this last month. "We won't talk about it anymore," she says. "We still have three hours yet. We won't even think about it."

He shrugs and looks past her towards the open windows with their blanket-like squares of white sky, out into the street, taking it all in. Dust covers the low, powdery buildings and fills the street.

"What will you wear?" he asks, not turning around.

"How can you talk about it so?" She slumps back in her chair, interlacing her fingers, twisting the lead ring around her index finger.

There are no other patrons on the patio and in the street nothing moves.

"I'll probably wear white, as usual. But, I might not. I won't!"

He smiles, then drains his cup, tasting, at the bottom, the almost bitter pieces of soft leaves that touch against his lips. "Should we go?"

He pays for the wine and counts out an additional five thousand pesos to the shopkeeper. "This is for you."

The old woman hesitates, looks at the younger woman and then with a birdlike frightened movement scrabbles up the bills and pushes them, crinkling, into a front pocket. "*Gracias.*" She bows stiffly, and respectfully touches her forehead.

The patio is dark and has a smell like rotting wood. There are squat black arches encircling it and one of these opens onto the street. It is noon. The pallid dead brilliance makes him dizzy for a minute. Heat ripples rise from the adobe walls that close in the narrow street. His eyes water and the air is dry and hot on his face.

"Are you all right?" She takes his arm.

"Yes. Just a minute." From a street very close to them, a band is playing. The music streams up and over the roofless buildings, melting against the heat over his head. "We should see this."

She frowns. It is the same frown she makes when someone tells her there are few young men interested in the Arena nowadays. "If you wish, darling."

"I do. Come on, aren't you going to indulge me on my last afternoon?"

She clutches his arm tighter and they go slowly down the street in the shade of a low wall, the music moving closer as they near the end of the street. When he was a child the band used to play several times a year, then twice a year for a long time, and now they play and march only one time in the year. Suddenly the soft, fluffed dust in front of his feet spouts, and he kicks up a brown spider that clings to the toe of his huarache before he kicks it away.

"Should we pretend?" he asks.

Her eyes have followed the spider and now they turn to him, flat and gray-filmed, motionless under her damp forehead. Her lips purse: "Pretend?"

On an impulse, he kisses her. Her lips are dry and cracked and he kisses her hard and presses her against the hot brick wall. The band shrieks and clangs and passes across at the end of the street, pauses, and moves on. Fainter now as it tramps along then turns off onto another street.

"Like it was when we first met and I was a struggling young disciple. You remember?" He remembers, anyway. Long, hot afternoons at the Arena; practicing, practicing, perfecting—every action, every thought, every grace. The blood thrill and rush of excitement as his compadres finished, one by one. He was one of the lucky ones and the dedicated. Then he'd moved up at last among the few eligibles, then above them even.

"I remember," she says.

This last year as his wife she might remember and perhaps

she might remember this afternoon. For a moment he lets himself think about the afternoon.

"It was good—it was," she says. Her eyes are cold and clouded, flat into her face like the eyes of a snake he'd killed once in the mountains in the blind season.

They come to the end of the street and stop. It is quiet and the only sound that reaches them is a dry rattling, gagging cough coming from somewhere down the street in the direction of the band. He looks at her and she shrugs before they turn down the street. They walk by some old men sitting in doorways, the doors boarded up behind them, their big dusty sombreros pulled down over their faces, legs drawn up tight and folded against their chests or sticking out into the street. The coughing starts again, dry and thick as if it comes from under the ground, the throat tubed full of dirt. He listens and looks closely at the men.

She points into a narrow passageway at a bareheaded small gray man squeezed in between the two buildings. The man opens his mouth . . . and makes a cough.

He turns her around to him. "How many of us have you lived with?"

"Why . . . five or six. I'd have to think. Why do you ask?"

He shakes his head. "Do you remember Luis?"

She pulls her arm out of his, her heavy bracelet making a dull chinking sound. "He was my first. I loved him."

"He taught me almost everything . . . I needed to know." He chews on his lip and the sun presses like a hot flat stone on his neck. "Do you remember Jorge?"

"Yes." They are walking again and she takes his arm once more. "A good man. Like you a little, but I didn't love him. Please, let's not talk about it anymore."

"All right. I think I'd like to walk down to the plaza."

Vacant-eyed men and women stare at them as they pass. They sag against the doors or crouch in the dark alcoves and some gaze dully at them from low windows. They walk farther, away from the town and out onto the plain. All around them are mortar blocks and chunks of old limed white cement and broken, grainy bits and pieces that crush under their feet. Over everything a thick coat of dust. The plated sun shimmers white and blinding above their heads, burning the garments into their sticky backs.

"We should go back," she says, squeezing his arm a little.

"Pretty soon." He points at the thin, wash-yellow flowers stretching up in the dark crack of a broken block of cement roadway. They are standing in the Zocalo, the Great Square, facing the ruins of the Metropolitan Cathedral. Bordering the square is a line of powdery brown mounds with a single hole in the side of each, facing them. Beyond the mounds, brown rows of adobe houses that run and spread toward the hills until only the tops of the tallest houses are visible. Then a long up-and-down line of gray humped hills that stretch as far as he can see down the valley. The hills have always reminded him of great-breasted reclining women but it all seems strange now, and dirty.

"Please, love," she says, "let's go back now and drink a little wine while there's time."

From the Arena the band has struck up, a few strains jagging over and across the plain to them. He listens. "Yes. We mustn't be late." He looks at the ground and stirs the dust with his heel. "All right, yes, let's go and have a little wine." He bends and picks the small cluster of yellow flowers for her.

They go to Manuel's and when Manuel sees them sit down at one of his tables he first salutes and then goes to the cellar and brings out their last bottle of dark wine.

"You will be at the Arena this afternoon, Manuel?"

Manuel studies a crack that runs down the length of the wall behind the table. "*Si*."

"Don't feel that way, my friend. It's not so bad. Look." He tilts his cup and lets the warm wine run down his throat. "I'm happy. What would be the sense of it if I were not happy? That the moment should be perfect, there should be joy and consent on the part of all persons concerned." He smiles at him; no hard feelings. "This is the way it has always been, so you see—I must be happy. And so should you, my friend. We're all in this together." He finishes another cup and wipes his sweaty palms on his pants. Then he gets up and shakes hands with Manuel. "We must go. Good-bye, Manuel."

At the entrance to their quarters she clings to him, whispering and stroking his neck. "I do love you! I love only you." She pulls him to her, her fingers digging into his shoulders, pulling his face to hers. And then she turns and runs for the entrance.

He shouts: "You'll have to hurry if you're going to dress!"

Now he is walking in the late afternoon green shadows and now crossing a deserted square, his sandaled feet settling into the hot crumbly dirt. For a moment the sun has gone behind a skein of white clouds and when he comes onto the street leading to the Arena, it is very pale and light and there are no shadows. Silent, small groups of people shuffle down the street but they keep their eyes away and show no recognition when he passes them. In front of the Arena a group of dusty men and women is already waiting. They stare at the ground or at the white-laced sky, and a few of them have their mouths open with the backs of their heads almost touching the shoulders, swaying back and forth like ragged stalks of corn as they follow the clouds. He uses a side entrance and goes directly to the dressing room.

He lies on the table, his face turned toward the dripping white candle, watching the women. Their distorted slow movements flicker on the wall as they undress him, rubbing his body with oils and scent before dressing him again in the white rough-textured garment. Dirt walls close in the narrow room and there is barely space for the table and the six women who hover over him. A wrinkled, oily brown face peers into his, blowing a wet breath of old food, the breath scraping in her throat. The lips crack farther until they part, open and close over hoarse ancient syllables. The others pick it up as they help him off the table and lead him into the Arena.

He lies down quickly on the small platform, closes his eyes and listens to the chanting of the women. The sun is bright against his face and he turns his head away. The band flares up, much closer, somewhere inside the Arena, and for a moment he listens to that. The chanting drops suddenly to a murmur, then stops. He opens his eyes and turns his head first to one side and then to the other. For an instant all the faces are focused on him, heads craning forward. He closes his eyes to the sight. Then the dull *chink* of a heavy bracelet close to his ear, and he opens his eyes. She is standing over him dressed in a white robe and holding the long shiny obsidian knife. She bends closer, the cluster of flowers woven into her hair—bending lower over his face as she blesses his love and devotion and asks his forgiveness.

"Forgive me."

"What is the use?" he whispers. Then, as the knife point touches his chest he screams, "I forgive you!"

And the people hear and settle back in their seats, exhausted, as she cuts out his heart and holds it up to the lustrous sun.

Poseidon and Company

H E saw nothing only suddenly the wind stiffened and blew mist up off the sea and over his face, taking him by surprise. He'd been dreaming again. Using his elbows, he worked a little closer to the edge that overlooked the beach and raised his face out toward the sea. The wind struck his eyes, bringing tears. Down below, the other boys were playing war but their voices sounded watery and far away, and he tried not to listen. Over the voices came the squeak of the gulls, out where the sea thundered on the rocks below the temple. Poseidon's temple. He lay again on his stomach and turned his face a little to one side, waiting.

On his back the sun slipped away and a chill broke over his legs and shoulders. Tonight he would lie wrapped in his cover and remember these few minutes of felt time, day fading. It was different than standing in Naiad's cave up in the hills, someone holding his hand under the water that trickled steadily out of the crack in the rock. It had been dripping for no one knows how long, they said. Different too than wading in the surf up to his knees, feeling the strange pull. That was time too, but not the same. They'd told him about that, about when to wade and when to stay off the beach. But this was something of his own and every afternoon he lay on his stomach up over the sea and waited for the change, the prickly passage of time across his back.

Out loud, tasting the sea salt on his lips as he did so, he said a few verses into the wind, new ones that he'd heard last night. Some of the words he liked he rolled over again in his mouth. Below, he heard Aias curse another boy and invoke one of the gods. Was it true, what men told of the gods? He remembered every song he'd heard, every story handed down and recited at night around the fire, as well as all the eyewitness accounts. Still, he had heard some men speak of the gods with disrespect, even disbelief, so that it was hard to know what to believe anymore. Someday he'd leave here and find out for himself. He'd walk over the hills to Eritrea where the trading ships came in. Maybe he'd even be able to board one of them and go wherever it was they go, the places men talked about.

Below, the voices were louder and one of the boys was crying jerkily against the clatter of their sticks on the shields. He raised up onto his knees to listen and swayed blindly, dizzy with memory and idea as the evening wind carried up the angry voices. He could hear Achilles yelling loudest of all as the two groups ran back and forth over the beach. Then his own name was called, and he lay down quickly to keep out of sight. Nearer, his sister called again. Now the steps behind him and he sat up all at once, discovered.

"There you are!" she said. "I had to walk all this way for you! Why didn't you come home? You never do anything you're supposed to." She came closer. "Give me your hand!"

He felt her hands take his and begin to pull him. "No!" he said, shaking. He jerked free and with the stick he sometimes called Spear began to feel his way down the trail.

"Well, you'll see, little man who thinks he's so big," she said. "Your time's coming, Mama said."

Bright Red Apples

I CAN'T make water, Mommy," Old Hutchins said, coming out of the bathroom with tears in his eyes.

"Close your barn door, Pa!" Rudy shouted. The old man disgusted him and his hand twitched in anger. He leaped out of his chair and looked around for his boomerang. "Have you seen my boomerang, Ma?"

"No, I haven't," Mother Hutchins said patiently. "Now you just behave yourself, Rudy, while I see to your pa. You just heard him say he can't make water. But close your barn door, Daddy, like Rudy says."

Old Hutchins sniffled but did as he was told. Mother Hutchins came over to him with a worried look, holding her hands in her apron.

"It's just what Dr. Porter said would happen, Mommy," Old Hutchins said, sagging against the wall and looking as if he were going to die right then. "I'll get up one morning, he said, and not be able to make water."

"Shut up!" Rudy shouted. "Shut up! Talk, talk, talk, dirty talk all day long. I've had enough of it!"

"You keep quiet now, Rudy," Mother Hutchins said feebly, moving back a step or two with Old Hutchins in her arms.

Rudy began stalking up and down the linoleum-covered floor of the sparsely furnished but tidy living room. His hands jumped in and out of his hip pockets as he threw menacing looks at Old Hutchins, who hung limply in Mother Hutchins's arms.

At the same time, a warm smell of fresh apple pie drifted in from the kitchen and made Rudy lick his lips hungrily, reminded him, even in the midst of his great anger, that it was nearly snack time. Now and then he glanced nervously out of the corner of his eye at his older brother Ben, who sat in a heavy oak chair in the corner near the treadle-operated sewing machine. But Ben never raised his eyes from his worn copy of *Restless Guns*.

Rudy couldn't figure Ben. He kept tramping up and down the living room, from time to time knocking over a chair or breaking a lamp. Mother Hutchins and Old Hutchins inched back toward the bathroom. Rudy stopped suddenly and glared at them, then looked at Ben again. He just couldn't figure Ben. He couldn't figure any of them, but he could figure Ben even less than the others. He wanted Ben to notice him sometimes, but Ben always had his nose in a book. Ben read Zane Grey, Louis L'Amour, Ernest Haycox, Luke Short. Ben thought Zane Grey, Louis L'Amour, and Ernest Haycox were all right, but not as good as Luke Short. He thought Luke Short was the best of the lot. He'd read Luke Short's books forty or fifty times. He had to have something to pass the time. Ever since his rigging had come loose seven or eight years ago when he was topping trees for Pacific Lumber, he'd had to have something to pass the time. Since then he could only move the upper part of his body; also, he seemed to have lost the power of speech. Anyway, he had never uttered a word since the day of the fall. But then he'd always been a quiet boy when he was living at home before; no bother at all. Still no bother, his mother maintained, if she was asked. Quiet as a mouse and needed very little seeing to.

Besides, on the first of each month Ben got a little disability check in the mail. Not much, but enough for them all to live on. Old Hutchins had quit work when the disability checks started coming. He didn't like his boss was the reason he gave at the time. Rudy had never left home. He'd never finished high school, either. Ben had finished high school but Rudy was a high school dropout. Now he was afraid of being drafted. The idea of being drafted made him very nervous. He didn't at all like the idea of being drafted. Mother Hutchins had always been a housewife and a homemaker. She was not very shrewd but she knew how to make ends meet. Once in a while, though, if they ran short before the end of the month, she had to walk into town with a nice box of apples on her back and sell them for a dime each on the corner in front of Johnson's Pharmacy. Mr. Johnson and the clerks knew her and she always gave Mr. Johnson and the clerks a shiny red apple that she polished against the front of her dress.

Rudy began making violent slashes and sword thrusts in the air, grunting as he gouged and chopped. He seemed to have forgotten about the old couple cowering in the passageway.

"Now, dear, don't you worry," Mother Hutchins said faintly to Old Hutchins. "Dr. Porter'll put you right. Why, a prostrate operation is, is an everyday occurrence. Look at Prime Minister MacMillian. Remember Prime Minister MacMillian, Daddy? When he was prime minister and had his prostrate operation he was up and around in no time. No time. Now you just cheer up. Why—"

"Shut up! Shut up!" Rudy made a frightening lunge toward them, but they drew back farther into the narrow passageway. Fortunately, Mother Hutchins had enough strength left to whistle up Yeller, a shaggy giant of a dog, who immediately ran into the room from the back porch and put his paws up on Rudy's narrow chest, pushing him back a step or two.

Rudy retreated slowly, appalled at the dog's rank breath. On his way through the living room he picked up Old Hutchins's prized possession, an ashtray made from the hoof and foreleg of an elk, and hurled the smelly thing out into the garden.

Old Hutchins began to cry again. His nerves were gone. Ever since Rudy's vicious attack upon his life a month ago, his nerves, which weren't good to begin with, had gone.

What had happened was this: Old Hutchins was taking a bath when Rudy sneaked up and threw the RCA Victrola into the bathtub. It could have been serious, fatal even, if in his haste Rudy hadn't forgot to plug it in. As it was, Old Hutchins had received a bad bruise on his right thigh when the Victrola had made its flying entry through the open door. That was just after Rudy had seen a movie in town called *Goldfinger*. Now they were more or less on guard at all moments, but especially whenever Rudy ventured into town. Who could tell what ideas he might pick up at the movies? He was very impressionable. "He's at a very impressionable age," Mother Hutchins said to Old Hutchins. Ben never said anything, one way or the other. Nobody could figure Ben, not even his mother, Mother Hutchins.

Rudy stayed in the barn just long enough to devour half the pie, then put a halter on Em, his favorite camel. He led her out the back door and safely through the elaborate network of snares, covered pits and traps, laid for the careless and the unwary. Once clear, he pulled Em's ear and commanded her to kneel, mounted, and was off.

He clop-clopped out across the back forty, up into the dry, sage-covered foothills. He stopped once on a little rise to look back at the old homestead. He wished he had some dynamite and a plunger to blow it right off the landscape—like Lawrence of Arabia had done with those trains. He hated the sight of it, the old homestead. They were all crazy down there anyway. They wouldn't be missed. Would he miss them? No, he wouldn't miss them. Besides, there would still be the land, the apples. Damn the land and the apples anyway! He wished he had some dynamite.

He turned Em into a dry arroyo. With the sun bearing down fiercely on his back, he cantered to the end of the box canyon. He stopped and dismounted and, behind a rock, uncovered the canvas that held the big Smith & Wesson service revolver, the burnoose and the headgear. He dressed and then stuck the revolver in his sash. It fell out. He stuck it in again and it fell out again. Then he just decided to carry it in his hand, though it was heavy and it would be hard to guide Em. It would call for a skillful bit of maneuvering on his part, but he thought he could do it. He thought he was up to it.

Back at the farm, he left Em in the barn and made his way to the house. He saw the elk-leg ashtray still in the garden, a few flies working away on it, and he sneered; the old man had been afraid to come out and retrieve it. But it gave him an idea.

He burst in on them in the kitchen. Old Hutchins, sitting rather comfortably at the kitchen table and stirring his coffee and cream, looked completely stunned. Mother Hutchins was at the stove, putting in another pie.

"Apples, apples, apples!" Rudy shrieked. He followed this outburst with a wild laugh, waving his Colt .45 around in the air, then herded them into the living room. Ben looked up with a slight show of interest, and then went back to his book. It was Luke Short's *Rawhide Trail*.

"This is it," Rudy said, his voice rising. "This is it, this is it, this is it!"

Mother Hutchins kept puckering her lips—almost as if expecting a kiss—trying to whistle up Yeller, but Rudy only laughed and hooted. He pointed at the window with the barrel of his Winchester. "There's Yeller," he said. Mother Hutchins and Old Hutchins both looked to see Yeller trotting into the orchard with the ashtray in his mouth. "There's your old Yeller," Rudy said.

Old Hutchins groaned and fell with a painful clump to his knees. Mother Hutchins got down beside him but cast an imploring look in Rudy's direction. Rudy was about four feet away from her, just to the right of the red Naugahyde footstool.

"Rudy, now you wouldn't do anything now, dear, you'd be sorry for later. You wouldn't hurt me or your pa, would you, Rudy?"

"He ain't a pa to me—ain't, ain't, ain't," said Rudy, dancing around the living room with an occasional glance at Ben, who, since his initial momentary flicker of interest in the proceedings, hadn't stirred himself again.

"Shouldn't say ain't, Rudy," Mother Hutchins gently reproved.

"Son," Old Hutchins stopped sniffling for a minute, "you wouldn't hurt a poor old helpless broken-down old man with a prostrate condition, would you? Huh?"

"Stick it out here, stick it out here and I'll blow it off for you," Rudy said, waving the ugly snub-nosed barrel of his .38 right under Old Hutchins's rather large nose. "I'll show you what I'll do for you!" He waved it there from side to side a minute longer, then danced off again. "No, no, I wouldn't shoot you. Shooting's too good for you." But he fired a burst from the BAR into the kitchen wall just to show them he meant business.

Ben raised his eyes. He had a soft, indolent look to his face. He stared at Rudy a minute without recognition, then went back to his book. He was in a fine room in a Virginia City hotel called The Palace. Downstairs there were three or four angry men waiting for him at the bar, but right now he was going to enjoy the first bath he'd had in three months.

Rudy faltered a minute, then looked around wildly. His eyes fell on the grandfather railroad ticktock clock that had been in the family seven years. "You see that clock there, Ma? When the b-big hand gets on the little hand there's going to be an explosion. Wham! Foom! Up she goes, everything! Ballou!" With this he bounded out the front door and jumped off the porch.

He sat down behind an apple tree a hundred yards from the

house. He intended to wait until they were all assembled on the front porch: Mother Hutchins, Old Hutchins, even Ben; all assembled there with the few pitiful accumulations they hoped to preserve, and then he would pick them off quickly, one by one. He swept the porch with his scope, putting the cross hairs on the window, a wicker chair, a cracked flowerpot drying in the sun on one of the porch steps. Then he took a long breath and settled down to wait.

He waited and waited, but they didn't come. A small band of California mountain quail began to work their way down through the orchard, stopping every now and then to pick at a fallen apple, or to look around the base of a tree for a nice juicy grub. He kept watching them and pretty soon was no longer watching the porch. He sat very still behind the tree, almost without breathing, and they didn't see him and came closer and closer, talking soft quail talk between themselves as they picked at the apples and sharply scrutinized the ground. He leaned forward slightly and strained his ears to overhear what they were saying. The quail were talking about Vietnam.

It was too much for Rudy. He could've cried. He flapped his arms at the quail, said "Who!" Ben, Vietnam, apples, prostrate: what did it all mean? Was there a connection between Marshal Dillon and James Bond? Oddjob and Captain Easy? If so, where did Luke Short fit it? And Ted Trueblood? His mind reeled.

With a last, forlorn glance at the empty porch, he placed the shiny, recently blued barrels of the 12-gauge double into his mouth.

from "The Augustine Notebooks"

OCTOBER II

"No way, sugar," she said, looking at him steadily. "No way at all. Not on your life."

He shrugged. He sipped from the glass of lemon fix without looking at her.

"You must be crazy, it's true." She looked around at the other tables. It was ten o'clock in the morning and, at this time of year, there were not many tourists left on the island. Most of the tables in the courtyard were empty and on some of the tables waiters had stacked chairs.

"Are you crazy? Is it really true, then?"

"Forget it," he said. "Let it alone."

A peacock had wandered in from the marketplace which was next to the nearly empty courtyard where they sat at their table drinking the lemon fixes. The peacock stopped at a spigot near the edge of the courtyard and held its beak under the dripping tap. As it drank, its throat rippled up and down. Then the peacock walked slowly around some empty tables and headed in their direction. Halprin threw a wafer onto the flagstones. The bird picked it to bits there on the flagstones and ate the pieces without once looking up at them.

"You remind me of that peacock," he said.

She stood up and said, "I think you might just as well stay here. I think you've had it, anyway. I think you've lost your mind. Why don't you just kill yourself and get it over with?" She waited a minute longer, holding her purse, and then she walked away between the empty tables.

He signaled the waiter, who had watched everything. In a minute the waiter put another bottle of lemon fix and a clean glass in front of him. After pouring what was left of her drink into his glass, the waiter took away her bottle and glass without saying anything.

Halprin could see the bay and their ship from where he sat. The harbor was too shallow for a ship of its size to enter, so it had anchored a quarter mile out, behind the breakwater, and they had come ashore that morning on a tender. The entrance to the bay was narrow and had, more than two thousand years ago, given rise to the legend that, in even more ancient days, the Colossus itself had straddled the entrance to the harbor— one mammoth bronze leg on either side of the harbor entrance. Some of the postcards for sale in the marketplace depicted a gigantic cartoon Colossus with boats going and coming between its legs.

In a little while, she came back to the table and sat down as if nothing had happened. Every day that passed, they hurt each other a little more. Every day now they grew more used to wounding each other. At night, with this knowledge, their lovemaking had become vicious and unbridled, their bodies coming together like knives clashing in the dark.

"You weren't serious, were you?" she said. "You didn't mean what you said? About staying here, you know, and all the rest?"

"I don't know. Yes, I said it, didn't I? I'm serious about it."

She continued to look at him.

"How much money do you have?" he asked.

"Not a cent. Nothing. You have everything, sugar. You're carrying it all. I can't believe this has happened to me, but I don't even have enough to buy cigarettes."

"I'm sorry. Well," he said after a minute, "if we just wouldn't look or act or even talk like broken-down Hemingway characters. That's what I'm afraid of," he said.

She laughed. "Jesus, if that's all you're afraid of," she said.

"You have your typewriter," she said.

"That's true, and they must sell paper here, and pens or pencils. Here, here's a pen, for instance. I have a pen right here in my pocket." He scribbled some sharp vertical lines on the paper coaster. "It works." He grinned for the first time.

"How long would it take?" she said and waited.

"I don't have any idea. Maybe six months, maybe longer. I've known people who . . . Probably longer. I've never done it before, as you know." He drank from his glass and didn't look at her. His breathing had slowed.

"I don't think we can make it," she said. "I don't think you, I don't think we have it in us."

"Frankly, I don't think we do, either," he said. "I'm not asking or forcing you to stay. The ship won't leave for another five or six hours, you can make up your mind before that. You don't

have to stay. I'll divide up the money, of course. I'm sorry
about that. I don't want you to stay unless you're sure you
want to stay. But I think I will stay. My life is half over, more
than half over. The only, the only really extraordinary thing to
happen to me in, I don't know, years, was to fall in love with
you. That's the only really extraordinary thing in years. That
other life is over now, and there's no going back. I don't
believe in gestures, not since I was a kid, before I married
Kristina, but this would be a gesture of some sort, I suppose.
Call it that, if you want. That is, if I pull it off. But I think I
might if I stay. I know it sounds crazy. I don't know, though,
about us. I'd like you to stay. You know what you mean to me.
But you must do what's right for you from now on. In my
more lucid moments"—he turned the glass in his hand— "I
think it's true, it's over for us. Why, just look at me! My hands
are shaking, for Christ's sake." He put his hands out over the
table so she could see. He shook his head. "In any case, there's
somebody out there waiting for you. If you want to go."

"Just like you were waiting."

"Yes, just like I was waiting, that's true."

"I want to stay," she said after a minute. "If it doesn't work,
if it isn't going to work, we'll know, we'll be able to see in a
little while, a week or two. I can always go then."

"Anytime," he said. "I won't try to hold you."

"You will," she said. "If I decide to go, one way or another
you'll try to hold me. You'll do that."

They watched a flock of pigeons turn with a rush of wings
overhead and then wheel toward the ship.

"Let's go for it, then," she said and touched the back of his
left hand where it held his glass. His right hand was in his lap,
clenched.

"You stay, I'll stay, we'll both stay together, okay? Then
we'll see. Sugar?"

"Okay," he said. He got up from the table and sat down
again. "Okay, then." His breathing was all right once more.
"I'll speak to someone about getting our stuff off the ship and
applying for a refund for the rest of the trip. Then I'll divide all
the money between us. We'll divide the money today. We'll
both feel better about that. We'll get a hotel for tonight, divide
the money, and then look for a place tomorrow. But you're

probably right, you know: I am crazy. Sick and crazy." He was serious as he said this.

She began to cry. He stroked her hand and felt tears come to his own eyes. He took her hands. She nodded slowly as the tears continued to run from her eyes.

The waiter turned his back on them abruptly. He moved to the sink and after a minute began to wash and dry some glasses and hold them up to the light.

A thin, moustached man with carefully combed hair—Halprin recognized him from the ship; the man had boarded with them at Piraeus—pulled out a chair and sat down at one of the empty tables. He hung his jacket over the back of one of the chairs, rolled the cuffs of his sleeves back once, and lighted a cigarette. He looked briefly in their direction—Halprin was still holding her hands, she was still crying—and then looked away.

The waiter arranged a small white towel over his arm and went over to the man. At the edge of the courtyard, the peacock turned its head slowly from side to side and regarded them all with cold, brilliant eyes.

OCTOBER 18

He sipped coffee and remembered beginnings. Imagine, he thought, and the next time he looked it was clearly noon. The house was quiet. He got up from the table and went to the door. Women's voices carried in from the street. Flowers of all kinds grew around the steps—big, puffy flowers, drooping red and yellow flowers mainly, with a few shapely purple ones as well. He shut the door and headed down the street for cigarettes. He didn't whistle, but he let his arms swing as he moved down the steep, cobbled street. The sun fell squarely off the sides of the white buildings and made him squint. *Augustine.* What else? Simple. No diminutive either, ever. He had never called her anything but: Augustine. He kept walking. He nodded at men, women, and horses alike.

He drew aside the bead curtains over the door and went inside. The young barman, Michael, wearing a black armband, was leaning on his elbows on the bar, a cigarette between his lips, talking to George Varos. Varos was a fisherman who had lost his left hand in an accident. He still went out now and then but since he was unable to handle the nets, he said he no longer felt right going out in the boats. He spent his days selling sesame rolls that looked like doughnuts. Two broomsticks stacked with sesame rolls leaned against the counter next to Varos. The men looked at him and nodded.

"Cigarettes and a lemon fix, please," he said to Michael. He took the cigarettes and his drink to a small table near the window where he could see the bay. Two small boats moved up and down with the motion of the waves. The men in the boats sat staring down into the water without moving or talking, while the boats moved up and down on the waves.

He sipped the drink and smoked and in a little while he took the letter out of his pocket and commenced to read. Now and then he stopped and looked out the window at the boats. The men at the counter went on talking.

"That's a start, for sure," she said. She had put her arms around his shoulders, her breasts just grazing his back. She was reading what he had written.

"It's not bad, sugar," she said. "No, it's not bad at all. But where was I when this was taking place? Was this yesterday?"

"What do you mean?" He glanced over the pages. "You mean this, *the house was quiet*? Maybe you were asleep. I don't know. Or out shopping. I don't know. Is it important? All I say is—the house was quiet. I don't need to go into your whereabouts right now."

"I never nap in the morning, or in the middle of the day either, for that matter." She made a face at him.

"I don't think I have to account in this for your whereabouts at every minute. Do you think? What the hell."

"No, I mean, I'm not making anything out of it. I mean, it's just strange, you know, that's what I mean." She waved her hand at the pages. "You know what I mean."

He got up from the table and stretched and looked out the window at the bay.

"Do you want to work some more?" she said. "Lord, we don't have to go to the beach. That was just a suggestion. I'd rather see you work some more, if that's what you want."

She had been eating an orange. He could smell the orange on her breath as she leaned over the table and looked seriously at the pages once more. She grinned and ran her tongue over her lips. "Well," she said. "So. Well, well."

He said, "I want to go to the beach. That's enough for today. That's enough for now, anyway. Maybe tonight I'll do something. I'll fool around with this tonight, maybe. I've started, that's the main thing. I'm the compulsive type; I'll go on now. Maybe it'll work itself out. Let's go to the beach."

She grinned again. "Good," she said. She put her hand on his cock. "Good, good, good. How is our little friend today?" She stroked his cock through his trousers. "I'd hoped you'd start today," she said. "I thought you might today for some reason, I don't know why. Let's go, then. I'm happy today, this minute. I can't tell you. It's as if . . . I feel happier today than I've felt in a long, long time. Maybe—"

"Let's not think maybe or anything," he said. He reached under the halter and touched her breast, took the nipple between his fingers and rolled it back and forth. "We'll take one day at a time, that's what we decided. One day, then the next day, then the next." The nipple began to stiffen under his fingers.

"When we come back from swimming we'll do things to each other," she said. "Unless, of course, you want to put off swimming until later?"

"I'm easy," he said. Then, "No, wait, I'll put my trunks on. When we're at the beach maybe we'll tell each other about what we're going to do to each other when we get back here. Let's go ahead and go to the beach now while the sun's out. It may rain. Let's go ahead and go."

She began to hum something as she put some oranges into a little bag.

Halprin slipped on his trunks. He put the sheets of paper and the ballpoint pen into the cupboard. He stared into the cupboard a minute and then, the humming gone, turned slowly.

She stood in front of the open door in her shorts and halter, the long black hair hanging down over her shoulders from under the white straw sun hat. She held the oranges and the straw-covered water bottle against her breasts. She looked at him a minute, and then she winked, grinned, and cocked her hip.

His breath went out of him and his legs felt weak. For a minute he was afraid of another seizure. He saw the wedge of blue sky behind her and the darker blue, shining blue, water of the bay, the small waves rising and falling. He closed his eyes and opened them. She was still there, grinning. *What we do matters, brother*, he remembered Miller saying long ago. There came to him an empty tugging in his stomach, then he felt his jaws simply tighten of their own accord until he ground his teeth and felt his face might tell her things he himself didn't yet know. He felt light-headed, but all senses on the alert: he could smell the broken orange in the room, could hear a fly drone and then bump the window near the bed. He heard flowers around the steps, their long stems moving against each other in the warm breeze. Gulls called and waves rose and then fell on the beach. He felt at the edge of something. It was as if things he had never understood before might now suddenly be made clear to him.

"Crazy about you," he said. "Crazy about you, baby. Baby." She nodded.

"Close the door," he said. His cock began to rise against the swimming trunks.

She put her things on the table and pushed the door shut with her foot. Then she took off her hat and shook her hair.

"Well, well, well," she said and grinned again. "Well, let me say hello to our friend," she said. "Not so little friend." Her eyes shone as she moved toward him and her voice had become languorous.

"Lie down," she said. "And don't move. Just lie down on the bed. And don't move. Don't move, hear."

Kindling

IT was the middle of August and Myers was between lives. The only thing different about this time from the other times was that this time he was sober. He'd just spent twenty-eight days at a drying-out facility. But during this period his wife took it into her head to go down the road with another drunk, a friend of theirs. The man had recently come into some money and had been talking about buying into a bar and restaurant in the eastern part of the state.

Myers called his wife, but she hung up on him. She wouldn't even talk to him, let alone have him anywhere near the house. She had a lawyer and a restraining order. So he took a few things, boarded a bus, and went to live near the ocean in a room in a house owned by a man named Sol who had run an ad in the paper.

Sol was wearing jeans and a red T-shirt when he opened the door. It was about ten o'clock at night and Myers had just gotten out of a cab. Under the porch light Myers could see that Sol's right arm was shorter than his other arm, and the hand and fingers were withered. He didn't offer either his good left hand or his withered hand for Myers to shake, and this was fine with Myers. Myers felt plenty rattled as it was.

You just called, right? Sol said. You're here to see the room. Come on in.

Myers gripped his suitcase and stepped inside.

This is my wife. This is Bonnie, Sol said.

Bonnie was watching TV but moved her eyes to see who it was coming inside. She pushed the button on a device she held in her hand and the volume went off. She pushed it again and the picture disappeared. Then she got up off the sofa onto her feet. She was a fat girl. She was fat all over and she huffed when she breathed.

I'm sorry it's so late, Myers said. Nice to meet you.

It's all right, Bonnie said. Did my husband tell you on the phone what we're asking?

Myers nodded. He was still holding the suitcase.

Well, this is the living room, Sol said, as you can see for

yourself. He shook his head and brought the fingers of his good hand up to his chin. I may as well tell you that we're new at this. We never rented a room to anybody before. But it's just back there not being used, and we thought what the hell. A person can always use a little extra.

I don't blame you a bit, Myers said.

Where are you from? Bonnie said. You're not from anywhere around town.

My wife wants to be a writer, Sol said. Who, what, where, why, and how much?

I just got here, Myers said. He moved the suitcase to his other hand. I got off the bus about an hour ago, read your ad in the paper, and called up.

What sort of work do you do? Bonnie wanted to know.

I've done everything, Myers said. He set the suitcase down and opened and closed his fingers. Then he picked up the suitcase again.

Bonnie didn't pursue it. Sol didn't either, though Myers could see he was curious.

Myers took in a photograph of Elvis Presley on top of the TV. Elvis's signature ran across the breast of his white sequined jacket. He moved a step closer.

The King, Bonnie said.

Myers nodded but didn't say anything. Alongside the picture of Elvis was a wedding picture of Sol and Bonnie. In the picture Sol was dressed up in a suit and tie. Sol's good strong left arm reached around Bonnie's waist as far as it would go. Sol's right hand and Bonnie's right hand were joined over Sol's belt buckle. Bonnie wasn't going anywhere if Sol had anything to say about it. Bonnie didn't mind. In the picture Bonnie wore a hat and was all smiles.

I love her, Sol said, as if Myers had said something to the contrary.

How about that room you were going to show me? Myers said.

I knew there was something we were forgetting, Sol said.

They moved out of the living room into the kitchen, Sol first, then Myers, carrying his suitcase, and then Bonnie. They passed through the kitchen and turned left just before the back door. There were some open cupboards along the wall, and a washer and dryer. Sol opened a door at the end of the little corridor and turned on the light in the bathroom.

Bonnie moved up and huffed and said, This is your private bathroom. That door in the kitchen is your own entrance.

Sol opened the door to the other side of the bathroom and turned on another light. This is the room, he said.

I made up the bed with clean sheets, Bonnie said. But if you take the room you'll have to be responsible from here on out.

Like my wife says, this is not a hotel, Sol said. But you're welcome, if you want to stay.

There was a double bed against one wall, along with a nightstand and lamp, a chest of drawers, and a pinochle table with a metal chair. A big window gave out onto the backyard. Myers put his suitcase on the bed and moved to the window. He raised the shade and looked out. A moon rode high in the sky. In the distance he could see a forested valley and mountain peaks. Was it his imagination, or did he hear a stream or a river?

I hear water, Myers said.

That's the Little Quilcene River you hear, Sol said. That river has the fastest per-foot drop to it of any river in the country.

Well, what do you think? Bonnie said. She went over and turned down the covers on the bed, and this simple gesture almost caused Myers to weep.

I'll take it, Myers said.

I'm glad, Sol said. My wife's glad too, I can tell. I'll have them pull that ad out of the paper tomorrow. You want to move in right now, don't you?

That's what I hoped, Myers said.

We'll let you get settled, Bonnie said. I gave you two pillows, and there's an extra quilt in that closet.

Myers could only nod.

Well, good night, Sol said.

Good night, Bonnie said.

Good night, Myers said. And thank you.

Sol and Bonnie went through his bathroom and into the kitchen. They closed the door, but not before Myers heard Bonnie say, He seems okay.

Pretty quiet, Sol said.

I think I'll fix buttered popcorn.

I'll eat some with you, Sol said.

Pretty soon Myers heard the TV come on again in the living room, but it was a very faint sound and he didn't think it would bother him. He opened the window all the way and heard the sound of the river as it raced through the valley on its way to the ocean.

He took his things out of the suitcase and put them away in the drawers. Then he used the bathroom and brushed his teeth. He moved the table so that it sat directly in front of the window. Then he looked at where she'd turned the covers down. He drew out the metal chair and sat down and took a ballpoint out of his pocket. He thought for a minute, then opened the notebook, and at the top of a blank white page he wrote the words *Emptiness is the beginning of all things.* He stared at this, and then he laughed. Jesus, what rubbish! He shook his head. He closed the notebook, undressed, and turned off the light. He stood for a moment looking out the window and listening to the river. Then he moved to get into bed.

Bonnie fixed the popcorn, salted it and poured butter over it, and took it in a big bowl to where Sol was watching TV. She let him help himself to some first. He used his left hand to good effect and then he reached his little hand over for the paper towel she offered. She took a little popcorn for herself.

What do you make of him? she wanted to know. Our new roomer.

Sol shook his head and went on watching TV and eating popcorn. Then, as if he'd been thinking about her question, he said, I like him all right. He's okay. But I think he's on the run from something.

What?

I don't know that. I'm just guessing. He isn't dangerous and he isn't going to make any trouble.

His eyes, Bonnie said.

What about his eyes?

They're sad eyes. Saddest eyes I ever saw on a man.

Sol didn't say anything for a minute. He finished his popcorn. He wiped his fingers and dabbed his chin with the paper towel. He's okay. He's just had some trouble along the way, that's all. No disgrace attached to that. Give me a sip of that, will you? He reached over for the glass of orange drink she was holding and took some. You know, I forgot to collect the rent from him tonight. I'll have to get it in the morning, if he's up. And I should have asked him how long he intends to stay. Damn, what's wrong with me? I don't want to turn this place into a hotel.

You couldn't think of everything. Besides, we're new at this. We never rented a room out before.

Bonnie decided she was going to write about the man in the notebook she was filling up. She closed her eyes and thought about what she was going to write. *This tall, stooped—but handsome!—curly headed stranger with sad eyes walked into our house one fateful night in August.* She leaned into Sol's left arm and tried to write some more. Sol squeezed her shoulder, which brought her back to the present. She opened her eyes and closed them, but she couldn't think of anything else to write about him at the moment. Time will tell, she thought. She was glad he was here.

This show's for the birds, Sol said. Let's go to bed. We have to get up in the morning.

In bed, Sol loved her up and she took him and held him and loved him back, but all the time she was doing it she was thinking about the big, curly headed man in the back room. What if he suddenly opened the bedroom door and looked in on them?

Sol, she said, is this bedroom door locked?

What? Be still, Sol said. Then he finished and rolled off, but he kept his little arm on her breast. She lay on her back and thought for a minute, then she patted his fingers, let air out through her mouth, and went off to sleep thinking about blasting caps, which is what had gone off in Sol's hand when he was a teenager, severing nerves and causing his arm and fingers to wither.

Bonnie began to snore. Sol took her arm and shook it until she turned over on her side, away from him.

In a minute, he got up and put on his underwear. He went into the living room. He didn't turn on the light. He didn't need a light. The moon was out, and he didn't want a light.

He went from the living room into the kitchen. He made sure
the back door was locked, and then he stood for a while outside the bathroom door listening, but he couldn't hear anything out of the ordinary. The faucet dripped—it needed a
washer, but then, it had always dripped. He went back
through the house and closed and locked their bedroom door.
He checked the clock and made sure the stem was pulled. He
got into bed and moved right up against Bonnie. He put his
leg over her leg, and in that way he finally went to sleep.

These three people slept and dreamed, while outside the house
the moon grew large, and seemed to move across the sky until
it was out over the ocean and growing smaller and paler. In his
dream, someone is offering Myers a glass of Scotch, but just as
he is about to take it, reluctantly, he wakes up in a sweat, his
heart racing.

Sol dreams that he is changing a tire on a truck and that he
has the use of both of his arms.

Bonnie dreams she is taking two—no, three—children to
the park. She even has names for the children. She named
them just before the trip to the park. Millicent, Dionne, and
Randy. Randy keeps wanting to pull away from her and go his
own way.

Soon, the sun breaks over the horizon and birds begin calling
to each other. The Little Quilcene River rushes down through
the valley, shoots under the highway bridge, rushes another
hundred yards over sand and sharp rocks, and pours into the
ocean. An eagle flies down from the valley and over the bridge
and begins to pass up and down the beach. A dog barks.

At this minute, Sol's alarm goes off.

Myers stayed in his room that morning until he heard them
leave. Then he went out and made instant coffee. He looked
in the fridge and saw that one of the shelves had been cleared
for him. A little sign was Scotch-taped to it: MR. MYERS SHELF.

Later, he walked a mile toward town to a little service station he remembered from the night before that also sold a few
groceries. He bought milk, cheese, bread, and tomatoes. That
afternoon, before it was time for them to come home, he left

the rent money in cash on the table and went back into his own room. Late that night, before going to bed, he opened his notebook and on a clean page he wrote, *Nothing*.

He adjusted his schedule to theirs. Mornings he'd stay in the room until he heard Sol in the kitchen making coffee and getting his breakfast. Then he would hear Sol calling Bonnie to get up and then they'd have breakfast, but they wouldn't talk much. Then Sol would go out to the garage and start the pickup, back out, and drive away. In a little while, Bonnie's ride would pull up in front of the house, a horn would toot, and Bonnie would say, every time, I'm coming.

It was then that Myers would go out to the kitchen, put on water for coffee, and eat a bowl of cereal. But he didn't have much of an appetite. The cereal and coffee would keep him for most of the day, until the afternoon, when he'd eat something else, a sandwich, before they arrived home, and then he'd stay out of the kitchen for the rest of the time when they might be in there or in the living room watching TV. He didn't want any conversation.

She'd go into the kitchen for a snack the first thing after she got in from work. Then she'd turn on the TV and wait until Sol came in, and then she'd get up and fix something for the two of them to eat. They might talk on the telephone to friends, or else go sit outside in the backyard between the garage and Myers's bedroom window and talk about their day and drink iced tea until it was time to go inside and turn on the TV. Once he heard Bonnie say to someone on the telephone, How'd she expect me to pay any attention to Elvis Presley's weight when my own weight was out of control at the time?

They'd said he was welcome anytime to sit in the living room with them and watch TV. He'd thanked them but said, No, television hurt his eyes.

They were curious about him. Especially Bonnie, who'd asked him one day when she came home early and surprised him in the kitchen, if he'd been married and if he had any kids. Myers nodded. Bonnie looked at him and waited for him to go on, but he didn't.

Sol was curious too. What kind of work do you do? he wanted to know. I'm just curious. This is a small town and I know people. I grade lumber at the mill myself. Only need one good arm to do that. But sometimes there are openings. I could put in a word, maybe. What's your regular line of work?

Do you play any instruments? Bonnie asked. Sol has a guitar, she said.

I don't know how to play it, Sol said. I wish I did.

Myers kept to his room, where he was writing a letter to his wife. It was a long letter and, he felt, an important one. Perhaps the most important letter he'd ever written in his life. In the letter he was attempting to tell his wife that he was sorry for everything that had happened and that he hoped someday she would forgive him. *I would get down on my knees and ask forgiveness if that would help.*

After Sol and Bonnie both left, he sat in the living room with his feet on the coffee table and drank instant coffee while he read the newspaper from the evening before. Once in a while his hands trembled and the newspaper began rattling in the empty house. Now and then the telephone rang, but he never made a move to answer it. It wasn't for him, because nobody knew he was here.

Through his window at the rear of the house he could see up the valley to a series of steep mountain peaks whose tops were covered with snow, even though it was August. Lower down on the mountains, timber covered the slopes and the sides of the valley. The river coursed down the valley, frothing and boiling over rocks and under granite embankments until it burst out of its confines at the mouth of the valley, slowed a little, as if it had spent itself, then picked up strength again and plunged into the ocean. When Sol and Bonnie were gone, Myers often sat in the sun in a lawn chair out back and looked up the valley toward the peaks. Once he saw an eagle soaring down the valley, and on another occasion he saw a deer picking its way along the riverbank.

He was sitting out there like that one afternoon when a big flatbed truck pulled up in the drive with a load of wood.

You must be Sol's roomer, the man said, talking out the truck window.

Myers nodded.

Sol said to just dump this wood in the backyard and he'd take care of it from there.

I'll move out of your way, Myers said. He took the chair and moved to the back step, where he stood and watched the driver back the truck up onto the lawn, then push something inside the cab until the truck bed began to elevate. In a minute, the six-foot logs began to slide off the truck bed and pile up on the ground. The bed rose even higher, and all of the chunks rolled off with a loud bang onto the lawn.

The driver touched the lever again and the truck bed went back to its normal place. Then he revved his engine, honked, and drove away.

What are you going to do with that wood out there? Myers asked Sol that night. Sol was standing at the stove frying smelt when Myers surprised him by coming into the kitchen. Bonnie was in the shower. Myers could hear the water running.

Why, I'm going to saw it up and stack it, if I can find the time between now and September. I'd like to do it before the rain starts.

Maybe I could do it for you, Myers said.

You ever cut wood before? Sol said. He'd taken the frying pan off the stove and was wiping the fingers of his left hand with a paper towel. I couldn't pay you anything for doing it. It's something I was going to do anyway. Just as soon as I get a weekend to my name.

I'll do it, Myers said. I can use the exercise.

You know how to use a power saw? And an ax and a maul?

You can show me, Myers said. I learn fast. It was important to him that he cut the wood.

Sol put the pan of smelt back on the burner. Then he said, Okay, I'll show you after supper. You had anything to eat yet? Why don't you have a bite to eat with us?

I ate something already, Myers said.

Sol nodded. Let me get this grub on the table for Bonnie and me, then, and after we eat I'll show you.

I'll be out back, Myers said.

Sol didn't say anything more. He nodded to himself, as if he was thinking about something else.

Myers took one of the folding chairs and sat down on it and looked at the pile of wood and then up the valley at the mountains where the sun was shining off the snow. It was nearly evening. The peaks thrust up into some clouds, and mist seemed to be falling from them. He could hear the river crashing through the undergrowth down in the valley.

I heard talking, Myers heard Bonnie say to Sol in the kitchen.

It's the roomer, Sol said. He asked me if he could cut up that load of wood out back.

How much does he want to do it? Bonnie wanted to know. Did you tell him we can't pay much?

I told him we can't pay anything. He wants to do it for nothing. That's what he said, anyway.

Nothing? She didn't say anything for a time. Then Myers heard her say, I guess he doesn't have anything else to do.

Later, Sol came outside and said, I guess we can get started now, if you're still game.

Myers got up out of the lawn chair and followed Sol over to the garage. Sol brought out two sawhorses and set them up on the lawn. Then he brought out a power saw. The sun had dropped behind the town. In another thirty minutes it would be dark. Myers rolled down the sleeves of his shirt and buttoned the cuffs. Sol worked without saying anything. He grunted as he lifted one of the six-foot logs and positioned it on the sawhorses. Then he began to use the saw, working steadily for a while. Sawdust flew. Finally he stopped sawing and stepped back.

You get the idea, he said.

Myers took the saw, nosed the blade into the cut Sol had started, then began sawing. He found a rhythm and stayed with it. He kept pressing, leaning into the saw. In a few minutes, he sawed through and the two halves of the log dropped onto the ground.

That's the idea, Sol said. You'll do, he said. He picked up the two blocks of wood and carried them over and put them alongside the garage.

Every so often—not every piece of wood, but maybe every fifth or sixth piece—you'll want to split it with the ax down the middle. Don't worry about making kindling. I'll take care of that later. Just split about every fifth or sixth chunk you have.

I'll show you. And he propped the chunk up and, with a blow of the ax, split the wood into two pieces. You try it now, he said.

Myers stood the block on its end, just as Sol had done, and he brought the ax down and split the wood.

That's good, Sol said. He put the chunks of wood by the garage. Stack them up about so high, and then come out this way with your stack. I'll lay some plastic sheeting over it once it's all finished. But you don't have to do this, you know.

It's all right, Myers said. I want to, or I wouldn't have asked.

Sol shrugged. Then he turned and went back to the house. Bonnie was standing in the doorway, watching, and Sol stopped and reached his arm around Bonnie, and they both looked at Myers.

Myers picked up the saw and looked at them. He felt good suddenly, and he grinned. Sol and Bonnie were taken by surprise at first. Sol grinned back, and then Bonnie. Then they went back inside.

Myers put another piece of wood on the sawhorses and worked awhile, sawing, until the sweat on his forehead began to feel chill and the sun had gone down. The porch light came on. Myers kept on working until he'd finished the piece he was on. He carried the two pieces over to the garage and then he went in, used his bathroom to wash up, then sat at the table in his room and wrote in his notebook. *I have sawdust in my shirtsleeves tonight*, he wrote. *It's a sweet smell.*

That night he lay awake for a long time. Once he got out of bed and looked out the window at the mound of wood which lay in the backyard, and then his eyes were drawn up the valley to the mountains. The moon was partially obscured by clouds, but he could see the peaks and the white snow, and when he raised his window the sweet, cool air poured in, and farther off he could hear the river coursing down the valley.

The next morning it was all he could do to wait until they'd left the house before he went out back to begin work. He found a pair of gloves on the back step that Sol must have left for him. He sawed and split wood until the sun stood directly over his head and then he went inside and ate a sandwich and drank some milk. Then he went back outside and began again. His shoulders hurt and his fingers were sore and, in spite of the gloves, he'd picked up a few splinters and could feel blisters rising, but he kept on. He decided that he would cut this wood and split it and stack it before sunset, and that it was a matter of life and death that he do so. I must finish this job, he thought, or else . . . He stopped to wipe his sleeve over his face.

By the time Sol and Bonnie came in from work that night—first Bonnie, as usual, and then Sol—Myers was nearly through. A thick pile of sawdust lay between the sawhorses, and, except for two or three blocks still in the yard, all of the wood lay stacked in tiers against the garage. Sol and Bonnie stood in the doorway without saying anything. Myers looked up from his work for a minute and nodded, and Sol nodded back. Bonnie just stood there looking, breathing through her mouth. Myers kept on.

Sol and Bonnie went back inside and began on their supper. Afterward, Sol turned on the porch light, as he'd done the evening before. Just as the sun went down and the moon appeared over the mountains, Myers split the last chunk and gathered up the two pieces and carried the wood over to the garage. He put away the sawhorses, the saw, the ax, a wedge, and the maul. Then he went inside.

Sol and Bonnie sat at the table, but they hadn't begun on their food.

You better sit down and eat with us, Sol said.

Sit down, Bonnie said.

Not hungry just yet, Myers said.

Sol didn't say anything. He nodded. Bonnie waited a minute and then reached for a platter.

You got it all, I'll bet, Sol said.

Myers said, I'll clean up that sawdust tomorrow.

Sol moved his knife back and forth over his plate as if to say, Forget it.

I'll be leaving in a day or two, Myers said.

Somehow I figured you would be, Sol said. I don't know why I felt that, but I didn't think somehow when you moved in you'd be here all that long.

No refunds on the rent, Bonnie said.

Hey, Bonnie, Sol said.

It's okay, Myers said.

No it isn't, Sol said.

It's all right, Myers said. He opened the door to the bathroom, stepped inside, and shut the door. As he ran water into the sink he could hear them talking out there, but he couldn't hear what they were saying.

He showered, washed his hair, and put on clean clothes. He looked at the things of his in the room that had come out of his suitcase just a few days ago, a week ago, and figured it would take him about ten minutes to pack up and be gone. He could hear the TV start up on the other side of the house. He went to the window and raised it and looked again at the mountains, with the moon lying over them—no clouds now, just the moon, and the snowcapped mountains. He looked at the pile of sawdust out in back and at the wood stacked against the shadowy recesses of the garage. He listened to the river for a while. Then he went over to the table and sat down and opened the notebook and began to write.

The country I'm in is very exotic. It reminds me of someplace I've read about but never traveled to before now. Outside my window I can hear a river and in the valley behind the house there is a forest and precipices and mountain peaks covered with snow. Today I saw a wild eagle, and a deer, and I cut and chopped two cords of wood.

Then he put the pen down and held his head in his hands for a moment. Pretty soon he got up and undressed and turned off the light. He left the window open when he got into bed. It was okay like that.

What Would You Like to See?

WE were to have dinner with Pete Petersen and his wife, Betty, the night before our departure. Pete owned a restaurant that overlooked the highway and the Pacific Ocean. Early in the summer we had rented a furnished house from him that sat a hundred yards or so back behind the restaurant, just at the edge of the parking lot. Some nights when the wind was coming in off the ocean, we could open the front door and smell the steaks being charbroiled in the restaurant's kitchen and see the gray flume of smoke rising from the heavy brick chimney. And always, day and night, we lived with the hum of the big freezer fans in back of the restaurant, a sound we grew used to.

Pete's daughter, Leslie, a thin blond woman who'd never acted very friendly, lived in a smaller house nearby that also belonged to Pete. She managed his business affairs and had already been over to take a quick inventory of everything—we had rented the house furnished, right down to bed linen and an electric can opener—and had given us our deposit check back and wished us luck. She was friendly that morning she came through the house with her clipboard and inventory list, and we exchanged pleasantries. She didn't take much time with the inventory, and she already had our deposit check made out.

"Dad's going to miss you," she said. "It's funny. He's tough as shoe leather, you know, but he's going to miss you. He's said so. He hates to see you go. Betty too." Betty was her stepmother and looked after Leslie's children when Leslie dated or went off to San Francisco for a few days with her boyfriend. Pete and Betty, Leslie and her kids, Sarah and I, we all lived behind the restaurant within sight of one another, and I'd see Leslie's kids going back and forth from their little place to Pete and Betty's. Sometimes the kids would come over to our house and ring the doorbell and stand on the step and wait. Sarah would invite them in for cookies or pound cake and let them sit at the kitchen table like grownups and ask about their day and take an interest in their answers.

Our own children had left home before we moved to this

northern coastal region of California. Our daughter, Cindy, was living with several other young people in a house on several rocky acres of ground outside of Ukiah, in Mendocino County. They kept bees and raised goats and chickens and sold eggs and goat's milk and jars of honey. The women worked on patchwork quilts and blankets too, and sold those when they could. But I don't want to call it a commune. I'd have a harder time dealing with it, from what I've heard about communes, if I called it a commune, where every woman was every man's property, things like that. Say she lived with friends on a little farm where everyone shared the labor. But, so far as we knew anyway, they were not involved in organized religion or any sort of sect. We had not heard from her for nearly three months, except for a jar of honey arriving in the mail one day, and a patch of heavy red cloth, part of a quilt she was working on. There was a note wrapped around the jar of honey, which said:

> Dear Mom and Dad
> I sewed this myself and I put this Honey up myself. I am learning to do things here.
>
> > Love,
> > Cindy

But two of Sarah's letters went unanswered and then that fall the Jonestown thing happened and we were wild for a day or two that she could be there, for all we knew, in British Guiana. We only had a post-office box number in Ukiah for her. I called the sheriff's office down there and explained the situation, and he drove out to the place to take a head count and carry a message from us. She called that night and first Sarah talked to her and wept, and then I talked to her and wept with relief. Cindy wept too. Some of her friends were down there in Jonestown. She said it was raining, and she was depressed, but the depression would pass, she said; she was where she wanted to be, and doing what she wanted to do. She'd write us a long letter and send us a picture soon.

So when Leslie's children came to visit, Sarah always took a large and real interest in them and sat them down at the table and made them cocoa and served them cookies or pound cake and took a genuine interest in their stories.

But we were moving, we had decided to separate. I was going to Vermont to teach for a semester in a small college and Sarah was going to take an apartment in Eureka, a nearby town. At the end of four and a half months, at the end of the college semester, then we'd take a look at things and see. There was no one else involved for either of us, thank God, and we had neither of us had anything to drink now for nearly a year, almost the amount of time we had been living in Pete's house together, and somehow there was just enough money to get me back east and to get Sarah set up in her apartment. She was already doing research and secretarial work for the history department at the college in Eureka, and if she kept the same job even, and the car, and had only herself to support, she could get by all right. We'd live apart for the semester, me on the East Coast, she on the West, and then we'd take stock, see what was what.

While we were cleaning the house, me washing the windows and Sarah down on her hands and knees cleaning woodwork, the baseboards and corners with a pan of soapy water and an old T-shirt, Betty knocked on the door. It was a point of honor for us to clean this house and clean it well before we left. We had even taken a wire brush and scoured the bricks around the fireplace. We'd left too many houses in a hurry in the past and left them damaged or in a shambles somehow, or else left owing rent and maybe having to move our things in the middle of the night. This time it was a point of honor to leave this house clean, to leave it immaculate, to leave it in better condition even than we had found it, and after we'd set the date we were going to leave, we had set to work with a passion to erase any signs of ourselves in that house. So when Betty came to the door and knocked, we were hard at work in different rooms of the house and didn't hear her at first. Then she knocked again, a little louder, and I put down my cleaning materials and came out of the bedroom.

"I hope I'm not disturbing you," she said, the color high in her cheeks. She was a little, compact woman with blue slacks and a pink blouse that hung out over her slacks. Her hair was short and brown and she was somewhere in her late forties, younger than Pete. She had been waitressing at Pete's restaurant and was friends with Pete and his first wife, Evelyn, Leslie's mother. Then, we had been told, Evelyn, who was only fifty-four, was returning home from a shopping trip into Eureka. Just as she pulled off the highway into the parking lot behind the restaurant and headed across the lot for her own driveway, her heart stopped. The car kept going, slowly enough, but with enough momentum to knock down the little wood rail fence, cross her flower bed of azaleas, and come to a stop against the porch with Evelyn slumped behind the wheel, dead. A few months later, Pete and Betty had married, and Betty had quit waitressing and become stepmother to Leslie and grandmother to Leslie's children. Betty had been married before and had grown children living in Oregon who drove down now and then to visit. Betty and Pete had been married for five years, and from what we could observe they were happy and well suited to each other.

"Come in, please, Betty," I said. "We're just cleaning up some around here." I moved aside and held the door.

"I can't," she said. "I have the children I'm looking after to-day. I have to get right back. But Pete and I were wondering if you could come to dinner before you leave." She spoke in a quiet, shy manner and held a cigarette in her fingers. "Friday night?" she said. "If you can."

Sarah brushed her hair and came to the door. "Betty, come in out of the cold," she said. The sky was gray and the wind was pushing clouds in off the sea.

"No, no, thank you, I can't. I left the children coloring, I have to get back. Pete and I, we just wondered if you two could come to dinner. Maybe Friday night, the night before you leave?" She waited and looked shy. Her hair lifted in the wind and she drew on her cigarette.

"I'd like that very much," Sarah said. "Is that all right with you, Phil? We don't have any plans, I don't think. Is it all right?"

"That's very nice of you, Betty," I said. "We'd be happy to come to dinner."

"About 7:30?" Betty said.

"Seven thirty," Sarah said. "This pleases us very much, Betty. More than I can say. It's very kind and thoughtful of you and Pete."

Betty shook her head and was embarrassed. "Pete said he's

sorry you're leaving. He said it's been like having more family here. He said it's been an honor having you here as renters." She started backing down the steps. The color was still high in her cheeks. "Friday night, then," she said.

"Thank you, Betty, I mean that," Sarah said. "Thank you again. It means a lot to us."

Betty waved her hand and shook her head. Then she said, "Until Friday, then," and the way in which she said it somehow made my throat tighten. I shut the door after she'd turned away, and Sarah and I looked at each other.

"Well," Sarah said, "this is a switch, isn't it? Getting invited to dinner by our landlord instead of having to skip town and hide out somewhere."

"I like Pete," I said. "He's a good man."

"Betty too," Sarah said. "She's a good kind woman and I'm glad she and Pete have each other."

"Things come around sometimes," I said. "Things work out."

Sarah didn't say anything. She bit her lower lip for a minute. Then she went on into the back room to finish scrubbing. I sat down on the sofa and smoked a cigarette. When I'd finished, I got up and went back to the other room and my mop bucket.

The next day, Friday, we finished cleaning the house and did most of our packing. Sarah wiped down the stove once more, put aluminum foil under the burners, and gave the counter a last going over. Our suitcases and few boxes of books stood in one corner of the living room, ready for our departure. We'd have dinner tonight with the Petersens and we'd get up the next morning and go out for coffee and breakfast. Then we'd come back and load the car; there wasn't all that much left after twenty years of moves and disorder. We'd drive to Eureka and unload the car and put things away in Sarah's efficiency apartment, which she'd rented a few days before, and then sometime before eight o'clock that night she'd drive me to the little airport where I would begin my trip east, planning to make connections with a midnight flight leaving San Francisco for Boston, and she would begin her new life in Eureka. She'd already, a month before, when we began discussing these matters, taken off her wedding ring—not so much in anger as just in sadness one night when we had been making these plans. She had worn no ring at all for a few days, and then she had bought an inexpensive little ring mounted with a turquoise butterfly because, as she said, that finger "felt naked." Once, some years before that, in a rage, she had twisted the wedding band off her finger and thrown it across the living room. I had been drunk and left the house and when we talked about that night a few days later and I asked about her wedding ring, she said, "I still have it. I just put it in a drawer. You don't really think I'd throw my wedding ring away, do you?" A little later she put it back on and she'd kept wearing it, even through the bad times, up until a month ago. She'd also stopped taking birth-control pills and had herself fitted with a diaphragm.

So we worked that day around the house and finished the packing and the cleaning and then, a little after six o'clock, we took our showers and wiped down the shower stall again and dressed and sat in the living room, she on the sofa in a knit dress and blue scarf, her legs drawn up under her, and me in the big chair by the window. I could see the back of Pete's restaurant from where I sat, and the ocean a few miles beyond the restaurant and the meadows and the copses of trees that lay between the front window and the houses. We sat without talking. We had talked and talked and talked. Now we sat without talking and watched it turn dark outside and the smoke feather up from the restaurant chimney.

"Well," Sarah said and straightened out her legs on the sofa. She pulled her skirt down a little. She lit a cigarette. "What time is it? Maybe we should go. They said 7:30, didn't they? What time is it?"

"It's ten after seven," I said.

"Ten after seven," she said. "This is the last time we'll be able to sit in the living room like this and watch it get dark. I don't want to forget this. I'm glad we have a few minutes."

In a little while I got up for my coat. On my way to the bedroom I stopped at the end of the sofa where she sat and bent and kissed her on the forehead. She raised her eyes to mine after the kiss and looked at me.

"Bring my coat too," she said.

I helped her into her coat and then we left the house and went across the lawn and the back edge of the parking lot to Pete's house. Sarah kept her hands in her pockets and I smoked a cigarette as we walked. Just before we got to the gate at the little fence surrounding Pete's house, I threw down my cigarette and took Sarah's arm.

The house was new and had been planted with a tough climbing vine that had spread over the fence. A little wooden lumberjack was nailed to the banister that ran around the porch. When the wind blew, the little man began sawing his log. He was not sawing at this moment, but I could feel the dampness in the air and I knew the wind would come soon. Potted plants were on the porch and flower beds on either side of the sidewalk, but whether they had been planted by Betty or the first wife, there was no way of telling. Some children's toys and a tricycle were on the porch. The porch light was burning, and just as we started up the steps Pete opened the door and greeted us.

"Come in, come in," he said, holding the screen door with one hand. He took Sarah's hands in his hands and then he shook hands with me. He was a tall thin man, sixty years old or so, with a full head of neatly combed gray hair. His shoulders gave the impression of bulk, but he was not heavy. He was wearing a gray Pendleton shirt, dark slacks, and white shoes. Betty came to the door as well, nodding and smiling. She took our coats while Pete asked us what we'd like to drink.

"What can I get you?" he said. "Name it. If I don't have it we'll send over to the restaurant for it." Pete was a recovering alcoholic but kept wine and liquor around the house for guests. He'd once told me that when he'd bought his first restaurant and was cooking sixteen hours a day he drank two fifths of whiskey during those sixteen hours and was hard on his help. Now he'd quit drinking, had been hospitalized for it, we'd heard, and hadn't had a drink in six years, but like many alcoholics, he still kept it around the house.

Sarah said she'd have a glass of white wine. I looked at her. I asked for a Coke. Pete winked at me and said, "You want a little something in the Coke? Something to help take the dampness out of your bones?"

"No thanks, Pete, but maybe you could toss a piece of lime in it, thanks," I said.

"Good fellow," he said. "For me it's the only way to fly anymore."

I saw Betty turn a dial on the microwave oven and push a button. Pete said, "Betty, will you have some wine with Sarah, or what would you like, honey?"

"I'll have a little wine, Pete," Betty said.

"Phil, here's your Coke," Pete said. "Sarah," he said, and gave her a glass of wine. "Betty. Now, there's lots more of everything. Let's go in where it's comfortable."

We passed through the dining room. The table was already set with four place settings, fine china, and crystal wineglasses. We went through to the living room and Sarah and I sat together on one of the sofas. Pete and Betty sat across the room on another sofa. There were bowls of cocktail nuts within reach on a coffee table, cauliflower heads, celery sticks, and a bowl of vegetable dip beside the peanuts.

"We're so glad you could come," Betty said. "We've been looking forward to this all week."

"We're going to miss you," Pete said, "and that's a fact. I hate to see you go, but I know that's life, people have to do what they have to do. I don't know how to say this, but it's been an honor having you over there in the house, you both being teachers and all. I have a great respect for education, though I don't have much myself. It's like a big family here, you know that, and we've come to look on you as part of that family. Here, here's to your health. To you," he said, "and to the future."

We raised our glasses and then we drank.

"We're so glad you feel that way," Sarah said. "This is very important to us, this dinner; we've been looking forward to it more than I can tell you. It means a great deal to us."

Pete said, "We're going to miss you, that's all." He shook his head.

"It's been very, very good for us living here," Sarah said. "We can't tell you."

"There was something about this fellow I liked when I first saw him," Pete said to Sarah. "I'm glad I rented the house to him. You can tell a lot from a man when you first meet him. I liked this fellow of yours. You take care of him, now."

Sarah reached for a celery stick. A little bell went off in the kitchen and Betty said, "Excuse me," and left the room.

"Let me freshen those up for you," Pete said. He left the

room with our glasses and returned in a minute with more wine for Sarah and a full glass of Coke for me.

Betty began carrying in things from the kitchen to put on the dining room table. "I hope you like surf and turf," Pete said. "Sirloin steak and lobster tail."

"It sounds fine, it's a dream dinner," Sarah said.

"I guess we can eat now," Betty said. "If you'd like to come to the table. Pete sits here always," Betty said. "This is Pete's place. Phil, you sit there. Sarah, you sit there across from me."

"Man who sits at the head of the table picks up the check," Pete said and laughed.

It was a fine dinner: green salad dotted with tiny fresh shrimp, clam chowder, lobster tail, and steak. Sarah and Betty drank wine, Pete drank mineral water, I stayed with the Coke. We talked a little about Jonestown after Pete brought it up, but I could see that conversation made Sarah nervous. Her lips paled, and I managed to steer us around to salmon fishing.

"I'm sorry we didn't have a chance to go out," Pete said. "But the sports fishermen aren't doing anything yet. It's only the fellows with the commercial licenses that are getting them, and they're going way out. In another week or two maybe the salmon will have moved in. Anytime now, really," Pete said. "But you'll be on the other side of the country then."

I nodded. Sarah picked up her wineglass.

"I bought a hundred and fifty pounds of fresh salmon from a guy yesterday, and that's what I'm featuring on the menu over there now. Fresh salmon," Pete said. "I put it right in the freezer and fresh-froze it. Fellow drove up with it in his pickup truck, an Indian, and I asked him what he was asking for it and he said $3.50 a pound. I said $3.25, and he said we had a deal. So I fresh-froze it and I have it over there on the menu right now."

"Well, this was fine," I said. "I like salmon, but it couldn't have been any better than what we had here tonight. This was delicious."

"We're so glad you could come," Betty said.

"This is wonderful," Sarah said, "but I don't think I've ever seen so much lobster tail and steak. I don't think I can eat all of mine."

"Whatever's left we'll put in a doggy bag for you," Betty

said and blushed. "Just like at the restaurant. But save room for dessert."

"Let's have coffee in the living room," Pete said.

"Pete has some slides we took when we were on our trip," Betty said. "If you'd care to see them, we thought we might put up the screen after dinner."

"There's brandy for those who want it," Pete said. "Betty'll have some, I know. Sarah? You'll have some. That's a good girl. It doesn't bother me a bit to have it around and have my guests drink it. Drinking's a funny thing," Pete said.

We had moved back into the living room. Pete was putting up a screen and talking. "I always keep a supply of everything on hand, as you noticed out there, but I haven't touched a drink of anything alcoholic myself for six years. Now this was after drinking more than a quart a day for ten years after I retired from the service. But I quit, God knows how, but I quit, I just quit. I turned myself over to my doctor and just said, Help me, doc. I want to get off this stuff, doc. Can you help me? Well, he made a couple of calls. Said he knew some fellows used to have trouble with it, said there'd been a time when he'd had trouble with it too. The next thing I knew I was on my way to an establishment down there near Santa Rosa. It was in Calistoga, California. I spent three weeks there. When I came home I was sober and the desire to drink had left me. Evelyn, that's my first wife, she met me at the door when I came home and kissed me on the lips for the first time in years. She hated alcohol. Her father and a brother both died from it. It can kill you too, don't forget it. Well, she kissed me on the lips for the first time that night, and I haven't had a drink since I went into that place at Calistoga."

Betty and Sarah were clearing the table. I sat on the sofa and smoked while Pete talked. After he'd put up the screen he took a slide projector out of a box and set it on an end table. He plugged in the cord and flicked a switch on the projector. Light beamed onto the screen and a little fan in the projector began to run.

"We have enough slides that we could look at pictures all night and then some," Pete said. "We have slides here from Mexico, Hawaii, Alaska, the Middle East, Africa too. What would you like to see?"

Sarah came in and sat down on the other end of the sofa from me.

"What would you like to see, Sarah?" Pete said. "You name it."

"Alaska," Sarah said. "And the Middle East. We were there for a while, years ago, in Israel. I've always wanted to go to Alaska."

"We didn't get to Israel," Betty said, coming in with the coffee. "We were on a tour that went only to Syria, Egypt, and Lebanon."

"It's a tragedy, what's happened in Lebanon," Pete said. "It used to be the most beautiful country in the Middle East. I was there as a kid in the merchant marines in World War II. I thought then, I promised myself then, I'd go back there someday. And then we had the opportunity, Betty and me. Didn't we, Betty?"

Betty smiled and nodded.

"Let's see those pictures of Syria and Lebanon," Sarah said. "Those are the ones I'd like to see. I'd like to see them all, of course, but if we have to choose."

So Pete began to show slides, both he and Betty commenting as the memory of the places came back to them.

"There's Betty trying to get on a camel," Pete said. "She needed a little help from that fellow there in the burnoose."

Betty laughed and her cheeks turned red. Another slide flashed on the screen and Betty said, "There's Pete talking with an Egyptian officer."

"Where he's pointing, that mountain behind us there. Here, let me see if I can bring that in closer," Pete said. "The Jews are dug in there. We could see them through the binoculars they let us use. Jews all over that hill. Like ants," Pete said.

"Pete believes that if they had kept their planes out of Lebanon, there wouldn't be all that trouble there," Betty said. "The poor Lebanese."

"There," Pete said. "There's the group at Petra, the lost city. It used to be a caravan city, but then it was just lost, lost and covered over by sand for hundreds of years, and then it was discovered again and we drove there from Damascus in Land Rovers. Look how pink the stone is. Those carvings in the stone are more than two thousand years old, they say. There used to be twenty thousand souls who lived there. And then the desert just covered it up and it was forgotten about. It's what's going to happen to this country if we aren't careful."

We had more coffee and watched some more slides of Pete and Betty at the souks in Damascus. Then Pete turned off the projector and Betty went out to the kitchen and returned with carameled pears for dessert and more coffee. We ate and drank and Pete said again how they would miss us.

"You're good people," Pete said. "I hate to see you leave, but I know it's in your best interests or you wouldn't be going. Now, you'd like to see some slides from Alaska. Is that what you said, Sarah?"

"Alaska, yes," Sarah said. "We'd talked once about going to Alaska, years ago. Didn't we, Phil? Once we were all set to go to Alaska. But we didn't go at the last minute. Do you remember that, Phil?"

I nodded.

"Now you'll go to Alaska," Pete said.

The first slide showed a tall, trim red-haired woman standing on the deck of a ship with a snow-covered range of mountains in the distance behind her. She was wearing a white fur coat and facing the camera with a smile on her face.

"That's Evelyn, Pete's first wife," Betty said. "She's dead now."

Pete threw another slide onto the screen. The same red-haired woman was wearing the same coat and shaking hands with a smiling Eskimo in a parka. Large dried fish were hanging on poles behind the two figures. There was an expanse of water and more mountains.

"That's Evelyn again," Pete said. "These were taken in Point Barrow, Alaska, the northernmost settlement in the U.S."

Then there was a shot of the main street—little low buildings with slanted metal roofs, signs saying King Salmon Café, Cards, Liquor, Rooms. One slide showed a Colonel Sanders fried-chicken parlor with a billboard outside showing Colonel Sanders in a parka and fur boots. We all laughed.

"That's Evelyn again," Betty said, as another slide flashed on the screen.

"These were made before Evelyn died," Pete said. "We'd always talked about going to Alaska, too," Pete said. "I'm glad we made that trip before she died."

"Good timing," Sarah said.

"Evelyn was a good friend to me," Betty said. "It was a lot like losing my sister."

We saw Evelyn boarding a plane back for Seattle, and we saw Pete, smiling and waving, emerging from that same plane after it had landed in Seattle.

"It's heating up," Pete said. "I'll have to turn off the projector for a little while to let it cool off. What would you like to see then? Hawaii? Sarah, it's your night; you say."

Sarah looked at me.

"I guess we should think about going home, Pete," I said. "It's going to be a long day tomorrow."

"Yes, we should go," Sarah said. "We really should, I guess." But she continued to sit there with her glass in her hand. She looked at Betty and then she looked at Pete. "It's been a very wonderful evening for us," she said. "I really have a hard time thanking you enough. This has meant a good deal to us."

"No, it's us who should be thanking you," Pete said, "and that's the truth. It's been a pleasure knowing you. I hope that the next time you're in this part of the country you'll stop by here and say hello."

"You won't forget us?" Betty said. "You won't, will you?" Sarah shook her head. Then we were on our feet and Pete was getting our coats. Betty said, "Oh, don't forget your doggy bag. This will make you a nice snack tomorrow."

Pete helped Sarah with her coat and then held my coat for me to slip my arm into.

We all shook hands on the front porch. "The wind's coming up," Pete said. "Don't forget us, now," Pete said. "And good luck."

"We won't," I said. "Thank you again, thanks for everything." We shook hands once more. Pete took Sarah by the shoulders and kissed her on the cheek. "You take good care of yourselves, now. This fellow too. Take good care of him," he said. "You're both good people. We like you."

"Thank you, Pete," Sarah said. "Thank you for saying that."

"I'm saying it because it's true, or else I wouldn't be saying it," Pete said.

Betty and Sarah embraced.

"Well, good night to you," Betty said. "And God bless you both."

We walked down the sidewalk past the flowers. I held the gate for Sarah and we walked across the gravel parking lot to our house. The restaurant was dark. It was after midnight. Wind blew through the trees. The parking lot lights burned, and the generator in back of the restaurant hummed and turned the freezer fan inside the locker.

I unlocked the door to the house. Sarah snapped on the light and went into the bathroom. I turned on the lamp beside the chair in front of the window and sat down with a cigarette. After a little while Sarah came out, still in her coat, and sat on the sofa and touched her forehead.

"It was a nice evening," she said. "I won't forget it. So different from so many of our other departures," she said. "Imagine, to actually have dinner with your landlord before you move." She shook her head. "We've come a long way, I guess, if you look at it that way. But there's a long way to go yet. Well, this is the last night we'll spend in this house, and I'm so tired from that big dinner I can hardly keep my eyes open. I think I'll go in and go to bed."

"I'm going too," I said. "Just as soon as I finish this."

We lay in bed without touching. Then Sarah turned on her side and said, "I'd like you to hold me until I get off to sleep. That's all, just hold me. I miss Cindy tonight. I hope she's all right. I pray she's all right. God help her to find her way. And God help us," she said.

After a while her breathing became slow and regular and I turned away from her again. I lay on my back and stared at the dark ceiling. I lay there and listened to the wind. Then, just as I started to close my eyes again, I heard something. Or, rather, something that I had been hearing I didn't hear anymore. The wind still blew, and I could hear it under the eaves of the house and singing in the wires outside the house, but something was not there any longer, and I didn't know what it was. I lay there a while longer and listened, and then I got up and went out to the living room and looked out the front window at the restaurant, the edge of moon showing through the fast-moving clouds.

I stood at the window and tried to figure out what was

wrong. I kept looking at the glint of ocean and then back to the darkened restaurant. Then it came to me, what the odd silence was. The generator had gone off over at the restaurant. I stood there a while longer wondering what I should do, if I should call Pete. Maybe it would take care of itself in a little while and switch back on, but for some reason I knew this wouldn't happen.

He must have noticed it too, for suddenly I saw a light go on over at Pete's, and then a figure appeared on the steps with a flashlight. The figure carrying the flashlight went to the back of the restaurant and unlocked the door, and then lights began to go on in the restaurant. After a little while, after I had smoked a cigarette, I went back to bed. I went to sleep immediately.

The next morning we had instant coffee, and washed the cups and packed them when we were finished. We didn't talk much. There was an appliance truck behind the restaurant, and I could see Betty and Leslie coming and going from the back door of the restaurant, carrying things in their arms. I didn't see Pete.

We loaded the car. We would be able to carry everything into Eureka in one load, after all. I walked over to the restaurant to drop off the keys, but just as I got to the office door, it opened and Pete came out carrying a box.

"It's going to rot," he said. "The salmon thawed out. It was just starting to freeze, then it began to thaw. I'm going to lose all this salmon. I'm going to have to give it away, get rid of it this morning. The fillets and prawns and scallops, too. Everything. The generator burned out, goddamn it."

"I'm sorry, Pete," I said. "We have to go now. I wanted to give you back the keys."

"What is it?" he said and looked at me.

"The house keys," I said. "We're leaving now. We're on our way."

"Give them to Leslie in there," he said. "Leslie takes care of the rentals. Give her your keys."

"I will, then. Good-bye, Pete. I'm sorry about this. But thanks again for everything."

"Sure," he said. "Sure, don't mention it. Good luck to you. Take it easy." He nodded and went on over to his house with his box of fillets. I gave the keys to Leslie, said good-bye to her, and walked back to the car where Sarah was waiting.

"What's wrong?" Sarah said. "What's happened? It looked like Pete didn't have the time of day for you."

"The generator burned out last night at the restaurant and the freezer shut down and some of their meat spoiled."

"Is that it?" she said. "That's too bad. I'm sorry to hear it. You gave them the keys, didn't you? We've said good-bye. I guess we can go now."

"Yes," I said. "I guess we can."

Dreams

M Y wife is in the habit of telling me her dreams when she wakes up. I take her some coffee and juice and sit in a chair beside the bed while she wakes up and moves her hair away from her face. She has the look that people waking up have, but she also has this look in her eyes of returning from somewhere.

"Well?" I say.

"It's crazy," she says. "This was a dream and a half. I dreamed I was a boy going fishing with my sister and her girl-friend, but I was drunk. Imagine that. Doesn't that beat everything? I was supposed to drive them fishing, but I couldn't find the car keys. Then, when I found the keys, the car wouldn't start. Suddenly, we were at the fishing place and on the lake in a boat. A storm was coming up, but I couldn't get the motor started. My sister and her friend just laughed and laughed. But I was afraid. Then I woke up. Isn't that strange? What do you make of it?"

"Write it down," I said and shrugged. I didn't have anything to say. I didn't dream. I hadn't dreamed in years. Or maybe I did but couldn't remember anything when I woke up. One thing I'm not is an expert on dreams—my own or anybody else's. Once Dotty told me she'd had a dream right before we got married when she thought she was barking! She woke herself up and saw her little dog, Bingo, sitting beside the bed looking at her in what she thought was a strange way. She realized she'd been barking in her sleep. What did it mean? she wondered. "That was a bad dream," she said. She'd added the dream to her dream book, but that was that. She didn't get back to it. She didn't interpret her dreams. She just wrote them down and then, when she had the next one, she wrote that one down too.

I said, "I'd better go upstairs. I need to use the bathroom."

"I'll be along pretty soon. I have to wake up first. I want to think about this dream some more."

I left her sitting up in bed, holding her cup, but not drinking from it. She was sitting there thinking about her dream.

I didn't have to go to the bathroom after all, so I took some coffee and sat at the kitchen table. It was August, a heat wave, and the windows were open. Hot, yes, it was hot. The heat was killing. My wife and I slept in the basement for most of the month. But it was okay. We carried the mattress down there, pillows, sheets, everything. We had an end table, a lamp, an ashtray. We laughed. It was like starting over. But all the windows upstairs were open, and the windows next door, they were open too. I sat at the table listening to Mary Rice next door. It was early, but she was up and in her kitchen in her nightgown. She was humming, and she kept it up while I listened and drank coffee. Then her children came into their kitchen. This is what she said to them:

"Good morning, children. Good morning, my loved ones."

It's true. That's what their mother said to them. Then they were at the table, laughing about something, and one of the kids was banging his chair up and down, laughing.

"Michael, that's enough," Mary Rice said. "Finish your cereal, honey."

In a minute, Mary Rice sent her kids out of the room to get themselves dressed for school. She began to hum as she cleaned a dish. I listened and, listening, I thought, I am a rich man. I have a wife who dreams something every night, who lies there beside me until she falls asleep and then she goes far away into some rich dream every night. Sometimes she dreams of horses and weather and people, and sometimes she even changes her sex in her dreams. I didn't miss dreaming. I had her dreams to think about if I wanted to have a dream life. And I have a woman next door who sings or else hums all day long. All in all, I felt quite lucky.

I moved to the front window to watch the kids next door when they went out of their house to go to school. I saw Mary Rice kiss each of the children on the face, and I heard her say, "Good-bye, children." Then she latched the screen, stood for a minute watching her children walk down the street, then turned and went back inside.

I knew her habits. She'd sleep in a few hours now—she didn't sleep when she came in from her job at night, a little after five in the morning. The girl who baby-sat for her— Rosemary Bandel, a neighbor girl—would be waiting for her and would leave and go across the street to her own house. And then the lights would glow over at Mary Rice's for the rest of the night. Sometimes, if her windows were open, like now, I'd hear classical piano music, and once I even heard Alexander Scourby reading *Great Expectations.*

Sometimes, if I couldn't sleep—my wife sleeping and dreaming away beside me—I'd get up out of bed and go up-stairs and sit at the table and listen to her music, or her talking records, and wait for her to pass behind a curtain or until I saw her standing behind the window shade. Once in a while the phone rang over there at some early and unlikely hour, but she always picked it up on the third ring.

The names of her children, I found out, were Michael and Susan. To my eye they were no different from any of the other neighborhood kids, except when I'd see them I'd think, you kids are lucky to have a mother who sings to you. You don't need your father. Once they came to our door selling bath soap, and another time they came around selling seeds. We didn't have a garden, of course not—how could anything grow where we lived—but I bought some seeds anyway, what the hell. And on Halloween they came to the door, always with their baby-sitter—their mother was working, of course—and I gave them candy bars and nodded to Rosemary Bandel.

My wife and I have lived in this neighborhood longer than anyone. We've seen almost everyone come and go. Mary Rice and her husband and children moved in three years ago. Her husband worked for the telephone company as a lineman, and for a time he left every morning at seven o'clock and returned home in the evening at five. Then he stopped coming home at five. He came home later, or not at all.

My wife noticed it too. "I haven't seen him home over there in three days," she said.

"I haven't either," I said. I'd heard loud voices over there the other morning, and one or both of the children were crying.

Then at the market, my wife was told by the woman who lived on the other side of Mary Rice that Mary and her husband had separated. "He's moved out on her and the children," was what this woman said. "The son of a bitch."

And then, not very long after, needing to support herself because her husband had quit his job and left town, Mary Rice had gone to work in this restaurant serving cocktails and, pretty soon, began staying up all night listening to music and talking records. And singing sometimes and humming other times. This same woman who lived next door to Mary Rice said she had enrolled in two correspondence courses from the university. She was making a new life for herself, this woman said, and the new life included her children too.

Winter was not so far away when I decided to put up the storm windows. When I was outside, using my ladder, those kids from next door, Michael and Susan, came charging out of the house with their dog and let the screen door bang shut behind them. They ran down the sidewalk in their coats, kicking piles of leaves.

Mary Rice came to the door and looked after them. Then she looked over at me.

"Hello there," she said. "You're getting ready for winter, I see."

"Yes, I am," I said. "It won't be long."

"No, it won't," she said. Then she waited a minute, as if she was going to say something else. Then she said, "It was nice talking to you."

"My pleasure," I answered.

That was just before Thanksgiving. About a week later, when I went into the bedroom with my wife's coffee and juice, she was already awake and sitting up and ready to tell me her dream. She patted the bed beside her, and I sat down.

"This is one for the book," she said. "Listen to this if you want to hear something."

"Go on," I said. I took a sip from her cup and handed it to her. She closed both hands around it as if her hands were cold.

"We were on a ship," she said.

"We've never been on a ship," I said.

"I know that, but we were on a ship, a big ship, a cruise ship, I guess. We were in bed, a bunk or something, when somebody knocked at the door with a tray of cupcakes. They came in, left the cupcakes and went out. I got out of bed and went to get one of the cupcakes. I was hungry, you see, but when I touched the cupcake it burned the tips of my fingers. Then my toes began to curl up—like they do when you're scared? And then I got back in bed but I heard loud music—it was Scriabin —and then somebody began to rattle glasses, hundreds of glasses, maybe thousands of glasses, all of them rattling at once. I woke you up and told you about it, and you said you'd go to see what it was. While you were gone I remember seeing the moon go by outside, go by the porthole, and then the ship must have turned or something. Then the moon came by again and lit up the whole room. Then you came back, still in your pajamas, and got back in bed and went back to sleep without saying a word. The moon was shining right outside the window and everything in the room seemed to gleam, but still you didn't say anything. I remember feeling a little afraid of you for not saying anything, and my toes started curling again. Then I went back to sleep—and here I am. What do you think of that? Isn't that some dream? God. What do you make of it? You didn't dream anything, did you?" She sipped from her coffee and watched me.

I shook my head. I didn't know what to say, so all I said was that she had better put it in her notebook.

"God, I don't know. They're getting pretty weird. What do you think?"

"Put it in your book."

Pretty soon it was Christmas. We bought a tree and put it up and on Christmas morning we exchanged gifts. Dotty bought me a new pair of mittens, a globe, and a subscription to *Smithsonian* magazine. I gave her a perfume—she blushed when she opened the little package—and a new nightgown. She hugged me. Then we drove across town to have dinner with some friends.

The weather became colder between Christmas and the first of the year. It snowed, and then it snowed again. Michael and Susan went outside long enough one day to build a snowman. They put a carrot in its mouth. At night I could see the glare of the TV in their bedroom window. Mary Rice kept going back and forth to work every evening, Rosemary came in to baby-sit, and every night and all night the lights burned over there.

On New Year's Eve we drove across town to our friends' for dinner again, played bridge, watched some TV and, promptly at midnight, opened a bottle of champagne. I shook hands with Harold and we smoked a cigar together. Then Dotty and I drove home.

But—and this is the beginning of the hard part—when we reached our neighborhood, the street was blocked off by two police cars. The lights on top of the cars revolved back and forth. Other cars, curious motorists, had stopped, and people had come out of their houses. Most of the people were dressed up and wearing topcoats, but there were a few people in night-clothes wearing heavy coats that they'd obviously put on in a hurry. Two fire engines were parked down the street. One of them sat in our front yard, and the other was in Mary Rice's driveway.

I gave the officer my name and said that we lived there, where the big truck was parked—"They're in front of our house!" Dotty screamed—and the officer said we should park our car.

"What happened?" I said.

"I guess one of those space heaters caught on fire. That's what somebody said, anyway. A couple of kids were in there. Three kids, counting the baby-sitter. She got out. The kids didn't make it, I don't guess. Smoke inhalation."

We started walking down the street toward our house. Dotty walked close to me and held my arm. "Oh my God," she said.

Up close to Mary Rice's house, under the lights thrown up by the fire trucks, I could see a man standing on the roof holding a fire hose. But only a trickle of water came out of it now. The bedroom window was broken out, and in the bedroom I could see a man moving around in the room carrying something that could have been an ax. Then a man walked out the front door with something in his arms, and I saw it was those kids' dog. And I felt terrible then.

A mobile TV unit from one of the local stations was there, and a man was operating a camera that he held over his shoulder. Neighbors huddled around. The engines in the trucks were running, and now and then voices came over speakers from inside the trucks. But none of the people watching were saying anything. I looked at them, and then I recognized Rosemary, who was standing with her mother and father with her mouth open. Then they brought the children down on stretchers, the firemen, big fellows wearing boots and coats and hats, men who looked indestructible and as if they could live another hundred years. They came outside, one on either end of the stretchers, carrying the children.

"Oh no," said the people who stood watching. And then again, "Oh no. No," someone cried.

They laid the stretchers on the ground. A man in a suit and wool cap stepped up and listened with a stethoscope for a heartbeat on each of the children, and then nodded to the ambulance attendants, who stepped forward to pick up the stretchers.

At that moment a little car drove up and Mary Rice jumped out of the passenger side. She ran toward the men who were about to put the stretchers into the ambulance. "Put them down!" she yelled. "Put them down!"

And the attendants stopped what they were doing and put the stretchers down and then stood back. Mary Rice stood over her children and howled—yes, there's no other word. People stepped back and then they moved forward again as she dropped to her knees in the snow beside the stretchers and put her hands on the face of one child and then the other.

The man in the suit with the stethoscope stepped forward and kneeled beside Mary Rice. Another man—it might have been the fire chief or else the assistant fire chief—signaled the attendants and then stepped up to Mary Rice and helped her up and put his arm around her shoulders. The man in the suit stood on the other side of her, but he didn't touch her. The person who'd driven her home now walked up close to see what was going on, but he was only a scared-looking kid, a busboy or a dishwasher. He had no right to be there to witness Mary Rice's grief and he knew it. He stood back away from people, keeping his eyes on the stretchers as the men put them into the back of the ambulance.

"No!" Mary Rice said and jumped toward the back of the ambulance as the stretchers were being put in.

I went up to her then—no one else was doing anything—
and took her arm and said, "Mary, Mary Rice."

She whirled on me and said, "I don't know you, what do
you *want*?" She brought her hand back and slapped me in the
face. Then she got into the ambulance along with the attendants, and the ambulance moved down the street, sliding, its
siren going off, as the people got out of the way.

I slept badly that night. And Dotty groaned in her sleep and
turned again and again. I knew she was dreaming that she was
somewhere far away from me all night. The next morning, I
didn't ask her what she'd dreamed, and she didn't volunteer
anything. But when I went in with her juice and coffee, she
had her notebook on her lap along with a pen. She closed the
pen up in the notebook and looked at me.

"What's happening next door?" she asked me.

"Nothing," I said. "The house is dark. There are tire marks
all over the snow. The children's bedroom window is broken
out. That's all. Nothing else. Except for that, the bedroom
window, you wouldn't know there'd been a fire. You wouldn't
know two children had died."

"That poor woman," Dotty said. "God, that poor, unfortu-
nate woman. God help her. And us, too."

From time to time that morning people in cars drove by
slowly and looked at her house. Or else people came up to the
front of the house, looked at the window, looked at how the
snow had been churned up in front of the house, and then
went on again. Toward noon I was looking out the window
when a station wagon drove up and parked. Mary Rice and her
former husband, the children's father, got out and went
toward the house. They moved slowly, and the man took her
arm as they went up the steps. The porch door stood open
from the night before. She went inside first. Then he went in.

That night on the local news we saw the whole thing going
on again. "I can't watch this," Dotty said, but she watched
anyway, just like I did. The film showed Mary Rice's house and
a man on the roof with a hose spraying water down through
the broken window. Then the children were shown being carried out, and again we watched Mary Rice dropping to her
knees. Then, as the stretchers are being put into the ambu-

lance, Mary Rice whirls on somebody and screams, "What do you *want*?"

At noon the next day the station wagon drove up in front of the house. As soon as it was parked, before the man could even turn off the engine, Mary Rice came down the steps. The man got out of the car, said "Hello, Mary," and opened the passenger's door for her. Then they went off to the funeral.

He stayed four nights after the funeral, and then the next morning when I got up, early as always, the station wagon was gone and I knew he'd left sometime in the night.

That morning Dotty told me about a dream she'd had. She was in a house in the country and a white horse came up and looked in through the window at her. Then she woke up.

"I want to do something to express our sorrow," Dotty said. "I want to have her over for dinner, maybe."

But the days passed and we didn't do anything, Dotty or I, about having her over. Mary Rice went back to work, only now she worked days, in an office, and I saw her leave the house in the morning and return home a little after five. The lights would go out over there around ten at night. The shade in the children's room was always pulled, and I imagined, though I didn't know, that the door was closed.

Toward the end of March, I went outside one Saturday to take down the storm windows. I heard a noise and looked and I saw Mary Rice trying to spade some dirt, to turn over some ground behind her house. She was wearing slacks, a sweater, and a summer hat. "Hello there," I said.

"Hello," she said. "I guess I'm rushing things. But I have all this time on my hands, you see, and—well, this is the time of year it says on the package." She took a packet of seeds out of her pocket. "My kids went around the neighborhood last year selling seeds. I was cleaning out drawers and found some of these packages."

I didn't mention the seed packets I had in my own kitchen drawer. "My wife and I have been wanting to ask you over for dinner for a long time," I said. "Will you come some night? Could you come tonight, if you're free?"

"I guess I could do that. Yes. But I don't even know your name. Or your wife's."

I told her and then I said, "Is six o'clock a good time?"

"When? Oh, yes. Six o'clock is fine." She put her hand on the spade and pushed down. "I'll just go ahead and plant these seeds. I'll come over at six. Thank you."

I went back into the house to tell Dotty about dinner. I took down the plates and got out the silverware. The next time I looked out, Mary Rice had gone in from her garden.

Vandals

CAROL and Robert Norris were old friends of Nick's wife, Joanne. They'd known her for years, long before Nick met her. They'd known her since back when she'd been married to Bill Daly. In those days, the four of them—Carol and Robert, Joanne and Bill—were newlyweds and graduate students in the university art department. They lived in the same house, a big house on Seattle's Capitol Hill, where they shared the rent, and a bathroom. They took many of their meals together and sat up late talking and drinking wine. They handed the work they'd done around to each other for criticism and inspection. They even, in the last year they shared the house together—before Nick appeared on the scene—bought an inexpensive little sailboat together that they used during the summer months on Lake Washington. "Good times and bad, high times and low," Robert said, for the second time that morning, laughing and looking around the table at the faces of the others.

It was Sunday morning, and they were sitting around the table in Nick and Joanne's kitchen in Aberdeen, eating smoked salmon, scrambled eggs, and cream cheese on bagels. It was salmon that Nick had caught the summer before and then had arranged to have vacuum packed. He'd put the salmon in the freezer. He liked it that Joanne told Carol and Robert that he'd caught the fish himself. She even knew—or claimed to know—how much the fish had weighed. "This one weighed sixteen pounds," she said, and Nick laughed, pleased. Nick had taken the fish out of the freezer the night before, after Carol had called and talked to Joanne and said she and Robert and their daughter, Jenny, would like to stop on their way through town.

"Can we be excused now?" Jenny said. "We want to go skateboarding."

"The skateboards are in the car," Jenny's friend, Megan, said.

"Take your plates over to the sink," Robert said. "And then

you can go skateboarding, I guess. But don't go far. Stay in the neighborhood," he said. "And be careful."

"Is it all right?" Carol said.

"Sure it is," Joanne said. "It's fine. I wish *I* had a skateboard. If I did, I'd join them."

"But mostly good times," Robert said, going on with what he'd been saying about their student days. "Right?" he said, catching Joanne's eye and grinning.

Joanne nodded.

"Those were the days, all right," Carol said.

Nick had the feeling that Joanne wanted to ask them something about Bill Daly. But she didn't. She smiled, held the smile a moment too long, and then asked if anybody would like more coffee.

"I'll have some more, thanks," Robert said. Carol said "Nope" and put the palm of her hand over her cup. Nick shook his head.

"So tell me about salmon fishing," Robert said to Nick.

"Nothing much to tell," Nick said. "You get up early and you go out on the water, and if the wind isn't blowing and it doesn't rain on you, and the fish are in and you're rigged up properly, you might get a strike. The odds are that, if you're lucky, you'll land one out of every four fish that hit. Some men devote their lives to it, I guess. I fish some in the summer months, and that's it."

"Do you fish out of a boat or what?" Robert said. He said this as if it was an afterthought. He wasn't really interested, Nick felt, but thought he had to say more since he'd brought it up.

"I have a boat," Nick said. "It's berthed down at the marina."

Robert nodded slowly. Joanne poured his coffee and Robert looked at her and grinned. "Thanks, babe," he said.

Nick and Joanne saw Carol and Robert every six months or so—more often than Nick would have liked, to tell the truth. It wasn't that he disliked them; he did like them. He liked them better, in fact, than any other of Joanne's friends he'd met. He liked Robert's bitter sense of humor, and the way he had of telling a story, making it seem funnier, probably, than it really was. He liked Carol, too. She was a pretty, cheerful woman who still did an occasional acrylic painting—Nick and

Joanne had hung one of her paintings, a gift, on their bed-room wall. Carol had never been anything but pleasant to Nick during the times they'd been in each other's company. But sometimes, when Robert and Joanne were reminiscing over the past, Nick would find himself looking across the room at Carol, who would hold his look, smile, and then give a little shake of her head, as if none of this talk of the past were of any consequence.

Still, from time to time when they were all together, Nick couldn't help feeling that an unspoken judgment was being made, and that Robert, if not Carol, still blamed him for breaking up Joanne's marriage with Bill and ending their happy foursome.

They saw each other in Aberdeen at least twice a year, once at the beginning of summer, and once again near the end. Robert and Carol and Jenny, their ten-year-old, made a loop through town on their way to the rain forest country of the Olympic Peninsula, heading for a lodge they knew about at a place called Agate Beach, where Jenny would hunt for agates and fill up a leather pouch with stones that she took back to Seattle for polishing.

The three never stayed overnight with Nick and Joanne—it occurred to Nick they'd never been asked to stay, for one thing, though he was sure that Joanne would have been pleased enough to have them, if Nick suggested it. But he hadn't. On each of their visits, they arrived in time for breakfast, or else they showed up just before lunch. Carol always called ahead to make the arrangements. They were punctual, which Nick appreciated.

Nick liked them, but somehow he was always made uneasy in their company, too. They'd never, not once, talked about Bill Daly in Nick's presence, or even so much as mentioned the man's name. Nevertheless, when the four of them were to-gether Nick was somehow made to feel that Daly was never very far from anyone's thoughts. Nick had taken Daly's wife away from him, and now these old friends of Daly's were in the house of the man who'd committed that callous indiscretion, the man who'd turned all their lives upside down for a while. Wasn't it a kind of betrayal for Robert and Carol to be friends with the man who'd done this? To actually break bread in the man's house and see him put his arm lovingly around the shoulders of the woman who used to be the wife of the man they loved?

"Don't go far, honey," Carol said to Jenny as the girls passed through the kitchen again. "We have to be leaving soon."

"We won't," Jenny said. "We'll just skate out in front."

"See that you do," Robert said. "We'll go pretty soon, you kids." He looked at his watch.

The door closed behind the children, and the grownups went back to a subject they'd touched on earlier that morning —terrorism. Robert was an art teacher in one of the Seattle high schools, and Carol worked in a boutique near the Pike Place Market. Between the two of them they didn't know anyone who was going to Europe or the Middle East that summer. In fact, several people, friends of theirs, had canceled their vacation plans to Italy and Greece.

"See America first, is my motto," Robert said. He went on to tell something about his mother and stepfather, who'd just come back from two weeks in Rome. Their luggage had been lost for three days—that was the first thing that'd happened. Then, the second night in Rome, walking down the Via Veneto to a restaurant not far from their hotel—the street patrolled by men in uniform, carrying machine guns—his mother had her purse snatched by a thief on a bicycle. Two days later, when they drove a rental car about thirty miles from Rome, somebody slashed a tire and stole the hood off the car while they were in a museum. "They didn't take the battery or anything, you understand," Robert said. "They wanted the hood. Can you beat it?"

"What'd they want with the hood?" Joanne asked.

"Who knows?" Robert said. "But in any case, it's getting worse for people over there—for tourists—since we bombed. What do you guys think about the bombing? I think it's just going to make things worse for Americans. Everybody's a target now."

Nick stirred his coffee and sipped it before saying, "I don't know any longer. I really don't. In my mind I keep seeing all those bodies lying in pools of blood in the airports. I just don't know." He stirred his coffee some more. "The guys I've talked to over here think that we should have dropped a few more bombs, maybe, while we were at it. I heard somebody say they should have turned the place into a parking lot, while they were at it. I don't know *what* we should or shouldn't do over there. But we had to do something, I think."

"Well, that's a little severe, isn't it?" Robert said. "A parking lot? Like, *nuke* the place—you know?"

"I said I don't know what they should have done. But some kind of response was necessary."

"Diplomacy," Robert said. "Economic sanctions. Let them feel it in their pocketbooks. Then they'll straighten up and fly right."

"Should I make more coffee?" Joanne said. "It won't take a minute. Who wants some cantaloupe?" She moved her chair back and got up from the table.

"I can't eat another bite," Carol said.

"Me neither," Robert said. "I'm fine." He seemed to want to go on with what they were talking about, and then he stopped. "Nick, sometime I'll come down here and go fishing with you. When's the best time to go?"

"Do it," Nick said. "You're welcome to come anytime. Come over and stay as long as you'd like. July is the best month. But August is good too. Even the first week or two of September." He started to say something about how swell it was fishing in the evenings, when most of the boats had gone in. He started to say something about the time he'd hooked a big one in the moonlight.

Robert seemed to consider this for a minute. He drank some of his coffee. "I'll do it. I'll come this summer—in July, if that's all right."

"It's fine," Nick said.

"What will I need in the way of equipment?" Robert said, interested.

"Just bring yourself," Nick said. "I have plenty of gear."

"You can use my pole," Joanne said.

"But then you couldn't fish," Robert said. And suddenly that was the end of the talk about fishing. Somehow, Nick could see, the prospect of sitting together in a boat for hours on end made Robert and him both feel uneasy. No, frankly he couldn't see any more for their relationship than sitting here in this nice kitchen twice a year, eating breakfast and lingering over coffee.

It was pleasant enough, and it was just enough time spent together. More than this was just not in the cards. Lately he'd even passed up an occasional trip to Seattle with Joanne, because he knew she'd want to stop at the end of the day at Carol and Robert's for coffee. Nick would make an excuse and stay home. He'd say he was too busy at the lumberyard that he managed. On one occasion, Joanne had spent the night with Carol and Robert, and when she came home, she seemed to Nick to be remote and thoughtful for a few days. When he asked her about the visit, she said it had been fine and that they'd sat up late after dinner talking. Nick knew they must have talked about Bill Daly; he was certain they had, and he found himself irritated for a few weeks. But so what if they'd talked about Daly? Joanne was Nick's now. Once he would have killed for her. He loved her still, and she loved him, but he didn't feel that obsessive now. No, he wouldn't kill for her now, and he had a hard time understanding how he'd ever felt that way in the first place. He didn't think that she—or anybody, for that matter—could ever be worth killing somebody else for.

Joanne stood up and began clearing the plates from the table.

"Let me help," Carol said.

Nick put his arm around Joanne's waist and squeezed her, as if vaguely ashamed of what he'd been thinking. Joanne stood still, close to Nick's chair. She let him hold her. Then her face reddened slightly and she moved a little, and Nick let go of her.

The children, Jenny and Megan, opened the door and rushed into the kitchen carrying their skateboards. "There's a fire down the street," Jenny said.

"Somebody's house is burning," Megan said.

"A fire?" Carol said. "If it's a real fire, stay away from it."

"I didn't hear any fire trucks," Joanne said. "Did you guys hear fire trucks?"

"I didn't either," Robert said. "You kids go play now. We don't have much longer."

Nick stepped to the bay window and looked out, but nothing out of the ordinary seemed to be happening. The idea of a house fire on the block in clear, sunny weather at eleven in the morning was incomprehensible. Besides, there had been no alarms, no carloads of rubberneckers or clang of bells, or wail of sirens and hiss of air brakes. It seemed to Nick it had to be a part of a game the children were playing.

"This was a wonderful breakfast," Carol said. "I loved it. I feel like I could roll over and go to sleep."

"Why don't you?" Joanne said. "We have that extra room upstairs. Let the kids play, and you guys take yourselves a nap before starting off."

"Go ahead," Nick said. "Sure."

"Carol's just kidding, of course," Robert said. "We couldn't do anything like that. Could we, Carol?" Robert looked at her.

"Oh, no, not really," Carol said and laughed. "But everything was so good, as always. A champagne brunch without the champagne."

"The best kind," Nick said. Nick had quit drinking six years ago after being arrested for driving under the influence. He'd gone with someone to an AA meeting, decided that was the place for him, and then went every night, sometimes twice in one night, for two months, until the desire to drink left him, as he put it, almost as if it'd never been there. But even now, though he didn't drink, he still went to a meeting every once in a while.

"Speaking of drinking," Robert said. "Jo, do you remember Harry Schuster—*Dr.* Harry Schuster, a bone-marrow-transplant man now, don't ask me how—but do you remember the Christmas party that time when he got into the fight with his wife?"

"Marilyn," Joanne said. "Marilyn Schuster. I haven't thought of her in a long time."

"Marilyn, that's right," Robert said. "Because he thought she'd had too much to drink and was making eyes at—"

He paused just long enough for Joanne to say, "Bill."

"Bill, that's right," Robert said. "Anyway, first they had words, and then she threw her car keys on the living-room floor and said, 'You drive, then, if you're so goddamn safe, sane, and sober.' And so Harry—they'd come in two cars, mind, he'd been interning at the hospital—Harry went out and drove her car two blocks, parked it, and then came back for *his* car, and drove that about two blocks, parked, walked back to her car, drove it two blocks, walked to his own car and drove it a little farther, and parked and walked back to her car and drove that a few blocks, et cetera, et cetera."

They all laughed. Nick laughed too. It *was* funny. Nick had heard plenty of drinking stories in his time, but he'd never heard one that had this particular spin on it.

"Anyway," Robert said, "to make a long story short, as they say, he drove both cars home that way. It took him two or three hours to drive five miles. And when he got to the house, there was Marilyn, at the table with a drink in her hand. Somebody had driven her home. 'Merry Christmas,' she said when Harry came in the door, and I guess he decked her."

Carol whistled.

Joanne said, "Anybody could see those two weren't going to make it. They were in the fast lane. A year later they were both at the same Christmas party, only they had different partners by then."

"All the drinking and driving I did," Nick said. He shook his head. "I was only picked up once."

"You were lucky," Joanne said.

"Somebody was lucky," Robert said. "The other drivers on the road were lucky."

"I spent one night in jail," Nick said, "and that was enough. That's when I stopped. Actually, I was in what they call detox. The doctor came around the next morning—his name was Dr. Forester—and called each person into this little examining room and gave you the once-over. He looked in your eyes with his penlight, he made you hold out your hands, palms up, he took your pulse and listened to your heartbeat. He'd give you a little talking-to about your drinking, and then he'd tell you what time of the morning you could be released. He said I could leave at eleven o'clock. 'Doctor,' I said, 'could I leave earlier, please?' 'What's the big hurry?' he said. 'I have to be at church at eleven o'clock,' I said. 'I'm getting married.'"

"What'd he say to that?" Carol said.

"He said, 'Get the hell out of here, mister. But don't ever forget this, do you hear?' And I didn't. I stopped drinking. I didn't even drink anything at the wedding reception that afternoon. Not a drop. That was it for me. I was too scared. Sometimes it takes something like that, a real shock to your nervous system, to turn things around."

"I had a kid brother who was nearly killed by a drunk driver," Robert said. "He's still wired up and has to use a metal brace to get around."

"Last call for coffee," Joanne said.

"Just a little, I guess," Carol said. "We really have to collect those kids and get on the road."

Nick looked toward the window and saw several cars pass by on the street outside. People hurried by on the sidewalk. He remembered what Jenny and the other child had said about a fire, but for God's sake, if there were a fire there'd be sirens and engines, right? He started to get up from the table, and then he didn't.

"It's crazy," he said. "I remember when I was still drinking and I'd just had what they call an alcoholic seizure—I'd fallen and hit my head on a coffee table. Lucky for me I was in the doctor's office when it happened. I woke up in a bed in his office, and Peggy, the woman I was married to at the time, she was leaning over me, along with the doctor and the doctor's nurse. Peggy was calling my name. I had this big bandage round my head—it was like a turban. The doctor said I'd just had my first seizure, but it wouldn't be my last if I kept on drinking. I told him I'd got the message. But I just said that. I had no intention of quitting then. I told myself and my wife that it was my nerves—stress—that had caused me to faint.

"But that night we had a party, Peggy and me. It was something we'd planned for a couple of weeks, and we didn't see how we could call it off at the last minute and disappoint everybody. Can you imagine? So we went ahead and had the party, and everybody came, and I was still wearing the bandage. All that night I had a glass of vodka in my hand. I told people I'd cut my head on the car door."

"How much longer did you keep drinking?" Carol said.

"Quite a while. A year or so. Until I got picked up that night."

"He was sober when I met him," Joanne said, and blushed, as if she'd said something she shouldn't.

Nick put his hand on Joanne's neck and rested his fingers there. He picked up some of the hair that lay across her neck and rubbed it between his fingers. Some more people went by the window on the sidewalk. Most of the people were in shirtsleeves and blouses. A man was carrying a little girl on his shoulders.

"I quit drinking about a year before I met Joanne," Nick said, as if telling them something they needed to know.

"Tell them about your brother, honey," Joanne said.

Nick didn't say anything at first. He stopped rubbing Joanne's neck and took his hand away.

"What happened?" Robert said, leaning forward.

Nick shook his head.

"What?" Carol said. "Nick? It's okay—if you want to tell us, that is."

"How'd we get onto this stuff, anyway?" Nick said.

"You brought it up," Joanne said.

"Well, what happened, you see, was that I was trying to get sober, and I felt like I couldn't do it at home, but I didn't want to have to go anyplace, like to a clinic or a recovery place, you know, and my brother had this summer house he wasn't using —this was in October—and I called him and asked him if I could go there and stay for a week or two and try to get myself together again. At first he said yes. I began to pack a suitcase and I was thinking I was glad I had family, glad I had a brother and that he was going to help me. But pretty soon the phone rang, and it was my brother, and he said—he said he'd talked it over with his wife, and he was sorry—he didn't know how to tell me this, he said—but his wife was afraid I might burn the place down. I might, he said, drop off with a cigarette burning in my fingers, or else leave a burner turned on. Anyway, they were afraid I would catch the house on fire, and he was sorry but he couldn't let me stay. So I said okay, and I unpacked my suitcase."

"Wow," Carol said. "Your own brother did that. He forsook you," she said. "Your own brother."

"I don't know what I'd have done, if I'd been in his shoes," Nick said.

"Sure you do," Joanne said.

"Well, I guess I do," Nick said. "Sure. I'd have let him stay there. What the hell, a house. What's that? You can get insurance on a house."

"That's pretty amazing, all right," Robert said. "So how do you and your brother get along these days?"

"We don't, I'm sorry to say. He asked me to lend him some money a while back, and I did, and he repaid me when he said he would. But we haven't seen each other in about five years. It's been longer than that since I've seen his wife."

"Where are all these *people* coming from?" Joanne said. She got up from the table and went over to the window and moved the curtain.

"The kids said something about a fire," Nick said.

"That's silly. There can't be a fire," Joanne said. "Can there?"

"Something's going on," Robert said.

Nick went to the front door and opened it. A car slowed and then pulled up alongside the curb in front of the house and parked. Another car drove up and parked across the street. Small groups of people moved past down the sidewalk. Nick went out into the yard, and the others—Joanne, Carol, and Robert—followed him. Nick looked up the street and saw the smoke, a crowd of people, and two fire engines and a police car parked at the intersection. Men were training hoses on the shell of a house—the Carpenter house, Nick saw at a glance. Black smoke poured from the walls, and flames shot from the roof. "My God, there's a fire all right," he said. "The kids were right."

"Why didn't we hear anything?" Joanne said. "Did you hear anything? I didn't hear anything."

"We'd better go down and see about the girls, Robert," Carol said. "They might get in the way somehow. They might get too close or something. Anything could happen."

The four of them started down the sidewalk. They fell in with some other people who were walking at an unhurried pace. They walked along with these other people. Nick had the feeling that they could have been on an outing. But all the while, as they kept their eyes on the burning house, they saw firemen pouring water onto the roof of the house, where flames kept breaking through. Some other firemen were holding a hose and aiming a stream of water through a front window. A fireman wearing a helmet with straps, a long black coat, and black knee-high boots was carrying an ax and moving around toward the back of the house.

They came up to where the crowd of people stood watching. The police car had parked sideways in the middle of the road, and they could hear the radio crackling inside the car, over the sound of the fire as it ripped through the walls of the house. Then Nick spotted the two girls, standing near the front of the crowd, holding their skateboards. "There they are," he said to Robert. "Over there. See them?"

They made their way through the crowd, excusing themselves, and came up beside the girls.

"We told you," Jenny said. "See?" Megan stood holding her skateboard in one hand and had the thumb of her other hand planted in her mouth.

"Do you know what happened?" Nick said to the woman beside him. She was wearing a sun hat and smoking a cigarette.

"Vandals," she said. "That's what somebody told me, anyway."

"If they can catch them, they ought to kill them, if you ask me," said the man standing next to the woman. "Or else lock them up and throw away the key. These people are traveling in Mexico and don't even know they won't have a house to live in when they come back. They haven't been able to get in touch with them. Those poor people. Can you imagine? They're going to come home and find out they don't have a house to live in any longer."

"It's going!" the fireman with the ax shouted. "Stand back!"

Nobody was close to him or to the house. But the people in the crowd moved their feet, and Nick could feel himself grow tense. Someone in the crowd said, "Oh my God. My God."

"Look at it," someone else said.

Nick edged closer to Joanne, who was staring intently at the fire. The hair on her forehead appeared damp. He put his arm around her. He realized, as he did it, that he'd touched her this way at least three times that morning.

Nick turned his head slightly in Robert's direction and was surprised to see Robert staring at him instead of the house. Robert's face was flushed, his expression stern, as if everything that had happened—arson, jail, betrayal, and adultery, the overturning of the established order—was Nick's fault and could be laid on his doorstep. Nick stared back, his arm around Joanne, until the flush left Robert's face and he lowered his eyes. When he raised them again, he didn't look at Nick. He moved closer to his wife, as if to protect her.

Nick and Joanne were still holding each other as they watched, but there was that familiar feeling Nick would have from time to time, as she absently patted his shoulder, that he didn't know what she was thinking.

"What are you thinking?" he asked her.

"I was thinking about Bill," she said.

He went on holding her. She didn't say any more for a minute, and then she said, "I think about him every now and then, you know. After all, he was the first man I ever loved."

He kept holding her. She let her head rest on his shoulder and went on staring at the burning house.

Call If You Need Me

W E had both been involved with other people that spring, but when June came and school was out we decided to let our house for the summer and move from Palo Alto to the north coast country of California. Our son, Richard, went to Nancy's grandmother's place in Pasco, Washington, to live for the summer and work toward saving money for college in the fall. His grandmother knew the situation at home and had begun working on getting him up there and locating him a job long before his arrival. She'd talked to a farmer friend of hers and had secured a promise of work for Richard baling hay and building fences. Hard work, but Richard was looking forward to it. He left on the bus in the morning of the day after his high school graduation. I took him to the station and parked and went inside to sit with him until his bus was called. His mother had already held him and cried and kissed him good-bye and given him a long letter that he was to deliver to his grandmother upon his arrival. She was at home now finishing last-minute packing for our own move and waiting for the couple who were to take our house. I bought Richard's ticket, gave it to him, and we sat on one of the benches in the station and waited. We'd talked a little about things on the way to the station.

"Are you and Mom going to get a divorce?" he'd asked. It was Saturday morning, and there weren't many cars.

"Not if we can help it," I said. "We don't want to. That's why we're going away from here and don't expect to see anyone all summer. That's why we've rented our house for the summer and rented the house up in Eureka. Why you're going away, too, I guess. One reason anyway. Not to mention the fact that you'll come home with your pockets filled with money. We don't want to get a divorce. We want to be alone for the summer and try to work things out."

"You still love Mom?" he said. "She told me she loves you."

"Of course I do," I said. "You ought to know that by now. We've just had our share of troubles and heavy responsibilities, like everyone else, and now we need time to be alone and work things out. But don't worry about us. You just go up there and have a good summer and work hard and save your money. Consider it a vacation too. Get in all the fishing you can. There's good fishing around there."

"Waterskiing too," he said. "I want to learn to water-ski."

"I've never been waterskiing," I said. "Do some of that for me too, will you?"

We sat in the bus station. He looked through his yearbook while I held a newspaper in my lap. Then his bus was called and we stood up. I embraced him and said, "Don't worry, don't worry. Where's your ticket?"

He patted his coat pocket and then picked up his suitcase. I walked him over to where the line was forming in the terminal, then I embraced him again and kissed him on the cheek and said good-bye.

"Good-bye, Dad," he said, and turned from me so I wouldn't see his tears.

I drove home to where our boxes and suitcases were waiting in the living room. Nancy was in the kitchen drinking coffee with the young couple she'd found to take our house for the summer. I'd met the couple, Jerry and Liz, graduate students in math, for the first time a few days before, but we shook hands again, and I drank a cup of coffee that Nancy poured. We sat around the table and drank coffee while Nancy finished her list of things they should look out for or do at certain times of the month, the first and last of each month, where they should send any mail, and the like. Nancy's face was tight. Sun fell through the curtain onto the table as it got later in the morning.

Finally, things seemed to be in order and I left the three of them in the kitchen and began loading the car. It was a furnished house we were going to, furnished right down to plates and cooking utensils, so we wouldn't need to take much with us from this house, only the essentials.

I'd driven up to Eureka, 350 miles north of Palo Alto, on the north coast of California, three weeks before and rented us the furnished house. I went with Susan, the woman I'd been seeing. We stayed in a motel at the edge of town for three nights while I looked in the newspaper and visited realtors. She watched me as I wrote out a check for the three months' rent. Later, back at the motel, in bed, she lay with her hand on her forehead and said, "I envy your wife. I envy Nancy. You hear people talk about 'the other woman' always and how the incumbent wife has the privileges and the real power, but I never really understood or cared about those things before. Now I see. I envy her. I envy her the life she'll have with you in that house this summer. I wish it were me. I wish it were us. Oh, how I wish it were us. I feel so crummy," she said. I stroked her hair.

Nancy was a tall, long-legged woman with brown hair and eyes and a generous spirit. But lately we had been coming up short on generosity and spirit. The man she'd been seeing was one of my colleagues, a divorced, dapper, three-piece-suit-and-tie fellow with graying hair who drank too much and whose hands, some of my students told me, sometimes shook in the classroom. He and Nancy had drifted into their affair at a party during the holidays, not too long after Nancy had discovered my own affair. It all sounds boring and tacky now—it is boring and tacky—but during that spring it was what it was, and it consumed all of our energies and concentration to the exclusion of everything else. Sometime in late April we began to make plans to rent our house and go away for the summer, just the two of us, and try to put things back together, if they could be put back together. We each agreed we would not call or write or otherwise be in touch with the other parties. So we made arrangements for Richard, found the couple to look after our house, and I had looked at a map and driven north from San Francisco and found Eureka, and a realtor who was willing to rent a furnished house to a respectable middle-aged married couple for the summer. I think I even used the phrase "second honeymoon" to the realtor, God forgive me, while Susan smoked a cigarette and read tourist brochures out in the car.

I finished storing the suitcases, bags, and cartons in the trunk and backseat and waited while Nancy said a final good-bye on the porch. She shook hands with each of them and turned and came toward the car. I waved to the couple, and they waved back. Nancy got in and shut the door. "Let's go," she said. I put the car in gear and we headed for the freeway. At the light just before the freeway we saw a car ahead of us come off the freeway trailing a broken muffler, the sparks flying. "Look at that," Nancy said. "It might catch fire." We waited and watched until the car managed to pull off the road onto the shoulder.

We stopped at a little café off the highway near Sebastopol. Eat and Gas, the sign read. We laughed at the sign. I pulled up in front of the café and we went inside and took a table near a window in the back. After we ordered coffee and sandwiches, Nancy touched her forefinger to the table and began tracing lines in the wood. I lit a cigarette and looked outside. I saw rapid movement, and then I realized I was looking at a hummingbird in the bush beside the window. Its wings moved in a blur of motion and it kept dipping its beak into a blossom on the bush.

"Nancy, look," I said. "There's a hummingbird."

But the hummingbird flew at this moment and Nancy looked and said, "Where? I don't see it."

"It was just there a minute ago," I said. "Look, there it is. Another one, I think. It's another hummingbird."

We watched the hummingbird until the waitress brought our order and the bird flew at the movement and disappeared around the building.

"Now that's a good sign, I think," I said. "Hummingbirds. Hummingbirds are supposed to bring luck."

"I've heard that somewhere," she said. "I don't know where I heard that, but I've heard it. Well," she said, "luck is what we could use. Wouldn't you say?"

"They're a good sign," I said. "I'm glad we stopped here."

She nodded. She waited a minute, then she took a bite of her sandwich.

We reached Eureka just before dark. We passed the motel on the highway where Susan and I had stayed and had spent the three nights two weeks before, then turned off the highway and took a road up a hill overlooking the town. I had the house keys in my pocket. We drove over the hill and for a mile or so until we came to a little intersection with a service station and a grocery store. There were wooded mountains ahead of us in the valley, and pastureland all around. Some cattle were grazing in a field behind the service station. "This is pretty country," Nancy said. "I'm anxious to see the house."

"Almost there," I said. "It's just down this road," I said,

"and over that rise." "Here," I said in a minute, and pulled into a long driveway with hedge on either side. "Here it is. What do you think of this?" I'd asked the same question of Susan when she and I had stopped in the driveway.

"It's nice," Nancy said. "It looks fine, it does. Let's get out."

We stood in the front yard a minute and looked around. Then we went up the porch steps and I unlocked the front door and turned on the lights. We went through the house. There were two small bedrooms, a bath, a living room with old furniture and a fireplace, and a big kitchen with a view of the valley.

"Do you like it?" I said.

"I think it's just wonderful," Nancy said. She grinned. "I'm glad you found it. I'm glad we're here." She opened the refrigerator and ran a finger over the counter. "Thank God, it looks clean enough. I won't have to do any cleaning."

"Right down to clean sheets on the beds," I said. "I checked. I made sure. That's the way they're renting it. Pillows even. And pillowcases too."

"We'll have to buy some firewood," she said. We were standing in the living room. "We'll want to have a fire on nights like this."

"I'll look into firewood tomorrow," I said. "We can go shopping then, too, and see the town."

She looked at me and said, "I'm glad we're here."

"So am I," I said. I opened my arms and she moved to me. I held her. I could feel her trembling. I turned her face up and kissed her on either cheek. "Nancy," I said.

"I'm glad we're here," she said.

We spent the next few days settling in, taking trips into Eureka to walk around and look in store windows, and hiking across the pastureland behind the house all the way to the woods. We bought groceries and I found an ad in the newspaper for firewood, called, and a day or so afterwards two young men with long hair delivered a pickup truckload of alder and stacked it in the carport. That night we sat in front of the fireplace after dinner and drank coffee and talked about getting a dog.

"I don't want a pup," Nancy said. "Something we have to clean up after or that will chew things up. That we don't need.

But I'd like to have a dog, yes. We haven't had a dog in a long time. I think we could handle a dog up here," she said.

"And after we go back, after summer's over?" I said. I rephrased the question. "What about keeping a dog in the city?"

"We'll see. Meanwhile, let's look for a dog. The right kind of dog. I don't know what I want until I see it. We'll read the classifieds and we'll go to the pound, if we have to." But though we went on talking about dogs for several days, and pointed out dogs to each other in people's yards we'd drive past, dogs we said we'd like to have, nothing came of it, we didn't get a dog.

Nancy called her mother and gave her our address and telephone number. Richard was working and seemed happy, her mother said. She herself was fine. I heard Nancy say, "We're fine. This is good medicine."

One day in the middle of July we were driving the highway near the ocean and came over a rise to see some lagoons that were closed off from the ocean by sand spits. There were some people fishing from shore, and two boats out on the water.

I pulled the car off onto the shoulder and stopped. "Let's see what they're fishing for," I said. "Maybe we could get some gear and go ourselves."

"We haven't been fishing in years," Nancy said. "Not since that time Richard was little and we went camping near Mount Shasta. Do you remember that?"

"I remember," I said. "I just remembered, too, that I've missed fishing. Let's walk down and see what they're fishing for."

"Trout," the man said, when I asked. "Cutthroats and rainbow trout. Even some steelhead and a few salmon. They come in here in the winter when the spit opens and then when it closes in the spring, they're trapped. This is a good time of the year for them. I haven't caught any today, but last Sunday I caught four, about fifteen inches long. Best eating fish in the world, and they put up a hell of a fight. Fellows out in the boats have caught some today, but so far I haven't done anything."

"What do you use for bait?" Nancy asked.

"Anything," the man said. "Worms, salmon eggs, whole-kernel corn. Just get it out there and leave it lay on the bottom. Pull out a little slack and watch your line."

We hung around a little longer and watched the man fish and watched the little boats *chat-chat* back and forth the length of the lagoon.

"Thanks," I said to the man. "Good luck to you."

"Good luck to you," he said. "Good luck to the both of you."

We stopped at a sporting goods store on the way back to town and bought licenses, inexpensive rods and reels, nylon line, hooks, leaders, sinkers, and a creel. We made plans to go fishing the next morning.

But that night, after we'd eaten dinner and washed the dishes and I had laid a fire in the fireplace, Nancy shook her head and said it wasn't going to work.

"Why do you say that?" I asked. "What is it you mean?"

"I mean it isn't going to work. Let's face it." She shook her head again. "I don't think I want to go fishing in the morning, either, and I don't want a dog. No, no dogs. I think I want to go up and see my mother and Richard. Alone. I want to be alone. I miss Richard," she said and began to cry. "Richard's my son, my baby," she said, "and he's nearly grown and gone. I miss him."

"And Del, do you miss Del Shraeder too?" I said. "Your boyfriend. Do you miss him?"

"I miss everybody tonight," she said. "I miss you too. I've missed you for a long time now. I've missed you so much you've gotten lost somehow, I can't explain it. I've lost you. You're not mine any longer."

"Nancy," I said.

"No, no," she said. She shook her head. She sat on the sofa in front of the fire and kept shaking her head. "I want to fly up and see my mother and Richard tomorrow. After I'm gone you can call your girlfriend."

"I won't do that," I said. "I have no intention of doing that."

"You'll call her," she said.

"You'll call Del," I said. I felt rubbishy for saying it.

"You can do what you want," she said, wiping her eyes on her sleeve. "I mean that. I don't want to sound hysterical. But I'm going up to Washington tomorrow. Right now I'm going to go to bed. I'm exhausted. I'm sorry. I'm sorry for both of us, Dan. We're not going to make it. That fisherman today. He wished us good luck." She shook her head. "I wish us good luck too. We're going to need it."

She went into the bathroom and I heard water running in the tub. I went out and sat on the porch steps and smoked a cigarette. It was dark and quiet outside. I looked toward town and could see a faint glow of lights in the sky and patches of ocean fog drifting in the valley. I began to think of Susan. A little later, Nancy came out of the bathroom and I heard the bedroom door close. I went inside and put another block of wood on the grate and waited until the flames began to move up the bark. Then I went into the other bedroom and turned the covers back and stared at the floral design on the sheets. Then I showered, dressed in my pajamas, and went to sit near the fireplace again. The fog was outside the window now. I sat in front of the fire and smoked. When I looked out the window again, something moved in the fog and I saw a horse grazing in the front yard.

I went to the window. The horse looked up at me for a minute, then went back to pulling up grass. Another horse walked past the car into the yard and began to graze. I turned on the porch light and stood at the window and watched them. They were big white horses with long manes. They'd gotten through a fence or an unlocked gate from one of the nearby farms. Somehow they'd wound up in our front yard. They were larking it, enjoying their breakaway immensely. But nervous, too; I could see the whites of their eyes from where I stood behind the window. Their ears kept rising and falling as they tore out clumps of grass. A third horse wandered into the yard, and then a fourth. It was a herd of white horses, and they were grazing in our front yard.

I went into the bedroom and woke Nancy. Her eyes were red and the skin around the eyes was swollen. She had her hair up in curlers, and a suitcase lay open on the floor near the foot of the bed.

"Nancy," I said. "Honey, come and see what's in the front yard. Come and see this. You must see this. You won't believe it. Hurry up."

"What is it?" she said. "Don't hurt me. What is it?"

"Honey, you must see this. I'm not going to hurt you. I'm sorry if I scared you. But you must come out here and see something."

I went back into the other room and stood in front of the

window, and in a few minutes Nancy came in tying her robe. She looked out the window and said, "My God, they're beautiful. Where'd they come from, Dan? They're just beautiful."

"They must have gotten loose from around here somewhere," I said. "One of these farm places. I'll call the sheriff's department pretty soon and let them locate the owners. But I wanted you to see this first."

"Will they bite?" she said. "I'd like to pet that one there, the one that just looked at us. I'd like to pat that one's shoulder. But I don't want to get bitten. I'm going outside."

"I don't think they'll bite," I said. "They don't look like the kind of horses that'll bite. But put a coat on if you're going out there; it's cold."

I put my coat on over my pajamas and waited for Nancy. Then I opened the front door and we went outside and walked into the yard with the horses. They all looked up at us. Two of them went back to pulling up grass. One of the other horses snorted and moved back a few steps, and then it, too, went back to pulling up grass and chewing, head down. I rubbed the forehead of one horse and patted its shoulder. It kept chewing. Nancy put out her hand and began stroking the mane of another horse. "Horsey, where'd you come from?" she said. "Where do you live and why are you out tonight, Horsey?" she said, and kept stroking the horse's mane. The horse looked at her and blew through its lips and dropped its head again. She patted its shoulder.

"I guess I'd better call the sheriff," I said.

"Not yet," she said. "Not for a while yet. We'll never see anything like this again. We'll never, never have horses in our front yard again. Wait a while yet, Dan."

A little later, Nancy was still out there moving from one horse to another, patting their shoulders and stroking their manes, when one of the horses moved from the yard into the driveway and walked around the car and down the driveway toward the road, and I knew I had to call.

In a little while the two sheriff's cars showed up with their red lights flashing in the fog and a few minutes later a fellow in a sheepskin coat driving a pickup with a horse trailer behind it. Now the horses shied and tried to get away, and the man with the horse trailer swore and tried to get a rope around the neck of one horse.

"Don't hurt it!" Nancy said.

We went back in the house and stood behind the window and watched the deputies and the rancher work on getting the horses rounded up.

"I'm going to make some coffee," I said. "Would you like some coffee, Nancy?"

"I'll tell you what I'd like," she said. "I feel high, Dan. I feel like I'm loaded. I feel like, I don't know, but I like the way I'm feeling. You put on some coffee and I'll find us some music to listen to on the radio and then you can build up the fire again. I'm too excited to sleep."

So we sat in front of the fire and drank coffee and listened to an all-night radio station from Eureka and talked about the horses and then talked about Richard, and Nancy's mother. We danced. We didn't talk about the present situation at all. The fog hung outside the window and we talked and were kind with one another. Toward daylight I turned off the radio and we went to bed and made love.

The next afternoon, after her arrangements were made and her suitcases packed, I drove her to the little airport where she would catch a flight to Portland and then transfer to another airline that would put her in Pasco late that night.

"Tell your mother I said hello. Give Richard a hug for me and tell him I miss him," I said. "Tell him I send love."

"He loves you too," she said. "You know that. In any case, you'll see him in the fall, I'm sure."

I nodded.

"Good-bye," she said and reached for me. We held each other. "I'm glad for last night," she said. "Those horses. Our talk. Everything. It helps. We won't forget that," she said. She began to cry.

"Write me, will you?" I said. "I didn't think it would happen to us," I said. "All those years. I never thought so for a minute. Not us."

"I'll write," she said. "Some big letters. The biggest you've ever seen since I used to send you letters in high school."

"I'll be looking for them," I said.

Then she looked at me again and touched my face. She turned and moved across the tarmac toward the plane.

Go, dearest one, and God be with you.

She boarded the plane and I stayed around until its jet engines started, and in a minute the plane began to taxi down the runway. It lifted off over Humboldt Bay and soon became a speck on the horizon.

I drove back to the house and parked in the driveway and looked at the hoofprints of the horses from last night. There were deep impressions in the grass, and gashes, and there were piles of dung. Then I went into the house and, without even taking off my coat, went to the telephone and dialed Susan's number.

SELECTED ESSAYS

My Father's Life

M Y dad's name was Clevie Raymond Carver. His family called him Raymond and friends called him C.R. I was named Raymond Clevie Carver Jr. I hated the "Junior" part. When I was little my dad called me Frog, which was okay. But later, like everybody else in the family, he began calling me Junior. He went on calling me this until I was thirteen or fourteen and announced that I wouldn't answer to that name any longer. So he began calling me Doc. From then until his death, on June 17, 1967, he called me Doc, or else Son.

When he died, my mother telephoned my wife with the news. I was away from my family at the time, between lives, trying to enroll in the School of Library Science at the University of Iowa. When my wife answered the phone, my mother blurted out, "Raymond's dead!" For a moment, my wife thought my mother was telling her that I was dead. Then my mother made it clear *which* Raymond she was talking about and my wife said, "Thank God. I thought you meant *my* Raymond."

My dad walked, hitched rides, and rode in empty boxcars when he went from Arkansas to Washington State in 1934, looking for work. I don't know whether he was pursuing a dream when he went out to Washington. I doubt it. I don't think he dreamed much. I believe he was simply looking for steady work at decent pay. Steady work was meaningful work. He picked apples for a time and then landed a construction laborer's job on the Grand Coulee Dam. After he'd put aside a little money, he bought a car and drove back to Arkansas to help his folks, my grandparents, pack up for the move west. He said later that they were about to starve down there, and this wasn't meant as a figure of speech. It was during that short while in Arkansas, in a town called Leola, that my mother met my dad on the sidewalk as he came out of a tavern.

"He was drunk," she said. "I don't know why I let him talk to me. His eyes were glittery. I wish I'd had a crystal ball." They'd met once, a year or so before, at a dance. He'd had girlfriends before her, my mother told me. "Your dad always

719

had a girlfriend, even after we married. He was my first and
last. I never had another man. But I didn't miss anything."

They were married by a justice of the peace on the day they
left for Washington, this big, tall country girl and a farmhand-
turned-construction worker. My mother spent her wedding
night with my dad and his folks, all of them camped beside the
road in Arkansas.

In Omak, Washington, my dad and mother lived in a little
place not much bigger than a cabin. My grandparents lived
next door. My dad was still working on the dam, and later,
with the huge turbines producing electricity and the water
backed up for a hundred miles into Canada, he stood in the
crowd and heard Franklin D. Roosevelt when he spoke at the
construction site. "He never mentioned those guys who died
building that dam," my dad said. Some of his friends had died
there, men from Arkansas, Oklahoma, and Missouri.

He then took a job in a sawmill in Clatskanie, Oregon, a
little town alongside the Columbia River. I was born there,
and my mother has a picture of my dad standing in front of the
gate to the mill, proudly holding me up to face the camera. My
bonnet is on crooked and about to come untied. His hat is
pushed back on his forehead, and he's wearing a big grin. Was
he going in to work or just finishing his shift? It doesn't
matter. In either case, he had a job and a family. These were his
salad days.

In 1941 we moved to Yakima, Washington, where my dad
went to work as a saw filer, a skilled trade he'd learned in
Clatskanie. When war broke out, he was given a deferment
because his work was considered necessary to the war effort.
Finished lumber was in demand by the armed services, and he
kept his saws so sharp they could shave the hair off your arm.

After my dad had moved us to Yakima, he moved his folks
into the same neighborhood. By the mid-1940s the rest of my
dad's family—his brother, his sister, and her husband, as well
as uncles, cousins, nephews, and most of their extended family
and friends—had come out from Arkansas. All because my dad
came out first. The men went to work at Boise Cascade, where
my dad worked, and the women packed apples in the canneries.
And in just a little while, it seemed—according to my mother—

everybody was better off than my dad. "Your dad couldn't keep money," my mother said. "Money burned a hole in his pocket. He was always doing for others."

The first house I clearly remember living in, at 1515 South Fifteenth Street, in Yakima, had an outdoor toilet. On Halloween night, or just any night, for the hell of it, neighbor kids, kids in their early teens, would carry our toilet away and leave it next to the road. My dad would have to get somebody to help him bring it home. Or these kids would take the toilet and stand it in somebody else's backyard. Once they actually set it on fire. But ours wasn't the only house that had an outdoor toilet. When I was old enough to know what I was doing, I threw rocks at the other toilets when I'd see someone go inside. This was called bombing the toilets. After a while, though, everyone went to indoor plumbing until, suddenly, our toilet was the last outdoor one in the neighborhood. I remember the shame I felt when my third-grade teacher, Mr. Wise, drove me home from school one day. I asked him to stop at the house just before ours, claiming I lived there.

I can recall what happened one night when my dad came home late to find that my mother had locked all the doors on him from the inside. He was drunk, and we could feel the house shudder as he rattled the door. When he'd managed to force open a window, she hit him between the eyes with a colander and knocked him out. We could see him down there on the grass. For years afterward, I used to pick up this colander —it was as heavy as a rolling pin—and imagine what it would feel like to be hit in the head with something like that.

It was during this period that I remember my dad taking me into the bedroom, sitting me down on the bed, and telling me that I might have to go live with my Aunt LaVon for a while. I couldn't understand what I'd done that meant I'd have to go away from home to live. But this, too—whatever prompted it —must have blown over, more or less, anyway, because we stayed together, and I didn't have to go live with her or anyone else.

I remember my mother pouring his whiskey down the sink. Sometimes she'd pour it all out and sometimes, if she was afraid of getting caught, she'd only pour half of it out and then add water to the rest. I tasted some of his whiskey once myself. It was terrible stuff, and I don't see how anybody could drink it.

After a long time without one, we finally got a car, in 1949 or 1950, a 1938 Ford. But it threw a rod the first week we had it, and my dad had to have the motor rebuilt.

"We drove the oldest car in town," my mother said. "We could have had a Cadillac for all he spent on car repairs." One time she found someone else's tube of lipstick on the floorboard, along with a lacy handkerchief. "See this?" she said to me. "Some floozy left this in the car."

Once I saw her take a pan of warm water into the bedroom where my dad was sleeping. She took his hand from under the covers and held it in the water. I stood in the doorway and watched. I wanted to know what was going on. This would make him talk in his sleep, she told me. There were things she needed to know, things she was sure he was keeping from her.

Every year or so, when I was little, we would take the North Coast Limited across the Cascade Range from Yakima to Seattle and stay in the Vance Hotel and eat, I remember, at a place called the Dinner Bell Cafe. Once we went to Ivar's Acres of Clams and drank glasses of warm clam broth.

In 1956, the year I was to graduate from high school, my dad quit his job at the mill in Yakima and took a job in Chester, a little sawmill town in northern California. The reasons given at the time for his taking the job had to do with a higher hourly wage and the vague promise that he might, in a few years' time, succeed to the job of head filer in this new mill. But I think, in the main, that my dad had grown restless and simply wanted to try his luck elsewhere. Things had gotten a little too predictable for him in Yakima. Also, the year before, there had been the deaths, within six months of each other, of both his parents.

But just a few days after graduation, when my mother and I were packed to move to Chester, my dad penciled a letter to say he'd been sick for a while. He didn't want us to worry, he said, but he'd cut himself on a saw. Maybe he'd got a tiny sliver of steel in his blood. Anyway, something had happened and he'd had to miss work, he said. In the same mail was an unsigned postcard from somebody down there telling my mother that my dad was about to die and that he was drinking "raw whiskey."

When we arrived in Chester, my dad was living in a trailer that belonged to the company. I didn't recognize him immediately. I guess for a moment I didn't want to recognize him. He was skinny and pale and looked bewildered. His pants wouldn't stay up. He didn't look like my dad. My mother began to cry. My dad put his arm around her and patted her shoulder vaguely, like he didn't know what this was all about, either. The three of us took up life together in the trailer, and we looked after him as best we could. But my dad was sick, and he couldn't get any better. I worked with him in the mill that summer and part of the fall. We'd get up in the mornings and eat eggs and toast while we listened to the radio, and then go out the door with our lunch pails. We'd pass through the gate together at eight in the morning, and I wouldn't see him again until quitting time. In November I went back to Yakima to be closer to my girlfriend, the girl I'd made up my mind I was going to marry.

He worked at the mill in Chester until the following February, when he collapsed on the job and was taken to the hospital. My mother asked if I would come down there and help. I caught a bus from Yakima to Chester, intending to drive them back to Yakima. But now, in addition to being physically sick, my dad was in the midst of a nervous breakdown, though none of us knew to call it that at the time. During the entire trip back to Yakima, he didn't speak, not even when asked a direct question. ("How do you feel, Raymond?" "You okay, Dad?") He'd communicate, if he communicated at all, by moving his head or by turning his palms up as if to say he didn't know or care. The only time he said anything on the trip, and for nearly a month afterward, was when I was speeding down a gravel road in Oregon and the car muffler came loose. "You were going too fast," he said.

Back in Yakima a doctor saw to it that my dad went to a psychiatrist. My mother and dad had to go on relief, as it was called, and the county paid for the psychiatrist. The psychiatrist asked my dad, "Who is the President?" He'd had a question put to him that he could answer. "Ike," my dad said. Nevertheless, they put him on the fifth floor of Valley Memorial Hospital and began giving him electroshock treatments. I was married by then and about to start my own family. My dad was still locked up when my wife went into this same hospital, just one floor down, to have our first baby. After she had delivered, I went upstairs to give my dad the news. They let me in through a steel door and showed me where I could find him. He was sitting on a couch with a blanket over his lap. *Hey*, I thought. *What in hell is happening to my dad?* I sat down next to him and told him he was a grandfather. He waited a minute and then he said, "I feel like a grandfather." That's all he said. He didn't smile or move. He was in a big room with a lot of other people. Then I hugged him, and he began to cry.

Somehow he got out of there. But now came the years when he couldn't work and just sat around the house trying to figure what next and what he'd done wrong in his life that he'd wound up like this. My mother went from job to crummy job. Much later she referred to that time he was in the hospital, and those years just afterward, as "when Raymond was sick." The word *sick* was never the same for me again.

In 1964, through the help of a friend, he was lucky enough to be hired on at a mill in Klamath, California. He moved down there by himself to see if he could hack it. He lived not far from the mill, in a one-room cabin not much different from the place he and my mother had started out living in when they went west. He scrawled letters to my mother, and if I called she'd read them aloud to me over the phone. In the letters, he said it was touch and go. Every day that he went to work, he felt like it was the most important day of his life. But every day, he told her, made the next day that much easier. He said for her to tell me he said hello. If he couldn't sleep at night, he said, he thought about me and the good times we used to have. Finally, after a couple of months, he regained some of his confidence. He could do the work and didn't think he had to worry that he'd let anybody down ever again. When he was sure, he sent for my mother.

He'd been off from work for six years and had lost everything in that time—home, car, furniture, and appliances, including the big freezer that had been my mother's pride and joy. He'd lost his good name too—Raymond Carver was someone who couldn't pay his bills—and his self-respect was gone. He'd even lost his virility. My mother told my wife, "All during that time Raymond was sick we slept together in the same bed, but we didn't have relations. He wanted to a few times, but nothing happened. I didn't miss it, but I think he wanted to, you know."

During those years I was trying to raise my own family and earn a living. But, one thing and another, we found ourselves having to move a lot. I couldn't keep track of what was going down in my dad's life. But I did have a chance one Christmas to tell him I wanted to be a writer. I might as well have told him I wanted to become a plastic surgeon. "What are you going to write about?" he wanted to know. Then, as if to help me out, he said, "Write about stuff you know about. Write about some of those fishing trips we took." I said I would, but I knew I wouldn't. "Send me what you write," he said. I said I'd do that, but then I didn't. I wasn't writing anything about fishing, and I didn't think he'd particularly care about, or even necessarily understand, what I was writing in those days. Besides, he wasn't a reader. Not the sort, anyway, I imagined I was writing for.

Then he died. I was a long way off, in Iowa City, with things still to say to him. I didn't have the chance to tell him goodbye, or that I thought he was doing great at his new job. That I was proud of him for making a comeback.

My mother said he came in from work that night and ate a big supper. Then he sat at the table by himself and finished what was left of a bottle of whiskey, a bottle she found hidden in the bottom of the garbage under some coffee grounds a day or so later. Then he got up and went to bed, where my mother joined him a little later. But in the night she had to get up and make a bed for herself on the couch. "He was snoring so loud I couldn't sleep," she said. The next morning when she looked in on him, he was on his back with his mouth open, his cheeks caved in. *Gray-looking*, she said. She knew he was dead—she didn't need a doctor to tell her that. But she called one anyway, and then she called my wife.

Among the pictures my mother kept of my dad and herself during those early days in Washington was a photograph of him standing in front of a car, holding a beer and a stringer of fish. In the photograph he is wearing his hat back on his forehead and has this awkward grin on his face. I asked her for it and she gave it to me, along with some others. I put it up on my wall, and each time we moved, I took the picture along and put it up on another wall. I looked at it carefully from time to time, trying to figure out some things about my dad, and maybe myself in the process. But I couldn't. My dad just kept moving further and further away from me and back into time. Finally, in the course of another move, I lost the photograph. It was then that I tried to recall it, and at the same time make an attempt to say something about my dad, and how I thought that in some important ways we might be alike. I wrote the poem when I was living in an apartment house in an urban area south of San Francisco, at a time when I found myself, like my dad, having trouble with alcohol. The poem was a way of trying to connect up with him.

PHOTOGRAPH OF MY FATHER IN HIS TWENTY-SECOND YEAR

October. Here in this dank, unfamiliar kitchen
I study my father's embarrassed young man's face.
Sheepish grin, he holds in one hand a string
of spiny yellow perch, in the other
a bottle of Carlsberg beer.

In jeans and flannel shirt, he leans
against the front fender of a 1934 Ford.
He would like to pose brave and hearty for his posterity,
wear his old hat cocked over his ear.
All his life my father wanted to be bold.

But the eyes give him away, and the hands
that limply offer the string of dead perch
and the bottle of beer. Father, I love you,
yet how can I say thank you, I who can't hold my liquor either
and don't even know the places to fish.

The poem is true in its particulars, except that my dad died in June and not October, as the first word of the poem says. I wanted a word with more than one syllable to it to make it linger a little. But more than that, I wanted a month appropriate to what I felt at the time I wrote the poem—a month of short days and failing light, smoke in the air, things perishing.

June was summer nights and days, graduations, my wedding anniversary, the birthday of one of my children. June wasn't a month your father died in.

After the service at the funeral home, after we had moved outside, a woman I didn't know came over to me and said, "He's happier where he is now." I stared at this woman until she moved away. I still remember the little knob of a hat she was wearing. Then one of my dad's cousins—I didn't know the man's name—reached out and took my hand. "We all miss him," he said, and I knew he wasn't saying it just to be polite.

I began to weep for the first time since receiving the news. I hadn't been able to before. I hadn't had the time, for one thing. Now, suddenly, I couldn't stop. I held my wife and wept while she said and did what she could do to comfort me there in the middle of that summer afternoon.

I listened to people say consoling things to my mother, and I was glad that my dad's family had turned up, had come to where he was. I thought I'd remember everything that was said and done that day and maybe find a way to tell it sometime. But I didn't. I forgot it all, or nearly. What I do remember is that I heard our name used a lot that afternoon, my dad's name and mine. But I knew they were talking about my dad. *Raymond*, these people kept saying in their beautiful voices out of my childhood. *Raymond*.

On Writing

B ACK in the mid-1960s, I found I was having trouble concentrating my attention on long narrative fiction. For a
time I experienced difficulty in trying to read it as well as in attempting to write it. My attention span had gone out on me; I
no longer had the patience to try to write novels. It's an involved story, too tedious to talk about here. But I know it has
much to do now with why I write poems and short stories. Get
in, get out. Don't linger. Go on. It could be that I lost any
great ambitions at about the same time, in my late twenties. If
I did, I think it was good it happened. Ambition and a little
luck are good things for a writer to have going for him. Too
much ambition and bad luck, or no luck at all, can be killing.
There has to be talent.

Some writers have a bunch of talent; I don't know any writers
who are without it. But a unique and exact way of looking at
things, and finding the right context for expressing that way of
looking, that's something else. *The World According to Garp*
is, of course, the marvelous world according to John Irving.
There is another world according to Flannery O'Connor, and
others according to William Faulkner and Ernest Hemingway.
There are worlds according to Cheever, Updike, Singer, Stanley Elkin, Ann Beattie, Cynthia Ozick, Donald Barthelme,
Mary Robison, William Kittredge, Barry Hannah, Ursula K.
LeGuin. Every great or even every very good writer makes the
world over according to his own specifications.

It's akin to style, what I'm talking about, but it isn't style
alone. It is the writer's particular and unmistakable signature
on everything he writes. It is his world and no other. This is
one of the things that distinguishes one writer from another.
Not talent. There's plenty of that around. But a writer who has
some special way of looking at things and who gives artistic expression to that way of looking: that writer may be around for
a time.

Isak Dinesen said that she wrote a little every day, without
hope and without despair. Someday I'll put that on a three-by-
five card and tape it to the wall beside my desk. I have some

three-by-five cards on the wall now. "Fundamental accuracy of statement is the ONE sole morality of writing." Ezra Pound. It is not everything by ANY means, but if a writer has "fundamental accuracy of statement" going for him, he's at least on the right track.

I have a three-by-five up there with this fragment of a sentence from a story by Chekov: ". . . and suddenly everything became clear to him." I find these words filled with wonder and possibility. I love their simple clarity, and the hint of revelation that's implied. There is mystery, too. What has been unclear before? Why is it just now becoming clear? What's happened? Most of all—what now? There are consequences as a result of such sudden awakenings. I feel a sharp sense of relief —and anticipation.

I overheard the writer Geoffrey Wolff say "No cheap tricks" to a group of writing students. That should go on a three-by-five card. I'd amend it a little to "No tricks." Period. I hate tricks. At the first sign of a trick or a gimmick in a piece of fiction, a cheap trick or even an elaborate trick, I tend to look for cover. Tricks are ultimately boring, and I get bored easily, which may go along with my not having much of an attention span. But extremely clever chi-chi writing, or just plain tomfoolery writing, puts me to sleep. Writers don't need tricks or gimmicks or even necessarily need to be the smartest fellows on the block. At the risk of appearing foolish, a writer sometimes needs to be able to just stand and gape at this or that thing—a sunset or an old shoe—in absolute and simple amazement.

Some months back, in the *New York Times Book Review*, John Barth said that ten years ago most of the students in his fiction writing seminar were interested in "formal innovation," and this no longer seems to be the case. He's a little worried that writers are going to start writing mom and pop novels in the 1980s. He worries that experimentation may be on the way out, along with liberalism. I get a little nervous if I find myself within earshot of somber discussions about "formal innovation" in fiction writing. Too often "experimentation" is a license to be careless, silly or imitative in the writing. Even worse, a license to try to brutalize or alienate the reader. Too often such writing gives us no news of the world, or else describes a desert landscape and that's all—a few dunes and lizards here and there, but no people; a place uninhabited by anything recognizably human, a place of interest only to a few scientific specialists.

It should be noted that real experiment in fiction is original, hard-earned and cause for rejoicing. But someone else's way of looking at things—Barthelme's, for instance—should not be chased after by other writers. It won't work. There is only one Barthelme, and for another writer to try to appropriate Barthelme's peculiar sensibility or *mise en scene* under the rubric of innovation is for that writer to mess around with chaos and disaster and, worse, self-deception. The real experimenters have to Make It New, as Pound urged, and in the process have to find things out for themselves. But if writers haven't taken leave of their senses, they also want to stay in touch with us, they want to carry news from their world to ours.

It's possible, in a poem or a short story, to write about commonplace things and objects using commonplace but precise language, and to endow those things—a chair, a window curtain, a fork, a stone, a woman's earring—with immense, even startling power. It is possible to write a line of seemingly innocuous dialogue and have it send a chill along the reader's spine—the source of artistic delight, as Nabokov would have it. That's the kind of writing that most interests me. I hate sloppy or haphazard writing whether it flies under the banner of experimentation or else is just clumsily rendered realism. In Isaac Babel's wonderful short story, "Guy de Maupassant," the narrator has this to say about the writing of fiction: "No iron can pierce the heart with such force as a period put just at the right place." This too ought to go on a three-by-five.

Evan Connell said once that he knew he was finished with a short story when he found himself going through it and taking out commas and then going through the story again and putting commas back in the same places. I like that way of working on something. I respect that kind of care for what is being done. That's all we have, finally, the words, and they had better be the right ones, with the punctuation in the right places so that they can best say what they are meant to say. If the words are heavy with the writer's own unbridled emotions, or if they are imprecise and inaccurate for some other reason—if the words are in any way blurred—the reader's eyes will slide right over them and nothing will be achieved. The reader's own artistic sense will simply not be engaged. Henry James called this sort of hapless writing "weak specification."

I have friends who've told me they had to hurry a book because they needed the money, their editor or their wife was leaning on them or leaving them—something, some apology for the writing not being very good. "It would have been better if I'd taken the time." I was dumbfounded when I heard a novelist friend say this. I still am, if I think about it, which I don't. It's none of my business. But if the writing can't be made as good as it is within us to make it, then why do it? In the end, the satisfaction of having done our best, and the proof of that labor, is the one thing we can take into the grave. I wanted to say to my friend, for heaven's sake go do something else. There have to be easier and maybe more honest ways to try and earn a living. Or else just do it to the best of your abilities, your talents, and then don't justify or make excuses. Don't complain, don't explain.

In an essay called, simply enough, "Writing Short Stories," Flannery O'Connor talks about writing as an act of discovery. O'Connor says she most often did not know where she was going when she sat down to work on a short story. She says she doubts that many writers know where they are going when they begin something. She uses "Good Country People" as an example of how she put together a short story whose ending she could not even guess at until she was nearly there:

When I started writing that story, I didn't know there was going to be a Ph.D. with a wooden leg in it. I merely found myself one morning writing a description of two women I knew something about, and before I realized it, I had equipped one of them with a daughter with a wooden leg. I brought in the Bible salesman, but I had no idea what I was going to do with him. I didn't know he was going to steal that wooden leg until ten or twelve lines before he did it, but when I found out that this was what was going to happen, I realized it was inevitable.

When I read this some years ago it came as a shock that she, or anyone for that matter, wrote stories in this fashion. I thought this was my uncomfortable secret, and I was a little uneasy with it. For sure I thought this way of working on a short story somehow revealed my own shortcomings. I remember being tremendously heartened by reading what she had to say on the subject.

I once sat down to write what turned out to be a pretty good story, though only the first sentence of the story had offered itself to me when I began it. For several days I'd been going around with this sentence in my head: "He was running the vacuum cleaner when the telephone rang." I knew a story was there and that it wanted telling. I felt it in my bones, that a story belonged with that beginning, if I could just have the time to write it. I found the time, an entire day—twelve, fifteen hours even—if I wanted to make use of it. I did, and I sat down in the morning and wrote the first sentence, and other sentences promptly began to attach themselves. I made the story just as I'd make a poem; one line and then the next, and the next. Pretty soon I could see a story, and I knew it was my story, the one I'd been wanting to write.

I like it when there is some feeling of threat or sense of menace in short stories. I think a little menace is fine to have in a story. For one thing, it's good for the circulation. There has to be tension, a sense that something is imminent, that certain things are in relentless motion, or else, most often, there simply won't be a story. What creates tension in a piece of fiction is partly the way the concrete words are linked together to make up the visible action of the story. But it's also the things that are left out, that are implied, the landscape just under the smooth (but sometimes broken and unsettled) surface of things.

V. S. Pritchett's definition of a short story is "something glimpsed from the corner of the eye, in passing." Notice the "glimpse" part of this. First the glimpse. Then the glimpse given life, turned into something that illuminates the moment and may, if we're lucky—that word again—have even further-ranging consequences and meaning. The short story writer's task is to invest the glimpse with all that is in his power. He'll bring his intelligence and literary skill to bear (his talent), his sense of proportion and sense of the fitness of things: of how things out there really are and how he sees those things—like no one else sees them. And this is done through the use of clear and specific language, language used so as to bring to life the details that will light up the story for the reader. For the details to be concrete and convey meaning, the language must be accurate and precisely given. The words can be so precise they may even sound flat, but they can still carry; if used right, they can hit all the notes.

Fires

INFLUENCES are forces—circumstances, personalities, irresistible as the tide. I can't talk about books or writers who might have influenced me. That kind of influence, literary influence, is hard for me to pin down with any kind of certainty. It would be as inaccurate for me to say I've been influenced by everything I've read as for me to say I don't think I've been influenced by any writers. For instance, I've long been a fan of Ernest Hemingway's novels and short stories. Yet I think Lawrence Durrell's work is singular and unsurpassed in the language. Of course, I don't write like Durrell. He's certainly no "influence." On occasion it's been said that my writing is "like" Hemingway's writing. But I can't say his writing influenced mine. Hemingway is one of the many writers whose work, like Durrell's, I first read and admired when I was in my twenties.

So I don't know about literary influences. But I do have some notions about other kinds of influences. The influences I know something about have pressed on me in ways that were often mysterious at first glance, sometimes stopping just short of the miraculous. But these influences have become clear to me as my work has progressed. These influences were (and they still are) relentless. These were the influences that sent me in this direction, onto this spit of land instead of some other—that one over there on the far side of the lake, for example. But if the main influence on my life and writing has been a negative one, oppressive and often malevolent, as I believe is the case, what am I to make of this?

Let me begin by saying that I'm writing this at a place called Yaddo, which is just outside of Saratoga Springs, New York. It's afternoon, Sunday, early August. Every so often, every twenty-five minutes or so, I can hear upwards of thirty thousand voices joined in a great outcry. This wonderful clamor comes from the Saratoga race course. A famous meet is in progress. I'm writing, but every twenty-five minutes I can hear the announcer's voice coming over the loudspeaker as he calls the positions of the horses. The roar of the crowd increases. It bursts over the trees, a great and truly thrilling sound, rising until the horses have crossed the finish line. When it's over, I feel spent, as if I too had participated. I can imagine holding pari-mutuel tickets on one of the horses who finished in the money, or even a horse who came close. If it's a photo finish at the wire, I can expect to hear another outburst a minute or two later, after the film has been developed and the official results posted.

For several days now, ever since arriving here and upon first hearing the announcer's voice over the loudspeaker, and the excited roar from the crowd, I've been writing a short story set in El Paso, a city where I lived for a while some time ago. The story has to do with some people who go to a horse race at a track outside of El Paso. I don't want to say the story has been waiting to be written. It hasn't, and it would make it sound like something else to say that. But I needed something, in the case of this particular story, to push it out into the open. Then after I arrived here at Yaddo and first heard the crowd, and the announcer's voice over the loudspeaker, certain things came back to me from that other life in El Paso and suggested the story. I remembered that track I went to down there and some things that took place, that might have taken place, that *will* take place—in my story anyway—two thousand miles away from here.

So my story is under way, and there is that aspect of "influences." Of course, every writer is subject to this kind of influence. This is the most common kind of influence—*this* suggests that, *that* suggests something else. It's the kind of influence that is as common to us, and as natural, as rain water.

But before I go on to what I want to talk about, let me give one more example of influence akin to the first. Not so long ago in Syracuse, where I live, I was in the middle of writing a short story when my telephone rang. I answered it. On the other end of the line was the voice of a man who was obviously a black man, someone asking for a party named Nelson. It was a wrong number and I said so and hung up. I went back to my short story. But pretty soon I found myself writing a black character into my story, a somewhat sinister character whose name was Nelson. At that moment the story took a different turn. But happily it was, I see now, and somehow knew at the time, the right turn for the story. When I began to write that story, I could not have prepared for or predicted the necessity for the presence of Nelson in the story. But now, the story finished and about to appear in a national magazine, I see it is right and appropriate and, I believe, aesthetically correct, that Nelson be there, and be there with his sinister aspect. Also right for me is that this character found his way into my story with a coincidental rightness I had the good sense to trust.

I have a poor memory. By this I mean that much that has happened in my life I've forgotten—a blessing for sure—but I have these large periods of time I simply can't account for or bring back, towns and cities I've lived in, names of people, the people themselves. Large blanks. But I can remember some things. Little things—somebody saying something in a particular way; somebody's wild, or low, nervous laughter; a landscape; an expression of sadness or bewilderment on somebody's face; and I can remember some dramatic things—somebody picking up a knife and turning to me in anger; or else hearing my own voice threaten somebody else. Seeing somebody break down a door, or else fall down a flight of stairs. Some of those more dramatic kinds of memories I can recall when it's necessary. But I don't have the kind of memory that can bring entire conversations back to the present, complete with all the gestures and nuances of real speech; nor can I recall the furnishings of any room I've ever spent time in, not to mention my inability to remember the furnishings of an entire household. Or even very many specific things about a race track—except, let's see, a grandstand, betting windows, closed-circuit TV screens, masses of people. Hubbub. I make up the conversations in my stories. I put the furnishings and the physical things surrounding the people into the stories as I need those things. Perhaps this is why it's sometimes been said that my stories are unadorned, stripped down, even "minimalist." But maybe it's nothing more than a working marriage of necessity and convenience that has brought me to writing the kind of stories I do in the way that I do.

None of my stories really *happened*, of course—I'm not writing autobiography—but most of them bear a resemblance, however faint, to certain life occurrences or situations. But when I try to recall the physical surroundings or furnishings bearing on a story situation (what kind of flowers, if any, were present? Did they give off any odor? etc.), I'm often at a total loss. So I have to make it up as I go along—what the people in the story say to each other, as well as what they do then, after thus and so was said, and what happens to them next. I make up what they say to each other, though there may be, in the dialogue, some actual phrase, or sentence or two, that I once heard given in a particular context at some time or other. That sentence may even have been my starting point for the story.

When Henry Miller was in his forties and was writing *Tropic of Cancer*, a book, incidentally, that I like very much, he talks about trying to write in this borrowed room, where at any minute he may have to stop writing because the chair he is sitting on may be taken out from under him. Until fairly recently, this state of affairs persisted in my own life. For as long as I can remember, since I was a teen-ager, the imminent removal of the chair from under me was a constant concern. For years and years my wife and I met ourselves coming and going as we tried to keep a roof over our heads and put bread and milk on the table. We had no money, no visible, that is to say, marketable skills—nothing that we could do toward earning anything better than a get-by living. And we had no education, though we each wanted one very badly. Education, we believed, would open doors for us, help us get jobs so that we could make the kind of life we wanted for ourselves and our children. We had great dreams, my wife and I. We thought we could bow our necks, work very hard, and do all that we had set our hearts to do. But we were mistaken.

I have to say that the greatest single influence on my life, and on my writing, directly and indirectly, has been my two children. They were born before I was twenty, and from beginning to end of our habitation under the same roof—some nineteen years in all—there wasn't any area of my life where their heavy and often baleful influence didn't reach.

In one of her essays Flannery O'Connor says that not much needs to happen in a writer's life after the writer is twenty years old. Plenty of the stuff that makes fiction has already happened to the writer before that time. More than enough, she says. Enough things to last the writer the rest of his creative life. This is not true for me. Most of what now strikes me as story "material" presented itself to me after I was twenty. I really don't remember much about my life before I became a parent. I really don't feel that anything happened in my life until I was twenty and married and had the kids. Then things started to happen.

In the mid 1960s I was in a busy laundromat in Iowa City trying to do five or six loads of clothes, kids' clothes, for the most part, but some of our own clothing, of course, my wife's and mine. My wife was working as a waitress for the University Athletic Club that Saturday afternoon. I was doing chores and being responsible for the kids. They were with some other kids that afternoon, a birthday party maybe. Something. But right then I was doing the laundry. I'd already had sharp words with an old harridan over the number of washers I'd had to use. Now I was waiting for the next round with her, or someone else like her. I was nervously keeping an eye on the dryers that were in operation in the crowded laundromat. When and if one of the dryers ever stopped, I planned to rush over to it with my shopping basket of damp clothes. Understand, I'd been hanging around in the laundromat for thirty minutes or so with this basketful of clothes, waiting my chance. I'd already missed out on a couple of dryers—somebody'd gotten there first. I was getting frantic. As I say, I'm not sure where our kids were that afternoon. Maybe I had to pick them up from someplace, and it was getting late, and that contributed to my state of mind. I did know that even if I could get my clothes into a dryer it would still be another hour or more before the clothes would dry, and I could sack them up and go home with them, back to our apartment in married-student housing. Finally a dryer came to a stop. And I was right there when it did. The clothes inside quit tumbling and lay still. In thirty seconds or so, if no one showed up to claim them, I planned to get rid of the clothes and replace them with my own. That's the law of the laundromat. But at that minute a woman came over to the dryer and opened the door. I stood there waiting. This woman put her hand into the machine and took hold of some items of clothing. But they weren't dry enough, she decided. She closed the door and put two more dimes into the machine. In a daze I moved away with my shopping cart and went back to waiting. But I remember thinking at that moment, amid the feelings of helpless frustration that had me close to tears, that nothing—and, brother, I mean nothing—that ever happened to me on this earth could come anywhere close, could possibly be as important to me, could make as much difference, as the fact that I had two children. And that I would always have them and always find myself in this position of unrelieved responsibility and permanent distraction.

I'm talking about real *influence* now. I'm talking about the moon and the tide. But like that it came to me. Like a sharp breeze when the window is thrown open. Up to that point in my life I'd gone along thinking, what exactly, I don't know, but that things would work out somehow—that everything in my life I'd hoped for or wanted to do, was possible. But at that moment, in the laundromat, I realized that this simply was not true. I realized—what had I been thinking before?—that my life was a small-change thing for the most part, chaotic, and without much light showing through. At that moment I felt— I knew—that the life I was in was vastly different from the lives of the writers I most admired. I understood writers to be people who didn't spend their Saturdays at the laundromat and every waking hour subject to the needs and caprices of their children. Sure, sure, there've been plenty of writers who have had far more serious impediments to their work, including imprisonment, blindness, the threat of torture or of death in one form or another. But knowing this was no consolation. At that moment—I swear all of this took place there in the laundromat —I could see nothing ahead but years more of this kind of responsibility and perplexity. Things would change some, but they were never really going to get better. I understood this, but could I live with it? At that moment I saw accommodations would have to be made. The sights would have to be lowered. I'd had, I realized later, an insight. But so what? What are insights? They don't help any. They just make things harder.

For years my wife and I had held to a belief that if we worked hard and tried to do the right things, the right things would happen. It's not such a bad thing to try and build a life on. Hard work, goals, good intentions, loyalty, we believed these were virtues and would someday be rewarded. We dreamt when we had the time for it. But, eventually, we realized that hard work and dreams were not enough. Somewhere, in Iowa City maybe, or shortly afterwards, in Sacramento, the dreams began to go bust.

The time came and went when everything my wife and I held sacred, or considered worthy of respect, every spiritual value, crumbled away. Something terrible had happened to us. It was something that we had never seen occur in any other family. We couldn't fully comprehend what had happened. It was erosion, and we couldn't stop it. Somehow, when we weren't looking, the children had got into the driver's seat. As crazy as it sounds now, they held the reins, and the whip. We simply could not have anticipated anything like what was happening to us.

During these ferocious years of parenting, I usually didn't have the time, or the heart, to think about working on anything very lengthy. The circumstances of my life, the "grip and slog" of it, in D. H. Lawrence's phrase, did not permit it. The circumstances of my life with these children dictated something else. They said if I wanted to write anything, and finish it, and if ever I wanted to take satisfaction out of finished work, I was going to have to stick to stories and poems. The short things I could sit down and, with any luck, write quickly and have done with. Very early, long before Iowa City even, I'd understood that I would have a hard time writing a novel, given my anxious inability to focus on anything for a sustained period of time. Looking back on it now, I think I was slowly going nuts with frustration during those ravenous years. Anyway, these circumstances dictated, to the fullest possible extent, the forms my writing could take. God forbid, I'm not complaining now, just giving facts from a heavy and still bewildered heart.

If I'd been able to collect my thoughts and concentrate my energy on a novel, say, I was still in no position to wait for a payoff that, if it came at all, might be several years down the road. I couldn't see the road. I had to sit down and write something I could finish now, tonight, or at least tomorrow night, no later, after I got in from work and before I lost interest. In those days I always worked some crap job or another, and my wife did the same. She waitressed or else was a door-to-door saleswoman. Years later she taught high school. But that was years later. I worked sawmill jobs, janitor jobs, delivery man jobs, service station jobs, stockroom boy jobs—name it, I did it. One summer, in Arcata, California, I picked tulips, I swear, during the daylight hours, to support us; and at night after closing, I cleaned the inside of a drive-in restaurant and swept up the parking lot. Once I even considered, for a few minutes anyway—the job application form there in front of me—becoming a bill collector!

In those days I figured if I could squeeze in an hour or two a day for myself, after job and family, that was more than good enough. That was heaven itself. And I felt happy to have that hour. But sometimes, one reason or another, I couldn't get the hour. Then I would look forward to Saturday, though sometimes things happened that knocked Saturday out as well. But there was Sunday to hope for. Sunday, maybe.

I couldn't see myself working on a novel in such a fashion, that is to say, no fashion at all. To write a novel, it seemed to me, a writer should be living in a world that makes sense, a world that the writer can believe in, draw a bead on, and then write about accurately. A world that will, for a time anyway, stay fixed in one place. Along with this there has to be a belief in the essential *correctness* of that world. A belief that the known world has reasons for existing, and is worth writing about, is not likely to go up in smoke in the process. This wasn't the case with the world I knew and was living in. My world was one that seemed to change gears and directions, along with its rules, every day. Time and again I reached the point where I couldn't see or plan any further ahead than the first of next month and gathering together enough money, by hook or by crook, to meet the rent and provide the children's school clothes. This is true.

I wanted to see tangible results for any so-called literary efforts of mine. No chits or promises, no time certificates, please. So I purposely, and by necessity, limited myself to writing things I knew I could finish in one sitting, two sittings at the most. I'm talking of a first draft now. I've always had patience for rewriting. But in those days I happily looked forward to the rewriting as it took up time which I was glad to have taken up. In one regard I was in no hurry to finish the story or the poem I was working on, for finishing something meant I'd have to find the time, and the belief, to begin something else. So I had great patience with a piece of work after I'd done the initial writing. I'd keep something around the house for what seemed a very long time, fooling with it, changing this, adding that, cutting out something else.

This hit-and-miss way of writing lasted for nearly two decades. There were good times back there, of course; certain grown-up pleasures and satisfactions that only parents have access to. But I'd take poison before I'd go through that time again.

The circumstances of my life are much different now, but now I *choose* to write short stories and poems. Or at least I think I do. Maybe it's all a result of the old writing habits from those days. Maybe I still can't adjust to thinking in terms of having a great swatch of time in which to work on something —anything I want!—and not have to worry about having the chair yanked out from under me, or one of my kids smarting off about why supper isn't ready on demand. But I learned some things along the way. One of the things I learned is that I had to bend or else break. And I also learned that it is possible to bend and break at the same time.

I'll say something about two other individuals who exercised influence on my life. One of them, John Gardner, was teaching a beginning fiction writing course at Chico State College when I signed up for the class in the fall of 1958. My wife and I and the children had just moved down from Yakima, Washington, to a place called Paradise, California, about ten miles up in the foothills outside of Chico. We had the promise of low-rent housing and, of course, we thought it would be a great adventure to move to California. (In those days, and for a long while after, we were always up for an adventure.) Of course, I'd have to work to earn a living for us, but I also planned to enroll in college as a part-time student

Gardner was just out of the University of Iowa with a Ph.D. and, I knew, several unpublished novels and short stories. I'd never met anyone who'd written a novel, published or otherwise. On the first day of class he marched us outside and had us sit on the lawn. There were six or seven of us, as I recall. He went around, asking us to name the authors we liked to read. I can't remember any names we mentioned, but they must not have been the right names. He announced that he didn't think any of us had what it took to become real writers—as far as he could see none of us had the necessary *fire*. But he said he was going to do what he could for us, though it was obvious he didn't expect much to come of it. But there was an implication too that we were about to set off on a trip, and we'd do well to hold onto our hats.

I remember at another class meeting he said he wasn't going to mention any of the big-circulation magazines except to sneer at them. He'd brought in a stack of "little" magazines, the literary quarterlies, and he told us to read the work in those magazines. He told us that this was where the best fiction in the country was being published, and all of the poetry. He said he was there to tell us which authors to read as well as teach us how to write. He was amazingly arrogant. He gave us a list of the little magazines he thought were worth something, and he went down the list with us and talked a little about each magazine. Of course, none of us had ever heard of these magazines. It was the first I'd ever known of their existence. I remember him saying during this time, it might have been during a conference, that writers were made as well as born. (Is this true? My God, I still don't know. I suppose every writer who teaches creative writing and who takes the job at all seriously has to believe this to some extent. There are apprentice musicians and composers and visual artists—so why *not* writers?) I was impressionable then, I suppose I still am, but I was terrifically impressed with everything he said and did. He'd take one of my early efforts at a story and go over it with me. I remember him as being very patient, wanting me to understand what he was trying to show me, telling me over and over how important it was to have the right words saying what I wanted them to say. Nothing vague or blurred, no smoked-glass prose. And he kept drumming at me the importance of using—I don't know how else to say it—common language, the language of normal discourse, the language we speak to each other in.

Recently we had dinner together in Ithaca, New York, and I reminded him then of some of the sessions we'd had up in his office. He answered that probably everything he'd told me was wrong. He said, "I've changed my mind about so many things." All I know is that the advice he was handing out in those days was just what I needed at that time. He was a wonderful teacher. It was a great thing to have happen to me at that period of my life, to have someone who took me seriously enough to sit down and go over a manuscript with me. I knew something crucial was happening to me, something that mattered. He helped me to see how important it was to say exactly what I wanted to say and nothing else; not to use "literary" words or "pseudo-poetic" language. He'd try to explain to me the difference between saying something like, for example, "wing of a meadow lark" and "meadow lark's wing." There's a different sound and feel, yes? The word "ground" and the word "earth," for instance. Ground is ground, he'd say, it means *ground*, dirt, that kind of stuff. But if you say "earth" that's something else, that word has other ramifications. He taught me to use contractions in my writing. He helped show me how to say what I wanted to say and to use the minimum number of words to do so. He made me see that absolutely everything was important in a short story. It was of consequence where the commas and periods went. For this, for that—for his giving me the key to his office so I would have a place to write on the weekends—for his putting up with my brashness and general nonsense, I'll always be grateful. He was an influence.

Ten years later I was still alive, still living with my children, still writing an occasional story or poem. I sent one of the occasional stories to *Esquire* and in so doing hoped to be able to forget about it for a while. But the story came back by return mail, along with a letter from Gordon Lish, at that time the fiction editor for the magazine. He said he was returning the story. He was not apologizing that he was returning it, not returning it "reluctantly," he was just returning it. But he asked to see others. So I promptly sent him everything I had, and he just as promptly sent everything back. But again a friendly letter accompanied the work I'd sent to him.

At that time, the early 1970s, I was living in Palo Alto with my family. I was in my early thirties and I had my first white-collar job—I was an editor for a textbook publishing firm. We lived in a house that had an old garage out back. The previous tenants had built a playroom in the garage, and I'd go out to this garage every night I could manage after dinner and try to write something. If I couldn't write anything, and this was often the case, I'd just sit in there for a while by myself, thankful to be away from the fracas that always seemed to be raging inside the house. But I was writing a short story that I'd called "The Neighbors." I finally finished the story and sent it off to Lish. A letter came back almost immediately telling me how much he liked it, that he was changing the title to "Neighbors," that he was recommending to the magazine that the story be purchased. It was purchased, it did appear, and nothing, it seemed to me, would ever be the same. *Esquire* soon bought another story, and then another, and so on. James Dickey became poetry editor of the magazine during this time, and he began accepting my poems for publication. In one regard, things had never seemed better. But my kids were in full cry then, like the race track crowd I can hear at this moment, and they were eating me alive. My life soon took another veering, a sharp turn, and then it came to a dead stop off on a siding. I couldn't go anywhere, couldn't back up or go forward. It was during this period that Lish collected some of my stories and gave them to McGraw-Hill, who published them. For the time being, I was still off on the siding, unable to move in any direction. If there'd once been a fire, it'd gone out.

Influences. John Gardner and Gordon Lish. They hold irredeemable notes. But my children are it. Theirs is the main influence. They were the prime movers and shapers of my life and my writing. As you can see, I'm still under their influence, though the days are relatively clear now, and the silences are right.

Author's Note to
Where I'm Calling From

I WROTE and published my first short story in 1963, twenty-five years ago, and have been drawn to short story writing ever since. I think in part (but only in part) this inclination toward brevity and intensity has to do with the fact that I am a poet as well as a story writer. I began writing and publishing poetry and fiction at more or less the same time, back in the early 1960s when I was still an undergraduate. But this dual relationship as poet and short story writer doesn't explain everything. I'm hooked on writing short stories and couldn't get off them even if I wanted to. Which I don't.

I love the swift leap of a good story, the excitement that often commences in the first sentence, the sense of beauty and mystery found in the best of them; and the fact—so crucially important to me back at the beginning and even now still a consideration—that the story can be written and read in one sitting. (Like poems!)

In the beginning—and perhaps still—the most important short story writers to me were Isaac Babel, Anton Chekhov, Frank O'Connor and V. S. Pritchett. I forget who first passed along a copy of Babel's *Collected Stories* to me, but I do remember coming across a line from one of his greatest stories. I copied it into the little notebook I carried around with me everywhere in those days. The narrator, speaking about Maupassant and the writing of fiction, says: "No iron can stab the heart with such force as a period put just at the right place."

When I first read this it came to me with the force of revelation. This is what I wanted to do with my own stories: line up the right words, the precise images, as well as the exact and correct punctuation so that the reader got pulled in and involved in the story and wouldn't be able to turn away his eyes from the text unless the house caught fire. Vain wishes perhaps, to ask words to assume the power of actions, but clearly a young writer's wishes. Still, the idea of writing clearly with authority enough to hold and engage the reader persisted. This remains one of my primary goals today.

My first book of stories, *Will You Please Be Quiet, Please?*, did not appear until 1976, thirteen years after the first story was written. This long delay between composition, magazine and book publication was due in part to a young marriage, the exigencies of child rearing and blue-collar laboring jobs, a little education on the fly—and never enough money to go around at the end of each month. (It was during this long period, too, that I was trying to learn my craft as a writer, how to be as subtle as a river current when very little else in my life was subtle.)

After the thirteen-year period it took to put the first book together and to find a publisher who, I might add, was most reluctant to engage in such a cockeyed enterprise—a first book of stories by an unknown writer!—I tried to learn to write fast when I had the time, writing stories when the spirit was with me and letting them pile up in a drawer; and then going back to look at them carefully and coldly later on, from a remove, after things had calmed down, after things had, all too regrettably, gone back to "normal."

Inevitably, life being what it is, there were often great swatches of time that simply disappeared, long periods when I did not write any fiction. (How I wish I had those years back now!) Sometimes a year or two would pass when I couldn't even think about writing stories. Often, though, I was able to spend some of that time writing poems, and this proved important because in writing the poetry the flame didn't entirely putter out, as I sometimes feared it might. Mysteriously, or so it would seem to me, there would come a time to turn to fiction again. The circumstances in my life would be right or at least improved and the ferocious desire to write would take hold of me, and I would begin.

I wrote *Cathedral*—eight of these stories are reprinted here —in a period of fifteen months. But during that two-year period before I began to work on those stories, I found myself in a period of stocktaking, of trying to discover where I wanted to go with whatever new stories I was going to write and how I wanted to write them. My previous book, *What We Talk about When We Talk about Love*, had been in many ways a watershed book for me, but it was a book I didn't want to duplicate or write again. So I simply waited. I taught at Syracuse University. I wrote some poems and book reviews, and an essay or two. And then one morning something happened. After a good night's sleep, I went to my desk and wrote the story "Cathedral." I knew it was a different kind of story for me, no question. Somehow I had found another direction I wanted to move toward. And I moved. And quickly.

The new stories that are included here, stories which were written after *Cathedral* and after I had intentionally, happily, taken "time out" for two years to write two books of poetry, are, I'm sure, different in kind and degree from the earlier stories. (At the least I think they're different from those earlier stories, and I suspect readers may feel the same. But any writer will tell you he wants to believe his work will undergo a metamorphosis, a sea change, a process of enrichment if he's been at it long enough.)

V. S. Pritchett's definition of a short story is "something glimpsed from the corner of the eye, in passing." First the glimpse. Then the glimpse given life, turned into something that will illuminate the moment and just maybe lock it indelibly into the reader's consciousness. Make it a part of the reader's own experience, as Hemingway so nicely put it. Forever, the writer hopes. Forever.

If we're lucky, writer and reader alike, we'll finish the last line or two of a short story and then just sit for a minute, quietly. Ideally, we'll ponder what we've just written or read; maybe our hearts or our intellects will have been moved off the peg just a little from where they were before. Our body temperature will have gone up, or down, by a degree. Then, breathing evenly and steadily once more, we'll collect ourselves, writers and readers alike, get up, "created of warm blood and nerves" as a Chekhov character puts it, and go on to the next thing: Life. Always life.

BEGINNERS

The Manuscript Version of
What We Talk About When We Talk About Love

Why Don't You Dance?

IN the kitchen, he poured another drink and looked at the bedroom suite in his front yard. The mattress was stripped and the candy-striped sheets lay beside two pillows on the chiffonier. Except for that, things looked much the way they had in the bedroom—nightstand and reading lamp on his side of the bed, a nightstand and reading lamp on her side. *His* side, *her* side. He considered this as he sipped the whiskey. The chiffonier stood a few feet from the foot of the bed. He had emptied the drawers into cartons that morning, and the cartons were in the living room. A portable heater was next to the chiffonier. A rattan chair with a decorator pillow stood at the foot of the bed. The buffed aluminum kitchen set occupied a part of the driveway. A yellow muslin cloth, much too large, a gift, covered the table and hung down over the sides. A potted fern was on the table, along with a box of silverware, also a gift. A big console-model television set rested on a coffee table, and a few feet away from this, a sofa and chair and a floor lamp. He had run an extension cord from the house and everything was connected, things worked. The desk was pushed against the garage door. A few utensils were on the desk, along with a wall clock and two framed prints. There was also in the driveway a carton with cups, glasses, and plates, each object wrapped in newspaper. That morning he had cleared out the closets and, except for the three cartons in the living room, everything was out of the house. Now and then a car slowed and people stared. But no one stopped. It occurred to him that he wouldn't either.

"It must be a yard sale, for God's sake," the girl said to the boy.

This girl and boy were furnishing a little apartment.

"Let's see what they want for the bed," the girl said.

"I wonder what they want for the TV," the boy said.

He pulled into the driveway and stopped in front of the kitchen table.

They got out of the car and began to examine things. The girl touched the muslin cloth. The boy plugged in the blender and turned the dial to MINCE. She picked up a chafing dish. He turned on the television set and made careful adjustments. He sat down on the sofa to watch. He lit a cigarette, looked around, and flipped the match into the grass. The girl sat on the bed. She pushed off her shoes and lay back. She could see the evening star.

"Come here, Jack. Try this bed. Bring one of those pillows," she said.

"How is it?" he said.

"Try it," she said.

He looked around. The house was dark.

"I feel funny," he said. "Better see if anybody's home."

She bounced on the bed.

"Try it first," she said.

He lay down on the bed and put the pillow under his head.

"How does it feel?" the girl said.

"Feels firm," he said.

She turned on her side and put her arm around his neck.

"Kiss me," she said.

"Let's get up," he said.

"Kiss me. Kiss me, honey," she said.

She closed her eyes. She held him. He had to prize her fingers loose.

He said, "I'll see if anybody's home," but he just sat up.

The television set was still playing. Lights had gone on in houses up and down the street. He sat on the edge of the bed.

"Wouldn't it be funny if," the girl said and grinned and didn't finish.

He laughed. He switched on the reading lamp.

She brushed away a mosquito.

He stood up and tucked his shirt in.

"I'll see if anybody's home," he said. "I don't think anybody's home. But if they are, I'll see what things are going for."

"Whatever they ask, offer them ten dollars less," she said. "They must be desperate or something."

She sat on the bed and watched television.

"You might as well turn that up," the girl said and giggled.

"It's a pretty good TV," he said.

"Ask them how much," she said.

Max came down the sidewalk with a sack from the market. He had sandwiches, beer, and whiskey. He had continued to drink through the afternoon and had reached a place where now the drinking seemed to begin to sober him. But there were gaps. He had stopped at the bar next to the market, had listened to a song on the jukebox, and somehow it had gotten dark before he recalled the things in his yard.

He saw the car in the driveway and the girl on the bed. The television set was playing. Then he saw the boy on the porch. He started across the yard.

"Hello," he said to the girl. "You found the bed. That's good."

"Hello," the girl said, and got up. "I was just trying it out." She patted the bed. "It's a pretty good bed."

"It's a good bed," Max said. "What do I say next?"

He knew he should say something next. He put down the sack and took out the beer and whiskey.

"We thought nobody was here," the boy said. "We're interested in the bed and maybe the TV. Maybe the desk. How much do you want for the bed?"

"I was thinking fifty dollars for the bed," Max said.

"Would you take forty?" the girl asked.

"Okay, I'll take forty," Max said.

He took a glass out of the carton, took the newspaper off it, and broke the seal on the whiskey.

"How about the TV?" the boy said.

"Twenty-five."

"Would you take twenty?" the girl said.

"Twenty's okay. I could take twenty," Max said.

The girl looked at the boy.

"You kids, you want a drink?" Max said. "Glasses in that box. I'm going to sit down. I'm going to sit down on the sofa."

He sat on the sofa, leaned back, and stared at them.

The boy found two glasses and poured whiskey.

"How much of this do you want?" he said to the girl. They were only twenty years old, the boy and girl, a month or so apart.

"That's enough," she said. "I think I want water in mine."

She pulled out a chair and sat at the kitchen table.

"There's water in that faucet over there," Max said. "Turn on that faucet."

The boy added water to the whiskey, his and hers. He cleared his throat before he sat down at the kitchen table too. Then he grinned. Birds darted overhead for insects.

Max gazed at the television. He finished his drink. He reached to turn on the floor lamp and dropped his cigarette between the cushions. The girl got up to help him find it.

"You want anything else, honey?" the boy said.

He took out the checkbook. He poured more whiskey for himself and the girl.

"Oh, I want the desk," the girl said. "How much money is the desk?"

Max waved his hand at this preposterous question.

"Name a figure," he said.

He looked at them as they sat at the table. In the lamplight, there was something about the expression on their faces. For a minute this expression seemed conspiratorial, and then it became *tender*—there was no other word for it. The boy touched her hand.

"I'm going to turn off this TV and put on a record," Max announced. "This record player is going, too. Cheap. Name a figure."

He poured more whiskey and opened a beer.

"Everything goes."

The girl held out her glass and Max poured more whiskey.

"Thank you," she said.

"It goes right to your head," the boy said. "I'm getting a buzz on."

He finished his drink, waited, and poured another. He was writing a check when Max found the records.

"Pick something you like," Max said to the girl, and held the records before her.

The boy went on writing the check.

"Here," the girl said, pointing. She did not know the names on these records, but that was all right. This was an adventure. She got up from the table and sat down again. She didn't want to sit still.

"I'm making it out to cash," the boy said, still writing.

"Sure," Max said. He drank off the whiskey and followed it with some beer. He sat down again on the sofa and crossed one leg over the other.

They drank. They listened until the record ended. And then Max put on another.

"Why don't you kids dance?" Max said. "That's a good idea. Why don't you dance?"

"No, I don't think so," the boy said. "You want to dance, Carla?"

"Go ahead," Max said. "It's my driveway. You can dance."

Arms about each other, their bodies pressed together, the boy and girl moved up and down the driveway. They were dancing.

When the record ended, the girl asked Max to dance. She was still without her shoes.

"I'm drunk," he said.

"You're not drunk," the girl said.

"Well, I'm drunk," the boy said.

Max turned the record over and the girl came up to him. They began to dance.

The girl looked at the people gathered at the bay window across the street.

"Those people over there. Watching," she said. "Is it okay?"

"It's okay," Max said. "It's my driveway. We can dance. They thought they'd seen everything over here, but they haven't seen this," he said.

In a minute, he felt her warm breath on his neck, and he said: "I hope you like your bed."

"I will," the girl said.

"I hope the both of you do," Max said.

"Jack!" the girl said. "Wake up!"

Jack had his chin propped and was watching them sleepily.

"Jack," the girl said.

She closed and opened her eyes. She pushed her face into Max's shoulder. She pulled him closer.

"Jack," the girl murmured.

She looked at the bed and could not understand what it was doing in the yard. She looked over Max's shoulder at the sky. She held herself to Max. She was filled with an unbearable happiness.

—

The girl said later: "This guy was about middle-aged. All his belongings right out there in his yard. I'm not kidding. We got drunk and danced. In the driveway. Oh, my God. Don't laugh. He played records. Look at this phonograph. He gave it to us. These old records, too. Jack and I went to sleep in his bed. Jack was hungover and had to rent a trailer in the morning. To move all the guy's stuff. Once I woke up. He was covering us with a blanket, the guy was. This blanket. Feel it."

She kept talking. She told everyone. There was more, she knew that, but she couldn't get it into words. After a time, she quit talking about it.

Viewfinder

A MAN without hands came to the door to sell me a photograph of my house. Except for the chrome hooks, he was an ordinary-looking man of fifty or so.

"How did you lose your hands?" I asked, after he'd said what he wanted.

"That's another story," he said. "You want this picture of your house or not?"

"Come on in," I said. "I just made coffee."

I'd just made some Jell-O too, but I didn't tell him that.

"I might use your toilet," the man with no hands said.

I wanted to see how he would hold a cup of coffee using those hooks. I knew how he used the camera. It was an old Polaroid camera, big and black. It fastened to leather straps that looped over his shoulders and around his back, securing the camera to his chest. He would stand on the sidewalk in front of a house, locate the house in the viewfinder, depress the lever with one of his hooks, and out popped the picture in a minute or so. I'd been watching from the window.

"Where'd you say the toilet was?"

"Down there, turn right."

By this time, bending and hunching, he'd let himself out of the straps. He put the camera on the sofa and straightened his jacket. "You can look at this while I'm gone."

I took the photograph from him. There was a little rectangle of lawn, the driveway, carport, front steps, bay window, kitchen window. Why would I want a photograph of this tragedy? I looked closer and saw the outline of my head, *my head*, behind the kitchen window and a few steps back from the sink. I looked at the photograph for a time, and then I heard the toilet flush. He came down the hall, zipped and smiling, one hook holding his belt, the other tucking his shirt in.

"What do you think?" he said. "All right? Personally, I think it turned out fine, but then I know what I'm doing and, let's face it, it's not that hard shooting a house. Unless the weather's inclement, but when the weather's inclement I don't work

757

except inside. Special-assignment type work, you know." He plucked at his crotch.

"Here's coffee," I said.

"You're alone, right?" He looked at the living room. He shook his head. "Hard, hard." He sat next to the camera, leaned back with a sigh, and closed his eyes.

"Drink your coffee," I said. I sat in a chair across from him. A week before, three kids in baseball caps had come to the house. One of them had said, "Can we paint your address on the curb, sir? Everybody on the street's doing it. Just a dollar." Two boys waited on the sidewalk, one of them with a can of white paint at his feet, the other holding a brush. All three boys had their sleeves rolled.

"Three kids were by here awhile back wanting to paint my address on the curb. They wanted a dollar, too. You wouldn't know anything about that, would you?" It was a long shot. But I watched him just the same.

He leaned forward importantly, the cup balanced between his hooks. He carefully placed the cup on the little table. He looked at me. "That's crazy, you know. I work alone. Always have, always will. What are you saying?"

"I was trying to make a connection," I said. I had a headache. Coffee's no good for it, but sometimes Jell-O helps. I picked up the photograph. "I was in the kitchen," I said.

"I know. I saw you from the street."

"How often does that happen? Getting somebody in the picture along with the house? Usually I'm in the back."

"Happens all the time," he said. "It's a sure sell. Sometimes they see me shooting the house and they come out and ask me to make sure I get them in the picture. Maybe the lady of the house, she wants me to snap hubby washing his car. Or else there's junior working the lawnmower and she says, *get him, get him*, and I get him. Or the little family is gathered on the patio for a nice little lunch, and would I please." His right leg began to jiggle. "So they just up and left you, right? Packed up and left. It hurts. Kids I don't know about. Not anymore. I don't like kids. I don't even like my own kids. I work alone, as I said. The picture?"

"I'll take it," I said. I stood up for the cups. "You don't live around here. Where do you live?"

"Right now I have a room downtown. It's okay. I take a bus out, you know, and after I've worked all the neighborhoods, I go somewhere else. There's better ways to go, but I get by."

"What about your kids?" I waited with the cups and watched him struggle up from the sofa.

"Screw them. Their mother too! They're what gave me this." He brought the hooks up in front of my face. He turned and started pulling into his straps. "I'd like to forgive and forget, you know, but I can't. I still hurt. And that's the trouble. I can't forgive or forget."

I looked again at the hooks as they maneuvered the straps. It was wonderful to see what he could do with those hooks.

"Thanks for the coffee and the use of the toilet. You're going through the mill now. I sympathize." He raised and lowered his hooks. "What can I do?"

"Take more pictures," I said. "I want you to take pictures of me and the house both."

"It won't work," he said. "She won't come back."

"I don't want her back," I said.

He snorted. He looked at me. "I can give you a rate," he said. "Three for a dollar? If I went any lower I'd hardly come out."

We went outside. He adjusted the shutter. He told me where to stand, and we got down to it. We moved around the house. Very systematic, we were. Sometimes I'd look sideways. Other times I'd look straight into the camera. Just getting outside helped.

"Good," he'd say. "That's good. That one turned out real nice. Let's see," he said after we'd circled the house and were back in the driveway again. "That's twenty. You want any more?"

"Two or three more," I said. "On the roof. I'll go up and you can shoot me from down here."

"Jesus," he said. He looked up and down the street. "Well, sure, go ahead—but be careful."

"You were right," I said. "They did just up and move out. The whole kit and caboodle. You were right on target."

The man with no hands said: "You didn't need to say word one. I knew the instant you opened the door." He shook his hooks at me. "You feel like she cut the ground right out from under you! Took your legs in the process. Look at this! This is what they leave you with. Screw it," he said. "You want to get up on that roof, or not? I've got to go," the man said.

I brought a chair out and put it under the edge of the carport. I still couldn't reach. He stood in the driveway and watched me. I found a crate and put that on the chair. I climbed onto the chair and then the crate. I raised up onto the carport, walked to the roof, and made my way on hands and knees across the shingles to a little flat place near the chimney. I stood up and looked around. There was a breeze. I waved, and he waved back with both hooks. Then I saw the rocks. It was like a little rock nest there on the screen over the chimney hole. Kids must have lobbed them up trying to land them in the chimney.

I picked up one of the rocks. "Ready?" I called.

He had me located in his viewfinder.

"Okay," he answered.

I turned and threw back my arm. "Now!" I called. I hooked that rock as far as I could, south.

"I don't know," I heard him say. "You moved," he said. "We'll see in a minute," and in a minute he said, "By God, it's okay." He looked at it. He held it up. "You know," he said, "it's good."

"Once more," I called. I picked up another rock. I grinned. I felt I could lift off. Fly.

"Now!" I called.

Where Is Everyone?

I'VE seen some things. I was going over to my mother's to stay a few nights, but just as I came to the top of the stairs I looked and she was on the sofa kissing a man. It was summer, the door was open, and the color TV was playing.

My mother is sixty-five and lonely. She belongs to a singles club. But even so, knowing all this, it was hard. I stood at the top of the stairs with my hand on the railing and watched as the man pulled her deeper into the kiss. She was kissing back, and the TV was going on the other side of the room. It was Sunday, about five in the afternoon. People from the apartment house were down below in the pool. I went back down the stairs and out to my car.

A lot has happened since that afternoon, and on the whole things are better now. But during those days, when my mother was putting out to men she'd just met, I was out of work, drinking, and crazy. My kids were crazy, and my wife was crazy and having a "thing" with an unemployed aerospace engineer she'd met at AA. He was crazy too. His name was Ross and he had five or six kids. He walked with a limp from a gunshot wound his first wife had given him. He didn't have a wife now; he wanted my wife. I don't know what we were all thinking of in those days. The second wife had come and gone, but it was his first wife who had shot him in the thigh some years back, giving him the limp, and who now had him in and out of court, or in jail, every six months or so for not meeting his support payments. I wish him well now. But it was different then. More than once in those days I mentioned weapons. I'd say to my wife, I'd shout it, "I'm going to kill him!" But nothing ever happened. Things lurched on. I never met the man, though we talked on the phone a few times. I did find a couple of pictures of him once when I was going through my wife's purse. He was a little guy, not too little, and he had a moustache and was wearing a striped jersey, waiting for a kid to come down the slide. In the other picture he was standing against a house—my house? I couldn't tell—with his arms crossed, dressed up, wearing a tie. Ross, you son of a bitch, I hope you're okay now. I hope things are better for you too.

The last time he'd been jailed, a month before that Sunday, I found out from my daughter that her mother had gone bail for him. Daughter Kate, who was fifteen, didn't take to this any better than I did. It wasn't that she had any loyalty to me in this—she had no loyalties to me or her mother in anything and was only too willing to sell either one of us down the river. No, it was that there was a serious cash-flow problem in the house and if money went to Ross, there'd be that much less for what she needed. So Ross was on her list now. Also, she didn't like his kids, she'd said, but she'd told me once before that in general Ross was all right, even funny and interesting when he wasn't drinking. He'd even told her fortune.

He spent his time repairing things, now that he could no longer hold a job in the aerospace industry. But I'd seen his house from the outside; and the place looked like a dumping ground, with all kinds and makes of old appliances and equipment that would never wash or cook or play again—all of it just standing in his open garage and in his drive and in the front yard. He also kept some broken-down cars around that he liked to tinker on. In the first stages of their affair my wife had told me he "collected antique cars." Those were her words. I'd seen some of his cars parked in front of his house when I'd driven by there trying to see what I could see. Old 1950s and 1960s, dented cars with torn seat covers. They were junkers, that's all. I knew. I had his number. We had things in common, more than just driving old cars and trying to hold on for dear life to the same woman. Still, handyman or not, he couldn't manage to tune my wife's car properly or fix our TV set when it broke down and we lost the picture. We had volume, but no picture. If we wanted to get the news, we'd have to sit around the screen at night and listen to the set. I'd drink and make some crack to my kids about Mr. Fixit. Even now I don't know if my wife believed that stuff or not, about antique cars and such. But she cared for him, she loved him even; that's pretty clear now.

They'd met when Cynthia was trying to stay sober and was going to meetings three or four times a week. I had been in and out of AA for several months, though when Cynthia met

Ross I was out and drinking a fifth a day of anything I could get my hands on. But as I heard Cynthia say to someone over the phone about me, I'd had the exposure to AA and knew where to go when I really wanted help. Ross had been in AA and then had gone back to drinking again. Cynthia felt, I think, that maybe there was more hope for him than for me and tried to help him and so went to the meetings to keep herself sober, then went over to cook for him or clean his house. His kids were no help to him in this regard. Nobody lifted a hand around his house except Cynthia when she was there. But the less his kids pitched in, the more he loved them. It was strange. It was the opposite with me. I hated my kids during this time. I'd be on the sofa with a glass of vodka and grapefruit juice when one of them would come in from school and slam the door. One afternoon I screamed and got into a scuffle with my son. Cynthia had to break it up when I threatened to knock him to pieces. I said I would kill him. I said, "I gave you life and I can take it away."

Madness.

The kids, Katy and Mike, were only too happy to take advantage of this crumbling situation. They seemed to thrive on the threats and bullying they inflicted on each other and on us—the violence and dismay, the general bedlam. Right now, thinking about it even from this distance, it makes me set my heart against them. I remember years before, before I turned to drinking full time, reading an extraordinary scene in a novel by an Italian named Italo Svevo. The narrator's father was dying and the family had gathered around the bed, weeping and waiting for the old man to expire, when he opened his eyes to look at each of them for a last time. When his gaze fell on the narrator he suddenly stirred and something came into his eyes; and with his last burst of strength he raised up, flung himself across the bed, and slapped the face of his son as hard as he could. Then he fell back onto the bed and died. I often imagined my own deathbed scene in those days, and I saw myself doing the same thing, only I would hope to have the strength to slap each of my kids, and my last words for them would be what only a dying man would have the courage to utter.

But they saw craziness on every side, and it suited their purpose, I was convinced. They fattened on it. They liked being able to call the shots, having the upper hand, while we bungled along letting them work on our guilt. They might have been inconvenienced from time to time, but they ran things their way. They weren't embarrassed or put out by any of the activities that went on in our house either. To the contrary. It gave them something to talk about with their friends. I've heard them regaling their pals with the most frightful stories, howling with laughter as they spilled out the lurid details of what was happening to me and their mother. Except for being financially dependent on Cynthia, who still somehow had a teaching job and a monthly paycheck, they flat out ran the show. And that's what it was too, a show.

Once Mike locked his mother out of the house after she'd stayed overnight at Ross's house. . . . I don't know where I was that night, probably at my mother's. I'd sleep over there sometimes. I'd eat supper with her and she'd tell me how she worried about all of us; then we'd watch TV and try to talk about something else, try to hold a normal conversation about something other than my family situation. She'd make a bed for me on her sofa—the same sofa she used to make love on, I supposed, but I'd sleep there anyway and be grateful. Cynthia came home at seven o'clock one morning to get dressed for school and found that Mike had locked all the doors and windows and wouldn't let her in the house. She stood outside his window and begged him to let her in—please, please, so she could dress and go to school, for if she lost her job what then? Where would he be? Where would any of us be then? He said, "You don't live here anymore. Why should I let you in?" That's what he said to her, standing behind his window, his face all stopped up with rage. (She told me this later when she was drunk and I was sober and holding her hands and letting her talk.) "You don't live here," he said.

"Please, please, please, Mike," she pleaded. "Let me in."

He let her in and she swore at him. Like that, he punched her hard on the shoulders several times—whop, whop, whop —then hit her on top of the head and generally worked her over. Finally she was able to change clothes, fix her face, and rush off to school.

All this happened not too long ago, three years about. It was something in those days.

I left my mother with the man on her sofa and drove around for a while, not wanting to go home and not wanting to sit in a bar that day either.

Sometimes Cynthia and I would talk about things—"reviewing the situation," we'd call it. But now and then on rare occasions we'd talk a little about things that bore no relation to the situation. One afternoon we were in the living room and she said, "When I was pregnant with Mike you carried me to the bathroom when I was so sick and pregnant I couldn't get out of bed. You carried me. No one else will ever do that, no one else could ever love me in that way, that much. We have that, no matter what. We've loved each other like nobody else could or ever will love the other again."

We looked at each other. Maybe we touched hands, I don't recall. Then I remembered the half-pint of whiskey or vodka or gin or scotch or tequila that I had hidden under the very sofa cushion we were sitting on (oh, happy days!) and I began to hope she might soon have to get up and move around—go to the kitchen, the bathroom, out to clean the garage.

"Maybe you could make us some coffee," I said. "A pot of coffee might be nice."

"Would you eat something? I can fix some soup."

"Maybe I could eat something, but I'll for sure drink a cup of coffee."

She went out to the kitchen. I waited until I heard her begin to run water. Then I reached under the cushion for the bottle, unscrewed the lid, and drank.

I never told these things at AA. I never said much at the meetings. I'd "pass," as they called it: when it came your turn to speak and you didn't say anything except "I'll pass tonight, thanks." But I would listen and shake my head and laugh in recognition at the awful stories I heard. Usually I was drunk when I went to those first meetings. You're scared and you need something more than cookies and instant coffee.

But those conversations touching on love or the past were rare. If we talked, we talked about business, survival, the bottom line of things. Money. Where is the money going to come from? The telephone was on the way out, the lights and gas threatened. What about Katy? She needs clothes. Her grades. That boyfriend of hers is a biker. Mike. What's going to happen to Mike? What's going to happen to us all? "My God," she'd say. But God wasn't having any of it. He'd washed his hands of us.

I wanted Mike to join the army, navy, or the coast guard. He was impossible. A dangerous character. Even Ross felt the army would be good for him, Cynthia had told me, and she hadn't liked him telling her that a bit. But I was pleased to hear this and to find out that Ross and I were in agreement on the matter. Ross went up a peg in my estimation. But it angered Cynthia because, miserable as Mike was to have around, despite his violent streak, she thought it was just a phase that would soon pass. She didn't want him in the army. But Ross told Cynthia that Mike belonged in the army where he'd learn respect and manners. He told her this after there'd been a pushing and shoving match out in his drive in the early morning hours and Mike had thrown him down on the pavement.

Ross loved Cynthia, but he also had a twenty-two-year-old girl named Beverly who was pregnant with his baby, though Ross assured Cynthia he loved her, not Beverly. They didn't even sleep together any longer, he told Cynthia, but Beverly was carrying his baby and he loved all his children, even the unborn, and he couldn't just give her the boot, could he? He wept when he told all this to Cynthia. He was drunk. (Someone was always drunk in those days.) I can imagine the scene.

Ross had graduated from California Polytechnic Institute and gone right to work at the NASA operation in Mountain View. He worked there for ten years, until it all fell in on him. I never met him, as I said, but we talked on the phone several times, about one thing and another. I called him once when I was drunk and Cynthia and I were debating some sad point or another. One of his children answered the phone and when Ross came on the line I asked him whether, if I pulled out (I had no intention of pulling out, of course; it was just harassment), he intended to support Cynthia and our kids. He said he was carving a roast, that's what he said, and they were just going to sit down and eat their dinner, he and his children. Could he call me back? I hung up. When he called, after an hour or so, I'd forgotten about the earlier call. Cynthia answered the phone and said "Yes" and then "Yes" again, and I knew it was Ross and that he was asking if I was drunk. I grabbed the phone. "Well, are you going to support them or not?" He said he was sorry for his part in all of this but, no, he guessed he couldn't support them. "So it's No, you can't support them," I said, and looked at Cynthia as if this should settle everything. He said, "Yes, it's no." But Cynthia didn't bat an eye. I figured later they'd already talked that situation over thoroughly, so it was no surprise. She already knew.

He was in his mid-thirties when he went under. I used to make fun of him when I had the chance. I called him "the weasel," after his photograph. "That's what your mother's boyfriend looks like," I'd say to my kids if they were around and we were talking, "like a weasel." We'd laugh. Or else "Mr. Fixit." That was my favorite name for him. God bless and keep you, Ross. I don't hold anything against you now. But in those days when I called him the weasel or Mr. Fixit and threatened his life, he was something of a fallen hero to my kids and to Cynthia too, I suppose, because he'd helped put men on the moon. He'd worked, I was told time and again, on the moon project shots, and he was close friends with Buzz Aldrin and Neil Armstrong. He'd told Cynthia, and Cynthia had told the kids, who'd told me, that when the astronauts came to town he was going to introduce them. But they never came to town, or if they did they forgot to contact Ross. Soon after the moon probes, fortune's wheel turned and Ross's drinking increased. He began missing work. Somewhere then the troubles with his first wife started. Toward the end he began taking the drink to work with him in a thermos. It's a modern operation out there, I've seen it—cafeteria lines, executive dining rooms, and the like, Mr. Coffees in every office. But he brought his own thermos to work, and after a while people began to know and to talk. He was laid off, or else he quit—nobody could ever give me a straight answer when I asked. He kept drinking, of course. You do that. Then he commenced working on ruined appliances and doing TV repair work and fixing cars. He was interested in astrology, auras, I Ching—that business. I don't doubt that he was bright enough and interesting and quirky, like most of our ex-friends. I told Cynthia I was sure she wouldn't care for him (I couldn't yet bring myself to use the word "love" then, about that relationship) if he wasn't, basically, a good man. "One of *us*," was how I put it, trying to be large about it. He wasn't a bad or an evil man, Ross. "No one's evil," I said once to Cynthia when we were discussing my own affair.

My dad died in his sleep, drunk, eight years ago. It was a Friday night and he was fifty-four years old. He came home from work at the sawmill, took some sausage out of the freezer for his breakfast the next morning, and sat down at the kitchen table, where he opened a quart of Four Roses. He was in good enough spirits in those days, glad to be back on a job after being out of work for three or four years with blood poisoning and then something that caused him to have shock treatments. (I was married and living in another town during that time. I had the kids and a job, enough troubles of my own, so I couldn't follow his too closely.) That night he moved into the living room with his bottle, a bowl of ice cubes and a glass, and drank and watched TV until my mother came in from work at the coffee shop.

They had a few words about the whiskey, as they always did. She didn't drink much herself. When I was grown, I only saw her drink at Thanksgiving, Christmas, and New Year's— eggnog or buttered rums, and then never too many. The one time she had had too much to drink, years before (I heard this from my dad, who laughed about it when he told it), they'd gone to a little place outside Eureka and she'd had a great many whiskey sours. Just as they got into the car to leave, she started to get sick and had to open the door. Somehow her false teeth came out, the car moved forward a little, and a tire passed over her dentures. After that she never drank except on holidays and then never to excess.

My dad kept on drinking that Friday night and tried to ignore my mother, who sat out in the kitchen and smoked and tried to write a letter to her sister in Little Rock. Finally he got up and went to bed. My mother went to bed not long after, when she was sure he was asleep. She said later she noticed nothing out of the ordinary except maybe his snoring seemed heavier and deeper and she couldn't get him to turn on his side. But she went to sleep. She woke up when my dad's sphincter muscles and bladder let go. It was just sunrise. Birds were singing. My dad was still on his back, eyes closed and mouth open. My mother looked at him and cried his name.

I kept driving around. It was dark by now. I drove by my house, every light ablaze, but Cynthia's car wasn't in the drive. I went to a bar where I sometimes drank and called home. Katy answered and said her mother wasn't there, and where was I? She needed five dollars. I shouted something and hung up. Then I called collect to a woman six hundred miles away whom I hadn't seen in months, a good woman who, the last time I'd seen her, had said she would pray for me.

She accepted the charges. She asked where I was calling from. She asked how I was. "Are you all right?" she said.

We talked. I asked about her husband. He'd been a friend of mine and was now living away from her and the children.

"He's still in Richland," she said. "How did all this happen to us?" she asked. "We started out good people." We talked a while longer, then she said she still loved me and that she would continue to pray for me.

"Pray for me," I said. "Yes." Then we said good-bye and hung up.

Later I called home again, but this time no one answered. I dialed my mother's number. She picked up the phone on the first ring, her voice cautious, as if expecting trouble.

"It's me," I said. "I'm sorry to be calling."

"No, no, honey, I was up," she said. "Where are you? Is anything the matter? I thought you were coming over today. I looked for you. Are you calling from home?"

"I'm not at home," I said. "I don't know where everyone is at home. I just called there."

"Old Ken was over here today," she went on, "that old bastard. He came over this afternoon. I haven't seen him in a month and he just shows up, the old thing. I don't like him. All he wants to do is talk about himself and brag on himself and how he lived on Guam and had three girlfriends at the same time and how he's traveled to this place and that place. He's just an old braggart, that's all he is. I met him at that dance I told you about, but I don't like him."

"Is it all right if I come over?" I said.

"Honey, why don't you? I'll fix us something to eat. I'm hungry myself. I haven't eaten anything since this afternoon. Old Ken brought some Colonel Sanders over this afternoon. Come over and I'll fix us some scrambled eggs. Do you want me to come get you? Honey, are you all right?"

I drove over. She kissed me when I came in the door. I turned my face. I hated for her to smell the vodka. The TV was on.

"Wash your hands," she said as she studied me. "It's ready."

Later she made a bed for me on the sofa. I went into the bathroom. She kept a pair of my dad's pajamas in there. I took them out of the drawer, looked at them, and began undressing. When I came out she was in the kitchen. I fixed the pillow and lay down. She finished with what she was doing, turned off the kitchen light, and sat down at the end of the sofa.

"Honey, I don't want to be the one to tell you this," she said. "It hurts me to tell you, but even the kids know it and they've told me. We've talked about it. But Cynthia is seeing another man."

"That's okay," I said. "I know that," I said and looked at the TV. "His name is Ross and he's an alcoholic. He's like me."

"Honey, you're going to have to do something for yourself," she said.

"I know it," I said. I kept looking at the TV.

She leaned over and hugged me. She held me a minute. Then she let go and wiped her eyes. "I'll get you up in the morning," she said.

"I don't have much to do tomorrow. I might sleep in awhile after you go." I thought: after you get up, after you've gone to the bathroom and gotten dressed, then I'll get into your bed and lie there and doze and listen to your radio out in the kitchen giving the news and weather.

"Honey, I'm so worried about you."

"Don't worry," I said. I shook my head.

"You get some rest now," she said. "You need to sleep."

"I'll sleep. I'm very sleepy."

"Watch television as long as you want," she said.

I nodded.

She bent and kissed me. Her lips seemed bruised and swollen. She drew the blanket over me. Then she went into her bedroom. She left the door open, and in a minute I could hear her snoring.

I lay there staring at the TV. There were images of uniformed men on the screen, a low murmur, then tanks and a man using a flamethrower. I couldn't hear it, but I didn't want to get up. I kept staring until I felt my eyes close. But I woke up with a start, the pajamas damp with sweat. A snowy light filled the room. There was a roaring coming at me. The room clamored. I lay there. I didn't move.

Gazebo

T HAT morning she pours Teacher's scotch over my belly and licks it off. In the afternoon she tries to jump out the window. I can't stand this anymore, and I tell her so. I go, "Holly, this can't continue. This is crazy. This has got to stop."

We are sitting on the sofa in one of the upstairs suites. There were any number of vacancies to choose from, but we needed a suite, a place to move around in and be able to talk. So we'd locked up the motel office that morning and gone upstairs to a suite.

She goes, "Duane, this is killing."

We are drinking Teacher's with ice and water. We'd slept awhile between morning and afternoon. Then she was out of bed and threatening to climb out the window in her undergarments. I had to get her in a hold. We were only two floors up, but even so.

"I've had it," she goes. "I can't take it anymore." She puts the back of her hand to her cheek and closes her eyes. She turns her head back and forth and makes this humming noise. I could die seeing her like this.

"Take what?" I go, though of course I know. "Holly?"

"I don't have to spell it out for you again," she goes. "I've lost self-control. I've lost my pride. I used to be a proud woman."

She's an attractive woman just past thirty. She is tall and has long black hair and green eyes, the only green-eyed woman I've ever known. In the old days I used to comment on her green eyes, and she'd tell me she knew she was meant for something special. And didn't I know it. I feel so awful from one thing and the other.

Downstairs in the office I can hear the telephone ringing again. It has been ringing off and on all day. Even when I was dozing earlier I could hear it. I'd open my eyes and look at the ceiling and listen to it ring and wonder at what was happening to us.

"My heart is broken," she goes. "It's turned to a piece of stone. I'm no longer responsible. That's what's as bad as anything, that I'm not responsible anymore. I don't even want to get up mornings. Duane, it's taken a long time to come to this decision, but we have to go our separate ways. It's over, Duane. We may as well admit it."

"Holly," I go. I reach for her hand, but she draws it away.

When we'd first moved down here and taken over as motel managers we thought we were out of the woods. Free rent and utilities plus three hundred a month, you couldn't beat it. Holly took care of the books, she was good with figures, and she did most of the renting of the units. She liked people and people liked her back. I saw to the grounds, mowed the grass and cut weeds, kept the swimming pool clean, did minor repairs. Everything was fine for the first year. I was holding down another job nights, a swing shift, and we were getting ahead, rich in plans. Then one morning, I don't know, I'd just laid some bathroom tile in one of the units when this little Mexican maid comes in to clean. Holly had hired her. I can't really say I'd noticed her before, though we spoke when we saw each other. She called me Mister. Anyway, one thing and the other, we talked. She wasn't dumb, she was cute and had a nice way about her. She liked to smile, would listen with great intent when you said something, and looked you in the eyes when she talked. After that morning I started paying attention when I'd see her. She was a neat, compact little woman with fine white teeth. I used to watch her mouth when she laughed. She started calling me by my first name. One morning I was in another unit replacing a washer for one of the bathroom faucets. She didn't know I was there. She came in and turned on the TV as maids are in the habit of doing while they clean. I stopped what I was doing and stepped outside the bathroom. She was surprised to see me. She smiled and said my name. We looked at each other. I walked over and closed the door behind her. I put my arms around her. Then we lay down on the bed.

"Holly, you're still a proud woman," I go. "You're still number one. Come on, Holly."

She shakes her head. "Something's died in me," she goes. "It took a long time for it to die, but it's dead. You've killed something, just like you'd take an ax to it. Everything is dirt now." She finishes her drink. Then she begins to cry. I make to hug her, but she gets up and goes into the bathroom.

I freshen our drinks and look out the window. Two cars with out-of-state plates are parked in front of the office. The drivers, two men, are standing in front of the office, talking. One of them finishes saying something to the other, looks around at the units and pulls his chin. A woman has her face up to the glass, hand shielding her eyes, peering inside. She tries the door. The phone begins ringing in the office.

"Even when we were making love a while ago you were thinking of her," Holly goes, as she returns from the bathroom. "Duane, this is so hurtful." She takes the drink I give her.

"Holly," I go.

"No, it's true, Duane." She walks up and down the room in her underpants and bra with the drink in her hand. "You've gone outside the marriage. It's our trust you've broken. Maybe that sounds old-fashioned to you. I don't care. Now I just feel like, I don't know what, like dirt, that's what I feel like. I'm confused. I don't have a purpose anymore. You were my purpose."

This time she lets me take her hand. I get down on my knees on the carpet and put her fingers against my temples. I love her, Christ, yes, I love her. But at that very minute too I'm thinking of Juanita, her fingers rubbing my neck that time. This is awful. I don't know what's going to happen.

I go, "Holly, honey, I love you." But I don't know what else to say or what else I can offer under the circumstances. She runs her fingers back and forth across my forehead as if she is a blind person being asked to describe my face.

In the lot someone leans on a horn, stops, starts again. Holly takes her hand away, wipes her eyes. She goes, "Fix me a drink. This one's too weak. Let them blow their horns, I don't care. I think I'll move to Nevada."

"Don't talk crazy," I go.

"I'm not talking crazy," she goes. "I just said I think I'll move to Nevada. Nothing's crazy about that. Maybe I can find someone there who'll love me. You can stay here with your Mexican maid. I think I'll move to Nevada. Either that or I'm going to kill myself."

"Holly!"

"Holly nothing," she goes. She sits on the sofa and draws

her knees up under her chin. It's getting dark outside and inside. I pull the curtain and switch on the table lamp.

"I said fix me another drink, son of a bitch," she goes. "Fuck those horn-blowers. Let them go down the street to the Travelodge. Is that where your Mexican girlfriend works now? The Travelodge? I'll bet she helps that Sleepy Bear get into his pajamas every night. Well, fix me another drink and put some scotch in it this time." She sets her lips and gives me a fierce look.

Drinking's funny. When I look back on it, all of our important decisions have been taken when we were drinking. Even when we talked about having to cut back on our drinking, we'd be sitting at the kitchen table or out at a picnic table in the park with a six-pack or a bottle of whiskey in front of us. When we decided to move down here and take this motel job, leave our town, friends and relations, everything, we sat up all night drinking and talking, weighing the pros and cons, getting drunk over it. But we used to be able to handle it. And this morning when Holly suggests we need a serious talk about our lives, the first thing I do before we lock the office and go upstairs for our talk is run to the liquor store for the Teacher's.

I pour the last of it into our glasses and add another ice cube and a little water.

Holly gets off the sofa and stretches out across the bed. She goes, "Did you make love to her in this bed, too?"

"I did not."

"Well, it doesn't matter," she goes. "Not much matters anymore, anyway. I've got to recover myself though, that much is for sure."

I don't answer. I feel wiped out. I give her the glass and sit down in the big chair. I sip my drink and think, What now?

"Duane?" she goes.

"Holly?" My fingers curl around the glass. My heart has slowed. I wait. Holly was my true love.

The thing with Juanita had gone on five days a week between the hours of ten and eleven for six weeks. At first we contrived to meet in one unit or another as she was making her rounds. I'd just walk in where she was working and shut the door behind me. But after a time that seemed risky and she adjusted her routine so that we began meeting in 22, a unit at the end of the motel that faced east, toward the mountains, whose front door couldn't be seen from the office window. We were sweet with each other, but swift. We were swift and sweet at the same time. But it was fine. It was entirely new and unexpected, that much more pleasure. Then one fine morning, Bobbi, the other maid, she walks in on us. These women worked together, but they were not friends. Like that she went to the office and told Holly. Why she'd do such a thing I couldn't understand then and still can't. Juanita was scared and ashamed. She dressed and drove home. I saw Bobbi outside a while later and sent her home too. I wound up putting the units in order myself that day. Holly kept to the office, drinking, I suspect. I stayed clear. But when I came into the apartment before I went to work she was in the bedroom with the door closed. I listened. I heard her asking the employment service for another maid. I heard her hang up the telephone. Then she began that hum. I was undone. I went on to work, but I knew there'd be a reckoning.

I think Holly and I could maybe have weathered that. Even though she was wild drunk when I got in from work that night and threw a glass at me and said awful things we could never either of us forget. I slapped her for the first time ever that night and then begged her forgiveness for slapping her and for getting involved with someone. I begged her to forgive me. There was a lot of crying and soul-searching, and more drinking; we were up most of the night. Then we went to bed exhausted and made love. It simply was not mentioned again, the business with Juanita. There'd been the outburst, and then we proceeded to act as if the other hadn't happened. So maybe she was willing to forgive me, if not to forget it, and life could go on. What we hadn't counted on was that I would find myself missing Juanita and sometimes unable to sleep nights for thinking about her. I'd lie in bed after Holly was asleep and think about Juanita's white teeth, and then I'd think about her breasts. The nipples were dark and warm to the touch and there were little hairs growing just below the nipples. She had hair under her arms as well. I must have been crazy. After a couple of weeks of this I realized I had to see her again, God help me. I called one evening from work and we arranged that

I would stop by. I went to her house that night after work. She was separated from her husband and lived in a little house with two children. I got there just after midnight. I was uncomfortable, but Juanita knew it and put me at ease right away. We drank a beer at the kitchen table. She got up and stood behind my chair and rubbed my neck and told me to relax, relax and let go. In her robe, she sat down at my feet and took my hand and began to clean under my fingernails with a little file. Then I kissed her and lifted her up, and we walked into the bedroom. In an hour or so I dressed, kissed her good-bye, and went home to the motel.

Holly knew. Two people who have been so close, you can't keep that kind of thing secret for long. Nor would you want to. You know something like that can't go on and on, something has to give. Worse, you know you're in a constant state of deception. It's no kind of life. I held on to the night job, a monkey could do that work, but things were going downhill fast at the motel. We just didn't have the heart for it any longer. I stopped cleaning the swimming pool, and it began to fill with algae so that guests couldn't use it. I didn't repair any more faucets or lay any more tile or do any touch-up painting. Even if we'd had the heart for it, there was just never enough time with one thing and the other, the drinking especially. That consumes a great deal of time and effort if you devote yourself to it fully. Holly began some very serious drinking of her own during this time. When I came in from work, whether I'd been by Juanita's or not, Holly would either be asleep and snoring, the bedroom smelling of whiskey, or else she'd be up at the kitchen table smoking her filter tip, a glass of something in front of her, eyes red and staring as I came in the door. She was not registering guests right either, charging too much or else, most often, not collecting enough. Sometimes she'd assign three people to a room with only one double bed, or else she'd put a single party in one of the suites that had a king-size bed and a sofa and charge the party for a single room only, that sort of thing. Guests complained and sometimes there were words. People would load up and go somewhere else after demanding their money back. There was a threatening letter from the motel management people. Then another letter, certified. Telephone calls. Someone was coming down from the city to look into matters. But we had stopped caring, and that's a fact. We knew things had to change, our days at the motel were numbered, a new wind was blowing—our lives fouled and ready for a shake-up. Holly's a smart woman, and I think she knew all this before I did, that the bottom had fallen out.

Then that Saturday morning we woke up with hangovers after an all-night rehashing of the situation that hadn't got us anywhere. We opened our eyes and turned in bed to look at each other. We both knew it at the same time, that we'd reached the end of something. We got up and dressed, had coffee as usual, and that's when she said we had to talk, talk now, without interruption, no phone calls, no guests. That's when I drove to the liquor store. When I came back we locked it up and went upstairs with ice, glasses, and the Teacher's. We propped up pillows and lay in bed and drank and didn't discuss anything at all. We watched color TV and frolicked and let the phone ring away downstairs. We drank scotch and ate cheese crisps from the machine down the hall. There was a funny sense of anything could happen now that we realized everything was lost. We knew without having to say it that something had ended, but what was about to begin and take its place, neither of us could think on yet. We dozed and sometime later in the day Holly raised herself off my arm. I opened my eyes at the movement. She sat up in bed. Then she screamed and rushed away from me toward the window.

"When we were just kids before we married?" Holly goes. "When we drove around every night and spent every possible minute together and talked and had big plans and hopes? Do you remember?" She was sitting in the center of the bed, holding her knees and her drink.

"I remember, Holly."

"You weren't my first boyfriend, my first boyfriend was named Wyatt and my folks didn't think much of him, but you were my first lover. You were my first lover then, and you've been my only lover since. Imagine. I didn't think I was missing that much. Now, who knows what I was missing all those years? But I was happy. Yes, I was. You were my everything, just like the song. But I don't know now what was wrong with me all those years loving just you and only you. My God, I've had the opportunities."

"I know you have," I go. "You're an attractive woman. I know you've had the opportunities."

"But I didn't take them up on it, that's the point," she goes. "I didn't. I couldn't go outside the marriage. It was beyond, beyond comprehension."

"Holly, please," I go. "No more now, honey. Let's not torture ourselves. What is it that we should do now?"

"Listen," she goes. "Do you remember that time we drove out to that old farm place outside of Yakima, out past Terrace Heights? We were just driving around, it was a Saturday, like today. We came to those orchards and then we were on a little dirt road and it was so hot and dusty. We kept going and came to that old farmhouse. We stopped and went up to the door and knocked and asked if we could have a drink of cool water. Can you imagine us doing something like that now, going up to a strange house and asking for a drink of water?"

"We'd be shot."

"Those old people must be dead now," she goes, "side by side out there in Terrace Heights cemetery. But that day the old farmer and his wife, they not only gave us a glass of water, they invited us in for cake. We talked and ate cake in the kitchen, and later they asked if they could show us around. They were so kind to us. I haven't forgotten. I appreciate kindness like that. They showed us through the house. They were so nice with each other. I still remember the inside of that house. I've dreamed about it from time to time, the inside of that house, those rooms, but I never told you those dreams. A person has to have some secrets, right? But they showed us around on the inside, those nice big rooms and their furnishings. Then they took us out back. We walked around and they pointed out that little—what did they call it? Gazebo. I'd never seen one before. It was in a field under some trees. It had a little peaked roof. But the paint was gone and weeds were growing up over the steps. The woman said that years before, before we were born even, musicians had come out there to play on Sundays. She and her husband and their friends and neighbors would sit around in their Sunday clothes and listen to music and drink lemonade. I had a flash then, I don't know what else to call it. But I looked at that woman and her husband and I thought, someday we'll be old like that. Old but dignified, you know, like they were. Still loving each other more and more, taking care of one another, grandchildren coming to visit. All those things. I remember you were wearing cutoffs that day, and I remember standing there looking at the gazebo and thinking about those musicians when I happened to glance down at your bare legs. I thought to myself, I'll love those legs even when they're old and thin and the hair on them has turned white. I'll love them even then, I thought, they'll still be *my* legs. You know what I'm saying? Duane? Then they walked with us to the car and shook hands with us. They said we were nice young people. They invited us to come back, but of course we never did. They're dead now, they'd have to be dead. But here we are. I know something now I didn't know then. Don't I know it! It's such a good thing, isn't it, a person can't look into the future? But now here we are in this awful town, a couple of people who drink too much, running a motel with a dirty old swimming pool in front of it. And you in love with someone else. Duane, I've been closer to you than to anyone on earth. I feel crucified."

I can't say anything for a minute. Then I go, "Holly, these things, we'll look back on them someday when we're old, and we will be old together, you'll see, and we'll go, 'Remember that motel with the cruddy swimming pool?' and then we'll laugh at the things we did crazy. You'll see. It'll be all right. Holly?"

But Holly sits there on the bed with her empty glass and just looks at me. Then she shakes her head. She knows.

I move over to the window and look from behind the curtain. Someone says something below and rattles the door to the office. I wait. I tighten my fingers on the glass. I pray for a sign from Holly. I pray without closing my eyes. I hear a car start. Then another. The cars turn on their lights against the building and, one after the other, pull away and out into the traffic.

"Duane," Holly goes.

In this, as in most matters, she was right.

Want to See Something?

I was in bed when I heard the gate unlatch. I listened carefully. I didn't hear anything else. But I had heard that. I tried to wake Cliff, but he was passed out. So I got up and went to the window. A big moon hung over the mountains that surrounded the city. It was a white moon and covered with scars, easy enough to imagine a face there—eye sockets, nose, even the lips. There was enough light that I could see everything in the backyard, lawn chairs, the willow tree, clotheslines strung between the poles, my petunias, and the fence enclosing the yard, the gate standing open.

But nobody was moving around outside. There were no dark shadows. Everything lay in bright moonlight, and the smallest things came to my attention. The clothespins standing in orderly rows on the line, for instance. And the two empty lawn chairs. I put my hands on the cool glass, hiding the moon, and looked some more. I listened. Then I went back to bed. But I couldn't sleep. I kept turning over. I thought about the gate standing open like an invitation. Cliff's breathing was ragged. His mouth gaped and his arms hugged his pale, bare chest. He was taking up his side of the bed and most of mine. I pushed and pushed on him. But he just groaned. I stayed in bed awhile longer until finally I decided it was no use. I got up and found my slippers. I went to the kitchen where I made a cup of tea and sat with it at the kitchen table. I smoked one of Cliff's unfiltereds. It was late. I didn't want to look at the time. I had to get up for work in a few hours. Cliff had to get up too, but he'd gone to bed hours ago and would be okay when the alarm went off. Maybe he'd have a headache. But he'd put away lots of coffee and take his time in the bathroom. Four aspirin and he'd be all right. I drank the tea and smoked another cigarette. After a while I decided I'd go out and fasten the gate. So I found my robe. Then I went to the back door. I looked and could see stars, but it was the moon that drew my attention and lighted everything—houses and trees, utility poles and power lines, the entire neighborhood. I peered around the backyard before I stepped off the porch. A little breeze came along that made me close the robe. I started toward the open gate.

There was a noise at the fence that separated our house from Sam Lawton's. I looked quickly. Sam was leaning with his arms on the fence, gazing at me. He raised a fist to his mouth and gave a dry cough.

"Evening, Nancy," he said.

I said, "Sam, you scared me. What are you doing up, Sam? Did you hear something? I heard my gate unlatch."

"I've been out here awhile, but I haven't heard anything," he said. "Haven't seen anything either. It might have been the wind. That's it. Still, if it was latched it shouldn't have come open." He was chewing something. He looked at the open gate and then he looked at me again and shrugged. His hair was silvery in the moonlight and stood up on his head. It was so light out I could see his long nose, even the deep lines in his face.

I said, "What are you doing up, Sam?" and moved closer to the fence.

"Hunting," he said. "I'm hunting. Want to see something? Come over here, Nancy, and I'll show you something."

"I'll come around," I said, and started along the side of our house to the front gate. I let myself out and went down the sidewalk. I felt strange, walking around outside in my nightgown and robe. I thought to myself that I must remember this, walking around outside in my nightgown. I could see Sam standing near the side of his house in his robe, his pajamas stopping just at the tops of his white and tan oxfords. He was holding a big flashlight in one hand and a can of something in the other. He motioned me with his light. I opened the gate.

Sam and Cliff used to be friends. Then one night they were drinking. They had an argument. The next thing, Sam had built a fence between the houses. Then Cliff decided to build his own fence. That was not long after Sam had lost Millie, remarried, and become a father again. All in the space of little more than a year. Millie, Sam's first wife, was a good friend of mine up until she died. She was only forty-five when she had heart failure. Apparently it hit her just as she turned their car into the driveway. She slumped over the wheel, the car kept going and knocked through the back of the carport. When Sam ran out of the house, he found her dead. Sometimes at night we'd hear a howling sound from over there that he must have been making. We'd look at each other when we heard that and not be able to say anything. I'd shiver. Cliff would fix himself another drink.

Sam and Millie had a daughter who'd left home at sixteen and gone to San Francisco to become a flower child. From time to time over the years she'd sent cards. But she never came back home. Sam tried but he couldn't locate her when Millie died. He wept and said he lost the daughter first and then the mother. Millie was buried, Sam howled, and then after a little while he started going out with Laurie something-or-other, a younger woman, a schoolteacher who did income tax preparations on the side. It was a brief courtship. They were both lonely and in need. So they married, and then they had a baby. But here's the sad thing. The baby was albino. I saw it a few days after they brought it home from the hospital. It was an albino, no question of that, right down to its poor little fingertips. Its eyes were tinged with pink around the iris instead of being white, and the hair on its head was as white as an old person's. Its head seemed overlarge too. But I haven't been around that many babies, so that could have been imagination on my part. The first time I saw it, Laurie was standing on the other side of its crib, arms crossed, the skin on the backs of her hands broken out, anxiety making her lips twitch. I know she was afraid I'd peep into the crib and gasp or something. But I was prepared. Cliff had already filled me in. In any case, I'm usually good at covering up my real feelings. So I reached down touched each of its tiny white cheeks and tried to smile. I said its name. I said, "Sammy." But I thought I would cry when I said it. I was prepared, but still I couldn't meet Laurie's eyes for the longest while. She stood there waiting while I silently gave thanks that this was her baby. No, I wouldn't want a baby like that for anything. I counted my blessings that Cliff and I had long ago decided against children. But according to Cliff, who's no judge, Sam's personality changed after the baby was born. He became short-tempered and impatient, mad at the world, Cliff said. Then he and Cliff had the argument, and Sam built his fence. We hadn't talked in a long while, any of us.

"Look at this," Sam said, hitching his pajamas and squatting down with the robe fanned over his knees. He pointed his light at the ground.

I looked and saw some thick white slugs curled on a bare patch of dirt.

"I just gave them a dose of this," he said, raising a can of something that looked like Ajax. But it was a bigger and heavier can than Ajax and had a skull and crossbones on the label. "Slugs are taking over," he said, working something in his mouth. He turned his head to one side and spit what could have been tobacco. "I have to keep at this nearly every night to just come close to staying up with them." He turned his light onto a glass jar that was nearly filled with the things. "I put bait out for them at night, and then every chance I get come out here with this stuff and hunt them down. Bastards are all over. Your backyard has them too, I'll bet. If mine does, yours does. It's a crime what they can do to a yard. And your flowers. Look over here," he said. He got up. He took my arm and moved me over to some rosebushes. He showed me little holes in the leaves. "Slugs," he said. "Everywhere you look around here at night, slugs. I lay out bait and then I come out and try to pick off the ones who don't eat the little banquet I've fixed up for them," he said. "An awful invention, a slug. But I save them up in that jar there, and when the jar is full and they're nice and ripe, I sprinkle them under the roses. They make good fertilizer." He moved his light slowly over the rosebush. After a minute he said, "Some life, isn't it?" and shook his head.

A plane passed overhead. I raised my eyes and saw its blinking lights and behind the lights, clear as anything in the night sky, the long white stream of its exhaust. I imagined the people on the plane as they sat belted into their seats, some of them involved in reading, some of them just staring out their windows.

I turned back to Sam. I said, "How're Laurie and Sam junior?"

"They're fine. You know," he said and shrugged. He chewed on whatever it was he was chewing. "Laurie's a good woman. The best. She's a good woman," he said again. "I don't know what I'd do if I didn't have her. I think if it wasn't for her I'd want to be with Millie, where she is. Wherever that is. I guess that's nowhere, as far as I can tell. That's my idea on the matter. Nowhere," he said. "Death is nowhere, Nancy. You can quote me if you want." He spat again. "Sammy's sick.

You know he gets these colds. Hard for him to shake them. She's taking him to the doctor again tomorrow. How're you folks? How's Clifford?"

I said, "He's fine. Same as ever. Same old Cliff." I didn't know what else to say. I looked at the rosebush once more. "He's asleep now," I said.

"Sometimes when I'm out here after these damn slugs, I'll glance over the fence in your direction," he said. "Once—," he stopped and laughed quietly. "Excuse me, Nancy, but it strikes me kind of funny now. But once I looked over the fence and saw Cliff out there in your backyard, peeing onto those petunias. I started to say something, make a little joke of some kind. But I didn't. From the looks of things, I think he'd been drinking so I didn't know how he'd take it, if I'd said anything. He didn't see me. So I just kept quiet. I'm sorry Cliff and me had that falling out," he said.

I nodded slowly. "I think he is too, Sam." After a minute I said, "You and he were friends." But the picture of Cliff standing unzipped over the petunias stayed in my head. I closed my eyes and tried to get rid of it.

"That's true, we were good friends," Sam said. Then he went on. "I come out here nights after Laurie and the baby are asleep. Gives me something to do, is one thing. You folks are asleep. Everybody's asleep. I don't sleep good anymore. And what I'm doing is worth doing, I believe that. Look there now," he said and drew a sharp breath. "There's one there. See him? Right there where my light is." He had the beam directed onto the dirt under the rosebush. Then I saw the slug move. "You watch this," Sam said.

I closed my arms under my breasts and bent over where he was shining his light. The slug stopped and turned its blind head from side to side. Then Sam was over it with the can, sprinkling, sprinkling. "Goddamn these slimy things," he said. "God, I hate them." The slug began to writhe and twist this way and that. Then it curled and then it straightened out. It curled again and lay still. Sam picked up a toy shovel. He scooped the slug into that. He held the jar away from him, unscrewed the lid, and dropped the slug into the jar. He fastened the lid once more and set the jar on the ground.

"I quit drinking," Sam said. "I didn't exactly quit, I just cut way back. Had to. For a while it was getting so I didn't know up from down. We keep it around the house still, but I don't have much to do with it anymore."

I nodded. He looked at me and he kept looking. I had the feeling he was waiting for me to say something. But I didn't say anything. What was there to say? Nothing. "I'd better get back," I said.

"Sure," he said. "Well, I'll continue with what I'm doing awhile longer, and then I'll head in too."

I said, "Good night, Sam."

"Good night, Nancy," he said. "Listen." He stopped chewing, and with his tongue pushed whatever it was behind his lower lip. "Tell old Cliff I said hello."

I said, "I will. I'll tell him you said hello, Sam."

He nodded. He ran his hand through his silvery hair as if he were going to make it lay down for once. "'Night, Nancy."

I went back to the front of the house and down the sidewalk. I stopped for a minute with my hand on our gate and looked around the still neighborhood. I don't know why, but I suddenly felt a long way away from everybody I had known and loved when I was a girl. I missed people. For a minute I stood there and wished I could get back to that time. Then with my next thought I understood clearly I couldn't do that. No. But it came to me then that my life did not remotely resemble the life I thought I'd have when I had been young and looking ahead to things. I couldn't remember now what I'd wanted to do with my life in those years, but like everybody else I'd had plans. Cliff was somebody who had plans too, and that's how we'd met and why we'd stayed together.

I went in and turned off all the lights. In the bedroom I took off the robe, folded it, put it within reach so I could get to it after the alarm went off. Without looking at the time, I checked again to make sure the stem was out on the clock. Then I got into bed, pulled the covers up, and closed my eyes. Cliff started to snore. I poked him, but it didn't do any good. He kept on. I listened to his snores. Then I remembered I'd forgotten to latch the gate. Finally I opened my eyes and just lay there, letting my eyes move around over things in the room. After a time I turned on my side and put an arm over Cliff's waist. I gave him a little shake. He stopped snoring for a minute. Then he cleared his throat. He swallowed. Something caught and rattled in his chest. He sighed heavily, then started up again, snoring.

I said, "Cliff," and shook him, hard. "Cliff, listen to me." He moaned. A shudder went through him. For a minute he seemed to have stopped breathing, to be down at the bottom of something. Of their own accord, my fingers dug into the soft flesh over his hip. I held my own breath, waiting for his to start again. There was a space and then his breathing, deep and regular once more. I brought my hand up to his chest. It lay there, fingers spread, then beginning to tap, as if thinking what to do next. "Cliff?" I said again. "Cliff." I put my hand to his throat. I found the pulse. Then I cupped his stubbled chin and felt the warm breath on the back of my hand. I looked closely at his face and began to trace his features with the tips of my fingers. I touched his heavy closed eyelids. I stroked the lines in his forehead.

I said, "Cliff, listen to me, honey." I started out everything I was going to say to him by saying I loved him. I told him I had always loved him and always would love him. Those were things that needed saying before the other things. Then I began to talk. It didn't matter that he was someplace else and couldn't hear any of what I was saying. Besides, in mid-sentence it occurred to me he already knew everything I was saying, maybe better than I knew, and had for a long time. When I thought that, I stopped talking for a minute and looked at him with new regard. Nevertheless, I wanted to finish what I'd started. I went on telling him, without rancor or heat of any sort, everything that was on my mind. I wound up by saying it out, the worst and last of it, that I felt we were going nowhere fast, and it was time to admit it, even though there was maybe no help for it.

Just so many words, you might think. But I felt better for having said them. And so I wiped the tears off my cheeks and lay back down. Cliff's breathing seemed normal, though loud to the point I couldn't hear my own. I thought for a minute of the world outside my house, and then I didn't have any more thoughts except I thought maybe I could sleep.

The Fling

IT'S October, a damp day outside. From my hotel room window I can look out and see much of this gray midwestern city; just now, lights are coming on here and there in some of the buildings, and smoke from the tall stacks at the edge of town is rising in a slow thick climb into the darkening sky. Except for a branch of the university campus located here—a poor relation, really—there isn't much to recommend the place.

I want to relate a story my father told me last year when I stopped over briefly in Sacramento. It concerns some sordid events that he was involved in nearly two years before that, before he and my mother were divorced. It could be asked that if it is important enough to warrant the telling—my time and energy, your time and energy—then why haven't I told it before this? I'd have no answer for that. In the first place, I don't know if it is that important—at least to anyone except my father and the others involved. Secondly, and perhaps more to the point, what business is it of mine? That question is more difficult to answer. I admit I feel that I acted badly that day with regard to my father, that I perhaps failed him at a time when I could have helped. Yet something else tells me that he was beyond help, beyond anything I could do for him, and that the only thing that transpired between us in those few hours was that he caused me—*forced* might be the better word —to peer into my own abyss; and nothing comes of nothing as Pearl Bailey says, and we all know from experience.

I'm a book salesman representing a well-known midwestern textbook firm. My home base is Chicago, my territory Illinois, parts of Iowa and Wisconsin. I had been attending the Western Book Publishers Association convention out in Los Angeles when it occurred to me, sheerly on the spur of the moment, to visit a few hours with my father on my way back to Chicago. I hesitated because, since his divorce, there was a very large part of me that didn't want to see him again, but before I could change my mind, I fished his address out of my wallet and proceeded to send him a telegram. The next morning I sent my things on to Chicago and boarded a plane for Sacramento.

The sky was slightly overcast; it was a cool, damp September morning.

It took me a minute to pick him out. He was standing a few steps behind the gate when I saw him, white hair, glasses, brown Sta-Prest cotton pants, a gray nylon jacket over a white shirt open at the throat. He was staring at me, and I realized he must have had me in view since I stepped off the plane.

"Dad, how are you?"

"Les."

We shook hands quickly and began to move toward the terminal.

"How's Mary and the kids?"

I looked at him closely before answering. Of course, he didn't know we'd been living apart for nearly six months. "Everyone's fine," I answered.

He opened a white confectionery sack. "I picked them up a little something, maybe you could take it back with you. Not much. Some Almond Roca for Mary, a Cootie game for Ed, and a Barbie doll. Jean'll like that, won't she?"

"Sure she will."

"Don't forget this when you leave."

I nodded. We moved out of the way as a group of nuns, flushed and talking excitedly, headed for the boarding area. He'd aged. "Well, shall we have a drink or a cup of coffee?"

"Anything you say. I don't have a car," he apologized. "Really don't need one around here. I had a cab bring me out."

"We don't have to go anyplace. Let's go to the bar and have a drink. It's early, but I could use a drink."

We located the lounge and I waved him into a booth while I went over to the bar. My mouth was dry and I asked for a glass of orange juice while I waited. I looked over at my father; his hands were clasped together on the table and he gazed out the tinted window that overlooked the field. A large plane was taking passengers and another was landing farther out. A woman in her late thirties, red hair, wearing a white knit suit, was sitting between two well-dressed younger men a few stools down. One of the men was close to her ear, telling her something.

"Here we are, Dad. Cheers." He nodded and we each took a long drink and then lighted cigarettes. "Well, how're you getting along?"

He shrugged and opened his hands. "So-so."

I leaned back in the seat and drew a long breath. He had an air of woe about him that I couldn't help but find a little irritating.

"I guess the Chicago airport would make three or four of this one," he said.

"More than that."

"Thought it was big."

"When did you start wearing glasses?"

"Not long ago. A few months."

After a minute or two I said, "I think it's time for another one." The bartender looked our way and I nodded. This time a slender pleasant girl in a red and black dress came to take our order. All the stools at the bar were taken now, and there were a few men in business suits sitting at the tables in the booths. A fishnet hung from the ceiling with a number of colored Japanese floats tossed inside. Petula Clark was singing "Downtown" from the jukebox. I remembered again that my father was living alone, working nights as a lathe operator in a machine shop, and it all seemed impossible. Suddenly the woman at the bar laughed loudly and leaned back on her stool, holding onto the sleeves of the men who sat on either side of her. The girl came back with the drinks, and this time my father and I clinked glasses.

"I liked to have died over it myself," he said slowly. His arms rested heavily on either side of his glass. "You're an educated man, Les. Maybe you can understand."

I nodded slightly, not meeting his eyes, and waited for him to go on. He began to talk in a low monotonous drone that annoyed me immediately. I turned the ashtray on its edge to read what was on the bottom: HARRAH'S CLUB RENO AND LAKE TAHOE. Good places to have fun.

"She was a Stanley products woman. A little woman, small feet and hands and coal black hair. She wasn't the most beautiful woman in the world, but she had nice ways about her. She was thirty years old and had kids but, but she was a decent woman, whatever happened.

"Your mother was always buying something from her, a broom or a mop, some kind of pie filling, you know your mother. It was a Saturday, and I was home alone and your mother was gone someplace. I don't know where she was. She wasn't working. I was in the front room reading the paper and drinking a cup of coffee, just taking it easy. There was a knock on the door and it was this little woman, Sally Wain. She said she had some things for my wife, Mrs. Palmer. 'I'm Mr. Palmer,' I said. 'Mrs. Palmer is not here right now.' I asked her just to step in, you know, and I'd pay her for the things. She didn't know whether she should or not, just stood there a minute holding this little paper sack and the receipt with it.

"'Here, I'll take that,' I said. 'Why don't you come in and sit down a minute till I see if I can find some money.'

"'That's all right,' she said. 'You can owe it. I can pick it up anytime. I have lots of people do that; it's all right.' She smiled to let me know it was all right.

"'No, no,' I said. 'I've got it, I'd rather pay it now. Save you a trip back and save me owing another bill. Come in,' I said again, and held open the screen door. 'It isn't polite to have you standing out there.' It was around eleven or twelve o'clock in the morning."

He coughed and took one of my cigarettes from the pack on the table. The woman at the bar laughed again, and I looked over at her and then back at my father.

"She stepped in then and I said, 'Just a minute, please,' and went into the bedroom to look for my wallet. I looked around on the dresser but couldn't find it. I found some change and matches, and my comb, but I couldn't find my wallet. Your mother had gone through that morning cleaning up. I went back to the front room and said, 'Well, I'll turn up some money yet.'

"'Please don't bother,' she said.

"'No bother,' I answered. 'Have to find my wallet, anyway. Make yourself at home.'

"'Look here,' I said, stopping by the kitchen door. 'You hear about that big holdup back east?' I pointed to the newspaper. 'I was just reading about it.'

"'I saw it on television last night,' she said. 'They had pictures and interviewed the cops.'

"'They got away clean,' I said.

"'Pretty slick of them, wasn't it?' she said.

"'I think everybody at some time or another dreams about pulling the perfect crime, don't they?'

"'But not many people get away with it,' she said. She picked up the paper. There was a picture of an armored car on the front page and the headlines said something like million-dollar robbery, something like that. You remember that, Les? When those guys dressed up as policemen?

"I didn't know what else to say, we were just standing there looking at each other. I turned and went on out to the porch and looked for my pants in the hamper where I figured your mother had put them. I found the wallet in my back pocket and went back to the other room and asked how much I owed.

"'We can do business now,' I said.

"It was three or four dollars, and I paid her. Then, I don't know why, I asked her what she'd do with it if she had it, all the money those guys got away with.

"She laughed out loud at that and showed her teeth.

"I don't know what came over me then, Les. Fifty-five years old. Grown kids. I knew better than that. This woman was barely half my age with little kids in school. She did this Stanley job just the hours they were in school, just to give her something to do. She got a little spending money from it, naturally, but mainly it was just to keep occupied. She didn't have to work. They had enough to get by on. Her husband, Larry, he, he was a driver for Consolidated Freight. Made good money. Teamster, you know. He made enough for them to live on without her having to work. It wasn't a have-to case."

He stopped and wiped his face. "I want to try and make you understand."

"You don't have to say any more," I said. "I'm not asking you anything. Anybody can make a mistake. I understand."

He shook his head. "I have to tell somebody this, Les. I haven't told this to anybody, but I want to tell you this and I want you to understand."

"She had two boys, Stan and Freddy. They were in school, about a year apart. I never met them, thank God, but later on she showed me some pictures of them. She laughed when I said that about the money, said she guessed she'd quit selling Stanley products, and they'd move to San Diego and buy a house there. She had relatives in San Diego, and if they had that much money, she said, they'd move down there and open a sporting goods store. That's what they'd always talked about doing, opening a sporting goods store, if they ever got enough ahead."

I lit another cigarette, glanced at my watch, and crossed and recrossed my legs under the table. The bartender looked over at us, and I raised my glass. He motioned to the girl who was taking an order at another table.

"She was sitting down on the couch now, more relaxed and just skimming the newspaper, when she looked up and asked if I had a cigarette. Said she'd left hers in her other purse, and she hadn't had a smoke since she left her house. Said she hated to buy from a machine when she had a carton at home. I gave her a cigarette and I held a match for her, but my fingers were shaking."

He stopped again and looked at the table for a minute. The woman at the bar had her arms locked through the arms of the man on each side of her, and the three of them were singing along with the music from the jukebox: *That summer wind, came blowin' in, a-cross the sea.* I ran my fingers up and down the glass and waited sadly for him to go on.

"It's kind of fuzzy after that. I remember I asked her if she wanted any coffee. Said I'd just made a fresh pot, but she said she had to be going, though maybe she had time for one cup. We never mentioned your mother the whole time, either of us, the fact she may just walk in any minute. I went out to the kitchen and waited for the coffee to heat, and by that time I had a case of the nerves so that the cups rattled when I brought them in . . . I'll tell you, Les, I'll swear before God, I never once stepped out on your mother the whole time we were married. Not once. Maybe there were times when I felt like it, or that I had the chance . . . You don't know your mother like I do. Sometimes she was, she could be—"

"That's enough of that," I said. "You don't have to say another word in that direction."

"I didn't mean anything by that. I loved your mother. You don't know. I just wanted you to try and understand . . . I brought in the coffee, and Sally'd taken off her coat by then. I sat down on the other end of the couch from her and we got to talking more personal. She said she had two kids in Roosevelt grade school, and Larry, he was a driver and was sometimes gone for a week or two at a time. Up to Seattle, or down to Los Angeles, or else to Phoenix, Arizona. Always someplace. Pretty soon we just began to feel good talking with one another, you know, and enjoying just sitting there talking. She said her mother and father were both dead and she'd been raised by an aunt there in Redding. She'd met Larry when they were both going to high school, and they'd gotten married, but she was proud of the fact she'd gone on to school till she finished. But pretty soon she gave a little laugh at something I'd said that could maybe be taken two ways, and she kept laughing, and then she asked if I'd heard the one about the traveling shoe salesman who called on the widow woman. We laughed quite a bit after she told that one, and then I told her one a little worse, and she giggled at that, and then smoked another cigarette. One thing was leading to another, and pretty soon I'd eased over beside her.

"I'm ashamed telling you this, my own flesh and blood, but I kissed her then. I guess I was clumsy and awkward, but I put her head back on the couch and kissed her, and I felt her tongue touch my lips. I don't, don't know quite how to say this, Les, but I raped her. I don't mean raped her against her will, nothing like that, but I raped her all the same, fumbling and pulling at her like a fifteen-year-old kid. She didn't encourage me, if you know what I mean, but she didn't do anything to stop me either . . . I don't know, a man can just go along, go along, obeying all the rules and then, then all of a sudden . . .

"But it was all over in a minute or two. She got up and straightened her clothes and looked embarrassed. I didn't really know what to do and I went out to the kitchen and got more coffee for us. When I came back in she had her coat on and was ready to leave. I put the coffee down and went over and squeezed her.

"She said, 'You must think I'm a whore or something.' Something like that, and looked down at her shoes. I squeezed her again and said, 'You know that isn't true.'

"Well, she left. We didn't say good-bye or see you later. She just turned and slipped out the door and I watched her get into her car down the block and drive off.

"I was all excited and mixed up. I straightened things around the couch and turned over the cushions, folded all the newspapers and even washed the two cups we'd used, and cleaned out the coffee pot. All the time I was thinking about how I was going to face your mother. I knew I had to get out for a while and have a chance to think. I went down to Kelly's and stayed there all afternoon drinking beer.

"That was the way it started. After that, nothing happened for two or three weeks. Your mother and I got along the same as always, and after the first two or three days I stopped thinking about the other. I mean, I remembered everything all right—how could I forget it?—I just stopped thinking about any of it. Then one Saturday I was out working on the lawn mower in the front yard when I saw her stop on the other side of the street. She got out of the car with a mop and a couple or three little paper bags in her hand, making a delivery. Now your mother was right in the house where she could see everything, if she just happened to look out the window, but I knew I had to have a chance to say something to Sally. I watched, and when she came out of the house across the street I sauntered over as ordinary-looking as I could, carrying a screwdriver and a pair of pliers in my hand like I might have some kind of legitimate business with her. When I walked up to the side of the car she was already inside and had to lean over and roll the window down. I said, 'Hello, Sally, how's everything?'

" 'All right,' she said.

" 'I'd like to see you again,' I said.

"She just looked at me. Not mad-like, or anything, just looked at me straight and even and kept her hands on the wheel.

" 'Like to see you,' I said again, and my mouth was thick. 'Sally.'

"She pulled her lip between her teeth and then let go and said, 'You want to come tonight? Larry's gone out of town to Salem, Oregon. We could have a beer.'

"I nodded and took a step back from the car. 'After nine o'clock,' she added. 'I'll leave the light on.'

"I nodded again, and she started up and pulled away, dragging the clutch. I walked back across the street, and my legs were weak."

Over near the bar a lean, dark man in a red shirt began to play the accordion. It was a Latin number and he played with feeling, rocking the big instrument back and forth in his arms, sometimes lifting his leg and rolling it over his thigh. The woman sat with her back to the bar and listened, holding a drink. She listened to him and watched him play and began to move back and forth on her stool in time with the music.

"Some live music," I said to distract my father, who merely glanced in that direction then finished his drink.

Suddenly the woman slid down off the stool, took a few steps toward the center of the floor, and commenced to dance. She tossed her head from side to side and snapped her fingers on both hands as her heels hit the floor. Everyone in the place watched her dance. The bartender stopped mixing drinks. People began to look in from outside and soon a little crowd had collected at the door to watch, and still she danced. I think people were at first fascinated, but a little horrified and embarrassed for her, too. I was, anyway. At one point her long red hair pulled loose and fell down her back, but she only cried out and stamped her heels faster and faster. She raised her arms above her head and began to snap her fingers and move about in a small circle in the middle of the floor. She was surrounded by men now, but above their heads I could see her hands and her white fingers, snapping. Then, with a last staccato stamping of her heels and a final yip, it was finished. The music stopped, the woman cast her head forward, hair flinging out over her face, and dropped to one knee. The accordion player led the applause, and the men nearest her backed away to give her room. She stayed there on the floor a minute, head bowed, taking long breaths, before she got to her feet. She seemed dazed. She licked the hair that clung to her lips and looked around at the faces. Men continued to applaud. She smiled and nodded slowly and formally, turning slowly until she had taken in everyone. Then she made her way back to the bar and picked up her drink.

"Did you see that?" I asked.

"I saw it."

He couldn't have appeared less interested. For a moment he seemed utterly contemptible to me, and I had to look away. I knew I was being silly, that I'd be gone in another hour, but it was all I could do to keep from telling him then what I thought of his dirty affair, and what it had done to my mother.

The jukebox started in the middle of a record. The woman sat at the bar still, only leaning on her elbow now, staring at herself in the mirror. There were three drinks in front of her, and one of the men, the one who had been talking to her earlier, had moved off, down toward the end of the bar. The other man had the flat of his hand against the lower part of her back. I drew a long breath, put a smile on my lips, and turned to my father.

"So that's the way it went for a while," he started in again. "Larry had a pretty regular schedule, and I'd find myself over there every night I had the chance. I'd tell your mother I was going to the Elks, or else I told her I had some work to finish up at the shop. Anything, anything to be gone a few hours.

"The first time, that same night, I parked the car three or four blocks away and walked up the street and then right on past her house. I walked with my hands in my coat and at a good pace and walked right on by her house, trying to get my nerve up. She had the porch light on all right, and all the shades pulled. I walked to the end of the block and then came back, slower, and walked up the sidewalk to her door. I know if I'd found Larry there to answer the door, that'd been the end of that. I'd have said I was looking for directions and gone on. And never come back. My heart was pounding in my ears. Just before I rang the bell, I worked the wedding ring off my finger and dropped it in my pocket. I guess, I guess right then, that minute on the porch before she opened the door, that was the only time I considered, I mean really considered, what I was doing to your mother. Just in that minute before Sally opened the door, I knew for a minute what I was doing, and that what I was doing was dead wrong.

"But I did it, and I must have been crazy! I must have been crazy all along, Les, and didn't know it, just laying in wait for me. Why? Why'd I do it? An old bastard like me with grown kids. Why'd she do it? That son-of-a-bitching slut!" He set his jaws and brooded for a minute. "No, I don't mean that. I was crazy about her, I admit it . . . I was even over there days when I had the chance. When I knew Larry'd be gone, I'd slip out of the shop in the afternoon and beat it over there. Her kids were always in school. Thank God for that, I never bumped into them. It'd be a lot harder now if I had . . . But that first time, that was the hardest time of all.

"We were both pretty nervous. We sat up for a long time in the kitchen drinking beer, and she began to tell me a lot about herself, secret thoughts, she called them. I began to relax and feel more at ease too, and I found myself telling her things. About you, for instance; you working and saving your money and going to school and then going back to Chicago to live. She said she'd been to Chicago on a train when she was a little girl. I told her about what I'd done with my life—not very much until then, I said. And I told her some of the things I still wanted to do, things that I still planned on doing. She made me feel that way when I was around her, like I didn't have it all behind me. I told her I wasn't too old to still have plans. 'People need plans,' she said. 'You have to have plans. When I get too old to make plans and look forward to something, that's when they can come and put me away.' That's what she said, and more, and I began to think I loved her. We sat there talking about everything under the sun for I don't know how long, before I put my arms around her."

He took off his glasses and shut his eyes for a minute. "I haven't talked about this to anybody. I know I'm probably getting a little tight, and I don't want any more to drink, but I've got to tell this to somebody. I can't keep it in any longer. So, so if I'm bothering you with all this you'll just have to, you'll just have to please oblige me by listening a little longer."

I didn't answer. I looked out at the field, then looked at my watch.

"Listen!—What time does your plane leave? Can you take a later one? Let me buy us another drink, Les. Order us two more. I'll speed it up, I'll be through with this in a minute. You don't know how much I need to get some of this off my chest. Listen.

"She kept his picture in the bedroom right by the bed . . . I want to tell it all, Les . . . First it bothered me, seeing his picture there as we climbed into bed, the last thing I saw before she turned out the light. But that was just the first few times. After a while I got used to having it there. I mean, I liked it, him smiling over at us, nice and quiet, as we got into his bed. I almost got to looking forward to it, and would have missed it if it hadn't been there. Got to where I was even liking to do it best in the afternoons, because there was always plenty of light then, and I could look over and see him whenever I wanted."

He shook his head and it seemed to wobble a little. "Hard to believe, isn't it? Don't hardly recognize your father anymore, do you? . . . Well, it all came to a bad end. You know that. Your mother left me, as she had every right to do. You know all that. She said, said she couldn't bear to look at me anymore. But even that's not so important."

"What do you mean," I said, "that's not important?"

"I'll tell you, Les. I'll tell you what's the most important thing here involved. You see there are things, things far more important than that. More important than your mother's leaving me. That's, in the long run, that's nothing . . . We were in bed one night. It must have been around eleven o'clock because I always made it a point to be home before midnight. The kids were asleep. We were just laying there in bed talking, Sally and me, my arm around her waist. I was kind of dozing, I guess, listening to her talk. It was pleasant just dozing and kind of half listening. At the same time, I was awake and I remember thinking that pretty soon I'd have to get up and go on home, when a car pulled into the driveway and somebody got out and slammed the door.

" 'My God,' she screams, 'it's Larry!' I jumped out of bed and was still in the hallway trying to get my clothes on when I heard him come onto the porch and open the door. I must have gone crazy. I seem to remember thinking that if I ran out the back door he'd pin me up against that big fence in the backyard and maybe kill me. Sally was making a funny kind of sound. Like she couldn't get her breath. She had her robe on but it was undone, and she stood in the kitchen shaking her head back and forth. All this was happening all at once. There I was, half naked with all my clothes in my hand, and Larry was opening the front door. I jumped. I jumped right into their big front-room window, right through the glass. I landed in some bushes, jumped up with the glass still falling off me, and started off running down the street."

You crazier than hell old son of a bitch, you. It was grotesque.

The whole story was insane. It would have been ludicrous, all of it, if it hadn't been for my mother. I looked at him steadily for a minute, but he didn't meet my eyes.

"You got away, though? He didn't come after you, or anything?"

He didn't answer, just stared at the empty glass in front of him, and I looked at my watch again. I stretched. I had a small insistent ache behind my eyes. "I guess I'd better be getting out there soon." I ran my hand over my chin and straightened my collar. "I guess that's all there is to it, huh? You and mother split up then, and you moved down here to Sacramento. She's still in Redding. Isn't that about it?"

"No, that's not exactly right. I mean, that's true, yes, yes, but—" He raised his voice. "You don't know anything, do you? You don't really know anything. You're thirty-two years old, but, but you don't know anything except how to sell books." He glared at me. Behind his glasses his eyes looked red and tiny and far away. I just sat there and didn't feel anything one way or the other. It was almost time to go. "No. No, that's not all . . . I'm sorry. I'll tell you what else happened. If, if he'd just beat her up or something, or else come after me, come looking for me at my home. Anything. I deserved it, whatever he had to dish out . . . But he didn't. He didn't do anything like that. I guess, guess he just broke up and went all to pieces. He just . . . went to pieces. He lay down on the couch and cried. She stayed out in the kitchen, and she cried too, got down on her knees and prayed to God out loud and said she was sorry, sorry, but after a while she heard the door close and came back out to the living room and he was gone. He didn't take the car, that was still there in the driveway. He walked. He walked downtown and rented a room there at the Jefferson, down on Third. He got hold of a paring knife at some all-night drugstore and went up to his room and began, began sticking it in his stomach, trying to kill himself . . . Somebody tried to get in there a couple of days later and he was still alive, and there were thirty or forty of those little knife wounds in him and blood all over the room, but he was still alive. He'd cut his guts all to pieces, the doctor said. He died up in the hospital a day or two later. The doctors said there was nothing they could do for him. He just died, never opened his mouth or asked for anybody. Just died and with his insides all cut to pieces.

"I feel like, Les, that I died up there. Part of me did. Your mother was right in leaving me. She should've left me. But they shouldn't have had to bury Larry Wain! I don't want to die, Les, it isn't that. I guess if you'd get right down to it, I'd rather it was him under the ground and not me. If there was a choice had to be made . . . I don't know what any of it's all about, life and death, those things. I believe you only have one life and that's that; but, but it's hard to walk around with that other on my conscience. It keeps coming back to me, I mean, and I can't get it out of my head that he should be dead for something I caused."

He started to say something else, but shook his head. Then he leaned forward slightly across the table, lips parted still, trying to find my eyes. He wanted something. He was trying to involve me in it someway, all right, but it was more than that, he wanted something else. An answer, maybe, when there were no answers. Maybe simply a gesture on my part, a touch on the arm, perhaps. Maybe that would have been enough.

I loosened my collar and wiped my forehead with my wrist. I cleared my throat, still unable to meet his eyes. I felt a shaky, irrational fear begin to work through me, and the pain behind my eyes grew stronger. He kept staring at me until I began to squirm, until we both realized I had nothing to give him, nothing to give to anyone for that matter. I was all smooth surface with nothing inside except emptiness. I was shocked. I blinked my eyes once or twice. My fingers trembled as I lighted a cigarette, but I took care not to let him notice.

"Maybe you think it isn't the right thing for me to say, but I think there must have been something wrong with the man to begin with. To do something like that just because his wife was chippying around. I mean, a man would have to be half crazy to begin with to do something like that . . . But you don't understand."

"I know it's terrible, having it on your conscience, but you can't go on blaming yourself forever."

"Forever." He looked around. "How long is that?"

We sat there for a few minutes longer without saying anything. We'd finished our drinks long ago, and the girl hadn't come back.

"You want another one?" I said. "I'm buying."

"You got time for another?" he asked, looking at me closely. Then: "No. No, I don't think we'd better. You've got a plane to catch."

We got up from the booth. I helped him into his coat and we started out, my hand guiding his elbow. The bartender looked at us and said, "Thanks, fellas." I waved. My arm felt stiff.

"Let's get a breath of air," I said. We walked down the stairs and outside and squinted in the bright afternoon glare. The sun had just gone behind some clouds and we stood outside the door and didn't say anything. People kept brushing past us. All of them seemed in a hurry except one man in jeans who carried a leather overnight kit and walked past us with a bloody nose. The handkerchief he held to his face appeared stiff with blood and he looked at us as he passed. A Negro cabbie asked if he could take us somewhere.

"I'll put you in a cab, Dad, and send you home. What's your address?"

"No, no," he said and took an unsteady step back from the curb. "I'll see you off."

"That's all right. I think it'd be better if we said good-bye here, out here in front. I don't like good-byes anyway. You know how that goes," I added.

We shook hands. "Don't worry about anything, that's the important thing right now. None of us, none of us is perfect. Just get back on your feet and don't worry."

I don't know if he heard me. He didn't answer anyway. The cabbie opened the rear door and then turned to me and said, "Where to?"

"He's okay. He can tell you."

The cabbie shrugged and shut the door and walked around to the front.

"Take it easy now and write, will you, Dad?" He nodded. "Take care of yourself," I finished. He looked back at me out of the window as the cab pulled away, and that was the last I've seen of him. Halfway to Chicago, I remembered I'd left his sack of gifts in the lounge.

He hasn't written, I haven't heard from him since then. I'd write to him and see how he's getting along, but I'm afraid I've lost his address. But, tell me, after all, what could he expect from someone like me?

A Small, Good Thing

SATURDAY afternoon she drove to the little bakery in the shopping center. After looking through a loose-leaf binder with photographs of cakes taped onto the pages, she ordered chocolate, his favorite. The cake she chose was decorated with a spaceship and launching pad under a sprinkling of white stars at one end of the cake, and a planet made of red frosting at the other end. His name, SCOTTY, would be in raised green letters beneath the planet. The baker, who was an older man with a thick neck, listened without saying anything when she told him Scotty would be eight years old next Monday. The baker wore a white apron that looked like a smock. Straps cut under his arms, went around in back and then back in front again where they were secured under his big waist. He wiped his hands on the front of the apron as he listened to her. He kept his eyes down on the photographs and let her talk. He let her take her time. He'd just come to work and he'd be there all night, baking, and he was in no real hurry.

She decided on the space cake, and then gave the baker her name, Ann Weiss, and her telephone number. The cake would be ready on Monday morning, just out of the oven, in plenty of time for Scotty's party that afternoon. The baker was not jolly. There were no pleasantries between them, just the minimum exchange of words, the necessary information. He made her feel uncomfortable, and she didn't like that. While he was bent over the counter with the pencil in his hand, she studied his coarse features and wondered if he'd ever done anything else with his life besides be a baker. She was a mother and thirty-three years old, and it seemed to her that everyone, especially someone the baker's age—a man old enough to be her father—must have children who'd gone through this special time of cakes and birthday parties. There must be that between them, she thought. But he was abrupt with her, not rude, just abrupt. She gave up trying to make friends with him. She looked into the back of the bakery and could see a long, heavy wooden table with aluminum pie pans stacked at one end, and beside the table a metal container filled with empty racks. There was an enormous oven. A radio was playing country-western music.

The baker finished printing the information on the special-order card and closed up the binder. He looked at her and said, "Monday morning." She thanked him and drove home.

On Monday afternoon, Scotty was walking home from school with a friend. They were passing a bag of potato chips back and forth and Scotty was trying to find out what his friend was giving him for his birthday that afternoon. Without looking, he stepped off the curb at an intersection and was immediately knocked down by a car. He fell on his side with his head in the gutter and his legs out in the road. His eyes were closed, but his legs began to move back and forth as if he were trying to climb over something. His friend dropped the potato chips and started to cry. The car had gone a hundred feet or so and stopped in the middle of the road. A man in the driver's seat looked back over his shoulder. He waited until the boy got unsteadily to his feet. They boy wobbled a little. He looked dazed, but okay. The driver put the car into gear and drove away.

Scotty didn't cry, but he didn't have anything to say about anything, either. He wouldn't answer when his friend asked him what it felt like to be hit by a car. He walked straight to his front door, where his friend left him and ran home. But after Scotty went inside and was telling his mother about it, she sitting beside him on the sofa, holding his hands in her lap and saying, "Scotty, honey, are you sure you feel all right, baby?" and thinking she would call the doctor anyway, he suddenly lay back on the sofa, closed his eyes, and went limp. When she couldn't wake him up, she hurried to the telephone and called her husband at work. Howard told her to remain calm, remain calm, and then he called an ambulance for Scotty and left for the hospital himself.

Of course, the birthday party was canceled. The boy was in the hospital with a mild concussion and suffering from shock. There'd been vomiting, and his lungs had taken in fluid which needed pumping out that afternoon. Now he simply seemed to be in a very deep sleep—but no coma, Dr. Francis had emphasized; no coma, when he saw the alarm in the parents' eyes.

At eleven o'clock that Monday night when the boy seemed to
be resting comfortably enough after the many X-rays and the
lab work, and it was now just a matter of his waking up and
coming around, Howard left the hospital. He and Ann had
been at the hospital with Scotty since that afternoon, and he
was going home for a short while to bathe and to change
clothes. "I'll be back in an hour," he said. She nodded. "It's
fine," she said. "I'll be right here." He kissed her on the forehead, and they touched hands. She sat in a chair beside the
bed, looking at Scotty. She kept waiting for him to wake up
and be all right. Then she could begin to relax.

Howard drove home from the hospital. He took the wet,
dark streets faster than he should have, then caught himself and
slowed down. Until now, his life had gone smoothly and to his
satisfaction—college, marriage, another year of college for the
advanced degree in business, a junior partnership in an investment firm. Fatherhood. He was happy and, so far, lucky—he
knew that. His parents were still living, his brothers and his
sister were established, his friends from college had gone out to
take their places in the world. So far he had kept away from any
real harm, from those forces he knew existed and that could
cripple or bring down a man, if the luck went bad, if things
suddenly turned. He pulled into the driveway and parked. His
left leg had begun to tremble. He sat in the car for a minute
and tried to deal with the present situation in a rational manner. Scotty had been hit by a car and was in the hospital, but he
was going to be all right. He closed his eyes and ran his hand
over his face. In a minute, he got out of the car and went up to
the front door. The dog, Slug, was barking inside the house.
The telephone kept ringing while he unlocked the door and
fumbled for the light switch. He shouldn't have left the hospital, he shouldn't have, he cursed himself. He picked up the receiver and said, "I just walked in the door! Hello!"

"There's a cake here that wasn't picked up," said the man's
voice on the other end of the line.

"What? What are you saying?" Howard asked.

"A cake," the voice said. "A sixteen-dollar cake."

Howard held the receiver against his ear, trying to understand. "I don't know anything about a cake," he said. "Jesus,
what are you talking about?"

"Don't give me that," the voice said.

Howard hung up the telephone. He went into the kitchen and poured himself some whiskey. He called the hospital, but Scotty's condition remained the same; he was still sleeping and nothing had changed there. While water poured into the tub, he lathered his face and shaved. He had stretched out in the tub and closed his eyes when the telephone began ringing again. He hauled himself out, grabbed a towel, and hurried through the house, saying, "Stupid, stupid," for having left the hospital. But when he picked up the receiver and shouted, "Hello!" there was no sound at the other end of the line. Then the caller hung up.

He arrived back at the hospital a little after midnight. Ann still sat in the chair beside the bed. She looked up at Howard and then she looked back at Scotty. The boy's eyes stayed closed, his head was still wrapped in the bandages. His breathing was quiet and regular. From an apparatus over the bed hung a bottle of glucose with a tube distending from the bottle to the boy's right arm.

"How is he?" Howard said. "What's all this?" waving at the glucose and the tube.

"Dr. Francis's orders," she said. "He needs nourishment. Dr. Francis said he needs to keep up his strength. Why doesn't he wake up, Howard?" she said. "I don't understand, if he's all right."

Howard put his hand at the back of her head and ran his fingers through the hair. "He's going to be all right, honey. He'll wake up in a little while. Dr. Francis knows what's what."

In a little while he said, "Maybe you should go home and get a little rest for yourself. I'll stay here. Just don't put up with this creep who keeps calling. Hang up right away."

"Who's calling?" she asked.

"I don't know who, just somebody with nothing better to do than call up people. You go ahead now."

She shook her head. "No," she said, "I'm fine."

"Really," he said. "Go home for a while, if you want, and then come back and spell me in the morning. It'll be all right. What did Dr. Francis say? He said Scotty's going to be all right. We don't have to worry. He's just sleeping now, that's all."

A nurse pushed the door open. She nodded at them as she

went to the bedside. She took the left arm out from under the covers and put her fingers on the wrist, found the pulse, and then consulted her watch. In a little while she put the arm back under the covers and moved to the foot of the bed, where she wrote something on a clipboard attached to the bed.

"How is he?" Ann said. Howard's hand was a weight on her shoulder. She was aware of pressure in his fingers.

"He's stable," the nurse said. Then she said, "Doctor will be in again shortly. Doctor's back in the hospital. He's making rounds right now."

"I was saying maybe she'd want to go home and get a little rest," Howard said. "After the doctor comes," he added.

"She could do that," the nurse said. "I think you should both feel free to do that, if you wish." The nurse was a big Scandinavian woman with blond hair, and heavy breasts that filled the front of her uniform. There was a trace of an accent in her speech.

"We'll see what the doctor says," Ann said. "I want to talk to him. I don't think he should keep sleeping like this. I don't think that's a good sign." She brought her hand up to her eyes and leaned her head forward a little. Howard's grip tightened on her shoulder, and then his hand moved to her neck where his fingers began to knead the muscles there.

"Dr. Francis will be here in a few minutes," the nurse said. Then she left the room.

Howard gazed at his son for a time, the small chest quietly rising and then falling under the covers. For the first time since the terrible minutes after Ann's telephone call at the office, he felt a genuine fear starting in his limbs. He began shaking his head, trying to keep it away. Scotty was fine, except instead of sleeping at home in his own bed, he was in a hospital bed with bandages around his head and a tube in his arm. But it was what he needed right now, this help.

Dr. Francis came in and shook hands with Howard, though they'd just seen each other a few hours before. Ann got up from the chair. "Doctor?"

"Ann," he said and nodded. "Let's just first see how he's doing," the doctor said. He moved to the side of the bed and took the boy's pulse. He peeled back one eyelid and then the other. Howard and Ann stood beside the doctor and watched.

Ann made a little noise as Scotty's eyelid rolled back and disclosed a white, pupilless space. Then the doctor turned back the covers and listened to the boy's heart and lungs with his stethoscope. He pressed his fingers here and there on the abdomen. When he was finished he went to the end of the bed and studied the chart. He noted the time on his watch, scribbled something on the chart, and then looked at Howard and Ann, who were waiting.

"Doctor, how is he?" Howard said. "What's the matter with him exactly?"

"Why doesn't he wake up?" Ann said.

The doctor was a handsome, big-shouldered man with a tan face. He wore a three-piece blue suit, a striped tie, and ivory cuff links. His gray hair was combed, and he looked as if he could have just come from a concert. "He's all right," the doctor said. "Nothing to shout about, he could be better, I think. But he's all right. Still, I wish he'd wake up. He should wake up pretty soon." The doctor looked at the boy again. "We'll know some more in a couple of hours, after the results of a few more tests are in. But he's all right, believe me, except for that hairline fracture of the skull. He does have that."

"Oh, no," Ann said.

"And a bit of a concussion, as I said before. Of course, you know he's in shock," the doctor said. "Sometimes you see this in shock cases."

"But he's out of any real danger?" Howard said. "You said before he's not in a coma. You wouldn't call this a coma then, would you, Doctor?" Howard waited and looked at the doctor.

"No, I don't want to call it a coma," the doctor said and glanced over at the boy once more. "He's just in a very deep sleep. It's a restorative, a measure the body is taking on its own. He's out of any real danger, I'd say that for certain, yes. But we'll know more when he wakes up and the other tests are in. Don't worry," the doctor said.

"It's a coma," Ann said. "Of sorts."

"It's not a coma yet, not exactly," the doctor said. "I wouldn't want to call it coma. Not yet, anyway. He's suffered shock. In shock cases this kind of reaction is common enough; it's a temporary reaction to bodily trauma. Coma—well, coma is a deep, prolonged unconsciousness that could go on for days, or weeks even. Scotty's not in that area, not as far as we can tell, anyway. I'm just certain his condition will show improvement by morning. I'm betting that it will, anyway. We'll know more when he wakes up, which shouldn't be long now. Of course, you may do as you like, stay here or go home for a while, but by all means feel free to leave for a while if you want. This is not easy, I know." The doctor gazed at the boy again, watching him, and then he turned to Ann and said, "You try not to worry, little mother. Believe me, we're doing all that can be done. It's just a question of a little more time now." He nodded at her, shook hands with Howard again, and left the room.

Ann put her hand on Scotty's forehead and kept it there for a while. "At least he doesn't have a fever," she said. Then she said, "My God, he feels so cold, though. Howard? Is he supposed to feel like this? Feel his head."

Howard put his hand on the boy's forehead. His own breathing slowed. "I think he's supposed to feel this way right now," he said. "He's in shock, remember? That's what the doctor said. The doctor was just in here. He would have said something if Scotty wasn't okay."

Ann stood there awhile longer, working her lip with her teeth. Then she moved over to her chair and sat down.

Howard sat in the chair beside her. They looked at each other. He wanted to say something else and reassure her, but he was afraid to. He took her hand and put it in his lap, and this made him feel better, her hand being there. He picked up her hand and squeezed it, then just held it. They sat like that for a while, watching the boy and not talking. From time to time he squeezed her hand. Finally, she took her hand away and rubbed her temples.

"I've been praying," she said.

He nodded.

She said, "I almost thought I'd forgotten how, but it came back to me. All I had to do was close my eyes and say, Please, God, help us—help Scotty; and then the rest was easy. The words were right there. Maybe if you prayed too," she said to him.

"I've already prayed," he said. "I prayed this afternoon— yesterday afternoon, after you called, while I was driving to the hospital. I've been praying," he said.

"That's good," she said. Almost for the first time, she felt they were together in it, this trouble. Then she realized it had only been happening to her and to Scotty. She hadn't let Howard into it, though he was there and needed all along. She could see he was tired. The way his head looked heavy and angled into his chest. She felt a good tenderness toward him. She felt glad to be his wife.

The same nurse came in later and took the boy's pulse again and checked the flow from the bottle hanging above the bed.

In an hour another doctor came in. He said his name was Parsons, from radiology. He had a bushy moustache. He was wearing loafers and a white smock over a western shirt and a pair of jeans.

"We're going to take him downstairs for more pictures," he told them. "We need to do some more pictures, and we want to do a scan."

"What's that?" Ann said. "A scan?" She stood between this new doctor and the bed. "I thought you'd already taken all your X-rays."

"I'm afraid we need some more," he said. "Nothing to be alarmed about. We just need some more pictures, and we want to do a brain scan on him."

"My God," Ann said.

"It's perfectly normal procedure in cases like this," the new doctor said. "We just need to find out for sure why he isn't back awake yet. It's normal medical procedure, and nothing to be alarmed about. We'll be taking him down in a few minutes," the doctor said.

In a little while two orderlies came into the room with a gurney. They were black-haired, dark-complexioned men in white uniforms, and they said a few words to each other in a foreign tongue as they unhooked the boy from the tube and moved him from his bed to the gurney. Then they wheeled him from the room. Howard and Ann got on the same elevator. Ann stood beside the gurney and gazed at the boy, who was lying so still. She closed her eyes as the elevator began its descent. The orderlies stood at either end of the gurney without saying anything, though once one of the men made a comment to the other in their own language, and the other man nodded slowly in response.

Later that morning, just as the sun was beginning to lighten the windows in the waiting room outside the X-ray department, they brought the boy out and moved him back up to his room. Howard and Ann rode up on the elevator with him once more, and once more they took up their places beside the bed.

They waited all day, but still the boy did not wake up. Occasionally one of them would leave the room to go downstairs to the cafeteria to drink coffee or fruit juice and then, as if suddenly remembering and feeling guilty, jump up from the table and hurry back to the room. Dr. Francis came again that afternoon and examined the boy once more and then left after telling them he was coming along and could wake up any minute now. Nurses, different nurses than the night before, came in from time to time. Then a young woman from the lab knocked and came into the room. She wore white slacks and a white blouse and carried a little tray of things which she put on the stand beside the bed. Without a word to them, she took blood from the boy's arm. Howard closed his eyes as the woman found the right place on the boy's arm and pushed the needle in.

"I don't understand this," Ann said to the woman.

"Doctor's orders," the young woman said. "I do what I'm told to do. They say draw that one, I draw. What's wrong with him, anyway?" she said. "He's a sweetie."

"He was hit by a car," Howard said. "A hit-and-run."

The young woman shook her head and looked again at the boy. Then she took her tray and left the room.

"Why won't he wake up?" Ann said. "Howard? I want some answers from these people."

Howard didn't say anything. He sat down again in the chair and crossed one leg over the other. He rubbed his face. He looked at his son and then he settled back in the chair, closed his eyes, and went to sleep.

Ann walked to the window and looked out at the big parking lot. It was night, and cars were driving into and out of the parking lot with their lights on. She stood at the window with her hands gripping the sill and knew in her heart that they were into something now, something hard. She was afraid, and her teeth began to chatter until she tightened her jaws. She saw a big car stop in front of the hospital and someone, a woman in a long coat, got into the car. For a minute she wished she were that woman and somebody, anybody, was driving her away from here to somewhere else, a place where she would find Scotty waiting for her when she stepped out of the car, ready to say *Mom* and let her gather him in her arms.

In a little while Howard woke up. He looked at the boy again, and then he got up from the chair, stretched, and went over to stand beside her at the window. They both stared out into the parking lot and didn't talk. They seemed to feel each other's insides now, as though the worry had made them transparent in a perfectly natural way.

The door opened and Dr. Francis came in. He was wearing a different suit and tie this time, but his hair was the same and he looked as if he had just shaved. He went straight to the bed and examined the boy once more. "He ought to have come around by now. There's just no good reason for this," he said. "But I can tell you we're all convinced he's out of any danger, we'll just feel much better when he wakes up. There's no reason, absolutely none, why he shouldn't come around and soon now. Oh, he'll have himself a dilly of a headache when he does, you can count on that. But all of his signs are fine. They're as normal as can be."

"Is it a coma, then?" Ann asked.

The doctor rubbed his smooth cheek. "We'll call it that for the time being, until he wakes up. But you must be worn out. This is hard to wait out. Feel free to go out for a bite," he said. "It would do you good. I'll put a nurse in here while you're gone, if you'll feel better about going. Go and have yourselves something to eat."

"I couldn't eat," Ann said. "I'm not hungry."

"Do what you need to do, of course," the doctor said. "Anyway, I wanted to tell you that all the signs are good, the tests are positive, nothing at all negative, and just as soon as he wakes up he'll be over the hill."

"Thank you, Doctor," Howard said. He shook hands with the doctor again, and the doctor patted his shoulder and went out.

"I suppose one of us should go home and check on things," Howard said. "Slug needs to be fed, one thing."

"Call one of the neighbors," Ann said. "Call the Morgans. Anyone will feed a dog if you ask them to."

"All right," Howard said. After a while he said, "Honey, why don't you do it? Why don't you go home and check on things, and then come back? It'll do you good. I'll be right here with him. Seriously," he said. "We need to keep up our strength on this. We may want to be here for a while even after he wakes up."

"Why don't you go?" she said. "Feed Slug. Feed yourself."

"I already went," he said. "I was gone for exactly an hour and fifteen minutes. You go home for an hour or so and freshen up, and then come back. I'll stay here."

She tried to think about it, but she was too tired. She closed her eyes and tried to think about it again. After a time she said, "Maybe I will go home for a few minutes. Maybe if I'm not just sitting right here watching him every second he'll wake up and be all right. You know? Maybe he'll wake up if I'm not here. I'll go home and take a bath and put on clean clothes. I'll feed Slug. Then I'll come back."

"I'll be right here," he said. "You go on home, honey, and then come back. I'll be right here keeping an eye on things." His eyes were bloodshot and small, as if he had been drinking for a long time, and his clothes were rumpled. His beard had come out again. She touched his face, and then took her hand back. She understood he wanted to be by himself for a while, to not have to talk or share his worry for a time. She picked up her purse from the nightstand, and he helped her into her coat.

"I won't be gone long," she said.

"Just sit and rest for a little while when you get home," he said. "Eat something. After you get out of the bath, just sit for a while and rest. It'll do you a world of good, you'll see. Then come back down here," he said. "Let's try not to worry ourselves sick. You heard what Dr. Francis said."

She stood in her coat for a minute trying to recall the doctor's exact words, looking for any nuances, any hint of something behind his words other than what he was saying. She tried to remember if his expression had changed any when he bent over to examine Scotty. She remembered the way his features had composed themselves as he rolled back the boy's eyelids and then listened to his breathing.

She went to the door and turned and looked back. She looked at the boy, and then she looked at the father. Howard nodded. She stepped out of the room and pulled the door closed behind her.

She went past the nurses' station and down to the end of the corridor, looking for the elevator. At the end of the corridor she turned to her right where she found a little waiting room with a Negro family sitting in wicker chairs. There was a middle-aged man in a khaki shirt and pants, a baseball cap pushed back on his head. A large woman wearing a house dress and slippers was slumped in one of the chairs. A teenaged girl in jeans, hair done in dozens of little braids, lay stretched out in one of the chairs smoking a cigarette, legs crossed at the ankles. The family swung their eyes to her as she entered the room. The little table was littered with hamburger wrappers and Styrofoam cups.

"Nelson," the large woman said as she roused herself. "Is about Nelson?" Her eyes widened. "Tell me now, lady," the woman said. "Is about Nelson?" She was trying to rise from her chair, but the man had closed his hand over her arm.

"Here, here," he said. "Evelyn."

"I'm sorry," Ann said. "I'm looking for the elevator. My son is in the hospital, and now I can't find the elevator."

"Elevator is down that way, turn left," the man said and aimed a finger down another corridor.

The girl drew on her cigarette and stared at Ann. Her eyes were narrowed to slits, and her broad lips parted slowly as she let the smoke escape. The Negro woman let her head fall down on her shoulder and looked away from Ann, no longer interested.

"My son was hit by a car," Ann said to the man. She seemed to need to explain herself. "He has a concussion and a little skull fracture, but he's going to be all right. He's in shock now, but it might be some kind of coma, too. That's what really worries us, the coma part. I'm going out for a little while, but my husband is with him. Maybe he'll wake up while I'm gone."

"That's too bad," the man said and shifted in the chair. He

shook! his head. He looked down at the table, and then he looked back at Ann. She was still standing there. He said, "Our Nelson, he's on the operating table. Somebody cut him. Tried to kill him. There was a fight where he was at. At this party. They say he was just standing and watching. Not bothering nobody. But that don't mean nothing these days. Now he's on the operating table. We're just hoping and praying, that's all we can do now." He gazed at her steadily and then tugged the bill of his cap.

Ann looked at the girl again, who was still watching her, and at the older woman, who kept her head down on her shoulder but whose eyes were now closed. Ann saw the lips moving silently, making words. She had an urge to ask what those words were. She wanted to talk more with these people who were in the same kind of waiting she was in. She was afraid, and they were afraid. They had that in common. She would have liked to have said something else about the accident, told them more about Scotty, that it had happened on the day of his birthday, Monday, that he was still unconscious. Yet she didn't know how to begin and so only stood there looking at them without saying anything more.

She went down the corridor the man had indicated and found the elevator. She stood for a minute in front of the closed doors, still wondering if she was doing the right thing. Then she put out her finger and touched the button.

She pulled into the driveway and cut the engine. Slug ran around from behind the house. In his excitement he began to bark at the car, then ran in circles on the grass. She closed her eyes and leaned her head against the wheel for a minute. She listened to the ticking sounds the engine made as it began to cool. Then she got out of the car. She picked up the little dog, Scotty's dog, and went to the front door, which was unlocked. She turned on lights and put on a kettle of water for tea. She opened some dog food and fed Slug on the back porch. He ate in hungry little smacks, between running back and forth to see that she was going to stay. As she sat down on the sofa with her tea, the telephone rang.

"Yes!" she said as she answered. "Hello!"

"Mrs. Weiss," a man's voice said. It was five o'clock in the morning, and she thought she could hear machinery or equipment of some kind in the background.

"Yes, yes, what is it?" she said carefully into the receiver. "This is Mrs. Weiss. This is she. What is it, please?" She listened to whatever it was in the background. "Is it Scotty, for Christ's sake?"

"Scotty," the man's voice said. "It's about Scotty, yes. It has to do with Scotty, that problem. Have you forgotten about Scotty?" the man said. Then he hung up.

She dialed the hospital's number and asked for the third floor. She demanded information about her son from the nurse who answered the telephone. Then she asked to speak to her husband. It was, she said, an emergency.

She waited, turning the telephone cord in her fingers. She closed her eyes and felt sick at her stomach. She would have to make herself eat. Slug came in from the back porch and lay down near her feet. He wagged his tail. She pulled his ear while he licked her fingers. Howard was on the line.

"Somebody just called here," she said. She twisted the telephone cord and it kinked back into itself. "He said, he said it was about Scotty," she cried.

"Scotty's fine," Howard was telling her. "I mean he's still sleeping. There's been no change. The nurse has been in twice since you've been gone. They're in here every thirty minutes or so. A nurse or a doctor, one. He's all right, Ann."

"Somebody called, he said it was about Scotty," she said.

"Honey, you rest for a little while, you need the rest. Then come back down here. It must be that same caller I had. Just forget it. Come back down here after you've rested. Then we'll have breakfast or something."

"Breakfast," she said. "I couldn't eat anything."

"You know what I mean," he said. "Juice, a muffin, something, I don't know. I don't know anything, Ann. Jesus, I'm not hungry either. Ann, it's hard to talk now. I'm standing here at the desk. Dr. Francis is coming again at eight o'clock this morning. He's going to have something to tell us then, something more definite. That's what one of the nurses said. She didn't know any more than that. Ann? Honey, maybe we'll know something more then, at eight o'clock. Come back here before eight. Meanwhile, I'm right here and Scotty's all right. He's still the same," he added.

"I was drinking a cup of tea," she said, "when the telephone rang. They said it was about Scotty. There was a noise in the background. Was there a noise in the background on that call you had, Howard?"

"I honestly don't remember," he said. "It must have been a drunk or somebody calling, though God knows I don't understand. Maybe the driver of the car, maybe he's a psychopath and found out about Scotty somehow. But I'm here with him. Just rest a little like you were going to do. Take a bath and come back here by seven or so, and we'll talk to the doctor together when he gets here. It's going to be all right, honey. I'm here, and there are doctors and nurses around. They say his condition is stable."

"I'm scared to death," she said.

She ran water, undressed, and got into the tub. She washed and dried quickly, not taking the time to wash her hair. She put on clean underwear, wool slacks, and a sweater. She went into the living room where Slug looked up at her and let his tail thump once against the floor. It was just starting to get light outside when she went out to the car. Driving back to the hospital on the damp, deserted streets, she thought back to the rainy Sunday afternoon nearly two years ago when Scotty had been lost and they'd been afraid he'd drowned.

The sky had darkened that afternoon and rain had begun to fall, and still he hadn't come home. They'd called all his friends, who were at home and safe. She and Howard had gone to look for him at his board-and-rock fort at the far end of the field near the highway, but he wasn't there. Then Howard had run in one direction beside the highway and she had run the other way until she came to what had once been a little stream of water, a drainage ditch, but its banks were filled now with a dark torrent. One of his friends had been with him there when the rain started. They had been making boats out of pieces of scrap wood, and empty beer cans that had been tossed from passing cars. They had been lining up the beer cans on the pieces of wood and sending them out into the stream. The stream ended on this side of the highway at a cul-

vert where the water boiled and could take anything under and
into the pipe. The friend had left Scotty there on the bank
when the first drops of rain had begun to fall. Scotty had said
he was going to stay and build a bigger boat. She had stood on
the bank and gazed into the water as it poured into the mouth
of the culvert and disappeared under the highway. It was plain
to her what must have happened—that he had fallen in, that
he must even now be lodged somewhere inside the culvert.
The thought was monstrous, so unfair and overwhelming that
she couldn't hold it in her mind. But she felt it was true, that
he was in there, in the culvert, and knew too it was something
that would have to be borne and lived with from here on, a life
without Scotty in it. But how to act in the face of this, the fact
of the loss, was more than she could comprehend. The horror of
the men and equipment working at the mouth of the culvert
through the night, that was what she did not know if she could
endure, that waiting while the men worked under powerful
lights. She would have to somehow get past that to the limit-
less sweep of emptiness she knew stretched beyond. She was
ashamed to know it, but she thought she could live with that.
Later, much later, maybe then she would be able to come to
terms with that emptiness, after the presence of Scotty had
gone out of their lives—then perhaps, she would learn to handle that loss, and the awful absence—she would have to, that's
all—but now she did not know how she could get through the
waiting part to that other part.

She dropped to her knees. She stared into the current and
said that if He would let them have Scotty back, if he could have
somehow miraculously—she said it out loud, "miraculously"—
escaped the water and the culvert, she knew he hadn't, but if
he had, if He could only let them have Scotty back, somehow
not let him be wedged in the culvert, she promised then that
she and Howard would change their lives, change everything,
go back to the small town where they had come from, away
from this suburban place that could ruthlessly snatch away your
only child. She had still been on her knees when she heard
Howard calling her name, calling her name from across the
field, through the rain. She had raised her eyes and seen them
coming toward her, the two of them, Howard and Scotty.

"He was hiding," Howard said, laughing and crying at

once. "I was so glad to see him I couldn't begin to punish him. He'd made a shelter. He'd fixed himself up a place under the overpass, in those bushes. He'd made like a nest for himself," he said. The two of them were still coming toward her as she got to her feet. She doubled her fists. " 'Forts leak,' the little nut said. He was dry as a bone when I found him, damn his hide," Howard said, the tears breaking. Then Ann was on Scotty, slapping him on the head and face with a wild fury. "You little devil, you devil you," she shouted as she slapped him. "Ann, stop it," Howard said, grabbing for her arms. "He's all right, that's the main thing. He's all right." She'd picked the boy up while he was still crying and she'd held him. She'd held him. Their clothes soaked, shoes squishing with water, the three of them had begun the walk home. She carried the boy for a while, his arms around her neck, his chest heaving against her breasts. Howard walked beside them saying, "Jesus, what a scare. God almighty, what a fright." She knew Howard had been scared and was now relieved, but he hadn't glimpsed what she had, he couldn't know. The quickness of how she had gone into the death and beyond it had made her suspect herself, that she hadn't loved enough. If she had, she would not have thought the worst so quickly. She shook her head back and forth at this craziness. She grew tired and had to stop and put Scotty down. They walked the rest of the way together, Scotty in the middle, holding hands, the three of them walking home.

But they hadn't moved away and they'd never talked about that afternoon again. From time to time she'd thought about her promise, the prayers she'd offered up, and for a while she'd felt vaguely uneasy, but they had continued to live as they had been living—a comfortably busy life, not a bad or a dishonest life, a life, in fact, with many satisfactions and small pleasures. Nothing more was ever said about that afternoon, and in time she had stopped thinking about it. Now here they were still in the same city and it was two years later, and Scotty was again in peril, an awful peril, and she began to see this circumstance, this accident and the not waking up as punishment. For hadn't she given her word that they'd move away from this city and go back to where they could live a simpler and quieter life, forget the jump in salary and the house which was still so new they hadn't put up the fence or planted grass yet? She imagined them all sitting around each evening in some big living room, in some other town, and listening to Howard read to them.

She drove into the parking lot of the hospital and found a space close to the front door. She felt no inclination to pray now. She felt like a liar caught out, guilty and false, as if she were somehow responsible for what had now happened. She felt she was in some obscure way responsible. She let her thoughts move to the Negro family, and she remembered the name "Nelson" and the table that was covered with hamburger papers, and the teenaged girl staring at her as she drew on her cigarette. "Don't have children," she told the girl's image as she entered the front door of the hospital. "For God's sake, don't."

She took the elevator up to the third floor with two nurses who were just going on duty. It was Wednesday morning, a few minutes before seven. There was a page for a Dr. Madison as the elevator doors slid open on the third floor. She got off behind the nurses, who turned in the other direction and continued the conversation she had interrupted when she'd gotten onto the elevator. She walked down the corridor to the little side room where the Negro family had been waiting. They were gone now, but the chairs were scattered in such a way that it looked as if people had just jumped from them the minute before. She thought the chairs might still be warm. The tabletop was cluttered with the same cups and papers, the ashtray filled with cigarette butts.

She stopped at the nurses' station just down the corridor from the waiting room. A nurse was standing behind the counter, brushing her hair and yawning.

"There was a Negro man in surgery last night," Ann said. "Nelson something was his name. His family was in the waiting room. I'd like to inquire about his condition."

A nurse who was sitting at a desk behind the counter looked up from a chart in front of her. The telephone buzzed and she picked up the receiver, but she kept her eyes on Ann.

"He passed away," said the nurse at the counter. The nurse held the hairbrush and kept on looking at her. "Are you a friend of the family or what?"

"I met the family last night," Ann said. "My own son is in

the hospital. I guess he's in shock. We don't know for sure what's wrong. I just wondered about Mr. Nelson, that's all. Thank you." She went on down the corridor. Elevator doors the same color as the walls slid open and a gaunt, bald man in white pants and white canvas shoes pulled a heavy cart off the elevator. She hadn't noticed these doors last night. The man wheeled the cart out into the corridor and stopped in front of the room nearest the elevator and consulted a clipboard. Then he reached down and slid a tray out of the cart, rapped lightly on the door, and entered the room. She could smell the unpleasant odors of warm food as she passed the cart. She hurried past the other station without looking at any of the nurses and pushed open the door to Scotty's room.

Howard was standing at the window with his hands together behind his back. He turned around as she came in.

"How is he?" she said. She went over to the bed. She dropped her purse on the floor beside the nightstand. She seemed to have been gone a long time. She touched the covers around Scotty's neck. "Howard?"

"Dr. Francis was here a little while ago," Howard said. She looked at him closely and thought his shoulders were bunched a little.

"I thought he wasn't coming until eight o'clock this morning," she said quickly.

"There was another doctor with him. A neurologist."

"A neurologist," she said.

Howard nodded. His shoulders were bunching, she could see that. "What'd they say, Howard? For Christ's sake, what'd they say? What is it?"

"They said, well, they're going to take him down and run more tests on him, Ann. They think they're going to operate, honey. Honey, they are going to operate. They can't figure out why he won't wake up. It's more than just shock or concussion, they know that much now. It's in his skull, the fracture, it has something, something to do with that, they think. So they're going to operate. I tried to call you, but I guess you'd already left the house."

"Oh, God," she said. "Oh, please, Howard, please," she said, taking his arms.

"Look!" Howard said then. "Scotty! Look, Ann!" He turned her toward the bed.

The boy had opened his eyes, then closed them. He opened them again now. The eyes stared straight ahead for a minute, then moved slowly in his head until they rested on Howard and Ann, then traveled away again.

"Scotty," his mother said, moving to the bed.

"Hey, Scott," his father said. "Hey, Son."

They leaned over the bed. Howard took Scotty's left hand in his hands and began to pat and squeeze the hand. Ann bent over the boy and kissed his forehead again and again. She put her hands on either side of his face. "Scotty, honey, it's Mommy and Daddy," she said. "Scotty?"

The boy looked at them again, though without any sign of recognition or comprehension. Then his eyes scrunched closed, his mouth opened, and he howled until he had no more air in his lungs. His face seemed to relax and soften then. His lips parted as his last breath was puffed through his throat and exhaled gently through the clenched teeth.

The doctors called it a hidden occlusion and said it was a one-in-a-million circumstance. Maybe if it could have been detected somehow and surgery undertaken immediately, it could have saved him, but more than likely not. In any case, what would they have been looking for? Nothing had shown up in the tests or in the X-rays. Dr. Francis was shaken. "I can't tell you how badly I feel. I'm so very sorry, I can't tell you," he said as he led them into the doctors' lounge. There was a doctor sitting in a chair with his legs hooked over the back of another chair, watching an early morning TV show. He was wearing a green delivery room outfit, loose green pants and green blouse, and a green cap that covered his hair. He looked at Howard and Ann and then looked at Dr. Francis. He got to his feet and turned off the set and went out of the room. Dr. Francis guided Ann to the sofa, sat down beside her and began to talk in a low, consoling voice. At one point he leaned over and embraced her. She could feel his chest rising and falling evenly against her shoulder. She kept her eyes open and let him hold her. Howard went into the bathroom but left the door open. After a violent fit of weeping, he ran water and washed his face. Then he came out and sat down at a little table that held a telephone. He looked at the telephone as though deciding what to do first. He made some calls. After a time, Dr. Francis used the telephone.

"Is there anything else I can do for the moment?" he asked them.

Howard shook his head. Ann stared at Dr. Francis as if unable to comprehend his words.

The doctor walked them to the hospital's front door. People were entering and leaving the hospital. It was eleven o'clock in the morning. Ann was aware of how slowly, almost reluctantly she moved her feet. It seemed to her that Dr. Francis was making them leave, when she somehow felt they should stay, when it would be more the right thing to do, to stay. She gazed out into the parking lot and then looked back at the front of the hospital from the sidewalk. She began shaking her head. "No, no," she said. "This isn't happening. I can't leave him here, no." She heard herself and thought how unfair it was that the only words that came out were the sorts of words on the TV shows where people were stunned by violent or sudden deaths. She wanted her words to be her own. "No," she said, and for some reason the memory of the Negro woman's head lolling on her shoulder came to her. "No," she said again.

"I'll be talking to you later in the day," the doctor was saying to Howard. "There are still some things that have to be done, things that have to be cleared up to our satisfaction. Some things that need explaining."

"An autopsy," Howard said.

Dr. Francis nodded.

"I understand," Howard said. "Oh, Jesus. No, I don't understand, Doctor. I can't, I can't. I just can't."

Dr. Francis put his arm around Howard's shoulders. "I'm sorry. God, how I'm sorry." Then he let go and held out his hand. Howard looked at the hand, and then he took it. Dr. Francis put his arms around Ann once more. He seemed full of some goodness she didn't understand. She let her head rest on his shoulder, but her eyes were open. She kept looking at the hospital. As they drove out of the parking lot, she looked back at the hospital once more.

At home, she sat on the sofa with her hands in her coat pockets. Howard closed the door to Scotty's room. He got the coffeemaker going and then he found an empty box. He had thought to pick up some of Scotty's things. But instead he sat down beside her on the sofa, pushed the box to one side, and leaned forward, arms between his knees. He began to weep. She pulled his head over into her lap and patted his shoulder. "He's gone," she said. She kept patting his shoulder. Over his sobs she could hear the coffeemaker hissing, out in the kitchen. "There, there," she said tenderly. "Howard, he's gone. He's gone and now we'll have to get used to that. To being alone."

In a little while Howard got up and began moving aimlessly around the room with the box, not putting anything into it, but collecting some things on the floor at one end of the sofa. She continued to sit with her hands in her pockets. Howard put the box down and brought coffee into the living room. Later, Ann made calls to relatives. After each call had been placed and the party had answered, Ann would blurt out a few words and cry for a minute. Then she would quietly explain, in a measured voice, what had happened and tell them about arrangements. Howard took the box out to the garage where he saw Scotty's bicycle. He dropped the box and sat down on the pavement beside the bicycle. He took hold of the bicycle awkwardly, so that it leaned against his chest. He held it, the rubber pedal sticking into his chest and turning the wheel across his trouser leg a little way.

Ann hung up the telephone after talking to her sister. She was looking up another number, when the telephone rang. She picked it up on the first ring.

"Hello," she said, and again she heard something in the background, a humming noise. "Hello! Hello!" she said. "For God's sake," she said. "Who is this? What is it you want? Say something."

"Your Scotty, I got him ready for you," the man's voice said. "Did you forget him?"

"You evil bastard!" she shouted into the receiver. "How can you do this, you evil son of a bitch?"

"Scotty," the man said. "Have you forgotten about Scotty?" Then the man hung up on her.

Howard heard the shouting and came in to find her with her

head on her arms over the table, weeping. He picked up the receiver and listened to the dial tone.

Much later, just before midnight, after they had dealt with many things, the telephone rang again.

"You answer it," she said. "Howard, it's him, I know." They were sitting at the kitchen table with coffee in front of them. Howard had a small glass of whiskey beside his cup. He answered on the third ring.

"Hello," he said. "Who is this? Hello! Hello!" The line went dead. "He hung up," Howard said. "Whoever it was."

"It was him," she said. "That bastard. I'd like to kill him," she said. "I'd like to shoot him and watch him kick," she said.

"Ann, my God," he said.

"Could you hear anything?" she said. "In the background? A noise, machinery, something humming?"

"Nothing, really. Nothing like that," he said. "There wasn't much time. I think there was some radio music. Yes, there was a radio going, that's all I could tell. I don't know what in God's name is going on," he said.

She shook her head. "If I could, could get, my hands, on him." It came to her then. She knew who it was. Scotty, the cake, the telephone number. She pushed the chair away from the table and got up. "Drive me down to the shopping center," she said. "Howard."

"What are you saying?"

"The shopping center. I know who it is who's calling now. I know who it is. It's the baker, the son-of-a-bitching baker, Howard. I had him bake a cake for Scotty's birthday. That's who's calling, that's who has the number and keeps calling us. To harass us about that cake. The baker, that bastard."

They drove out to the shopping center. The sky was clear and stars were out. It was cold, and they ran the heater in the car. They parked in front of the bakery. All of the shops and stores were closed, but there were still cars at the far end of the lot in front of the twin cinemas. The bakery windows were dark, but when they looked through the glass they could see a light in the back room and, now and then, a big man in an apron moving in and out of the white, even light. Through the glass she could see the display cases and some little tables with chairs. She tried the door. She rapped on the glass. But if the baker heard them he gave no sign. He didn't look in their direction.

They drove around behind the bakery and parked. They got out of the car. There was a lighted window too high up for them to see inside. A sign near the back door said, "The Pantry Bakery, Special Orders." She could hear faintly a radio playing inside and something—an oven door?—creaking as it was pulled down. She knocked on the door and waited. Then she knocked again, louder. The radio was turned down and there was a scraping sound now, the distinct sound of something, a drawer, being pulled open and then closed.

The door was unlocked and opened. The baker stood in the light and peered out at them. "I'm closed for business," he said. "What do you want at this hour? It's midnight. Are you drunk or something?"

She stepped into the light that fell through the open door, and he blinked his heavy eyelids as he recognized her. "It's you," he said.

"It's me," she said. "Scotty's mother. This is Scotty's father. We'd like to come in."

The baker said, "I'm busy now. I have work to do."

She had stepped inside the doorway anyway. Howard came in behind her. The baker had moved back. "It smells like a bakery in here. Doesn't it smell like a bakery in here, Howard?"

"What do you want?" the baker said. "Maybe you want your cake? That's it, you decided you wanted your cake. You did order a cake, didn't you?"

"You're pretty smart for a baker," she said. "Howard, this is the man who's been calling us. This is the baker man." She clenched her fists. She stared at him fiercely. There was a deep burning inside her, an anger that made her feel larger than herself, larger than either of these men.

"Just a minute here," the baker said. "You want to pick up your three-day-old cake? That it? I don't want to argue with you, lady. There it sits over there, getting stale. I'll give it to you for half of what I quoted you. No, you want it? You can have it. It's no good to me, no good to anyone now. It cost me time and money to make that cake. If you want it, okay, if you don't, that's okay too. Just forget it and go. I have to get back to work." He looked at them and rolled his tongue behind his teeth.

"More cakes," she said. She knew she was in control of it, of what was increasing her. She was calm.

"Lady, I work sixteen hours a day in this place to earn a living," the baker said. He wiped his hands on his apron. "I work night and day in here, trying to make ends meet." A look crossed Ann's face that made the baker move back and say, "No trouble, now." He reached to the counter and picked up a rolling pin with his right hand and began to tap-tap it against the palm of his other hand. "You want the cake or not? I have to get back to work. Bakers work at night," he said again. His eyes were small, mean looking, she thought, nearly lost in the bristly flesh around his cheeks. His neck around the collar of his T-shirt was thick with fat.

"We know bakers work at night," Ann said. "They make phone calls at night too. You bastard," she said.

The baker continued to tap the rolling pin against his hand. He glanced at Howard. "Careful, careful," he said to them.

"My boy's dead," she said with a cold, even finality. "He was hit by a car Monday afternoon. We've been waiting with him until he died. But, of course, you couldn't be expected to know that, could you? Bakers can't know everything. Can they, Mr. Baker? But he's dead. Dead, you bastard." Just as suddenly as it had welled in her the anger dwindled, gave way to something else, a dizzy feeling of nausea. She leaned against the wooden table that was sprinkled with flour, put her hands over her face and began to cry, her shoulders rocking back and forth. "It isn't fair," she said. "It isn't, isn't fair."

Howard put his hand at the small of her back and looked at the baker. "Shame on you," Howard said to him. "Shame."

The baker put the rolling pin back on the counter. He undid his apron and threw it on the counter. He stood a minute looking at them with a dull, pained look. Then he pulled a chair out from under a card table that held papers and receipts, an adding machine, and a telephone directory. "Please sit down," he said. "Let me get you a chair," he said to Howard. "Sit down now, please." The baker went into the front of the shop and returned with two little wrought-iron chairs. "Please sit down, you people."

Ann wiped her eyes and looked at the baker. "I wanted to kill you," she said. "I wanted you dead."

The baker had cleared a space for them at the table. He shoved the adding machine to one side, along with the stacks of notepaper and receipts. He pushed the telephone directory onto the floor, where it landed with a thud. Howard and Ann sat down and pulled their chairs up to the table. The baker sat down too.

"I don't blame you," the baker said, putting his elbows on the table and shaking his head slowly. "First. Let me say how sorry I am. God alone knows how sorry. Listen to me. I'm just a baker. I don't claim to be anything else. Maybe once, maybe years ago I was a different kind of human being, I've forgotten, I don't know for sure. But I'm not any longer, if I ever was. Now I'm just a baker. That don't excuse my offense, I know. But I'm deeply sorry. I'm sorry for your son, and I'm sorry for my part in this. Sweet, sweet Jesus," the baker said. He spread his hands out on the table and turned them over to reveal his palms. "I don't have any children myself, so I can only imagine what you must be feeling. All I can say to you now is that I'm sorry. Forgive me, if you can," the baker said. "I'm not an evil man, I don't think. Not evil, like you said on the phone. You must understand that what it comes down to is I don't know how to act anymore, it would seem. Please," the man said, "let me ask you if you can find it in your hearts to forgive me?"

It was warm in the bakery and Howard stood up from the table and took off his coat. He helped Ann from her coat. The baker looked at them for a minute and then nodded and got up from the table. He went to the oven and turned off some switches. He found cups and poured them coffee from an electric coffeemaker. He put a carton of cream on the table, and a bowl of sugar.

"You probably need to eat something," the baker said. "I hope you'll eat some of my hot rolls. You have to eat and keep going. Eating is a small, good thing in a time like this," he said.

He served them warm cinnamon rolls just out of the oven, the icing still runny. He put butter on the table and knives to spread the butter. Then the baker sat down at the table with them. He waited. He waited until they each took a roll from the platter and began to eat. "It's good to eat something," he said, watching them. "There's more. Eat up. Eat all you want. There's all the rolls in the world in here."

They ate rolls and drank coffee. Ann was suddenly hungry and the rolls were warm and sweet. She ate three of them, which pleased the baker. Then he began to talk. They listened carefully. Although they were tired and in anguish, they listened to what the baker had to say. They nodded when the baker began to speak of loneliness, and the sense of doubt and limitation that had come to him in his middle years. He told them what it was like to be childless all these years. To repeat the days with the ovens endlessly full and endlessly empty. The party food, the celebrations he'd worked over. Icing knuckle-deep. The wedding couples stuck to each other's arms, hundreds of them, no, thousands by now. Birthdays. Just the candles from all those cakes if you thought you could see them all burning at once. He had a necessary trade. He was a baker. He was glad not to be a florist. It was better to be feeding people. Not giving them something that sat around for a while until it was thrown out. This was a better smell than flowers.

"Here, smell this," the baker said, breaking open a dark loaf. "It's a heavy bread, but rich." They smelled it, then he had them taste it. It had the taste of molasses and coarse grains. They listened to him. They ate what they could. They swallowed the dark bread. It was like daylight under the fluorescent trays of light. They talked on into the early morning, the high pale cast of light in the windows, and they did not think of leaving.

Tell the Women We're Going

BILL JAMISON had always been close with Jerry Roberts. The two grew up in the south area, near the old fair-grounds, went through grade school and junior high together, and then on to Eisenhower where they took as many of the same classes and teachers as they could manage, wore each other's shirts and sweaters and pegged pants, and dated or ganged the same girl—whichever came up as a matter of course.

Summers they took jobs together—swamping peaches, picking cherries, stringing hops, anything they could do that paid a little money to see them through to fall, something where they didn't have to worry about a boss breathing down their necks every five minutes. Jerry didn't like to be told what to do. Bill didn't mind; he liked it that Jerry was the sort of take-charge guy he was. The summer just before their senior year, they chipped in and bought a red '54 Plymouth for $325. Jerry would keep it a week at a time, then Bill. They were used to sharing things, and it worked out fine for a while.

But Jerry got married before the end of the first semester, kept the car, and dropped out of school to go to work steady at Robby's Market. That was the only time there was a strain in their relationship. Bill liked Carol Henderson—he'd known her a couple of years, almost as long as Jerry had—but after Jerry and she got married, things were just never the same between the two friends. He was over there a lot, especially at first—it made him feel older, having married friends—for lunch or dinner, or else late evenings to listen to Elvis Presley, and Bill Haley and the Comets, and there were a couple of Fats Domino records he liked, but it always embarrassed him when Carol and Jerry started kissing and near making out in front of him. Sometimes he'd have to excuse himself and take a walk to Dezorn's service station to get some Coke because there was only the one bed in the apartment, a hideaway that let down right in the middle of the living room. Other times Jerry and Carol would simply head off in a clumsy leg-hugging walk to the bathroom, and Bill would move to the kitchen and pretend to busy himself looking in the cupboards and refrigerator, trying not to listen.

So he stopped going over so much; and then June he graduated, took a job at the Darigold Milk plant, and joined the National Guard. In a year he had a milk route of his own and was going steady with Linda Wilson—a good, clean girl. He and Linda dropped in at the Roberts' once a week or so, drank beer and listened to records. Carol and Linda got along fine. Bill was flattered when Carol said that, confidentially, she thought Linda was "a real person." Jerry liked Linda too. "She's a great little chick," he told Bill.

When Bill and Linda married, Jerry was best man, of course; and at the reception later at the Donnelly Hotel, it was a little like old times, Jerry and Bill cutting up together and linking arms and tossing off glasses of spiked punch. But once, in the midst of his happiness, Bill looked at Jerry and thought how much older he looked, a lot older than just twenty-two. His hair was beginning to recede, just like his father's, and he was getting heavy around the hips. He and Carol had two kids, and she was pregnant again. He was still with Robby's Market, though now an assistant manager. Jerry got drunk at the reception and flirted with both bridesmaids, then tried to start a fight with one of the ushers. Carol had to drive him home before he made a real scene.

They saw each other every two or three weeks, sometimes oftener, depending on the weather. If the weather was good, like now, they might get together on Sunday at Jerry's, barbecue hot dogs or hamburgers, and turn all the kids loose in the wading pool Jerry had got for next to nothing from one of the women checkers at the store.

Jerry had a comfortable house. He lived in the country on a hill overlooking the Naches River. There were a half-dozen other houses scattered around, but he was by himself, too, compared to in town anyway. He liked his friends to come to his place; it was just too much trouble getting all the kids washed, dressed, and into the car—a red '68 Chevy hardtop. He and Carol had four kids now, all girls, and Carol was pregnant again. They didn't think they'd have any more after this one.

Carol and Linda were in the kitchen washing dishes and straightening up. It was around three in the afternoon. Jerry's four little girls were playing with Bill's two boys, down below the house near a corner of the fence. They had a big red plastic ball they kept throwing into the wading pool and, yelling, splashed after. Jerry and Bill sat in reclining lawn chairs on the patio, drinking beer.

Bill had to do most of the talking—things about people they both knew, the power play going on at the Darigold head office in Portland, about a new four-door Pontiac Catalina he and Linda were thinking of buying.

Jerry nodded now and then, but most of the time just stared at the clothesline or at the garage. Bill thought he must be depressed, but then he'd noticed Jerry had gotten deep the last year or so. Bill moved in his chair, lighted a cigarette, finally said, "Anything wrong, man?"

Jerry finished his beer and then mashed the can. He shrugged. "What say we get out for a while? Just drive around a little, stop off and have a beer. Jesus, a guy gets stale just sitting around all his Sundays."

"Sounds good to me. Sure. I'll tell the women we're going."

"By ourselves, remember. By God, no family outing. Say we're going to have a beer or something. I'll wait for you in the car. Take my car."

They hadn't done anything together for a long while. They took the Naches River highway out to Gleed, Jerry driving. The day was warm and sunny, and the air blew through the car and felt good on their necks and arms. Jerry was grinning.

"Where we going?" Bill said. He felt a whole lot better just seeing Jerry brighten up.

"What say we go out to old Riley's, shoot a little rotation?"

"Fine with me. Hey, man, we haven't done anything like this in a long time."

"Guy's got to get out now and then or he gets stale. Know what I mean?" He looked at Bill. "Can't be all work and no play. You know what I mean."

Bill wasn't sure. He liked to get out with the guys from the plant for the Friday night bowling league, and he liked to stop off once or twice a week after work with Jack Broderick and have a few beers, but he liked being at home too. No, he wouldn't say he felt stale exactly. He looked at his watch.

"Still standing," Jerry said, pulling up onto the gravel in front of the Gleed Recreation Center. "Been by here now and then, you know, but I haven't been inside for a year or so. Just no time anymore." He spat.

They went inside, Bill holding the door for Jerry. Jerry punched him lightly in the stomach as he went by.

"Heeey there! How you boys doing? I haven't seen you boys around in I don't know how long. Where you been keeping yourselves?" Riley started around from behind the counter, grinning. He was a heavy bald-headed man wearing a short-sleeved print shirt that hung outside his jeans.

"Ah, dry up you old coot and give us a couple of Olys," Jerry said, winking at Bill. "How you been?"

"Fine, fine, just fine. How you boys doing? Where you been keeping yourselves? You boys getting any on the side? Jerry, the last time I seen you, your old lady was six months pregnant."

Jerry stood a minute and blinked his eyes. "How long's that been, Riley? Has it been that long?"

"How about the Oly?" Bill said. "Riley, you have one with us."

They took stools near the window. Jerry said, "What kind of place is this, Riley, that don't have any girls on a Sunday afternoon?"

Riley laughed. "I guess there just ain't enough to go around, boys."

They had five cans of beer each and took two hours to play three games of rotation and two games of snooker. Riley didn't have anything to do and came around from behind the counter and sat on a stool and talked and watched them play.

Bill kept looking at his watch, then at Jerry. Finally, he said, "You think we should be going now, Jerry? I mean, what d'you think?"

"Yeah, okay. Let's finish this beer, then go." In a little while Jerry drained his can, mashed it, and then sat there on the stool a minute turning the can in his hand. "See you around, Riley."

"You boys come back now, you hear? Take it easy."

Back on the highway Jerry opened it up some—little spurts of eighty-five and ninety—but there were other cars, people returning from the parks and the mountains, and he mostly had to be satisfied with a quick pass now and then, and then a slow creeping along at fifty with the rest.

They'd just passed an old pickup loaded with furniture when they saw two girls on bicycles.

"Look at that!" Jerry said, slowing. "I could do for some of that."

He drove on by, but both of them looked back. The girls saw them and laughed, kept pedaling along the shoulder of the road.

Jerry drove another mile and then pulled off the road at a wide place. "Let's go back. Let's try it."

"Jesus. Well, I don't know, man. We should be getting back. That stuff's too young anyway. Huh?"

"Old enough to bleed, old enough to . . . You know that saying."

"Yeah, but I don't know."

"Christ sake. We'll just have some fun with 'em, give 'em a bad time."

"All right. Sure." He glanced at his watch and then at the sky. "You do the talking."

"Me! I'm driving. You do the talking. Besides, they'll be on your side."

"I don't know, man, I'm rusty."

Jerry hooted as he whipped the car around, started back the way they'd come.

He slowed when he came nearly even with the girls, pulled onto the shoulder across the road from them. "Hey, where you going? Want a lift?"

The girls looked at each other and laughed, but kept riding. The girl on the inside, nearest the road, was seventeen or eighteen, dark-haired, tall and willowy as she leaned over her bicycle. The other girl was the same age, but smaller and with light hair. They both wore shorts and halters.

"Bitches," Jerry said. "We'll get 'em, though." He was waiting for the cars to pass so he could pull a U. "I'll take the brunette, you take the little one. Okay?"

Bill moved his back against the front seat and touched the bridge of his dark glasses. "Hell, we're wasting our time any-way—they're not going to do anything."

"Christ, man! Jesus, don't go in there already defeated."

Bill lighted a cigarette.

Jerry pulled across the road, and in a minute or two drove up behind the girls. "Okay, do your stuff," he said to Bill. "Turn on your charms now. Hustle 'em in for us."

"Hi," Bill said as they drove slowly alongside the girls. "My name's Bill."

"That's nice," the brunette said. The other girl laughed, and then the brunette laughed too.

"Where are you going?"

The girls didn't answer. The little one tittered. They kept riding and Jerry drove along slowly beside them.

"Oh, come on now. Where you going?"

"No place," the little one answered.

"Where's no place?"

"Just no place."

"I told you my name. What's yours? This is Jerry."

The girls looked at each other and laughed again. They kept riding.

A car came up from behind, and the driver leaned on the horn.

"Ah, cram it!" Jerry said. He pulled off a little farther onto the shoulder, though; and after a minute, seeing his chance, the driver of the other car shot around them.

They pulled up alongside the girls again.

"Let us give you a lift," Bill said. "We'll take you wherever you want to go. That's a promise. You must be tired riding those bicycles. You look tired. Too much exercise isn't good for you, you know."

The girls laughed.

"Come on now, tell us your names."

"My name's Barbara, hers is Sharon," the little one said. She laughed again.

"Now we're getting someplace," Jerry said to Bill. "Ask 'em again where they're going."

"Where you girls going? Barbara, . . . where you going, Barb?"

She laughed. "No place," she said, "just down the road."

"Where down the road?"

"D'you want me to tell them?" she said to the other girl.

"I don't care. It doesn't make any difference; I'm not going to go anyplace with them anyway."

"Well, I'm not either," she said. "I didn't mean that."

"Christ sake," Jerry said.

"Where you going?" Bill asked again. "Are you going to Painted Rocks?"

The girls began laughing.

"That's where they're going," Jerry said. "Painted Rocks." He picked up a little speed then and pulled off onto the shoulder ahead of the girls so that they had to come by on his side of the car to get around.

"Don't be that way," Jerry said. "Come on, get in. We're all introduced. What's the matter anyway?"

The girls just laughed as they rode by, and laughed even more when Jerry said, "Come on, we won't bite."

"How do we know?" the little one called back over her shoulder.

"Take my word for it, sister," Jerry said under his breath.

The brunette glanced back, caught Jerry's eyes, and looked away with a frown.

Jerry pulled back onto the highway, dirt and rocks spurting from under the rear tires. "We'll be seeing you," Bill called as they sped by.

"It's in the bag," Jerry said. "See the look that bitch gave me? I tell you, we got it made."

"I don't know," Bill said. "Maybe we should cut for home."

"No, no, we got it made! Just take my word for it."

He pulled off the road under some trees when they came to Painted Rocks. The highway forked here, one road going on to Yakima, the other, the main highway, heading for Naches, Enumclaw, the Chinook Pass, Seattle. A hundred yards off the road was a high sloping black mound of rock, part of a low range of hills honeycombed with footpaths and small caves with a sprinkling of Indian sign-painting here and there on several of the cave walls. The cliff side of the rock, facing the highway, carried announcements and warnings like NACHES 67—GLEED WILDCATS—Jesus Saves—Beat Yakima, flat irregular letters for the most part, in red or white paint.

They sat in the car smoking cigarettes, watching the highway and listening to the intermittent tat-tat of a woodpecker back in the trees. A few mosquitoes flew into the car and hovered over their hands and arms.

Jerry tried to pick up something on the radio and rapped the dashboard sharply. "Wish we had another beer now! Damn, I could sure go for a beer."

"Yeah," Bill said. He looked at his watch. "Almost six, Jerry. How much longer we going to wait?"

"Christ, they'll be along any minute. They'll have to stop when they get where they're going, won't they? I'll bet three bucks, all I got, they'll be here in two or three minutes." He grinned at Bill and bumped his knee. Then he began to tap the head of the gear shift.

When the girls came into view, they were on the opposite side of the highway, facing the traffic.

Jerry and Bill got out of the car and leaned against the front fender, waiting.

When the girls turned off the shoulder into the trees, they saw the men and began to pedal faster. The little one was laughing as she raised up from the seat to push harder.

"Remember," Jerry said, starting away from the car, "I'll take the brunette, you take the little one."

Bill stopped. "What're we going to do? Man, we'd better be careful."

"Hell, we're just having some fun. We'll get 'em to stop and talk awhile, that's all. Who cares? They aren't going to say anything; they're having fun. They like to be paid attention to."

They began sauntering over to the cliff. The girls dropped their bicycles and commenced running up one of the paths. They disappeared around a corner and then reappeared again, a little higher up, where they stopped and looked down.

"What're you guys following us for?" the brunette called down. "Huh? What d'you want?"

Jerry didn't answer, just started up the path.

"Let's run," Barbara said, still laughing and a little out of breath. "Come on."

They turned and started going up the path at a trot.

Jerry and Bill climbed at a walking pace. Bill was smoking a cigarette, stopping every ten feet or so to get a good inhale. He was beginning to wish he were home. It was still warm and clear, but shadows from the overhead rocks and trees were starting to lengthen out over the trail in front of them. Just as the path turned, he looked back and caught a last glimpse of the car. He hadn't realized they were so high.

"Come on," Jerry snapped. "Can't you keep up?"

"I'm coming," Bill said.

"You go right, I'll go straight on. We'll cut 'em off."

Bill angled to the right. He kept climbing. He stopped once and sat down to catch his breath. He couldn't see the car, nor the highway. Over on his left he could see a strip of the Naches River, the size of a ribbon, sparkling beside a stand of miniature white spruce. To the right he could look down the valley and see the apple and pear orchards neatly laid out against the ridge and on down the sides of the ridge into the valley, with here and there a house, or the sun-gleam of an automobile moving on one of the little roads. It was very still and quiet. After a minute he got up, wiped his hands on his pants, and began following the trail again.

He went higher, and then the path began to drop, turning left, toward the valley. When he came around a bend he saw the two girls crouched behind an outcrop of rock, looking down over another path. He stopped, tried casually to light a cigarette, but noticed with a little shock his trembling fingers, and then began to walk toward the girls as nonchalantly as he could.

When they heard a rock turn under his foot, they jerked around, saw him, and jumped up, the little one squealing.

"Come on, wait a minute! Let's sit down and talk this over. I'm tired of walking. Hey!"

Jerry, hearing the voices, came jogging up the path into sight. "Wait, goddamn it!" He tried to cut them off and they broke in another direction, the little one squealing and laughing, both of them running barefoot across the shale and dirt in front of Bill.

Bill wondered where they'd left their shoes. He moved to the right.

The little one turned sharply and cut up the hill; the brunette whirled, paused, and then took off down a path that led toward the valley, along the side of the hill. Jerry went after her.

Bill looked at his watch and then sat down on a rock, took off his dark glasses and looked again at the sky.

—

The brunette kept running, hopping, until she came to one of the caves, a large overhang of rock with the interior hidden in the shadows. She climbed in as far as she could, sat down and dropped her head, breathing hard.

In a minute or two she heard him coming down the path. He stopped when he came to the overhang. She held her breath. He picked up a piece of shale, sailed it back into the dark. It whacked against the wall just over her head.

"Hey, what d'you want to do—put my eye out? Quit throwing rocks, you damn jerk."

"Thought you might be hiding out in there. Come out with your hands up, or I'm coming in for you."

"Wait a minute," she said.

He jumped up onto a little ledge under the rock and peered into the dark.

"What d'you want?" she said. "Why don't you leave us alone?"

"Well," he said, looking at her, letting his eyes move slowly over her body, "why don't you stop running, and we will."

She came up close to him, and then with a darting movement tried to slip by, but he put his hand out to the wall, blocking her way. He grinned.

She grinned, then bit her lip and tried to go by on the other side.

"You know you're cute when you smile." He tried to grab her around the waist but she turned, slipped away from him.

"Come *on*! Stop it! Let me out of here."

He moved in front of her again, touched her breast with his fingers. She slapped his hand down, and he grabbed her breast, hard.

"Oh," she said. "You're hurting me. Please, please, you're hurting me."

He relaxed his grip, but didn't let go. "All right," he said. "I'm not going to hurt you." Then he let go.

She pushed him off balance and jumped past onto the path, running downhill.

"Goddamn you," he yelled, "come back here!"

She took a path to the right that began to climb again. He slipped on some bunchgrass, fell, scrambled up and started running again. Then she turned into a narrow defile, a hundred feet long, with light and a view of the valley at the other end. She ran, her bare feet smacking the rock and echoing to him above his own hoarse breathing. At the end she turned and yelled, "Leave me *alone!*" her voice breaking.

He saved his breath. She turned and ducked out of sight. When he got to the end he looked up over his shoulder and saw her climbing steadily on her hands and knees. They were on the valley side, and she was climbing towards the top of a knoll. He knew if she made it he'd probably lose her; he couldn't go much farther. He put everything he had into it, scrabbling up the side, using rocks and bushes for handholds, his heart pounding and his breath coming in sharp cutting gasps.

Just as she reached the top he grabbed her ankle and they crawled onto the little plateau at the same time.

"Damn you," he sobbed. He still had her ankle when she kicked him as hard as she could in the head with her other foot, jarred him so that his ear rang and lights flashed behind his eyes.

"Son, son of a bitch you," his eyes streaming water. He threw himself down over her legs and grabbed her by the arms.

She kept trying to bring her knees up but he turned slightly, kept her pinned down.

They lay like for a while, gasping. The girl's eyes were large and rolling with fear. She kept turning her head from side to side and biting her lips.

"Listen, I'll let you go. You want me to let you go?"

She nodded quickly.

"Okay, I will. First I want it though. Understand? Without any trouble. Okay?"

She lay without speaking.

"Okay? Okay, I said?" he shook her.

After a moment she nodded.

"Okay. Okay."

He turned loose her arms and raised up, began fumbling with her shorts, trying to unzip them and slide them over her hips.

She moved quickly and caught him on the ear with a clenched fist, rolling to the side in the same motion. He lunged after her. She was yelling now. He jumped onto her back and drove her face into the ground. He held onto the nape of her neck. In a minute, when she stopped struggling, he began slipping her shorts down.

He stood up, turned his back to her and began brushing his clothes. When he looked at her again she was sitting up, staring at the scuffed ground and rubbing a few strands of hair against her forehead.

"You going to tell anybody?"

She did not speak.

He wet his lips. "I wish you wouldn't."

She leaned forward and began to cry, quietly, holding the back of her hand against her face.

Jerry tried to light a cigarette but dropped the matches and started to walk off without picking them up. Then he stopped and looked back. For a minute he couldn't understand what he was doing there, or who this girl was. He glanced uneasily across the valley, the sun just starting to sink into the hills. He felt a slight breeze against his face. The valley was being tipped in with the dark ground-covering shadows of ridges, rocks, trees. He looked at the girl again.

"I said I wish you wouldn't say anything. I'm . . . Jesus! I'm sorry, I really am."

"Just . . . go away."

He came closer. She started to get up. He stepped forward quickly and hit her on the side of the head with his fist, just as she got to one knee. She fell back with a scream. When she tried to get to her feet again, he picked up a rock and slammed it into her face. He actually heard her teeth and bones crack, and blood came out between her lips. He dropped the rock. She went down heavily, and he crouched over her. When she began moving he picked up the rock and hit her again, not very hard this time, on the back of the head. Then he dropped the rock and touched her shoulder. He began to shake her, and after a minute he turned her over.

Her eyes were open, glassy, and she began turning her head slowly from side to side, rolling her tongue thickly in her mouth as she tried to spit out blood and splinters of teeth. As she moved her head slightly from side to side, her eyes kept focusing on him, then slipping off. He got up and walked a few feet, then came back. She was trying to sit up. He knelt, put his hands on her shoulders and tried to make her lie down again. But his hands slipped to her throat, and he began to choke her. He couldn't go through with it, though, just enough so that when he released his hands her breath came scraping hysterically up her windpipe. She sank back, and he stood up. Then he bent over and worked loose from the ground a big rock. Loose dirt fell from the bottom of the rock as he raised it up even with his eyes and then over his head. Then he dropped it on the girl's face. It sounded like a slap. He picked up the rock again, trying not to look at her, and dropped it once more. Then he picked up the rock again.

Bill made his way through the defile. It was very late now, almost evening. He saw where somebody had gone up the hill, turned and retraced his steps to go a different, easier way.

He'd caught up with the little one, Barbara, but that was all; he hadn't tried to kiss her, much less anything else. He honestly just hadn't felt like it. Anyway, he was afraid. Maybe she was willing, maybe she wasn't, but he had too much at stake to take a chance. She was down at the bicycles now, waiting for her friend. No, he just wanted to round up Jerry, get back before it got any later. He knew he was going to catch hell from Linda, and she was probably worried sick besides. It was too late, they should have been back hours ago. He was very nervous and sprinted the last few feet up the hill, onto the little plateau.

He saw them both at the same time, Jerry standing to the other side of the girl, holding the rock.

Bill felt himself shrinking, becoming thin and weightless. At the same time he had the sensation of standing against a heavy wind that was cuffing his ears. He wanted to break loose and run, run, but something was moving towards him. The shadows of the rocks as the shape came across them seemed to move with the shape and under it. The ground seemed to have shifted in the odd-angled light. He thought unreasonably of the two bicycles waiting at the bottom of the hill near the car, as though taking one away would change all this, make the girl stop happening to him in that moment he had topped the hill.

But Jerry was standing now in front of him, slung loosely in his clothes as though the bones had gone out of him. Bill felt the awful closeness of their two bodies, less than an arm's length between. Then the head came down on Bill's shoulder. He raised his hand, and as if the distance now separating them deserved at least this, he began to pat, to stroke the other, while his own tears broke.

If It Please You

EDITH PACKER had the tape cassette cord plugged into her ear and was smoking one of his cigarettes. The TV played without any volume as she sat on the sofa with her legs tucked under her and turned the pages of a news magazine. James Packer came out of the guest room which he'd fixed up as an office. He was wearing his nylon windbreaker and looked surprised when he saw her, and then disappointed. She saw him and took the cord from her ear. She put the cigarette in the ashtray and wiggled the toes of one stockinged foot at him.

"Bingo," he said. "Are we going to play bingo tonight or not? We're going to be late, Edith."

"I'm going," she said. "Sure. I guess I got carried away." She liked classical music, and he didn't. He was a retired accountant, but he did tax returns for some old clients and he'd been working tonight. She hadn't wanted to play her music so that he'd hear it and be distracted.

"If we're going, let's go," he said. He looked at the TV, and then went to the set and turned it off.

"I'm going," she said. "Just let me go to the bathroom." She closed the magazine and got up. "Hold your old horses, dear," she said and smiled. She left the room.

He went to make sure the back door was locked and the porch lamp on, then came back to stand in the living room. It was a ten-minute drive to the community center, and he could see they were going to be late for the first game. He liked to be on time, which meant a few minutes early, so he'd have a chance to say hello to people he hadn't since last Friday night. He liked to joke with Frieda Parsons as he stirred sugar into his Styrofoam cup of coffee. She was one of the club women who ran the bingo game on Friday nights and during the week worked behind the counter of the town's only drugstore. He liked getting there with a little time to spare so he and Edith could get their coffee from Frieda and take their places at the last table along the wall. He liked that table. They'd occupied the same places at the same table every Friday night for months now. The first Friday night that he'd played bingo there, he'd won a forty-dollar jackpot. He'd told Edith afterwards that now he was hooked forever. "I've been looking for another vice," he'd said and grinned. Dozens of bingo cards were piled on each table, and you were supposed to pick through and find the cards you wanted, the cards that might be winning cards. Then you sat down, scooped a handful of white beans from the bowl on the table, and waited for the game to get under way, for the head of the women's club, stately white-haired Eleanor Bender, to commence turning her basket of numbered poker chips and begin calling numbers. That's the real reason you had to get there early, to get your place and pick out your particular cards. You had cards you favored and even felt you could recognize from week to week, cards whose arrangements of numbers seemed more inviting than those of other cards. Lucky cards, maybe. All of the cards had code numbers printed in the upper right-hand corner, and if you'd won a bingo on a certain card in the past, or even come close, or if you just had a feeling about certain cards, you got there early and went through the piles of cards for your cards. You started referring to them as your cards, and you'd look for them from week to week.

Edith finally came out of the bathroom. She had a puzzled expression on her face. There was no way they were going to be on time.

"What's the matter?" he said. "Edith?"

"Nothing," she said. "Nothing. Well, how do I look, Jimmy?"

"You look fine. Lord, we're just going to a bingo game," he said. "You know about everybody there anyway."

"That's the point," she said. "I want to look nice."

"You look nice," he said. "You always look nice. Can we go now?"

There seemed to be more cars than usual parked on the streets around the center. In the place where he normally parked, there was an old van with psychedelic markings on it. He had to keep going to the end of the block and turn.

"Lots of cars tonight," Edith said.

"There wouldn't be so many if we'd gotten here earlier," he said.

"There'd still be as many, we just wouldn't have seen them," she corrected, teasing. She pinched his sleeve.

"Edith, if we're going to play bingo we ought to try to get there on time," he said. "First rule of life is get where you're going on time."

"Hush," she said. "I feel like something's going to happen tonight. You watch and see. We're going to hit jackpots all night long. We're going to break the bank," she said.

"I'm glad to hear it," he said. "I call that confidence." He finally found a parking space near the end of the block and turned into it. He switched off the engine and cut the lights. "I don't know if I feel lucky tonight or not. I think I felt lucky earlier this evening for about five minutes when I was doing Howard's taxes, but I don't feel very lucky right now. It's not lucky if we have to start out walking half a mile just to play bingo."

"You stick close to me," she said. "We'll do fine."

"I don't feel lucky," he said. "Lock your door."

They began walking. There was a cold breeze and he zipped the windbreaker to his neck. She pulled her coat closer. He could hear the surf breaking on the rocks at the bottom of the cliff down behind the community center.

She said, "I'll take one of your cigarettes, Jimmy, before we get inside."

They stopped under the streetlamp at the corner. The wires supporting the old streetlamp swayed in the wind, and the light threw their shadows back and forth over the pavement. He could see the lights of the center at the end of the block. He cupped his hands and held the lighter for her. Then he lit his own cigarette. "When are you going to stop?" he said.

"When you stop," she said. "When I'm ready to stop. Maybe just like when you were ready to stop drinking. I'll just wake up some morning and stop. Like that. Like you. Then I'll find a hobby."

"I can teach you to knit," he said.

"I guess I don't think I have the patience for that," she said. "Besides, one knitter in the house is enough."

He smiled. He took her arm and they kept walking.

When they reached the steps in front of the center, she threw down her cigarette and stepped on it. They went up the steps and into the foyer. There was a sofa in the room, along with a scarred wooden table and several folding chairs. On the walls of the room hung old photographs of fishing boats and a naval vessel, a frigate from before the First World War, that had capsized off the point and been driven ashore onto the sandy beaches below the town. One photograph that always intrigued him showed a boat turned upside down on the rocks at low tide, a man standing on the keel and waving at the camera. There was a sea chart in an oak frame, and several paintings of pastoral scenes done by club members: rugged mountains behind a pond and a grove of trees, and paintings of the sun going down over the ocean. They passed through the room, and he took her arm again as they entered the hall. Several of the club women sat to the right of the entrance behind a long table. There were thirty or so other tables set up on the floor, along with folding chairs. Most of the chairs were filled. At the far end of the hall was a stage where Christmas programs were put on, and sometimes amateur theatrical productions. The bingo game was in progress. Eleanor Bender, holding a microphone, was calling numbers.

They didn't stop for coffee but walked quickly along the wall toward the back, toward their table. Heads bent over the tables. No one looked up at them. People watched their cards and waited for the next number to be called. He headed them toward their table, but tonight starting out the way it had already, he knew someone would have their places, and he was right.

It was a couple of hippies, he realized with a start, a man and a young woman, a girl really. The girl had on an old faded jeans outfit, pants and jacket, and a man's denim shirt, and was wearing rings and bracelets and long dangling earrings that moved when she moved. She moved now, turned to the long-haired fellow in the buckskin jacket beside her and pointed at a number on his card, then pinched his arm. The fellow had his hair pulled back and tied behind his head, and a scruffy bunch of hair on his face. He wore little steel-frame spectacles and had a tiny gold ring in his ear.

"Jesus," James said and stopped. He guided them to another table. "Here's two chairs. We'll have to take these places and take our chances. There's hippies in our place." He glared over in their direction. He took off his windbreaker and helped Edith with her coat. Then he sat down and looked again at the pair sitting in their place. The girl scanned her cards as the numbers were called. Then she leaned over next to the bushy fellow and looked his cards over, as if, James thought, she were afraid he might not have sense enough to mark his own numbers. James picked up a stack of bingo cards from the table and gave half to Edith. "Pick some winners for yourself," he said. "I'm just going to take these first three on top. I don't think it matters tonight which cards I choose. I don't feel very lucky tonight, and there's nothing I can do to change the feeling. What the hell's that pair doing here? They're kind of off their beaten path, if you ask me."

"Don't pay them any attention, Jimmy," she said. "They're not hurting anybody. They're just young, that's all."

"This is regular Friday night bingo for the people of this community," he said. "I don't know what they want here."

"They want to play bingo," she said, "or they wouldn't be here. Jimmy, dear, it's a free country. I thought you wanted to play bingo. Let's play, shall we? Here, I've found the cards I want." She gave him the stack of cards, and he put them with the other cards they wouldn't use in the center of the table. He noticed a pile of discards in front of the hippie. Well, he'd come here to play bingo and by God he was going to play. He fished a handful of beans from the bowl.

The cards were twenty-five cents each, or three cards for fifty cents. Edith had her three. James peeled a dollar bill from a roll of bills he kept for this occasion. He put the dollar next to his cards. In a few minutes one of the club women, a thin woman with bluish hair and a spot on her neck—he knew her only as Alice—would come around with a coffee can picking up quarters, dollar bills, dimes, and nickels, making change from the can when necessary. It was this woman, or another woman named Betty, who collected the money and paid off jackpots.

Eleanor Bender called "I-25," and a woman at a table in the middle of the room yelled, "Bingo!"

Alice made her way between the tables. She bent over the woman's card as Eleanor Bender read out the winning numbers. "It's a bingo," Alice said.

"That bingo, ladies and gentlemen, is worth twelve dollars,"

Eleanor Bender said. "Congratulations to you!" Alice counted
out some bills for the woman, smiled vaguely, and moved away.

"Get ready now," Eleanor Bender said. "Next game in two
minutes. I'll set the lucky numbers in motion right now." She
began turning the basket of poker chips.

They played four or five games to no purpose. Once James
was close on one of his cards, one number away from a bingo.
But Eleanor Bender called five numbers in succession, none of
them his, and even before someone else in the hall had found
the right number and called out, he knew she wouldn't be
calling the number he needed. Not for anything, he was convinced, would she have called his number.

"You were close that time, Jimmy," Edith said. "I was
watching your card."

"Close doesn't count," he said. "It may as well have been a
mile. She was teasing me, that's all." He turned the card up
and let the beans slide into his hand. He closed his hand and
made a fist. He shook the beans in his fist. Something came to
him about a kid who'd thrown some beans out of a window. It
had something to do with a carnival, or a fair. A cow was in
there too, he thought. The memory reached to him from a
long way and was somehow disturbing.

"Keep playing," Edith said. "Something's going to happen.
Change cards, maybe."

"These cards are as good as any others," he said. "It just
isn't my night, Edith, that's all."

He looked over at the hippies again. They were laughing at
something the fellow had said. He could see the girl rubbing
his leg under the table. They didn't seem to be paying attention to anyone else in the room. Alice came around collecting
money for the next game. But just after Eleanor Bender had
called the first number, James happened to glance in the direction of the hippies again. He saw the fellow put a bean down
on a card he hadn't paid for, a card that was supposed to be
with the discard pile. But the card lay so that the fellow could
see it and play it along with his other cards. Eleanor Bender
called another number, and the fellow placed another bean on
the same card. Then he pulled the card over to him with the
intention of playing it. James was amazed at the act. Then he

got mad. He couldn't concentrate on his own cards. He kept looking up to see what the hippie was doing. No one else seemed to have noticed.

"James, look at your cards," Edith said. "Watch your cards, dear. You missed number thirty-four. Here." She placed one of her beans on his number. "Pay attention, dear."

"That hippie over there who has our place is cheating. Doesn't that beat all?" James said. "I can't believe my eyes."

"Cheating? What's he doing?" she said. "How's he cheating at bingo, Jimmy?" She looked around, a little distracted, as if she'd forgotten where the hippie was sitting.

"He's playing a card that he hasn't paid for," he said. "I can see him doing it. My God, there's nothing they won't stop at. A bingo game! Somebody ought to report him."

"Not you, dear. He's not hurting us," Edith said. "One card more or less in such a roomful of cards and people. Let him play as many cards as he wants. There're some people here playing six cards." She spoke slowly and tried to keep her eyes on her cards. She marked a number.

"But they've paid for them," he said. "I don't mind that. That's different. This damned fellow is cheating, Edith."

"Jimmy, forget it, dear," she said. She extracted a bean from her palm and placed it on a number. "Leave him alone. Dear, play your cards. You have me confused now, and I've missed a number. Please play your cards."

"I have to say it's a hell of a bingo game when they can get away with murder," he said. "I resent that. I do."

He looked back at his cards, but he knew he might as well write this game off. The remaining games as well, for that matter. Only a few numbers on his cards had beans. There was no way of telling how many numbers he'd missed, how far behind he'd fallen. He clenched the beans in his fist. Without hope, he squeezed a bean out onto the number just called, G-60. Someone yelled, "Bingo!"

"Christ," he said.

Eleanor Bender said they would take a ten-minute break for people to get up and move around. The game after the break would be a blackout, one dollar a card, winner take all. This week's pot, Eleanor announced, was ninety-eight dollars. There was whistling and clapping. He looked over at the hippies. The fellow was touching the ring in his ear and looking around the room. The girl had her hand on his leg again.

"I have to go to the bathroom," Edith said. "Give me your cigarettes. Maybe you'd get us one of those nice raisin cookies we saw, and a cup of coffee."

"I'll do that," he said. "And, by God, I am going to change cards. These cards I'm playing are born losers."

"I'll go to the bathroom," she said. She put his cigarettes into her purse and stood up from the table.

He waited in line for cookies and coffee. He nodded at Frieda Parsons when she made some light remark, paid, then walked back to where the hippies were sitting. They already had their coffee and cookies. They were eating and drinking and conversing like normal people. He stopped behind the fellow's chair.

"I see what you're doing," James said to him.

The man turned around. His eyes widened behind his spectacles. "Pardon me?" he said and stared at James. "What am I doing?"

"You know," James said. The girl seemed frightened. She held her cookie and fixed her eyes on James. "I don't have to spell it out for you," James said to the man. "A word to the wise, that's all. I can see what you're doing."

He walked back to his table. He was trembling. Damn all the hippies in this world, he thought. It was enough of an encounter so that it made him feel he'd like to have a drink. Imagine wanting to drink over something happening at a bingo game. He put the coffee and cookies down on the table. Then he raised his eyes to the hippie, who was watching him. The girl was watching him too. The hippie grinned. The girl took a bite of her cookie.

Edith came back. She handed him the cigarettes and sat down. She was quiet. Very quiet. In a minute James recovered himself and said, "Is there anything the matter with you, Edith? Are you all right?" He looked at her closely. "Edith, has something happened?"

"I'm all right," she said and picked up her coffee. "No, I guess I should tell you, Jimmy. I don't want to worry you, though." She took a sip of her coffee and waited. Then she said, "I'm spotting again."

"Spotting?" he said. "What do you mean, Edith?" But he knew what she meant, that at this age and happening with the kind of pain she'd said it did, it might mean what they most feared. "Spotting," he said quietly.

"You know," she said, picking up some cards and beginning to sort through them. "I'm menstruating a little. Oh dear," she said.

"I think we should go home. I think we'd better leave," he said. "That isn't good, is it?" He was afraid she wouldn't tell him if the pain started. He'd had to ask her before, watching to see how she looked. She'd have to go in now. He knew it.

She sorted through some more cards and seemed flustered and a little embarrassed. "No, let's stay," she said after a minute. "Maybe it's nothing to worry about. I don't want you to worry. I *feel* all right, Jimmy," she said.

"Edith."

"We'll stay," she said. "Drink your coffee, Jimmy. It'll be all right, I'm sure. We came here to play bingo," she said and smiled a little.

"This is the worst bingo night in history," he said. "I'm ready to go anytime. I think we should go now."

"We'll stay for the blackout, and then it's just forty-five minutes or so. Nothing can happen in that time. Let's play bingo," she said, trying to sound cheerful.

He swallowed some coffee. "I don't want my cookie," he said. "You can have my cookie." He cleared away the cards he was using and took two cards from the stack of bingo cards that weren't in use. He looked over angrily at the hippies as if they were somehow to blame for this new development. But the fellow was gone from the table and the girl had her back to him. She had turned in her chair and was looking toward the stage.

They played the blackout game. Once he glanced up and the hippie was still at it, playing a card he hadn't paid for. James still felt he should call the matter to someone's attention, but he couldn't leave his cards, not at a dollar a card. Edith's lips were tight. She wore a look that could have been determination, or worry.

James had three numbers to cover on one card and five numbers on another card, a card he'd already given up on, when the hippie girl began screaming. "Bingo! Bingo! Bingo! I have a bingo!"

The man clapped and shouted with her. "She's got a bingo! She's got a bingo, folks! A bingo!" He kept clapping.

Eleanor Bender herself went to the girl's table to check her card against the master list of numbers. Then she said, "This young woman has just won herself a ninety-eight-dollar jackpot. Let's give her a round of applause. Let's hear it for her."

Edith clapped along with the rest of the players, but James kept his hands on the table. The hippie fellow hugged the girl. Eleanor Bender handed the girl an envelope. "Count it if you want to," she said with a smile. The girl shook her head.

"They'll probably use the money to buy drugs," James said.

"James, please," Edith said. "It's a game of chance. She won fair and square."

"Maybe she did," he said. "But her partner there is out to take everyone for all he can get."

"Dear, do you want to play the same cards again?" Edith said. "They're about to start the next game."

They stayed for the rest of the games. They stayed until the last game was played, a game called Progressive. It was a bingo game whose jackpot was increased each week if no one had bingoed on a fixed amount of numbers. If no one had hit a bingo when the last number was called, that game was declared closed and more money, five dollars, was added to the pot for the next week's game, along with another number. The first week the game had started, the jackpot was seventy-five dollars and thirty numbers. This week it was a hundred and twenty-five dollars and forty numbers. Bingos were rare before forty numbers had been called, but after forty numbers you could expect someone to bingo at any time. James put his money down and played his cards without any hope or intention of winning. He felt close to despair. It wouldn't have surprised him if the hippie had won this game.

When the forty numbers had been called and no one had cried out, Eleanor Bender said, "That's bingo for tonight. Thank you all for coming. God bless you, and if He's willing we'll see you again next Friday. Good night and have a nice weekend."

James and Edith filed out of the hall along with the rest of the players, but somehow they managed to get behind the hippie couple, who were still laughing and talking about her big jackpot. The girl patted her coat pocket and laughed again. She had an arm around the fellow's waist under his buckskin jacket, fingers just touching his hip.

"Let those people get ahead of us, for God's sake," James said to Edith. "They're a plague."

Edith kept quiet, but she hung back a little with James to give the couple time to move ahead.

"Good night, James. Good night, Edith," Henry Kuhlken said. Kuhlken was a graying heavyset man who'd lost a son in a boating accident years before. His wife had left him for another man not long afterwards. He'd turned to serious drinking after a time and later wound up in AA, where James had first met him and heard his stories. Now he owned one of the two service stations in town and sometimes did mechanical work on their car. "See you next week."

"'Night, Henry," James said. "I guess so. But I feel pretty bingoed out tonight."

Kuhlken laughed. "I know just exactly what you mean," he said and moved on.

The wind was up and James thought he could hear the surf over the sound of automobile engines starting. He saw the hippie couple stop at the van. He might have known. He should have put two and two together. The fellow pulled open his door and then reached across and opened the door on the woman's side. He started the van just as they walked by on the shoulder of the road. The fellow turned on his headlamps, and James and Edith were illumined against the walls of the nearby houses.

"That dumbbell," James said.

Edith didn't answer. She was smoking and had the other hand in her coat pocket. They kept walking along the shoulder. The van passed them and shifted gears as it reached the corner. The streetlamp was swinging in the wind. They walked on to their car. James unlocked her door and went around to his side. Then they fastened the seat belts and drove home.

—

Edith went into the bathroom and shut the door. James took off his windbreaker and threw it across the back of the sofa. He turned on the TV and sat down and waited.

In a little while Edith came out of the bathroom. She didn't say anything. James waited some more and tried to keep his eyes on the TV. She went to the kitchen and ran water. He heard her turn off the faucet. In a minute she came to the kitchen doorway and said, "I guess I'll have to see Dr. Crawford in the morning, Jimmy. I guess something's happening down there." She looked at him. Then she said, "Oh, damn it, damn it, the lousy, lousy luck," and began to cry.

"Edith," he said and moved to her.

She stood there shaking her head. She covered her eyes and leaned into him as he put his arms around her. He held her.

"Edith, dearest Edith," he said. "Good Lord." He felt helpless and terrified. He stood with his arms around her.

She shook her head a little. "I think I'll go to bed, Jimmy. I am just exhausted, and I really *don't* feel well. I'll go to see Dr. Crawford first thing in the morning. It'll be all right, I think, dear. You try not to worry. If anyone needs to worry tonight, let me. Don't you. You worry enough as it is. I think it'll be all right," she said and stroked his back. "I just put some water on for coffee, but I think I'll go to bed now. I feel worn out. It's these bingo games," she said and tried to smile.

"I'll turn everything off and go to bed too," he said. "I don't want to stay up tonight either, no sir."

"Jimmy, dear, I'd rather be alone right now, if you don't mind," she said. "It's hard to explain. It's just that right now I want to be alone. Dear, maybe that doesn't make any sense. You understand, don't you?"

"Alone," he repeated. He squeezed her wrist.

She reached up to his face and held him and studied his features for a minute. Then she kissed him on the lips. She went into the bedroom and turned on the light. She looked back at him, and then she shut the door.

He went to the refrigerator. He stood in front of the open door and drank tomato juice while he surveyed its lighted interior. Cold air blew out at him. The little packages and cartons of foodstuffs on the shelves, a chicken covered in plastic wrap, the neat foil-wrapped bundles of leftovers, all of this suddenly repelled him. He thought for some reason of Alice, that spot on her neck, and he shivered. He shut the door and spit the last of the juice into the sink. Then he rinsed his mouth and made himself a cup of instant coffee which he carried into the living room where the TV was still playing. It was an old Western. He sat down and lit a cigarette. After watching the screen for a few minutes, he felt he'd seen the movie before, years ago. The characters seemed faintly recognizable in their roles, and some of the things they said sounded familiar, as things to come often did in movies you'd forgotten. Then the hero, a movie star who'd recently died, said something—asked a hard question of another character, a stranger who'd just ridden into the little town; and all at once things fell into place, and James knew the very words that the stranger would pick out of the air to answer the question. He knew how things would turn out, but he kept watching the movie with a rising sense of apprehension. Nothing could stop what had been set in motion. Courage and fortitude were displayed by the hero and the townsmen-turned-deputies, but these virtues were not enough. It took only one lunatic and a torch to bring everything to ruin. He finished the coffee and smoked and watched the movie until its violent and inevitable conclusion. Then he turned off the set. He went to the bedroom door and listened, but there was no way of telling if she was awake. At least there was no light showing under the door. He hoped she was asleep. He kept listening. He felt vulnerable and somehow unworthy. Tomorrow she'd go to Dr. Crawford. Who knew what he would find? There'd be tests. Why Edith? he wondered. Why us? Why not someone else, why not those hippies tonight? They were sailing through life free as birds, no responsibilities, no doubts about the future. Why not them then, or someone else like them? It didn't add up. He moved away from the bedroom door. He thought about going out for a walk, as he did sometimes at night, but the wind had picked up and he could hear branches cracking in the birch tree behind the house. It'd be too cold anyway, and somehow the idea of a solitary walk tonight at this hour was dispiriting.

He sat in front of the TV again, but he didn't turn on the set. He smoked and thought of the way the hippie had grinned at him across the room. That sauntering, arrogant gait as he moved down the street toward his van, the girl's arm around his waist. He remembered the sound of the heavy surf, and he thought of great waves rolling in to break on the beach in the dark at this very minute. He recalled the fellow's earring and pulled at his own ear. What would it be like to want to saunter around like that fellow sauntered, a hippie girl's arm around your waist? He ran his fingers through his hair and shook his head at the injustice. He recalled the way the girl looked as she yelled her bingo, how everyone had turned enviously to look at her in her youth and excitement. If they only knew, she and her friend. If he could only tell them.

He thought of Edith in there in bed, the blood moving through her body, trickling, looking for a way out. He closed his eyes and opened them. He'd get up early in the morning and fix a nice breakfast for them. Then, when his office opened, she would call Dr. Crawford, set a time for seeing him, and he would drive her to the office and sit in the waiting room and page through magazines while he waited. About the time Edith came out with her news, he imagined that the hippies would be having their own breakfast, eating with appetite after a long night of lovemaking. It wasn't fair. He wished they were here now in the living room, in the noontime of their lives. He'd tell them what they could expect, he'd set them straight. He would stop them in the midst of their arrogance and laughter and tell them. He'd tell them what was waiting for them after the rings and bracelets, the earrings and long hair, the loving.

He got up and went into the guest room and turned on the lamp over the bed. He glanced at his papers and account books and at the adding machine on his desk and experienced a welling of dismay and anger. He found a pair of old pajamas in one of the drawers and began undressing. He turned back the covers on the bed at the other end of the room from his desk. Then he walked back through the house, turning off lights and checking doors. For the first time in four years he wished he had some whiskey in the house. Tonight would be the night for it, all right. He was aware that twice now in the course of this evening he had wanted something to drink, and he found this so discouraging that his shoulders slumped. They said in

AA never to become too tired, or too thirsty, or too hungry—or too smug, he might add. He stood looking out the kitchen window at the tree shaking under the force of the wind. The window rattled at its edges. He recalled the pictures down at the center, the boats going aground on the point, and hoped nothing was out on the water tonight. He left the porch lamp on. He went back to the guest room and took his basket of embroidery from under the desk and settled himself into the leather chair. He raised the lid of the basket and took out the metal hoop with the white linen stretched tight and secured within the hoop. Holding the tiny needle to the light, he threaded the eye with one end of the blue silk thread. Then he set to work where he'd left off on the floral design a few nights before.

When he'd first stopped drinking he'd laughed at the suggestion he'd heard one night at AA from a middle-aged businessman who said he might want to look into needlework. It was, he was told by the man, something he might want to do with the free time he'd now have on his hands, the time previously given over to drinking. It was implied that needlework was something he might find good occupation in day or night, along with a sense of satisfaction. "Stick to your knitting," the man had said and winked. James had laughed and shaken his head. But after a few weeks of sobriety when he did find himself with more time than he could profitably employ, and an increasing need for something to do with his hands and mind, he'd asked Edith if she'd shop for the materials and instruction booklets he needed. He was never all that good at it, his fingers were becoming increasingly slow and stiff, but he had done a few things that gave him satisfaction after the pillowcases and dishcloths for the house. He'd done crocheting too —the caps and scarves and mittens for the grandchildren. There was a sense of accomplishment when a piece of work, no matter how commonplace, lay finished in front of him. He'd gone from scarves and mittens to create little throw rugs which lay on the floor of every room in the house now. He'd also made two woolen ponchos which he and Edith wore when they walked on the beach; and he'd knitted an afghan, his most ambitious project to date, something that had kept him busy for the better part of six months. He'd worked on it every evening, piling up the small squares, and had been happy with the feeling of regular industry. Edith was sleeping under that afghan right now. Late nights he liked the feel of the hoop, its taut holding of the white cloth. He kept working the needle in and out of the linen, following the outline of the design. He tied little knots and clipped off bits of thread when he had to. But after a while he began to think about the hippie again, and he had to stop work. He got mad all over again. It was the principle of the thing, of course. He realized it hadn't helped the hippie's chances, except maybe by a fraction, just by cheating on a single card. He hadn't won, that was the point, the thing to bear in mind. You couldn't win, not really, not where it counted. He and the hippie were in the same boat, he thought, but the hippie just didn't know it yet.

James put the embroidery back into the basket. He stared down at his hands for a minute after he did so. Then he closed his eyes and tried to pray. He knew it would give him some satisfaction to pray tonight, if he could just find the right words. He hadn't prayed since he was trying to kick the drink, and he had never once imagined then that the praying would do any good, it just seemed to be one of the few things he could do under the circumstances. He'd felt at the time that it couldn't hurt anyway, even if he didn't believe in anything, least of all in his ability to stop drinking. But sometimes he felt better after praying, and he supposed that was the important thing. In those days he'd prayed every night that he could remember to pray. When he went to bed drunk, especially then, if he could remember, he prayed; and sometimes just before he had his first drink in the morning he prayed to summon the strength to stop drinking. Sometimes, of course, he felt worse, even more helpless and in the grip of something most perverse and horrible, after he'd say his prayers and then find himself immediately reaching for a drink. He had finally quit drinking, but he did not attribute it to prayer and he simply hadn't thought about prayer since then. He hadn't prayed in four years. After he'd stopped drinking, he just hadn't felt any need for it. Things had been fine since then, things had gotten good again after he'd stopped drinking. Four years ago he'd awakened one morning with a hangover, but instead of pouring himself a glass of orange juice and vodka, he decided he wouldn't. The vodka had still been in the house, too, which made the situation all the more remarkable. He just didn't drink that morning, nor that afternoon or evening. Edith had noticed, of course, but hadn't said anything. He shook a lot. The next day and the next were the same: he didn't drink and he stayed sober. On the fourth day, in the evening, he found the courage to say to Edith that it had been several days now since he'd had a drink. She had said simply, "I know that, dear." He remembered that now, the way she'd looked at him and touched his face, much in the manner she'd touched his face tonight. "I'm proud of you," she'd said, and that was all she'd said. He started going to the AA meetings, and it was soon after that he took up needlework.

Before the drinking had turned bad on him and he'd prayed to be able to stop, he'd prayed on occasions some years before that, after his youngest son had gone off to Vietnam to fly jet planes. He'd prayed off and on then, sometimes during the day if he thought about his son in connection with reading something in the newspaper about that terrible place; and sometimes at night lying in the dark next to Edith, turning over the day's events, his thoughts might come to rest on his son. He'd pray then, idly, like most men who are not religious pray. But nevertheless he'd prayed that his son would survive and come home in one piece. And he had returned safely too, but James hadn't ever for a minute really attributed his return to prayer—of course not. Now he suddenly remembered much farther back to a time when he'd prayed hardest of all, a time when he was twenty-one years old and still believed in the power of prayer. He'd prayed one entire night for his father, that he would recover from his automobile accident. But his father had died anyway. He'd been drunk and speeding and had hit a tree, and there was nothing that could be done to save his life. But even now he still remembered sitting outside the emergency room until sunlight entered the windows and praying and praying for his father, making all kinds of promises through his tears, if only his father would pull through. His mother had sat next to him and cried and held his father's shoes which had unaccountably come along in the ambulance beside him when they'd brought him to the hospital.

He got up and put his basket of embroidery away for the

night. He stood at the window. The birch tree behind the house was fixed in the little area of yellow light from the back porch lamp, the treetop lost in the overhead darkness. The leaves had been gone for months, but the bare branches switched in the gusts of wind. As he stood there he began to feel frightened, and then it was on him, a real terror welling in his chest. He could believe that something heavy and mean was moving around out there tonight, and that at any minute it might charge or break loose and come hurtling through the window at him. He moved back a few steps and stood where a corner of light from the porch lamp caused the room to brighten under him. His mouth had gone dry. He couldn't swallow. He raised his hands toward the window and let them drop. He suddenly felt he had lived nearly his whole life without having ever once really stopped to think about anything, and this came to him now as a terrible shock and increased his feeling of unworthiness.

He was very tired and had little strength left in his limbs. He pulled up the waist of his pajamas. He barely had energy to get into bed. He pushed up from the bed and turned off the lamp. He lay in the dark for a while. Then he tried praying again, slowly at first, forming the words silently with his lips, and then beginning to mutter words aloud and to pray in earnest. He asked for enlightenment on these matters. He asked for help in understanding the situation. He prayed for Edith, that she would be all right, that the doctor wouldn't find anything seriously wrong, not, please not, cancer, that's what he prayed for strongest. Then he prayed for his children, two sons and a daughter, scattered here and there across the continent. He included his grandchildren in these prayers. Then his thoughts moved to the hippie again. In a little while he had to sit up on the side of the bed and light a cigarette. He sat on the bed in the dark and smoked. The hippie woman, she was just a girl, not much younger or different-looking than his own daughter. But the fellow, him and his little spectacles, he was something else. He sat there for a while longer and turned things over. Then he put out his cigarette and got back under the covers. He settled onto his side and lay there. He rolled over onto his other side. He kept turning until he lay on his back, staring at the dark ceiling.

The same yellow light from the back porch lamp shone against the window. He lay with his eyes open and listened to the wind buffet the house. He felt something stir inside him again, but it was not anger this time. He lay without moving for a while longer. He lay as if waiting. Then something left him and something else took its place. He found tears in his eyes. He began praying again, words and parts of speech piling up in a torrent in his mind. He went slower. He put the words together, one after the other, and prayed. This time he was able to include the girl and the hippie in his prayers. Let them have it, yes, drive vans and be arrogant and laugh and wear rings, even cheat if they wanted. Meanwhile, prayers were needed. They could use them too, even his, especially his, in fact. "If it please you," he said in the new prayers for all of them, the living and the dead.

So Much Water So Close to Home

$\mathbf{M}$Y husband eats with good appetite but seems tired, edgy. He chews slowly, arms on the table, and stares at something across the room. He looks at me and looks away again, and wipes his mouth on the napkin. He shrugs, goes on eating. Something has come between us though he would like to believe otherwise.

"What are you staring at me for?" he asks. "What is it?" he says and lays his fork down.

"Was I staring?" I say and shake my head stupidly, stupidly.

The telephone rings. "Don't answer it," he says.

"It might be your mother," I say. "Dean—it might be something about Dean."

"Watch and see," he says.

I pick up the receiver and listen for a minute. He stops eating. I bite my lip and hang up.

"What did I tell you?" he says. He starts to eat again, then throws the napkin onto his plate. "Goddamn it, why can't people mind their own business? Tell me what I did wrong and I'll listen! It's not fair. She was dead, wasn't she? There were other men there besides me. We talked it over and we all decided. We'd only just got there. We'd walked for hours. We couldn't just turn around, we were five miles from the car. It was opening day. What the hell, I don't see anything wrong. No, I don't. And don't look at me that way, do you hear? I won't have you passing judgment on me. Not you."

"You know," I say and shake my head.

"What do I know, Claire? Tell me. Tell me what I know. I don't know anything except one thing; you hadn't better get worked up over this." He gives me what he thinks is a meaningful look. "She was dead, dead, dead, do you hear?" he says after a minute. "It's a damn shame, I agree. She was a young girl and it's a shame, and I'm sorry, as sorry as anyone else, but she was dead, Claire, dead. Now let's leave it alone. Please, Claire. Let's leave it alone now."

"That's the point," I say. "She was dead—but don't you see? She needed help."

"I give up," he says and raises his hands. He pushes his chair away from the table, takes his cigarettes and goes out to the patio with a can of beer. He walks back and forth for a minute and then sits in a lawn chair and picks up the paper once more. His name is there on the first page along with the names of his friends, the other men who made the "grisly find."

I close my eyes for a minute and hold onto the drainboard. I must not dwell on this any longer. I must get over it; put it out of sight, out of mind, etc., and "go on." I open my eyes. Despite everything, knowing all that may be in store, I rake my arm across the drainboard and send the dishes and glasses smashing and scattering across the floor.

He doesn't move. I know he has heard, he raises his head as if listening, but he doesn't move otherwise, doesn't turn around to look. I hate him for that, for not moving. He waits a minute, then draws on his cigarette and leans back in the chair. I pity him for listening, detached, and then settling back and drawing on his cigarette. The wind takes the smoke out of his mouth in a thin stream. Why do I notice that? He can never know how much I pity him for that, for sitting still and listening, and letting the smoke stream out of his mouth . . .

He planned his fishing trip into the mountains last Sunday, a week before the Memorial Day weekend. He and Gordon Johnson, Mel Dorn, Vern Williams. They play poker, bowl, and fish together. They fish together every spring and early summer, the first two or three months of the season, before family vacations, Little League baseball, and visiting relatives can intrude. They are decent men, family men, responsible at their jobs. They have sons and daughters who go to school with our son, Dean. On Friday afternoon these four men left for a three-day fishing trip to the Naches River. They parked the car in the mountains and hiked several miles to where they wanted to fish. They carried their bedrolls, food and cooking utensils, their playing cards, their whiskey. The first evening at the river, even before they could set up camp, Mel Dorn found the girl floating face down in the river, nude, lodged near the shore against some branches. He called the other men and they all came to look at her. They talked about what to do. One of the men—Stuart didn't say which—perhaps it was Vern Williams, he is a heavyset, easy man who laughs often—one of them thought they should start back to the car at once. The others stirred the sand with their shoes and said they felt inclined to stay. They pleaded fatigue, the late hour, the fact that the girl "wasn't going anywhere." In the end they all decided to stay. They went ahead and set up the camp and built a fire and drank their whiskey. They drank a lot of whiskey and when the moon came up they talked about the girl. Someone thought they should do something to prevent the body from floating away. Somehow they thought that this might create a problem for them if she floated away during the night. They took flashlights and stumbled down to the river. The wind was up, a cold wind, and waves from the river lapped the sandy bank. One of the men, I don't know who, it might have been Stuart, he could have done it, waded into the water and took the girl by the fingers and pulled her, still face down, closer to shore, into shallow water, and then took a piece of nylon cord and tied it around her wrist and then secured the cord to tree roots, all the while the flashlights of the other men played over the girl's body. Afterwards, they went back to camp and drank more whiskey. Then they went to sleep. The next morning, Saturday, they cooked breakfast, drank lots of coffee, more whiskey, and then split up to fish, two men upriver, two men down.

That night, after they had cooked their fish and potatoes and had more coffee and whiskey, they took their dishes down to the river and washed them a few yards from where the girl lay in the water. They drank again and then they took out their cards and played and drank until they couldn't see their cards any longer. Vern Williams went to sleep but the others told coarse stories and spoke of vulgar or dishonest escapades out of their past, and no one mentioned the girl until Gordon Johnson, who'd forgotten for a minute, commented on the firmness of the trout they'd caught, and the terrible coldness of the river water. They'd stopped talking then but continued to drink until one of them tripped and fell cursing against the lantern, and then they climbed into their sleeping bags.

The next morning they got up late, drank more whiskey, fished a little as they kept drinking whiskey, and then, at one o'clock in the afternoon, Sunday, a day earlier than they'd planned, decided to leave. They took down their tents, rolled their sleeping bags, gathered their pans, pots, fish and fishing gear, and hiked out. They didn't look at the girl again before they left. When they reached the car they drove the highway in silence until they came to a telephone. Stuart made the call to the sheriff's office while the others stood around in the hot sun and listened. He gave the man on the other end of the line all of their names—they had nothing to hide, they weren't ashamed of anything—and agreed to wait at the service station until someone could come for more detailed directions and individual statements.

He came home at eleven o'clock that night. I was asleep but woke when I heard him in the kitchen. I found him leaning against the refrigerator drinking a can of beer. He put his heavy arms around me and rubbed his hands up and down my back, the same hands he'd left with two days before, I thought.

In bed he put his hands on me again and then waited, as if thinking of something else. I turned slightly and then moved my legs. Afterwards, I know he stayed awake for a long time, for he was awake when I fell asleep; and later, when I stirred for a minute, opening my eyes at a slight noise, a rustle of sheets, it was almost daylight outside, birds were singing, and he was on his back smoking and looking at the curtained window. Half-asleep, I said his name, but he didn't answer. I fell asleep again.

He was up that morning before I could get out of bed, to see if there was anything about it in the paper, I suppose. The telephone began to ring shortly after eight o'clock.

"Go to hell," I heard him shout into the receiver. The telephone rang again a minute later, and I hurried into the kitchen. "I have nothing else to add to what I've already said to the sheriff. That's right!" He slammed down the receiver.

"What is going on?" I said, alarmed.

"Sit down," he said slowly. His fingers scraped, scraped against his stubble of whiskers. "I have to tell you something. Something happened while we were fishing." We sat across from each other at the table, and then he told me.

I drank coffee and stared at him as he spoke. I read the account in the newspaper that he shoved across the table . . . unidentified girl eighteen to twenty-four years of age . . . body three to five days in the water . . . rape a possible motive . . . preliminary results show death by strangulation . . . cuts and bruises on her breasts and pelvic area . . . autopsy . . . rape, pending further investigation.

"You've got to understand," he said. "Don't look at me like that. Be careful now, I mean it. Take it easy, Claire."

"Why didn't you tell me last night?" I asked.

"I just . . . didn't. What do you mean?" he said.

"You know what I mean," I said. I looked at his hands, the broad fingers, knuckles covered with hair, moving, lighting a cigarette now, fingers that had moved over me, into me last night.

He shrugged. "What difference does it make, last night, this morning? You were sleepy, I thought I'd wait until this morning to tell you." He looked out to the patio; a robin flew from the lawn to the picnic table and preened its feathers.

"It isn't true," I said. "You didn't leave her there like that?"

He turned quickly and said, "What'd I do? Listen to me carefully now, once and for all. Nothing happened. I have nothing to be sorry for or feel guilty about. Do you hear me?"

I got up from the table and went to Dean's room. He was awake and in his pajamas, putting together a puzzle. I helped him find his clothes and then went back to the kitchen and put his breakfast on the table. The telephone rang two or three more times and each time Stuart was abrupt while he talked and angry when he hung up. He called Mel Dorn and Gordon Johnson and spoke with them, slowly, seriously, and then he opened a beer and smoked a cigarette while Dean ate, asked him about school, his friends, etc., exactly as if nothing had happened.

Dean wanted to know what he'd done while he was gone, and Stuart took some fish out of the freezer to show him.

"I'm taking him to your mother's for the day," I said.

"Sure," Stuart said and looked at Dean, who was holding one of the frozen trout. "If you want to and he wants to, that is. You don't have to, you know. There's nothing wrong."

"I'd like to anyway," I said.

"Can I go swimming there?" Dean asked and wiped his fingers on his pants.

"I believe so," I said. "It's a warm day so take your suit, and I'm sure Grandmother will say it's okay."

Stuart lighted another cigarette and looked at us.

Dean and I drove across town to Stuart's mother's. She lives in an apartment building with a pool and a sauna bath. Her name is Catherine Kane. Her name, Kane, is the same as mine, which seems impossible. Years ago, Stuart has told me, she used to be called Candy by her friends. She is a tall, cold woman with white-blond hair. She gives me the feeling that she is always judging, judging. I explain briefly in a low voice what has happened (she hasn't yet read the newspaper) and promise to pick Dean up that evening. "He brought his swimming suit," I say. "Stuart and I have to talk about some things," I add vaguely. She looks at me steadily from over her glasses. Then she nods and turns to Dean, saying, "How are you, my little man?" She stoops and puts her arms around him. She looks at me again as I open the door to leave. She has a way of looking at me without saying anything.

When I returned home Stuart was eating something at the table and drinking beer . . .

After a time I sweep up the broken dishes and glassware and go outside. Stuart is lying on his back on the grass now, the newspaper and can of beer within reach, staring at the sky. It is breezy but warm out and birds call.

"Stuart, could we go for a drive?" I say. "Anywhere."

He rolls over and looks at me and nods. "We'll pick up some beer," he says. "I hope you're feeling better about this. Try to understand, that's all I ask." He gets to his feet and touches me on the hip as he goes past. "Give me a minute and I'll be ready."

We drive through town without speaking. Before we reach the country he stops at a roadside market for beer. I notice a great stack of papers just inside the door. On the top step a fat woman in a print dress holds out a licorice stick to a little girl. In a few minutes we cross Everson Creek and turn into a picnic area a few feet from the water. The creek flows under the bridge and into a large pond a few hundred yards away. There are a dozen or so men and boys scattered around the banks of the pond under the willows, fishing.

So much water so close to home, why did he have to go miles away to fish?

"Why did you have to go there of all places?" I say.

"The Naches? We always go there. Every year, at least once."
We sit on a bench in the sun and he opens two cans of beer
and gives one to me. "How the hell was I to know anything
like that would happen?" He shakes his head and shrugs, as if
it had all happened years ago, or to someone else. "Enjoy the
afternoon, Claire. Look at this weather."

"They said they were innocent."

"Who? What are you talking about?"

"The Maddox brothers. They killed a girl named Arlene
Hubly near the town where I grew up, and then cut off her
head and threw her into the Cle Elum River. She and I went to
the same high school. It happened when I was a girl."

"What a hell of a thing to be thinking about," he says.
"Come on, get off it. You're going to get me riled in a minute.
How about it now? Claire?"

I look at the creek. I float toward the pond, eyes open, face
down, staring at the rocks and moss on the creek bottom until
I am carried into the lake where I am pushed by the breeze.
Nothing will be any different. We will go on and on and on
and on. We will go on even now, as if nothing had happened. I
look at him across the picnic table with such intensity that his
face drains.

"I don't know what's wrong with you," he says. "I don't—"

I slap him before I realize. I raise my hand, wait a fraction of
a second, and then slap his cheek hard. This is crazy, I think as
I slap him. We need to lock our fingers together. We need to
help one another. This is crazy.

He catches my wrist before I can strike again and raises his
own hand. I crouch, waiting, and see something come into his
eyes and then dart away. He drops his hand. I drift even faster
around and around in the pond.

"Come on, get in the car," he says. "I'm taking you home."

"No, no," I say, pulling back from him.

"Come on," he says, "Goddamn it."

"You're not being fair to me," he says later in the car. Fields
and trees and farmhouses fly by outside the window. "You're
not being fair. To either one of us. Or to Dean, I might add.
Think about Dean for a minute. Think about me. Think about
someone else besides yourself for a change."

There is nothing I can say to him now. He tries to concen-

trate on the road, but he keeps looking into the rearview mirror. Out of the corner of his eye, he looks across the seat to
where I sit with my knees doubled under me. The sun blazes
against my arm and the side of my face. He opens another beer
while he drives, drinks from it, then shoves the can between his
legs and lets out breath. He knows. I could laugh in his face. I
could weep.

2.

Stuart believes he is letting me sleep this morning. But I was
awake long before the alarm sounded, thinking, lying on the
far side of the bed, away from his hairy legs and his thick,
sleeping fingers. He gets Dean off for school, and then he
shaves, dresses, and leaves for work himself soon after. Twice
he looks into the bedroom and clears his throat, but I keep my
eyes closed.

In the kitchen I find a note from him signed "Love." I sit in
the breakfast nook in the sunlight and drink coffee and make a
coffee ring on the note. The telephone has stopped ringing,
that is something. No more calls since last night. I look at the
paper and turn it this way and that on the table. Then I pull it
close and read what it says. The body is still unidentified, un-
claimed, apparently unmissed. But for the last twenty-four
hours men have been examining it, putting things into it, cutting, weighing, measuring, putting back again, sewing up,
looking for the exact cause and moment of death. And the evidence of rape. I'm sure they hope for rape. Rape would make
it easier to understand. The paper says she will be taken to
Keith & Keith Funeral Home pending arrangements. People
are asked to come forward with information, etc.

Two things are certain: 1) people no longer care what happens to other people, and 2) nothing makes any real difference
any longer. Look at what has happened. Yet nothing will change
for Stuart and me. Really change, I mean. We will grow older,
both of us, you can see it in our faces already, in the bathroom
mirror, for instance, mornings when we use the bathroom at
the same time. And certain things around us will change,
become easier or harder, one thing or the other, but nothing
will ever really be any different. I believe that. We have made

our decisions, our lives have been set in motion, and they will go on and on until they stop. But if that is true, what then? I mean, what if you believe that, but you keep it covered up, until one day something happens that should change something, but then you see nothing is going to change after all. What then? Meanwhile, the people around you continue to talk and act as if you were the same person as yesterday, or last night, or five minutes before, but you are really undergoing a crisis, your heart feels damaged . . .

The past is unclear. It is as if there is a film over those early years. I cannot be sure that the things I remember happening really happened to me. There was a girl who had a mother and father—the father ran a small café where the mother acted as waitress and cashier—who moved as if in a dream through grade school and high school and then, in a year or two, into secretarial school. Later, much later—what happened to the time in between?—she is in another town working as a receptionist for an electronic parts firm and becomes acquainted with one of the engineers who asks her for a date. Eventually, seeing that's his aim, she lets him seduce her. She had an intuition at the time, an insight about the seduction that later, try as she might, she couldn't recall. After a short while they decide to get married, but already the past, her past, is slipping away. The future is something she can't imagine. She smiles, as if she has a secret, when she thinks about the future. Once during a particularly bad argument, over what she can't now remember, five years or so after they were married, he tells her that someday this affair (his words: "this affair") will end in violence. She remembers this. She files this away somewhere and begins repeating it aloud from time to time. Sometimes, she spends the whole morning on her knees in the sandbox behind the garage playing with Dean and one or two of his friends. But every afternoon at four o'clock her head begins to hurt. She holds her forehead and feels dizzy with the pain. Stuart asks her to see a doctor and she does, secretly pleased at the doctor's solicitous attention. She goes away for a while to a place the doctor recommends. His mother comes out from Ohio in a hurry to care for the child. But she, Claire, Claire spoils everything and returns home in a few weeks. His mother moves out of the house and takes an apartment across town and perches there, as if waiting. One night in bed when they are both near sleep, Claire tells him that she heard some women patients at DeWitt discussing fellatio. She thinks this is something he might like to hear. She smiles in the dark. Stuart is pleased at hearing this. He strokes her arm. Things are going to be okay, he says. From now on everything is going to be different and better for them. He has received a promotion and a substantial raise. They have even bought another car, a station wagon, her car. They're going to live in the here and now. He says he feels able to relax for the first time in years. In the dark, he goes on stroking her arm . . . He continues to bowl and play cards regularly. He goes fishing with three friends of his.

That evening three things happen: Dean says that the children at school told him that his father found a dead body in the river. He wants to know about it.

Stuart explains quickly, leaving out most of the story, saying only that, yes, he and three other men did find a body while they were fishing.

"What kind of a body?" Dean asks. "Was it a girl?"

"Yes, it was a girl. A woman. Then we called the sheriff." Stuart looks at me.

"What'd he say?" Dean asks.

"He said he'd take care of it."

"What did it look like? Was it scary?"

"That's enough talk," I say. "Rinse your plate, Dean, and then you're excused."

"But what'd it look like?" he persists. "I want to know."

"You heard me," I say. "Did you hear me, Dean? Dean!" I want to shake him. I want to shake him until he cries.

"Do what your mother says," Stuart tells him quietly. "It was just a body, and that's all there is to tell."

I am clearing the table when Stuart comes up behind and touches my arm. His fingers burn. I start, almost losing a plate.

"What's the matter with you?" he says, dropping his hand. "Tell me, Claire, what is it?"

"You scared me," I say.

"That's what I mean. I should be able to touch you without you jumping out of your skin." He stands in front of me with a little grin, trying to catch my eyes, and then he puts his arm around my waist. With his other hand he takes my free hand and puts it on the front of his pants.

"Please, Stuart." I pull away and he steps back and snaps his fingers.

"Hell with it, then," he says. "Be that way if you want. But just remember."

"Remember what?" I say quickly. I look at him and hold my breath.

He shrugs. "Nothing, nothing," he says and cracks his knuckles.

The second thing that happens is that while we are watching television that evening, he in his leather reclining chair, I on the couch with a blanket and magazine, the house quiet except for the television, a voice cuts into the program to say that the murdered girl has been identified. Full details will follow on the eleven o'clock news.

We look at each other. In a few minutes he gets up and says he is going to fix a nightcap. Do I want one?

"No," I say.

"I don't mind drinking alone," he says. "I thought I'd ask."

I can see he is obscurely hurt, and I look away, ashamed and yet angry at the same time.

He stays in the kitchen for a long while, but comes back with his drink when the news begins.

First the announcer repeats the story of the four local fishermen finding the body, then the station shows a high school graduation photograph of the girl, a dark-haired girl with a round face and full, smiling lips, then a film of the girl's parents entering the funeral home to make the identification. Bewildered, sad, they shuffle slowly up the sidewalk to the front steps to where a man in a dark suit stands waiting and holding the door. Then, it seems as if only a second has passed, as if they have merely gone inside the door and turned around and come out again, the same couple is shown leaving the mortuary, the woman in tears, covering her face with a handkerchief, the man stopping long enough to say to a reporter, "It's her, it's Susan. I can't say anything right now. I hope they get the person or persons who did it before it happens again. It's all this violence . . ." He motions feebly at the television camera.

Then the man and woman get into an old car and drive away into the late afternoon traffic.

The announcer goes on to say that the girl, Susan Miller, had gotten off work as a cashier in a movie theater in Summit, a town 120 miles north of our town. A green late-model car pulled up in front of the theater and the girl, who according to witnesses looked as if she'd been waiting, went over to the car and got in, leading authorities to suspect that the driver of the car was a friend, or at least an acquaintance. The authorities would like to talk to the driver of the green car.

Stuart clears his throat, then leans back in the chair and sips his drink.

The third thing that happens is that after the news Stuart stretches, yawns, and looks at me. I get up and begin making a bed for myself on the couch.

"What are you doing?" he says, puzzled.

"I'm not sleepy," I say, avoiding his eyes. "I think I'll stay up awhile longer and then read something until I fall asleep."

He stares as I spread a sheet over the couch. When I start to go for a pillow, he stands at the bedroom door, blocking the way.

"I'm going to ask you once more," he says. "What the hell do you think you're going to accomplish?"

"I need to be by myself tonight," I say. "I just need to have time to think."

He lets out breath. "I'm thinking you're making a big mistake by doing this. I'm thinking you'd better think again about what you're doing. Claire?"

I can't answer. I don't know what I want to say. I turn and begin to tuck in the edges of the blanket. He stares at me a minute longer and then I see him raise his shoulders. "Suit yourself, then. I could give a fuck less what you do," he says and turns and walks down the hall scratching his neck.

This morning I read in the paper that services for Susan Miller are to be held in Chapel of the Pines, Summit, at two o'clock the next afternoon. Also, that police have taken statements from three people who saw her get into the green Chevrolet, but they still have no license number for the car. They are getting warmer, though, the investigation is continuing. I sit for a long while holding the paper, thinking, then I call to make an appointment at the hairdresser's.

I sit under the dryer with a magazine on my lap and let Millie do my nails.

"I'm going to a funeral tomorrow," I say after we have talked a bit about a girl who no longer works there.

Millie looks up at me and then back at my fingers. "I'm sorry to hear that, Mrs. Kane. I'm real sorry."

"It's a young girl's funeral," I say.

"That's the worst kind. My sister died when I was a girl, and I'm still not over it to this day. Who died?" she says after a minute.

"A girl. We weren't all that close, you know, but still."

"Too bad. I'm real sorry. But we'll get you fixed up for it, don't worry. How's that look?"

"That looks . . . fine. Millie, did you ever wish you were somebody else, or else just nobody, nothing, nothing at all?"

She looks at me. "I can't say I ever felt that, no. No, if I was somebody else I'd be afraid I might not like who I was." She holds my fingers and seems to think about something for a minute. "I don't know, I just don't know . . . Let me have your other hand now, Mrs. Kane."

At eleven o'clock that night I make another bed on the couch and this time Stuart only looks at me, rolls his tongue behind his lips, and goes down the hall to the bedroom. In the night I wake and listen to the wind slamming the gate against the fence. I don't want to be awake, and I lie for a long while with my eyes closed. Finally I get up and go down the hall with my pillow. The light is burning in our bedroom and Stuart is on his back with his mouth open, breathing heavily. I go into Dean's room and get into bed with him. In his sleep he moves over to give me space. I lie there for a minute and then hold him, my face against his hair.

"What is it, Mama?" he says.

"Nothing, honey. Go back to sleep. It's nothing, it's all right."

I get up when I hear Stuart's alarm, put on coffee and prepare breakfast while he shaves.

He appears in the kitchen doorway, towel over his bare shoulder, appraising.

"Here's coffee," I say. "Eggs will be ready in a minute."

He nods.

I wake Dean and the three of us have breakfast. Once or twice Stuart looks at me as if he wants to say something, but each time I ask Dean if he wants more milk, more toast, etc.

"I'll call you today," Stuart says as he opens the door.

"I don't think I'll be home today," I say quickly. "I have a lot of things to do today. In fact, I may be late for dinner."

"All right. Sure." He wants to know, he moves his briefcase from one hand to the other. "Maybe we'll go out for dinner tonight? How would you like that?" He keeps looking at me. He's forgotten about the girl already. "Are you . . . all right?"

I move to straighten his tie, then drop my hand. He wants to kiss me good-bye. I move back a step. "Have a nice day, then," he says finally. Then he turns and goes down the walk to his car.

I dress carefully. I try on a hat that I haven't worn in several years and look at myself in the mirror. Then I remove the hat, apply a light makeup, and write a note for Dean.

> Honey, Mommy has things to do this afternoon, but will be home later. You are to stay in the house or in the backyard until one of us comes home.
>
>   Love

I look at the word "Love" and then I underline it. As I am writing the note I realize I don't know whether backyard is one word or two. I have never considered it before. I think about it and then I draw a line and make two words of it.

I stop for gas and ask directions to Summit. Barry, a forty-year-old mechanic with a moustache, comes out from the rest-room and leans against the front fender while the other man, Lewis, puts the hose into the tank and begins to slowly wash the windshields.

"Summit," Barry says, looking at me and smoothing a finger down each side of his moustache. "There's no best way to get to Summit, Mrs. Kane. It's about a two-, two-and-a-half-hour drive each way. Across the mountains. It's quite a drive for a woman. Summit? What's in Summit, Mrs. Kane?"

"I have business," I say, vaguely uneasy. Lewis has gone to wait on another car.

"Ah. Well, if I wasn't all tied up there"—he gestures with his thumb toward the bay—"I'd offer to drive you to Summit and back again. Road's not all that good. I mean it's good enough, there's just a lot of curves and so on."

"I'll be all right. But thank you." He leans against the fender. I can feel his eyes as I open my purse.

Barry takes the credit card. "Don't drive it at night," he says. "It's not all that good a road, like I said, and while I'd be willing to bet you wouldn't have car trouble with this, I know this car, you can never be sure about blowouts and things like that. Just to be on the safe side I'd better check these tires." He taps one of the front tires with his shoe. "We'll run it onto the hoist. Won't take long."

"No, no, it's all right. Really, I can't take any more time. The tires look fine to me."

"Only takes a minute," he says. "Be on the safe side."

"I said no. No! They look fine to me. I have to go now, Barry . . ."

"Mrs. Kane?"

"I have to go now."

I sign something. He gives me the receipt, the card, some stamps. I put everything in my purse. "You take it easy," he says. "Be seeing you."

Waiting to pull into traffic, I look back and see him watching. I close my eyes, then open them. He waves.

I turn at the first light, then turn again and drive until I come to the highway and read the sign: SUMMIT 117 miles. It is ten thirty and warm.

The highway skirts the edge of town, then passes through farm country, through fields of oats and sugar beets and apple orchards, with here and there a small herd of cattle grazing in open pastures. Then everything changes, the farms become fewer and fewer, more like shacks now than houses, and stands of timber replace the orchards. All at once I'm in the mountains and on the right, far below, I catch glimpses of the Naches River.

In a little while a green pickup truck comes up behind me and stays behind for miles. I keep slowing at the wrong times, hoping he will pass, and then increasing my speed, again at the wrong times. I grip the wheel until my fingers hurt. Then on a long clear stretch he does pass, but he drives along beside for a minute, a crew-cut man in a blue workshirt in his early thirties, and we look at each other. Then he waves, toots the horn twice, and pulls ahead of me.

I slow down and find a place, a dirt road off of the shoulder, pull over and shut off the ignition. I can hear the river somewhere down below the trees. Ahead of me the dirt road goes into the trees. Then I hear the pickup returning.

I start the engine just as the truck pulls up behind me. I lock the doors and roll up the windows. Perspiration breaks on my face and arms as I put the car in gear, but there is no place to drive.

"You all right?" the man says as he comes up to the car. "Hello. Hello in there." He raps the glass. "Are you okay?" He leans his arms on the door then and brings his face close to the window.

I stare at him and can't find any words.

"After I passed I slowed up some," he says, "but when I didn't see you in the mirror I pulled off and waited a couple of minutes. When you still didn't show I thought I'd better drive back and check. Is everything all right? How come you're locked up in there?"

I shake my head.

"Come on, roll down your window. Hey, are you sure you're okay? Huh? You know it's not good for a woman to be batting around the country by herself." He shakes his head and looks at the highway and then back at me. "Now come on, roll down the window, how about it? We can't talk this way."

"Please, I have to go."

"Open the door, all right?" he says, as if he isn't listening. "At least roll down the window. You're going to smother in there." He looks at my breasts and legs. The skirt has pulled up over my knees. His eyes linger on my legs, but I sit still, afraid to move.

"I want to smother," I say. "I am smothering, can't you see?"

"What in the hell?" he says and moves back from the door. He turns and walks back to his truck. Then, in the side mirror, I watch him returning, and close my eyes.

"You don't want me to follow you toward Summit, or anything? I don't mind. I got some extra time this morning."

I shake my head again.

He hesitates and then shrugs. "Have it your way, then," he says.

I wait until he has reached the highway, and then I back out. He shifts gears and pulls away slowly, looking back at me in his rearview mirror. I stop the car on the shoulder and put my head on the wheel.

The casket is closed and covered with floral sprays. The organ begins soon after I take a seat near the back of the chapel. People begin to file in and find chairs, some middle-aged and older people, but most of them in their early twenties or even younger. They are people who look uncomfortable in their suits and ties, sports coats and slacks, their dark dresses and leather gloves. One boy in flared pants and a yellow short-sleeved shirt takes the chair next to mine and begins to bite his lips. A door opens at one side of the chapel and I look up and for a minute the parking lot reminds me of a meadow, but then the sun flashes on car windows. The family enters in a group and moves into a curtained area off to the side. Chairs creak as they settle themselves. In a few minutes a thick, blond man in a dark suit stands and asks us to bow our heads. He speaks a brief prayer for us, the living, and when he finishes he asks us to pray in silence for the soul of Susan Miller, departed. I close my eyes and remember her picture in the newspaper and on television. I see her leaving the theater and getting into the green Chevrolet. Then I imagine her journey down the river, the nude body hitting rocks, caught at by branches, the body floating and turning, her hair streaming in the water. Then the hands and hair catching in the overhanging branches, holding, until four men come along to stare at her. I can see a man who is drunk (Stuart?) take her by the wrist. Does anyone here know about that? What if these people knew that? I look around at the other faces. There is a connection to be made of these things, these events, these faces, if I can find it. My head aches with the effort to find it.

He talks about Susan Miller's gifts: cheerfulness and beauty, grace and enthusiasm. From behind the closed curtain someone clears his throat, someone else sobs. The organ music begins. The service is over.

Along with the others I file slowly past the casket. Then I

move out onto the front steps and into the bright, hot afternoon light. A middle-aged woman who limps as she goes
down the stairs ahead of me reaches the sidewalk and looks
around, her eyes falling on me. "Well, they got him," she says.
"If that's any consolation. They arrested him this morning. I
heard it on the radio before I came. A guy right here in town.
A longhair, you might have guessed." We move a few steps
down the hot sidewalk. People are starting cars. I put out my
hand and hold on to a parking meter. Sunlight glances off polished hoods and fenders. My head swims. "He's admitted
having relations with her that night, but he says he didn't kill
her." She snorts. "You know as well as I do. But they'll probably put him on probation and then turn him loose."

"He might not have acted alone," I say. "They'll have to be
sure. He might be covering up for someone, a brother, or
some friends."

"I have known that child since she was a little girl," the
woman goes on, and her lips tremble. "She used to come over
and I'd bake cookies for her and let her eat them in front of
the TV." She looks off and begins shaking her head as the tears
roll down her cheeks.

3.

Stuart sits at the table with a drink in front of him. His eyes are
red and for a minute I think he has been crying. He looks at
me and doesn't say anything. For a wild instant I feel something has happened to Dean, and my heart turns.

Where is he? I say. Where is Dean?

Outside, he says.

Stuart, I'm so afraid, so afraid, I say, leaning against the door.

What are you afraid of, Claire? Tell me, honey, and maybe I
can help. I'd like to help, just try me. That's what husbands
are for.

I can't explain, I say. I'm just afraid. I feel like, I feel like, I
feel like . . .

He drains his glass and stands up, not taking his eyes from
me. I think I know what you need, honey. Let me play doctor,
okay? Just take it easy now. He reaches an arm around my

waist and with his other hand begins to unbutton my jacket, then my blouse. First things first, he says, trying to joke.

Not now, please, I say.

Not now, please, he says, teasing. Please nothing. Then he steps behind me and locks an arm around my waist. One of his hands slips under my brassiere.

Stop, stop, stop, I say. I stamp on his toes.

And then I am lifted up and then falling. I sit on the floor looking up at him and my neck hurts and my skirt is over my knees. He leans down and says, You go to hell, then, do you hear, bitch? I hope your cunt drops off before I touch it again. He sobs once and I realize he can't help it, he can't help himself either. I feel a rush of pity for him as he heads for the living room.

He didn't sleep at home last night.

This morning, flowers, red and yellow chrysanthemums. I am drinking coffee when the doorbell rings.

Mrs. Kane? the young man says, holding his box of flowers.

I nod and pull the robe tighter at my throat.

The man who called, he said you'd know. The boy looks at my robe, open at the throat, and touches his cap. He stands with his legs apart, feet firmly planted on the top step, as if asking me to touch him down there. Have a nice day, he says.

A little later the telephone rings and Stuart says, Honey, how are you? I'll be home early, I love you. Did you hear me? I love you, I'm sorry, I'll make it up to you. Good-bye, I have to run now.

I put the flowers into a vase in the center of the dining room table and then I move my things into the extra bedroom.

Last night, around midnight, Stuart breaks the lock on my door. He does it just to show me that he can, I suppose, for he does not do anything when the door springs open except stand there in his underwear looking surprised and foolish while the anger slips from his face. He shuts the door slowly and a few minutes later I hear him in the kitchen opening a tray of ice cubes.

He calls today to tell me that he's asked his mother to come stay with us for a few days. I wait a minute, thinking about this, and then hang up while he is still talking. But in a while I dial his number at work. When he finally comes on the line I say, It doesn't matter, Stuart. Really, I tell you it doesn't matter one way or the other.

I love you, he says.

He says something else and I listen and nod slowly. I feel sleepy. Then I wake up and say, For God's sake, Stuart, she was only a child.

Dummy

MY father was very nervous and disagreeable for a long time after Dummy's death, and I believe it somehow marked the end of a halcyon period in his life, too, for it wasn't much later that his own health began to fail. First Dummy, then Pearl Harbor, then the move to my grandfather's farm near Wenatchee, where my father finished out his days caring for a dozen apple trees and five head of cattle.

For me, Dummy's death signaled the end of my extraordinarily long childhood, sending me forth, ready or not, into the world of men—where defeat and death are more in the natural order of things.

First my father blamed it on the woman, Dummy's wife. Then he said, no, it was the fish. If it hadn't been for the fish it wouldn't have happened. I know he felt some to blame for it, because it was Father showed Dummy the advertisement in the classified section of *Field and Stream* for "live black bass shipped anywhere in the U.S." (It may be there now, for all I know.) That was at work one afternoon and Father asked Dummy why not order some bass and stock that pond in back of his house. Dummy wet his lips, Father said, and studied the advertisement a long while before laboriously copying the information down on the back of a candy wrapper and stuffing the wrapper down the front of his coveralls. It was later, after he received the fish, he began acting peculiarly. They changed his whole personality, Father claimed.

I never knew his real name. If anyone else did, I never heard it called. Dummy it was then, and Dummy I remember him by now. He was a little wrinkled man in his late fifties, bald headed, short but very muscular arms and legs. If he grinned, which was seldom, his lips furled back over yellow, broken teeth and gave him an unpleasant, almost crafty expression; an expression I still remember very clearly, though it's been twenty-five years ago. His small watery eyes always watched your lips when you were speaking, though sometimes they'd roam familiarly over your face, or your body. I don't know why, but I had the impression he was never really deaf. At least, not as deaf as he made out. But that isn't important. He couldn't speak, that was certain enough. He worked at the sawmill where my father worked, the Cascade Lumber Company in Yakima, Washington, and it was the men there who had given him the nickname "Dummy." He had worked there ever since the early 1920s. He was working as a cleanup man when I knew him, though I guess at one time or another he'd done every kind of common-labor job around the plant. He wore a grease-spotted felt hat, a khaki work shirt, and a light denim jacket over a bulging pair of coveralls. In his top front pockets he nearly always carried two or three rolls of toilet paper, as one of his jobs was to clean and supply the men's toilets; and the men on nights used to walk off after their shift with a roll or two in their lunchboxes. He also carried a flashlight, even though he worked days, as well as wrenches, pliers, screwdrivers, friction tape, all the things the millwrights carried. Some of the newer men like Ted Slade or Johnny Wait might kid him pretty heavily in the lunchroom about something, or tell him dirty jokes to see what he'd do, just because they knew he didn't like dirty jokes; or Carl Lowe, the sawyer, might reach down and snag Dummy's hat as he walked under the platform, but Dummy seemed to take it all in stride, as if he expected to be kidded and had gotten used to it.

Once, though, one day when I took Father his lunch at noon, four or five of the men had Dummy off in a corner at one of the tables. One of the men was drawing a picture and, grinning, was trying to explain something to Dummy, touching here and there on the paper with his pencil. Dummy was frowning. His neck crimsoned as I watched, and he suddenly drew back and hit the table with his fist. After a moment's stunned silence, everyone at the table broke up with laughter.

My father didn't approve of the kidding. He never kidded Dummy, to my knowledge. Father was a big, heavy-shouldered man with a crew haircut, a double chin, and a paunch—which, given the chance, he was fond of showing off. He was easy to make laugh, just as easy, only in a different way, to get riled. Dummy would stop in the filing room where he worked and sit on a stool and watch Father use the big emery-wheel grinders on the saws, and, if he wasn't too busy, he'd talk to Dummy as he worked. Dummy seemed to like my father, and

Father liked him too, I'm certain. In his own way, Father was probably as good a friend as Dummy had.

Dummy lived in a small tarpaper-covered house near the river, five or six miles from town. A half mile behind the house, at the end of a pasture, lay a big gravel pit that the state had dug years before when they were paving the roads in that area. Three good-sized holes had been scooped out and over the years they had filled with water. Eventually, the three separate ponds had formed one really large pond, with a towering pile of rocks at one side, and two smaller piles on the other. The water was deep with a blackish-green look to it; clear enough at the surface, but murky down toward the bottom.

Dummy was married to a woman fifteen or twenty years younger than he, who had the reputation of going around with Mexicans. Father said later it was busybodies at the mill that helped get Dummy so worked up at the end by telling him things about his wife. She was a small stout woman with glittery, suspicious eyes. I'd seen her only twice; once when she came to the window the time Father and I arrived at Dummy's to go fishing, and one other time when Pete Jensen and I stopped there on our bicycles to get a glass of water.

It wasn't just the way she made us wait out on the porch in the hot sun without asking us in that made her seem so distant and unfriendly. It was partly the way she said, "What do you want?" when she opened the door, before we could say a word. Partly the way she scowled, and partly the house, I suppose, the dry musty smell that came through the open door and reminded me of my aunt Mary's cellar.

She was a lot different than other grown women I'd met. I just stared for a minute, before I could say anything.

"I'm Del Fraser's son. He works with, with your husband. We were just on our bicycles and thought we'd stop for a drink . . ."

"Just a minute," she said. "Wait here."

Pete and I looked at each other.

She returned with a little tin cup of water in each hand. I downed mine in a single gulp and then ran my tongue around the cool rim. She didn't offer us any more.

I said, "Thanks," handing back the cup and smacking my lips.

"Thanks a lot!" Pete said.

She watched us without saying anything. Then, as we started to get on our bicycles, she walked over to the edge of the porch.

"You little fellas had a car now, I might catch a ride into town with you." She grinned; her teeth looked shiny white and too large for her mouth from where I stood. It was worse than seeing her scowl. I turned the handle grips back and forth and stared at her uneasily.

"Let's go," Pete said to me. "Maybe Jerry'll give us a pop if his dad ain't there."

He started away on his bicycle and looked back a few seconds later at the woman standing on the porch, still grinning to herself at her little joke.

"I wouldn't take you to town if I had a car!" he called.

I pushed off hurriedly and followed him down the road without looking back.

There weren't many places you could fish for bass in our part of Washington: rainbow trout, mostly, a few brook trout and Dolly Varden in some of the high mountain streams, and silvers in Blue Lake and Lake Rimrock; that was mostly it, except for the migratory runs of steelhead and salmon in several of the freshwater rivers in the late fall. But if you were a fisherman, it was enough to keep you occupied. No one I knew fished for bass. A lot of people I knew had never seen a real bass, only pictures now and then in some of the outdoor magazines. But my father had seen plenty of bass when he was growing up in Arkansas and Georgia: back home, as he always referred to the South. Now, though, he just liked to fish and didn't care much what he caught. I don't think he minded if he caught anything; I believe he just liked the idea of staying out all day, eating sandwiches and drinking beer with friends while sitting in a boat, or else walking by himself up or down a riverbank and having time to think, if that's what he felt like doing that particular day.

Trout, then, all kinds of trout, salmon and steelhead in the fall, and whitefish in the winter on the Columbia River. Father would fish for anything, at any time of the year, and with pleasure, but I think he was especially pleased that Dummy was going to stock his pond with black bass, for of course, Father assumed that when the bass were large enough, he'd be able to

fish there as often as he wished, Dummy being a friend. His
eyes gleamed when he told me one evening that Dummy had
sent off in the mail for a supply of black bass.

"Our own private pond!" Father said. "Wait till you tie into
a bass, Jack! You'll be all done as a trout fisherman."

Three or four weeks later the fish arrived. I'd gone swimming at the city pool that afternoon and Father told me about
it later. He'd just gotten home from work and changed clothes
when Dummy pulled up in the driveway. With hands trembling he showed Father the wire from the parcel post he'd
found at home that said three tanks of live fish from Baton
Rouge, Louisiana, were waiting to be picked up. Father was
excited too, and he and Dummy went down right then in
Dummy's pickup.

The tanks—barrels, really—were each crated in white, clean-
smelling new pine boards, with large rectangular openings cut
on the sides and at the top of each crate. They were standing in
the shade around at the back of the train depot, and it took my
father and Dummy both to lift each crate into the back of the
truck.

Dummy drove very carefully through town and then twenty-
five miles an hour all the way to his house. He drove through
his yard without stopping, down to within fifty feet of the
pond. By that time it was nearly dark, and he had his headlights on. He had a hammer and tire iron under the seat and
jumped out with them in his hand as soon as they stopped.
They lugged all three tanks down close to the water before
Dummy started to open the first crate. He worked in the headlights from his truck, and once caught his thumb with the claw
side of the hammer. The blood oozed thickly out over the
white boards, but he didn't seem to notice. After he'd pried
the boards off the first tank, he found the barrel inside covered
thickly with burlap and a kind of rattan material. A heavy
board lid had a dozen nickel-sized holes scattered around.
They raised the lid and both of them moved up over the tank
as Dummy took out his flashlight. Inside, scores of little bass
fingerlings finned darkly in the water in the tank. The beam of
light didn't bother them, they just swam and circled darkly
without seeming to go anywhere. Dummy moved his light

around the tank several minutes before he snapped it off and dropped it back in his pocket. He picked up the barrel with a grunt, started down to the water.

"Wait a minute, Dummy, let me help you," Father called to him.

Dummy set the tank at the water's edge, again removed the lid, and slowly poured the contents into the pond. He took out his flashlight and shined it into the water. Father went down, but there was nothing to be seen; the fish had scattered. Frogs croaked hoarsely on all sides, and in the overhead dark, nighthawks wheeled and darted after insects.

"Let me get the other crate, Dummy," Father said, reaching as if to take the hammer from Dummy's coveralls.

Dummy pulled back and shook his head. He undid the two crates himself, leaving dark drops of blood on the boards, stopping long enough with each tank to shine his light through the clear water to where the little bass swam slowly and darkly from one side to the other. Dummy breathed heavily through his open mouth the whole time, and when he was through he gathered up all the boards and the burlap mesh and the barrels and threw everything noisily into the back of the truck.

From that night, Father maintained, Dummy was a different person. The change didn't come about all at once, of course, but after that night, gradually, ever gradually, Dummy moved closer to the abyss. His thumb was swollen and still bleeding some, and his eyes had a protruding, glassy look to them in the light from the dashboard, as he bounced the truck across the pasture, and then drove the road taking Father home.

That was the summer I was twelve.

Dummy wouldn't let anyone go there now, not after Father and I tried to fish there one afternoon two years later. In those two years Dummy had fenced all the pasture behind his house, then fenced the pond itself with electrically charged barbed wire. It cost him over five hundred dollars for materials alone, Father said to my mother in disgust.

Father wouldn't have any more to do with Dummy. Not since that afternoon we were out there, toward the end of July. Father had even stopped speaking to Dummy, and he wasn't the sort to cut anyone.

One evening just before fall, when Father was working late and I took him his dinner, a plate of hot food covered with aluminum foil, and a mason jar of ice tea, I found him standing in front of the window talking with Syd Glover, the millwright. Father gave a short, unnaturally harsh laugh just as I came in and said, "You'd guess that fool was married to them fish, the way he acts. I just wonder when the men in white coats will come to take him away."

"From what I hear," Syd said, "he'd do better to put that fence round his house. Or his bedroom, to be more exact."

Father looked around and saw me then, raised his eyebrows slightly. He looked back at Syd. "But I told you how he acted, didn't I, the time me and Jack was out to his house?" Syd nodded, and Father rubbed his chin reflectively, then spat out the open window into the sawdust, before turning to me with a greeting.

A month before, Father had finally prevailed upon Dummy to let the two of us fish the pond. Bulldozed him might be the better word, for Father said he decided he simply wasn't going to take any more excuses. He said he could see Dummy stiffen up when he kept insisting one day, but he went on talking fast, joking to Dummy about thinning out the weakest bass, doing the rest of the bass a favor, and so on. Dummy just stood there pulling at his ear and staring at the floor. Father finally said we'd see him tomorrow afternoon, then, right after work. Dummy turned and walked away.

I was excited. Father had told me before that the fish had multiplied crazily and it would be like dropping your line into a hatchery pond. We sat at the kitchen table that night long after Mother had gone to bed, talking and eating snacks and listening to the radio.

Next afternoon when Father pulled into the drive, I was waiting on the front lawn. I had his half-dozen old bass plugs out of their boxes, testing the sharpness of the treble hooks with my forefinger.

"You ready?" he called to me, jumping out of the car. "I'll go to the toilet in a hurry, you put the stuff in. You can drive us out there, if you want."

"You bet!" I said. Things were starting out great. I'd put everything in the backseat and started toward the house when

Father came out the front door wearing his canvas fishing hat and eating a piece of chocolate cake with both hands.

"Get in, get in," he said between bites. "You ready?"

I got in on the driver's side while he went around the car. Mother looked at us. A fair-skinned, severe woman, her blond hair pulled into a bun at the back of her head and fastened down with a rhinestone clip. Father waved to her.

I let off the hand brake and backed out slowly onto the road. She watched us until I shifted gears, and then waved, still unsmiling. I waved, and Father waved again. He'd finished his cake, and he wiped his hands on his pants. "We're off!" he said.

It was a fine afternoon. We had all the windows down in the 1940 Ford station wagon, and the air was cold and blew through the car. The telephone wires alongside the road made a humming noise, and after we crossed the Moxee Bridge and swung west onto Slater Road, a big rooster pheasant and two hens flew low across the road in front of us and pitched into an alfalfa field.

"Look at that!" Father said. "We'll have to come out here this fall. Harland Winters has bought a place out here somewheres, I don't know exactly where, but he said he'd let us hunt when the season opens."

On either side of us, green wavy alfalfa fields, with now and then a house, or a house with a barn and some livestock behind a rail fence. Farther on, to the west, a huge yellow-brown cornfield and behind that, a stand of white birch trees that grew beside the river. A few white clouds moved across the sky.

"It's really great, isn't it, Dad? I mean, I don't know, but everything's just fun we do, isn't it?"

Father sat in the seat cross-legged, tapping his toe against the floorboards. He put his arm out the window and let the wind take it. "Sure, it is. Everything." Then, after a minute, he said, "Sure, you bet it's fun! Great to be alive!"

In a few minutes we pulled up in front of Dummy's, and he came out of the house wearing his hat. His wife looked out the window.

"You have your frying pan out, Dummy?" Father called to him as he came down the porch steps. "Fillet of bass and fried potatoes."

Dummy came up to where we stood beside the car. "What a

day for it!" Father went on. "Where's your pole, Dummy? Ain't you going to fish?"

Dummy jerked his head back and forth, No. He moved his weight from one bandy leg to the other and looked at the ground and then at us. His tongue rested on his lower lip, and he began working his right foot into the dirt. I shouldered the wicker creel and immediately felt Dummy's eyes on me, watching, as I gave Father his pole and picked up my own.

"We ready?" Father said. "Dummy?"

Dummy took off his hat and, with the same hand, wiped his wrist over his bald head. He turned abruptly, and we followed him over to the fence, about a hundred feet behind his house. Father winked at me.

We walked slowly across the spongy pasture. There was a fresh, clean smell in the air. Every twenty feet or so snipe flew up from the clumps of grass at the edge of the old furrows, and once a hen mallard jumped off a tiny, almost invisible puddle of water, and flew off quacking loudly.

"Probably got her nest there," Father said. A few feet farther on he began whistling, but then stopped after a minute.

At the end of the pasture the ground sloped gently and became dry and rocky with a few nettle bushes and scrub oak trees scattered here and there. Ahead of us, behind a tall stand of willows, the first pile of rocks rose fifty or seventy-five feet in the air. We cut to the right, following an old set of car tracks, going through a field of milkweed that came up to our waists. The dry pods at the tops of the stalks rattled as we pushed through. Dummy was walking ahead, I followed two or three steps behind, and Father was behind me. Suddenly I saw the sheen of water over Dummy's shoulder, and my heart jumped. "There it is!" I blurted out. "There it is!" Father said after me, craning his neck to see. Dummy began walking even slower and kept bringing his hand up nervously and moving his hat back and forth over his head.

He stopped. Father came up beside him and said, "What do you think, Dummy? Is one place as good as another? Where should we come onto it?"

Dummy wet his lower lip and looked around at us as if frightened.

"What's the matter with you, Dummy?" Father said sharply. "This is your pond, ain't it? You act like we was trespassing or something."

Dummy looked down and picked an ant off the front of his coveralls.

"Well, hell," Father said, letting out his breath. He took out his watch. "If it's still all right with you, Dummy, we can fish for forty-five minutes or an hour. Before it gets dark. Huh? What about it?"

Dummy looked at him and then put his hands in his front pockets and turned toward the pond. He started walking again. Father looked at me and shrugged. We trailed along behind. Dummy acting the way he was took some of the edge off our excitement. Father spat two or three times without clearing his throat.

We could see the whole pond now, and the water was dimpled with rising fish. Every minute or so a bass would leap clear of the water and come down hugely in a great splash, sending the water across the pond in ever-widening circles. As we came closer we could hear the ker-splat-splat as they hit the water. "My God," Father said under his breath.

We came up to the pond at an open place, a gravel beach fifty feet long. Some shoulder-high water tules grew on the left, but the water was clear and open in front of us. The three of us stood there side by side a minute, watching the fish come up out toward the center.

"Get down!" Father said as he dropped into an awkward crouch. I dropped down too and peered into the water in front of us, where he was staring.

"Honest to God," he whispered.

A school of bass cruised slowly by, twenty or thirty of them, not one under two pounds.

The fish veered off slowly. Dummy was still standing, watching them. But a few minutes later the same school returned, swimming thickly under the dark water, almost touching one another. I could see their big, heavy-lidded eyes watching us as they finned slowly by, their shiny sides rippling under the water. They turned again, for the third time, and then went on, followed by two or three stragglers. It didn't make any difference if we sat down or stood up; the fish just weren't frightened of us. Father said later he felt sure Dummy came down there afternoons and fed them, because, instead of shying away from us as fish should do, these turned in even closer to the bank. "It was a sight to behold," he said afterwards.

We sat there for ten minutes, Father and I, watching the bass come swimming up out of the deep water and fin idly by in front of us. Dummy just stood there pulling at his fingers and looking around the pond as if he expected someone. I could look straight down the pond to where the tallest rock pile shelved into the water, the deepest part, Father said. I let my eyes roam around the perimeter of the pond—the grove of willows, the birch trees, the great tule bed at the far end, a block away, where blackbirds flew in and out, calling in their high, warbling summer voices. The sun was behind our backs now, pleasantly warm on my neck. There was no wind. All over the pond the bass were coming up to nuzzle the water, or jumping clear of the water and falling on their sides, or coming up to the surface to cruise with their dorsal fins sticking out of the water like black hand-fans.

We finally got up to cast and I was shaky with excitement. I could hardly take the plug hooks from the cork handle of the rod. Dummy suddenly gripped my shoulder with his big fingers, and I found his pinched face a few inches from mine. He bobbed his chin two or three times at my father. He wanted only one of us to cast, and that was Father.

"Shh-Jesus!" Father said, looking at us both. "Jesus Kayrist!" He laid his pole on the gravel after a minute. He took off his hat and then put it back on and glared at Dummy before he moved over to where I stood. "Go ahead, Jack," he said. "That's all right, go ahead, Son."

I looked at Dummy just before I cast; his face had gone rigid and there was a thin line of drool on his chin.

"Come back hard on the son of a bitch when he strikes," Father said. "Make sure you set the hooks; their mouths are as hard as a doorknob."

I flipped off the drag lever and threw back my arm, lurched forward and heaved the rattling yellow plug out as far as I could. It splatted the water forty feet away. Before I could begin winding to pick up the slack, the water boiled.

"Hit him!" Father yelled. "You got him! Hit him! Hit him again!"

I came back hard, twice. I had him, all right. The steel casting rod bowed over and sprung wildly back and forth. Father kept yelling, "Let him go, let him go! Let him run with it! Give him more line, Jack! Now wind in! Wind in! No, let him run! Woo-ee! Look at him go!"

The bass jump-jumped around the pond and every time it came up out of the water it shook its head, and we could hear the plug rattle. And then the bass would take off on another run. In ten minutes I had the fish on its side, a few feet from shore. It looked enormous, six or seven pounds, maybe, and it lay on its side, whipped, mouth open and gills working slowly. My knees felt so weak I could hardly stand, but I held the rod up, the line tight. Father waded out over his shoes.

Dummy began sputtering behind me, but I was afraid to take my eyes away from the fish. Father kept moving closer, leaning forward now, his arm reaching lower, trying to gill it. Dummy suddenly stepped in front of me and began shaking his head and waving his hands. Father glanced at him.

"Why, what the hell's the matter with you, you son of a bitch? This boy's got hold the biggest bass I've seen; he ain't going to throw him back. What's wrong with you?"

Dummy kept shaking his head and gesturing toward the pond.

"I'm not about to let this boy's fish go. You've got another think coming if you think I'm going to do that."

Dummy reached for my line. Meanwhile the bass had gained strength and turned over and started swimming back out again. I yelled and then, I lost my head, I guess; I slammed down the brake on the reel and started winding. The bass made a last, furious run, and the plug flew over our heads and caught in a tree branch.

"Come on, Jack," Father said, grabbing up his pole. "Let's get out of here before we're crazy as this son of a bitch. Come on, goddam him, before I knock him down."

We started away from the pond, Father snapping his jaws he was so angry. We walked fast. I wanted to cry but kept swallowing rapidly, trying to hold back the tears. Once Father stumbled over a rock and ran forward a few feet to keep from falling. "Goddam the son of a bitch," he muttered. The sun was almost down and a breeze had come up. I looked back over my shoulder and saw Dummy still down at the pond, only now he'd moved over by the willows and had one arm wrapped around a tree, was leaning over and looking down into the water. He looked very dark and tiny beside the water.

Father saw me look back, and he stopped and turned. "He's talking to them," he said. "He's telling them he's sorry. He's crazy as a coot, that son of a bitch! Come on."

That February the river flooded.

It had snowed heavily throughout our part of the state during the first weeks of December, and then the weather had turned very cold just before Christmas, the ground froze, and the snow remained fast on the ground. Toward the end of January the Chinook wind struck. I woke up one morning to hear the house being buffeted by the wind, and the steady drizzle of water running off the roof.

It blew for five days, and on the third day the river began to rise.

"It's up to fifteen feet," Father said one evening, looking up from the newspaper. "Three feet over flood level. Old Dummy's going to lose his fish."

I wanted to go down to the Moxee Bridge to see how high the water was running, but Father shook his head.

"A flood is nothing to see. I've seen all the floods I want to see."

Two days later the river crested, and after that the water slowly began to subside.

Orin Marshall and Danny Owens and I bicycled the five or six miles out to Dummy's one Saturday morning a week later. We parked the bicycles off the road before we got there and walked across pastureland that bordered Dummy's property.

It was a damp, blustery day, the clouds dark and broken, moving fast across the gray sky. The ground was soppy wet and we kept coming to puddles in the thick grass that we couldn't go around and so waded through. Danny was just learning how to cuss and filled the air with a wild string of profanities every time he stepped in over his shoes. We could see the swollen river at the end of the pasture, the water still high and out of its channel, surging around the trunks of trees and eating away at the edge of the land. Out toward the middle, the water moved heavily and swiftly, and now and then a bush floated by, or a tree with its branches sticking up.

We came to Dummy's fence and found a cow wedged in against the wire. She was bloated and her skin was slick-looking and gray. It was the first dead thing of any size any of us had seen. Orin took a stick and touched the open jelly eyes, then raised the tail and touched here and there with the stick.

We moved on down the fence, toward the river. We were afraid to touch the wire because we thought it might still carry an electric shock. But at the edge of what looked like a deep canal, the fence came to an abrupt end. The ground had simply dropped into the water here, and this part of the fence as well. We crossed through the wire and followed the swift channel that cut directly into Dummy's land and headed straight for his pond. Coming closer we saw that the channel had cut lengthwise into the pond, forced an outlet for itself at the other end, then twisted and turned several times, and rejoined the river a quarter of a mile away. The pond itself now looked like a part of the main river, broad and turbulent. There was no doubt that most of Dummy's fish had been carried away, and those that might remain would be free to come and go as they pleased when the water dropped.

Then I caught sight of Dummy. It scared me, seeing him, and I motioned to the other guys and we all got down. He was standing at the far side of the pond, near where the water rushed out, gazing into the rapids. In a while he looked up and saw us. We broke suddenly and fled the way we'd come, running like frightened rabbits.

"I can't help but feel sorry for old Dummy, though," Father said at dinner one night a few weeks later. "Things are going all to hell for him, that's for sure. He brought it on himself, but you can't help feeling sorry for him anyway."

Father went on to say George Laycock saw Dummy's wife sitting in the Sportsman's Club with a big Mexican fellow last Friday night. "And that ain't the half of it—"

Mother looked up at him sharply and then at me, but I just went on eating like I hadn't heard anything.

"Damn it to hell, Bea, the boy's old enough to know the facts of life! Anyway," he said after a minute, to no one in particular, "there's liable to be some trouble there."

He'd changed a lot, Dummy had. He was never around any of the men now, if he could help it. He didn't take his breaks at the same time, nor did he eat his lunch with them anymore. No one felt like joking with him any longer, either, since he chased Carl Lowe with a two-by-four stud after Carl knocked his hat off. He was missing a day or two a week from work on the average, and there was some talk of his being laid off.

"He's going off the deep end," Father said. "Clear crazy if he don't watch out."

Then on a Sunday afternoon in May, just before my birthday, Father and I were cleaning the garage. It was a warm, still day and the dust hung in the air in the garage. Mother came to the back door and said, "Del, there's a call for you. I think it's Vern."

I followed him inside to wash up, and I heard him take the phone and say, "Vern? How are you? What? Don't tell me that, Vern. No! God, that ain't true, Vern. All right. Yes. Good-bye."

He put the phone down and turned to us. His face was pale and he put his hand on the table.

"Some bad news . . . It's Dummy. He drowned himself last night and killed his wife with a hammer. Vern just heard it on the radio."

We drove out there an hour later. Cars were parked in front of the house, and between the house and the pasture. Two or three sheriff's cars, a highway patrol car, and several other cars. The gate to the pasture stood open, and I could see tire marks that led toward the pond.

The screen door was propped open with a box, and a thin, pock-faced man in slacks and sports shirt and wearing a shoulder holster stood in the doorway. He watched us get out of the station wagon.

"What happened?" Father asked.

The man shook his head. "Have to read about it in the paper tomorrow night."

"Did they . . . find him?"

"Not yet. They're still dragging."

"All right if we walk down? I knew him pretty well."

"Don't matter to me. They might chase you off down there, though."

"You want to stay here, Jack?" Father asked.

"No," I said, "I guess I'll go along."

We walked across the pasture, following the tire marks, taking pretty much the same route as we had the summer before.

As we got closer we could hear the motorboats, could see the dirty fluffs of exhaust smoke hanging over the pond. There was only a small trickle of water coming in and leaving the pond now, though you could see where the high water had cut away the ground and carried off rocks and trees. Two small boats with two uniformed men in each cruised slowly back and forth over the water. One man steered from the front, and the other man sat in the back, handling the rope for the hooks.

An ambulance was parked on the gravel beach where we'd fished that evening so long ago, and two men in white lounged against the back, smoking cigarettes.

The door was open on the sheriff's car parked a few feet the other side of the ambulance, and I could hear a loud crackling voice coming over the speaker.

"What happened?" Father asked the deputy, who was standing near the water, hands on hips, watching one of the boats. "I knew him pretty well," he added. "We worked together."

"Murder and suicide, it appears," the man said, taking an unlit cigar from his mouth. He looked us over and then looked back at the boat again.

"How'd it happen?" Father persisted.

The deputy hooked his fingers under his belt, shifted the large revolver a little more comfortably on his broad hip. He spoke from the side of his mouth, around his cigar.

"He took the wife out of a bar last night and beat her to death in the truck with a hammer. There was witnesses. Then . . . whatever his name is . . . he drove to this here pond with the woman in the truck still, and just jumped in over his head. Beats all. I don't know, couldn't swim, I guess, but I don't know that . . . But they say it's hard for a man to drown himself, just give up and drown without even trying, if he knows how to swim. A fellow named Garcy or Garcia followed them home. Had been chasing after the woman, from what we gather, but he claims he saw the man jump in from off that rock pile, and then he found the woman in the truck, dead." He spat. "A hell of a mix-up, ain't it?"

One of the motors suddenly cut. We all looked up. The man in back of one of the boats stood up, began pulling heavily on his rope.

"Let's hope they got him," the deputy said. "I'd like to get home."

In a minute or two I saw an arm emerge out of the water; the hooks had evidently struck him in the side, or the back. The arm submerged a minute later and then reappeared, along with a shapeless bundle of something. It's not him, I thought for an instant, it's something else that has been in the pond for months.

The man in the front of the boat moved to the back, and together they hauled the dripping bundle over the side.

I looked at Father, who'd turned away, lips trembling. His face was lined, set. He looked older, suddenly, and terrified. He turned to me and said, "Women! That's what the wrong kind of woman can do for you, Jack."

But he stammered when he said it and moved his feet uncomfortably, and I don't think he really believed it. He just didn't know what else to say at the time. I'm not sure what he believed, I only know he was frightened with the sight, as I was. But it seemed to me life became more difficult for him after that, that he was never able to act happy and carefree anymore. Not like he used to act, anyway. For myself, I knew I wouldn't forget the sight of that arm emerging out of the water. Like some kind of mysterious and terrible signal, it seemed to herald the misfortune that dogged our family in the coming years.

But that was an impressionable period, from twelve to twenty. Now that I'm older, as old as my father was then, have lived awhile in the world—been around some, as they say—I know it now for what it was, that arm. Simply, the arm of a drowned man. I have seen others.

"Let's go home," my father said.

Pie

ER car was there, no others, and Burt gave thanks for that. He pulled into the drive and stopped beside the pie he'd dropped last night. It was still there, the aluminum pan upside down, the pumpkin splattered on the pavement. It was Friday, almost noon, the day after Christmas.

He'd come on Christmas Day to visit his wife and children. But Vera told him before he came that he had to be gone before six o'clock when her friend and his children were coming for dinner. They had sat in the living room and solemnly opened the presents he had brought. The lights on the Christmas tree blinked. Packages wrapped in shiny paper and secured with ribbons and bows lay stuffed under the tree waiting for six o'clock. He watched the children, Terri and Jack, open their gifts. He waited while Vera's fingers carefully undid the ribbon and tape on her present. She unwrapped the paper. She opened the box and took out a beige cashmere sweater.

"It's nice," she said. "Thank you, Burt."

"Try it on," Terri said to her mother.

"Put it on, Mom," Jack said. "All *right*, Dad."

Burt looked at his son, grateful for this show of support. He could ask Jack to ride his bicycle over some morning during these holidays and they'd go out for breakfast.

She did try it on. She went into the bedroom and came out running her hands up and down the front of the sweater. "It's nice," she said.

"It looks great on you," Burt said and felt a welling in his chest.

He opened his gifts: from Vera a certificate for twenty dollars at Sondheim's men's store; a matching comb and brush set from Terri; handkerchiefs, three pair of socks, and a ballpoint pen from Jack. He and Vera drank rum and Coke. It grew dark outside and became five-thirty. Terri looked at her mother and got up and began to set the dining room table. Jack went to his room. Burt liked it where he was, in front of the fireplace, a glass in his hand, the smell of turkey in the air. Vera went into the kitchen. Burt leaned back on the sofa.

Christmas carols came to him from the radio in Vera's bedroom. From time to time Terri walked into the dining room with something for the table. Burt watched as she placed linen napkins in the wine glasses. A slender vase with a single red rose appeared. Then Vera and Terri began talking in low voices in the kitchen. He finished his drink. A little wax and sawdust log burned on the grate, giving off red, blue, and green flames. He got up from the sofa and put eight logs, the entire carton, into the fireplace. He watched until they began to flame. Then, making for the patio door, he caught sight of the pies lined up on the sideboard. He stacked them up in his arms; there were five of them, pumpkin and mincemeat—she must think she was feeding a soccer team. He got out of the house with the pies. But in the drive, in the dark, he'd dropped a pie as he fumbled with the car door.

Now he walked around the broken pie and headed for the patio door. The front door was permanently closed since that night his key had broken off inside the lock. It was an overcast day, the air damp and sharp. Vera was saying he'd tried to burn the house down last night. That's what she'd told the children, what Terri had repeated to him when he called the house this morning to apologize. "Mom said you tried to burn the house down last night," Terri had said and laughed. He wanted to set the record straight. He also wanted to talk about things in general.

There was a wreath made out of pinecones on the patio door. He rapped on the glass. Vera looked out at him and frowned. She was in her bathrobe. She opened the door a little.

"Vera, I want to apologize for last night," he said. "I'm sorry I did what I did. It was stupid. I want to apologize to the kids, too."

"They're not here," she said. "Terri is off with her boyfriend, that son of a bitch and his motorcycle, and Jack is playing football." She stood in the doorway and he stood on the patio next to the philodendron plant. He pulled at some lint on his coat sleeve. "I can't take any more scenes after last night," she said. "I've had it, Burt. You literally tried to burn the house down last night."

"I did not."

"You did. Everybody here was a witness. You ought to see the fireplace. You almost caught the wall on fire."

"Can I come in for a minute and talk about it?" he said. "Vera?"

She looked at him. She pulled the robe together at her throat and moved back inside.

"Come in," she said. "But I have to go somewhere in an hour. And please try to restrain yourself. Don't pull anything again, Burt. Don't for God's sake try to burn my house down again."

"Vera, for heaven's sake."

"It's true."

He didn't answer. He looked around. The Christmas tree lights blinked off and on. There was a pile of soft tissue papers and empty boxes at the end of the sofa. A turkey carcass filled a platter in the center of the dining room table. The bones were picked clean and the leathery remains sat upright in a bed of parsley as if in a kind of horrible nest. The napkins were soiled and had been dropped here and there on the table. Some of the dishes were stacked, and the cups and wine glasses had been moved to one end of the table, as if someone had started to clean up but thought better of it. It was true, the fireplace had black smoke stains reaching up the bricks toward the mantel. A mound of ash filled the fireplace, along with an empty Shasta cola can.

"Come out to the kitchen," Vera said. "I'll make some coffee. But I have to leave pretty soon."

"What time did your friend leave last night?"

"If you're going to start that you can go right now."

"Okay, okay."

He pulled a chair out and sat down at the kitchen table in front of the big ashtray. He closed his eyes and opened them. He moved the curtain aside and looked out at the backyard. A bicycle without a front wheel rested on its handlebars and seat. Weeds grew along the redwood fence.

"Thanksgiving?" she said. She ran water into a saucepan. "Do you remember Thanksgiving? I said then that was the last holiday you'd ever ruin for us. Eating bacon and eggs instead of turkey at ten o'clock at night. People can't live like that, Burt."

"I know it. I said I'm sorry, Vera. I meant it."

"Sorry isn't good enough anymore. It just isn't."

The pilot light was out again. She was at the stove trying to light the gas burner under the pan of water. "Don't burn yourself," he said. "Don't catch yourself on fire."

She didn't answer. She lit the ring.

He could imagine her robe catching fire and himself jumping up from the table, throwing her down onto the floor and rolling her over and over into the living room where he would cover her with his own body. Or should he run to the bedroom first for a blanket to throw over her?

"Vera?"

She looked at him.

"Do you have anything to drink around the house? Any of that rum left? I could use a drink this morning. Take the chill off."

"There's some vodka in the freezer, and there is rum around here somewhere, if the kids didn't drink it up."

"When did you start keeping vodka in the freezer?"

"Don't ask."

"Okay, I won't."

He took the vodka from the freezer, looked for a glass, then poured some into a cup he found on the counter.

"Are you just going to drink it like that, out of a cup? Jesus, Burt. What'd you want to talk about, anyway? I told you I have someplace to go. I have a flute lesson at one o'clock. What is it you want, Burt?"

"Are you still taking flute?"

"I just said so. What is it? Tell me what's on your mind, and then I have to get ready."

"I just wanted to say I was sorry about last night, for one thing. I was upset. I'm sorry."

"You're always upset at something. You were just drunk and wanted to take it out on us."

"That's not true."

"Why'd you come over here then, when you knew we had plans? You could have come the night before. I told you about the dinner I planned yesterday."

"It was Christmas. I wanted to drop off my gifts. You're still my family."

She didn't answer.

"I think you're right about this vodka," he said. "If you have any juice I'll mix this with some juice."

She opened the refrigerator and moved things around. "There's cran-apple juice, that's all."

"That's fine," he said. He got up and poured cran-apple juice into his cup, added more vodka, and stirred the drink with his little finger.

"I have to go to the bathroom," she said. "Just a minute."

He drank the cup of cran-apple juice and vodka and felt better. He lit a cigarette and tossed the match into the big ashtray. The bottom of the ashtray was covered with cigarette stubs and a layer of ash. He recognized Vera's brand, but there were some unfiltered cigarettes as well, and another brand—lavender-colored stubs heavy with lipstick. He got up and dumped the mess into the sack under the sink. The ashtray was a heavy piece of blue stoneware with raised edges they'd bought from a bearded potter on the mall in Santa Cruz. It was as big as a plate and maybe that's what it'd been intended for, a plate or a serving dish of some sort, but they'd immediately started using it as an ashtray. He put it back on the table and ground out his cigarette in it.

The water on the stove began to bubble just as the phone rang. She opened the bathroom door and called to him through the living room: "Answer that, will you? I'm just about to get into the shower."

The kitchen phone was on the counter in a corner behind the roasting pan. It kept ringing. He picked the receiver up cautiously.

"Is Charlie there?" a flat, toneless voice asked him.

"No," he said. "You must have the wrong number. This is 323-4464. You have the wrong number."

"Okay," the voice said.

But while he was seeing to the coffee, the phone rang again. He answered.

"Charlie?"

"You have the wrong number. Look here, you'd better check your numbers again. Look at your prefix." This time he left the receiver off the hook.

Vera came back into the kitchen wearing jeans and a white sweater and brushing her hair. He added instant coffee to the cups of hot water, stirred the coffee, and then floated vodka onto his coffee. He carried the cups over to the table.

She picked up the receiver, listened, and said, "What's this about? Who was on the phone?"

"Nobody," he said. "It was a wrong number. Who smokes lavender-colored cigarettes?"

"Terri. Who else would smoke such things?"

"I didn't know she was smoking these days," he said. "I haven't seen her smoking."

"Well, she is. I guess she doesn't want to do it in front of you yet," she said. "That's a laugh, if you think about it." She put down the hairbrush. "But that son of a bitch she's going out with, that's something else. He's trouble. He's been in and out of scrapes ever since he dropped out of high school."

"Tell me about it."

"I just did. He's a creep. I worry about it, but I don't know what I can do. My God, Burt, I've got my hands full. It makes you wonder sometimes."

She sat across the table from him and drank her coffee. They smoked and used the ashtray. There were things he wanted to say, words of devotion and regret, consoling things.

"Terri also steals my dope and smokes that too," Vera said, "if you really want to know what goes on around here."

"God almighty. She smokes dope?"

Vera nodded.

"I didn't come over here to hear that."

"What did you come over here for then? You didn't get all the pie last night?"

He recalled stacking pie on the floorboards of the car before driving away last night. Then he'd forgotten all about pie. The pies were still in the car. For a minute he thought he should tell her.

"Vera," he said. "It's Christmas, that's why I came."

"Christmas is over, thank God. Christmas has come and gone," she said. "I don't look forward to holidays anymore. I'll never look forward to another holiday as long as I live."

"What about me?" he said. "I don't look forward to holidays either, believe me. Well, there's only New Year's now to get through."

"You can get drunk," she said.

"I'm working on it," he said and felt the stirrings of anger. The phone rang again.

"It's someone wanting Charlie," he said.

"What?"

"Charlie," he said.

Vera picked up the phone. She kept her back to Burt as she talked. Then she turned to him and said, "I'll take this call on the phone in the bedroom. Would you please hang up this phone after I've picked it up in there? I can tell, so hang it up when I say."

He didn't answer, but he took the receiver. She left the kitchen. He held the receiver to his ear and listened, but he couldn't hear anything at first. Then someone, a man, cleared his throat at the other end of the line. He heard Vera pick up the other phone and call to him: "Okay, you can hang it up now, Burt. I have it. Burt?"

He replaced the receiver in its cradle and stood looking at it. Then he opened the silverware drawer and pushed things around inside. He tried another drawer. He looked in the sink, then went into the dining room and found the carving knife on the platter. He held it under hot water until the grease broke. He wiped the blade dry on his sleeve. Then he moved to the phone, doubled the cord in his hand, and sawed through the plastic coating and the copper wire without any difficulty. He examined the ends of the cord. Then he shoved the phone back into its corner near the canisters.

Vera came in and said, "The phone went dead while I was talking. Did you do anything to the phone, Burt?" She looked at the phone and then picked it up from the counter. Three feet of green cord trailed from the phone.

"Son of a bitch," she said. "Well, that does it. Out, out, out, where you belong." She was shaking the phone at him. "That's it, Burt. I'm going to get a restraining order, that's what I'm going to get. Get out right now, before I call the police." The phone made a *ding* as she banged it down on the counter. "I'll go next door and call them if you don't leave now. You're destructive is what you are."

He had picked up the ashtray and was stepping back from

the table. He held the ashtray by its edge, his shoulders bunched. He was poised as if he were going to hurl it, like a discus.

"Please," she said. "Leave now. Burt, that's our ashtray. Please. Go now."

He left through the patio door after telling her good-bye. He wasn't certain, but he thought he'd proved something. He hoped he'd made it clear that he still loved her, and that he was jealous. But they hadn't talked. They'd soon have to have a serious talk. There were matters that needed sorting out, important things that still had to be discussed. They'd talk again. Maybe after these holidays were over and things were back to normal.

He walked around the pie in the drive and got into his car. He started the car and put it into reverse. He backed out into the street. Then he put the car in low gear and went forward.

The Calm

IT was Saturday morning. The days were short and there was chill in the air. I was getting a haircut. I was in the chair and three men were sitting along the wall across from me, waiting. Two of the men I'd never seen before, but one of them I recognized though couldn't place. I kept looking at him as the barber worked on my hair. He was moving a toothpick around in his mouth. He was heavyset, about fifty years old and had short wavy hair. I tried to place him, and then I saw him in a cap and uniform, wearing a gun, little eyes watchful behind the glasses as he stood in the bank lobby. He was a guard. Of the two other men, one was considerably the older, but with a full head of curly gray hair. He was smoking. The other, though not so old, was nearly bald on top, and the hair at the sides of his head hung in dark lanks over his ears. He had on logging boots and his pants were shiny with machine oil.

The barber put a hand on top of my head to turn me for a better look. Then he said to the guard, "Did you get your deer, Charles?"

I liked this barber. We weren't acquainted well enough to call each other by name, but when I came in for a haircut he knew me and knew I used to fish, so we'd talk fishing. I don't think he hunted, but he could talk on any subject and was a good listener. In this regard he was like some bartenders I've known.

"Bill, it's a funny story. The damnedest thing," the guard said. He removed the toothpick and laid it in the ashtray. He shook his head. "I did and yet I didn't. So yes and no to your question."

I didn't like his voice. For a big man the voice didn't fit. I thought of the word "wimpy" my son used to use. It was somehow feminine, the voice, and it was smug. Whatever it was it wasn't the kind of voice you'd expect, or want to listen to all day. The two other men looked at him. The older man was turning the pages of a magazine, smoking, and the other fellow was holding a newspaper. They put down what they were looking at and turned to listen.

"Go on, Charles," the barber said. "Let's hear it." He turned my head again, held the clippers a minute, then went back to work.

"We were up on Fikle Ridge, my old man and me and the kid. We were hunting those draws. My old man was stationed at the head of one draw, and me and the kid were on another. The kid had a hangover, goddamn his hide. It was in the afternoon and we'd been out since daybreak. The kid, he was pale around the gills and drank water all day, mine and his both. But we were in hopes of some of the hunters down below moving a deer up in our direction. We were sitting behind a log watching the draw. We'd heard shooting down in the valley."

"There's orchards down there," said the fellow with the newspaper. He fidgeted a lot and kept crossing a leg, swinging his boot for a time, and then crossing the other leg. "Those deer hang out around those orchards."

"That's right," the guard said. "They'll go in there at night, the bastards, and eat those green apples. Well, we'd heard shooting earlier in the day, as I said, and we were just sitting there on our hands when this big old buck comes up out of the underbrush not a hundred feet in front of us. The kid saw him the same time I did, of course, and threw down and started banging at him, the knothead. The old buck wasn't in any danger from the kid as it turns out, but at first he couldn't tell where the shots were coming from. He didn't know which way to jump. Then I got off a shot, but in all the commotion I just stunned him."

"Stunned him," the barber said.

"You know, stunned him," the guard said. "It was a gut shot. It just stunned him, like. He dropped his head and began trembling. He trembled all over. The kid was still shooting. I felt like I was back in Korea. I shot again but missed. Then old Mr. Buck moves off into the brush once more, but now, by God, he didn't have any what you'd call bounce left in him. The kid had emptied his gun by this time to no purpose, but I'd hit him. I'd rammed one right in his guts and that took the wind out of his sails. That's what I meant by stunning him."

"Then what?" The fellow had rolled his newspaper and was tapping it against his knee. "What then? You must have trailed him. Invariably, they'll find a hard place to die."

I looked at this fellow again. I still recall those words. The older man had been listening all the while, watching as the guard told his story. The guard was relishing his limelight.

"But you trailed him?" the older man asked, though it wasn't really a question.

"I did. Me and the kid, we trailed him. But the kid wasn't good for much. He got sick on the trail. Slowed us down, that knothead." He had to laugh now, thinking about that situation. "Drinking beer and chasing all night, then thinking he can hunt deer the next day. He knows better now, by God. But we trailed him. A good trail, too. There was blood on the ground and blood on the leaves and honeysuckle. Blood everywhere. There was even blood on those pine trees he leant against, resting up. Never seen an old buck with so much blood. I don't know how he kept going. But it started to get dark on us, and we had to go back. I was worried about the old man, too, but I needn't have worried, as it turns out."

"Sometimes they'll just go forever. But invariably they'll find them a hard place to die," the fellow with the newspaper said, repeating himself for good measure.

"I chewed the kid out good for missing his shot in the first place, and when he started to say something back, I cuffed him I was so mad. Right here." He pointed to the side of his head and grinned. "I boxed his ears for him, that damn kid. He's not too old. He needed it."

"Well, the coyotes'll have that deer now," the fellow said. "Them and the crows and buzzards." He unrolled his newspaper, smoothed it out and put it off to one side. He crossed a leg again. He looked around at the rest of us and shook his head. But it didn't look like it mattered much one way or the other to him.

The older man had turned in his chair and was looking out the window at the dim morning sun. He lit a cigarette.

"I figure so," the guard said. "It's a pity. He was a big old son of a bitch. I wish I had his horns over my garage. But so, in answer to your question, Bill, I both got my deer and didn't get him. But we had venison on the table anyway, it turns out. The old man had got himself a little spike in the meantime. He already had him back to camp, hanging up and gutted slick as a whistle. Had the liver, heart, and kidneys wrapped in waxed paper and placed in the cooler already. He heard us coming down and met us just outside of camp. He held out his hands just all covered with dried blood. Didn't say a word. Old fart scared me at first. I didn't know for a minute what'd happened. Old hands looked like they'd been painted. 'Looky,' he said"—and here the guard held out his own plump hands— "'Looky here at what I've done.' Then we stepped into the light and I seen his little deer hanging there. A little spike. Just a little bastard, but the old man, he was tickled to death. Me and the kid didn't have anything to show for our day, except the kid, he was still hungover and pissed off and had a sore ear." He laughed and looked around the shop, as if remembering. Then he picked up his toothpick and stuck it back into his mouth.

The older man put his cigarette out and turned to Charles. He drew a breath and said, "You ought to be out there right now looking for that deer instead of in here getting a haircut. That's a disgusting story." Nobody said anything. A look of wonderment passed over the guard's features. He blinked his eyes. "I don't know you and I don't want to know you, but I don't think you or your kid or your old man ought to be allowed out in the woods with other hunters."

"You can't talk like that," the guard said. "You old asshole. I've seen you someplace."

"Well, I haven't seen you before. I'd recollect if I'd seen your fat face before."

"Boys, that's enough. This is my barbershop. It's my place of business. I can't have this."

"I ought to box *your* ears," the older man said. I thought for a minute he was going to pull up out of his chair. But his shoulders were rising and falling, and he was having a visible difficulty with his breathing.

"You ought to try it," the guard said.

"Charles, Albert's a friend of mine," the barber said. He had put his comb and scissors on the counter and had his hands on my shoulders now, as if I was thinking to spring from the chair into the middle of it. "Albert, I've been cutting Charles's head of hair, and his boy's too, for years now. I wish you wouldn't pursue this." He looked from one man to the other and kept his hands on my shoulders.

"Take it outside," the Invariably fellow said, flushed and hoping for something.

"That'll be enough," the barber said. "I don't want to have to be calling the law. Charles, I don't want to hear anything more on the subject. Albert, you're next in line, so if you'll just hold on a minute until I'm finished with this man. Now," he turned to Invariably, "I don't know you from Adam, but it would help things if you'd not put your oar in again."

The guard got up and said, "I think I'll come back for my cut later, Bill. Right now the company leaves something to be desired." He went out without looking at anybody and pulled the door closed, hard.

The older man sat there smoking his cigarette. He looked out the window for a minute, and then he examined something on the back of his hand. Then he got up and put on his hat.

"I'm sorry, Bill. That guy pushed a button, I guess. I can wait a few more days for a haircut. I don't have any engagements but one. I'll be seeing you next week."

"You come around next week then, Albert. You take it easy now. You hear? That's all right, Albert."

The man went outside, and the barber stepped over to the window to watch him go. "Albert's about dead from emphysema," he said from the window. "We used to fish together. He taught me everything there is to know about salmon fishing. The women. They used to just flock after him, that old boy. He's picked up a temper, though, in his later years. But I can't say, in all honesty, if there wasn't some provocation this morning." We watched him through the window get into his truck and shut the door. Then he started the engine and drove away.

Invariably couldn't sit still. He was on his feet and moving around the shop now, stopping to examine everything, the old wooden hat rack, photos of Bill and his friends holding stringers of fish, the calendar from the hardware store showing pictures of outdoor scenes for each month of the year—he flipped every page and came back to October—even going so far as to stand and scrutinize the barber's license, which was up on the wall at the end of the counter. He stood first on one foot and then the other, reading the fine print. Then he turned to the barber and said, "I think I'm going to get going too and come back later. I don't know about you, but I need a beer." He went out quickly, and we heard his car start.

"Well, do you want me to finish barbering this hair or not?" the barber said to me in a rough manner, as if I was the cause of this.

Somebody else came in then, a man wearing a jacket and tie. "Hello, Bill. What's happening?"

"Hello, Frank. Nothing worth repeating. What's new with you?"

"Nothing," the man said. He hung his jacket on the hat rack and loosened his tie. Then he sat down in a chair and picked up Invariably's newspaper.

The barber turned me in the chair to face the mirror. He put a hand on either side of my head and positioned me a last time. He brought his head down next to mine and we looked into the mirror together, his hands still encircling my head. I looked at myself, and he also looked at me. But if he saw something, he didn't ask any questions or offer any comment. He began then to run his fingers back and forth through my hair, slowly, as if thinking of something else the while. He ran his fingers through my hair as intimately, as tenderly, as a lover's fingers.

That was in Crescent City, California, up near the Oregon border. I left soon after. But today I was thinking of that place, Crescent City, and my attempt at a new life there with my wife, and how even then, in the chair that morning, I had made up my mind to leave and not look back. I recalled the calm I felt when I closed my eyes and let the fingers move through my hair, the sadness in those fingers, the hair already starting to grow again.

Mine

DURING the day the sun had come out and the snow melted into dirty water. Streaks of water ran down from the little, shoulder-high window that faced the backyard. Cars slushed by on the street outside. It was getting dark, outside and inside.

He was in the bedroom pushing clothes into a suitcase when she came to the door.

I'm glad you're leaving, I'm glad you're leaving! she said. Do you hear?

He kept on putting his things into the suitcase and didn't look up.

Son of a bitch! I'm so glad you're leaving! She began to cry. You can't even look me in the face, can you? Then she noticed the baby's picture on the bed and picked it up.

He looked at her and she wiped her eyes and stared at him before turning and going back to the living room.

Bring that back.

Just get your things and get out, she said.

He did not answer. He fastened the suitcase, put on his coat, and looked at the bedroom before turning off the light. Then he went out to the living room. She stood in the doorway of the little kitchen, holding the baby.

I want the baby, he said.

Are you crazy?

No, but I want the baby. I'll get someone to come by for his things.

You can go to hell! You're not touching this baby.

The baby had begun to cry and she uncovered the blanket from around his head.

Oh, oh, she said, looking at the baby.

He moved towards her.

For God's sake! she said. She took a step back into the kitchen.

I want the baby.

Get out of here!

She turned and tried to hold the baby over in a corner behind the stove as he came up.

He reached across the stove and tightened his hands on the baby.

Let go of him, he said.

Get away, get away! she cried.

The baby was red-faced and screaming. In the scuffle they knocked down a little flowerpot that hung behind the stove.

He crowded her into the wall then, trying to break her grip, holding onto the baby and pushing his weight against her arm.

Let go of him, he said.

Don't, she said, you're hurting him!

He didn't talk again. The kitchen window gave no light. In the near-dark he worked on her fisted fingers with one hand and with the other hand he gripped the screaming baby up under an arm near the shoulder.

She felt her fingers being forced open and the baby going from her. No, she said, just as her hands came loose. She would have it, this baby whose chubby face gazed up at them from the picture on the table. She grabbed for the baby's other arm. She caught the baby around the wrist and leaned back.

He would not give. He felt the baby going out of his hands and he pulled back hard. He pulled back very hard.

In this manner they decided the issue.

Distance

SHE's in Milan for Christmas and wants to know what it was like when she was a kid. Always that on the rare occasions when he sees her.

Tell me, she says. Tell me what it was like then. She sips Strega, waits, eyes him closely.

She is a cool, slim, attractive girl. The father is proud of her, pleased and grateful she has passed safely through her adolescence into young womanhood.

That was a long time ago. That was twenty years ago, he tells her. They're in his apartment in the Via Fabroni near the Cascina Gardens.

You can remember, she says. Go on, tell me.

What do you want to hear? he asks. What else can I tell you? I could tell you about something that happened when you were a baby. Do you want to hear about their first real argument? It involves you, he says and smiles at her.

Tell me, she says and claps her hands with anticipation. But first get us another drink, please, so you won't have to interrupt halfway through.

He comes back from the kitchen with drinks, settles into his chair, begins slowly:

They were kids themselves, but they were crazy in love, this eighteen-year-old boy and his seventeen-year-old girlfriend when they married, and not all that long afterwards they had a daughter.

The baby came along in late November during a severe cold spell that just happened to coincide with the peak of the waterfowl season in that part of the country. The boy loved to hunt, you see, that's part of it.

The boy and girl, husband and wife now, father and mother, lived in a three-room apartment under a dentist's office. Each night they cleaned the upstairs in exchange for their rent and utilities. In summer they were expected to maintain the lawn and the flowers, and in winter the boy shoveled snow from the walks and spread rock salt on the pavement. Are you still with me?

917

I am, she says. A nice arrangement for everyone, dentist included.

That's right, he says. Except when the dentist found out they were using his letterhead stationery for their personal correspondence. But that's another story.

The two kids, as I've told you, were very much in love. On top of this they had great ambitions and they were wild dreamers. They were always talking about the things they were going to do and the places they were going to go.

He gets up from his chair and looks out the window for a minute over the slate rooftops at the snow that falls steadily through the weak late afternoon light.

Tell the story, she reminds gently.

The boy and girl slept in the bedroom and the baby slept in a crib in the living room. The baby was about three weeks old at this time and had only just begun to sleep through the night.

On this one Saturday night after finishing his work upstairs, the boy went into the dentist's private office, put his feet up on his desk, and called Carl Sutherland, an old hunting and fishing friend of his father's.

Carl, he said when the man picked up the receiver, I'm a father. We had a baby girl.

Congratulations, boy, Carl said. How is the wife?

She's fine, Carl. The baby's fine too, the boy said. We named her Catherine. Everybody's fine.

That's good, Carl said. I'm glad to hear it. Well, you give my regards to the wife. If you called about going hunting, I'll tell you something. The geese are flying down there to beat the band. I don't think I've ever seen so many of them and I've been going there for years. I shot five today, two this morning and three this afternoon. I'm going back in the morning and you come along if you want to.

I want to, the boy said. That's why I called.

You be here at five thirty then and we'll go, Carl said. Bring lots of shells. We'll get some shooting in all right, don't worry. I'll see you in the morning.

The boy liked Carl Sutherland. He had been a friend of the boy's father, who was dead now. After the father's death, maybe trying to replace a loss they both felt, the boy and Sutherland had started hunting together. Sutherland was a bluff, heavyset, balding man who lived alone and was not given to casual talk. Once in a while when they were together the boy felt uncomfortable, wondered if he had said or done something wrong because he was not used to being around people who kept still for long periods of time. But when he did talk the older man was often opinionated, and frequently the boy didn't agree with the opinions. Yet the man had a toughness about him and a woods knowledge that the boy liked and admired.

The boy hung up the telephone and went downstairs to tell the girl about going hunting the next morning. He was happy about going hunting, and he laid out his things a few minutes later: hunting coat and shell bag, boots, woolen socks, brown canvas hunting cap with fur earmuffs, 12-gauge pump shotgun, long john woolen underwear.

What time will you be back? the girl asked.

Probably around noon, he said, but maybe not until after five or six o'clock. Would that be too late?

It's fine, she said. Catherine and I will get along just fine. You go and have some fun, you deserve it. Maybe tomorrow evening we'll dress Catherine up and go visit Claire.

Sure, that sounds like a good idea, he said. Let's plan on that.

Claire was the girl's sister, ten years older. She was a striking woman. I don't know if you've seen pictures of her. (She hemorrhaged to death in a hotel in Seattle when you were about four.) The boy was a little in love with her, just as he was a little in love with Betsy, the girl's younger sister who was only fifteen then. Joking once he'd said to the girl, if we weren't married I could go for Claire.

What about Betsy? the girl had said. I hate to admit it but I truly feel she's better looking than Claire or me. What about her?

Betsy too, the boy said and laughed. Of course Betsy. But not in the same way I could go for Claire. Claire is older, but I don't know, there's something about her you could fall for. No, I believe I'd prefer Claire over Betsy, I think, if I had to make a choice.

But who do you really love? the girl asked. Who do you love most in all the world? Who's your wife?

You're my wife, the boy said.

And will we always love each other? the girl asked, enormously enjoying this conversation, he could tell.

Always, the boy said. And we'll always be together. We're like the Canadian geese, he said, taking the first comparison that came to mind, for they were often on his mind in those days. They only marry once. They choose a mate early in life, and then the two of them stay together always. If one of them dies or something the other one will never remarry. It will live off by itself somewhere, or even continue to live with the flock, but it will stay single and alone amongst all the other geese.

That's a sad fate, the girl said. It's sadder for it to live that way, I think, alone but with all the others, than just to live off by itself somewhere.

It is sad, the boy said, but it's a part of nature like everything else.

Have you ever killed one of those marriages? she asked. You know what I mean.

He nodded. Two or three times I've shot a goose, he said, then a minute or two later I'd see another one turn back from the rest and begin to circle and call over the goose that lay on the ground.

Did you shoot it too? she asked with concern.

If I could, he answered. Sometimes I missed.

And it didn't bother you? she asked.

Never, he said. You can't think about it when you're doing it. I love everything there is about hunting geese. And I love to just watch them even when I'm not hunting them. But there are all kinds of contradictions in life. You can't think about all the contradictions.

After dinner he turned up the furnace and helped her bathe the baby. He marveled again at the infant who had half his features, the eyes and mouth, and half the girl's, the chin, the nose. He powdered the tiny body and then powdered in between the fingers and toes. He watched the girl put the baby into its diaper and pajamas.

He emptied the bath into the shower basin and went upstairs. It was overcast and cold outside. His breath steamed in the air. The grass, what there was of it, reminded him of canvas, stiff and gray under the streetlight. Snow lay in piles beside the walk. A car went by and he heard sand grinding under the tires. He let himself imagine what it might be like tomorrow, geese milling in the air over his head, shotgun plunging against his shoulder.

Then he locked the door and went downstairs.

In bed they tried to read but both of them fell asleep, she first, letting the magazine sink to the quilt after a few minutes. His eyes closed, but he roused himself, checked the alarm, turned off the lamp.

He woke to the baby's cries. The light was on out there, and the girl was standing beside the crib rocking the baby in her arms. In a minute she put the baby down, turned out the light, and returned to bed.

It was two o'clock in the morning and the boy fell asleep again.

But half an hour later he heard the baby once more. This time the girl continued to sleep. The baby cried fitfully for a few minutes and stopped. The boy listened, then began to doze.

Again the baby's cries woke him. The living room light was burning. He sat up and turned on the lamp.

I don't know what's wrong, the girl said, walking back and forth with the baby. I've changed her and given her something more to eat, but she keeps crying. She won't stop crying. I'm so tired I'm afraid I might drop her.

You come back to bed, the boy said. I'll hold her for a while.

He got up and took the baby, and the girl went to lie down again.

Just rock her for a few minutes, the girl said from the bedroom. Maybe she'll go back to sleep.

The boy sat on the couch and held the baby, jiggling it in his lap until its eyes closed. His own eyes were near closing. He rose carefully and put the baby back in the crib.

It was quarter to four and he still had forty-five minutes. He crawled into bed and dropped off.

But a few minutes later the baby began to cry once more, and this time they both got up, and the boy swore.

For God's sake, what's the matter with you? the girl said to him. Maybe she's sick or something. Maybe we shouldn't have given her the bath.

The boy picked up the baby. The baby kicked its feet and

smiled. Look, he said, I really don't think there's anything wrong with her.

How do you know that? the girl said. Here, let me have her. I know that I ought to give her something, but I don't know what.

Her voice had an edginess that caused the boy to look at her closely.

After a few minutes and the baby had not cried, the girl put her down again. He and the girl looked at the baby, then looked at each other as the baby opened its eyes once more and began to cry.

The girl took the baby. Baby, baby, she said with tears in her eyes.

Probably it's something on her stomach, the boy said.

The girl didn't answer. She went on rocking the baby in her arms, paying no attention now to the boy.

The boy waited a minute longer, then went to the kitchen and put on water for coffee. He drew on his woolen underwear over his shorts and T-shirt, buttoned up, then got into his clothes.

What are you doing? the girl said to him.

Going hunting, he said.

I don't think you should, she said. Maybe you could go later on in the day if the baby is all right then, but I don't think you should go this morning. I don't want to be left alone with her like this.

Carl's planning on me going, the boy said. We've planned it.

I don't give a damn about what you and Carl have planned, she flared. And I don't give a damn about Carl either. I don't even know the man. I don't want you to go is all. I don't think you should even consider wanting to go under the circumstances.

You've met Carl before, you know him, the boy said. What do you mean you don't know him?

That's not the point and you know it, the girl said. The point is I don't intend to be left alone with a sick baby. If you weren't being selfish you'd realize that.

Now wait a minute, that's just not true, he said. You don't understand.

No, you don't understand, she said. I'm your wife. This is

your baby. She's sick or something, look at her. Why else is she crying? You can't leave us to go hunting.

Don't get hysterical about it, he said.

I'm saying you can go hunting anytime, she said. Something's wrong with this baby and you want to leave us to go hunting.

She began to cry then. She put the baby back in the crib, but the baby started again. The girl dried her eyes hastily on the sleeve of her nightgown and picked her up once more.

The boy laced his boots slowly, put on his shirt, sweater, and coat. The kettle whistled on the stove in the kitchen.

You're going to have to choose, the girl said. Carl or us, I mean it, you've got to choose.

What do you mean? the boy said slowly.

You heard what I said, the girl answered. If you want a family you're going to have to choose. If you go out that door you're not coming back, I'm serious.

They stared at each other. Then the boy took his hunting gear and went upstairs. He started the car after some difficulty, went around to the car windows and, making a job of it, scraped away the ice.

The temperature had dropped during the night, but the weather had cleared so that stars had come out, and now they gleamed in the sky over his head. Driving, the boy glanced up once at the stars and was moved when he considered their bright distance.

Carl's porch light was on, his station wagon parked in the drive with the motor idling. Carl came outside as the boy pulled to the curb. The boy had decided.

You might want to park off the street, Carl said as the boy came up the walk. I'm all ready, just let me hit the lights. I feel like hell, I really do, he went on. I thought maybe you had overslept so I just this minute finished calling your place. Your wife said you had left. I feel like hell calling.

It's okay, the boy said, trying to pick his words. He leaned his weight on one leg and turned up his collar. He put his hands in his coat pockets. She was already up, Carl. We've both been up for a while. I guess there's something wrong with the baby, I don't know. She keeps crying, I mean. The thing is, I guess I can't go this time. He shivered against the cold and looked away.

You should have stepped to the phone and called me, boy, Carl said. It's okay. Shoot, you know you didn't have to come over here to tell me. What the hell, this hunting business you can take it or leave it. It's not that important. You want a cup of coffee?

No thanks, I'd better get back, the boy said.

Well, since I'm already up and ready I expect I'll go ahead and go, Carl said. He looked at the boy and lit a cigarette.

The boy kept standing on the porch, not saying anything.

The way it's cleared up, Carl said, I don't look for much action this morning anyway. It sure is cold though.

The boy nodded. I'll see you, Carl, he said.

So long, Carl said. Hey, don't let anybody ever tell you otherwise, Carl called after him. You're a lucky boy and I mean that.

The boy started his car and waited, watched Carl go through the house and turn off all the lights. Then the boy put the car in gear and pulled away.

The living room light was on, but the girl was asleep on the bed and the baby was asleep beside her.

The boy took off his boots, pants, and shirt and, in his socks and woolen underwear, sat on the couch and read the Sunday paper.

Soon it began to turn light outside. The girl and the baby slept on. After a while the boy went to the kitchen and began to fry bacon.

The girl came out in her robe a few minutes later and put her arms around him without saying anything.

Hey, don't catch your robe on fire, the boy said. She was leaning against him but touching the stove too.

I'm sorry about earlier, she said. I don't know what got into me, why I said those things.

It's all right, he said. Here, honey, let me get this bacon.

I didn't mean to snap like that, she said. It was awful.

It was my fault, he said. How's Catherine?

She's fine now. I don't know what was the matter with her earlier. I changed her again after you left, and then she was fine. She was just fine then and went right off to sleep. I don't know what it was. Don't be mad with us though.

The boy laughed. I'm not mad with you, don't be silly, he said. Here, let me do something with this pan.

You sit down, the girl said. I'll fix the breakfast. How does a waffle sound with this bacon?

Sounds great, he said. I'm starved.

She took the bacon out of the pan and then made waffle batter. He sat at the table, relaxed now, and watched her move around the kitchen.

She left to close their bedroom door, then stopped in the living room to put on a record that they both liked.

We don't want to wake that one up again, the girl said.

She put a plate in front of him with bacon, a fried egg, and a waffle. She put another plate on the table for herself. It's ready, she said.

It looks swell, he said. He spread butter and poured syrup over the waffle, but as he started to cut into the waffle he turned the plate into his lap.

I don't believe it, he said, jumping up from the table.

The girl looked at him, then at the expression on his face, and she began to laugh.

If you could see yourself in the mirror, she said and kept laughing.

He looked down at the syrup that covered the front of his woolen underwear, at the pieces of waffle, bacon, and egg that clung to the syrup. He began to laugh.

I was starved, he said, shaking his head.

You were starved, she said, still laughing.

He peeled off the woolen underwear and threw it at the bathroom door. Then he opened his arms and she moved into them. They began to move very slowly to the recorded music, she in her robe, he in his shorts and T-shirt.

We won't fight anymore, will we? she said. It's not worth it, is it?

That's right, he said. Look how it makes you feel after.

We'll not fight anymore, she said.

When the record ended he kissed her for a long while on the lips. This was about eight o'clock in the morning, a cold Sunday in December.

He gets up from his chair and refills their glasses.

That's it, he says. End of story. I admit it's not much of one.

I was interested, she says. It was very interesting, if you want to know. But what happened? she asks. Later, I mean.

He shrugs and carries his drink over to the window. It's dark now but still snowing.

Things change, he says. Kids grow up. I don't know what happened. But things do change and without your realizing it or wanting them to.

Yes, that's true, only— But she does not finish.

She drops the subject then. In the window's reflection he sees her study her nails. Then she raises her head, asks brightly if he is, after all, going to show her something of the city.

Absolutely, he says. Put your boots on and let's get under way.

But he continues to stand at the window, remembering that gone life. After that morning there would be those hard times ahead, other women for him and another man for her, but that morning, that particular morning, they had danced. They danced, and then they held to each other as if there would always be that morning, and later they laughed about the waffle. They leaned on each other and laughed about it until tears came, while outside everything froze, for a while anyway.

Beginners

My friend Herb McGinnis, a cardiologist, was talking. The four of us were sitting around his kitchen table drinking gin. It was Saturday afternoon. Sunlight filled the kitchen from the big window behind the sink. There were Herb and I and his second wife, Teresa—Terri, we called her—and my wife, Laura. We lived in Albuquerque, but we were all from somewhere else. There was an ice bucket on the table. The gin and the tonic water kept going around, and we somehow got on the subject of love. Herb thought real love was nothing less than spiritual love. When he was young he'd spent five years in a seminary before quitting to go to medical school. He'd left the Church at the same time, but he said he still looked back to those years in the seminary as the most important in his life.

Terri said the man she lived with before she lived with Herb loved her so much he tried to kill her. Herb laughed after she said this. He made a face. Terri looked at him. Then she said, "He beat me up one night, the last night we lived together. He dragged me around the living room by my ankles, all the while saying, 'I love you, don't you see? I love you, you bitch.' He went on dragging me around the living room, my head knocking on things." She looked around the table at us and then looked at her hands on her glass. "What do you do with love like that?" she said. She was a bone-thin woman with a pretty face, dark eyes, and brown hair that hung down her back. She liked necklaces made of turquoise, and long pendant earrings. She was fifteen years younger than Herb, had suffered periods of anorexia, and during the late sixties, before she'd gone to nursing school, had been a dropout, a "street person" as she put it. Herb sometimes called her, affectionately, his hippie.

"My God, don't be silly. That's not love, and you know it," Herb said. "I don't know what you'd call it—madness is what I'd call it—but it's sure as hell not love."

"Say what you want to, but I know he loved me," Terri said. "I know he did. It may sound crazy to you, but it's true just the same. People are different, Herb. Sure, sometimes he may have acted crazy. Okay. But he loved me. In his own way, maybe, but he loved me. There *was* love there, Herb. Don't deny me that."

Herb let out breath. He held his glass and turned to Laura and me. "He threatened to kill *me* too." He finished his drink and reached for the gin bottle. "Terri's a romantic. Terri's of the 'Kick-me-so-I'll-know-you-love-me' school. Terri, hon, don't look that way." He reached across the table and touched her cheek with his fingers. He grinned at her.

"Now he wants to make up," Terri said. "After he tries to dump on me." She wasn't smiling.

"Make up what?" Herb said. "What is there to make up? I know what I know, and that's all."

"What would you call it then?" Terri said. "How'd we get started on this subject anyway?" She raised her glass and drank. "Herb always has love on his mind," she said. "Don't you, honey?" She smiled now, and I thought that was the last of it.

"I just wouldn't call Carl's behavior love, that's all I'm saying, honey," Herb said. "What about you guys?" he said to Laura and me. "Does that sound like love to you?"

I shrugged. "I'm the wrong person to ask. I didn't even know the man. I've only heard his name mentioned in passing. Carl. I wouldn't know. You'd have to know all the particulars. Not in my book it isn't, but who's to say? There're lots of different ways of behaving and showing affection. That way doesn't happen to be mine. But what you're saying, Herb, is that love is an absolute?"

"The kind of love I'm talking about is," Herb said. "The kind of love I'm talking about, you don't try to kill people."

Laura, my sweet, big Laura, said evenly, "I don't know anything about Carl, or anything about the situation. Who can judge anyone else's situation? But, Terri, I didn't know about the violence."

I touched the back of Laura's hand. She gave me a quick smile, then turned her gaze back to Terri. I picked up Laura's hand. The hand was warm to the touch, the nails polished, perfectly manicured. I encircled the broad wrist with my fingers, like a bracelet, and held her.

"When I left he drank rat poison," Terri said. She clasped

her arms with her hands. "They took him to the hospital in Santa Fe where we lived then and they saved his life, and his gums separated. I mean they pulled away from his teeth. After that his teeth stood out like fangs. My God," she said. She waited a minute, then let go of her arms and picked up her glass.

"What people won't do!" Laura said. "I'm sorry for him and I don't even think I like him. Where is he now?"

"He's out of the action," Herb said. "He's dead." He handed me the saucer of limes. I took a section of lime, squeezed it over my drink, and stirred the ice cubes with my finger.

"It gets worse," Terri said. "He shot himself in the mouth, but he bungled that too. Poor Carl," she said. She shook her head.

"Poor Carl nothing," Herb said. "He was dangerous." Herb was forty-five years old. He was tall and rangy with wavy, graying hair. His face and arms were brown from the tennis he played. When he was sober, his gestures, all his movements, were precise and careful.

"He did love me though, Herb, grant me that," Terri said. "That's all I'm asking. He didn't love me the way you love me, I'm not saying that. But he loved me. You can grant me that, can't you? That's not much to ask."

"What do you mean, 'He bungled it'?" I asked. Laura leaned forward with her glass. She put her elbows on the table and held her glass in both hands. She glanced from Herb to Terri and waited with a look of bewilderment on her open face, as if amazed that such things happened to people you knew. Herb finished his drink. "How'd he bungle it when he killed himself?" I said again.

"I'll tell you what happened," Herb said. "He took this twenty-two pistol he'd bought to threaten Terri and me with —oh, I'm serious, he wanted to use it. You should have seen the way we lived in those days. Like fugitives. I even bought a gun myself, and I thought I was a nonviolent sort. But I bought a gun for self-defense and carried it in the glove compartment. Sometimes I'd have to leave the apartment in the middle of the night, you know, to go to the hospital. Terri and I weren't married then and my first wife had the house and kids, the dog, everything, and Terri and I were living in this apartment. Sometimes, as I say, I'd get a call in the middle of the night and have to go in to the hospital at two or three in the morning. It'd be dark out there in the parking lot and I'd break into a sweat before I could even get to my car. I never knew if he was going to come up out of the shrubbery or from behind a car and start shooting. I mean, he was crazy. He was capable of wiring a bomb to my car, anything. He used to call my answering service at all hours and say he needed to talk to the doctor, and when I'd return the call he'd say, 'Son of a bitch, your days are numbered.' Little things like that. It was scary, I'm telling you."

"I still feel sorry for him," Terri said. She sipped her drink and gazed at Herb. Herb stared back.

"It sounds like a nightmare," Laura said. "But what exactly happened after he shot himself?" Laura is a legal secretary. We'd met in a professional capacity, lots of other people around, but we'd talked and I'd asked her to have dinner with me. Before we knew it, it was a courtship. She's thirty-five, three years younger than I am. In addition to being in love, we like each other and enjoy one another's company. She's easy to be with. "What happened?" Laura asked again.

Herb waited a minute and turned the glass in his hand. Then he said, "He shot himself in the mouth in his room. Someone heard the shot and told the manager. They came in with a passkey, saw what had happened, and called an ambulance. I happened to be there when they brought him in to the emergency room. I was there on another case. He was still alive, but beyond anything anyone could do for him. Still, he lived for three days. I'm serious though, his head swelled up to twice the size of a normal head. I'd never seen anything like it, and I hope I never do again. Terri wanted to go in and sit with him when she found out about it. We had a fight over it. I didn't think she'd want to see him like that. I didn't think she should see him, and I still don't."

"Who won the fight?" Laura said.

"I was in the room with him when he died," Terri said. "He never regained consciousness, and there was no hope for him, but I sat with him. He didn't have anyone else."

"He was dangerous," Herb said. "If you call that love, you can have it."

"It was love," Terri said. "Sure it was abnormal in most people's eyes, but he was willing to die for it. He did die for it."

"I sure as hell wouldn't call it love," Herb said. "You don't know what he died for. I've seen a lot of suicides, and I couldn't say anyone close to them ever knew for sure. And when they claimed to be the cause, well I don't know." He put his hands behind his neck and leaned on the back legs of his chair. "I'm not interested in that kind of love. If that's love, you can have it."

After a minute, Terri said, "We were afraid. Herb even made a will out and wrote to his brother in California who used to be a Green Beret. He told him who to look for if something happened to him mysteriously. Or not so mysteriously!" She shook her head and laughed at it now. She drank from her glass. She went on. "But we did live a little like fugitives. We *were* afraid of him, no question. I even called the police at one point, but they were no help. They said they couldn't do anything to him, they couldn't arrest him or do anything unless he actually *did* something to Herb. Isn't that a laugh?" Terri said. She poured the last of the gin into her glass and wagged the bottle. Herb got up from the table and went to the cupboard. He took down another bottle of gin.

"Well, Nick and I are in love," Laura said. "Aren't we, Nick?" She bumped my knee with her knee. "You're supposed to say something now," she said and turned a large smile on me. "We get along really well, I think. We like doing things together, and neither of us has beaten up on the other yet, thank God. Knock on wood. I'd say we're pretty happy. I guess we should count our blessings."

For answer, I took her hand and raised it to my lips with a flourish. I made a production out of kissing her hand. Everyone was amused. "We're lucky," I said.

"You guys," Terri said. "Stop that now. You're making me sick! You're still on a honeymoon, that's why you can act like this. You're still gaga over each other yet. Just wait. How long have you been together now? How long has it been? A year? Longer than a year."

"Going on a year and a half," Laura said, still flushed and smiling.

"You're still on the honeymoon," Terri said again. "Wait a

while." She held her drink and gazed at Laura. "I'm only kidding," she said.

Herb had opened the gin and gone around the table with the bottle. "Terri, Jesus, you shouldn't talk like that, even if you're not serious, even if you are kidding. It's bad luck. Here, you guys. Let's have a toast. I want to propose a toast. A toast to love. True love," Herb said. We touched glasses.

"To love," we said.

Outside, in the backyard, one of the dogs began to bark. The leaves of the aspen tree that leaned past the window flickered in the breeze. The afternoon sunlight was like a presence in the room. There was suddenly a feeling of ease and generosity around the table, of friendship and comfort. We could have been anywhere. We raised our glasses again and grinned at each other like children who had agreed on something for once.

"I'll tell you what real love is," Herb said finally, breaking the spell. "I mean I'll give you a good example of it, and then you can draw your own conclusions." He poured a little more gin into his glass. He added an ice cube and a piece of lime. We waited and sipped our drinks. Laura and I touched knees again. I put a hand on her warm thigh and left it there.

"What do any of us really know about love?" Herb said. "I kind of mean what I'm saying too, if you'll pardon me for saying it. But it seems to me we're just rank beginners at love. We say we love each other and we do, I don't doubt it. We love each other and we love hard, all of us. I love Terri and Terri loves me, and you guys love each other. You know the kind of love I'm talking about now. Sexual love, that attraction to the other person, the partner, as well as just the plain everyday kind of love, love of the other person's being, the loving to be with the other, the little things that make up everyday love. Carnal love then and, well, call it sentimental love, the day-to-day caring about the other. But sometimes I have a hard time accounting for the fact that I must have loved my first wife too. But I did, I know I did. So I guess before you can say anything, I *am* like Terri in that regard. Terri and Carl." He thought about it a minute and then went on. "But at one time I thought I loved my first wife more than life itself, and we had the kids together. But now I hate her guts. I do. How do you figure that? What happened to that love? Did that love just get erased from the big board, as if it was never up there, as if it never happened? What happened to it is what I'd like to know. I wish someone could tell me. Then there's Carl. Okay, we're back to Carl. He loved Terri so much he tries to kill her and winds up killing himself." He stopped talking and shook his head. "You guys have been together eighteen months and you love each other, it shows all over you, you simply glow with it, but you've loved other people too before you met each other. You've both been married before, just like us. And you probably loved other people before that. Terri and I have been together five years, been married for four. And the terrible thing, the terrible thing is, but the good thing, too, the saving grace, you might say, is that if something happened to one of us—excuse me for saying this—but if something happened to one of us tomorrow, I think the other one, the other partner, would mourn for a while, you know, but then the surviving party would go out and love again, have someone else soon enough and all this, all of this love—Jesus, how can you figure it?—it would just be memory. Maybe not even memory. Maybe that's the way it's supposed to be. But am I wrong? Am I way off base? I know that's what would happen with us, with Terri and me, as much as we may love each other. With any one of us for that matter. I'll stick my neck out that much. We've all proved it anyhow. I just don't understand. Set me straight if you think I'm wrong. I want to know. I don't know anything, and I'm the first to admit it."

"Herb, for God's sake," Terri said. "This is depressing stuff. This could get very depressing. Even if you think it's true," she said, "it's still depressing." She reached out to him and took hold of his forearm near the wrist. "Are you getting drunk, Herb? Honey, are you drunk?"

"Honey, I'm just talking, all right," Herb said. "I don't have to be drunk to say what's on my mind, do I? I'm not drunk. We're just talking, right?" Herb said. Then his voice changed. "But if I want to get drunk I will, goddamn it. I can do anything I want today." He fixed his eyes on her.

"Honey, I'm not criticizing," she said. She picked up her glass.

"I'm not on call today," Herb said. "I can do anything I want today. I'm just tired, that's all."

"Herb, we love you," Laura said.

Herb looked at Laura. It was as if he couldn't place her for a minute. She kept looking at him, holding her smile. Her cheeks were flushed and the sun was hitting her in the eyes, so she squinted to see him. His features relaxed. "Love you too, Laura. And you, Nick. I'll tell you, you're our pals," Herb said. He picked up his glass. "Well, what was I saying? Yeah. I wanted to tell you about something that happened a while back. I think I wanted to prove a point, and I will if I can just tell this thing the way it happened. This happened a few months ago, but it's still going on right now. You might say that, yeah. But it ought to make us all feel ashamed when we talk like we know what we were talking about, when we talk about love."

"Herb, come on now," Terri said. "You are too drunk. Don't talk like this. Don't talk like you're drunk if you're not drunk."

"Just shut up for a minute, will you?" Herb said. "Let me tell this. It's been on my mind. Just shut up for a minute. I told you a little about it when it first happened. That old couple who got into an accident out on the interstate? A kid hit them and they were all battered up and not given much chance to pull through. Let me tell this, Terri. Now just shut up for a minute. Okay?"

Terri looked at us and then looked back at Herb. She seemed anxious, that's the only word for it. Herb handed the bottle around the table.

"Surprise me, Herb," Terri said. "Surprise me beyond all thought and reason."

"Maybe I will," Herb said. "Maybe so. I'm constantly surprised with things myself. Everything in my life surprises me." He stared at her for a minute. Then he began talking.

"I was on call that night. It was in May or June. Terri and I had just sat down to dinner, when the hospital called. There'd been an accident out on the interstate. A drunk kid, a teenager, had plowed his dad's pickup into a camper with this old couple in it. They were up in their mid-seventies. The kid, he was eighteen or nineteen, he was DOA when they brought him in. He'd taken the steering wheel through his sternum and must have died instantly. But the old couple, they were still alive, but just barely. They had multiple fractures and contusions, lacerations, the works, and they each had themselves a concussion. They were in a bad way, believe me. And, of course, their age was against them. She was even a little worse off than he was. She had a ruptured spleen and along with everything else, both kneecaps were broken. But they'd been wearing their seatbelts and, God knows, that's the only thing that saved them."

"Folks, this is an advertisement for the National Safety Council," Terri said. "This is your spokesman, Doctor Herb McGinnis, talking. Listen up now," Terri said and laughed, then lowered her voice. "Herb, you're just too much sometimes. I love you, honey."

We all laughed. Herb laughed too. "Honey, I love you. But you know that, don't you?" He leaned across the table, Terri met him halfway, and they kissed. "Terri's right, everybody," Herb said as he settled himself again. "Buckle up for safety. Listen to what Doctor Herb is telling you. But seriously, they were in bum shape, those old people. By the time I got down there the intern and nurses were already at work on them. The kid was dead, as I said. He was off in a corner, laid out on a gurney. Someone had already notified the next of kin, and the funeral home people were on the way. I took one look at the old couple and told the ER nurse to get me a neurologist and an orthopedic man down there right away. I'll try and make a long story short. The other fellows showed up, and we took the old couple up to the operating room and worked on them most of the night. They must have had incredible reserves, those old people, you see that once in a while. We did everything that could be done, and toward morning we were giving them a fifty-fifty chance, maybe less than that, maybe thirty-seventy for the wife. Anna Gates was her name, and she was quite a woman. But they were still alive the next morning, and we moved them into the ICU where we could monitor every breath and keep a twenty-four-hour watch on them. They were in intensive care for nearly two weeks, she a little longer, before their condition improved enough so we could transfer them out and down the hall to their own rooms."

Herb stopped talking. "Here," he said, "let's drink this gin. Let's drink it up. Then we're going to dinner, right? Terri and

I know a place. It's new place. That's where we'll go, this new place we know about. We'll go when we finish this gin."

"It's called The Library," Terri said. "You haven't eaten there yet, have you?" she said, and Laura and I shook our heads. "It's some place. They say it's part of a new chain, but it's not like a chain, if you know what I mean. They actually have bookshelves in there with real books on them. You can browse around after dinner and take a book out and bring it back the next time you come to eat. You won't believe the food. And Herb's reading *Ivanhoe*! He took it out when we were there last week. He just signed a card. Like in a real library."

"I like *Ivanhoe*," Herb said. "*Ivanhoe*'s great. If I had it to do over again, I'd study literature. Right now I'm having an identity crisis. Right, Terri?" Herb said. He laughed. He twirled the ice in his glass. "I've been having an identity crisis for years. Terri knows. Terri can tell you. But let me say this. If I could come back again in a different life, a different time and all, you know what? I'd like to come back as a knight. You were pretty safe wearing all that armor. It was all right being a knight until gunpowder and muskets and twenty-two pistols came along."

"Herb would like to ride a white horse and carry a lance," Terri said and laughed.

"Carry a woman's garter with you everywhere," Laura said.

"Or just a woman," I said.

"That's right," Herb said. "There you go. You know what's what, don't you Nick?" he said. "Also, you'd carry around their perfumed hankies with you wherever you rode. Did they have perfumed hankies in those days? It doesn't matter. Some little forget-me-not. A token, that's what I'm trying to say. You needed some token to carry around with you in those days. Anyway, whatever, it was better in those days being a knight than a serf," Herb said.

"It's always better," Laura said.

"The serfs didn't have it so good in those days," Terri said.

"The serfs have never had it good," Herb said. "But I guess even the knights were vessels to someone. Isn't that the way it worked in those days? But then everyone is always a vessel to someone else. Isn't that right? Terri? But what I liked about knights, besides their ladies, was that they had that suit of armor, you know, and they couldn't get hurt very easy. No cars in those days, man. No drunk teenagers to run over you."

"Vassals," I said.

"What?" Herb said.

"Vassals," I said. "They were called *vassals*, Doc, not *vessels*."

"Vassals," Herb said. "Vassals, vessels, ventricles, vas deferens. Well, you knew what I meant anyway. You're all better educated in these matters than I am," Herb said. "I'm not educated. I learned my stuff. I'm a heart surgeon, sure, but really I'm just a mechanic. I just go in and fix things that go wrong with the body. I'm just a mechanic."

"Modesty somehow doesn't become you, Herb," Laura said, and Herb grinned at her.

"He's just a humble doctor, folks," I said. "But sometimes they suffocated in all that armor, Herb. They'd even have heart attacks if it got too hot and they were too tired and worn out. I read somewhere that they'd fall off their horses and not be able to get up because they were too tired to stand with all that armor on them. They got trampled by their own horses sometimes."

"That's terrible," Herb said. "That's a terrible image, Nicky. I guess they'd just lay there then and wait until someone, the enemy, came along and made a shish kabob out of them."

"Some other vassal," Terri said.

"That's right, some other vassal," Herb said. "There you have it. Some other vassal would come along and spear his fellow knight in the name of love. Or whatever it was they fought over in those days. Same things we fight over these days, I guess," Herb said.

"Politics," Laura said. "Nothing's changed." The color was still in Laura's cheeks. Her eyes were bright. She brought her glass to her lips.

Herb poured himself another drink. He looked at the label closely as if studying the little figures of the beefeater guards. Then he slowly put the bottle down on the table and reached for the tonic water.

"What about this old couple, Herb?" Laura said. "You didn't finish that story you started." Laura was having a hard time lighting her cigarette. Her matches kept going out. The light inside the room was different now, changing, getting weaker. The leaves outside the window were still shimmering, and I stared at the fuzzy pattern they made on the pane and the Formica counter under it. There was no sound except for Laura striking her matches.

"What about that old couple?" I said after a minute. "The last we heard they were just getting out of intensive care."

"Older but wiser," Terri said.

Herb stared at her.

"Herb, don't give me that kind of look," Terri said. "Go on with your story. I was only kidding. Then what happened? We all want to know."

"Terri, sometimes," Herb said.

"Please, Herb," she said. "Honey, don't always be so serious. Please go on with the story. I was joking, for God's sake. Can't you take a joke?"

"This is nothing to joke about," Herb said. He held his glass and gazed steadily at her.

"What happened then, Herb?" Laura said. "We really want to know."

Herb fixed his eyes on Laura. Then he broke off and grinned. "Laura, if I didn't have Terri and love her so much, and Nick wasn't my friend, I'd fall in love with you. I'd carry you off."

"Herb, you shit," Terri said. "Tell your story. If I weren't in love with you, I damn sure well wouldn't be here in the first place, you can bet on it. Honey, what do you say? Finish your story. Then we'll go to The Library. Okay?"

"Okay," Herb said. "Where was I? Where am I? That's a better question. Maybe I should ask that." He waited a minute, and then began to talk.

"When they were finally out of the woods we were able to move them out of intensive care, after we could see they were going to make it. I dropped in to see each of them every day, sometimes twice a day if I was up doing other calls anyway. They were both in casts and bandages, head to foot. You know, you've seen it in the movies even if you haven't seen the real thing. But they were bandaged head to foot, man, and I mean head to foot. That's just the way they looked, just like those phony actors in the movies after some big disaster. But this was the real thing. Their heads were bandaged—they just had eye holes and a place for their mouths and noses. Anna Gates had to have her legs elevated too. She was worse off than he was, I told you that. Both of them were on intravenous and glucose for a time. Well, Henry Gates was very depressed for the longest while. Even after he found out that his wife was going to pull through and recover, he was still very depressed. Not just about the accident itself, though of course that had gotten to him as those things will. There you are one minute, you know, everything just dandy, then blam, you're staring into the abyss. You come back. It's like a miracle. But it's left its mark on you. It does that. One day I was sitting in a chair beside his bed and he described to me, talking slowly, talking through his mouth hole so sometimes I had to get up to his face to hear him, telling me what it looked like to him, what it felt like, when that kid's car crossed the center line onto his side of the road and kept coming. He said he knew it was all up for them, that was the last look of anything he'd have on this earth. This was it. But he said nothing flew into his mind, his life didn't pass before his eyes, nothing like that. He said he just felt sorry to not be able to see any more of his Anna, because they'd had this fine life together. That was his only regret. He looked straight ahead, just gripped the wheel and watched the kid's car coming at them. And there was nothing he could do except say, 'Anna! Hold on, Anna!' "

"It gives me the shivers," Laura said. "Brrrr," she said, shaking her head.

Herb nodded. He went on talking, caught up in it now. "I'd sit a while every day beside the bed. He'd lay there in his bandages staring out the window at the foot of his bed. The window was too high for him to see anything except the tops of trees. That's all he saw for hours at a stretch. He couldn't turn his head without assistance, and he was only allowed to do that twice a day. Each morning for a few minutes and every evening, he was allowed to turn his head. But during our visits he had to look at the window when he talked. I'd talk a little, ask a few questions, but mostly I'd listen. He was very depressed. What was most depressing to him, after he was assured his wife was going to be all right, that she was recovering to everyone's satisfaction, what was most depressing was the fact they couldn't be physically together. That he couldn't see her and be with her every day. He told me they'd married in 1927 and since that time they'd only been apart from each other for any time on two occasions. Even when their children were born, they were born there on the ranch and Henry and the missus still saw each other every day and talked and were together around the place. But he said they'd only been away from each other for any real time on two occasions—once when her mother died in 1940 and Anna had to take a train to St. Louis to settle matters there. And again in 1952 when her sister died in Los Angeles, and she had to go down there to claim the body. I should tell you they had a little ranch seventy-five miles or so outside of Bend, Oregon, and that's where they'd lived most of their lives. They'd sold the ranch and moved into the city of Bend just a few years ago. When this accident happened, they were on their way down from Denver, where they'd gone to see his sister. They were going on to visit a son and some of their grandchildren in El Paso. But in all of their married life they'd only been apart from each other for any length of time on just those two occasions. Imagine that. But, Jesus, he was lonely for her. I'm telling you he *pined* for her. I never knew what that word meant before, *pined*, until I saw it happening to this man. He missed her something fierce. He just longed for her company, that old man did. Of course he felt better, he'd brighten, when I'd give him my daily report on Anna's progress—that she was mending, that she was going to be fine, just a question of a little more time. He was out of his casts and bandages now, but he was still extremely lonely. I told him that just as soon as he was able, maybe in a week, I'd put him into a wheelchair and take him visiting, take him down the corridor to see his wife. Meanwhile, I called on him and we'd talk. He told me a little about their lives out there on the ranch in the late 1920s and during the early thirties." He looked around the table at us and shook his head at what he was going to say, or just maybe at the impossibility of all this. "He told me that in the winter it would do nothing but snow and for maybe months at a time they couldn't leave the ranch, the road would be closed. Besides, he had to feed cattle every day through those winter months. They would just be there together, the two of them, him and his wife. The kids hadn't come along yet. They'd come along later. But month in, month out, they'd be there together, the two of them, the same routine, the same everything, never anyone else to talk to or to visit with during those winter months. But they had each other. That's all and everything they had, each other. 'What would you do for entertainment?' I asked him. I was serious. I wanted to know. I didn't see how people could live like that. I don't think anyone can live like that these days. You think so? It seems impossible to me. You know what he said? Do you want to know what he answered? He lay there and considered the question. He took some time. Then he said, 'We'd go to the dances every night.' 'What?' I said. 'Pardon me, Henry,' I said and leaned closer, thinking I hadn't heard right. 'We'd go to the dances every night,' he said again. I wondered what he meant. I didn't know what he was talking about, but I waited for him to go on. He thought back to that time again, and in a little while he said, 'We had a Victrola and some records, Doctor. We'd play the Victrola every night and listen to the records and dance there in the living room. We'd do that every night. Sometimes it'd be snowing outside and the temperature down below zero. The temperature really drops on you up there in January or February. But we'd listen to the records and dance in our stocking feet in the living room until we'd gone through all the records. And then I'd build up the fire and turn out the lights, all but one, and we'd go to bed. Some nights it'd be snowing, and it'd be so still outside you could hear the snow falling. It's true, Doc,' he said, 'you can do that. Sometimes you can hear the snow falling. If you're quiet and your mind is clear and you're at peace with yourself and all things, you can lay in the dark and hear it snow. You try it sometimes,' he said. 'You get snow down here once in a while, don't you? You try it sometimes. Anyway, we'd go to the dances every night. And then we'd go to bed under a lot of quilts and sleep warm until morning. When you woke up you could see your breath,' he said.

"When he'd recovered enough to be moved in a wheelchair, his bandages were long gone by then, a nurse and I wheeled him down the corridor to where his wife was. He'd shaved that morning and put on some lotion. He was in his bathrobe and hospital gown, he was still recovering, you know, but he held himself erect in the wheelchair. Still, he was nervous as a cat, you could see that. As we came closer to her room, his color rose and he got this look of anticipation to his face, a look I can't begin to describe. I pushed his chair, and the nurse walked along beside me. She knew something about the situation, she'd picked up things. Nurses, you know, they've seen everything, and not much gets to them after a while but this one was strung a little tight herself that morning. The door was open and I wheeled Henry right into the room. Mrs. Gates, Anna, she was still immobilized, but she could move her head and her left arm. She had her eyes closed, but they snapped open when we entered the room. She was still in bandages, but only from the pelvic area down. I pushed Henry up to the left side of her bed and said, 'You have some company, Anna. Company, dear.' But I couldn't say any more than that. She gave a little smile and her face lit up. Out came her hand from under the sheet. It was bluish and bruised-looking. Henry took the hand in his hands. He held it and kissed it. Then he said, 'Hello, Anna. How's my babe? Remember me?' Tears started down her cheeks. She nodded. 'I've missed you,' he said. She kept nodding. The nurse and I got the hell out of there. She began blubbering once we were outside the room, and she's a tough lot, that nurse. It was an experience, I'm telling you. But after that, he was wheeled down there every morning and every afternoon. We arranged it so they could have lunch and dinner together in her room. In between times they'd just sit and hold hands and talk. They had no end of things to talk about."

"You didn't tell me this before, Herb," Terri said. "You just said a little about it when it first happened. You didn't tell me any of this, damn you. Now you're telling me this to make me cry. Herb, this story better not have an unhappy ending. It doesn't, does it? You're not setting us up, are you? If you are, I don't want to hear another word. You don't have to go any farther with it, you can stop right there. Herb?"

"What happened to them, Herb?" Laura said. "Finish the story, for God's sake. Is there more? But I'm like Terri, I don't want anything to happen to them. That's really something."

"Are they all right now?" I asked. I was involved in the story too, but I was getting drunk. It was hard to keep things in focus. The light seemed to be draining out of the room, going back through the window where it had come from in the first place. Yet nobody made a move to get up from the table or to turn on an electric light.

"Sure, they're all right," Herb said. "They were discharged a while later. Just a few weeks ago, in fact. After a time, Henry was able to get around on crutches and then he went to a cane and then he was just all over the place. But his spirits were up now, his spirits were fine, he just improved every day once he got to see his missus again. When she was able to be moved, their son from El Paso and his wife drove up in a station wagon and took them back down there with them. She still had some convalescing to do, but she was coming along real fine. I just had a card from Henry a few days ago. I guess that's one of the reasons they're on my mind right now. That, and what we were saying about love earlier.

"Listen," Herb went on. "Let's finish this gin. There's about enough left here for one drink all around. Then let's go eat. Let's go to The Library. What do you say? I don't know, the whole thing was really something to see. It just unfolded day after day. Some of those talks I had with him . . . I won't forget those times. But talking about it now has got me depressed. Jesus, but I feel depressed all of a sudden."

"Don't feel depressed, Herb," Terri said. "Herb, why don't you take a pill, honey?" She turned to Laura and me and said, "Herb takes these mood elevator pills sometimes. It's no secret, is it, Herb?"

Herb shook his head. "I've taken everything there is to take at one time or another. No secret."

"My first wife took them too," I said.

"Did they help her?" Laura said.

"No, she still went around depressed. She cried a lot."

"Some people are born depressed, I think," Terri said. "Some people are born unhappy. And unlucky too. I've known people who were just plain unlucky in everything. Other people—not you, honey, I'm not talking about you, of course —other people just set out to make themselves unhappy and they stay unhappy." She was rubbing at something on the table with her finger. Then she stopped rubbing.

"I think I want to call my kids before we go eat," Herb said.

"Is that all right with everybody? I won't be long. I'll take a quick shower to freshen up, then I'll call my kids. Then let's go eat."

"You might have to talk to Marjorie, Herb, if she answers the phone. That's Herb's ex-wife. You guys, you've heard us on the subject of Marjorie. You don't want to talk to her this afternoon, Herb. It'll make you feel even worse."

"No, I don't want to talk to Marjorie," Herb said. "But I want to talk to my kids. I miss them real bad, honey. I miss Steve. I was awake last night remembering things from when he was little. I want to talk to him. I want to talk to Kathy too. I miss them, so I'll have to take the chance their mother will answer the phone. That bitch of a woman."

"There isn't a day goes by that Herb doesn't say he wishes she'd get married again, or else die. For one thing," Terri said, "she's bankrupting us. Another is that she has custody of both kids. We get to have the kids down here just for a month during the summer. Herb says it's just to spite him that she won't get married again. She has a boyfriend who lives with them, too, and Herb is supporting him as well."

"She's allergic to bees," Herb said. "If I'm not praying she'll get married again, I'm praying she'll go out in the country and get herself stung to death by a swarm of bees."

"Herb, that's awful," Laura said and laughed until her eyes welled.

"Awful funny," Terri said. We all laughed. We laughed and laughed.

"Bzzzzzz," Herb said, turning his fingers into bees and buzzing them at Terri's throat and necklace. Then he let his hands drop and leaned back, suddenly serious again.

"She's a rotten bitch. It's true," Herb said. "She's vicious. Sometimes when I get drunk, like I am now, I think I'd like to go up there dressed like a beekeeper—you know, that hat that's like a helmet with the plate that comes down over your face, the big thick gloves, and the padded coat. I'd like to just knock on the door and release a hive of bees in the house. First I'd make sure the kids were out of the house, of course." With some difficulty, he crossed one leg over the other. Then he put both feet on the floor and leaned forward, elbows on the table, chin cupped in his hands. "Maybe I won't call the kids right now after all. Maybe you're right, Terri. Maybe it isn't such a hot idea. Maybe I'll just take a quick shower and change my shirt, and then we'll go eat. How does that sound, everybody?"

"Sounds fine to me," I said. "Eat or not eat. Or keep drinking. I could head right on into the sunset."

"What does that mean, honey?" Laura said, turning a look on me.

"It just means what I said, honey, nothing else. I mean I could just keep going and going. That's all I meant. It's that sunset maybe." The window had a reddish tint to it now as the sun went down.

"I could eat something myself," Laura said. "I just realized I'm hungry. What is there to snack on?"

"I'll put out some cheese and crackers," Terri said, but she just sat there.

Herb finished his drink. Then he got slowly up from the table and said, "Excuse me. I'll go shower." He left the kitchen and walked slowly down the hall to the bathroom. He shut the door behind him.

"I'm worried about Herb," Terri said. She shook her head. "Sometimes I worry more than other times, but lately I'm really worried." She stared at her glass. She didn't make any move for cheese and crackers. I decided to get up and look in the refrigerator. When Laura says she's hungry, I know she needs to eat. "Help yourself to whatever you can find, Nick. Bring out anything that looks good. Cheese in there, and a salami stick, I think. Crackers in that cupboard over the stove. I forgot. We'll have a snack. I'm not hungry myself, but you guys must be starving. I don't have an appetite anymore. What was I saying?" She closed her eyes and opened them. "I don't think we've told you this, maybe we have, I can't remember, but Herb was very suicidal after his first marriage broke up and his wife moved to Denver with the kids. He went to a psychiatrist for a long while, for months. Sometimes he says he thinks he should still be going." She picked up the empty bottle and turned it upside down over her glass. I was cutting some salami on the counter as carefully as I could. "Dead soldier," Terri said. Then she said, "Lately he's been talking about suicide again. Especially when he's been drinking. Sometimes I think he's too vulnerable. He doesn't have any defenses. He doesn't have defenses against anything. Well," she said, "gin's gone. Time to cut and run. Time to cut our losses, as my daddy used to say. Time to eat, I guess, though I don't have any appetite. But you guys must be starving. I'm glad to see you eating something. That'll keep you until we get to the restaurant. We can get drinks at the restaurant if we want them. Wait'll you see this place, it's something else. You can take books out of there along with your doggie bag. I guess I should get ready too. I'll just wash my face and put on some lipstick. I'm going just like I am. If they don't like it, tough. I just want to say this, and that's all. But I don't want it to sound negative. I hope and pray that you guys still love each other five, even three years from now the way you do today. Even four years from now, say. That's the moment of truth, four years. That's all I have to say on the subject." She hugged her thin arms and began running her hands up and down them. She closed her eyes.

I stood up from the table and went behind Laura's chair. I leaned over her and crossed my arms under her breasts and held her. I brought my face down beside hers. Laura pressed my arms. She pressed harder and wouldn't let go.

Terri opened her eyes. She watched us. Then she picked up her glass. "Here's to you guys," she said. "Here's to all of us." She drained the glass, and the ice clicked against her teeth. "Carl too," she said and put her glass back on the table. "Poor Carl. Herb thought he was a schmuck, but Herb was genuinely afraid of him. Carl wasn't a schmuck. He loved me, and I loved him. That's all. I still think of him sometimes. It's the truth, and I'm not ashamed to say it. Sometimes I think of him, he'll just pop into my head at any old moment. I'll tell you something, and I hate how soap opera a life can get, so it's not even yours anymore, but this is how it was. I was pregnant by him. It was that first time he tried to kill himself, when he took the rat poison. He didn't know I was pregnant. It gets worse. I decided on an abortion. I didn't tell him about it either, naturally. I'm not saying anything Herb doesn't know. Herb knows all about it. Final installment. Herb gave me the abortion. Small world, isn't it? But I thought Carl was crazy at the time. I didn't want his baby. Then he goes and kills himself. But after that, after he'd been gone for a while and there was no Carl anymore to talk to and listen to his side of things and help him when he was afraid, I felt real bad about things. I was sorry about his baby, that I hadn't had it. I love Carl, and there's no question of that in my mind. I still love him. But God, I love Herb too. You can see that, can't you? I don't have to tell you that. Oh, isn't it all too much, all of it?" She put her face in her hands and began to cry. Slowly she leaned forward and put her head on the table.

Laura put her food down at once. She got up and said, "Terri. Terri, dear," and began rubbing Terri's neck and shoulders. "Terri," she murmured.

I was eating a piece of salami. The room had gotten very dark. I finished chewing what I had in my mouth, swallowed the stuff, and moved over to the window. I looked out into the backyard. I looked past the aspen tree and the two black dogs sleeping in amongst the lawn chairs. I looked past the swimming pool to the little corral with its gate open and the old empty horse barn and beyond. There was a field of wild grass, and then a fence and then another field, and then the interstate connecting Albuquerque with El Paso. Cars moved back and forth on the highway. The sun was going down behind the mountains, and the mountains had gotten dark, shadows everywhere. Yet there was light too and it seemed to be softening those things I looked at. The sky was gray near the tops of the mountains, as gray as a dark day in winter. But there was a band of blue sky just above the gray, the blue you see in tropical postcards, the blue of the Mediterranean. The water on the surface of the pool rippled and the same breeze caused the aspen leaves to tremble. One of the dogs raised its head as if on signal, listened a minute with its ears up, and then put its head back down between its paws.

I had the feeling something was going to happen, it was in the slowness of the shadows and the light, and that whatever it was might take me with it. I didn't want that to happen. I watched the wind move in waves across the grass. I could see the grass in the fields bend in the wind and then straighten again. The second field slanted up to the highway, and the wind moved uphill across it, wave after wave. I stood there and waited and watched the grass bend in the wind. I could feel my heart beating. Somewhere toward the back of the house the shower was running. Terri was still crying. Slowly and with an effort, I turned to look at her. She lay with her head on the table, her face turned toward the stove. Her eyes were open, but now and then she would blink away tears. Laura had pulled her chair over and sat with an arm around Terri's shoulders. She murmured still, her lips against Terri's hair.

"Sure, sure," Terri said. "Tell me about it."

"Terri, sweetheart," Laura said to her tenderly. "It'll be okay, you'll see. It'll be okay."

Laura raised her eyes to mine then. Her look was penetrating, and my heart slowed. She gazed into my eyes for what seemed a long time, and then she nodded. That's all she did, the only sign she gave, but it was enough. It was as if she were telling me, Don't worry, we'll get past this, everything is going to be all right with us, you'll see. Easy does it. That's the way I chose to interpret the look anyway, though I could be wrong.

The shower stopped running. In a minute, I heard whistling as Herb opened the bathroom door. I kept looking at the women at the table. Terri was still crying and Laura was stroking her hair. I turned back to the window. The blue layer of sky had given way now and was turning dark like the rest. But stars had appeared. I recognized Venus and farther off and to the side, not as bright but unmistakably there on the horizon, Mars. The wind had picked up. I looked at what it was doing to the empty fields. I thought unreasonably that it was too bad the McGinnises no longer kept horses. I wanted to imagine horses rushing through those fields in the near dark, or even just standing quietly with their heads in opposite directions near the fence. I stood at the window and waited. I knew I had to keep still a while longer, keep my eyes out there, outside the house as long as there was something left to see.

One More Thing

L.D.'s WIFE, Maxine, told him to leave one night after she came home from work and found him drunk again and being abusive with Bea, their fifteen-year-old. L.D. and his daughter were at the kitchen table, arguing. Maxine didn't have time to put her purse away or take off her coat.

Bea said, "Tell him, Mom. Tell him what we talked about. It's in his head, isn't it? If he wants to stop drinking, all he has to do is tell himself to stop. It's all in his head. Everything's in the head."

"You think it's that simple, do you?" L.D. said. He turned the glass in his hand but didn't drink from it. Maxine had him in a fierce and disquieting gaze. "That's crap," he said. "Keep your nose out of things you don't know anything about. You don't know what you're saying. It's hard to take anybody seriously who sits around all day reading astrology magazines."

"This has nothing to do with *astrology*, Dad," Bea said. "You don't have to insult me." Bea hadn't attended high school for the past six weeks. She said no one could make her go back. Maxine had said it was another tragedy in a long line of tragedies.

"Why don't you both stop?" Maxine said. "My God, I already have a headache. This is just too much. L.D.?"

"Tell him, Mom," Bea said. "Mom thinks so too. If you tell yourself to stop, you can stop. The brain can do anything. If you worry about going bald and losing your hair—I'm not talking about you, Dad—it'll fall out. It's all in your head. Anybody who knows anything about it will tell you."

"How about sugar diabetes?" he said. "What about epilepsy? Can the brain control that?" He raised the glass right under Maxine's eyes and finished his drink.

"Diabetes, too," Bea said. "Epilepsy. Anything! The brain is the most powerful organ in the body. It can do anything you ask it to do." She picked up his cigarettes from the table and lit one for herself.

"Cancer. What about cancer?" L.D. said. "Can it stop you from getting cancer? Bea?" He thought he might have her there. He looked at Maxine. "I don't know how we got started on this," he said.

"Cancer," Bea said and shook her head at his simplicity. "Cancer, too. If a person wasn't afraid of getting cancer, he wouldn't get cancer. Cancer starts in the *brain*, Dad."

"That's crazy!" he said and hit the table with the flat of his hand. The ashtray jumped. His glass fell on its side and rolled toward Bea. "You're crazy, Bea, do you know that? Where'd you pick up all this crap? That's what it is too. It's crap, Bea."

"That's enough, L.D.," Maxine said. She unbuttoned her coat and put her purse down on the counter. She looked at him and said, "L.D., I've had it. So has Bea. So has everyone who knows you. I've been thinking it over. I want you out of here. Tonight. This minute. And I'm doing you a favor, L.D. I want you out of the house now before they come and carry you out in a pine box. I want you to leave, L.D. Now," she said. "Someday you'll look back on this. Someday you'll look back and thank me."

L.D. said, "I will, will I? Someday I'll look back," he said. "You think so, do you?" L.D. had no intention of going anywhere, in a pine box or otherwise. His gaze switched from Maxine to a jar of pickles that had been on the table since lunch. He picked up the jar and hurled it past the refrigerator through the kitchen window. Glass shattered onto the floor and windowsill, and pickles flew out into the chill night. He gripped the edge of the table.

Bea had jumped away from her chair. "*God*, Dad! *You're* the crazy one," she said. She stood beside her mother and took in little breaths through her mouth.

"Call the police," Maxine said. "He's violent. Get out of the kitchen before he hurts you. Call the police," she said.

They started backing out of the kitchen. For a moment L.D. was insanely reminded of two old people retreating, the one in her nightgown and robe, the other in a black coat that reached to her knees.

"I'm going, Maxine," he said. "I'm going, right now. It suits me to a tee. You're nuts here, anyway. This is a nuthouse. There's another life out there. Believe me, this is not the only life." He could feel the draft of air from the window on his face. He closed his eyes and opened them. He still had his hands on the edge of the table and was rocking the table back and forth on its legs as he spoke.

"I hope not," Maxine said. She'd stopped in the kitchen doorway. Bea edged around her into the other room. "God knows, every day I pray there's another life."

"I'm going," he said. He kicked his chair and stood up from the table. "You won't see me again, either."

"You've left me plenty to remember you by, L.D.," Maxine said. She was in the living room now. Bea stood next to her. Bea looked disbelieving and scared. She held her mother's coat sleeve in the fingers of one hand, her cigarette in the fingers of her other hand.

"*God*, Dad, we were just talking," she said.

"Go on now, get out, L.D.," Maxine said. "I'm paying the rent here, and I'm saying go. Now."

"I'm going," he said. "Don't push me," he said. "I'm going."

"Don't do anything else violent, L.D.," Maxine said. "We know you're strong when it comes to breaking things."

"Away from here," L.D. said. "I'm leaving this nuthouse."

He made his way into the bedroom and took one of her suitcases from the closet. It was an old brown Naugahyde suitcase with a broken clasp. She used to pack it full of Jantzen sweaters and carry it with her to college. He'd gone to college too. That had been years ago and somewhere else. He threw the suitcase onto the bed and began putting in his underwear, trousers and long-sleeved shirts, sweaters, an old leather belt with a brass buckle, all of his socks and handkerchiefs. From the nightstand he took magazines for reading material. He took the ashtray. He put everything he could into the suitcase, everything it would hold. He fastened the one good side of the suitcase, secured the strap, and then remembered his bathroom things. He found the vinyl shaving bag up on the closet shelf behind Maxine's hats. The shaving bag had been a birthday gift from Bea a year or so back. Into it went his razor and shaving cream, his talcum powder and stick deodorant, his toothbrush. He took the toothpaste too. He could hear Maxine and Bea in the living room talking in low voices. After he washed his face and used the towel, he put the bar of soap into the shaving bag. Then he added the soap dish and the glass from over the sink. It occurred to him that if he had some cutlery and a tin plate, he could keep going for a long time. He couldn't close the shaving bag, but he was ready. He put on his coat and picked up the suitcase. He went into the living room. Maxine and Bea stopped talking. Maxine put her arm around Bea's shoulders.

"This is good-bye, I guess," L.D. said and waited. "I don't know what else to say except I guess I'll never see you again," he said to Maxine. "I don't plan on it, anyway. You too," he said to Bea. "You and your crackpot ideas."

"*Dad*," she said.

"Why do you go out of your way to keep picking on her?" Maxine said. She took Bea's hand. "Haven't you done enough damage in this house already? Go on, L.D. Go and leave us in peace."

"It's in your head, Dad. Just remember," Bea said. "Where are you going, anyway? Can I write to you?" she asked.

"I'm going, that's all I can say," L.D. said. "Anyplace. Away from this nuthouse," he said. "That's the main thing." He took a last look around the living room and then moved the suitcase from one hand to the other and put the shaving bag under his arm. "I'll be in touch, Bea. Honey, I'm sorry I lost my temper. Forgive me, will you? Will you forgive me?"

"You've made it into a nuthouse," Maxine said. "If it's a nuthouse, L.D., you've made it so. You did it. Remember that, L.D., as you go wherever you're going."

He put the suitcase down and the shaving bag on top of the suitcase. He drew himself up and faced them. Maxine and Bea moved back.

"Don't say anything else, Mom," Bea said. Then she saw the toothpaste sticking out of the shaving bag. She said, "Look, Dad's taking the toothpaste. Dad, come on, don't take the toothpaste."

"He can have it," Maxine said. "Let him have it and anything else he wants, just so long as he gets out of here."

L.D. put the shaving bag under his arm again and once more picked up the suitcase. "I just want to say one more thing, Maxine. Listen to me. Remember this," he said. "I love you. I love you no matter what happens. I love you too, Bea. I love you both." He stood there at the door and felt his lips begin to tingle as he looked at them for what, he believed, might be the last time. "Good-bye," he said.

"You call this love, L.D.?" Maxine said. She let go of Bea's hand. She made a fist. Then she shook her head and jammed her hands into her coat pockets. She stared at him and then dropped her eyes to something on the floor near his shoes.

It came to him with a shock that he would remember this night and her like this. He was terrified to think that in the years ahead she might come to resemble a woman he couldn't place, a mute figure in a long coat, standing in the middle of a lighted room with lowered eyes.

"Maxine!" he cried. "Maxine!"

"Is this what love is, L.D.?" she said, fixing her eyes on him. Her eyes were terrible and deep, and he held them as long as he could.

CHRONOLOGY

NOTE ON THE TEXTS

CHRONOLOGICAL BIBLIOGRAPHY

NOTES

Chronology

Raymond Clevie Carver is born in Clatskanie, Oregon,
on May 25, first child of Ella Beatrice Casey and Clevie
Raymond (C.R.) Carver. (Ella, born in Magnet Cove,
Arkansas, on July 11, 1913, was the youngest of four children of William Casey [1882–1962] and Katherine Guyse
[1886–1976]. C.R., called "Raymond" by his family, was
born in Gifford, Arkansas, on September 17, 1913, the
youngest of three children of Edwin Frank Carver [1877–
1948] and Mary Green [1880–1951]. Carver descended
from settlers and farmers who moved westward from the
Carolinas, Georgia, Alabama, Tennessee, and Mississippi.
Abraham Carver [1815–1860] arrived in Arkansas around
1855 with his family and a few slaves, purchased several
hundred acres in south-central Arkansas, and was considered prosperous. His eldest son, Robert Hosea Carver
[1835–1902], C.R.'s grandfather, acquired a homestead
west of the Saline River near Leola, adjacent to the farm
owned by William Jenkins [1814–1859] and his wife, Jane
McWhorter [1818–1899], who together operated Jenkins'
Ferry, site of a noted Civil War battle on April 29–30, 1864.
Robert married two Jenkins daughters, the second of
whom, Elizabeth Ann Jenkins [1842–1916], was C.R.'s
grandmother. Robert and his younger brother John M.
Carver [1841–1901], who married a third Jenkins daughter, fought for the Confederacy in 1862–63 and for the
Union after November 1863. "He fought for both sides!"
Carver later marveled, repeating C.R.'s story about his
grandfather. "He was a turncoat." In May 1929, in response to economic hardship in Arkansas caused by the
floods of 1927, the loss of farms, collapse of cotton and
timber prices, and widespread unemployment, C.R., aged
16, set out from Leola and traveled to Omak, Washington, with his parents and two older siblings, Fred [1903–
1984] and Violet LaVonda [1910–2001], and their families,
to find work in the apple orchards and sawmills of the
Pacific Northwest. On a trip back to Arkansas in 1935,
C.R. married Ella Casey, whom he had met only briefly,
on December 24. She returned with him to Omak, where
he worked at the Biles-Coleman Lumber Company. The
mill was a hotbed of labor disputes in the 1930s, and

when union workers went out on strike in spring 1936, C.R. took a job 50 miles away at the construction site of the Grand Coulee Dam. In 1938 C.R. and his pregnant wife followed his relatives to Wauna, Oregon, a mill town for the Crossett Western Company, part of an Arkansas-based timber conglomerate. C.R. was employed as a saw filer at the Wauna lumber mill on the Columbia River, 12 miles west of Clatskanie, where Ella gave birth to a boy in Dr. James Wooden's obstetrical offices on the second floor of a brick building on Nehalem Street, then known as the Clatskanie Hospital.)

1941   The Carvers and members of their extended family move 200 miles northeast to Yakima, Washington, where C.R. takes a job as a saw filer for the Cascade Lumber Company. C.R., Ella, and their young son live in a rented house at 1515 South 15th Street in the rundown Fairview section, opposite the Central Washington Fairgrounds. The house lacks an indoor toilet and is the first home that Carver will remember.

1943   Carver's only sibling, James Franklin Carver, is born in Yakima on August 18.

1944   Carver enters the first grade at Jefferson School, a Yakima public elementary school, which he attends from September 1944 to June 1950. He is an excellent reader, an indifferent arithmetic student, and a fun-loving boy easily distracted in class. His father buys him books and tells him stories about relatives in Arkansas and Depression-era adventures. Carver writes "little stories about monsters, ants, laboratories, and mad doctors." The family has no car, and C.R. travels by bus to his job at the mill on the Yakima River northeast of town. Carver often waits at the bus stop for his dad to come home from work. Periodically, C.R. fails to arrive, having instead gone out drinking with friends. "I still remember the sense of doom and hopelessness that hung over the supper table when my mother and I and my kid brother sat down to eat."

1950   In September, Carver begins seventh grade at Washington Junior High School, where he is a student until June 1953. Before he enters junior high, his parents buy a small house in a modest middle-class neighborhood on 11th Avenue, near Mead Avenue, in Yakima. The family's years in this house are the happiest period of his childhood. He and his father hunt ducks and geese in the woods and fish for bass and perch in the ponds and streams around

Yakima. Among Carver's haunts are Sportsman Park, Wenas Lake, Athanum Creek, and Bachelor Creek— places that will figure in his poems and stories. "That's what excited me in those days, hunting and fishing. That's what made a dent in my emotional life, and that's what I wanted to write about." His other passion is books. Once a week he walks to the Yakima Public Library. "I wanted to be a writer, and I mostly followed my nose as far as reading was concerned." He reads science fiction, westerns, jungle adventures, and history books. "My favorite author was Edgar Rice Burroughs. I read all of his books, and most of them five, six, and eight times."

1953   Carver enters tenth grade at Yakima Senior High School in September. His father pays for him to enroll in a correspondence course in creative writing offered by the Palmer Institute of Authorship in Los Angeles. He works part-time as a delivery boy for Woolf's Pharmacy, one of three drugstores owned by pharmacist Albert B. Kurbitz, who offers to pay Carver's college tuition if he promises to study pharmacy and return to Yakima to manage a drugstore, an offer Carver declines. On one delivery he meets "an anonymous and lovely old gentleman" who talks to him about writing and gives him an issue of *Poetry* magazine and Margaret Anderson's *Little Review Anthology* (1953). Carver recalled this meeting as a "pole-star" in his literary education. "I had the distinct feeling my life was in the process of being altered in some significant and even, forgive me, magnificent way."

1955   C.R. sells the family's home on 11th Avenue and rents a larger house at 3515 Summitview Avenue in a more prosperous part of Yakima. In the summer between Carver's junior and senior years of high school he works at a grocery store three miles south of Yakima in Union Gap, where his mother is a waitress at the Spudnut Shop. (Spudnuts are doughnuts made from potato flour, and franchise Spudnut Shops proliferated in the 1950s.) Also working at the shop is 14-year-old Maryann Elsie Burk (born August 7, 1940, in Bellingham, Washington), the middle child among the three daughters of Yakima schoolteacher Alice Ritchey and her former husband Valentine R. ("Val") Burk, who owns a farm in Blaine, Washington. The teenagers begin dating, although Maryann is slated to move 130 miles away in September to resume her studies at Saint Paul's School for Girls, an Episcopalian boarding school in Walla Walla, Washington.

That summer C.R. moves to Chester, a logging town 600 miles south of Yakima, on the shore of Lake Almanor in northeastern California, and takes a job at the Collins Pine Company sawmill, where his brother, Fred, has found better-paying work. Ella and her two sons remain in Yakima so Carver can finish high school.

1956   Carver graduates from high school on June 7. He relocates with his mother and brother to Chester, where they discover C.R. to be seriously ill with what family members believe is blood poisoning caused by an injury on the job. Carver joins the "chain gang" at the Collins Pine mill, hauling freshly cut lumber away from the saws. Maryann visits the family in Chester during summer vacation before going back to school. After briefly enlisting in the Army National Guard of California, Carver returns to Yakima in November to be closer to Maryann, staying with his aunt Von (LaVonda Carver) and uncle Bill (William T.) Archer, and working at Woolf's Pharmacy.

1957   Inspired by H. Rider Haggard's adventure novel *King Solomon's Mines* (1885) and its 1950 movie adaptation, Carver sets out with two friends to hunt for diamonds in South America, getting as far as Guaymas in northern Mexico before the three fall ill, quarrel, and separate. He returns to Chester, then to Yakima. In the spring Maryann learns that she and Carver are expecting a child. Shortly after her high school graduation the couple are married on June 7 at St. Michael's Episcopal Church, the oldest church in Yakima. The wedding is followed by a reception at Playland, a popular dance hall in the nearby town of Selah, and a one-week honeymoon in Seattle. C.R.'s health has badly deteriorated in Chester. His physical ailments, compounded by depression and substance abuse, render him unable to work, and he returns with his wife and son James to Yakima, where they live on the charity of relatives. Carver and Maryann are also living in Yakima, in a basement apartment below a doctor's office, which they clean at night in lieu of paying rent. In the fall Carver takes two classes at Yakima Valley Community College. Their daughter, Christine LaRae, is born on December 2 at Yakima Valley Memorial Hospital. C.R., whose depression has become acute, is a patient in the same hospital. Carver visits his father and his wife on different floors on the day his first child is born. Confined for weeks in the psychiatric ward, C.R. undergoes electroshock therapy and will be unable to hold a steady job for six years after his release.

1958   In August, Carver, his wife, and daughter move to Paradise, California, in the northern foothills of the Central Valley, where they live in a house that Maryann's mother has purchased as a future retirement property on Roe Road. He begins working at a drugstore and taking classes at Chico State College, 12 miles to the west. The second of the couple's two children, Vance Lindsay, is born at Enloe Hospital in Chico on October 19. Carver's first publication appears in the Chico State student newspaper, *The Wildcat*, on October 31. It is a letter to the editor headed "Where Is Intellect?" lamenting student apathy on campus.

1959   In the spring Carver moves with his family to Chico, where Maryann begins working as a telephone operator. That fall he enrolls in Creative Writing 101 taught by a new faculty member at Chico State, John Gardner, who takes a special interest in his work. "He'd take one of my early efforts at a story and go over it with me. . . . He made me see that absolutely everything was important in a story." Gardner gives Carver a key to his faculty office to use as a private place for writing.

1960   During the spring term Carver and fellow student Nancy Parke edit and publish the first issue of the Chico State literary magazine, *Selection*. To launch it memorably, Carver asks his "greatest hero," William Carlos Williams, for a submission and receives the previously unpublished poem "The Gossips." In June the Carvers move 200 miles northwest to Eureka, California, where Maryann works during the day at the local telephone company and Carver finds night work in area sawmills; each takes care of the children while the other is away. They rent a small house on Artino Road. In the fall he begins classes at Humboldt State College, eight miles north of Eureka in the foggy woods of Arcata. Among his teachers is a new instructor, Richard Cortez ("Dick") Day, who becomes a lifelong friend. Stories written for Day's classes include "The Hair" and "The Night the Mill Boss Died." The second issue of *Selection* contains Carver's first published story, "The Furious Seasons," written under Gardner's mentorship at Chico State.

1961   "The Father," a story written for Day's class, appears in
            the spring issue of *Toyon*, the Humboldt State literary
            journal. In the summer, seeking a change of pace, the
            Carvers drive 700 miles north to Blaine, Washington,
            near the Canadian border. There Maryann's father, Val
            Burk, and her paternal aunt May (Mary K. Burk) operate
            a farm that has been owned by the Burk family since 1886.
            They plan to stay a year, but Carver soon feels anxious
            and unproductive in the isolated rural setting. In August
            he returns with his family to northern California, renting
            a house on I Street in the Northtown section of Arcata.
            In the fall he and Maryann take classes at Humboldt State
            while holding jobs, she as a waitress and he as an assistant
            in the college library. They socialize with Dick Day, Dave
            Palmer (a college reference librarian and poet), and their
            wives, as well as with Amy Burk, Maryann's younger
            sister, who is an aspiring actress.

1962   In the spring, to shore up the family's finances, Carver
            takes a second part-time job at a sawmill. His curriculum
            at Humboldt State includes an independent study in
            Russian literature with Thelwall Proctor and a modern
            drama course with longtime Oregon Shakespeare Festival
            director Jerry Turner. On May 11, Carver's absurdist one-
            act play *Carnations* is performed on campus. "The audi-
            ence had the chance to meet the author after the play, but
            what happened was more like a public hanging." That ex-
            perience is offset when, on a single "red-letter day," two
            works he has submitted to off-campus literary magazines
            are accepted for publication: his poem "The Brass Ring"
            appears in the September issue of *Targets*, and his story
            "Pastoral" is published early the next year in *Western Hu-
            manities Review*.

1963   On February 1, Carver receives his B.A. in English from
            Humboldt State. He edits the spring issue of *Toyon*,
            which includes his stories "Poseidon and Company" and
            "The Hair" and two works under the pseudonym John
            Vale: his poem "Spring, 480 B.C." and his Hemingway
            satire, "The Aficionados." With Dick Day's help, he re-
            ceives a $1,000 fellowship in support of a year's study at
            the Iowa Writers' Workshop, beginning in the fall. For
            the spring and summer he accepts a job in a library at the
            University of California, Berkeley, nearly 300 miles away.
            Maryann remains in Arcata with the children to complete
            spring classes at Humboldt State. When her semester
            ends, the family reunites in Berkeley. In late summer they

drive to Iowa City, where Carver enrolls in the Workshop's two-year M.F.A. program. They move into Hawk-
eye Trailer Park, then into Finkbine Park, a complex of
World War II–era Quonset huts that serves as married-
student housing. While Carver takes classes with R. V.
Cassill and other writers, Maryann works as a waitress at
the University Athletic Club. "The Furious Seasons," revised and published in the fall issue of the little magazine
December, is listed among the "Distinctive Short Stories
in American and Canadian Magazines, 1963" in *Best American Short Stories 1964*.

1964   Isolation from family and friends, coupled with the frigid
        Iowa winter, takes a toll on the Carvers' morale. When
        Maryann's father dies unexpectedly in January in Blaine,
        Washington, she and the children travel west by train for
        the funeral, leaving Carver to his classes for the next
        month. Under the mentorship of Irish short-story writer
        Bryan McMahon, he drafts several new stories, including
        "The Student's Wife," "Sixty Acres," and "Will You
        Please Be Quiet, Please?" The burst of creativity strength-
        ens his desire to leave school and write full time but also
        underscores his sense that a writer's life is beyond his
        grasp, given his "position of unrelieved responsibility and
        permanent distraction" as the father of two children. In
        June, after he completes his first year at the Writers'
        Workshop, the family returns to California. They settle in
        Sacramento, where his parents are living on C.R.'s dis-
        ability payments and intermittent income from Ella's jobs
        in eateries and retail stores. Maryann works as a waitress
        and restaurant hostess. Carver has a hard time finding
        work that allows him time to write. He takes a series of
        "crap jobs" and is eventually hired as a custodian at Sacra-
        mento's Mercy Hospital, a post he will hold for two years.
        C.R. finds steady work after six years of illness and unem-
        ployment. He is offered a job at a sawmill 350 miles to the
        north in California's redwood country, near the town of
        Klamath. In time, Ella joins him, and they move to Cres-
        cent City, 20 miles north of Klamath.

1965   In January Maryann begins working for the Parents Cul-
        tural Institute, an educational-products subsidiary of *Par-
        ents* magazine. She sells instructional kits for children
        door-to-door, produces good sales figures, and is pro-
        moted, first to team manager, then to regional manager.
        She is given a red Pontiac convertible to make sales calls
        from her base in Sacramento. The Carvers rent a small

house at 2641 Matheson Way, then a larger one at 2642 Larkspur Lane. They hire a housekeeper and enjoy a period of relative economic stability. After a year on the day shift at Mercy Hospital, Carver transfers to the night shift. He can finish his duties quickly, go home to sleep, and write the next day. In time, instead of returning home from work, he begins going out to drink with friends.

1966   The poet Dennis Schmitz joins the faculty of Sacramento State College, and in the fall Carver sits in on Schmitz's undergraduate course in creative writing. In the class is Gary Thompson, a poet who, like Schmitz, becomes Carver's close friend. "Will You Please Be Quiet, Please?" is published in *December*.

1967   Maryann's success at the Parents Cultural Institute brings an offer of further advancement. The post will require extended travel, and Carver objects to her taking it. She yields to his wishes but falls into a sales slump, severely reducing her income. Borrowing and overspending on credit worsen the couple's financial woes. On April 14 they file for bankruptcy protection. Maryann resigns from her job, and the Carvers vacate their rental home. She secures a position as a live-in manager of the Riviera Apartments, a poolside complex at 940 Fulton Avenue in Sacramento, where the family can stay rent-free. Carver quits his job at Mercy Hospital, decides to become a librarian, and is accepted into the master's program of the University of Iowa's School of Library Science. He drives with Gary Thompson to Iowa City in June, but the trip is cut short when he receives word that his father, aged 53, has died on June 17 in Crescent City, California. He flies back to the West Coast and drives north to his parents' home. His mother arranges for C.R.'s body to be transported 500 miles to Yakima for burial. (Ella Carver will survive her husband for 25 years and die in Sacramento County on April 18, 1993.) Carver abandons his plan to attend library school and returns to Sacramento. He is hired for his "first white-collar job" as a textbook editor at the educational publishing firm of Science Research Associates (SRA) in Palo Alto, California, where the family rents a house at 886 Loma Verde Avenue. Maryann takes classes at Foothill College, a two-year institution in nearby Los Altos Hills. Curt Johnson, publisher of *December*, visits Carver to celebrate the selection of "Will You Please Be Quiet, Please?" by editor Martha Foley for *Best American Short Stories 1967*. "It was the most momentous thing in regard to my writing that had ever happened to me." Johnson introduces Carver to Gordon Lish, a *December* contributor and founding editor of the avant-garde journal *Genesis West*, then working at another textbook company in Palo Alto.

1968   In the spring Carver's first book, the poetry collection *Near Klamath*, is published by the English Club of Sacramento State College. To pursue a bachelor's degree in English, Maryann transfers to San Jose State College. There she receives a one-year $5,000 fellowship to study in Israel, beginning in the summer. Carver arranges a year's leave from SRA, and in June the family flies to Tel Aviv. The accommodations at the University of Tel Aviv fall far short of expectations. "They promised us a villa on the Mediterranean. . . . Instead the house was awful, the kids were miserable, and we ran out of money." In October the Carvers leave Israel and return to the United States by way of a cruise on the Aegean and a tour of Greece, Italy, and France. In November they arrive in Hollywood, California, where they stay in a rented house on Gregory Avenue near Maryann's sister Amy and her husband, Michael Wright. To support themselves while seeking jobs as actors, Amy and Michael hawk souvenir movie programs on Hollywood Boulevard. Carver joins them for a time, attempting to sell programs for Stanley Kubrick's *2001: A Space Odyssey*. Maryann makes good money as a cocktail waitress at a storied Hollywood restaurant, Edna Earle's Fog Cutter.

1969   The Carvers move to San Jose, California, in January. They rent an apartment on 7th Street in Spartan Village, a student housing complex at San Jose State College, where Maryann resumes her undergraduate studies. In February Carver is rehired at SRA, this time as advertising director. During quarterly "collating parties" at the San Francisco home of George Hitchcock, founding editor of *Kayak* magazine, Carver meets fellow writers and lifelong friends Morton Marcus and James D. Houston. Both men live 70 miles south of San Francisco, in Santa Cruz. Hitchcock moves there, bringing with him *Kayak* and his small press, Kayak Books. Gordon Lish, now fiction editor of *Esquire* magazine, writes to Carver in November, urging him to submit stories.

1970   Carver receives a promotion at SRA, but his goal remains to be a full-time writer. In March he wins a $3,000

Discovery Award for poetry from the National Endowment for the Arts. *Winter Insomnia*, his second book of
poems, is published by Kayak Books in the spring. While
representing SRA at a teachers conference in Seattle,
Carver meets Montana-based writer William Kittredge,
who becomes a lasting friend. In June the Carvers move
to Sunnyvale, California, 12 miles west of San Jose. They
rent a house on Wright Avenue from a high school
teacher on a year's sabbatical in Germany, a situation
adapted for the story "Put Yourself in My Shoes." In the
summer Maryann completes her B.A. in English at San
Jose State and enters an accelerated teacher-certification
program. In August she is hired as an English teacher at
Los Altos High School, a position she will hold for eight
years. During the summer Carver rents a room in Palo
Alto as a writing studio, where he drafts a story called
"The Neighbors." Its idea comes from an experience he
had in Tel Aviv, when he was given private access to the
apartment of neighbors who were out of town. In August
he submits "The Neighbors" to Lish, who line-edits the
text, shortens the title to "Neighbors," and accepts the
story for publication in *Esquire*. Carver is "bowled over"
and expresses his gratitude to Lish. "This is a milestone, a
turning point." The friendship between writer and editor
is supportive and productive. "One of the things that was
so helpful about Gordon was that he believed in me as a
writer when I needed that, when I had no other contact
with the great world, living as I was in Sunnyvale and Cupertino, California." On September 25, Carver's job at
SRA is eliminated in a reorganization. A year's severance
pay, supplemented by his NEA award and Maryann's
teaching salary, enables him to write full-time. "Sixty
Acres" is included in *Best Little Magazine Fiction, 1970*.

1971   Unencumbered by a job, Carver writes many of the stories that make up his first trade-press book, *Will You
Please Be Quiet, Please?* (1976). "Something happened
during that time in the writing, to the writing. It went
underground and then it came up again, and it was
bathed in a new light for me. I was starting to chip away,
down to the image, then the figure itself. And it happened during that period." In the spring he shares the
San Francisco Foundation's annual Joseph Henry Jackson
Award for the most promising young writer in northern
California. "Neighbors" is published in *Esquire* in June.
George Hitchcock joins the faculty of the University of

California, Santa Cruz. He recommends Carver to James B. Hall, a writer who has been appointed provost of College V, a new arts unit within the university. Hall hires Carver for his first teaching post, as a visiting lecturer in creative writing, beginning in the fall. In August the Carvers leave Sunnyvale and rent a home in Ben Lomond, a rustic community among the redwoods of the San Lorenzo Valley, 12 miles north of Santa Cruz. The story "Fat" is published in *Harper's Bazaar* in September; "A Night Out" is included in *Best Little Magazine Fiction, 1971*. When classes begin at UC Santa Cruz, Carver serves as founding editor of the journal *Quarry* (later *Quarry West*). The first issue contains poems by Morton Marcus, a story by William Kittredge, contributions by Leonard Michaels, Richard Hugo, and John Haines, and Gordon Lish's essay "How I Got to Be a Big-Shot Editor and Other Worthwhile Self-Justifications."

1972   Carver holds multiple academic positions simultaneously without informing his employers about his obligations to the others. In the spring, while teaching at UC Santa Cruz, he accepts a Wallace E. Stegner Fellowship at Stanford University that requires him to attend classes in Palo Alto. He also accepts an appointment, to begin in the fall, as a visiting lecturer at the University of California, Berkeley. In July the Carvers make their first and only home purchase, a ranch-style house with a circular driveway at 22272 Cupertino Road in Cupertino, California. Cupertino is near San Jose, but it is at least an hour's drive from Berkeley and almost two hours from Santa Cruz. In August, Carver drives to Montana without Maryann to celebrate William Kittredge's 40th birthday. Kittredge introduces him to several hard-drinking Missoula writers, including novelists James Crumley, James Welch, and Chuck Kinder. Carver and Kinder have previously met at Stanford, and they become good friends. At Kittredge's party Carver meets Diane Cecily, with whom he begins a sexual liaison that, unlike his earlier flings, continues for several years. His persistent infidelity, coupled with his and Maryann's heavy drinking, leads to violent arguments. Late in the year he rents an apartment in Berkeley, where he stays for part of each week. Having a pied-à-terre cuts down on his driving time and facilitates his affair with Cecily.

1973   Constant shuttling between universities and residences earns Carver the nickname "Running Dog." When he

accepts an appointment as visiting lecturer at the Iowa
Writers' Workshop for the fall term, he resigns his position at UC Berkeley but retains his job at UC Santa Cruz.
His commitment to teach classes each week in Iowa and
California entails tightly scheduled air travel, with the
house in Cupertino serving as a hub. When in Iowa City,
he lives on campus in the Iowa House and befriends fellow resident and visiting faculty member John Cheever.
Carver and Cheever meet their classes but otherwise do
little except drink, sometimes together in Cheever's
room. "I don't think either of us ever took the covers off
our typewriters. We made trips to a liquor store twice a
week in my car," Carver recalled. "What Is It?" is included in the O. Henry Awards annual *Prize Stories 1973*.
Five of Carver's poems are reprinted in *New Voices in
American Poetry*.

1974   Carver resigns from UC Santa Cruz and, for the spring
semester, moves alone to Iowa City, where he continues
teaching at the Writers' Workshop. He returns to Cupertino in May. Overspending has again put the Carvers deep
in debt, and they file for bankruptcy protection a second
time. He accepts a visiting lectureship at the University of
California, Santa Barbara, for the academic year 1974–75.
Maryann arranges a year's leave from Los Altos High
School to accompany him. They rent out their house in
Cupertino and move 300 miles south to Goleta, a coastal
town near the Santa Barbara campus. During the fall
term, both Carver and Maryann are arrested for driving
while intoxicated. Symptoms of alcoholism force him to
resign from UC Santa Barbara at the end of the semester.
In December the couple return to Cupertino. "Put Yourself in My Shoes" is included in *Prize Stories 1974* and is
printed as a chapbook by Santa Barbara–based Capra
Press, founded by Noel Young, who remains Carver's
friend and publisher for many years.

1975   Out of work, unable to write, and morbidly ill, Carver
lives with his wife and teenage children in Cupertino. His
drinking and extramarital affairs continue, leading to domestic turmoil and occasional violence. On leave from her
teaching job, Maryann works as a cocktail waitress.
Carver is admitted to a short-term treatment center in
San Jose, where he suffers an alcohol-withdrawal seizure.
"Are You a Doctor?" is included in *Prize Stories 1975*.

1976   As Carver's health declines, his literary profile rises, thanks to the appearance of older writings. His third book of poetry, *At Night the Salmon Move*, is published in February by Capra Press. In New York, Lish's advocacy of Carver's work bears fruit. In March, under the newly established Gordon Lish imprint, McGraw-Hill publishes Carver's first book of fiction, *Will You Please Be Quiet, Please?* It contains 22 stories, all previously published in periodicals, each further edited by Lish with Carver's approval. The book receives a short but positive review by Geoffrey Woolf in *The New York Times* on March 7. A story not in the collection, "So Much Water So Close to Home," is selected for the first annual *Pushcart Prize* anthology. During the year Carver undergoes multiple hospitalizations for acute alcoholism. In October the house on Cupertino Road is sold, and Maryann rents a home on nearby Carmen Road. After Thanksgiving the couple live apart. Carver rents an apartment but soon moves in with his former secretary from SRA. He ends the year at Duffy's, a residential treatment center in Calistoga, California, in the Napa Valley, 70 miles north of San Francisco. "I was completely out of control and in a very grave place. . . . I was dying from it, plain and simple, and I'm not exaggerating."

1977   Carver's self-imposed confinement at Duffy's extends into the new year. (The setting is recalled in his story "Where I'm Calling From.") When he leaves the facility in January, he attempts to limit his drinking but relapses around social drinkers. He stays briefly in San Francisco with Maryann's sister Amy and her second husband, the novelist Douglas Unger. In February Dick Day arranges for him to rent a house in the relatively isolated community of McKinleyville, California, eight miles north of Arcata, near the Pacific Ocean. The house at 1131 Henry Lane is behind a restaurant off Bella Vista Road. Both the house and the Bella Vista restaurant are owned by Edward ("Pete") Peterson, who operates the establishment with his second wife, Betty. "Chef's House" is one of three stories set in this locale. (The others are "What Would You Like to See?" and "Call If You Need Me.") During the spring Carver lives alone and tries to quit drinking. His efforts collapse in late May, when he goes to San Francisco for a meeting with Fred Hills, editor-in-chief at McGraw-Hill. At a party Carver drinks and blacks out. He wakes up drunk and sick but manages to keep his appointment with Hills, who offers him an advance on a proposed novel. (A portion of this never-completed book, likely its entirety, is published as "From *The Augustine Notebooks*" in 1979.) Returning to McKinleyville, he briefly continues to drink. On June 2, the day he will call "the line of demarcation," he stops drinking. Sick for four days afterward, he emerges shaky but sober, and he never drinks again. "I'm prouder of that, that I've quit drinking, than I am of anything in my life." Participation in Alcoholics Anonymous helps him maintain sobriety. Carver and Maryann reunite for their 20th anniversary on June 7. She takes a leave from Los Altos High School, and they live together in McKinleyville through the summer and fall. The first published interview with Carver, "Accolade-Winning Author Returns to Humboldt," appears in the Eureka *Times-Standard* on July 24. During this time he applies for fellowships and teaching jobs, and he writes two new stories, "View Finder" and "Why Don't You Dance?" In November he attends a conference at Southern Methodist University in Dallas, Texas, where he meets two key figures, both writers, of his post-alcoholic "second life." One is Richard Ford, with whom he has previously corresponded and who becomes a close friend. The other is Tess Gallagher. Born Theresa Jeanette Bond in Port Angeles, Washington, on July 21, 1943, she shares Carver's southern heritage, northwestern upbringing, and working-class background. She is the oldest of five children of Leslie Bond and Georgia Morris (a Missouri native), both of whom have worked as loggers. Twice divorced, Gallagher is a poet, essayist, and creative-writing teacher. She and Carver will begin an association that leads to literary collaboration, reciprocal influence, and intimate partnership. Carver's second collection of fiction, *Furious Seasons and Other Stories*, is published in November by Capra Press. It contains eight stories, none of which had appeared in *Will You Please Be Quiet, Please?*

1978   Carver and Maryann leave McKinleyville in January. He is hired to teach in the creative-writing program of Goddard College in Plainfield, Vermont. She rents a room in Arcata and continues working as a cocktail waitress while on leave from teaching. It is unclear when they will resume living together. He travels to northern Vermont for the two-week campus-based portion of the program; other instructors include Donald Hall, Tobias Wolff, and Stephen Dobyns. After the session, Carver goes to Illinois and remains for a week in Curt Johnson's remote vacation cabin. Freezing weather and isolation prompt him to depart for Iowa City. There he stays first with Dobyns, who is teaching at the Writers' Workshop, then in a rented room. Carver's application for a Guggenheim Fellowship is approved, and he receives an appointment as visiting distinguished writer-in-residence at the University of Texas, El Paso, beginning in the fall. In March he flies to California, then drives back to Iowa City with Maryann, who resigns from her position at Los Altos High School. They move out of his rented room and into the Park Motel on Interstate 80. He reads at the Writers' Workshop on April 18. In late spring they rent an apartment in town, but he soon takes separate quarters where he lives and writes. Maryann moves back to California on July 24, the date that marks their separation. In August, Carver leaves Iowa City for El Paso. His car breaks down in the desert at Van Horn, Texas, and he continues by Greyhound bus, arriving in El Paso with a single suitcase. He stays with a faculty couple, the writers Bruce and Patricia Dobler, and participates in a two-week literary conference then in progress at the university, where he meets Tess Gallagher for the second time. They socialize with other attendees, dine together, and attend a bullfight in Juárez, Mexico, with the Doblers. In the fall, when Gallagher returns to her cabin on Discovery Bay in northwest Washington state, she and Carver correspond, and he visits her on holidays. His book reviews begin appearing in the *Chicago Tribune, Texas Monthly*, and the *San Francisco Review of Books*.

1979   On January 1, Carver and Gallagher, who is a Guggenheim Fellow, begin living together in a rented house in El Paso near the Mexican border. A critical study, "*Will You Please Be Quiet, Please?*: Voyeurism, Dissociation, and the Art of Raymond Carver" by David Boxer and Cassandra Phillips, appears in the summer issue of *Iowa Review*. Carver accepts an appointment as professor of English at Syracuse University in upstate New York. He defers the position for a year, during which he will hold his Guggenheim Fellowship and write stories. Gallagher and he spend the summer in a cabin in Chimacum, Washington, on the Olympic Peninsula. In the fall they move to Tucson, where she has a teaching appointment at the University of Arizona. They live in a house she has purchased at

2905 East 23rd Street. There Carver works on new stories, including "Gazebo," "One More Thing," "Pie," "If It Please You," "Where Is Everyone?" and "Beginners."

1980   Carver is awarded a Literature Fellowship for fiction by the National Endowment for the Arts. Unexpectedly, he assumes his teaching post at Syracuse University in late January, departing Tucson a semester early to replace George P. Elliott, senior professor of English and creative writing, who has fallen ill. Gallagher remains in Arizona during the spring term. In Syracuse Carver takes up temporary residence at 1064 Westmoreland Avenue, in a house originally rented by poet Hayden Carruth, and continues working on new stories, including "Want to See Something?" and "A Small, Good Thing." On February 15 he writes Gordon Lish, now a book editor at Alfred A. Knopf, to say he has completed a number of new stories, perhaps enough for a book, when added to previously uncollected fiction. "I've been writing stories these last six months, steadily. A few good ones, I think. I have a long one in the works now, forty pages. . . ." In early May they meet in New York City, and Carver gives Lish an untitled manuscript of stories. In Syracuse Carver and Gallagher jointly purchase a two-story, wood-shingled house at 832 Maryland Avenue. In mid-June they travel to the University of Alaska at Fairbanks to participate in the Midnight Sun Writers' Conference. During May and June, Lish edits Carver's manuscript aggressively, reducing its overall length by more than half. Carver returns alone to Syracuse, and on July 7 he reads the edited stories for the first time. He writes to Lish at 8 A.M. on July 8 expressing profound dismay at the alterations. The stories are central, he says, to his recovery from alcoholism. Despite Lish's "genius" as an editor, Carver insists that publication of the book, now entitled *What We Talk About When We Talk About Love*, be canceled. Lish convinces him that the changes are improvements, and production of the book goes forward. Carver rejoins Gallagher in Port Angeles, Washington, on July 15. When they return to Syracuse University later that summer, Gallagher begins an appointment as professor of English and coordinator of the creative-writing program. The faculty includes Tobias Wolff, Stephen Dobyns, and Douglas Unger. Among the students are Jay McInerney and Mary Bush. Carver edits a sampler of student writings, *Syracuse Poems and Stories 1980*. In his foreword (collected under the title "Steering by the Stars") he writes, "We have here the makings of a literary community."

1981   Carver's essay "A Storyteller's Shoptalk" (later retitled "On Writing") appears in *The New York Times Book Review* on February 15. *What We Talk About When We Talk About Love* is published by Knopf on April 20 and receives a favorable front-page review by Michael Wood in *The New York Times Book Review* on April 26. In the June issue of *The Atlantic*, James Atlas offers a less positive assessment but says of the elliptical, enigmatic narratives, "their very minimality gives them a certain bleak power." Unaware that the stories have been shortened by Lish, critics label Carver a minimalist. He chafes at the description. "There's something about 'minimalist' that smacks of smallness of vision and execution that I don't like." New stories appear in the fall. They include "Cathedral," "Vitamins," and Carver's first publication in *The New Yorker*, "Chef's House." In style and scale these stories differ markedly from those in his "minimalist" collection. Two stories in *What We Talk About When We Talk About Love* win awards: the title story is included in *The Pushcart Prize, VI*, and "The Bath" wins *Columbia* magazine's Carlos Fuentes Fiction Award.

1982   Under the guest editorship of poet Donald Hall, *Ploughshares* publishes a restored version of "A Small, Good Thing." Hall, who had read several stories before they were edited for *What We Talk About When We Talk About Love*, asked Carver to submit "the original story about the baker." On June 23, Carver files for divorce from Maryann in New York state court. Their divorce becomes final on October 18. Carver and Gallagher travel in Europe during the summer, visiting Germany, Switzerland, and France. He is elected a member of the Corporation of Yaddo, an artists' retreat in Saratoga Springs, New York. His autobiographical essay "Fires," written while in residence at Yaddo, appears in the autumn issue of *Antaeus*. In September, film director Michael Cimino and producer Carlo Ponti commission Carver and Gallagher to rewrite a screenplay based on the life of Fyodor Dostoevsky. (The film is never produced.) With his share of the proceeds, Carver purchases what Gallagher calls "the Mercedes that Dostoevsky bought." Guest editor John Gardner includes "Cathedral" in *Best American Short Stories 1982*. On September 14, Gardner dies in a motorcycle accident. In October "The Pheasant"

is published in book form by William Ferguson's Metacom Press. Carver and Gallagher spend the winter holidays in her newly built home in Port Angeles. Her
glass-walled "Sky House" overlooks the Strait of Juan de
Fuca, the 22-mile-wide waterway that separates the U.S.
from Canada.

1983   Carver continues publishing new stories and restored ver-
sions of older ones that had appeared in *What We Talk
About When We Talk About Love*. His miscellany *Fires:
Essays, Poems, Stories* is published by Capra Press on April
14. It includes a full-length version of "So Much Water So
Close to Home" and restorations of "Distance" and
"Where Is Everyone?" On May 18 the American Academy
and Institute of Arts and Letters awards Carver and Cynthia Ozick its first Mildred and Harold Strauss Livings.
The renewable five-year fellowships carry annual tax-free
stipends of $35,000 to support full-time writing. As a con-
dition of the award, he resigns his professorship at Syracuse. His essay "John Gardner: Writer and Teacher"
appears in the summer issue of *Georgia Review*. It serves
as the foreword to Gardner's posthumous book *On
Becoming a Novelist*. A long interview with Carver by
Mona Simpson and Lewis Buzbee appears in the summer
issue of *The Paris Review*. In it, for the first time, he talks
publicly about his alcoholism. He also contrasts the stories in *What We Talk About When We Talk About Love*
with his more recent fiction, notably "Cathedral." "There
was an opening up when I wrote the story. I knew I'd
gone as far the other way as I could or wanted to go, cutting everything down to the marrow, not just to the
bone." Lish remains his editor at Knopf, but Carver insists on complete control of his stories, restricting Lish to
standard copyediting. Their professional and personal relationship ends abruptly in the spring. Robert Gottlieb,
editor-in-chief of the firm, becomes Carver's titular editor. Knopf publishes *Cathedral* in September. The collection includes 12 stories, 11 of them written in the past two
years. The longest is "A Small, Good Thing," a full-
length restoration of its Lish-edited counterpart "The
Bath" in *What We Talk About When We Talk About Love*.
On September 11 a review of *Cathedral* by Irving Howe
appears on the front page of *The New York Times Book
Review*. Based on a close comparison of "The Bath" and
"A Small, Good Thing," he concludes that the longer
version is the better story and that the new collection is

Carver's best book. "*Cathedral* shows a gifted writer struggling for a larger scope of reference, a finer touch of nuance." Guest editor Anne Tyler includes "Where I'm Calling From" in *Best American Short Stories 1983*. "A Small, Good Thing" appears in the eighth annual *Pushcart Prize* anthology and wins first-place honors in *Prize Stories 1983: The O. Henry Awards*. *Cathedral* is nominated for the National Book Critics Circle Award and a Pulitzer Prize.

1984   Carver retreats to Port Angeles in January to secure privacy to write. He lives alone in Sky House after Gallagher returns to Syracuse to teach. His plan is to write a work of long fiction, but instead he begins writing poetry and continues doing so for ten weeks. "I've never had a period in which I've taken such joy in the act of writing as I did in those two months." He also writes nonfiction. His review of Sherwood Anderson's *Selected Letters* appears in *The New York Times Book Review* on April 22. He contributes a foreword to William Kittredge's story collection *We Are Not in This Together*. "Raymond Carver: A Chronicler of Blue-Collar Despair," a 5,000-word feature article by Bruce Weber, appears in *The New York Times Magazine* on June 28. In the summer Carver and Gallagher make a reading tour of Brazil and Argentina under the auspices of the U.S. Information Agency. They are visited in Port Angeles by the novelist Haruki Murakami, who will translate Carver's writings into Japanese. "My Father's Life," Carver's essay on C.R., appears in the September issue of *Esquire*. His story "If It Please You," restored to full length after Lish's cuts, is published as a limited edition book by Lord John Press. Seven of Carver's poems appear in William Heyen's anthology *The Generation of 2000*. His story "Careful" is included in *The Pushcart Prize, IX*.

1985   In January Carver purchases a home at 602 South B Street in Port Angeles. The renovated Victorian-era farmhouse is in a working-class neighborhood above the harbor and the Rayonier pulp mill. He and Gallagher share their two residences. Five of his poems appear in the February issue of *Poetry*. His poetry collection *Where Water Comes Together with Other Water* is published by Random House on May 1. In the spring two books by Carver are published in England: an expanded edition of *Fires*, published by Collins Harvill on April 15, and *The Stories of Raymond Carver*, a collection of three books in one

volume published by Pan/Picador on May 16. Carver and
Gallagher fly to London for promotional appearances.
Dostoevsky: A Screenplay, the couple's coauthored film
script, is published by Capra Press in the fall. His review
of two biographies of Ernest Hemingway appears in *The
New York Times Book Review* on November 17. That
month he wins *Poetry* magazine's annual Levinson Prize.
The winter issue of *Mississippi Review*, guest-edited by
Kim Herzinger, includes a special section on "Minimalist
Fiction" and contains a long interview with Carver by
Larry McCaffery and Sinda Gregory. At year's end he re-
turns to writing fiction.

1986   During the winter Carver continues writing stories. Four
are published in *The New Yorker* between February and
July: "Boxes," "Whoever Was Using This Bed," "Elephant," and "Blackbird Pie." "Intimacy" appears in *Esquire* in August. The stories explore new subject matter
and approach it in new ways. "I feel I'm just beginning to
make some discoveries about what I can do with a short
story, about what I want to do with *my* short stories. I'm
more or less verging on finding out something, and that's
exciting." In May he and Gallagher attend the 50th anniversary reunion of the Writers' Workshop in Iowa City.
He serves as guest editor of *Best American Short Stories
1986*, contributing an introduction and including stories
by Richard Ford, Tess Gallagher, and Tobias Wolff,
among others. "Together in Carver Country," a profile of
Carver and Gallagher in Port Angeles by Tom Jenks, appears in the October issue of *Vanity Fair*. Random House
publishes a second book of his poems, *Ultramarine*, on
November 7. On the same date he and Gallagher are fea-
tured readers at the Modern Poetry Association's annual
Poetry Day celebration in Chicago.

1987   The story "Menudo" appears in the spring issue of
Granta, and "Errand" is published in *The New Yorker* of
June 1. From April through June, Carver and Gallagher
visit Paris, Wiesbaden, Zürich, Rome, Milan, London,
Dublin, and Belfast. On April 3, *American Short Story
Masterpieces*, an anthology edited by Carver and Jenks, is
published by Delacorte Press. In May, Raven Editions
publishes *Those Days: Early Writings by Raymond Carver*.
On June 1, *In a Marine Light*, a selection of poems from
Where Water Comes Together with Other Water and *Ultra-
marine*, is published in London by Collins Harvill.
Carver is interviewed by Kasia Boddy for *The London Re-*

view of Books on June 10. "It's a good time in my life right now. I'm writing stories and I'm writing poems." He and Gallagher return to the U.S. and spend the rest of the summer in Port Angeles. "*Esquire*'s Guide to the Literary Universe" by editor Rust Hills appears in August, and Carver is among those listed at "The Red-Hot Center." (Also in the center are his editors Gordon Lish, Robert Gottlieb, and Gary Fisketjon, as well as his literary agent, Amanda "Binky" Urban of International Creative Management.) Of his recovery from alcoholism and "second chance at my life again," he tells interviewer Michael Schumacher in late summer, "Every day is a bonus. Every day now is pure cream." Twenty years earlier, in his first published interview, he had described himself as "a cigarette with a body attached to it." In September he experiences pulmonary hemorrhages. The diagnosis is cancer. On October 2, at St. Joseph's Hospital in Syracuse, two-thirds of his left lung is removed. On November 11 he is honored at the New York Public Library's annual "Literary Lions" gala, where he meets fellow honoree Harold Pinter. Ann Beattie includes "Boxes" in *Best American Short Stories 1987*.

1988   Carver and Gallagher move into a spacious new contemporary home they have purchased east of Port Angeles. Situated on the slopes of the Olympic Mountains, "Ridge House" is three miles inland from Sky House. Carver's study overlooks the woods above Morse Creek, which flows into the strait. He serves as guest judge for the short story annual *American Fiction 88*. In March, his cancer reappears, this time in his brain. The couple take temporary quarters in Seattle, where he undergoes seven weeks of radiation therapy at the Fred Hutchinson Cancer Research Center. Gary Fisketjon, his editor at Random House, has recently become editorial director of Atlantic Monthly Press. Carver signs a three-book contract with the firm. The first volume is a collection of stories, slated for publication in May. In advance of the book, interviews with Carver appear in major newspapers, including *The Boston Globe* and *The New York Times*. "I can't think of anything else I'd rather be called than a writer, unless it's a poet," he tells *Publishers Weekly*. "Short-story writer, poet, occasional essayist." In May he and Gallagher travel to the East Coast, where honors await him. He receives a Creative Arts Award Citation for Fiction from Brandeis University on May 4. The University of Hartford confers on him the honorary degree of Doctor of Letters at its commencement on Sunday, May 15. That day his book *Where I'm Calling From: New and Selected Stories* receives front-page coverage in *The New York Times Book Review* in a highly positive review by novelist Marilynne Robinson; equally favorable notices appear in *The Washington Post, The Los Angeles Times, Newsweek*, and other national publications. He is inducted into the American Academy and Institute of Arts and Letters in New York City on May 18. Despite his illness, he reads from his new collection to a packed house at Endicott Booksellers in Manhattan. He and Gallagher fly back to Seattle, where they both read at the Elliott Bay Book Company on May 24 to an overflowing audience. On June 6 cancer is found in his right lung. Carver and Gallagher are married in the Heart of Reno Chapel in Reno, Nevada, on June 17. They return to Port Angeles and work on his poetry collection *A New Path to the Waterfall*. (It is published by Atlantic Monthly Press in 1989 with an introduction by Gallagher.) In mid-July they take a fishing trip to Alaska. On returning to Seattle, he enters Virginia Mason Hospital. He is released to go home with Gallagher to Ridge House. There he dies at 6:20 A.M. on August 2. After a private wake in the home, he is buried in Ocean View Cemetery in Port Angeles on August 4. That same day, a collection of his seven most recent stories is published in London by Collins Harvill under the title *Elephant*. His valedictory poem "Gravy" appears in *The New Yorker* on August 20, and his essay "Friendship" is published in the autumn issue of *Granta*. His last work of fiction, "Errand," is selected for inclusion in *Best American Short Stories 1988*. It also appears in *Prize Stories 1988: The O. Henry Awards*, where it wins first prize. On September 22 a public memorial service for him is held at Saint Peter's Church on Lexington Avenue in New York City. The black granite monument on Carver's grave above the Strait of Juan de Fuca bears the words "Poet, Short Story Writer, Essayist."

Note on the Texts

This volume contains 90 short stories by Raymond Carver. These include the complete contents of his books *Will You Please Be Quiet, Please?* (1976), *What We Talk About When We Talk About Love* (1981), and *Cathedral* (1983). Also included are the stories in his collections *Furious Seasons and Other Stories* (1977), *Fires: Essays, Poems, Stories* (1983), and *Where I'm Calling From: New and Selected Stories* (1988) that do not appear in his other books; four early stories uncollected in his lifetime; and five stories discovered after his death in 1988. This volume contains the fragment "From *The Augustine Notebooks*," and four of his personal and literary essays. Finally, it publishes for the first time in English *Beginners: The Manuscript Version of* What We Talk About When We Talk About Love.

Will You Please Be Quiet, Please?

Carver's first collection of short fiction was *Will You Please Be Quiet, Please?* This book of 22 stories, all of which had previously appeared in periodicals, was published by McGraw-Hill in March 1976. The back flap of the first-edition dust jacket states that *Will You Please Be Quiet, Please?* is "A McGraw-Hill Book in Association with Gordon Lish." Lish had been Carver's friend since they both worked as textbook editors in California in the late 1960s. Hired as fiction editor of *Esquire* in 1969, Lish had published Carver's stories "Neighbors," "What Is It?" and "Collectors" in the magazine between 1971 and 1975. An influential figure in the New York literary scene who dubbed himself "Captain Fiction," Lish was instrumental in convincing McGraw-Hill, a firm specializing in nonfiction, to publish a volume of short stories by a relatively unknown writer who had not established himself with a novel.

In November 1974 Carver learned of the publisher's willingness to bring out a collection and signed the contract for *Will You Please Be Quiet, Please?* in February 1975. During this period his alcoholism was worsening, leading to extended unemployment and multiple hospitalizations the following year. Deeply grateful to Lish, Carver participated in the book's editing but for the most part deferred to Lish's judgments about its final form. "About the editing necessary in some of the stories," he wrote Lish in a letter of November 11, 1974, "tell me which ones and I'll go after it, or them. Tell me which ones. Or I will leave it up to you & you tell me what you think needs done or doing. Whatever or both."

Lish had edited seven of the stories when Carver submitted them in manuscript to *Esquire*. He edited the 15 other stories from photocopies of their appearances in print between 1963 and 1973. His alterations included changes of words and phrases, deletions of sentences and paragraphs, and changes of titles. In a letter of September 28, 1975, Carver expressed his thanks for "all the blood, sweat and so on" his editor had invested in the book. He also gave his considered approval of the outcome. "I think, all in all, you did a superb job w/ cutting and fixing on the stories."

This volume prints the text of the 1976 McGraw-Hill edition. Following is a list of the first periodical appearances of the 22 stories, nine under alternate titles, in the order of their sequence in the book: "Fat" (*Harper's Bazaar*, September 1971); "Neighbors" (*Esquire*, June 1971); "The Idea" (*Northwest Review*, Fall-Winter 1971–72); "They're Not Your Husband" (*Chicago Review*, Spring 1973); "Are You a Doctor?" (*Fiction*, 1973); "The Father" (*December*, 1968); "Nobody Said Anything" (as "The Summer Steelhead," *Seneca Review*, May 1973); "Sixty Acres" (*Discourse*, Winter 1969); "What's in Alaska?" (*Iowa Review*, Spring 1972); "Night School" (as "Nightschool," *North American Review*, Fall 1971); "Collectors" (*Esquire*, August 1975); "What Do You Do in San Francisco?" (as "Sometimes a Woman Can Just About Ruin a Man," *Colorado State Review*, Summer 1967); "The Student's Wife" (*Carolina Quarterly*, Fall 1964); "Put Yourself in My Shoes" (*Iowa Review*, Fall 1972); "Jerry and Molly and Sam" (as "A Dog Story," *Perspective*, Summer 1972); "Why, Honey?" (as "The Man Is Dangerous," *Sou'wester Literary Quarterly*, Winter 1972); "The Ducks" (as "The Night the Mill Boss Died," *Carolina Quarterly*, Winter 1963); "How About This?" (as "Cartwheels," *Western Humanities Review*, Autumn 1970); "Bicycles, Muscles, Cigarets" (as "Bicycles, Muscles, Cigarettes," *Kansas Quarterly*, Winter 1972–73); "What Is It?" (*Esquire*, May 1972; retitled "Are These Actual Miles?" in *Where I'm Calling From*, 1988); "Signals" (as "A Night Out," *December*, 1970); "Will You Please Be Quiet, Please?" (*December*, 1966). The story "Put Yourself in My Shoes" was also separately published by Noel Young's Capra Press in Santa Barbara, California, in 1974, in a trade edition of 500 copies and a limited edition of 75 signed, numbered copies.

From *Furious Seasons and Other Stories*

Carver's second collection of short fiction, *Furious Seasons and Other Stories*, was published by Capra Press in November 1977, in a limited edition of 100 signed, numbered copies and a trade edition of 1,200 unsigned copies. The book contained eight stories in the following sequence: "Dummy"; "Distance"; "The Lie"; "So Much

Water So Close to Home"; "The Fling"; "Pastoral"; "Mine"; "Furious Seasons." Revised versions of "Dummy," "Distance," "The Lie," "So Much Water So Close to Home," "The Fling," and "Mine" appear in later sections of this volume, and the texts in *Furious Seasons* are omitted here.

The texts of the two remaining stories in *Furious Seasons* are taken from the Capra Press edition. "Pastoral" was originally published in the winter 1963 issue of *Western Humanities Review*. In 1982 Carver revised extensively the text of "Pastoral" as collected in *Furious Seasons*, changed its title, and published the resulting story as "The Cabin" in the winter 1983 issue of *Indiana Review*. That same year "The Cabin" was included in his Capra Press collection *Fires*. Comparing "Pastoral" and "The Cabin" reveals changes in Carver's treatment of a single story over the course of 20 years. For that reason, both "Pastoral" and "The Cabin" are included in this volume. The second story from *Furious Seasons* in this section is the title story, which appeared in no other book in Carver's lifetime. An early version, entitled "The Furious Seasons," was written for John Gardner's creative-writing class at Chico State College in 1959 and was Carver's first published work of fiction when it appeared in the winter 1960–61 issue of *Selection*, the literary magazine that he and fellow student Nancy Parke founded at Chico State in 1960. A revision of the story, with the title shortened to "Furious Seasons," was published in the fall 1963 issue of *December*. The version in *December* is the basis of the text in *Furious Seasons*, which is printed here.

What We Talk About When We Talk About Love

Carver's third story collection, *What We Talk About When We Talk About Love*, was published in hardcover by Alfred A. Knopf on April 20, 1981, and in London by Collins in January 1982. All 17 of the stories in *What We Talk About When We Talk About Love* had appeared in periodicals between 1967 and 1981. Several had been published in more than one version, some under alternate titles. Five had been collected, albeit in different forms, in *Furious Seasons*.

In the years since the publication of *Will You Please Be Quiet, Please?* Carver had stopped drinking and begun his association with fellow writer Tess Gallagher. After surviving the alcoholism that had incapacitated him during the mid-1970s, he began writing new stories in the summer of 1977. During the same period Gordon Lish had left *Esquire* and become a fiction editor at the publishing house of Alfred A. Knopf. Carver and Lish had corresponded, and in early May 1980 they met in New York City. At the meeting Carver delivered to Lish a book-length manuscript of new and revised stories for possible publication by Knopf.

How the manuscript of those stories came to be published in significantly altered form as *What We Talk About When We Talk About Love* is detailed below in the note on the text of *Beginners: The Manuscript Version of* What We Talk About When We Talk About Love. As explained there, Lish more than halved the length of Carver's manuscript and radically altered many of the stories. Carver had initially been deeply distressed by Lish's aggressive editing, going so far as to request in a letter of July 8, 1980, that Knopf halt production of *What We Talk About When We Talk About Love*. Lish had assured him that the cuts were for the good, and Carver had acquiesced, as in the past, to his editor's judgment. But soon after the publication of *What We Talk About When We Talk About Love* in April 1981, Carver restored several stories to their original forms in *Fires*, *Cathedral*, and the limited-edition book *If It Please You* (Northridge, Calif.: Lord John Press, 1984).

This volume prints the text of the 1981 Knopf edition of *What We Talk About When We Talk About Love*. The note on *Beginners* below gives the complete history of the stories included in the collection.

From *Fires: Essays, Poems, Stories*

The first edition of *Fires: Essays, Poems, Stories* was published by Capra Press on April 14, 1983. In addition to a trade edition, 250 copies, each supplemented with a numbered limitation leaf signed by Carver, were printed. The first edition of *Fires* included two essays, 50 poems, seven short stories, and an afterword by the author. Later American and British versions of *Fires* published by Vintage Books (1984), Harvill (1985), and Vintage Contemporaries (1989) altered the table of contents by adding (and subsequently deleting) an interview, increasing the number of essays, and omitting the afterword.

In all editions of *Fires* the stories appear in the following sequence: "Distance"; "The Lie"; "The Cabin"; "Harry's Death"; "The Pheasant"; "Where Is Everyone?"; "So Much Water So Close to Home." Three stories in *Fires* are restorations of stories edited, shortened, and in two cases retitled by Gordon Lish for publication in *What We Talk About When We Talk About Love*. The versions of "Distance," "Where Is Everyone?" and "So Much Water So Close to Home" in *Fires* are not included here; the texts of these stories as Carver submitted them to Lish in the spring of 1980 are printed in *Beginners: The Manuscript Version of* What We Talk About When We Talk About Love. The notes on *Beginners* below give the publication history of these stories, as well as an account of their editing by Lish and their subsequent restoration by Carver in *Fires*.

The texts of the four other stories in *Fires*—"The Lie," "The Cabin," "Harry's Death," and "The Pheasant"—are printed in this section from the Capra Press edition. "The Lie" was first published in the winter 1971 issue of *Sou'wester Literary Quarterly* and was collected in *Furious Seasons*. Carver later revised "The Lie" and published the revision in the November-December 1982 issue of *American Poetry Review*. That version was collected in *Fires* and is printed here. "The Cabin," Carver's extensive revision of his early story "Pastoral," was first published in the winter 1963 issue of *Western Humanities Review* (as "Pastoral") and was collected in *Furious Seasons* in 1977. Because differences between "Pastoral" and "The Cabin" cast light on developments in Carver's writing over two decades, both "Pastoral" and "The Cabin" are included in this volume. The two remaining stories in this section, "Harry's Death" and "The Pheasant," made their sole collected appearances in *Fires* and are printed from that book. "Harry's Death" was originally published in the winter 1975–76 issue of *Eureka Review*. "The Pheasant" made its first appearance in *Occident* in 1973. Carver later revised "The Pheasant" and published the revision in the autumn-winter 1982 issue of *New England Review/Bread Loaf Quarterly*. That same year a signed, limited edition, *The Pheasant*, was published by Metacom Press. The 1982 *Fires* version of "The Pheasant" is printed here.

Cathedral

The first edition of Carver's short story collection *Cathedral* was published in hardcover by Alfred A. Knopf in New York on September 15, 1983, and in London by Collins on January 30, 1984. In September 1984 a softcover version of *Cathedral* was published as one of the first volumes in the Vintage Contemporaries trade paperback series launched by Random House editor Gary Fisketjon.

Of *Cathedral*'s 12 stories, all but "A Small, Good Thing" had been written during 1981–82 and published in periodicals. "A Small, Good Thing" was the restoration and revision of a story that Carver had completed in 1980 but had not at that time submitted to a periodical. Instead, he had included "A Small, Good Thing" in the manuscript of stories he gave to Gordon Lish in May 1980 for possible publication in book form by Knopf, which after being edited by Lish was published in April 1981 as *What We Talk About When We Talk About Love*. (A detailed account of the editing is given below in the discussion of *Beginners: The Manuscript Version of* What We Talk About When We Talk About Love.)

"A Small, Good Thing" was the newest and longest story Carver had submitted to Lish in 1980. The original typescript, preserved in the Lilly Library of Indiana University, runs to 37 double-spaced pages. Over the course of two rounds of line-editing, Lish shortened "A Small, Good Thing" from 11,000 words to fewer than 2,500, the

largest cut to any story in the manuscript. Lish also changed the title
to "The Bath," the title under which a version of the story as edited
by Lish appeared in the spring-summer 1981 issue of *Columbia*,
which awarded it the journal's annual Carlos Fuentes Fiction Award.

Several writers who had read some of Carver's stories in manuscript before Lish edited them for *What We Talk About When We
Talk About Love*, including "A Small, Good Thing," were not convinced that Lish's changes were improvements. One of these readers
was the poet, essayist, and anthologist Donald Hall, who was scheduled to edit an issue of the journal *Ploughshares* devoted to short fiction in 1982. Hall requested and received Carver's permission to
publish in *Ploughshares* a fuller version of "A Small, Good Thing,"
which Carver revised somewhat from the 1980 manuscript version.
The *Ploughshares* text of the story was awarded first place in the annual O. Henry Awards anthology *Prize Stories 1983*.

Although "The Bath" had been published in Carver's previous
Knopf book only two years earlier, he insisted that a full-length version of "A Small, Good Thing" be included in *Cathedral*. He made
a few more changes to the *Ploughshares* text for *Cathedral*. With "A
Small, Good Thing," as with all the stories in the new book, Carver
made it clear that no editorial alterations could be made without his
consent. In a letter of August 11, 1982, he informed Lish that the stories in *Cathedral* would not be uniform in style or size. "But, Gordon, God's truth, and I may as well say it out now, I can't undergo
the kind of surgical amputation and transplant that might make
them someway fit into the carton so the lid will close. There may
have to be limbs and heads of hair sticking out. My heart won't take
it otherwise. It will simply burst, and I mean that." Aware of Lish's
distaste for some of the stories in the new book, in particular "A
Small, Good Thing," Carver recognized that this collection would
challenge expectations about "what a Carver short story ought to
be—yours, mine, the reading public at large, the critics." "But I'm
not them," he added, "I'm not us, I'm me." He was emphatic that
the stories in *Cathedral* would be "*fuller* than the ones in the earlier
books." He acknowledged that his work would benefit from copyediting. This time, however, he would scrutinize every proposed
change. "Gordon, the last book passed as if in a dream for me. This
one can't go that way, and we both know it."

Carver's trust in Lish had been eroded by the peremptory editing
of *What We Talk About When We Talk About Love*. On October 3,
1982, as he prepared to submit the completed manuscript of *Cathedral*, he minced no words about control. "You know I want and
have to have autonomy on this book and that the stories have to
come out looking very essentially the way they look right now." In a

letter of October 29 he underscored the point: "My biggest concern, as you know, is that the stories remain intact." As late as February 23, 1983, when he asked to see the galley proofs of *Cathedral*, he repeated the caution: "I don't need to tell you that it's critical for me that there not be any messing around with titles or text." In the end, Carver accepted only minor corrections from Lish. This volume prints the text of the 1983 Knopf edition of *Cathedral*.

The stories in *Cathedral* made their first appearances in American and British periodicals as follows: "Feathers" (*The Atlantic*, September 1982); "Chef's House" (*The New Yorker*, November 30, 1981); "Preservation" (*Grand Street*, Spring 1983); "The Compartment" (*Antioch Review*, Spring 1983, and *Granta* [London], 1983); "A Small, Good Thing" (*Ploughshares*, 1982); "Vitamins" (*Esquire*, October 1981, and *Granta* [London], 1981); "Careful" (*The Paris Review*, Summer 1983); "Where I'm Calling From" (*The New Yorker*, March 15, 1982); "The Train" (*Antaeus*, Spring-Summer 1983); "Fever" (*North American Review*, June 1983); "The Bridle" (*The New Yorker*, July 19, 1982); "Cathedral" (*The Atlantic*, September 1981, and *The London Magazine*, February-March 1984).

New Stories from *Where I'm Calling From*

Where I'm Calling From: New and Selected Stories was published by Atlantic Monthly Press in May 1988. Founded in 1917 as an affiliate of the Boston-based *Atlantic Monthly* magazine, the press had been sold in 1986. Its editorial director was Gary Fisketjon, who had previously overseen Carver's books as published by Random House and reprinted by its Vintage Books division. Among the first projects contracted under his directorship was what would be Carver's longest book to date, a 400-page volume of new and selected stories.

Publication of *Where I'm Calling From* coincided with Carver's 50th birthday on May 25, 1988. To mark the occasion, Atlantic Monthly Press published *Where I'm Calling From* in both trade and limited editions. A privately printed first edition was also published by the Franklin Library for members of its Signed First Edition Society. An undisclosed number of copies were bound in stamped leather with marbled endpapers and page edges gilt. Each included a leaf signed by Carver, a specially commissioned illustration by Steve Johnson, and "A Special Message for the First Edition" by the author. This 1,000-word essay appeared in no other edition of *Where I'm Calling From* published in Carver's lifetime. Under the title "Introduction to *Where I'm Calling From*," it is included among the "Selected Essays" in this volume.

The "New Stories" section of *Where I'm Calling From* consisted of seven stories written during 1985–86 and published in periodicals during 1986–87. All made their first appearances in book form in *Where I'm Calling From*. In England, these stories were collected in a separate volume entitled *Elephant and Other Stories*, published in hardcover by Collins Harvill in London on August 4, 1988, two days after Carver's death. Following is a list of the first American and British periodical appearances of the seven previously uncollected stories in *Where I'm Calling From* and *Elephant*: "Boxes" (*The New Yorker*, February 24, 1986); "Whoever Was Using This Bed" (*The New Yorker*, April 28, 1986); "Intimacy" (*Esquire*, August 1986); "Menudo" (*Granta* [London], Spring 1987); "Elephant" (*The New Yorker*, June 9, 1986, and *Fiction Magazine* [London], October 1986); "Blackbird Pie" (*The New Yorker*, July 7, 1986); "Errand" (*The New Yorker*, June 1, 1987). Two of the stories were also separately published as limited editions: *Intimacy* by William B. Ewert (1987) and *Elephant* by Jungle Garden Press (1988). The texts printed in the present volume of the "New Stories" from *Where I'm Calling From* are taken from the 1988 Atlantic Monthly Press edition.

The "Selected Stories" section of *Where I'm Calling From* was made up of 30 stories chosen by Carver, in consultation with Tess Gallagher and Gary Fisketjon, from his earlier trade-press books. Twelve came from *Will You Please Be Quiet, Please?* (McGraw-Hill, 1976); eight came from *What We Talk About When We Talk About Love* (Knopf, 1981); two came from *Fires* (Capra Press, 1983; Vintage Books, 1984); and eight came from *Cathedral* (Knopf, 1983). An "Editor's Note" prefaced to *Where I'm Calling From* stated, "The stories in this collection are arranged, generally, in chronological order. A number of them have been revised for this edition, and in a few cases titles have been changed." The order followed the stories' chronological appearance in collections rather than the dates of their composition or first appearances in periodicals. The revisions in *Where I'm Calling From* were principally changes of names previously assigned to various characters: Jack to Carl and vice-versa; Carl to Dick or Earl; Jack to Bill. In addition, some corruptions were introduced into the text, including typographical errors and the rendering of dialect and colloquialisms into standard English. The titles of two stories that appeared in earlier books were changed in *Where I'm Calling From*. First, the story that Lish had edited and titled "What Is It?" for publication in *Esquire* and in *Will You Please Be Quiet, Please?* was renamed "Are These Actual Miles?" In *What It Used to Be Like: A Portrait of My Marriage to Raymond Carver* (St. Martin's Press, 2006), Maryann Burk Carver reported that "Are These Actual Miles?" was the original title under which Carver had submitted the story to Lish. Second, the story that Lish had edited and titled "Popular Mechanics" for inclusion in *What We Talk*

About When We Talk About Love was renamed "Little Things." Under that title Carver had previously published the story in *Fiction* in 1978.

None of the "Selected Stories" as printed in *Where I'm Calling From* is included in this volume. Instead, the texts of these stories are taken either from the books in which they were first collected or from *Beginners: The Manuscript Version of* What We Talk About When We Talk About Love. In *Where I'm Calling From*, the 30 "Selected Stories" appear in the following sequence: "Nobody Said Anything"; "Bicycles, Muscles, Cigarettes"; "The Student's Wife"; "They're Not Your Husband"; "What Do You Do in San Francisco?"; "Fat"; "What's in Alaska?"; "Neighbors"; "Put Yourself in My Shoes"; "Collectors"; "Why, Honey?"; "Are These Actual Miles?" ("What Is It?" in *Will You Please Be Quiet, Please?*); "Gazebo"; "One More Thing"; "Little Things" ("Popular Mechanics" in *What We Talk About When We Talk About Love*); "Why Don't You Dance?"; "A Serious Talk"; "What We Talk About When We Talk About Love"; "Distance"; "The Third Thing That Killed My Father Off"; "So Much Water So Close To Home"; "The Calm"; "Vitamins"; "Careful"; "Where I'm Calling From"; "Chef's House"; "Fever"; "Feathers"; "Cathedral"; "A Small, Good Thing."

Other Fiction

This volume includes, in a section entitled "Other Fiction," nine short stories and a fictional fragment. Four early stories and the fragment "From *The Augustine Notebooks*" were published in periodicals during Carver's lifetime. Five unpublished stories were found in manuscript a decade after his death and appeared in American and British periodicals during 1999–2000. All ten "Other Stories" were included in *Call If You Need Me*, a posthumous collection of Carver's writings edited by William L. Stull. The British edition, *Call If You Need Me: The Uncollected Fiction & Prose*, was published in hardcover by Harvill Press in 2000. An American softcover publication, *Call If You Need Me: The Uncollected Fiction and Other Prose*, identical to the British edition except for its title, title page, and copyright notice, was published by Random House under its Vintage Contemporaries imprint in 2001.

The text of "The Hair," written for a creative-writing class taught by Richard Cortez Day at Chico State College in the early 1960s, is printed from its first periodical appearance, in the spring 1963 issue of the Chico State literary magazine *Toyon*. That issue was edited by Carver and included four works by him. Two of these, the stories "The Hair" and "Poseidon and Company," appeared under his own name. Two others, the poem "Spring, 480 B.C." and the story "The

Aficionados," appeared under the pseudonym John Vale. Carver subsequently published a revision of "The Hair" in the January 7–20, 1972, issue of the Santa Cruz, California, alternative newspaper *Sundaze*. The later version is not included in this volume. It can be read in *Those Days: Early Writings by Raymond Carver*, a limited-edition book edited by William L. Stull and published by Raven Editions in Elmwood, Connecticut, in 1987. Carver contributed a preface to *Those Days* in which he reassessed "The Hair" and other early works he had not read in many years. "Not bad, considering," was his opinion of them:

> The thing is, if a writer is still alive and well (and he's always well if he's still writing) and can look back from a great distance to a few early efforts and not have to feel *too* abashed or discomfited, or even ashamed of what he finds he was doing then—then I say good for him. And good, too, whatever it was that pushed him along and kept him going. The rewards being what they are in this business, few enough and far between, he ought perhaps even be forgiven if he takes some little satisfaction in what he sees: a continuity in the work, which is of course to say, a continuity in the life.

The second early story, "The Aficionados," a satire on Hemingway's tales about doomed bullfighters, is printed from its sole appearance in Carver's lifetime. Carver published "The Aficionados" under his pseudonym John Vale in the spring 1963 issue of *Toyon*. That issue is also the source for the text printed here of the story "Poseidon and Company," which Carver published in *Toyon* under his own name. A slightly different text of "Poseidon and Company" appeared in the spring 1964 issue of *Ball State Teachers College Forum*. The 1964 revision of "Poseidon and Company" is excluded from this volume in favor of the first published version of the story. The last of Carver's early stories, "Bright Red Apples," appeared once in his lifetime. It was published in the spring-summer 1967 issue of *Gato Magazine*, and the text printed here is taken from that periodical.

Only one source exists for the fragment of Carver's uncompleted novel. "From *The Augustine Notebooks*" appeared in the summer 1979 issue of *Iowa Review* and is printed from that source. In the spring of 1977, while living in McKinleyville, California, and struggling to quit drinking, Carver had accepted an advance on an unwritten novel from McGraw-Hill, the publisher of his 1976 story collection *Will You Please Be Quiet, Please?* In an interview in the *Times-Standard* of Eureka, California, on July 24, 1977, he described the planned book as "an *African Queen* sort of thing" set in German East Africa after World War I. Five years later he admitted he had stopped working on the novel after two weeks. "I just lost interest in it," he told Jim Spencer of the Norfolk *Virginian-Pilot* in an interview published on October 1, 1982. "I may write a novel someday, but I have no pressure on me, because I'm successful as a short story writer."

This section of "Other Fiction" ends with five stories not published in Carver's lifetime. Files relating to "Kindling," "Vandals," and "Dreams" were found in March 1999 by Tess Gallagher and Jay Woodruff, then a senior editor at *Esquire*, in Carver's writing desk at Ridge House in Port Angeles, Washington. Gallagher and Woodruff transcribed the three stories from typescripts and handwritten drafts. They were then published in *Esquire* as follows: "Kindling" (July 1999), "Vandals" (October 1999), and "Dreams" (July 2000). On July 15, 1999, two more unpublished stories were found by William L. Stull and Maureen P. Carroll among the Raymond Carver papers housed in the William Charvat Collection of American Fiction at the Ohio State University Library. "What Would You Like to See?" and "Call If You Need Me" are each preserved in a single ribbon typescript marked with Carver's holograph corrections. These two stories made their first appearances in British periodicals. "Call If You Need Me" was published in the winter 1999 issue of *Granta*, and "What Would You Like to See?" appeared in *The Guardian Weekend* on June 24, 2000. The texts of the five unpublished stories are printed from *Call If You Need Me* (2000), where they made their first appearance in book form.

Selected Essays

This volume includes, under the heading "Selected Essays," four pieces of Carver's expository writing. The first of these, "My Father's Life," was originally published in the September 1984 issue of *Esquire* and is printed from that source.

The essay appeared under the title "Where He Was: Memories of My Father" in the winter 1984 issue of *Granta*, with variants made in accordance with British and house-style conventions. It was included as "My Father's Life" in the first British edition of *Fires*, which was published in London by Collins Harvill on April 15, 1985. In 1986 *My Father's Life* was separately published by Babcock & Koontz of Derry, New Hampshire, and Ridgewood, New Jersey, in a signed, limited edition of 240 copies. The second and third essays, "On Writing" and "Fires," are printed from the 1983 Capra Press edition of *Fires*. "On Writing" made its first appearance as "A Storyteller's Shoptalk" in *The New York Times Book Review* on February 15, 1981. As submitted, the essay was untitled, and the title in the *Book Review* was supplied by an editor. In preparing the essay for inclusion in *Fires* Carver titled it "On Writing." The essay "Fires" was first published in the autumn 1982 issue of *Antaeus.* It appeared in slightly different form in the fall 1982 issue of *Syracuse Scholar.* Carver had written "Fires" at the request of editors Ted Solotaroff and Stephen Berg for inclusion in the Harper & Row anthology *In Praise of What Persists*, and it appeared in that book in 1983. The fourth essay, "Introduction to *Where I'm Calling From*," originally appeared as "A Special Message for the First Edition" prefaced to the signed, limited edition of *Where I'm Calling From: New and Selected Stories* published by the Franklin Library in 1988. For descriptive purposes the essay was editorially renamed "On *Where I'm Calling From*" when it was posthumously included among Carver's uncollected writings in *No Heroics, Please* (1991) and *Call If You Need Me* (2000). This volume prints the essay from the Franklin Library edition under the title "Author's Note to *Where I'm Calling From*."

Beginners: The Manuscript Version of
What We Talk About When We Talk About Love

Beginners is the manuscript version of the 17 stories that were published in book form as *What We Talk About When We Talk About Love* by Alfred A. Knopf on April 20, 1981. The manuscript, which Carver's editor Gordon Lish shortened to less than half its original length in two rounds of close line-editing, is preserved in the Lilly Library of Indiana University. The editors of this volume have restored the stories to their original forms by transcribing Carver's typewritten words that lie beneath Lish's alterations in ink on the typescripts. For ease of comparison, and because Carver's manuscript included no title page or table of contents, the stories in this section are arranged in the same sequence as in *What We Talk About When We Talk About Love*. The title, *Beginners*, has been provided by the editors because the story "Beginners" corresponds to the title story of *What We Talk About When We Talk About Love*.

Lish was a literary mainstay during Carver's alcoholic years of the 1970s. He published Carver's fiction in *Esquire*, recommended him to editors and agents in New York City, and made possible the publication of his first collection of stories, *Will You Please Be Quiet, Please?*, in 1976. In the years that followed, Carver's life changed. On June 2, 1977, he stopped drinking. In 1978 his first marriage ended in separation (divorce would follow in 1982), and in 1979 he began living with the writer Tess Gallagher. After years of temporary jobs and unemployment he was appointed senior professor of English at Syracuse University, where he began teaching in January 1980. During these same years Lish left *Esquire* and joined the publishing firm of

Alfred A. Knopf. The two men kept in contact by letter and discussed the possibility of publishing a new collection of Carver's fiction under Lish's editorship at Knopf. In early May 1980 they met in New York City, where Carver gave Lish a manuscript of new and revised short stories.

From Carver's perspective, the manuscript he gave Lish was substantially complete. Lish had previously edited several of the stories, and the bulk of them had been published in periodicals and/or small-press books. Nonetheless, shortly after returning to Syracuse, Carver evidently received a query. In a letter dated May 10, 1980, he told Lish "not to worry about taking a pencil to the stories if you can make them better." He added, "If you see ways to put more muscle in the stories, don't hesitate to do so." He valued his editor's skills so highly that he offered to pay the cost of retyping if the marked-up manuscript required it.

While Carver finished the semester in Syracuse and prepared to travel to the Pacific Northwest for the summer, Lish edited the manuscript. As he later said, what struck him in Carver's writing was "a peculiar bleakness." To foreground that bleakness, he cut the stories radically, reducing plot, character development, and figurative language to a minimum. Some stories were shortened by a third, several by more than a half, and two by three-quarters of their original length. The overall reduction of the manuscript in word count was 55%.

Lish worked quickly, cutting the stories to his pattern for the book. The project was on a fast track. Five weeks after receiving the manuscript, he mailed a revised and retyped version to Syracuse. It arrived just as Carver and Gallagher were departing for Alaska. After failing to reach Lish by telephone, Carver mailed him a note on June 13, 1980, and promised to call later. "The collection *looks* terrific, though I haven't been able to read more than the title page—which title is fine, I think." He enclosed payment for the typist, gave a mailing address in Fairbanks, and left without examining the edited manuscript.

While Carver and Gallagher participated in the Midnight Sun Writers' Conference, Lish edited the collection a second time. Once again he had the manuscript retyped. At the end of June, while Gallagher remained in Port Angeles, Carver briefly returned to Syracuse. There he awaited the second edited version of the manuscript, apparently without having read the first revision. On July 4, 1980, he wrote Lish that the "revised collection" had not yet arrived. Time was short, since he was scheduled to fly back to Washington State in ten days. To cover the second round of typing costs, he enclosed a blank check. On July 7 he received what Lish presented as the finished text of the book. When he read the edited manuscript he was shocked by the extensive changes that he found. "A Small, Good Thing," a 37-page story, had been cut to 12 pages and renamed "The Bath." A 26-page story, "If It Please You," had been cut to 14 pages and renamed "Community Center." (Lish later changed the title to "After the Denim.") A 15-page story, "Where Is Everyone?" had been shortened to five pages and renamed "Mr. Coffee and Mr. Fixit." "Beginners," a 33-page story, had been cut to 19 pages and renamed "What We Talk About When We Talk About Love." Even "Mine," a 500-word story previously edited by Lish and published twice, had been further condensed and renamed "Popular Mechanics."

After a sleepless night, early on the morning of July 8, 1980, Carver wrote an anguished letter.

July 8, 8 a.m.

Dearest Gordon,

I've got to pull out of this one. Please hear me. I've been up all night thinking on this, and nothing but this, so help me. I've looked at it from every side, I've compared both versions of the edited mss—the first one is better, I truly believe, if some things are carried over from the second to the first—until my eyes are nearly to fall out of my head. You are a wonder, a genius, and there's no doubt of that, better than any two of Max Perkins, etc. etc. And I'm not unmindful of the fact of my immense debt to you, a debt I can simply never, never repay. This whole new life I have, so many of the friends I now have, this job up here, everything, I owe to you for WILL YOU PLEASE. You've given me some degree of immortality already. You've made so many of the stories in this collection better, far better than they were before. And maybe if I were alone, by myself, and no one had ever seen these stories, maybe then, knowing that your versions are better than some of the ones I sent, maybe I could get into this and go with it. But Tess has seen all of these and gone over them closely. Donald Hall has seen many of the new ones (and discussed them at length with me and offered his services in reviewing the collection) and Richard Ford, Toby Wolff, —Geoffrey Wolff, too, some of them. This new issue of TRI-QUARTERLY, out a few days ago, has a story by Toby W, one by Ford, Kittredge, McGuane, and "Where Is Everyone?" ("Mr. Fixit"). How can I explain to these fellows when I see them, as I will see them, what happened to the story in the meantime, after its book publication? Maybe if the book were not to come out for 18 months or two years, it would be different. But right now, everything is too new. Why TRI-

QUARTERLY has just taken another one, but that will not, cannot, come out until Fall-Winter 1981–1982. Gordon, the changes are brilliant and for the better in most cases—I look at "What We Talk About . . ." ("Beginners") and I see what it is that you've done, what you've pulled out of it, and I'm awed and astonished, startled even, with your insights. But it's too close right now, that story. Now much of this has to do with my sobriety and with my new-found (and fragile, I see) mental health and well-being. I'll tell you the truth, my very sanity is on the line here. I don't want to sound melodramatic here, but I've come back from the grave here to start writing stories once more. As I think you may know, I'd given up entirely, thrown it in and was looking forward to dying, that release. But I kept thinking, I'll wait until after the election to kill myself, or wait until after this or that happened, usually something down the road a ways, but it was never far from my mind in those dark days, not all that long ago. Now, I'm incomparably better, I have my health back, money in the bank, the right woman for this time of my life, a decent job, blah, blah. But I haven't written a word since I gave you the collection, waiting for your reaction, that reaction means so much to me. Now, I'm afraid, mortally afraid, I feel it, that if the book were to be published as it is in its present edited form, I may never write another story, that's how closely, God Forbid, some of those stories are to my sense of regaining my health and mental well-being. As I say, maybe if I had 18 months or two years, some distance from these pieces and a good deal more writing under my belt, I could and would go with it. Likely so. But I can't now. I just can't, I don't know what else to say.

Please help me with this, Gordon. I feel as if this is the most important decision I've ever been faced with, no shit. I ask for your understanding. Next to my wife, and now Tess, you have been and are the most important individual in my life, and that's the truth. I don't want to lose your love or regard over this, oh God no. It would be like having a part of myself die, a spiritual part. Jesus, I'm jabbering now. But if this causes you undue complication and grief and you perhaps understandably become pissed and discouraged with me, well, I'm the poorer for it, and my life will not be the same again. True. On the other hand, if the book comes out and I can't feel the kind of pride and pleasure in it that I want, if I feel I've somehow too far stepped out of bounds, crossed that line a little too far, why then I can't feel good about myself, or maybe even write again; right now I feel it's that serious, and if I can't feel absolutely good about it, I feel I'd be done for. I do. Lord God I just don't know what else to say. I'm awash with confusion and paranoia. Fatigue too, that too.

Please, Gordon, for God's sake help me in this and try to understand. Listen. I'll say it again, if I have any standing or reputation or credibility in the world, I owe it to you. I owe you this more-or-less pretty interesting life I have. But if I go ahead with this as it is, it will not be good for me. The book will not be, as it should, a cause for joyous celebration, but one of defense and explanation. All this is complicatedly, and maybe not so complicatedly, tied up with my feelings of worth and self-esteem since I quit drinking. I just can't do it, I can't take the risk as to what might happen to me. I know that the discomfort of this decision of mine is at its highest now, it's rampant, I feel nearly wild with it. But I know it will cause you grief as well, explanations, more work, stopping everything in its tracks and coming up with valid reasons for why. But, eventually, my discomfort and yours, will go away, there'll be a grieving, I'm grieving right now, but it will go away. But if I don't speak now, and speak from the heart, and halt things now, I foresee a terrible time ahead for me. The demons I have to deal with every day, or night, nearly, might, I'm afraid, simply rise up and take me over.

Of course I know I shouldn't have signed the contract without first reading the collection and making my fears, if any, known to you beforehand, before signing. So what should we do now, please advise? Can you lay it all on me and get me out of the contract someway? Can you put the book off until Winter or Spring of 1982 and let them know I want to have the stories in the collection published in magazines first (and that's the truth, several of them are committed to places with publication way off next year)? Tell them I want the magazine publications first, and then the book out when I'm up for tenure here that spring of 1982? And then decide next year what, for sure, to do? Or else can or should everything just be stopped now, I send back the Knopf check, if it's on the way, or else you stop it there? And meanwhile I pay you for the hours, days and nights, I'm sure, you've spent on this. Goddamn it, I'm just nearly crazy with this. I'm getting into a state over it. No, I don't think it should be put off. I think it had best be stopped.

I thought the editing, especially in the first version, was brilliant, as I said. The stories I can't let go of in their entirety are these. "Community Center" (It Please You) and "The Bath" (A Small Good Thing) and I'd want some more of the old couple, Anna and Henry Gates, in "What We Talk About When We Talk About Love" (Beginners). I would not want "Mr. Fixit" (Where Is Everyone?) in the book in its present state. The story "Distance" should not have its title changed to "Everything Stuck to Him." Nor the little piece "Mine" to "Popular Mechanics." "Dummy" should keep its title. "A Serious Talk" is fine for "Pie." I think "Want to See Something?" is fine, is better than "I Could See the Smallest Things." Otherwise, with the exception of little things here and there, incorporating some of the changes from version #2 into #1, I could live with and be happy with. That little business at the end of "Pie" (A Serious Talk) him leaving the house with the ashtray, that's just inspired and wonderful. There are so many places like that the ms is stronger and clearer and more wonderful. But I could not have "Mr. Fixit" published the way it is in the present collection. Either the whole story, the one that's in TRIQUARTERLY now, or at least the better part of it, or else not at all.

I'm just much too close to all of this right now. It's even hard for me to think right now. I think, in all, maybe it's just too soon for me for another collection. I know that next spring is too soon in any case. Absolutely too soon. I think I had best pull out, Gordon, before it goes any further. I realize I stand every chance of losing your love and friendship over this. But I strongly feel I stand every chance of losing my soul and my mental health over it, if I don't take that risk. I'm still in the process of recovery and trying to get well from the alcoholism, and I just can't take any chances, something as momentous and permanent as this, that would put my head in some jeopardy. That's it, it's in my head. You have made so many of these stories better, my God, with the lighter editing and trimming. But those others, those three, I guess, I'm liable to croak if they came out that way. Even though they may be closer to works of art than the originals and people be reading them 50 years from now, they're still apt to cause my demise, I'm serious, they're so intimately hooked up with my getting well, recovering, gaining back some little self-esteem and feeling of worth as a writer and a human being.

I know you must feel angry and betrayed and pissed off. God's sake, I'm sorry. I can pay you for the time you've put in on this, but I can't begin to help or do anything about the trouble and grief I may be causing there in the editorial and

business offices that you'll have to go through. Forgive me for
this, please. But I'm just going to have to wait a while yet for
another book, 18 months, two years, it's okay now, as long as
I'm writing and have some sense of worth in the process. Your
friendship and your concern and general championing of me
have meant, and mean still, more to me than I can ever say. I
could never begin to repay you, as you must know. I honor
and respect you, and I love you more than my brother. But
you will have to get me off the hook here Gordon, it's true. I
just can't go another step forward with this endeavor. So
please advise what to do now. I'm going out of town tomorrow, but I will be back Saturday. Monday morning I'm leaving
for the West Coast, Bellingham and Pt. Townsend, as I think
I mentioned, and I'll hook up with Tess out there and return
here on the 30th of July. My address here is

832 Maryland Avenue
Syracuse, NY 13210

As I say, I'm confused, tired, paranoid, and afraid, yes, of the
consequences for me if the collection came out in its present
form. So help me, please, yet again. Don't, please, make this
too hard for me, for I'm just likely to start coming unraveled
knowing how I've displeased and disappointed you. God
almighty, Gordon.

Ray [signed]

Please do the necessary things to stop production of the book.
Please try and forgive me, this breach.

Not long afterward, Carver spoke to Lish by telephone. No record
of their conversation is preserved, but Lish's point of view prevailed.
The contract remained in force, and production of the book proceeded at full speed. By this time the mechanisms of publication
were out of Carver's hands. He may not have realized this, because
he spent July 10, 1980, belatedly comparing the first and second
edited versions of the book. That evening he wrote Lish a letter filled
with equivocations. On the one hand, he was thrilled at the prospect
of a book with Knopf and deeply grateful to his editor. "It's a beauty
for sure," he began, "it is, and I'm honored and grateful for your attentions to it." On the other hand, he had nagging doubts about the
cuts made to the stories. He proposed specific changes to the edited
text, "small enough" but "significant." These were largely restorations of material Lish had deleted during the second editing. "I have
serious questions or reservations," Carver wrote, "or I wouldn't
have marked the things I did." His fear was that the pared-down stories would make his writing seem disjointed. "I'm mortally afraid of

taking out too much from the stories, of making them too thin, not enough connecting tissue to them."

Rather than attempt to salvage "Where Is Everyone?" which had been cut by more than three-quarters and renamed "Mr. Coffee and Mr. Fixit," Carver requested that it be dropped from the collection. The original story was in press at *TriQuarterly*, and he understood that the editor was submitting it for a possible O. Henry Award. Moreover, as a story about an alcoholic just beginning to face his problems, "Where Is Everyone?" marked a turning point in his own recovery. "I have a lot of rampant and complicated feelings about that story," he explained, "no matter if it is never included in a book in any form whatsoever." He finished the letter the next morning, restating that he was "thrilled with this book and that you're bringing it out with Knopf." Eager to rejoin Gallagher in Port Angeles, he focused on endorsements and publicity. To build anticipation for the new book, the previously unpublished stories would need to be rushed into magazines. By the end of the letter, Carver had slipped back into the deferential posture he had assumed toward Lish during his drinking years. "I once told you I thought I could die happy after having a story in *Esquire*," he wrote. "Now a book out with Knopf —and such a book! And there'll be more, you'll see. I'm drawing a long second wind." He closed "with my love" and promised he would write again "sometime or another" in the future.

By the eve of Carver's departure from Syracuse, the night of July 14, 1980, he had left the form of the book to his editor's discretion. "I know you have my best interests at heart," he said in a letter, "and you'll do everything and more to further those interests." Not wanting to be "a pest of an author," he asked only that Lish "please look at" the restorations he had proposed: "if you think I'm being my own worst enemy, you know, well then, stick to the final version of the second edited version." The resistance he had voiced a week earlier had collapsed, as had his self-confidence. "Maybe I am wrong in this, maybe you are 100% correct, just please give them another hard look. That's all." His only firm directive was that "Mr. Coffee and Mr. Fixit" should not be included in the book.

How did Lish respond to Carver's unease about the editing of *What We Talk About When We Talk About Love*? In August 1998 he told *The New York Times Magazine*, "My sense of it was that there was a letter and that I just went ahead." In due course he sent Carver proofs of *What We Talk About When We Talk About Love*. "I still haven't done anything but glance at the galleys you sent up," Carver wrote on October 6, 1980. "Took the wind out of my sails some when you said to send them back to you so soon without reading them even." Had he read them, he would have found that the stories conformed to Lish's second edited version, to which a few more cuts had been made. Virtually none of the changes Carver proposed were incorporated, and the book included "Mr. Coffee and Mr. Fixit."

On February 15, 1980, Carver had written Lish to say he had on hand three groups of stories. One group had previously appeared in little magazines or small-press books but had never been published in a trade-press book. A second group either had appeared or would soon appear in periodicals. A third group consisted of newly written stories still in typescript.

The *Beginners* manuscript as presented in this volume comprises these three groups of stories. In preparing the stories for submission to Knopf, Carver revised a number of them that had appeared in books or magazines. These authorial revisions, including handwritten corrections, are reflected in the text. Obvious word omissions, misspellings, and inconsistencies in punctuation in the manuscript have been silently corrected. What follows is a publication history of each story in the *Beginners* manuscript, including an account of its editing by Lish and its subsequent appearances, if any, in books by Carver.

Abbreviations

Beginners	*Beginners*, untitled manuscript preserved among the Gordon Lish papers in the Lilly Library of Indiana University as "Raymond Carver, *What We Talk About When We Talk About Love*, Manuscript—First Draft." Net editorial reduction of word-count of each story in the manuscript is expressed as a percentage.
Cathedral	*Cathedral*, first edition (New York: Alfred A. Knopf, 1983)
Fires	*Fires: Essays, Poems, Stories*, first edition (Santa Barbara: Capra Press, 1983)
FS	*Furious Seasons and Other Stories* (Santa Barbara: Capra Press, 1977). The papers of Capra Press are housed at the Lilly Library.
WICF	*Where I'm Calling From: New and Selected Stories*, first edition (New York: Atlantic Monthly Press, 1988)
WWTA	*What We Talk About When We Talk About Love*, first edition (New York: Alfred A. Knopf, 1981)

Why Don't You Dance? *Beginners*: 8-page manuscript cut by 9% for inclusion in *WWTA* as "Why Don't You Dance?" PREVIOUS PUB-

LICATION: "Why Don't You Dance?" *Quarterly West*, Autumn 1978; *The Paris Review*, Spring 1981. The version in *The Paris Review* was the product of Lish's first editing of *Beginners*. In 1977 Carver had submitted a story entitled "Why Don't You Dance?" to *Esquire*. Lish had edited it and changed the title to "I Am Going to Sit Down," but no version ever appeared in *Esquire*. As published in *Quarterly West* the story included many but not all of Lish's suggested changes and is nearly identical to the text in *Beginners*. SUBSEQUENT PUBLICATION: "Why Don't You Dance?" was collected in *WICF* as it appeared in *WWTA*.

Viewfinder. *Beginners*: 6-page manuscript cut by 30% for inclusion in *WWTA* as "Viewfinder." PREVIOUS PUBLICATION: As "View Finder," *Iowa Review*, Winter 1978, and *Quarterly West*, Spring-Summer 1978. These two versions, which are virtually identical, included many of Lish's suggested changes to "The Mill," an earlier story by Carver that remains unpublished. The title "The Mill" was based on the handless man's observation: "You're going through the mill now." Lish deleted that sentence and renamed the story "Viewfinder" based on a word that occurs twice in the original text. Efforts to publish "Viewfinder" in *Esquire* came to a halt when Lish ceased to be fiction editor in September 1977. The text in *Quarterly West* is identical to the text in *Beginners*. SUBSEQUENT PUBLICATION: None.

Where Is Everyone? *Beginners*: 15-page manuscript cut by 78% for inclusion in *WWTA* as "Mr. Coffee and Mr. Fixit." PREVIOUS PUBLICATION: "Where Is Everyone?" *TriQuarterly*, Spring 1980. The text in *TriQuarterly* is identical to the text in *Beginners* except for differences in punctuation. NOTE ON *WWTA*: In Lish's first editing of the story he changed the daughter's name from Kate to Melody, changed the wife's name from Cynthia to Myrna, and eliminated all references to the son, Mike. He renamed the story "Mr. Fixit" but later changed that to "Mr. Coffee and Mr. Fixit." SUBSEQUENT PUBLICATION: As "Where Is Everyone?" in *Fires*. The text in *Fires* is identical to the text in *TriQuarterly* except for light editing by Carver, including his deletion of the line "I don't know where everyone is at home." As a result, the line appears only in *TriQuarterly* and *Beginners*.

Gazebo. *Beginners*: 13-page manuscript cut by 44% for inclusion in *WWTA* as "Gazebo." PREVIOUS PUBLICATION: A version of "Gazebo" that was the product of Lish's first editing of *Beginners* appeared in *Missouri Review*, Fall 1980. SUBSEQUENT

PUBLICATION: "Gazebo" was collected in *WICF* in a version nearly identical to that in *WWTA*.

Want To See Something? *Beginners*: 11-page manuscript cut by 56% for inclusion in *WWTA* as "I Could See the Smallest Things." PREVIOUS PUBLICATION: A version of "Want to See Something?" that was the product of Lish's first editing of *Beginners* appeared in *Missouri Review*, Fall 1980. In the first editing Lish deleted most of the story's original ending; in the second editing he changed the title to "I Could See the Smallest Things." SUBSEQUENT PUBLICATION: None.

The Fling. *Beginners*: 21-page manuscript cut by 61% for inclusion in *WWTA* as "Sacks." PREVIOUS PUBLICATION: "The Fling," *Perspective: A Quarterly of Modern Literature*, Winter 1974; collected in *FS*. The texts in *Perspective* and *FS* are nearly identical to the text in *Beginners*. SUBSEQUENT PUBLICATION: None.

A Small, Good Thing. *Beginners*: 37-page manuscript cut by 78% for inclusion in *WWTA* as "The Bath." PREVIOUS PUBLICATION: A version of "The Bath" that was the product of Lish's first editing of *Beginners* appeared in *Columbia: A Magazine of Poetry and Prose*, Spring-Summer 1981. SUBSEQUENT PUBLICATION: As "A Small, Good Thing" in *Ploughshares*, 1982. The version in *Ploughshares* followed the *Beginners* manuscript except for minor changes in diction and phrasing and the deletion of a 4-page flashback section. None of Lish's changes in "The Bath" were incorporated into the *Ploughshares* text except for a few rephrasings in the opening paragraphs. Carver collected "A Small, Good Thing" in *Cathedral*, in the process lightly editing the version in *Ploughshares* and incorporating into it several revisions suggested to him by Tess Gallagher. "A Small, Good Thing" was collected in *WICF* as it appeared in *Cathedral*.

Tell the Women We're Going. *Beginners*: 19-page manuscript cut by 55% for inclusion in *WWTA* as "Tell the Women We're Going." PREVIOUS PUBLICATION: As "Friendship," *Sou'wester Literary Quarterly*, Summer 1971. In 1969 Carver had submitted "Friendship" to Lish for consideration at *Esquire*, but the story was not accepted. He later submitted it to Noel Young, publisher of Capra Press, for inclusion in *FS*, but Young deemed it "too gruesome for my quavering senses" and excluded it (Capra Press mss., letter of April 24, 1977). The text of "Tell the Women We're Going" in *Beginners* is very similar to the text of "Friendship" in *Sou'wester*. In revising the story Carver changed the title, altered a few words, and expanded the final paragraph. SUBSEQUENT PUBLICATION: None.

If It Please You. *Beginners*: 26-page manuscript cut by 63% for inclusion in *WWTA* as "After the Denim." PREVIOUS PUBLICATION: "If It Please You," *New England Review*, Spring 1981. The text in *New England Review* is nearly identical to the text in *Beginners*. NOTE ON *WWTA*: In Lish's first editing he changed the title to "Community Center" and canceled the last 6 pages. He later renamed the story "After the Denim." SUBSEQUENT PUBLICATION: *If It Please You* was published in a signed, limited edition of 226 copies by Lord John Press of Northridge, California, in 1984. The text in the limited edition agrees with the text in *New England Review* except for a few changes in phrasing. Carver revised the final sentence of the story several times:

> "If it please you," he said in the new prayers for all of them, the living and the dead. ~~Then he slept.~~ (*Beginners*, second sentence hand-canceled by Carver)

> "If it please you," he said in the new prayers for all of them, the living and the dead. (*New England Review*)

> "If it please you," he said in the new prayers for all of them. (Lord John Press limited edition)

So Much Water So Close To Home. *Beginners*: 27-page manuscript cut by 70% for inclusion in *WWTA* as "So Much Water So Close to Home." PREVIOUS PUBLICATION: "So Much Water So Close to Home," *Spectrum*, 1975; collected in *FS*. The texts in *Spectrum* and *FS* are identical. An abridged version of the story was published in *Playgirl*, February 1976. The *Playgirl* editor made extensive cuts and added two final sentences that appear nowhere else: "I begin to scream. It doesn't matter any longer." The texts in *Spectrum* and *FS* are identical to the text in *Beginners* except for differences in punctuation. SUBSEQUENT PUBLICATION: "So Much Water So Close to Home" was included in *Fires* in a text nearly identical to that in *FS*. The version in *Fires* was collected in *WICF*.

Dummy. *Beginners*: 24-page manuscript cut by 40% for inclusion in *WWTA* as "The Third Thing That Killed My Father Off." PREVIOUS PUBLICATION: "Dummy," *Discourse: A Review of the Liberal Arts*, Summer 1967; collected in *FS*. The source of the text in *FS* was an offprint from *Discourse* on which Carver had made incidental corrections. The text in *FS* is virtually identical to the text in *Beginners*. NOTE ON *WWTA*: In Lish's second editing he changed the title from "Dummy" to "The First Thing That Killed My Father Off" after adding and then canceling the title "Friendship." He later changed the title to "The Third Thing That Killed My Father Off." SUBSEQUENT PUBLICATION: "The Third Thing That Killed My Father Off" was collected in *WICF* in a version nearly identical to that in *WWTA*.

Pie. *Beginners*: 11-page manuscript cut by 29% for inclusion in *WWTA* as "A Serious Talk." PREVIOUS PUBLICATION: A version of "A Serious Talk" that was the product of Lish's first and partial second editing of "Pie" appeared in *Missouri Review*, Fall 1980. In December 1980 a version of "Pie" that was nearly identical to the version in *Beginners* was published in *Playgirl*. (The story takes place at Christmastime, and the magazine had held it for the holiday issue.) SUBSEQUENT PUBLICATION: "A Serious Talk" was collected in *WICF* as it appeared in *WWTA*.

The Calm. *Beginners*: 9-page manuscript cut by 25% for inclusion in *WWTA* as "The Calm." PREVIOUS PUBLICATION: "The Calm," *Iowa Review*, Summer 1979. The text in *Iowa Review* is identical to the text in *Beginners*. NOTE ON *WWTA*: In editing the last sentence of "The Calm" Lish changed Carver's description of the barber's touch from "sadness" to "tenderness" and later to "sweetness." SUBSEQUENT PUBLICATION: "The Calm" was collected in *WICF* in a version nearly identical to that in *WWTA*.

Mine. *Beginners*: "Mine" is the only story for which no typescript is preserved in the manuscript of *Beginners*. The story is included in the second revised manuscript of *WWTA*, which corresponds to Lish's second editing of the book. The 3-page typescript of "Mine" was cut by only 1%. PREVIOUS PUBLICATION: "Mine" made its first appearance in *FS*. An identical version was published under the title "Little Things" in *Fiction*, 1978. In June 1978 "Mine" was reprinted unchanged from *FS* in *Playgirl*. In April 1977 Carver had sent "a three-page mini-story" titled "A Separate Debate" to Noel Young of Capra Press, together with the signed contract for *FS*. Carver simultaneously submitted the story to Lish, who edited it for possible publication in *Esquire*. Lish cut "A Separate Debate" by 7% and asked Carver to change the title. Carver renamed the story "Little Things," then "Mine," but it never appeared in *Esquire*. The text published as "Mine" in *FS* incorporated many but not all of Lish's editorial suggestions and is virtually identical to the text in *Beginners*. NOTE ON *WWTA*: Lish changed the title from "Mine" to "Popular Mechanics" in his second editing of the *Beginners* manuscript. SUBSEQUENT PUBLICATION: The text of the story was collected in *WICF* as it appeared in *WWTA*, but Carver changed the title from "Popular Mechanics" to "Little Things."

Distance. *Beginners*: 13-page manuscript cut by 45% for inclusion in *WWTA* as "Everything Stuck to Him." PREVIOUS PUBLICATION: "Distance," *Chariton Review*, Fall 1975; collected in *FS*. The source of the text in *FS* was a photocopy of pages from *Chariton Review* on which Carver had made incidental corrections. "Distance" was reprinted from *FS* in *Playgirl*, March 1978. The text in *FS* is identical to the text in *Beginners*. SUBSEQUENT PUBLICATION: "Distance" as collected in *Fires* is for the most part a restoration of the text in *FS*. In addition, the text in *Fires* incorporates a few of Lish's revisions of the story in *WWTA* and several changes suggested in marginalia by Tess Gallagher. The version in *Fires* was collected in *WICF*.

Beginners. *Beginners*: 33-page manuscript cut by 50% for inclusion in *WWTA* as "What We Talk About When We Talk About Love." PREVIOUS PUBLICATION: A version of "What We Talk About When We Talk About Love" that was the product of Lish's second editing of *Beginners* and his corrections to the printer's manuscript of *WWTA* appeared in *Antaeus*, Winter-Spring 1981. NOTE ON *WWTA*: The *Beginners* manuscript of "Beginners" bears corrections in Carver's hand, including his cancellation of the two final sentences: "Then it would get better. I knew if I closed my eyes, I could get lost." In Lish's first editing of the story he cut the last five pages. In his second editing he changed the title from "Beginners" to "What We Talk About When We Talk About Love" and deleted the names of the old couple "Anna" and "Henry [Gates]." SUBSEQUENT PUBLICATION: "What We Talk About When We Talk About Love" was collected in *WICF* as it appeared in *WWTA*. "Beginners" was published in *The New Yorker* of December 24–31, 2007, as it appeared in the *Beginners* manuscript.

One More Thing. *Beginners*: 7-page manuscript cut by 37% for inclusion in *WWTA* as "One More Thing." PREVIOUS PUBLICATION: "One More Thing," *North American Review*, March 1981. The text in *North American Review* is nearly identical to the text in *Beginners*. NOTE ON *WWTA*: In the course of editing the story Lish changed the name of the daughter from Bea to Rayette and later, at Carver's suggestion, to Rae. SUBSEQUENT PUBLICATION: "One More Thing" was collected in *WICF* as it appeared in *WWTA*.

For texts taken from printed sources, this volume does not attempt to reproduce features of typographic design, such as display capitalization. The texts are printed without change, except for the correction of obvious typographical errors. Spelling, punctuation, and capitalization are often expressive features, and they are not altered, even when inconsistent or irregular. For texts taken from the manuscript of *Beginners*, the treatment of the text is described above. The following errors have been corrected: 15.10, out; 41.4, end tightened; 63.3, "Sure,; 96.23, huh?; 97.6, promise?; 107.11, one his; 108.34, "Mr.; 111.20, *a*; 113.31, *Consider!*; 136.31, bed.; 164.3, little; 179.7, it?; 187.28, nothing"; 196.39, cigaret; 203.5, you? the; 207.2, is—eighteen; 246.8, says.; 325.5, From,; 356.39, knowck; 435.14, hemself; 534.6, out; 570.19, any more; 575.36, anymore; 636.31, happy?; 651.25, now.; 696.27, 'They; 733.1, langage.

Chronological Bibliography

The following list indicates the first American and English periodical publications of Carver's stories, as well as their published revisions, separate editions, and inclusions in collections. Alternate titles are given in brackets.

Abbreviations

Beginners	*Beginners* (Unpublished original manuscript of *WWTA*, 1980)
Call	*Call If You Need Me: The Uncollected Fiction and Prose* (Harvill Press, 2000)
Cathedral	*Cathedral* (Knopf, 1983)
Fires	*Fires: Essays, Poems, Stories* (Capra Press, 1983)
FS	*Furious Seasons and Other Stories* (Capra Press, 1977)
WICF	*Where I'm Calling From: New and Selected Stories* (Atlantic Monthly Press, 1988)
WWTA	*What We Talk About When We Talk About Love* (Knopf, 1981)
WYPBQP	*Will You Please Be Quiet, Please?* (McGraw-Hill, 1976)

1960
  "The Furious Seasons" ["Furious Seasons"]
    "The Furious Seasons," *Selection* 2 (Winter 1960–61): 1–18.
    ——, *December* 5.1 (Fall 1963): 31–41.
    "Furious Seasons," *FS* 94–110.
    ——, *Call* 129–45.
1961
  "The Father," *Toyon* 7.1 (Spring 1961): 11–12.
    ——, *December* 10.1 (1968): 32.
    ——, *WYPBQP* 39–40.
1963
  "The Aficionados," signed "John Vale," *Toyon* 9.1 (Spring 1963): 5–9.
    ——, *Call* 150–55.
  "Poseidon and Company," *Toyon* 9.1 (Spring 1963): 24–25.
    ——, *Ball State Teachers College Forum* 5.2 (Spring 1964): 11–12.
    ——, *Call* 156–57.
  "The Hair," *Toyon* 9.1 (Spring 1963): 27–30.
    ——, *Sundaze* 2.6 (Jan. 7–20, 1972): n. pag.

——, *Those Days: Early Writings by Raymond Carver*
(Elmwood, Conn.: Raven Editions, 1987): 19–23.

——, *Call* 146–49.

"Pastoral" ["The Cabin"]

"Pastoral," *Western Humanities Review* 17.1 (Winter 1963):
33–42.

——, *FS* 79–91.

"The Cabin," *Indiana Review* 6.1 (Winter 1983): 4–13.

——, *Fires* 127–38.

——, *Granta* 12 (1984): 99–110.

"The Night the Mill Boss Died" ["The Ducks"]

"The Night the Mill Boss Died," *Carolina Quarterly* 16.1
(Winter 1963): 34–39.

"The Ducks," *WYPBQP* 175–82.

1964

"The Student's Wife," *Carolina Quarterly* 17.1 (Fall 1964): 19–29.

——, *WYPBQP* 120–29.

——, *WICF* 26–32.

1966

"Will You Please Be Quiet, Please?" *December* 8.1 (1966): 9–27.

——, *WYPBQP* 225–49.

1967

"Bright Red Apples," *Gato Magazine* 2.1 (Spring-Summer 1967):
8–13.

——, *Call* 158–64.

"Sometimes a Woman Can Just About Ruin a Man" ["What Do
You Do in San Francisco?"]

"Sometimes a Woman Can Just About Ruin a Man,"
Colorado State Review 2.3 (Summer 1967): 35–40.

"What Do You Do in San Francisco?" *WYPBQP* 109–19.

——, *WICF* 40–47.

"Dummy" ["The Third Thing That Killed My Father Off"]

"Dummy," *Discourse* 10.3 (Summer 1967): 241–56.

——, *FS* 9–26.

"The Third Thing That Killed My Father Off," *WWTA* 89–103.

——, *WICF* 149–59.

"Dummy," *Beginners* (884–900 in this volume).

1969

"Sixty Acres," *Discourse* 12.1 (Winter 1969): 117–27.

——, *WYPBQP* 60–74.

1970

"A Night Out" ["Signals"]

"A Night Out," *December* 12.1–2 (1970): 65–68.

"Signals," *WYPBQP* 217–24.

"Cartwheels" ["How About This?"]
    "Cartwheels," *Western Humanities Review* 24.4 (Autumn 1970): 375–82.
    "How About This?" *WYPBQP* 183–92.

1971

"Neighbors," *Esquire* (June 1971): 137–39.
    ——, *WYPBQP* 7–14.
    ——, *WICF* 65–70.

"Friendship" ["Tell the Women We're Going"]
    "Friendship," *Sou'wester Literary Quarterly* (Summer 1971): 61–74.
    "Tell the Women We're Going," *WWTA* 57–66.
    ——, *Beginners* (831–44 in this volume).

"Fat," *Harper's Bazaar* (Sept. 1971): 198–99, 228.
    ——, *WYPBQP* 1–6.
    ——, *WICF* 48–52.

"Nightschool" ["Night School"]
    "Nightschool," *North American Review* 256 [n.s. 8].3 (Fall 1971): 48–50.
    "Night School," *WYPBQP* 92–99.

"The Idea," *Northwest Review* 12.1 (Fall-Winter 1971–72): 81–84.
    ——, *WYPBQP* 15–19.

"The Lie," *Sou'wester Literary Quarterly* (Winter 1971): 56–59.
    ——, *FS* 37–40.
    ——, *Playgirl* (May 1978): 92.
    ——, *American Poetry Review* 11.6 (Nov.-Dec. 1982): 7.
    ——, *Fires* 123–25.

1972

"What's in Alaska?" *Iowa Review* 3.2 (Spring 1972): 28–37.
    ——, *WYPBQP* 75–91.
    ——, *WICF* 53–64.

"What Is It?" ["Are These Actual Miles?"]
    "What Is It?" *Esquire* (May 1972): 134–37.
    ——, *WYPBQP* 206–16.
    "Are These Actual Miles?" *WICF* 96–103.

"A Dog Story" ["Jerry and Molly and Sam"]
    "A Dog Story," *Perspective* 17.1 (Summer 1972): 33–47.
    "Jerry and Molly and Sam," *WYPBQP* 151–67.

"Put Yourself in My Shoes," *Iowa Review* 3.4 (Fall 1972): 42–52.
    ——, *WYPBQP* 130–50.
    ——, *WICF* 71–84.

"The Man Is Dangerous" ["Why, Honey?"]
    "The Man Is Dangerous," *Sou'wester Literary Quarterly* (Winter 1972): 53–62.

"Why, Honey?" *WYPBQP* 168–74.

——, *WICF* 91–95.

"Bicycles, Muscles, Cigarettes" ["Bicycles, Muscles, Cigarets"]

"Bicycles, Muscles, Cigarettes," *Kansas Quarterly* 5.1 (Winter 1972–73): 17–23.

"Bicycles, Muscles, Cigarets," *WYPBQP* 193–205.

"Bicycles, Muscles, Cigarettes," *WICF* 17–25.

1973

"Are You a Doctor?" *Fiction* 1.4 (1973): 27–28.

——, *WYPBQP* 29–38.

"The Pheasant," *Occident* 7 [n.s.] (1973): 76–81.

——, *New England Review/Bread Loaf Quarterly* 5.1–2 (Autumn-Winter 1982): 5–10.

The Pheasant. Worcester, Mass.: Metacom Press, 1982.

"The Pheasant," *Fires* 147–53.

"They're Not Your Husband," *Chicago Review* 24.4 (Spring 1973): 101–7.

——, *WYPBQP* 20–28.

——, *WICF* 33–39.

"The Summer Steelhead" ["Nobody Said Anything"]

"The Summer Steelhead," *Seneca Review* 4.1 (May 1973): 60–75.

"Nobody Said Anything," *WYPBQP* 41–59.

——, *WICF* 3–16.

1974

"The Fling" ["Sacks"]

"The Fling," *Perspective* 17.3 (Winter 1974): 139–52.

——, *FS* 62–78.

"Sacks," *WWTA* 37–45.

"The Fling," *Beginners* (788–803 in this volume).

1975

"So Much Water So Close to Home," *Spectrum* 17.1 (1975): 21–38.

——, *Playgirl* (Feb. 1976): 54–55, 80–81, 110–11.

——, *FS* 41–61.

——, *WWTA* 79–88.

——, *Fires* 167–86.

——, *WICF* 160–77.

——, *Beginners* (864–83 in this volume).

"Collectors," *Esquire* (Aug. 1975): 95–96.

——, *WYPBQP* 100–108.

——, *WICF* 85–90.

"Distance" ["Everything Stuck to Him"]

"Distance," *Chariton Review* 1.2 (Fall 1975): 14–23.

———, *FS* 27–36.

———, *Playgirl* (Mar. 1978): 101–4.

"Everything Stuck to Him," *WWTA* 127–35.

"Distance," *Fires* 113–21.

———, *WICF* 140–48.

———, *Beginners* (917–26 in this volume).

"Harry's Death," *Eureka Review* 1 (Winter 1975–76): 21–28.

———, *Iowa Review* 10.3 (Summer 1979): 28–32.

———, *Fires* 139–45.

1977

"Mine" ["Little Things"] ["Popular Mechanics"]

"Mine," *FS* 92–93.

"Little Things," *Fiction* 5.2–3 (1978): 241–42.

"Mine," *Playgirl* (June 1978): 100.

"Popular Mechanics," *WWTA* 123–25.

"Little Things," *WICF* 114–15.

"Mine," *Beginners* (915–16 in this volume).

1978

"View Finder" ["Viewfinder"]

"View Finder," *Iowa Review* 9.1 (Winter 1978): 50–52.

———, *Quarterly West* 6 (Spring-Summer 1978): 69–72.

"Viewfinder," *WWTA* 11–15.

———, *Beginners* (757–60 in this volume).

"Why Don't You Dance?" *Quarterly West* 7 (Autumn 1978): 26–30.

———, *Paris Review* 23.79 (Spring 1981): 177–82.

———, *WWTA* 3–10.

———, *WICF* 116–21.

———, *Beginners* (751–56 in this volume).

1979

"The Calm," *Iowa Review* 10.3 (Summer 1979): 33–37.

———, *WWTA* 115–21.

———, *WICF* 178–82.

———, *Beginners* (909–14 in this volume).

"From *The Augustine Notebooks*," *Iowa Review* 10.3 (Summer 1979): 38–42.

———, *Call* 167–74.

1980

"Where Is Everyone?" ["Mr. Coffee and Mr. Fixit"]

"Where Is Everyone?" *TriQuarterly* 48 (Spring 1980): 203–13.

"Mr. Coffee and Mr. Fixit," *WWTA* 17–20.

"Where Is Everyone?" *Fires* 155–65.

———, *Beginners* (761–71 in this volume).

"A Serious Talk" ["Pie"]

"A Serious Talk," *Missouri Review* 4.1 (Fall 1980): 23–28.

"Pie," *Playgirl* (Dec. 1980): 72–73, 83, 92, 94–95.

"A Serious Talk," *WWTA* 105–13.

——, *WICF* 122–27.

"Pie," *Beginners* (901–8 in this volume).

"Want to See Something?" ["I Could See the Smallest Things"]

 "Want to See Something?" *Missouri Review* 4.1 (Fall 1980): 29–32.

 "I Could See the Smallest Things," *WWTA* 31–36.

 "Want to See Something?" *Beginners* (781–87 in this volume).

"Gazebo," *Missouri Review* 4.1 (Fall 1980): 33–38.

——, *WWTA* 21–29.

——, *WICF* 104–9.

——, *Beginners* (772–80 in this volume).

1981

"What We Talk About When We Talk About Love" ["Beginners"]

 "What We Talk About When We Talk About Love," *Antaeus* 40–41 (Winter-Spring 1981): 57–68.

 ——, *WWTA* 137–54.

 ——, *WICF* 128–39.

 "Beginners," *New Yorker* (Dec. 24–31, 2007): 100–109.

 ——, *Beginners* (927–48 in this volume).

"One More Thing," *North American Review* 266.1 (Mar. 1981): 28–29.

 ——, *WWTA* 155–59.

 ——, *WICF* 110–13.

 ——, *Beginners* (949–53 in this volume).

"If It Please You" ["After the Denim"]

 "If It Please You," *New England Review* 3.3 (Spring 1981): 314–32.

 "After the Denim," *WWTA* 67–78.

 If It Please You. Northridge, Calif.: Lord John Press, 1984.

 "If It Please You," *Beginners* (845–63 in this volume).

"The Bath" ["A Small, Good Thing"]

 "The Bath," *Columbia* 6 (Spring-Summer 1981): 32–41.

 ——, *WWTA* 47–56.

 "A Small, Good Thing," *Ploughshares* 8.2–3 (1982): 213–40.

 ——, *Cathedral* 59–89.

 ——, *WICF* 280–301.

 ——, *Beginners* (804–30 in this volume).

"Cathedral," *The Atlantic* (Sept. 1981): 23–29.

 ——, *Cathedral* 209–28.

 ——, *London Magazine* (Feb.-Mar. 1984): 3–18.

 ——, *WICF* 266–79.

"Vitamins," *Esquire* (Oct. 1981): 130–39.
———, *Granta* 4 (1981): 215–30.
———, *Cathedral* 91–109.
———, *WICF* 183–96.
"Chef's House," *New Yorker* (Nov. 30, 1981): 42–43.
———, *Cathedral* 27–33.
———, *WICF* 222–26.

1982
"Where I'm Calling From," *New Yorker* (Mar. 15, 1982): 41–51.
———, *Cathedral* 127–46.
———, *WICF* 208–21.
"The Bridle," *New Yorker* (July 19, 1982): 30–39.
———, *Cathedral* 187–208.
"Feathers," *The Atlantic* (Sept. 1982): 62–69.
———, *Cathedral* 3–26.
———, *WICF* 248–65.

1983
"The Compartment," *Antioch Review* 41.2 (Spring 1983):
133–41.
———, *Granta* 8 (1983): 67–77.
———, *Cathedral* 47–58.
"Preservation," *Grand Street* 2.3 (Spring 1983): 7–16.
———, *Cathedral* 35–46.
"The Train," *Antaeus* 49–50 (Spring-Summer 1983): 151–57.
———, *Cathedral* 147–56.
"Fever," *North American Review* 268.2 (June 1983): 11–19.
———, *Cathedral* 157–86.
———, *WICF* 227–47.
"Careful," *Paris Review* 25.88 (Summer 1983): 222–34.
———, *Cathedral* 111–25.
———, *WICF* 197–207.

1986
"Boxes," *New Yorker* (Feb. 24, 1986): 31–37.
———, *WICF* 305–16.
"Whoever Was Using This Bed," *New Yorker* (Apr. 28, 1986):
33–40.
———, *WICF* 317–30.
"Elephant," *New Yorker* (June 9, 1986): 38–45.
———, *Fiction Magazine* (Oct. 1986): 15–20.
Elephant. Fairfax, Calif.: Jungle Garden Press, 1988.
"Elephant," *WICF* 351–64.
"Blackbird Pie," *New Yorker* (July 7, 1986): 26–34.
———, *WICF* 365–80.
"Intimacy," *Esquire* (Aug. 1986): 58–60.

Intimacy. Concord, N.H.: William B. Ewert, 1987.
"Intimacy," *WICF* 331–37.

1987
"Menudo," *Granta* 21 (Spring 1987): 157–71.
——, *WICF* 338–50.
"Errand," *New Yorker* (June 1, 1987): 30–36.
——, *WICF* 381–91.

1999
"Kindling," *Esquire* (July 1999): 72–77.
——, *Call* 7–20.
"Vandals," *Esquire* (Oct. 1999): 160–65.
——, *Call* 49–62.
"Call If You Need Me," *Granta* 68 (Winter 1999): 9–21.
——, *Call* 63–74.

2000
"What Would You Like to See?" *Guardian Weekend*
(June 24, 2000): 14–20.
——, *Call* 21–37.
"Dreams," *Esquire* (Aug. 2000): 132–37.
——, *Call* 38–48.

Notes

In the notes below, the reference numbers denote page and line of this volume (the line count includes headings). No note is made for material included in standard desk-reference books such as Webster's *Collegiate, Biographical,* and *Geographical* dictionaries. Quotations from Shakespeare are keyed to *The Riverside Shakespeare*, ed. G. Blakemore Evans (Boston: Houghton Mifflin, 1974). References to the Bible have been keyed to the King James version. For references to other studies and further biographical background than is contained in the Chronology, see Maryann Burk Carver, *What It Used to Be Like: A Portrait of My Marriage to Raymond Carver* (New York: St. Martin's Press, 2006); Raymond Carver, *All of Us: The Collected Poems*, ed. William L. Stull, with introduction by Tess Gallagher (New York: Knopf, 1998), and *Carver Country: The World of Raymond Carver*, with photographs by Bob Adelman and introduction by Tess Gallagher (New York: Scribner's, 1990); Richard Ford, *Good Raymond* (London: Harvill Press, 1998); Tess Gallagher, *Soul Barnacles: Ten More Years with Ray*, ed. Greg Simon (Ann Arbor: University of Michigan Press, 2000); Marshall Bruce Gentry and William L. Stull (eds.), *Conversations with Raymond Carver* (Jackson: University Press of Mississippi, 1990); Sam Halpert, *Raymond Carver: An Oral Biography* (Iowa City: University of Iowa Press, 1995); William L. Stull. "Raymond Carver, 1938–1988." *Dictionary of Literary Biography Yearbook: 1988*, ed. J. M. Brook (Detroit: Gale Research, 1989), 199–213; William L. Stull and Maureen P. Carroll (eds.), *Remembering Ray: A Composite Biography of Raymond Carver* (Santa Barbara: Capra Press, 1993); and William L. Stull and Maureen P. Carroll (eds.), *Tell It All* (Rome: Leconte, 2005).

WILL YOU PLEASE BE QUIET, PLEASE?

8.1   *Neighbors*]   The following short essay about this story was included in *Cutting Edges: Young American Fiction for the '70s*, ed. Jack Hicks (New York: Holt, Rinehart and Winston, 1973), 528–29:

> "Neighbors" first hit me as an idea for a story in the fall of 1970, two years after returning to the United States from Tel Aviv. While in Tel Aviv, we had for a few days looked after an apartment belonging to some friends. Though none of the high jinks in the story really occurred in the course of our apartment watching, I have to admit that I did do a bit of snooping in the refrigerator and liquor cabinet. I

found that experience of entering and leaving someone else's empty apartment two or three times a day, sitting for a while in other people's chairs, glancing through their books and magazines and looking out their windows, made a rather powerful impression on me. It took two years for the impression to surface as a story, but once it did I simply sat down and wrote it. It seemed a fairly easy story to do at the time, and it came together very quickly after I went to work on it. The real work on the story, and perhaps the art of the story, came later. Originally the manuscript was about twice as long, but I kept paring it on subsequent revisions, and then pared some more, until it achieved its present length and dimensions.

In addition to the confusion or disorder of the central personality in the story—the main theme at work, I guess—I think that the story has captured an essential sense of mystery or strangeness that is in part due to the treatment of the subject matter, in this case the story's style. For it is a highly "stylized" story if it is anything, and it is this that helps give it its value.

With each subsequent trip to the Stones' apartment, Miller is drawn deeper and deeper into an abyss of his own making. The turning point in the story comes, of course, when Arlene insists that this time she will go next door alone and then, finally, Bill has to go and fetch her. She reveals through words and through appearance (the color in her cheeks is high and there is "white lint clinging to the back of her sweater") that she in turn has been doing pretty much the same kind of rummaging and prowling that he has been engaging in.

I think the story is, more or less, an artistic success. My only fear is that it is too thin, too elliptical and subtle, too inhuman. I hope this is not so, but in truth I do not see it as the kind of story that one loves unreservedly and gives up everything to; a story that is ultimately remembered for its sweep, for the breadth and depth and lifelike sentiment of its characters. No, this is a different kind of story—not better, maybe, and I surely hope no worse, different in any case—and the internal and external truths and values in the story do not have much to do, I'm afraid, with character, or some of the other virtues held dear in short fiction.

As to writers and writing that I like, I tend to find much more around that I like than dislike. I think there is all kinds of good stuff getting written and published these days in both the big and little magazines, and in book form. Lots of stuff that's not so good, too, but why worry about that? To my mind Joyce Carol Oates is the first writer of my generation, perhaps any recent generation, and we are all going to have to learn to live under that shadow, or spell—at least for the foreseeable future.

36.12–13   *The Princess of Mars*]   *A Princess of Mars* (1917), science-fiction novel by Edgar Rice Burroughs.

146.2 Ghelderode] Visionary Belgian playwright Michel de Ghelderode (1898–1962), whose plays include *La Balade du grand macabre* (*The Ballad of the Great Macabre*, 1934) and *La Mort du Docteur Faust* (*The Death of Dr. Faust*, 1928).

159.9 Blue Chip stamps] Trading stamps given away with purchases at supermarkets and gas stations, redeemable for merchandise.

168.20 *Une cuiller, s'il vous plaît*] French: a spoon, please.

172.31 *casita*] Spanish: little house.

178.6–7 Strindberg . . . *Miss Julie*] *Miss Julie* (1888), play by Swedish dramatist August Strindberg (1849–1912).

178.8 Norman Mailer . . . breast] In November 1960, novelist Mailer (1923–2007) stabbed his wife, Adele, in the back and abdomen with a penknife at the end of a party in which he had announced his intention to run for mayor of New York City.

181.25 Shrine circus] Traveling circus mounted by the Shriners, an American Masonic fraternity.

STORIES FROM FURIOUS SEASONS

205.2–4 *That duration* . . . Browne] From Browne's *Hydriotaphia, or Urn-Burial* (1658), chapter 5.

STORIES FROM FIRES

329.37 *Blow-up*] Film (1966) by Italian director Michelangelo Antonioni (1912–2007), based loosely on a Julio Cortázar short story.

331.26 muzhik] Russian: peasant.

CATHEDRAL

400.37 POUSSEZ] French: push.

434.31 Johnny Hodges] Hodges (1906–1970), longtime alto saxophonist for the Duke Ellington Orchestra, led his own big band from 1950 to 1955.

470.12 *amico mio*] Italian: my friend.

492.17 Colette did that . . . fever] See "Fever" in *Journal à rebours* (*Looking Backwards*, 1941) by the French writer Colette, pen name of Sidonie-Gabrielle Colette (1873–1954).

519.38 Barry Fitzgerald] Irish stage and movie actor (1888–1961) whose films include *Going My Way* (1944) and *The Quiet Man* (1952).

STORIES FROM WHERE I'M CALLING FROM

598.29 Council of Trent] Roman Catholic council (1545–63) convened by Pope Paul III to address church doctrine and institutional reform in the wake of the Protestant Reformation.

598.29 Treaty of Utrecht] Treaty signed in 1713 marking the end of the War of the Spanish Succession.

598.34–35 First Silesian War] Fought from 1740 to 1742, the first of two wars between Prussia and Austria (and its allies) for control of the central European region of Silesia.

598.37–599.1 Thermopylae, Shiloh] Thermopylae, site in Greece of several battles in antiquity, most notably the two-day standoff in 480 BCE between Greek troops and a far more numerous force of Persian forces; Shiloh, Civil War battle (April 6–7, 1862) fought in western Tennessee.

599.1 Maxim Gun] Machine gun invented in 1884 by Hiram Stevens Maxim (1840–1916).

599.1 Tannenberg] The name of two notable battles: the First Battle of Tannenberg (1410), also known as the Battle of Grunwald, resulted in the knights of the Teutonic Order being soundly defeated by Polish and Lithuanian forces; the Second Battle of Tannenberg (1914) was a German victory against the Russians early in World War I.

599.2–3 famous four and twenty . . . king] From the nursery rhyme "Sing a Song of Sixpence": "Sing a song of sixpence, / A pocketful of rye. / Four and twenty blackbirds / Baked in a pie. / When the pie was opened, / The birds began to sing. / Wasn't that a dainty dish / To set before the king?"

604.18–20 Lancelot . . . Barnacle] Famed lovers: Lancelot and Guinevere, legendary adulterous couple of Arthurian literature; French theologian Pierre Abélard (1079–1142) and his pupil Héloïse, who fell in love, secretly married, and conceived a child together before Abelard was castrated by Héloïse's brothers (their story was recalled in works such as Alexander Pope's 1717 poem "Eloisa to Abelard"); Troilus, son of Trojan king Priam, and his beloved Cressida, who during the Trojan War is sent to the Greeks and has an affair with the Greek warrior Diomedes, a legend treated in a poem by Chaucer (c. 1380–87) and a play by Shakespeare (c. 1603), among others; Pyramus and Thisbe, lovers in Greek mythology who, forbidden by their parents to marry, arrange a meeting that turns disastrous when Pyramus assumes Thisbe has been killed by a wild beast and kills himself, prompting her to do the same when she discovers his corpse; Irish novelist James Joyce (1882–1941) and his wife Nora, née Barnacle (1884–1951).

605.18–19 Just so did Darius . . . Alexander the Great] At the Battle of the Granicus (334 BCE), Alexander the Great defeated Persian forces under the command of satraps (provincial governors) serving Persian king Darius III; Darius himself was not at the battle.

607.13–14   blameless . . . first stone]   See Jesus' discussion with the
scribes and Pharisees about the stoning of an adulterous woman at John 8:7:
"So when they continued asking him, he lifted up himself, and said unto
them, He that is without sin among you, let him first cast a stone at her."

614.1   *Errand*]   When "Errand" was included in *The Best American Short
Stories 1988*, selected from U.S. and Canadian magazines by Mark Helprin
with Shannon Ravenel (Boston: Houghton Mifflin, 1988), it was published
with the following note by Carver:

> In early 1987 an editor at E. P. Dutton sent me a copy of the newly
> published Henri Troyat biography, *Chekhov*. Immediately upon the
> book's arrival, I put aside what I was doing and started reading. I
> seem to recall reading the book pretty much straight through, able, at
> the time, to devote entire afternoons and evenings to it.
>
> On the third or fourth day, nearing the end of the book, I came to
> the little passage where Chekhov's doctor—a Badenweiler physician
> by the name of Dr. Schwöhrer, who attended Chekhov during his last
> days—is summoned by Olga Knipper Chekhov to the dying writer's
> bedside in the early morning hours of July 2, 1904. It is clear that
> Chekhov has only a little while to live. Without any comment on the
> matter, Troyat tells his readers that this Dr. Schwöhrer ordered up a
> bottle of champagne. Nobody had asked for champagne, of course; he
> just took it upon himself to do it. But this little piece of human busi-
> ness struck me as an extraordinary action. Before I really knew what I
> was going to do with it, or how I was going to proceed, I felt I had
> been launched into a short story of my own then and there. I wrote a
> few lines and then a page or two more. How did Dr. Schwöhrer go
> about ordering champagne and at that late hour at this hotel in Ger-
> many? How was it delivered to the room and by whom, etc.? What
> was the protocol involved when the champagne arrived? Then I
> stopped and went ahead to finish reading the biography.
>
> But just as soon as I'd finished the book I once again turned my at-
> tention back to Dr. Schwöhrer and that business of the champagne. I
> was seriously interested in what I was doing. But what *was* I doing?
> The only thing that was clear to me was that I thought I saw an op-
> portunity to pay homage—if I could bring it off, do it rightly and
> honorably—to Chekhov, the writer who has meant so much to me for
> such a long time.
>
> I tried out ten or twelve openings to the piece, first one beginning
> and then another, but nothing felt right. Gradually I began to move
> the story away from those final moments back to the occasion of
> Chekhov's first public hemorrhage from tuberculosis, something that
> occurred in a restaurant in Moscow in the company of his friend and
> publisher, Suvorin. Then came the hospitalization and the scene with
> Tolstoy, the trip with Olga to Badenweiler, the brief period of time
> there in the hotel together before the end, the young bellman who

makes two important appearances in the Chekhov suite and, at the end, the mortician who, like the bellman, isn't to be found in the biographical account.

The story was a hard one to write, given the factual basis of the material. I couldn't stray from what had happened, nor did I want to. As much as anything, I needed to figure out how to breathe life into actions that were merely suggested or not given moment in the biographical telling. And, finally, I saw that I needed to set my imagination free and simply invent within the confines of the story. I knew as I was writing this story that it was a good deal different from anything I'd ever done before. I'm pleased, and grateful, that it seems to have come together. (318–19)

623.33   *Comprenez-vous?*]   French: do you understand?

OTHER FICTION

641.35   *Restless Guns*]   Western novel (1929) by William Colt MacDonald (1891–1968).

642.6–7   Zane . . . Short]   Prolific writers of Western novels and pulp stories: Zane Grey (1872–1939); Louis L'Amour (1908–1988); Ernest Haycox (1899–1950); and Luke Short, pen name of Frederick Dilley Glidden (1908–1975).

643.4–5   MacMillian . . . operation]   British Prime Minister Harold Macmillan (1894–1986) underwent surgery for an enlarged prostate on October 10, 1963, a day after he informed the Queen of his intention to resign as Prime Minister.

643.27   *Goldfinger*]   Third film in the James Bond series, released in 1964.

645.24   BAR]   Browning Automatic Rifle.

646.23   Marshal Dillon]   Marshal Matt Dillon, lead character in *Gunsmoke,* popular radio (1952–61) and television (1955–75) Western series.

646.23   Oddjob . . . Easy]   Characters, respectively, in *Goldfinger* and the syndicated newspaper comic strip *Captain Easy, Soldier of Fortune* (1933–1988), created by cartoonist Roy Crane (1901–1977).

646.24   Ted Trueblood]   Hunter, fisherman, and outdoorsman writer (1913–1982), author of several handbooks and a columnist and editor at *Field & Stream* magazine.

668.24   Jonestown]   In November 1978, 909 members of the Peoples Temple cult, led by Jim Jones (1931–1978), committed mass suicide at Jonestown, their jungle settlement in Guyana.

685.5   Alexander Scourby]   Stage, film, radio, and television actor (1913–

1985) who made numerous audio recordings of classics such as *War and Peace* as well as the King James Bible in its entirety.

SELECTED ESSAYS

719.27   Grand Coulee Dam]   Dam built on the Columbia River, one of the massive public works projects of the New Deal.

729.1–2   "Fundamental accuracy . . . Pound]   From "The Quality of Mr. Joyce's Work," essay collected in *Pound/Joyce: The Letters of Ezra Pound and James Joyce* (1967).

730.11   Make It New, as Pound urged]   Title of Ezra Pound's 1934 essay collection; the phrase is a credo of Pound's attempt to revitalize tradition.

730.29   Evan Connell]   Novelist, short-story writer, and biographer Evan S. Connell (b. 1924), author of *Mr. Bridge* (1958), *Mrs. Bridge* (1969), *Custer: Son of the Morning Star* (1984), and many other books.

731.2–3   Henry James . . . "weak specification."]   See James's 1908 preface to *The Turn of the Screw*: "Make him think the evil, make him think it for himself, and you are released from weak specifications."

732.7–9   For several days . . . rang."]   Cf. the opening line of "Put Yourself in My Shoes" (see 101.2–3): "The telephone rang while he was running the vacuum cleaner."

740.20–21   "grip and slog" of it, in D.H. Lawrence's phrase]   In Lawrence's story "Mother and Daughter" (1929).

748.33–34   "created of warm blood and nerves"]   See Chekhov's story "Ward No. 6" (1892): "I only know that God has created me of warm blood and nerves, yes, indeed!"

THE LIBRARY OF AMERICA SERIES

The Library of America fosters appreciation and pride in America's literary heritage by publishing, and keeping permanently in print, authoritative editions of America's best and most significant writing. An independent nonprofit organization, it was founded in 1979 with seed funding from the National Endowment for the Humanities and the Ford Foundation.

1. Herman Melville: *Typee, Omoo, Mardi*
2. Nathaniel Hawthorne: *Tales and Sketches*
3. Walt Whitman: *Poetry and Prose*
4. Harriet Beecher Stowe: *Three Novels*
5. Mark Twain: *Mississippi Writings*
6. Jack London: *Novels and Stories*
7. Jack London: *Novels and Social Writings*
8. William Dean Howells: *Novels 1875–1886*
9. Herman Melville: *Redburn, White-Jacket, Moby-Dick*
10. Nathaniel Hawthorne: *Collected Novels*
11. Francis Parkman: *France and England in North America*, Vol. I
12. Francis Parkman: *France and England in North America*, Vol. II
13. Henry James: *Novels 1871–1880*
14. Henry Adams: *Novels, Mont Saint Michel, The Education*
15. Ralph Waldo Emerson: *Essays and Lectures*
16. Washington Irving: *History, Tales and Sketches*
17. Thomas Jefferson: *Writings*
18. Stephen Crane: *Prose and Poetry*
19. Edgar Allan Poe: *Poetry and Tales*
20. Edgar Allan Poe: *Essays and Reviews*
21. Mark Twain: *The Innocents Abroad, Roughing It*
22. Henry James: *Literary Criticism: Essays, American & English Writers*
23. Henry James: *Literary Criticism: European Writers & The Prefaces*
24. Herman Melville: *Pierre, Israel Potter, The Confidence-Man, Tales & Billy Budd*
25. William Faulkner: *Novels 1930–1935*
26. James Fenimore Cooper: *The Leatherstocking Tales*, Vol. I
27. James Fenimore Cooper: *The Leatherstocking Tales*, Vol. II
28. Henry David Thoreau: *A Week, Walden, The Maine Woods, Cape Cod*
29. Henry James: *Novels 1881–1886*
30. Edith Wharton: *Novels*
31. Henry Adams: *History of the U.S. during the Administrations of Jefferson*
32. Henry Adams: *History of the U.S. during the Administrations of Madison*
33. Frank Norris: *Novels and Essays*
34. W.E.B. Du Bois: *Writings*
35. Willa Cather: *Early Novels and Stories*
36. Theodore Dreiser: *Sister Carrie, Jennie Gerhardt, Twelve Men*
37a. Benjamin Franklin: *Silence Dogood, The Busy-Body, & Early Writings*
37b. Benjamin Franklin: *Autobiography, Poor Richard, & Later Writings*
38. William James: *Writings 1902–1910*
39. Flannery O'Connor: *Collected Works*
40. Eugene O'Neill: *Complete Plays 1913–1920*
41. Eugene O'Neill: *Complete Plays 1920–1931*
42. Eugene O'Neill: *Complete Plays 1932–1943*
43. Henry James: *Novels 1886–1890*
44. William Dean Howells: *Novels 1886–1888*
45. Abraham Lincoln: *Speeches and Writings 1832–1858*
46. Abraham Lincoln: *Speeches and Writings 1859–1865*
47. Edith Wharton: *Novellas and Other Writings*
48. William Faulkner: *Novels 1936–1940*
49. Willa Cather: *Later Novels*
50. Ulysses S. Grant: *Memoirs and Selected Letters*
51. William Tecumseh Sherman: *Memoirs*
52. Washington Irving: *Bracebridge Hall, Tales of a Traveller, The Alhambra*
53. Francis Parkman: *The Oregon Trail, The Conspiracy of Pontiac*
54. James Fenimore Cooper: *Sea Tales: The Pilot, The Red Rover*
55. Richard Wright: *Early Works*
56. Richard Wright: *Later Works*
57. Willa Cather: *Stories, Poems, and Other Writings*
58. William James: *Writings 1878–1899*
59. Sinclair Lewis: *Main Street & Babbitt*
60. Mark Twain: *Collected Tales, Sketches, Speeches, & Essays 1852–1890*
61. Mark Twain: *Collected Tales, Sketches, Speeches, & Essays 1891–1910*
62. *The Debate on the Constitution: Part One*
63. *The Debate on the Constitution: Part Two*
64. Henry James: *Collected Travel Writings: Great Britain & America*
65. Henry James: *Collected Travel Writings: The Continent*

To subscribe to the series or to order individual copies, please visit www.loa.org or call (800) 964–5778.

This book is set in 10 point Linotron Galliard,
a face designed for photocomposition by Matthew Carter
and based on the sixteenth-century face Granjon. The paper
is acid-free lightweight opaque and meets the requirements
for permanence of the American National Standards Institute.
The binding material is Brillianta, a woven rayon cloth made
by Van Heek–Scholco Textielfabrieken, Holland. Composition
by Dedicated Book Services. Printing and binding
by Edwards Brothers Malloy, Ann Arbor.
Designed by Bruce Campbell.